MW00577933

The 'Beyond' Trilogy

Novels By:

J. Winfield Currie

Beyond All Reason
Book I

Beyond All Odds
Book II

Beyond the Horizon
Book III

The 'Beyond' Trilogy

A Refreshing Approach to Historical Fiction

New Edition 2012

abbott press®
A DIVISION OF WRITER'S DIGEST

Cover concept by J. Winfield Currie
Graphic Arts by: Rana Graphics
26 Stafford Street, Plymouth, MA 02360 USA
www.ranagraphics.com

Rings courtesy of King Jewelry, Cohasset, MA

For information contact the Author:
J. Winfield Currie
P. O. Box 223, Rockland, MA 02370 USA
E-mail: joan@jwinfieldcurrie.com
www.jwinfieldcurrie.com

Abbott Press books may be ordered through booksellers or by contacting:

Abbott Press
1663 Liberty Drive
Bloomington, IN 47403
www.abbottpress.com
Phone: 1-866-697-5310

ISBN: 978-1-4582-0506-3 (e)
ISBN: 978-1-4582-0508-7 (sc)

Library of Congress Control Number: 2012913099

Printed in the United States of America

Abbott Press rev. date: 07/31/2012

Author's Note:
"The 'Beyond' Trilogy" is a work of fiction. Please accept artistic license used in my interpretations of any formerly living individuals portrayed in this historical fiction in an attempt to bring each character to life. This novel was written for your enjoyment. My fictitious characters are just that, bearing no resemblance (other than accidentally) to any persons alive today. Enjoy.

For Stacey

My Daughter … My Dearest Friend

The Beyond Trilogy - Table of Contents

The 'Beyond' Trilogy

Novels by **J. Winfield Currie**

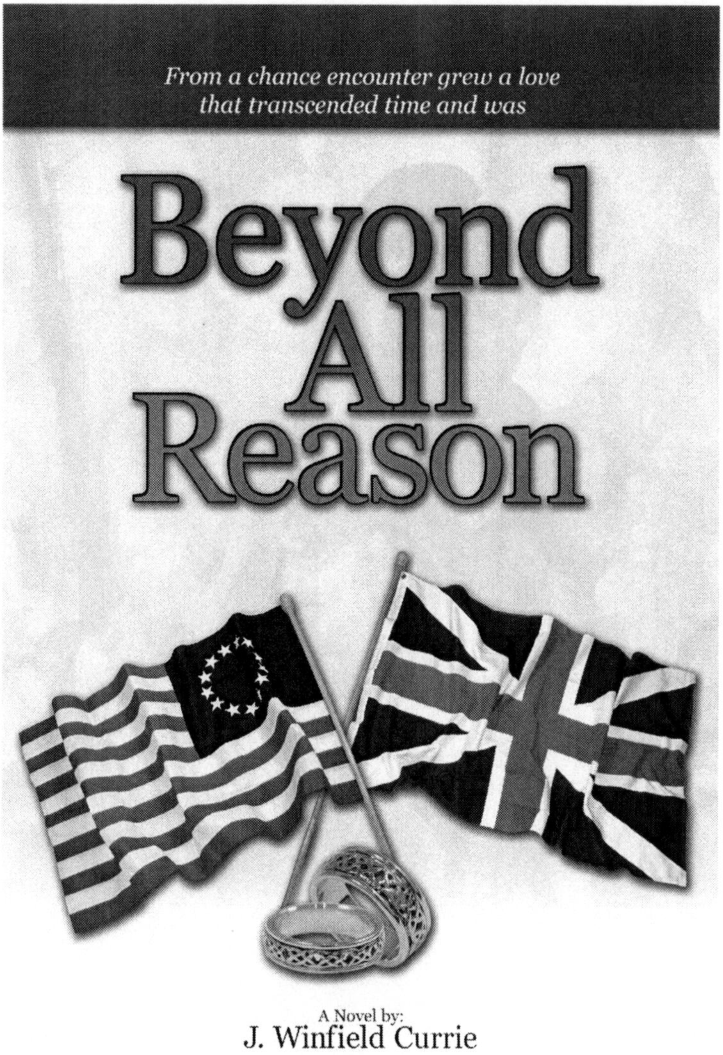
From a chance encounter grew a love
that transcended time and was
Beyond
All
Reason
A Novel by:
J. Winfield Currie

Beyond All Reason

Book I

Awakening Passion

Prologue

Kathryn leisurely traversed a narrow, woodsy trail just north of Charleston, South Carolina. It was summer of 1776, the weather as always this time of year: steamy, sultry.

"Lord, will this heat ever cease?" she muttered, swiping her perspiring brow with the back of an already damp sleeve. Reining her faithful mare, Beauty, to a halt, she snatched her canteen and took a long pull—instantly annoyed at finding it almost empty. Just ahead the trail split, either way eventually leading to the Charleston Path and ultimately, the Cherokee village of Keowee.

Swatting distractedly at an irritating mosquito, she contemplated her choices. The roundabout trail would delay reaching Keowee and an eagerly awaited visit with Anna: longtime friend and noted Cherokee healer. But the longer route offered a chance of finding and perhaps reconnecting with her brother.

"Ahh, Jamie," she sighed. His angry words still echoed clearly. "Ye'll be back—just like always," he had flung at her receding form as she galloped towards the woods, refusing to so much as look back, equally as stubborn as he. *How long have I been gone this time?* She no longer recalled.

"Ye aire right, Jamie, yet again," she muttered.

Maybe they could permanently 'mend broken fences'—heal the angry words which had motivated her impetuous journey of *'seeking'* in the first place. *Seeking what?* After weeks of introspection, drifting with no particular direction in mind—just drifting—she felt no closer to discovering what she wanted or needed from life. *Is my 'journey' purely for the sake of adventure? Or to let Jamie know I am more than capable of taking care of myself without him constantly telling me what to do? Or perhaps ...* She shook her head sadly. *Will I ever be able to forget memories of Black Raven and bury a haunted past?*

Swarming insects were driving her to distraction. This on-going quandary could wait until later. She recalled a little brook nearby, a perfect place to slake their thirst, replenish water, and treat herself to a relaxing bath. Decision made, with a gentle nudge she headed Beauty down the longer trail.

After a bath and a bite to eat Kathryn remounted, refreshed and eager to be back on the trail. Yes, it *was* hot, but a gentle breeze had sprung up and felt good. Relaxing into her mare's familiar gait, she hummed a bright tune, smiling as Beauty's ears pricked with interest. Knowing this area like the back of her hand, she rode completely at ease. Not long ago, there had been a beehive of activity nearby when British dragoons attacked the Fort on Sullivan Island. However, much to their chagrin, its feisty commander, William Moultrie, soundly repelled them. Rumor had it that British militia were still in the vicinity, 'worrying' rebel colonials to keep them under control, but Kathryn had yet to see any signs. As a matter of fact the area seemed too quiet—except for the cicadas, of course.

Cresting a small hill, Kathryn reined her mare to an abrupt halt, and with gentle nudges edged her back out of sight. Hastily dismounting, she crept closer to the ridge and secreted herself in low bushes, confident she could observe without risk of being discovered. She stared openly—surprised and intrigued. Below her spread an encampment of British dragoons, their tents laid out with exacting precision. *How fascinating, the rumor is obviously true.* She smiled, eyes a twinkle.

Curiosity winning out over caution and good judgment, she immersed herself in watching them as they set the cooking fires, curried their horses and practiced their .... A terse warning conveyed in her mother's lilting tones unexpectedly flickered through her mind: *'curiosity killed the cat', my dear.* However, the rippling tingle of imminent danger proved exhilarating—she could not turn away.

Intensely focused on her 'game', she heard not so much as a twig snap *until* ... Large hands grabbed her roughly from behind, and yanked her from hiding.

"And just what do you think you are doing?" a gruff voice hissed against her ear as strong fingers dug painfully into her shoulders; and with a violent twist her arm wrenched behind her in a viselike grip.

Suddenly it struck her. *You really pressed your luck too far this time, Kathryn ...*

Chapter One

Striking a Bargain

"Colonel, pardon the interruption …" Lieutenant Jackson ducked his head cautiously under the open flap of the field tent.

"What is it, Lieutenant?" growled the British officer sitting behind a desk strewn with paperwork. Arching a reproachful eyebrow, he eyed his officer.

"We seized a rebel on the ridge above the campsite, sir."

"Well, bring him in, Lieutenant, so we may determine what he knows of their troop movements."

The lieutenant hesitated, shifting uncomfortably, but at his commanding officer's continued steely gaze blurted, "It is a woman, sir, and she is rather difficult to handle."

"Well then, Lieutenant, bring *her* in," he snapped. "Rebels are rebels regardless of their sex. Let us see what she knows of their plans."

Nodding obediently, the lieutenant backed out of the tent. Returning shortly, he prodded a somewhat disheveled woman ahead of him. With hands trussed behind her and clad in the typical dress of colonial men—laced shirt, greatcoat, leather boots and breeches—a forceful shove sent her stumbling to one knee in front of the colonel's desk. Pulling herself up awkwardly, she spun about, skewering the lieutenant with a poisonous look. "Damn it. Keep your hands off me." Breathing heavily from the exertion of resisting her captors, her greatcoat hung askew and loose blonde strands trailed from her once tidy bun.

"Well, now—and just what do we have here?" the colonel remarked acidly.

She turned abruptly riveting full attention on the officer behind the desk.

"Lieutenant Jackson is correct. You certainly have a nasty temper, a rather unladylike characteristic, I might add."

Drawing herself up to her full height, she glared unwaveringly as he looked her over slowly taking note of her long, lean figure. After several moments of contemplation he rose from his chair, and casually taking his pistol off the papers on the corner, walked leisurely around the desk. He wore the brilliant red jacket, black pants and tall, leather riding boots of the fearsome British Green Dragoons. Even the bright color of his tailored jacket did nothing to dispel the overwhelming sense of menace he presented.

Standing a full head taller, his jet-black hair tied in a neat queue, he boldly appraised her with piercing blue eyes, noting the smallest detail. She watched as he approached, her attention never leaving his face even when he stopped directly in front of her. Despite handsome chiseled features, his steely eyes were devoid of warmth or caring. "Untie her, Lieutenant," he commanded.

Locking eyes with him, she squared her shoulders defiantly. A flick of his thumb cocked the hammer back as he thrust the muzzle against her forehead. She barely flinched, impressing him.

"Have you checked her for weapons?" His gaze shifted to his men, who stood in uneasy silence.

"She had these, sir." A young corporal stepped forward holding a pistol, well-maintained flintlock and finely honed tomahawk. With intricate engraving on the blade, the latter caught his attention—an unusual weapon for her to be carrying; he made mental note to pursue that item later.

"Have you checked her person?" he asked tartly, uttering each word slowly and succinctly.

The corporal cleared his throat uneasily, intimidated and at a loss for words.

"Always check a colonial thoroughly," he snarled. Circling slowly, pistol still aimed at her head, he patted her down with his free hand. Feeling small lumps in the pocket of her greatcoat he withdrew several pieces of hard sugar. "You have a sweet tooth, madam?" He flashed a surly grin.

"Not I. However my mare does," she said acidly, refusing to be intimidated.

Ignoring her smart retort, he continued his search. "Drop your coat, madam," he demanded, yanking it back from her shoulders.

Shrugging out of the heavy garment, she allowed it to fall at her feet.

"Arms out to your sides," he demanded.

Wordlessly complying, she watched as he moved slowly behind her. Through the thin material of her shirt she felt his hand drift lightly across the underside of one arm before dipping to the edge of her breast. Continuing in a leisurely fashion, he trailed his fingers sensuously across her shoulder blades to the underside of the opposite arm where his touch lingered, creating tingling warmth. Almost tenderly, he began tracing an intimate path along her spine, slowly down to her buttocks.

Sucking a quick intake of breath, she tensed as his hand cupped, pausing before continuing his exploration along the inner edge of her thighs, then lower, tapping her knees to nudge legs further apart. Disturbing warmth lingered where his hand had traced so knowingly, shocking her. Tingling sensations spread, his touch creating conflicting emotions.

Noting her reaction he smiled and continued sliding his hand along her calf. Tucked into the side of her right boot, he retrieved a small dirk. "This is a common practice of these colonials, Corporal." Abruptly standing, he drove the dirk into the desktop. Swinging his pistol up, he aimed at the young dragoon's head. "I trust you will not forget again," he spat, eyeing the visibly shaken young man.

Suddenly lowering his weapon, he leisurely sat back on the edge of the desk, arms folded, pistol resting casually against his thigh. "I will handle it from here." With a curt nod he dismissed his men.

She stood assessing him. He was cold, calculating, and dangerous. She would have to play for time in order to create a plan of escape.

"What is your name?" His clipped words abruptly interrupted her thoughts.

"Kathryn," she answered coolly, attempting to appear unconcerned.

"Your full name," he retorted, fixing her with a steely, blue gaze.

"Kathryn Cameron," she shot back, returning his icy stare.

"What were you doing on the ridge?" he asked in lilting singsong, questioning as though she were a naughty child.

She met his stare with narrowed eyes and icy silence.

Standing away from the desk, he tapped the pistol muzzle menacingly against his hand and moved closer, lowering his face to within inches of hers. "Do you live in this area?" Circling slowly, he studied her intently, continuing his game of 'cat and mouse'.

"Not now." She stared straight ahead, ignoring him.

"Do you have family nearby?"

She shrugged. "Perhaps, but with you English everywhere—probably not." Unmistakable defiance flared.

Patience worn thin, he pressed the pistol to her forehead, again impressed by her cool demeanor as she unflinchingly watched him pull the hammer back. "Are you riding with the rebel militia?"

"Do I look like I am?" she sneered.

This interrogation was going nowhere; he had more important things on his agenda than expending time with this stubborn female. Easing the hammer down, he lowered his pistol. "You are wasting my time, madam." He moved to his desk. "Do you have any idea of who I am?" He turned to face her, a haughty sneer curling his lip.

She hesitated, recalling hearsay about the battle at Fort Moultrie; how soundly the dragoons had been beaten, and their colonel—a man of unbelievable violence. "Yes, Colonel Tarrington, I am aware of your reputation." Her gaze held unwavering contempt.

"Then I am sure you realize that I *never* take prisoners." He paused for effect. "However, I do think that shooting you is not the answer: too quick—too easy." He shrugged indifferently.

Oh, God, how can I ever …? He is cold as ice. Despite outward composure her insides constricted violently at his veiled threat, his methods of interrogation unnerving. *How much more …?*

Setting the pistol on his desk, he paused as if immersed in thought, allowing tension to build. Grasping her dirk he tweaked it from the desktop, and stepping forward, pressed the finely honed weapon against her collarbone. She barely tensed. "You have nerves of steel, madam, a rather unusual quality in a woman."

He smiled coldly. "Hmm, I wonder what it would take to break that insolent streak." With a quick flick of the dirk he cut the laces of her blouse. Pausing, he waited for her reaction. As she continued her bold stance, he slid the blade under the edge of the garment and with deft strokes—ever so slowly—opened the front to her waist. Her chest rose and fell in quick, shallow breaths. The oversized shirt had hidden an exquisite body; much to his chagrin he experienced instant response. "Perhaps pain, madam, hmm?" Placing the dirk against the base of her throat, he leaned in close arching a questioning eyebrow—but expected no answer.

She held her silence as he slowly trailed the flat of the blade between her breasts, then casually around one, adding pressure at the nipple yet never breaking the skin. *He is the devil incarnate.* Sheer willpower retained her outward confidence, yet deep within she experienced a sudden prick of fear.

With slow deliberation calculated to shatter her resolve, he continued his tracings, suddenly pressing the point against her breastbone, drawing blood. "There is no rebel movement of which I have knowledge—nothing I can tell you," she hissed.

He searched her face, momentarily deep in thought. Noticing a trickle of blood at her hairline, he brushed the hair back. "Hmm," he flashed a callous smile, "my men are not always gentle." Abruptly stabbing the dirk back into the desktop, the colonel reached behind her head. Loosening the pins holding her unruly golden curls, he allowed them to tumble in billows around her shoulders. Running his lean fingers through the honey-golden mass, he observed her silently.

She eyed him warily as he took his time, prolonging the game. Despite unbearable tension, she was acutely aware of the electricity tracking between them, his proximity: exciting—and disturbing.

Angling his head, he contemplated his next move with unveiled pleasure. Slowly and distinctly he informed her: "I do believe I may have just the answer to break your insolence." Abruptly twisting his fingers in her thick hair, he jerked her head back. Grasping her chin, he studied her face thoughtfully. Despite his unsettling touch, her eyes met his and held.

"You really are quite beautiful," he purred. "What a shame." He shook his head, the feral quality of his tone immediately increasing her uneasiness. "My men have been on the road for some time now. I am afraid that by the time they are finished with you ..." He trailed off leaving the statement hanging between them and stepped back, slowly folding his arms across his chest. She visibly paled, awarding him a sense of satisfaction in finally detecting her weakness. She quickly collected herself, but not before a moment of stark terror flickered in her eyes. Leaning back against his desk, he quietly studied her, curious as to her next reaction.

Lowering her eyes for the first time, her haughty stance visibly sagged. After a long pause, she looked directly at him, her emotions again in control, he noted approvingly.

"Colonel," she began tentatively, "why share me with your men?"

Eyes narrowed, he scrutinized her silently—annoyed. His own lack of immunity to the exhilarating energy between them was disconcerting.

"How long has it been since you were with a woman?" With a slight shrug her blouse shifted, exposing more of her breast.

He glanced momentarily at her perfect body; then lifted icy blue eyes to hers—assessing.

"There is passion to your anger, Colonel," she said softly. "Are you as passionate ... when you make love?" All bravado gone, her voice dropped to a whisper. As she searched his face, warmth purled low in her belly and her body began its final betrayal. Color washed across her cheeks with the quickening of her pulse, forcing her to take slow, even breaths—none of which went unnoticed.

Maintaining steely control had become difficult. His desire, which until now had been precariously held in cheque, continued to build—much to his physical discomfort.

"Colonel," her voice had a breathless edge. "Is your schedule so busy that you cannot allow yourself a few minutes of pleasure?"

A sardonic grin twisted his mouth as the last traces of her defiant facade crumbled. Within moments she would be pleading. The fleeting thought of somehow reaching the dirk and taking her life seemed a reasonable solution. "Colonel..." Her eyes changed, softened, earlier challenge replaced by conflicting emotions: anguish, desire ... confusion.

Abruptly he pulled her to him. Clutching the mass of curling hair at the nape of her neck, he forced her head back to stare into wide, green eyes that did not falter. His breath came in ragged bursts, his desire—obvious.

"You may regret your offer, madam, before we are through," he growled. His mouth closed over hers, hard and demanding as he encircled her in a crushing embrace. Begun as an act of control demanding submission, the kiss, in its infancy, lacked warmth or caring, but quickly changed as caressing lips met his willingly. She did not recoil as expected, startling him as she met his desire with an equal passion of her own.

The kiss intensified yet softened, evolving into an act of seeking, neither comprehending what ... or why. Both vulnerable from pasts which continued to haunt them, they sensed longing need in each other. Perhaps, somewhere amidst these exquisite sensations lay an answer.

Taken aback by the unexpected depth of their mutual attraction they paused, breathing erratic, eyeing each other warily, both clinging to a façade of indifference, yet craving more: neither one able to deny the unfathomable bond.

He eased his crushing embrace, searching her face as he gently stroked back tangled blonde curls. Reaching to encircle his neck her hand paused touching a tanned cheek, lingering in a soft caress. Eyes closed, she inhaled the scent of him: an intoxicating mixture of warm wool, leather, tang of male sweat and the hint of English lavender. The thudding of his heart against her breast echoed her own as heat and pleasure spiraled through her. His touch, his nearness filled an aching void—yet overwhelmed her.

Her breath wafted warm and sweet across his cheek in a sigh of inexorable hunger as she molded herself against him. He claimed her lips almost gently. But captured by the delicious taste, deepened the kiss as his strong, yet gentle hands caressed the length of her spine.

Expecting her to react as all others, intimidated and pleading for gentleness, her response left him awestruck. He had broken women in his past; she would not be the last—just one more. But that was before he had kissed her, before emotions long forgotten began to rekindle. She did not shrink from him. Meeting his passion with an unquenchable one of her own, she returned his possessive kiss fervently in a flash-fire of emotion which threatened to engulf her. *Proprieties be damned.* Right or wrong, she ached for him … wanted him. With uncontained desire, she arched hungrily to meet him. Tracing the palm of her hand slowly along his lean abdomen, she slipped questing fingers under tight breeches to caress his burgeoning arousal, drawing a gasp of pleasure—or surprise—she was unsure which.

Quickly shedding constrictive clothing, he forced her back onto blankets snatched from his cot and flung in a random heap, pinning her firmly beneath him. Bending close, he began tracing the fullness of her breasts creating molten paths, flicking his tongue to capture first one nipple and then the other. Slowly at first, then building feverishly, she became a willing captive to his exquisite tenderness. Gasps of pleasure burst unbidden, their shared passion: all consuming, wild, and uninhibited. But without warning he changed, efforts at gentleness abandoned as he took his pleasure callously. This was no longer an attempt at making love, merely a savage act of possession demanding submission. Startling him somewhat, she matched his rhythm in mutual need demanding satisfaction. She embraced her pain—an exquisite affirmation of being alive; she needed that. All in good time their mutual gratification brought both to shattering fulfillment: powerful, satisfying … complete.

Rolling aside, breathing heavily, body slick with sweat, he eyed her as she sat up and met his steely gaze. Locking eyes they appraised each other like wary animals, neither able, nor willing, to speak for the moment. Quirking an eyebrow he sneered, "Was that passion up to your standards, madam?" He inhaled deeply, eyeing her with icy reserve.

"Not bad for a first attempt." She shrugged noncommittally, refusing to be intimidated or forced to confess the truth.

He needed no confirmation. Both understood what had passed between them. She glanced away, hoping he would not humiliate her by forcing the issue. She maintained smug defiance, but was inwardly aghast at the feelings he had aroused.

Well aware of the pleasure she had experienced, he ignored her barb. Standing slowly, he eyed her with cool disdain. As he began to dress he turned and casually informed her, "I have business that requires my attention. However, I *will* take this matter up with you again later, madam."

"How chivalrous of you, Colonel," she said tartly. Casting a baleful glance in his direction, she began retrieving her clothes.

"You have five minutes to freshen yourself." He indicated a washbasin in the corner of the tent, and at her hesitation added, "I will avert my eyes, but be quick."

As she tucked in her shirt, he turned to watch. Turning away she proceeded to coil her long, honey-colored hair into a bun.

"Leave it down," he demanded, stepping towards her. Running his fingers through the long tendrils he studied her, amused by her irritated look. Abruptly pulling her close, he startled her with a firm kiss; rekindling warmth took her by surprise. But as quickly as it had begun, the kiss ended.

"Turn around," he ordered. Taking a short piece of rope, he bound her wrists behind her back. "Now, stay put." Picking up her boots, he headed for the tent entrance.

"Colonel ..."

Turning at the sound of her voice, he regarded her with cool interest.

"My boots, if you do not mind," she demanded, tilting her chin defiantly.

"But I *do* mind, madam." He paused for effect. "Without your boots you will not go far, nor at least not fast, should you decide to try something foolish." Angling his head, he arched an eyebrow. An amused expression washed over his face, and he had the unmitigated gall to grin.

Slow burning fury smoldered in her eyes as she faced him. With a chuckle, he shook his head and turned to leave. Looking back over his shoulder, his eyes fairly twinkled. "If looks could kill, madam, you would be halfway to freedom by now."

As he disappeared through the tent opening carrying her boots, she could see him still shaking his head in amusement.

He strode from his tent feeling somewhat confused. Besides her obvious appeal, she amused him. That was unusual. He had found absolutely nothing to amuse him since his arrival in this God-forsaken country several months earlier. Intolerable summer heat, over abundant insects, and the endless fetid swamps of these southern colonies were unbearable. Add to that his recent defeat at Fort Moultrie, SC, a loss which had failed to set well with headquarters, and ... As a matter of fact, he could not recall having smiled once since his arrival—not until today.

She watched through narrowed eyes as he ducked through the tent flap with her boots tucked snuggly under his arm. She stood where he had left her in the middle of the tent, fuming at his annoying cleverness. Turning slowly she scrutinized her surroundings, searching for possibilities of immediate escape. Without his constant supervision, she would eventually find a way to elude him, of that she was sure. However, at the moment her mind refused to focus. His lovemaking, albeit rough and demanding, made her feel more alive than she had in months. Her passion matched his. Beyond being an unnerving discovery, it was ... *confusing.*

Shaking her head to clear it of incongruous thoughts, she forced herself to concentrate on a means of escape. Slowly pacing the inside walls of the tent she attempted to formulate a plan. Nearing the opening, a picket standing at attention moved his hand ever so slightly, tightening his grip on the hilt of a sabre. *Not a pleasant way to die.* She moved back into the depths of her 'canvas prison', bleak thoughts filling her mind. The colonel, though arrogant, seemed not blinded by self-importance. He was vividly aware of events occurring around him, not missing the tiniest detail. Yes, he would be difficult to elude—a real challenge. Her mood lightened with that thought. She always enjoyed a challenge, invariably eager and more than able to take on any new adventure. Could she escape? *Absolutely: well, probably with effort.* At this point did she care? Again her spirits plummeted.

What had life become? For weeks she had ridden Beauty, her faithful mare and only companion, throughout South Carolina trying to forget angry parting words with her brother, Jamie. She missed him, missed his children and was unsure as to their whereabouts—or if they were still alive. What had become of her friend, Anna, and her former Cherokee family? And what of Soaring Eagle's resentment, she wondered with nagging discomfort. *Has he finally forgiven me?*

Should she seek death at the hands of the colonel? She had no misconception as to his ability to end her life with little more than momentary regret for the loss of a good bedmate; she had been that. If only she could be certain he would end it quickly and cleanly. *Stop this train of thought* she scolded. Weariness was defeating her ability to think clearly. Clumsily lowering herself to the floor, she leaned back against the colonel's desk. From that viewpoint, she could see some of the campsite through the open tent flap. Drawing her legs up, she rested her head on her knees and, despite the discomfort of trussed hands, fell asleep almost instantly.

The colonel found her still asleep when he returned much later with a plate of food. He started to rouse her but stopped. Her face was turned towards him relaxed in sleep, her cheek resting on her knee. He leaned against the edge of his desk studying her features. There was no denying her beauty: curling blonde lashes, high cheekbones and a delicate nose. But her lips—they caught and held his attention: full and sensuous. What was she doing alone in the wilderness, well armed and obviously self-sufficient? Such fiery spirit—so unlike any woman he had known. She did not shrink from his passion, her needs matching his, a fact which gave pause for thought. Yes, she piqued his interest.

Captivated by the mass of silky, golden curls tumbling about her shoulders, he moved to her side. Without thought, he reached to push a stray curl off her forehead, but quickly stopped himself, disconcerted by what he had been about to do. Although her passion was astounding, there was more than that, something deeper. *What is it about her?* He frowned in consternation.

A soft moan as she shifted with discomfort, snapped him back.

"Madam," he said firmly, startling her out of sleep.

Momentarily confused, her large, green eyes swept the tent anxiously, returning to rest on him.

Reaching down, he took her arm to assist her in rising.

"I can get up by myself," she snapped. Tucking her long legs in cross-legged fashion, she leaned forward and rose to her full height in one fluid motion, impressing him with her agility and strength.

Ignoring her, he proceeded lighting the oil lamps, delaying untying her wrists merely to see her reaction. Would she complain? But she watched in glowering silence. She would never admit the burning pain in her shoulders; she would not give him the satisfaction.

When he finally removed the rope her arms dropped limply to her sides. Shooting him a baleful look she turned away. Grimacing slightly, she allowed her stiffened limbs to loosen a bit before gingerly flexing sore shoulder muscles, hoping he would not notice her discomfort. But she did not fool him, impressing him yet again. She certainly was not one to complain.

Pulling a chair to the desk, he indicated the food. She continued to ignore him. Again he gestured towards the chair, more assertively this time. "Sit and eat," he ordered.

Grudgingly she sat down, eyeing him over her shoulder, anger bubbling just below the surface.

"Eat, madam." There was no mistaking the veiled threat in his tone.

Although extremely hungry, unable to remember when she had eaten last, she stubbornly hesitated, refusing to comply until ready. "What about you, Colonel?" she asked softly as she began picking idly at her plate, unwilling to give him the satisfaction of knowing how hungry she was.

"I ate with my dragoons. Is that a problem?" he replied curtly, and moved to the opposite side of the desk.

She shook her head, shrugging. "I find it feels impolite to eat in front of you." She ate slowly, casting furtive glances in his direction through curling lashes, trying to discern his next move. For there would be one; she was positive.

Reaching into his desk drawer, he withdrew a flask and small glass. Pouring himself a brandy, he lounged back sipping slowly, but within moments set the glass down with a soft thunk and stood. Placing both hands on the desk, he leaned forward bringing his face to within inches of hers. Warm breath, pleasantly scented with brandy, accosted her senses as he spoke. "I believe, madam, if I understood you correctly, I have been requested to improve my performance."

His words held sarcasm, but he was not truly angry. Rather than unleashing the cold fury for which he was well known, her game that afternoon had amused him. Rebel action had been almost non-existent for several weeks now, allowing the dragoons to enjoy a lengthy stay in their present encampment. Frayed nerves from long days in the saddle, and the arduous setting-up and breaking down of campsites had been eased, along with his chronic ill temper.

Sensing her forthcoming response to be caustic, he leaned closer and silenced her with a kiss, clamping his mouth fiercely over hers, taking her by surprise. Grasping her shoulders he continued the kiss, pausing just long enough to move around the desk and pull her up into his arms. Strong hands cupped her face as he deepened the kiss, his tongue meeting hers in a caress so seductive she could not resist—did not want to resist. Within moments she relented, all intention of remaining immune to his touch, abandoned.

This time it was more ... so very much more than their earlier union. With gentle experienced caresses, he robbed her of the ability to think coherently. Breathless and confused in the aftermath, she struggled to re-center and re-focus.

"Does that meet your expectations, madam?" he asked softly, gazing down into a face glowing with fulfillment.

"Better, sir," she gasped, wishing her pounding heart would return to normalcy.

Had any other woman made that remark, he would have been incensed. But passion-glazed eyes belied her words, all the answer he required. He had felt the instant she relinquished all control to him, a sensation which had brought exquisite pleasure—uniquely fulfilling, unlike any former experience. 'Fine ladies' in his past had been famous for their games of make believe, and he despised them for that. But not this one, she was forthright and honest in her needs, and he found that honesty refreshing.

As Kathryn drifted back to reality, it shocked her to realize her body took what it required, denying all she had been taught of propriety and etiquette. There was no time for self-recrimination at this point as he suddenly arose and systematically began collecting her clothes. Taking his time he carefully folded them, enjoying her curiosity and rising irritation. She watched in silence as he tucked them under the covers on his side of the bed, and then looked up with an engagingly cool smile.

"Sir …" She was perplexed. "You would leave me naked?"

"It would seem rather late to play shy with me now, madam." Again, she amused him, and he found the sensation quite pleasant.

"But it often gets cold at night." She glared angrily.

"Madam," his voice dripped with sarcasm, "I do believe I have proven my ability to warm you, have I not?" He paused, waiting for an answer he knew she would not give.

"But, sir …"

"Silence, madam," he snarled. "Else I will be forced to bind and gag you, hmm?" He arched a thick dark brow, a now familiar gesture annoying her further. As he settled himself beside her, she made a great show of turning her back and moving to the outermost edge of the bed.

"Come, now. I would not want you to be cold." With that statement, he pulled her forcefully to his side. "Besides, I rather enjoy the feel of your warm body against me." Patting her bottom, he placed his arm snuggly around her and immediately dropped off to sleep.

She lay awake for some time, annoyed with the fact that he could fall asleep so easily, then turned to wracking her brain for ways to escape. She must devise a plan … *soon*. The longer she remained in captivity, the more difficult it would be for a successful getaway. She recalled that after gathering her clothes, he had taken his pistol and placed it at the head of the bed. If she could just get to the pistol, perhaps she could force him to relinquish her clothes and release her. It was not a very good plan, but it was all she had. Feigning deep, even breathing, she waited until sure he was soundly asleep.

Turning towards him, she slowly raised herself on one elbow. Holding her breath, she reached across his chest. As her hand brushed the pistol his arm moved quickly, strong fingers clamping painfully around her wrist. *He must sleep with one eye open*, she grimaced at his unrelenting grip.

"Was there something you needed, madam?" he purred.

At her hesitation, he twisted her wrist sharply, causing her breath to catch. But she made no complaint, earning his grudging respect.

"No, sir," she ground out through gritted teeth, silently chiding herself for believing such a ridiculous plan could succeed against a man of his astute awareness.

"Then get some sleep, dawn comes early."

He lay with his lean body molding itself against her back, pulling her snugly against him so as to sense her every move. Maybe his loosely draped arm encircling her waist was not a sign of affection, but it still felt good. And *that* fact was rather unsettling. Escape would not be easy, perhaps not even possible. But all was not lost yet. She would bide her time, lull him into a false sense of security. *At that point I will ...*

Lying within his snug grip, she listened to his deep, even breathing. But despite exhaustion, it was some time before she could finally give in to sleep.

Chapter Two

Dangerous Diversion

The next morning she awoke feeling chilled, missing the warmth of his body. Dawn was breaking and he was already gone. Quickly donning her clothing, she looked down and shrugged; nothing could be done with the tattered blouse other than tucking it into her breeches. She briskly splashed fresh water onto her face and had just begun running fingers through her long hair, attempting to tame the unruly tangle, as he strode into the tent.

He looked her up and down, slowly appraising. "An early riser, I see." He nodded approvingly.

"Morning is the best part of the day," she answered softly.

He watched in silence as she continued to tug at her hair.

"If I might have a brush from my saddlebags this would be an easier task, sir."

Although succinctly polite, he noticed the hint of sarcasm. Moving to her side he stilled her hands, and with deft strokes smoothed the wild curls; then turning her, untangled the back.

She eyed him over her shoulder, startled, as his touch ignited renewed desire. Sensing her response, he raised a heavy mass of curls and pressed his lips against her neck, enjoying the warmth and smell of her—pleased with her reaction. *She feels it too*, he mused. *Yesterday was not a fluke.* From past experience, he had expected he would have to rouse her and wait, patiently if possible, while she dressed. However, this was not the case. She was not your 'usual' woman—far from it. Perhaps therein lay the reason she had piqued his interest from the moment he laid eyes on her. What an intriguing challenge: *to break her or …* Allowing that thought to drop he traced his lips along the rim of her ear, smiling as she trembled, enjoying the power he held over her.

Reaching up she pulled his head down, turning to claim his mouth passionately, as she slid her hand slowly down his muscled abdomen. He sucked in a sharp breath, his body instantly responding to her caressing touch, leaving him wondering who truly wielded the power. Women had caressed him before, some more satisfying than others, but none like this one. She touched a chord somewhere deep within, and he wanted her again … *her.*

This too will pass as all things do given time, he realized. *I will use her, enjoy the passion, and when tired of the game—will at that point determine her …* Having resolved the problem, he decided to be more pleasant, perhaps even charming. *After all, I learned from the very best—trained in the art of deception at my father's knee.* Refusing to drag up unpleasant memories, he focused on pleasing her. Her body spoke to him of untapped mysteries and limitless possibilities as he crushed her in a savage embrace—to which she responded fully: her arms encircling his neck, their lips meeting in a demanding kiss.

Stepping back, he cupped her face, observing with eyes so intense it took her breath away. Slowly slipping his hands inside her blouse he opened the front, sliding the fabric off her shoulders to drop in a bulky mass encircling her waist. As his lips brushed her throat, his fingers trailed sensuously across her breasts. Hands that could wield a sword with the power to cleave a man in two touched her as delicately as fluttering butterfly wings. He studied her face, pleased with his efforts, as her eyes slowly closed, her head lolling sideways. His lips, so demanding moments before, caressed upwards along the arched curve of her neck, reaching her ear where his tongue lingered and played. His strong arms encircled her as she swayed against him. With absolute control he seduced her, coaxed her, his practiced hand gradually building exquisite sensations unlike any she had experienced. Eventually relieved of her entangling blouse, she reached for him seeking release in shared need.

Bracing himself on one elbow, he stroked damp curls back from her forehead. Their eyes locked, both silent—both appraising—both disturbed at the intensity of feelings. Brushing his lips against hers he arose and faced her, unashamed of his nakedness. The glow of dawn's first rays entering through the open tent flap played across his muscular frame, making it difficult to tear her eyes away as he began dressing. Not wanting to incur curt words or break the peaceful mood, she followed his lead and dutifully tidied herself as best she could, curious as to what he had in store for the day.

"I will return shortly with your breakfast and another shirt." A grin played about his lips. Scanning her tousled, glowing appearance, unexpected warmth filled him—warmth he forcefully pushed aside; it confused him. "Do not go anywhere, madam, my men are just outside." He eyed her sharply, waiting for questions … or comments.

She nodded, meeting his gaze. He could have sworn he detected the slightest smile—perhaps an effect of the early morning light—but he thought not.

He returned shortly with coffee, a light breakfast, fresh water and a bundle tucked under his arm. "I took the liberty of going through your saddlebags," he said, placing clean clothes and her hairbrush on the desk. This considerate act, along with extended time allowed for privacy to attend personal needs, surprised and confused her.

She sat cross-legged on the floor of the tent, coffee mug grasped in both hands, inhaling the aroma. Strong, piping hot and delicious, she savored every sip.

Watching her enjoying her coffee, he was amused to discover that she was perfectly content where she sat. He could not think of another woman who would be remotely happy under these primitive circumstances. She was without guile, accepting and honest.

Observing him over the edge of her coffee, she found herself surprisingly content. *If this is to be my last day on earth, perhaps it is enough to have experienced this.*

"Where did you get the tomahawk?" His sharp question startled her from her reverie.

She eyed him with new respect. He could lose himself to the passion—for he was as consumed by it as she—but he also maintained focus on the duty at hand. She must not be lulled into a sense of false security by this man. He had not gained his reputation for nothing.

"That seems a simple enough question, hmm?" His features hardened.

"Why do you want to know? It seems of little importance." Inquisitive but not rude, she stood to face him, taking careful note of the imposing figure he presented—a man in control at all times.

"The importance of a question is not for your determination." He shot her a warning glance.

What could she tell him without revealing more than she wished to divulge? Her initials, carved into the blade in a lavish style, were difficult to read. Hopefully, he would not discern the last initial, for that could create a serious problem. "It belonged to a friend and was given to me as a gift," she said matter-of-factly.

A quick glance proved there was more to the story than that. Her face displayed feelings openly, her striking green eyes mirroring every thought. He doubted she could deceive effectively, but did he wish to force the issue? "Can you handle the weapon well?" He changed his approach, attempting to unsettle her.

She nodded, eyes meeting his commanding gaze without faltering.

"Rather an unusual talent for a woman, would you not agree?"

With just the slightest hint of insolence she said: "I have no idea what other women can or cannot do, sir."

God, she is feisty and so cool under questioning. His admiration increased. Someday he would put her to the test, determine her capabilities—but not today. Abruptly turning, he sat down at his desk and began to peruse a stack of papers; the interrogation over for the time being. "I have things to do. Settle yourself over there." With a sharp jerk of his chin, he indicated a far corner of the tent.

She did as told without comment, surprised by his quick change of attitude. She sat quietly watching him until boredom overtook her. Then, pulling her legs up tightly and resting her forehead against her knees, she dozed.

Her quiet presence made it difficult to focus on paperwork, an irritating fact. Clenching his fist, he grabbed the top document, shut her forcefully from his mind and began to read.

Kathryn awoke to an empty tent. Standing slowly, she stretched to relieve cramped muscles. With the tent flap tied back, guards were highly visible. There was no question as to where he expected to find her upon his return. She paced the length of the tent slowly, back and forth—back and forth. In time, an officer approached with a plate of food, a man she recognized as one of her captors. He was tall, well muscled and quite good-looking, but quiet.

Entering the tent, he went directly to the desk and set her food down. "Colonel Tarrington will return later, Miss Cameron." He was curt but not impolite.

"I did not get your name, Lieutenant." His uniform indicated him to be the colonel's lieutenant-at-arms—or whatever the English called them. *If I can entice him to talk about the dragoon's camp life, he might inadvertently divulge something useful in planning my escape.* However, he was non-communicative, ignoring all attempts at conversation, most likely needing the colonel's permission to speak. She neither knew nor cared—he thoroughly annoyed her.

She ate slowly leaning propped against the desk, watching the goings on of the encampment from within her limited view. The atmosphere amongst the men appeared relaxed; some busy cleaning weapons while others lounged under nearby trees engaging in idle conversation. A small group of dragoons rode by, their prancing horses kicking up dust. Apprehension nagged as the image of her little mare sprang to mind. *I do hope my Beauty is being well cared for, but that too is beyond my ability to control.* She shook her head, disheartened.

"Damn it," she muttered, her thoughts turning to an honest appraisal of her situation. *This cannot last, but I see no easy escape. The encampment is well secured, and the constant coming and going of dragoons makes it difficult for any unobserved moves.* She released a long sigh—the beginning of resignation, perhaps?

It was the end of one more interminably long day. Their evening meal over, she stalled taking great pains brushing her hair and washing her face. The colonel, annoyed with her dawdling, moved to the bed. Standing in silence, he loosened his jabot and stripped off his shirt. Glancing at his muscular frame, clad only in boots and black breeches, creeping warmth began coiling low in her belly.

"Madam ..." He nodded towards the bed in a wordless, insistent command.

"You have all the charm of a snake," she quipped, glowering at him.

"Perhaps," he stated coldly, "but I might remind you, a snake who controls your fate. Tread lightly," he paused for emphasis. "Do not try my patience."

Narrowing angry green eyes, she stubbornly stood her ground as he again indicated the bed.

"If I recall correctly, this was *your* bargain. Do you wish to reconsider your offer, madam?" His icy blue gaze impaled her unnervingly.

Removing pins from her hair, she shook it out allowing curls to fall in a golden tangle. "No, sir," she sighed. "Once given, I never default on a bargain, or words stated in promise." Stepping out of her breeches, she dropped them on the desk and moved towards him. She stood before him searching his face for several moments then stripped her blouse off to drop at her feet.

He studied her openly—wordlessly. Abruptly reaching out, he pulled her forcefully against him. She had gone to him grudgingly, but when he touched her all anger was forgotten, her traitorous body relinquishing itself to his seduction. She claimed his mouth, relishing the hint of brandy as his tongue caressed, finding her an eager partner.

Just who is in command on this battlefield? Amidst the heat of passion that thought flickered, but he no longer found it of importance.

Each day passed much the same as the previous one—time rapidly moving on. Some mornings she awoke to an empty bed; others he lingered before bringing coffee and breakfast. He would then sit watching her eat, making occasional conversation before disappearing for the day—always tying her hands loosely in front of her. His cleverness irked her. He secured the knots on the inner side of her wrists making it almost impossible to untie with her teeth. She gathered that to be an act of consideration on his part: the manner in which she was trussed causing little discomfort.

Her life took on a predictable pattern, verbal sparring comprising a good part of it. At times his anger flared, barely held in control. He had yet to do any physical harm, but she did not rule out the possibility. As time passed, she realized she truly enjoyed his companionship.

The lieutenant always brought her midday meals and upon occasion, fresh coffee in the afternoon. Their talking amounted to small talk initiated by her. Though hoping to gather helpful information, she desperately needed to ease the deadly boredom. Continued inactivity weighed heavily. Endless hours of pacing, dozing fitfully or watching the dragoons from her limited viewpoint provided meager respite. In time she found herself eagerly awaiting what moments the lieutenant shared with her—enjoying the meager friendship he might offer.

In truth, although it annoyed her, as time passed she began anticipating the limited hours spent with the colonel. Often during daylight hours he passed their tent sitting ramrod-straight astride a high-strung black stallion, riding out with a large number of dragoons. Were they scouting and encountering rebels? Was Jamie alive and traveling with the colonials? She had so many questions, yet no answers; he refused to discuss his whereabouts or duties, sharing nothing more than bits of chit-chat; at least it served as communication.

This particular night, after finishing a quiet meal, she casually inquired about her mare and then worked the conversation into subtle questions about his day. Skirting her queries he turned to questioning her, and she evaded likewise, a game of sorts: at least a form of companionship.

After finishing his brandy, he began preparing for his nightly ritual. She sat regarding him coldly, making no move to undress and join him. She was not in the mood to give in graciously tonight.

"Madam, I would act more eager to come to my bed if I were you." His eyes narrowed threateningly. It had been a long day and he was not about to put up with her choler.

Rising slowly, she straightened her shoulders, planted hands firmly on her hips and returned his steely gaze. "My bargain did not specify eagerness or enjoying—only willingness to comply," she snapped.

Eyes flashing, he rested his palm over the ever-present pistol on his desk—a silent warning.

"Kill me if you like, that is your prerogative." Her acid tone earned a malevolent stare. They locked eyes, both furious. "You might consider proving yourself worthy of—eagerness on my part." She flung the challenge, and for the briefest moment thought he would strike her.

He stepped closer breathing heavily, as she stubbornly stood her ground. Suddenly realizing her game, well aware of the uninhibited passion he instilled in her, he took deep breaths, calming himself—then forced a smile. "Worthy, hmm?" His grin widened. Pulling her into a crushing embrace he claimed her mouth fiercely, yet within moments eased his hold and leaned back.

"That, madam, is to get your attention. Now let me see what I can do about the *'worthy'* part of your complaint." His kiss was deep, lingering—his lips coaxing, enticing. His hands caressed so gently, her thoughts began to shred and tumble crazily. *What is happening? Is this an answer or…?* Painful memories flooded back: bitter words with her brother—and the death of Black Raven.

Brushing his lips along the rim of her ear, he meandered lower tracing the slender arch of her neck, across her collarbone, and outward to her shoulder … where he nipped gently. It was then that all ability to formulate thoughts ceased as she surrendered, giving herself to him completely. *Worthy … so very worthy,* her last cognizant thought as she relinquished her mind and body to him.

Chapter Three

Seeds of Change

Each morning as he prepared to leave, she donned her greatcoat before he tied her wrists. He was unsure why the coat was of comfort, but found it harmless if she insisted. She had made no further attempts at escape, but she would; it was merely a game of 'biding time'. He continued tying her hands, keeping the bindings loose to ease any discomfort. After all this time, why did he still perform this ritual? The answer eluded him—perhaps only a subtle reminder of his ultimate control.

The weather had been cooler than usual, the midday temperature in the tent bearable. But in the past day or two a sultry heat had settled in, bringing with it hazy humidity—so typical of the South.

"I would not wear my coat, madam; the cicadas annoying din promises midday heat."

"I am fine, sir, but thank you for your consideration."

"Well then, enjoy your day." Smiling tightly he turned to leave. She had been warned.

By midday the heat and oppressive humidity had become unbearable. Even sitting under the shade of trees, the dragoons found it necessary to unbutton their woolen jackets, breaking from formality. The colonel paused in drinking from a shared jug of water being passed among them, his eye catching the lieutenant's. Seeing his uneasiness, sure of the reason, he signaled to him. "Put together some food and water, Lieutenant. I will check on our prisoner."

The heat was beyond bearing. *Why did I assert myself in such a stupid way?* At first she paced—as always. But as the day progressed, stifling heat exacted its toll. Perspiration rolled freely down her face and neck soaking her shirt, causing it to cling uncomfortably. Dizziness overwhelmed her, the throbbing of her head matching each pulse of her heart. Bile rose at the back of her throat as weakness drove her stumbling towards his desk. Dropping her forehead onto her trussed wrists, she clung to the edge for support. "Thirsty … so very thirsty … should have listened …" she mumbled.

He entered the tent and finding her slumped over his desk strode to her side, quickly setting the food down. He placed a hand against her perspiring forehead, disconcerted by her lack of response. Grabbing a basin of water and towel from the far corner of the tent, he returned to her side, glad for his lieutenant's efficiency. Pulling the chair close, he eased her into it. She was barely aware as her wrist restraints were removed, quickly followed by her coat being slipped from her shoulders and flung forcefully aside.

Crouching down, he pulled her against him. Brushing aside saturated curls, he soaked the towel and bathed her face repeatedly attempting to lower the cascading waves of heat. Refreshing the towel, he sponged her neck, sliding his hand under her clinging shirt, splashing cooling water liberally. She moaned softly, head lolling weakly against him as she began to rouse.

"You are a stubborn one, I give you that." His voice was not unkind.

Barely focused green eyes gazed up into his concerned face as he set the cloth aside and pressed a cup of water to her lips. She struggled to sit upright, grasping the cup in trembling hands and gulping water.

"Not so fast," he cautioned, pulling the cup away, "you will be sick." He paused, forcing her to wait before putting the cup to her lips. "Slowly, hmm?"

That chastising *'look'* of his; she grimaced at his arched brow, grateful he was there—*'look'* or no.

"Oh, God, I feel awful," she gasped. "I think I am going to ..."

"Put your head between your knees and take slow, deep breaths," he instructed. Gently rubbing her back in comforting circles, he guided her head.

Eventually struggling upright, she studied him thoughtfully. "I should have listened, sir."

He smiled, pushing the plate of food towards her. "Eat, you will feel better in a few minutes."

As she picked up a piece of bread and took a small bite, he paid careful attention to her appearance. Pausing in chewing, she offered a piece to him. Shaking his head, he gently chided. "You really do have a problem with eating in front of me."

She shrugged, slightly embarrassed. But within a few more minutes, as he had said, she did feel better. "Thank you, sir," she said gratefully; well aware how serious the outcome could have been, if he had not checked on her when he did. As he stood to leave, she held her arms out obediently.

"No more ropes. Come sit outside under the trees where it is cooler." She took his offered arm, allowing him to steady her. After a long pause he turned to her. "Tonight, I think you might relish a bath, madam."

Her eyes lit up at the suggestion, his offer too good to be true. After all the days of washing her long hair and maintaining a modicum of cleanliness with only a bucket of water, a real bath would feel wonderful. How long had it been? A week—perhaps two—no, longer; she wanted that bath.

"There is a small stream nearby," he said quietly. "It looks to be a nice night. I thought we might take a walk ..." He left his thought unfinished.

His warmth created a twinge of guilt as *escape* immediately crossed her mind. He had been concerned by her earlier distress, relaxing his guard. The timing was right. *Tonight I will make my try.*

A few dragoons in the immediate area watched with interest as the colonel bid her sit under nearby trees. Leaving a canteen of water, he advised she continue sipping slowly and returned to sit with his men. Despite her lingering pallor, she seemed to be recovering rapidly. The lieutenant took note and was pleased. He found himself quite drawn to her, in spite of all good intentions. He liked this bold, young woman.

She leaned against a tree, relaxing and continuing to sip water. But as she felt more like herself, she became anxious. She stood and began pacing in small circles, until a look from the colonel advised her to sit. Crouching, she picked up a stick and began drawing in the dirt. As she searched her immediate vicinity seeking sticks to vary the thickness of lines, she found one which appealed in a different way. She remembered how Jamie had taught her to flip a knife, catching it between thumb and forefinger, always making her practice with sticks until she became proficient. Balancing the newfound stick in her hand, she tested it for weight. A quick flick of her wrist brought it in a perfect arc ending caught between two fingers. She had not lost her touch. She continued flipping the stick with deadly accuracy—never missing.

The colonel sat quietly observing this display, her sense of balance and timing absolutely perfect. He doubted she reserved this talent for sticks only and was impressed. Well aware his men were watching her with increasing interest, he decided to end her little display. Rising slowly, he excused himself. He moved to her side and stood quietly as she flipped the stick again. Although intensely aware of his proximity, she never lost focus, easily catching the stick between thumb and forefinger.

"Time to have a drink, madam." Surprised by his suggestion, she tossed the stick aside.

"I thought I might join you for dinner tonight. Do you have any objections?"

"None, sir." Her mind worked rapidly. *What is this new game? Tonight is the night.* That was all there was to it; she would make her try at escape—*tonight.*

"You have excellent timing and balance," he complimented, passing her a glass of brandy.

She paused before taking the offered drink, eyeing him inquisitively.

"You earned it," he said, pursing his lips slightly in thought.

She was not sure if he was referring to her heat prostration or display of dexterity but would not ask. She had no wish to soften her feelings—not with what she had in mind for tonight.

The lieutenant announced himself shortly, arriving with their evening meal. After setting the plates on the desk, he stayed long enough to talk quietly at the tent opening with the colonel. Then, with clipped acknowledgment to his superior officer, inclined his head with a tight smile and left.

She remained quiet as they ate, speculating about his conversation with the lieutenant—that try as she might—had been unable to overhear. Positive that her trip to the stream had been discussed, she became concerned. Their collaboration could create a problem, but she would try anyway.

"I thought you preferred not to eat alone," he commented drily.

"That is true, sir." She smiled pleasantly.

"You are quiet, madam. As I am trying to fulfill your request, I thought you might be more talkative."

"I am pleased with your effort, Colonel, but perhaps not feeling my best tonight." She hoped a bit of sympathy might act as diversion.

However, he recognized her 'quiet' for exactly what it was. She would make her try at escape; of that he was sure. *She is working things out in that pretty head of hers*—a fact which amused him. *She will not give in gracefully, nor will she quit without another try. Well, we shall just see about that.*

Making an attempt at conversation, she asked, "How is Beauty, sir? Is she eating well? Have you given her the sugar cubes yet?"

"I did just yesterday."

"But I gave them to you two days ago with instructions…" she trailed off as his eyebrow rose reproachfully and softened her statement. "With the request that you please …"

"That sounds better, madam." He smiled agreeably, taking pleasure in watching her try not to anger him. After a long pause, allowing her to 'stew' a bit, he rose from his chair. "Are you feeling up to taking a walk to the stream—and a bath?"

"Yes, that is exactly what I need." She smiled prettily and slowly stood, hoping not to appear overly anxious.

Picking up a bar of soap and a towel he ushered her from the tent, nodding at his lieutenant as they headed for the stream. She knew the stream he mentioned from having traveled throughout this area many times. It meandered in the open for a short distance and then disappeared into a small wooded area with a heavy covering of low brush. *If I am careful, this should work perfectly.*

As they walked in silence, he studied her closely. Her mind had not stopped working since he had made the offer. Completely wrapped in her thoughts, she failed to notice his close scrutiny.

Depositing her at the edge of the stream he smiled, disarming her slightly. "You have fifteen minutes of privacy, milady. Do not try anything foolish as I will be nearby."

She bathed quickly luxuriating in the soaps clean smell as it clung to her damp curls, then washed her shirt and pants, donning them as rapidly as possible. They hung like sodden lumps from her wet frame, but she paid that no mind; she felt clean and refreshed once again. Wading downstream while toweling her hair, she picked her way carefully amongst the sharp stones wishing she had her boots. She slogged along for some distance until sure she could reach the woods undetected. Having wasted no time in bathing, she assumed there should be several minutes before he checked on her.

As she gingerly climbed the small embankment near the woods, so close to freedom she could almost taste it, the metallic click of a pistol hammer cocking stopped her in her tracks. Looking up, a pair of black boots came into view at eye level. Continuing her gaze upwards, she eyed a pair of long, lean legs, and a little higher—a pistol aimed directly at her.

"Going somewhere, madam?" He cocked an eyebrow as the corners of his mouth lifted in a grin; her heart sank. She eyed him angrily as he scolded her like a child. "I am truly disappointed in you, madam. I believe we had a bargain struck on … *your word*." He stressed the last, remembering those words.

Calf deep in water, she drew herself up to her full height. Beyond furious, she thumped balled fists on her hips and spat: "If I give my word, sir, I am completely trustworthy." She glared at him. "I never said I would not try to escape."

"Ahh, I see." His eyes sparkled with amusement as he reached down and grabbed her under the arm, pulling her up the embankment to stand before him. "I stand corrected, madam." He paused, his eyes holding hers. "Shall we exact that specific promise so we may enjoy the rest of the evening?"

She was incredibly beautiful: her face glistening with sparkling droplets of water, wet curls lying tangled about her shoulders and her blouse—clinging to her stunning body. He wanted her desperately. Holstering his pistol, ignoring her angry glare, he gently cupped her breasts, his thumbs teasing. Inhaling sharply, she swayed, her eyes changing … softening. Moving closer, he caressed gently, bending to brush his lips the length of her neck as she began surrendering to the promise of passion. His body pressed close and hardened in arousal, kindled a fire threatening to engulf her.

Tracing a heated trail along her throat he paused at her ear. "Do I have that promise we mentioned … from you?" Breathing escalating, he spoke haltingly. "Do I have that promise?" He pressured, nuzzling insistently.

"Yes … yes," she ground out breathlessly.

"Say it," he demanded.

His touch, incredibly enticing and gentle, caused a rapid relinquishing of sanity to the demands of her body. She could not resist … *did not want to resist.* Gazing into his unyielding blue eyes, she knew: despite aching need, he required—no, demanded—an answer.

"Yes, damn you, I will not … try to … escape." Her words tumbled out barely coherent. "I promise." He had won. She was his—and they both knew it.

Deny all you want, milady, but your beautiful eyes mirror your very soul. With a barely discernible nod of satisfaction, he swept her into his arms and strode towards his tent.

Over coffee the next morning she chastised him. "That was not playing fair last night."

At his feigned look of innocence she added, "You know what I mean. To exact such a promise under those conditions was unfair."

He found her umbrage amusing. "That may be true, madam." His face suddenly became serious. "But life is not always fair, is it?"

"No," she answered simply.

They sat assessing each other, both aware that they could answer from personal experience in that area.

"Do you wish to retract that promise?" he asked softly.

"You know I cannot do that, I have given my word." His question annoyed her. "But what if the situation had been different and it was *I*, who demanded that promise from you? What would you have done?"

So incredibly bold, so little that frightens her—an unusual woman. The corners of his eyes crinkled as he answered quite honestly. "Under those same set of circumstances, I would have done exactly as you." Moving to her side, he bent and kissed the top of her head. "You smell delicious, madam. I wish I had more time to …"

"But you do not," she said tartly eyeing him with annoyance, still irked by the way he had extracted her promise—although she had to admit it was quite clever.

"But, unfortunately, I do not." He brushed a chaste kiss to her forehead. "However, tonight is a different matter, madam." He started for the tent flap.

"You are not going to tie my wrists or take my boots?"

"That will no longer be necessary, milady. You have given your word." With that statement and a brilliant smile, he exited the tent leaving her fuming.

Although the day promised not to be as hot as the previous one, she decided her coat really was unnecessary. She paced—she brushed her hair—she paced. Lack of activity was becoming intolerable. As the heat rose within the tent, she ventured outside. The lieutenant greeted her, asking if she needed anything.

"May I see my horse, sir?"

Her beautiful, green eyes were mesmerizing, causing him to hesitate before answering. "I believe the colonel would prefer you stay near the tent, Miss Cameron," he hedged. But at her obvious disappointment added, "I will mention your request when he returns."

Where has he gone now? The campsite had been quiet, or seemed so from her limited viewpoint. No sizable interaction with the rebels had occurred. What was going on and how much longer would they be in this encampment? News of angry differences between the colonies and England had been sketchy before her capture; but now she was completely shielded from all input.

"Might I at least stay outside, sir?" There was no use arguing with the lieutenant, he had his orders. At his nod, she settled herself beside the tent and smiled. Of late, he had become more relaxed. They conversed with comparative ease, on quickly broadening subject matter. He helped make the long days pass more quickly; it was time to attempt building a friendship of sorts.

Shortly before dusk as she tidied for supper, the hoof beats of several horses announced the colonel's return. Within a few minutes he strode in, and after tossing his helmet and gloves onto the desk, turned to appraise her. He was dusty from the ride but seemed in good humor. Eyeing her freshly brushed hair coiling about her shoulders, he began slowly unbuttoning the numerous buttons on his red jacket. "Your day was pleasant, I trust." His eyes held a hint of humor.

She stood with hands on hips, flashing an irritated look—still upset with him.

Before she could formulate a tart retort the lieutenant arrived with their supper.

"Well, a good meal should improve your sense of humor, madam."

Inclining his head in dismissal to his officer, he sat down at his desk indicating for her to join him. He ate with relish, hungry from his long day on horseback. Glancing at her from time to time as she picked at the food he was amused. *Such stubbornness; she acts as if she is doing me a favor to eat.*

Putting his fork down, he leaned back in his chair. "Is the food unacceptable, madam?"

"Your cook could use some helpful hints, but it will do."

Giving in gracefully was not part of her nature—and that amused him. "And what hints might those be?" he asked, actually interested. He found her feisty spirit admirable in the face of an uncertain future. He would play her game.

Having cooked meals over a campfire most of her life, his question had opened a door into one of her areas of expertise. Without hesitation she began talking in animated fashion, describing preparation and cooking of wild game, and the correct herbs for seasoning. Deeply immersed in this comfortable subject, she moved to another area of expertise—making snares and trapping game. Suddenly realizing she had become lost in her own private world, she shut her mouth mid-sentence and returned to eating her meal.

He watched in fascination, pleased to see animation and excitement wash across her features. *She glows, absolutely glows.* He waited a few minutes, studying this enigmatic woman—so child-like in many ways—and realized he wanted to hear more. Her voice was pleasing and unpretentious. He could not recall a time when he had dined with anyone, be it man or woman, without talking military matters—this conversation was refreshing. "You like to hunt?" He nudged.

Is he making fun of me? She eyed him cautiously but seeing genuine interest, nodded slowly. "I like fishing, also."

"Are you going to tell me about that?"

At the shake of her head he raised a questioning eyebrow. Reaching into his desk drawer he brought out two glasses and a bottle of brandy. Filling both glasses, he pushed one towards her and began sipping his own.

"And why will you not talk about hunting or fishing?" He eyed her, waiting for an answer as he moved to sit on the corner of the desk. Setting his glass down, he removed his jacket and tossed it on the cot. He continued to sit there sipping his brandy; well aware he was sending a silent promise.

She watched him, unable to draw her eyes away, enjoying the play of firm muscles rippling under the thin material of his shirt as he moved.

"Hmm?" He interrupted her silence, pleased to notice her eyes following him.

"Tomorrow," she said softly, almost shyly. Her eyes were green, an indescribable green in the lantern light as she looked up smiling. "Could we go for a walk?" Her question caught him off guard. "I hear the wind blowing softly in the trees and the moon is full and ..." Her eyes were pleading.

He searched her face for only a moment before pulling her up into his arms. As they stepped out into the cool night air, she gazed up at the sky, breathing deeply of the windborne aromas. "There's the North star," she said softly as she pointed, "ever constant." She grinned, eyes asparkle.

"Where do you have in mind to walk?"

"May I see my little mare, sir?"

Placing a hand in the middle of her back, he guided her towards the holding area. As she neared the horses her soft whistle brought an answering whinny. Seeing Beauty, she broke from the colonel and ran ahead. Throwing her arms around the animal's neck, she clung to her crooning lovingly, and at her insistent nuzzling, laughed. "I did not forget you, Beauty, my spoiled little girl."

He watched as she pulled a sugar cube from her pocket and offered it to the eager animal, fascinated by their shared devotion.

"Perhaps, if we behave, the colonel will allow us to go riding someday." She nuzzled Beauty's velvety nose, knuckling her forehead, continuing to speak quietly.

"She's a fine looking animal," he commented as he stroked the mare's neck, causing her to flatten her ears.

"Behave," Kathryn snapped, and Beauty's ears perked upright—thoroughly amusing him.

Placing an arm about her shoulder, he headed her towards a small group of trees at the far end of the encampment. "Feeling better about your mare?" he asked softly as he leaned back against a tree enjoying her quiet presence, studying her profile as she gazed up at the star-filled sky.

Eyeing him over her shoulder, face aglow in the moonlight, she nodded happily.

"We will go riding if you like."

She turned quickly, not sure if she had heard correctly.

"Soon," he added softly.

Growing affection moved her to his side. His body exuded welcoming warmth and felt good in the chilly night air. A sudden gust of wind rustled the leaves overhead and sent a shiver across her shoulders. Pulling her into his warmth, he held her close. Tentatively placing her hand against the middle of his back, she caressed lightly. They stood this way for several minutes watching the sky, enjoying each other's comforting touch.

"Let us not have you chilled, madam," he said, breaking the mood and heading towards the tent.

Stopping abruptly she faced him and asked, "How did you know last night, sir? Her foiled escape attempt still confounded her, though she was no longer angry.

With that question his smile widened. "Your incredible eyes mirror your every thought. If ever I need question your motive, I will watch your eyes." Lifting a hand to her face, he traced a finger gently along the edge of her cheek. "Come now, it is late." With a quick hug, he guided her back towards their quarters.

Much later that night, lying beside him as he slept, she was deeply content, yet confused by her feelings. He had been considerate, actually kind tonight. *What are these emotions I seem unable to control?* As she drifted into sleep her final thoughts were of him. *He disarms me with a look, and his touch ... his touch.* He had been easier to deal with in the beginning ... when she thought she hated him.

Before leaving at dawn the next morning he tarried longer, enjoying her presence. As he bent to exit the tent he turned and smiled, intense warmth radiating for a brief unguarded moment. "Enjoy your day, madam. I will return early."

Watching his imposing figure stride proudly towards the corral she felt a sense of pride. Yes, oddly enough … pride.

Lieutenant Jackson, she finally knew his name, arrived shortly and with breakfast the day proceeded like every other day since her capture. But it was all about to change.

She wished she could brew some willow bark tea to ease the dull ache that had settled across her temples. It was late afternoon of another interminably long day as she sat cross-legged beside his desk staring glumly at the floor. Suddenly a pair of black boots stepped into her peripheral vision. Grimacing from the nagging pain, she looked up to see him standing there observing her silently, irritation apparent.

"Are you ill?" he asked.

"Just a headache." She rubbed her forehead willing the pain to go away.

He walked to his desk, and pulling a flask from his drawer held it out. "Sip some brandy, it may relax you." Annoyance bristled in his tone.

"No thank you." Standing up slowly, she turned and moved away from the desk.

Shrugging, he sat down and began rifling through papers. Quiet and distant, he apparently had important matters on his mind. His moods, so changeable and contrary at times, confounded her.

Looking up abruptly, he gave a sharp jab of his chiseled chin towards the far side of the tent, indicating: sit there and be quiet. She did as instructed, but within minutes stood and began pacing.

"Sit," he demanded.

She tried again to do as ordered. But she had spent hours sitting all day, every day. Her head ached, and his irritability failed to help the situation. She had never been one to stay put for long, pent up energies always demanding some form of release. Frustration building, she stood and began pacing in a distracted fashion.

"I told you to sit. I am trying to concentrate." His voice held a raw edge as he touched the ever present pistol lying on his desk.

Sure he would never use that on her, she was unconcerned. "Colonel, I am unused to long hours of inactivity. I have endured many weeks of exactly that and …"

He angled his head towards the corner of the tent, narrowing his eyes threateningly. Obediently she sat down once again, but was soon fidgeting.

"Madam, can you read?" He was thoroughly irritated with her interruptions.

"Of course," she retorted angrily.

With that, he pulled a small book from his desk drawer and flipped it to her. She caught it neatly, and upon reading the title her face wreathed in smiles, headache all but forgotten. "Poetry by James Beattie," she breathed with reverence. "*The Minstrel* is one of my favorites—and *you* have his works?" She could not suppress her surprise. "But he is considered to be a romantic poet."

He regarded her thoughtfully ignoring the barb. Pallor gone, her face visibly glowed with happiness. Once again it stunned him how little it had taken to please her.

"You thought me totally unfeeling, madam?" A smile played at the corners of his mouth.

"Not at all, sir—merely surprised and pleased." This was a considerate gesture and she had not meant to sound insulting. However, she did find it highly unusual for a colonel in the British Green Dragoons to enjoy reading poetry so much, that he had brought the book with him when he came to the colonies to fight a war.

"Then perhaps you will also enjoy James MacPherson's translations from the ancient bard Ossian. Maybe your days will not seem so interminably long if you have a diversion."

"Oh, yes, thank you." She began thumbing through the pages carefully. "*Fingal,* this is the poem which has caught the attention of King George, if memory serves me correctly." Her innocent enthusiasm was captivating.

"I see you are well-read," he said, sounding surprised and impressed with her literary knowledge.

Glancing up from the page she was reading she narrowed her eyes—thoroughly irritated. "If you think all colonials are ignorant and unread, sir," she stated curtly, "you have much to learn." With a dismissive shrug she turned to the book, leaving him suspecting she was absolutely correct.

He went back to his paperwork but found it difficult to refocus. With each insight into her personality, he became more interested in the fascinating puzzle she presented. His mind was not truly on the matters at hand; he had a serious choice to make … and soon.

As dusk fell the lieutenant brought supper. She had been reading avidly but set the poetry book down to greet the officer. He nodded in response to her bright greeting, noting her animated expression and subtle overall changes. "Enjoy your meal, sir—milady." He placed their plates on the desk and bid them 'good evening', heading out to join the dragoons around the evening campfire.

Lieutenant Jackson walked away from the tent somewhat disconcerted. He was unsure how he felt about this situation with the girl, curious as to how long it might last. Although she had been here for many weeks, that fact in itself unusual, he had no desire to know her better or perhaps come to truly like her if she was only temporary entertainment for the colonel. However, despite his vow to remain aloof, he found himself enjoying her company more each day—actually looking forward to the time they spent in quiet conversation during lunch. Making a soft sound at the back of his throat, he shook his head. *I guess it will all sort itself out in time.*

Flowing eagerly into the colonel's arms after dinner, she smiled as he gently cupped her face before kissing her. She was passionate, anxious to please: their night, one of ardent giving and taking which left both sated and deeply content.

With each kindness he showed she responded with new softness, pleasing him immensely. He reveled in the comforting feel of her beside him, lying contentedly in his arms. Since her arrival, long forgotten feelings had begun to reawaken—surprising him. He had never known another woman who seemed less concerned and so at ease with primitive living conditions. She actually enjoyed his lifestyle when he was treating her kindly. A complex, interesting creature, she was beginning to get under his skin. His growing feelings were disturbing, yet felt right—the endless numbing emptiness which had engulfed him for so long slowly receding as his caring deepened.

He knew nothing of her life, her family or ties to this looming war. Yet, none of that would be relevant if he could come to trust her. Could he risk that? She seemed to want that conviction from him too—that and more. They answered a profound need in each other, a fact of which they were both aware. Hugging her close, he pressed a kiss to her forehead and slowly relaxed into sleep.

Lying within his arms, lulled by the comforting rhythm of his heart pulsing against her cheek, she felt complete and safe—a fascinating enigma. At times anger pushed him to the brink of violence, yet his gentle consideration often brought tears to her eyes. He was proud and arrogant, though she sensed that to be more a protective façade hiding deep inner hurt. From the moment they met, an invisible bond had drawn them to each other like magnets unable to resist. Although they had both fought these feelings, neither could deny them now. Like it or not, the incredible bond existed.

At times he appeared on the verge of reaching out and offering more, but quickly shied away, suddenly afraid. Afraid of what? Entering into a commitment, daring to entrust the safekeeping of your heart to another? There was much she wanted to know about him. *He has been hurt ... as have I. We share common ground, of that, I am sure.*

As she drifted into sleep, she snuggled against him pressing her lips to his chest in a soft kiss ... and he smiled.

Chapter Four

Desperate Plea

For the next several days Kathryn spent endless hours reading, thoroughly enjoying MacPherson's and Beattie's literary works, but of greater importance, examining her feelings. She would make a commitment to this man if he would only ask. Decidedly an irrational decision, but after months of searching for something … *anything* … to ease her inner ache, perhaps she had found it. Was it purely lust, or the meager beginnings of a meaningful relationship? An unfathomable connection held them *both* captive, but … With him, there would be passion beyond her wildest expectations; excitement, danger and adventure: elements which equally appealed to her independent and, at times, wild nature. Time would tell, but for her that was rapidly running out.

She had come to grips with her inability to escape long before he exacted her promise; but how could there be a future? Comforting possibilities seemed almost believable when drifting in the aftermath of lovemaking—but in the harsh reality of dawn's breaking rays? He was as obsessed with 'their game' as she, but how much longer could it last? As a colonel in the Green Dragoons, could he justify a rebel companion and continue his career? Doubtful—but how would he rid himself of the entanglement? She was sure that after all this time, throwing her to his men would not be an option. Could he bring himself to kill her? If so, how would it be accomplished? Dying did not upset her, only the method of getting there. These tumbling, nonstop thoughts slowly dashed all optimism, driving her deeper into depression.

Kathryn lowered herself to the floor beside his desk. Pulling her knees up, she stared bleakly out the tent opening, attempting to focus on the organized buzz of the encampment. A willful tear rolled down her cheek; quickly swiped aside with her sleeve. But another followed … then another. *I am lost … lost.* Uncontrollable sobs racked her body as she buried her face against her knees.

Much to his chagrin, she had become increasingly silent—withdrawn. It struck him how much he looked forward to her lively dinner conversation. Although occasionally feisty, she tempered those qualities to suit his mood. During their time together she had slowly opened up to him, sharing small glimpses into her life. She was independent, intelligent, and honest—and he missed all that.

In an attempt to elevate her mood, aware of how much Beauty meant to her, he had offered to take her riding. At her quiet refusal and sorrowful expression, he recognized how deeply withdrawn she had become. His inability to alleviate the situation was frustrating; to be honest, he was deeply concerned. Admittedly, his initial plan had been to enjoy himself, break her and then cast her aside when he became bored. But that had not happened—would not happen. He found himself more irresistibly drawn to her with each passing day. Her incredible passion had come as a surprise, something unexpected … and enchanting. Her past, gathered from bits of conversation, appeared equal in pain to his, although identical methods of infliction probably unlikely. *What am I going to do with this woman? Time is playing out.*

He walked into his tent earlier than usual and stopped abruptly, startled by the scene before him. She sat on the floor beside his desk, legs drawn up, face hugged to her knees, rocking slowly and humming a plaintive melody. He watched as she cried, occasionally drawing deep sobbing breaths. In their time together, with all the grief he had put her through, she had never cried; he was stunned.

"The accommodations are not to your liking, madam?" He flinched at his pompous insensitivity, wishing he could recall the words.

Startled, she quickly swiped at her cheeks, embarrassed. Looking away, she stammered softly, "No, sir. They are more than adequate."

Chiding himself for adding to her distress, he moved to her side. *What do I want from her? In truth, do I want her beaten into submission?* The resounding answer: *No.* He was irresistibly drawn to her bold, independent nature, and to find her so distraught she could not be provoked into a feisty bit of anger was distressing. *What has happened?* Her despondency had nothing to do with their lovemaking, of that he was sure. In the past few days his touch had been all she responded to—with unashamed, uninhibited ardor.

Placing his hands gently on her cheeks, he turned her to face him. Tear filled eyes met his, so bleak their beautiful green appeared flat and lackluster. "Come have supper and talk to me," he said, gently coaxing her into a chair. She sat obediently, but began staring at her hands.

"Are you ill?" he asked softly. At the shake of her head he added, "Eat, perhaps you will feel better."

"I could not keep it down, sir." A willful tear spilled over and trickled along her cheek where he stopped it tenderly with his thumb. Placing a hand on her shoulder, he leaned close. "I have watched you become more withdrawn over the last few days," he said tenderly, pausing to gently trace his finger along one of the dark smudges under her eyes. "Talk to me. We have come to know each other quite well. I had not thought you to be that unhappy."

"I am not, sir," she murmured.

"Then what is it?" Irritated by his inability to understand, he sounded curter than he wished.

"What is to become of me, Colonel?" Her choice had been made … but how could *he* make this situation work? There was no possibility.

Taken aback, he eyed her in silence, trying to answer that question himself.

"I am not afraid of your ultimate decision, sir, rather the method in which it is carried out." She faced him bravely, albeit sadly, noting his confusion.

Struck by her courage, he was at a loss of words for the first time in his life.

"Colonel," she interrupted his thoughts. "Would you take a ride with me?" She rushed on before her courage failed. "I grew up in this area; there is a place I would like to show you, a special place I would like to see once more before …" She inhaled a shuddering breath.

He searched her upturned face thoughtfully.

"I am unarmed, you could easily overpower me. But you know I will not try to escape, I have given my word." Her eyes implored he grant this one final wish.

This situation must be resolved, one way or the other; he made his decision. "Let us go then," he said briskly, and taking her hands, pulled her up from the chair.

Snagging her coat from its resting place on the floor, and guided by his firmly placed hand in the small of her back, they headed out into the encampment, aglow with the light of a full moon.

Lieutenant Jackson quickly fell in step beside the colonel.

"Ready Diablo, Lieutenant."

"And the lady's horse also?"

"No, I believe she might like to do that herself."

She looked up smiling almost shyly, pleased by his sensitivity. Seeing a sparkle returning to her eyes, he allowed himself the flicker of a smile. What passed between them was not lost on Lieutenant Jackson but he made no outward indication. *Something is not right, but what?*

As they approached the horses holding area, she heard an insistent nicker and moved quickly to her mare's side. Reaching up, she rubbed Beauty's forelock and patted her nose as the little horse snuffled happily against her cheek. Her bright laughter rang with pure joy, pleasing him.

"My little girl," she whispered, hugging her. Placing a sugar cube on her upturned palm, she laughed again as the mare gobbled the treat. But her laughter ended abruptly as she glanced down and saw hobbles. "Hold, Beauty," she crooned as she crouched to investigate. Quickly removing the restraints she turned to the colonel. "These are not necessary, sir, she will not leave without me." Deeply concerned, she stroked her mare's legs, caressing the abrasions created by the fetters.

"I will see that does not happen again," he said quietly. Grasping her elbow, he eased her up. "Would you like a hand saddling Beauty?"

"If you would like," she replied, accepting his attempted apology.

They rode in silence, the colonel allowing her to lead the way. A short ride took them to a narrow stream, its dark water rippling slowly, sparkling beneath the brilliant moonlight. Speaking softly, she reined her mare to an obedient stop and slid to the ground letting her reins fall. Bringing his charger to a halt beside her the colonel dismounted, also dropping his reins in a silent, universal command.

He said nothing, but she sensed his eyes upon her, watching intently. She reached out tentatively, and taking his hand urged him to follow. Ducking occasionally to maneuver through low brush, they eventually emerged in a small well hidden glen. Stepping aside she watched his reaction. Beautiful crystal falls splashed wetly into an indigo pool bathed in golden moonlight, sending out circle after circle of sparkling ripples, moving ever outward, almost beckoning. The pristine beauty of this spot awed him, and for the briefest moment his expression softened.

Shedding her clothing, she dove into the pool—not asking permission—he would not hurt her. Surfacing several yards out, she began strong, measured strokes propelling her towards the falls. Nearing them, she re-submerged in a quick graceful arc, the last few feet accomplished in an underwater glide creating barely a ripple on the sparkling surface. Bursting clear of the invigorating wetness, she gulped a breath of air, shook wet hair back from her eyes, and quickly steadied herself on the rocky base at the edge of the falls.

A big splash, a gulped breath—she whipped about, surprised to find him immediately behind her, toeing the bottom for a good foothold.

"I see there is a great deal we do not know of each other," he said. Arching a dark brow he added, "You are a powerful swimmer, madam, a rather uncommon ability for a woman."

She shrugged, a grin slowly spreading, "There is much to learn, sir. I see you are also a powerful swimmer."

Edging into the falls, they held each other enjoying the sensation of falling water assaulting their bodies. Reaching up she untied his queue and with deft strokes fanned his long, black hair across his shoulders, an act of intimacy which struck a deep chord pleasing him. He turned and ran his fingers slowly through her tangled tresses, watching her face intently, assessing her feelings … and his.

Well-hidden behind the falls lay a small cave—a quiet spot where slowly smoldering passion ignited like tinder to a match, where, in quiet desperation, they tasted the essence of each other for the last time. In the aftermath, sitting side-by-side, they gazed out through the liquid screen of water as it cascaded into the dazzling pool, alight with magical moonbeams. The soft fringes of that very same light played across her body mesmerizing him.

Changes in his demeanor were evident; she sensed true caring. But this must come to an end; they both understood that reality. Without warning, she rose and moved towards the back of the shallow cave. Curious, he watched but made no attempt to stop her. Reaching behind a rock she brought out a towel, and returning to his side sat down smiling. *She has been here before*, he realized, *but when and why?*

She began toweling him dry, enjoying the feeling of his well-muscled body. The night air was warm, the cold water chilling—the gentle buffing of his flesh creating a delicious sensation. After a few minutes he took the towel, and draping it across her shoulders slowly massaged her back, studying her reactions in an attempt to discern her feelings, and examining his own. She relaxed back against him, her eyes flickering closed … enjoyment or deep thought, he was not sure which.

With a sigh of resignation, decision reached, she sat up producing a small dirk. He instantly tensed. But quickly flipping the knife with practiced dexterity, she caught the blade between thumb and forefinger, extending it to him handle first. He remembered having watched her practice with a stick and was doubly impressed. "You handle a knife well, madam," he complimented, taking the weapon.

"For all the good it does me." She smiled ruefully, her eyes twin pools of anguish. "You have beaten me at my own game, sir."

"I am afraid I do not follow your train of thought, madam," he said curtly, attempting to cover his confusion, but she sensed the truth.

"Before I gave my promise I was positive that given time, I could elude you. But it cannot be done. You are too good at what you do." She held his bewildered stare, unfaltering. "If you thought I would share more information as time passed," she paused shaking her head, "there is nothing I know that could help you." Honesty shone in her eyes. "And you will tire of the game, sir, incredible as it has been."

"You are sure of that, madam?" He could not take his eyes from her.

"Please do not toy with me, Colonel, I do not fear your ultimate decision, only the method in which you carry it out. I can face death." Unshed tears shimmered in the dim light. "It would be a peaceful ending; no one will even miss me." Her voice dropped to a whisper as she touched the knife he held in his hand. "Do it now … cleanly; please do not make me suffer."

As he made no immediate response she added, "I doubt you will share me with your men. *You* do not share what belongs to you." She searched his face. "And I have to believe you would not subject me to that agony after our time together."

He was completely taken aback. How could a beautiful young woman be so tormented she would ask for death? But then, he remembered a time when he would have accepted it gratefully himself.

She was not unlike him—tired of fighting inner furies, aching from a haunted past. He watched this woman who read him so well, who could make him forget so much of the bitterness that had haunted him … and felt emptiness at the thought of losing her.

She reached out and touched his face, studying his features as if to etch them in her mind permanently. "Do it quickly, sir, I beg you; and please take care of my Beauty. Do not forget her sugar." A single tear slid slowly down her cheek.

My God, she is facing death and yet, is concerned for her mare—how astounding. Setting the knife down between them he gently took her hand. "I cannot do that, Kathryn, for *I* would miss you," he said quietly, the hard angles of his face softening with compassion.

"Jason …" Placing her hand over his, she swallowed convulsively.

He heard unmistakable hunger as she spoke his name for the first time … and with that simple utterance, long forgotten emotions ignited catching him off-guard. Decision made—perhaps not the wisest for his career but best for him personally—he pulled her to him. The kiss began fiercely, softening as his last shreds of resistance crumbled, giving way to final acceptance.

For the first time in many long months she experienced deep, healing inner peace.

Wordlessly, he led her from the cave. "Get dressed, Kathryn," he commanded hoarsely.

Neither spoke as they quickly donned clothing—she finishing before him. Shrugging into her coat, she whistled sharply. He glanced up from buttoning his jacket, surprised to see her mare trotting towards them with his black charger at her side. The mare came to a halt and snuffled into Kathryn's hand, then began nuzzling her pocket insistently.

"You are so spoiled, little girl." Laughing, she took a lump of sugar from her pocket, and breaking it in two, fed one piece to her mare. Beauty's soft lips tickled her palm and she smiled. "You are my Beauty." She knuckled her forehead fondly. "But we must not forget your friend." She extended her hand palm up with a sugar cube for the big charger. Sniffing cautiously at first, he gently mouthed her hand and began chomping as she scratched his forelock and spoke softly.

Jason watched, fascinated, or more aptly—shocked. His charger had come by his name for good reason. A temperamental stallion that responded poorly to anyone but himself, Diablo could be quite ugly upon occasion. Yet, there he stood quite literally 'eating out of her hand'. He saw her interaction with the horses, noting the pleasure she received, and was reminded; how very little it required to make her happy.

So passionate, unafraid, intelligent, startling in beauty; yes, I want you with me always … my Kathryn. A fleeting image of the 'fine ladies' attending General Cornwallis's parties darted through his mind. How they paled in comparison. Several had fawned over him seeking status through alliance with his family name but caring nothing for him. He had never enjoyed their games, but that no longer mattered. That part of his life was over. Brushing these thoughts aside, he stepped to Diablo's side.

"Let us go, Kathryn," he said a bit stiffly. Before he could offer assistance in mounting, she flung herself onto the saddle in a graceful motion, stunning him with her agility. There was so much he wanted to understand about this fascinating, challenging woman—a woman he would not, or truth be known, *could not* let go. Reality struck; he admired her spirit and bravery and would not wish her to be any other way.

Her high-strung, mare started to prance and paw. "Hold, Beauty," she crooned, patting the sleek neck, quieting her immediately. They rode back to the encampment in silence, each immersed in private thoughts. Something had changed between them, of that he was well aware, a 'beginning' of sorts and, she sensed it too.

As they entered the campsite, a soldier stepped forward to take the horses, greeting the colonel and nodding politely to her. Jason watched as she deftly swung her leg over the mare's head, slid to the ground and stood quietly awaiting his command. He gestured towards the tent, stepping aside at the entrance, allowing her to enter first. As she turned to face him, he was relieved to see her emerald eyes more at peace. "I shall return shortly," he said softly, and tipping her chin up, brushed a gentle kiss to her lips.

"I will be here, sir." And with just the hint of a smile, he withdrew from the tent.

The oil lamps had been lit, most assuredly the work of Lieutenant Jackson. He was extremely conscientious in his duties and becoming friendlier with each passing day—a rather pleasant man. Turning slowly she took a quiet assessment of the tent, her home for many weeks and now perhaps indefinitely. She could see Jason's piercing blue eyes, feel his presence and found it comforting. Recalling the exquisite beauty of the waterfalls, the moonlight and his tender words, she knew him to be as confused as she by these growing feelings. Now the only nagging disquiet in the back of her mind was Jamie; but she could not think of him now. She sat down in 'Jason's' chair, and found it pleasant to have him in her thoughts by 'name'. Kicking off her boots, she curled her feet under her to wait for his return, and fell into an exhausted sleep.

As Jason left the tent, Lieutenant Jackson approached with two steaming cups of coffee.

"I will tend the horses, sir," he assured. But at the colonel's gesture to accompany him to the holding area, he quickly set the cups on the ground.

"Do not hobble her horse, Lieutenant. That little mare will not leave without her."

"Yes, sir," he answered. Noting a new attitude towards the lady, he was both curious and surprised. Having trained many months under Colonel Tarrington's command in England, prior to sailing to the colonies, he knew him quite well. This was out of character. *She must be very special to have affected him so.* From the time he shared with her on a daily basis, he had already begun to suspect that.

"The lady will be joining us shortly for meals and I will expect her to be treated with utmost respect." He arched a brow at his lieutenant, who, snapping out of his reverie, answered with a curt nod. With brief orders for the following day, the colonel bid 'goodnight' and headed into the dark.

Lieutenant Jackson watched him go, pondering his commanding officer's changes. He would have laid odds nothing like this could happen. *Will wonders never cease?* He shook his head and grinned.

Jason entered his quarters with the warm coffee. Finding her curled in his chair, asleep, he placed the cups quietly on the desk. As he watched her sleep, so childlike and innocent, his thoughts turned to his decision at the waterfall; he had no regrets. She stirred, coming slowly awake, momentarily disoriented. As her eyes came to rest on him, confusion vanished and she smiled.

"Luke warm coffee our specialty." He returned her smile. Picking up the cups, he handed her one and leaned back against the desk. Sipping his coffee he watched her quietly, unsure of how to broach the topic he needed to discuss.

"We need to talk of trust, Jason." She paused in sipping her coffee.

He eyed her sharply. "You are perceptive Kathryn. As I am usually the one dictating terms, perhaps you would like the opportunity to speak first." *What will she have to say*? He was curious.

She remained silent for several moments, her expression thoughtful. "I told you before; when I give my word I never default. I give you my word, Jason; I will never betray your trust. Never..."

"I need that from you, Kathryn if we are to ..." He struggled with the words.

"Build a relationship," she answered softly, loving the sound of her name rolling from his tongue with a distinct British accent.

"I fear we may be kindred souls. You caught me off-guard tonight when you handed me the knife. I have been where you were, where you have been for the past few days. I would not wish that desolation for you." He touched her cheek where a single tear slowly tracked. "We both have pasts that haunt us. Perhaps sharing will help lay them to rest—but all in good time. For the moment, let us proceed with 'no questions asked, no answers given,' hmm?" Again, he arched his eyebrow in a look she was beginning to find endearing.

Standing quickly, she moved into his arms, reaching up to kiss him. As the kiss deepened, his hands slid under her blouse caressing.

His touch, his touch ... she sighed deeply.

"You never tire of my touch, do you?" He sounded pleased, almost surprised.

"Never ... never," she declared, a distinct sparkle returning to her eyes.

"Later, my vixen, you have had a rough day. Let us get some sleep." At her pout, he trailed a thumb down the bridge of her nose, tipping her chin up to kiss her tenderly.

After readying for the night, he led her to their bed and pulling her against him, cradled her head on his shoulder. Draping her arm across him, she snuggled against his chest. *Jamie forgive me, I want this man so. And I, too, need a chance at happiness.* With that last waking thought, she relaxed into sleep.

The next morning there was an imperceptible difference—newfound respect. They shared a quiet breakfast but lingered over coffee.

"I am glad to see you in a better frame of mind, Kathryn," he said softly, relieved to see her smiling, her face at peace.

They chatted noncommittally for awhile, Kathryn well aware that he was girding himself to tell her something. "I will be working here at my desk for part of the day." He paused.

"I will entertain myself, sir." But there was more he had to say, of that she was sure.

"Tomorrow I will be making preparations to ride north for a meeting."

Her face registered dismay, though she tried to hide it. "When do you leave, sir?

"The day after tomorrow, just after dawn." He studied her face, reading her thoughts. "I will be gone for two days, but Lieutenant Jackson will be sure you are not inconvenienced in any way." Aware of her unrest, he attempted reassurance. "Tonight you will join the men for supper—to become more accustomed to them."

She looked away hastily, lost in tangled thoughts.

"It will be all right, Kathryn." He took her hand, squeezing gently. "They do not bite unless I give them the order," he quipped lightly, hoping to lessen her anxiety.

She spent much of the afternoon sitting just outside the tent entrance reading, while he worked at his desk.

Lieutenant Jackson came by and made an effort at light conversation to ease her tension. *She might feel uneasy about this situation, but she should try viewing it from my standpoint*, he thought. They would both have to work at adapting while the colonel was away. Perhaps, if conversation became lacking, he would bring that point up for her consideration.

That evening just before supper, she sat working the tangles from her hair, fussing with her clothing.

"Kathryn, relax. Talk to the men or remain quiet." He cocked his eyebrow and grinned.

She gave him a long look; she was allowing herself to be upset for no reason. After all, Jason would be there tonight. *Save the panic for when he is away.*

Moving to his desk, he opened a drawer and took out her dirk. Holding it out, he nodded for her to take it. "Tuck that into your boot." She did so quickly, smiling gratefully. "There now, feel better?"

"Yes, sir," She brightened but then became serious. "I will not betray this trust."

"See to it, madam. I do not relish a knife in the back." He eyed her with mock severity.

At her horrified expression and assurance of reliability, he took her into his arms laughing out loud. Tucking wild strands of tawny gold hair behind her ears, he absorbed her childlike expression. She could turn him inside out with just a look. "When I come back we will discuss the return of the rest of your weapons. For now, I do not want to make the men nervous in my absence."

She was now grinning openly at his attempted humor.

"Let us get this over with. Perhaps then, you will relax and enjoy the time we have left before I head out." Brushing a kiss to her lips, he placed a firm hand in the middle of her back and ushered her towards the campfires.

"Gentlemen," he announced, "Miss Cameron will be joining us for supper. Please make her feel welcome." His eyes swept the circle of dragoons, watching as they responded with polite nods.

Lieutenant Jackson immediately brought two plates of food and joined them at the colonel's invitation. The colonel sat down upon a log, but Kathryn settled herself on the ground cross-legged near his feet, feeling more comfortable and less ill-at-ease in that position. Jason eyed her with amusement but said nothing. If she found it easier to relax sitting in that fashion, he had no argument. The meal was uneventful, the dragoons making small talk around her, Lieutenant Jackson conversing with the colonel, and occasionally trying to include her.

After the meal was finished a tin whistle appeared in the hands of a young cornet. Being quite adept with the instrument, in short order he had the men singing loudly, thoroughly enjoying the camaraderie. Kathryn listened carefully to the tunes, imprinting them on her mind. If she was to fit in, she must learn their ways.

Lieutenant Jackson, although polite, seemed stiff in her presence. Suddenly realizing he was not being helpful in making her feel welcome, he turned to her. "My apologies, Miss Cameron, for my lack of conversation," he said, smiling with genuine warmth. *Hopefully we will get to know each other better while the colonel is away, making future instances easier for us both.* He would make a concerted effort. "Be assured your safety will be well guarded in the colonel's absence."

Acknowledging his sincerity, she relaxed into the mood of the evening, enjoying the music and watching the star-filled skies.

Later that night, as she splashed water onto her face preparing for bed, Jason moved to her side. Sensing him watching she turned, shiny droplets of water clinging enticingly to her long lashes. Her cheeks held a light flush, her breathing having … changed. *A mere look, or a touch, my love …* Flashing a brilliant smile, she moved into his embrace.

"I told you all would be well, did I not." He breathed softly into her hair as they rested in the afterglow. At her nod, he added, "Lieutenant Jackson has never failed me before; he will not now."

As feared, the next day passed all too quickly. Thankfully, the evening meal with the dragoons turned out to be more relaxed than the previous one. Having given the situation some thought, she refused to worry further about things over which she had no control. This would be just another adventure of sorts. Decision made, she joined the men in singing jaunty after dinner tunes, some of which were already beginning to sound familiar, and thoroughly enjoyed herself.

Much to her chagrin, dawn arrived too soon. She stood quietly watching him dress, already feeling the encircling emptiness. All in readiness, he came to her side. Brushing his thumb along the bridge of her nose, he tipped her chin up to receive a lingering kiss.

"I will be here waiting for your return, Jason. Go safely," she whispered. Holding his gaze, she smiled bravely, blocking out thoughts of the next two days.

She stood outside their tent and watched until he disappeared out of sight, riding straight and proud astride Diablo, flanked by four of his officers.

Turning to reenter the tent, she felt the loneliness surround her. *It would be a long two days.*

Chapter Five

An Unpleasant Meeting

The next morning Kathryn awakened to an empty bed, immediately feeling a sense of loss. Touching the empty space Jason usually occupied, she missed him. Pushing aside unhappy thoughts, she dressed, tidied up their living quarters and waited to see what the day would bring. She heard Lieutenant Jackson's shouted greeting as he entered the tent carrying steaming coffee and a bowl of gruel. Curled up in the colonel's chair, barefoot and reading poetry, she immediately closed her book, placed it on the desk and greeted him pleasantly.

Lieutenant Jackson wished her a 'good day', and to enjoy her reading. But as he turned to leave, he stopped. Glancing at the cover of the book she had set aside he said: "I hope you will not find me rude, but I was curious as to what you were reading."

"Not rude at all, Lieutenant." She quickly handed him the book.

"Ahh, MacPherson. Perchance are you reading *Fingal*?"

She nodded excitedly pleased they had stumbled upon a unique common interest; one which could provide hours of friendly discussion. "I understand it is a favorite of your King George."

For a moment, he appeared dumbstruck. *How can she possibly be aware of that little known fact?*

"Lieutenant," she laughed, "I am not ignorant, despite being a colonial—a fact your colonel has finally accepted." As he appeared somewhat uncomfortable, she softened her statement by asking, "Do you think MacPherson was quoting the ancient bard Ossian? Or is it only an interesting ruse?"

Lieutenant Jackson eyed her with new respect. He was beginning to understand how the colonel could spend so much time with this woman. She was fascinating and possessed a sharp mind.

"Every author needs a premise on which to base his words. Who can say?" He shrugged, weighing his thoughts. "But I, personally, prefer the idea that Ossian really existed."

And that was how their friendship began. They spent the afternoon in good-natured argument about the worthiness of different selections before breaking for a late afternoon snack, both having forgotten lunch in their avid conversation. By the time she accompanied him to Cook's wagon, she was more at ease. They stopped along their way to speak with several dragoons, each acknowledging her with polite consideration. After eating, the lieutenant suggested they sit under the trees and enjoy the beautiful weather.

I am beginning to really like this man. The next two days might not be as bad as I had feared. "Shall I get the poetry book, Lieutenant?"

Grinning widely, he threw out a challenge. "I know Macpherson's work quite well by heart. I believe I can hold my own with a fellow poetry lover." *Why did I ever dread having to spend two days with her? She is charming.*

"All right," she countered. "What about James Beattie? He is a Scot. I may have the upper hand there." She grinned cocking an eyebrow, startling him, her expression so similar to the colonel's.

"Let me see," he paused. "Although I do not know you well, yet, I imagine one of your favorites might be *The Minstrel*." He had caught *her* totally off-guard. Noting her surprised reaction, he laughed. "We English are not a totally ignorant lot either, Miss Cameron."

"Touché, Lieutenant, I stand corrected."

He liked her laughter: unpretentious, genuine. They spent the rest of the afternoon relaxing, arguing poets and poetry. Supper was ready before they realized, causing both to agree how easily the time had passed. Around the campfire, the dragoons were as Jason had promised, somewhat distant but polite. She ate quietly and joined in their singing for a while; but not wanting to put a damper on their games and talk, begged-off at an early hour.

As Lieutenant Jackson left her at the tent opening, he thanked her. "In all truthfulness, miss, I was worried as to how we would get through these two days. But I find you easy to be with."

She smiled, amused by his candor. "We share the same thoughts, Lieutenant. Perhaps tomorrow we can discuss herbal remedies or hunting—unless, of course, you have other duties."

Shaking his head he said, "I will bring an early breakfast and we shall see how the day unfolds."

She lay in 'their' bed staring at the ceiling watching flickering shadows cast by the oil lamp, again engulfed by loneliness. *How strange*, she thought, *I spent months on my own never bothered by being alone. But a few weeks with him and my life has turned completely upside down.*

When Lieutenant Jackson returned the next morning, she asked when he expected the colonel to return. But at his brief, non-committal reply, realized he would be honor bound not to reveal such information. With a shrug she brightened, setting her mind to enjoying the day. Where Jason had gone or what he was doing was irrelevant, at least for now.

Today their topic of discussion shifted from poetry to herbal remedies. Although well versed in many common cures for diseases, Lieutenant Jackson found Kathryn's knowledge of plants and their usage far better: when to use a decoction instead of an infusion to coax the best properties from each herb, where to find specific plants, and best time to pick them for optimum strength—and more.

"Let me show you how to make what I call willow bark tea," she offered, excited at the prospect of doing something useful. "There are willow trees by the stream; you can help me collect the bark."

At first hesitant, he quickly relented, deciding there would be no imminent danger that close to camp. After grabbing a haversack from his tent they headed for the stream, chatting amiably as they went. Upon returning, she taught him the proper brewing of willow bark tea: explaining each step in the process. "This tea works well in treating fever or pain, I like to keep it on hand at all times. It may be slightly less potent if not fresh, but it beats having nothing."

He smiled as he cautiously sipped the beverage. "Not bad." He nodded approval then found containers to store the liquid.

"Perhaps tomorrow we should gather some herbs for drying," she suggested eagerly.

"I would like that, miss. Your knowledge of herbs and medicine is impressive. Where did you ever learn all this?"

"A little here and there over the years." She gave a dismissive shrug: too soon to mention her time spent with the Cherokees.

His compliment provided the first hint of acceptance, and she was glad for their newfound friendship. Again the next day flew by, the evening meal ready before they realized. They sat near the campfire sipping coffee with the dragoons. Although she tried to relax, the lieutenant noted her dinner plate remained untouched, and she appeared distracted. Within moments, she stood and excused herself. "Lieutenant, I fear I am not very good company tonight. Perhaps I will wait for the colonel in his quarters."

He made a friendly effort to dissuade her, but at her insistence walked her back to the tent.

Accompanied by four officers, the colonel had ridden out two days earlier in answer to General Cornwallis's summons. The general's expressed displeasure with his progress in dispersing these Southern rebels, promised their meeting would be less than pleasant. His orders had been specific: keep bands of colonials from grouping into a major force: complete destruction preferable; leastwise limit their numbers substantially.

His lordship failed to understand the unique abilities of these so-called 'ignorant farmers'—a wily bunch inspired to loyalty by their stubborn leader: a man of iron determination, a man who fought like a rabid dog, instilling the same principles in his followers. This rebel leader had a nasty habit of intercepting English supply wagons, using no set pattern, making him difficult to intercept or capture. Identity unknown, he moved about quickly and freely. By the time his whereabouts was discovered, he had moved on.

Apparently well known to the Cherokees, this cunning rebel disappeared as if into thin air, wandering in and out of Indian lands without confrontation. Although the Cherokees held no particular aversion to the Redcoats, neither did they feel compulsion to aid them. When questioned about this man they remained non-committal. Jason referred to this elusive rebel as 'devil's spawn' and wanted him out of the way—preferably dead. Without their leader, the rebel bands would lose courage and disappear back into the obscurity from whence they had come.

As a diversion from brooding, Jason focused on Kathryn—the feel of her warm body pressed against him, eager to match passion. His choice was made, but as a British Green Dragoon colonel—perhaps not one of his better decisions. *Would I ever have appealed to her had she not been facing rape and imminent death?* As this speculation brought no peace of mind, he dashed all thoughts and surrendered to the satisfaction derived from Diablo's even paced gait. At least that pleasure never diminished.

As expected, their meeting was extremely tense. Cornwallis, arrogant and failing to comprehend the ghostlike qualities of the rebel bands, dictated ultimatums—perhaps attainable in fighting regular militia—but impossible to accomplish against these cunning rebels. The session was short, their words angry and terse.

Meeting adjourned, Jason strode to his waiting charger. Immersed in a black mood, he summoned his men and headed back to their encampment at breakneck speed. His mind churned as he urged Diablo to pick up the pace. *Damn this 'devil's spawn'. Who is he? Where does he come from? Does Kathryn know who he is? And why was she spying on my encampment? Honestly out of curiosity—or with purpose?* He would get answers from her the minute he returned to the encampment.

Hours later they galloped into camp: hot, tired and dusty. The colonel flung himself from the lathered and panting Diablo before fully reining to a stop. Throwing his reins to his lieutenant, he stormed silently towards his tent leaving the men eyeing one another with curiosity.

As he approached he heard her singing one of the tunes sung regularly around the evening campfire. Pleasantly surprised by the lustrous quality of her full, rich voice he hesitated, anger beginning to subside. His fierce temper had created devastating results in the past, however, attempts to control that part of his personality were still greatly lacking. Striding into the tent unannounced, he flung his helmet onto the cot. As he stood silently appraising her, he slowly removed one glove then the other. Slapping them sharply against the palm of his hand, he tossed them beside his helmet.

She sat braiding her tawny hair into a long plait over one shoulder, happily content. At his abrupt entrance she stopped: shocked. Raw fury and exhaustion etched his features, the air surrounding him crackling with tension. He stood rigid, drawing deep breaths, fighting to control his temper.

She remained sitting, quietly assessing and trying to understand what had happened while he was away. Apparently it involved her in some way. Aware that saying anything or approaching him would make matters worse, she sat in respectful silence.

"I have just ridden eight hours straight, madam. After the meeting I went through this morning, I have a good mind to have you flogged—or do whatever necessary to get honest answers from you." The menace in his tone was unnerving. "I want the truth from you."

Hands clenched by his sides he studied her face, watching as her eyes filled with distress and confusion—but not the slightest hint of guilt or deceit. Blinded by anger, had he misjudged? "Kathryn, I need answers," he ground out, the raw edge to his voice betraying inner turmoil.

"What do you need to know, Jason?" she asked quietly. "I have given you my word that I will not betray you, and I will not … ever."

"Upon occasion, as I recall, if the promise is not worded in specific terms …"

"I will answer all your questions with absolute honesty," she interrupted, hurt but tolerant as she tried to determine the cause.

"What is your real name?" He eyed her with unsettling intensity.

"Kathryn Cameron … MacLean."

She would not lie, her word had been given. Although 'Cameron' was a family name, it failed to reveal the complete truth. Would Jason be familiar with the name 'MacLean'? If so, could he trust her knowing to whom she was related? Was Jamie involved with the rebels, or even still alive? She honestly did not know. After witnessing hideous atrocities in the French and Indian War, he had sworn never to be involved in any conflict again. How would Jason react; what consequences would he inflict upon her? *Better to determine that now*, she decided.

"MacLean?" He eyed her with renewed interest. He recalled having heard that name mentioned in the past but was unsure of the context in which it had been disclosed. He would find out.

She nodded, watching him closely, trying to discern whether this disclosure was of relevance.

"Ahh, that accounts for the 'M' on your tomahawk. I *was* curious."

"You never miss the slightest detail, Jason." She regarded him with complete respect.

His voice softened; he was calmer now. "Do you have any family in this area?"

"Yes, perhaps, but I really do not know. My parents are both dead. My brother and his children may be alive," she murmured, shaking her head and shrugging, sadness returning to her eyes. "It has been many months since I last spoke to him, our angry words—difficult—unpleasant at best. I suspect Jamie is alive but have no proof."

He listened carefully to catch her soft words, the memories clearly painful. "Where were you coming from; where were you heading when my men captured you?" he asked more gently.

"I came from the upper part of this state and was heading south. I had no specific plans. I had heard the English burned our farm in Georgetown and was intending to see if it was true," she explained in a matter-of-fact tone, as if not giving in to emotion she could deny the hurt. "I was actually headed for the Charleston Path, then south towards Keowee."

Now this bit of information did arouse interest. "Why would you be heading there, Kathryn?"

"I have friends—Cherokees." She wished he would stop the questions before she was forced to say too much. "I was not spying, Jason. I really did happen upon your encampment quite by accident and thought it would be an adventure." She looked up with a sheepish smile. "I have often gotten myself into difficulties with this inane sense of—whatever you wish to call it."

The hint of a smile played at the corners of his mouth as the last shreds of anxiety fell away.

"I really am not aware of any information that will be of help to the English or the rebel cause for that matter." Her eyes were twin pools of green shimmering in the lantern light.

Relieved that nothing in her background appeared to pose immediate threat, he moved to her side. Her brother was of great interest, but her words indicated they were on bad terms. The Cherokees: also of interest, but not a particular threat.

As he pulled her gently forward, she went willingly into his arms. He had been rough on her, forcing her to discuss things she had not been ready to divulge. There was more to her story, of that he was sure, but nothing of a foreboding nature. It could wait until she was ready.

"I owe you an apology, Kathryn," he breathed softly into her hair. "I said there would be no questions asked, and there will not be again, I promise." Scrutinizing her expressive face for several moments, he resolved any lingering shreds of indecision, satisfied with her answers and honesty.

She gazed at him, deeply relieved. "Come, sit down, Jason. I will ask Lieutenant Jackson to bring you some food."

He started to protest, but she urged him into the chair and quickly left the tent, returning within moments. Smiling at his perplexed expression, she filled two glasses with brandy and handed him one. He sipped slowly watching her, realizing he had missed their daily companionship.

Setting her glass down, she moved behind him and began unplaiting his queue. Recognizing his exhaustion, she set her mind to easing his stress. Her hands were soothing as she worked his hair, her fingers gently massaging his scalp and temples. With a sigh he leaned back, his eyes closing, surrendering to the luxury of her ministrations.

At the sound of the lieutenant's voice, she quickly moved away so as not to seem overly familiar—impressing Jason with her sensitivity to appearances.

Lieutenant Jackson entered with two plates of food and hot coffee. "I thought you might be hungry too, miss," he explained, smiling as she thanked him.

"How is Diablo, Lieutenant?" Jason asked, concerned. He had pushed his faithful charger hard.

"Toweled down and fed, sir."

Kathryn reached into her coat pocket and handed him a cube of sugar. "Please see that he gets this, and…" Digging into her pocket again, she handed him a second cube. "I better not forget Beauty." The lieutenant glanced to the colonel.

Rolling his eyes he nodded, relaxing his demeanor for the briefest moment, surprising his officer.

As Lieutenant Jackson turned to leave, Kathryn stopped him. "Would you please bring me some willow bark tea we brewed today—for my headache?"

"Of course, miss." Inclining his head, he hid a grin.

She returned to massaging Jason's temples as he picked at his food.

"Are you all right?" he asked, concerned.

"Yes." She bent down, smiling. "It is for you, sir." He looked up, surprised.

"I believe you have a headache," she commented, and continued working his scalp with capable fingers.

"How did you know?" he asked, somewhat mystified. Her smiling silence caused him to remark, "It would appear that you and Lieutenant Jackson are no longer at odds."

"We were never at odds, just uncomfortable, thinking we had no common ground."

"I gather you have found things of shared interest, then?"

"Yes, it helped the time pass in your absence; I will share that with you when you are more rested; but not tonight."

Lieutenant Jackson soon returned with the tea, and setting it on the desk bid them a 'goodnight'. Stopping abruptly, he turned to the colonel. "She certainly is a wealth of knowledge, sir."

"I have discovered that myself, Lieutenant," he replied with just the hint of a smile.

When they were alone, she pressed the cup into Jason's hand. At her insistent urging he sipped tentatively, finding the flavor not unpalatable.

"I am not trying to poison you, Colonel," she assured, grinning impishly.

Funny, he thought, *that is one of the things so attractive about her. She amuses me.*

Unbuttoning his jacket, she eased it off his shoulders and folded it neatly. As he sat watching her straighten their living quarters, his headache eased, her concoction bringing needed relief. Returning to his side, she moistened a cloth and proceeded to bathe his face. As she untied his jabot, opening his shirt to the waist, he took her hands and began gently turning them in his.

Weeks ago when he first questioned her ability with the tomahawk, he had had nothing with which to compare. However, having witnessed the expert way she controlled a knife, he now did. Continuing to turn her hands in his, he studied them carefully. "Can you handle that tomahawk as well as you do a knife?" he asked suddenly.

She eyed him closely, caught off-guard then grinned, amused—*His mind never ceases working, a bit like a dog with a bone, gnawing until satisfied.* Planting both hands on her hips she stated cockily, "Sir, I only carry weapons on my person that I can handle with ability."

With that statement, he burst out laughing. "Of that, I have absolute proof, madam." Arching an eyebrow, a wide grin spread across his face.

Aware of his inner meaning, she smiled shyly, a pink haze rushing to her tan cheeks.

"Why, I believe you are blushing, madam." He found that fact irresistibly charming.

"Are you making fun of me, sir?" She looked away, obviously distressed.

Surprised by her abrupt change of mood, he cupped her face forcing her to meet his intense gaze. "No not at all." *Who has been so insensitive to your feelings of sexuality that mild teasing hurts so deeply?* Bold and brash one minute; sensitive and easily hurt the next. She carried deep scars, as did he, of that, he was certain. "Smile," he whispered. Taking the cloth from her hand he tossed it aside, and pulling her into his arms, began nuzzling the side of her neck.

Conscious of his exhaustion, she shook her head, resisting his urgently whispered suggestions. "Come to bed to sleep," she said firmly.

Starting to undress, he grinned, indicating for her to also disrobe.

"Not unless you are willing to just sleep. We have lots of time ahead of us, my colonel; you are exhausted."

"I did not sleep well last night, Kathryn," he admitted, recalling the empty bed, missing her.

"Nor did I, Jason." She brushed him a kiss, cleverly evading his encircling arms. "Roll over onto your stomach," she commanded, amused by his grimace. "Do as I say, sir."

"I am not sure I can, madam, in the state in which you have put me." Despite his words, he slowly complied. Folding his elbows, he rested on his forearms as she gently began working tension from his shoulder muscles.

As her hands worked he groaned, overwhelmed by the sheer pleasure of her touch. *Absolutely no one has ever cared enough to consider my discomfort, let alone attempt to ease it ... up until now.* Her hands were magic, deliciously soothing—exactly what he needed. Within moments he relaxed into sleep, his last thoughts before peaceful oblivion: of Kathryn—and her caring touch.

Listening to his deep, even breathing, she smiled. Leaning down, she placed a kiss on his muscled back. When satisfied she had eased the soreness of his muscles, she quickly undressed, and molding her body against his, dropped into sleep, pleased to have him beside her.

He slept soundly, coming awake the next morning to find her still asleep curled snugly against him. He stretched languorously, feeling completely restored and relaxed.

Sensing him move, she roused. With her golden hair in a riot of tousled curls and a sleepy grin, she reached for him.

"I feel like a new man. How did you ever learn to do that?" He stroked her hair pushing wild curls back from her face.

"All in the hands, sir." She wriggled her fingers, grinning.

"It certainly is, madam, another one of your excellent weapons," he replied, watching for adverse reaction. But she was no longer sensitive to his teasing, beginning to feel secure and trusting of him.

"Kathryn," he gasped as her hand abruptly slid along his torso, moving lower to caress gently, finding him more than attentive. Taking control, she traced a sensuous exploration with her tongue along the length of his lean body,

"Kathryn," he choked, sucking air through clenched teeth as he tangled his fingers in her golden mane, surrendering completely, lost amidst the pleasures of her exquisite touch.

Aware of new respect blossoming between them, she understood that he would never berate her for inadequacies or boldness in any area. At last, they had begun to trust on more than one level. With that knowledge instilling a sense of confidence, she fell to pleasing him.

When he could speak without gasping, he murmured, "That was incredible, but seemed terribly one-sided, Kathryn."

Resting her head on his chest, she said, "You had a bad day yesterday and I was part of it."

"Kathryn ..." He uttered her name with reverence.

"Do you want to talk about yesterday? Would it help?" she asked, raising herself on one elbow to gaze into his piercing blue eyes.

Her lovely eyes, not hazel but an indescribable green, reveal her thoughts like an open book. He doubted she could lie if her life depended upon it. Each glimpse of her complex personality drew him closer, wanting more. "Not today ... but some day." He cupped her cheek gently, taken aback by his depth of feelings. Smoothing her tangle of golden curls, he murmured softly. "I am afraid our destinies were sealed from the moment I saw you standing in my tent. We both have much to share, but all in good time." A bargain had been struck: both understanding that their lives were taking an untried direction which strangely felt right.

Sometime later as he sat at his desk shaving, he glanced over at her, thinking what a fascinating woman, and this ... only the beginning. They had barely begun to discover each other. His thoughts drifted ahead, realizing he wanted more than victories on the battlefield—so much more. Confident of her honesty, he would dare to trust her. This new emotion would take time to become an integral part of him, but the prize would be worth every bit of effort.

This brother of hers was a factor to be dealt with—his instincts told him that. He believed her avowal of ignorance as to his whereabouts; but 'who' is he? For now, he would give her the benefit of doubt.

She sat watching him shave, silently taking it all in.

"You appear deep in thought," he said softly, eyeing her over the edge of his razor as he paused in shaving.

"I was just thinking how much I would like to do that for you."

He hesitated only a moment before holding the razor out. As she stepped behind him preparing to shave his cheek, she was conscious of the trust he was extending.

"Please take care not to nick me, madam, or I will be forced to confess that I allowed a woman to shave me," he teased, grinning up at her in the mirror.

"Then say no more so I can concentrate." Returning his smile, she took the razor. After studying his profile carefully, she made a clean, gentle swipe. If he was nervous, he never let her know. She made a neat job of it and soon handed the razor back suggesting, "Until I get a little more adept, I think you should finish your upper lip."

After rinsing and toweling his face, she placed a hand on each side of his temple and massaged, gently working her fingers back and down through his long hair, smoothing and plaiting it into a queue. Checking the results in the small mirror she held, he nodded approval.

Pushing his chair back, he stood and turned. "My apologies, my lady, but I must put business before pleasure today. However, I will make it up to you this evening." He touched her cheek, eliciting a smile.

"I will hold you to that promise, Colonel."

Grinning back over his shoulder, he exited the tent.

The day seemed to pass more quickly, possibly due to knowing that Jason, albeit busy, was somewhere in camp, or perhaps newly emerging trust and respect providing her inner contentment. She spent some time with Lieutenant Jackson talking, of all things, about fishing. He had been an avid fly fisherman back in England, a fact she found fascinating. He was beginning to share more of himself, and she enjoyed that.

Jason returned late afternoon. Finding her sitting cross-legged deeply engrossed in a book, he grinned. "I believe these belong to you, milady." He held her rifle, pistol and tomahawk in his arms. "I imagine you could carry on your own personal war with all this artillery, madam."

Dropping the book, she came to her feet in shocked pleasure. In answer to her eager look, he nodded. "You may carry them, now. The dragoons will not question you, but please… "

"I will only use them in an appropriate manner, sir," she interrupted happily, then with eyes twinkling, added, "I promise not to terrorize your men, Colonel."

He burst out laughing. "As it is early yet, why not share a brandy while you tell me how you entertained yourself when I was away?"

They relaxed, enjoying their drinks and each other's company as Kathryn related all that had gone on during his absence. Jason was unaware of Lieutenant Jackson's interest in poetry. Obviously there was more to his lieutenant than he had originally perceived. Having sheltered himself from becoming close to anyone, he had rarely extended common courtesy to him, yet had always been served well. He would begin correcting that injustice; perhaps make an effort to know him better.

Jason watched her expressive face as she talked, her hands gesturing happily, illustrating explanations visually. The longer he watched, the more demanding his need. Setting his glass down, he pulled her up into his arms. "If we are terribly efficient, madam, we may have just enough time before supper …" he trailed off seductively, a devilish glint flashing in his eyes.

Without hesitation, she tossed boots and blouse in the corner, the rest of her clothing abandoned callously as she moved towards their bed. She watched intently as the last of his more complicated garb was discarded; anticipation and rising passion barely held in cheque.

As he moved towards her, the intensity of his gaze held her spellbound. Abruptly he knelt at her feet, and working from her toes upward, traced nipping kisses along her legs. Turning her leg to place a kiss on the back of her right knee, he discovered a well-healed but good-sized scar.

"How did this happen, Kathryn?" he asked in passing, touching the old wound gently, studying it curiously.

Terrifying memories, forcefully pushed back from conscious thought, flashed before her. She was there, again … reliving the fear, reliving the agony as a sturdy branch, snatched burning from the roaring fire, was slammed against her back driving her to her knees. And as she desperately struggled to grab her tomahawk in self-defense, that same glowing branch was plunged into the back of her leg … the agony unbearable. "No, Black Raven, no!"

Jason's head snapped up at her piteous cry. One look at her terrified face brought immediate realization: *she is reliving some past horror.*

"Kathryn." He shook her shoulders gently. "Kathryn," he said louder, shaking her harder, attempting to rouse her from the black place into which she had retreated. "Stay with me." Cradling her in his arms, he spoke her name repeatedly whispering words of comfort, rocking her gently for what seemed an eternity.

Eventually, gulping deep breaths, she began slowly clawing her way back to reality. As the wild terror in her eyes receded he was flooded with relief. She finally recognized him, aware that *he* was the one holding her, sure beyond doubt: *not him … thank God … not him.*"

"Jason, oh, Jason." Tears coursed down her cheeks.

"You are safe now, Kathryn. Safe." He held her tight, stroking her hair and rocking gently.

"Please do not make me go there. Not yet, not yet." Voice hoarse, ragged with emotion, she clung to him, trembling. "Too soon … I may not … be able to come back. I … am so… " Sobbing uncontrollably, she could not finish.

"Hush, now," he crooned. "Hush, love, you are safe."

Who hurt her so—and why? Physically and mentally she had been abused. Her brother was one culprit, but who was Black Raven? The answers must wait. He dared not risk having her retreat back into this black hell; perhaps have it claim her mind permanently. Again and again, like crashing waves, it impacted on him: *her past is as haunted as mine.*

He held her tenderly, crooning soft words, until she again became calm. Remembering his endearments, he was surprised but not sorry. *My Kathryn … oh my Kathryn.* He watched as she tried bravely to smile, mumbling apologies, embarrassed by her weakness.

"I have been where you were, Kathryn."

Her eyes searched his, recognizing the truth in his words.

"We will work this out in time, *together.*" He kissed her tenderly, feeling her relax. "Let us take a ride out to the falls," he whispered.

Explanations were unnecessary, the underlying significance of returning to the beautiful crystal falls, their place of 'beginnings', brought gratitude, inner calm and … *love.*

Lieutenant Jackson noted exhaustion and melancholy as she quietly allowed the colonel to give her a 'leg up' onto her saddle—sparking his concern. She never accepted anyone's assistance. He liked this young woman more with each passing day, admiring her strength and spirit. To see her so bereft was disconcerting. The pinched expression around the colonel's eyes also bore witness—whatever had happened impacted on both equally.

As they prepared to ride out, Lieutenant Jackson handed the colonel a package. "I thought you could both use a bite to eat, sir."

Jason inclined his head, again aware that he had overlooked this man's capabilities too long.

Although extremely late when they returned, Lieutenant Jackson, having waited up to see them back and tend their horses, greeted them with a warm smile. He noticed, deeply relieved, that the sparkle had returned to her eyes and the colonel appeared more relaxed. As he walked the horses back to the holding area his mind started to wander. *Strange,* he thought. *They are such an unlikely pair, and yet …*

Chapter Six

Military Protocol?

Shortly after daybreak he sat sipping coffee, watching her sleep as he mulled over the previous night's events. In fear and need she had cried out, trusting him to be there ... and he had been. She reached for him ... and he responded. Finally, after years of haunting memories, he could give of himself without reprisal or rejection ... *to her alone.* This was the beginning of healing for both of them, common ground on which to build a solid foundation. He smiled, surprised that he considered such thoughts. Yes, he was going through a lot of reassessment; he was changing.

She moaned, bringing him immediately alert. Sleepily rolling over, her hand blindly searched the area he usually occupied.

"I am here, Kathryn," he softly reassured, pleased to see her instantly relax as she came fully awake and rolled to face him.

Crouching by her side, he stroked her tangled curls. "I brought coffee," he murmured.

Peaceful eyes met his smile. "I thought you had left when I reached for ..."

He did not let her finish. Taking her hand gently, he shook his head and bent to kiss her forehead. "I will always tell you before I leave, Kathryn, always."

Her eyes sought his and held. "Are you riding out today?" she asked, reaching for the coffee.

"No, that business can wait another day. I thought we might take a ride, let the horses run." He would remain close today, guarding against lingering repercussions from the previous night's terror.

She scanned his face to be sure she had not misunderstood. His chiseled features softened as he smiled, nodding slightly—a smile which deepened as her face brightened. Throwing the covers aside, she quickly made herself presentable for the day.

As they cantered through grassy meadows dotted with clusters of trees, her whole being came alive.

"May I run with her, sir?" she yelled over her shoulder.

"Of course, enjoy yourself. You know I am an excellent shot."

She laughed gleefully at his beaming face and attempted humor. Needing no further encouragement, she gave Beauty her head. Having had little exercise for many weeks, she bubbled with raw energy. Leaping forward, she ran free, her mane and tail flying, proud head held high.

Needing no reins for security, Kathryn flung her arms wide, angling her head back. Eyes closed, in complete harmony with her animal, she drifted blissfully in another world.

Jason reined Diablo back slightly to watch the pair. Kathryn's long, thick curls billowed behind her in a golden tangle, not unlike Beauty's red-gold mane. She rode as if an integral part of the little mare's back, entirely relaxed—the two completely in tune with each other. What an incredible sight. *There is so much I want to know about you, Kathryn ... so very much.*

They arrived back at their campsite late afternoon, both smiling and refreshed. As Lieutenant Jackson came forward to take the horses, he noted the happy aura she exuded, her sun kissed face glowing as she swung her leg over the mare's shoulder and dropped gracefully to the ground.

"What a beautiful day, Lieutenant." Kathryn laughed, slapping dust from her coat and breeches.

Observing the colonel sitting astride Diablo, absorbing Kathryn's exuberance, Lieutenant Jackson was aware of a pronounced softening in his usually cold exterior.

"I concur." He nodded fighting a smile, the harsh lines of his face easing.

Lieutenant Jackson knew him well enough by now; this formality for show only. Yes, he was changing—becoming decidedly more human.

As the colonel walked Kathryn back to their tent, he reflected upon the effortlessness of their day—Kathryn as always, uncomplaining, happy and conversational. Their ride had been what they both needed, a chance to set aside everyday routine for a few hours, and share time together.

Recalling her passion-glazed eyes as she lay beneath him beside the narrow woodland stream, and her childlike joy in splashing him as they bathed, he smiled in spite of himself. With each passing day, they became more attuned to each other's whims and moods, but of greater importance: to each other's needs.

"I do believe you had a pleasant ride today, sir." Breaking his reverie, she smiled impishly.

Stopped short in his tracks, he aimed an arched eyebrow and laughed out loud. "You, madam, are a tart. And for that, I am thankful." Ushering her quickly inside, he wrapped her in strong arms, kissing her soundly. "I have a few things that need tending, but I will return in time for the evening meal." He searched her face, cupping her cheek.

"I am fine, now," she said quietly, reading his thoughts. "Truly, I am."

He walked into the tent at suppertime and found her mending a torn cuff on one of his shirts. "You never cease to amaze me, Kathryn." He eyed her appreciatively as he stepped to the washbasin and splashed water on his face.

Breaking the thread with her teeth and folding the shirt carefully, she gave him a sidelong glance. "It may not be a chore of preference but it has to be done," she said cheerfully.

Wiping his face with a towel, he turned to face her and paused. "I will be talking with my officers during the meal tonight, but will join you for coffee afterwards." Although he and his dragoons had not encountered rebel activity for several days, his outriders had just brought new information.

More accustomed to him with each passing day, a raw edge to his voice brought her fully alert. Apparently, the temporary peace within the campsite was about to change. Perhaps someday she would be included in his plans rather than left to wonder—but all in good time.

Pulling her against him for a quick hug, he then took her elbow and guided her out to the campfire. As they approached, the dragoons sat up a little straighter paying heed to their colonel.

"Gentlemen," He inclined his head acknowledging a small group. "As I will be engaged with my officers during the meal, please make Miss MacLean feel welcome."

Glances passed surreptitiously between them. That was not the name they recalled when she had been introduced.

"Lieutenant Jackson will see that you get something to eat, Miss MacLean," he said curtly, all business now, as he moved to join his officers.

Noticing the curious looks, she smiled uncomfortably, hoping this change of name would not create more distrust than already existed.

"Come, sit here, Miss MacLean." Lieutenant Jackson stressed her name with a welcoming smile.

He appeared not to be surprised. As close as he was to the colonel, at least in performing duties, perhaps he had been informed of the name change earlier. He gestured her to a spot on a large log where two soldiers were sliding over to make room.

Smiling tentatively and thanking them, she sat down. Within moments, the lieutenant placed a plate of something indiscernible, but not bad tasting, in front of her, along with a cup of hot coffee. Each time she joined them the same recurring thought popped into her head. As soon as she was allowed, she would venture into nearby woods and shoot some grouse or snare a few rabbits to help make their meals more interesting. She ate in silence, listening to their friendly banter as they soon forgot her presence and relaxed—but not completely. Their talk remained light, centered on topics of no great import. Nothing was mentioned about troop movements or the rebels.

The colonel glanced over and returned to the discussion with his officers, satisfied she was handling herself well.

Lost in thought, she was startled as Lieutenant Jackson returned to her side after taking food to Jason and the officers.

"I did not mean to come up on you so quietly," he apologized.

She shook her head. "I am 'wool gathering', Lieutenant, pay me no mind."

After finishing a quiet meal she sat sipping her coffee, enjoying the warmth of the lieutenant's company. He tried nudging her into the campfire conversation more than once, but with little or no success. She remained unsure of herself with the dragoons in general.

But her relationship with the lieutenant was changing. When they had been abruptly thrown together during the colonel's two-day absence, they had not known each other well enough to touch upon questions of a personal nature. But with each passing day, he had become more comfortable in asking her about herself. He showed no attempt to pry, only genuine interest in getting to know her better; she liked the man.

Sitting side-by-side sharing their coffee, she relaxed and began chatting. But the cheerful sound of a tin whistle trilling from farther out in the campsite brightened her face, stopping her mid-sentence as she paused to listen.

"You play the tin whistle, miss?" The lieutenant smiled, noticing how animated she became when happy.

She nodded, paused a moment then shook her head, confusing him. At his quizzical look she explained, "I do, but not yet. I … I want to feel more a part of …" She shrugged apologetically.

"All in good time," he assured, making her grateful for his understanding.

She continued to drink coffee while listening to the music and watching the sky. Sunset was upon them, the heavens putting on a brilliant show of oranges, reds, golden yellows and a glistening halo as the last rays of sunlight kissed the edges of deep indigo clouds. Awestruck by the magnificence of nature's handiwork, she temporarily forgot where she was. Standing quickly, she stepped over to the group of men huddled together in talk, stopping at Jason's side.

"Look at the sky, gentlemen." She was spellbound, her voice breathless. "Oh, excuse me." For a moment she remembered her manners, realizing she had interrupted. "But just look at that sky: the oranges and yellows, the black silhouettes of the fir trees …" She bubbled with exuberance. "And, Colonel …" Without thinking she crouched by his side, placing her hand on his shoulder, gesturing towards the sunset. "The halo around the clouds is so magnificent." She turned to him thoroughly entranced. But at his officers' shocked expressions, and more importantly, Jason's, her face fell.

"I … I …" she stammered. Thoroughly embarrassed, she removed her hand and stood. Dropping her head, unable to meet their eyes, she slowly began backing away.

The colonel arose, turning slowly and deliberately to face her, his features awash with cold fury, restraining his temper by sheer willpower.

She met his eyes then, her face contrite. "I fear I have much to learn about military protocol, sir. I am truly sorry for the interruption."

All eyes had been on her, waiting for the colonel to erupt furiously, his usual reaction to interference. But at a stern look from Lieutenant Jackson both conversation and music resumed.

The colonel returned to his conversation as if nothing had happened, his demeanor making it obvious he would brook no comments. But his mind struggled with odd emotions which caused difficulty in regaining concentration. *You are such an enigma, Kathryn. Your childlike tendencies are in such contrast to your boldness—you fascinate me.*

Kathryn was truly taken aback. The powerful beauty of nature always moved her; she assumed others shared the same feelings. Heading for their tent, humiliated and not ready to rejoin the men, she stopped beside a large tree. Muttering under her breath, she slammed both fists against the trunk. Angrily swiping her foot at a small patch of fallen leaves, she leaned in bracing herself, pressing her forehead against the rough bark.

"Damn it!" Straightening, she struck the trunk with her fist. "Damn it, you fool." She struck again in exasperation.

At the sound of a twig snapping, she whirled to find the lieutenant standing directly behind her with an amused expression and a mug of coffee.

"Oh …" she blurted, startled. "Not you, sir. I was not referring to you or …" she stammered.

His smile broadened. "You did not finish your coffee, Miss MacLean." He held the cup out to her. "Please stay awhile. The sky *is* beautiful tonight," he said softly, hoping to alleviate the sting of her earlier rebuke.

Attempting a smile, she accepted the coffee and began sipping slowly. They were both silent for a moment, as he studied her intently.

"Lieutenant, would you teach me protocol? I obviously have much to learn if I am ever to fit in. Tonight I learned that one does not interrupt the colonel's meetings for any reason, but…"

"There is not a lot to know, miss. Merely live by the creed: 'Do not offend or antagonize Colonel Tarrington' and you will have no problems."

She arched a questioning eyebrow accompanied by a lopsided grin, and again he found the similarities of their gestures intriguing. *Yes, you could be good for the colonel—very good.* Then, on a more serious vein, he talked in detail of British protocol: correct behavior in regards to officers, 'regulars' and prisoners—the latter being an unlikely situation upon which he did not elaborate.

Finishing her coffee she handed him the empty cup, thanked him kindly, and bid goodnight.

The colonel, ever aware of actions going on around him, had not missed Kathryn's show of temper. He knew her well enough to realize it had been aimed it at herself; she wanted desperately to be accepted by his dragoons. Her open display of anger had thoroughly amused him. That particular emotion was one he could easily understand—one which he had problems with himself.

The feeling irking him at the moment was a twinge of jealousy at seeing her response to his lieutenant. They had stood talking for some time; nothing inappropriate in either of their actions. Why did it bother him? Because, he realized, she had been absolutely correct, and very perceptive, when she had told him some time ago that he would never share her. Breaking his meeting earlier than planned, he headed towards the campfire to confer with Lieutenant Jackson.

As she walked slowly into their tent, many thoughts rushed through her head. She must learn their ways; she did not enjoy feeling like a fool or embarrassing Jason.

After freshening up she stood by the desk brushing her hair, her back turned to the tent entrance. Jason entered quietly and stood watching her stroke the long, honey colored curls. Sensing his presence she turned, immediately dropping the brush on the desk.

"Colonel, I apologize for tonight." She rushed on, "I … I completely forgot myself." Contrite and trying to atone for her mistake, her eyes filled with distress. "I am now aware of how I should purport myself and will make every effort to …"

He moved closer and touched a silencing finger to her lips. Picking up the hairbrush, he began stroking her hair, saying nothing for the moment. Setting the brush down and placing his hands gently on her shoulders, he turned her to face him. Pushing tawny curls aside, he studied her face.

"I spoke with Lieutenant Jackson," he said—his way of accepting her misdemeanor. "The sunset was beautiful, but it could not hold a candle to you, Kathryn."

Flowing into his welcoming arms, she savored the feel of him, enjoying his strength. Having fully expected to take the brunt of his wrath, she was surprised and pleased. There would be time to ponder his more controlled reaction later. For now, she would lose herself to him once again.

Chapter Seven

Rebel Encounter

As time passed, the dragoons became more receptive. Kathryn did not force herself on them and did not use being in the colonel's favor to exact special consideration—thus earning their grudging respect. She accepted the fact that it would require more time before they fully trusted her, and worked hard to earn their confidence. At least they no longer exhibited trepidation at her carrying a dirk in her boot—and she certainly felt more at ease having it there. Her tomahawk rode comfortably against the small of her back, tucked into her belt underneath her greatcoat. Good to his word, Jason had not questioned her further about its history after that dreadful night. Although curious, he let the subject drop. She would share more of her past when ready, as he would he … but not yet.

On the advice of loyalist informants, Jason had moved their encampment further south. Kathryn loved the sight of the field tents being dismantled, the dusty road, the smell of horses and worn leather, long hours in the saddle, Jason's passion at days end and falling asleep encircled within his arms. To her, the anticipation of picking up and moving on was invigorating and exciting.

They had followed the rambling curve of the Big Snake River for days and were now encamped near Charlesville, an area known to harbor rebel militia. During the arduous journey southward, Kathryn had been ready, on several occasions, to sidetrack into the woods to hunt rabbits. But Jason kept a tight rein on her; they were in rebel territory. Several heated 'discussions', as she called them, had arisen—but he would brook no argument. She was informed of her place in the event of an attack, and as to hunting … "You will not." She would remain far from the firing lines as instructed. When the battle was over, he expected to find her where he had left her. *End of discussion.* During a fit of pique, she had accused him of not trusting her. To his credit, he held his temper, brushing a light kiss to her forehead before admonishing her not to forget his orders.

Their 'love' strengthened daily, abusive characteristics of earlier trysts replaced by a shared desire to please each other. She looked forward to the end of each day: enjoying camaraderie with the dragoons, sharing events over a brandy with Jason—impatient to be in his arms again. His personality was gradually changing, the violent temper of his past having moderated to an occasional flare-up. As his former fear tactics were steadily replaced with stern, but fair, judgments, even the dragoons showed new respect for their colonel.

Gunfire in the distance startled her from reverie. Having kissed her soundly, Jason had ridden out earlier with his dragoons, leaving the lieutenant and a handful of soldiers to protect the campsite. She had paced like a caged animal, back and forth in front of their tent, lost in thought. Lieutenant Jackson brought food and coffee but she would have none of it.

"He will return unharmed," he assured, and matching her pace continued to talk.

"I cannot stand not knowing where he is or if he is hurt, or …" Raising anxious eyes to the lieutenant she exclaimed, "I want to be out there with him." Distressed and without thinking, she divulged strong feelings.

In a moment of fleeting concern, Lieutenant Jackson hoped he would not hurt her too badly. "You know I have been given my orders, miss," he apologized. "Perhaps you might try to read or …" For the life of him he could not think of any suggestions.

"Ignore me, Lieutenant, I really am not at my best today," she mumbled and continued pacing.

After what seemed an interminable amount of time, the gunfire quieted to occasional erratic bursts—then edgy silence. At the sound of hoof beats approaching she stopped pacing and stood riveted, eyes scanning the horizon, desperate for him to come into sight. He was suddenly there, cresting the hill sitting tall and proud astride Diablo, flanked by two columns of dragoons. Flooded with relief, fearful her knees would give out she ducked into their tent and collapsed onto the chair, gulping deep breaths and mouthing prayers of gratitude.

Jason reined to a stop and dismounted, immediately removing his helmet and gloves. The lieutenant stepped forward offering assistance, noting a spot of drying blood on the colonel's neck.

"Is Kathryn all right?" he demanded, concerned by her sudden disappearance.

Lieutenant Jackson nodded, noticing the colonel's familiarity—no longer Miss MacLean—a definite relaxing of protocol. "She has paced like a restless mountain lion, sir."

"I am not surprised." Eyeing his officer with a slight smile, he turned abruptly and headed towards his tent.

"I will bring bandaging for your neck right away, sir," he called after him.

As the colonel entered the tent she flung herself into his arms. "Jason," she cried, relieved to touch him, hold him. Planting a firm kiss on his smiling lips, she trembled noticeably. Abruptly standing back she looked him over, paling at the blossom of red adorning his collar and a dark smudge along his hairline. "Sit down, let me take a look," she instructed, and hurriedly began unfastening his jacket.

"Relax, Kathryn, it is no more than a scratch." Waving his hand dismissively, he watched her clumsy attempts. "Kathryn …" He stayed her frantic hands. "I am fine," he stated, quietly insistent.

Her eyes met his as he smiled reassuringly. "I understand you wore out a perfectly good pair of boots today." Angling his head, he arched a quizzical brow.

She nodded, smiling sheepishly at her overreaction. "I will have to speak to Lieutenant Jackson about giving my secrets away," she said with mock severity, her composure beginning to return.

Announcing himself, the lieutenant entered with bandaging and medical supplies. Setting the supplies on the desk, he moved closer to be of assistance, but made no move to interfere: Kathryn was more than capable.

Opening Jason's shirt, baring his neck, she was relieved to see no more than a minor graze from a bullet by the looks, and a small cut on his forehead. After cleaning both wounds, using some of his best brandy to sterilize them, she turned to the lieutenant. Before she could form the question, he handed her a mug of willow bark tea. "I am impressed by your perception, Lieutenant; thank you."

"I see you have Lieutenant Jackson well trained with your herbal remedies," Jason observed, accepting the soothing tea without hesitation.

The lieutenant's face eased into a smile. He had appraised her competence in tending the colonel's wounds while handing her supplies as needed. If she were willing, she could be very helpful in the medical tent, a place where competent hands often determined the outcome in a wounded man's recovery. After picking up leftover supplies and clearing the desk he headed out, calling back over his shoulder that he would return shortly with food.

Kathryn turned to Jason. "I would like to hear about your day—about the skirmish."

He had not intended to broach the subject, unsure whether she wanted to know the details. But at her insistence, he described the small band of rebels who had fled for the woods in full retreat after a brief encounter. Casualties were minimal, only two dragoons having sustained injuries no worse than his—a successful outcome all in all.

He intended to crush these renegade bands of militia; keep them on the run preventing them from joining the larger forces of General Gates or Major Beldon. Without reinforcements, the Americans would be hard pressed to stand up to British forces when both sides clashed head on: the eventual reality of this irritating situation. These colonials were a tough bunch that tried his patience. Extremely wily, and knowing the area like the back of their hand, they were running his dragoons ragged in constant pursuit.

Lieutenant Jackson returned shortly with food and drink, leaving almost immediately. Having worked up an appetite Jason ate hungrily but Kathryn picked at her food, watching him in silence.

"You are very quiet," he commented, curious. *Are former ties giving you second thoughts my Kathryn?*

She quickly turned away, but not before he saw a tear slowly tracking down her cheek.

Immediately on his feet, he moved to her side and drew her up into his arms. Ragged breaths proved she was crying. Did she feel torn between loyalties after this encounter with fellow colonials?

"Kathryn, what is it?" Women had often cried in his presence, and having often been the object of their distress he callously dismissed it. But Kathryn's tears were genuine, disturbing. "Have I hurt you in some way?" Long pause … no answer. "Are you ill?"

She shook her head.

"Kathryn, please … Look at me." Touching her cheek, he searched her face for a clue. "If you feel you have made a bad decision and want to leave … You must know by now that I could never harm you. You are free to go if that is what you want." Raw emotion lent a husky edge to his voice.

With that statement, her cheeks were instantly awash with fresh tears, her shoulders heaving with anguished sobs as she watched his tormented face.

"God knows I do not want you to go, but …"

Pulling his head down, she kissed him deeply. "Oh, Jason, I … I do not want to leave you. I cannot for …" murmured so softly he was hard pressed to hear, "I love you … with all my heart."

Unprepared for this open declaration he was momentarily speechless. She had often spoken of need, of their intense passion, of enjoying his touch, but this sudden avowal forced him to confront his own feelings. *Where can this relationship go? Where do I want it to go?* "Then what has saddened you to tears, Kathryn?"

"Another inch and your injury could have been …" She could not complete her statement.

"But that did not happen. It is no more than a scratch." He shrugged. "It is nothing."

"Perhaps today meant nothing to you but what if …"

"Kathryn, I would make assurances if I could, but realistically, I can promise you nothing long term." He breathed into her hair, stroking the long curls. "I can offer you today only, and hope I will be able to do the same tomorrow." Pausing, he allowed her time to digest his words. "I am no bargain, Kathryn; you deserve better." He searched her face, his intense blue gaze capturing hers and holding: a kaleidoscope of emotions openly displaying the answers she so desperately sought.

"You are my life," she whispered.

"You honor me, milady." At her confused look, he added huskily, "No one has shown such concern for me before—no one."

Who has treated this man so callously, she wondered. Perhaps someday he would share his hurt with her, as she would with him, but not now … later.

He stood holding her close, his hands automatically beginning to rove. Cupping her bottom, he drew her against him, needing her more than he needed air to breath. He could no longer deny the fact. He loved her—even more with each passing day.

Love was a frightening new emotion. He had spent his life shielding himself from hurt, refusing to care, remaining detached within a self-imposed suit of protective armor. A lifetime of hurt had been dealt him at the hand of his father. Caring for anyone or anything courted disappointment and pain. He had joined the British Green Dragoons because of their intense training and brutal battle techniques, the perfect career for him—one in which he could vent inner rage. But Kathryn was changing all this, creating chinks in his armor, making it worth the risk to care … to love her.

Jason could promise her nothing but today. It was a foolish waste of time to shed tears for a situation beyond her control to alter. Then and there, she promised: *From this day forth, I will take each day as it comes, love him in all ways and cherish whatever time we are able to share.* Although he had yet to voice it, she knew he loved her too. Head sorted out emotionally and heart overflowing with passion, she concentrated on loving him.

In the middle of the night she awoke momentarily melancholy and reached for him.

"Are you all right, Kathryn?" he whispered, gently touching her shoulder.

"Umm, with you beside me," she murmured, rolling to face him and snuggling against his chest.

Kissing her forehead, he stroked her arm in a comforting gesture.

"No one has ever loved you enough to cry for you?" she asked, finding that hard to accept.

Silence … then the slightest shake of his head.

"All that has changed," she said firmly. "Let the past go, Jason." As she began drifting sleepily, he kissed her ear and whispered, somewhat hesitantly, "I love you, Kathryn Cameron MacLean."

He felt her lips curve in a smile against his chest and was surprised at himself. He had never spoken those words to anyone before … yet he knew he meant them.

It felt so very right.

Chapter Eight

Relapse of Attitudes

The colonel's band of dragoons headed northwards loosely following the Savannah River. They moved at a moderate pace, side-tracking in fanlike maneuvers to flush out small groups of rebel militia. Kathryn enjoyed the picked-up pace of life—being on the move; it appealed to her independent, adventurous nature. She relished the challenge of cooking on the trail—having had plenty of experience in that area. Tactfully suggesting changes and additions to Cook, she hoped to create more variety in their everyday fare. Recently she had shared her favorite bread recipe with him; one which required pounding acorns into a fine powder and adding it to the dough. Baked on hot stones, the unusual nutty flavor of the loaves had drawn favorable comments from the dragoons.

Cook was more than glad to have help with his demanding job. Besides, he enjoyed her companionship and intelligence. In addition to hunting and cooking abilities, he found her well versed on the benefits of certain local vegetation: nutritionally valuable vegetables which would maintain a high level of health amongst the men. Being well read, Cook's curiosity was piqued. *How does she know so much about Indian lore—specifically, her knowledge of the Cherokees?* When questioned she shrugged, flashing a disarming smile, remaining non-committal. Busy with meal preparations at that time, he did not pursue the question.

This particular morning, after Jason and the dragoons had ridden out for the day, she talked Lieutenant Jackson into accompanying her on a short hunting trip in woods near their camp. While setting her snares along well-used rabbit trails, she patiently explained the process. He watched closely, impressed by her ability. Within a short time, they retraced their steps and collected several rabbits for the evening meal.

She also dug up large clusters of what she called 'u la tli ya', roots which looked a bit like beets. As she washed them in the little brook, she described a type of bread she would make after the roots were dried and pounded into meal. "They are also tasty served by themselves, Lieutenant, and the dough is delicious fried, baked or sometimes boiled—in my opinion a rather versatile vegetable. You will see," she assured, holding them out for him to carry.

Kathryn's knowledge of Indian fare intrigued him. He knew the area was populated with Cherokees who, although not enamored with the English, were not outright enemies. Might she have contacts that could prove useful in tracking this errant rebel leader the colonel so despised? Not as easily put off as Cook, he was insistent upon some answers.

However, she cleverly sidestepped his queries with a simple shrug. "I have friends with Cherokee ties, but it really is too long a story to start at this hour. We had best get back before the colonel returns." She flashed her most charming smile, knowing that statement would weigh heavily. "But I will tell you someday." Her eyes sparkled with humor as she thrust another bundle of green vegetation into his hand and headed towards the horses. Grimacing at the dripping vegetation in his hand, he followed her lead.

Cook was pleasantly surprised by her afternoon of trapping and gathering fresh vegetables, but more impressed when she gutted and skinned the rabbits herself. In no time, they were spitted over the campfire, browning quite nicely and emitting a delicious aroma. Inhaling deeply, she sat down on a fallen log, sipping coffee while she kept a vigilant eye on the roasting rabbits. She was no longer considered an oddity around the campfire. The dragoons appreciated her efforts and looked forward to her singing and playing the tin whistle each evening. On the surface, they appeared to have relaxed their guard while in her presence, though little of their plans were discussed within her earshot.

Kathryn understood their reserve; there had been no opportunity permitting her to prove she could be trusted. They acknowledged her as the colonel's lady, but had not accepted her for herself. On a positive note, however, they appeared to soften a little more each day. Lately, by listening carefully, she overheard repeated reference to a band of rebel militia whose leader was particularly adept at antagonizing the English troops. He specifically targeted their supply wagons, stealing much needed provisions on a regular basis—his attacks silent and swift.

Might this have been the individual to blame for that 'black day' several weeks ago when Jason returned to camp in a violent temper? She was aware that his superiors continued their bullying demands, reproaching him for his lack of ability—an emotional toll unjustly inflicted. His mood often reflected this constant frustration, his temper flaring violently upon occasion. Time and patience would eventually convince him of her trustworthiness and help him to control his anger better.

She sat by the campfire surrounded by dragoons sharing a light supper. The rabbit, cooked to perfection, was obviously appreciated from their forthright comments.

Jason had ridden in late with three of his officers just before supper, greeting her offhandedly in a distracted manner. At times like this she maintained a low profile, allowing him to sort things out. He sat at a campfire off to one side picking at his food, discussing the territory with Lieutenant Jackson and a handful of officers. Frustration accented the angular quality of his face; a muscle twitched in his lower jaw.

As he bit into a piece of rabbit he paused looking it over; it was not the usual fare. The lieutenant mentioned Kathryn's contribution to the meal and her hunting abilities. Nodding in her direction with a tight smile, he continued with the business at hand. "I want this 'devil's spawn' brought to heel," he growled.

Though unable to hear more than bits and pieces of their conversation, Kathryn easily overheard that vehement statement and perked up her ears.

"Where can we ford the Catawba River without trouble?" Lieutenant Jackson asked.

Jason turned to her. "Get the maps off my desk," he demanded curtly, then resumed talking with his officers. Realizing she had made no move to do as ordered, he turned an icy glare in her direction. "I told you to get the maps, woman. I will not tell you again."

The officers turned, eyeing her silently. Lieutenant Jackson held his breath willing her to *back down, back down.* Having shared many hours with her over the past months, he knew her better than they. Spirited and strong willed, she was not one to bend to demands.

She stood, but did not budge in the direction of the tent. Returning his icy glare, she casually put two fingers to her lips and whistled sharply.

"Madam ..." He did not get to finish his sentence as Beauty trotted up—surprising all but him.

Grabbing the halter rope, she flung herself onto the mare's bare back, and with a pat to her neck and soft words, quieted her.

"Just what do you think you are doing?" Squaring his shoulders, he strode towards her. "I told you to get the maps."

"I am going for a ride," she answered, her voice ragged with controlled anger.

Locking eyes in a war of wills, they glared in frosty silence. Not a sound could be heard, the dragoons holding their breath as one, silently watching this tense drama unfold.

"Get down," he demanded furiously reaching unconsciously for his pistol, abruptly stopping as he realized what he had been about to do. Breathing heavily, eyes narrowed, his smoldering gaze impaled her.

Knowing the restraint he had exacted upon himself and what it cost him, she made her decision. Sliding her leg over Beauty's neck, she dropped to the ground, and handing the halter rope to Lieutenant Jackson, turned to face the colonel. A tense silence hung between them as they eyed each other angrily. She would not embarrass him further by continuing her defiance, but it irked her.

"Go to the tent," he ordered. "I will be there shortly to deal with you."

At his veiled threat, she eyed him heatedly for a long moment. "I would have a word with you *now*, sir. I have obeyed your order and respect your authority, Colonel, but I need a word with you … now." She spoke quietly but vehemently, her look and tone sending a warning message; she, too, was holding her temper by sheer will power.

After a moment's contemplation, he nodded, gesturing her towards the tent.

"Lieutenant, break for coffee, I will join you shortly." He turned and stalked after her.

The men eyed each other, no one uttering a word. Lieutenant Jackson breathed a sigh of relief as tension eased and they returned to their coffee. He also noticed, with acute interest, certain changes in his commanding officer—changes that he would never have thought to be possible.

She entered the tent fuming. Stalking behind his desk, she turned to face him as he strode in behind her, arrogant and furious. Planting both hands firmly on the maps, she met his angry glare with a smoldering intensity of her own.

He stepped quickly towards her, stopped abruptly and slammed both fists heavily on his side of the desk. "You need a lesson in humility and obedience," he hissed leaning forward, their faces mere inches apart.

If he thought to intimidate her, he was sorely mistaken. With a violent slam, she brought both fists down on the maps, and leaned in closer. "I may not be traveling with you through benefit of title or definition, but I am neither your slave nor your whore. Do not treat me so in front of your men." Her voice shook. Abruptly straightening, she moved swiftly around the desk.

Making no retort he watched her approach, absorbing her anger. As he turned to meet her, she struck his face with force mustered from fury. "How dare you treat me like that?" she spat.

Grabbing her wrist before she could strike again, with a swift practiced motion he twisted her arm painfully behind her back, and clamping his arm across her chest, trapped her in a viselike grip. Digging strong fingers painfully into her flesh, he yanked her back against him, forcing her steadily downwards.

"Do not ever strike me again!" he snarled.

Struggling to stand upright, refusing to be forced to her knees, her strength surprised him.

"You will have to break it, sir," she gasped as pain tore through her shoulder. "I will not—be brought to my knees by you—or any man for that matter," she panted, her words coming in ragged breaths. She grimaced as he maintained steady, painful pressure.

Without warning she ceased her struggle, sagging limply against him, allowing just enough leeway to turn and look up into his face. "Except of course: by choice, Colonel." There was no mistaking the sparkling humor in her eyes despite her intense discomfort.

She had pierced his unmanageable fury, returning him to reality. *How can she possibly find humor amidst such anger and pain? This woman: ... my woman.* He released her immediately, desperately sorry for his actions. Turning her towards him he gently massaged her shoulder, attempting to ease the pain he had inflicted.

"What have I done to deserve this treatment from you?" Her eyes filled with question and confusion. "I was ready to ride away—to defy you." She held his gaze. "The only reason I dismounted was to show obedience and respect for *you* in front of your men, so as not to undermine your authority; and no other reason. I *do* try to live up to your expectations, but you treated me as if I were ..."

His mouth closed gently over hers stopping her mid-sentence. Holding her against him, he breathed softly against her ear, "I was wrong." He had never admitted that to anyone before. Tipping her chin up, he gazed into her sad eyes and felt guilt—a new and discomforting emotion.

"I will endeavor to treat you with more consideration from now on. I do not consider you my slave nor my whore, and I will not give you cause to think that again. You have often made concessions affording me respect in front of my men, I owe you better."

She easily sensed his discomfort and distinct wariness at what her next reaction might be. Touching a finger to his lips she said quietly, "Go finish your meeting, Jason." Turning to the desk, she picked up the maps and handed them to him with a warm smile. "We will talk later."

"I shall return soon," he assured, still somewhat uneasy.

"And I will be here, Jason, waiting for you." Her eyes softened. "When you love someone, you do not leave because of a rough spot." Brushing a kiss to his cheek, she whispered, "You stay and work it out."

With a smile of gratitude, he took the maps and left.

Lieutenant Jackson, concerned for Kathryn's welfare, studied the colonel's face as he approached. As he neared the lieutenant, he paused long enough to say, "I have been thoroughly chastised for my bad manners." A hint of a grin played at the corners of his mouth.

"You know, sir, she is the best thing that ever happened to you," he murmured.

The colonel tensed and Lieutenant Jackson braced himself, expecting a well-deserved reprimand for his impertinence.

"You are right, Lieutenant, and I must make an effort to remember that—often."

They walked to the campfire where the men greeted their commanding officer as if nothing had happened. Lieutenant Jackson made no outward acknowledgement of the bright mark on the colonel's cheek, but realized it must have been an extremely heated discussion. *She has more guts than any woman I have ever known, more than many men*—and was duly impressed.

The hour was late, their planning having taken longer than expected. Jason entered the tent quietly so as not to wake her. She was asleep on their bed, covered with a light blanket, her chest rising and falling in deep even breaths.

Sitting on the edge of his desk, he watched her for several minutes. She could be so damned stubborn and defiant and yet—even when right—would back down to protect him from losing face with his dragoons. *You are such an unusual woman, my Kathryn … and I love you.*

As he continued to watch, her eyes suddenly fluttered open. Partially awake, she smiled sleepily and reached out welcoming him to bed. Bare shoulders indicated she was naked, surprising him. She did not hold on to anger; she fought and made up, then put all the unpleasantness behind her.

He knelt down and with great tenderness, brushed curls back from her face. Previous experience had proven that women withheld favors when displeased. Kathryn was unique, unlike other woman he had known, but how would she react if he …

"Come to bed, love," she whispered, smiling enigmatically. "I am chilled and miss your warmth."

As he touched her face, she reached for the buttons on his jacket, no longer sleepy.

"Kathryn, Kathryn," he whispered, breathing deeply, enjoying the intoxicating scent of her.

Tossing his jacket aside, he began trailing heated kisses across her taut stomach, working ever lower. As his tongue began an insistent and intimate exploration, a delicious shudder coursed through her. "Jason," she gasped, attempting to sit up, shy for the first time.

"Stay put," he smiled reassuringly. Considerate of her insecurities he proceeded slowly, allowing her to become accustomed at her own pace.

"Jason … is that pleasant for you?"

"Go with it, my pet, do not fight me," he murmured, pleased to find her a novice in this area. He nuzzled gently, relishing her sharp inhalation of breath. "If I do this correctly, my love," he said lightly, hoping to ease her tension, "I will introduce you to pleasures you have never experienced before." Continuing cautiously he watched her reaction "Do you trust me?" he asked softly, and reaching for her hand squeezed gently.

Nodding slightly, her dreamy eyes met his reflecting that trust. With her hand clasped firmly in his she surrendered, allowing herself to become immersed in a world of absolute ecstasy.

She drifted in endless delight, slowly returning from sensuous oblivion. Stroking her damp curls back he smiled—blue eyes filled with tenderness. "Was it as I said it would be?" Arching a questioning eyebrow, he softly traced his finger along the bridge of her nose.

Nodding in dazed wonderment, she kissed him hungrily and began working the buttons on his breeches. Within moments, rid of all constrictive garments, he slid naked beneath the covers. The hour may have been late, but he made no polite refusals.

In the afterglow, entwined in each other's arms, they touched playfully, enjoying being together—anger resolved.

"Kathryn, help me keep a tight rein on my emotions. It seems you are the only one who can."

Wincing, she reached to touch the lingering mark on his cheek. His eyes expressed concern and regret as he massaged her shoulder gently, wishing he could undo his hurtful action.

"It is nothing more than a reminder that I, too, must learn to curb my temper." She shrugged. "What a pair we make." Her eyes sparkled.

As she drifted towards sleep within the comforting circle of his arms, she studied his faintly flushed face.

"Jason ..." her voice was soft with wonderment.

He turned a questioning look her way.

"You were incredible."

"I had hoped you would see it that way." He grinned.

Chapter Nine

New Revelations

Morning found them enjoying hot coffee while she plaited his queue. He sat at his desk watching her in a small standing mirror. She had treated him to a relaxing shave earlier, and he had to admit she was so adept with the straightedge razor that he could do no better.

Quietly content since she awoke, obviously lost in thought, she hummed happily as she smoothed his hair.

"If I did not know better, my pet, I would not be surprised to hear you purr like a contented kitten at any moment." He watched with smiling eyes as she blushed, somewhat embarrassed. "Now, to what might we attribute that fact, I wonder?" But at the uncomfortable expression creeping across her face, he ceased his teasing.

"Jason, are you making light of my feelings?" she asked uncertainly.

Instantly up and out of his chair, he encircled her in his arms. "No, love," he shook his head vehemently. "I am pleased to have found a way to give you such obvious pleasure."

She looked up hesitantly, eyes wide with shy innocence. "I have never experienced anything like that before."

Chucking her under the chin tenderly he whispered, "Then we will have to try that more often, hmm?"

At his familiar arched brow, she nodded eagerly.

"Now, would you help me finish this?" Indicating his hair he sat back down. "Then we can enjoy our morning coffee before it gets cold."

She sat on the edge of his desk swinging her legs, bare feet dangling, savoring her coffee and grinning at him.

Jason enjoyed these private moments with Kathryn. She presented an endless enigma, a mixture of complete opposites: strong—yet possessed of a tender vulnerability, bold—yet often timid, passionate in her needs and yet—ultimately shy. And at times, a picture of innocence that never ceased to charm him. He watched her quietly, his mind awhirl with the pleasures she brought to him.

Quite abruptly his expression changed, an ever-vigilant sense of duty interrupted his musings. Questions forced aside for the time being, suddenly came unbidden to the forefront.

"You are thinking too much," she commented. "You have moved on to different ground. Well, ask what you will."

She read him all too well, easily sensing his changing thoughts.

"Cook has been thoroughly impressed with your cooking skills, and ..."

She watched him, eyes alert and smiling. "And you would like to know how I come by such an extensive knowledge of Indian customs."

Folding his arms across his chest, he leaned back in his chair shaking his head, amused at her ability to know his mind.

"Actually, most are Cherokee customs." She was quiet for a moment. "I lived with the Cherokees for many months, the Bird Clan to be more specific." She observed him closely relieved to see no negative reaction. "It is a rather long story that you do not have time for now."

"Kathryn, I once said, 'No questions asked and no answers need be given.' I will stand by that statement, but you have piqued my curiosity."

"I will share all of it with you, but may I choose the appropriate time?" she asked quietly. "My relationship with the Cherokees," she paused deciding what, if anything needed to be said at this time, "...will not hurt *our* cause in any way that I can foresee." Her statement reinforced a commitment to him and his military duty, pleasing him. "It may actually help that I know a great deal about the territory we are heading into. As a matter of fact, I know this area like the back of my hand."

He studied her intently, his mind working quickly.

"I am sure you sometimes wonder about the dirk and the towel left in the cave at the falls."

She had his complete attention at this point.

"I was there many months ago." She shrugged as to the exact timing. "Alone," she said in answer to his unasked question. "I had been through a rather difficult time and was headed deeper into South Carolina." Beginning to anxiously twist a loose curl around her finger, she scrutinized him. "I just ... left them there. I am not quite sure why, maybe to make the statement: 'I exist'; more to prove that fact to myself than to anyone else."

The longer she talked the more serious and quiet she became, as if reliving whatever had happened back then. "May we talk of this another time?" she asked softly.

He remembered only too well, that night not so long ago when she had called out Black Raven's name in overwhelming terror. He would not push her to talk until she was ready, if or when that time ever came. Taking her hand, he squeezed gently. "Whenever you are ready, Kathryn." Leaning forward, he placed a comforting kiss on her forehead.

Looking up, her expression pained, she twisted the curl more tightly.

"My ... brother ..."

Again, his attention riveted on her. *Is this to be a day of confessions?*

"I honestly do not know if he is alive, but ..." She remained quiet for so long he wondered if she had decided not to share her thoughts. "I overheard small talk around the campfire about this rebel—this 'devil's spawn' you speak of so vehemently."

Her confession to eavesdropping brought a grin.

"It could be Jamie—my brother." She tugged her hair anxiously. "But that fact changes nothing ... not my feelings for you, or the choice I have made." Gripping his arms, she beseeched him: "If *we* find this to be true, please do not mistrust my loyalty."

"We have come too far to take a step backwards, Kathryn. You know, that thought had actually occurred to me before," he added dryly. "We will weather this storm too, if it should arise."

Setting her away from him, hands placed lightly on her shoulders, he searched her face. "Enough talk for this morning. Let us get some breakfast and then perhaps go over a couple of the maps." He shot her a cautious, sideways glance.

"You are a brave man, Colonel," she teased. "You dare to tread on dangerous ground."

He chuckled at her good humor, marveling at how rapidly her moods could change. She never stayed angry or 'down' for long; just put things behind her and moved on.

Chapter Ten

Honorable Recruits?

Days piled quickly one upon another becoming weeks, which in their good turn became months. Kathryn was amazed at how quickly time had passed and how attuned she had become to her life on the move.

In the beginning, Jason's band of dragoons had treated her respectfully in deference to their colonel: polite but distant. Now, they knew her better. She was considerate and co-operative, never shirking her share of tasks at hand. Much to her satisfaction, they had begun to respect her for herself. She enjoyed being included in their card games and singing around the campfire. Often the lilting notes of her tin whistle could be heard drifting across the encampment as she entertained them with English ditties and lively airs from her Scottish ancestry.

Absorbing the beauty of the new day she hunkered down beside the hot coals of the morning's breakfast fire, enjoying her second cup of Cook's steaming coffee. Fog lay in thick blankets across the meadow in which they were camped, adding a sense of mystery to the early morning hour. A buzz of excitement filled the air as plans were finalized for their next campaign and supplies readied for the move.

Lost in the enjoyment of private thoughts, she pressed the cup between her palms and brought it to her face, savoring its warmth and aroma, reflecting on her relationship with Jason, and how their love continued to grow. He had changed considerably, as had she—for the better she hoped. Each day brought deeper trust and a greater sense of peace. Recently, he had even begun to share bits of his past, a sure sign that he finally felt *safe* with her. Their boundless passion never diminished, each encounter retaining the 'thrill' and fulfillment of all previous encounters—both wanting and *needing* to touch the other. As feelings intensified, deep understanding and appreciation drew them closer—often sharing identical thoughts and voicing them in unison.

The dragoons also exhibited a new-found respect for their commanding officer. With all former bullying and brutal tactics replaced by stern but fair judgment, they co-operated fully. Camp life flowed more smoothly, the severity of absolute protocol relaxing somewhat—occasionally even abandoned. He even smiled while within sight of his dragoons, albeit not frequently. But when alone with her, his smile reached the depth of his striking, blue eyes and set them sparkling.

She was proud to be with him and made that fact obvious. Although openly friendly with the dragoons, she never allowed any misinterpretation to arise.

"You are somewhere far away, Kathryn," Jason whispered into her ear, startling her as he sat down with his coffee.

Grinning sheepishly, she nodded. "I was thinking how very content I am being here with you, and how much we have both changed," she said, her voice a soft caress. Smiling, she looked out across the meadow to where the fog was lifting leaving wisps clinging tenaciously in spots.

He sipped his coffee, enjoying the inner calm her quiet companionship always afforded him, and watched the day awaken.

Lieutenant Jackson was heading in their direction with his own cup of coffee.

"Good morning, Lieutenant." She smiled warmly at his sleepy nod. "Did you win or lose?" she chided good-naturedly.

"Let us not talk about it," he groaned.

"I will loan you my lucky rabbit's foot," she teased. "But I shall want to share in your winnings."

The colonel arched an eyebrow, eyeing them both, but said nothing.

"Would you like to join us?" She pointed to the tree stump opposite them.

The lieutenant looked momentarily unsure, but Kathryn nodded firmly and flashed a welcoming smile. Pleasantly surprised, he sat down. For a few moments, they sat quietly sipping their coffee, watching the last curls of mist dissipate.

"What do you think of the two new recruits?" Jason broke their silence, glancing first at Lieutenant Jackson and then Kathryn.

The lieutenant shrugged. "They seem rather quiet and rarely interact with the others."

Jason nodded, turning to Kathryn.

"It is not for me to judge; to like them or not. It is a matter of how efficiently they do their job."

"You are hedging, Kathryn." Jason turned a sharp eye on her.

"You never miss a thing, sir," she admitted. Hesitating briefly, she tried to think exactly how to express her uneasiness. As one was too forward, she avoided him as much as possible. Truth be known, she did not care for either of them; they made her nervous. "Something is nagging in the back of my mind about one of them, but I can not put my finger on it." She looked perplexed. "But it will come to me, I am sure."

"Do you recognize them?" Jason asked.

"I am not really sure, maybe—maybe not."

She remained thoughtful for a long moment and gave up. Her face suddenly brightened as she turned to Lieutenant Jackson. "Please tell us about your home in England, Lieutenant." She wanted Jason to get to know him better.

"There is not a great deal to tell." He pursed his lips in thought. "I lived with my sister and her husband on a lovely estate in England, not far from the Scottish border. After my nephew was born, I thought it time for me to move on and allow my sister and her family more privacy." He paused, sipping his coffee. "As there were problems in both Scotland and America I had a choice. Travel to the colonies offered more possibilities for adventure, so I joined the colonel's dragoons." His lips curved in a crooked smile. "I will return when the war is over; England is my home."

"I hope to see England someday," she said eagerly. "I have always wanted to trace the roots of my forefathers in Scotland, and see where my parents lived before they came to the colonies; maybe I will do both." Kathryn wished Jason would open up about his boyhood in England, but he remained silent. *Too soon,* she realized, and would not press him further.

As much needed to be accomplished before they broke camp, the lieutenant excused himself, allowing Kathryn and Jason to finish their coffee together. She expected to be left on her own while Jason organized this evening's meeting with his officers. But he surprised her, as he often did of late, wanting to exercise the horses and spend the day enjoying her company. He spent too many long hours caught up in the military responsibilities of managing his dragoons. As they would soon be moving deeper into rebel territory, more demands were going to be placed upon him by Lord Cornwallis. Today belonged to Kathryn and him.

They rode into camp late-afternoon, relaxed and refreshed, just in time for dinner. This day had been a wonderful gift. Allowing the horses to run, they had galloped through streams, splashing water into rainbow shimmers, allowing reality to fall away and enjoy being alive … and together. Completely happy, Kathryn was at one with Jason and the beautiful gifts bestowed by nature.

That evening as they ate together in the privacy of their tent she bubbled with excitement, chatting happily, her face aglow. She kidded with him suggesting what he might expect if he shortened this evening's meeting.

Jason came around the desk, and pulling her up into his warm embrace kissed her thoroughly. "Maybe I will have to cancel this meeting, madam," he breathed seductively into her ear.

"Now, Colonel, you know duty comes first, but I *will* make it up to you later."

After a hug and lingering kiss, she left the tent with dinner plates and mugs in hand, mouthing: "I will be back after your meeting is over."

He smiled warmly and watched as she disappeared in the direction of Cook's wagon. Their day together had done them both a world of good, but now he must focus on the plans at hand.

After leaving their dinner utensils with Cook, she headed to the far corner of the encampment, already imagining the little brook with its dark water rippling in the soft light of a crescent moon. Childlike, she loved the freedom of being barefoot and could already feel the cool water swirling about her feet.

Kathryn enjoyed walking the perimeters of their campsite on nights when Jason met with his officers, savoring her private moments, and the crisp evening air. She always returned, refreshed and alert, knowing he would be in need of diversion after frequently tense and tiring meetings.

As she neared the creek a dark figure stepped from the shadows and approached. Although appearing to be a dragoon, she sensed danger and wished she had brought her tomahawk and pistol.

He moved swiftly, grabbing her by the shoulders and yanking her firmly against him before she could react. She recognized him instantly: the overly forward new recruit. Crushing his mouth over hers, he prevented her startled protest. "How dare you?" she gasped when able to break free of his kiss. She swung at him, struggling instinctively, until a large fist sent her thoughts reeling dizzily.

Clamping a large hand over her nose and mouth, cutting off her air—and a scream for help—he crushed her in a viselike grip. As her struggles weakened, he began dragging her farther away from the safety of the campsite. Reaching a more secluded spot he stopped, and with a deft move, caught her behind the knees with a sharp jab, throwing her to the ground. Her lungs burned, spots of color pulsed before her eyes and she experienced true fear.

"Relax, missy, an' this'll go easier," he hissed. Dropping astride, he pinned her effectively. As he tore at her blouse, readjusting his grip over her mouth, she bit down hard.

"You bitch," he yelped, rewarding her with a savage backhander, his ring slicing her temple.

Pain rocketed up the side of her face as a steady trickle of blood coursed along her cheek. At least he had released her nose; she could breathe. Gulping air, her mind began to clear. She fought frantically, bucking and trying to roll out from under him, but to no avail—no match for his brute strength. A vicious slap, then another, slowed her struggles. With a burst of cruel laughter he leaned in close, accosting her with fetid, whiskey-laden breath. "I don't see why the good colonel should have you all to himself. With a fighting little vixen like you, there's plenty to go around."

Clamping his hand back over her mouth, he bent and savagely bit her breast, stifling her anguished cry in his cupped hand. Her struggles were futile, her pinned arms making all attempts ineffectual as he struck her … again and again. Blood poured from her nose.

Her blouse lay open baring her body to his lustful gaze. Starting at the base of her throat, he trailed the fingers of one hand slowly downwards. Seizing her breast he kneaded cruelly, enjoying her muffled whimpers. Then, as if a gentle lover, he bent to tease her nipple with a rough tongue. He kept her mouth blocked stifling any cries—and a scream flung from the depths of agony as he sank his teeth deeply into her flesh. With a sadistic laugh he nuzzled upwards along the side of her neck, tracing slobbering kisses. The soft spot at the base of her throat became his next target for a searing bite, causing smarting tears and another smothered cry.

Be calm. Think! Think! She struggled to focus, block the agony. She must not surrender to the encircling dizziness … must not. Terror overwhelmed her as he unbuckled her belt, and tossing it aside, began cupping her crotch. Mere moments—and it would be too late.

Centering her attention on what must be done, she relaxed. *Be calm. Regain control,* she repeated over and over as her head slowly cleared. Ceasing her struggle brought renewed strength and more. Feeling the fight go out of her, he came to false conclusions. "I think you really want it, you little vixen," he panted. "And I can take much better care of you than the colonel, any day." Fondling her crotch, he ground his fingers deeply into the fabric of her clothing. Confident of attaining his goal he relaxed his hold, allowing her to ease her hand free.

Reaching up, she ran her fingers tentatively along the side of his face, his reaction—just as she had hoped. In arrogance and over eagerness, he actually thought she would give in to his advances. Sprawling across her, he removed his hand to kiss her, as she slowly wrapped one leg around his back. "Why you cheeky bitch, you little tease." He grinned lasciviously as her other leg wrapped around him, then kissed her fiercely, sure of his trophy.

Excited to the point of intense discomfort and fumbling to unbutton his breeches, he inadvertently loosened his grip further, failing to see her hand slide into her boot—and slowly withdraw the dirk. In one swift motion, she raked a deep gash across the side of his neck.

With a shocked yelp, he pitched backwards clutching his throat—blood pouring around the edges of his fingers. Rolling up onto her feet and into a low crouch she lunged, knocking him to the ground—all in one fluid motion.

Before he could comprehend or prevent what was about to happen, she dropped down straddling his chest. Slashing in a wide arc with all her remaining strength, she slit his throat from ear to ear. An expression of surprise froze on his face as his life's blood puddled onto the ground forming a darkening crimson pool. She scrambled up weakly and stood over him, her sides heaving from exertion, dizzy with pain. She stared at the front of her blouse, saturated with blood, then the gore-covered knife clutched in her hand, and gorge rose in her throat.

Dropping the dirk, she staggered down the embankment to the edge of the brook and collapsed, vomiting until no more would come. When the dry heaves finally subsided she plunged her face into the cool water and began frantically rinsing her mouth, spitting repeatedly to remove the filth and taste of him. After splashing copious amounts on her chest to rid it of lingering saliva, she gulped and spit more water, desperate to erase all residue of his touch.

As her labored breathing slowed she paused to survey the situation, the horror of it all. Suddenly panic seized her. She had killed an English soldier, a dragoon. She was a colonial. This would destroy the precious trust she had worked so hard to build. *What will Jason do? How will the dragoons react?* Whatever the repercussions she had a responsibility to fulfill: make the camp secure by alerting Jason that the guard was dead. Sucking in a shuddering breath, she picked up her bloody knife and headed for his tent.

She paused at the entrance of the tent, breathing heavily, dizziness overtaking her. The evening was cold, her wet clothing clinging heavily and chilling her to the bone. Shivering visibly, she drew a deep breath for courage and entered the tent.

"Please, excuse … the interruption," she spoke haltingly.

Jason's look of annoyance was instantly replaced with concern.

"The left quadrant … is unprotected, sir. I … have killed the guard … near the brook." She swayed unsteadily as she approached his desk.

The officers parted to let her through, their faces registering shock as light from the oil lantern bared the visible extent of her injuries. Clutching her bloody shirt to her chest, she staggered but reached his desk. Dropping the gory knife she grasped the edge for support. Lieutenant Jackson reached to steady her, fighting the urge to take her in his arms and comfort her—aghast at her obvious suffering.

Jason paled visibly and quickly moved to her side. The lieutenant immediately relinquished her and grabbing a chair, steadied it as Jason gently lowered her sagging body.

"What happened?" he demanded. Grabbing a towel the lieutenant handed him, he pressed it firmly against her bleeding forehead.

She sat mute, numb, in shock; eyes bleak, her teeth chattering uncontrollably. Quickly grabbing the blanket, offered by his ever-efficient lieutenant, Jason wrapped it snuggly about her shoulders.

"How severely are you hurt?" he asked, inspecting her face, assessing her visible injuries.

She stared forlornly, all traces of earlier happiness vanished.

"It is his blood. I … I killed … a dragoon." Her chin quivered as she bit down on her lower lip.

Jason turned and spoke quietly with his lieutenant, then with a curt nod, dismissed the rest of his officers, who up to this point had looked on, speaking in hushed tones amongst themselves.

"I will handle everything, sir," Lieutenant Jackson answered softly, and casting a concerned look towards Kathryn, he departed.

Dizziness circling, she leaned forward resting her head in her lap, groaning slightly. Jason crouched at her side placing a hand on her shoulder.

"Are you going to be sick?"

"I have already been so sick there is nothing left." Lackluster eyes met his as she struggled to sit upright.

Speaking soothingly, he gently pried her trembling fingers apart and opened her shirt. The sight of her injuries created such blinding fury, if she had not already killed this man he would have done the deed himself: painfully and slowly.

"My God, Kathryn ..." He swept her from the chair and carried her to the cot. "Talk to me. What happened? Did he ...?"

"Rape me?" She supplied the repugnant word for him. "No," she stated adamantly. "If he had ..." She paused, eyes filled with sad determination. "If he had, I would have killed myself."

"Kathryn." Cradling her head in hands that shook slightly, he searched her distraught face. Realizing the conviction of her statement he was horrified. Dumbstruck, at a loss for words, he picked small debris from her disheveled curls. Just as he started to counter her remark, the lieutenant returned with medical supplies.

"You could use some brandy," he murmured. She remained silent, continuing to stare straight ahead. With a gentle squeeze to her hand he moved towards his desk, sidetracking to speak with the lieutenant.

Outside, Lieutenant Jackson quietly confirmed that she had indeed killed one of the new recruits. There were all the signs of an incredible struggle. She had slashed his throat, killing him almost instantly. "He was a brute, sir. It took tremendous courage to do what she did." He sucked air softly through his teeth, shocked by what he had seen.

Jason swallowed his anger with difficulty. As they reentered the tent, he paused to pour a brandy and returned to her side. Crouching close, he pressed the glass to her lips. "Sip this, Kathryn; it will help with your chills."

Lieutenant Jackson stood quietly watching as Jason talked soothingly, urging her to take more brandy. Under his firm insistence, she finally gave in, wordlessly obeying.

She remained unresponsive, bravely silent as he commenced gently cleaning trickling blood from her face. It required no astute observation to verify how severely she had been beaten, her swollen face hinting at worse to be revealed.

As the lieutenant handed him a freshly wrung out cloth, Jason asked, "What have we got to stop the bleeding?"

"In my saddle bag—a leather pouch—mountain alum." She grimaced with the effort.

Relieved to find her consciously aware, Jason turned to his lieutenant, finding instruction unnecessary; he was already ducking under the tent flap and headed out.

As Jason applied the alum powder she flinched, but the bleeding quickly stopped.

"I have killed an English soldier," she mumbled more to herself than to him, shaking her head, horrified at the gravity of her perceived crime.

"Focus, Kathryn." She made no move to comply. "Focus on me now," he said more firmly.

She turned her head slowly, willing herself to meet his gaze.

"If I had been there, I would have killed him myself. You did the right thing." She searched his face then glanced to the lieutenant, who nodded, agreeing wholeheartedly. Jason turned to tending the painful bites on her neck. With a sharp intake of breath she winced, a whimper escaping.

To have killed such a powerfully built, well-trained dragoon—her desperation must have been overwhelming. Jason fought for control, furious that one of his men could have treated her in this manner. *Be gentle with her, stay calm*, he told himself, *you can deal with the men later.*

"How can you trust me after what I have done?" Her voice caught, her eyes pooling and threatening to spill over.

"Did he offend you?" His curious phrasing resulted as he had hoped. She riveted her attention on him, puzzled. "Did he hurt you? Were you at the point of being violated?"

She nodded, chin quivering.

"If the man had been a colonial and treated you in the same manner, would you have done anything differently?"

"No, I would have killed him without hesitation," she said with certainty.

"The fact that he was one of my men does nothing to lessen my trust in you. My regret and concern is that any man in my regiment would hurt you so. And I will deal with them later."

She eyed him cautiously, the vehemence of his statement startling. At his nod, the lieutenant handed him the brandy and he once again put it to her lips. She sipped obediently, the warming effects of the amber liquid beginning to relax her.

"But what of the men, sir, they have had nothing on which to base trust in me—and now this?"

"There will be no problem with the men," Lieutenant Jackson interjected firmly, compassion etched on his strong features.

"Please, Colonel …" a panicking thought occurred. "Do not berate the men on my account. I would not have them like me any less." Her eyes implored he understand. After a moment's consideration, he nodded, unwilling to upset her further.

"I just snapped," she blurted offhandedly, surprised by her own revelation.

Jason, having just finished treating her easily visible wounds, was about to dismiss Lieutenant Jackson so as not to embarrass Kathryn as he cared for her more personal injuries. But at her unusual statement he paused, eyeing her quizzically.

"He was rude—brutal. I reached my dirk and slashed him. He stumbled backwards, gripping his neck in surprise. I lunged, shoving him to the ground and—cut his throat." She shuddered.

Jason and the lieutenant swapped astounded looks.

"He had to die. I could not allow him to bring shame upon you, sir, through me." She spoke so softly they were hard pressed to hear.

"I am in your debt, Kathryn, you amaze me. Where did you learn to handle yourself so well under such frightening circumstances? And the way you wield a dirk …" He eyed her with complete respect.

She glanced from one to the other. "My brother …" she looked directly at Jason, "is an expert with a knife."

A long moment of silence hung between them as Jason considered the import of that information. Lieutenant Jackson had been quietly absorbing the unnerving reality of the situation, but that statement caught his attention. She seemed calmer now. The colonel needed to tend to her more personal injuries—details could be discussed later.

He cleared his throat. "Colonel, with your leave, I will await your instructions at a later time." He stepped towards the tent flap, but abruptly stopped and turned. "Permission to speak freely, sir."

At his crisp nod, Lieutenant Jackson stepped closer, addressing Kathryn. "Milady, you accomplished an extremely brave deed tonight." He smiled kindly. "I regret none of us was there to protect you. I will take personal responsibility for correcting our inadequacy."

Turning to the colonel he said, "I shall speak to the men tonight, sir, and relieve you of the burden."

"However …" he turned to Kathryn with a wink that caused Jason to stiffen, "I believe you now command new respect within our ranks and will not have any further problems."

She smiled for the first time that evening, albeit wanly, murmuring her gratitude.

"I have also left some willow bark tea," he added, and at that remark she smiled anew.

When they were alone, Jason stroked her hair back and asked softly, "How are you feeling?".

Her eyes were brimming as she mouthed 'all right', but that was far from the truth. Opening her blouse, he fought to keep his expression neutral at the sight of her vicious injuries.

She stared blankly at the ceiling as he cleaned and sterilized the wounds on her breasts. Her mental anguish engulfed them like a thick fog, her suffering well beyond physical discomfort. There was more to it than that.

"Kathryn, absolutely nothing has changed between us," he said emphatically. "I alone, am responsible for your ordeal. The fact that one of my dragoons dared to harm you …" he trailed off, his expression pained as he recalled his callous threat many months ago—vicious words that had brought her to heel—words that promised brutal rape if she did not bend to his wishes. He fully understood the severity of her trauma, both then and now, and cringed at what he had done to her emotionally at that time.

"Almost done, love," he said softly in a voice that caressed. "You have been so very brave."

She gnawed her lower lip, her large green eyes meeting his gaze unwaveringly. By now, so attuned to her strengths and insecurities, he recognized her need for reassurance that he would still want her, even after this awful experience. And he knew within his heart, that he would want her … no, need and love her … even if she had suffered the ultimate degradation of rape. As she started to speak, he touched her lips silencing her; he must be the one to initiate the request.

"Kathryn." Leaning forward, he grasped her hand and began slowly tracing the backs of her fingers. "If you will allow me …" He began again, trying to express himself meaningfully. "I will be very gentle, if you …"

Realization struck; she reached to clasp his face. He had never asked permission before. Awestruck by the implication, she kissed him fervently. "Oh, Jason, make me forget everything; make it all go away."

He tasted salty tears as she responded hungrily to his ardent kiss. Despite physical discomfort, she needed *him* to make it right, to allay her fears and reassure her.

He took his time, loving her gently and completely, slowly bringing her back to reality to sleep encircled within his arms.

But sleep did not come easily for him this night. He lay wakeful long after she slept, quieting her once in a nightmare that brought her awake in terror.

"I am here, my love, you are safe now. I will not let anything harm you," he crooned softly.

Comforted, she drifted back into sleep. But his mind remained active, sleep continuing to elude him. For the first time in his life he was frightened for someone else, terrified by what could have been lost. Understanding her fearful reaction when he had been injured, he vowed to be more open, to reveal his feelings often, to reassure her of his love—never allow her to be fraught with doubts. *For I need that also,* he realized.

Another turning point had been reached. This brave, feisty woman had brutally slain a man because he had attempted to dishonor her, and in that vicious act, also bring shame on him. Jason finally understood how fiercely she loved him … and the revelation was astounding. *Oh my Kathryn, you are such a delightful mystery: shy and insecure, brave and feisty, childlike—but most interesting of all—deadly with a knife.* That last image brought to mind this elusive brother of hers, a point of real interest. As various thoughts continued to tumble through his head, he unexpectedly recalled Lieutenant Jackson's reactions to Kathryn's ordeal. It dawned on him how deeply his lieutenant cared for her, a fact which caused him a rare and unpleasant emotion: jealousy.

It was a very long night of wakefulness. But Kathryn slept peacefully in his arms with no further nightmares, and for that he was thankful.

The next morning, he was up early and headed out to the campfire. Breakfast in bed would be good for her. As he stepped from the tent, Lieutenant Jackson came forward, his face etched with concern.

"How is Miss MacLean?" he inquired.

She is still sleeping." He took the coffee the lieutenant offered. "Thank you for last night, Jackson. That tea really helped ease Kathryn's discomfort."

The lieutenant shook his head dismissively. "I have spoken to every man here, sir. They will all be much more protective of her from this time forward."

Seeking them out at their guard posts or in individual groups as they relaxed for the evening, he had talked to every dragoon. Having been amongst the group of witnessing officers, he could discuss the severity of Kathryn's injuries, stressing the fact that this must never happen again. News had traveled rapidly within the campsite, the dragoons well aware of how she had dispatched her attacker. Many of them, finding it difficult to believe, had viewed the body. Although greatly impressed with her ability, they realized she should never have been subjected to such abuse.

Jason appreciated the underlying reason his lieutenant had handled the situation so rapidly and approved. He was a good man, one who had both his and Kathryn's best interests in mind. He must express his gratitude more often.

"The other new recruit was oddly disinterested. I am not quite sure what I make of him yet," Lieutenant Jackson reported, somewhat disconcerted.

"Well, keep an eye on him, he is still an unknown entity," Jason remarked. He started towards the campfire but stopped abruptly. Eyeing his officer thoughtfully, he decided to view the body and get this whole nasty business out of the way before Kathryn was up and about.

At Jackson's suggestion, he followed him to the spot where the attack had taken place. Viewing the evidence brought the full horror of her struggle crashing home. And this powerfully built military man, known for his iron façade, was visibly shaken. He returned to the campfire and picked up their breakfast, stopping momentarily to converse with several officers who had witnessed the previous evening's event, then headed back to their tent.

As he entered, he caught her sitting at his desk with a light blanket draped around her, gingerly examining her wounds in his shaving mirror. At the sound of his step, she looked up and winced.

"I know it is only a woman's false vanity, but I really am a mess." She smiled weakly. "I have some horehound and wild plantain that may help with healing, but I doubt they can handle all this."

He smiled and set the food down as he perched on the edge of the desk. "You are always beautiful to me," he whispered, kissing her gently. "This will be gone shortly. I have heard of those herbs you mentioned. Show me how to prepare them after breakfast, hmm?"

She nodded, taking the coffee he offered, inhaling its rich aroma, enjoying the warmth. Before she could ask what was topmost in her mind, he slid off the desk and came around to her. There was a new intensity about him as he took her coffee and set it on the desk

"Come to me, my Kathryn." The tenderness in his voice moved her as she was drawn gently up into his arms and held close. "This morning I have seen where …" he began huskily but was unable to finish—his throat constricting as he fought back tears. Clinging tightly, he caressed the length of her back, up over her shoulders, along her arms—touching frantically, needing to be sure she was truly here in his arms. "How I do love you, Kathryn." His voice cracked.

She understood completely, suffering his anguish as it had been hers at another time … and would be so again, many times over in the course of their life together … for both of them.

"Do not fret, love, I am better now." She caressed his face, kissing him repeatedly. "All of this is nothing and will be gone in a matter of days."

They stood wrapped in each other's arms drawing strength. Finally he released her, admonishing that she eat breakfast before it became cold, embarrassed by his show of emotion. But she loved him all the more.

"What is the reaction of your dragoons?" she asked.

"Impressed with your abilities; eager to see you up and about."

"But look at me," she said grimacing.

"Never be ashamed of battle scars won in defending one's honor," he reassured.

He and Lieutenant Jackson had discussed the attack in detail after viewing the body, both agreeing she was lucky to be alive. He hoped she would eventually share the details. But that could wait, she needed time to heal.

He examined her wounds cleansing them thoroughly, pleased to see no sign of infection. Certain areas were obviously painful but she withstood his ministrations stoically.

Suddenly she smiled. "You saved me last night." He looked puzzled as to her meaning. "I needed your *'attentions'* to erase the horror, and you did not fail me." Her eyes misted. "You never do."

He smiled as he traced a finger along the bridge of her nose. "I would like to spend a quiet day in camp. Would you please join me?"

She looked up, surprised. "But I thought we needed to be on the road."

"Nothing so pressing that it cannot be delayed one more day. Now, throw on some clothes, the day is beautiful."

She dressed quickly, combed her tangled tresses and within minutes they emerged from the tent. His arm surrounded her protectively as he greeted his men. They nodded respect but made no embarrassing display, for which she was grateful. Those who had not seen her the night before were taken aback by the severity of the visible injuries, general knowledge from attending officers divulging there was much more.

After infusing a concoction of herbs and applying it liberally, she and Jason walked to a nearby grove of trees. He spread a blanket under a large tree near the brook and sat reading some of her favorite Scottish poems. She never tired of hearing him read, his crisp English articulation and subtle expressions always bringing endless pleasure.

In time she dozed, her head resting in his lap. Setting the book aside, he leaned back watching her; she needed sleep to regain her strength. Exhausted from his sleepless night, he joined her, dozing intermittently but remaining alert. She slept contentedly for several hours, awaking refreshed.

"How do you feel?" he asked.

She stretched slowly. "Better." She started to sit up but he stayed her effort.

"Relax," he grinned. "I rather like the feel of you lying in my lap."

Her face lit up happily for a moment, then settled into a serious expression. "I will give you the details, Jason. Then I can lay it aside once and for all."

Taking her hand, he listened intently as she related the horrors of the previous evening. When she had finished, he hugged her close. "Put it behind you, love. That will never happen again." Picking up the poetry book he resumed reading.

By late afternoon, she felt greatly refreshed. Feeling up to a quiet ride, they returned to camp and saddled their horses. As they rode out she felt eyes on her and noticed the remaining recruit watching her with an odd expression. She said nothing to Jason, dismissing it as over reaction or slight paranoia due to her attack.

They returned to camp as the campfires were being lit and shared a quick supper; anxious to enjoy a bath. Darkness was falling as Jason accompanied her to the brook. Guards had been set farther out for their privacy and protection, Lieutenant Jackson, as expected, good to his word about increased security.

Jason examined her wounds, pleased to see she was healing quickly and experiencing less discomfort. Kathryn's recuperative abilities were remarkable, her herbal remedies working well.

After washing her hair he began gently laving water over her shoulders and back, enjoying the delicious feel of tracing his hands over her body.

"Madam, we had best return to our tent lest we embarrass ourselves here so close to camp."

"That would certainly make tongues wag," she giggled impishly.

Her laughter was music to his ears; she would be fine.

Much later, happily content within each other's arms, they drifted into sleep. He roused in the middle of the night, startled momentarily, and found her already awake. "What is troubling you?" he asked softly.

Her cheek moved against his chest as she murmured, "There is something about that other recruit that bothers me." She paused trying to fathom the cause. "He was watching us closely as we rode out today." She shook her head, perplexed. "He seems familiar. I feel I have met him, but can not quite put the pieces together."

"Sleep now, love," he whispered. "We move camp tomorrow and I want you rested." He traced a finger along the bridge of her nose and touched her lips. "Do not try to think so hard, perhaps it will come to you. However, I will speak to Lieutenant Jackson and see that he is watched closely to help ease your mind."

Cuddling back against the warmth of him, within moments they both slept soundly.

Chapter Eleven

Spy Within

Kathryn and Jason slept soundly until first light and then were up, dressed, and ready to travel in short order. After a light breakfast and coffee, the main band of dragoons mounted their horses and took formation, waiting patiently to move out. Those bringing up the rear with tents, food wagon and other various supplies, were busily making final preparations to break camp.

As Jason rode to the front of his dragoons, he stopped momentarily by Kathryn's side as she sat astride her mare. Her usual place was somewhat farther back in the lines for more protection. But today he felt the area they would be traversing was secure enough.

"Would you care to ride up front with me today, milady?" he asked formally, then smiled at her beaming face.

"It would be an honor, sir." She could hardly contain her excitement as she moved into place beside him.

Lieutenant Jackson smiled a greeting from his usual position flanking the colonel, noticing how cheerful and animated she looked at his side, her injuries healing rapidly.

Jason stood in his stirrups looking back over his shoulder, checking the readiness of his men. With a crisp forward motion of his gloved hand, the dragoons stepped off in organized columns.

Kathryn was comfortable in her surroundings, at peace with the world, as they rode for several hours across land she knew so well. The day was bright and warm with a delicious mix of odors: new grass, wild meadow flowers, worn leather and horses. Giddy with delight, she even welcomed the occasional gust of wind that brought an accompanying cloud of dust. Out of respect for Jason's position and appearance in the eyes of his men, she remained quiet. But this feat required great self-discipline; she wanted to point out sights of interest and share her past. The time to divulge more than he might wish to hear was near at hand—but must be done. As the day was too beautiful to think of anything other than enjoying the moment, she forced that thought aside.

Occasionally she allowed Beauty to fall back a step or two before nudging her back to the colonel's side. As she pulled abreast this time, he eyed her in a bemused fashion.

"May I inquire as to what you are doing, madam?"

Struggling to look serious she said lightly, "I never tire of watching how well you sit your saddle, sir." She grinned impishly as he arched a reproachful eyebrow.

Lieutenant Jackson caught what passed between them and stifled a grin.

"You, my dear, are a tart." Jason's eyes spoke softly in wordless volumes. Then in concern for her injuries, he asked more seriously, "Would you like to take a break?"

"Only when the troops are ready, sir, I really am fine now."

He stood in his stirrups, looking back down the columns assessing their temperament. "We will break shortly," he decided. "By the way, any problems with that recruit?"

"No. I saw him watching us, or me," she amended, looking thoughtful. "But he is keeping his distance."

Jason remained quiet, giving the situation some thought before pushing onward. By dusk they had covered a good distance and paused to spend the night in an open meadow dotted with clusters of low trees. As they would be heading out early the following morning a full campsite was not erected—only a rapidly raised, small travel tent for the colonel in deference to his title—and privacy.

After a hot dinner with the men, which although filling was uninteresting, she decided she must be allowed some hunting time. She mentioned that fact to Jason as they headed towards the tent, but he said nothing, remaining noncommittal until they were inside. "My little huntress," he murmured taking her in his arms. "Where did you learn all this? From your brother?" She shrugged and proceeded to distract him with a lingering kiss.

She felt restored, more herself, her bruises fading rapidly, her mood inventive and playful. As he moved towards the small traveling desk he removed his jacket and began undoing his shirt. Maps left for his perusal by the lieutenant caught his eye. Sitting down, he scanned the route for their next day's march as he continued removing his clothes in a rather distracted manner.

Kathryn had been freshening up in a water-filled basin left by Lieutenant Jackson, and made a mental note to tell him how much they appreciated his thoughtfulness. Finished with toweling her face, she approached Jason quietly and leaning close, draped her arms around his shoulders. Putting the maps aside he turned, and placing both hands on her waist, eased her astride his lap. Beginning a trail of kisses upwards along his neck she lingered at his ear lobe, her tongue playing lightly. Relishing the firm response pressed against her thigh, she reinforced her efforts.

Placing fervent kisses at the base of her throat, his hands began a teasing exploration, a throaty chuckle erupting as he caressed her bottom, finding her soft, warm and—naked. "How did I find such a wanton as you?" he groaned, urgent need building.

"As I recall, I found you. And I was pretty sure I had a man who was up to the task." She eyed him pertly, and they both laughed.

"Well now, I believe the maps can wait until later," he chuckled, as he swept her into his arms and headed for their blankets.

Shortly after midnight she came fully awake. "Jason." She touched his shoulder bringing him instantly alert and reaching for his pistol. "I remember who he is."

He knew immediately to whom she referred and listened intently as her story tumbled out in panic-filled words. "A few years ago, I recall going into Georgetown with my family. He burned straw effigies of English officers, bragging how he would kill them all—drawing a spiteful crowd. I was much younger then, and was forced to watch from a safe distance. But he is no loyal recruit; he is one of the rebels, likely a spy."

"You seem positive that he would not change his allegiance," he stated.

The inference lying beneath his words annoyed her. "Unless he harbors the same feelings for you that I do, sir, he would not change." As her reply sounded terser than she had meant it to be, she added, "And if that were the case, I guess we would have a problem of a different kind."

He gave her a long look, aware his remark had been tactless, regretting the way he had phrased it.

"Jason, I have this terrible gut feeling … something is very wrong." Standing abruptly, she reached for her clothes.

Picking up on her apprehension, he dressed and armed himself, listening carefully as she rapidly provided more detail about this man's past.

"If he is not in the campsite right now, he is up to no good. A surprise attack maybe? I do not know exactly what, but something is about to happen; I feel it."

Her foreboding quickly transferred itself to him. Grasping her elbow, he ushered her out of the tent. Lieutenant Jackson approached, intercepting them. Jason spoke hurriedly, and with a quick explanation, sent him to locate the recruit. Returning to her side, he declared, "If this situation is what it appears to be, we will be in your debt." He tucked an errant curl behind her ear. "Any lingering shreds of doubt concerning trust between you and my men will be over … hmm?"

She searched his face, his familiar arched brow indicating he expected an answer.

"Yes," she agreed softly.

Anything he might have added further was interrupted by the return of his lieutenant, slightly winded from running. "He is nowhere to be found, sir."

"Rouse the men immediately," Jason commanded as he loosened the strap on his sabre.

By now several officers surrounded them, curious as to the disturbance. Suddenly dropping to her knees, Kathryn leaned down placing her ear to the ground. At the onset of questions, she threw her hand up in a sharp gesture commanding silence. Within moments she rocked back onto her heels and stood, turning full attention on Jason before scanning the circle of officers. "A group of riders is coming fast, not far from here," she warned.

"To arms," Jason shouted, sending the dragoons bolting for their positions of defense.

Piercing yells and staccato gunfire from the far side of their encampment indicated her words were true. Glancing about uneasily, Jason realized there was no safe place to send Kathryn—too late for that. But before he could voice his concern, she broke his train of thought. "Jason, concentrate on what is at hand. Forget I am here," she demanded.

At that moment, several men hurdled out of the darkness, and she thanked the instincts that had prodded her to grab a small sword in addition to her other arms. Drawing that sword, she slipped sideways and behind him.

"Concentrate; I have your back." With an eerie war whoop, she plunged at her opponent, quickly bringing him down, his startled expression frozen in death. As her hair loosened, she shook it out—long and wildly curling about her shoulders—momentary distraction allowing her to deal another killing blow to her next opponent. Within her peripheral vision, she noted Jason was easily holding his own. Reassured, she moved aggressively forward.

"I have this side, Kathryn." Lieutenant Jackson's voice came from her right.

She thrust on defiantly, surprising and slowing each opponent: momentary confusion, when confronted by this wild woman, gaining her the upper hand. As the rebels fell back, she realized that Jason and Lieutenant Jackson—as they continued fighting the retreating enemy—had been pulled farther out. Quickly scanning all sides, she eased her posture, resting for a moment, arms dangling across her knees in a semi-crouch, catching her breath.

It was then that he came at her out of the brush. "You bitch, you traitorous, bitch!" His sabre sliced the air, barely missing her as she swiftly dodged the blow. "You killed my brother."

"Your brother was a pig who deserved to die," she hissed. Lunging forward she slashed a small cut on his chest.

Feigning a move in the opposite direction he spun about, catching her upper arm with his blade. The searing pain and force of the blow brought her stumbling to a half crouch, her sword dropping to the ground. *This is it, do or die.* She grabbed instinctively for the dirk in her boot. Her sword had fallen beyond her reach, no time to draw the pistol tucked in her belt. She prayed the little dirk would not fail her now. She sensed, as well as heard, his approach from behind.

"I'll do the Rebs a favor in killing you," he gloated.

As he closed in, bringing his blade up for the killing slash, she abruptly spun thrusting her dirk upwards under his ribs with all her strength. Dropping his weapon, he clutched frantically at himself, a look of startled disbelief transforming his face. She used this moment to follow through, taking him to the ground, twisting the dirk deeper. Face contorted in a dreadful grimace, he moaned as a slow trickle of blood started from the corner of his mouth.

Though aware that Jason and Lieutenant Jackson were returning, she remained doggedly focused on her purpose: get information from this man before he died. Crouching at his side, she kept one hand on the dirk imbedded in his gut as she drew the pistol from her belt. Aiming it at the suffering man's face, she slowly brought the hammer back to half cock.

"Tell me who you are riding with: places, names, time frames for attacks," she demanded.

He coughed, spraying flecks of blood. "I am done for anyway—go ahead and shoot me."

"I know you are dying," she hissed, "but I can give you pain—unlike any you have ever known—while you wait … and pray for a rapid death. You still have a while yet to live." With that terse remark, she pulled the hammer to full-cock and jabbed him painfully in the groin. He gasped, fear creeping across his face as he imagined the horror of what she threatened.

"We do not have a lot of time. Talk," she demanded, prodding him painfully again.

He turned pleading eyes to the colonel and Lieutenant Jackson, who stood nearby observing. But both remained silent and unsympathetic, their faces stony.

"Look at me, you son-of-a-bitch and talk. There is nothing that would give me greater pleasure than to neuter you here and now." Her face was fierce, unrelenting.

As he started to speak, slowly and painfully, she added. "I know who you are, Brandon Gordon."

Surprised, he paused eyeing her closely, not answering rapidly enough. "This is the last time I will ask." Pressing the pistol more forcefully, she scowled, narrowing her eyes menacingly. Suddenly he started blurting the truth, intermingled with painful gasps.

"Rebel militia … going to join … Major … Beldon."

"Where is he heading?" she prodded.

"North to meet … Gates and … cut you … to ribbons." He flung the information with all the defiance he could muster, his breathing now labored, his coloring having paled substantially. "Your … brother will … kill you, bitch." He coughed painfully.

"My brother has nothing to do with this war," she spat.

He sneered, then suddenly convulsed and was gone.

She had wanted to ask him about Jamie; his statement had been unsettling. She must tell Jason about her past. It could not be put off any longer, but she dreaded the telling. Looking up, she found Jason and the lieutenant watching her with respect bordering on awe. Momentarily flustered at having been caught in such an unladylike act, she stood and faced them, shrugging with embarrassment. "My apologies for using bad language, gentlemen."

Jason shook his head, amused that she did not think the rest of her display unusual in any way. What an incredible woman.

"You are not hurt?" She scanned Jason and gave a 'once-over' to Lieutenant Jackson before turning back to Jason.

As the adrenaline of battle waned, she became aware of intense throbbing in her arm and was suddenly unsteady on her feet. Absentmindedly she clutched her arm to ease the stabbing pain. Blood that had been running freely made contact with her oversized sleeve, soaking it crimson.

At the sight of her bloodied sleeve, Jason's attention was drawn to the puddle of sticky red gathering at her feet. "Kathryn." Stepping to her side, he steadied her as she faltered. "Lieutenant, get a quick status and get back here ..."

"With medical supplies," he finished, as Jason nodded grimly.

"This is getting to be a bad habit of yours, my love." He held her tight as she paled visibly, swaying against him.

"I can walk," she protested as he whipped her off her feet and headed back towards their tent.

After placing her carefully on the chair, he elbowed everything off the desktop to make room for the medical supplies.

"I am just fine—it is no more than a knick." She cradled her arm gingerly. "I can elaborate on Gordon's remarks and perhaps help you, Jason." She looked up, wincing slightly as another stabbing spasm traveled the length of her arm.

"No more talk until we get you patched up, hmm?" Gently he opened her shirt, dropping the sleeve from her left shoulder, grimacing at what he saw: a deep wound bleeding heavily. Quickly making a wadding of towel, he pressed it firmly over the gash, impressed with her courage. He fixed her a brandy and was just pressing it to her lips when the lieutenant returned with bandages and other medical paraphernalia.

"How bad, sir?" he asked, setting the supplies on the desk.

"Not good, although she would have us believe it is only a knick." He gave her a chastising look. "She has lost a lot of blood."

"Stop talking as if I were not present," she grumbled. She had been resting her head on the desk warding off dizziness, but quickly sat upright, tugging her shirt closed as they came to her side.

Jason accommodated her with a draped towel, and gently pulled the compress away, baring her wound for the lieutenant's appraisal.

With a sharp inhalation of breath, he flashed Jason a concerned look. "I do believe I would consider that a bit more than a 'knick', Kathryn," he said softly.

"Drink up, my love." Jason held out a glass full of brandy but had no need to coax her; she gulped the fiery liquid knowing how bad this was going to be.

"I will need you to hold her, Jackson."

Despite the encircling fogginess, Kathryn noticed his lowering of formality.

"This gash must be cleaned thoroughly—and you will need stitches," Jason said softly, apologetically. "I will be as gentle as I can."

With those words the agony began. She was bound she would not cry out—she would not. She leaned back into the strong arms of Lieutenant Jackson, afraid she might lose consciousness any moment. She moaned, struggling to remain alert as Jason poured brandy into the wound. As the excruciating pain subsided, she gasped, attempting a smile, "… a waste of perfectly good brandy."

"Brace yourself," he warned. Concentrating on what must be done, he started to sew small, neat stitches, hoping to minimize the eventual scar. Closing her eyes, she willed herself to remain quiet, not pass out or worse—vomit.

Jackson held her firmly. "You are doing fine, Kathryn," he said quietly, forgetting himself in his concern.

Jason's head snapped up, surprised by his lieutenant's familiarity in using her name. He took a long look at his officer, causing him momentary embarrassment.

The final stitch brought a yelp. "Are you not done yet?" she demanded, so close to caving in it scared her.

Jason took a cold, wet cloth from the basin and squeezed out excess water. As Jackson released his grip, Jason grasped her chin and gently started bathing her perspiring face. "The worst is over," he whispered "I have seen many men not nearly as brave as you."

Breathing soft words into her hair, he finished bandaging her arm and slipped his jacket over her shoulders. "I will have some of your tea made ready, and brew more of those herbal concoctions that worked so well before. You will be back to normal in no time."

"What are our casualties, Lieutenant?" He turned to face his officer.

"We have no deaths and only five with negligible wounds, thanks to Miss MacLean." A warm, reassuring smile crossed his face. "In case it has been of concern, there is not a man in this unit who would doubt your loyalty after tonight."

She smiled weakly, appreciating his thoughtfulness. "Please call me Kathryn, when we are together in private." Sitting up, she faced him. "You are too good a friend, Jack—to both of us—to hang on such formalities." She glanced to Jason, who answered with a firm nod.

"The rebel count?" she asked.

"Ten dead and four captives with minor wounds, he said. Turning to address the colonel—all business now, he added, "We will await your orders on handling the rebel casualties, sir. The captives will be thoroughly questioned."

"Perhaps Kathryn should do the questioning." Jason grinned. "Her methods are—how shall I put it—more directly to the point than most men would accomplish." He noticed her pale skin and sheen of perspiration glistening across her face. With initial shock wearing off real throbbing was setting in. "How about some coffee, Jackson, and lots of water, she needs to get fluids into her."

Lieutenant Jackson left, returning rapidly with steaming mugs for both of them. She had said nothing while he was gone, just leaned quietly against Jason as he held her gently. He was shaken by the severity of her injury, aghast at what could have happened and, having been there himself, well aware of her severe pain. "You scared me," he whispered. "I would rather it were me, I hate to see you hurt like this." Her hand found his and squeezed.

She sipped her coffee, smiling weakly at the lieutenant. But as he started to leave, she stopped him. "Stay a minute, Jack, and I will tell you about Brandon Gordon." She proceeded slowly, relating the same facts she had shared with Jason. "Probably by killing his brother I inadvertently forced his hand sooner than intended. I never knew he had a brother," she said, shrugging. "They were obviously spying for Major Beldon—trying to plot our moves."

As Jason's dragoons were headed in a northerly direction, and knowing the territory well, she outlined what the rebel militia's moves might be, suggesting how they could use this knowledge to their advantage.

"Set an officer's meeting for tomorrow after breakfast, Lieutenant, and we will plan our course of action," Jason said. "I believe the next surprise attack will be ours."

Jackson started to back out of the tent, nodding goodnight to both of them.

"Please wait, I need to explain about my—brother."

"Perhaps I should leave, sir. This is between you and the lady." He slipped back into formality when it came to business.

"No," she said softly, shaking her head sadly. "You have the most direct knowledge of the dragoon's feelings, Lieutenant. What I have to tell you involves not only the colonel, but how the men will feel about me being in their company."

They watched closely as she cradled her injured arm, massaging gently before beginning to speak.

"Have either of you ever heard of Colonel James Douglas MacLean? Of his exploits involving the Cherokees during their capturing of Fort Loudon from the English—and other escapades?"

Both men nodded, neither one taking their eyes from her pained face.

"Kathryn," Jason interrupted gently. "Long ago, if you recall, I decided our relationship was more important than the past. No questions would be asked, nor answers given." She touched his arm and smiled.

"I know, but the dragoons should be told in case it changes my relationship with them. I do not wish to deceive them, especially now when they trust me." She looked apprehensively towards the lieutenant. "I gave the colonel my real name long ago, but never said much about my brother. I honestly did not know if he was alive. But it has been weighing heavily on me for some time, especially since I continually overhear bits and pieces about this elusive rebel you seek."

She rushed on before she lost her courage. "Lieutenant, I am Kathryn Cameron MacLean: Colonel MacLean's sister. And according to Brandon Gordon, he is very much alive."

She waited for this disclosure to sink in thoroughly. No one spoke, the silence hanging heavily.

"Discouraged after endless bloody skirmishes, and disgusted with the atrocities committed in the French and Indian War—in which he played a large part—he put military life aside. At that time he had small children and a sickly wife. So, he returned to his farm vowing never to fight again. His wife died, leaving him with four children to rear alone. I have not spoken with him in many months. However, in my travels I did hear rumors: when problems with England's King George escalated, and troubles began encroaching on his family's well being, he considered joining the militia again."

She paused a moment eyeing them both, her large, green eyes begging they trust her and understand. "I was looking for him when your men found me."

"And you suspect from what Gordon said, that he may be working with Beldon's troops?" Jason asked.

"There is a strong possibility." She winced, readjusting her injured arm.

"I am not following the significance of what you are trying to tell me, Kathryn," Jason said patiently, taking her anguished expression into consideration.

"My brother would be a fearsome adversary; I can not have you, Lieutenant, or the men—ever question my loyalties if things become difficult. I have made my choice and nothing will change that," she declared vehemently. "Besides, if my brother is in the militia he will kill me for my betrayal as fast as he would kill any English soldier." She shrugged, wincing as that move chased shooting pains the length of her arm.

The lieutenant spoke first assuring her: "I can speak for the others without question. After what you have done for us tonight, if there had been lingering doubts, they are gone. And I am not convinced this information needs to become general knowledge. Let it lie." As Jason nodded, agreeing, he added, "I feel privileged that you shared this with me, but will keep it between the three of us for now." His smile was comforting.

"Thank you," she mouthed softly.

"I will take my leave now, sir. But if you need anything …"

"Thank you, Jack," Jason said appreciatively.

When they were alone, he put his arm around her carefully. She was trembling and a tear had begun slowly gliding down the side of her face. Turning her to him, he traced its wet trail with his finger. Without her saying a word, he knew the internal turmoil she was experiencing.

"Kathryn, my love," he breathed against her ear. "I would trust you with my life. I know you have chosen; I have a very good idea of what a painful choice that has been. I hope your brother and I never face each other on the battlefield. But if we do," he added with deep feeling, "… that you will be able to *forgive* whoever wins."

The enormity of what he said overwhelmed her.

"Oh, Jason," half choke, half sob. Tears flowed freely as she pressed against him.

Stroking her hair, he kissed the top of her head. "I pray I will always be worthy in your eyes, so that you never regret the price you have had to pay."

"Jason." Her gaze was unfaltering. "You are … and always will be … my very life."

"As you are mine," he murmured, and smiled that look she loved so in him.

"There is one more thing I need to discuss." She looked troubled and her increasing physical discomfort was obvious.

"I meant what I said when Jack was here, no questions or answers necessary."

She stood a little shakily but steadied quickly with sheer willpower. He watched silently as she paced a few steps before turning to face him. She deemed their relationship strong enough to withstand almost anything at this point, but she needed to make him totally aware of her past. With his military career, he had much more to lose than she if her past came back to haunt them both. It was time to bring everything out in the open, for him to judge.

"I see you look inquisitive, at times, when I do things of a somewhat unusual nature, for instance: listen for hoof beats with my ear to the ground, my knowledge of Indian hunting methods, herbal medicines and … my war whoops." She watched him wanting to be sure he was following her train of thought. "And that awful time when I relived the horror of …"

"Kathryn, please …" Jason became immediately concerned; he could not risk her revisiting that black morass which had nearly claimed her several months ago.

She smiled weakly and continued. "I am strong enough now, Jason. Your love shields me."

He started to move to her side but she gestured for him to sit and hear her out. "I mentioned this once before but asked if we could delay the conversation until a later date." She paused giving him a moment to recall the incident. "I lived with the Cherokees, the Bird Clan, for several months." She searched his face for any reaction. He smiled but appeared confused. "They called me Ugilohi, or 'Long Hair'."

"That seems a rather unusual choice to have made. What prompted that decision?"

She paced a few steps, holding her injured arm, before turning to look him squarely in the eye. He indicated the chair, concerned by exhaustion reflected in her eyes. But she was oblivious, concentrating only on what she had to divulge.

"I sometimes decide I need to test my independence." At that statement, he started to chuckle and she grinned, despite her pain. "I had become close to a woman I call Anna. She is a healer, or 'Ku ni a ka ti', the person who taught me so much of herbal remedies. My family was unhappy with the friendship and Jamie took it upon himself to stop me from spending time with the Cherokees. He is my only sibling; mother lost several children before they took their first breath and was overly protective of me: fearful she might lose me too." She continued pacing, and watching his expression.

"In a fit of defiance I stole away one night, proud that I had outsmarted my brother. Through prior agreement Anna was waiting, ready to take me to her Clan. The Cherokees are a wonderful people and taught me a great deal. Though it is a very different way of life, I was content—at least for a while."

"What happened?" he asked. Her expression indicated something distressing had occurred.

She hesitated, uncertain how he would react to what she was about to say. But he had to be sure his commitment to her was the right choice. "After I had been part of their community for a while, a young brave chose me as his wife—we married in their tribal custom."

"Black Raven?" Jason inquired, his eyes narrowing.

Anguished eyes met his, bringing him instantly to her side, anger barely contained. "Where is he now?" he demanded, his voice harsh with emotion.

"He is dead."

Jason gave her a sharp look.

"He was young and arrogant and wanted a quiet, obedient wife." Her voice was so low he had to lean in to hear. "I do not believe there was one thing about me he approved of—or liked. One day he taunted an English officer while in town. I do not even recall why he had gone there. And the officer killed him." She looked at Jason.

"He tortured you." Jason's gaze held hers, watching any signs of her retreating into her hurtful past, but he could see she was stronger now. He slipped an arm around her waist as she leaned against him.

"He … was not kind." She had no wish to recall the mental and physical anguish he had subjected her to, despite Anna's constant intercession and pleading in her favor "I was relieved when he died," she admitted hesitantly.

Jason stroked her hair, continuing to hold her gently.

"By Cherokee custom a wife is required to mourn for many months, during which time she cannot bathe, change clothes or wash her hair."

At Jason's look of distaste, she nodded agreement.

"Somehow Jamie discovered what had happened and arrived shortly after the fact, snatched me onto his horse and took me home." Her eyes brightened a little. "And for his interference in my life that time, I was actually quite thankful." A smile played at the corners of her mouth. "I am sure you remember the towel and dirk I had squirreled away in the cave."

He nodded, remembering his curiosity at the time, realizing how much had changed between them in these last months.

"Jamie and I stopped there so that I could take a much needed bath. I do not know why I left those things, perhaps to make the statement that I had been there shedding one life for another."

"Did you love him?" Jason asked, startling her, causing her to think for a moment.

"I was so wrapped up in making a statement to my family, asserting my complete independence, that I married him for spite." She paused. "I was fond of him before he became cruel, but love? No." Shaking her head sadly, she continued. "Jamie took me home, where I stayed for awhile. But after our mother's death, I drifted. We had serious words—made angry accusations. I was irritated with his interference in my life even though he had rescued me. We have always been like that—constantly bickering and fighting. There is very little we agree upon. But in time I missed his children: two boys and two little girls. I guess I even missed his bad temper and bossy ways. For whatever reason, I had decided to 'bury the hatchet', so to speak, when I bumped into your camp."

His arms stayed gently around her, his nearness and strength a soothing balm.

"I am so sorry, Kathryn. You have had some big hurts." He rested his cheek against her hair.

"No more than most," she murmured, "and probably less than you."

He remained silent for a few moments, working through this information, surprised it did not particularly bother him once he got past the initial shock of her confession. Her past was irrelevant, of that he was sure. His own past certainly was not one of which to be proud.

"I have never experienced enduring love before you, Jason," she murmured, breaking into his thoughts. "There are no adequate words to express the depth of my feelings."

"Oh, my Kathryn, you show me in so many ways, each and every day." Stroking her hair back, he studied the beauty of her face, absorbing every angle, each tiny detail. His eyes drifted to hers and held, sharing myriads of emotions without the utterance of a single word.

"Marry me, Kathryn," a fervent demand, sounding far too blunt.

Arm throbbing, unsure if she had heard correctly, she eyed him quizzically.

"Kathryn, I am no good with speeches. I did not mean that to sound like a command. But I have thought on this often of late …" He hesitated but quickly rushed on. "Will you be my wife?"

She answered with a lingering kiss. "I would be honored but I am surprised, and just a little confused."

He kissed the bridge of her nose, then her lips. "It feels right—as simple as that," he replied. "I am proud to have you at my side; I want it known to one and all that you are mine beyond doubt."

She hugged him happily.

"Besides, I have noticed the way some of the men look at you." His eyes held a sparkling intensity. "It is time to make an honest woman of you."

"You never cease to amaze me, sir." She shook her head, grinning.

Gently taking her chin, he tipped her face up capturing her gaze, and in a more serious tone said, "You are right about my past, Kathryn, but you have changed me; made me realize that someone could love me without guile or motive. Someday I *will* talk to you about …" he trailed off, "but not tonight."

"When you are ready, I will always listen. That is part of what love and trust are about; just a small part." Her luminous, green eyes held a misty shimmer.

"I have something I want to show you," he said eagerly as he headed for his desk. Reaching far back, he pulled a small package from his desk drawer. Scooping her into his arms, he ensconced himself on the chair and carefully settled her on his lap.

"In case you are afraid that I have put no thought into tonight's request," he said softly as he opened the package, "What do you think?" He held in his hand, two of the most beautiful rings she had ever seen.

"Oh," she gasped, touching the intricate, gold pattern of the matching rings. "Celtic knotwork representing eternal love," she whispered, regarding him with wonderment. "How did you …?" She was speechless, unable to take her eyes from them. "They are exquisite, Jason. When did you …?"

Seeing joy reflected in her eyes, he was relieved. He had made the right choice, given her pleasure; he could ask for no greater reward.

"A while back, when we were camped outside Camden for two weeks, I found a Scottish craftsman and had him make them for me. They are the only two of their kind in existence; quite large enough, I think, to make just the right statement and hopefully … perfect for my Scottish lass."

He had never referred to her heritage before and she was touched. "They are perfect." She was awestruck.

"I had to guess at the size but I think it looks right." Hugging her close, he held it up. "Would you like to try it on?"

"Oh no, Jason," She drew back—shocked. "That would bring bad luck."

My brave warrior is superstitious. "As I do not want you to have time to change your mind, we will find a preacher in the next town." He grinned widely.

"Not a chance." Her green eyes caressed.

Seeing her fatigue, he pulled her to him, cradling her head against his chest. He caressed her thick, tawny hair, whispering tender words and within minutes felt her relax into him, her breathing even and deep.

Many thoughts rushed through his head as he held her. Dawn was near and he would have to make some serious decisions as to how to thwart Major Beldon's plans, but they could wait. His adrenaline rush waning, he nodded off in the chair, content to feel her safe in his arms.

Lieutenant Jackson poked his head through the tent flap and stopped, the tender scene before him created a lasting impression, one confirming the incredible changes in Colonel Tarrington—all because of this unusual woman.

Dozing lightly, Jason sensed his presence and looked up with a silencing gesture, to which the lieutenant smiled and nodded. Carefully gathering Kathryn, so as not to create further pain, he settled her on the cot. She mumbled his name as he covered her with a blanket but did not awaken.

"Rest now, love." He kissed her forehead then went to join Lieutenant Jackson outside the tent.

"How is she doing, sir?" he asked, offering a mug of coffee which Jason gratefully accepted.

"Although she is strong and feisty, I want to delay moving for at least today—to give her a few hours to bounce back."

Jackson nodded and handed him a small flask. At the colonel's raised eyebrow, he explained, "I made some of that herbal infusion Kathryn used recently. Hopefully it will help."

Jason smiled, pleased by his consideration. "As soon as she wakes, I will start that treatment."

"Cook is also working on a poultice made of comfrey, or at least I think that is what he said. I gather it is supposed to draw out the poison and infection."

"Whatever will get her back to full strength quickly," Jason said, glancing at her peacefully sleeping form. "Let us head over to the holding area and talk to the prisoners before she awakens."

"I doubt we will get much information." Jackson shook his head. "They are a surly lot."

"Kathryn informed me she knows this area well. When she recovers a bit, I am sure she will have some useful input which may save us time and distance. I want to be sure we cut Beldon off from Gates's army."

As they headed for the prisoner's area, he turned to face his lieutenant and abruptly paused, shy for the first time in his life. "Kathryn has agreed to marry me," he announced, sounding proud, pleased and slightly surprised.

Lieutenant Jackson stopped and turned to face the colonel with an inquisitive look.

"I caught her in a weak moment," he said somewhat self-consciously.

"Congratulations, sir, it is about time." He grinned widely. "I was almost ready to ask her myself."

He resumed walking, leaving the colonel standing there, momentarily unsure as to just how much truth there might be in his statement.

Chapter Twelve

Recovering

Kathryn awoke sometime later, relieved to find herself decidedly better, thankful for her excellent recuperative powers. Never one to require a great deal of sleep; she was refreshed, alert and already dressed when Jason walked into their tent with coffee and a late breakfast. She moved quickly into his arms as he set the food down on the desk.

"Count your final hours of freedom, madam. Jack informed me that there is a town within two days ride."

He brushed a light kiss to her brow as she grinned up at him, her eyes sparkling. "I was about to give you the same warning, sir," she retorted happily.

When breakfast was finished he cleared desk space, preparing to examine her arm. As he went for the brandy and bandages, she rolled her eyes and groaned. Flashing a look of severity, he sat her down and stepped behind her for support. Reaching around, he uncovered the wound. As he flushed the area with brandy she pressed back against him, sucking in a small gasp. The final bathing of the gash with an infusion Jackson had concocted, was nothing in comparison. When satisfied it was clean, Jason applied a gooey poultice of pounded comfrey root, finishing with fresh linen binding.

"It looks good, no inflammation or warmth," he said quietly against her ear.

Though the pain had been severe, she tolerated it without complaint, and when able to speak without a hitch, her sense of humor returned. "I have a very good doctor to thank for that."

"Now, I want you to get some rest."

"But I just got up and feel quite refreshed," she grumbled, pouting prettily.

He shook his head chuckling, but on a more serious note added, "I need you to be ready to ride early tomorrow. I hate to push you, but …"

"I can save you a lot of time, Jason," she interrupted. "Let me show you on the map."

Needing no further urging, he unrolled it on his desk. He had not wanted to ask, and was pleased she had brought the subject up first. Moving quickly would be to their advantage.

She offered interpretations of Gordon's dying statements in regards to Beldon's plan of attack, the confessions of a dying man apt to hold some truth. She pointed out familiar shortcuts which could eliminate hours of travel. Although their ride would be long and hard, they could catch the rebel militia off-guard in about two weeks time, and drive them back before they joined General Gates's.

Jason absorbed every word, proud and impressed by her excellent strategy. Finishing her summarization, she glanced up to determine his thoughts.

"I have never given you sufficient recognition for your intelligence; I stand corrected."

"I have learned a great deal watching you, Jason," she countered, sharing the credit.

"Never sell yourself short, Kathryn, never. Your help has been invaluable, and I thank you." His eyes flashed pride, making her truly feel a part of his life—at long last.

Relenting on her required nap, he took her hand and led her outside. "Come, get some fresh air and talk with my officers. They are concerned about you."

As she deemed Cook's poultice to be a major contributing factor in her rapid recovery, she made a point to visit him first. At his gruff response to her show of appreciation, she winked and added, "I think that rough exterior of yours hides a very beautiful heart." Leaning forward, she planted a light kiss on his cheek, embarrassing him thoroughly.

Later, as Kathryn relaxed against a tree trunk talking with a few of the men, she realized she had been accepted as part of the team. Jack was there, relieved to see her rebounding quickly. She thanked him for concocting her herbal remedy and helping Cook with the poultice; the herbs were rapidly doing their work. Several dragoons came and went greeting her warmly, making it a relaxing afternoon. She discussed the prisoners with Jason, but there was not much to tell. They were uncooperative, refusing to divulge any information, especially one young man who was especially defiant.

"He must be related to me," she laughed and gave it no further thought.

"They will be kept under heavy guard until we reach Camden, and then be left for possible swapping of prisoners," he explained.

Not that long ago, according to hearsay, they all would have been tortured or shot. However, that information no longer held credence, Jason had changed.

Later that afternoon, while reclining on a soft patch of grass within their campsite, she drifted into sleep. Jason rolled her sleeve up, and removing the bandage, exposed her wound to the healing rays of sunlight. Those who saw the severity of her injury whispered amongst themselves, passing it on to others: she had been extremely courageous and lucky to be alive.

Jason left Lieutenant Jackson watching her while he briefed his officers on the next few days moves, explaining their ultimate goal.

By suppertime, freshly awakened and feeling more herself, she ate heartily. They sat with the men for a brief time and she joined in their singing around the campfire.

"You need to get some rest before tomorrow's long ride," Jason said softly as darkness fell.

"If you are going to send me to bed early, Colonel …" she purred, leaning closer for his hearing only. "It had better be with you."

He shot her an amused look and quickly stood, offering her a hand up.

Alone in their tent, he pulled the chair out from the desk and bid her sit down.

"My arm is much better." She narrowed her eyes.

Ignoring her look, he indicated with an expression she recognized all too well—'do as instructed without argument'. She complied, grudgingly; she would not win this contest of wills—this time.

Jason redressed her arm, pleased to see the herbal concoctions had worked rapidly, her wound sore, but looking much better. When he finished, she stood and walked towards their bed, loosening clothing as she went.

"Kathryn," he said firmly, "We leave early tomorrow; tonight we shall sleep. I am well able to control my carnal urges." Catching her frown, he added lightly, "However, a penance of my choosing shall be imposed for my inconvenience—one that I shall eagerly collect at a later time." That brought a delighted peal of laughter and a saucy retort.

Although morning came quickly, she had slept soundly and awoke refreshed. Finding Jason's side of the bed empty, she roused and quickly prepared for travel so as not to keep the troops waiting, or worse, be relegated to ride in one of the wagons in the rear. She was stronger, the throbbing in her arm reduced to a dull ache.

As she stepped out of the tent, Lieutenant Jackson approached with biscuits and coffee.

"The colonel said to take it slowly; he is talking to the men. We can join him shortly."

She smiled and took the hot coffee, inhaling deeply, savoring its delicious smell.

"How is your arm?" he asked.

She arched a non-committal eyebrow. "Oh, it is very much there, but better."

"May I get anything for you?"

She shook her head, but on second thought said, "Yes, my mare, so that I will not hold things up." She smiled prettily, hoping he would not give her an argument.

"Are you sure you are up to a long day in the saddle? You took a nasty wound the other night. No one would think any less of you if you chose an easy day. Why not join Cook in the wagon? He would love the company."

"I appreciate your concern, Jack. But I really would like to ride today." Her eyes conveyed a quiet plea.

"How can I refuse when you give me a look like that?" He shook his head. "The colonel will probably have my hide." However, against his better judgment, he had Beauty saddled and brought up.

The little mare pranced in her usual high-strung manner, but quieted as Kathryn began patting her neck and talking soothingly. Thanking the dragoon, she turned at Beauty's insistent nuzzling, and reaching into her pocket, brought out a sugar cube, scolding her lovingly. Without thinking, she reached to grab the saddle and fling herself astride. Excruciating pain shot the length of her arm. Groaning, she clutched the throbbing limb to her side and leaned into Beauty's neck, on the verge of fainting. "Hold, Beauty," she gasped, and the mare immediately stood still, supporting her mistress.

"Are you going to pass out or be sick?" It was Jackson at her shoulder, a touch of ill-concealed humor in his question.

She rolled to face him, leaning heavily against Beauty. His interruption helped her focus on something other than her spinning head; she smiled weakly. "Not sure, maybe both."

"Take deep breaths," he advised, and after a moment asked, "Ready to try again?"

At her nod, he knelt and gave her the traditional 'leg up' just as Jason headed in their direction astride his black charger.

"Not a word, please," she beseeched. Healthy color was returning, and the pinched look about her eyes had lessened.

"Your secret is safe with me," he assured, flashing a grin.

"Thank you," she mouthed, turning to greet Jason as he brought Diablo to a halt at her side.

He noticed lingering pallor. But at his questioning look, she stated firmly, "I am fine."

He looked to his lieutenant, but receiving no answer to the contrary, decided not to squash her pride with more questions. Without further delay, they rode to the front of the formation and stepped off together. Nods of acknowledgment, as she moved to the head of the column, provided a decided lift to her spirits, her wound all but forgotten.

They journeyed in silence for some time as Jason observed her surreptitiously. She kept 'working' the injured arm, the discomfort this action caused, easily discernable. Exasperated, he confronted her.

"Kathryn, I can see you are in pain. What are you doing to your arm?"

"I am afraid it will stiffen, sir. I need to have use of that arm," she said firmly, attempting to defend her action.

"It will not stiffen if you take it easy for a couple of days, and is far less apt to bleed," he answered curtly, frustrated by her stubbornness.

Flashing a look of annoyance, she ceased flexing her arm.

Within a short time, he halted for a break in a small wooded glen. Quickly dismounting, he removed his helmet and moved to her side. From her pallor, it was obvious she was hanging on by sheer will power; which appeared to be fading rapidly. Reaching outspread arms, he indicated he would catch her. With a thin smile she accepted, and swinging her leg over Beauty's neck, slid down.

With his arm around her waist, he propelled her to a big oak tree by the edge of the brook.

"Sit," he commanded.

She did as told and leaned back against the tree trunk. She gave no argument as he slid the shirt off her shoulder and began removing the bandage. He eyed the wound closely, a little disconcerted at the seepage of blood. The wound looked clean; and no warmth was present indicating infection.

Lieutenant Jackson approached with food and bandaging and crouched to be of assistance. But she was too tired to even attempt light conversation.

Ignoring her resistance, Jason put a flask of brandy to her lips. The wound had bled slightly, it would be painful. At his stern insistence, she sipped the burning liquid, but eyed him crossly.

"This will hurt, but I will try to be quick about it." Moistening a cloth with brandy, he daubed her wound; his planned admonitory words, dying on his lips when he saw her suffering.

Clutching her lower arm, she leaned back weakly against the tree, eyes pinched closed, her mouth twisted in a grimace. Hastily finishing with the salve and bandaging, he turned to sponging her perspiring forehead.

"Better?" he asked.

She nodded forcing a smile, but could do no more than nibble the light meal Jackson had brought—too exhausted to eat.

"Come here," he breathed into her hair as he pulled her against his chest, for once completely unconcerned with appearances.

She nestled against him, asleep before he could advise her to do so. He sat stroking her hair, enjoying the feel of the silky tresses beneath his fingers, and the warmth of her pressed against his side. Relaxing, he dozed for a short time, awaking to find her still asleep and her hand resting lightly on his chest; peaceful within the safety of his arms. He studied her face thoughtfully. This incredible child-woman would soon be his wife—and was thankful. *Will I even begin to know you, my Kathryn, if I have two lifetimes to devote to the task?*

His reverie was interrupted by hushed murmurings as she stretched and looked up. "Jason, my love, just touching you renews my strength."

"Feeling better, I gather," he confirmed, smiling warmly.

"Very much so, but I would say I felt terrible if I could spend the rest of the day in your arms."

"Now you sound more like my Kathryn," he chuckled, giving her a hug.

Looking up, he saw Lieutenant Jackson approaching, and to his unasked question answered, "Kathryn is better; we move out in one half hour."

Chapter Thirteen

Wedding Vows

By evening, they were on the outskirts of a small town. Tired, but feeling more like her self, Kathryn sat watching the men pitch tents for a two-day layover. With shortcuts she had provided along their route, they were making excellent time.

Sipping hot coffee, she awaited Jason's company for dinner. When he appeared somewhat later bearing two plates of something less than distinguishable, she smiled weakly, silently vowing to go hunting—soon.

"I have sent Jack into town to find a preacher." Sparkling blue eyes belied the matter-of-fact delivery of his statement.

"You are a brave man, sir," she chuckled.

"I believe you are correct, madam." He winked, causing her to grin at his unusual gesture.

As they ate, she teased about the state of their dinner fare. "You really do need something more fit for human consumption. It is time for me to go hunting again."

"We are in enemy territory now. Do not, under any circumstances, try any surprises." He fixed her with a serious look, and that same arched brow that conveyed far more than words.

She remained quiet, judging how she could word her hunting proposal to make him agreeable.

He eyed her in stony silence, awaiting an answer, annoyance increasing at her willfulness. "Kathryn, a simple: 'no, I will not disappear into the woods without your knowledge'—will suffice quite nicely."

She timed her answer, judging his level of irritation—testing her parameters. "All right, I will tell you *before* I go hunting. But you treat me like a child," she complained, eyeing him peevishly.

He shook his head, laughing. "That is one of the many things I love about you, Kathryn, your damnable need for independence."

Rising from her chair, she moved around the desk and into his welcoming embrace. Ensconcing herself on his lap, she rested her forehead against his, hugging him quietly. Although she desired freedom to make her own decisions, she also wanted to make him happy. Some instances were more difficult than others; this was one of the easy ones. She kissed his cheek.

"Let us join the men. A cup of coffee, a few songs and a smoky campfire would be a perfect way to top off the evening, hmm?"

Setting her on her feet, he ushered her out into the fresh evening air.

Lieutenant Jackson returned before dark with a preacher, who at first seemed reluctant to accept the task at hand. However, he immediately warmed to Kathryn: her exuberance and obvious love for this man, rapidly winning him over.

He talked with both of them at length, observing their interaction with each other. Though not entirely understanding their odd set of circumstances, he could condone this marriage with good conscience. With his blessings, plans were put together for their wedding the following afternoon.

That night she was happy, excited and playful—their earlier 'discussion' put behind them. Jason paced himself, providing her the ultimate pleasure of slow, sensual moves, watching as she lost herself to the moment, a flush of color rushing to her beautiful face—savoring the deep inner satisfaction at the 'giving' process he had learned with her; no longer taking what he needed without regard, as he had so often been wont to do in the past.

In the afterglow of passion spent, they slept soundly in each other's arms, awaking refreshed just before dawn.

As she prepared for the day's festivities, he handed her a wrapped parcel. She took it hesitantly, with a look of surprise. "But I have nothing to give you," she protested.

"*You* are my gift," he assured. Stroking her hair back, he traced a finger gently along her cheek, studying her face—and then kissed her deeply. Abruptly breaking the contact, he gestured for her to open the brown wrapping paper, anxious to see her reaction.

Untying the string, she pushed the paper carefully aside and gasped with pleasure at the new breeches and dressy, full-sleeved blouse. "Oh, Jason," she murmured, clutching the garments, her face wreathed in smiles.

"Are those to your liking, Kathryn?" Stepping forward, he quickly swept her into his arms, crushing both her and the new garments against him.

"Oh, yes," she exclaimed, nodding eagerly. "They are beautiful, but …" with a somewhat contrite smile she added, "But I would have worn a dress if you asked."

"Actually, I prefer pants on you, madam. I can better appreciate your beautiful, long legs and lovely bottom." Cupping her behind, he caressed sensuously—satisfied as her breathing heightened. "As much as I would like to accommodate you, milady, we have a preacher and my officers expecting us. However, I will make it up to you later."

He kissed the pout from her lips and before she could protest, quickly rolled up her sleeve. "Let me take a look at your arm. I am glad you seem to be in less pain today."

Arguing would accomplish nothing. With a sigh of resignation, she sat quietly watching as he removed the bandage. The wound looked substantially better: no bleeding and healing rapidly. "Your herbal remedies work exceptionally well," he said thoughtfully. "Perhaps you might consider helping in the medical tents when we have need."

"Oh yes," she bobbed her head eagerly, pleased to have finally been asked to be a participating member of this group.

After gently redressing her arm he pressed a kiss to her forehead, smiled and exited the tent, calling back over his shoulder: "Get ready, my Kathryn, I will be back for you shortly."

She hastily readied herself, donning her new clothes and combing her hair, allowing it to fall in a cascade of tangled curls billowing about her shoulders—exactly the way he loved to see her. Good to his word, he returned shortly and stopped abruptly in his tracks.

"You take my breath away, Kathryn." Slowly turning her, he examined her appreciatively from all angles.

Eyes aglow, she adjusted his jabot and reached to touch his cheek. "My Colonel," she said tenderly, her eyes caressing.

"Come, love, time to make an honest woman of you." Placing his arm protectively around her shoulder, they headed towards the small assembly of men in the center of camp.

Lieutenant Jackson stood smiling, watching them approach. Behind him, he overheard one of the sergeants speak softly to a fellow officer. "I would never have believed it. He is lethal in battle; there are none tougher. But around her, he is a different man. He sure does love that girl."

His companion nodded remarking, "But it is obviously so very mutual."

Lieutenant Jackson agreed. Even the preacher smiled at the devoted couple as they approached.

As the ceremony proceeded, they were both calm, relaxed.

"Do you, Colonel Jason William Tarrington, take Kathryn Cameron MacLean, to be your lawfully wedded wife? To love her, honor her and cherish her until death do you part?"

Gazing into her beautiful green eyes, Jason took her hands in his and stated fervently: "Kathryn, I will love, honor and cherish you … always." He paused, and then continued quietly. "Even death will not part us." He squeezed her hands and she returned the gesture.

She heard the preacher's words, asking her the questions, but could not take her eyes from Jason.

"Kathryn," the preacher droned on. "Do you take Colonel Tarrington to be your lawfully wedded husband? Wilt thou love him, honor him, cherish and obey him until death do you part?"

Clinging tightly to his hands, she fastened emotionally charged green eyes on his piercing blue ones. "Jason. I will love you, honor you and cherish you … always. Even in death we will be as one."

The preacher nudged verbally. "And, Kathryn …" He paused, waiting for her to finish her vows.

With extreme discomfort, she searched Jason's face, then the preacher's and back to Jason, who allowed just the hint of a smile to play at the corner of his lips. "And I will try my best to always—obey you," she finally answered, looking somewhat pained.

Jason chuckled as his officers struggled to conceal smirks.

"Kathryn," the preacher said firmly, beginning a quiet reprimand.

"Reverend," Jason interrupted, never losing a moment's eye contact with her, holding her hands, his blue eyes dancing. "I accept Kathryn's answer as it stands. She is far too honest to agree to a promise she may not be able to keep at all times." He winked as she mouthed, "I really will try."

Although taken somewhat aback, the preacher continued with the ring ceremony.

Lieutenant Jackson had been entrusted to hold the rings, which he now handed to each in turn. Jason took Kathryn's hand, feeling it tremble slightly as he threaded the golden knotwork onto her finger with the appropriate words.

"Oh, Jason …" she breathed, her eyes moist and threatening to spill over.

He smiled warmly, both hands encasing her ring hand. Raising it to his lips, he brushed a light kiss. An errant tear did spill down her cheek at that point and he traced it with his thumb.

Never taking her eyes from Jason's face, lower lip quivering ever so slightly, she reached back to Lieutenant Jackson for the ring. She slid the Celtic knotwork slowly onto his finger, speaking the ceremonial rite with firm assurance. Raising his hand, she cradled it to her breast.

"You are my life," she whispered.

The preacher stood spellbound at this point, almost forgetting his final line. "I now pronounce you man and wife."

They turned, facing each other. At this moment in time, no one existed but the two of them. Gazing at Jason with deepest reverence, she touched his chest with the flat of her hand. "Your heart," she murmured, curling her hand into a fist and placing it against her heart, "and mine … will always beat as one."

With a gently placed kiss to her forehead, he began slowly tracing his thumb from her brow, along the bridge of her nose to her chin, and tilting her chin up, kissed her tenderly. "Always," he whispered, his eyes capturing hers.

They stood as if completely alone, lost in each other.

Lieutenant Jackson noted that a ritual had been born: one that he would witness many times, a powerful ritual that never failed to move him each time it was repeated.

Having never experienced this side of their colonel, the officers watched in fascination, but rather than perceiving it as weakness, they regarded him with new admiration.

By now the preacher's insistent, "You may kiss the bride," jolted them from their reverie.

She looked about at the smiling faces, somewhat embarrassed. But Jason, with complete disregard, bent to her in earnest, kissing her deeply. Slowly her arms snaked around his neck, ignoring the lingering pain of her wound. Clinging, she returned his kiss fervently. There was no mistaking the raw hunger existing between this unusual pair.

"I think the heat between those two could light the cook fire," the sergeant chortled, nudging a fellow officer who grinned, nodding agreement.

Kathryn broke first, her eyes capturing Jason's meaningfully, easily reading his thoughts and urgency to share matching desire.

"Our claims …" he whispered huskily.

"Yes," a breathless murmur, "… when we have honored our dragoons."

"Agreed," he squeezed her hand, comprehending fully.

Turning quickly, he grinned. "Crack the keg, gentlemen, the party has just begun."

Lieutenant Jackson promptly handed each of them a brimming mug.

"To my beloved husband," Clicking the side of his cup, she smiled devotedly.

"To my cherished wife," he answered.

They drank deeply, eyeing each other over their mugs. As the sun sank lower in the sky on that most perfect day, their matching rings flashed shards of glittering golden light for all to see.

"Now there's a statement that will not fail to be noticed," the sergeant commented.

"More of a warning, I suspect, knowing the colonel as we do," was the retort. "No one had better make a move on that lady if he wants to live to see another day." They grinned, agreeing wholeheartedly.

Jason lowered his mug, casting a glance skyward, appreciating the changing shades of color as late afternoon edged closer to sunset's glorious hues. "This certainly is beautiful time of day."

"Yes, my love." She smiled at the sensitivity which had become a part of him.

"But not nearly as beautiful as you, Mrs. Tarrington." His hand traced her cheek as he bent to kiss her.

At that moment, Lieutenant Jackson approached. "If I might interrupt for just a minute..." Banging the side of his mug with a large soup ladle, he yelled loudly, grabbing the dragoon's attention. "I would like to propose a toast to the newly married couple."

The dragoons turned in unison as he lofted his mug of ale.

"To our colonel and his very special lady, may your love continue to grow, and may you always find solace in each other's arms." Jackson smiled warmly at both of them.

"Here, here," came the loud and rowdy chorus.

Kathryn grinned, mouthing a sincere 'thank you'.

Several toasts followed as everyone relaxed, enjoying the festivities. Much to Kathryn's surprise and pleasure, Lieutenant Jackson produced what he called—a wedding cake.

"How did you ever manage this beautiful creation?" she asked, thrilled.

He shrugged, somewhat embarrassed, becoming more so as she gave him a quick hug. Although not your customary Scottish wedding bannock, it tasted marvelous as she and Jason followed proper traditional dictates—each feeding the other, accompanied by loud cheers.

They socialized amongst the dragoons, chatting amiably for a while longer, enjoying the party. As sunset began her brilliant display, Jason bent to his wife's ear.

"Kathryn, we have ..." a serious edge to his tone caught her attention.

"Yes, it *is* time."

Jason stepped aside to quickly confer with Jack.

"Enjoy your evening, sir. All will be handled as you wish."

Arching an eyebrow, Jason smiled. "You and I both know my wife would not miss the evening camaraderie. I am sure we will see you later." He started to turn away, but added softly, "Our heartfelt thanks, Jack. This day has meant a great deal ... to *both* of us."

Ducking into their tent, they were greeted by a small bouquet of wild daisies arranged in a tin cup, sitting beside the blankets—more of Jackson's thoughtfulness.

With a sharp yank Jason dropped the tent flap, and moving to Kathryn's side, began slowly removing her clothing—one piece at a time—enjoying his self-imposed torture of resisting the urge to ravish her.

Momentarily submissive, she lay back absorbing each expressive nuance chasing across his features. When finally freed from her last article of clothing, she reached up and pulled him firmly against her nakedness, nibbling his ear, teasing of what was to come. Then it was her turn. Undressing him slowly, she allowed her fingers the merest breath of a touch in areas selected to tantalize, thrilled as his eyes followed her every move, his breath rapidly quickening.

Guiding her back onto the blankets, he placed his nakedness the full length of her, pinning her gently. Neither moved—both relishing the heightened emotional energy pulsating about them as they enticed each other, their passionate need to become one, escalating.

With his firm arousal spiking increasing shivers of anticipation, she could deny no longer—reaching for him first. But he gently pinned her arms, aware of her wound even in his need. His tongue caressed and teased each nipple in turn, forcing soft whimpers and his name whispered fervently, over and over in aching want.

Passion escalated to a fever pitch, their needs identical, each wanting to possess the other. Nudging her legs apart he entered slowly, in complete control, a shudder rippling through both—simultaneously.

"Jason …" Insatiable yearning threatened to engulf her.

Rising up on one elbow, he caressed her hair, taking note of her green eyes dilated with passion.

"Kathryn." Despite a ragged edge to his voice, he maintained absolute control. "You belong to me, now and forever … and to no other." His look demanded she fully understand: from this day forward, he claimed her as his alone.

"Always," she answered fervently.

Never losing eye contact, slowly wrapping her legs snuggly, she brought him deep within. A sharp intake of breath and low moan were the answers she sought as he finally lost his battle for self-control.

"As you are mine alone … and for no other, Jason," she whispered tersely, the intensity of her emerald eyes making it impossible to look away.

"Always," he answered firmly, voice husky with desire.

Claims staked, they could no longer contain themselves. She arched against him as he responded in kind. Their personalities were such that neither would countenance the slightest hint of infidelity—they drove that fact home again and again in a fierce rite of mutual possessiveness. Eventually, both completely content and sated, they lay encircled in each other's arms. Resting against his chest, waiting for her wildly beating heart to return to normalcy, she absolutely glowed.

When his breathing slowed he tipped her chin up, capturing her attention with piercing blue eyes. "We have now consummated our marriage, milady. I am afraid it is too late for you to back out of our bargain."

"Thank heavens," she breathed, planting a kiss at the base of his neck. Resisting the strong urge to remain within the comfort of his arms, she arose. Smiling over her shoulder as she freshened and began dressing, she commented: "I would really enjoy playing the tin whistle tonight and …"

Jason chuckled at that remark. "I told Jack we would be returning, my love."

"Well, it *would* be a nice way to round out this day. The men have treated me well, although I am sure it has often been inconvenient. And—'it is their duty'—does not count." At her mock severity, he shook his head and chuckled, *amused.*

Full darkness rapidly approached, the glowing campfires and delicious aromas of Cook's stew, beckoning. Lacing her arm through his, she tugged him towards the noisy group. Singing had already begun—an accompanying tin whistle trilling crisply throughout the campsite.

"May I play?" she asked, ignoring the low growl of her empty stomach.

The officer immediately offered it up with a grin, carefully wiping the mouthpiece on his sleeve. After a couple of practice trills, she turned to address the group. "How about a little tune I learned down home?"

They whooped and cheered as she started a lilting Scottish aire, followed in quick succession by a rebel jig. The men, clapping in time with the music, watched as she gracefully skipped an accompanying two-step, enthralled by this captivating woman. And Jason beamed with pride.

Far at the back of the encampment, the rebel prisoners caught bits and pieces of the festivities which floated back to them on the quiet night air. They muttered rude slurs under their breath, quietly so as not to be overheard by the guards.

At the easily recognizable musical notes, one young rebel took particular interest and listened more carefully to the lilting melody of the tin whistle. He recognized that song, as well as all the others he had heard tonight—and was confused. He had seen the colonel's woman upon occasion, just quick glimpses from a distance. Nagging at the back of his mind was something remembered—and vaguely familiar.

The celebration continued on into early evening, a quick meal being thrown together by Cook to help sober up those who had to return to duty. This had been an event they would talk about for years to come: the unlikely meeting and pairing of this couple, and their incredible devotion, was not an everyday occurrence.

A full moon chased the darkness, illuminating their tent, as she lay within his arms drifting sleepily, reliving his incredible touch: like molten fire kissing her flesh, igniting an all-consuming inferno. She needed him as he needed her—equally—as necessary to life as the air they breathed. At long last, as Mrs. Jason William Tarrington, she was truly happy. Jason completed her—supplying the missing piece she had been seeking most of her life. *Our journey is just beginning, my love.*

"My husband," she murmured, snuggling closer.

He awoke in the middle of the night, reassured to feel the warmth of her at his side. She lay snuggled against him drifting, barely awake. With her face pressed close, her warm breath caressing his skin, he was hard-pressed to hear her contented whisper: *"My husband,"* as her hand touched his chest.

He watched her sleeping peacefully, acutely aware of how deeply he loved this woman ... *his wife*, and was filled with contentment for the first time in his life.

The demons of his past were finally vanquished.

Chapter Fourteen

Gabriel

They roused early the next morning, happy in their first day as man and wife, a good amount of time being devoted to enjoying their new status. They both sensed a deepened bond of respect, devotion and inner contentment. By mid-morning, Jason and Kathryn turned to more pressing matters. They pored over the maps of the area while enjoying their coffee, discussing routes and timing to intercept Major Beldon's forces.

Advanced word had finally reached them: preparations were being formulated for British divisions to move southward into the Carolinas. If they could successfully scatter Beldon's incoming reinforcements, it would allow Clinton and Cornwallis greater potential for a rapid victory.

"Enough." Jason suddenly planted both hands firmly in the middle of the map.

Kathryn glanced up from the area she had been studying and focused on her husband. At her questioning look, he smiled. "Tomorrow we leave for several days on the road, this can wait." Drawing her up into his arms he added, "We are well ahead of schedule, let us take the horses out and give them a run, hmm?"

Her face lit up with excitement.

"Bring along a book and I shall read to you, if you like. Just allow me a few minutes to speak to Jack and get the horses ready."

With childlike glee, she kissed his cheek and reached for her favorite poetry book.

As Jason approached, the lieutenant greeted him with a smile. "Good morning, sir. It certainly was a splendid party yesterday."

Jason returned his smile. "Thank you again for your part in our wedding, Jack, especially the cake. Kathryn was touched."

Lieutenant Jackson shrugged, a bit embarrassed. A show of appreciation from the colonel was a rare occurrence, yet recently, that, too, had been changing.

"My wife and I would like to spend this afternoon away from camp," he said, and proceeded to outline necessary details.

Jason returned to their tent shortly leading Beauty and Diablo. Kathryn stood outside the entrance, smiling and eager to be on their way.

"Jackson and three other men will ride point for us," he said.

"I know you warned me yesterday not to go hunting alone, but do you really feel there is a threat with both of us together?"

"Word travels fast, love. The prisoners we hold have probably been missed by now." Cupping her cheek, he gave her a long, meaningful look. "I will never knowingly put you at risk, Kathryn, even if you think I am being overly cautious."

"I know you would not," she acknowledged, kissing him softly.

"Jackson has been advised to give us room for privacy. However, madam, we will have to be chaste." He winked, his playful expression of admonition making her giggle.

"Are you throwing out a challenge to me, sir?" She raised an eyebrow.

"Actually, my wife, it will be a challenge for me not to ravish you amongst the wild flowers and sweet meadow grass." With a quickly brushed kiss, he gestured towards the patiently waiting horses.

Tossing her saddlebag up onto Beauty, she smiled a warm greeting to Lieutenant Jackson and the others. Jason held back, waiting to see if she would care for assistance in mounting.

"Let me see if I can do it," she said lightly, grinning as she flung herself astride her little mare.

Her arm obviously gave some pain, but he pretended not to notice. With a quick pat to her thigh, he mounted Diablo. She was proud and stubborn; and he would have her be no other way. With a waved signal to his men, they took off at a gallop.

The two horses raced across the open fields surrounding their campsite. Being spirited animals, they sensed the exuberant mood of their riders and leaped forward eagerly. Kathryn took Beauty on a series of jumps over low bushes and fallen logs with Diablo close on her heels. The day was beautiful, the air rich with pungent aromas of grass, flowers, leather and horses.

Eventually they reined to a halt in a small cluster of trees where a brook widened into a shallow pool. There they dismounted, allowing the horses to graze and slake their thirst. Kathryn immediately found a sizable rock at the edge of the water and quickly sat down to tug off her boots. The pool, although not deep enough for swimming, felt deliciously cool as she sat paddling her feet in the crystal clear water.

Jason moved to her side and placed his hand lightly on her shoulder, smiling indulgently into her upturned face. She leaned back against his thigh, enjoying his nearness as she watched the ever widening ripples created by her splashing.

"Come sit with me." He gestured towards a big tree nearby, offering her a hand up.

They settled themselves comfortably, sharing some bread and ale before he began to read. With the book held in one hand propped on his knee, and an arm draped loosely around her shoulder, they relaxed together. They could see Lieutenant Jackson and the other men stationed discreetly at a distance, but all seemed well. Jason read for some time as she watched his changing expressions, hanging upon every word. She never tired of listening to his eloquent English—or having him near.

After awhile he put the book aside and just held her, his cheek resting lightly atop her head. Taking her hand, he began tracing her fingers with his much larger ones.

Such strong hands—yet so gentle, she thought as she enclosed them in hers. She sensed his unease; something disturbing him deeply. But she would not press for details; he would share, when ready.

"Kathryn," he said softly, pausing to collect his thoughts. "I want to tell you—about me. Once it is said, I can lay all my demons to rest … or at least try."

Her expressive eyes met his and held, understanding completely.

"My father," he began hesitantly, "drank himself into oblivion every night. He beat me daily, sometimes for reason, more often for the sheer delight." A muscle twitched along his jaw as he continued—noncommittally—as if relating a story about someone else. By remaining detached, he could forcefully contain his emotions, refusing to relive the inner ache. "With my mother, he used sex as punishment," he stated bitterly and went silent.

Squeezing his hand gently, she hugged him, listening compassionately as he attempted to expunge his past.

"Many nights I lay in my bed hearing her cry out, but was helpless to go to her aid." Huskiness in his voice reflected his emotional torment.

Kathryn placed her hand over his and looked up into his stricken eyes.

"I loved her, my quiet, gentle mother," his voice caught, "… but she died and I was left alone, abandoned to the likes of him. In my child's mind, I blamed her for leaving me to my father's abuse." He sighed deeply, shaking his head. "Like a chameleon, he presented the perfect image in the public eye: loving father, bereaved husband." He laughed bitterly. "He was a monster, Kathryn." He spat the last with such rancor, it was easy to comprehend how traumatized he had been as a child. She understood what had driven him to such hatred in his past, and how deeply scarred he had been by boyhood abuse. This proud man—her beloved husband—had bared his soul. Recognizing the faith it had taken for him to entrust her with that painful knowledge, she loved him all the more.

Turning, arms reaching to encircle his neck, she pulled his head against her shoulder. "I will always love you, Jason. You are my life," she whispered fiercely, then kissed him ardently.

As his hands reached to tangle in her long curls, his eyes caressed, and in their depths she easily recognized both gratitude and relief.

"My wife," he breathed softly, realizing that this woman, *his wife*, had saved him in many ways. Seething anger no longer consumed him, newly acquired respect flashed in the eyes of his men, and—of greater importance—Lieutenant Jackson was becoming a good friend.

Glancing down at Kathryn, he caught her observing him intently, concern furrowing her brow as his silence continued.

"Just thinking how much I love you," he whispered, and she grinned. "I feel a need to return to camp, my love. Would you join me?" Standing, he offered his hand and reached to brush her bottom, taking longer than necessary.

"I believe you are sending me a discreet message, my husband," she replied, laughing happily.

She allowed Jason to give her a leg up onto Beauty before he mounted his charger. Turning the prancing Diablo, he waved to signal his men.

"Race you to camp," he challenged. With a sharp nudge, Diablo leaped forward and galloped towards camp.

Grinning, she shouted to Beauty who bolted after the big black charger, needing no coaxing.

Jason raced into the campsite, reining his panting steed to a skidding stop. He sat astride his dancing charger and watched her galloping towards him, hair streaming behind her in wild tangles.

Only moments behind, she leaped to the ground before her little mare came to a complete stop and strode towards him. Hands on hips, she stood glaring up at him.

"You cheated, sir," she accused.

"You are correct, madam—I did." He eyed her with a wicked grin. Dismounting quickly, he lifted her into the air and spun her in a circle as she burst into laughter. The intolerable weight of the world had been lifted from his shoulders at last … and he rejoiced. They held each other, laughing uproariously as Lieutenant Jackson and his guards sat astride their panting horses, smirking and taking it all in.

"She says I cheated, Jackson," he said with feigned innocence, and kissed her soundly.

They decided to share a private dinner in their tent before striking camp the next morning. Sitting on opposite sides of the desk, they enjoyed a mug of ale. Every so often she looked at her ring finger, turning it so the lantern light would catch the warm sparkle of the gold knotwork.

Smiling lovingly, he looked at his own, thoroughly pleased.

"We really did it," she breathed, her voice a mixture of joy, awe and devotion.

He reached across the desk to touch her cheek. "I consider myself a lucky man, Kathryn. Who knows what the future may hold? At times I dare think ahead to the day this war will be over."

"Today is our day," she interrupted quietly, "… and perhaps tomorrow. I have learned to accept that, Jason. I dream of more, but the reality is now."

Refusing to have their evening become too serious, he grinned lasciviously and encouraged, "Eat up my Scottish lass. Let us finish this meal; I have some interesting ideas for dessert."

Laughing gaily, she rose from their makeshift table. "Hold that thought just long enough for me to get some fresh water."

He quickly reached to take the bucket, but she gave him her familiar upraised hand stopping him, she would brook no discussion.

"Relax, my colonel; allow me to wait on you." She smiled and disappeared into the night.

Returning a few minutes later with her water, she saw a dark shape move menacingly towards the back of their tent, where Jason's outline was dimly visible from the lamplight inside. The threatening figure, clutching a knife in one hand, moved with stealthy agility. Concentration focused completely on the tent and his intended victims, he had failed to see her.

Setting the bucket down, she drew her pistol and began silently stalking him. As she closed the distance between them, she recognized the blue rebel coat; one of the prisoners must have slipped the guard. Realizing there would have been many more of this ones kind if it were an attack, she relaxed slightly. From his stance and silhouette, he appeared to be a youth.

The young rebel paused, trying to build courage to slash through the tent and take the colonel and his 'wife'—the latter term offensive—completely by surprise. Having spent long hours in decisive thought, he planned to kill the colonel first and then her, if she did not recant her vile support for him and the English.

The metallic click of a pistol hammer cocking, and firm pressure against the base of his skull caused him to freeze in his tracks.

"Drop that knife or you will die where you stand," she growled. "Colonel, bring a lantern quickly."

Having sprung to alert with her first words, Jason was just rounding the tent, pistol drawn and lantern held high. He found her gingerly patting down the rebel for weapons, his back turned towards them and hands raised above his head. She quickly found an additional dirk in his boot and tossed it out of his range.

"Turn around," she demanded, glancing to Jason for reassurance.

Jason's imperceptible nod and grim smile bolstered her courage as the young soldier turned. She had never gone near the prisoners taken in the recent attack on their camp, nor caught a glimpse of any of them; they were kept at the rear of the entourage. It had been a long time, but there was no mistaking her brother's oldest son. Suddenly she recalled joking with Jason about the defiant young rebel—and her heart lurched.

"Gabriel," she gasped.

At her side, Jason tensed. She did not lower her pistol even briefly, keeping it half-cocked and aimed at his chest, although Jason noticed a slight tremor to her arm.

"Yes, *Aunt* Kathryn," he spat, emphasizing the word, 'aunt'.

Seeing the two of them together, Gabriel realized he would not have been saving her, even if he killed the colonel. Apparently this was where she wanted to be, but needing to be sure he asked her. "At one time you were fiercely patriotic, but now? Now you are with *him*; by your own choice?"

She stayed Jason with a gesture.

"Absolutely," she answered firmly.

"You traitorous bitch."

Moving swiftly, she stepped within inches of her nephew, blocking Jason from striking him down in front of her. Resisting the urge to slap him for his insolence, she thumbed the pistol hammer to full cock and shoved it forcefully against his chest. Almost his height, she faced him boldly, holding his angry glare unflinchingly.

"Take a deep breath," she commanded. "I said—take a deep breath." She pressed the pistol more firmly into his flesh.

When he visibly began to relax, enough so that she was sure he would listen, she spoke with deadly calm, her voice more lethal than a striking snake.

Jason watched Kathryn's commanding presence as she stood up to her own flesh and blood, awestruck. *My wife, my wife …* no adequate words came to mind.

"Nephew, I will say this only once, I want you to listen carefully."

Gabriel nodded slowly.

"This man, my husband, is my very life. I would gladly die for him if that were necessary. And I will be at his side if ever that time comes." She paused, waiting while he digested that information. "Now, if Colonel Tarrington is good enough, after this foolish attempt of yours, to drop you in Camden where you may possibly be traded back to your side, go to Jamie and make him aware of these facts."

"I … I do not understand, Aunt," he said haltingly, softly.

She relented slightly, but never lowered the pistol. "You are young, Gabriel. Perhaps someday, if you are incredibly lucky, you will understand."

As the prisoner's disappearance had rapidly become known, Lieutenant Jackson and several dragoons joined the scene and stood watching with interest.

There was so much Kathryn wished she could explain to ease the hurt evident in her nephew's eyes, so much she would have liked to ask him. The child she had grown up with was maturing into a handsome, young man and… "Get him out of my sight," she spat, slowly lowering her gun and backing away.

Her eyes sought Jason's as he pulled her against him, brushing a kiss to her forehead, unashamed with his show of pride in his wife. The gesture was not lost on Gabriel, but he had no more time to think about it as the dragoons roughly prodded and shoved him back towards the confinement area. They were overly forceful, due to embarrassment. This defiant young man's determination had allowed him to cleverly escape a well-trained guard. In grim amusement, Kathryn realized family traits do prevail. She could not allow herself to think of what they would do to him once out of her sight, and quickly turned away. Retrieving the two knives, she handed them to Jason. He studied her carefully, understanding the thoughts going through her mind. With each passing day, he found he could read her better, their souls becoming truly entwined as one.

"Go pour a brandy for us both, hmm?" Touching her shoulder, he lowered his head capturing her gaze. "I will see to it that he is not hurt." Giving her hand a comforting squeeze, he turned to follow his men.

He strode into the middle of the circled dragoons as they took turns shoving and punching Gabriel, bent on teaching him a lesson.

"Enough lessons for one day, gentlemen." Jason elbowed a couple of overzealous dragoons, quickly backing them off, leaving Gabriel cursing under his breath. He was down on one knee, blood trickling from the corner of his mouth, glaring at the colonel as he struggled to rise.

"Light chain will be adequate to hold this young rebel," he commented, gesturing to Lieutenant Jackson.

The other men kept their distance, menacing with angry glares. Jason turned back to the defiant young man and actually smiled at the arrogant youth standing before him, brushing dust from his blue coat.

"I see that proud, defiant streak runs in the family," he said without rancor. "Your aunt just saved your life, young man."

At Gabriel's confused look, he added, "There was a time when I did not take prisoners, especially ones as disrespectful as you. They never lived long enough to have an opportunity for exchange—and perhaps return to their own side."

Gabriel, having calmed considerably, listened carefully.

Lieutenant Jackson returned with the chains and stood awaiting orders. Jason turned, and taking them, put the cuffs on Gabriel himself, checking to be sure they did not cut the lad's wrists.

Eyeing him thoughtfully for several moments, he finally said. "Kathryn showed me—how did she put it exactly—the error of my ways," he said softly with a wry grin. "Do not forget that when we reach Camden." He took several steps, but stopped, turning to face the lad. "And take this knowledge with you also, Gabriel."

The use of his given name by this 'black villain' was unsettling.

"She is my whole life. And I, too, would gladly die protecting her if ever there is need." *God, how I hope you or your father will never constitute that need*, he thought.

Gabriel's look softened as he was led away.

Looking directly at his lieutenant Jason instructed: "Be sure he is not manhandled, Lieutenant. And keep him at the very back of the dragoons until we reach Camden."

Lieutenant Jackson nodded understanding, and as the colonel turned to leave said quietly, "Sir, no offense intended, but your wife is one incredible woman."

"Yes, she certainly is that—and no offense taken."

He entered their tent silently, finding her sitting at the desk toying with the glasses of brandy. She looked up as he entered, quiet anguish reflected in her eyes. Moving to the desk, he picked up his brandy and handed her a glass. They sipped in silence for a few moments, while he stood at her side, his hand resting lightly on her shoulder.

"I talked to Gabriel," he said simply, breaking the silence. "Jackson will be sure he is not harmed." He touched her hair, caressing the long curls.

"Thank you," she whispered. "I could not have brought myself to ask that of you." She gazed up with huge doe eyes.

"You did not have to, my love. I would not see you hurt in any way, if it is within my power to control. If there were not a war…" he trailed off. They could not pursue this line of thought. No amount of wishing would change the facts.

Suddenly an unsettling thought crossed his mind. Abruptly his blue eyes changed, the comforting look for her, replaced by one mirroring his own pain from lingering insecurities … and a question not yet asked.

"Absolutely not," she stated fiercely.

He stared in surprise, confused.

"You were going to ask me if I had any regrets, or felt that I had made the wrong choice, or something of that nature, were you not."

"You read me all too well, love." A weak smile played at the corners of his mouth, relief flooding his face as he nodded.

"As you do with me," she reminded. She rose, stepping around the desk into his waiting arms. "My only wish is that circumstances could be different so that you could know my family, but regrets—never."

Their kiss was passionate, demanding and rough as he tangled his fingers in her golden hair, hugging her to him.

"Jason." Breathlessly she leaned back placing a finger on his lips. "Wait." Unmistakable passion glittered in her eyes, but much to his confusion and discomfort she said: "I will get the horses; you bring the brandy and a blanket." Her grin was that of a devilish child as she rushed from the tent, leaving him uncomfortable in his need.

Lieutenant Jackson, ever available to tend them, stepped forward as she grabbed Beauty's saddle.

"May I be of service, milady?"

"Would you please ready Diablo?"

She noticed his concerned expression as she cinched the mare's saddle snugly and slipped the halter over her ears. Jackson moved quickly, matching her sense of urgency, the black charger ready as she finished with Beauty. Grabbing the reins of both animals she nodded her 'thanks', and looking back over her shoulder, to his unasked question answered quietly, "All is well, do not lose any sleep tonight, Jack."

He smiled sheepishly, wondering if she could read every one's mind as easily as she read his and the colonel's.

Jason waited outside the tent with a look of grim resolve. "You will pay dearly, madam, for the discomfort you have put me through." Grabbing her around the waist, he whisked her up onto the saddle and with a pat to her knee, took Diablo's reins and quickly mounted.

"That was my intention, sir. Follow me."

As they left the encampment, she urged Beauty into a gallop. They rode a short distance, slowing the pace as they approached a narrow river, allowing the horses to pick their way over ground strewn with stones and gullies. Water tumbled from the side of a small rocky outcropping into a pool that rippled in the soft light of a full moon, beautiful in its silvery magnificence.

Jason was awestruck. *Kathryn does know this area like the back of her hand* he realized, and sensing no tension in her demeanor, knew she was sure they would be unobserved. She dismounted, dropping the mare's reins to stay her and walked around to Jason's side, reaching a hand up to him. Grasping it firmly, he stepped down, encircling her in his arms relishing her sensitivity—recalling the rejuvenating effect of waterfalls in their relationship.

"Kathryn, my Kathryn," he breathed into her hair as he cupped her bottom, pulling her tightly against him. He sought her mouth, claiming it in an ardent kiss. It required only moments of anxious fumbling to discard the fabric standing between them.

Picking her up he waded into the water, smiling as she trailed her fingers bringing up handfuls of the cool liquid to trickle over his muscular chest. Stopping directly under the falls, he set her down, steadying her until she found firm footing. Reaching up she deftly released his long hair, allowing the wet strands to fan out across his shoulders.

Her upturned face glistened with sparkling droplets of water—he could resist no longer. Murmuring his name, soft as a caress, her mouth found his. This time there would be no interruptions. Unsure quite how they arrived there, they found themselves on the embankment, driven by matching desire—a passionate giving and taking that left them gasping as final tremors subsided.

"No regrets, no doubts between us ever," she whispered.

"Absolutely none," he answered fervently, as he began tracing the shapes of her eyebrows with his fingertip—first one, then the other—watching the moonlight play across her delicate features. Tugging the blanket over them, he leaned back with her head resting on his shoulder. "What is it about waterfalls and us?" he wondered.

"To the Cherokees, waterfalls and thunderstorms are symbols of power, restoration and rebirth, perhaps it is universal. However, for us they have nourished the soul and healed the heart."

"Kathryn, tell me more about you—about your family," he said, abruptly changing the mood.

Watching the moonlight play across the angular planes of his face, she grew pensive.

"What do you wish to know, love?"

At this point, she would not have broached the topic herself, of that he was certain. This first involvement with one of her family was upsetting, justifiably so. It would only be a matter of time before similar encounters occurred. Unfortunately, this was just the beginning.

"Gabriel is so like you in some ways and your brother, James—Jamie. In my interactions with him, now that I know you, I see the same defiant proud heritage, the same wily courage."

He traced his finger along her nose, down to touch her lips. "Talk to me over a brandy," he suggested, coaxing her to relax and share more of her life.

She watched him go to the saddle packs, remove a flask and return to her side. Dropping down beside her, he poured the fiery liquid into two tin cups.

"How very uncouth, my dear," she giggled, accepting a cup as he pulled the blanket around their shoulders. She sat sipping in silence, unsure exactly where to begin.

"Your father was a Scot—and your mother?" He nudged gently, giving her a starting point.

"Ian Dougal MacLean: my father. Now there was a man who set the standards for stubbornness in the nationality." She smiled at the remembrance of him.

"My mother was a soft-spoken, gentle lady: Mairi Gordon Cameron. That is why I called myself 'Kathryn Cameron' when I first met you; it is my middle name."

He nodded, recalling that day.

"Obviously I am more like my father," she admitted, glancing to see if he would tease her, but he just smiled.

"My father was one of the very few Scots to survive Culloden in '46. And with the 'Act of Proscription' compounding hardships the following year, he came to America with the hope of being better able to provide for his wife and son. I believe Jamie was about eight at the time. They lived in North Carolina for a while, but later moved to South Carolina where I was born in '52. Jamie and I are the only two children."

Watching the memories flit across her face, Jason was fascinated.

"Father had a mind of his own, a rather unusual individual," she grinned. "That is why my name is spelled in an odd fashion: 'K-a-t-h-r-y-n'. He insisted I was unique and my name should reflect that fact."

"You loved your father very much," Jason said tenderly.

She nodded, smiling at the memories. "He taught me how to be self-sufficient—how to shoot, ride, handle a dirk. He expected me to respect life, but be able to defend myself without guilt if the occasion arose. Actually, he taught me only about as much as you can teach a twelve year old child."

Jason looked puzzled.

"He was always involved in one cause or another, helping those in need. When it became common knowledge that Sir Jeffrey Amherst had supplied the Indians with smallpox infested blankets, my father was furious. He had always been friendly with the Cherokees, especially the Bird Clan ..." she trailed off, her face clouding with sad recollection.

Jason gently took her hand, and she continued. "The disease killed him; his death destroyed my mother. She was never the same without him and died a few years later."

"I guess that brings us to Jamie." She continued on doggedly, wishing to be done with the telling. "He married Mairi MacDonald and they had three children before dad died. Their youngest, Caitlin, did not come along until after he was gone. Jamie took over the care of the farm and tried to help mother raise me, attempting to be both father and older brother—which of course, I resented."

She paused, taking a sip of her brandy. "He was the one who taught me so much. The tomahawk is not a skill I learned from the Cherokees—but from Jamie. As I have mentioned before, he is equally as stubborn and proud as our father and always right—or so *he* thought. I joined the Bird Clan because I wanted to let him know, in no uncertain terms, that he was not my boss."

Suddenly her demeanor changed, softening with the memory. "Even with four children and a sickly wife, he watched out for me." She searched Jason's face, seeking understanding and acceptance, and was not disappointed by the compassion reflected there. "He loved his wife with a passion similar to ours. There were times when I doubted he could go on another day after her death, but he is a feisty survivor, the way we were taught to be. Mother showed us the gentler lessons, or at least tried to. With me, it was always 'make an effort to be a lady at all times', but it never quite took."

"Never apologize, Kathryn, you are you—and I would have you no other way." He gazed into her beautiful green eyes for several moments then kissed her.

This brief recap of her life provided Jason with a better understanding of this complex woman he loved so deeply. Obviously Jamie had meant a great deal to her—still did, though she refused to admit that fact—perhaps a subconscious attempt to make the pain more bearable. She was a survivor, a product of many hurts and hard lessons. She had freely chosen to give herself entirely to him—renouncing both family and a former life—a profound revelation which left Jason awestruck.

They arrived back at camp very late, quietly elated. Lieutenant Jackson had waited up to tend their horses and bid them 'good evening'. He was inwardly relieved to see their obvious serenity. Kathryn, with her husband's help, had apparently come to some means of acceptance in regards to her nephew's capture. *He is becoming a better man every day.* Jackson headed away with the horses to settle them in and catch some sleep. Dawn would be here all too soon, and they would be on the road again.

They lay together on their bed, Jason's arms encircling her gently, her back cuddled against him. As his hand caressed her stomach she stopped him. "Wait a minute, Jason." He felt a slight movement against the palm of his hand. "There, do you feel that?" It happened again with more intensity.

He rolled her to face him, eyeing her incredulously. "Kathryn ...?'

"Our baby, Jason." He heard her loving tone and was thunderstruck.

For a moment, in the brightness of the moonlit tent, her eyes reflected panic. He understood the complexity of her—her fear of his reaction. A baby was to be expected at some point, he guessed. After all, they had been together for many months, and with the intensity of their relationship it was surprising it had not happened sooner.

It would not be the easiest of lives traveling with a baby, always on the move. But he would not waste his breath attempting to convince her to stay in a safe house with the child, while he continued this aggravating war. Besides, he could not allow her away from him; she had become his whole life, he refused to give her up—for anything or anyone. Somehow, they would work this out together.

"Our child," Placing his cheek against her stomach, he was rewarded with another tiny kick. "Already proud and defiant, just like its mother."

He smiled reassuringly relieved to see her eyes become calm and happy once again. Holding her gently, he trailed a finger along the bridge of her nose, one of his favorite gestures. "I am complete, Kathryn. First you come into my life and now a child ... our child. I could not be happier, or more proud." He held her tenderly, instilling comfort; somehow all would be well.

They broke camp the next morning. Lieutenant Jackson joined them for a quick cup of coffee, noticing their mood to be different today. Kathryn, as always, was beautiful, happy. It was the colonel who caught his attention, the slightest difference in his demeanor. His eyes always followed his wife, emotions unguarded when they were alone with Jack. But today his look bore even more intense pride than usual. Jackson's curiosity was piqued, causing him to ponder possibilities as he watched them over the edge of his coffee cup.

Jason eyed his wife, and at her nod of consent, leaned towards Jack and whispered somewhat conspiratorially: "My wife is with child, Jackson." Nodding eagerly at his lieutenant's surprised look, he reached for Kathryn's hand.

"I… Congratulations, I am speechless." Lieutenant Jackson tried to absorb the implications of this announcement.

Eager to be on the road, their coffee finished, within a few minutes all three stood and headed for their waiting horses.

"Keep an eye on her, Jack," Jason said quietly as fleeting concern flashed in his eyes.

"Depend on it, sir," he answered firmly.

Lieutenant Jackson reeled with mixed emotions—surprised by the inner ache this news brought. Immediately, he forced his forbidden feelings aside. He dared not analyze them—must not think of them. Instead, he turned his thoughts towards the increased protection and aid that would be necessary for the colonel and … *his wife*, he reminded himself firmly. *A child: … their child … Kathryn's child.* He would protect her with his life if that became necessary.

They rode out, Kathryn joining Jason at the front of the dragoons, with Jackson flanking her other side for protection. Jason wanted to keep her separated as far as he could from the prisoners—and Gabriel. She did not see Gabriel again, and chose not to ride into Camden when Jason delivered the prisoners into custody the next day.

Chapter Fifteen

An Invitation

Lieutenant Jackson and a handful of dragoons stayed with Kathryn at their campsite while the prisoners were escorted, under heavy guard, into Camden.

Jason had ridden out after their 'farewell salute'. This gesture of devotion, created on their wedding day, had become as much of a tradition with the dragoons as their daily coffee around the campfire—the men anticipating this moment, as it set the tone of the day.

She felt the emptiness immediately and was silent, withdrawn.

"He will return soon." Jackson broke into her thoughts with a proffered mug of coffee. "It is not a long trip."

"Thanks, Jack," she said quietly, accepting the steaming mug and attempting a smile. "Without him I feel incomplete, as if a major part of me was missing." Shaking her head sadly she added, "And that feeling does not lessen with time."

"You two share something unique, the likes of which I have never seen—nor experienced," he added pensively.

"However, it is a double edged sword, Jack: exquisite passion … acute pain."

For a moment she was lost within her own thoughts but abruptly returned to the present, somewhat embarrassed, as he began speaking. "I can appreciate that, Kathryn, and yet I doubt there is a man among us who does not privately envy the way you two look at each other."

She murmured something he did not quite catch, and again withdrew to her personal thoughts.

Not wanting to intrude, he left her alone but remained close, never allowing his protective vigil to lapse when the colonel was away from the campsite; or anytime actually. It troubled him to see her so disconcerted. Perhaps the baby weighed heavily on her mind. As a diversion, he returned later with two apples, a rare delight he had begged from Cook 'for a good cause'.

"I thought this might be a treat for both you and Beauty." He grinned as he gave a quick swipe of his sleeve over the bright red surface adding luster.

At his show of consideration, she roused herself from her doldrums. "I would say I have spent more than enough time feeling sorry for myself today." Taking the offered apple, she buffed it on her shirt and took a bite. "Delicious," she managed, around a mouthful of apple, her eyes coming alive, her dazzling smile touching him deeply.

"Ready for a ride?" he asked as a corporal approached with their two horses.

With an eager nod, she stepped to Beauty's side and stood stroking the little mare's neck while she eagerly chomped the apple core.

"How I do love this little horse. We have been through a lot together." She rubbed her nose fondly and then, without giving thought to her still recovering wound, flung herself into the saddle.

"Damn it," she swore softly, immediately embarrassed, and gave Jack a sidelong glance as she rubbed her arm grimacing.

He laughed out loud but leaned forward with a questioning look—concerned.

"I will be so glad when this arm …" Recovering rapidly, she nudged Beauty and took off at a gallop, grinning back over her shoulder.

Beauty wanted to run and Kathryn allowed her the freedom to pick the trail, the little horse sidetracking to leap small objects and play. It was a beautiful day and Kathryn reveled in the pleasure of being alive, in love and carrying Jason's child. She threw her head back and rode with arms flung wide, her face turned to the sun until the mare eventually slowed. Kathryn leaned forward and hugged Beauty's strong, sleek neck as they came to a stop.

Lieutenant Jackson had kept pace on the crazy ride and pulled up beside her. "Kathryn," he panted, slightly out of breath, his horse blowing and frothing at the bit. "The colonel will have my hide if anything …"

"I know," she interrupted, "but it feels so good."

"Time to go back now," he coaxed. "Your husband will return soon and we should be there to greet him." He hoped the manner in which he phrased the request would convince her to comply.

"Beat you back," she challenged, and with a kneed signal, the mare wheeled pawing the air, and plunged forward.

Jackson smiled, shaking his head as he wheeled his mount, urging him into a gallop. As the long legs of his big horse could eat up ground faster than Beauty's, she barely beat him, and by a small margin at that.

Leaping down from her saddle, Kathryn laughed gleefully as a pair of dragoons approached to take their horses. But she refused, thanking them kindly for their consideration, choosing to brush and towel Beauty herself while the lieutenant looked on.

Jason returned mid-afternoon, sooner than expected, with a dozen new recruits he had picked up in Camden. "I missed you," was his smiling reply to her curious, but pleased, look. Kissing her forehead, he quipped, "Do not disappear, madam. I have a surprise for you; I will be right back."

She watched his muscular form as he strode over to confer with Jackson, appreciating his graceful, easy gait. *Strange how time works changes, certain inferences with words being one,* she thought. At one time, his use of the word, 'madam', had held a cold, intimidating edge, but now: merely his way of teasing lovingly.

He quickly returned to her side with a package retrieved from his saddlebags and ushered her into their tent. Once inside, he watched her carefully untie the twine while he removed his sabre and stripped off his gloves, tossing them on the desk.

Opening the wrapping paper she brought out an elegant dress. Surprised and somewhat confused, she turned to him frowning.

"Duty calls both of us this time, I am afraid." He grinned rakishly. "Lord Cornwallis has commanded our presence at his party next week."

"Oh, Jason, I do not think so. You, perhaps: definitely not me." She felt a little out of her element at the thought.

"Oh, yes, *you*, my love. He heard that the evil, Colonel Tarrington has been married. I gather he wishes to meet the unfortunate victim." His blue eyes twinkled gleefully.

"This is not amusing, Jason," she chastised. "I will not be a cause of embarrassment for you."

"Kathryn?" He was truly taken aback by her answer. "You are beautiful, intelligent and …"

"Look at me, Jason," she spluttered.

"I am looking." He eyed her lustfully.

"Look beyond that," she scowled. "I am too tall, too tanned, freckles on my nose, no powdered wig—and do not get me one," she admonished, pointing a warning finger. "The sleeves on the gown are short; a healing scar on my arm is definitely *not* something a lady should have." She faced him with hands on hips and chin jutting stubbornly.

"Kathryn," he cajoled as he swept her into his arms. "You are a real person, unlike those pampered, powdered dolls that will be in attendance. I am more concerned that I may have to fight to defend your honor when the officers see you." He kissed her neck, nuzzling tenderly.

"You have no intention of letting me out of this, do you?" Pushing away, she crossed her arms pouting prettily.

"Never." He kissed her soundly.

"We shall delay this conversation for the moment," she hedged and began re-wrapping the dress, taking care to fold it neatly.

Abruptly her demeanor changed. Looking up, her expression became serious. "How did it go? Any exchange?"

"Surprisingly smoothly," he answered softly, well aware of the basis for her question. "I removed Gabriel's chains before we reached town."

She was touched by his effort to save her nephew's pride, allowing him to ride in as the other prisoners: well guarded but without fetters.

"Did he say anything?" she asked.

"He watched me like a hawk, as if trying to etch my face permanently into his memory. But other than that, we exchanged no words."

"I hope it is over," she sighed. She remained silent, trying to dispel disconcerting thoughts careening in her head.

"What are you thinking, Kathryn?"

"Jamie will be informed soon and …" She shook her head.

"And …" he nudged.

"I fear the die is cast, Jason. I just wish I could get inside his head—know his thoughts."

"When his cards are put into play, we will handle those we are dealt at that time. Do not worry, my Kathryn." His finger traced her cheek gently. "Now," abruptly changing the mood he said, "I understand you had quite a pleasant ride today." Eyeing her over the top of the decanter, he poured them both a brandy.

Taking the offered glass she sipped slowly, looking somewhat guilty. "I must talk to Jack about giving away all my secrets." She frowned, but was not truly upset.

They dined with the men that evening, the atmosphere around the campfire relaxed and buoyant—excitement building at the prospect of breaking camp the following day. Although Kathryn was coaxed into playing the tin whistle and singing, Jack noticed a distinct 'quietness', her usual uninhibited élan lacking, drawing his concern.

"Is Kathryn ailing tonight?" he asked Jason under the pretense of bringing him coffee.

"She is worried about Jamie's reaction when Gabriel gets back to their camp. All we can do is reassure her, Jack."

Jack understood all too well, no further discussion necessary.

As the hour grew late, Jason nudged gently. "Tomorrow will be a long day, my love."

Without further discussion, she bid the men 'goodnight' and headed for the tent with her husband.

"I think we have time for a quick bath, milady." He eyed her lustfully.

"I suppose we will have to eat a lot of dust tomorrow—might as well start off clean," she answered innocently, as the hint of a grin played at the corners of her mouth.

"We will not need the horses as Jackson has set a guard for privacy, allowing us to remain close and make it an early night."

"Why an early night?" She pierced him with a stern look. "Do not start to coddle me, sir."

"Because tonight *I* am tired," he lied in deference to her pride. However, she saw right through his excuse, grateful for his consideration—it had been a day of emotional ups and downs.

They lay in their bed like a pair of 'cupped' spoons. Kathryn's breathing slow and deep. Jason lay awake, as yet unable to capture the elusive peacefulness of slumber. His mind raced, revisiting 'their bath', a trip of intimate pleasures. Kathryn had given herself completely to him, loving him selflessly without reserve or imposed conditions. He was awestruck. As realization continued to wash over him in endless waves, he was reminded of just how empty his life had been before Kathryn. He held her tenderly, kissing her softly.

"There are no words, my Kathryn."

"I know, my love," she whispered, responding to his touch.

His hand rested on her abdomen and within moments, he felt the expected 'nudge'. "Our child," he breathed, as he gently caressed.

"Our child," she answered. "Our immortality: our everlasting love."

She lay contentedly within his arms, drifting sleepily, secure in the knowledge that nothing could come between them. Somehow, *together*, they would work through every obstruction thrown in their path.

They broke camp the next day and headed north to intercept Major Beldon and his men. With the time they had saved through Kathryn's shortcuts, they were confident of catching him by surprise, preventing him from joining the Continentals moving down from Pennsylvania.

Each day's ride was dusty and long, but she rode proudly at Jason's side, thoroughly enjoying his nearness. Lieutenant Jackson flanked her, his permanently assigned position. And she took pleasure in his quiet presence, appreciating the fact that Jason was providing all the protection he could.

Her only discomfort was the pending party with Cornwallis. With each day, as they drew closer to his headquarters, her enthusiasm lessened. But each evening, as Jason passionately claimed her, she knew she would get through this too.

Chapter Sixteen

Lord Cornwallis's Party

The dreaded day finally arrived. Lord Cornwallis's party was a command performance this evening.

The dragoons were awake and on the road at dawn, having spent the previous night under deep indigo skies. It had been a beautiful warm evening with bright stars and a full moon; Kathryn regretted their lack of privacy in such a romantic setting. Jason had decided not to set up a campsite, foregoing even their small travel tent. As they had not stopped for a break until well after dark, and would be gone before daylight, they slept under the stars with the rest of the men.

Shortly after mid-day, the colonel chose an open area dotted with thickets and a stand of trees and brought the dragoons to a halt, giving orders to set up camp. A small brook meandered past the site with good possibilities for fishing; a thought that thoroughly pleased Kathryn. She would also venture into the small forest that loomed in the distance to see if bathing opportunities would be *'adequate'*. She smiled as she stood observing the men working efficiently about her, already feeling Jason's touch, his body sensuously slick with dripping water.

"And what thoughts are making my lovely wife smile?" Having come up quietly from behind, he spoke softly against her ear, startling her.

"Thoughts I shall refrain from mentioning until after I have you completely to myself, sir, in privacy." She eyed him over her shoulder suggestively.

Reading her easily, he brushed a light kiss to her forehead, and flashing an intimate smile, headed off to see that the campsite was being set up to his satisfaction.

In short order their encampment looked as if it had always sat on this spot. Only a few miles from Cornwallis's headquarters, and not that far from their planned interception of Beldon's troops, they would remain here for several days.

Having watered and toweled down both horses, she sat perched on a large rock. Diablo had become almost as spoiled as her Beauty when it came to sugar cubes, but Kathryn had an ever ready rationalization: "They work hard and deserve their treats." She took turns scratching their forelocks, talking to each one lovingly.

"They will get fat and lazy," he chided, startling her again.

"Jason. That is the second time you surprised me today. I must be losing my edge."

"Not to worry, lass, ye're merely a wee distracted." A distinct burr rolled across his tongue as he put on his best Scottish accent, eliciting a chuckle.

"Tonight will not be as bad as you think." He knew her well; she radiated increasing tension over this evening's party.

She turned a disbelieving eye to him.

"Kathryn." He took her hand, looking her squarely in the eye. "You would not allow me to go into battle alone, if I said I needed you at my side."

She knew what he was getting at, but remained silent.

"Hmm?" he nudged, taking her chin in his hand. "Visualize this as a battle and believe me when I say … I do need you at my side." Cocking an eyebrow, he pulled her gently into his arms and held her. "However, right now I think you could use some rest."

Draping his arm loosely around her shoulder, he headed her towards their tent. Looking back at the horses, she hesitated.

"Do not fret so," he said gently knowing she was tired. "Jackson will take care of them."

She eyed him thoughtfully for a long moment. He was probably right, but she would not admit that fact out loud. Yes, she was tired. Perhaps it was her body getting used to a new life within; she had not been feeling herself these past few days.

Ignoring her protests of wanting him to join her, he tucked her in on the cot. "There are times, my pet, when you will do as I ask." He kissed her nose, amused by her childlike scowl.

Moving to his desk, he removed a book from the drawer. Returning to her side, he sat down on the floor, and turned smiling eyes up to her.

"I think Beattie's poetry would be quieting, hmm?" Without waiting for an answer, he began to read in his soft, clipped English she loved so well.

Barely into the second page, he realized her breathing had become deep and even. After setting the book on his desk, he stood watching her sleeping peacefully. She needed this brief rest, whether she would admit it or not—his stubborn love. Bending down, he brushed a kiss to her forehead and left to talk to Jack.

She awoke sometime later to the sound of splashing water and stretched languorously; long rays of sun hitting the side of the tent indicated late afternoon.

"It is late; I cannot believe I slept so long." Yawning sleepily, she sat up and swung her feet onto the floor, struggling to come fully awake.

Jason merely smiled as he emptied another steaming bucket of water into a large galvanized washtub in the middle of the tent.

"There is a crystal pool in the woods that I have already investigated." His eyes held unmistakable promise. "Tomorrow night we will have to make an exploration together."

That explained the damp hair hanging limply on his naked shoulders, and a towel knotted at a seductively low angle on his hips, threatening to slip to the floor at any moment.

"However, as it is still afternoon, I am not willing to share the vision of your exquisite body with any of my men." Testing the temperature of the tub water, he beckoned her to him. She came quickly into his arms, reaching up to kiss him.

"You look well rested, my love." Untying the laces of her blouse, he peeled it back from her shoulders allowing it to drop.

Closing her eyes, she stood quietly enjoying his touch as he slowly disrobed her. With a sudden brush of warm lips across her breast, her eyes flew open. "Jason," she gasped, "play fair, do not torture …"

But he ignored her, continuing to trace endless patterns with the tip of his tongue. A flick of her wrist released his towel sending it to the floor.

"Let the games begin, my love, I am more than ready."

Kathryn was the first to realize how low the sun had traveled in the sky and quickly scrambled up. She sat down in the tub of now tepid water, relishing the luxury as Jason scrubbed her back and washed her long curls—forcefully ignoring the delightful sensations his touch created. No time for further dalliance—they would have to hurry so as not to be late. *He is enjoying what he does to me quite thoroughly,* her ready smile answering his devilish grin.

She stood before him completely attired, needing only to have his assistance in closing the back of her dress. As he finished with the last of the buttons on his jacket he turned, and seeing her, his breath caught.

"Is it all right? Do I look …?" She tugged nervously at the décolletage that showed much more of her than she deemed appropriate.

He remained silent for so long she became unsure of herself. "This shows way too much of what should be for your eyes only," she said with growing distress.

"Kathryn." He went to her quickly, staying her nervous hands. "You are so incredibly beautiful. You …" He paused, awestruck. "You take my breath away."

At her questioning glance, he nodded touching her cheek. "And this," he traced a finger along the top edge of her gown, "is all the style. You will not be out of place." He grinned as her composure returned. "I may, however, find myself defending you from aspiring new beaus."

She shook her head, smiling, and turned so he could fasten all the little pearl buttons on the back of her gown. She found it amazing that a man with hands as large and strong as his could fasten something so small and delicate with such agility.

"Thank you, love," she whispered, as she pinched color into her cheeks and put the finishing touches to her cascade of honey-gold curls.

Jason stepped to the desk still watching her, finding it difficult to take his eyes away. As she turned to pick up her shawl, he came up behind her.

"Hold your hair up in back, and be still for just one minute."

She did as asked, somewhat curious. He fastened a delicate chain around her neck and then turned her to face him. Looking down at where it rested just above her breasts, she inhaled sharply: a beautiful single pearl snugly set within a tiny heart of gold.

"Jason," she exclaimed breathlessly. "It is beautiful."

To her questioning look, he said quietly with deep feeling, "It belonged to my mother." Before she could say a word, he silenced her lips with his finger. "I want you to have it, to wear it, always." His voice was husky as he searched the depths of her eyes.

The incredible underlying meaning of this exquisite gift awed her; it represented so much more than just a beautiful piece of jewelry. He had loved his mother dearly.

"It was a gift from her mother, given to her in love and happiness. She was the 'pearl' of her mother's eye," he said quietly, his voice redolent with tender memories. "I think it helped her through some of the despicable times with my father … until eventually she could take no more." His voice trailed to a whisper of regret as his arms encircled her.

"I am honored, my love, and will treasure it always." Her eyes welled with tears as she gently clasped the necklace, studying its beautiful simplicity.

"Do not … please. I cannot bear it if you cry." He clung to her, caressing her curls. "My mother wore it in happiness, and that is what I want for you … always."

He stepped back, thumbing a tear from the corner of her eye with great tenderness.

"Now, we must go or we risk being late." His demeanor changed abruptly. Placing the shawl around her shoulders, he nudged her towards the tent flap with a hand placed firmly in the small of her back.

She would treasure this moment and relive it often, remembering his incredible display of love and sensitivity until the day she died.

As they stepped from the tent, a rousing applause sounded from the group of officers waiting patiently to escort them to Cornwallis's headquarters. Lieutenant Jackson was thunderstruck, although he tried to cover his reaction. She was radiant—absolutely radiant—it struck with a slight pang. The colonel displayed an inner peace that he had never witnessed before. He had to admit they certainly were a handsome couple, obviously in complete harmony with each other.

Lord Cornwallis had been thoughtful enough to send a small open carriage to convey them to his headquarters; although Jason was not fooled. It was the general's way of being assured they would attend the festivities. During the carriage ride Kathryn remained silent, visibly nervous. She struggled to control the thoughts running rampant in her head, but was failing miserably. Even the beautiful sunset could not interrupt the gloomy possibilities she imagined.

"No more, Kathryn." Jason placed a hand on hers to stay it from fidgeting. "Cease beating yourself." His warm gaze conveyed reassurance.

Forcing a thin smile, she made a concentrated effort to relax. By the time they arrived at the large southern mansion where his lordship was currently residing, she was again in control, much calmer.

As the groom held the horse's reins, Jason stepped from their carriage. Walking around to Kathryn's side, he reached up offering his hand. Lieutenant Jackson and his accompanying officers watched as she gracefully stepped down, holding the colonel's hand and smiling into his eyes.

Jason felt her hesitation as she took his arm and began walking up the wide steps to the grand hallway. "Relax, my pet, all will be well." He patted her arm, holding it tighter, not completely sure that she would not try to flee.

"This is a mistake," she hissed, her stricken tone belying the sweet smile glued to her face. "If I dishonor you in anyway, I will never forgive …"

"Kathryn," his voice was a stern caress. Pausing on the top step, he turned her to face him. Lightly running his thumb along the bridge of her nose and bringing it to rest on her chin, he tipped her head up ever so slightly. "Always … always, hmm?" His blue eyes spoke to her.

"Always," her answering whisper, as she visibly relaxed.

As they were ushered into the main salon, the butler's voice rang out over the noisy crowd of guests, loudly and clearly. "Colonel and Mrs. Jason Tarrington."

The assemblage turned in unison, curious to see the colonel's new wife: a colonial so it had been rumored.

Kathryn took a deep breath, and smiling prettily, started down the receiving line exchanging small pleasantries as she proceeded. Jason's hand, gently placed in the small of her back imbued her with the strength she needed to get through this ordeal. He was proud, pleased, and not just a little surprised at the ease with which his wife handled herself once she set her mind to it. She conversed easily with the officers; their appreciation displayed openly—much to Jason's irritation. The 'fine ladies', however, were aloof, politely cool, assessing her in all ways. Undaunted, she held her head high, returning their assessment in a polite but detached manner.

Finally, they were nearing the end of the reception line where they would greet his lordship. Cornwallis had been watching their slow progress, greatly impressed by the colonel's wife. He took special notice of how easily she conversed with strangers, many of whom shared quite different backgrounds, if rampant rumors held any truth.

Stopping in front of Lord Cornwallis and a rather dour looking major stationed beside him, Jason immediately spoke up. "Lord Cornwallis, Major Ferguson, I would like you to meet my wife, Kathryn."

They each took her hand in turn, kissing it in gentlemanly fashion.

Pausing before his lordship, she dropped into a deep curtsy, surprising Jason.

"Milord, I am deeply honored to have been included in your party." Her eyes held Cornwallis's, unfaltering.

Taking her hand, he enclosed it in both of his. "Colonel, your wife is not only beautiful, she is charming as well," he commented, squeezing her hand gently, a warm smile curving his lips.

"Thank you for noticing, milord." Jason inclined his head.

"I would like to get to know you better, Mrs. Tarrington. Perhaps you would allow me a few minutes of your time—possibly a dance, or two?"

She felt Jason tense as she smiled graciously and nodded. "I have heard much about you and your brilliant strategies on the battlefield, milord. I would enjoy hearing more about your many successful encounters."

Lord Cornwallis raised an eyebrow at Jason. "Beautiful, charming and a sharp mind: where did you find such a unique woman?"

Turning to Kathryn, he squeezed her hand again. "I look forward to chatting with you, milady."

She returned his smile and moved on, breathing a sigh of relief. They—or rather she—had survived running the gauntlet. Jason, appearing polished and at ease, was more used to the duty. She now viewed his patient acceptance of protocol with greater respect.

"You were incredible, my love." Jason bent to her ear speaking softly. "He is quite taken with you, as I knew he would be."

"He really is quite brilliant in many ways. It will be interesting to get to know him better."

Jason caught a tone of reservation in her accolades and was curious, but this was neither the time nor place for that particular conversation—the walls always had ears. They proceeded to a long table laden with drinks and pastries where Jason greeted fellow officers, introducing his wife and including her in their conversations.

Kathryn sensed open hostility from the beautifully coifed ladies, many regarding her with undisguised haughtiness while others—openly jealous—eyed her husband surreptitiously. The latter looks bothered her most.

One overly powdered and perfumed woman glided towards Jason, her bosom almost bursting from her extremely low bodice. Pushing rudely in front of Kathryn, she placed her back to her, as if she did not exist. Leaning against Jason, she draped herself seductively, purring like a feral cat. "I do so hope you have saved some dances for an old friend, Colonel," she enticed, her voice dripping liquid honey.

Kathryn tensed, struggling to restrain her rising temper, but Jason quickly took polite control of the situation, disengaging his arm from the woman and stepping away. Pulling Kathryn forward, he spoke pleasantly, but firmly, in a tone forbidding discussion.

"Lady Antonia. I would like you to meet my wife, Kathryn."

Lady Antonia eyed her balefully, her color rising.

"My apologies, milady, but Kathryn has already reserved every dance." Abruptly turning, he ushered his wife away leaving the spluttering Lady Antonia in a fit of pique.

As delightful tones from the orchestra began to fill the hall, Jason smiled down at his wife. "I do hope you like to dance, my pet, I want an excuse to put my arms around you."

"I have always loved to dance, Jason," she whispered.

The upset of moments before was instantly forgotten in anticipation of dancing to the enchanted, lilting rhythms that blossomed within the hall. Taking her in his arms, Jason swept her out onto the dance floor. Dancing came naturally and she easily picked up the steps. Eyes sparkling and face aglow, she gazed at her husband with obvious devotion. His eyes flashed unmistakable answer as a slow grin spread across his face, amazed at how un-worldly and innocent she could be at times—thankful she belonged to him.

As they danced, lost in each other, her shoulder wrap slipped enough to reveal the newly healing wound on her arm, a fact noticed by many. The rumor circulating about her participation in quelling a rebel attack on their encampment was obviously true. The gentlemen viewed her with respect, the dignified ladies, on the other hand, were horrified. As the music drew to a close, Lord Cornwallis approached.

"Colonel, might I borrow your wife for the next dance?"

Jason nodded assent as was his duty, but obviously not to his pleasure.

"Come, come now, Colonel. I will return her to your side shortly," he stated with a wry grin.

A somewhat slower tune began playing as his lordship ushered her out onto the dance floor.

Jason joined a group of fellow officers to share a drink, but his eyes followed his wife closely.

"Your husband is very protective of you," Cornwallis observed.

"He is that, milord," she answered politely.

"How did you two meet? There are rumors, of course."

She smiled in ladylike fashion, pausing before answering. Detecting a certain mysterious quality, he wondered what she was truly thinking.

"One should never accept rumors as complete truth, milord. They usually distort the facts."

"Then, just what is the truth in this instance?" His curt tone indicated that despite a friendly appearance, he wanted answers.

"It is a rather long, involved story, milord, one which should be saved for a later discussion when we have more time than just mere minutes of a dance." Her eyes fixed unfalteringly on his. "But in answer to your underlying question,"—he watched intently trying to read her—"this wound on my arm, which has not gone unnoticed tonight, was received in a fight while defending our camp from a surprise rebel attack."

"It is said that you actually alerted the camp, effectively averting a major disaster." He noted her embarrassment at his compliment. *An interesting reaction from a fascinating woman,* he thought. "And that you dispensed with a few of the rebels yourself," he added, pressing for more information.

"That is true, milord. If you ask me, I will always give you truth. However, at times you may not find that to your liking." A small grin played at the corner of her mouth, and a definite twinkle of amusement danced in her eyes.

As the music ended, he placed his hand delicately on her back and guided her over to Jason.

"I meant what I said, Mrs. Tarrington. You have piqued my interest, and I want to get to know you better."

She nodded, immediately turning to smile at her husband as he strode forward.

"Your wife is a breath of fresh air, Colonel. I will expect you both to join me for a luncheon soon."

"As you wish, milord," Jason answered agreeably, inclining his head politely. Taking her arm, he headed for the dance floor just as the music resumed playing. They enjoyed several more dances, Jason allowing no others to share Kathryn's attentions.

"Are you thirsty? Would you care for some wine, love?"

She nodded, pushing damp curls back from her moist brow. "It is either very warm in here, or perhaps the nearness of you." Her eyes sparkled with deviltry.

Indicating the wide stairs circling to the second floor lounge area he said, "Wait there by the stairwell, madam, where we may share a little more privacy. I will be right back."

As she stood where Jason had indicated, a figure sauntered out from under the staircase where, hidden from view, he had obviously been observing the dance floor, paying special attention to her.

"Good evening, Mrs. Tarrington. Lieutenant Colonel Banastre Tarleton—'Ban', to my friends."

Having startled her, she eyed him in coolly, remaining silent. She did not care for his excessively friendly manner or the fact that he had been lurking under the stairwell.

Taking her hand with mock gallantry, he proceeded to kiss it—overly long in her estimation. "I assume Colonel Tarrington has spoken of me," he purred unctuously.

Although she found his arrogance and enormous ego annoying, she must hold her temper, he was a fellow officer of Jason's. Yes, she knew of him, knew of his total lack of mercy in giving quarter to prisoners, knew he was referred to as 'Bloody Ban', and did not want to know him better. He and Jason were not particularly friendly, although they had fought in some of the same skirmishes. However, Jason had been recently informed by Cornwallis, that he would be putting them together on the battlefield more often as the war escalated. Tarleton's present lifestyle was as Jason's had been in the past. She was glad her husband had reassessed himself and made changes. But that appeared not be an option for Tarleton, he delighted in his notoriety.

Eyeing her necklace and lower, he reached out seductively.

Her hand flew to her breast in a protective gesture. "Do not touch me, sir," she demanded, angry at his impertinence.

He shrugged innocently. "I merely noticed your lovely necklace, and wished to take a closer look."

"Do not presume to take liberties with me, Colonel Tarleton," she retorted angrily, not believing his ruse for a moment.

Jason, approaching with food and drink, did not have to see Kathryn's face to detect discord.

"Your wife has spirit, Colonel—I like that in a woman."

But his rakish smile ended abruptly with Kathryn's next statement. "It has been our distinct pleasure Colonel Tarleton," she said tartly, inclining her head and effectively dismissing him.

Tarleton, taken aback at her bold effrontery, realized he had been dismissed. Quickly regaining his composure, he nodded politely and moved off to another part of the room.

Jason eyed her, questioning.

"Later, my love," With a slight smirk, she took the wine he offered.

In his distraction, as Colonel Tarleton strode from the hall, he almost slammed into Major Ferguson. Barely repressed anger and a fixed scowl caused Ferguson to stop him and ask questions.

"What a hellcat," he spat.

At Ferguson's sustained look of confusion, Tarleton retorted sharply, "Tarrington's wife," he muttered. "I do not doubt the rumors about the men she has killed, probably by breaking their damn backs."

"I would be cautious with any observations in reference to her character, Ban. It seems our hardened colonel has a tender spot for his wife, and will brook no injury to her name, or person." He flashed Tarleton a concerned look. "Take that as fair warning, my friend," he urged, and with a slap on Tarleton's back, moved off to find Cornwallis.

Jason stood by the stairwell drinking wine with his wife. Seeing that she was in good spirits after her encounter with Colonel Tarleton, he did not pursue the matter. Banastre was rude and brash, not a person Jason particularly admired. Everything he took upon himself to accomplish, turned into a competition, and Tarleton hated to lose. Kathryn had certainly taken the wind out of his sails—it was about time.

"I can see we will have much to discuss tomorrow, madam," he teased.

"As a matter of fact, we will, Colonel. I have a couple of questions to put to you." She shot him a sidelong glance as he wrapped his arm around her shoulder.

"I hear the orchestra beginning, would you do me the honor, milady?"

"I would love to, sir, but please allow me a few minutes upstairs." She looked pained at having to leave his watchful eye for even a short time.

"Do not look so uneasy, love. I will wait for you right here."

With a reassuring hug, she hurried up the long staircase before she lost courage, glancing back over her shoulder once or twice for support. Approaching the garderobe, she heard raucous laughter. Several women talked rapidly in hushed tones, interrupting one another excitedly to add more fuel to the gossip. Lady Antonia's whiny voice was easily recognizable, her venomous spite not surprising.

"What does he see in her? She is too tall, and her skin is so dark from the sun."

"Oh, but I heard he was coerced into marriage as part of his duties to help control the rebels," another voice added but was quickly squelched.

"Oh, for heaven's sake, that sounds farfetched. But did you see her arm? How unladylike."

"And her hair," yet another added insult.

"Ladies, ladies, these are only surface blemishes," a forceful voice spoke up.

For a moment, Kathryn thought she might have one person who would give her a chance. But the next remark quickly crushed that hope.

"She is a rebel, a colonial, uneducated and ignorant," her voice dripped with disgust.

"She must be after the colonel's money and good name," they chorused in absolute agreement.

Kathryn was taken aback, and deeply hurt at these unfounded insults.

"I hear she is one of the worst kind—a Scots-Irish immigrant from that wild, unruly bunch at Wautauga Settlement—on the other side of the mountains."

They all went silent, in horror, she imagined.

"What do they call them?" Another voice spoke up. "Over the mountain men? How vulgar. I cannot understand …"

All conversation stopped mid-sentence as the door slammed back, startling them. Kathryn stepped into the room glowering, pinning each individual with an icy stare. She wanted to shout, to refute the hateful accusations, but that would make her no better than them. Besides, why bother? They had already prejudged her.

Squaring her shoulders, she stood tall refusing to cower. Inhaling long even breaths, she eyed them balefully as they stood rooted in silence—not even one offering an apology. "Fancy trappings to cover bad manners; how shallow you are."

The 'fine' ladies, indignant, flustered and offended, began hushed whisperings amongst themselves.

"If you women are an example of polite society, then I am glad to be a rude colonial." With that statement, she pushed through them to attend to her needs. When she reappeared, they were gone. Looking into the mirror, sad eyes stared back as she attempted pinching color into her cheeks. Making a practiced smile, she bit her lip so as not to cry.

Jason, as promised, was waiting for her. Hearing her footsteps, he looked up, his smiling face immediately becoming serious. Her attempted smile was forced, the gaiety of a few minutes before, now gone. Having seen a group of women come down the stairs moments before, talking into their hands while eyeing him, he suspected it was not a good sign. Setting his wine glass down, he took the stairs in twos, concerned she might trip and fall in her distracted state. With a firm grasp of her hand and a steadying arm, he guided her to the bottom of the steep stairs.

Afraid she would break down and tears, once begun—unstoppable, she refused to meet his eyes. She could not risk such damaging embarrassment for Jason, or herself. He felt her shoulders heave as she gulped air fighting for control, and quickly escorted her out through a side door, across the terrace, and down onto the lawn well away from the house.

Once away from prying eyes, he bent to her in deep concern, pulling her snugly against him. "Talk to me, love," he encouraged in comforting tones.

"Later." A single word whispered painfully as she shook her head, pressing her face to his chest.

"Kathryn, this cannot wait," he said, voice taut with barely concealed anger. Resting his chin lightly against the top of her head he asked, "What did those bitches say that cut you so deeply?"

Her head came up sharply at his choice of words, sensing his growing anger. She must regain control of her emotions, and calm him before he erupted in unmanageable rage—perhaps causing serious repercussions.

"Jason," she whispered, reaching to touch his cheek, seeing barely controlled fury seething just below the surface. "I will be all right now." Her green eyes implored him to let go of his anger. "It … hurt so, at the time."

He held her close as she slowly repeated all that had transpired in a quiet, composed manner, her emotions finally under control. He wasted no time on inadequate apologies, as there were no words to excuse this misconduct. He merely held her close.

After a few minutes of silence, he tipped her chin up and brushed her lips in a kiss of utmost tenderness. With relief, she saw he was again calm.

"I am afraid, Kathryn, that for past misdeeds, it is my punishment to love you … beyond all reason." His thumb gently removed a remaining tear at the corner of her eye.

At the grating sound of a throat being cleared, they turned in unison to see Lord Cornwallis quietly observing them with interest. Kathryn wondered just how long he had been standing there unannounced.

"Is everything all right, Mrs. Tarrington?" His intense gaze was somewhat disconcerting.

She forced gaiety into her tone, turning to face him with a charming smile. "Certainly, milord, I merely have a bit of dust in my eye. We will be back inside in a few minutes."

"Hmm," he mused, regarding her thoughtfully. Well aware of her unpleasant encounter from the indignant babbling of the offenders as they returned to the ballroom, he had searched her out. She had the ability to rebound and cover herself quite well. He liked that.

"I will see you inside then. I look forward to sharing another dance with you, milady." He eyed the colonel, pleased to see irritation flare once again. Colonel Tarrington had never been an easy man to deal with; they had crossed swords more than once. It could be very interesting to see how this woman would influence him. Changes were already evident in his demeanor.

As Lord Cornwallis turned to head back to the ballroom, Kathryn spoke up. "Milord, please wait."

As she stepped towards him, Cornwallis turned, eyeing her with mild curiosity.

"I fear I have offended some of your guests," Kathryn stated softly.

Although caught off-guard, the general quickly decided to play ignorant of any earlier discord. "I doubt that Mrs. Tarrington," he said, smiling as he watched her eyes, noticing the unusual green coloring they reflected in the light of the moon.

Gnawing her lower lip, brow furrowed, she attempted conveying what she wished to say in a proper manner. Jason's hand moved to the small of her back and rested gently, providing courage.

"I felt they spoke—*unfairly*." She searched for a word that would not sound too condemning.

"They treated you rudely." Cornwallis made a statement of fact.

She eyed him, unblinking. "Yes, milord, and I pointed that fact out to them in a less than polite manner myself."

A slight smile played at the corners of the general's mouth.

Jason's hand caressed her back in a series of small circles, sending a message of approval.

"And for that indiscretion, I do apologize," she said softly, never losing eye contact.

How well spoken and forthright she is, and honest to a fault … excellent qualities. Cornwallis was impressed. *Yes, I definitely want to get to know you better, Mrs. Tarrington.* This should be a very interesting couple to watch.

"I believe it is I, who am grateful for your forbearance in this matter. It is an unfortunate incident, milady, which will not happen again." He reached out, and taking both her hands, kissed each in turn. "You are a delight, a breath of fresh air." He turned to the colonel. "And you, sir, are a lucky man."

Jason nodded in complete agreement.

"I will expect that dance shortly, milady," he insisted, inclining his head as he started back towards the terrace.

Suddenly concerned, Kathryn turned to her husband. "Was I wrong to tell him?"

"On the contrary, my pet, it was a bold and forthright move on your part, attributes his lordship reveres. I am sure he was well aware of the incident and was merely testing you."

At her concerned look, he smiled reassuringly. "You have passed his test, Kathryn. He will always let you know if you displease him," he added with a wry grin. "You can trust me on that account." Putting an arm around her, he tucked her head into his shoulder. "You met him head on with honesty. He will never fault that, nor forget that in your character."

"In the event that anything else ever concerns him about me," she interjected, understanding full well the inference.

"You, madam, are extremely astute in your judgment and comprehension, and I am proud of you." Jason kissed the top of her head then moved lower. His mouth found hers in a demanding kiss, their passion building.

"If we do not stop now, it will be too late," she said breathlessly.

"Later then, my love?" He arched an eyebrow, breathing with some difficulty.

"Later," she smiled.

As they reentered the ballroom, Cornwallis was waiting. He extended a hand to Kathryn.

"I would like to claim my dance, milady." His smile was charming, belying a look that commanded obedience.

Jason tensed, irritated, but this was a matter of duty. She curtsied prettily and accepted. "It would be my pleasure, milord."

With a warm smile to Jason, she stepped onto the dance floor to the notes of a lilting waltz, arm in arm with Lord Cornwallis.

"Do not allow the 'fine ladies'," he emphasized the words, "to cause you concern. They will accept you in time, Mrs. Tarrington."

Having recovered from earlier stung pride, she shrugged indifferently. "I know who I am, milord. I was caught off-guard but their remarks will not be of concern again." She eyed him boldly.

"Perhaps another dance would be helpful," he suggested, but she read him perfectly. It had nothing to do with helping her gain acceptance—or dancing.

"If I may be so bold, milord. It would seem you derive great pleasure from irritating my husband."

He chuckled, taking careful note of her expressive face. "You are very perceptive, milady. I like that."

At her questioning look, he explained. "We have had our differences. The colonel can be difficult." He paused unsure as to how much he wanted to discuss.

"But he is not the same man he was six months ago, or even three months past, milord. I would ask that you remain unbiased in your appraisal." Softly she added, "He is a good man, milord, in military duties and otherwise."

The music was slowing to a finale.

"I do believe you truly love him." He sounded rather skeptical.

"He is my life," she stated fiercely, her green eyes filled with passion.

Such intensity of feelings and obvious pride in her husband were admirable qualities. He liked her more with each passing minute. As the music slowly drifted to a close, Cornwallis bowed, and purposely taking her left hand, kissed it. He touched the exquisite, golden knotwork of her wedding ring, marveling at the complexity and craftsmanship. "With the patent statement of this ring, milady, perhaps I had best return you to your husband." He glanced over at Jason's unsmiling face and uneasy stance. "However, I do want to know more about you, Mrs. Tarrington. Anyone who can influence one of my most successful, but difficult officers, is a person I need to understand."

He took her elbow and began escorting her back to where Jason stood, his impatience barely concealed. "I think a luncheon after this next campaign would be appropriate—in about three weeks, hmm? I will send word."

"Should I expect an inquisition rather than a luncheon, milord?" She appraised him with an unfaltering eye.

Hearing this last statement as they stopped in front of him, Jason struggled to remain straight-faced. He hated to see her hurt in any manner, but she had rebounded quickly, once again her independent self.

"Your wife is extremely perceptive and honest in her appraisal, Colonel." He smiled effusively at Kathryn. "No, my dear, let us make it a luncheon."

"Thank you, General. Then I shall look forward to it."

He turned, assessing Jason with a more acute eye, perceiving the smallest nuance of change in his manner. *Perhaps she is right*, he mused. *I will watch him.* "Your wife is charming, Colonel." Without further adieu he moved away, making polite conversation as he went.

The orchestra began playing a slow song, the violins bowing with feeling as Jason moved Kathryn onto the dance floor.

"I was afraid he would keep you all night, love, a rather unsettling thought as I thoroughly enjoy the feel of you dancing within my arms." He looked down into smiling, green eyes that spoke of love.

"You are all right?" Her beaming countenance relieved his concern. "We will talk later," he murmured against her ear, pulling her closer. "For now, I merely want to enjoy the music, and you."

They lost themselves completely, floating gracefully, perfectly in tune with each other and the lyrical notes of the orchestra, existing in a world of their own. Completely oblivious, Jason encircled his wife, pulling her body to mold tightly against his. His hand reached to tangle in her cascading mass of golden curls as he tipped her face up gently to receive his kiss. Her arms floated up, encircling his neck, pulling him to her. Completely lost in each other—no one else existed. Their kiss deepened, rooting them to the floor in a passionate embrace.

Boisterous yells and the booming voice of Lord Cornwallis announcing: "Congratulations to the newlyweds", brought them crashing back to reality.

Kathryn, flustered and self-conscious, was unaware the music had ended—or how long ago. Jason, on the other hand, in more typical male-like fashion, merely smiled—unabashed.

Leaning close he whispered conspiratorially, "Well, Mrs. Tarrington, perhaps that will relieve certain faction's anguish over my being unhappily burdened with you."

The orchestra began another slow tune and Jason, somewhat uncomfortable in his desire, whisked his wife back onto the dance floor and stepped into the rhythm. The guests began dancing once again, many of the ladies clinging to the last vestiges of shock, but most of the men grinning.

Their massive wedding rings, glinting brightly as they held each other, made a statement for all to see. Jason bent to kiss her lightly again, openly displaying his feelings for his wife and her importance to him. He had shown his peers, beyond doubt.

"Madam," his voice was husky with desire. "We must go home soon, as I have an extremely important need to discuss with you." Urgency added a raspy edge to his voice as he gazed into green eyes sparkling with promise.

They started the rounds of polite leave-takings. As they approached Lord Cornwallis, he made an aside to Major Ferguson. "Contrary to popular rumor, Major, I fail to see that we have any unfortunate victims here. They seem quite besotted with each other."

The major looked slightly puzzled. "You know, milord, the colonel seems somehow changed. I cannot quite grasp what is different but ..." He let the thought drop as the Tarringtons stopped in front of them to pay their respects.

As Cornwallis took her hand, he smiled directly at Kathryn. "I will look forward to our luncheon in three weeks." He wanted to get to know this unusual woman. There was a unique depth and passion he needed to comprehend.

"It will be our pleasure," she said, curtsying gracefully, as Jason looked on with pride.

When they reached their carriage, Lieutenant Jackson was waiting, a light robe ready for Kathryn's bare shoulders in the cooler night air. He smiled in greeting. "It appears that all went well."

At that comment they laughed in unison.

"It will be a great tale for around the campfire some evening," she giggled.

"What I wish to know, madam, is where you learned to curtsy in such a gracious manner," Jason teased lightly.

"I told you, sir. My mother was a genteel lady. I must have absorbed some of her manners." She shrugged—her grin impish. "However, I try not to make a common practice of it."

Both men shook their heads, amused. But Jason viewed her with heightened respect, aware of just how attuned she was to his military position, rising to the occasion as required. As she stepped up into the carriage, her skirts hiked up to show her lower leg.

"Kathryn, you wore your boots," Jason exclaimed, laughing wholeheartedly, causing her minor discomfit at his drawing attention to her idiosyncrasy in front of his men.

Jackson grinned widely, although the other officers tried to be somewhat more subtle.

"And your dirk, madam?" Jason was still laughing.

"In my boot, of course," she said innocently, grinning back as he stood shaking his head.

With that statement, Jackson guffawed, but squelched it rapidly at her stern look. She stood in the carriage, hands on hips, surveying the group with mock severity. "Well, you never know when it might come in handy," she said defensively, her eyes sparkling with deviltry.

After a few minutes of additional banter, Jason settled her into the carriage, placing the robe gently over her shoulders. With a protective arm around her and a hand on the reins, they headed back to their encampment, Lieutenant Jackson and six dragoons falling in on both sides of the carriage.

Within moments, Jason felt the weight of her against him and her steady, even breathing. He smiled to himself, grateful for the contentment she brought into his life. He would not rouse her when they got back to their encampment. It had been an evening of exhausting, mixed emotions; she had earned a good night's sleep. They had much to discuss, but it could definitely wait until morning.

Clucking to the horse, he urged it to make a faster pace.

Chapter Seventeen

False Calm

Yawning and stretching, she came awake slowly, momentarily confused. She remembered Jason teasing about her boots as he settled her into the carriage, but that was all. She must have fallen asleep as soon as her head touched his shoulder. A quick look revealed he had, indeed, undressed her and removed her boots. *Lord, I must have been tired not to have roused a little. But why did he not wake me?*

She quickly washed and dressed, unsettled. Where was he? She did not have long to wait for an answer. Within moments he entered the tent with a plate full of food and two mugs of coffee.

"Ahh, sleepy head," he teased, but stopped abruptly at her look of distress. Setting their breakfast on the desk, he pulled her to him, holding her gently. "You were so soundly asleep I did not have the heart to wake you, my love." He kissed her tenderly.

"Why am I so tired all of a sudden?" she asked, concerned.

"Kathryn." Stepping back, he looked her directly in the eye—incredulous. "Last night was extremely exhausting emotionally. I slept deeply myself. We have also been under great strain, pushing hard to intercept Beldon's forces." He saw she was considering his words, accepting that possibility as being true. "You are always too demanding of yourself."

He handed her a cup of coffee and took one for himself. She sipped slowly watching him over the edge of the cup. "And do not forget our little one," he said, softly caressing her stomach. "Jackson noted your exhaustion last night and commented that it was the same with his sister when she was first with child. It will soon pass; you will feel more like yourself again." He reached for her hand and held it as they drank their coffee.

She smiled distractedly deep in thought. She must find Anna before their child was born. As a healer, she would know what to do when it came time for her to deliver. But of utmost importance, she must not appear sensitive or too tired. She made an additional mental note to talk to Jackson about his sister's childbirth when it was closer to her time. Her mind churned. *This is a natural part of life, many women have done this before me, and many will after. I can survive this too.*

"Do not fret, hmm?" He interrupted her musings, his arched brow bringing a smile as she nodded, feeling better. Imagining how difficult it must be to deal with internal changes while carrying a baby, he was determined to make every effort to support her emotionally. Handing her a plate of food, he suggested: 'eat before it becomes cold'.

She ate slowly, eyeing him silently as he stood leaning casually against the desk, a smile curving his mouth. As they would not be breaking camp today, he had dressed less formally: jacket open, lace jabot untied and hanging loosely. His long hair hung in lustrous black strands about his shoulders. There was no other man quite as handsome, of that she was sure. Just looking at him, dressed in this fashion, never failed to start an inner aching need.

Setting her plate down she moved to him and with gentle nudging, insinuated herself seductively between his legs. "Why did you not wake me?" Her eyes searched his.

Setting his coffee down, he kissed her lightly. "I could not very well take advantage of you in your exhausted condition, madam. However ..." His hand slid under her blouse, cupping her breast. "You seem well recovered this morning."

Pressing closer, moving slowly, purposefully, she felt instant response as he sucked in a sharp breath, groaning deeply.

"You are a vixen, my wife," he murmured huskily, cupping her face. He drew her close, claiming her lips passionately in a kiss which abruptly changed as she took control—loving him slowly, exquisitely, her touch deliciously insistent, coaxing him to surrender completely.

Much later, lying in each other's arms, enjoying the final moments of euphoria, he gazed into her glowing face and seeing his love returned in full measure, felt complete.

Rolling up onto one elbow she gazed down into his incredible blue eyes. "Next time, you wake me," she said with playful sternness.

"Yes, madam," he answered, looking thoroughly chastised, causing both to laugh.

He pulled her down for another kiss. Then, fingering his mother's necklace where it lay between her breasts, he said softly, "It looks as if it were always meant to be there. Wear it for all time, my Kathryn ... in happiness."

Her hand automatically touched the gold heart with reverence, her eyes misting.

"That reminds me, love. What was on Colonel Tarleton's mind last night?" Raising a questioning eyebrow, he abruptly changed direction in subject and mood.

"Whatever was on his mind, I gave him no time to express it. He is rude and impertinent, but I doubt he will seek my company if there is another occasion."

Jason noticed the smug glint in her eye and smiled, satisfied she could handle herself well even with some of the most hardened officers in the English cavalry. Settling back comfortably on a pile of blankets, he pulled her snugly against his side and held her while they discussed the events of the previous evening. In talking her through the extremely cruel treatment of the 'fine ladies', he was relieved to find that, that with the light of a new day, they had both put the incident into its proper perspective.

With no immediate demands for the day they relaxed, enjoying each other's company, eventually dozing contentedly. Kathryn roused first, and seeing Jason beginning to stir, realized that he, too, had been tired, and was glad for this idle time to restore their energy. With the bright noonday sun, the tent became uncomfortably hot. Jason brushed a kiss to her forehead and rose, pulling her up with him.

"I think fresh fish for supper might be in order. What say you, madam?" He pressed a dampened cloth to her warm cheek, enjoying her eager nod and twinkling eyes.

"Last one dressed has to saddle the horses," she teased, winking at him.

Within minutes they strode out into the bright summer day. Kathryn struggled to maintain decorum; childishly giddy over the prospect of investigating the stream for fishing and ..." Her mind wandered to other pleasurable areas.

Having been watching for them, Lieutenant Jackson approached with bread and cheese, attentive to their needs as always.

"Good morning, Lieutenant. I guess, more accurately—good afternoon."

He eyed her closely; noting she appeared rested her face luminous, reassuring him she would be fine. As he began to smile, she warned, "I do not want to hear one word about my boots." She grinned, quirking an eyebrow.

"Of course not, milady," he answered in a dignified manner, his eyes full of good humor. "That was the farthest thing from my mind."

Jason chuckled at their light banter, no longer experiencing jealousy over their friendship. With Kathryn's deep, abiding love, he could accept Jackson's honest feelings for her. *Actually, it is good to know he will always be there if ever...* But he refused to dwell on such thoughts, wasting precious moments of this beautiful day.

Taking the food Jackson had provided, they readied the horses and cantered off towards the nearby woods. As Diablo and Beauty were filled with high-spirited energy, they sidetracked across the grassy fields, permitting both to run before heading to the stream for fishing. Later, sitting beside the secluded stream, Jason leaned back on his elbows thoroughly enjoying himself, watching his wife catch several large trout.

"Look, Jason." She jerked her head towards the horses. Diablo nipped Beauty playfully, causing her to dance away but quickly return to his side. "I believe she has tamed the wild beast in him."

"As her mistress has tamed me," he whispered against her ear, creating delightful shivers.

"Not tamed in the least, my love," she purred, "and very much to my liking."

"Is there something I may do for you, madam?"

Narrowing her eyes, she grinned. "I thought you would never ask, my love."

Some time later, they awoke to lengthening shadows and the sun having shifted much lower in the sky—the promise of a beautiful sunset slowly beginning to insinuate itself across the horizon.

Stretching languorously, Jason grinned. "Judging by the sun, my love, I fear we had best return to camp if you want to surprise the men with trout for supper."

"If you had not sidetracked me, sir, there would have been more fish. I am afraid it will be a rather meager meal and you will have to explain," she challenged playfully.

"I can do that if you like, madam."

"I bet you would." She laughed aloud at his devilish look, throwing her arms around his neck, hugging him.

They rode into camp to the smell of campfires beginning the evening meal. As Kathryn threw her leg over Beauty's head and slid to the ground, she handed the string of slimy fish to Lieutenant Jackson.

"Thank you ... I think," he commented dryly, taking them with a slightly distasteful expression. Handing them to a nearby corporal and sending him off to Cook's wagon, he looked for somewhere to wipe his hands. Turning back, he caught Kathryn grinning, hands placed jauntily on her hips, the colonel at her side looking on with amusement.

Lieutenant Jackson was pleased to see them both looking relaxed and well rested. The approaching battle with Major Beldon would be far more serious than previous skirmishes. Thankfully they had rebounded quickly, something they seemed to easily accomplish, as long as they could claim intimate time together.

They spent two more days of unstructured pleasure allowing whim to guide their actions. Kathryn took Jason into the forest and shared her expertise in setting rabbit snares, captivating him with her extensive knowledge in the skills of self-preservation. He could easily understand how she had managed on her own for so many months before they met.

They rarely talked of her time spent with the Cherokees or with Jamie, other than in passing. But he could detect the influences of both in many of her abilities. He often read poetry while propped against a tree trunk, Kathryn encircled in his arms and sharing a glass of brandy. She never tired of *The Minstrel*, and he never tired of the joy reflected in her upturned face as she listened to him read.

Their nights and sometimes their days, found them sharing various levels of passion as dictated by the moment: often quietly within their tent, but occasionally with fierce intensity in the cool, rejuvenating waters of the nearby stream. By touching and being near, it seemed none of this idyllic existence would come to an end.

The afternoon of the third day found them relaxing by the stream. Hot, heavy, air, with its promise of rain, made her sleepy as he read. She settled against him, arm flung loosely across his waist, unaware that she had slept, until awaking to find him writing on a piece of paper atop the poetry book. She was curious, but would not pry; he would tell her when he was ready.

"Sleep well?" he asked, smiling down at her. "I am doing something I should have done many months ago."

At her inquisitive look, he explained. "My mother's mother is a lovely woman—my grandmother." He shook his head, disconcerted. "I have not thought to call her that for so long."

"She is still alive?" Kathryn asked.

"Yes, she is about seventy, I believe. She has written within the last year or so, but I have never answered. I did not wish to share the life I was living, knowing it would bring her no solace; perhaps better she remember me as an unhappy, young man who left to lose himself in battle."

Kathryn eyed him sympathetically, recalling the sadness he had endured as a child.

"However, now I have much to relate to her." His face brightened, his brilliant, blue eyes smiling into hers. "About my beloved wife, our expected child, the necklace—I want to share all of this with her. Perhaps she will find pleasure in knowing her daughter raised a son who could finally find happiness despite all the bad times." He paused, holding her gaze. "I want her to know of you, Kathryn." He kissed the top of her head and held the letter out for her perusal.

At her protest that it was personal, he disagreed. "No, my love, anything concerning us is for your eyes also."

She read slowly, devouring every word. It was not only his broad, well-formed penmanship that astounded her, but the eloquent manner in which he conveyed simple truths to his grandmother.

"It is beautiful, Jason," she breathed softly, pleased to see his questioning look change to one of relief.

"Write something to her," he encouraged, handing her the pen. "Please." He nodded towards the letter.

She thought for a long moment and then penned, in her more delicate handwriting:

'Dear Grandmother,
Our love and devotion is beyond all reason.
Jason is my whole life and a credit to both his mother and you.
With deepest affection, Kathryn.'

She handed the letter back and watched as he read her additional message, his eyes filling with gratitude. Folding the letter neatly, he put it safely into his inner jacket pocket and encircled her in his arms, enjoying the feel of her, the peaceful companionship. "These past three days have been a gift," he murmured.

"Yet, it will feel good to be on the move again," she said quietly, knowing they were of one mind in this, as in most things.

When duties commanded his presence elsewhere, he often thought about her and their life together. He found it astounding that she truly enjoyed the rigors of long days on horseback and primitive camp life—ever grateful for her positive, uncomplaining attitude. Even now, after only a short delay, she was as eager as he to be on the move once again. That knowledge filled him with inner contentment; they had truly been blessed in finding each other.

Pulling his head down, she brushed his lips softly with hers. "What say you to a quick ride before we head in?" She stood and began collecting their things. "That will still give you enough time to prepare for your officers' meeting tonight."

She extended her hand down to him, but he continued to sit there, silently drinking in her beauty, enjoying her feline grace as she moved.

"Come now, sir, duty calls, I will not have it said that your wife has kept you from those duties."

"You never miss a thing, Mrs. Tarrington." He took her proffered hand and stood, bending to her ear he said softly, "And for that, and many more endearing qualities, I adore you."

Sparkling eyes met his as she kissed him deeply; abruptly pushing away before it was too late to stop the inevitable. Grabbing their blanket she headed for the horses, eyeing him lustfully over her shoulder as she flung herself into Beauty's saddle.

"Keep the meeting short tonight, sir, and you may be rewarded."

Shaking his head he chuckled, and quickly mounted Diablo.

Once back within the encampment, all returned to the business at hand. After a brief chat with Jackson, they retired to their tent. Jason immediately pulled maps out to study, spreading them across the top of his desk. Kathryn moved closer and traced her finger rapidly over the mapped area where they were now encamped, trying to determine Major Beldon's most likely route of travel. She also considered alternatives he might choose; discussing each possibility thoroughly with her husband.

"The success of this encounter depends on the precise timing of our attack," he mused.

Looking up, face serious, she nodded agreement.

"I had Lieutenant Jackson send men out on reconnaissance two nights ago to determine their exact position and hopefully establish their direction."

She eyed him respectfully, a knowing glance passing between them.

"They should be back by tonight in time for the meeting. However, I foresee no major difficulties," he said matter-of-factly.

"Then, depending upon the information you receive tonight, we should be able to determine how soon we move into battle," she deduced.

Draping his arm about her shoulder, he gave her a reassuring hug as they continued poring over every conceivable possibility—working out the finest details.

"Enough, my love." He took her hand and headed for the tent opening. "Let us join the men for dinner." With a wry grin he added: "As we have not been too visible these last few days, they might appreciate our company."

There had been a time when this would have been far from the truth—but no longer. Many things had changed between the colonel and his men.

The reconnaissance riders returned as supper was drawing to a close, weary from their long ride. Their horses, bearing obvious signs of the journey, were immediately led away to be toweled down and fed. Although the two men had a great deal of information to impart, Jason made sure they had time to refresh themselves and have a bite to eat first.

Kathryn looked up from where she and Jason had been re-examining the maps as the fairly refreshed riders entered their tent, arriving early to brief their colonel prior to the officer's meeting. After a quick greeting, she politely excused herself.

"Do not go too far, Kathryn," Jason advised.

She nodded, somewhat curious.

To her obvious, but unasked question, he added, "I may want your input once I have established Beldon's position."

Her face registered surprise; he had never included her before. He certainly knew his men better than she, but would they appreciate her suggestions? At her hesitation, his eyebrow raised.

"Yes sir, of course." She noticed the hint of a smile; he read her completely.

Standing outside the tent, she greeted the officers with quiet dignity, but extended a bright smile to Lieutenant Jackson—the last to enter. Even the newly relaxed atmosphere within the campsite demanded proper decorum in important situations.

She entertained herself watching the patterns of stars in the brightly lit sky, the threatening rain of late afternoon having never arrived. From within the tent the officer's voices droned on, but she did not bother to sort the words for understanding. She was pacing, as was her habit, when Jackson approached, amusement flickering in his eyes as he bid her softly, "The colonel wishes your presence, milady."

Quietly entering the tent, she stood at the back beside the lieutenant, awaiting Jason's instructions. The colonel immediately looked up, beckoning her to his desk. She approached, sensing the polite skepticism of his officers as they parted, allowing her to pass through.

"Beldon's troops are here," he stated, pointing to a position on the map.

He watched as she hesitated, carefully weighing all odds, remaining silent until sure of her assessment.

"What is your opinion?" he asked, his eyes encouraging her to speak freely.

"The colonel feels," she stressed his title to capture their attention, "that a somewhat more difficult approach across here . . ." she indicated on the map as they crowded closer, "would serve us better for a surprise attack than the alternative route through here—which although safer—affords them advance knowledge of our presence." She slowly traced the map with her finger, demonstrating both possibilities as the men watched, impressed with the strategy; well aware her familiarity with this area must have influenced these decisions.

"Also, if Beldon tries to approach from this direction, we can still catch him at a disadvantage." Her finger moved lightly across the map in further explanation.

Jason watched intently, noting the growing respect of his officers as they listened to her logical, concise explanation of different possibilities. Outlining in careful, thorough detail, she ended with her reiteration of Beldon's most likely route of approach. She stood up looking to Jason for approval, and was rewarded with his proud gaze. He surveyed his officers as they talked amongst themselves, waiting for them to quiet.

"While my wife is too self-effacing to take any credit, I am sure you gentlemen can appreciate the excellent strategy proposed here, and realize it was born of an excellent knowledge of this area—and a clever mind."

Although deeply pleased with the honor her husband had bestowed, she was embarrassed. However, the new respect reflected in the eyes of his most hardened officers compensated for any momentary discomfort. They finally realized her full commitment, accepting her as one of their own.

Lieutenant Jackson stood at the back of the tent watching her intently throughout the whole discussion of strategy, and was deeply impressed. This woman was one of a kind; there would never be another like her, not in his lifetime, of that he was sure.

Suddenly she glanced towards him, his approval also important. Flattered by this gesture, he flashed a look of praise in answer. *If only she knew how it pleases me to be included in her thoughts. But then, perhaps she does.*

After the meeting, Jason shared more of the outriders' report, both agreeing they had made the best plan with the knowledge available at this time. Major Beldon was closer, having moved faster than expected. The thought that Jamie might be riding with him, his extensive knowledge of the area putting Beldon's forces on a more even keel with Jason's dragoons, was disturbing. She voiced this thought openly; Jason merely shrugged, replying that he would deal with the hand dealt at that time.

Removing books from the corners of the map, he allowed it to roll up as he began untying the laces of her blouse, resisting her protests of other possibilities to be discussed.

"I believe I exacted a promise from you earlier, madam. I intend to hold you to your bargain."

He started at her ear with great tenderness, working soft kisses along the length of her throat. Quickly surrendering to the pleasure of his touch, she wanted to forget tomorrow when they would head into … She did not want to think about it.

Naked together in the privacy of their tent, her body responded automatically. But fight it as she may, Kathryn was distracted.

"Stop thinking out loud, my pet."

Worried green eyes met his, taken aback at his words. She started to speak, but he placed a silencing finger to her lips. "Hush, hush, love, do not fret so. We have made our plans and they are sound. I realize this will be our first major encounter, I am well aware of your concerns."

He stroked her tawny curls, watching her face. "Kathryn, I will not go … will not ever leave … without you. Together, always, remember?"

At the depth of his meaning, her eyes filled. Clinging tightly, she whispered fervently, "Promise me, my love. Promise me."

Feeling her tremble, he gathered her closer. "I promise you, Kathryn MacLean Tarrington," he breathed softly against her ear.

She saw his promise reflected in those magnificent, piercing blue eyes that captured hers, and felt overwhelming relief.

An inner voice with far greater knowledge had spoken, and Jason knew beyond the shadow of a doubt, these were more than idle words. *But not yet … not yet, our 'time' is not now.*

With extreme patience and understanding he eased her distress, slowly enticing her back into their world of passion, reclaiming her for himself. Her mind finally ceded the battle to sensuous pleasure as she closed all thoughts to the worries at hand, reveling in his exquisite touch.

"Better, now?" he murmured, nuzzling her cheek as they lay together peacefully much later.

She nodded, thankful for his forbearance. Snuggling closer, safe within his arms, she whispered, "It will go well, it will," as she drifted into sleep.

Chapter Eighteen

Successful Interception

Just before the first rays of dawn slipped over the horizon, they claimed each other fiercely, clinging silently in the afterglow. As he gently stroked her tangled mass of golden curls, she settled beside him, inwardly calm and sensing all would go as planned.

As they dressed in preparation for the day's battle, she turned and asked: "Is there anything I can say that will convince you to …"

"No, my pet." He stopped her mid-sentence, well aware of her request.

Reaching to touch her chin, amused at her pout, he kissed her tenderly. "Today is not the day to have you anywhere near the fighting." He held up a silencing hand as she started to argue her abilities. "Your arm is not yet as strong as it should be; I will not risk having you injured." He hoped she would accept that reasoning without further argument.

"As you well know, we must stop Beldon's forces from joining Gates if we hope to bring the South under our thumb. I cannot do what needs to be done if I must worry about you, hmm?"

She gazed into blue eyes that spoke so eloquently of abiding love. Knowing his judgment to be valid she conceded, and kissing him whispered, "Come back to me unharmed, my husband. I will be watching for you."

He kissed her deeply, meaningfully. Slowly releasing her, he grasped her hand firmly in his and walked her from their tent to join the men for a quick breakfast.

Excitement and activity bubbled throughout the encampment as the dragoons ate quickly, eager to be on the road. Lieutenant Jackson greeted them warmly, but purposely joined a small group of officers off to one side to allow the colonel and his wife some privacy. His consideration did not go unnoticed, Kathryn immediately flashing him a smile of sincere appreciation.

"Will you be back by tonight?" she asked Jason, almost afraid of his reply.

His look was thoughtful in trying to give her a fair answer. "I will do my best, love. If we chase them farther south it may be sometime tomorrow, so do not worry." With a reassuring smile, he added, "It may be bad for our little one."

She returned his smile bravely, refusing to have him ride out to battle, upset and distracted because of her.

All too quickly the dragoons moved into formation, focused and eager, prepared to ride. Jason made a final check of Diablo's trappings and then turned to her. The men watched with quiet respect as she gently placed her hand over his heart and began their salute.

"Your heart and my heart beat as one," she whispered, her eyes never leaving his.

"Always," he answered, brushing a kiss to her forehead and beginning to trace his thumb down the bridge of her nose to her chin, tipping it up to receive his kiss.

Smiling with reassurance, she moved back to a place where she could watch the men parade by as they headed out to intercept Major Beldon.

Jason's demeanor changed abruptly as he stepped to the head of his column and mounted Diablo. He was now their colonel, sitting proud and straight astride his charger, his complete focus dedicated to the task lying ahead. With a forward motion of his gloved hand, the troops began to move.

The vision of gallant horses and well-trained men in striking uniforms never failed to move her each time she watched them ride out, ready for battle. As the colonel approached where she stood, she smiled and curled a fist to her heart. With the slightest inclining of his helmeted head, he acknowledged her tribute. After he passed, she lowered her hand but continued to address each man as he rode by with a solemn smile. Many of the dragoons tipped their head ever so slightly in respect, especially the officers who felt well prepared for the day's engagement due to her help the previous evening.

She watched quietly, mouthing small prayers for the success of their mission, but especially for Jason's safety, never taking her eyes away until they were completely out of sight. Reluctantly turning away, lost in thought, she almost collided with Lieutenant Jackson. Startled by his close proximity, she was momentarily flustered.

To his earnest apologies, she shook her head. "It is just me, Jack. Will it ever become easy to see him ride away and wonder ...?"

"Not easier, but you will become more accustomed," he assured, offering her a mug of coffee.

Accepting gratefully, she stood sipping the hot liquid in silence.

Jack watched her thoughtfully for several moments. Kathryn," he said abruptly. "You can help me with a project."

Rousing from her musings, she eyed him with interest.

"We need to prepare for possible injuries. As you know, seriously wounded will be shipped to the surgeons in Winnsboro. But there is much we can accomplish here in the field."

At the prospect of making herself useful, her eyes came to life. This would be much more satisfying than pacing uselessly, 'wearing out boots', as they often teased her. "Prepare bandages and the like?" she asked.

"Yes, but more important, you have a great knowledge of herbal medicines."

She eyed him curiously. They had often talked of her time spent with the Cherokees. Actually, as a result of their many long hours together, Jack knew almost as much about her as Jason did.

"What can be prepared while staying close to camp for safety's sake?"

Without hesitation she replied, "Inner bark from fir trees, black cherry if we can find some, and willow—that should be easy as I know of two by the stream. Perhaps rhododendron, some sphagnum moss and ..."

They worked together gathering the necessary materials, Kathryn instructing Jackson on making an infusion, mashing fir bark for poultices, willow bark tea and more. It pleased him to see her spirits soar as she worked happily, finally feeling needed.

"Did your sister have a difficult pregnancy?" she paused abruptly while crushing fir bark into a pulpy mass, her question taking him completely by surprise.

This was an area not usually discussed between men and women, but then, there was nothing usual about Kathryn. Not wanting to upset her, as his sister had almost died during the birth, he remained silent.

"Jack?" her voice held an edge that demanded an answer. She would not let it drop.

"No. It was normal and she felt well."

Sensing from his tone that he was withholding information, she pushed harder. "You are not telling me something." She pierced him with a look. "And you are not shy, as we know each other too well after all these months."

She reads people way too easily he thought, and found the fact disconcerting.

"The birth was difficult." He hesitated, hoping she would stop there, but knowing Kathryn as he did, realized that would not be the case.

At her sharp look of interest, and refusal to change the subject, he continued, "My nephew was breached."

Briefly taken aback, Kathryn became thoughtful. "Anna told me of one such birth she was aware of in the Bird Clan. Both the child and mother died," she added softly.

"Well, my sister is alive and well, thankfully, and I have a handsome nephew," he assured.

"Were you there?" Needing some sense of security if they could not find Anna in time, she wanted to know. He was silent for so long, she repeated the question, "Were you there, Jack?"

"Kathryn." He felt ill-at-ease, but her look demanded an answer. The only way of moving on to another subject was to give her the truth and be done with it.

"Yes," he hesitated. "She began labor quite suddenly and no doctor was available."

"You saved her life," a statement rather than a question.

"I suppose you could say that."

Seeing him obviously uncomfortable and having gained the information she wanted, Kathryn ended the discussion.

"Thanks, Jack." She squeezed his arm and returned to mashing fir bark. "Do you think we could talk Cook into another cup of coffee?"

Relieved to be out of the line of fire, he took their empty mugs and headed for the food wagon.

Kathryn watched him walk away, shaking her head. *Men*, she thought, *can be so touchy about certain subjects.*

By noontime, Kathryn had become edgy. Everything she could prepare for the wounded was ready. Distant rumbling indicated gunfire several miles away, pulsing like a living thing—growing louder, then softer, then louder once more. She could not determine if the fighting was actually moving in different directions, or whether myriads of misdirected sounds merely drifted on a changing wind, but she wanted it to be over.

Telling Lieutenant Jackson she would return later, she turned and walked back to their tent. Once inside, she immediately felt Jason's comforting presence. Moving to his desk she sat down, unrolled the maps and began scrutinizing them once again. She repeated the day's strategy over and over, trying to be sure she had forgotten nothing—had not possibly misjudged.

"Mrs. Tarrington." Lieutenant Jackson interrupted her brooding thoughts as he entered the tent carrying a light luncheon for them both of them.

She looked up slightly startled.

"The plans are sound. Second guessing yourself only causes undue concern, and will change nothing." He smiled understanding completely, as he moved the maps and placed the food in front of her. "You really need to eat, Kathryn." His tone was gentle, his look, insistent.

She regarded him silently for so long, he was sure she would refuse. Eventually, taking a piece of bread, she began to eat. Pulling the other chair closer to the desk, she gestured him to be seated.

"Tell me more about your home, Jack."

"There really is not much to tell. My youth was normal to the point of boredom. We lived just outside of London on a modest estate where my parents still live today. Father has always done well in banking and provided generously for mother, my sister and me. My sister, Eugenie, and her husband, Thomas, live a few miles away with their son, Robert. Eugenie loves to 'dig in the dirt' as she calls it, and has some of the most prized gardens in the area." He paused trying to think of more to relate.

"Knowing you would leave all that behind, for who knows how long, why did you volunteer for the dragoons?" Kathryn asked, truly curious.

"Perhaps for some of the same reasons you left home." He grinned. "Just to prove to myself that I could actually walk away from all that and survive on my own."

Regarding him thoughtfully, she pushed the chair back from the desk and stood, and he followed suit. "Let us go for a walk, Jack," she urged, and quickly gathering their plates, headed for the doorway.

They walked towards Cook's tent in mutual silence. Gunfire continued to rumble in the distance but was becoming less and less noticeable. Handing the plates to Cook with a smile and word of 'thanks,' she headed for the outer edge of the encampment.

"How did you meet Jason?" she asked, as they continued to walk.

"Not far from my hometown, Jason was training a band of dragoons in preparation to embark for the colonies. He had created quite a reputation for himself—which aroused my curiosity. Under King George's orders, they were to suppress an insurrection over taxation with the colonials."

Kathryn listened with great interest; this was an area she and Jason had talked very little about.

"Jason demanded unquestioning loyalty and exacting military skills. His intense training, and an innate ability to lead, quickly raised him to the rank of colonel."

She stopped walking and faced Jack. He met her intense gaze with one of extreme sincerity.

"Jason demands perfection in himself and will tolerate no less from his men." He hesitated, his expression displaying admiration. "He is the best of the best, Kathryn."

"Yes," she murmured fingering her wedding ring, briefly losing herself to private thoughts.

"At one time, he commanded their loyalty through fear."

She looked up sharply, but knew he spoke the truth.

"Fear of humiliation, of physical pain ..." He shrugged, shaking his head. "But all that has changed. They now follow him out of deep respect—actually, respect for both of you."

The smile she flashed was twofold: pride in her husband and gratitude for Jack's honest words.

"Strange how fates interweave," Kathryn mused. "Jason arrived in Charleston to put a stop to the rebel uprisings just in time to join Clinton's English soldiers in their unfortunate attack on Sullivan's Island. As I had no sense of direction in my life at that time, I was headed towards Keowee to rebuild relations with my Cherokee friend, Anna, and perhaps find my brother and his family—or at least discover whether they were still alive."

Lieutenant Jackson watched varying expressions chase across her face, enjoying the strength and beauty reflected there.

"A day or two, one way or the other, and all this would have been lost," she said wistfully.

"Somehow, somewhere you two would have met—it was destined to be," he answered fervently.

Looking up, he saw a young corporal heading their way with mugs of coffee. Kathryn was vaguely aware that distant gunshots had finally ceased, and the sun was sitting low in the sky.

"Milady... sir," the corporal extended the mugs in greeting. "A rider has just arrived with word from the colonel."

Jack felt Kathryn go rigid at his side.

"He is unharmed, milady, and bids you rest easy."

For the slightest moment her knees weakened, threatening to give out. Gulping deep breaths, she struggled to maintain composure—relief and joy flooding throughout her body. *He is safe. He is safe.*

As any physical gesture on his part would appear inappropriate, or be misinterpreted by this new recruit, Jackson was helpless to offer a strong arm for support. But she steadied herself and pressed the young soldier for information, eager to know any further news he could provide.

"Colonel Tarrington is on his way back to camp, but will be delayed while he organizes the return of those injured, and prisoners." At her silence, he glanced at the lieutenant and then uneasily back to her, unsure of what to say. "Would you care to speak directly to the rider, milady?" he asked, somewhat uncomfortable in the presence of the colonel's wife.

Finally finding her voice, Kathryn assured him that would be unnecessary, and after thanking him for his consideration, began sipping coffee in a distracted fashion—pacing in earnest.

Lieutenant Jackson leaned back against a tree and watched her purposeful step, shaking his head with a wry grin as he drank his coffee.

She stared constantly in the direction the dragoons would be returning, continuing to sip coffee and ... pace. After some time had passed, she noticed small clouds of dust on the horizon. Abruptly handing her almost empty mug to the lieutenant she dropped to her knees, and pressing an ear to the ground, listened intently. In a flash, she was up and walking rapidly. "They are coming in," she yelled back over her shoulder, never breaking her stride.

Several soldiers looked up from where they crouched around the campfire, and then stood to greet the returning dragoons.

Nearing the crest of the hill, she stopped and waited, rigid with anxiety, clasping her hands behind her so as not to wring them.

Despite long hours of battle, Jason crested the hill sitting straight and proud atop Diablo, his men in perfect formation behind him. Her fist curled against her heart as she watched him approach—sure she would burst from the thrill that just seeing him always evoked. She stood shakily, fighting an overwhelming urge to fling herself into his arms regardless of how it would look in front of his men. No one existed ... but him.

Catching sight of her, he sheared off from the troops and reined Diablo to an abrupt halt. Stepping down from his saddle, he removed his helmet and gloves as he strode forward, a slight smile curving his lips.

With trembling chin, she faced him trying valiantly to smile.

"Sir..." One word uttered—gratitude, relief and love.

"Sir, nothing," he exclaimed, his intense gaze devouring her. "Come to me, my wife." His arms opened in welcome; enveloping her in a crushing embrace he quickly gentled so as not to hurt her.

"My husband, my love," she murmured, tears of joy bathing her cheeks as she clung to him.

Jason tipped her face up, absorbing her beauty, inhaling the essence of her, his blue eyes caressing. "Am I to understand you missed me, madam?"

A tear-streaked face, wreathed in smiles met his, as he lowered his mouth to hers, claiming it passionately. Pausing to remove pins from her hair, he stroked the long curls, allowing them to tumble onto her shoulders. Drinking in her glowing face, he gently wiped her tears, smiling with reassurance.

"You are not hurt?" Her anxiety required reassurance.

Shaking his head, he wrapped an arm around her shoulder and headed down into the encampment with Diablo following.

Lieutenant Jackson had waited near the campfires while they greeted each other, but now stepped forward to tend the colonel's horse.

"Colonel," Jackson inclined his head in greeting. "All went as planned?"

"Yes, the strategy was perfect." He hugged Kathryn. "We have scattered their forces and successfully cut them off from Gates. For the next few days we will harry them, drive them further south." He looked thoughtfully at his wife. "I believe they were quite surprised by our attack."

"If Jamie was with them and caught off-guard, he knows beyond doubt where my loyalties lie." She kept her tone neutral. "Be cautious, Jason. He will be furious—and humiliated."

Jason followed her line of thought, agreeing completely. "I did not happen to confront him, but he was seen by others—and he exacted his toll on our men," he answered truthfully, knowing she would demand nothing less.

Kathryn's eyes clouded with concern. In answer to her unasked question he added solemnly, "We have a few serious injuries, a handful of minor ones, but we have lost Blake, Stearns and Wilson."

"Oh, Jason …" Shaking her head sadly, she glanced first at him, and then Lieutenant Jackson.

"All good men," Jackson said. "We will feel their loss."

"Have the wounded been brought in yet?" she asked.

"If not already here, they will be shortly," Jason replied. Resisting Kathryn's offer of refreshment until later, he added, "I would like to see the injured men before darkness falls." Placing a guiding hand in the small of her back, he headed towards the medical tent with Lieutenant Jackson falling in step beside them.

Nearing the tent, Jackson spoke up. "Your wife has made preparations for the wounded, sir."

Jason eyed her with interest. "Really now, you have given up on pacing, my love?" He arched an amused eyebrow.

"I will not justify that remark with any comment, sir." She shot him a sidewise grin. "Actually, Jack was extremely helpful. We have material for poultices as well as herbs to help ease pain."

"Good, I fear we will need them."

As they entered the tent, anguished moans of the injured, in different stages of discomfort, tore at Kathryn. Oil lanterns bathed the wounded in a mellow glow, vividly displaying the extent of their pain. At her sharp intake of breath, Jason turned, his eyes following the direction of her stare.

Moving quickly to the side of a young corporal's stretcher, she knelt and gently opened his jacket to examine the gaping wound in his chest. Lieutenant Jackson handed her a towel, which she pressed firmly, attempting to staunch some of the blood flow. Moaning piteously, his eyes fluttered open … eyes that no longer focused.

"Mother, Mother?" he whimpered.

Kathryn looked to Jason, distress etching her features. At his grim nod, she gently raised the young man's head, cradling him in her lap. Stroking his hair with great tenderness, she talked softly.

"I have ... missed ... you so," he rasped, his voice rapidly weakening, but not his pain.

She could do nothing to ease that, and it frustrated her.

"You have made me proud, Samuel, my dearest son," she crooned, gently squeezing his hand, surprised at the lack of warmth. Humming softly, she began picking out words to an English tune the dragoons sang around the campfire, singing as she rocked him gently. That seemed to calm him, as he smiled ever so slightly and weakly grasped her hand.

At the touch of a hand on her shoulder, she looked up to see Jason's slight headshake, and realized the young man was beyond caring.

"He was no more than a boy, Jason." Tears welled as she struggled for control.

With a light touch, acknowledging her sorrow, he helped cover the young dragoon.

"Come, love." He guided her away from the body with a firm hand at her elbow. "You helped ease his dying; others need your attention now."

As she saw the next soldier struggling to sit up in the colonel's presence, she quickly wiped her tears and forced a smile.

Jason crouched down to take a look at the bleeding gash on Sergeant Gilson's forehead. Kathryn quickly knelt opposite her husband, handing him the bandaging and disinfectant Jackson had supplied. Having bled freely, the wound looked to be clean, but painful.

"Colonel, please allow me to try some fir resin to ease his discomfort."

Jason watched as she took a gooey substance and gently dabbed it on the sergeant's forehead. "That will help ease your pain," she assured, mopping excess blood from his cheek and neck as her husband applied bandaging.

At Gilson's inquisitive look she answered, "Fir tree resin helps ease pain. However, Lieutenant Jackson will bring you some willow bark tea; I want you to drink it all, hmm?" She raised an eyebrow, eliciting a smile and fleeting observation: *She is so like the colonel in many ways.*

"You will be fine, Gilson," Jason concurred, as he took his wife's hand and stood.

Across the tent lay Lieutenant McCrae, his startling pallor evident even in the dim lamplight. She and Jason had enjoyed his brash Scottish wit around the campfire many evenings. He possessed the unusual ability of seeing a positive aspect to any event. Kathryn could not recall a time she had seen him depressed. Kneeling at his side, she took his hand and squeezed gently, studying him, seeking the source of his obvious pain.

"How aire ye doin', McCrae?" she greeted with a slight Scottish burr.

His eyes flickered open, and seeing her smiling face he grinned, coughing slightly. Jason crouched beside his wife and nodded to his officer, a man he held in highest regard. Lieutenant Jackson stood ready with medical supplies, but as Kathryn glanced up she was met with a grim look.

Noticing the torn and bloody leg of McCrae's breeches, she gently laid the fabric back to examine his wound. Although it was deep, there had to be more than this to cause such pallor and the glistening sheen of perspiration that bathed his face.

"Not too bad, Danny," she smiled reassuringly, but was disconcerted. Reaching out, she gently turned his chin to expose the cut along his hairline and began bathing his face with a cool cloth.

His sad eyes met hers. "Dinna waste yer time, lass." He coughed, a trickle of blood starting at the corner of his mouth. "T'is the musket ball ... in me back."

It was then she noticed his shortness of breath.

"Danny, we have an excellent surgeon ..." Her face filled with anguish as Jason leaned forward and placed a comforting hand on McCrae's arm.

"It's ... tae late ... sir," he gasped, his words coming with more difficulty.

"What can we do to ease your pain?" Kathryn's eyes glistened with unshed tears. She took his hand and gently sponged his face as he watched her, absorbing her presence.

"Dinna fash yerself, lass, t'is wurth it." Smiling at the confusion his statement had created, he continued somewhat breathlessly, "Jist last week ... I says ter Jackson, here ..." Grinning weakly at the lieutenant he coughed, then turned his eyes back to her. "T'would be wurth the dyin' ... jist ter feel ... yer gentle touch."

"Oh, Danny," she sobbed, moving closer.

Jason's hand, resting on her shoulder, gave her strength as she stroked McCrae's cheek, pushing his hair back.

"Do not go; please," a soft but futile plea.

"Dan," Jason's voice caught as he reached to touch McCrae's shoulder. "You have been a good officer and ... a friend."

McCrae had been watching Kathryn's stricken face, his breathing quickly becoming more pained and shallow. But as the colonel spoke, his eyes drifted to his commanding officer.

"Ye're ... a better man, sir ... fer all ... her lovin' you." A fit of coughing left him gasping, blood now flowing heavily from his mouth.

"Tak ye care ... o' each other." His eyes fixed on them both as he began to fade.

Kathryn leaned forward and kissed his forehead with great tenderness.

"Thank ye ... lass," were his last words.

Kathryn searched her husband's face, noticing his open grief at the loss of McCrae. Grasping her hands he held tight, neither one speaking. This encounter with Beldon's forces and *Jamie*—although a victory—had come at a high price.

Jason carefully draped a blanket over Lieutenant McCrae. Standing slowly, he pulled his wife to him, holding her for comfort.

"He was a good man, sir."

At Lieutenant Jackson's words, Jason looked up, taking note of his lieutenant's solemn face. "They are all good men," he replied, shaking his head sadly.

"Milady," Jackson spoke directly to Kathryn. "There is a young rebel over there," he gestured towards the far corner of the tent "... who has requested speaking with you."

"Jason?" She looked up, perplexed. "Rebels, here?"

He nodded. "We took a handful of prisoners, one or two requiring immediate medical attention."

She looked in the direction Jackson indicated and saw the form of a slender young man.

"Not Gabriel?" she asked, relieved when Jackson shook his head.

"Any weapons?"

Jack flashed a wry grin. "A dirk in his boot."

"I am not surprised." She rolled her eyes, shaking her head in grim amusement.

Jason's arm remained protectively around his wife as Jackson handed her the intricately engraved knife. As she admired the craftsmanship, a sense of familiarity with its detailing nagged her. With an uneasy foreboding, she turned it over slowly to examine the other side.

"Oh my God." Her eyes widened with disbelief.

Jason quickly scanned the name etched on the deadly blade. 'Ian Hamish MacLean'. "Gabriel has a brother in this war?" he asked.

"I do not see how." She counted mentally. "He cannot be more than fifteen years old."

Visibly dismayed, she slowly walked towards the prone figure with Jason at her side, his arm placed protectively on her shoulder.

"How badly is he hurt, Jack?" Glancing at his grim face, she did not want to hear the answer.

"He has little time left, Kathryn," he answered, quietly eyeing her sympathetically.

Faltering for a moment, she felt Jason's arm tighten about her and steeled herself to do what must be done. Kneeling beside her nephew, she gently lifted him and placed a rolled blanket under his head for comfort.

Frightened green eyes flew open, darting to scan the area. But as they came to rest on her, his fear fled—replaced by inner calm.

"Aunt Kathryn," he whispered. His tremulous voice held more than physical pain, and tore at her painfully.

Touching his pale cheek with utmost compassion, she bent low murmuring, "Ian … Ian." Her grief was such she could find no appropriate words.

Sensitive to his wife's anguish, Jason smiled kindly at the lad, leaning closer to touch his shoulder. "You are a brave, young man, Ian—a credit to your family."

Kathryn clasped his hand. "It has been so many years, Ian. You have become a man. But I remember when … I remember."

His breathing, although shallow, was not labored—shock having eased his pain momentarily.

"Are you warm enough, Ian?"

It was the colonel who addressed the young man's comfort, and he nodded in answer, surprised at the caring from this supposed 'black villain'.

"Your hair …" Ian hesitated, studying her in recollection. "It was always so long—curls everywhere."

Realizing she had swept it behind her head into her collar, she smiled, tugging it all forward into a tangled mass.

"Yes," he whispered, reaching weakly to touch the golden tresses, memories washing across his young face.

"I remember how you used to tug my curls." Her heart ached as his small laugh became a racking cough.

Jackson leaned down offering a cup of water, which Jason took and pressed to Ian's lips. "This will help, son."

Ian sipped slowly, his eyes never leaving the colonel's face. "You are not what they say, sir." He turned to Kathryn, gazing at her with the devotion of a child. "Aunt, you are so kind … so gentle. I have watched you with the others."

Placing her cheek against his forehead, she was distressed by the coolness, it would not be long.

"Thank you, Ian." Kissing him tenderly, she tucked the blanket closer around him.

Suddenly he turned, staring directly at the colonel. "You love my aunt very much," more a statement of fact than question.

"I do, son, she is my life," he answered with absolute honesty.

Jack stood quietly, deeply moved as he watched this child trying to die like a man—attempting to sort through his thoughts and make things right before he departed.

"Take care of her, sir," he choked, wincing with discomfort.

Kathryn held both his hands in hers, willing him to live, but knowing it to be futile.

"They will ... try to kill her ... and you." There was a long pause as he gathered strength to finish what he had to say. "They do not ... know you ... as I do."

Kathryn's eyes brimmed with tears as she met Jason's compassionate gaze across the slender form of her nephew briefly, then turned her attention back to Ian's pallid face.

"Would you play for me ... like you used to?" he managed, so weak now, his voice was barely audible.

"Anything, Ian, anything you ask." She fought to maintain control.

"Remember ... the tin whistle ... the campfire?" His breathing was short and labored.

She looked desperately to Jack, who stepped away, quickly returning with the little instrument.

Jason tucked another blanket around Ian to combat his chill, and the boy looked up smiling wanly. "What shall your aunt play?" he asked softly.

"Something ... happy." His eyes crinkled slightly in an attempted smile.

Kathryn nodded, stroking his shaggy hair back from his forehead. "I love you, Ian." She kissed him tenderly then began to play.

His eyes held hers, calm and unafraid as her lilting notes wafted through the encampment. But before the tune ended ... he was gone. Unable to contain the agony of this loss, she sobbed uncontrollably, tears rolling freely down her cheeks as Jason reached for her, and held her tenderly.

"He knew us for who we are Kathryn, and was not disappointed," he breathed softly against her ear. Never had he felt so helpless. No words could heal the sorrows of this day ... only time, maybe.

"Take her home, Jason," Jack said kindly, greatly concerned. "I will see that he is cared for properly and returned to his family."

Unable to speak, Kathryn's distraught eyes met his with gratitude. Jackson was always there whenever needed ... always there.

As Jason ushered her out of the medical tent, she turned for one last look at the young boy she hardly knew, a boy so mature for his years, robbed of time in the prime of life—a brave, young lad she would never have the opportunity of knowing.

Pausing outside the medical tent, Jason encircled her within loving arms. "Come walk with me a bit, love." At the start of a protest, he pressed a silencing finger to her lips. "Hush, now, no one will think the less of you for taking a break for a few minutes."

Her sad eyes tore at him.

"I ..." he paused, "need your company right now."

Glancing into his troubled eyes, she realized that he, too, felt the losses deeply. With a slight nod, her arm slid around his waist, and they headed towards a small grouping of trees.

Lowering himself onto a fallen tree trunk, he pulled her gently down beside him.

"I have so much for which to be thankful." She spoke first, taking his hands in hers, caressing gently as she searched his face with shimmering, green eyes. "You have returned unharmed to me. Your plan was a success. The enemy has been forced southward ... but the price has been 'dear'."

He bent forward, resting his forehead against hers as she continued speaking softly, his tension easing at her words.

"I weep for not having known Ian and now, to never have that chance. For Samuel and Danny: the knowing of them both, and the great sense of loss." She searched his face.

"Your pain and grief are also mine, Kathryn. Do not forget that." His gaze held hers, unblinking.

"We need to go back," she said firmly. "There will be time for grieving later."

"You have touched men's lives today and eased their pain, love."

"No, we have, *together*," she corrected, pressing her lips to his forehead. Smiling grimly at each other, they stood and headed back to the medical tent.

Lieutenant Jackson looked up as they entered relieved to see Kathryn calmer. "We seem to be under control here, everyone has been tended. Oh …" he suddenly remembered a message for Kathryn. "Sergeant Gilson is somewhat surprised, and very pleased to be out of intense pain."

"We will make believers of them yet, Jack." She forced lightness to her voice that she did not truly feel.

"There is another young rebel in the corner—somewhat feisty." He gave her an amused look.

The three of them walked to the far side of the tent together. As they approached the young soldier, he scowled defiantly. Kathryn knelt down to check his boots, pleased to find no dirk.

"They already found my knife," he said sullenly.

Noticing his swollen cheek, bloodied by an angry cut, she moved closer. Taking his chin in her hand, she turned his face for a better look. But, scooting up onto his elbows, he twisted away.

Annoyance flaring, she studied him for a long silent moment before speaking. "It is a minor wound; I will leave it then. You certainly will not die from that."

As Jason and Lieutenant Jackson watched, she proceeded to move down the length of his leg to where the trouser was soaked with blood. Carefully slitting the material with her dirk, she said. "This, however, could use some attention."

"Not from you, turncoat," he sneered.

"Do not disrespect my wife." Jason moved closer, his angry tone sending unmistakable warning.

Kathryn smiled, staying his arm as he reached for the young soldier, her look indicating she would handle this arrogant whelp.

Crossing his arms, the angry young man glared at her, issuing a derisive sound from the back of his throat.

"Enough," she hissed, and with a quick motion, pressed the point of her dirk against the base of his neck. "I have lost friends and kin today. Do not aggravate me further."

Arching an eyebrow, she narrowed her eyes fiercely at the young rebel, causing Jason and Jackson to eye each other with barely concealed humor.

"I owe you nothing, other than resisting the urge to kill you where you lie." Her intense gaze had a withering effect; he began regarding her with a look bordering on respect.

"I can make you more comfortable—or not—your choice."

He paled considerably at her lethal tone, combined with the sharp point of the dirk still pressed against his throat.

"If you need to say anything further, talk to me of Major Beldon's future plans, or do not speak."

He swallowed convulsively, nodding vehemently, causing her a moment's guilt as fear leapt into his eyes. Sliding the dirk back into her boot, she proceeded to examine his leg thoroughly, taking care not to cause undo pain.

"I think we could use some willow tea and a poultice, Lieutenant," she suggested, catching his eye with the hint of a smile.

Jack angled his head, smiling inwardly at her command of the situation, and stepped away to get the items she requested.

Holding the cup of tea to the young lad's lips, she ignored his protestations about the taste. One look at her icy glare, and he complied with no further argument. She stirred the mashed fir bark into a wet pulp, allowing the tea a few minutes to take the edge off his pain. She then tended his wound deftly, while her husband and Jackson looked on, handing her supplies as needed. The young rebel remained uncomplaining, watching intently as she worked on his leg.

"You are cut from the same cloth, milady," he said politely, all earlier malice gone.

Looking up, she eyed him sharply, curious at his words.

"Bold and brash like all the MacLeans." A wry grin tugged at his lips. "But Ian always remembered you as the compassionate one," he added quietly, all rancor now gone.

"You are a friend of Ian's?" she asked, searching his face.

He nodded, unblinking.

"I am truly sorry, lad." She tucked his torn pant leg back into his boot carefully. "You are both too young to have been involved in this war."

Scrutinizing him thoughtfully, she searched for a clue to his identity. "What is your name, soldier?" She extended him a bit of pride to hold onto in a difficult situation.

"Hamish MacGregor, ma'am," he said softly, his quiet appraisal of her less critical than earlier.

"That name has a familiar sound, but it has been a very long time." As she started to rise, his next question caught her off guard.

"What will happen to me?" His large, innocent eyes conveyed the fear he had hidden earlier with false bravado.

"You will be questioned," Jason answered not unkindly, as he placed his wife's arm in his, "and then taken to Camden with the other prisoners." He gave the boy a thoughtful look, and noting the flicker of apprehension in the young man's eyes, softened his tone. "You will not be harmed while under my command."

Kathryn leaned against her husband, suddenly extremely tired. As his arm slid up around her shoulder in a comforting gesture, the young soldier watched with particular interest. *Ian was correct … there is deep caring,* he realized, and in youthful inexperience, was confused.

"I will handle things from here, sir," Lieutenant Jackson assured.

Their faces registered gratitude as they turned to leave. Lieutenant Jackson: always competent, always considerate.

"Milady …"

They turned in unison at the young rebel's soft voice, and studied his serious face.

"For what you did for Ian and for me, I—thank you." He looked directly at this fierce colonel, a man well known for his cruelty, and added, "I saw what you *both* did for him."

Hamish was not prepared for the very human smile that crossed the colonel's face as he turned and ushered his wife from the tent. Then and there, he vowed he would always remember; and be less apt to rush to judgment in the future.

Back in their tent, Jason stood watching her splash water on her face as he poured them both a brandy. Turning towards him, still toweling her face, she smiled warmly.

"Can I get you something to eat? You must be famished, love."

He shook his head as he handed her a glass. "All I need is time with my beautiful wife," he murmured as he stroked the curls back from her face, nuzzling the side of her neck.

Heedless of the sloshing brandy, she forcefully set her glass on the desktop. Clasping his face, she claimed his mouth fiercely.

His glass followed hers, as they began a frenzied reclaiming … both craving the ultimate consolation always found in each other's arms … needing desperately to experience the exquisite pain of being alive.

Just before dawn, in a tender moment, he gently fingered his mother's pearl necklace where it lay delicately against Kathryn's throat, watching as her eyes caressed, speaking of everlasting love.

"Words are so inadequate …" he murmured.

Her finger silenced him, a look of deep understanding passing between them. *So many words and yet, never enough*, she thought.

Comforted within the protective circle of each other's arms, they finally relinquished themselves to a deep, healing sleep.

Chapter Nineteen

Following Up

At daybreak, and only half awake, she rolled over reaching for him and found he was gone. Instantly awake, she quickly flung aside the bed covers and began dressing, upset that he had not waked her when he arose, upset that he might have ridden out already—*upset.*

She splashed cold water on her face and began the task of taming her unruly curls. She was fighting with the tangled mass, becoming more distressed by the moment, when he walked in with coffee. Instantly aware of her agitation, he stepped behind her to gently work his fingers through her long curls. Bending to kiss her neck, he felt her tension begin to ease.

"I thought you had left." Her voice was pained … almost frail.

"Why would you think that, love?" She was upset, overtired, he would not tease her. "You know I would never ride out without seeing you first."

She eyed him over her shoulder somewhat discomfited, knowing the truth of his statement. His arms encircled her gently, his hands tenderly stroking her stomach. Placing her hands atop his, she relaxed back into him.

Resting his chin comfortingly against the top of her head, he commented, "Our little one is quiet this morning."

"Umm," she mused, enjoying the strength of his protective arms.

"Are you all right, Kathryn?"

She nodded silently, and for several minutes they remained this way, enjoying the inner peace always derived from touching each other. Finally, Kathryn steeled herself to ask the question she dreaded.

"How soon will you ride out, Jason?"

Stepping away to reach the coffee, he offered her a mug and answered quietly, "I told the men about half an hour." He paused as her exquisite, green eyes met his bravely. "Is that enough time for you to have some breakfast and be ready to ride with us?" he asked.

For a second she was not sure she had heard correctly, and stood just staring.

He smiled and kissed her cheek. "The expression on your face is priceless, my pet."

"You are not teasing, are you?" she demanded.

He could see her excitement building as he shook his head in answer. Quickly setting her coffee down, she armed herself with her dirk and pistol.

"I believe you could use the diversion, Kathryn. And quite honestly, if your brother does intend to retaliate, it would make sense for him to strike our camp, looking for you, while he thought I was gone."

"One never knows what Jamie is thinking," she replied, as she tucked her tomahawk into its customary resting place at the small of her back. "But to ride with you for a purpose is a special privilege." She smiled gratefully, reaching up to kiss him.

"You may not want to thank me tonight, after having ridden long miles and eaten lots of trail dust. But it is good to see you smile." His hand brushed her cheek, then wrapped around her shoulder as they headed out to join the men.

Kathryn rode out, flanked by Lieutenant Jackson and her husband. She pushed all thoughts of yesterday from her mind, concentrating on the business at hand. As there could easily be colonial stragglers, she must not risk being lost in sad memories. Plenty of time for that later—and yet, no amount of wishful thinking, or 'if only', would change what already was.

Breathing deeply of the wonderful aromas of a warm, summer day, her heart filled with appreciation for what she did have in life. Her glowing face was not lost on either her husband or Lieutenant Jackson. High spirits seemed to be the order of the day. Even the horses sensed the mood as Beauty playfully nipped at Diablo, causing the big charger an amount of discomfort at being harassed by the little mare. Kathryn chastised Beauty, reminding her that this was business, she must act accordingly if she wanted to be included again—a reprimand that thoroughly amused both men.

Then and there, Jason made a decision: include Kathryn on more of these minor forays. She handled herself well under duress, and her skill with weapons could match many men. What other woman would find such intense happiness under these conditions? *She is truly amazing, my wife.* Smiling to himself, he vowed to make a concentrated effort not to worry over her.

Midday they broke for refreshment in a small wooded glen, a lazy brook providing fresh water for drinking, as well as washing some of the grime from their perspiring faces. In almost no time, they were on their way again, covering large areas in a zigzag pattern. Late afternoon, as they turned north towards their encampment, they had their first encounter with the rebels.

Gunshots erupted, scudding up puffs of dirt several feet in front of Diablo. Beauty's shorter legs allowed her to immediately rein to a standstill, and Kathryn's pistol, braced across her forearm for accuracy, fired with deadly accuracy. A colonial staggered from his hiding place in the low bushes, dropped his rifle and fell to the ground.

Jason and Jackson, astride their two big chargers, were slower to rein to a halt. As they whirled to protect Kathryn, guns drawn, she waved them forward into the chase as Beauty closed the gap between them.

The dragoons, having plunged ahead, were heavily in pursuit of the snipers, the attack almost over before it had begun. There were about a dozen rebels, of which three were taken prisoner, the rest slain outright.

Kathryn sat astride Beauty, working at controlling her prancing horse, while Jason shouted orders to his dragoons and checked the identities of the dead.

"Very nice shooting, Mrs. Tarrington," Lieutenant Jackson praised, a wide grin spreading across his face.

Kathryn faced him, ignoring the compliment—deadly serious. "If only I can prove myself, assure him that I will not be a hindrance, and that he does not have to worry about me. I want so desperately to be part of these men's lives."

"Kathryn," he exclaimed with gentle exasperation, attempting tolerance at her repeated concern. "Jason has absolute faith in your abilities. The only thing he must learn to control is worrying over your safety. That is a valid concern and to be expected when you care deeply about another person." He gave her a long look. "If you may recall, I watch you pace when he is gone."

"Leave it to you, Jack, to point out my frailties." But her statement held no rancor. "You do have a way of reminding me to confront life honestly," she remarked, grinning.

As Jason approached, she turned to greet him, her brow furrowed—questioning.

"Jamie is not with them," he said, much to her relief. "Although they profess not to have seen him, I suspect he visited our encampment today."

She shrugged. "I refuse to worry about him, Colonel. We will encounter him at some point—or we will not. I shall deal with that situation, if and when it occurs."

"By the way, excellent shot today, madam. Remind me never to irritate you." He grinned widely, but beneath the teasing words lay a deeper understanding; his eyes flashed praise, thrilling her.

They arrived back at their campsite well after dark, not overly surprised to find that the 'devil's spawn' had been there. The sudden attack had ended rapidly when it became obvious to Jamie that the targets of his ire were missing, along with most of the dragoons.

***

Jamie had ridden in with a handful of men, sure that after the previous day's victory the colonel would be relaxing on his laurels. He was certain he would take them by surprise, knowing beyond doubt he would kill Tarrington outright, but as yet—reserving judgment as to his sister.

When he found the colonel had left camp, taking Kathryn with him, Jamie's fury, mostly at himself, could hardly be contained. In complete disgust, he called his men off and headed back into the woods, deeming it no sport to kill a cook and a handful of young recruits.

As he rode away from the dragoon's encampment, it struck Jamie like a thunderbolt: *That son-of-a-bitch is as wily as she.* The intricate strategies which had caused Major Beldon's fiasco had her name written all over them. But this protective move of keeping Kathryn with him, knowing Jamie would dare to come for her out of embarrassment at being outmaneuvered by his sister—that was all Tarrington's doing. He cursed fluently. *They are strong as individuals, but as a team are formidable.*

Twice in two days running, they had caught him unprepared, having assessed his moves and countering them perfectly. He had been humiliated in front of his men, although they would never voice such a thought out loud. And yes, he had to admit, he was hurt. *How can my little sister turn against me?* Embarrassment or hurt—he was not sure which emotion was more repugnant—but neither set well. He hoped the possibility of talking to her would present itself at some point; if not, he would accept what he saw at face value … and deal with her accordingly.

With a great deal of work rebuilding Beldon's forces still ahead of him, and much lost ground to regain, he tabled his anger with Kathryn for the time being. There was no doubt in his mind that the day would come when the colonel, and Kathryn if need be, would be his for the taking; he would bide his time until then. With that thought firmly placed in mind, he kicked his horse into a gallop, signaling his men to keep up the pace.

***

Supper was jubilant as the dragoons bantered amongst themselves, pleased with the day's outcome. Continued weakening of Beldon's scattered troops, added to the previous day's success, was good reason for high spirits. But when they began singing her praises, Kathryn squelched them gently.

"Every man here does a good job, and does not expect to be singled out for praise. Please treat me no differently."

Extremely uncomfortable, although each dragoon's face reflected only appreciation for her acknowledgment, she asked for the tin whistle and started to play. Within moments, all had returned to normal and she relaxed, enjoying the evening surrounded by 'her family'.

That night, as Jason and Kathryn sat having a brandy in their tent, they eyed each other smiling.

"What are you thinking?" she asked.

"Many things," he mused. "How very good it felt to have you with me today. How proud I am at the way you handled yourself—both on the field and around the campfire tonight. And, you *are* 'handling'... Jamie."

She rose slowly and moved around the desk. Pushing his chair back, he extended his arms, encircling her waist as she settled herself astride his lap. Draping her arms casually on his shoulders, she began releasing his long hair from its queue. As she massaged his temples, gently running her fingers slowly back through the full length of the silky, black mass, he studied her face. Despite the sorrow of the previous day, there was an undeniable inner serenity and warm glow about her.

"You were happy out there today." He brushed a stray curl behind her ear.

She closed her eyes and smiled, remembering the feel of Beauty beneath her, her husband's strong presence as he rode straight and proud beside her, and breathed a whispered, "Yes ... oh yes."

He eyed her thoughtfully, shaking his head. "I was afraid that would happen, my love." He sighed deeply.

Placing both hands on her bottom, he picked her up and deposited her on their bed. "Is there something that I might do for you, madam?" His words held a playful lilt.

Within the breath of two sentences, their teasing entertainment turned to a much more fulfilling game of carnal pleasure.

Later on, as they relaxed contentedly, Kathryn snuggled into his shoulder trailing loving fingers across his chest.

"He will be furious," she stated.

"You are reading my mind again." Running a finger along the bridge of her nose, he watched the changing expressions on her upturned face. "Twice now, within two days, we have out-maneuvered him, Kathryn; that fact will not set easy with a man of his pride."

They were both silent for a minute.

"Perhaps I should speak to our men, to explain the situation." Her eyes held his, deeply concerned. "He will target me as well as you from now on."

As Jason began to disagree, she interrupted, "Jamie has been embarrassed and hurt. I know him, Jason; he is slow to forgive ... or forget."

He hugged her, accepting her statement. "I will talk to the dragoons, Kathryn. That is not something you must do." He stroked her hair idly with great tenderness. "At times I wish ... But that only achieves frustration." The sadness in his tone touched her.

Shifting up onto one elbow, she gazed down with love-filled eyes and whispered, "Heart of my heart, always."

"Will you join me tomorrow?" He doubted the threat of Jamie being close would daunt her, but felt he should ask.

"After today do you really think I could stay happily in camp?" Her sparkling eyes met his.

"There will be occasions, Kathryn, when I shall not ask you to accompany me, and I will brook no argument at that time."

"We shall discuss that at the time, sir," she answered dutifully, not wishing to irritate him.

His serious look, and all further discussion, was cleverly diverted as she placed his hand against her stomach to feel a new life asserting its presence.

As she settled beside him sleepily, he whispered, "I do believe you are putting on a little weight Mrs. Tarrington."

Glancing at her stomach, she wrinkled her nose. "I hope you will like a plump wife, sir. I really am beginning to round out a bit."

"Never fret, Kathryn." With a light kiss to her forehead, he became serious. "I think we should tell the men in the near future."

She would realize his underlying reason, heightened safety for her, but would not compromise her independence by voicing the fact.

"I leave that to your judgment, love." She yawned sleepily as he hugged her, happy at the thought of having her ride with him on the morrow.

The next morning Jason left her brushing her hair while he went to get coffee for them to enjoy in privacy, after which they would join the men at breakfast. Whatever information he had shared, when they arrived at the campfire a little later, the men greeted her with warm smiles.

Leaning close, speaking quietly, she asked, "May I assume this reaction from the men is not a result of information about my brother?"

"Actually, their reaction to that was not one of concern," he assured. "But they found our other bit of news quite fascinating."

Lieutenant Jackson approached and sat down obviously pleased with the way the day had started.

The dragoons rode out for another full day of eating dust, and a quick meal on the trail. They fanned out to cover an even larger area than the previous day, but found the rebels had successfully disappeared into the 'forests and mists'.

"We are near Keowee, Jason." Kathryn eyed him with disquiet. "I am sure Jamie has gone to friends."

"Why are they still friendly with him, after he rescued you ..." He left the thought unfinished; she understood his underlying question.

"Their fight is not with him but with me. I did not return to fulfill my obligation after I left Jamie. Though perhaps, it is not even with me. It was not I, who killed Black Raven." Her eyes clouded with memory.

"It is of no matter, love. However, do you feel that continuing to chase the rebels in this direction will gain us any advantage?" He rested his hand gently on her arm.

"He has gone, at least for now. I fear our time is wasted here. It might serve us better to turn towards Charleston and discover what awaits us there. We may still find stragglers along the way."

"My thoughts, exactly," he replied.

Nodding agreement, he signaled the dragoons to head for 'home'.

Arriving back at camp in late evening, the aroma of a pungent stew filled the air. Cook had kept the fires going and a hot meal waiting. The horses were quickly bedded down, and then the men met for a much-deserved meal. The dragoons ate with relish, their spirits high, despite the lack of rebel encounter—there would be more opportunities in the near future.

As they relaxed to the music of the tin whistle, and played a few hands of cards around the fire, they were suddenly interrupted by an approaching rider accompanied by one of the dragoon pickets. Jason stood to receive the soldier, who identified himself as a messenger from Cornwallis's headquarters.

Kathryn looked slightly nonplussed as she turned to Lieutenant Jackson. "Inquisition time," she muttered, and at his questioning look added, "Mark my word; Cornwallis will expect us to join him for luncheon within the week."

Jason broke the seal, opening the official looking correspondence from his lordship. He looked it over slowly, his face betraying none of his inner thoughts. Nodding 'thanks' to the rider he indicated refreshments and bedding would be provided, then moved to Kathryn's side.

"Your invitation, milady." He smiled, extending the neatly written parchment for her perusal.

"Duty calls," she sighed, turning to Lieutenant Jackson. "What did I tell you? We are expected in three days time for a one o'clock meal."

"We break camp tomorrow and head north. Let us call it a day, gentlemen; get some rest." Extending a hand to his wife, he drew her up to his side. Bidding his lieutenant 'good evening', he and Kathryn headed for their tent, arm-in-arm.

"This may not go too badly, Jason. I will answer any questions with honesty and hope my words will convince him of my loyalty. He will have to decide for himself."

Jason toyed with her necklace as she spoke. "I am not concerned, Kathryn. He has already indicated he likes and respects you."

He smiled into her upturned face as he removed the pins from her hair, uncoiling it to lie in a golden mass on her shoulders. "Come, love, tomorrow will be a busy day; let us get some sleep."

But seductive eyes peered up through curling lashes, capturing his heart and dashing all his good intentions.

Eventually they slept, his hand gently placed on her slightly rounding stomach in a protective gesture for his child.

Chapter Twenty

Lunch with his Lordship

By habit, Kathryn awoke early the next morning, a fact which allowed her plenty of time to pay special attention to her appearance. With Jason's approval, she was wearing her wedding day outfit: dressy, lace-front blouse and crisp, tan breeches. Pretty dresses were a useless commodity in her lifestyle, his lordship might as well get used to that fact early on. As she finished patting her long curls into place and began pinching color into her cheeks, Jason entered the tent.

Setting their breakfast on the desk, he folded his arms and leaned back appraising his wife, his immediate smile easing the concern reflected on her furrowed brow.

"You are lovely, Kathryn," he assured, grimacing, adjusting himself to ease his discomfort.

"I gather you approve," she chuckled, grinning devilishly.

Casting a chastising look from under an arched brow, he slid a mug of coffee towards her. "Eat your breakfast, madam, so we may be on our way. I fear we shall not get there at all, if I am closeted with you alone much longer."

As he held the chair for her to sit, she smiled up over her shoulder, laughter twinkling in her eyes at his look of feigned severity.

"Somehow you have a way of diverting my attention from the duties at hand." He placed a light kiss on the top of her head.

"Tonight, sir, you will pay for looking so handsome—and for rushing me."

With a quick hug, he moved to take his seat.

Sitting opposite his wife, sharing a simple breakfast, he recalled their recent wedding vows: their acknowledgment of abiding love, and was unable to take his eyes from her. Seeing his mother's pearl necklace lying against the lace at her breast filled him with inner contentment. Glancing up, their eyes met, caressing openly.

As if by prior arrangement, both abruptly stood. Stepping around the desk into a welcoming embrace each murmured the other's name.

"Are you happy, Kathryn?" he paused, breathing into her hair. "Happy with me?"

She stared into his startling blue eyes, surprised by his question.

"You are my life, Jason, you and no other. Yet how do I find adequate words, my love, to express the depth of my feelings?"

"I see it reflected in your beautiful eyes every time you look at me, my Kathryn. And know always, it is returned to you tenfold."

Their kiss was tender, lingering, as they connected emotionally. For a few moments longer, they relished the joy of merely holding, touching. Finally separating, they stood back eyeing each other.

"I am afraid we really must be on our way, Kathryn. I would not purposely displease his lordship."

"Well, at least not on our first invitation to lunch," she said.

With a gentle pat to her bottom, he ushered her from the tent. Immediately outside, Lieutenant Jackson was waiting patiently with their horses saddled and ready. At his concerned questioning for their safety, Jason assured they would keep to the main trails and return before dark. "However, Jackson, if it eases your mind, meet us halfway with several dragoons late this afternoon."

Jackson nodded, greatly relieved. He would not put it past Kathryn's brother to try another attempt at taking her, or even both of them. He would be there at the appointed time for the return ride back to camp.

The morning displayed cloudless, blue skies, but promised a hot day to come. Retaining the coolness of the previous night, the air as yet, was still fresh and new. They cantered out across the dew-covered fields, the horses anxious to run. Kathryn glanced over at her husband as he turned to her, smiling. Inhaling deeply, she sorted the different aromas wafting on the slight breeze, enjoying each one fully: leather, warm horses, sweet grass and the tangy scent of tall pine trees dotting the nearby slope—all so familiar yet newly appreciated.

As the beautiful mansion housing Lord Cornwallis's temporary headquarters loomed into view, she found herself sorry to have arrived so quickly. The warm companionship she and Jason shared was ending all too soon, quiet treasured moments, which she clung to protectively.

As they entered the library, Lord Cornwallis looked up from the papers he had been discussing with Ferguson. Appearing not to be surprised by her attire, he smiled warmly. Major Ferguson's expression, however, was one of barely concealed dismay.

"Good day, milord," she greeted brightly. "And to you also, Major Ferguson."

As she approached his desk, Cornwallis observed her feline grace appreciatively. He could easily understand the colonel's attraction to her mode of dress, one that so well accentuated her long, lean form.

After a few superficial pleasantries and time allotted for them to freshen up, their luncheon was served around a pristine, linen-covered table on the verandah. Before sitting down, Kathryn moved to the porch railing and stood for a few moments, drinking in the beauty of the estate. Manicured lawns sloped to a small pond where ducks and geese swam in slow, lazy circles. Delicate weeping willows gracing the water's edge, trailed myriads of drooping boughs along the mirror-like surface, creating a memorable pastoral scene.

Their luncheon was excellent, obviously planned with great care for their visit—a flattering realization for Kathryn. With a silent prayer to her mother for having taught her excellent dining manners, and pleased at having retained them, she relaxed and enjoyed the veritable feast. Table conversation was benign, of no lasting importance; but that would not last. There would be questions, of that she was sure.

As they sipped tea after the final plate had been cleared, Cornwallis finally got to the crux of the matter.

"Colonel, would you allow me to speak to your wife—alone?"

It was not a request.

Kathryn quickly stood. The moment she dreaded had arrived.

Pushing his chair back, Jason started to rise, but she stayed him with a gently placed hand on his shoulder. "Please, your Lordship, I request that Colonel Tarrington remain here while we talk."

Lord Cornwallis appeared somewhat disconcerted, but eyed her with growing interest. However, regarding her bold audacity contemptuously, Major Ferguson's shocked look turned steely.

"I do not ask for the colonel's sake, milord. As an officer under your command, he will leave as requested, and later accept my word for what is discussed between us." She met his look with an unwavering one of her own.

Cornwallis pushed his chair away from the table and leaned back, keenly interested in what she was about to say.

"I ask for my *husband's* sake," she stressed the word, "that he be allowed to join us. A bond of trust exists between us that has been tested in the past, continues to be tested—and prevails. Yet it is a new and fragile bond that I would protect at all cost."

She glanced momentarily at Ferguson, and then returned full attention to Lord Cornwallis.

"As words may be so easily misconstrued by a simple inference or gesture, I would have my husband judge for himself the content of our conversation today—rather than by interpretation from another party at a later time."

Jason squeezed her hand gently under the table. Major Ferguson looked slightly aghast at her boldness, but Cornwallis sat in deep thought, studying her. "You are fiercely devoted to the colonel."

She detected surprise in his statement. "Unashamedly, milord; he is my life."

"As Kathryn is mine, milord," Jason said firmly, the depth of feeling in his tone not lost on the general.

"Your wife is as eloquent as she is beautiful, Colonel." He regarded Jason thoughtfully. "Join us, then; I see she has nothing to hide."

Jason sat down, but Kathryn remained standing. The general indicated her chair, but smiling prettily she declined.

"She paces milord," Jason interjected, smiling up at her.

At Cornwallis's amused stare, she leaned slightly forward placing both hands flat on the table. Looking first at the major, and then back to the general, she asked politely, "What do you wish to know?"

"There are so many rumors about you two, that out of my own curiosity, I would hear the truth of the matter from you."

"We have talked before of the questionable reliability of rumors, milord." She straightened, placing her hands loosely in her pockets, completely relaxed, enchanting the general with her boldness.

"Let me see if I can guess what piques your curiosity most." Starting to pace, she paused frequently to make eye contact with one or the other of the two English officers.

"I was caught spying on the colonel's encampment, rather innocently as it were," she paused sending her husband a private look. "I had been searching for any members of my family who might possibly be still alive, and just happened upon his camp." She decided it was unnecessary to mention the other part of her mission—ultimately ending up in the Cherokee village of Keowee—it had no direct bearing on her English loyalties.

"My presence was quickly brought to the colonel's attention." Grinning widely, she looked down at Jason as he sat with fingers tented, looking rather amused.

"How can I put this delicately, now?" She paused. "After we shared a brief discussion, it became necessary to strike a bargain. Fortunately, he accepted my offer; we have been together ever since."

Stepping back to the table, she again leaned forward and placed both hands flat on the cloth.

"You see that beautiful forest over there, General?" He looked where she indicated and then returned his attention to her. "I was born not far from here, just beyond that forest. My family is small, honest, hard-working—well-read." Her hesitation was lengthy as she thought through her next words carefully.

"Patriots, rebels, colonials, call us by whatever term you choose."

Cornwallis hung on every word, fascinated by her confident, honest manner. Major Ferguson, however, stared intently distancing himself, as he dissected her words, forming pointed questions of his own.

"I understand our farm has been burned, although I have not seen it for myself as yet. My father and mother are both dead. My brother, whom I had thought dead, seems to be very much alive; or so I have been told. Though I have not seen him in many months, he would be a formidable foe if not on your side." Discussing Jamie made her uneasy, but she had to be honest for Jason's sake as well as her own.

"And just what side is he on?" Major Ferguson's sarcastic question interrupted her train of thought.

Jason tensed, but Kathryn moved behind his chair and placed a calming hand on his shoulder before she answered. "He is with the rebel militia: Colonel James Douglas MacLean. I am sure you have heard of his exploits."

"And you would have us believe that you would renounce your past and be true to the English cause with a brother like that?" Major Ferguson interrupted sharply.

Jason started to rise, angry at the uncalled for attack on his wife. Placing both hands on his shoulders, Kathryn stayed him with light pressure.

Lord Cornwallis turned, piercing his major with a withering glance. "That tone of voice is out of line, Major. Mrs. Tarrington is here for a luncheon—not an interrogation." He turned back to Kathryn. "However, that is not a totally inappropriate question when phrased with less hostility. Go on, milady."

Feeling Jason relax under her reassuring hands, she continued, "You will believe what you wish, gentlemen, no matter what I say. But for what it is worth, I have proven myself committed to the English cause more than once."

As Jason started to speak in her defense, she interrupted softly, moving around the chair to look him directly in the eyes. "Please allow me, Colonel, to defend myself that they may judge me alone, thereby casting no reflection—either good or bad—upon you." Her warm smile acknowledged gratitude; he inclined his head ever so slightly in answer.

"Major Ferguson, I sense you wish to know if guilt and regrets, or family pressure would change my choice. Guilt is a self-deprecating emotion on which I have no time to waste. As to any regrets? Only that were there not a war dividing us, I truly believe we could all be friends. Would I conveniently take up their rebel cause under direct pressure from my brother or …" She trailed off, moving to stand beside Jason, again placing a hand on his shoulder.

"There is one reason, and only one, that I am here."

Jason's hand slid up to rest on hers, the wide gold knotwork of their wedding bands throwing shards of light and creating a bold statement.

"This man alone; as long as he is with me I will defend him, and his cause, with my life … even against my brother."

At that statement, Jason stood up and encircled her waist with his arm. "Kathryn," he murmured softly against her ear.

But Major Ferguson was not done yet; she was too cocky, too self-assured. "You claim you are loyal to our cause," he challenged with a malicious grin, disbelieving.

"Despite my heritage, I have proven my loyalty beyond doubt, sir. You have no right to question me in such a manner."

"I have every right, madam." His voice turned surly.

Bristling at his use of that term in addressing her, she leaned closer, planting both fists firmly on the table that separated them, pinning him with a fierce glare. Jason tensed, remembering the violent eruption this gesture had precluded a few months back.

Lord Cornwallis started to intervene, but thinking it more interesting to watch her in action, sat back quietly to observe.

"I have been informed that you played a most important role in the planning of the recent encounter with Major Beldon's troops," Ferguson stated coldly.

She nodded, eyeing him uneasily. Where was he going with this line of questioning?

"I understand we lost several excellent men. Was that due to poor planning or perhaps some other reason?" His voice held an accusing edge.

Furious beyond words, unable to contain her rage, she slammed both fists on the table, causing plates and silverware to clatter, startling all but Jason. Leaning in close to the major, a muscle twitched in her jaw as she hissed, "Yes, plans which ultimately caused the death of my nephew, a fifteen year old boy with his whole life ahead of him," she spat. "... and I watched him die." Her last words were no more than a hoarse whisper.

Jason moved quickly to her side, placing a comforting hand gently in the small of her back. For the briefest instant, her fury lingered as she glowered at the speechless major. Then she straightened slowly and stepped back from the table, taking measured even breaths—fighting for restraint, struggling to regain her composure. Glancing quickly at Jason, assuring him she was again in control, she turned her attention once more to the major.

"Major Ferguson, dislike me as a person; that is acceptable. But never question my loyalty again—never!" she hissed, skewering him with a withering gaze.

General Cornwallis sat mesmerized. *What an incredible temper—such passion she displays. And yet, with no more than a gentle touch and knowing look from her husband, she quells that fiery temper, suppresses her outrage.*

He had seen her do the same for the colonel's violent nature upon occasion. *An incredible couple; and what a dynamic bond unifies them.* He watched Kathryn face her husband, noting what silently passed between them ... a look of such intensity the air surrounding them seemed to fairly crackle ... and marveled at the strength of their devotion.

Major Ferguson, aware of their deep feelings for each other, found the fact annoying. Was he angry with this man who regularly bested him in many areas? Was he jealous of the fact that the colonel had a prize he, himself, had never been able to attain? Or was he angered that a colonial, the term was offensive to his finer sensibilities, could command the respect of Lord Cornwallis? He was not sure which aggravated him more but decided, at least for the moment, to cease analyzing further.

"My apologies, milord, for my inappropriate actions, there is no excuse for such a display of temper ..."

Cornwallis stepped around the table, interrupting her. "I am truly sorry about your nephew, Kathryn. It must be a bitter pill to swallow." With a quick hug, he took her arm.

"Let us enjoy tea down by the pond. A little walk and fresh air would be in order, I believe."

As they headed out across the lawn, Cornwallis spoke with sincerity. "I believe in you completely, my dear. Major Ferguson will do the same, because I say so." He eyed Ferguson meaningfully, creating a cool truce between them.

"I had to be sure of your loyalties, milady, as your influence with the colonel of our dragoons is of utmost importance," Ferguson said softly, almost apologetically.

Kathryn nodded, not particularly believing his explanation, but ready to take the conversation in a different direction. They paused, taking fresh tea offered by the butler, and watched the ducks paddling contentedly in the pond. Kathryn sipped slowly, absorbing the beauty surrounding her for several minutes before turning to Cornwallis.

"Milord, I have read a great deal about your battle strategies and am fascinated."

Jason watched her closely, not entirely sure where this conversation was going.

"You have had great success, so far," a quiet statement of fact.

"Madam?" His lordship was piqued.

Undaunted, she proceeded to explain, "You have a tendency towards arrogance, milord."

Jason tensed as the general's color began to rise. But Kathryn was not intimidated by either the major's angry look, or his lordship's high color.

"Do not underestimate the rebels," she warned. "They are far more than ignorant farmers. They believe in their cause wholeheartedly, and will fight with the tenacity of bulldogs against all odds. I know this for a fact; I know my brother and those who follow him. Our schooling may not be that of fine English officers; perhaps more aptly described: an education gleaned from hard work, constant struggle to survive in a new land, and a devout love of freedom for that land."

They all listened intently.

"Do not sell them short, milord. Pride and arrogance go hand in hand, often preventing one from seeing the truth of a situation, until sometimes … it is too late."

"How dare you insult his lordship in such manner?" Major Ferguson stepped towards her in a menacing gesture, but Jason moved between them shielding his wife.

"I do not presume to insult, Major," she answered calmly. Standing tall, she placed both hands on her hips and moved to face him without fear. "I merely point out a truth which may help you in battle, if you can step back and analyze with an unbiased mind."

At that moment, Cornwallis spoke up. Initially angered by the perceived insult, he slowly acknowledged her words. He had not become a great general through ineptitude or lack of attention to statements that rang of truth.

"You are correct, Mrs. Tarrington," he said, as all three turned to face him. "You anger me because you have pricked my pride." His look softened. "You are an incredibly perceptive woman: discerning, fearless, defiant." He studied her intently.

"All the qualities of a rebel, milord, do not disregard that fact." Her smile was friendly, filled with warmth.

"I will consider all we have discussed here today," he said thoughtfully. "I would also like to make a request that your *husband*," he emphasized the word, "and you, will return for a visit in the near future; one of fewer questions and far less intensity."

Jason nodded as his arm slid around his wife's waist.

"Come, let us take a walk, it is such a delightful day." His lordship turned to his major who still looked somewhat nonplussed. "Swallow your pride, Major, and join us."

Nodding assent, Ferguson actually allowed himself to smile at the couple.

"You know, Colonel, you are a lucky man."

"I am that, milord."

"You are also a changed man, and those changes are good," he said thoughtfully.

The general smiled at Kathryn. With her directness and candor, she was a multi-faceted gem. He would weigh her words and try to heed her reprimand. Yes, he found himself already looking forward to their next visit.

"Perhaps, when I next see you, Kathryn, we might spend time discussing how to impress upon Colonel Tarleton the necessity for change." He shot a sidewise glance to his major, Tarleton's best friend, before turning back to Kathryn and adding, "As your husband will be riding more often with his cavalry in the future, I think you may find it easier if you can come to terms with the man."

At the anxious look spreading across her face, he patted her arm.

"But we shall worry about that next time."

"It has been a delightful day, milord, but it is time for us to return to camp. Might we take our leave?" Jason asked formally, more than ready to end the visit. Kathryn, with that last bit of information about Banastre, would be extremely anxious to be on her way.

As their horses were brought around, Kathryn strode to Beauty and reached to grasp her saddle.

"Madam," Jason stepped quickly to her side, his tone causing her to pause. "Do allow me to assist you, Mrs. Tarrington." Cocking an eyebrow and flashing a wicked grin, he dropped to one knee, basketing his hands.

At his humorous expression, she laughed out loud and stepped into his cupped hands, quickly mounting Beauty. "You are bound and determined you will make a lady out of me yet," she pouted, leaning down to kiss him.

Shaking his head, he patted her thigh and moved to Diablo's side.

General Cornwallis turned to Major Ferguson as they watched the pair trot down the gracefully arching driveway.

"I do believe they write books about such relationships."

"If I had not seen with my own eyes, I would never have believed the changes in the colonel," Ferguson said, having softened his opinion some.

"She is absolutely correct Major. She irked us because she was bold enough to point out our faults. We have been given a chance to reassess our views of the enemy. If we are attentive, we may learn a great deal from this woman."

Cornwallis remained quiet for a moment, then looking directly at Ferguson said firmly, "When she returns, there will be no further questions as to her loyalty. Do you understand?"

Well aware that she had represented herself flawlessly and convincingly, Ferguson nodded grudgingly.

"We had best remember she has a brother out there, and a nephew, if all we hear is true. I fear they are all cut from the same cloth as this passionate woman. And we had best not dismiss their threat too easily." Cornwallis became pensive.

"Rumors are often exaggerated your Lordship. However, in Mrs. Tarrington's case, I suspect that what we have heard of her fierce loyalty and defense of her husband is probably a great understatement."

The more Ferguson thought about her, the more impressed he became.

"Yes, Major, let us wish the colonel a long life. I fear she would become a formidable enemy if he were gone."

Having experienced it himself, Cornwallis knew of devoted love. His thoughts suddenly drifted to his ever-faithful wife, Jemima, and their two children back in England, missing them—especially his beloved wife. Her last correspondence had been extremely disconcerting, having informed him of a strange and lingering illness that continued to hold her in its unrelenting grip. Yes, he loved her dearly, but the incredible oneness of the colonel and his wife was rare, and beyond his comprehension.

As the two men turned to reenter the mansion, the major reached out and touched Cornwallis's sleeve.

"Look, milord," he directed the general's attention to the fields beyond the house where Kathryn and Jason could be seen galloping their horses.

Kathryn's mare raced ahead leaping a log with the colonel's charger in close pursuit. Suddenly the little mare slowed and Kathryn, arms flung wide, hair tumbling wildly about her shoulders, turned her face up to the sun with eyes closed, absorbing its warmth. With no perceptible instruction from her mistress, the little horse performed various sidesteps and turns as Jason watched, enthralled. Arms flung wide and face aglow, Kathryn sat her saddle with ease as Beauty reared prancing, and then dropped into a bow.

"Look how she manages her horse," Major Ferguson said, impressed. "That looks to be ..."

"Dressage," Cornwallis answered.

"Yes, but how would a colonial ..." He stopped mid-sentence.

"Major, the next time Mrs. Tarrington speaks of arrogance blinding us to the truth, please *do* listen."

The major nodded somewhat embarrassed. Both men stood, continuing to watch, mesmerized by the grace and ability of both Kathryn and her little mare.

As Jason and Kathryn had left the mansion, anxious to be away, they trotted their horses along the gracefully curving driveway—both silent—each immersed in their own thoughts.

With an abrupt change of mood, needing to release pent up emotions, Kathryn decided to take Jason on a merry chase. Flashing him a challenging look, she 'yipped' to Beauty. Both horses, always eager to run, needed no encouragement. Relieved that their command performance was finally over, elated to share his wife's zest for life, Jason seized the moment and rose to her challenge. Putting the tension of the luncheon behind him, he charged after her at a breakneck pace. That was all the inspiration Kathryn needed; the performance was on.

"Showing off, my pet?" Jason laughed as he nudged his charger forward.

She grinned impishly, nodding eagerly. As he came abreast of her mare, she stood in her stirrups, leaning to throw her arms around her husband's neck, kissing him soundly.

With one smooth motion, he lifted her from her saddle and settled her on his lap. Tangling his fingers in her long hair, he returned the passionate kiss. She thrilled to his taste and touch, reveling in the instant arousal pressed boldly against her thigh.

"My God, wife," he gasped. "Get back on your mare; else I will be forced to take you right here in this field—in front of the major and his lordship." He chuckled, nuzzling the arch of her neck.

Grasping his hand, she placed it against her stomach, eyeing him over her shoulder. Bending somewhat awkwardly, he kissed her abdomen with extreme tenderness, and with a pat to her bottom, settled her back onto Beauty.

Speaking softly to the prancing, high-strung animal, Kathryn reined her in tightly beside Diablo.

"Then I have a promise when we return to camp, sir? You are not angry with me?"

His eyes captured hers as he reached to cup her cheek. "Angry or not, you always have a promise, my love." He caressed her cheek with his thumb. "But angry about today? Never; how could I possibly be, when you honor me so? Come, let us get home."

"Yes, Jackson will be worried." Thoughts of his unwavering selflessness brought a smile.

As they disappeared over the crest of the hill, Cornwallis turned to Major Ferguson and shook his head, grinning.

"They cannot keep their hands off each other, and I guess it is no wonder. She is child-like one moment then defiant; passionate, courageous and decidedly intelligent—an unusual woman. Who could not love her?"

Stroking his chin, momentarily deep in thought, he suddenly remembered a gesture of the colonel's which finally registered; his face wreathed in smiles.

"Well, I will be damned."

At his lordship's unusual expletive, Major Ferguson paused, regarding him inquisitively.

"She is carrying his child—amazing."

He was still shaking his head, pleasantly surprised and content with the knowledge as they reentered the manse.

The low slanting rays of the sun indicated the day had grown old. It would be well after dusk by the time they reached their encampment. As they approached a copse of mixed pine and oaks, Lieutenant Jackson and four dragoons rode forward.

"I am glad to see you, Lieutenant; our day ran much longer than expected." Jason's smile softened the slight formality he still maintained with Jackson in front of his other officers.

Kathryn pulled abreast, pleased with Jackson's constant concern for their safety. "You are a welcome sight, Lieutenant, thank you." Her smile flashed gratitude and affection. "It was an interesting visit. We will have much to discuss over coffee."

The lieutenant and the dragoons fell into a protective formation flanking their colonel and his wife as they turned towards home. The trip was fast paced and uneventful, a fact for which they were all grateful.

Riding into camp well after dusk, they were pleased that Cook had saved a hot meal. A spicy stew answered one of their needs; bidding an early 'goodnight' to the dragoons, they headed to their tent to answer the other.

Within the quiet walls of their tent, Jason encircled his wife in a loving embrace, drawing her snuggly against him. Sparkling, green eyes sought his as her breathing escalated in response to his touch.

"I believe I recall a promise, milord husband." Her voice was breathy with anticipation.

"As always; you are correct, my love."

His lips traced the arch of her neck, eliciting a small groan.

"I intend to fulfill that promise … thoroughly."

And he did.

Chapter Twenty-One

Jamie

Several weeks had passed since their luncheon with Lord Cornwallis. Kathryn rode with Jason on a regular basis in their continued effort to keep the rebels fragmented, and unable to group in significant numbers to pose a threat. Her reputation was growing along with that of her husband, a fact which pleased Jason, yet caused greater concern for her safety. She was not to be denied on these small forays; as long as she could sit astride Beauty, she would ride with him. *End of discussion.* And he had to concede, her expert marksmanship had served them well more than once. Extremely successful in their strategies, encounters with rebel factions became fewer and ended quickly, with minimal injuries and no further fatalities amongst the dragoons.

Several prisoners had been taken to Camden after questioning by the colonel. Interrogation of these stubborn rebels was futile and frustrating, producing no useful information. Though often urged by fellow officers to use a means of torture Jason resisted: he had put aside that phase of his life.

Strangely, nothing had been heard of Jamie: as if he had vanished into thin air. Neither Kathryn nor Jason was fooled. He was biding his time, waiting. Several raids on English supply wagons bore his signature style, though none of the captured rebels would admit to knowing him.

Cornwallis maintained his efforts further north, continuing regular communication with Jason. His lordship was being unduly pressured by Commander-in-Chief Clinton, who wished to be relieved of command. Frustrated from lack of supplies, empty promises of new troops, lingering fevers and general ill health continually plaguing his army, Clinton took out his angst on Cornwallis. Attempting to maintain control in New York, while keeping a vigilant eye on situations in Canada, was becoming an overwhelming task. And now, to add to his woes, trouble had begun to escalate in the south.

As if that were not enough, the powers in England failed to understand the difficulties of the American situation. Unable to comprehend the wily character of these colonial upstarts, his superiors back home continued making absurd demands he could never fulfill. All in all, Clinton was more than ready to withdraw from his post with his dignity, more or less, in tact.

Ever confident in his own abilities, Cornwallis was confident he could improve the situation by taking over the command, but had pressing matters of his own—matters he wished to discuss with Colonel Tarrington. Each correspondence to Jason included a personal message for Kathryn, and she never failed to send a response. There was much to admire in this man, albeit he annoyed her upon occasion. His lordship's most recent communiqué requested they return north for an important meeting. Beyond alluding to discussions involving future campaigns in the south, she sensed there was something pressing—something of a more personal nature.

Aware that Colonel Tarleton would be present, Kathryn was less than eager to attend, and conspired to do everything in her power to delay that inevitability. She could still hear the silky arrogance in Tarleton's voice, overly confident of the handsome figure he had presented at Cornwallis's ball—and it irked her.

Kathryn had become acutely aware of her growing girth. Although rapidly approaching her time, her stomach appeared only modestly rounded, a greatcoat and billowing shirt usually covering her condition. She smiled thinking of Jason and his reaction to her blossoming shape. He loved to lie beside her in the evening, his head resting with utmost care against her stomach, rubbing its fullness gently 'for good luck'. Unwilling to have her suffer insecurities or doubts, he regularly reinforced his love—constantly reassuring, and sharing his thoughts on coping with an infant—as well as their military duties.

They sat enjoying a brandy after dinner, having chosen to eat within the privacy of their tent; they would be on the road north to meet Cornwallis before dawn. Kathryn had toyed with her food, overly quiet and reserved, her tension emanating in waves.

"Kathryn, dinna fash yerself, lass." His Scottish lilt drew a tight smile; he had her attention.

"What troubles you so, love?" Taking her hand, he gently traced her fingers with his thumb.

At a non-communicative shake of her head, he pressed for an answer. "Talk to me, Kathryn." He lowered his head to meet her eye-to-eye, capturing her gaze and holding it with concerned blue eyes. "Do not shut me out, love, please."

She shook her head, eyeing him in silence.

"Our baby?" he asked quietly, stressing mutual responsibility to relieve thoughts she might harbor of the 'problem' being hers alone. He waited for an answer, his consternation growing, but still no response. She could be so damned stubborn upon occasion.

"Kathryn."

From his exasperated tone, she knew his patience was wearing thin. He was not thrilled about making this long journey north either, and she was not helping the situation. Reaching out, she touched his cheek tenderly. "Lots of little things of no consequence, I guess," she muttered.

He took both her hands, cradling them between his, rolling her wedding band slowly as he watched her expressive face.

"Jamie …"

At mention of her brother's name he tensed. "What of him?" he asked gently.

"I have not 'sensed' him in months, but suddenly I feel him … here." Retrieving one of her hands, she placed it against her chest. "Do not chide me, Jason," she warned, silencing him before he could form his answer. "Over the years, we have 'sensed' things about each other. Somehow, he knew when I was in trouble at Keowee. I never contacted him; he just knew." She shrugged. "I 'sensed' that his wife, Mairi, was dying when I was still many weeks journey from their home. We 'sense' each other, not only in times of need …"

Jason eyed her intently before speaking. "I actually do understand, love. There have been times before we met, when I would have inexplicable feelings of being a part of something, or someone. I used to think perhaps it was my grandmother sending encouraging thoughts."

It was now Kathryn's turn to scrutinize her husband.

"More than once, I have experienced a second sense, a premonition, gut feeling or whatever you wish to call it—it has served me well in battle."

Her look of pure relief touched him.

"As you know, my pet, you and I also share the same unusual 'connection'. We read each other all too well … and often."

Quickly she moved to him, accepting outstretched arms welcoming her onto his lap. Their kiss was tender, reassuring and comforting as she snuggled against his shoulder. Stroking her hair gently, he rocked her.

"When do you think we might hear from Grandmother?" she asked softly.

"Soon, I hope. But we will write again after our child is born, whether we have heard or not."

Both sat quietly content, holding each other and drawing inner strength. His fingers slowly began tracing small circles on her round stomach, and within moments, an insistent kick rewarded him.

"I will be sure you have a long, extremely elegant shawl to drape around your shoulders at any required dinners while we are at Cornwallis's headquarters. Do not fret so, love."

He cupped her face with utmost tenderness and brushed a kiss to her forehead. Feeling the path of a tear on her cheek, he hugged her closer, holding her until she relaxed against him limply, her breathing having become deep and even. Carrying her to their bed, he covered her with a light blanket, leaving her fully clothed so as not to disturb her much needed sleep.

Later, as she lay cradled in his arms, many thoughts flooded his mind. She was tired. The child took what it needed, often leaving her energies spent, the closer she came to giving birth. Being so adoringly stubborn, she never knew when to give in. Cornwallis's demands for this military meeting came at a bad time. As soon as they completed that obligation, it was imperative they turn south and head down the Charleston Path to find Anna. Just tonight, he noticed the child had shifted lower. He knew nothing about childbirth, but this did seem to be an indication that her time was drawing near.

Aware of Jackson's experience in this area, he would catch him alone when they could talk privately. If the child would not wait, at least there was a doctor at 'The 96', about one hundred miles closer than Keowee. As Kathryn was relying heavily on Anna for courage during the birth, and act as a nursemaid afterwards, he would do everything in his power to find her. He nestled against her back, breathing in the scent of her, more at peace than any time in his life. The Charleston Path had brought him salvation before, in the form of Kathryn. He was certain it would be their salvation once again, either with the arrival of Anna, or finding a good doctor, when her time made it necessary.

Murmuring his name, she turned sleepily, reaching for him. "Why am I still dressed, love?" she mumbled against his chest, beginning to come awake.

"Sleep now, my pet," he crooned. "I will make it up to you in the morning." He hugged her closer as she faded slowly back into sleep.

Well before dawn, she slipped out of her clothes and pressed the warmth of her nakedness against her husband. Sleepily he reached for her, his hands caressing. "I love you, my Kathryn," he breathed huskily against her throat … and fell to loving her properly.

It was late afternoon as they approached the stockade fence of Cornwallis's headquarters. It had been a long, dusty ride at a rapid pace, and Kathryn was feeling the effects. Jason flanked her right side, Lieutenant Jackson her left, four officers brought up the rear.

The gates stood open as a man, a colonial officer from his dress, strode through them preparing to join a small group of mounted men waiting immediately outside.

Jason leaned closer to Kathryn. "This must be the result of Clinton's new rule of pardon," he said disgustedly.

At inquisitive looks from both Kathryn and Jackson, he explained, "Any captured colonial or loyalist, who swears loyalty to King George, will be pardoned." He rolled his eyes for effect.

"Why that is the most naïve statement I have ever heard. Does he truly think the likes of my brother and his followers would ever swear allegiance—and actually hold to it?"

Kathryn was incredulous, but Jackson merely smirked. Engrossed in the absurdity of it all, she failed to pay more than a cursory glance to the small gathering by the gate. But Jason had taken note: that particular colonial looked familiar.

They reined to a stop just inside the gates where Major Ferguson stood watching the departing colonial. To Jason's questioning look he replied, "Clinton's pardon." Shaking his head in disgust, he shrugged, but remembering his manners, greeted Kathryn and the others pleasantly. "General Cornwallis is expecting you." He smiled his customary tight-lipped smile.

Attention focused on Ferguson, Kathryn failed to see the colonial officer turn, watching intently as they prepared to dismount. At a sharp whistle, Beauty's ears instantly pricked. Rearing, she spun abruptly, trying to locate the source of the familiar sound. Had Kathryn been any less competent a rider, she would have been thrown.

Jason fought to control Diablo as he sidled nervously away from the agitated mare.

"Hold, Beauty, hold," Kathryn commanded sternly, grasping her mane as the little mare began to respond. "Hold!" she hissed sharply. As the mare turned towards the gate reacting to another shrill whistle, Kathryn spotted the colonial officer, hands on hips, grinning widely at her. Finally obeying her mistress, Beauty ceased her prancing and stood calmly, continuing to watch the man at the gate.

"Damn you, Jamie," she spat.

Kathryn's leg swung over the mare's head as she slid to the ground. Dropping Beauty's reins, she strode towards her brother. Hair bouncing, long curls swinging with each step, she closed the distance between them.

"Remember, Mrs. Tarrington, they rode in under a white flag and have been pardoned," the major admonished, as she brushed past ignoring him.

As she approached her brother, his hand slid quickly inside the back of his coat. In a swift motion she, too, reached to the small of her back, seizing her tomahawk. Snatching their weapons in unison, they both dropped into a threatening crouch, facing off against each other.

Jason leaped from his charger, pistol drawn, quickly moving to his wife's side as all eyes turned towards the menacing pair.

With a laugh, the colonial officer suddenly stood and tucked the tomahawk back into his breeches, a grin spreading across his face. "Ahh, Kathryn, lass, I taught ye well. You are fast." He nodded approvingly.

Continuing to glower, she relaxed her stance and thrust her tomahawk back into her belt.

"I taught your mare well too, didn't I?" he chuckled, drinking in his sister's presence, slipping easily into their familiar Scottish brogue.

"I am not amused, Jamie." She scanned his face, a face she had not seen in many months, a face she would probably never see again—except behind a rifle.

Jason holstered his pistol and stepped to her side, placing his hand on her shoulder in a protective gesture. Glancing up, she flashed a brief smile of gratitude.

Complete silence reigned as all watched, mesmerized by the scene unfolding before them—tension escalating. Jamie observed the look which passed between his sister and the colonel with bitterness. "Then it is true what Gabriel has told me," he stated with a mixture of resignation and confusion.

Placing her hand on Jason's chest, displaying the wide gold knotwork of her wedding band, she nodded. No further words were necessary.

"Then you have chosen, Kathryn," he said icily, his eyes suddenly changing, reflecting smoldering fury as he glanced to Jason, and back to her. Beneath his fury, anguish was evident. They locked eyes, years of love and memories passing wordlessly between them.

"Jamie, remember how it was between you and Mairi? Your love was such you could not look at each other without the need to touch." She spoke quietly, her eyes never leaving his.

He regarded her sadly, precious memories playing across his face, and nodded ever so slightly.

"It is so between us. We do not choose where we find love, Jamie. It chooses us." Her eyes beseeched him to understand.

Only the pawing of fretful horses broke the tense silence as all stood riveted, unable to tear their eyes from the drama unfolding. Without warning, Jamie moved forward, abruptly clutching her to him in a bear hug. Briefly, he allowed his hand to tangle in the mass of golden curls he had always loved to tousle, resting his cheek against hers. Jason stood aside allowing the contact; but remained watchful for any indication of harm aimed towards his wife.

As Jamie held her, he became aware of the roundness of her belly; abruptly his expression changed to outraged shock. "You carry his child," he gasped, on a swallowed sob.

"Yes, proudly," she answered fiercely.

For a moment his icy control failed him, his steely visage collapsing, and eyes distraught. Then, just as suddenly, he regained his composure. "I love you, Kathryn," he choked hoarsely.

"As I do you, Jamie," she whispered, encircling his neck in loving arms. Returning the hug, she placed a soft kiss on his cheek.

With a brush of his lips across her forehead, he broke from her, knowing in one more moment he would weaken, beg her to reconsider and come with him.

"For what you did for Ian," He could not bring himself to face the colonel and thank him. "I will be forever grateful. But for what you did to me with Beldon's forces ..." His face contorted with pain at the remembrance of that deceit, but quickly changed: his eyes hardening with icy resolve.

"When we meet again, I will kill you." His voice dripped pure venom. With a fierce uncompromising stare, he scanned from Kathryn to the colonel, then back to his sister.

"Aye, MacLean." The Scottish burr rolled easily off her tongue. "Or perhaps, I will kill you." She met his unwavering glare with one of her own.

Jason watched compassionately as the drama played out. These two fiercely proud individuals, who loved each other desperately, would turn their backs on each other for a far greater need and passion: Jamie's passion—gaining freedom for his fledgling country, and Kathryn's—for the love of her colonel. *For him*—the enormity of this disclosure washed over him in waves. This woman he loved so dearly, stood strong in the face of all odds. Somehow, she had found strength to cope with losing her nephew, Gabriel. She deeply mourned the death of his younger brother, Ian, yet had rebounded—and now this, a final 'goodbye' to her only brother. He admired her incredible strength and fortitude; but how much more she could withstand?

Kathryn and Jamie stared, unblinking, mixed emotions chasing across their faces. *This is forever.* The finality cut like a knife and both, though suffering visibly, fought to conceal it.

Jason moved closer, and placing an arm around her shoulder, pulled her to his side. Jamie watched with open resentment as she leaned against her husband. Damning protocol, Jason bent to kiss the top of his wife's head, hugging her gently.

Sliding her arm around his waist, she returned his hug. Looking up, she searched his face; tormented blue eyes stared back.

"Always, my love, never doubt," she reassured.

"Kathryn," his voice faltered, husky with emotion as realization struck. Despite bidding a final 'goodbye' to her brother, her first concern was for him—reiterating her absolute commitment.

When she turned back, Jamie was just swinging up into his saddle—so like her. It was then that she saw Gabriel, watching her with open compassion. His intense gaze captured hers and held as he inclined his head ever so slightly. Eyes never faltering, forcing a thin smile, she returned the gesture, grateful for his understanding.

"Jamie …" Her voice broke as she suddenly called out to him.

Reining his horse in, he turned, impaling his sister with smoldering intensity.

Making an outward motion of her hand from her heart, she spoke in fluent Cherokee. Wincing, he repeated the phrase and gesture. With one last sorrowful look, he spun his horse and galloped from the enclosure with his men in close pursuit.

Jason moved to her side. Feeling her tremble, aware of the toll this farewell had exacted, he encircled her in a firm grip.

The English soldiers commenced talking in hushed tones amongst themselves as they watched the rebels disappear over the horizon. But Kathryn, unable to watch Jamie's departure, not wishing to be questioned lest she break down, headed for the main house.

Jackson's face searched hers with concern as she approached. Pausing beside him, she forced a smile. "Would you take care of Beauty for me?"

"Of course, milady."

For some reason, his necessary formality broke the tension of the past few minutes; she found she could actually smile.

"I am all right … I am," she assured, and turned to her husband as he reached to take her arm.

"What was that all about?" Major Ferguson demanded acidly, flustered at the colonel's disregard for protocol: showing open familiarity with his wife in front of the troops.

Kathryn stopped in her tracks, glaring at Ferguson. Before she could say anything, Jason interjected curtly, "I believe it was rather obvious, Major Ferguson. My wife was saying a final 'goodbye' to her brother."

He then ushered Kathryn up the steps into headquarters. In the vestibule, away from prying eyes, he took her in his arms. Nothing he could do or say would diminish her hurt. She clung to him, quietly drawing strength. Despite extreme emotional turmoil, she was acutely aware of the incredible changes in her husband. He was compassionate, loving, and supportive, but of greater importance: trusted her implicitly. She looked up, her eyes proclaiming her abiding love, as he bent to kiss her.

Major Ferguson came up behind them, and clearing his throat loudly, growled, "I will announce your arrival to the general." He remained dispassionate, haughty.

"Allow us a few minutes of privacy, Major. My wife needs my consideration at the moment."

Making a disparaging sound, Ferguson headed for Cornwallis's office.

Kathryn reached to touch Jason's cheek. Searching his eyes, she detected the barest hint of uncertainty reflected there, despite his attempt to conceal it. Their love was still new, untried; she would not have him worry.

"Never doubt my love for you, Jason; it will only deepen with time. I have made the right choice in *you*." Her eyes caressed. "I have no regrets, none."

He leaned close, running his fingers repeatedly through her long, golden curls, studying her beautiful face. "May I ask you about one thing?" he said softly.

"That was a Cherokee phrase; but our own hand-sign." So attuned to each other's needs, she did not have to hear Jason's question in order to voice the answer.

"*Good bye. My heart travels with you.*" She shrugged. "Over the years, we fought, parted and made up so often, we created our own parting tribute."

"Much like you and I share," he said softly against her hair.

"Similar, my love, but nowhere near the depth of what we share." She paused in deep thought. "He is my brother and I love him."

Reaching up with both hands, she gently cupped Jason's face, holding his gaze. "But what you and I share goes way beyond love. You, my husband, are my heart, my soul, my whole life. Never forget; never doubt." Pulling his head down, she claimed his mouth passionately.

"The general will see you now," Major Ferguson interrupted brusquely.

Jason stiffened, but Kathryn forcefully calmed her breathing and stepped back. Smiling her gratitude, she turned a beaming face to the major, astounding him.

"We are coming now, Major," she said pleasantly, and linking arms with her husband, followed him down the hall.

Lord Cornwallis observed them sharply as they entered. He sat at a long, highly polished table with brandy glasses and decanter close at hand. His glass, partially empty, attested to the fact he had observed her from the window, her display having caused concern.

She would correct his unrest immediately. It had been one thing to attend a private luncheon and speak her mind. However, they were here by direct order attending a meeting of military importance concerning her husband's command: she would not risk impairing his career.

"Milord, it is good to see you, would that it had been under less stressful conditions," she spoke up quickly, hoping to open the subject for immediate discussion: to settle and put behind them.

Lord Cornwallis, with a quick nod of greeting to Jason, returned his attention to Kathryn. "Might I be so bold as to inquire just what, exactly, transpired between you and that colonial officer?"

His lordship's tone was curt. He was playing games; she must be cautious and get it over with quickly. If she thought too much, she might break down.

"I am sure you are aware that man was my brother, your Lordship." She met his gaze, resolutely.

"He used the name, Cameron, I believe." His voice sounded constricted, and though obviously annoyed, he attempted to keep a level tone. He suspected he had been duped by the colonial, but awarded her time to explain, and defend herself.

"I am not surprised, milord. I have used that name myself." She shot a sidelong glance at her husband as he squelched a smile. "That was our mother's maiden name."

"Why would he do that?" Cornwallis looked to be at a complete loss.

"My brother was attempting to create dishonor for Colonel Tarrington and myself, milord."

"I do not follow your line of thought Mrs. Tarrington."

"Jamie was here claiming loyalty to the Crown in order to receive a pardon, for himself and the others, under Clinton's new dictate. Am I correct?"

His lordship nodded, disgusted with the premise.

"If he had used his real name, you would have ignored the dictate and hanged him on the spot." She looked to Cornwallis, pausing as he gave a quick nod, agreeing. "Jamie was sure his pardon would eventually come to my attention. I would recognize his ruse and be placed in an awkward position. If I claimed ignorance in knowing his identity, I would soon be exposed for my deceit: many are familiar with my background. Having proven my absolute loyalty, I have not felt it necessary to hide my identity. He hoped I would be branded traitor. That would take care of me, and my husband's career would be forfeit … or worse."

Cornwallis admired her honest appraisal—nothing held back. Her face was pale, a haggard look about her eyes giving testimony to the afternoon's trauma.

"In Jamie's mind, he would at least accomplish embarrassment for me and my husband. And he has done that, for which I am truly sorry if it reflects in any way upon you, milord." She paused, her face crumbling slightly. Taking a deep breath, she regained composure and continued. "What he did not count upon was my being here. It was a difficult meeting … a final 'goodbye'." Her voice was hushed, threatening to falter altogether.

Jason stepped immediately to her side and rested his hand on her shoulder. Automatically she reached up, covering his hand with her own, displaying the beautiful rings the general found so fascinating. He regarded them in silence, thinking what a magnificent couple they made. He truly admired this woman and surprisingly, was beginning to reassess and *like* the colonel.

Having known Colonel Jason Tarrington for some time, he had often been witness to his callous treatment of both men and women alike. The display he had observed from his window this afternoon, a vantage point from which he could easily discern reactions of all three involved, had shown the colonel to be quite a different man. He possessed an inner calm and obvious compassion. Yes, he liked this 'new man'.

Already aware that Kathryn was with child, he had scrutinized her carefully as she entered; she was close to term. He needed their cooperation, hers especially. Now was not the time to add to her grief, her distress would impact upon the colonel. He would see to it that no further mention was made of this day. Clinton's dictate was unenforceable and ridiculous. Cornwallis found it gratifying, that although they both realized that fact, they were too polite to make mention of it.

He smiled and poured more glasses of brandy, offering each a drink. "I am afraid I am not a good host. Come, sit down Kathryn." He took her hand and escorted her to the settee. "You must be exhausted from the long ride."

Jason stood beside her, his hip touching her shoulder lightly as they talked of superficial pleasantries. Cornwallis watched her quietly sipping the brandy, slowly beginning to re-center and relax—a result of her husband's proximity rather than the brandy, he was sure.

Major Ferguson watched Kathryn intently, finding her silence irritating. "Mrs. Tarrington, you would have us believe …"

"Major," Cornwallis interrupted sharply, stopping Ferguson mid-sentence.

Kathryn closed her eyes, shaking her head sadly. "What do you want from me, Major?" she asked, so tired that Jason leaned closer in a protective stance. "I cannot believe you still question my loyalties. Why would you request my help in discussing details of the areas around Charleston, Savannah and Camden if you honestly think me a traitor? Would you not be concerned that I might send your armies into the wilderness or into Cherokee lands, thereby stressing your questionable truce? Or perhaps lead you into the hands of the rebel militia—or, worse yet, to Jamie?" She was calm, patient, as if explaining to a child.

"Well, Major, do you have an answer for Mrs. Tarrington?" Cornwallis was curt, embarrassing Ferguson with his fierce scrutiny. But he had warned him not to attack her.

As Major Ferguson had no suitable answer, he picked at her again. "What was that language you spoke with your brother?"

"We said farewell in Cherokee. Having lived with the Bird Clan for many months, I speak the language fluently." Noting his spark of interest at that disclosure, she stated crisply, "And I do not intend to discuss that part of my life today, or soon for that matter."

"You never cease to amaze me, Mrs. Tarrington," Cornwallis said admiringly as he refilled her glass. "Sometime I would like to hear more about the Cherokees, but only on a non-military level, and only what you choose to share." Inclining his head with a smile he added, "You *are* allowed to retain some modicum of privacy—although it is small." He chuckled, his attempt at light humor finally breaking the tension.

Acutely aware of Jason's hip pressed against her shoulder, proud of his adherence to protocol dictated by this situation, her courage rebounded.

"Major." She eyed him narrowly, a confident edge returning to her voice.

She stood slowly and removed her coat, boldly displaying the roundness of her figure. She had observed the general's glances to her waistline earlier; he was aware of her condition. Jason watched proudly, knowing what she was about to say.

"My loyalties lie with those of my husband. I carry his child—our child."

She grinned at Lord Cornwallis who sat studying her, smiling benevolently, having thrown protocol to the wind. "I believe you were already aware, milord, you never miss the smallest detail."

She returned her focus to Ferguson, the blush rising on his square-set face washing his pale complexion to a rosy pink. "You cannot truly believe, Major, that I would consider endangering the father of my child—or any of the rest of you for that matter." Her eyes held his, demanding he trust her, causing Major Ferguson to turn away—flustered and at a loss for words.

"Major Ferguson."

At her crisp tone he turned, and confronting eyes twinkling with deviltry, was taken aback.

"I believe you enjoy sparring with me." She placed her hands jauntily on her hips facing him with a wide grin. "And I imagine that once we get past this 'loyalty issue', we will have much to debate."

The slightest smile began to play at the corner of his lips as he softened.

"You are a worthy opponent, sir," she complimented, continuing to smile as she donned her coat with Jason's assistance.

Cornwallis stepped forward chuckling, smiling first at Jason, then Kathryn. "You are honest and forthright as always, Kathryn." His eyes conveyed genuine warmth. "Congratulations to you both."

He then turned to Jason. "Colonel, cocktails will be at seven. I have invited several officers and their guests to join us for dinner."

"Yes, milord," Jason inclined his head with appropriate dignity.

"I believe your wife needs time to rest," he suggested. "I will have you shown to your room. Tomorrow will be soon enough to talk of business."

"Thank you, milord. I look forward to dining with both you and Major Ferguson," Kathryn said lightly, her eyes dancing mischievously as she glanced at the slightly disgruntled officer.

As the general's aide opened the door to their room, gesturing politely for them to enter, it was all Kathryn could do not to gasp audibly. She maintained dignity barely long enough for the man to leave.

"Good heavens, Jason, people really live like this?" She turned, scanning the opulence of their quarters. Their saddlebags sat on a low settee centered between two large windows swathed in drapery running from floor to ceiling; yards of cascading elegance. The incongruity of their rough leather bags and the rich fabric was striking—almost humorous.

To the far right, on a low sideboard, stood pitchers of fresh, cool water and drinking glasses. Slightly set apart sat two hand-painted, porcelain basins of steaming water, accompanied by heaps of soft towels and two bars of imported English soap. Kathryn shook her head in disbelief.

An elegant cut-glass decanter of brandy, surrounded by delicate snifters, sat dwarfed by a bouquet of exquisite roses on a highly polished table. Stepping to the flowers, she inhaled deeply, enjoying their delicious fragrance.

Turning in a circle, observing carefully, she struggled to grasp the need for such wasteful luxuries. The room boasted of Georgian refinement from the canopied bed to the mounds of soft pillows piled amidst numerous comforters; tasteful colors of understated elegance. The top covers lay folded neatly at an angle displaying silky sheets that beckoned to be touched, and that is exactly what she did—awestruck at the fine quality.

Turning to her husband, she announced solemnly, "I do not see how we can possibly consider sleeping in our tent again."

His expression proved she had caught him off guard. With a laugh, she moved into his arms, hugging him. "How can people live like this—so much excess?"

"For a moment I feared you might demand a change of lifestyle, my pet."

"Never," she shot back, leaning into him, suddenly exhausted—the afternoon's trauma exacting its toll.

"Oh, Jason," a ragged sobbed escaped. "I … hold me tight, I cannot bear the thought …" She searched his face, her distraught eyes revealing deep aching loss and overwhelming fear: fear of recrimination from Jamie's idiocy, fear for their babe, fear that Jason might be forced to … All consuming fear.

"I shall never let you go, my Kathryn … never." He understood completely. "I will not give you up, nor lose you under any circumstances."

Tears began to chase in wet rivulets as she buried her face into the protective warmth of him, losing herself to his comforting embrace. Her shoulders shook with deep wracking sobs as he held her, crooning softly. Lifting her, he strode to the bed, settled her carefully and joined her. Pulling her snuggly against him, he held her as she cried. Her anguish was his also, to be shared as one, but despite sharing, cut so deeply. He grieved for her, and struggled to select words which might provide solace … if any could.

"*Gv ge yu a*, my Kathryn, always," he whispered. "*Gv ge yu a*, I love you with all my heart."

His use of Cherokee … *I love you* … caught her attention, calming her.

She reached for him and held tightly, needing him desperately, his enduring love and immeasurable strength, her *'safe port'* in every storm. "*Gv ge yu a*," she murmured over and over, "my husband, my heart and soul."

"*We* will survive, my love," he assured. Dropping his forehead to hers, he murmured, "We are as one, my Kathryn, always."

Yanking a comforter over them, he began softly quoting from *The Minstrel* and within moments felt her steady, even breathing. *Damn Jamie straight to hell.* There were no words to soothe this wound, only the sweet mercy of time. All he could offer was assurance of his abiding love, and pray that would help.

They slept soundly, both needing to recuperate from the exhausting demands of the day. The sun was low in the sky as she roused. Scanning their room, momentarily vague as to the lavish surroundings, her eyes came to rest on her husband. Jason stood across the room, clad only in boots and breeches as he leaned into an ornate mirror, shaving.

"Feeling more rested, love?" he asked, eyeing her in the mirror. Turning, he smiled at her sleepy appearance as he toweled his face, deeply relieved to see her again serene and composed. Her recuperative powers never failed to amaze him.

"Umm." She stretched languorously, her eyes showering warmth.

Moistening a cloth, he wrung out the excess and moved to her side. Pushing straggling curls back from her forehead, he gently sponged her face.

"This too will pass," she whispered, touching his cheek. "I have you; I need no other."

Taking her outstretched hands, he drew her up into his arms.

"*Gv ge yu a,*" she whispered. "How did you know?"

He grinned. "There is much I have learned, my Kathryn, yet I have barely scratched the surface."

"I fear you are doomed to spend several lifetimes with me, my love … and thankfully so." She glanced towards the window. "However, I had best hurry," she said ruefully, breaking from his embrace. "I would not want to give the fodder mills a chance to grind further."

Tugging her new dress down over her shoulders, she settled it about her hips. Turning to eye herself in the full-length mirror, she watched how the skirts billowed. This had been Jason's surprise to her recently; he had chosen well. Although the bodice clung, enhancing her obvious attributes, the skirt was voluminous, masking her pregnancy quite effectively. The gown was a shimmering fabric of indescribable green that matched her eyes flawlessly. Although she hated to dress up, she had to admit it did look stunning. Her husband never ceased to amaze her.

Jason sat on the edge of the bed watching as she smoothed the new gown into place on her shoulders, pleased to see her happy with his choice, and the way it fit.

"Well, I suppose if we have to go down into the lion's den, you had best help me with these infernal buttons." She pouted beautifully.

Stepping behind her, he nuzzled her neck. "You smell delicious, my pet. I do believe his lordship brought that soap from England."

She smiled happily. English Lavender was one of her favorites; an exquisite and rare treat. "The buttons, sir, we are running late," she reminded, turning her back and grinning over her shoulder.

With a delicate touch, he trailed his fingers ever so seductively along the ridge of her spine causing shivers to cascade in delicious ripples.

"Colonel, if I recall, it was a similar move that got you into this situation in the first place."

He laughed heartily, wrapping her in a warm embrace. "How I do love you, Kathryn."

Although savoring his nearness she ducked out of his arms, sending a stern look before turning again, allowing him to fasten the buttons. "Our social obligations come first, sir," she chastised.

This time he started to work at the small pearl orbs in earnest. With the closure of the last one, he signaled her to pirouette so he might appraise the overall effect. Her hair was swept back from her face, fastened to tumble in a single long, curling ringlet over one shoulder.

"Something to go with your gown, madam." He pulled a small package from his jacket and opened it.

"Jason," she gasped. The earbobs were delicate, green stones twinkling within gold settings.

"They match your eyes," he stated proudly.

"And the gold matches my necklace." Her hand encircled the ever-present pearl that had belonged to his mother. "I … I do not know what to say."

"Your eyes say it all, my love, words are not necessary."

Her face glowed, all traces of sadness and exhaustion gone. Quickly fastening them to her ears she angled her head, showing them off.

"You really do take my breath away, Kathryn."

Her smile continued as she put finishing touches on his lace jabot, tweaking it into perfection just as a knock came on the door and a succinctly proper British voice announced: 'cocktails within ten minutes'.

As Jason started buttoning his jacket, he saw his wife reach under a chair, grab her boots and begin to tug one on. "Kathryn, really now …" He shot her a look, arching an eyebrow.

"Are you forbidding me to wear my boots?"

Plunking her fists on her hips, she eyed him sharply.

"I would not dare forbid you my dearest wife, merely requesting that you wear your party shoes." His grin was wide, infectious.

"Oh, all right, because you asked nicely." Returning his grin, she slipped into the delicate slippers which matched her gown. "I will never understand why women choose to wear these pinched things. Besides, as I am not supposed to show my ankles in polite company, no one would have known."

Silencing her with a laughing kiss, he placed a light shawl of exceptional detail and length across her shoulders and nudged her towards the door.

"Know that I will never allow you to feel insecure or be hurt by any given situation if it is within my power to change it." Seeing a single tear tarry at the edge of her eye, he gently thumbed it away.

Swallowing deeply, she took his arm properly. Then, casting a chastising sidelong glance, she said, "If you have occasion to ride into town again, sir, I must request permission to accompany you. You are too extravagant when you decide you must spoil me."

Eyes turned as they were ushered into Cornwallis's library for cocktails. Kathryn was slightly taken aback at the thirty or more officers and ladies that mingled about the room. That was not her idea of 'a few' guests. But she took a deep breath, and with her hand resting lightly on her husband's arm, rose to the occasion. With the arrival of what seemed to be the last of the invited guests, she breathed a quiet sigh of relief that, at least, Lady Antonia was not present.

"I am pleased to see you looking more rested, Mrs. Tarrington." Lord Cornwallis approached and bent to kiss her hand.

She curtsied deeply, smiling with genuine caring. For all his pomp, she liked the man. But something was slightly amiss. Although smiling, she sensed an inner sorrow that had not been present on their last visit, one that with her own trauma, she had failed to notice. She met his gaze, her eyes, questioning. With the slightest inclining of his head, he indicated they would talk later.

"Your wife is radiant, Colonel. Care for her well, life is too short."

Jason acknowledged the statement, somewhat confused, taken aback. Something was not right. But there was no time to ponder his lordship's words further as Major Ferguson stepped forward. He took Kathryn's hand with new warmth and definite respect, inclining his head to both of them. *Perhaps he has finally decided upon a truce*, she thought. *Now we can enjoy arguing merely for the sport.* She would like that.

As they worked their way around the room, greeting people they knew and making introductions to others, Jason's hand rested protectively in the small of her back—*right where my tomahawk should be*—she smiled at her inappropriate thought. Would she ever get used to this?

Jason caught her look, knowing her thoughts, and bent to speak softly. "I am afraid you would find occasion to use it before this evening is done, madam. Hence, your dirk remains in our room."

She shot him a sidelong glance. *He senses my thoughts all too accurately.*

Nudging him discreetly, he followed her line of vision, noting Lieutenant Jackson standing at the far corner of the library, drink in hand and a lovely, young lady standing at his side—obviously quite taken with his good looks. Kathryn was pleased he had been included; Cornwallis was not always so magnanimous in his invitations. However, Jackson was watching them, immune to the young lady's charms, definitely uncomfortable.

Kathryn smiled broadly as Jason greeted Lieutenant Jackson and his 'companion'.

"You look beautiful tonight, Mrs. Tarrington," he said quietly as she blushed, and Jason's eyes narrowed. "Beauty is well attended, as well as Diablo, sir," he added quickly, attempting a new topic for discussion while trying to tear his eyes away from Kathryn.

Kathryn stepped in; graciously including the smitten young woman in their conversation as she stood quietly hanging on Jackson's every word. Jason silently applauded his wife's attempt to find the lieutenant a partner. Much to his chagrin, despite his best efforts, he was still *jealous*—and of all people. Of course Jackson loved Kathryn; he had known that for some time—confident he would never compromise her in any way. But *knowing* did not stop jealousy from rearing its ugly head upon occasion.

Scanning the room, he noticed several others eyeing his wife with open admiration. But one look at her love-filled eyes, following only him amidst all this temptation, made it obvious she was immune to all others, as was he. They had staked their claims on their wedding day. A lesson had been learned tonight, one he must remember and adhere to: do not waste time on jealousy: a useless emotion. Being so attuned, she sensed what had taken place; no discussion necessary. She had learned that particular lesson, only sooner, the evening of Cornwallis's party—with Lady Antonia.

A loud greeting, hailed from halfway across the room, suddenly interrupted her thoughts. There was no need to turn; it could be none other than Colonel Tarleton. He swept to her side, all but ignoring Jason, and kissed her hand flamboyantly.

"Colonel Tarleton; how pleasant to see you." She almost bit her tongue in trying not to hiss.

Jason greeted him politely, although coolly. One way or another, she must learn to work with this man. Though Jason slightly outranked Tarleton, they agreed it would go more smoothly if he was not reminded of that fact. Better to have him watching their back, than trying to put a knife in it.

Dinner was eventually served, sumptuous and lasting overly long with several courses. But Kathryn's patience was rewarded as dancing followed. Gliding gracefully around the ballroom floor, she gazed up at her husband. "This is one part of 'polite society' I truly enjoy."

He scooped her close, enjoying the feel of her, vividly aware of their child. "Are you all right, my love?"

"Yes—and no." At his anxious look, she grinned. "My feet hurt; boots are better for dancing."

Unable to resist, he bent and kissed her soundly.

At the side of the hall Cornwallis watched, melancholy filling his heart with the thoughts of what lay ahead for him. Trying to rise above that feeling and enjoy the music and camaraderie, he leaned towards Major Ferguson. "An amazing couple, when in each other's arms they are completely unaware the rest of us exist." He shrugged, smiling. "She is a good woman, Major. Cross swords with her if you must, but do not step over the line. I will hear of it, and will not be pleased."

Ferguson inclined his head, accepting his superior's demand.

The evening finally drew to a close. Kathryn had watched Lieutenant Jackson's young lady hang on him all evening despite Jack's lack of enthusiasm. Tarleton, on the other hand, had relished playing the role of carefree bachelor. He flirted outrageously, bending to whisper in innocent ears—as well as several not so innocent. Missing for some time earlier in the evening, he eventually returned, face flushed and wearing a self-satisfied smile.

That man has such unmitigated gall carrying on his dalliances during the party. As she stood, waiting for Jason to return with a glass of wine, Tarleton suddenly appeared at her side.

"Would you care to dance, Mrs. Tarrington?" He was ever so polite.

"No, thank you." She eyed him balefully, finding it difficult to remain civil.

Suddenly he laughed. "Mrs. Tarrington, would you please do me the favor of not disliking me quite so openly? I fear it does not serve my reputation well with the ladies."

"I have not noticed you having any problem in that area, Colonel, my liking or disliking obviously irrelevant."

With her curt retort, he chose to tweak her. "That could not possibly be a hint of jealousy I detect in your tone, madam?" He winked boyishly.

Grateful she did not have her tomahawk, afraid she would have killed him where he stood, she breathed deeply trying to control her temper.

"You, sir, are insufferable."

Looking up, she saw Lieutenant Jackson approaching and was glad.

"Ahh, the watchdog approaches." Tarleton was glib.

This rude banter had to stop, too much was at stake; it was up to her.

"Colonel," with a deep breath, she forced a thin smile. "Banastre."

At her addressing him quietly, using his first name, he eyed her with interest.

"Let us begin again, call a truce, whatever is necessary. We must set aside differences and work towards our common goal. Either we convince the colonials to support England in reality, not word only, or we defeat them. With the likes of my brother fighting with the rebel militia, it will be a long war." She paused, allowing him time to digest her words. "I would have it peaceful between us, Banastre."

She spoke further of their cause and her brother without hesitation, so he could not chide her as to loyalties. She had been forced to withstand way too much of that already.

Colonel Tarleton regarded her with newfound respect. Well aware of the traumatic meeting with her brother, he gave her credit. She was honest ... and courageous. Not many could experience what she had, then attend a dinner looking calm and in control a few hours later.

Lieutenant Jackson paused beside Kathryn just as Tarleton took her hand and shook it in agreement. Tarleton ignored him, all interest fixed on her.

"I have no doubt we will still fail to see eye to eye in many instances, Mrs. Tarrington. However, I will make an attempt to refrain from openly antagonizing you. I accept your truce."

Kissing her hand politely for once, he acknowledged Jackson. As he backed away, his smile was charming, almost sincere.

"My regards to the colonel: your husband." Flashing a wide grin, he spun on his heel and disappeared out onto the verandah.

"What was that all about, Kathryn?" Jackson was concerned, she looked peaked.

"Oh, Jack, hopefully, I have put Colonel Tarleton on our side. At least I am making an effort to cope with his obnoxious personality. We cannot remain at odds, there is too much at stake."

At that moment, Jason returned with wine. He had seen Kathryn in serious conversation with Tarleton. They had seemed to part on reasonably good terms, he would wait until later to discuss the outcome. His wife could be incredibly diplomatic once she set her mind to a cause.

"Sorry it took so long, love, Major Ferguson cornered me; and by the way, Jackson, where is your lady friend?" But at his disgusted look, Jason dropped the issue.

As the evening dragged on, Jason, felt his wife's weight against his shoulder, leaning slightly, exhausted. From what little information he had coaxed out of Major Ferguson, it would be a long meeting the next morning; time to get Kathryn to bed. Nodding to Jack, they began edging towards the door, eventually working their way to their host's side.

As Cornwallis took Kathryn's hand bidding 'goodnight', it was easy to see, that despite his steady smile, his eyes were noticeably haggard.

Noting her concern, he found it oddly comforting. "You and I will talk together before you leave tomorrow. I have a personal favor to request."

"I shall look forward to our conversation, milord." She curtsied graciously, complimenting him on his delightful party.

Lieutenant Jackson walked them to the end of the stairwell, and bidding 'good evening', left to check the horses before retiring to the officer's quarters.

Jason lay in the big bed, Kathryn nestled against his side. She talked of her conversation with Tarleton, encouraged that the outcome seemed agreeable, at least for the time being.

"That man is absolutely incorrigible. But we, or rather I, must make it work." Her eyes sparkled as she commented lightly, "I understand why you do not allow me to carry my tomahawk to these necessary functions."

He smiled proud of her efforts. Banastre Tarleton was not an easy man to understand or like.

Suddenly she became serious. "I am truly concerned with his lordship. I cannot imagine what favor he could request of me; but I will do my best to fulfill whatever he asks."

"Major Ferguson talked to me at length, but made no mention of any specific problem. It appears you will have to wait until our meeting." Taking her hand, he kissed each finger in turn. "Tomorrow you and I have an early breakfast with Cornwallis, after which I will meet with his lordship and Colonel Tarleton, perhaps making it a long meeting. Then we head south to find Anna."

Placing his hand gently on her stomach, within moments he felt an answering kick.

"How did it fare with your mother when she gave birth?" he asked suddenly.

She would not worry him with details of difficult births, stillborn children and deaths way too young; she hedged. "I am afraid the only one to answer that, would be Jamie. I was not there for his birth and too young to remember mine. But I doubt he would have much to say to me at this time."

She was glib, too much so, causing immediate concern.

"Would you read to me, love?" Quickly disengaging herself, she crossed the room to rummage in her saddlebag. With a satisfied sound, she held up the small Scottish poetry book.

To his smiling nod, she returned to their bed, inched under the covers and ensconced herself within the circle of his awaiting arms.

"Any special requests, my wife?"

"You choose, my love."

She snuggled close, listening to his eloquent pronunciation of the beautiful words, adoring him, the searing emotional pain of the day held at bay with his enduring love.

He cherished the feel of her, the delicate aroma of lavender clinging to her hair, replete in the knowledge he was bringing her comfort. Within a few minutes she rolled in close, arm flung loosely across his waist, her fingers caressing softly in idle patterns. He felt her become heavier against his side as her breathing deepened.

Her lips brushed his chest ever so gently. "Thank you, my love, for being you … and for loving me." She trailed off to a whisper, falling into exhausted sleep.

He continued to read, glancing frequently at her face, so beautiful and serene in sleep: thankful for his salvation … for Kathryn … and their child.

Chapter Twenty-Two

Dangerous Journey

Jason awoke well before Kathryn, a fact attesting to her exhaustion. He would let her to sleep until the very last minute. He was a man used to being in control at all times. *Well, at least most of the time where his wife was concerned.* Watching her sleeping peacefully, hair amassed in a golden tangle about her face, curling lashes dusting her cheeks, he smiled. So much had changed—so much more was about to change. A soft sound from their bed nudged him from his reverie. As sleepy, green eyes met his, a smile lighted her face and she stretched languorously.

"More rested, love?" Crossing the room to her side, he leaned down and kissed her soundly.

Nodding contentedly, she reached to stroke his cheek, drinking in his handsome features. "I assume sir, that if you have allowed me to sleep this long, it must be late and I will have to hurry." She narrowed her eyes in reprimand.

Standing, he offered her a hand up. "You read me well, madam. I have hot water ready, coffee and about one half hour before we are due at breakfast."

Aiming a pillow she tossed it, laughing delightedly as he ducked adroitly. Yes, she felt more herself this morning—thankfully. Awakened in the night with disquieting thoughts of her brother, she had drawn strength and comfort from the warmth of Jason's body snug against her back, his arm draped gently around her waist. *Jamie, oh, Jamie. We have both made our choice.* Wishing the situation to be otherwise, served no useful purpose. A small jab against her lower belly reminded: life is precious. She would put this behind her and move on. Lying within her husband's arms feeling his soft, steady breathing against her shoulder, she had drifted back to sleep.

Cornwallis's aide ushered them into a small office and quietly closed the door. His lordship sat busily attending to paperwork at his desk, a deep frown settled upon an already troubled face. At their entrance he stood, forcing a bright smile.

"Good morning, Kathryn—Jason," he said lightly, his informality setting the tone of their meeting. "Come, join me outside." Gesturing them to the verandah where a table had been set in preparation for their morning repast he added, "Major Ferguson will join us shortly."

It was unusual for the major not to be present at all times—Kathryn searched Cornwallis's face for a clue. He wasted no time in getting to the point.

"I am going home to England," he said somewhat sadly.

Thoroughly taken aback, Kathryn set her coffee cup down, almost dropping it.

"This is why I wanted to talk to you, Kathryn."

"I would be glad to allow you privacy milord," Jason said, pushing his chair back to stand.

"I appreciate your offer, Colonel … Jason, but you are welcome to stay."

With a slight nod he remained seated, studying the general closely, concerned.

"Are you ill, milord?" Kathryn reached to touch his sleeve, her eyes troubled.

Placing his hand atop hers he smiled, grateful for her caring and intrigued: her eyes mirrored her every thought.

"No, my dear, it is Lady Cornwallis. I have known for some time that she was not well. Recently I have been informed that she languishes with a curious illness for which a cure seems questionable." Within the depth of his sad eyes, Kathryn detected guilt.

"You will return, milord, when she recovers." Jason tried to sound encouraging.

"No, this is the end of my time in the colonies, Colonel." Continuing to hold Kathryn's hand, he turned full attention on Jason. "I will not leave her again. She is a good woman, always accepting my career without complaint; but I have left her too long and miss her greatly."

Having never witnessed this side of the general, Kathryn and Jason remained silent, awestruck by his announcement ... and the deep feelings he harbored for his wife.

Eventually Kathryn found her voice. "How may we best serve you, milord? You made mention of requesting a favor."

"My wife, Jemima, has qualities that remind me of you, Kathryn, brave, outspoken, brash upon occasion. She was beautiful in her youth, and even now after all these years, still beautiful to me. She learned to accept the strict regime of my office, as have you, Kathryn, as the wife of a colonel in the dragoons."

He paused, eyeing both of them. "I have been made aware of how well you handled Colonel Tarleton yesterday. Not an easy accomplishment, but it had to be done." He smiled pointedly at her.

"Allow me to get directly to the point so that we may put this discussion behind us and enjoy our meal." He refilled her coffee cup himself. "Kathryn, would you write to my wife, a letter I could carry with me?" At her astonished look he added. "I would like to return home with more than discouraging tales of the war to relate. You converse eloquently and, I expect, write well."

"Milord, I ..." she hesitated, somewhat puzzled by his request.

"Merely tell her of you, the colonel and your forthcoming child—anything you are willing to share. I daresay she will be fascinated by the lifestyle you lead. It is, after all, somewhat irregular."

"I am flattered, milord, and shall do my best, it will be done before we head south."

Giving her arm a light squeeze, he offered a soft word of 'thanks' and turned to Jason.

"When I first requested our meeting, I had planned to have you both provide details of the Carolinas—especially you, Kathryn, as you are so familiar with the area. That is no longer necessary as it will be up to Clinton to determine all future plans. He may contact you—or not. He seems to feel quite capable of handling the command alone, although he does not particularly relish the responsibility. The South will figure heavily in the future. Nothing immediate, but its vital importance is at last being realized. I have requested Colonel Tarleton join us after breakfast, Jason, at which time we will discuss some of Clinton's views and what your future may entail."

"When will you leave, milord?" Mixed emotions roiled through Jason's mind.

"By weeks end; I must get home."

"We shall be sorry to see you leave, milord," Kathryn said quickly. "I will keep you apprised of life in the colonies and of our little one, who will join us all too soon. Would you do me a favor?"

"You have but to ask, Kathryn."

"Colonel Tarrington has an elderly grandmother ..."

Sensing her forthcoming request, he did not allow her to finish. "I will find her, tell her of you, and share news of her grandson's success and blessings. Now, let us dine. I detest sad farewells, we shall say no more." And with those words, he gave a nod to his aide.

Within moments, Major Ferguson joined them and a scrumptious repast was served. He greeted them with genuine warmth, surprising Kathryn somewhat. She had never given the man credit for sensitivity. Obviously he had tarried elsewhere, allowing them time alone with his lordship. As Lord Cornwallis was known to speak freely in front of the major, she doubted he had been forbidden to be present: Ferguson's choice alone. *Will wonders never cease?*

Kathryn eyed the delicious meal: sweet rolls, mounds of butter, fresh hens' eggs, ham, an urn of hot coffee and so much more. All this delicious food—and if the rumor mills rang true—their army hard put to have more than one good meal most days. She winced at the thought, but this was neither the time nor place for that discussion.

"I do believe you are trying to fatten me up, your Lordship."

They all laughed, even Ferguson, she noticed. Perhaps her truce with his friend Tarleton had softened his rough edges. Who could tell? *Men are certainly impossible at times.*

Colonel Tarleton arrived for the appointed meeting just as Kathryn was leaving. She glanced towards him keeping her expression neutral, curious to see his response.

"Good morning, Mrs. Tarrington, you look lovely as always." He kissed her hand politely, good to his word so far, and she greeted him in a likewise manner.

Back in their bedroom, she packed their saddlebags with quick efficiency and set them out in the hall. Sitting down at the lady's desk, she pulled several sheets of parchment from a small drawer. Picking up a quill pen, she paused for several moments, playing idly with the edge of the paper, deep in thought. Taking a deep breath, she dipped the quill in the ink jar and began. '*Dear Lady Cornwallis, allow me to introduce myself…*'

As Kathryn and Jason stood beside their horses, Lieutenant Jackson and his officers having already mounted, Lord Cornwallis bid them safe travel. As he took Kathryn's letter and tucked it into his inner coat pocket, he assured her he would remain in contact.

"I shall truly miss you, milord," she said softly, her eyes misting.

With a quick kiss on her cheek, and a firm handshake to Jason, he bid them goodbye. "I shall expect to hear soon of the babe. Travel safely." He smiled and stepped back.

Finally, they were on their way home. Relief washed over her as she nudged Beauty into a fast trot to stay apace of Diablo. It had been an emotional visit in so many ways, especially this morning—one of many surprises. She was anxious for nightfall and a chance to discuss the import of all that had occurred with Jason. For now, she merely relished the fact that their lives could return to some sense of normalcy, at least for a while. Thankfully, it was a clear, dry day, the customary unrelenting humidity, so apt to plague her in her present condition, held at bay.

Her thoughts drifted ahead. She had missed the evening campfires with the dragoons: singing, playing cards and helping Cook with the meals. This wonderful group of men, her *only* family since Jamie had … *Stop that. Put it behind you, it is done,* she chided.

Looking over at Lieutenant Jackson and catching his eye, she winked, causing him to color slightly. She wondered if he had spent any more time with his lady friend, sure he had not, and felt a twinge of guilt; suspecting the reason.

They rode for a couple of hours before Jason called a rest. The day was not overly hot and Kathryn was not uncomfortable.

"Do not coddle me, sir," she chastised, eyeing her husband.

"Well, madam, if you are not in need of some relief from all the coffee we drank, then I admire your constitution, especially in your condition."

After a short rest, they turned south again, following now familiar trails. Jason made excuses to stop on a regular basis, a fact causing no undue concern with the dragoons, this leisurely pace—unusual and rather pleasant.

A makeshift camp was set up well before dusk, a campfire lit in preparation for the evening meal. Kathryn, insistent upon providing fresh game to supplement the provisions Lord Cornwallis had graciously supplied, cajoled Jason into hunting nearby. A small copse of mixed trees and low-lying brush bordered by a small streamlet, seemed a likely spot.

Before long, she beamed proudly as she held up three rabbits for his approval.

"You are incredible, my wife." Pulling her close, he kissed her forehead.

"Is that all the reward I receive for this good dinner?" Cocking her head, she pouted prettily.

"For now, madam, yes, we are all hungry. Perhaps later, yon streamlet beckons, hmm?" He winked.

Arm in arm, they returned to the camp. In short order, she had the rabbits cleaned, skewered and sizzling over the fire, the delicious aroma causing all their stomachs to complain loudly. She crouched down, moving each skewer in turn, browning the meat evenly—pleased she could still maintain this position with relative ease despite her rapidly growing belly.

Lieutenant Jackson, rummaging through the supplies, brought out a bottle of brandy and whistled appreciatively. "Now this is a pleasant surprise, one which I am sure his lordship planned for you and your wife, Colonel."

Thoroughly engrossed in watching his wife prepare their meal, Jason merely nodded distractedly at the bottle he held high. *Lady Cornwallis and Kathryn might share similar characteristics, but I doubt she, or his lordship, could exist happily in this lifestyle. My Kathryn is unique.*

Kathryn momentarily diverted her attention from cooking, curious as to Jason's reaction. "Jason …?" she said softly.

Snapping out of his reverie, he realized Jackson was still holding the bottle of fine brandy. "It would seem you gentlemen have traveled as long and hard as we." With a gesture of his hand indicating they all partake, he extended a tin cup and added, "We will all share in the gift."

His eyes met Kathryn's as she happily nodded approval, cautioning them all, "Just remember to save a drink for the cook if you expect any supper tonight, gentlemen." Narrowing her eyes in warning, she grinned as each officer immediately leaned forward offering his cup.

Jason moved to her side and crouching down, offered her a cup; watching closely as she sipped the fine liquor—searching her face—questioning silently.

"Supper will be ready in ten minutes, sir, and I feel wonderful," she assured patiently.

Brushing a stray curl behind her ear, he continued studying her, seeking the truth of that statement. Smiling, she contemplated the fascinating complexity of her husband, and of all these men: brutal in battle, yet freely revealing a softer side in their consideration for her.

The meal, cooked to perfection, was mouth-watering, Kathryn having outdone herself. The men ate with relish, devouring every bite as if they had not touched food in days, gnawing the bones, wasting nothing. After chatting casually for awhile, Jason enlightened them about Cornwallis's plans. This announcement aroused much supposition as to the direction the war would take in the South. With this additional responsibility being placed on Commander-in-Chief Clinton's already overburdened shoulders, action would likely progress slowly—a fact pleasing Jason, considering his present circumstances.

Kathryn leaned against Jason's side as the men spread out around the campfire relaxing with their coffee, and the distinct notes of a tin whistle filled the air. Jason snugged his wife close, resting his cheek against her head, allowing himself more informality with this small group of officers: his regular attendants.

In a short while, with a subtle probably prearranged signal to Lieutenant Jackson, Jason stood, helping his wife to her feet. Wrinkling her nose, she shook her head. "I do not like being portly."

"Come, madam, a refreshing bath awaits you," he said softly.

Inclining his head to his officers, he grasped her elbow and guided her away from the campfire. Beside the gently trickling water, he produced towels and the English lavender soap she so coveted. Solicitous of her condition, he pampered her, much to her delight. Not feeling very independent at the moment, she indulged herself without complaint, reveling in his attention, feeling loved and desired, despite her growing belly. She was truly weary, more than ready to have this birth behind her. *If only we can find Anna.*

"We will find Anna," he stated with conviction.

His words startled her, interrupting her quiet thoughts. She turned, eyeing him with wide-eyed surprise. Leaning down, his mouth sought hers with infinite tenderness, his hands caressing her rounded belly. Eagerly returning his kiss, she clung to him … wanting him, needing him.

His first thought was to refuse gently; she was too close to term. But of late, she had become overly sensitive and insecure—constantly needing his reassurance.

"Kathryn," he mouthed against her ear, caressing her breast with the palm of his hand, his own desire escalating. *God, how I want her, always want her. My need never diminishes; never.*

Fleetingly he thought of Cornwallis's words regarding his own wife's beauty even now, and hoped he and Kathryn might be blessed with enough time to grow old together—time to see their child mature.

Maintaining control of his growing urgency, he guided her backwards. Pressing her carefully against a large oak at waters edge, he loved her gently; sating her needs without risking injury to their babe. It came to him, a somewhat startling revelation—this more gentle form of lovemaking was also deeply satisfying and pleasurable.

They lay together near the campfire with the others, wrapped snugly in their bedroll to ward off the chilly night air. All thoughts of sharing a more in-depth discussion of the surprising, and somewhat unsettling, events of their morning meeting with his lordship were forgotten as Kathryn fell immediately into a happy, exhausted sleep within her husband's arms.

None of what Cornwallis had divulged would impact upon their present activities. Once they rejoined the main body of dragoons, approximately two days hence, they would head deeper south. Due to minimal camp setup while on the trail, privacy would be substantially limited. For once, this did not upset her. Alone together, their conversation might drift towards talk of Jamie, at present the scar was too fresh, still hurt too deeply.

The next two days although arduous, were nothing out of the ordinary. There was no sign of rebel activity, a disconcerting fact which surprised both of them. Jamie should have headed south to rebuild his numbers in an area of future importance. He understood the 'game' perfectly. It took time and lots of friendly persuasion—or even a little coercion—to build a formidable force. Where had he gone? And why had he not taken this opportunity to strike at them?

Kathryn almost hoped Jamie might seek her out just once more, but to what purpose? Nothing would change—nothing could change. Their choices had been made. *Move on with your life,* she ordered sternly, but still wondered.

Kathryn's face broke into a smile as their encampment came into view and the outer pickets hailed them enthusiastically. They were finally home. Tonight she could fall asleep in her husband's arms and wake to his gentle touch in the privacy of their own tent. This trip had been extremely difficult, and taken a heavy toll—a fact not lost on Jason.

He delayed their trip south to Keowee for one more day, allowing Kathryn much needed rest, and him more time to meet with his officers. He required briefing on problems during his absence, but of greater importance, the present status of rebel movements. In turn, he outlined the unusual changes at Headquarters.

After a quiet breakfast the following morning, Kathryn spent her day replenishing herbal supplies and readying for their journey. She took particular care in being well prepared each time they took to the trail, especially when heading farther south. The constant heat and humidity of that area made the chance of snakebite, fever, or simply the risk of infection much greater.

Late morning, Lieutenant Jackson stopped by the tent with a fresh cup of coffee for both of them. He stood watching, as she wrapped a particularly unusual root carefully in a clean cloth.

"What is that odd thing?" he asked, wrinkling his nose as he offered her a mug of coffee.

"Snakeroot, Jack, for treating snakebite." She looked up with a humorous expression, accepting the hot coffee gratefully, then added, "This is an example of the 'doctrine of signatures', or an instance of the cure somewhat resembling the cause. There are other herbs, such as wild horehound and plantain that will do the trick, but I prefer this one."

Eyeing another clump of the long snakelike roots, he easily understood the connection.

"I have a decoction of willow bark tea almost ready to add to your supplies. And I thought you might like these, Kathryn." Removing a loosely rolled cloth tucked in his belt, he handed it to her, watching for her reaction.

Opening it carefully, she gasped, surprised and pleased. "Jack. Leaves of feverwort; how did you know? When did you …"

"You, milady, are an excellent teacher. I have watched you in the medical tent, observing your success in treating fever. I thought it might be useful." His eyes danced at having pleased her.

"You amaze me, Jack; this is a perfect addition."

Carefully re-rolling the leaves, she set them with her supplies, as Jack hunkered down beside her.

"How are you faring, Kathryn?" His question caught her off guard.

"I am fine," she declared, but did not make eye contact.

"That is an unacceptable answer, Kathryn."

She eyed him sharply. "I may be closer to delivery than I originally thought, Jack. But I *am* fine."

Looking her over carefully, he accepted her assessment—for the moment.

"Do not make mention of this to Jason, please. He has enough on his mind. And I do remember much of Anna's birthing instructions. I should be able to manage even if we do not find her in time and you …" Her voice trailed off, unsure.

"I will be there for you, if you need me." He sucked in a deep breath, pinning her with a stern gaze. "Kathryn, allow yourself to give in to your pregnancy; do not fight it so. Everyday, I see you exhaust yourself trying to prove you are still 'worthwhile'. Each of us, to the very last man, knows your abilities and values your addition. You need no longer prove yourself. *We* do not judge you harshly—do not judge yourself so. Save your strength for the birth."

Noting her crestfallen look at his harsh reprimand, he added quietly, "You will need your strength."

He had never lectured her before—never. Dropping her head, she became engrossed in rewrapping the snakeroot, but not before he saw a tear escape and begin its slow journey. He offered a handkerchief, forcefully stopping himself from catching the shimmering droplet. He wanted desperately to comfort her, and regretted causing her grief. But it was not his place to console her.

"Do not fret, Kathryn," he said softly as she swiped her cheeks. "This, too, is all part of it."

She eyed him through curling lashes dotted with sparkling tears, disbelieving.

"It is true. My sister lived—still lives, on a beautiful estate surrounded by a loving husband, devoted family and numerous house servants to answer her every whim. Well fed and content with life, she still cried constantly during her pregnancy. On numerous occasions, you have had valid reason to break down, yet rarely permit yourself the privilege. This will pass," he said firmly. "Now, dry your eyes. Your husband is approaching, and I do not want him to accuse me of beating you." That statement encouraged a smile. "Trust me to finish packing your medical supplies. Get some rest so we may enjoy your voice around the campfire tonight."

With a hand under her arm, he helped her to her feet, his eyes meeting the colonel's over her head, nodding in answer to his concerned expression. "Your wife is tired, sir."

"I can speak for myself, Lieutenant." Momentarily curt, she felt immediate remorse, but his smile carried no recrimination.

"Come with me, love. I have left you longer than intended." Jason snaked his arm around her shoulder.

Before she could begin to scold him for coddling, he held out the Scottish poetry book concealed in his hand. Her face beamed as she reached for the book, a smile returning to her eyes. Flashing a look of gratitude to Jackson, he guided her towards the brook.

Relaxing against her husband, she closed her eyes enjoying the familiar aromas: moist earth, moss, warm wool, leather, and the masculinity of him. A warm breeze kissed her cheeks, causing wisps of tawny gold hair to dance as she leaned heavily, relishing the feel of him against her. As she began thumbing through the worn pages, searching for a special passage, he held a battered parchment out for her perusal.

"Grandmother?" she whispered with disbelief.

"Yes," he breathed softly against her cheek.

"Is she well? What did she say? About you? About us? About the babe?" She could barely contain her excitement.

"We shall have to open it to determine all that," he chuckled. "I saved it to enjoy with you. It arrived just after we headed north and Jenkins kept it safe for us."

It was then that she noticed the ribbon and seal were still intact. Turning the worn parchment over, she saw the decorative script created with a hand firm and adept at the art of writing.

To: Colonel and Mrs. Jason William Tarrington
Camden, South Carolina

Her hand shook slightly as she carefully slipped the ribbon and unfolded the missive. Scanning the beautiful script, she held it up to him, her eyes misting. "Please …"

Placing his hand over hers, he began to read in a voice husky with emotion.

My dearest Grandson and Kathryn,

You have given me reason to continue my life, to cease railing against the unfairness of the hand that was dealt you and your dear mother. There have been moments when I wished it over; convinced I had failed you both, but no more. You have finally found well-deserved happiness despite your difficult career. Your father still lives, a wretched, unhappy man receiving his punishment here in life … as he so deserves. Justice is served.

But you, my dearest Jason, at last have found the true meaning and essence of life. I sense from your words, through this beautiful woman … your Kathryn … that you have discovered inner peace. I shall thank the Lord each and every day for bringing her to you. I hold dear the words she penned and pray we shall one day meet. For now, I rest content knowing she wears your mother's necklace in happiness. I wait impatiently to hear of Kathryn's well being and the birth of your child, my great grandchild. Kiss Kathryn for me.

With deepest love and affection,
Grandmother

Neither one spoke. Kathryn held his hand as she re-read the letter quietly to herself, thrilled for Jason's sake; he needed to hear those words: perhaps a very old and deep wound could finally begin to heal. They sat contentedly holding each other, as he rocked her gently, humming softly.

Much later, she awoke with a start, momentarily forgetting where she was.

"Ahh, my sleepy head." He smiled, brushing a light kiss to her forehead. "Relax, my love. It is still a while before supper."

Horrified by the lengthy time she had slept, she awkwardly tried to rise. Offering his hand, he grinned as she eyed her rounding belly grimacing.

"For your extreme forbearance, my husband, and so much more, I love you dearly."

"Always, my beautiful wife," he answered, brushing a chaste kiss to her lips. "That is from Grandmother." Then, kissing her fervently, he added, "And that, my love, is from me."

Their eyes met, sparkling, alive—desperately happy.

A sharp 'poke' caught Kathryn by surprise, and she grabbed her belly laughing. Jason's hand reached to caress, and within moments felt the strength behind the kick.

"Exactly like its mother," he announced, ducking as she playfully swung at him.

The sun had dipped closer to the horizon, beginning to display its palette of exquisite brilliance as it set—time to head back to camp.

"We must write Grandmother soon, my love. She is a wonderful lady, and you have made her happy."

"Oh, I am not so sure it was I who did that, Kathryn." Tucking his grandmother's letter carefully into his jacket, they headed back towards the encampment, arm in arm.

She felt refreshed, more like herself. Tonight she intended to play rebel jigs, sing English tunes, and enjoy the camaraderie around the campfire before retiring to the familiar feel of their own bed for one last night. Tomorrow, they headed south in search of Anna. She hoped this child would wait; it had seemed to drift slightly lower with each passing day. *It will not be long now.*

Her last thoughts, much later that night as she dropped into sleep, were of Grandmother: grateful for her letter and the deep healing she had provided Jason.

They broke camp early next morning and headed south, Kathryn riding at ease flanked on one side by her husband and the other by Jack. She made a special effort to smile brightly at him, and compliment the organized way in which he had packed the medical supplies, his beaming smile registering no resentment at her moods of late.

They traveled for several days, covering a great deal of distance. Kathryn discovered the lack of privacy was not as unbearable as she had anticipated. Jason, ever vigilant to both her physical and emotional needs, found quiet moments of an evening that they could talk, touch, and love each other in gentle ways.

"Kathryn, there is more to us than this," he explained quietly one night as she bemoaned her size. Although she would never admit her discomfort, he was well aware of the fact. "Do not misunderstand, my pet. Loving you is exquisite, but I can wait. Grandmother always told me that 'absence makes the heart grow fonder'. However ..." his grin was devilish, "when this is over, I may require your 'understanding' for some very long nights. Be prepared."

Smoke signals had been seen drifting on the horizon for the past two days. They were on the Charleston Path, still three days hard ride from 'The 96', pressing ever southward to Keowee. Kathryn voiced her concern one evening to both Jason and Jack as they hunkered around the campfire at dinner. She sat on a large stone, her expression pinched, obviously uncomfortable. Both men traded glances but said nothing.

"They know of us and are nearby. I do not understand why they have not made contact." Kathryn was distracted and unsettled. Realizing her weariness, Jason decided to make it an early evening. A long journey still lay ahead, and dawn would come early.

She lay within his arms in their bedroll, wracking her brain for an answer. *I did not kill my husband. They do not seek me.* Suddenly, chilling apprehension clutched her heart—though she could not voice it until sure of her thoughts. She had not killed Black Raven. He had been slain by an English officer. *They could not possibly hold Jason accountable—could they?* She searched her mind for Cherokee customs and law, unwilling to accept the possible answer. She slept fitfully and awoke the following morning still tired.

Jason had left a few minutes earlier to speak to Lieutenant Jackson, his pretense being to coordinate travel plans, but she was not fooled. They had yet to find Anna, although frequent smoke signals indicated the Cherokees were well aware of their presence: something was definitely amiss.

Her girth was growing rapidly, the additional bulk extremely uncomfortable for one so used to being slender. She felt awkward. *How in the world do women make this appear so easy?* Chiding herself for dwelling on the inconvenience, rather than the happily awaited outcome, she turned to watching the dragoons prepare for the day's journey.

The child rested even lower this morning, kicking insistently. With a grimace, she edged forward, trying to gain purchase and heave herself up from the log where she perched. She needed to relieve herself—again. This was becoming a chore.

A large hand unexpectedly reached down offering assistance. Somewhat startled, she was surprised to see the grinning face of the Loyalist captain.

"Allow me, Mrs. Tarrington."

Accepting his proffered hand, she smiled. "Captain Hodges, I do believe you are a godsend. Thank you."

He was a large man, taller than Jason. Despite appearing quiet and unpretentious, he was known to be ruthless on the battlefield. Having seen him in action, she knew that for a fact. It suddenly struck her; he was actually quite shy, as he quickly colored at her remark. Having come to know all the dragoons over time, she was amazed at the diverse individuals comprising their 'family'.

"None of us will ever press you, milady. But if you need help, we are all at your disposal." He smiled kindly, and at her look of surprise nodded confirmation, continuing his shy grin.

"I …" She was at a loss for words. This young man's statement reinforced their acceptance, no matter what her condition. "Thank you, Captain; you make me feel as if I am part of the 'family'."

She had been aware of their sidelong glances for some time, and assumed them to be merely curious as to how close to term she was. But Captain Hodges's statement made it obvious they were keeping an eye on her in case she needed assistance; that revelation filled her with joy.

She scanned the faces of those sitting around the morning campfire and beamed, green eyes alive and sparkling. Several of the men, catching her look, returned her smile.

"You have made my day, Captain, but please excuse me. I …" She trailed off, aware of his sensitivities.

Inclining his head, he colored slightly as he backed away.

Jason saw her head for the copse and followed shortly to be sure she was all right. He had also noted Hodge's interaction and was curious.

He never misses a thing, that husband of mine. She grinned as Jason asked her about the incident.

"Finally I am truly a part of the group," she bubbled happily.

"Are you surprised, my pet? Why should they not accept you? You keep them well fed."

She eyed him with uncertainty, frowning. Gently chucking her under the chin he became serious.

"Everything takes time, my Kathryn." He stroked her hair gently. "You have won their hearts, as I knew you would." His eyes caressed; "As you have won mine."

Their kiss was tender and lingering as he held her tightly to him.

"Come, love, let us find Anna."

Within minutes they were underway, Beauty, as always, prancing and eager. But as morning waned and the sun climbed higher in the sky, the day became overly warm, heavy with humidity, a 'weather-breeder' as her father used to say. She drank water frequently; she had little choice with Jason and Lieutenant Jackson offering their canteens on a regular basis. Even with her heavy greatcoat flung across Beauty's rump, and her shirt bloused for cooling, her strength was flagging by mid-morning.

Jason studied her quietly. Raising a gloved hand, he gestured towards a cluster of trees, signaling the dragoons to a halt. Dismounting quickly, he handed Diablo's reins to Jackson and moved directly to her side. Slowly she inched her leg over Beauty's head and slid down into his waiting arms.

"Sit for awhile, love." He guided her to a large boulder. "Hungry?"

At her nod and bright smile, he touched her shoulder. "I will be back shortly to ease that problem, madam." He winked.

She watched the dragoons settle themselves in a relaxed fashion, some talking together, others rummaging through knapsacks for edibles, a few settling back against tree trunks to nap.

Lieutenant Jackson stepped over to greet her, chatted a few minutes, and then moved to sit on a half decayed log in the sun, just beyond the shadowed protection of the trees. He never seemed to mind heat or brilliant sunshine, much to Kathryn's envy. She sat quietly tired, the heat and humidity weighing heavily on her spirits. The child was especially active today, kicking vigorously, and she was uncomfortable.

At the insidious rattle of a 'sidewinder' about to strike, her head snapped up. Reacting instantaneously, all fatigue fell away as she spun towards the sound, her pistol clearing its holster and firing with deadly accuracy—all in one fluid motion.

The dragoons' heads whipped up in unison, their hands grasping for various weapons. Staying their defensive actions, they watched in fascination as the large snake writhed in continuous, coiling death throes. Her bullet had shattered its spinal column just as the lethal fangs sank into Jackson's thigh, its life ended before the body was aware of any change. Jamie had taught her well; if only there had been a few more seconds of warning.

In three strides, she reached Jackson's side. Crouching quickly, she took note of his pallor, vague look of surprise and noticeable pain.

"Do not move," she commanded.

Carefully timing the snake's continued spiraling she waited, tense with anticipation. Abruptly her hand shot out, catching the rattler firmly behind its head. Working within the patterns of its death throes, she coaxed the fangs, ever so gently, from Jackson's thigh so as not to force more venom into the wound. Despite the large bullet hole which had almost severed its body, the snake continued to coil slowly as she flung it away.

Scanning Jackson's face, she grinned, attempting to ease his apprehension. "You have choices to make, Lieutenant. Either I cut your breeches—or you remove them."

He eyed her narrowly, his smile tight with pain. "Cut the pants, milady," he ground out through clenched teeth.

However, needing to move rapidly before the poison spread, she had quickly slid the dirk from her boot and sliced his breeches before giving him time to answer. Laying the fabric back, she examined the puncture wounds, and whipping her belt off, snugged it into a tourniquet on his upper thigh.

By now she had an audience of concerned men surrounding her. At her request, Captain Hodges stepped closer to maintain the tourniquet pressure. Jason, having gone to fetch her saddlebag, was just returning.

"Whiskey and water, quickly, please."

Holding her dirk out, a nearby officer sloshed it thoroughly with whiskey.

"Sorry I cannot offer you whiskey at the moment, Lieutenant." She squeezed his hand offering encouragement, noting the clamminess there.

"I am about to show you firsthand how snakeroot works, Jackson."

Jason moved behind Lieutenant Jackson for support, and to still him, under the pain she would be inflicting.

Drawing a deep breath, she instructed: "Brace yourself, Lieutenant, this will hurt." With a deft move, she slashed across the twin punctures in Jackson's thigh. A thin sheen of perspiration bathing his face, and a sharply sucked inhalation were the only indication of his pain. With a quick look to see if he was still conscious, she pressed her mouth firmly over the open wound and sucked deeply, turned to spit, then sucked again.

Reaching her hand out, a cup of water and small towel were thrust towards her. Rinsing her mouth thoroughly, she spit and absentmindedly wiped her face, angling her head in 'thanks' to the sergeant. At her sharp nod, Hodges released the tourniquet allowing the blood to flow freely. Watching Jack intently, she rummaged in her saddlebag, hurriedly withdrawing the snakeroot. Pulling the strange looking tuber from its wrapping, she cut a piece and pressed it to his lips.

"Chew this, Lieutenant—thoroughly. Swallow some juice, but keep chewing it into a pulp."

At her unyielding frown and narrowed eyes, he hastily did as instructed, glad for the diversion and for his pain. As she gently touched his thigh again, he struggled to keep his mind blank lest he embarrass himself.

She cut another hunk of the root and began chewing it herself, wrinkling her nose. "Not very tasty, hmm?"

Catching Jason's eye, she flashed a reassuring look; they had caught it in time.

"Spit," she commanded. Talking around her own mouthful of pulp, she cupped her hand under his lip. At his hesitation, she grinned. "Do not be shy with me now, Lieutenant."

Several of the dragoons smirked, admiring her ability to defuse a tense situation with her calm demeanor and sense of humor.

Jackson spat into her palm and she immediately pressed the sticky mass against his thigh, kneading gently. The blood flow slowed considerably, pleasing her. After applying her own gooey wad of snakeroot, she carefully bandaged his thigh.

"I think Lieutenant Jackson could use some of that whiskey now."

She angled her head at Captain Hodges who immediately brought a flask and stood awaiting her next order. Inching closer—somewhat clumsily with her well-rounded form—she reached for the flask, and placed it to Jack's lips. Although ashen, pain obvious in the pinched look about his eyes, he would be fine—she was positive.

After a few sips, she set the whiskey aside and sloshed water on a towel. As she bathed Jackson's face she gazed up at Jason, pleased to see pride shining unashamedly back at her.

"By tomorrow at this time, you will feel much better. Trust me, Jack," she said softly, the informality for his ears only, grabbing his attention.

"Thank you, I hope to return the favor someday." Despite the weakness of his voice, he managed a thin smile.

"I believe the score sheet shows us to be greatly in your debt, Lieutenant." Jason said as he reached to put a hand on his wife's shoulder.

She pressed more whiskey to Jackson's lips, eyeing him affectionately. Then turning to her husband suggested, "We had best stay put tonight, sir, even set a few tents; it looks like rain."

With Kathryn's work finished, Jason took over. "Hodges. Samuels. Give me a hand; make the lieutenant as comfortable as possible."

He then turned to his wife. "And you, madam, go sit in the shade and relax. I am not ready to learn how to deliver a child today." Grinning, he bent near, speaking quietly. "You never cease to amaze me, my love. You have done a remarkable thing today."

Smiling weakly, she moved back into the shade of a big tree and dropped unceremoniously to the ground, exhaustion engulfing her. Burying her face against her knees, she began to shake. She could still hear Jamie's strident voice, ever insistent, demanding that she learn. *"You can do this, Kathryn. Pay attention."* Jamie had always been more convinced of her abilities than she. *"Be alert to the sound: locate it, fire quickly—but be accurate."*

Blindfolded, she had concentrated, straining to hear as he moved around her shaking the rattles of an old snakeskin. Turning quickly, taking aim where she had last heard the clatter, she fired an empty pistol as he watched. He had made her repeat the exercise over and over until she wanted to scream and walk away. *Damn you, Jamie. Damn you.* The remembrance still angered her, but she had learned—as he had known she would.

"Oh, Jamie," the whispered sob was hers, she realized. "Jamie." Would she ever be able to put him from her mind? Tears trickled down her cheeks as she hugged her knees.

A gentle hand came to rest on her shoulder, a loving touch which could only be that of her husband.

"Do not deny the memories, Kathryn. He is as much a part of you, as you are of him. Treasure those memories … treasure him." His voice was a caress.

She could not look up, could not stop the tears.

"Oh my love, my Kathryn," he murmured, his strong arms surrounding her. Pulling her up with great tenderness, he held her, crooning softly as she wept.

"What Jamie ingrained in you has saved Jackson's life. I have just left him; he rests easy now."

Eyes swimming with tears met his, as he kissed her salty cheeks. With great dexterity, he maneuvered her onto his lap, ignoring her protests of bulk and additional weight. Encircling her in strong arms, he hugged her to him, breathing softly against her hair, quoting bits and pieces from some of her favorite Scottish poems until she finally slept.

Captain Hodges took it upon himself to organize the setup of camp in the absence of Lieutenant Jackson, and did so in an efficient manner, impressing Jason. By the time the first few warning drops of rain had begun to fall, there were enough tents to provide cover for everyone.

Kathryn looked up groggily, just coming awake as the captain arrived to inform the colonel his tent was ready, their horses unsaddled and fed. As rain was beginning to pelt in earnest, he reached out politely to help Kathryn rise. Murmuring 'thanks', Jason ushered her in the direction of their tent.

"Is Lieutenant Jackson under cover?" she asked, pausing to glance over her shoulder at Captain Hodges.

"Yes, he rests comfortably, milady. He drank some willow bark tea, and it eased the pain greatly."

With a sigh of relief, she hurried for the dry comfort of their tent.

After a hearty meal, she fell asleep within her husband's arms, lulled by the steady drumming of rain on the tent's canvas roof. She slept soundly throughout the night, awaking at morning's first light feeling deeply refreshed—and concerned for Jack.

Quickly dressing, Kathryn headed for Lieutenant Jackson's tent. Jason walked her most of the way, but detoured towards the morning campfire, promising to bring coffee for the three of them shortly.

After yelling 'good morning' from outside his tent, she was welcomed by a firm voice from within.

"Jack, you sound so much better today." Her face wreathed in smiles as she walked to the cot where he lay propped on a pile of blankets. Placing her hand gently on his forehead, she could detect no hint of fever, and his color was good.

"May I?" she asked, indicating his leg under the blanket.

At his slow nod, she folded the blanket back carefully. Eyeing his torn breeches with approval, she teased, "I see you have made this easy for me to examine your wound."

"I have only so many breeches issued, milady." He grimaced. "I thought not to have you cut another pair." He frowned, attempting to hide a grin.

"As I recall, Lieutenant, I did offer you a choice." Her wide grin held a bit of deviltry, earning her a look of feigned consternation.

Unwrapping the bandaging, she felt him tense and realized his concern.

"Think of me as your sister, Jack. I will try to be quick."

Immediately she became all business. Her practiced hands deftly prodded his thigh for signs of swelling or infection, her eyes never glancing above his wound as she applied more pulverized snakeroot, and then re-bandaged his thigh.

"Perfect," she announced with a smile. "Take it easy today. By tomorrow, other than a sore thigh, you will feel more like yourself." She squeezed his hand warmly. "Snakeroot is a great antidote, thank heavens."

At that point, Jason arrived with breakfast for the three of them. During their meal, and at Kathryn's insistence, it was decided they would camp here one more day. She looked more rested this morning and claimed to feel well. One more day could not hurt.

They would break camp tomorrow, very early, and press ever southward in search of Anna.

Chapter Twenty-Three

Gabrielle

Once again, they headed towards the distant smoke signals, but still no sign of the Cherokee Clan she had once known so well. Beauty was easily visible, prancing with barely contained energy at the front of the column. They would surely recognize the little mare and her indomitable spirit. Kathryn's condition, rather than being concealed, was well known to those who would be in a position to make the Bird Clan aware: Jamie for one. Her concern grew daily, although she made no mention to Jason.

Lieutenant Jackson's wound improved rapidly, as Kathryn had assured him it would. By the end of the third day, he no longer favored the leg, annoyed only by the constant itching of healing flesh.

"That is a good sign, Jack," she declared, turning in her saddle to face him, aware he was rubbing the thigh fretfully. "Do not worry at it, or I will have to tend it again, and you know what that entails."

Narrowing his eyes, he ceased the action immediately. Jason merely smiled, pleased by the warm friendship existing between the pair.

As to her own physical condition, Kathryn was concerned. Just this morning, stabbing pains had radiated across her belly, excruciating pains which brought her close to tears. Jason had been busy shaving at the time, unaware of her distress; and she intended to keep him that way as long as possible. Perhaps today they would find Anna.

As they rode, Kathryn's mind drifted thinking of Anna: a renowned and highly revered Cherokee healer. From the moment they first met, a solid, loving friendship had blossomed. When Anna had been unable to prevent Jamie from spiriting her away after Black Raven's death … The remembrance of her distraught face lingered painfully. *She will come to me, she will … When she is allowed,* the thought suddenly struck.

It would be an easy birth once they found Anna, and after seeing the child she would join them to act as nanny, of that Katherine was sure. Although not the traditional way of raising a child, as much as she would love Jason's baby, boy or girl—her husband came first. He always would, he was her destiny. Through the healing of past wounds they had brought sanity and inner peace to each other, their love increasing daily. They cherished each moment shared, eager for more but able to accept what fate had pre-destined. *Today, they held in the palm of their hand … but tomorrow? Who knew?*

She and Jackson had also developed a close bond of friendship, a relationship she cherished in a different sense. In talking with him recently of the pending birth and her intention to engage Anna as caregiver, she had felt guilty.

She could still hear his laughing tone. "Ahh, Kathryn, I see by the look on your face that you have found yet another way to beat yourself up." Rolling his eyes, he had said without hesitation, "That is a rather common British approach; you will fit in very nicely back home after the war is over." With a warm smile and light touch to her arm he had once again instilled courage.

Amidst the late afternoon heat, her pains began again. Something felt … different. Although she tried to conceal her condition, Jason read her well. She had been 'drifting' mentally during the day—so very unlike her when on the trail.

"Kathryn." Jason eyed her, concerned. "Kathryn," he repeated sharply.

Yanked from her reverie by his tart tone, she flashed what she hoped would be a convincing smile, but the effort was almost too great. Pain which had been easily bearable now girdled her belly with an unrelenting hold.

Making eye contact with Jackson over her head, both agreed, time to set up camp—quickly. Scanning the surroundings, Jason indicated an area just ahead which offered cooling shade trees, and directed his men to set up camp.

"How long have you been in pain, Kathryn?" Jason's voice was sharper than intended. Annoyed with her stubborn independence, he reached to help her down from her saddle.

Her face paled as another spasm gripped fiercely. Clutching her middle, she shook her head, barely managing to whisper, "Wait, please."

As the pain eased, she began sliding down to him, all usual grace deserting her.

"Kathryn." Jason's voice caught. Gripping her firmly, he guided her to a mossy spot under a large pine tree and eased her down.

"I am better now, love." She saw the spark of fear recede in his eyes. "Just the heat," she assured, squeezing his hand gently.

Lieutenant Jackson crouched beside her at that moment, handing Jason a mug of cool water. As Jason placed the cup to her lips, he shot a questioning look at Jackson.

"Your tent will be ready shortly, sir. Preparations are being made for a layover."

Kathryn eyed him over the lip of the mug, pausing from slaking her thirst. "I planned to trap …"

She was not allowed to finish her statement.

"You will trap nothing, Mrs. Tarrington, and I will brook no argument. Do you understand?" Jason had reached the limit of his patience.

Rolling her eyes, she nodded dutifully. He was right. She *was* stubborn, and did not feel very well at the moment—though she would never admit it.

"Rest easy, milady. Captain Hodges has volunteered to bring in fresh meat for dinner." Jackson smiled as she fretted.

Within the hour, campfires were lit and tents dotted the field in a surprisingly structured manner, the dragoons moving about tending horses and unpacking saddlebags.

Her pains had miraculously receded and Kathryn, sure she had been given a reprieve, decided to attend supper with the men. The smell of roasting rabbit and partridge wafting throughout the campsite, indicated that Hodges's hunting venture had been successful, the aroma mouthwateringly delicious as she approached the campfire with Jason's arm around her waist.

As she stood complimenting the captain on his catch, insidious pain struck like a sledgehammer's blow. With a gasp she faltered, eyes pinched shut in agony. The captain immediately stepped forward, but Jason already had her in his arms, despite her protestations of being able to walk. As he strode towards his tent, he yelled for Jackson to make ready—an unnecessary order as the lieutenant had begun preparing needed supplies the moment they had set up camp.

"Is there any way I can find Anna?" he asked as he set her gently on the cot. "We cannot be that far from her people."

She shook her head slowly, then convulsed as another hammer-like blow struck.

"They have seen Beauty, they choose not to acknowledge …" Unable to finish, she clutched her belly, curling into a ball.

Immediately at her side, Jason sponged her forehead with the cooling water Jackson had left.

"What can I do, Kathryn?"

She shook her head, trying to smile.

"The nearest village is about a day's ride. I could …"

"Do not leave me, Jason." Her pain-laced voice breathed panic.

"I have towels, plenty of water, what else?"

"Jackson will know. It will be …" Another vicious pain arched her up into a sitting position.

As she struggled to discard her clothing, Jason crouched to help ease her boots off. Stripped down to her voluminous shirt, she suddenly rocked forward off the edge of the cot and pushed past him. Dropping to her knees, she grasped the edge of his desk. Jason crouched at her side, rubbing her back. Breathing deeply between spasms, she eyed him, noting his puzzled expression.

"Cherokees use this position …" Her voice cracked as the unrelenting cramps began again. She clung to the edge of the desk, bearing down as Anna had counseled during other births. Her hair clung in damp rivulets along both sides of her face, a face grown ashen as she bravely worked at bringing this new life into being.

Jason was beside himself. This was far worse than any battle. This was his Kathryn suffering—and he hated himself for being the cause of her pain.

"Something is wrong," she barely managed the words as insistent, non-stop pains increased in magnitude.

With a small cry, and a sudden gush of warmth, her water broke. Jason immediately applied towels, horrified at the amount of blood. As she pushed away from the desk struggling to stand, he caught her and carefully lowered her to the floor.

"Can you see the baby?" she gasped.

Holding a lantern close, he investigated then looked up, his face lined with concern.

"Yes, but I do not believe that is the head." He sounded confused.

"Oh, God," she groaned, "find Jack." She clutched her abdomen as a violent spasm seized her. "Help me, please. Please."

She was exhausted and visibly fading, but as Jason arose, she grasped his hand feebly. "Tell him the baby is breeched," she choked, swallowing a scream as another fierce contraction wracked her body.

Lieutenant Jackson intercepted Jason just as he was exiting their tent. His fearful expression answered the question Jack had been poised to ask.

"She is in terrible pain, Jack. She said to tell you the baby is breeched." He looked unsure as to the implication of that statement.

"Hodges," Jackson yelled authoritatively. "Bring all the supplies we spoke of immediately."

Turning to Jason, he asked, "How far has she progressed?"

"I can see the baby, but not the head." He paused at the tent entrance. "Jack," he pleaded as choking sobs erupted from within. "Save her. Please … save her."

"Colonel," Jack turned deadly serious—assertive. "When we go into that tent, I need you to understand: I am the one in command. Do not question anything I may do to help Kathryn."

His steely features portrayed firm authority, complete control, and demanded that his superior officer comply.

"Do what must be done, Lieutenant, I understand."

Captain Hodges arrived shortly bringing all the necessary supplies, and setting them down, quickly left—but remained close at hand.

Jackson stepped into the tent, and rolling up his sleeves, moved to Kathryn's side. She was ghastly pale, half out of her head with the hammering pain.

"Whiskey," he ordered, and Jason quickly handed him a decanter.

After sloshing the amber liquid over his hands and arms, he scrubbed it thoroughly into his skin, drying the excess.

"Clear the desk, Colonel, I need Kathryn on a hard surface," Jackson instructed as he knelt beside her.

Caught in the grips of another agonizing spasm, he waited for it to subside before attempting to get her attention.

"Kathryn." He touched her forehead with the back of his hand gently.

Her eyes fluttered open, momentarily unfocused and closed again, her head lolling sideways.

Jason cleared the desk with a sweep of his arm, covered it with blankets, and then moved another lantern closer for better lighting. At the lieutenant's nod, he picked his wife up and lifted her carefully onto the desktop.

"Jason." Her frightened eyes searched wildly for him as she tried to rise.

"Jack is here, Kathryn, he knows what to do." He kissed her cheek and gently pressed her back down. But she gave no acknowledgement, her eyes closing—trying desperately to block the agony.

Lubricating his fingers with lard from the supply wagon, Jackson ran his hand up under her blouse. While probing gently to judge her progress, he placed his other hand on her distended belly, kneading in a close pattern trying to ascertain the child's exact position. At his invading touch, her eyes flew open, pupils dilated in pain. Uttering soothing words, he made a quick visual inspection, reinforcing what he already knew.

"Kathryn," he said tersely. "Kathryn, look at me and focus."

She gasped as another wave of pain swept violently over her.

"Do not push," he demanded, but did not have her attention as yet. She was drifting. "Kathryn," he hissed angrily, hating what he was about to do. Leaning in close, he swore fiercely. "God damn it, Kathryn. Look at me and focus now!"

Startled by his fierce anger, she struggled to rise from her pain-filled haze, attempting to center on him—but quickly glanced to Jason for comfort.

"Kathryn. Look at me," he insisted. Grasping her chin firmly, he forced her to face him. "The baby is breeched. This is between you and me—and no one else. Focus on me now, and keep that focus!"

Startled eyes searched his face—hurt mingled with torment.

He had never treated her this way, not even in the beginning before he came to know her … to love her. He waited, angry eyes burning into hers, until she slowly nodded comprehension. Again her face contorted in agony, but she immediately refocused on him when the wave passed.

"I have to turn the baby." He sounded less angry now. "The pain will be excruciating, far worse than your knife wound. It is vital that you understand what you will be facing." He needed to paint a realistic image before asking his question.

Jason watched, conflicting emotions roiling through him. He dared not interfere, but struggled to control his temper. He watched Lieutenant Jackson, a man he thought he knew well, become unsympathetic in his demands, and was reminded of himself before there was Kathryn … before there was Kathryn. *She must not die.* Whatever was necessary to save her must be done.

"I need to know if you can bear the pain without being restrained." Jack's voice had become almost tender as he watched her tortured face.

"Kathryn, there is no time, decide now." He was fierce again—angry at the necessity of what he was about to do.

"This is your life hanging in the balance, not the baby's … but *yours.* If you move, if I tear you in any way inside … you will die." His voice cracked slightly, his distress obvious. "I will not have you die." He held her chin, his face mere inches from hers. "I need you conscious and unmoving. Can you do that?" His eyes were intense.

"Jack. Jack?" questioning—frightened.

"Yes or no, Kathryn?" he demanded. He had already begun to lubricate his hand and arm heavily. If there was any chance of saving both lives, he must act now.

She nodded, her terrified eyes holding his, entrusting herself to him, ready to do as he requested.

"Focus on me at all times. Do exactly as I tell you."

Her head bobbed slightly as she visibly struggled to comply, making him proud.

"Colonel, get her semi-upright. Stand behind her and grip her arms tightly."

Jason moved to do as directed, refraining from kissing her and whispering words of endearment. She must not lose her focus. He understood what Jackson was attempting, and the enormous responsibility which had been thrust upon the man.

As the lieutenant's hand slid into her and began steadily pushing against the child's bottom, she tensed, moaning, then gasped at the brutal assault being inflicted on her tormented body. A massive contraction started her instinctively bearing down, trying to rid herself of her painful burden.

"Do not bear down," he hissed, attempting to focus his full concentration on what he must do.

As the spasm released her momentarily he continued to push, steadily guiding the baby back into her womb where it could be turned—and then make its entrance into the world.

She trembled violently, her body rigid in horrendous agony.

"Focus on me, Kathryn. Breathe deeply. Take deep breaths. Scream, if it makes this bearable … but *do not* move."

The sound of his voice, even angry, helped her. She could do this. She could.

Without warning, Jack's arm slid deeply into her, ending her battle for silence in an anguished cry—somewhat akin to that of a maimed animal. Jason clung tightly trying to block her pain, willing her strength and courage. Her fingers dug deeply into his arms, but her body barely moved as she visibly fought for control.

"Do not push. Focus, Kathryn, stay with me," he ordered, deep in concentration. "It is almost over."

He turned the baby, feeling his way slowly, careful not to tear her delicate inner flesh. Distractedly swiping his perspiring forehead across his sleeve, he wondered how much more she could take. This was worse than when his sister's child had been born.

He saw her intense suffering, saw her begin to fade. "Kathryn," he growled, loud and insistent.

She snapped back, refocusing on his face as another contraction ripped through her. But he felt her fight it, her legs trembling with the exertion.

"Breathe, breathe," he ordered; she panted in answer.

"All right, Kathryn." He withdrew his blood-covered arm slowly. "With the next contraction, I want you to push. The worst is over." His eyes caressed her unashamedly.

The next contraction caught her unaware, tearing through her with a vengeance.

"Push now, Kathryn. Bear down."

With a gasped sob she bore down, her face contorting with the effort, as the baby's head suddenly crowned.

"Again!" he commanded.

And with a final effort, the baby slid free.

"You have a beautiful little girl, Kathryn." He beamed at her as he gave a quick slap to the tiny, pink bottom, the resulting angry squall filling the tent.

Kathryn fell limply back against her husband, who immediately began crooning soft words of endearment, pride and endless devotion, as he pushed aside drenched hair to nuzzle her neck.

Lieutenant Jackson allowed them a few moments of quiet words. He carefully cut the umbilical cord and bathed the indignant infant, all the while admiring her incredible set of lungs. They would not have to announce this baby to the dragoons. She had done that quite competently on her own.

Wrapping the tiny bundle in a soft towel, he brought her to Kathryn's side and held her out for their inspection.

"Look what we have created, my love." Jason's voice held wonder.

Kathryn smiled through her exhaustion at her husband. The intensity of their incredible love gave Jackson a moment's inner pang. But he could never begrudge her that; she was far too dear.

"Jason, hold your daughter for a few minutes." He smiled at the colonel's sudden lack of composure as he placed the squalling infant in his arms. "She will not break, Jason, relax."

Lieutenant Jackson then turned to Kathryn, his voice tender as he said. "Kathryn and I have one last phase of this birth to get through."

But she gestured him to wait for a minute while she watched her husband. As Jason's tension eased, he bounced the little bundle gently in the crook of his arm and extended a large hand towards the flailing fists. A small fist glanced off his hand then returned. This time her tiny fingers opened to grasp the large finger he had extended. Loud squalls became tentative sobs that finally quieted as she clung to her father's finger. Striking blue eyes brimming with tears, stared at the large face bending close, crooning with a soft British lilt—a face that melted as his baby daughter hiccupped and gripped his finger tighter.

"Poppet," he breathed, his voice breaking. For a moment, his eyes closed as he dropped his head to rest against his little girl's forehead—awestruck. This tiny package represented both of them … their immortality. Suddenly so many bits and pieces fell into place, all the unhappiness of his earlier life no longer of importance. He would protect this bit of fluff with his very life … as he would her mother.

When he could speak again, he whispered, "You gave your mother a difficult time, little one. Do not make this a habit, for I love her dearly, and will brook no insolence on your part."

Kathryn smiled contentedly at the beautiful scene her husband and baby presented before turning to eye Jackson. "Let us be done with this, Jack, for I am truly exhausted."

"All right, Kathryn, focus on me for a few more minutes. I am going to press on your abdomen while you bear down, we have to finish this." As he began kneading gently, applying heavy pressure with his palm, he added softly, "This will not be bad, I promise."

She groaned but did as asked, the aftermath of the pregnancy discarding itself with no further difficulty. It was truly over.

She closed her eyes, trembling from shear exhaustion, too tired to feel embarrassment as Jackson deftly tended her aching body. He was casual, yet tender, as she had been with him just days before; she relaxed easily under his gentle ministrations.

Jason continued to become acquainted with his baby daughter as he watched Jack gently bathing Kathryn's face and pushing back damp strands of golden hair. Her eyes flickered open, lucid and free of intense pain, regarding Jack with a depth of feeling that warmed him to his very core.

"Come, Mrs. Tarrington, let us get you into a clean bed." With that brief warning, Jack picked her up in strong arms and carried her to the cot. Setting her down carefully, he turned towards the colonel.

"Jason, I will hold ..." He paused eyeing both of them, curious as to the little girl's name.

Kathryn smiled at her husband as he said proudly, "Gabrielle Elizabeth Tarrington, meet your Uncle Jack."

Jason placed the quiet, but squirming bundle in the lieutenant's arms and turned to his wife, his eyes filled with tenderness. "A clean shirt and warm blanket are what you need, love." He sat down on the edge of the cot, bending to brush a kiss to her forehead as he began easing her blouse off, taking consideration to conceal her nudity.

"I can wait outside with Gabrielle," Jackson suggested, sensing Jason's concern.

But with that remark, she laughed out loud despite her exhaustion. "Jack, after where we have been tonight, I am afraid there is little more of importance to see."

She quickly shrugged out of the soiled garment as Jason dropped a clean shirt over her head, adjusting it around her for comfort. Covering her with a warm blanket, he smiled, his face finally beginning to relax.

"Her sense of humor is restored, Jason. She is going to be just fine."

As Jackson moved to the cot and crouched down with Gabrielle, the baby's face screwed up into an angry little storm cloud. She thrust her small fist into her mouth and began sucking loudly. Kathryn reached for her, and placing the baby to her breast, watched intently as she began to suckle noisily; Jason and Jackson looking on, mesmerized.

Jason studied Jack thoughtfully, surprised he harbored no jealousy in sharing this private moment with his lieutenant ... no, his 'friend'.

"Everyone is going to be fine." Jack sounded relieved and very tired. "You were extremely brave, Kathryn. After my sister gave birth to my nephew, she informed me that the pain was so terrible, she would have killed me if only she had had a knife."

"Ahh," she grinned up at him, "that is why you were checking to see if I had my boots on when you first arrived."

Both men chuckled; her strength was improving with each passing moment.

Jackson stood, sweeping up all the soiled blankets as he rose. "I will return shortly with hot broth and willow bark tea that Cook made for you, Kathryn, and coffee for you, Jason?"

Nodding appreciatively, he stood to accompany Jackson outside the tent. At Kathryn's sudden unsettled look, he smiled, explaining, "I just want to thank Jack. I will only be a moment, love."

Her tired eyes followed him as he exited, then returned to her daughter's tiny face, watching her small mouth as it worked at filling her stomach.

Outside their tent, Jason stopped and placed his hand on Jackson's arm. "Jack. I cannot even begin to thank ..."

Jack smiled, interrupting him with a shake of his head. "No 'thanks' are necessary, Jason. Kathryn saved my life the other day, and very likely will again. It all works out in the end."

He shrugged, then turning to leave advised, "Keep a close eye on her for a couple of days. If the bleeding does not stop, or there are any changes, let me know. I doubt she will tell you, she is so stubborn ..."

He looked quickly to be sure no offense had been taken, but Jason merely grinned. "I do believe you know her almost as well as I, Jack."

Reentering the tent, he found her dozing with the baby asleep in her arms. His love for her and this new little life they had created was overwhelming. He sat on the edge of the desk, unable to take his eyes from her. After a few moments, he leaned down and picked up his daughter, carefully so as not to wake Kathryn. Tenderly he opened her blanket, absorbing the petite perfection of her tiny toes and long delicate fingers. Caressing her silky, black hair, he murmured soft words but paused, looking up with wonderment and almost boyish exuberance, as Jackson entered with refreshments.

"Look, Jack, so tiny, so perfect." He was awestruck.

Jack grinned at the complete pleasure reflected in Jason's face. "I gather there have never been any babies in your family, Jason."

Shaking his head, he answered quietly, "I asked my mother once, when I was about six, if I would ever have a brother or sister. She told me I had had a twin brother who died shortly after birth. She never had another child, and we never spoke of it again."

Rewrapping Gabrielle's blanket, he placed her in a large basket before accepting the hot coffee Jack offered. Both men sat sipping slowly, each immersed in private thoughts as they watched Kathryn dozing.

With a little groan, she roused, a smile chasing at the corners of her mouth. "I feel weak as a newborn kitten," she murmured, as she gazed lovingly at the two most important men in her life.

Jack moved to her side and sat down with a bowl of hot broth, pressing her to take nourishment.

"Within a day or two, you will feel quite yourself again," he assured. "But do not take things too fast. You have been through a lot tonight."

Suddenly tears began to roll uncontrolled down her cheeks. "Jack, I ..." She reached to touch his arm as he put shushing fingers against her lips.

"I owe you an apology for the way I had to treat you," he said softly.

"My God, Jack, you saved my life—Gabrielle's life. There should be no apologies." Her eyes caressed with utmost gratitude and warmth. Observing his love reflected so openly, she reached up and gently touched his cheek. "Thank you," she whispered.

"Time for everyone to get some much needed sleep." Deeply moved, Jackson quickly stood and turned to leave, but not before she saw the glistening moisture in his eyes.

After he had gone, Jason sat by her side caressing her cheek with his finger. "I believe he loves you as much as I," he said softly.

"Perhaps even more, if that is possible," she mused.

Jason looked at her, his eyebrow arched in question.

"He puts my need for you ahead of his own, always considering *our* needs first. He is a very special man, a dear friend."

Jason thought for a moment. "You are right, my love. Feeling as I do, and suspecting Jack shares identical sentiments, how is he able to manage those emotions? I could never bear to give you up or see you with another—never."

Standing and stepping back, he began the arduous task of unbuttoning his jacket. As she swallowed the strong broth, she watched him, her eyes unwavering. Knowing he would be up tending the babe in the night, he stripped only to his breeches before helping her tend to her own necessities. Settling her back onto the cot, he handed her a cup of willow bark tea and tucked the blankets snuggly about her. With a glance over at his daughter, to assure himself she was truly 'real', he kissed Kathryn gently.

"There is much to discuss tomorrow, my Kathryn. But tonight, please sleep. I wish to see you fully recovered soon." He paused. "You frightened me." His eyes narrowed slightly. "You frightened me."

With a final kiss, he settled himself on blankets arranged on the floor nearby; where he could be roused instantly if she needed him.

She had already begun to nod drowsily, fight it though she tried, still wanting to hold him and talk of their child. The willow tea was taking affect, her aching body quickly reduced to mild discomfort.

She slept fitfully on the cot, drifting half awake, feeling at loss without Jason beside her. Within a short time she was nudged fully awake, urgently needing to relieve her bladder. Weakly, she forced herself out of bed and tended the problem quietly so as not to disturb her husband. Seeing that Jason was sleeping the much needed, deep sleep of emotional exhaustion, she smiled tenderly; witnessing the birth had been difficult for him.

Instead of returning to her cot after looking in on Gabrielle, she cuddled in beside him. Automatically, even in sleep, his arms surrounded her as he breathed softly, 'love you', into her hair, his nearness and warmth giving her a sense of security.

Her body ached, but from far more than the birth. She had missed him these last days, hungering for their special physical connection. The possibility of Jason finding her no longer attractive after having born a baby weighed heavily. She had heard of instances where this happened, a disconcerting and silly notion perhaps, but one she could not get out of her head. Overly emotional and exhausted in the aftermath of birth, this thought persisted insidiously.

Suddenly he awoke, startled to find her at his side. "Kathryn, you should have waked me." His eyes filled with concern. "Are you in pain?" Propping himself up on one elbow, he gazed at her as he smoothed golden tangles back from her forehead. "Do you need help with Gabrielle?"

"I needed to feel you beside me, my husband," she whispered, pressing her cheek against his chest.

Petulant whimpers sounded from the corner, escalating rapidly into a demanding squall.

"With lungs like that, little one, you will wake the whole camp." Jason rose, moving quickly to pick up his daughter and quiet her distress.

Placing the indignant bundle in his wife's arms, he sat down and cradled Kathryn between his knees, pulling her back to rest against his chest while she nursed the baby.

"She is truly beautiful, just like her mother."

He kissed the top of Kathryn's head as he stroked Gabrielle's cheek with his finger, watching her suckle with feisty determination.

"She has your coloring, my love. Look at all that black hair, and the striking blue of her eyes. There will never be any question as to who is her father." She squeezed his hand, relaxing back against his shoulder.

With a sigh and a full belly, Gabrielle soon became heavy against her mother's breast, drifting into sleep, her small fists curled tightly. Gently, so as not to awaken her, Kathryn changed her soiled linen. Grinning at her husband's look of perplexity, she assured: "This is not a chore I will request you perform, Colonel, you may relax your concern."

"Thank you, madam, for small favors."

He smiled as he picked up his daughter, and with a light kiss to the top of her sleeping head, tucked her into her basket. Returning to his wife's side, he slid beneath the blankets beside her. Kathryn reached for him, caressing his face, her emerald eyes searching his, needing answers.

"What concerns you, my pet?"

As she made no immediate reply he kissed her gently, then with more fervor. Responding hungrily, quiet desperation cloaked within her kiss was not lost on him. She pressed against the full length of him, his firm desire immediately noticeable, much to her relief.

"I can hear your mind working, my pet. What is troubling you?"

He rolled up onto one elbow to better see her face. In the light of the oil lantern, he saw tears. Kissing her forehead, he traced his thumb down her nose and tipped her chin up, meeting her mouth with his in their well-known ritual of devotion.

"Talk to me, we have no secrets. I am at such a loss when you are upset."

She touched his face, her green eyes swimming with tears. "I have been so afraid that you would not …" Her voice trailed into silence.

"Would not what?" Momentarily confused, he searched her face. Then suddenly it struck him. Knowing her as well as he did, he realized the fears she needed to address. Having fears of his own, he understood the difficulty it often took to voice them aloud. This tiny child was a new responsibility in their lives, creating new concerns and insecurities they both needed to address. He would allay her fears tonight; his could be dealt with later.

"Becoming a mother, the mother of my child, our child—makes me love you all the more, if that is possible."

At his reassuring words, strain began to ease from her face.

"Lying beside you, touching you … requires all my willpower to refrain from making love to you. My passion for you, Kathryn, grows with each passing day, and that will never change. But …" His eyes caressed. "I shall wait until you have healed, I have hurt you enough already." His face fell with guilty remorse.

"You have given me what I needed to hear, my love." Her green eyes flashed inordinate relief as her fingers stroked his long hair. "But you, also, need to hear some things from me."

He, too, craved reassurance as remnants of his unhappy past still nagged at the far recesses of his mind. This would be a night of talk, to settle all concerns and move on. Before he could speak, to protest the late hour or her need for rest, she continued. "It is not your fault that I had difficulty in the birth. It just happened. There is always a certain amount of pain, but never more than can be borne for the gift of immortality it brings us. Everything has a price in life, as we both realize."

He hung on each word, listening intently.

"Would you deny our daughter, a chance for life?" She touched his cheek, and reaching to encircle his neck, hugged him close. "For I would not, I love her dearly."

He cradled her against his shoulder stroking her tangled curls, murmuring softly. "No, Kathryn, I could never deny her. But I wish it could have been easier for you. I am …"

"Enough, my love, put all that behind us." She shushed him gently. "The look on your face when you first held her, made it more than worth the effort."

She hesitated before continuing, choosing her words carefully. "However, I need you to understand, Jason, you come first and foremost: now … always. And that shall remain so. As much as I will cherish our daughter, I must find Anna soon. For I cannot give up *our* life—all that we share together. I *cannot*. Will not."

She watched his reaction to her vehement statement, comforted by the absolute relief displayed in his eyes. He had been questioning where Kathryn would place the child in their relationship, had been fearful of her answer, but unable to voice his fears.

"I love you more than life itself, my Kathryn. You understand me better than I understand myself." He hugged her closer. With a few well-chosen words, she had assuaged his fears. In their months of loving each other and growing together, they had truly become one: united in mind, body, and soul.

He placed his hand gently over hers, their large, knotwork rings touching. *Yes,* he thought, *our existence is as uniquely interwoven and complex as our beautiful, golden wedding bands. Our love: everlasting, eternal … always.*

"You are my heart and soul," she murmured. Inhaling the familiarity of him, she relaxed into much needed sleep, knowing that all was well between them.

When Gabrielle stirred in the wee hours of the morning, Jason arose and brought her to Kathryn's side. Sleepily she cradled the baby, allowing her to suckle noisily, while he cradled her within his strong arms, his face buried against the warm arch of her neck.

"Our daughter has the manners of a little piglet," she chuckled. "We must correct that so she may make a proper wife for a colonel in the dragoons someday."

"If that is her choice—as long as she is happy. We shall rear her with love. I fear she will find pain on her own, as life has a way of supplying that, but not through us.

Jason waited until late morning to walk down to the food wagon for breakfast and coffee. Cook had taken special efforts to make a healthy porridge for her. Lieutenant Jackson was there and accompanied him back to look in on Kathryn.

He smiled at Jason, taking note of his tired eyes. "You will get more sleep eventually," he grinned.

"My concern is that the men get some sleep. The only saving grace is the fact we have no active forays to pursue at the moment," Jason countered.

"Do not worry about the men, Colonel. You may see them move their tents a little farther out, but do not be overly concerned."

The two men entered the tent still chuckling.

"And just what amuses you two this morning?"

Jackson noted how quickly she had rebounded. Despite looking tired, her skin glowed. With her hair brushed and coiling in shiny waves on her shoulders, she looked jaunty in clean breeches and blouse. She was sitting at the desk holding the baby, but immediately stood to thrust Gabrielle into Jackson's waiting arms.

"I fear the men received as little sleep as we."

"Not to fret. They will survive, as will you." Jack grinned.

She watched him rock the child in the crook of his arm, talking to the warm, little bundle with the electric blue eyes who peered steadily up at him. Kathryn held Jason's hand as she sipped her coffee. She would tackle Cook's porridge when she was more awake.

"You will make a good father someday, Jack. You are a natural." Seeing his love for their little girl it struck her, she and Jason should make decisions regarding her rearing in the event of …

She could not complete the thought, though it was not the first time it had crossed her mind. *Yes, Jack would be the one.* At some point, they must approach him, but not yet, there was plenty of time.

"Take it very easy today, Kathryn. Sleep," Jack broke into her thoughts. "You really do need rest … and you must eat." He eyed her with concern.

"Well, perhaps coming from you, she will comply," Jason interjected. "It is not considered a sign of weakness to relax after a difficult time, my love." He squeezed her hand gently.

"I will do as you have both requested, gentlemen. We have a lot of ground to cover if we are to find Anna. But of greater importance, we must make ourselves available to aid Archie Campbell if he needs our assistance in securing Savannah. That may take some planning."

As she returned Gabrielle to her basket, the men eyed each other shaking their heads. This woman made no attempt to understand the meaning of the word, 'relax'. It was just not in her nature.

Jason spent the day helping her with the baby, assisting in tending her physical needs, reading favorite excerpts from her books or dozing with her, relishing the touch of her newly slender body against his. At times, he just sat and watched her sleep. He continued to marvel at the tiny perfection of his daughter, gently uncurling her long fingers to examine the small fingernails, and sweeping her mass of black, wavy hair back from her petite face.

Lieutenant Jackson brought their meals but quickly left, leaving them to their privacy. It was after a quiet supper together that night, that she bid Jason spend some time with his men. She could smell the wafting smoke of the campfires clinging to the evening air and hear the buzz as they talked amongst themselves.

"I would not have your dragoons think you softening towards duty, my love." She smiled. "Go. I will be fine."

After he left, she washed her face, changed into fresh clothing and battled her errant curls into submission. Pinching her cheeks for color, she peeked at herself in Jason's shaving mirror. *Not too bad considering everything.* She smiled at her weary reflection. The effort to look presentable had made her a little lightheaded, but that would pass.

With Gabrielle sleeping in the crook of one arm, she stepped out of the tent to a pleasant surprise. Ever concerned for her safety, Jason had posted Captain Hodges and a young corporal immediately outside. They both greeted her politely, Captain Hodges offering his arm.

"May I be of assistance, Mrs. Tarrington?"

Smiling up at his concerned face, she noticed he was eyeing the tiny bundle she held.

"Would you like to meet the cause of your lack of sleep last night, Captain?"

She pushed the blanket back from the little face just as Gabrielle's pink bowed mouth opened in a wide yawn. With eyes squeezed tightly shut, she thrust a tiny fist into her mouth and began sucking with eager anticipation. Kathryn watched as the captain's large face broke into a wide grin. The young corporal looked on, somewhat abashed, not quite certain what his proper reaction should be.

"She is a bonnie one, milady. Already I see the look of both of you in her." Taking her arm he added, "We had best get you to the colonel. He will want to know you are up and about."

Although it was only a short distance to the ring of men grouped around the campfire, she was relieved to have the captain's support; her legs lacked their usual strength.

Out of the corner of his eye, Jason saw her and immediately strode to her side, grasping her arm as the captain stepped away. After inclining his head in a quick nod of 'thanks', he turned full attention on his wife. His expression was stern as he spoke her name with exasperation. She merely gazed up through curling, golden lashes smiling innocently, an expression never failing to disarm him, a fact of which she was well aware.

"Gentlemen," she scanned the group, her eyes coming to rest on Jack. "I want to publicly thank Lieutenant Jackson for helping me through a rather difficult time last night."

The uncomfortable expressions on the faces of both Jack and her husband did not daunt her in the least.

"Perhaps this is not proper British protocol. Lord knows I have been guilty of that more than once." She grinned at the men as they tried to cover smirks.

"However," she looked first at her husband, and then with warmth at Jackson, "his gift to us is too precious to be overlooked."

She would not further embarrass him by making mention of his having saved her life—sure the men were quite aware of that fact.

At that moment, Gabrielle found her fist no longer of comfort and let out a loud wail.

"Allow me to present our daughter, gentlemen: Gabrielle Elizabeth Tarrington. She is somewhat assertive, a bit like her mother, I am proud to say." Jason's eyes were dancing.

If any of the men were curious about their daughter's first name, not one made the slightest indication. Jason and she had discussed several names prior to the birth. But it had been Jason's suggestion, knowing it would please his Kathryn, which prompted them to choose the feminine version of 'Gabriel'. Elizabeth had been his mother's name, and Kathryn was insistent that she be remembered.

Glancing at his wife and seeing she was beginning to show fatigue, Jason handed the baby to Lieutenant Jackson and proceeded to get Kathryn seated.

"Do you feel up to joining us, my love?" His words were soft, for her ears only, as he scrutinized her. "I will gladly accompany you …"

Gabrielle had ceased her wailing as Lieutenant Jackson bounced her lightly. Crooning quietly, he extended a finger for her to suck upon.

"Jackson is working his magic with our child. I would really like to stay a bit. She will need to be fed soon, but for the moment I am going to enjoy the campfire."

Happily ensconced on a log and completely at ease, she sipped her coffee and chatted with the dragoons, a sense of normalcy returning to her life. As a tin whistle's lilting melody filled the air, the men began humming and singing. Kathryn eagerly joined in, trilling a lively tune or two on the little tin whistle, until Gabrielle demonstrated the power of her tiny lungs, much to the dragoons' amusement.

Bidding 'goodnight' to his men, Jason walked her back to their tent. Completely exhausted, she dropped heavily onto the desk chair and bared her breast for an impatient little mouth. Jason cast a reprimanding look her way, his eyes narrowing.

"Do not chastise me, my husband. I am exhausted, admittedly so, but it did wonders for me to join the men, even for a short while."

Her look pleaded for patient understanding, and he did … completely. He knew her so very well.

As they lay in each other's arms after Gabrielle was contentedly sleeping, she trailed gentle kisses the length of his neck and lower. As her tongue traced across his chest barely touching, he inhaled sharply.

"Enough, my wanton wife, you require sleep, as do I."

He was light and teasing but knew her underlying need, one that matched his own so well. His voice was a husky growl as he pulled her tightly to him.

"Soon, my love, very soon," he promised.

Kissing her pouting mouth, he settled her into his shoulder and began humming a fondly remembered bedtime tune from his childhood. It took only moments before he felt her relax against him, her breathing deep and even.

My stubborn love, he smiled. *It is contrary to your nature to give in gracefully.*

His final thoughts before drifting into sleep were of how much she amused him, even now. After all this time—she still amused him.

Chapter Twenty-Four

Soaring Eagle's Vengeance

"Damn it all to Hell!" Kathryn swore vehemently, fighting to tame her wild curls: frustrated with her hair, frustrated with not finding Anna—just plain frustrated. As she angrily jerked her hairbrush back mid-fling, her wrist was gently curbed by her husband. Reaching deftly around her, setting coffee cups on the desk, he smoothly restrained her fit of temper.

"Jason." She jumped. "Damn it, you startled me." Her eyes blazed defiantly as he pried the brush from her curled fingers, grinning widely.

"Good morning, my love. Do allow me," he said brightly.

Slowly stroking her tangled curls, he brought them into some semblance of order and tied them with a leather strap she held out. Taking her in his arms, he eased her back against him. Resisting only momentarily, with a soft sigh she relaxed, responding to his touch, irritation suddenly forgotten.

"I see you are full of pent up energies today, my pet," he breathed softly against her ear.

She remained silent, her hands resting lightly atop his.

Two weeks, perhaps a little more, had passed since Gabrielle's birth. One day was like the next: evening flowing into day, flowing into evening. Gabrielle was healthy and happy, not a difficult child in any way. But she required much of Kathryn's time and attention. Unless they could find Anna, she saw no relief in sight. She loved her daughter and relished their unique 'connection' as the babe suckled at her breast. She delighted in Jason's loving acceptance and joy in his tiny poppet, his pet name for his little girl. But the monotony of their seemingly endless, new day-to-day routine weighed heavily upon each—although he tried to hide that fact. They both needed action, be it as simple as a wild horseback race across the surrounding fields.

"Do you think you could be packed by mid-morning?" he interrupted her musings.

"Jason, do you mean it?" She spun about eyeing him sharply; had she heard correctly? At his answering smile, she kissed him soundly.

"Sooner than that, Colonel." Executing a quick salute, she started towards her saddlebag, only to be brought up short by her husband's capturing of her arm.

"There is time, my love. Join me first with coffee. I wish to discuss plans with you."

Had he asked her to join him for coffee only, she could not have concealed her impatience. However, he had opened an important door; she needed to discuss some of her concerns, preparing them in the event of …

She moved to the desk and sat down, sipping from the hot cup he offered.

"As it has been months since I last spoke with Colonel Cruger, and we are near 'The 96', we will stop at Star Redoubt." At her look of disappointment he added, "We will stay no more than one night, but I must talk with John. We need to know if he has heard news of Archie Campbell and Savannah—or Clinton's plans for us."

Though agreeing with his decision, she regretted the further delay in their search for Anna.

"Perhaps Colonel Cruger would be good enough to relay our mail on to Lord Cornwallis and Grandmother," she said, her spirits brightening. She thought of the letters they had composed together, eager to share news of Gabrielle's birth and bring happiness to both parties, especially Lady Cornwallis, who hopefully was on her way to recovery by now.

"You read my mind, Kathryn," he murmured, reaching across the desk to take her hand. "I also thought John Cruger might have knowledge of the Bird Clan: information which may help in finding Anna."

As he drank his coffee, he watched her over the rim of his cup, noting the return of good color to her face. Though tired from too few hours of sleep, physically she was again her robust self.

"I have sensed your uneasiness over our lack of communication from Anna, especially as the Cherokees seem to be nearby. Talk to me of what you suspect," he coaxed.

Thankfully, he had opened the conversation to disturbing possibilities she needed to share. "Have you ever heard of 'blood vengeance', Jason?" she asked, observing him with a troubled look.

He shook his head, pursing his lips in consideration.

"When a Cherokee is killed, it becomes the sworn duty of the older brother, or nearest male family member, to avenge his death. They do not cease their quest until they have taken the scalp of the offender—or one from another member of his clan."

Jason digested her words, watching her intently.

"Although the Cherokees were not happy when Jamie dragged me away from my mourning period after Black Raven's death, it seemed, at least on the surface, they understood and accepted. Moreover, it was my brother's decision, an act beyond my control. I doubt they could hold that against me; at least not a punishment deserving of death. After all, Jamie is their friend. He has fought for, and supported their rights against the colonials. They would forgive him almost anything."

She talked rapidly, weighing the pros and cons of her thoughts for his consideration.

"As the British officer who killed Black Raven was no blood relation of yours, you should not be a target for vengeance either. After all, the Cherokees are not entirely innocent of taking the life of an occasional British soldier. Why would their need for vengeance not have been fulfilled elsewhere, or abandoned?" She paused, frowning. "I have wracked my brain trying to see how it could possibly concern us—but I am sure it does, somehow. Anna would have come to me long ago if she were able."

"Do not worry, Kathryn. We will travel with the dragoons at all times and be cautious."

"There is only one other possibility," she mumbled more to herself, deep in thought as she worked at the solution—oblivious to anything he had to say.

Relieved to see her able to talk freely of Black Raven, he hoped her past had finally been laid to rest. He would listen while she sorted things out, and then work at allaying her fears.

"Soaring Eagle is Black Raven's older brother; sometimes hot-tempered—more often a slow-burning fuse. Although aware of Black Raven's ill treatment of me, he never once came to my aid. He revered his younger brother and thought he could do no wrong." She grimaced at the remembrance. "I would not put it past him to invent *insult* where none even existed."

A spark of understanding abruptly lit her eyes. "He knows I have married a British officer and borne him a child. Soaring Eagle would perceive that to be the ultimate insult to his precious brother's memory."

"Although we have not hidden those facts Kathryn, how can you be sure that particular news would have traveled back into Cherokee country?"

"My brother would make sure." She winced, pained at the thought.

Jason eyed her quizzically. "Jamie's words of hatred would have been tempered once his immediate anger passed, Kathryn. There is too much love shared between you. I saw that for myself," he said softly.

"Jamie, God love him, can be hot-tempered, often acting hastily on impulse only—not thinking through all the reactions that might arise from a simple statement placed in the wrong ears. In anger, he could easily have informed Soaring Eagle of my despicable behavior, hoping you would be killed and perhaps your child—not giving thought that I, too, would likely be forfeit in the process. But, then again, perhaps that is what he wishes." Her voice caught on that painful thought.

"I do not believe he wants you dead, love, not for a moment. Unfortunately, I think your premise makes great sense. He merely failed to realize the ultimate consequences." Moving around the desk, he drew her up into his arms, kissing her gently.

A tiny whimper suddenly demanded their attention and they separated, eyeing each other with lopsided grins.

"I will tend your daughter, milord, and be ready to travel within the hour."

Touching her cheek in a tender gesture, he headed towards the tent flap. Abruptly turning, he silently regarded her. Intense pride and respect for her intelligence and the ability to dissect problems accurately, showed openly in his eyes.

"Knowledge of the enemy is strength, Kathryn," he reminded. "It is our sorry lot in life not to allow the likes of you to become a general. Hell, the war would be already won, with us on a ship sailing to England or Scotland by now." Inclining his head with a wink, he left to organize breaking camp.

In two days time they arrived at Star Redoubt. Kathryn's mood was light-hearted, pleased that her stamina had fully returned. During their journey, Jason had observed her carefully, relieved to see her riding at ease without any discomfort. Knowing she would vehemently refuse riding in Cook's wagon, he had not wasted his breath. When one's wife was as stubborn as Kathryn, you chose your battles carefully, opting for those of extreme import only—preferably ones you might have a chance at winning. He smiled to himself, loving her desperately.

Gabrielle was a good baby, usually cheerful when riding in her blanket sling. Anna had always preached the Cherokee method of placing a sling across the mother's back. But Kathryn felt more assured of Gabrielle's safety carrying her cradled in front where she could see her at all times. As well as making it easier for her to be fed and bodily needs tended, Kathryn enjoyed talking to her daughter when she was awake. Gabrielle already showed interest in sights and sounds, her startling blue eyes becoming more focused with each passing day, as she gazed up at her mother, swinging her fists and cooing happily. Jason and Lieutenant Jackson took turns reining in close to Beauty, offering assistance, and taking a few moments to talk to the little bundle with the full head of black wavy hair.

When they arrived at Star Redoubt, Colonel Cruger received Jason as if he were a long, lost friend, the men doing their share of back slapping and laughing. Colonel Cruger, a seemingly pleasant man, was extremely solicitous of Kathryn, mouthing all the appropriate niceties while extending a warm welcome. As she was shown about the fort, she found it a point of interest that this part of the base was manned almost completely by Loyalists—including its colonel.

Even with short notice, Colonel Cruger had organized a delicious meal that night, a pleasant departure from their trail fare of the past two days. When they found Anna, Kathryn was definitely returning to hunting on a regular basis.

Although Colonel Cruger's young wife was pleasant enough, Kathryn had nothing in common with the woman and quickly became bored by her frivolous, light-headed chatter. Lieutenant Jackson shot her one or two surreptitious glances from across the table during dinner, smiling sympathetically, well aware Kathryn's enthusiasm was lacking. Following traditional custom, as dinner came to an end the men excused themselves and taking their brandy and cigars, headed for a separate room to talk of 'important matters'—further annoying her.

Jason eyed her apologetically, trusting that her ability to adhere to protocol would not desert her, despite her desire to be included. "Courage, my love, I will make this up to you," he whispered as he excused himself.

She did not disappoint him. Maintaining perfect ladylike manners, she conversed amiably with the small group of officer's wives stationed at the fort; all the while wishing for any diversion to rescue her from this atrocious example of polite society. With luck, perhaps the young maid in charge of Gabrielle might require her aid. But it was not to be.

Touching her hand lightly to the pearl necklace that had belonged to Jason's mother, she prayed it would impart courage. Perhaps it did, as she found herself beginning to relax. She acted her role as the wife of a British colonel with perfection—a frightening thought. *I even look the part in this damn dress.* In struggling to maintain her sense of humor, she turned to formulating plans of how she would torment Jason when they retired for the evening.

Later in their room, as he helped unbutton the tiny pearls at the back of her dress and ease the gown to the floor, he nuzzled her neck voicing apologies. She moved to sit on the edge of the comfortable bed, taking note of their accommodations. Although not as elaborate as those at Lord Cornwallis's headquarters, they were still a far cry from a tent encampment on the road.

As Jason reached to help free her from her feminine underpinnings, their daughter demanded she be fed, loudly and insistently. Within moments, Gabrielle suckled noisily, her small fists kneading her mother vigorously. While watching her nurse, Jason related highlights from the after dinner discussion with Cruger and his officers.

"There was a lot of idle talk, merely supposition, rumors in which I take little stock. However, it appears Archie Campbell has been delayed in New Jersey. Savannah will not be a target until this fall at the earliest, or more likely the end of the year. Tarleton presses the importance of Camden and is making overtures about heading south. Clinton wants, and needs, to take Charleston—but can only accomplish that when he finally rids himself of duties in the North." Jason shook his head. "All the maneuvers Lord Cornwallis talked of are delayed due to his unexpected return to England. And word is unsettling from his lordship. His wife continues to languish in the clutches of the same damnable illness."

Detecting deep concern, Kathryn scrutinized her husband. At another point in time he would have relished Cornwallis's pain. Yes, her husband had changed. They both had.

"And what of us—what orders?"

"Stay put for the moment." He smiled at her. "Allow our daughter to grow—allow me to love my wife."

Kissing his daughter, he settled her into the small crib John Cruger's wife had provided. She was soundly asleep with a full belly and dry bottom, her small fists curled at either side of her face.

He turned to find Kathryn watching him with odd intensity. He moved towards her, unbuttoning his jacket as he closed the distance between them. Her face was moist with the water she had just splashed there, her breasts rising and falling in a heavy rhythm, her green eyes holding his, unblinking.

"Am I to be chastised for the bad manners of all men, madam?" His piercing gaze impaled her as his body responded—denying any indifference he might claim in trying to refrain from touching her, concerned for her well being.

"Yes." Her voice was smoky—seductive.

With a few swift moves, her remaining clothing settled in a small heap on the floor. Her eyes slowly roved the full length of his muscular body, taking note of his obvious arousal, before returning to his face. "Make love to me, Jason," a plea—a demand—her voice filled with yearning.

Clothing no longer existed as he reached her, held her, felt her supple warmth. He wanted her, needed her, to the point of desperation. Concerned he might cause pain, his caresses were, at first, tentative.

She felt his indecision and deep within understood—but refused to accept. As desire rose to an overwhelming inner ache, she clasped his face firmly in her hands. "Like the first time," she purred, her voice hoarse with need, her luminous, green eyes boring into his, almost through his, with the intensity of her desire. They had been apart way too long.

He arched a questioning brow, struggling to control his fierce urgency at the vivid remembrance of uninhibited passion shared on their first encounter.

"Yes," she demanded, claiming his mouth violently.

He was lost, no longer able to control his aching desire. At first rough and demanding as requested, he was then alternately violent … and gentle. He played her with an expertise gleaned from months of intimate knowledge of her uniqueness, until she feared she would scream with the overwhelming intoxication of his touch.

Using her knowledge of his innermost desires, she encouraged and enticed … driving him to the very precipice before luring him back, prolonging his exquisite torment. Suckling her breast, he was fascinated as pale droplets emerged increasing the throbbing intensity of his need.

They rode their wild, uninhibited tempest until unable to deny longer, the momentary cessation of time and excruciating bliss gleaned from a total merging of body and soul. Needing to possess and reclaim each other, they clung fiercely, yielding to the violent spasms of complete surrender.

She lay gasping beneath him, sure the world had ceased to exist, elated beyond her wildest dreams.

Bending to her ear he hissed, "Was that passion up to your standards, madam?"

"Not bad for a first attempt, sir, but it may require years of practice."

With a low growl, he pushed damp curls back from her forehead to smile into her expressive passion glazed eyes. Roguishly planting nipping kisses along her arched neck, rough mutual satisfaction turned to gentle play, both laughing in unison.

She felt renewed, complete, relishing the ache of flesh still tender from childbirth, and strained muscles not yet fully recovered, at one with her husband. Lying within the circle of his arms, gently caressing and teasing, his desire renewed, demanding further release.

"As I recall, Colonel, you required that I must wait until evening for our next encounter. Rather rude of you to have denied a lady, I might add." She arched an eyebrow, grinning widely.

"You, madam, are a wanton temptress. Tread lightly, or I may call you to task yet again," he warned as his hands began moving seductively in secret places.

"Are you throwing out a challenge to me, sir?" Her look and tone were of laughing innocence.

"To no other, my pet," he growled, as his mouth found her breasts, sweet droplets causing him to linger before drifting lower.

"Jason." Raw emotion etched her face.

"Gently this time, my love," he murmured against her newly flat belly, as his tongue became the tender instrument of her torture.

She arched against him, unable to deny. Teasing, coaxing he seduced with utmost patience until her complete being splintered into tiny shards spinning out of control … eventually reclaiming her soul, her heartbeat slowing, she murmured breathlessly, "My love, my love …" *He was hers and hers alone, as she was his … for all time.*

Deeply engrossed in each other's presence at breakfast the following morning, they had difficulty participating in the conversation bubbling around them. Lieutenant Jackson took one look at their relaxed, happy faces knowing all was well. He had been concerned by the escalating tension apparent between them of late, but that was obviously over. They were a unique couple—allowing discord to proceed just so far, before one or the other took measures to correct the problem.

The dragoons sat astride their mounts in crisp formation awaiting their colonel's signal. As they prepared to mount, Jason handed Colonel Cruger the two letters he had mentioned the night before.

"I will be sure they are sent ahead with dispatches by the end of the week, Jason. I know of your approximate whereabouts and will be in touch."

He inclined his head towards Kathryn remembering the polite amenities in 'goodbyes'. As he was her husband's friend, she would never make rude comments, though it irked her: he obviously found women a necessary evil with but one purpose in life—one having nothing to do with their mind.

As they headed south towards Keowee, Jason informed her that a small party of Cherokees had been seen traveling in a somewhat erratic pattern about two day's ride from Star Redoubt. Colonel Cruger's reconnaissance riders had spotted them the previous week. The description of a large warrior, appearing to be the leader, sounded close to that of Soaring Eagle.

"We will soon have answers, Kathryn." He smiled pointedly, but had no need to elaborate.

They rode three days out from 'The 96' before stopping to set up their encampment for a few days layover near a group of mixed pines and oaks. A brook gurgled from the copse, meandering across an open field before pooling into a shallow pond in a small wooded glen. Kathryn took special note, pointing it out to her husband with a suggestive glint to her eye.

Acutely aware of increased smoke signals as they traveled southward, Kathryn assured Jason that the sound of a hooting owl their first evening in camp was not an owl. The Bird Clan took pride in its ability to mimic nature, and was extremely clever at it. But having spent time with them, she could recognize the difference, as well as create the same cries from nature herself.

The first night in their new camp, she and Jason sat in their tent sipping glasses of brandy from a coveted bottle Kathryn had set aside. Lieutenant Jackson had been asked to join them; their plan directly involved him. They needed to discuss suspicions about Soaring Eagle and wanted his input.

He sat, savoring his drink as he bounced Gabrielle gently in the crook of his arm. Despite her full belly and clean bottom she remained wakeful, happily watching her Uncle Jack. Setting his glass down, he ruffled his fingers through her soft, black curls, eliciting a tiny smile and gurgle of pleasure. He continued stroking Gabrielle's soft hair as he eyed Kathryn inquisitively.

"What is the plan, milady?" His smile was warm, his expression curious.

Kathryn began slowly discussing all the theories she had shared with Jason. As Jack had been only vaguely aware of her former husband and his treatment of her, she touched lightly on her past. Wanting to be done with the conversation and move on to possible solutions, she began speaking more rapidly. As she talked, Jason watched her intently.

"I knew you had spent time with the Cherokees, Kathryn. I had not realized you …" Jackson stopped mid-sentence.

Kathryn's face had become still, a haunted look darting across her features. Jason moved to her side with such abruptness, he startled Jackson. Taking her hand, he squeezed gently, leaning close and speaking softly in her ear. Her eyes searched his, acknowledging his words, composure returning as she gripped his hand. "I am all right, love," she assured. "Truly I am."

"Forgive me, Kathryn, I had no intention of prying." Lieutenant Jackson silently cursed himself for his insensitivity and having hurt her.

Interrupting him with a wave of her hand she said quietly, "It is no fault of yours, Jack. It is a part of my life I occasionally have difficulty in discussing, but I am better."

Gabrielle's eyes grew heavy as she snuggled happily in Jack's arms. At Jason's suggestion she be put in her bed, Jack waved him off, enjoying the warmth of the little bundle he never tired holding.

Jason remained by Kathryn's side, hand resting gently on her shoulder as she began speaking. "It is a pity we need you in other areas, Jack. I daresay you are as easy with the babe as Anna will be, once we find her."

"We *will* find her," Jason assured, then turned to Jack. "Jack." He fixed him with a long look. "Soaring Eagle and his braves will not show themselves if we travel with the whole company of dragoons. Kathryn knows him well; he will make himself known to us *alone*. He wants us to be fully aware of his reason for vengeance, for he will demand strict justice—in what form, we are not yet sure. But he will not stop until he has achieved his goal. His threat must be ended so Anna may join us, and we can stop looking back over our shoulder at the Cherokees.

"When do we ride out?" Jack asked without hesitation.

"Jack, it is a tremendous risk." Kathryn's face creased with worry. "I cannot tell you how Soaring Eagle will react until I see him … talk to him. The danger is in his response. We could all be …"

"When do we leave?" His eyes held hers for a long moment before glancing to Jason.

"Tomorrow just after dawn, plan on two or three day's supplies, hopefully less, but who knows."

"If that is the case, perhaps we had all best get some rest." Handing his empty glass to Kathryn, he rose slowly, caressed Gabrielle's cheek, and placed her in her father's arms.

"And Gabrielle?" From the look on their faces, he had known the answer before he had asked.

"I fear Soaring Eagle wants our daughter as badly as he wants us, Jack. But I *will* take him down. I remember his weaknesses, his habits. I only hope his remembrance of me is less clear."

Jack eyed her, deeply concerned, impressed with her courage.

"When we have made contact, I believe everything will happen fast. There will be no time for conversation between us—just action. You both must do as I say, immediately and without question." There was no faltering in her tone, only icy determination.

Before Jack could voice an opinion, Jason spoke up. "Kathryn and I have talked at length … rather heatedly upon occasion." A private look passed between them. "I do not like the idea of placing her in such danger, but neither of us can see any alternative."

The two men eyed each other, unspoken feelings understood and shared.

"We will both back you, Kathryn; I will protect Gabrielle so your husband may focus on you." He noticed a slight quiver of her lower lip as she flashed a look of gratitude.

"Goodnight, Jack, and thank you," she whispered.

He smiled as he left; etching the three of them together in his mind, knowing he would do whatever it took to preserve that picture.

After Jason's quick briefing with Captain Hodges, they were on their way just after dawn as planned, Gabrielle sleeping peacefully in her blanket sling with her little belly full. They rode steadily southward in silence, each immersed in personal thoughts.

They broke for a light breakfast followed later by lunch—still no sign of Soaring Eagle. There was little conversation between them, tension increasing with each passing hour. Gabrielle created no additional burden; she was a natural at traveling, happily content in her sling cuddled against her mother, even when awake.

By mid afternoon, Kathryn had all but given up hope. As they neared a small outcropping of woodland, having decided to make camp for the night—suddenly he was there: appearing out of nowhere as if by magic. Soaring Eagle sat bold and straight astride his pony, flanked by four warriors whom Kathryn recognized, but could not immediately recall by name: fearsome in his painted grandeur, as were his companions.

Swiftly reining in, they faced off with the warriors, Kathryn's heart pounding like a trip hammer. Jason and Jackson watched the Indians intently, waiting for Kathryn's instruction.

Gently handing Gabrielle to Jackson, a steely form of control changed her whole demeanor.

"Stay here, he will talk first," she said just loud enough for the two men to hear.

As if by agreed signal, she and Soaring Eagle both urged their horse forward, stopping midway.

Jason's body tensed as he surreptitiously flipped his holster strap aside for quicker access. Other than his child's birth, he had never felt so helpless in his life, and the feeling was not to his liking.

All watched as the conversation escalated. Kathryn spoke fluent Cherokee expressing confusion, indignation and rage. Soaring Eagle's voice rose to a bellow as he countered with fierce, threatening gestures, none of which intimidated Kathryn.

Pounding her chest, she swept her arm in a wide arc gesturing to Jason, the lieutenant and her child. Growling angry retorts, fearless in his presence, her eyes bored into Soaring Eagle's with an intensity that would have made most men flinch unashamedly. Jackson watched, mesmerized, the likeness of a lioness protecting her own, the only image that came to mind.

Suddenly Soaring Eagle sawed on his pony's rope halter, whirling away—then circled back, and nudging into the space left by his warriors, turned to face her.

With light knee pressure, she backed Beauty into the space between her husband and Jack's chargers, not willing to turn her back on the imminent danger.

Both sides sat regarding one another in silence. It was then, in a subtle motion, that Soaring Eagle adjusted his arrow quiver, moving it from behind his shoulder to a spot tucked just under his left arm. Nodding to her in apparent 'farewell', he began to swing away as if to leave.

Jackson breathed an audible sigh of relief. But Gabrielle, upset from unaccustomed angry voices, and sensing Uncle Jack's tension, began to whimper.

Jason, the air surrounding him fairly crackling with intense energy, touched a trained hand to his pistol butt.

"He will turn and fire," a clipped whisper. "At my signal, wheel aside so I may finish this," she hissed.

Quickly, accurately she judged the timing.

"Now!" she yelled. Flinging her left arm wide in signal, her pistol cleared its holster smoothly—in complete control.

With loud commands to their horses, Jason and Jackson both wheeled in opposite directions, a tactic which succeeded in throwing Soaring Eagle's judgment slightly off as he spun his horse, arrow nocked and ready to fly.

Kathryn's bullet smashed into his upper chest just as the arrow loosed his bow, deflecting its lethal path, allowing it to fall harmlessly, far from target.

As he toppled from his pony, Kathryn flung herself from her saddle and strode towards the injured man. A quick scan of his companions showed them observing quietly, making no threatening moves. It was Soaring Eagle's vengeance—not their place to interfere.

Soaring Eagle tried valiantly to rise as a low moan clawed its way from the depths of his throat, his face a mask of pain. Whipping the tomahawk from the small of her back, Kathryn forcefully shoved the big warrior flat, a feat accomplished through the momentum of her fierce approach.

Quickly straddling him, she dropped to her knees, pinning his arms painfully. With a vicious swing, her tomahawk thunked into the ground barely an inch from his head, momentarily startling him out of his pain. His eyes flew open, the air whooshing from his lungs, as she brought her full weight down onto his chest.

Yanking his topknot roughly, she slipped her dirk smoothly from her boot and pressed its keen edge flat against his hairline. His eyes held no fear as they met hers, the grimace of his mouth changing ever so slightly into a thin smile.

"You are a worthy foe, Ugilohi," he gasped painfully.

Her eyes never leaving Soaring Eagle's face, and ignoring his compliment, she jerked her head sharply towards the spot where Jason sat astride Diablo. "My English husband has nurtured my spirit and made me whole with the gift of his child." Pride edged the fierce quality of her tone.

Gabrielle's whimpering could be heard faintly, enforcing her statement.

Soaring Eagle's breathing was thready and becoming more difficult with each inhalation.

"I will have him—and no other. End this vengeance, end it now," she demanded.

Her voice held a lethal edge, her presence fearsome in her determination. She lowered her face to within inches of his, eliciting a groan from the suffering man as her weight shifted closer to his open wound. With pressure on her dirk, she started a trickle of blood flowing at his hairline.

Wincing, he appraised the strength now present in her whole being, a strength that had never existed under Black Raven's heavy hand.

"Tell them," she spat, gesturing towards his companions who sat astride their ponies, watching and waiting for the final outcome. Her lip curled back, her next words a fierce snarl. "Tell them or I will take your scalp while you yet live."

His eyes widened, an odd look flashing across his face—distinct uneasiness—or perhaps fear.

"I will wear your scalp on my belt for all to see your disgrace. Or I will return you to your companions to ride away—perhaps to live—or at least to die a proud man having ended an unjust vengeance. It is your choice."

He was visibly fading.

"End this now," she hissed.

His voice, though weak as he finally spoke, was audible to his companions. "The vengeance is done, I am satisfied." He regarded her with newfound respect. "You are now wise … and strong." A slight smile played at the corner of his mouth.

Sliding the dirk smoothly back into her boot, she rocked her tomahawk free, returning it to its customary resting place against the small of her back, then slowly stood. Backing away, she indicated for his companions to come forward and assist their injured leader.

With quiet alacrity, they surrounded Soaring Eagle and helped him onto a pony. Eyeing her, quietly resigned, he slumped painfully against one of his fellow warriors.

"You will not die Soaring Eagle," she assured, scrutinizing him through narrowed eyes, assessing the visible damage to his chest. "Anna, your 'Ku ni a ka ti', will work her magic." Their eyes met and held. "Send her to me when your danger has passed."

He nodded weakly, understanding and agreeing.

Jason and Lieutenant Jackson dismounted and stepped forward to flank her. Kathryn gathered Gabrielle lovingly into her arms, the baby's mewling ceasing at her mother's soft words. She swayed against Jason, weariness suddenly overcoming her, but with the reassuring touch of his hand, steadied, drawing herself up to her full height.

Inclining their heads in acknowledgement and respect, the Cherokees spun their ponies and quickly slipped back into the woods as quietly as they had come.

As she stood watching them depart, her adrenalin rush abruptly deserted her. Reaching out, she grasped blindly for Jason's sleeve, needing his support.

"I … I need to sit down," she choked, weakness overcoming her.

Instantly encircling her in his arms he lowered her gently onto the soft grass. Leaning forward, she rested her head against her baby, waiting for the dizziness to subside.

Gabrielle began to cry with determination as her father reached to take her. "Hush now, little one, your mother needs my attention," he said softly. Stroking her hair gently, he handed her to Jackson, who proceeded to croon to the angry little bundle in an attempt to quiet her.

"She is hungry, love, and frightened. Just give me a minute, I will be fine." Kathryn's face was pale as she tried gamely to smile.

Jason cupped her cheek with extreme tenderness. "She must learn, even now, as little as she is: you come first, my Kathryn … always." Sitting down beside his wife, he gently pulled her against him, brushing a soft kiss to her forehead.

Shuddering violently, she buried her face against his chest, inhaling deeply of his familiar scent, feeling his strong body and presence, needing reassurance that he was alive, and here with her.

"I was so frightened, so very frightened." She stifled a muffled cry against his jacket. "If my timing had been misjudged …"

"My love, my very brave love," he interrupted. "We are all safe; it is over."

Well aware that her tough exterior concealed an inner softness and compassion, her exhaustion came as no surprise. She tackled every confrontation with fierce determination, accomplishing what must be done—but took no joy at causing pain to others, even when justified.

He held her close until her trembling eased, until she turned large, tired eyes to his hoping for approval … or forgiveness. Running a hand through her hair, she looked from her husband to Jack.

"I am so sorry for what I put you both through. I never realized …"

Jason shook his head, silencing her with a gently pressed finger.

"You are to be commended, Kathryn," Jackson stated firmly, his eyes meeting hers with warmth.

Gabrielle continued fussing, quietly but insistently. Kathryn chuckled as she reached for her child, smiling at her husband as some of her usual vitality returned with all danger finally past.

"Good luck with trying to teach your daughter, sir. I am truly afraid she has a touch of the MacLean stubborn streak when she wants something."

She sat nursing Gabrielle, grimacing as this hungry little being suckled with vengeance.

"May I ask a question, Kathryn?" It was Jackson, a frown wrinkling his brow. At her smiling nod, he asked, "How did you know that it was all a ruse—that they were not going to leave in peace?"

"When Soaring Eagle shifted his quiver from where he customarily carried it against his back, I knew we had trouble. It is a common Cherokee custom used when hunting or in battle. Moving the arrow quiver down to their side, provides easier access for drawing an arrow and firing rapidly. Either he thought I learned nothing during my stay with his people … or that I had forgotten."

"You are amazing, Kathryn." Jack smiled, awestruck.

She then shared a loose translation of all that had been said between Soaring Eagle and herself, watching the men's faces as she spoke. "Do you now understand why I was unable to tell you in advance what he would do? I had no way of determining his mood or—his plan. It had to 'play itself out' according to his decision of that moment."

"I gather we have Jamie to thank for your admirable abilities in self-defense, Kathryn," Jason remarked as he touched her shoulder; his meaningful look sending an unspoken reminder: hold dear the memories of your brother.

"But he is very likely the one who …" she began to protest.

"Curse him for having put you in this difficult position if it is easier for you to accept, but be thankful he taught you the skills to survive such a predicament. I wonder if he has realized that yet," Jason mused. "If so, I imagine *he* is most likely the one cursing."

For a split second her eyes filled, grateful for his sensitivity. Then, setting her blouse in place, she accepted a hand up from her grassy seat with her now sleeping daughter.

"Let us return to our encampment. If we hurry, perhaps we can make a late supper." She headed for the horses, anxious to be on their way. "The men will be worried, and I actually find myself quite hungry for one of Cook's meals, perhaps some singing and laughter to help put this all behind us."

"What of Anna?" Jason asked, stopping her mid-stride.

Kathryn looked a little discomfited, hesitantly admitting, "I told Soaring Eagle to use Anna's healing abilities. When his immediate danger is over, he is to send her to me at the encampment."

She shrugged apologetically. "I know I have been extremely anxious to have her with us, but it was the least I could do. He suffered a grave injury; it will take Anna's expertise to heal him. What are a few more days of waiting?" She glanced at Jason through curling lashes, pleading for patience.

"How I do love you," he said quietly, as he helped her onto her saddle. "Rest easy, love, I will carry our daughter."

He quickly mounted Diablo, taking the baby from his wife. His usually restive horse quieted immediately, as if aware of his important cargo.

They cantered across fields and woodlands in a smooth, rolling gait that ate up the miles quickly, Gabrielle sleeping soundly against the warmth of her father. As they neared the encampment Kathryn reined to a halt, causing both men to slow their mounts and circle back to her.

Jason looked concerned as he approached his wife, but at his raised eyebrow, she smiled.

"I am fine, Colonel. However, I will carry Gabrielle the rest of the way."

He gave her a long, thoughtful look and carefully passed his daughter to her. So perfect was their understanding, no discussion was necessary. Informal as they had become, it was important that Jason maintain a position of authority befitting his rank when they rode into camp to reunite with his dragoons. His fatherhood must never be perceived as a weakening of his ability to command.

Well-placed pickets waved them into camp just at dusk, the delicious aroma of food roasting and tangy wood smoke greeting them in warm welcome.

"Home," Jason heard Kathryn murmur happily.

Captain Hodges's greeting was appropriately military although underlying warmth made it obvious he was pleased they were returned unharmed. He reported that all smoke signals had ceased; and no further indication that the Cherokees were still in the area.

"Good," Kathryn nodded eyeing the colonel. "Then it is truly over, they are gone. Soaring Eagle would never announce defeat; only his continued vengeance."

Hodges looked mildly confused at mention of 'vengeance', but made no comment. The reason for the colonel's foray had not been explained beyond expressing dire necessity of their action. It was none of his business, or anyone else's for that matter. He too, was protective of the colonel and his family.

Kathryn's exhaustion fell away as they all gathered around the familiar campfire in a comforting atmosphere she found so healing. Watching the many unique individuals that comprised the dragoons as the firelight played across their faces, she knew beyond doubt: this was her home; this was where she belonged.

Jason interacted with his men chatting conversationally, but maintained close scrutiny of his wife, deeply heartened at her rapidly returning vitality. It never ceased to amaze him how much she enjoyed their arduous lifestyle, a unique woman indeed, this wife of his.

Eventually the colonel bid 'good evening' to his men and escorted his wife towards their tent. Lieutenant Jackson accompanied them a short distance, getting just beyond hearing distance before he spoke.

"I have no desire to sleep yet, sir." His eyes danced. "Perhaps, once the little one is fed you might care to take your wife for a walk."

Jason raised a surprised eyebrow, marveling at his intuitive thoughtfulness.

"Give me about fifteen minutes, Jack," Kathryn said happily as she headed the last few feet to the tent, rousing Gabrielle as she went.

Having been entertained by the cheerful voices around the campfire, Gabrielle had stayed contentedly awake, her small fists waving and gurgling happily. A composite of them both, with each passing day she became more attuned to their lifestyle, causing Kathryn to wonder why she had ever entertained misgivings in the first place.

A few minutes later, she gently placed Gabrielle in Jackson's waiting arms. Although eager to share some private moments with her husband, she lingered a bit, watching the two of them together. Suddenly she leaned up and brushed a light kiss to his cheek, startling him slightly, but not disturbing Jason in the least.

"Thank you for everything, Jack." Her eyes met his and held, conveying wordless volumes.

He smiled with great tenderness, his eyes answering with perception … and inner peace gleaned from absolute acceptance. What an incredible man this lieutenant of theirs, this dear friend.

Much later, as they returned from their 'walk', a visit to the stream obvious from their still damp hair, Jackson greeted them with their daughter happily asleep in his arms.

"You spoil her, Jack," Jason chided, grinning at his friend.

"That is what uncles are for," he chuckled as he handed the little bundle to Kathryn and headed for the tent flap.

Pausing, he turned, eyeing both of them. "Perhaps 'lady luck' will provide us a few days of quiet so we may all be spoiled."

That night Kathryn slept serenely, her body stretched the length of Jason's muscular frame, savoring his nearness. With arms wrapped around each other, immersed in deep sleep, neither roused to Gabrielle's soft whimpers much later, whimpers that quickly ceased as she dropped back into sleep.

Perhaps it was the deep, even breathing of her parents nearby that lulled her, or perhaps the effect of an overwhelming sense of tranquility that permeated their living quarters on this particular evening. But Gabrielle slept through until dawn before her stomach finally demanded attention.

Chapter Twenty-Five

Anna

Within a week, just before dusk one evening, Anna suddenly appeared. She was ushered into camp with utmost courtesy, the pickets having been forewarned of her pending arrival, and explicitly instructed as to the proper respect to be afforded this esteemed Cherokee healer.

The colonel and Kathryn strode from their tent to welcome Anna with Gabrielle tucked in the crook of her mother's arm. Kathryn remained calm, speaking quietly in fluent Cherokee, adhering to age-old protocol in demonstrating respect for her mentor—only her sparkling green eyes belying outward control.

Jason studied Anna closely, impressed by this striking woman sitting astride a small, dark pony. She looked to be taller than average, of about middle age. Raven colored hair pulled into two precisely woven plaits hung evenly, one over each shoulder. Wide, identical, silver streaks sweeping back from her temples added an air of distinction and austerity. Her skin, creased and tanned from years of living in harmony with the elements, bore the look of aged leather. But her eyes … those piercing jet-black orbs missed nothing. They were alive with a passion for life: curious, discerning, and extremely shrewd. Although making an appearance of talking directly to Kathryn, she assessed him with an intensity that made him slightly uneasy.

Jason noted her patent fascination for adornment: beads, brightly colored feathers, small tinkling bells, bangles on her wrists and ankles. Her soft doeskin dress and leggings were ornately trimmed and immaculate.

A talented healer of repute, she was a proud woman and had every right to be. She had passed his muster. Now, if only he could pass hers, strong critic that she looked to be. The idea that he should be the one to worry about acceptance actually amused him.

Kathryn spoke his full name in introduction, startling him from his thoughts. He greeted Anna with his usual precise English inflection, welcoming her, acknowledging her reputation, and 'inviting' her to join them. Kathryn had carefully warned him that no one dictated to Anna, they suggested or invited.

This should be interesting he thought, curious as to how much English she actually understood.

"I sense you are a good man." She cocked her head, narrowing her eyes … judging. "Yes, I believe you are good for my Ugilohi." She continued openly evaluating him, making no pretense of doing otherwise. "Yes." She slowly nodded approval.

With that one terse word, Jason caught himself releasing his breath—relieved—*actually relieved*: he had been accepted. As to her command of the English language—excellent, he noted, impressed.

Suddenly she broke into a wide smile displaying small, even white teeth. The myriads of tiny lines etched into her face from years of hardship suddenly fell away, leaving her youthful in appearance. She watched him intently, holding her silence—perhaps reading his thoughts—amused at his mistaken perception of her, understanding him better than he did himself: a rather unnerving observation which left him feeling naked and somewhat lacking in the eyes of this venerable woman.

Decision made, she quickly dismounted. Taking Gabrielle gently from Kathryn, she proceeded to systematically check their daughter for any hidden imperfections while they both looked on, curious as to the outcome of her observations.

Gabrielle was alert, her striking blue eyes watching this dark stranger, unafraid. Suddenly she cooed, her tiny fists waving, reaching towards Anna with her little bowed mouth pursed in a smile.

"Ahh, you are bold, tiny bird, as are your parents. You have the look of my Kathryn, but the coloring of your father." She nodded approvingly, passing her carefully to Jason.

With all proper greetings complete, she turned and threw her arms around Kathryn, clasping her tightly, speaking rapidly in Cherokee. Tears flowed freely down both women's cheeks as they continued to hug, breaking only long enough for Anna to step back and take a long, perceptive look at her 'white daughter' before encircling her again.

Whatever the exact words that transpired between them, it was easy for an observer to read Anna's explanation and Kathryn's acceptance, of all that had happened since they had last met. The love and mutual respect between these two was not lost on Jason, or any of the dragoons. While trying to appear busy with preparation for the evening meal, they observed quietly from a distance.

Jason's eyes met Lieutenant Jackson's over the top of Kathryn's head, gratified to see no hint of reservation. With the slightest smile, Jackson gave further ease to any lingering misgivings. Jason trusted his excellent abilities in character judgment, and ever-accurate assessment of both their needs—often before they came to any realization themselves. *Yes. This will work. Kathryn will be at my side again.* Their idyllic world of the moment could not go on endlessly; a few weeks at best. This infernal war was about to escalate—directly on the South's doorstep. He needed Kathryn at his side.

After her initial indoctrination into the daily regimen of the dragoons, Anna rapidly established her own pace of daily living, adapting easily. Both women had much to share, a great deal of 'catching up' to accomplish, and spent many hours together the first few days after Anna's arrival.

Although Kathryn had no wish to discuss Black Raven, she was pleased to hear that Soaring Eagle had survived his wound and held her in high esteem. Jamie, as Kathryn had suspected, was well protected by the Bird Clan, drifting in and out of Cherokee land, as necessary, to elude the English. Anna, always fond of Jamie too, would not discuss him further—their boundaries for conversation had now been clearly established.

Lieutenant Jackson occasionally offered to watch Gabrielle so the two women could hunt together, an offer that benefited the whole camp. With the addition of Anna's expertise in hunting and cooking, the dragoons had never eaten so well. No one could bake a loaf of bread as tasty as Anna's. Once Cook was able to rise above the initial affront to his perceived title, they became fast friends.

After several weeks of living within the structure of dragoon life, Anna felt comfortable with their customs. One morning just before dawn, she quietly set out to hunt with Gabrielle snuggled sleepily into her blanket sling, securely anchored across her back. Staying near the encampment, she was unconcerned about danger. The rebel militia had moved farther south in recent weeks, that she knew for a fact. Besides, if she encountered Jamie, he would not harm her or Kathryn's child, despite what he had avowed.

When Anna returned from her successful expedition shortly after sunrise, Jason was aghast, furious, but Kathryn, after the initial shock wore off, remembered her time spent with the Bird Clan; their daughter could not be in more trustworthy hands. This was a normal way of life for Anna.

With that knowledge, and a great deal of patient explanation, she was able to moderate her husband's point of view, easing his fear for their daughter.

"Do you question Anna's love for our little girl, Jason?" Kathryn asked calmly.

Their words had been heated up to this point.

"No," he stated after consideration, trying to contain his anger. "She loves Gabrielle as much as we. I do believe that." He was becoming calmer, more able to think rationally.

"Then she will protect our child as she would her own, of that I am positive. Although her way is different from ours, she would never knowingly bring danger to our little girl, Jason."

On that point, he had to agree.

"We have a choice, love, we either trust in Anna's judgment or I must ..."

"No," he cut her short. "I will have you at my side. There will be no further discussion on that matter." Arching his brow he angled his head, his blue eyes crackling with intensity.

Flowing into his arms, she kissed him deeply. "There will be no discussion on that matter, my love—none."

Moving close as he sat down at his desk, she gently cupped his face, capturing his gaze.

"Our daughter will grow strong and beautiful with a rich background: English, Scot and Cherokee. More children should be so blessed." Their first misgivings had been addressed and soothed. This would work.

Although never openly rude, as word of this infraction would bring the colonel's wrath down upon their backs, the dragoons were, at first, not overly solicitous of the Cherokee healer. But in time, as a soldier had an irritated eye, sore stomach, congestion or fever, Anna's incredible abilities with herbs won them over. Only an ignorant man would continue clinging to false pride, denying relief from common ailments found on the trail because the 'doctor' was an Indian woman.

Relishing the freedom afforded by Anna's presence, Kathryn and Jason worked at accepting the eccentricities of this unusual woman. There was no denying her growing respect for Jason, her love for Kathryn, or her absolute devotion for their child. And Gabrielle's love for her 'Nana' was second only to that of her Uncle Jack.

Time galloped on: days becoming weeks—weeks becoming months. Gabrielle had begun testing her small legs with cheerful determination, chortling happily as she plopped down and picked herself up, yet again, undaunted by the pull of gravity. She was an absolute delight for Jason and Kathryn: a happy, loving child with a 'will of iron'.

Anna's presence allowed them much leisure time: hours allotted to discussions of their future military involvement in this war, hours of shared pleasure in watching the daily changes in their beautiful, little girl. But of even greater importance, private times of shared intimacy: unstructured moments of poetry, loving, and growing together. It was becoming difficult to determine a line of delineation between the two, where one's existence ended and the other's began—or perhaps, one unique and inseparable existence.

Early fall brought a dispatch rider from Colonel Cruger's headquarters. Good to his promise, given during their spring visit at Star Redoubt, he had sent their letters on to Jason's grandmother and Lord Cornwallis. Cruger's rider was now carrying correspondence from both parties, along with a communiqué of his own.

It was just before supper and Kathryn was helping Gabrielle show off her rapidly improving walking abilities to Lieutenant Jackson. Jack held his arms out, encouraging her to come to him. Gleeful shrieks of laughter drew attention to the happy child as she eagerly tottered towards her Uncle Jack with arms spread wide, and black, curly hair bouncing. Losing her balance often and landing on her plump little behind, she pushed herself up giggling happily. Then, with feisty determination, began once again, bound she would reach her destination.

Jason joined them at this point, his meeting with the recently arrived dispatch carrier now over. He moved to stand beside his wife, their shoulders touching, quietly watching his daughter with pride; so like his Kathryn. His wife smiled acknowledging him, and turned to watch their daughter's progress.

Gabrielle, suddenly seeing her father, veered in his direction, her unsteady legs tangling to dump her in a heap at his feet. "Poppa, up, up," she demanded, her small arms reaching for him.

"Ahh, my poppet." He gently whipped her up over his head as she giggled and cooed "poppa", her tiny hands pulling at his hair as he lowered her to rest in the crook of his arm.

Kathryn smiled, regarding them both warmly.

"Greetings, my colonel." Her eyes caressed as she moved closer. Gabrielle immediately leaned and clutched a handful of her mother's hair, giggling impishly.

"This fascination for hair must stop, little one. You are much too strong to tug like that." With that reproof, she gently uncurled the small fist, releasing the hank of hair pulled from her bun.

As Gabrielle stubbornly reached for her mother's hair again, Kathryn arched an eyebrow sternly, gently but firmly restraining the tiny fist. For a moment the two eyed each other, 'waging a war of wills'. Gabrielle finally accepted her mother's instruction, and pulling her chubby hand free, reached to pat her face before following with a wet kiss.

"Momma," she cooed.

Kathryn hugged the black, curly-haired head to her shoulder, whispering, "I love you little one."

When Jason set her down on the grass, she continued pursuit of her original target. Finally reaching Jack and grasping his knee for support, she babbled happily.

Sweeping her onto his lap, he talked softly, calming her exuberance. Cuddling against his chest quietly, she watched the dragoons group together for their evening meal.

"Jack is so good with her, love," Kathryn commented softly, watching Jackson stroke the child's unruly curls, her daughter's hair so very like her own.

They retired early after seeing their little girl into her bed in Anna's tent. As was their evening ritual, both parents related a bedtime tale to their daughter, each cuddling and kissing her with a tender 'goodnight' before returning to their own tent.

"I cannot stand the suspense any longer." Kathryn splashed water on her face and turned towards her husband, toweling herself dry. "What news?"

Jason sat on the edge of his desk, observing his wife, a grin curving the corners of his mouth.

"There are two letters and a package." His air was nonchalant, almost teasing. "However, I thought we might wait until …"

"Jason." Tossing the towel aside, she reached him in three strides. "Stop torturing me."

She slid into his waiting arms, warm tingles spreading immediately as his lips brushed her neck and nipped. "Not now," she gasped, returning his gleeful grin.

"Ahh, but I do have a promise for later this evening, my pet?" he coaxed, his grin quickly bordering on devilish. "As I recall, madam, I must word my requests precisely with you."

As his eyebrow arched rakishly, her eyes narrowed. "Jason," she muttered a teasing growl of warning. "Of course you have a promise this evening." Her tone turned light, laughing. "Read me the news now, rapidly please; you have created a sense of urgency I can not long deny."

Brushing a kiss to her forehead, he pulled her up onto the desk beside him, and removed two wrinkled letters from inside his jacket. Holding them out, he waited for her to decide the order in which they should be read. Wanting to savor the news from Grandmother, she chose the parchment bearing Lord Cornwallis's bold handwriting first.

Leaning against her husband, his arm draped about her shoulders, they read the letter together. The news was not happy. Although still alive at the time of writing, Lady Cornwallis's health mysteriously continued to fail. He congratulated them on the birth of Gabrielle, spoke of his wife's appreciation for Kathryn's thoughtful letters, talked a little of his home, but made no mention of future plans—of any kind.

"The situation could be gravely changed by now, Jason. Is it not two or three months, even by fast packet, to traverse the ocean between here and England?" Kathryn eyed her husband solemnly.

"About that time, I would say. I wonder if his lordship would consider returning to the colonies. His letter indicates he fears his wife's death to be imminent. With her loss, I believe he would seek solace by immersing himself in what he does best. If he does return, and Henry Clinton gives him the South, that will impact directly upon us."

"We have been truly blessed, my love."

He shot her a sideways glance, curious at her statement.

"The months have passed so quickly," she explained. "Do you realize we have been together for over two years now? Months in which the pressure of war was heavy in the North, but here we have had time to come to know each other, love each other, enjoy watching our beautiful little girl grow … all without the heavy cannons of war sounding on the horizon."

Removing the pins from her hair, he loosed it to coil onto her shoulders and held her close, wordlessly stroking the golden mass. For long moments, he was silent before stating softly, "These last two years have been more meaningful than any other in my life, Kathryn. *You* are my blessing."

They held each other quietly, assimilating emotions unable to express verbally.

"Words are such frail vehicles," she whispered, and felt him nod.

"There will be much more time for us, but I sense drastic changes in our future." He grasped her chin, and turning her mouth to meet his, grazed her lips in a touch so incredibly tender, she gasped. Not wishing the mood to become too heavy, he sat up and handed her the letter from Grandmother.

"Let us see how Grandmother fares."

They pored over the beautiful script, smiles erupting in unison. It was a lengthy letter describing Jason's home in England with detailed reminiscences of his childhood. She was thrilled to be a great grandmother, talking of the time when this dreadful war would end. Jason could then return to England and bring his wife and child home for her to meet. She pressed Kathryn for more information about her great grandchild, and to write often. Then, as she wished them happiness and love, she mentioned the package.

Jason leaned backwards, and reaching into his desk drawer, brought out a brown bundle that looked to have been passed through numerous hands—callously—yet was still intact.

Nudging his wife to do the honors, he watched as she tossed the paper aside to reveal a delicate dress, embroidered exquisitely with intricate detail and tiny seed pearls. The outer skirt opened to reveal an under panel of startling blue with ribbons of the same shade adorning the delicate bodice and matching bonnet.

"It is beautiful. Grandmother must have made this herself. I am honored."

Jason smiled as he opened the small parcel that had been tucked inside the skirt. At his sharp inhalation of breath, Kathryn turned from examining the delicate material to discover the cause.

In his hand, he held a small wooden horse mounted on a platform with bright red wheels, the remnants of a string with which to pull the toy still visible.

"It was mine," was all he could manage, so deeply touched by his grandmother's thoughtfulness.

His large hands traced over every detail of the toy lovingly, fleeting memories of his childhood darting in moist eyes. Kathryn reached to touch the carved toy, placing it in her lap as his arms encircled her with a hug. Needing comfort he sought her lips, her mouth claimed his answering an urgent need within them both.

John Cruger's communiqué could wait.

Murmuring soft words she took control, her warm lips caressing and tongue tracing molten patterns of delicious excitement. Focusing on his needs and desires, she took her time, slowly bestowing unutterable pleasure—coaxing a final release which left him shaking from sheer ecstasy.

Lying beside him, she stroked his forehead with fingers of silk. Kissing the sheen of perspiration lingering there, her eyes searched his, finding within their blue depth the answers she sought.

Shifting up onto an elbow, he rolled to cover her, accepting none of her protestations out of consideration for him. The delicate flick of his tongue against a taut nipple elicited a gasped whimper. She was his to love, to fulfill … and he would do so. *Yes. John Cruger's message could wait until tomorrow.*

The next morning she sat eyeing him over the rim of her coffee, a self-satisfied gleam in her eyes.

"I sense you are about to purr, my pet." His statement caused her to giggle.

"I just may," she sighed, "I just may."

After a leisurely breakfast, they headed for Anna's tent. Finding it vacant, they approached Lieutenant Jackson and received the answer they both suspected.

"At least now, she tells me when she is going hunting." He shrugged, shaking his head.

Jason tensed, but feeling Kathryn's hand in the small of his back, relaxed. "If events change, as I suspect they may, Jack, her hunting will have to be curbed. I will need your help on that one."

"Yes, sir," he said dutifully, always the consummate officer when within the dragoon's hearing. He cast a curious eye to his commanding officer, and at Jason's gesture to follow them, fell in step beside Kathryn.

They stood talking beside a small group of trees. Captain Hodges brought fresh coffee and stayed just long enough to share pleasantries before leaving.

"Did you ask him to bring us fresh coffee, Jack? I saw no indication …" Kathryn was curious but Jackson merely grinned, leaving her wondering.

After explaining his thoughts as to Cornwallis's possible future actions, Jason talked of Cruger's communiqué. "Archibald Campbell is on his way from New Jersey. It is now fact, no longer hearsay. Cruger thinks he should be in Savannah by the end of December."

"And that will be just the beginning," Jack finished solemnly, understanding the implications.

"We also had an extremely nice invitation from Colonel Cruger which my wife has begged me to refuse." Kathryn eyed him balefully as he continued. "When you arise from your tent, chilled in the winter dawn, you may thank her."

"We were invited to winter over at Star Redoubt with those simpering ..."

Jack shook his head, laughing. "After considering the alternative, milady, I shall look forward to spending many invigorating winter mornings in our encampment."

At that, they all chuckled and continued drinking their coffee.

"Ahh, here they come now." Gulping the last of her coffee, Kathryn gestured towards the woods where Anna could be seen just emerging.

A bulging haversack indicated her usual luck when it came to hunting. As she neared, they could hear the happy babbling of their daughter. Handing her cup to Jason, she strode out to meet Anna, and relieved her of the chattering bundle on her back.

"Come say 'good morning' to poppa and Uncle Jack, little one."

As her mother blew raspberry sounds against her chubby, little cheeks, Gabrielle squirmed, giggling uncontrollably. Chirping first at her father, then at Jack, she entertained the two with her antics while they finished their coffee.

Kathryn gazed at the peaceful scene, allowing it to imprint on her memory, sensing there would be times when she would relish reliving this moment dearly.

Yes, it was all about to change.

Chapter Twenty-Six

Chance Encounter

As Kathryn urged Beauty to a slow canter, she wondered if perhaps this had not been one of her better ideas. She patted the pocket of her greatcoat, smiling with satisfaction. She had traded some of her carefully dried herbs at a small shop in town, and now carried blue hair ribbons for Gabrielle, and a few cubes of sugar for the horses. The ribbons matched the blue in the beautiful dress Grandmother had sent from England perfectly, and she was pleased.

She had left their encampment three hours earlier on a spur-of-the-moment whim, slipping out undetected, wanting to find ribbons to control Gabrielle's thick curls. Actually, that was more an excuse than reality. She had a compelling need to distance herself from the day-to-day peace of the campsite for a few hours. Their life had been so quiet lately—so predictable.

With the dragoons encamped within close proximity to town, she had given no thought to the possibility of encountering rebel militia. However, as she flung herself onto Beauty's, back preparing to return to camp, she noticed several men entering a small inn. They sported the familiar garb of colonial militia, outfits so like Jamie's the memory was instantly painful. Extremely uneasy and needing to distance herself from danger, she urged her mare to a fast pace. She wanted no time-delaying confrontations now. Jason would be concerned, more than likely thoroughly annoyed, if he found her missing when he returned from his meeting with John Cruger.

Approaching a narrow, rocky area on the wooded trail, she reined Beauty in, slowing to a brisk walk so as not to risk injuring her legs. Without warning, a large figure hurtled from the underbrush, directly into her path. Grabbing the reins and slamming his shoulder into the startled mare's chest, he brought her to an abrupt standstill. Before a cognizant thought could form, Kathryn was yanked from her saddle and thrown forcefully to the ground, the air whooshing from her lungs leaving her gasping. A cruel backhander followed, jerking her head sideways, her forehead striking a rock and opening a bloody gash—none of which brought the slightest consideration. He meant business; a prick of fear grabbed Kathryn.

Lungs burning, she gasped for air in a panicked attempt to combat her faltering awareness, and regain her feet. Quickly straddled by the big man, her efforts to rise were thwarted. Coarse hands tugged her coat off, hands that continued groping carelessly, removing her tomahawk and pistol. Hauling her up, limp as a rag doll, he slammed her back against a large tree. Chest heaving, she sucked air in deep gulps, slowly regaining her senses as he moved in close pinning her tightly, his leering face almost touching hers.

"Well, now, seems we have decisions ta' make here," he mumbled drunkenly.

Disgusted, she shoved him, wrinkling her nose at his fetid breath.

"I ken see she don't think yer as pretty as the colonel, Bentley." The second man, having released his hold on Beauty, swayed closer pushing his friend aside. Pressing his palm against the tree beside her head, he lowered his face to meet her on eye level, a feral glint to his eye. Gripping her chin with his free hand, dirty nails biting into her skin, he forced her to face him.

"I kin make you forget 'im, ma' pretty," he slobbered. As he leaned closer, his lips nearly brushing hers, her knee jerked up—connecting sharply with her target.

"Jeezus, you bitch," he gasped, reeling away clutching himself.

At that, his companion released a high-pitched, drunken giggle. "Don't seem like she thinks much o' you either, Boggs," he guffawed.

"Yew jest ain't wurth the trouble," he spat. Staggering, still clutching his aching groin, he turned and clamped his hand around her throat. "We'll jest take ya with us, let the rest of the men l'arn ya sum manners. See how that sets wit' ya." Leaning even closer, he squeezed his fingers tighter, closing off her air.

Kathryn's struggling weakened, as dancing spots and encircling darkness closed in.

"Take your hands off her and back away."

An authoritative voice pierced the enclosing darkness as she gasped for air, uncertain whether ... *reality or cruel delusion?*

"But, sir," the two men whined in unison.

"I said to let her go." The deadly click of a pistol hammer reinforced his order, and they grudgingly complied. "Get back to camp and sober up."

As they scrabbled away, Kathryn sank to her knees, eyes closing momentarily as weakness claimed her. *Gabriel? ... Gabriel?* She was afraid to look, certain it was no more than a wishful vision.

As she labored to regain her feet, a large hand reached down. Looking up she met eyes filled with mixed emotions. But with a slight nod, he urged her to accept his help. Taking the proffered hand, she stood shakily.

"Oh, Kathryn," he murmured, immediately slipping a strong arm around her waist for support.

"You are a lieutenant," she stated dumbly, not knowing what to say.

He merely smiled and took her arm as he bent to pick up her weapons and whistled to Beauty. Guiding her off the path into dense shrub covering, he indicated for her to sit on an old tree stump. Moving to his horse, he returned within moments carrying a canteen and flask. Kathryn sat watching, absorbing his commanding presence, rubbing her throat to ease the ache.

Handing the tomahawk and pistol back to her, he crouched at her side. Gently pushing her hand aside, he inspected her throat. Then, stroking her hair back to appraise her injured forehead, said somewhat acerbically: "I trust you will not use those weapons; at least not until after I have left."

He eyed her meaningfully for long moment, before turning concentration to her bloody cheek.

Making a soft negative sound in her throat, she searched his face wanting to imprint every nuance of him on her mind. He had grown more handsome, his boyish qualities having given way to robust manhood. He exuded an air of confidence, inner satisfaction and a certain 'totality' which had not been present before.

"Why?" she asked quietly.

Briefly pausing in his ministrations, he eyed her thoughtfully then offered a drink from his canteen; which she accepted gratefully, swallowing with obvious difficulty.

"Your throat will ease within a day or two," he said, hedging.

"Why?" she repeated softly, pressing for an answer.

He shrugged. "I owed you that: for me, for Ian, for all the memories of our youth."

A tear slowly tracked down her cheek, stopped with a gentle touch of his thumb before she could swipe it away.

"I love you, my feisty, little aunt. I always will, for I understand you now."

He remained silent, ignoring her puzzled expression as he bathed her face gently with a water-soaked handkerchief, a smile flickering at the corners of his mouth.

"Remember that Sunday dinner with the vicar? When you rushed in late, your face filthy, dressed in men's clothes, a brace of rabbits dangling from your belt, as usual smiling in all innocence?"

"Oh yes, how I remember that. Your father was speechless at my disgraceful appearance, for the first time in his life, I believe." She grinned and both started to laugh, their eyes interlocking, so many warm recollections flowing between them.

Pouring whiskey onto a cloth, he reached for her head. "This will hurt."

She grimaced as he applied the cloth, creating fierce burning along her hairline.

"You understand me?" she ground out.

"You spoke to me of your love for the colonel, which I can now accept, but still must ask, why him? It was not the best of choices for your family or for your country." His tone held no accusation or anger, just a need to understand fully.

"Love chooses us, Gabriel, not the other way 'round. Many times, it is not a choice of convenience."

She paused, well aware this would likely be the last time they would be together, and wanted to explain. "I chose Black Raven for spite, at the time angry with your father, and paid dearly for that indiscretion—yet he forgave me. This time, love chose me. Jason is my heart and soul; I am nothing without him." His name rolled softly as a caress from her tongue, moving Gabriel with the intensity of her devotion.

She searched his face, noting his thoughtful expression as a glimmer of comprehension dawned. "Not out of spite, nor necessarily a wise decision, but a passion for this man that I have no power to deny, have no wish to deny, although I realize the pain I have caused elsewhere. Perhaps one day Jamie will find it in his heart to forgive me yet again."

Reaching up, she touched his cheek tenderly. "What of you, Gabriel? I see the beginnings of acceptance in you."

"I have married a beautiful, young woman who carries my child as we speak, a woman who makes me complete; one my father has finally accepted although she would not have been his first choice. Ours will not be the easiest of lives even when this damned war is finally over."

Kathryn's eyes widened as she tilted her head—surprised and curious.

"Silver Fox," he said softly, his thoughts drifting homewards at mentioning his wife's name.

"Soaring Eagle's daughter? But she is just a child, is she not?"

Issuing a derisive sound, he angrily retorted, "She is now a woman of seventeen summers, but there is more to your look than that. MacLeans never could hide true feelings. I see it in your eyes."

"You misread me, Gabriel," she assured, grabbing his shoulder, not allowing him to back away in anger. "My first reaction is exactly as you stated. This will be a difficult marriage, a life not easy for your child ... for your children. Seek solace and hold fast to each other at all times, for others will forsake you."

He read her well, seeing deep pain reflected from personal experience, knowing he had chosen a rough route as well.

"Secondly, I am truly thankful that my dealings with Soaring Eagle did not leave you without a father-in-law. I fear that would have been an unbearable burden to add to your lives. I am extremely happy for you."

With a quick kiss to his cheek she added, "MacLeans also tend to make hasty assumptions, to which they often cling with indignant tenacity."

An embarrassed flush rising to his cheeks made her grin.

"I will try to remember that in the future, Aunt," he said softly, eyeing her with tenderness. "Soaring Eagle has great respect for you and deeply regrets your treatment at the hands of his brother. He has voiced a wish that perhaps some day you will sit down again and talk together."

She nodded, but silently questioned that possibility ever arising.

"Anna did not tell you of my marriage?" Gabriel was surprised at the firm shake of her head.

"There are certain areas we do not discuss; it is less painful that way."

"What of your child?"

She was glad he had asked; she needed a favor.

"We have a beautiful little girl. She looks like me, but with her father's jet-black hair and piercing blue eyes. Jason suggested we name her Gabrielle." She searched her nephew's face, noticing his surprise. "He thought it might be of comfort to me … and it is." She fought the stinging tears which threatened.

"We both adore our daughter. She is not part of all this, Gabriel. If there is ever a time when it becomes necessary …" she trailed off having difficulty with what she needed to ask. "Promise me you will keep Gabrielle from harm if anything happens to us." There—she had laid it all out to him to accept or deny.

She started to stand, knowing their luck of being undetected could not hold out much longer.

"And someday, when Jamie, your father, can forgive me, tell him how much I miss him … how very much I love him." Her last words were barely audible.

She turned abruptly, but not before he saw the trembling chin, the eyes pressed tight so as not to cry. He swept her into his arms, clasping her tightly to him. Pressing her head gently to his shoulder, he held her while she sobbed.

"My beautiful, Kathryn, you have endured so much pain." He stroked her hair, tangling his fingers in the riot of curls he had always loved to tug as a boy. "I pray the time will never come when I will be called upon to carry out your request, but rest assured, I shall protect Gabrielle from any harm if there is ever need. You have my sworn word."

Stepping back, he raised her chin and tenderly wiped her tears. Placing a soft kiss to her lips, he whistled for Beauty.

"We have tarried too long. You must go now before we are discovered. As a lieutenant, I have no authority to save you if one of my superiors happens by. You have a reputation that grows daily, along with that of your husband. That fact both frightens me … and fills me with pride." He smiled gently. "I fear I will not be able to defend you further."

"By putting my fears for our daughter at rest, you have done far more for me than you realize, Gabriel. Take care of your wife … and your father."

Holding her coat out, he helped her shrug into it. "The tales this thing could tell if only it could talk," he laughed.

The answering smile that spread across her face was rich and warm. Brushing her lips to his cheek, she turned to Beauty and flung herself into the saddle in a familiar graceful motion that brought a smile to Gabriel's face. For the briefest of moments, she gazed at him, her face reflecting a mixture of raging emotions: gratitude, sadness, pride and love. With one last look, she spun Beauty and galloped away, leaving him staring after her, filled with sudden emptiness and regret.

***

Much later that evening, in a small camp lodged deep within the swamps, Gabriel dismounted and strode through the lounging men towards a campfire set off from the rest. A lone man slouched there, alternately sipping wine and pouring hot lead into a mold creating ammunition for his pistol.

"Your sister misses you," he said quietly to the crouched figure

"I have no sister," his quiet retort without looking up.

"You do," Gabriel stated forcefully, "and she misses you."

At that remark, his father turned tired eyes to him. "I understand you two met today." He made a statement expecting no further explanation, and Gabriel offered none.

The details of what had been said were between Kathryn and him, the business of no one else.

"She has chosen her bed. If it is cold, it is of her making," he said tersely.

"Far from cold, father." His intent was to shock, to break the icy barrier erected by his father to prevent the pain of feeling.

"It is over two years, and she loves that man with devotion so intense … so intense." He was at a loss to find words expressing his thoughts appropriately. "He cannot be all bad."

Jamie eyed his son with fierce anger burning, but after a moment calmed himself and returned to the task at hand.

Gabriel watched silently then turned to go. As he stepped away, he heard the soft, painful inquiry.

"She is well … and the child?"

***

Kathryn rode back into camp just as Jason was readying to ride out in search of her. Having returned from his meeting with Colonel Cruger, and not in the best frame of mind, he had erupted in uncontrolled fury when informed of her disappearance. Not only was she gone, no one—including Lieutenant Jackson—had any idea of where or how long she had been out of camp.

Anna stepped forward carrying Gabrielle, attempting to placate Jason with assurances of Kathryn's abilities. Sensing something was terribly wrong, his little girl wanted desperately to be held and reached for him. In his distraction, he barely nodded in her direction, speaking her name quickly. But her broken-hearted sobs halted him.

"Poppet, I must find your mother."

He kissed her gently, gesturing to Anna to take her back to their tent.

Lieutenant Jackson sat in formation with the dragoons, ready to ride out the moment Jason finished speaking with Anna. Jason noticed his ghostly pallor, recognizing it for fear, knowing himself to be a mirror image of Jack. For he was afraid, he admitted freely to himself. If anything had happened to Kathryn …

A loud yell abruptly ceased that thought.

"She is coming in!" Captain Hodges bellowed from the back of the formation.

The men turned in unison, relief flooding their faces. With a quick gesture of his gloved hand, Jason dismissed the dragoons and dismounting, stood rigidly waiting for his wife to reach his side.

She reined to a stop, immediately swung her leg over Beauty's neck and slid to the ground.

"Colonel, I …"

"Where have you been?" he demanded, interrupting her. "There is rebel activity in this area. What ever possessed you …?" He could not finish his statement.

She remained silent; she had no excuse for what she had done. Having put herself in such danger, she was lucky to be alive. Fear shone in his eyes and she ached for him, ashamed by her thoughtlessness in assuaging her own needs without thought for others.

"Wife, you have truly tried my patience this time. We will talk inside." A curt jerk of his head indicated their tent.

Handing Beauty's reins to Jackson, she mouthed, "I am so sorry."

As he took the mare's reins, Jack's attention was drawn to her forehead, his face remaining rigid as he eyed the large purple lump and crusted blood. Noticing the extent of bruises on her chin and neck, he sucked in a deep breath, thankful for whatever incredible luck had brought her safely back to the encampment.

She stood holding the edge of Jason's desk, somewhat unsteady in the aftermath of her ordeal. At the sound of his step she turned, her contrite eyes meeting his. He strode towards her, angrily removing his gloves as he approached. Flinging his gloves onto the desk, he clenched white-knuckled fists at his sides. Furious beyond words, he faced her, his rage so close to the surface she could almost see it rippling beneath his skin. He fought for control, trying not to strike her—momentarily afraid he might finish the job someone else had started if he gave in to his emotions.

"What ever possessed you, Kathryn?" he ground out through clenched teeth.

She saw it all in his eyes: fear so intense at what could have been, and dark fury that anyone would have hurt her so. Her eyes held his, knowing she had no appropriate words, no suitable defense for such stupidity and thoughtlessness. His face was deathly pale, the depth of pain reflected in his eyes, unbearable. She looked away, then down at the floor.

Abruptly he turned and stalked to the tent opening where he stopped, his labored breaths coming in painful bursts. Her eyes followed him as he suddenly turned and strode back to stand quietly in front of her. With hands that shook slightly, he pushed the hair back from her forehead to examine the purple swelling, and then gently touched the bruises on her chin, finally inspecting the heavy bruising on her neck.

"Jason," her voice broke on a quiet plea for forgiveness, a cry of need.

"Hush now, love," he murmured softly, again in control of his violent temper.

Pulling her firmly against him, he buried his face against her neck.

"Kathryn ..." A sob wrenched free as his tears fell unashamedly on her shoulder. The dam had finally burst allowing him to cry for all that had been lost in his past—what had almost been lost today—this incredible woman, his wife, all being celebrated in one cataclysmic release. Her tears mingled with his as they clung to each other.

"We have come too far together, my beloved Kathryn. I ... do not believe I could go on without you," his voice faltered, breaking on the last words.

"Nor I, without you," she sobbed.

He needed to hold her, to know she was real. Later he would need her in a carnal way to reclaim all that could have been lost, but now ... just to hold, to savor, was enough.

"Tell me what happened, Kathryn," he said, when finally able to talk.

Holding her gently, he listened to her story, at first haltingly, then building with intensity as she spoke proudly of Gabriel, and his promise to protect their daughter.

"He has not chosen an easy life either and is to be admired."

Jason remained silent for several moments, absorbing her words. "Then I will feel confidant in whatever he must decide regarding our daughter's safety, if that need should ever arise." Sensing his words brought Kathryn inner peace pleased him ... he could at least afford her that.

They talked of Soaring Eagle, Silver Fox and the difficulties lying ahead for the young couple. They addressed the recent increase of rebel militia in the area, a fact which had been abruptly and violently brought to their attention. And they spoke of Jamie and his continued bitterness. But her voice softened with tenderness as she discussed Gabriel's understanding and acceptance of their situation, despite wishing it could be otherwise.

Jason hoped this chance meeting with Gabriel might ease some of the ache she carefully concealed within her heart: devastating pain which occasionally overwhelmed her with grief. With the additional gift of his wife's life on this day, he owed Gabriel more than he could ever repay … he would not forget that.

They stood quietly within each others arms for several minutes. With a soft sigh, he separated and moved to the desk drawer for salve and his flask of brandy. As he started to tend her forehead, she winced.

"Please, Gabriel already scrubbed whiskey into it."

"It looks nasty, Kathryn, and I do not want any infection to set in."

As he began to cleanse the wound she looked up, watching as he concentrated, deciding whether to use stitches.

"I would feel better if you had struck me," she said softly, grabbing his attention. "I was thoughtless. I made a snap …"

His fingertip silenced her. "It is over, my love, and will never happen again, will it?"

She shook her head, biting her lower lip.

"It was not Jack's fault; you must know that."

He smiled ruefully. "I will talk to him later and make amends. I am sure he is brewing willow tea for you at this moment. I saw the look on his face at the sight of your injuries."

With that statement, he rolled her head back gently. Eyeing the bruises along her throat, he leaned close and traced his lips tenderly up one side and down the other, sending shivers racing to the pit of her stomach and lower.

"That medicine is all I can provide for those bruises, but I will apply it often so that you will not forget how important you are to me, nor take careless risks again."

"Let us go assure our daughter that all is well," she said, pulling the ribbons from her coat pocket and handing them to him apologetically.

"After supper we need to talk of John Cruger's meeting and the real reason for your trip into town today." He arched an eyebrow meaningfully, his intense gaze capturing hers—reading her so completely it was unnerving.

Within moments of gathering at supper, all tension eased as it became obvious the colonel and his wife had come to terms with each other. Gabrielle sat happily ensconced in her father's lap, the new blue ribbons adorning her hair. Jason, not always as overtly affectionate in front of his men, wanted to reassure his daughter lest she become insecure, compensation for his earlier abruptness.

Kathryn sat observing them together, but turned to smile at Jack as he handed her a large cup of willow tea, his eyes concerned and questioning.

"What pains me most is the distress I caused all of you today." She winced, contrite.

"That is unimportant, as long as you were not seriously harmed."

With eyes that could conceal neither his love, nor his intense relief at her safe return, he moved closer and added, "You frightened me, Kathryn."

Her eyes stung from barely contained tears as she mumbled quiet regrets.

"My wife bids me apologize for my bad manners, Lieutenant."

Setting Gabrielle in her mother's lap Jason moved closer, speaking quietly to Jack so as to not be overheard. But his eyes conveyed feelings far stronger than those expressed.

As Gabrielle touched her mother's forehead, she questioned in her baby voice. "Mama hurt. Why?" Her large blue eyes searched for an answer.

Both men turned to Kathryn, curious what her answer to the child would be.

"Mama was careless, little one. I forgot your father's warning. Heed him well; his decisions are wise and just. Your poppa is a good man."

Chucking her daughter under the chin, she kissed her button nose.

Some time later in their tent, she sat across the desk from Jason, observing a series of emotions track across his face as he talked. The nagging ache in her head was rapidly dissipating as a result of the willow tea she had sipped while around the campfire and the cup she was just finishing now.

Jason laid out all the reasons behind her questionable behavior in a series of precise observations, open to discussion if she could find any incongruities in his logic. But she could not. He knew her as well as he knew himself, identical needs driving them both.

Her mounting desire for action and inability to accept complacency as a way of life had been the catalyst for leaving camp. She was so like him, and for that he was thankful, although her boldness often scared him. Gabriel's comment about her growing reputation and increased risk of becoming a more obvious target had not set well. But she immediately made light of that comment; the only alternative solution would be unacceptable to both of them.

"As of tomorrow, my love, you shall be at my side every time we ride out. I will make it my personal responsibility to ingrain a sense of respect for caution in that bold heart of yours."

His intense gaze brought a rapid, "As you wish, my husband."

Their eyes met and held, teeming with passion far beyond that of mere physical gratification.

"John brought it to my attention that the rebel militia is working with renewed effort to build its numbers in this area. They are well aware of the importance the South is about to play in the future outcome of the war. Up until now, our dealings with the rebels have amounted to no more than swatting at flies, but that is about to change."

He paused, smiling at his wife, one eyebrow raised. "However, I gather you discovered that for yourself through firsthand experience today."

She grinned sheepishly; she deserved the additional 'tweak'.

"We are to scatter them, and you are very good at that, my pet. Now, when you and Gabriel talked, did he give any indication where Jamie and his men are hiding?"

"I did not ask, nor did Gabriel press me for information regarding our position and plans. None of that had any place in our conversation today." Her tone took on a slight edge. "I am sure they are lurking back in the swamps. However, it is not worth the risk to follow them in there."

She shrugged, and at his unfathomable look added, "You are not presuming my reluctance to chase them has any bearing on ..."

Jason cut her short with a denial she considered inadequate.

Still reeling emotionally from her ordeal, she was overly sensitive and deeply irritated by his implication.

"You were furious with me earlier, and had every right to be, what with my irresponsible ride into town without telling anyone. But at that time, I was unaware of any rebel militia in the area. I certainly had no idea that I might see any member of my family again—other than on the battlefield."

"And, Jason," her voice took on an emotional, raspy timbre, "I never, in my wildest dreams, envisioned a chance meeting with Gabriel—especially one of such warmth. I had thought all likelihood of that long past. But do not even hint, after all our time together, that I might play you false, that I would do less than what is expected of me because of family …"

She stood abruptly, knowing she was overreacting yet unable to prevent the angry tears spilling across the planes of her distraught face—incapable of stopping her continued diatribe. "I have proven myself time and again, and damn it, I chose you over all else. You!" Her voice softened as she added, "And I have never regretted that decision for one moment … not ever."

Before she could draw another tearful breath, he moved around the desk and swept her into his arms, his kiss fierce and demanding—her resistance, momentary, before melting into his embrace. Her tears continued to fall wetly on his jacket as he held her, experiencing searing pangs of guilt. *How could I have allowed her to sense the slightest doubt for even a moment?*

They were both irrational at this point, exhausted in the aftermath of inordinate relief at her safe return, suffering from lingering fear at what could have been … if not for Gabriel.

"I am concerned our dragoons might succumb to fever in those dismal, bug infested swamps, Jason—nothing more."

She sniffled, hiccupping, as she tried to explain, continuing even as he shook his head and placed a finger to her lips. "Jamie and his men are used to the swamps and have built immunity to many diseases. Our dragoons have not, and I fear for them. We must remain strong to contend with what lies ahead," she finished quietly.

"I trust your loyalty and judgment with the same assurance I would have at putting my life in your hands, my love …"

He was not allowed to finish as her mouth crushed against his.

His hands slid up under her blouse, cupping her breasts, his thumbs teasing gently.

Already working her fingers beneath his shirt she caressed seductively, and began tracing lower.

"I need you, my Kathryn, in so many ways; God, how I need you."

"Oh Jason," she mouthed softly against his cheek. "Make me yours alone, my love, make me complete." Searching his face, she finally admitted what he already knew. "I was terrified while they held me—certain my selfish foolhardiness would hurt you, hurt our daughter, regretting my …"

"No more, my love, it is over. I have you now, and may never let you out of my sight again."

With the final pieces of clothing discarded, he pulled her naked warmth against him, relishing the feel of her anxious response. Sweeping her into his arms, he strode towards their bed.

Tender in his reclaiming, he loved her with a depth of feeling that brought tears … tears that he kissed into nonexistence. Reassuring himself she was truly alive and whole, he explored gently, maintaining iron control until she trembled, begging for completion. Then, and only then, he filled her, unable to deny their mutual hunger longer.

Chapter Twenty-Seven

Rebirth

Sitting across the desk from each other the next day, enjoying their morning coffee, he held her hand, electricity tracking between them, small ripples cascading in private places. Their night had been one of little sleep—hours of talking quietly and surrendering to rekindling passion, the healing properties of their physical love working its magic. Both glowed with vitality, the energy surrounding them humming almost audibly, neither appearing tired.

"Jason," her soft tone and large, expressive eyes captured his attention. "I will wear the red jacket and uniform of the dragoons from now on."

He eyed her silently, his brow furrowing at the quiet determination in her tone ... and the magnitude of what she proposed.

"We must have extra uniforms in the supply wagon," she reasoned, studying him closely as he nodded, somewhat distractedly, deep in thought. "As it would be perceived far less offensive than my colonial attire, I cannot foresee criticism coming from headquarters. I *will* miss my greatcoat, however." She paused, touching the front of her coat with such reverence his lips twitched into a tight smile, which quickly faded. At his continued silence she added, "I will be a credit to the uniform. No one will ever have cause to doubt my loyalties then."

He eyed her wordlessly, myriads of conflicting emotions coursing through him.

"Please, Jason, I rarely ask for favors. But this is something I need to do for me ... for us."

"Kathryn." He squeezed her hand gently, searching her face, seeking the correct words to begin a gentle denial.

"Do you fear reprimand from headquarters?" she interrupted his thoughts. "I am well able to hold my own in combat. Besides, we will be skirmishing regularly for at least two weeks—plenty of time for me to be ready for Savannah. I will bring no shame to your good name."

"My love, hush for a moment, hear me out." He took both her hands in his. "I am not concerned with what headquarters will think, one way or the other. I am well aware of your abilities. And for God's sake, I know you will never bring shame to me; only credit and honor."

"What then? Why do you hesitate so? I know you are sitting there trying to determine how to phrase a quiet denial; one you hope will be convincing enough for me to accept."

At that declaration, he grinned, shaking his head. She read him like an open book.

"For none of the reasons you have stated, Kathryn, rather one of concern for your safety. Attired as a dragoon you will become an even greater target, and I fear ..."

Quickly interrupting to prevent his putting that fear into words, she pointed out: "We will soon be joining British contingencies that do not know me yet. My rebel garb would send mixed messages, and rightfully so. And if the time comes when I must take a musket ball, I would rather it be at the hands of a rebel while proudly wearing this uniform, than by one of our own in error." Grasping his hands, she added softly, "As both Jamie and Gabriel will become much more visible, I must prove beyond doubt ..."

Shaking his head he inhaled sharply, a protest forming on the tip of his tongue, but she was insistent.

"I must, my love, for me, for you, and for our daughter. Do you not feel the energy surging between us, the vitality … the invincibility? We are as one, Jason—always have been—but even more so now," she exclaimed passionately, eyes ablaze.

"Last night you claimed you wanted me by your side, did you not," a terse statement rather than a question, one to which he only nodded, unable to answer as she rushed on. "That does not mean that when our battles become more serious I am told to remain in camp, wearing out my boots while awaiting your safe return."

At this flare of temper, he smiled, remembering her habit of pacing.

"Your risks are my risks, our destinies so intricately entwined they cannot be separated," she declared. Her voice softened. "Our strength lies in *us* … *together* as a team, and I refuse to sit idly by while you march into battle. Whatever our destiny, I will not deny it. We have spoken often of this. Today is ours … perhaps tomorrow. I can accept that, for I will not allow you to go alone; I will never allow that." Her voice broke on a stifled sob.

With that passionate statement his breath caught—the dual meaning of her few simple words—staggering. Rising quickly, he moved around the desk and pulled her up into the circle of his arms. Stroking her hair, he brushed a kiss into the tangle of curls.

"My beautiful, stubborn, determined wife," he replied huskily, "Do I feel the passion? Yes, I am more certain every day that this is what we are all about, our destinies inseparable. Your words, your feelings, are mine exactly."

"Then why are you hesitant, my beloved?"

"Your boldness frightens me. I dread the thought of one day …"

"I share the same thoughts about you, but we must not give voice to them. Voicing makes them all too real. We have made a practice of living and loving for the moment, yet always looking ahead, and we shall continue to do so … always," she ended upon a soft whisper.

Resting his cheek against the top of her head, he remained silent for several moments, wrestling with his emotions. With a long sigh, he finally spoke. "I will return shortly, stay put." With a quick kiss, he disengaged himself and strode resolutely from the tent.

Upon his return a few minutes later, he found her sitting where he had left her.

"I am glad to see you are able to follow orders, madam, one of the first requirements of a dragoon."

Her eyes met his expectantly; excitement building as she fully digested his words.

"Are these the items you requested?" he asked succinctly, placing red jackets, black breeches, even a black bear fur helmet in her lap.

She touched the fabric of the uniforms with reverence, shaking slightly as she separated the pieces, finding white shirts with lace jabots tucked between the layers. She nodded, biting her lower lip, unable to speak.

Drawing a deep, ragged breath of resignation, he took the articles, and setting them on the desk, pulled her into his arms.

"Kathryn, my love, it would not be considered weakness for you to change …"

"Never, never." She pulled his head down to meet her fierce kiss.

"Then we are as one, no turning back, God help us," his warm breath whispered against her ear, as she murmured undying love.

She stood with her back to him, putting final touches to the loose coil of her hair as he watched. Shifting himself in discomfort he grimaced, wanting her, again, with such intense desire only his sense of duty, and knowing the dragoons were ready and waiting, forced him to push the need aside.

She turned and smiled, hands on her hips. "Well?" Her expression was hopeful, anxious.

"I am honored and so very proud of you." His words were a welcome caress.

She went into his outstretched arms eagerly, returning his kiss fervently. He held her quietly for a few moments, enjoying her touch. Then, stepping back he instructed, "Get your weapons and helmet, madam, we have a group of men anxious to be on the way."

His eyes held a roguish glint. "If we tarry longer, you will find yourself having to dress yet again."

With a chuckle, she tucked the dirk into her boot, slipped the tomahawk into its familiar spot against the small of her back and snugged the leather belt holding the regulation, holstered pistol. For good measure, she forced her own pistol into her belt beside it.

He watched her arm herself, shaking his head, smiling. "Perhaps I should feel sympathy for the enemy. They have no idea what awaits them."

As they exited the tent, she looked up quickly. "Perhaps the men may have your permission to call me by my name, sir? It would be easier in a situation demanding immediate attention; and I would not feel it disrespectful."

At his silence, she added, "Just think on it, love. Now, let us bid 'good morning' to our daughter and be on our way."

Lieutenant Jackson stood holding their horses at the ready while the dragoons made final adjustments to their weapons and harnessing. As they stepped from the tent in unison, the smile on his lips froze as he saw Kathryn's attire. Recovering rapidly, he bid them both 'good day'.

Each carried a helmet in the crook of their arm and nodded greetings to the men as they made a quick detour to Anna's quarters to see their daughter, a now familiar pattern to which they strictly adhered: always finding time for their little girl. They loved greeting her each morning before the sleepy glow left her face, and tucking her into bed with a song or story at the end of the day.

Having arrived later than usual, Gabrielle greeted her parents boisterously, already wide awake and full of playful energy. Kathryn crouched down to the little girl's level, her arms outstretched in greeting. Eyeing her mother's new attire, she flung her small body into the waiting arms, touching the red jacket in awe. Kathryn balanced her helmet atop the curly-haired head, eliciting a high-pitched giggle from the happy child as it slid sideways, covering one eye.

Anna watched the three of them, her mind working, nodding as she pondered the situation.

"You have truly found each other."

She caught Jason's eye and held his gaze. Kathryn paused in playing with Gabrielle to eye her friend and mentor, paying heed to her words.

"I sensed it from the first, Colonel. You are the one for my Ugilohi. No longer two separate individuals, you exist as one, *only one*. One life … one destiny." Her smile held warmth directed at both. "You merely needed time to accept and understand yourselves."

With loving hugs to their daughter, they instructed she behave for Anna and headed towards the saddled and waiting dragoons. Kathryn, gazing up at her husband's smiling face, adjusted her helmet as they walked.

"Anna's observation reinforces all we have discussed, my love. I value her opinion; she has 'the sight'. On some occasions she sees more clearly than at other times, yet her decisions are always wise; she does not make quick judgments. I gather we have her seal of approval."

Murmuring agreement, he stopped beside Beauty and faced his wife, his eyes capturing hers.

With a gently placed hand on his chest, their familiar ritual began. *Your heart and mine are as one.* Her fist curled against her breast as his thumb traced the bridge of her nose: a tilted chin, a tender brush of lips … *'always'*, they breathed.

For a long moment, he continued cupping her chin, searching her face for uncertainty—finding only eager anticipation and a slight smile lifting the corners of her mouth. Inclining his head, he stepped back.

As she turned to grasp her saddle, the utterance of her name halted her.

"Mrs. Tarrington, please allow me."

All eyes watched in fascination as he dropped to one knee, basketing his hands.

"Colonel, please, I…" she began, caught off-guard by such an incredible gesture.

"It is my distinct honor, milady." Proud and wishing to express that fact, he allowed his voice to carry back through the rows of men. "Please permit me, just this once, to mark our new beginning."

Biting her lower lip, eyes brimming, she stepped into his cupped hands allowing him to boost her into the saddle. With a pat to her knee and a private look, he strode to Diablo and quickly mounted.

Not so much as an eyebrow had been raised. At this point in time, nothing surprised the dragoons about this unusual woman or her dynamic husband—they would protect this feisty pair with their lives, if necessary.

Lieutenant Jackson scanned the formation assessing each man's reaction, disappointed to see only nods of approval and admiration. Finding support for his arguments against Kathryn's decision, and Jason's acceptance, would not be forthcoming from these men. He mounted his horse and moved into formation, his mouth set in a severe line.

As he reined in beside Kathryn, she smiled, adjusting her helmet.

"Will I ever get used to wearing this thing?" Furrowing her brow, she grinned, attempting to ease his concern through distraction.

There was no mistaking the message displayed for all to see in her luminous green eyes: vitality, spirit, determination and the incredible bond she shared with her husband.

Jackson had been standing close, had witnessed the indescribable look passing between them, a sense of 'oneness', an inner calm borne of strength and shared passion—two lives so entwined there would be no turning back.

With a rueful sigh, he worked at acceptance. As he watched Kathryn, this incredible woman he loved so deeply, he willed himself to trust in her decision. Pushing his fears for her, and the path she had chosen, into the far recesses of his mind, he attempted to focus on the business at hand.

As they approached a swampy area suspected of concealing Jamie's hideout, Kathryn felt trepidation. *What if Jamie or Gabriel …? I must not allow those thoughts, must not …* she forcefully pushed them aside, far from conscious awareness. The love and understanding Gabriel had bestowed at their 'chance meeting' was a precious gift to hold dear and close to her heart, but that was where it must remain.

A sideways glance caught her husband watching her, concern etching the corners of his piercing, blue eyes. Squaring her shoulders, she winked—and he winked back, surprising her.

A puff of smoke and a loud report from within the reeds, instantly whipped her back to the present. With no other warning, a musket ball streaked their way. The soft 'thunk' as it found a target just behind her, accompanied by Captain Hodges's cry of pain, threw Kathryn into action.

At the colonel's brusque command, the dragoons immediately fanned out to flush the attackers from hiding. But Kathryn effortlessly spun Beauty, quickly turning aside to aid the stricken captain.

"Watch the colonel's back. I have Hodges," she yelled, gesturing to Jackson.

Waving two dragoons back to aid her, he galloped after his commanding officer.

Rifle fire filled the air as she leaped from Beauty's back at a run. Captain Hodges, thrown from his horse with the impact of the musket ball, struggled valiantly to right himself. The rebel who had brought him down raced towards his victim, crashing through the reeds with focused intent, sabre drawn—sure of his quarry. That misplaced focus was his downfall.

She judged the distance, carefully timing her throw. Her eerie war whoop split the air startling him, slowing his deadly attack. The rebel straightened, head snapping in her direction—that momentary pause all she needed as her tomahawk found its target with deadly accuracy.

Screaming as blood seeped ever faster from the deep wound in his chest the rebel stumbled in small circles, clutching the handle of her tomahawk, trying desperately to dislodge it. Before the two dragoons riding to her assistance could reach her, reluctant to fire lest they harm the colonel's wife, she strode to the staggering man's side. Halting him mid-circle, she shoved him to the ground, planting a knee forcefully in his gut. It was then she recognized him: one of her attackers from the previous day.

Grabbing his hair, she brutally yanked his head up, and with a practiced motion, slid the dirk smoothly from her boot and pressed it against the base of the terrified man's throat; his eyes widened in fear ... and recognition.

"How does it feel to be on the receiving end, you son-of-a-bitch?" she hissed, lowering her angry face to within inches of his. "Enjoy your trip to hell." With that she slashed savagely, laying his neck wide-open, blood spraying copiously.

Standing slowly, eyes never leaving the body, she stood dispassionately watching his life ebb away. As she leaned down and rocked her tomahawk from the dead man's chest, she became aware of the dragoons standing at her side, realizing they must have witnessed the whole scene. Her breathing had slowed, her heart once again beating at a manageable pace. Expelling a deep breath, she turned to face them, her expression changing to one of confusion as their faces went pale.

"What, Sampson? What is the matter?" She frowned, impatient. She needed to tend Captain Hodges's wound; yet they stood gaping.

"Your face, milady." Sergeant Bartlett pulled a bandanna from his pocket. "You are covered with blood." He held the cloth out to her.

"Oh," she said, shrugging dismissively. "Do not worry, gentlemen, the blood belongs to that bastard." She gestured towards the fallen rebel as she crouched down beside the captain.

"He was one of the men who attacked me yesterday. I would say he got what he deserved."

With a quick swipe of her face, she turned her attention to the injured captain.

Relieved, they knelt to be of help with Hodges. Gunfire had all but ceased, a rapid glance to the edge of the swamp showing Jason and Lieutenant Jackson heading her way at full gallop.

Captain Hodges was barely conscious, a gaping wound to his shoulder. But his eyes widened with concern as she bent close.

"Rest easy, Captain, it is not my blood." She smiled reassuringly.

Opening his shirt, she examined the damage gently. Cutting the jabot from his collar, she wadded it against his injury to stanch the flow of blood.

"You will be fine, Captain Hodges, but let us get you back to camp where I can take better care of your wound."

As the dragoons started to move the injured captain, Jason and Jackson reined to a halt and joined them, the rest of the dragoons having rapidly regrouped, were not far behind. Kathryn scanned the men noticing one or two minor injuries, relieved to see no one was missing.

"Jesus, Kathryn," Jason rasped. Flinging himself from his saddle, he strode to his wife's side. Grasping her chin, he brushed back wisps of hair escaping wildly around the edges of her helmet, searching for the wound.

Seeing the alarmed look on his commanding officer's face, Sampson quickly spoke up. "It is not her blood, sir, it is his." He jerked his head in the direction of the rebel's body. "He was one of the men who attacked her yesterday."

Kathryn was grateful for Sampson's explanation, Jason's firm grip on her chin made it difficult to speak.

Jackson moved to her side, sloshing water from his canteen onto a rag and handed it to the colonel. Not until Jason had removed all the red stickiness, sure that none of it belonged to his Kathryn, did his tension ease on a sigh of relief.

"We must attend Captain Hodges, sir," she reminded firmly, drawing his attention to the wounded captain.

She took a step backward, needing some form of action. As her adrenaline abruptly waned, her legs became a bit shaky. This was neither the time nor place to throw her arms around her husband's shoulders for comfort. With a final glance at the dead rebel, she headed for Beauty.

Recalling distinct pleasure as she slashed that individual's throat, she was shocked and quite concerned at her lack of guilt. *Is this a normal way to feel? Or do I suffer from some sort of lewd depravity?*

She would have to discuss this troubling thought with Jason tonight.

Back in the encampment, Kathryn immediately bent to the task of making Hodges more comfortable. Further investigation showed the bullet still imbedded in his shoulder, resting against the bone in a place of reasonable accessibility—the bone miraculously still intact.

"Sip some of this, Captain." She held an infusion of black cherry to his lips. "Not too much, now." She talked calmly, scrubbing her hands with whiskey as she waited for the liquid to take effect.

Jackson stood at her side with necessary supplies while Jason observed. Two more dragoons would need minor attention, but the severity of the captain's injury had to be addressed first.

"I will work my magic on you, Captain," she assured as she stroked his hair back. "Later, I will be sure that Anna inspects my work. Nothing but the best care for you, sir."

She could see his focus fading as she reached for the sterile knife. Indicating for Jack to hold the captain's shoulders, and two others to restrain his legs, she began her task. Her work went quickly, aided by the captain's ability to bear extreme pain while remaining almost motionless. After a few minutes of probing, Kathryn held the lead ball up to show Hodges.

"There it is, Captain. Now, brace yourself," she warned, hating what must be done.

Before he realized her next move, she splashed raw alcohol into the bleeding wound.

His eyes flew open, yet he remained motionless by sheer willpower. After that assault, mountain alum for cauterizing seemed easy to withstand.

After pressing a gooey poultice gently into place and bandaging his wound, Kathryn sat back to wash the gore from her hands and forearms as she appraised her patient. Wringing a cool cloth from the water basin, she sponged the beading perspiration from his forehead. At her gentle ministrations, his eyes flickered open, the beginning of a smile playing about his lips.

"You are an angel, milady," he sighed and drifted into sleep.

The wounds of the other two men were minor and easily cared for, with both bandaged and headed to the campfire to await the evening meal.

As she washed up, she watched her husband smiling benevolently, waiting patiently for her to finish so he could claim some of her time. However, they had one last important stop to make. Having not had a chance to see Gabrielle, both were anxious lest she fret. They headed towards Anna's quarters, Jason's arm draped loosely around her shoulder.

Neither had spoken of the attack as yet, but her question pressed so hard, it could not wait.

"Why do I feel no remorse over that man, Jason? I was furious at what he did to Captain Hodges, but when I recognized him—I was brutal."

She stopped and looked up into his understanding gaze.

"You did what needed to be done, Kathryn. That is the main reason I agreed to your becoming a member of the dragoons."

She looked slightly confused.

"Because I know you have both the physical strength, as well as mental ability to do what is required of you. Guilt in our line of work is a useless sentiment which cannot be allowed. It merely eats at one until it destroys the ability to function. Feel momentary remorse if you must, but quickly put it aside, knowing they would do the same to you—to us. War is a nasty business, my love."

He touched her cheek scrutinizing carefully before asking, "Do you wish to ...?"

"Absolutely not," she replied heatedly. "And I will thank you to make this the last time you ask me that question."

She eyed him narrowly, knuckles pressed against her hips, glaring with mock severity. Tilting her head, she shrugged and added softly, "I thought there must be something wrong with me, that is all. I just surprised myself."

Right there in the middle of the path to Anna's tent, he scooped her into his arms and nuzzled her neck.

"How I do love you, my Kathryn. Come, let us greet our daughter and then go to supper. Tonight, Mrs. Tarrington, you may tell the dragoons you wish to be called: *Kathryn*."

"Momma, Poppa." They turned abruptly at the bubbly, high-pitched greeting from an elated little girl.

Gabrielle toddled towards them on sturdy little legs, arms flailing, delighted to see them home, her toy horse tied with a blue ribbon to her wrist. Kathryn crouched down, opening her arms in greeting and smiled, how that child loved her father's toy horse.

Supper around the campfire was especially boisterous that evening, with tales of the skirmish being told and retold to those who had remained in camp. Kathryn sat on a log placed near the fire feeding her daughter from her tin plate. She blew a visible breath of frosty, fall air, followed by a puff of warm air against her ear as Gabrielle patted her face, giggling happily. Jason sat by her side enjoying their company, and absorbing the surrounding banter. He was distinctly proud of the praise being lavished on his wife, although she suffered extreme discomfiture at being singled out.

Finally, unable to stand it longer, she spoke up. "I did no more or less than any of the rest of you today. Please do not …" She shook her head, embarrassed.

Needing to divert their attention in another direction, she suddenly flashed a beaming smile. "I wish for all of you to call me Kathryn. In the heat of battle, I feel it will roll more easily from the tongue than 'Mrs. Tarrington', although I am extremely proud of that title." She turned warm eyes to her husband as she reached to touch his hand.

As the colonel stood, he purposefully scanned the individual faces of his men. "Always use her name with utmost respect, gentlemen, for I will not permit the slightest disregard for her … ever."

His look demanded absolute compliance, but there would never be cause to worry. These men knew her loyalties and abilities, and were proud to call her one of their own.

Music began at the far corner of the encampment, spreading inward on a gentle wave that gained in intensity as it moved towards them, many happy voices joining in loud song. As Jason sat down beside his wife, she touched his thigh surreptitiously, communicating loving gratitude. With an answering squeeze, he began chuckling, amused by his daughter as she scrambled onto his lap, showering him with wet kisses intermingled with garbled, broken sentences.

"Kathryn, do I detect Cherokee interspersed in our daughter's chatter?"

"It sounds like that to me, sir. She will certainly have quite a vocabulary someday."

"That is not necessarily a bad thing," he replied honestly. Hugging his little girl, he placed a kiss on her forehead. "Just be sure I am familiar with the words." He grinned at his wife. "As she has your independent spirit, I want to be sure I always understand exactly what she is saying."

Her answering smirk brought a chuckle.

They sat quietly, shoulders touching, enjoying the music as Gabrielle became sleepy, and cuddled against her father for warmth.

"I shall put poppet to bed. Go speak with Jack, love."

His suggestion surprised her. She eyed him thoughtfully, and slowly nodded. "He is so quiet tonight, Jason; actually has been all day. Clearly, he is unhappy with my decision … our decision."

"He is afraid for you, my love. Take a walk with him. I trust you will find the words to ease his concerns. He wants … no needs, to hear them from you." He eyed her with deep understanding.

With a light kiss to him and a hugged 'good night' to her little one, she picked up her coffee, and walked to where Lieutenant Jackson sat keeping an eye on Captain Hodges, the latter having insisted on joining the campfire despite his injury.

Jackson rose immediately, smiling somewhat tensely.

"I see Lieutenant Jackson has plied you with willow bark tea, Captain. Are you comfortable enough?" At his smile and quick nod, she advised him to take care not to push himself too hard.

"Do you mind if I steal Lieutenant Jackson for a few minutes?"

"Not at all, I shall retire shortly; I expect to be back in the foray by weeks end."

"I have no doubt of that, what with your will power, Captain. I witnessed your fortitude earlier and admire your ability to maintain self-control, despite intense pain."

Her compliment brought a smile and a rush of color to his cheeks, evident even in the dim light. As she turned towards Jackson, his soft-spoken words drew her attention back.

"I would prefer to call you 'Lady Kathryn', if that would be permitted."

Her glowing smile was his answer as she bade him 'good night'.

"Would you walk with me, Jack?" she invited, scanning his sad eyes. Without waiting for an answer, she hooked her arm loosely into his and steered him away from the main campfire. Beside a small group of trees she paused, and turning to face him, relaxed back against one of the rough trunks. Sipping her coffee, she watched him, her eyes soft with understanding.

"Talk to me, Jack."

His look was one of discomfort as he sipped his coffee in silence.

"We have been too close for way too long. Please do not remain silent when you are obviously angry with me." Her eyebrow arched in question.

"I am not angry, Kathryn. I am afraid for you, the added risk you take wearing a British uniform." His words were hesitant, pained.

"We will be riding with large numbers of English military and Loyalists in the near future, men who do not know me, but are well aware of my brother's reputation. I will not have my loyalties questioned, Jack, nor do I wish to risk being shot by our own side while in a rebel greatcoat."

She watched him closely as he digested her logic.

"We must always maintain a positive outlook, as difficult as it may be to watch those people we love putting themselves in danger. Does it not occur to you that I worry for both *you* and Jason? But I cannot allow myself to be overwhelmed by those fears, and will not contemplate negative possibilities even for a moment … or I will be unable to do what must be done."

She searched his face, waiting for a response.

"Jack," her voice held a husky, emotional edge. "You must know by now that you hold a large piece of my heart in your hands, and that I would try to respect your wishes in most instances. But in this one, I cannot. For Jason holds my soul, my complete being, our destiny in his. And I will follow that path with him … wherever it takes us."

Her eyes shimmered as she continued to watch him struggle with warring emotions. She could not bear his pained silence much longer; if he did not speak soon … She would give it one last try.

"I desperately need your support and understanding, Jack. I need your strength too. Perhaps I have no right to ask this of you, but …"

His hand suddenly reached out, his fingers brushing her cheek with great tenderness.

"You have every right, my 'Lady Kathryn'. I do understand and accept your decision, but I do not have to be happy about it, aye?" He smiled his familiar smile for the first time that day, and she breathed a sigh of relief.

Giving him a quick hug, she started back towards the campfire with Jack close by her side.

"I was at far greater risk when I gave birth, Jack. And you brought me through that. We will succeed together—all of us."

"You wear the uniform well, Kathryn. I have watched the dragoons for some time now, noting their growing pride and admiration for you." He paused, then added softly, "Be assured, those are my feelings also."

Her chin quivered slightly as she smiled up at him.

"Now, milady, let us return you to your husband before he forces me to ride with Cook for having kept you out so long."

As she approached their tent with soundless steps, she could see Jason engrossed in MacPherson's interpretation of Ossian, the badly worn corners of the book making it easily identifiable. Smiling, she began unbuttoning her jacket, slowing her step, enjoying the play of lantern light across his handsome features. Tingling warmth spread within her creating a molten trail of delicious sensations which brought her up short, her breathing quick and shallow.

He sensed her presence but remained focused on the book in his hands as tension escalated, hot pressure building. The game had begun. This was a part of the enigma that was his Kathryn: alternately wife, mother to his child, companion, seductive lover and so much more. She fulfilled all his needs.

Stepping into the tent, she tossed her jacket onto the cot, and with a quick flick of her wrist, released the canvas ties, dropping the tent flap behind her.

At the soft sound of her jacket hitting the bed he looked up, his eyebrow arched. Laying the book down, he slowly pushed away from the desk and leaned casually back into his chair, watching intently as she approached.

With nimble fingers she loosened her jabot, opening the lace front of her shirt almost to the waist, revealing a round lushness that caused him immediate, painful response. Removing the pins from her hair, she allowed the heavy, tawny mass to tumble freely about her shoulders. Her eyes flashed a bold, seductive invitation, her intense gaze never leaving his face. With hands resting loosely on her hips, she abruptly dropped her head, shaking the curls out, making eye contact through a screen of tangled blonde tresses.

"Colonel," she purred huskily.

His eyes raked boldly over her figure with feigned casualness. But his body betrayed that seeming indifference; his breath caught raggedly, the raw hunger smoldering in those emerald green eyes holding him captive.

"You wish to speak with me, madam?" he growled.

Angling his head, he scrutinized her through narrowed eyes.

"That is not what I had in mind, sir."

Her piercing gaze followed him as he rose, slowly.

"I would remind you, madam, I am a very busy man," he hurled savagely through tight lips.

"Make the time, Colonel, you will not regret it, that I promise," she purred with a sensuality that tortured him with delicious implications.

With measured steps, he moved around the desk, pausing at the corner. Keeping his eyes riveted on her, he slowly unholstered his pistol and placed it precisely on top of the papers piled there.

Her breath caught sharply, every inch of her screaming for his touch.

A slight smile played about his lips as he approached, so close now she could inhale the delicious scent of him, feel the heat emanating from his muscular body.

Grasping her chin, he raised her face to meet his. Tangling fingers in her long mane, he pulled her head back slowly and brought his warm lips to the base of her throat. His tongue traced a languid, enticing pattern upwards, sending radiating shivers as she flowed against him.

"Do not forget, for even one moment, Mrs. Tarrington, you belong to me alone, and to no other … as I belong to you."

His throaty growl against her ear was stated with such vehemence, it struck her suddenly: this was not part of their game.

"Always my love, always." Without hesitation, she answered in a tone matching his in intensity, understanding his meaning completely.

His wife had been kept overly long on a beautiful fall night, with a man who loved her as much as he—perhaps more, if that were possible. He trusted them implicitly, but was only human, wanting her tender words shared with no other. The length of time she had been gone nagged at him.

With her fervent answer, he knew she understood his unrest, as she always did. Needing reassurance of her abiding love, he claimed her mouth violently, her response, passionate and reassuring. His strong arms encircled her in a crushing embrace as her hands slid the length of his lean hips pulling him closer, savoring the strength of his muscular body, thrilling to his intense arousal.

"You may regret your offer by the time we are through, madam," he whispered harshly against her ear, as his hands explored and teased ruthlessly.

"Never, my Colonel, never," she gasped, needing him with unbearable urgency.

With a low groan, he dampered the oil lamp and fell to loving her in earnest.

"Kathryn, my Kathryn," he kissed her gently as she lay beneath him much later, his voice a soft caress as he fingered the pearl necklace at her throat.

Searching her face, he traced a finger tenderly over its angles and planes.

She sensed he was troubled by having expressed a moment's insecurity, but could not voice it.

"Jason, you hold my soul, my destiny … *our destiny* … in your hands, my love. I will follow you wherever that path leads."

She stroked damp tendrils of hair back from his face.

"That is what I told Jack," she murmured.

His finger stopped tracing as his eyes met hers. *Is there ever a time when she cannot read me?*

She continued to caress his cheek, adding quietly, "I also told him …"

Jason interrupted, shaking his head. "It is not necessary, my love, I …"

Touching a finger to his lips, she smiled warmly and began again. "I explained all the reasons why I must do this *with you*; it is *our destiny.* I told him he also holds a large piece of my heart, for he does—as a dear friend. He remained silent for so long I almost walked away to allow him time to sort things out. But he finally accepted how important it is to me to have his strength and support so that I may focus on what needs to be done, although he admitted it does not truly please him."

Enjoying the lean firmness of her husband pressed against her, she stayed him as he began to shift up and away, concerned for any discomfort he might cause.

"Do not move yet, my love. I would enjoy the weight of you against me longer."

As his lips brushed hers, she murmured, "You are my heart, my soul, Jason, and will remain so even after we cross into eternity. Hold that truth close and never forget … not even for a moment."

"You always know my thoughts before I can voice them, Kathryn." His striking blue eyes sparkled as he toyed with a blonde curl. "Even eternity cannot separate us, my Kathryn … when we eventually take that step together."

Although barely a whisper, she caught the depth of passion in his terse statement.

They clung to each other, comforting energies flowing between them in wordless comprehension. Her hands began caressing tentatively, his flesh quickening in vehement answer to her touch. Sensuously his fingers, so attuned to her needs, began once again to entice, capturing her slowly.

It would be a long, exquisite night: one establishing a new sense of inner peace and serenity between the two—one that would mark a positive new direction they were taking ... *together.*

Chapter Twenty-Eight

On to Savannah

She came awake slowly, enjoying the comfortable feeling of his muscular body molded against her naked back.

"Good morning, my pet."

His warm breath against the nape of her neck sent a thrill darting the length of her spine. Stretching languorously, she rolled to face him, snuggling against his chest.

"Umm, good morning to you, my love," she whispered sleepily. Kissing his chest, she glided warm lips over a nipple that tightened with the flick of her tongue.

"None of that, my sweet vixen." Throwing the blanket off, he patted her bottom allowing the cool morning air to hit her naked flesh, spiking goose bumps and a quick intake of breath.

"Jason," she squeaked, grasping for the blanket.

"Up we get, my pet, we are breaking camp this morning." At her inquisitive look, he grinned. "I had planned to discuss this with you last night, but somehow my attention was diverted."

As he stood, he reached for her hand and pulled her up against him. Hugging her tightly, he said quietly, "I had also wanted to tell you how proud I was of the way you handled yourself in the skirmish yesterday."

He noted the pleasure his compliment provided, and was glad he had remembered to acknowledge her. Unseasoned to heavy conflict, as yet, she needed reassurance for her actions.

"I am quite sure it has become obvious, madam, that I am having difficulty in getting today's duties begun while standing in such close proximity to you." Brushing his lips along the arch of her neck, he slowly disengaged himself. "Dress quickly, for there is much to be done."

Laughing happily, she touched a soft kiss to his lips and began dressing.

"Good morning, poppet," Jason greeted his daughter brightly as he reached down to pick her up.

Already wide-awake, she grinned up at him, the little wooden horse cradled lovingly in her lap. It was her favorite toy and could usually be found tucked under her arm, or being towed with a long, blue ribbon.

Kathryn stood beside Anna, watching her husband share a piece of bread with the happily chattering Gabrielle, love for his little girl shining openly in his eyes. He took great pride in this beautiful miniature of his wife, so intelligent and mature for her age. It never ceased to amaze him that she was a creation of his loins, Kathryn's genes obviously responsible for the delightful result.

Anna spoke in her soft, musical native Cherokee. Smiling at Kathryn, she gestured towards Jason, scrutinizing him with a keen eye and approving nod.

Somewhat bemused, Jason turned, raising a questioning eyebrow to his wife. Kathryn's eyes displayed warmth as she answered softly, "She says we become stronger, more confident and unified with each passing day; success will be ours."

Anna nodded solemnly, eyeing Jason with respect.

Standing, he smiled at the healer as he placed Gabrielle in Kathryn's arms.

"I believe momma has a surprise for you, poppet. You and your mother are going for a ride while poppa readies the camp for a move."

Catching Anna's curious look he added, "We head south. If all goes well, Anna, we may be close enough for you to visit your people if you wish."

Anna nodded 'thanks', pleased for his consideration; but she could not go home now. She, too, had had to make choices when she decided to stay with the dragoons. Walking a tightrope between the two worlds of Kathryn and her brother created far too great a risk for her Ugilohi; she would not do that. Kathryn had come into her life many moons past, shortly after the vicious small pox disease had taken her own child. She loved Kathryn as if she were of her own flesh and was determined to protect her, and those she loved.

Gabrielle bounced excitedly as they approached the spot where Lieutenant Jackson held Beauty saddled and waiting. Her small arms reached eagerly for Uncle Jack as he kissed the top of her head, hugging her close.

Beauty nickered, her soft nose snuffling against Kathryn as she sought her usual sugar treat. Two cubes of sugar later, amidst squeals of delight from the eager little girl, Kathryn flung herself gracefully into the saddle, and reaching for her bubbly child, settled her carefully on her lap.

Jason patted his wife's knee. "Stay close, milady, we should be on the move shortly."

With a bright smile, she clucked to Beauty. Childish prattle turned to avid concentration as the little girl attempted to emulate her mother's confident posture, amusing passing dragoons. Some day this youngster would be a delightful handful for some lucky man—just like her mother.

After a few minutes of riding, Kathryn realized she must spend more time with her daughter on horseback. The child was a natural, unafraid and completely at ease, much like herself at that age.

***

"Look how she spoils that child," Jamie spat, as he observed Kathryn through his looking glass.

Still licking wounds over the loss of one good man and three others injured during the previous day's encounter, his temper was not to be tested. However, Gabriel spoke up, undaunted by his father's peevishness.

"It seems to me she is doing for her daughter exactly what you did for your baby sister long ago; teaching her to sit a horse well at a young age."

Jamie growled an oath low in his throat, but could not take his eyes from the pair, noting how well the little girl already sat the small mare. Forgotten memories swept unbidden through his mind, the lump in his throat creating momentary difficulty in swallowing.

"Come, father, they are obviously preparing to break camp. If we stay longer, we run the risk of being seen."

He tugged Jamie's coat sleeve impatiently.

"Let us rejoin our men and be ready to follow."

***

Within two hours, a signal from Jason's gloved hand headed the dragoons south in an orderly fashion. Gabrielle was riding in Cook's wagon with Anna, a cookie grasped in her small hands, still sniffling occasionally in her discontent. Sobs of protest, as she had been handed down from Beauty's back to Anna, had brought a sharp reprimand from both parents. But once underway Anna relented, allowing the child a sweet as diversion.

As the colonel and Kathryn had moved into position beside Lieutenant Jackson at the head of the column, they exuded raw energy and confidence for all to see. They were heading south to meet Archibald Campbell within two weeks time. A hum of excitement thrummed amongst the ranks.

The following week they set up camp near Savannah, far enough out to avoid immediate suspicion, yet near enough for rapid access when orders came. This was the first time they had traveled at such a pace and distance with Gabrielle. Kathryn's initial concerns rapidly dissipated as it soon became evident her daughter, like herself, took to the trail with ease, always eager for new sights, enjoying the adventure. Although not surprised, Anna was impressed by how little effort it required to care for this unique child, and loved her all the more.

***

High on a scrub-covered hillcrest, well hidden from the pickets' view, two men observed the dragoon campsite through a looking glass.

"She continues to spoil that child." Jamie made a disgusted sound at the back of his throat.

Gabriel took the glass from his father's hand and looked for himself. Dusk was now falling rapidly. Kathryn held Gabrielle on her hip, bouncing her lightly in a quick two-step around the freshly lit campfire. Although the crisp notes of a tin whistle were almost inaudible at such distance, the child's happiness was evident as she clung to her mother's long curls, her small face aglow with laughter.

"She loves her daughter, father. That is apparent even viewed from this distance. And your niece is beautiful."

Jamie made another sound of disgust as he reclaimed the looking glass and scanned the campsite. "They certainly are here for a reason. Rumors about Campbell coming south must be true," he groused.

Gabriel maintained a silent, thoughtfulness as he observed his father.

"Look. She even dresses as one of them now," Jamie growled.

"Let us be gone before we are missed at camp," Gabriel admonished, eager to be away. His father's tendency to throw caution to the wind where his sister was concerned made him nervous.

As they turned to leave, the colonel suddenly came into view. Approaching Kathryn with a wide smile, he swept their eager child into his arms, hugging her with a kiss.

"Obviously he loves their little girl, too. I regret they are not on our side; I feel he is a good man in many ways."

"God damn it, Gabriel." Jamie's voice rose as his hand tightened on the barrel of his musket.

"We have seen what we came to see," Gabriel interrupted. "Come now." Ducking low, he crept back through the underbrush.

Jamie hesitated one more moment before following on his son's heels.

***

Pre-dawn, December 29th: Kathryn came awake suddenly, excitement thrumming through her being, not surprised that Jason had already roused.

"Our first major encounter today, Kathryn." He ran a finger along the curve of her cheek, searching her face for any hint of apprehension, knowing he would find none.

Smiling, she cupped his face and drawing him close, claimed his lips with a fierce kiss.

"Savannah will be ours," she avowed, eyeing her husband with confidence and determination as she quickly arose to prepare for the day.

"Momma and poppa will return in three days time, little one, be good for Anna."

With what lay ahead, it was a hurried 'goodbye'. As this was the first time they would be gone for an extended period of time, Kathryn tarried a few minutes longer giving final instructions to her child. With a loving hug and tender farewell kiss, she strode out to meet her husband and the waiting dragoons. Flinging herself astride Beauty, she nodded to the colonel then smiled greetings to Lieutenant Jackson.

"Finally Jack: some real action."

He returned her grin, but mouthed a small, silent prayer as the formation moved out.

As the dragoons reined to a halt at Girardeau's Plantation, Archie Campbell watched Colonel Tarrington and his wife approach with particular interest, their reputation having preceded them. Kathryn was equally intrigued at the sight of the hearty, heavyset Scot as they walked forward to meet him, glad he was on their side; he would make a fearsome enemy.

"Colonel Archibald Campbell: my wife, Kathryn MacLean Tarrington." Jason proudly introduced her as they shook hands on the front porch of the main house.

Although it had been a long, exhausting trip from Sandy Hook, New Jersey for Campbell and his troops, no one would have realized that to look at the energetic presence of the man. Campbell possessed an unusual vitality and exuberance which carried over to his men, who all looked equally refreshed and ready for battle.

"A Scottish lass: an excellent choice, Colonel." He mouthed polite niceties, but Kathryn sensed his reticence as he eyed her uniform.

"Might I make a request, Colonel Campbell?" Kathryn spoke up quietly.

Slightly taken aback by her boldness, he eyed her curiously for a long moment before speaking.

"And what might that be, Mrs. Tarrington?" His eyes narrowed slightly, regarding her with interest, an unusual woman to say the least.

"Withhold your judgment of me until after our encounter. I promise you will not be disappointed."

Her statement was not prideful or arrogant in any way and Campbell took no offense. The determination and courage reflected in her earnest face impressed him. Yes, he had heard of her brother, but he would extend her the benefit of doubt. After all, her husband's reputation was well known and beyond reproach. Campbell had also heard whispers of their unusual teamwork, their success in skirmishes having earned them grudging respect, even from such officers as Banastre Tarleton, himself formidable in battle, albeit his means of victory sometimes questionable.

"Agreed, milady," he replied without hesitation. Taking her hand, he squeezed firmly.

Jason stood close, his hand placed securely against the small of her back, amused to feel the tomahawk's ever-constant presence.

"Colonel Tarrington." Campbell turned full attention to Jason. "General Provost is marching up from Florida to meet us. But I have it on good authority that General Howe and Savannah are ours for the taking if we move quickly. I say we do not wait for Provost. How say you?"

A short while later, as they stood beside their horses watching the dragoons take formation, Jason leaned close to his wife. "Be careful, my love," he said softly. His eyes searched hers. "You have nothing to prove to those of us who already know your abilities and love you." His arched brow demanded she heed his words—words that touched her deeply.

Within moments, Jason's dragoons sat astride their horses quietly awaiting his orders. Kathryn stepped to Beauty's side and reached up to grasp her saddle.

"Kathryn." Her husband's tone was intense, stopping her instantly.

Turning, she eyed him with question. She had not given consideration to enacting their 'salute' amongst these strangers, perhaps allowing cause for embarrassment.

Jason placed a hand on her shoulder. "I care not what others think, my Kathryn," he stated with feeling.

Moving closer, his piercing gaze locked on her upturned face, capturing her sparkling emerald green eyes as she began their familiar salute. When his lips brushed hers tenderly in closure, his hand remained soft on her shoulder.

"Be careful, my love."

"Yes, my husband, and you, also."

Flinging herself into the saddle, she nudged Beauty into place and sat in formation with the dragoons awaiting his command.

As Lieutenant Jackson pulled abreast, she felt his eyes scrutinizing. For the briefest moment she resisted looking at him, not wanting to address any insecurity he might harbor in this, their first battle of size and consequence. But she could not ignore him … not Jack. Her eyes met his, surprised to see warmth, confidence and pride reflected as he nodded encouragement. But most of all, she saw his deep caring … and felt his love.

"Be careful, Jack," she mouthed softly, unable to hide her feelings for him.

Buoyed up by his support, she moved out with utmost confidence. She would prove herself today, to those who knew her as well as those who did not—as yet.

The day's encounter was fast and furious; injuries almost nonexistent on the British side, the battle quickly ended as Howe's Continentals were caught by surprise and vastly outnumbered. The American units retreated rapidly in a fairly organized manner, all but a group of Georgia militia. Jason's dragoons took chase, successfully cutting them off from the causeway that crossed Musgrove Swamp, forcing them to retreat directly into the quagmire.

"Colonel Tarrington." Kathryn pulled Beauty alongside Diablo. "This time of year the water will be very high; some of our men could drown. We had best not follow them in there."

Nodding appreciation, he signaled the men back to Girardeau's Plantation where they rejoined Archie Campbell.

Kathryn remained on horseback with the dragoons as Jason dismounted to talk to Campbell. She cast Jack a sidelong glance, a smile playing at the corners of her mouth.

"I shall no longer worry about you, Kathryn," he said softly as she turned happy eyes on him, nodding a quick 'thanks'.

Returning her gaze to Jason, she was surprised to see Archie Campbell striding in her direction. He was a large man, and did not have far to look up as he stopped beside Beauty, grinning openly.

"Glad I am, that I didna' judge ye afore the encounter, Mrs. Tarrington. For I would ha' been mistakin'. I ha' seen men who could not manage themselves as ye ha' today."

His face broke into a broad grin.

"Now, why should tha' surprise me; ye aire a highland lass." His burr became more pronounced. "I shall be headin' North tomorrow, leavin' you and the colonel to keep these rebels back in the swamps and under control. But tonight let's ferget all that; join us fer the evenin' meal, aye?"

Dinner was a boisterous affair, full of congratulations and friendly banter. Midway through the meal, almost as if by prearranged cue, Jason's eyes met Kathryn's with such intense intimacy, Archie Campbell felt the intruder for having observed.

Oblivious of their noisy surroundings, they had eyes only for each other, the raw emotion leaping between them astounding Campbell. Their fervor had been exhibited in their incredible teamwork on the battlefield, and he recognized it for what it was: passion borne of deep, abiding love and mutual respect, passion they could not conceal and of which they were not ashamed. He had never witnessed anything like it before, probably never would again.

During the battle earlier in the day, they had been dynamic, their love in no way enervating. Totally attuned to each other, both were strong, adept with weapons and driven to succeed. He regretted his duties called him north as he truly wished more time to get to know them better. But he could move on with utmost confidence, they would hold Savannah secure in British hands, crushing any further renegade attacks.

Kathryn's complete loyalty and commitment to her husband's cause was obvious, despite 'wagging tongues' that claimed her false due to her brother's rising importance in the rebel militia. Campbell was not sure how she coped emotionally, but somehow she did; a truly amazing lass.

As the meal came to an end, Campbell stood slowly. Taking a cigar from an inner pocket of his coat, he bit the tip off cleanly and popped it into his mouth. Casually, lighting a match, he touched it to the end, puffing deeply until it glowed brightly and rich aroma wafted from the smoky circles he exhaled.

"I believe we have brandy awaiting us in the library, gentlemen, and Mrs. Tarrington?" He left the question of her joining them hanging, somewhat ambiguous.

"I thank you for your kind invitation, sir. However, with so little time left before you take your leave, you and your officers must have much to discuss. Perhaps more could be accomplished without my distraction." Smiling prettily, she excused herself.

Jason's hand, lingering in the small of her back as he held the chair for her to rise, sent a private message—and a promise.

As the officers headed towards the library, Campbell moved to Jason's side, addressing him with a quiet aside. "Your wife is perceptive and diplomatic, Colonel, a woman of rare talents." His eyes narrowed slightly. "You are a very lucky man, sir."

Much later that evening she lay within her husband's arms amidst soft pillows and thick comforters, the brazier in the fireplace throwing warmth and flickering shadows.

"I feel guilty, Jason. All this comfort while our men are huddled around campfires in the open tonight."

"None of them would begrudge you, my love." He kissed the damp curls clinging along her neck. "I do believe you impressed Archie tonight when you refused to join us. A woman who knows her place is a rare jewel." He chuckled devilishly as she elbowed him playfully in the ribs.

He would not lavish praise as it caused her discomfort; but he had kept a cautious eye on her, as had Jack. They had spoken together earlier in the evening, both agreeing she had handled herself proficiently despite the pressure of encountering large enemy numbers, and working with unknown British troops.

"This is just the beginning, my pet. Whether you like to hear it or not, you have made me proud, yet again."

"I did no more or less …"

He silenced her mid-sentence with a deep kiss.

"Hush, now, love, get some sleep. It has been a busy day and early tomorrow we head back to our encampment."

As she snuggled into his shoulder he whispered softly, "I find I miss our little girl."

She nodded sleepily, suddenly extremely tired. It had been an invigorating and emotionally charged day, and all had gone well.

"Was Jamie seen?" she asked suddenly, thoughts of him jarring her from drifting into sleep.

"Several of Campbell's men chased a man who fit his description into the swamp with some of the Georgia militia. I am sure those who are with him will certainly live to fight another day."

"He knows those swamps like the back of his hand, Jason," she mumbled, yawning sleepily. "Our success today will make him furious; we had best be cautious."

She fit herself tighter to him, her fingers curling against his chest, asleep before she could make an effort to entice him further.

The following morning they bid a warm farewell to Colonel Campbell and his troops and headed back to the encampment; it would be their home for several weeks to come.

Ever since Kathryn's brush with death at the hands of Gabriel's men, Jason had barely allowed her out of his sight. Yet, rather than finding this fact constricting or threatening to her independence, she reveled in the constant closeness with her husband. As the weeks passed, they became more visible as a dynamic team, their reputation growing. Kathryn watched his back like a protective lioness, and Lieutenant Jackson watched hers. They pushed the rebel militia inexorably, not allowing them a moment's peace. Savannah was theirs and they would keep it so.

Weeks passed quickly, one after another. Spring arrived with its warmth, life renewing itself in soft shades of color, heady aromas and sun-drenched afternoons. As always, fighting with the rebels was scattered and abrupt. They chose a mode of quick encounters: shoot and run, then slip back into the forests leaving barely a ripple in the grass to indicate from whence they had come.

It was another somewhat quiet time in Jason and Kathryn's lives, and they reveled in watching Gabrielle grow into a healthy, active child. She now rode with confidence beside her parents on a small pony of her own, their joy and pride in their little girl knowing no bounds.

Jack spent countless hours with his beloved godchild, reading to her and teaching her to prepare medicinal herbs, as Kathryn had taught him. They rode through the surrounding fields where Gabrielle practiced jumping her pony, and occasionally wandered to the nearby stream to fish. But it was under Anna's careful tutelage that she learned to set snares and trap small game.

In the months to come, Jason and Kathryn would often look back, thankful for having had this idyllic period: limitless hours of unstructured time spent with their child … and each other.

Chapter Twenty-Nine

Hamish

As the dragoons swept down upon the fleeing rebels, Kathryn's eye caught motion off to her right. Veering in that direction, she watched as a wounded rebel slid limply from his horse into the grass. Leaping from Beauty, she strode towards the fallen soldier, dirk at the ready to strike a killing blow. Nearing the still figure, she noticed he was slight of build—probably young. Stunned and in pain, he offered no resistance as she grabbed his shoulder, yanking him over onto his back. Frightened eyes met hers as her knife pressed against his throat: sudden recognition stopping the motion instantly.

"Hamish!" She was horrified at what she had almost done. "I thought you would go home after Ian's …" She could not finish. "You are so young."

Cursing under her breath, she flipped her dirk catching the blade close to the hilt. "I am so sorry, son." She grimaced, biting her lower lip.

As his frightened eyes widened, bracing for the killing blow, she slammed the handle against his forehead. With a low moan, he slumped to the ground. A hurried assessment showed a flesh wound high on his shoulder; nothing serious. He would live if Jamie's men found him soon.

Seeing Lieutenant Jackson headed in her direction, not wishing him to come closer, she quickly moved to intercept him. Taking a hurried step towards Beauty she winced, faltering slightly, suddenly recalling the rock that had slipped under foot as she leaped to the ground. Cursing softly, she flung herself astride Beauty, clucking to her to make haste. Pulling abreast of the lieutenant, she noted his questioning look. How much had he witnessed? He remained silent, studying her thoughtfully, saying nothing for the moment.

"How is your ankle, Kathryn?" he finally asked.

"It is nothing," she said dismissively. Nodding towards the regrouping band of dragoons, she kneed Beauty and headed off to join them.

As she and Jackson reined in, Jason gave them a quick onceover assuring all was well, then stood in his stirrups to take a head count, before glancing again at his wife. Though he could see no visible injury, something was amiss. He sensed it, rising uneasiness behind her calm façade.

Arriving back at their camp, she rode directly into the holding area, distancing herself from Jackson and dismounting carefully so as not to jar her ankle. Beauty nuzzled her pockets in search of a treat and was rewarded with her usual sugar. With soft words of praise, Kathryn toweled the animal dry and then replaced her heavy bridle with a light rope halter.

Jack eyed her over the withers of his horse, but had no wish to interrupt her private thoughts. Besides, Jason was approaching, concern etching his features. Stopping at her side, he placed a hand on her shoulder startling her.

"Colonel …" Startled, she stepped back twisting her injured ankle. Facing her husband, somewhat abashed, she tried to hide a grimace.

"Might I offer a hand?" His tone was light, neutral, but held underlying concern. Stepping to her side, he unfastened Beauty's stomach cinch. With practiced ease, he removed the saddle and carried it to the covered storage area, then returned to his wife's side.

"Colonel, I would request a few moments of your time." Her large, serious eyes sought his.

"What, madam, no tender words for your husband after a well fought skirmish?"

"Sir, I really must …"

"Ahh, I see how it is." He gave her a long intense look before turning to Jackson.

"Lieutenant, would you finish here, please?"

Whatever was bothering his Kathryn, it was important he address the situation with propriety.

"Come to my quarters, Kathryn," he said officially, gesturing for her to precede him.

Though she attempted to conceal her limp, pain was evident. As they entered the tent, he marveled at how brave and stubborn she could be. He ached to take her in his arms—but could not. She would never accept that from her commanding officer.

While she stood quietly at attention, he moved behind his desk and pulled the chair out. Inclining his head, he indicated for her to sit.

"Colonel, I am …"

"You are limping," he said quietly.

"It is nothing, sir, I twisted it slightly." She shrugged as he indicated the chair again.

"Sit down, Kathryn, that is an order," he reiterated firmly.

She did as commanded but looked uncomfortable.

Bending down he lifted her foot, bracing her leg against his knee as he eased her boot off.

"Sir, this is not necessary."

"Mrs. Tarrington, the well-being of my dragoons is of utmost importance. I wish to examine your injury."

At the beginning of a protest, he silenced her with a look. "Remain quiet, hmm? Whatever you need to discuss will keep for a few minutes."

Raw tension emanated in waves as he tenderly examined her ankle, massaging with knowledgeable fingers. She winced but remained still and silent.

"The swelling is not bad." He placed his warm hands on either side of her ankle and leaned back against his desk. "A day or two of rest should have you as good as new."

She opened her mouth to speak.

"Does this help ease the pain?" he interrupted patiently.

A quick nod was her only answer as his warm hands cupped the injury. As his thumbs continued kneading, some of her anxiety began to fall away.

"I will ask Jack to brew some willow bark tea; that may help ease your discomfort."

He continued massaging for another minute or two—studying her closely, until he could see she was again becoming anxious, needing to address her problem.

"Now, what has upset you so, Mrs. Tarrington?"

She attempted to pull her leg back to stand, but he held it firmly, distressing her further.

"Sir, I must tell you about today. And I feel that …"

"As your commanding officer, I insist you talk to me while sitting in that chair, in deference to your injury received in the line of duty," he said firmly, he would brook no argument.

"Duty," she murmured. "I fear I did not do my duty today; that pains me more than the ankle."

"Why not permit me be the judge, Kathryn? You are often overly harsh in assessing yourself."

He continued gently massaging attempting to impart comfort and reassurance as she slowly related her incident with Hamish.

"I am well aware that he is the enemy, sir. But he is no more than a boy. I looked into his frightened eyes and could not kill him. Nor could I take him as prisoner: to what purpose? I fear he will be brought down soon enough; but not by my hand."

She sat ramrod straight, eyes bravely holding his, ready to comply with his decision.

"Was I wrong?" Her voice broke as she fought for control. Would he demand she cease to wear the proud uniform of a dragoon?

"I have seen you in battle, Kathryn. I know you do not falter in duty, nor do you award favors negligently." He understood her fear; as her colonel, what might her penalty be?

"No," he said softly, "you were not wrong."

Her eyes closed momentarily upon a sigh.

"I am not sure I could have stopped in the heat of battle, but you were not wrong. Perhaps it may even help our image."

Confused, she looked up to find him smiling.

"Twice now, this lad has received kindness at your hands. It would be rather pleasant not to be perceived with such animosity as your friend, Tarleton," he teased, flashing a broad grin.

With her look of shocked horror, he chuckled. Gently setting her foot down, he pulled her into his arms. "Now, I wish to be your husband, so I may comfort and assure you I would never demand your uniform be forfeit, my love."

"I was so afraid," she whispered.

"Fret no longer, my pet. Who knows, perhaps historians may some day give us the benefit of doubt and portray us fairly. It is never easy to make life and death decisions with so many variables. However, you made a wise and fair choice today."

"I care not what others think, Jason, historians or otherwise, only how *you* see me."

He tipped her chin up to meet his thoughtful gaze.

"I see a beautiful, compassionate, brave woman who shares my heart and soul." Stroking back errant curls, he whispered against her ear, "I love you, my Kathryn."

Before she could murmur an answer, his mouth claimed hers, his hands reaching to cup her bottom and pull her against the firmness of his desire.

"There is only one instance in which I would request you forfeit your uniform." His grin was devilish, his breathing heightened. "And you would not be refused donning it again—much later."

"Yes, sir," she said smartly, returning his grin. "I believe this might be one of those instances you spoke of, sir."

"Yes," he sucked through clenched teeth as his hands skimmed up under her shirt.

***

"God damn it," Jamie swore softly as he bandaged Hamish's shoulder by the light of a small campfire.

Hidden well back in the swamps, he was unconcerned with the possibility of attack. The dragoons would never venture this far, even with Kathryn's help—*Kathryn's help.*

"Damn her," he ground out furiously, unable to contain his anger.

Gabriel watched in silence, allowing his father to vent his fury.

"She spared my life, sir," Hamish ventured, flinching as Jamie's eyes narrowed impaling him, his expression icy.

"And that is the second time, sir," he added doggedly.

Before Jamie could become more agitated, Gabriel crouched to offer Hamish a cup of willow tea and with a slight nod indicated his approval. He then turned to face his father. Eyes smoldering with intensity, he stated quietly, "She does what she must for love of her husband and his cause, but she still cares … she still remembers."

***

Chapter Thirty

Cornwallis Returns

Kathryn strode into their tent shaking her hair out and running her fingers through the thick mass, stopping abruptly at finding Jason with company. Immediately her face lit up in recognition.

"Why, Major Ferguson, what an unexpected and pleasant surprise."

She was actually pleased; it had been some time since she had had anyone to cross swords with verbally. But what purpose had brought him this far south to visit their encampment?

"How nice to see you again, Mrs. Tarrington," he replied, sounding equally pleased.

Standing quickly, he moved to take her hand, clasping it firmly in both of his.

"Do join us." His smile held genuine warmth.

Slightly taken aback, she stepped closer eyeing Jason curiously as he sat watching her reaction from behind his desk, a smile playing at the corners of his mouth.

As soft light from the oil lamp washed over her, Ferguson scanned her outfit, nodding approval.

"I have heard of your exploits. You and your husband have become quite a dynamic team. Rather unusual, but it seems to work."

She murmured a quiet 'thank you', but he continued. "I do believe my friend, Tarleton, is jealous of your recognition. And I, too, am somewhat out of sorts."

At her arched brow and puzzled look, he smiled again. "With your obvious dedication to our cause, I fear it will be more difficult for me to find subject matter over which to cross swords with you, milady. However, I will make every effort to do so."

Grinning at his humorous remark, she glanced to her husband in amused confusion. Ferguson's mood was light—extremely out of character—for what reason?

"Tell her, Colonel. I see my glib attitude has confused your lovely and perceptive wife.

"Lord Cornwallis is returning, Kathryn. Mrs. Cornwallis was taken in her illness … and he no longer wishes to remain on their estate without her."

"I am deeply sorry for his loss, but pleased we will see him again. When might we expect his lordship?" Kathryn asked eagerly.

"You really do like the man," Ferguson commented, sounding somewhat surprised.

Taking immediate umbrage at his insulting tone, she scowled, readying a caustic retort.

Throwing his hands up in mock surrender, he shook his head chuckling. "I see you have lost none of that feisty spark. I do believe Lord Cornwallis will be impressed. Becoming a mother has not softened you in any way."

As her eyes narrowed he quickly added, "That is a compliment, Mrs. Tarrington, perhaps the only one you may ever hear cross my lips, treasure it." An unmistakable twinkle in his eye gave proof he, too, was pleased with the change in events.

"Would you like to meet our daughter Major?" Kathryn asked, taking the conversation in a different direction, again relaxing.

At his nod, she excused herself. Within minutes, she returned with a tousle-haired little girl whose bright, alert eyes gave no hint of having been picked up from her bed just as she nodded into sleep. That was a talent she had inherited equally from both parents.

"Poppa," she squealed, reaching for her father as he swept her proudly into his arms, his eyes lingering softly on his wife before turning to Ferguson.

As the lanterns glow highlighted the little girl's features the major's eyes widened. "My God, there is no question as to her parentage. Why, she is absolutely charming."

Smiling, he stretched his arms out, surprising Kathryn. "Will she come to me?"

Gabrielle eyed both parents for approval as Jason set her down. At their nods, she toddled to the major, and stopping in front of him, demanded: "Up. Up."

With a laugh, he swung her up onto his lap. Once there, she immediately became fascinated with the gold buttons on his jacket.

"She is the spitting image of you, Kathryn, but with Jason's coloring, how extraordinary."

"Like poppa." Gabrielle swung around in Ferguson's lap, pointing towards her father, gesturing at the gold buttons of his jacket.

Kathryn grinned then spoke to her daughter in Cherokee. Ferguson angled his head inquisitively as Gabrielle turned and babbled to him in what sounded to be a foreign dialect.

"Loosely translated, Major, she bids you 'goodnight'. Her nurse is teaching her Cherokee."

"Ahh," he nodded, appreciating the uniqueness of this child. "Well then, 'good night' to you, Gabrielle." Touching a light kiss to her forehead, he was somewhat nonplussed as she grasped his collar and placed a sloppy kiss on his chin.

Both parents shrugged, grinning.

As Kathryn reached for her daughter, she resisted being picked up.

"No. Want to walk," she pouted, stubbornly digging in her heels.

Kathryn rolled her eyes at her husband and groaned. "She is your daughter, sir." Flashing him a quick wink, she then took the small hand offered and left the tent.

"I see you have your hands full, Colonel, with two quite independent women."

"Yes, Major, I am a very fortunate man."

Jack sat beside Cook's wagon lingering over a cup of coffee, retelling some of their tales from past skirmishes.

"Uncle Jack," a small voice shrilled.

Gabrielle babbled happily as she pulled away from her mother's side and took rolling steps towards the lieutenant. Instantly setting his coffee aside, Jack extended welcoming arms. Hugging her close, he inhaled the sweet smell of this child he loved as if she were his own.

"What brings Ferguson this far a field, Kathryn?" He looked up offering her his coffee, which she gladly accepted, sipping as she watched Gabrielle curl against his chest, her sleepy eyes fighting to stay open.

"Actually, I am truly excited. Lord Cornwallis is coming back to the colonies. I expect that all he talked of months ago will now become reality."

Jack's expression became thoughtful. "He is an excellent strategist. If England will give him the men and funding he needs ..." The statement hung between them unfinished.

"You ought to get back, Kathryn. I will put my little princess to bed."

With a quick squeeze to his shoulder, and a kiss to her sleeping child, she murmured a warm 'thanks' and headed back to the tent.

She found Jason and Ferguson chatting over a brandy, one having also been poured for her. She was to be included in the conversation, an interesting change of status while in Ferguson's presence. They talked at length of the importance of the British taking Charleston, Cornwallis's first target upon return, and his lordship's relationship with Commander-in-Chief Clinton. As the British would begin a sweep northwards once South Carolina was taken—and there was no doubt of that being accomplished—talk eventually turned to other necessary conquests to bring this war to a close.

Major Ferguson spoke warmly of his friend, Banastre Tarleton, discussing at length, the man's aspirations and idiosyncrasies. He also talked about the probable impact on them in the near future, when they would be teamed together in the conflict. Kathryn found it necessary, more than once, to bite her tongue in order to maintain silence, grateful that Ferguson could not read minds.

With some hesitation, recalling her unpleasant experience at the hands of the 'Southern Belles' at his lordship's party, she brought up the Wautauga Settlement in the South Carolina Blue Ridge.

"They are some of the most independent, determined Irish-Scots you will ever encounter, Major. They make me look tame by comparison." She eyed him gravely and continued before he could interject any comments. "Never sell their abilities short or count on them to embrace tenets they have no conviction to support. If they can be brought to our side, what a boon, if not ..."

Eyeing him solemnly, she left that particular thought hanging, not wishing to pursue it further, but advised: "If you become involved with them, whatever you do, never make idle threats. You may receive more than you bargained for."

Having said all she deemed appropriate in apprising Ferguson of the dangers of Wautauga, she settled back with her brandy to listen and absorb the implications of what the two men discussed.

Ferguson departed for 'The 96' the following morning to meet with Colonel Cruger and await Cornwallis's arrival, leaving Jason and Kathryn to continue their duties until further orders arrived.

Within three weeks after Major Ferguson's unexpected visit, their orders arrived directly from his lordship, commanding them to meet him at Star Redoubt in 'The 96' before month's end. As they were requested to bring Gabrielle, and the journey was long, Jason decided to break camp and relocate closer to Charleston.

Gabrielle changed almost daily, her chubby, baby form stretching into what would eventually become a tall, lean child. Much to her parents' amusement, she spoke with an ever-broadening range of words in both English and Cherokee.

Kathryn was excited to be 'on the trail' again, proud of their daughter and eager to show her off to his lordship. She hoped Lord Cornwallis had brought news of Jason's grandmother from England. Although Jason was eager to see his old friend, John Cruger, Kathryn lacked enthusiasm. However, duty called—and she knew all about that. Besides, her impatience to see his lordship again, overcame any downside to the rest of their 'command visit'. It would be interesting to observe Cornwallis's reaction to her participation in the fighting; she doubted he would be surprised.

Jason opened the door to the large study, stepping back to allow his wife to enter first. Visually striking in her uniform, he watched with pride as she took precise, measured steps in approaching his lordship's desk. Cornwallis and Ferguson were poring over papers but immediately rose in greeting as Kathryn and Jason came to a standstill, inclining their heads in appropriate acknowledgment. They stood, their shoulders nearly touching, waiting for his lordship's demeanor to set the tone of the meeting. He had lost weight, Kathryn noticed, lines of sadness etched the corners of his eyes yet he looked well; she was glad to see him.

Coming around the desk, he moved towards Kathryn, his face serious. "Is there truth to the rumors, Mrs. Tarrington?"

Eyeing him thoughtfully, she answered softly, "We have discussed the relevance of rumors, milord. Of which do you speak?"

His hand made a wide sweep indicating her uniform. "It is said your loyalties are beyond reproach, despite the higher visibility of your brother."

Jason's hand moved to the small of her back, and feeling her tomahawk smiled to himself.

"That is true, milord."

"Both you and the colonel have established quite a reputation on the battlefield. The colonel's abilities have been known for some time, but you, madam …" he paused scrutinizing her intently. "It is said, you are the equal of most men when on the field."

Kathryn's cheeks flared pink as she shifted uncomfortably, murmuring quiet denial.

"She is that and more, milord," Jason concurred, as his thumb scrolled small circles on her back.

"So, Kathryn, it is as rumored. I am not surprised; I expected no less of you." He eyed her uniform, noticing her lean fitness and proud, confident stance. "You are an unusual woman," he complimented, his eyes crinkling slightly at the corners.

Without warning, he strode forward, and pulling her against him in a warm embrace, abandoned further protocol.

"Your wife never ceases to amaze me, Colonel." He stood back extending a hand to Jason. "And I do believe she is even more beautiful than I remembered."

Though she had dreaded this obligation their extended visit turned out to be enjoyable. As Kathryn's newly acquired reputation had preceded her, Colonel Cruger treated her with new respect. The ladies of 'The 96' were polite, although distant, a fact which did not bother Kathryn—they had no common ground on which to converse.

She and Jason spent many pleasurable hours talking with Lord Cornwallis: subjects of a personal nature as well as the escalating war. He had made a special effort to meet Jason's grandmother before returning; the letter he carried, being read many times over in the privacy of their quarters. Cornwallis talked at length about the gentle lady, relating all he had told her of them: their incredible love and the favorable changes in Jason, a result of old wounds healing under Kathryn's caring guidance.

Gabrielle was on best behavior and inexplicably drawn to the general. Kathryn enjoyed watching them interact, a respected military strategist sitting with their curly-haired little girl on his knee, singing nonsense rhymes as she giggled—amazing. Kathryn better understood his lordship's doting, when in a private moment, he shared the fact that he had a son and daughter he adored, but out of necessity had left back in England.

He idolized Gabrielle and showered her with attention. When not in military meetings, he could often be found walking the premises of the fort with her clinging to his hand, Gabrielle babbling in a combination of English and Cherokee while his lordship paid rapt attention.

Although she still carried her father's wooden horse tucked carefully under her arm, a new cloth doll had been added—brought all the way from England by a considerate general, and sent by a loving great grandmother.

Chapter Thirty-One

Confident Beginnings

By the time they entered into the battle to take Charleston, Kathryn had reached her stride: confidant, physically strong, an accomplished marksman, outstanding in close combat and seemingly tireless. She and Jason fed on each other's energies and passions, each completely attuned to the other's needs. Their familiar 'salute' prior to any conflict always inspired the dragoons. Riveting their attention on the couple, they observed the ritual solemnly, absorbing their passion—riding out for the day's foray with a unified, positive mindset.

Confident of her abilities, Jason no longer worried when Kathryn was out of his sight. Driven by a unified quest, neither would accept nor contemplate negative possibilities. Their passion increased daily encompassing all areas of their existence. But above all else—culminated in a physical need of mutual sharing that left them clinging, often shaken at the incredible depth of their passionate joining, be it that of exquisite tenderness or a cataclysmic union of wild, untamed energies.

Charleston was theirs for the taking—and take it, they did. Although forced to work together, she found riding with Banastre Tarleton not as intolerable as imagined, finding she could distance herself emotionally from the man, remaining aloof without being openly offensive. Jason, on the other hand, seemed more able to tolerate him; after consideration, Kathryn concluded it must be part of the elusive male ability to cope. Despite her intense dislike for the man, he was an excellent soldier on the field, the battle for Charleston a decisive victory, the fall of this important city a great coup for the British.

***

"She was magnificent in battle; you have to give her that."

His father remained silent feigning deep interest in the lead ball he was casting.

"I said she was …" Gabriel started to repeat.

"I am well aware of that; I saw her, I trained her, but why? Why? Fighting for a cause so foreign to all she used to hold dear." Jamie felt angry, hurt … betrayed.

"She loves her husband. It is his cause … therefore hers. If not for him, I doubt she would take that side. Under the circumstances, she has no choice" Gabriel countered, justifying his aunt's actions. "She did not take up his side to hurt you, father, or out of spite. She fights solely in support of her husband. I doubt she even considers the actual cause any longer."

"Well, perhaps if he were gone …"

Gabriel forced a bowl of stew into his father's hand trying to divert his attention.

"There will be many more encounters, father, eat your dinner. Forget it for tonight, we have wounded to attend."

***

The victory celebration would be large, loud and festive. Charleston was only the beginning. All of South Carolina would be secured in short order, then on to North Carolina. Cornwallis was self-assured, positive of future success, and in over self-confidence became arrogant. *Yes, this successful battle demands acknowledgement of my officers' expertise. A regal ball will be an appropriate means to honor them—and a perfect way to allow the Charlestonians to understand their defeat.* Lord Cornwallis smiled proudly.

Lieutenant Jackson stood lost amidst his own thoughts, holding the bridle of the carriage horse as it snorted anxiously. The sound of Kathryn's throaty chuckle snapped his attention to the opening of their tent. His heart lurched, his breath catching at the back of his throat. 'Exquisite': the only word that slammed through his mind.

She was gazing up into her husband's intense, blue eyes as he guided her towards the carriage with a gently placed hand at her waist. Her gown, carefully chosen by him, was of a rich emerald green that shimmered in the rays of the setting sun, throwing shards of light matching those of her eyes. The simplicity of the gown enhanced the beautiful heart shaped necklace she always wore. Delicate earbobs dangled saucily, peaking below the billow of her tawny hair. Drawn up high on both sides of her head, it cascaded in heavy ringlets of golden honey, interwoven carefully with emerald green, satin ribbons, an effect obviously having required assistance to achieve.

This was another side of the complex man Jackson had known for so long, yet in many ways, hardly knew. Though a hardened dragoon colonel, with a sensitive touch and deep caring, he had obviously dressed his wife's hair. Jason walked beside his wife, pride and devotion displayed unashamedly, handsome in his crisp uniform—the pair making a dramatic, bold statement. Jackson smiled as they approached. *He loves her more deeply with each passing day,* the thought struck with a pang, but he could accept no less for her.

As Jack stood aside to allow Jason to assist her into the carriage he murmured polite greetings, but stopped mid-sentence as she set foot on the carriage step revealing a boot toe peeking from under the edge of her gown. At his stifled chuckle, she paused, eyeing him with mock irritation.

"Yes, I am wearing my boots and yes, I have my dirk. And I would thank you not to notice, Lieutenant, as the colonel and I have already had a 'discussion' about my feet." Her eyes danced gleefully as she glanced at her husband.

"My wife assures me, Lieutenant, she will not use her dirk on any of the fine ladies at the ball."

"Think back on my exact words, sir. Are you absolutely certain of what I promised?" With a devilish grin she touched his cheek gently and moved gracefully into the carriage. At her husband's perplexed expression and arched brow, she flashed a look of complete innocence.

Captain Hodges stood on the opposite side of the carriage with four additional officers waiting to act as escort, their heads ducked to cover smiles as they tried to maintain a sense of decorum. This was a facet of their colonel and his wife they thoroughly enjoyed, one seen more frequently with passing time. Their playful banter was in such contrast to the passion and ruthless pursuit of their common goal displayed on the battlefield.

Slipping onto the seat beside his wife, he brushed a quick kiss to the top of her head and settled a shawl around her shoulders.

"Let us be on our way, gentlemen, and get this duty over with."

Clucking to the horse with a quick snap of the reins, they headed out.

***

"My God, she is beautiful." Gabriel said softly as he offered the looking glass to his father.

"For Christ's sake, Gabriel, they go to celebrate our defeat. South Carolina will belong to the British in short order at this rate. If only my rifle was accurate at this distance, I would take him now."

Gabriel would not waste words. His father had closed his mind to all reason. Killing the colonel would not bring Kathryn rushing back into his arms, grateful for his having saved her from a horrible fate. This was her husband, the man she loved possessively, fiercely ... loved so deeply Gabriel doubted she could survive the loss.

Often in the quiet of night, Gabriel lay sleepless thinking of his beloved wife, Silver Fox, waiting for him back home. While pondering difficulties the future held for both of them and their child, his thoughts frequently turned to his Aunt Kathryn. He refused to project events beyond a daily basis, but knew he would never seek her out on the battlefield—nor her husband.

His father, however, was a different matter. Jamie followed the dragoons obsessively, often watching their encampment from a dangerously close position. Dragoon pickets were vigilant in keeping a tight, protective circle around their camp at all times, an irritating fact relegating him to brief looks through his long distance glass; and well beyond rifle range.

Gabriel tried to temper his father's moods and actions, careful not to overplay his stance lest he innocently goad him into some rash action. He would be glad when this war was over; healing could begin on all sides and life would hopefully resume some semblance of normalcy.

Often he wished his father would find love again. His mother's death had left Jamie inconsolable, with Kathryn his only solace. Many times as a young boy, Gabriel had come upon the two of them sitting quietly on the porch stoop, her arm draped about his shoulder murmuring comforting words as she wiped his tear streaked face.

Yes, Jamie missed his sister, missed her companionship desperately. But Gabriel understood. Kathryn had a right to her life too, even if it was not one of Jamie's choosing.

***

Jason turned and reached to assist his wife from the carriage as it came to a stop in front of the lovely southern plantation house where Lord Cornwallis's celebration was being held.

Winking at Jack, she mouthed, "Wish us well."

As they started up the long walk to the main entrance, Kathryn smiled up at her husband. "I am afraid your choice of gown may draw much attention, my love."

"It merely accentuates you, Kathryn—bold, beautiful and belonging to me."

At her arched brow he added, "... as I belong to you. But that goes without saying."

Piercing him with a sharp look, she slowed her pace so as not to reach the main door where she could be overheard. "No, Jason, the saying of it is important to both of us."

Pausing on the top step, their eyes met and held, a silent understanding passing between them.

"I stand corrected, my love," he said sincerely.

Tipping her chin up, he kissed her tenderly as she murmured soft, intimate words against his lips.

Cornwallis nudged Major Ferguson as they stood in the receiving line. Following his lordship's gaze, he turned towards the door just as Jason ran his finger tenderly across his wife's cheekbone, tracing a line along the side of her face, his eyes speaking wordless devotion.

"I wonder what gentle words she whispered," Cornwallis mused.

They watched the colonel slip his arm through his wife's as they gracefully entered the grand hallway.

"I have seen for myself, Major. Unleash that pair in battle and they are invincible, fierce, feeding upon each other's strengths. Yet look at them here … the incredible tenderness they display openly."

If Ferguson had been planning an answer, it was silenced as Kathryn extended her hand, inclining her head in pleasant greeting. Lord Cornwallis reached for her hand, drawing it to his lips in a light kiss as she dropped into a deep curtsy.

"It is good to see you, milord. This is certainly an auspicious occasion. Our recent victory is a credit to your exceptional military skills, and I am proud to be part of all this." Her eyes held his, her sincerity easily read in her candid expression.

"You honor me with your kind words, Kathryn." He squeezed her hand, placing it between both of his and smiling.

"Your wife grows lovelier each time I see her, Colonel."

Jason nodded 'thanks' as Kathryn blushed, never comfortable with compliments. Suddenly his lordship reached out, and grasping Jason's hand shook it firmly, taking him by surprise. "I saw the way you handled your men in battle—an excellent job. Well done Colonel."

Kathryn bit her lip trying to maintain composure. This was the first time Cornwallis had given credit to Jason's abilities so openly, and it filled her with pride. She moved back a step to allow Jason to bask in the praise, but he pulled her to his side into an encircling arm.

"And your wife, Colonel, is truly the most incredible woman I have had the pleasure to know."

Kathryn smiled appreciatively, but was relieved he had the sensitivity to say no more—aware of mixed feelings amongst some of the guests. Her loyalties were indisputable, but riding beside her husband in battle raised quite a few eyebrows from those who did not know her well.

Finally, with a sigh of relief, they reached the end of the receiving line and moved into the main ballroom. Jason immediately picked up drinks and after a quick sip, both smiled and began their required 'stroll' about the room exchanging dubious pleasantries demanded by proper etiquette.

As they headed for the dance floor, Lieutenant Colonel Banastre Tarleton abruptly stepped into their path "Good evening, Colonel, Mrs. Tarrington. Fine work on the field the other day."

His smile smacked of insincerity, irking her, but she held her tongue.

"You look very lovely tonight, Mrs. Tarrington. Your gown enhances your eyes and …"

Kathryn felt Jason stiffen at her side, his fists balling.

"Thank you for noticing, Colonel Tarleton," she said curtly.

Immediately turning to Jason, she pulled him towards the dance floor. "Come, love, the orchestra sounds wonderful."

"Someday he will push me too far," Jason ground out through tightly clenched teeth.

They glided as one, fluid grace in motion. This was a part of polite society that Kathryn truly enjoyed: the music and being in her husband's arms. After one or two officers were politely turned down in requesting a dance, there were no further attempts—clearly the couple had eyes only for each other.

Cornwallis had been kept so busy with accolades and greetings from guests that he had not approached, but Kathryn knew he would be at her side before the evening ended.

"I must make a trip upstairs, love," she whispered, smiling at Jason with no hint of trepidation. "I will be fine," she assured.

He walked her to the bottom of the stairwell, and insisting that he wait, stood watching her lithe form glide up the stairs amidst the soft rustling of petticoats. As she disappeared from view, Banastre stepped from a small partially concealed alcove where he had been observing them: obviously a regular practice of his. Jason's hackles began to rise at his audacity.

"Jason, my good man ..."

Tarleton's broad grin was infuriating; he strode casually forward, drink in hand, stopping in front of Jason.

"And you must be good, because she only has eyes for you. God knows I have watched for any weakness, and tried more than once to ..."

He never finished his sentence, never saw the punch coming. Jason's fist collided with his jaw, staggering him backwards against the handrail.

Recovering his balance, he rubbed his chin ruefully and shrugged. "I guess I had that coming. I do hope you realize what a lucky man you are, Colonel."

Jason's eyes narrowed, nostrils flaring on a sharp inhalation; Tarleton quickly backed away.

"I fear I must be going, the evening is yet young and many tender treats await me." Striding away, he turned briefly with a glib wave. "See you at Camden, Colonel ... Oh, good evening, Kathryn." He smiled, glancing to the top of the stairs where she was beginning her descent, but at Jason's icy stare, quickly continued walking.

Kathryn hastily glided to her husband's side.

"That man is insufferable," Jason spat.

"He is that, but we must ignore his boorishness. It is far better to have him protecting our backs, my love. Now, are you going to ask me about my trip to the garderobe?" she asked, diverting his attention to a less dangerous subject. "Two 'ladies' actually spoke to me, rather politely, I might add."

Murmuring apologies for having lost his temper, he touched her cheek, pleased there had been no repetition of his lordship's previous party.

Suddenly she took his hand, turning it to examine the split skin and raw knuckles. "That looks to be rather painful, my love." Her eyes searched his face, concerned.

"It is nothing." He shook his head dismissively.

Abruptly she grinned. "Do you feel better?"

"Absolutely, madam." His eyes twinkled with merriment. "Let us dance."

Cornwallis intercepted them as they stepped onto the dance floor. "I am sure, Colonel, you will allow me just one dance with your wife." His look brooked no refusal and Jason backed away forcing a smile, trying valiantly to cover his annoyance.

As they moved about the dance floor Cornwallis grinned at her. "He hates to let you go for even an instant, Kathryn."

"I am the same with him, milord."

For a moment he remained silent. "It gave my wife great pleasure to hear of you, to read your letters, Kathryn. She felt you to be a kindred spirit in many ways, and empathized with the choices you have had to make."

Sensing his statement was founded on underlying guilt at having spent little time with his dying wife, she hoped to ease his conscience. "I have never regretted any of my choices, milord, nor did your wife, of that I am sure. Love makes hardships easier to bear in many ways."

"Thank you, Kathryn," he said softly.

Gratitude for more than the dance misted his eyes as he returned her to Jason's side.

"Colonel, allow me to ask one last favor."

Jason's demeanor was guarded as he eyed the general.

"Bring your beautiful daughter to see me before we move on to Camden."

"Gladly, milord," he said and reached for his wife's hand as the lilting strains of a waltz began.

As they moved onto the dance floor, Cornwallis leaned to speak quietly into Kathryn's ear. "Tend your husband's hand, milady. The cause was more than justifiable, but it looks to be sore."

"That man does not miss a thing," she chuckled as she flowed into her husband's arms.

Encircling her waist firmly, Jason pulled her snugly against him. With a sigh, her arms drifted up about his neck. Lost in the music, lost in each other they glided blissfully, eyes closed shutting out the rest of the world, barely managing to return to their present surroundings as the last note sounded.

Ferguson stood beside Cornwallis watching the colonel and his wife as they circled the dance floor—oblivious to all others.

"There is such raw hunger between them, your Lordship, such passion. Mayhap, therein lays the key to their success, both on and off the battlefield."

"We need to go home, my love," Kathryn whispered urgently, her voice ragged, breathless from the intense thrill charging through her body.

"Your wish is my command, Mrs. Tarrington." His breath was warm against her ear as he ushered her quickly off the dance floor and towards the hallway to bid their farewells.

Camden fell next, a decidedly British win due to the teamwork of Banastre's cavalry and Jason's dragoons; but at a heavy loss of men. There were several grave injuries amongst the dragoons that needed Kathryn's expert attention and four of their best had been slain—Kathryn and Jason quietly grieving the loss. Kathryn sought solace within the arms of her husband, the deaths of fellow dragoons bringing back, all too clearly, memories of the battle with Beldon's troops so long ago when they had lost several other men so dear to her … and her nephew, Ian.

Early in the battle, Jason had seen Jamie at close range. Although wounded by one of Banastre's men, he had seen him limping from the field aided by one of his cohorts, still very much alive.

Kathryn's jacket sleeve had saved her from a serious sabre wound, a shallow knick to her wrist the only damage. Both Jackson and the colonel were initially concerned, but she merely brushed the injury off without further thought; so many others needed her attention.

Later that night as she lay quietly in her husband's arms, the trip-hammer beat of her heart slowing to its normal pace once again, happily sated and feeling renewed, she clung to him as he gently whispered words of love and praise—urging her to be cautious.

Much to Cornwallis's delight, South Carolina was now in the hands of the British. The time had come to move northwards. Breaking camp, they proceeded towards North Carolina fanning out in three columns spanning the state. Ferguson struck out towards the Wautauga settlement to entice, if possible—or threaten if necessary—the wily frontiersmen into joining him. Banastre's cavalry and Jason's dragoons formed another column, while Cornwallis took his main forces up the center of the state.

Jason and Kathryn spent many an evening over a hot cup of coffee with Lieutenant Jackson in the aftermath of their victory at Camden, pondering how the removal of Gates as commander of the American troops would impact on future encounters. It was rumored General Washington had replaced the inefficient leader with Nathanael Greene, a man whose reputation preceded him: a man to be taken seriously.

Kathryn spoke to Ferguson before he left, reminding him again about the feisty Irish-Scots immigrants. He had bid farewell with a smile and glib words of assurance—but he had not listened.

Angering the brash Irish-Scots with violent threats he was unable to fulfill, Ferguson and his troops were chased for miles, the 'over the mountain boys' snapping at their heels all the way. Finally, with nowhere else to turn, he halted his men and dug himself in at King's Mountain. As Ferguson's desperate requests to 'The 96' for immediate assistance remained unanswered, Jason's dragoons and Tarleton's cavalry raced back to give aid.

The fury of the Irish-Scots was incredible, their 'run and hide' style of fighting not at all what Ferguson's British soldiers were used to, or expected. Being in their element, surrounded by woodlands which allowed them to attack in their favorite manner, the rebels took their toll on the British. Although the victory technically belonged to Cornwallis's troops, the battle was bloody and brutal—Ferguson being brought down in a hail of bullets.

Tarleton, infuriated by the loss of his friend, gave no quarter when the battle finally came to an end, lashing out with brutality that would eventually brand him 'butcher'.

Kathryn was winded but unscathed as final gunshots faded and the area became quiet, except for the groans of injured men and screams of dying horses. Although she had lost track of both Lieutenant Jackson and Jason early in the encounter, she had not been concerned ... until now. They were taking too long to regroup. Many dragoons had drifted to her side to assure themselves she was uninjured, and to look for their colonel.

Lieutenant Jackson suddenly came into view, approaching at full gallop, closing the distance between them rapidly. She stood dumbfounded, watching his frantic approach. Flailing his reins viciously side-to-side across his charger's rump, he urged more speed from the faithful beast—an act so out of character, her heart skipped a beat—growing panic and fear gripping her.

Sawing at the reins, he brought his lathered horse abreast of her, foaming and blowing, trembling from the exertion of a vicious ride.

"Where is the colonel?" she demanded, panic-filled eyes meeting his.

"He is alive, Kathryn; but his injury is severe."

All color instantly drained from her face.

"They have him in a medical tent not far from here, awaiting a surgeon to remove his leg." Before he could add, "... come quickly," she had kneed Beauty and sped off.

The rapidly gathering dragoons quickly followed: Kathryn might need their help.

She strode into the medical tent just ahead of Lieutenant Jackson. In the farthest corner, so as to afford a modicum of privacy, she saw Jason. His face mirrored the agony of his wound as he struggled weakly against the burly pair of men trying to restrain him.

"Do not take my leg off," he demanded weakly in a voice husky with pain and anger.

The doctor stood impassively with scalpel in hand, and a vicious looking array of other medical instruments resting on the small wooden platform beside him.

"Lord Cornwallis instructed me to do whatever was necessary to save you," the doctor said matter-of-factly. Having seen too much gore during years of practice, he had become inured to the pain of others—unable to summon the least bit of compassion.

"The leg must come off, Colonel," he stated unemotionally.

"Put that scalpel down and back away from the colonel," she growled.

Thumbing the hammer back, she aimed her pistol directly at the doctor's chest, in full command of the situation. Jackson knew there would be hell to pay, but his pistol was drawn and cocked, ready to back her move.

"Out," she yelled, swinging her pistol towards the two burly attendants.

Startled, they turned to the doctor for instruction.

"I said get out." She strode towards them menacingly. "If you think to stop me as I have but one bullet—think again." Whipping the tomahawk from the small of her back, she swung in a sweeping arc driving it forcefully into the table holding the 'butcher's' instruments—causing implements to clatter and startling the men. Mouth set in a grim line, she rocked the tomahawk free, and fixing them with a fearless, steely gaze, stood watching as they quickly moved around the colonel, avoiding the doctor's angry glare, and hastily headed for the tent flap.

"You cannot do that, madam," the doctor stated indignantly.

"I just did," she spat, eyeing him caustically as she moved to Jason's side and took his hand.

Jason struggled to remain conscious, calmer once aware she was there.

"Do not let them take my leg, Kathryn."

He was weak, so very weak it panicked her.

"They will not take your leg, my love." Squeezing his hand, she brushed a kiss to his moist forehead, all the while eyeing the doctor—her gun trained on his chest.

Jackson stood quietly, his presence commanding, backing her to the hilt.

"He will die, madam," the doctor retorted. "If not from the wound, from lead poisoning; the ball is lodged against the main artery in his thigh." His smugness and lack of empathy infuriated her.

"Then at least he will die a whole man." Glaring unblinking she added, "Your arrogance has robbed you of judgment and compassion, sir. Now get out of my sight."

"As you wish, madam," he stated haughtily, and pulling himself up to his full height, backed away shrugging. "Be assured I will report your actions to his lordship."

Her eyes flicked over him disdainfully, then immediately turned to Jack.

"Get my saddlebags and four of our biggest men, please. Make one of them Hodges."

"Right away, Kathryn, you did just fine." His eyes flashed admiration as he left to do her bidding.

Turning back to Jason, tears started at the sight of him. His face was deathly pale, eyes tightly closed, his broad chest rising and falling in a shallow rhythm.

"Jason," she whispered urgently. Taking his hand in both of hers, she spoke his name repeatedly.

He roused slowly, turning pain-darkened eyes to search her face as she gently stroked his forehead. But as she started speaking, she was interrupted.

"Excuse me, 'Lady Kathryn'."

Captain Hodges, always soft-spoken, stood with three of Jason's officers grouped in a semi-circle. Jack had wasted no time—nor had they.

"How may we be of help?" Hodges voiced deep concern.

"I need you to stand guard while I take a bullet out of the colonel's leg," she said firmly, attempting to sound self-assured. "No one—absolutely no one," she stated emphatically, "is to come near him."

Scanning each man's face, her look conveyed her expectations, and they nodded in unison. Immediately placing themselves shoulder to shoulder, hands resting on loosed holsters, they faced out towards the main entrance—anyone approaching would be seen. Jackson had been precise in his instructions; they quickly complied without need of further explanation.

The doctor stormed from the tent, indignantly marching the full length of the medical field tents, stopping abruptly as he saw Cornwallis coming towards him.

"Who does that woman think she is?" he hissed.

Cornwallis grinned slightly. "I see you have met Mrs. Tarrington."

"His wife?" The doctor was incredulous. "Why, she is rude and unschooled and ignorant," he spat, deeply affronted.

"A bit rash, perhaps, but neither unschooled nor ignorant, doctor."

"The colonel's leg must come off if he is to live. She informed me my ability and compassion were blinded by arrogance. How dare she?"

"She dares because she loves that man with a fierce passion, protectively ... almost like a lioness defending a cub," he mused, speaking the latter more to himself. "She is correct about arrogance, doctor. She and I," he paused reflectively "have spoken of that vice before."

Vanity pricked, the doctor countered somewhat curtly. "Well, she certainly cannot help him; he will be dead by nightfall."

"Do not count on that, doctor. If anyone can save him, I think perhaps she can. It is an unusual, mutual devotion they share; they are an amazing couple."

Spotting Lieutenant Jackson heading for the medical tent, he excused himself and hastily strode to intercept him.

"How is Colonel Tarrington, Lieutenant? How badly is he injured?"

"Serious, milord, but Mrs. Tarrington will save his leg," he said hastily, anxious to get back inside, but hesitant to offend his lordship.

"She has enough to provoke and worry her, and time is of the essence. Please inform her," he weighed his words carefully, "I have complete confidence in her abilities."

As Jackson inclined his head politely, he noticed Banastre Tarleton approaching at a rapid pace.

"My God, he looks terrible. I wonder what bad news he has to impart." Shaking his head, Cornwallis moved out to meet him.

Kathryn had explained to Jason what she intended to do, attempting to instill confidence. Having stripped off her jacket, she was scrubbing her hands and assorted implements with alcohol as he hazily watched, trying to remain focused. As Jackson set her saddlebags down, she nodded 'thanks'.

"Black cherry?" he asked, pulling a small vial from her assortment of herbs.

She nodded slowly, clearly weighing what she was about to do. Gently sliding her arm under Jason's neck, she cradled him against her shoulder and pressed the vial to his lips. "Only a little to take the edge off, love," she assured.

His eyes sought hers: seeking … drifting … beginning to lose focus. "Jason," she said urgently, preparing to take on the challenge of her life. "I cannot allow …" she trailed off, searching for the correct words. Beginning again she said more assertively, "I need you to be conscious. It will be bad, but we can do it." She rushed on while he remained alert. His pain would be overwhelming—he needed to understand

"The bullet is lodged against your artery. If you move … you cannot move. With that willpower of yours, you must keep your leg still."

He nodded ever so slightly.

"Jackson will help." Her eyes searched his, seeking comprehension.

"Do what you must," he rasped.

As she started to cut his pant leg away, she turned at the touch of his hand on her sleeve.

"Whatever happens … know I love you always." His hand dropped away weakly.

She bent and kissed his forehead fervently, then forcefully willed herself to get on with it. Baring his leg, she examined the angry entrance wound. Using some of the tools left by the doctor, she cleaned and disinfected the area thoroughly. Scanning the table where Jackson had laid out her herbs, she pointed to a mallet and asked him to have one of the dragoons collect bark from a pine or hemlock tree.

"I need some of the inner bark and …"

"I will show them how to prepare it properly. You concentrate on what you need to do here." He smiled kindly. "I almost forgot …" he briefly relayed Lord Cornwallis's message.

Inhaling a deep breath, she mouthed a small prayer for courage and gently coaxed a thick leather strap between Jason's lips. "You will need this, love."

Jackson came to her side and began scrubbing his hands thoroughly as she rinsed hers again, needing to be sure they were clean.

Jason's leg had been immobilized with a board, the tight bands biting into his flesh. Loosening the bands, she eased an additional leather strap under his thigh close to the wound, and handed both ends to Jack.

"My thoughts are these, Jack." Her gaze followed him as he moved to the opposite side of the table, turning to face her over Jason's prone form.

"I shall have to make a deep incision so I can get at the lead ball."

His eyes held hers as he nodded complete understanding.

"When I begin to remove the shot, tighten the tourniquet, the artery should stop pulsing, allowing me enough leeway to safely …" She could not voice the disastrous possibilities if she should nick that artery.

"Let us do it." Jack took a deep breath

Picking up a scalpel, she paused considering. If she attempted to be gentle, she would put her husband at greater risk. She must be decisive: determine the cut, commit to it, and slice with conviction.

Jackson sensed her anxiety, knew what she faced. "Kathryn," he said softly. "You can do it." Amber eyes met hers with assurance.

Muttering another small prayer for guidance, she took a deep breath.

"Hold tight, Jason."

Jackson held his leg firmly as she quickly gauged her cut and sliced deeply. Jason released a deep groan but remained still. She could not look at his face, could not bear to think of his pain—she must focus. Her opening was perfect, wide and deep enough, she was certain.

"Now," she nodded and Jack immediately tightened the tourniquet.

Jason moaned, perspiration beading his forehead heavily, but his iron will did not fail. His leg remained motionless as she slid her little finger deep into the wound, gently probing, smiling grimly at finding what she sought.

As the pulsing artery slowed, the tiniest amount of space allowed her finger easy access. Perhaps it was imagination, or that she willed it so, but she could retrieve that musket ball. Quickly, and with great dexterity, she slid the narrow point of the small scalpel under the lead, pushing it up and out of the wound. Jason's leg trembled from the exertion of remaining still, but the worst was over.

"Good work," Jack praised, reaching to wipe her perspiring brow.

"Slowly release that," she said, indicating the tourniquet and scrutinizing the wound as he did so. Although bleeding heavily, no gushing spurt indicated a nicked artery. Greatly relieved, she allowed it to bleed a few moments to flush out as much contamination as possible.

Reaching for her saddlebag, she removed a small bladder and quill. Jason lay with eyes closed, face contorted in agony, rapidly losing his battle to remain conscious. He had helped through the critical part of the surgery; now pain and loss of blood were exacting their toll. Fervently hoping he would quickly give in to peaceful oblivion on this next assault, she filled the bladder with alcohol and poised it over his thigh.

"The bullet is out, love, but I have to sterilize the wound. Brace yourself."

She doubted he realized what she was about to do, perhaps that was for the best. With a sure and gentle hand, she spread the wound and squeezed alcohol through the quill.

Jason's hand clutched spasmodically at the table edge, as he bit deeply into the leather strap, shuddering as he collapsed.

"Thank God," she breathed, scanning his face, pallid but relaxed in unconsciousness.

Swiping her sleeve across her perspiring forehead, she finished flushing the wound.

Jackson reached for her next herb. "Alum root?" he asked.

"You are getting good at this, Jack," she said, and actually smiled. "Now the poultice."

Before she could ask, Jack rose and disappeared around the guards, who stood steadfastly maintaining their positions, keeping vigil over their colonel.

Within minutes, he returned with a pulpy mass that met with her critical approval.

"I need your input, Jack. If I spread this pulp on a piece of woven hemp, it will do its work while the material shrinks and closes the wound."

She eyed him, unsure. "Or do I dare stitch the wound closed, and hope I have gotten it clean?" She shook her head, becoming distressed. "If I do not stitch it, the scar will be large. I am so …" She turned exhausted eyes to him, pleading for him to help her make the right decision.

"I would not worry about a scar." He weighed his thoughts. "If the wound remains open it will have a better chance to drain if infection does set in."

Flashing a look of gratitude, she rummaged in her bag, and finding a section of hemp, spread it out on the small side table. She smoothed the gummy bark paste evenly on the material then carefully placed it over Jason's thigh. Loosening the restraining board under his leg, she secured the poultice with clean strips of linen.

"For the time being, perhaps I should not remove the splint. I want him to stay as still as possible. That artery may still be at risk ..." she trailed off, her thoughts jumbling in her tired mind.

Jack touched her shoulder, gently drawing her attention. The pallor and exhaustion etching her beautiful features concerned him. There was no use asking when she had eaten last; she would refuse food as being unimportant. But he could see she was fading physically and emotionally.

"I have an infusion of willow bark that should be ready. Relax, I will be right back."

Moving closer to her husband, she took his hand, caressing gently, watching him intently. Jackson touched her shoulder, but received only a distracted nod.

"Keep an eye on both of them," he advised Hodges as he moved past the guards.

Kathryn began moistening a cloth to wash Jason's face, but looking down, realized she was covered in blood. That would not do. *I must clean myself up.* She tried to focus, but her mind no longer cooperated. *No, that is not important.* Swiping her hands on her shirt, she began bathing his face, paying close attention for any sign of movement.

"Jason, oh Jason, I pray I have done the right thing." Cradling him to her, she placed a blanket under his head. Unbraiding his queue, she lovingly spread his long black hair smoothly over his shoulders, needing to touch him, to breathe in his essence.

As she placed another blanket over him for warmth, her hands started to shake. Suddenly chilled, she trembled, emotional agony finally taking its toll. Her knees buckled, and with an exhausted sob, she slid to the floor. Burying her face in her hands, she began to rock back and forth on her knees, sobbing uncontrollably.

Jason's officers eyed one another uneasily. Indicating for them to maintain their vigil, Captain Hodges stepped back.

"Lady Kathryn." Crouching beside her, he touched her shoulder. "How may I be of help?"

Keeping her face buried in her hands, she shook her head, unable to speak. He had never seen her so beside herself and was relieved to see the lieutenant returning.

"I think she has had about all she can take for one day, Lieutenant." Hodges stepped aside, making room for Jackson to set down the food and coffee he was carrying.

"Thank you, Captain. As soon as I get Kathryn squared away, I will see that you men get some relief. It has been a long day."

"No rush, sir." Hodges smiled and returned to his post.

Jackson held the coffee mug close to her face hoping the aroma would help rouse her. Bending to her ear, he whispered, "Kathryn, listen to me." He wanted to take her in his arms and hold her, caress her hair, comfort her. But he could do none of these. "You need to eat."

Not looking up, she shook her head, but the racking sobs quieted.

"You need to be strong for your husband," he said slowly and distinctly, allowing her to absorb the import of what he was saying. "He needs you more than ever right now. You must be strong for him, help him heal and rebuild that leg."

Slowly she raised a tear stained face, large droplets glistening in her blonde lashes, eyes drained of their usual sparkle. Fighting to regain control, she swiped her hand across one cheek and then the other, brushing aside tears.

Again Jack held the coffee out, and noticing the tremor of her hands, placed the cup to her lips. Closing her eyes, she sipped the hot liquid, savoring the taste and aroma in spite of herself. Picking up the cloth she had used on Jason's face, he wiped hers quickly, trying to remain detached. Breaking a piece of bread, he put it in her hand, glad to see it steadier. With a shuddering breath, she gave in and began to eat; Jack, as always, was right.

"Take it slowly; you will be all right," he crooned, crouching at her side and sharing a hunk of bread, willing her to relax.

Jason swam back to consciousness from his quagmire of pain, struggling to return to reality and regain control. Hearing Jackson's troubling words, despite his suffering, he was concerned for her.

"My wife?" His voice sounded weak, hoarse with the exertion of controlling his agony. "Is she all right?" From where he lay, all he could glimpse was Jackson's back as he bent over her.

With the first sound he uttered, she scrambled up and reached to touch his cheek with trembling fingers.

"Kathryn ..." His eyes were clear and responsive, albeit dark with pain. "You look tired, love."

"I am better now," she assured, holding his hand to her cheek and then bringing it to her lips.

Jackson quietly moved to join the officers, but Kathryn had eyes only for her husband and never noticed. Reaching into her pocket, she withdrew the black cherry sedative.

"What you need is sleep to help you heal." She pressed the vial to his lips, but allowed very little of the potent fluid, well aware of the dangers of overuse. "I am going to get you moved to someplace more comfortable."

His eyes met hers warily.

"Someplace where I will not have to let you out of my sight," she said lovingly, pleased to see unspoken relief as she held his hand, watching for the sedative to work.

"My leg is it ...?" he trailed into a whisper, fearful of her answer.

"I am afraid, sir, that you will have no excuse to miss his lordship's next ball." She smiled into eyes that were rapidly becoming heavy, expecting no answer.

Suddenly aware that Lieutenant Jackson had cleared his throat loudly, she turned to see the reason. Lord Cornwallis stood appraising her.

"What have we here, Mrs. Tarrington?" With a sweep of his hand, he indicated the dragoon officers, who stood by looking uneasy.

Squaring her shoulders, she faced the general.

"They are here at my request, milord, for the colonel's protection and privacy."

Cornwallis eyed her pallor, taking note of the dark smudges under her eyes.

"A well thought out decision, milady." He nodded agreeably.

"With your permission, milord, I will dismiss these good men so they may get some refreshment. It has been a very long day."

He nodded acquiescence as she moved closer to the dragoons, individually thanking each officer in turn. Cornwallis watched with interest, as each officer smiled in deference. The influence she had with these men was astounding. These dragoons, belonging to one of England's most feared military units, and capable of extreme violence, stood there smiling, with looks bordering on tenderness, at their colonel's wife.

"I will await your orders, milady." Lieutenant Jackson was the last to leave, and stepping close, gave her a reassuring smile.

She smiled gratefully and turned to the general, noticing his features bore certain sadness. But it was not her place to question, and her husband's health took precedence.

"How fares your husband, Kathryn?" Without prying eyes and ears, he relaxed protocol.

"He will live, milord, and he will have a leg that will be strong again in no time."

"I have arranged for his transportation to my headquarters so that he may be more comfortable, and enjoy complete privacy as he recovers. That is with your permission, of course." He smiled slightly at her bold, sharp scrutiny, momentarily envisioning a wary lioness, yet again, as she weighed her answer.

"Kathryn," he said familiarly, "you and no other, unless chosen by you, will be in charge of his care." At her continued thoughtful silence, he added in a quiet voice, "We have lost Ferguson; I would have your company for awhile."

Her expression turned to one of shock and sadness, but he held up a silencing hand before she could ask the questions he saw forming in her mind.

"We will speak of him later. For now, let us get your husband to safety."

Within a matter of minutes, Jason's men moved him carefully into the back of a wagon. He was only partially aware as the potent sedative had done its work. Kathryn stepped aside to speak briefly with Lieutenant Jackson and co-ordinate plans; he would follow as soon as her herbs and infusions were repacked.

Understanding her need to be with her husband, Lord Cornwallis had given orders that Kathryn be made comfortable in the wagon beside the colonel. He offered her a hand up just as Jason began to speak. Turning immediately at the sound of her husband's voice, she completely forgot all protocol in excusing herself properly. Under the circumstances, his lordship was not offended and waited patiently while she reassured Jason.

"How is he, Kathryn?" His expression demanded an honest answer, not words spoken for the ears of his men.

"He will live, milord. The leg will mend with time and exercise." Her voice had lost its fierce edge, yet still held confidence.

"Ahh, then I will definitely expect you at my next ball."

At his knowing grin, she looked somewhat embarrassed.

"Yes, milord, we would not think of missing that."

Settling herself beside her husband, they began the bumpy ride. Jason roused occasionally, but reassured by her presence and with a comforting touch of her hand, drifted back into sleep.

After what seemed an interminable amount of time, they arrived at an elegant, old house, Cornwallis's latest seat of operation.

Jason's men moved him gently into a room set aside for their extended stay. Kathryn preceded them, moving to the wide bed and quickly throwing back the comforters, indicating they place the colonel directly on the sparkling sheets. Captain Hodges eyed her with a grin and quick wink at her boldness. The impish expression she flashed in answer was a relief; she was calm and in control again. He stayed long enough to help remove the splint from his commander's leg, excusing himself at Lieutenant Jackson's arrival.

Jackson, thorough as always, had retrieved Jason's sabre, pistol and both their saddlebags. She smiled gratefully and accepted his offer to help ease Jason's boots off. Eyeing the sparkling sheets he, too, grinned at her audacity.

"And what would you have me do, Lieutenant?" she demanded with mock severity. "Place your commanding officer on the floor?"

Joining her in laughter, he hugged her to him, holding her for a moment, stating with utmost sincerity, "You were incredible today. I am truly humbled by your bravery and your abilities."

At her look of denial, he touched her cheek. "I have been placed down the hall, if you need me."

Her brow arched, pleased but confused, it was unusual for a lower officer to be housed within headquarters.

He shrugged. "I gather his lordship wanted me nearby if you need my assistance. He mentioned he would be up shortly with refreshments and lots of fluids for the colonel. Perhaps even a hot tub of water for you." Jackson indicated her shirt.

She had not given it any thought up until now; looking down at her attire, she shrugged. "I guess I am a mess."

With a sharp rap on the door, and minimal announcement, Lord Cornwallis entered their room followed by several house servants. Smiling politely, Jack abruptly stepped out of the way.

"Mrs. Tarrington, I have hot broth for both of you, plenty of fresh water, a light repast, a bit of brandy which I feel you are in definite need of—and a tub of hot water."

"Thank you, milord." Her voice sounded gravelly with fatigue.

"Anything you require, merely ring the bell." He indicated a decorative bell-pull near the door.

Stepping to the bed, he looked down at the colonel, taking note of the crisp sheets beneath his dirty uniform. Eyeing her with a hint of glee, he added, "Food, then rest for you, Kathryn. That is an order." Patting her shoulder, he bid her 'goodnight'.

As he turned at the door, his face once again displayed his earlier sadness. "We will talk of all else tomorrow."

She was beginning to fade rapidly, yet there was much to do before she could lie down and rest. While Jason slept, she took a quick bath, donning a clean shirt and brushing her hair. At least she would now look more presentable for her husband. Sitting at his side, she ate some bread, discovering she really was hungry. The rich broth tasted delicious, its warming effects rejuvenating.

Feeling more herself, she proceeded to give Jason a sponge bath, discarding his soiled clothes in a heap. His skin felt cool to the touch, reassuring that no infection had begun to set in yet. They were not completely out of the woods but this, at least, took on a more positive note. As she pulled a clean shirt down over his torso, her ministrations roused him from his stupor.

"Try this, love," she urged, raising his head to place the cup of broth to his dry lips. "You have lost a lot of blood, Jason. Please, I must insist." She nudged him patiently.

He made the effort for her, but truly thirsted for water—which she quickly provided, helping him as he drank heavily. After tending his needs and making him as comfortable as she could under the circumstances, she poured some of the willow bark tea. He eyed it suspiciously and she smiled.

"This will only help dull the pain, not sedate you." He hated not having complete control of any given situation at all times, but with her assurance, drank fully before settling back onto the pillows, his eyes quickly closing from the exertion.

Tucking the comforter carefully around him and placing a light kiss to his forehead, she settled into the chair beside him, reaching to hold his hand. Within moments, he rolled his head to face her.

"Come to bed, Kathryn … please," he said softly. His eyes were clear, the pain having abated somewhat. At the beginning of a protest, he said firmly. "Join me, my love; I need you by my side."

She rose but hesitated.

"Do not worry, you will not hurt me."

Carefully she eased under the covers beside his uninjured leg. Pulling her close to snuggle against his shoulder, he kissed her forehead. Exhausted with the effort, he became silent for a few minutes.

"You are an incredible woman, my wife. I love you," he whispered softly, fading rapidly, on the verge of sleep.

"You are my life, my husband," she whispered, cuddling closer, nearly asleep from exhaustion herself.

His gentle hug was the last thing she remembered as she drifted off, thanking the powers that be for guiding her hand that day. They slept deeply, rousing only to answer Jason's need for more soothing willow tea.

Kathryn awoke early the next morning, and feeling substantially restored, began making herself presentable, sure that Jackson would arrive shortly with his customary hot coffee. Unbeknownst to her, Jason had roused—in pain but clearheaded. While staring into the dressing table mirror, working at taming her wild curls, she suddenly caught sight of him just as he swung his injured leg over the edge of the bed, preparing to stand.

"No, Jason," she cried, alarmed by what he was attempting.

Stopping mid-action, agonizing pain shot through his thigh, twisting his face into a mask of agony. Instantly at his side, she blurted, "I did not stitch the wound and it is deep. You cannot …" she explained her reasoning somewhat remorsefully. "It will probably leave a scar." Unhappy eyes met his, confusing him somewhat.

"I agree with your choice, love, and will be more careful for a few days."

Her deeply concerned look brought instant understanding, and a hearty chuckle.

"As you will be the only person to ever see it, madam, I do not foresee any problem, hmm?" He arched an eyebrow and winked, a good night's rest having done him a world of good.

Lieutenant Jackson arrived shortly with the hot coffee she had hoped for, and a fresh batch of willow tea. Jason dutifully drank the potion, although he detested the taste. The three of them sat drinking coffee and eating fresh bread Jackson had filched from the kitchen to tide them over until mid-morning breakfast. He was impressed with their recuperative powers, especially Jason's, and pleased to see Kathryn looking more at ease and rested. He considered conveying detailed news about Ferguson, but decided to give them more time to focus on healing. News like that could wait. Jason would have to know soon enough.

"Well," she eyed the two men, "let us see how it looks."

After scrubbing her hands with the brandy she had failed to drink the night before, she gently placed moist compresses on Jason's thigh, to soften the hemp poultice. Thankfully, his leg was cool and continued to show no signs of infection. As the willow tea was quickly taking affect, he was not unduly uncomfortable. Testing the edges of the hemp cautiously, she slowly peeled the poultice aside as both men watched, fascinated at how well the wide gash had pulled together.

"I am impressed, Kathryn." Jack pursed his lips thoughtfully.

With a sudden rap on the door, it opened—his lordship striding in, not waiting on invitation.

"And how fares the colonel today?" He forced himself to appear happy and robust. "I have a visitor who would like to inquire how the injury is progressing."

With that announcement he stepped aside, ushering the doctor into the room before she could form a protest. Jason felt her tense and reached quickly for her hand. The doctor, Kathryn observed happily, appeared distinctly uncomfortable having been most assuredly goaded into the visit by his lordship.

"Good morning," he said somewhat stiffly as he walked across the room to the bed.

As he eyed the wound, no one spoke until he instinctively reached to investigate more thoroughly.

"Do not touch his leg," Kathryn warned icily, moving to intercept him.

"What did you use?" he asked in amazement.

"Why?" she demanded.

Jason and Jack stifled amusement at her choler.

"Because it is obviously working, he should have been feverish from infection or dead by now."

She eyed him warily, but with a gentle touch of her husband's hand, relented somewhat.

"Indian remedies, rebel potions, common sense, a bit of luck and the fierce need to keep my husband alive and whole." She paused, then continued acidly, "None of which will be of interest to you with your arrogant perception of medicine."

Cornwallis choked back a chuckle, enjoying the doctor's discomfort as he spluttered wordlessly, shocked by her audacity.

"Madam," he stated haughtily, but quickly caught himself. Rethinking his words, he took a deep breath and began again. "Mrs. Tarrington," he said courteously. "I do not wish to cross swords with you. I came to apologize. Now that I see what you have accomplished, I am genuinely interested."

Softening her stance a bit, she granted him permission to stay. "Then you may watch if you like. Lieutenant Jackson and I were about to redress the colonel's wound."

She proceeded to smear a new piece of hemp with freshly mashed fir tree bark, but paused, eyeing Jack with consideration.

"If I soak the hemp in willow infusion first, might that help even more in lessening the pain?"

"It certainly cannot hurt," he answered, giving the idea some thought.

The doctor started to interrupt, but silencing him with a sharp look, she continued preparing the poultice, all the while watching Jason, aware he was beginning to tire. He had settled back against the pillows with a slight smile, his blue eyes watching her intently, as she began swabbing his thigh with more of the willow bark solution.

"This may hurt some," she cautioned softly.

But he shook his head, never taking his eyes from her.

Cornwallis watched the interplay between them, their eyes speaking to each other as if they were the only two in the room.

As she placed the poultice, gently forming it over his wound, a twitching muscle along the edge of his jaw was the only indication of his pain. Lieutenant Jackson stepped to her side and raised the colonel's leg carefully so she could secure the gooey mass with clean linen strips; a resultant sharp intake of breath hinting at his discomfort.

Reaching for his hand, she cradled it in both of hers and murmured, "In a few minutes you will be more comfortable, my love."

At his sideways glance she shot him a long look.

"You are my beloved husband, and I care not that my actions, or terms of endearment, may be deemed inappropriate in present company."

"Laudanum, perhaps?" the doctor suggested, hoping to ease momentary tension and have a little input due his professional status.

"No," she declared firmly without giving reason.

Turning to the lieutenant she asked, "Would you please collect some fresh resin from a fir tree?"

She pursed her lips deliberating mentally, testing a better solution. "I believe it will have longer lasting effects than the willow."

"Yes, thicker and slower to evaporate; I believe you are right." Jackson smiled at her logical suggestion as he began to clean up the medical supplies. "I will get some resin and return shortly. Is there anything else you will need?"

"Please send word to Anna and our little girl." Her eyes were far away, filled with concern.

"I did that last night, milady, as you were rather busy," he replied, conveying a look of deep caring, pleased to see warmth and heartfelt gratitude answering in hers.

Excusing himself, he departed, taking much of the clutter with him.

Glancing at her husband, seeing him struggle to remain awake, she turned to Cornwallis. "Milord, may I request some time alone for my husband to sleep?"

"Of course, Kathryn, I will have food sent up later. Whatever you need," he trailed off, "you have but to ask."

His sincere kindness pleased her and she softened.

"And, doctor," she turned to offer her hand in truce. "I will sit down with you and answer all your questions. Just not today, please."

"I look forward to that, Mrs. Tarrington." He squeezed her hand. "There is a great deal I wish to discuss with you."

After they had gone, she returned to Jason's side and gently examined the poultice. His eyes were closed, his breathing even as she ran her fingers over his thigh, pleased at the continued coolness.

"If you touch me like that once more, madam, there will be no chance of getting any sleep." He pulled her close to meet his kiss. "Soon, very soon, my love," he promised.

She shook her head grinning widely; he would be fine.

"Come lie with me, Kathryn, you need rest too."

Tugging off her boots, she crept carefully under the covers, happily content as he snugged her against his chest, encircling her protectively in his arms.

"I am very proud of you, love, the way you handled the doctor—absolutely perfect."

With a soft sigh, he drifted into sleep.

She awoke a short while later, and finding Jason still sleeping peacefully, was careful not to disturb him as she arose. Leaving Jack to watch over him, and call her on a moment's notice, she sought out his lordship to talk of Major Ferguson.

She had to bite her tongue to keep from blurting her utter frustration to Cornwallis. Ferguson had disregarded her warnings, sure of himself in his conceit. She was angry and saddened: angry at the loss of a good man, deeply saddened by the loss of a friend. Cornwallis offered to accompany her to the lower level where Ferguson's body awaited burial orders. But to say her 'goodbye', she wanted to be alone.

Kneeling beside his body, she scanned Ferguson's still form covered by clean sheeting, his face peaceful and unscathed in death. Easing his cold hand from under the edge of the covering, she held it gently, wishing she could will warmth and life back into him.

"You were a worthy opponent and I shall miss you, my friend," she said quietly as she leaned forward, placing a kiss to his brow.

"Paying last respects to the enemy, Mrs. Tarrington?"

Banastre Tarleton startled her reverie with his caustic appraisal. He stood directly behind her, although she had not heard him approach.

"Have you ever shown one moment of compassion in your life?" she spat, eyeing him angrily.

"Compassion is an emotion denoting weakness." He eyed her haughtily. "A useless sentiment that hinders getting the job done."

She ignored him, turning back to Ferguson and rising slowly.

"Kathryn," speaking with a soft familiarity which caused her to bristle at his audacity, he stopped her angry retort with an abrupt gesture. "If it is of any comfort, Patrick told me not long ago, that he has trusted your complete loyalty for some time. He merely liked your style when it came to sparring. I gather he felt you had an intelligent mind."

His smile, for once seemed genuine, catching her by surprise.

At his kind words, her eyes softened.

"Thank you, Banastre," she murmured, noting his smile actually reached his eyes.

"And how fares your husband?" he asked almost gently.

"He will be fine; he will be."

Detecting unmistakable exhaustion in her tone, he experienced a pang of momentary compassion, an odd and distasteful emotion upon which he refused to dwell.

"You despise my ethics, Mrs. Tarrington," he said lightly, in a tone conveying the glib façade of minutes before.

She eyed him silently, irked by his callousness.

"Because my actions reflect on your husband," he continued, goading her slightly.

Not wanting an angry confrontation, she pushed past him attempting to leave.

"You are like a lioness protecting a cub where he is concerned." His tone was liquid honey, insulting.

"What do you want from me, Tarleton?" She spun on him, eyes narrowed.

"Did you see what they did to Patrick?" he demanded. "Take a look—a good look."

Gripping her shoulder firmly, he forced her to Ferguson's side. Without a word of warning, Tarleton yanked the sheet back, exposing the major's bullet-riddled body … his pent-up anger so intense, it startled her.

Her hand flew to her mouth, stifling a sob. Had it not been for Banastre's strong arm she would have staggered, as her knees suddenly buckled. A single tear rolled down her cheek as she looked up at him, her eyes forlorn.

"He was my only true friend," he uttered brokenly. "What would you have done differently?" At her silence, he rushed on angrily. "Yes, I slew as many rebels as I could, in a frenzy, like a wild man. I gave no quarter, damned right." He turned away abruptly, but not before she saw his face crumble.

He stood there in silence, shoulders slumped, a slight tremor rippling across the muscles of his upper back "He was my friend." His voice broke. "He forgave my—idiosyncrasies."

For the briefest moment he visibly sagged, then squaring his shoulders, he turned back to her. "Now do you understand?" His voice softened to a desperate plea.

"Yes," her answer was thin, pained.

He hesitated at the gentleness of her tone, fighting for composure.

Having never witnessed this side of him, she was taken aback. His reputation was well documented: boyish good looks belying unwarranted cruelty, flagrant callous sex, unmitigated arrogance and yet … he grieved deeply too.

"I am so sorry, Banastre." Her hushed voice rang with undeniable sincerity.

For a moment, he stood in silence, watching her through narrowed eyes.

"What would *you* have done differently?" he asked quietly, his anger dissolving.

"I would have given quarter, trusting they would do the same if circumstances had been reversed; that had Jason been forced to surrender, he would live and eventually be returned to me … safe and sound."

"Kathryn!" His throat closed convulsively in exasperation. He stood ramrod stiff—speechless, battling to control his emotions.

Without warning, he spun on his heel and rapidly moved away, his boots striking a staccato beat on the highly polished floor as he disappeared down the hallway.

She breathed deeply willing inner calm to return, then with mouthed 'goodbyes' and a final touch to Ferguson's pale cheek, left to seek much needed comfort in her husband's presence.

Jason sat propped against pillows discussing the previous day's battle with Lieutenant Jackson. King's Mountain had been their first major loss, and they spoke with determined resolve of future encounters. This was no more than a temporary setback, partially due to Ferguson's pigheaded stance with the Wautauga immigrants. From her husband's clear-eyed expression and seemingly minor discomfort, Jack had been plying him with willow bark tea. Both men turned as she entered: Jack immediately standing and offering his chair, Jason wincing as he moved to the edge of the bed.

"You stay put, Jason Tarrington, or I will have to bring out that vial of black cherry."

Beneath her light teasing, he read sorrow, her green, lack-luster eyes staring at him from a pale face. Patting the bed beside him, he extended his hand.

"Jack told me about the major, love."

She moved to his side as uncontrolled tears began to flow.

Jack excused himself, and stood to leave.

"Do not go, Jack. Please … just give me a moment."

Jason wrapped his arm about his wife, easing her back against the pillows. "I wish you had wakened me." He kissed the top of her head.

Accepting Jack's offer of a handkerchief, she mopped her face unceremoniously and then, in a hiccupping voice, related her meeting with Tarleton.

"I … have never seen him so … stricken." She paused, searching first Jason's face and then Jack's. "But what they did to Patrick … There was no need for that."

"I am sorry you had to see him that way, Kathryn," Jack said softly.

Tears started afresh as Jason pulled her close, holding her tenderly.

"Rest now, that goes for both of you." Jack's eyes locked meaningfully on hers. "I need to make more willow tea and prepare another poultice, but I will return shortly before the evening meal."

With a quivering lip, she watched as the door shut softly behind him, then buried her face against her husband's chest, drawing much needed strength and consolation.

Much later, a light rapping on the door brought them both instantly awake, Kathryn scanning her surroundings to reestablish reality after a moment's confusion. Jack's head poked around the edge of the door, his face breaking into a wide grin as he saw her sleepy tousled appearance.

"I slept like a log," she exclaimed. Running fingers through her tangled curls, she swung her feet to the floor and stood.

Jason nodded greetings, stretching with a grimace, in need of more willow tea.

"English tea for both of you, some of his lordships very own I might add, a light repast to stave off hunger pangs, and this ..." he said, setting a dish of fir bark pulp on the bedside stand.

"You are a gem, Jack. I never tell you often enough," she said quietly, taking a cup of tea and leaning back beside her husband.

"For you, sir, a special brew first."

With a smile, Jack handed the colonel a cup of willow tea, which he dispatched without complaint, anxious for its pain deadening effects.

"Cornwallis is planning to join you for dinner tonight, about 7 o'clock here in your room, perhaps the doctor also. I thought you might appreciate fair warning." He grinned and shrugged. "No chance of escape that I can see."

The next morning found her reticent, going through necessary motions, but obviously deep in thought.

"Kathryn," Jason interrupted her silence. "What has you so quiet?" With his continued improvement, he knew he was not the focus of her unrest. As she remained silent, busily preparing his poultice, he nudged again. "Kathryn?"

"Who will care for Gabrielle if the time ever comes when we are ..." She left the question hanging, not wishing to voice the thought.

His attention riveted on her; those thoughts had crossed his mind more than once since his close brush with death.

"Anna? She loves our daughter dearly, but the future for the Cherokees promises to be unsettled ... and that concerns me deeply."

She eyed him thoughtfully before suggesting: "Perhaps your grandmother?"

"Not as long as my father lives," he declared.

"What of your brother?" he asked. "Gabriel has given his word he will protect our daughter."

But she shook her head vehemently, surprising him somewhat.

"Jamie would look at her and see you and me—not Gabrielle. I am not sure he could forgive me enough to be fair to our child, although he would try."

She was right about Jamie, but he sensed she had come to an alternative decision.

"You have someone else in mind, Kathryn." It was a statement. "Jack?" he ventured.

"Yes," she said with conviction. "He loves her as his own, and would do anything for us. He has family members in England that I am sure would come to his aid, if it were necessary. She would lack for nothing."

She searched his face for an indication of his feelings.

"I truly doubt it will come to that, but I agree. If he will accept the challenge of raising our daughter, we may rest easy. I can have his lordship draw up the papers for guardianship while we are here."

"Yes," she said firmly. "That way there would never be any question as to our intent."

Moving to sit beside him on the bed, she took both his hands, and squeezing gently, smiled. Acutely aware of their mortality, a fact hammered home by the severity of Jason's injury, their unified decision provided deep relief.

Lieutenant Jackson, arriving a little later with breakfast and medical supplies, took note of their contented smiles; something was afoot.

"Jack," Jason greeted, waving his friend to a nearby chair. He wanted to settle the situation, put it behind them and move ahead with a positive mindset.

"Yes sir?" He was immediately attentive, picking up on the underlying tone of Jason's voice as he set the tray on the bedside table and began serving coffee.

"Kathryn and I would like to ask a favor; give it some thought before making a final decision."

Jack eyed them with a bemused expression.

"In the event of our ..." Jason hesitated, not liking the sound of that statement and began again, rephrasing his request. "If there ever comes a time when we cannot raise our daughter, would you be her legal guardian?" There, he had said it.

Lieutenant Jackson was surprised, flattered and pleased by their request. "I need no time to make that decision; I am honored. I would raise her as my own." He hesitated before adding softly, "However, I do not expect to be called upon to fulfill your request."

"We are both eternally grateful, Jack. This has been on our minds for some time." Kathryn moved close, hugging him with a quiet, heartfelt 'thank you'. "Jason will have the legalities taken care of before we leave."

Placing her hands at a jaunty angle on her hips, she took a deep breath. "Now that that is settled, let us move ahead. We have much to accomplish, and a great deal to look forward to in the future."

Their talk turned to the state of the dragoons and care of the horses, continuing their idle chat while Jason's bandaging was changed. His wound was healing rapidly, the pain lessening with each passing day.

Over the next few days, when not spending time reading with her husband and trying to bolster his spirits, Kathryn visited with the doctor and Cornwallis. Doctor Jacobs, she had finally made the effort to remember his name, was interested in her herbal remedies and theories on healing. She remained polite at all times, but found his personality not particularly to her liking.

After Major Ferguson's quiet burial, his lordship spent more time with both of them, their positive attitude an inspiration during this difficult time. He searched Kathryn out on a regular basis, needing to talk, relishing her candid views. Many times, he found her chatting over coffee with the dragoons, keeping them apprised of their colonel's recovery. On more than one occasion, he sat in the background quietly enthralled as she played the tin whistle to the accompaniment of the dragoons' boisterous singing and cheering.

As Jason's health continued to improve, Cornwallis shared more meals with them. The conversation often turned to the future, their forthright determination a tonic for his occasionally flagging spirit. Kathryn was curious as to Tarleton's whereabouts; but his name never came up in conversation, and that was probably for the best. They would be riding with him soon enough.

With each passing day, Jason became more frustrated—his endless inactivity combined with inability to tend to duty, tested his patience sorely. Kathryn and Jackson began working the muscles in his thigh to rebuild its strength, pushing him to the limits of endurance. Hopefully, it might also divert his attention from the boredom. He could now stand without intolerable pain, and take several tentative steps out to the balcony to enjoy the sun's healing rays.

Inactivity grated on both of them, Kathryn finding further irritation in having to watch every word she said so as not to offend. Socializing and protocol were necessary while accepting his lordship's hospitality, but the toll exacted was becoming intolerable. She pined for their camp life: sleeping in their own tent, enjoying their own bed and playing with their little girl. She missed Jason's touch, feeling empty—incomplete. She wanted to fling herself astride Beauty and race across the fields with Jason and Diablo, to enjoy the wind tangling her hair into wild curls, and savor Jason's strength as he swung her in a circle, laughing happily at the end of their wild ride.

"Soon," she kept telling herself, "soon."

It had been over a week, days of Jason pushing himself to the limit, his leg substantially stronger from constant exercise and Kathryn's exacting ministrations. Yet, he was still a long way from full recovery.

He awoke early one morning, ill-tempered and tense. Kathryn quietly accepted his mood, curbing a sharp retort at his grumbling, and began her morning regimen of exercising his thigh muscles. Gently kneading and massaging, she inadvertently probed a more painful spot

"This is doing no good. It is not working fast enough," he erupted angrily.

"Jason," she said calmly, "It has been scarcely over a week, your injury was severe. Give yourself time to ..."

"You do not understand, Kathryn. How could you possibly?" He cut her off sarcastically.

She slowly arose, and placing her hands on her hips, fixed him with an angry glare.

"I? I do not understand pain and frustration?" she replied acidly.

For seconds she clung to her anger, then suddenly it left her. She would not fight when he was down; she understood all too well and ached for him. Eyes softening, she turned away, shrugging.

"Perhaps you are right, Jason. When I can be of some solace ..."

She took a step but stopped, turning back at the sound of her name called out in anguish. Frustration impelled him to strike out, but not at her, of all people, not at her; he was ashamed.

"Kathryn," he begged, his voice ragged. "Please stay."

He stood up carefully and started towards her.

Immediately returning to his side, she flowed into his arms as he buried his face against her neck. Firm hands caressed the length of her spine, down to its base then back up to tangle in her golden curls. Cupping her face, he kissed her slowly, deeply.

"I need you, my love," he whispered hoarsely. "Do not go."

His hands trailed along her neck and then lower to gently cup her full breasts, kissing each in turn. Deftly removing her blouse, he trailed heated kisses along the arch of her neck, as his thumbs tantalized taut nipples. Her body was alive, electric, trembling as the familiar heat rose within. She would utter no words of caution, following his lead as he set the pace, savoring each delicious touch, aching to feel complete again.

Her hands skimmed slowly up under his shirt, stroking the firm curve of his hardened chest muscles, her fingers lingering playfully before creeping lower, drawing a sharp gasp as she caressed the heat of him.

Edging her down amidst soft comforters, his knowledgeable fingers coaxed and aroused until she thought she would go mad from aching want. Unable to match his iron reserve, she pulled him to her and rolled atop, ever careful of his injury. He filled her eagerly, watching the passion take her: a gentle rocking, gathering in momentum, spiraling them both to shuddering, gasping fulfillment.

The solid pounding of his heart against her cheek was reassuring as she savored the delicious sensation of him beneath her, feeling calm and complete once more.

Stroking the damp hair away from her forehead and smoothing the tangled curls, he whispered, "We have been apart too long, my love, I have needed you desperately."

Sliding down beside him, she propped herself up on one elbow, eyes aglow as her fingers gently traced the planes of his face. Her kiss was tender as her luminous, green eyes searched his. A tear started, but he caught it with a light brush of his thumb.

"We need to go home, my Kathryn, it is as simple as that." His hands cupped her cheeks. "Will you help me? It may not be easy."

She nodded vigorously, stifling a sob. "Whatever you need, you will have, my love." Kissing him happily, she quickly began dressing. "I will be packed and ready within a half hour—less than that."

With a happy grin, she began moving quickly about the room hastily putting their things in order, excitement pounding in her chest.

"No longer than that, madam, we have our daughter to see and a need to become reacquainted with our own bed." A sparkle, missing far too long, had returned to his piercing blue eyes.

"Enter." Jason yelled, at the sudden rap on their door, turning to grin at his wife and wink.

Lieutenant Jackson elbowed the door open bringing breakfast. "I am sorry to be late this morning." He looked briefly confused at the sideways glance they gave each other, a definite sparkle evident in their eyes. But noticing the blushing glow of their faces—his timing had been perfect.

"Do not apologize, Jack." Jason smiled taking two cups of coffee and handing one to his wife.

"I am glad to see you both in such high spirits today," Jack quipped as he leaned casually against an elegant chair observing the two closely. Something was afoot.

"We are going home, Jack," Kathryn exclaimed.

At his questioning look, Jason nodded enthusiastically. "Just as soon as we finish our coffee."

"Well, I am certainly thankful for that. I know the dragoons are restless and anxious to be on the road again. I will ready the men and horses immediately."

Setting his coffee down without finishing, he headed for the door humming a bright tune.

Within twenty minutes, they stood in his lordship's office. Cornwallis was disappointed to have them leave, but not surprised. Reaching into his desk drawer, he removed a large envelope and handed it to Jason.

"These are the papers you requested for Lieutenant Jackson. If the time comes when they are needed, I will enforce all we have discussed. However, I doubt that will be necessary. I hope to see all of us return to England when this is over. The war is moving in a positive direction, I feel it. I miss Major Ferguson, but King's Mountain was no more than an unfortunate setback, a thorn in our side but nothing insurmountable."

Taking Kathryn's hand, he brought it to his lips. "Take your husband home and restore his health. Winter will be upon us soon, but before it is too cold, I would like to see Gabrielle once more; perhaps a quick personal visit before we continue to head north?"

Kathryn hugged him, assuring they would return soon, thanking him for his kindness and promising to bring herbs to help assuage cold weather ailments which so often plagued the troops.

She had plied Jason with willow bark tea to ease the ache in his thigh. As they left their room she pressed a small vial of cherry bark into his hand, and upon meeting with resistance, reminded him: a small amount would merely take the edge off his pain, and in no way impair his abilities.

Tucking it into his jacket pocket, he kissed her exuberantly. "We are finally going home, love."

Grasping her hand, they took a final look around their room and stepped into the main hallway—neither one pausing to look back.

Lieutenant Jackson and Kathryn flanked the colonel, providing substantial support as he walked slowly to Diablo. His dragoons stood at attention, every face alert, each pleased to see their commanding officer doing so well. Kathryn had bandaged the wound with fresh linen just before they left, hoping that if he were careful, it would not reopen. She must try to temper his actions, without appearing to fret over him.

She watched proudly as he mounted Diablo with no assistance, masking any discomfort. He would be in pain tonight, she was positive, but they would be home. That fact alone was a powerful, healing medicine for both of them. Sitting straight and tall, he took command of his men. With a forward motion of his gloved hand, they moved out in proud formation.

Cornwallis stood with Doctor Jacobs watching them depart. The doctor shook his head, smiling. Kathryn had stopped to speak to him before they left, amazing him at how his opinion had changed in such short time.

"An unusual woman," he mused. "By all rights, that man should not be able to sit a horse, let alone mount one unassisted in this short time."

"I think stubbornness has a good deal to do with it, doctor. And it is an interesting question as to which one of them holds the title better."

His smile flashed total respect for the pair as he watched them disappear over the horizon.

Chapter Thirty-Two

Beyond King's Mountain

They left Lord Cornwallis's headquarters riding at a slow and steady pace, with Diablo maintaining an even gait. Being a highly intelligent animal, he appeared to sense his master's injury. Jason's leg, bent tautly in the stirrup for long hours would create enough pain; he did not need the additional stress of a rough ride. Kathryn would reward the magnificent steed with an extra lump of sugar when they returned to camp that night.

She continuously shot sidelong glances at her husband: watching for signs of discomfort, noting his coloring, judging his level of exhaustion.

After having been in the saddle for some time, he turned to her flashing a wry grin.

"Do not worry so, madam. I will give you fair warning if I am about to fall from my saddle."

She bit her lower lip, thoroughly chastised, embarrassed at having been caught in over-vigilant concern. She must not fuss over him like 'an over protective lioness'; Banastre's words echoed in her mind, much to her chagrin.

As she turned away he noticed her hurt expression, and within minutes raised a gloved hand to stay his dragoons, indicating a shady copse where they could take a break.

Lieutenant Jackson moved immediately to Jason's side offering assistance in dismounting, a gesture he accepted gratefully, cramped muscles and knifing pains gripped him. Limping slowly with great effort, he moved to a large tree and leaned back against its rough bark. Breathing heavily from exertion, he steadied himself and cautiously began massaging his thigh to ease the throbbing ache.

Kathryn kept her distance, for once unsure of herself, and not wanting to offend him. He watched her, reading her perfectly, a smile slowly beginning to creep across his face.

"Kathryn." He reached his hand out, bringing her instantly to his side. Quickly encircling her in his arms, he kissed her tenderly. "I do hope your sense of humor will improve, love, when we are home again." Arching an expressive brow, he gently grasped her chin and kissed her again.

She eyed him apologetically, nodding. "I guess I would expect you to treat me with deference if it were my leg," she reasoned, beginning to brighten.

"Would expect?" he chided playfully. "You have 'expected'—no—demanded so, in the past if you will recall."

"I stand corrected, sir" she quipped, her smiling eyes raking his handsome face.

When his leg had eased, he sat beside her on a fallen tree, joining the rest of the dragoons for a light repast. Accepting willow tea, he decided to forego the cherry bark solution for now; it would be far more welcome tonight after a long day in the saddle.

They entered the welcome familiarity of their camp late that evening, surprised by the boisterous greeting from those who had remained at the site. Exhaustion etched both their faces, hers more from worry over her husband. He had endured the rigors of the long ride well, but was beginning to suffer the effects of his stubborn determination.

In a subtle move, Jackson edged closer to his commanding officer on the pretense of checking Diablo's saddle cinch. Kathryn understood his ploy, thankful he was at hand if Jason's leg failed to co-operate after so many hours in one cramped position. But with that obstinate resolve she so loved in him, he dismounted slowly without assistance. Jason stood a little unsteadily beside Diablo testing his leg cautiously, needing to be sure it would not collapse under him.

"Poppa. Momma." A happy shriek grabbed their attention as their little girl came running towards them, her nightshirt flapping and black curls bouncing as Anna followed in rapid pursuit: chastising the overly eager child loudly.

She flung herself into her father's arms as he precariously held his balance. Diablo stood firmly, pressing closer offering support. Tears streamed down the child's face as she hugged her father's neck, kissing him soundly.

"You are all better." she demanded.

"Almost, poppet, thanks to your mother." He glanced towards her, his eyes filled with devotion.

Kathryn moved closer as Gabrielle leaned to hug her.

"Let us get poppa off that leg, little one, he has had a very long ride today.

***

"That son-of-a-bitch has the nine lives of a cat. By all rights, he should be dead. Watkins's shot would have been good, if his damned horse had not swung away so fast." Jamie swore under his breath, rubbing his hip tenderly, his own wound still causing pain.

Watching intently through his looking glass, he noted how the light of the campfire played across the planes of sister's delighted face as she hugged her child—and grimaced.

Gabriel and his father had kept a close watch on the dragoon's progress after they left Cornwallis's headquarter, following at a distance all too close for Gabriel's comfort. He had tried to keep his father on an even keel; but there were times when he wondered how much longer this obsession of his could go on.

"Damn it, that lead ball in his thigh should have killed him," Jamie grumbled loudly.

"You know, father, it is as if you have a personal vendetta with this man, rather than a war to win. I sometimes feel you lose sight of the overall picture, and yet you criticize Kathryn for having done the same where her husband is concerned."

"Whose side are you on, anyway?" he growled. His hip was giving him severe pain tonight, his temper shorter than usual. "If he were gone …"

"If he were gone, father, there are others who would follow in his footsteps, many more dangerous than he: Tarleton for example. Now, there's a man who would not give his own mother quarter."

"Well, at least the Wautauga boys got Ferguson," he retorted.

Gabriel made a low sound in his throat. "Yes, but now the English may retaliate more fiercely." He shook his head. "Only time will tell."

"Well, it is fall now; they will lay low for awhile."

Jamie collapsed the looking glass against his palm and tucked it back into his saddlebag. "Hell, this time of year, what with the raw, damp cold and lack of good food, maybe they will all die of fever or dysentery. They can starve, for all I care."

Gabriel bit his tongue. His father's wound was not healing. Hopefully a few weeks in hiding—away from the battlefield—would give him a better perspective. He knew his father well. Beneath his callous exterior breathed a man who still grieved over the loss of his sister, a man who desperately wanted to talk to her … even after all these months.

***

"Our own bed," Kathryn sighed, stretching languorously, her white shirt clinging seductively as she grinned up at her husband.

Returning her smile, he slowly levered himself down beside her.

"We have answered several needs in the last couple of hours." He paused, eyeing her meaningfully.

Raising an eyebrow, she listened closely as he leisurely ticked each one off.

"Seeing our little girl, visiting Anna, reviewing problems that occurred while we were gone …" His eyes locked on hers. "However, there is one particular need that can wait no longer."

Opening her blouse, he brought his lips to her breast, his tongue gently teasing as she arched against him, relinquishing herself in complete abandon. *How splendid to be home in our own bed in Jason's arms. How magnificent.*

Kathryn relished the peacefulness of the next three months spent within the campsite. Their orders to move northward had been unexpectedly delayed, allowing them more time to enjoy Gabrielle, and share many hours as a family. Pride in their little girl showed openly on their faces. She was tall for her age, unusually graceful and at almost four years old, could ride a full-sized horse with confidence. Her smattering of Cherokee had grown into a full vocabulary, allowing her to speak equally at ease in either language.

The dragoons fared well, throughout the winter months, as Kathryn and Anna maintained a strict vigilance: hunting daily to keep food adequate and fresh. Medicine concoctions, insisted upon as a daily regimen, kept illness to a minimum, the majority of men remaining in good health and high spirits. Occasional fevers, even dysentery, responded quickly to an oil Anna brewed from red cedar berries; life moved on at a slower pace.

Cornwallis's army had not fared as well. He visited their campsite several times, spending hours talking with both Jason and Kathryn, many evenings late into the night, rehashing never-ending problems: lack of understanding received from the English homeland, constant rebel attacks, captured supply wagons and his deep disappointment with their recent lack of success.

"My God," he spluttered, "I cannot convince Lord George Germain or the King, of the vacillating loyalties encountered here in the colonies. With Loyalists—one minute they are with us and the next …"

He threw his hands up in exasperation.

"And England tires of the funding. I need supplies and more men."

But no matter his level of frustration, he always looked forward to his time spent with Gabrielle. He missed his own children, Charles and Mary, back home in England, and she helped ease the ache in his heart. How he loved this intelligent, independent little girl—so like her parents. After each visit, he returned to headquarters in far better spirits, along with a satchel full of herbal remedies to help control the outbreaks of raging fever his troops were constantly experiencing.

Towards the beginning of January, Jason and Kathryn found themselves back patrolling the area on a regular basis. Much to their chagrin, Daniel Morgan, the wily American sent by Nathanael Greene to harass their western South Carolina positions, proved to be very efficient at his job.

Although Jason's leg was still mending and often uncomfortable, he refused to let that keep him from his duties. Cornwallis needed every man he could muster. Even Banastre Tarleton, barely recovered from a bout with dysentery, was back in action, kept upright in his saddle by Kathryn's medicinal herbs, a fact he readily admitted, impressed with her abilities. An unspoken understanding existed between them, one that had blossomed slowly after Ferguson's death. Tarleton treated her with newfound respect, grateful she had never exposed him to ridicule by revealing his momentary weakness that sad day.

Banastre arrived late one afternoon, just as Kathryn and Jason had ridden into camp with a small group of dragoons. They had flushed out several rebel raiders and were in high spirits. Within a few days, they would be moving against Greene—or so they thought.

However, Tarleton had brought official word from his lordship: Jason was to 'sit this one out'. Although not stated in those exact words, their orders were explicit. Cornwallis expected them to join him on the sidelines, a fact met with vehement displeasure by both Jason and Kathryn.

"For Christ's sake, Jason, I can take Morgan with one hand tied behind my back. His lordship misses Ferguson's company. If he wants you two at his side watching the battle—so be it. Your dragoons will follow me."

Tarleton risked a quick look at the two of them. "Well, if you tell them to follow me, they will," he amended. "Besides, I can show you how it is done." He flashed his infectious grin, thoroughly irritating both of them.

By the time he rode out the following morning, they were relieved to see him go. More than once Kathryn was sure her husband would come to blows with the arrogant young man. Jack had even stepped in with coffee and brandy on two separate occasions, trying to defuse rising tension.

"Thankfully, he has finally gone." Kathryn breathed a sigh of relief.

However, the Battle of Cowpens was not the success of which Banastre had bragged—or Cornwallis had been so sure of. Kathryn and Jason chafed at having to sit astride their horses on the sideline with Cornwallis, watching Banastre's brash carelessness threaten defeat. Arrogant and cocky, he had charged across the battlefield, over zealously and in poor order.

When it became apparent their help was gravely needed, it was too late. Morgan's clever military tactics ripped apart Tarleton's cavalry along with his contingency of dogged Highlanders and Jason's dragoons.

Although he never exposed Tarleton to either public or private censure, Cornwallis confided his deep disappointment to Kathryn and Jason, and after a few days rest, broke camp to continue his march northward, his mood greatly dampened.

Traveling with minimal equipment, Kathryn and Jason broke camp with their dragoons, joining Cornwallis's army in pursuit of Greene and Morgan, moving ever deeper into North Carolina. They maintained high spirits while on the road, playing with Gabrielle, enjoying each other's company, and imbuing the dragoons with indefatigable confidence: all would go well in their next encounter.

Even the discouraging fact that the Americans always remained ahead of them—just out of reach—could not flag their confidence. They *would be* victorious. Perhaps it would take more time than originally planned, but they would succeed.

Cornwallis drew back to Hillsboro with the largest part of his army, hoping to enlist more Loyalists, needing to gather strength. The chase had been exhausting. He was tired, discouraged and—his troops were hungry.

Jason's dragoons fared better. Being comprised of a much smaller band of men, Kathryn was able to keep them healthy and reasonably well fed. Fireside camaraderie, evenings of singing and playing the tin whistle, helped buoy their spirits. But it was to their colonel and his wife that they looked to set the tone of daily living and confidence in battle: their unflagging determination a tonic for every member.

Kathryn and Jason might confide their concerns to each other within the privacy of their tent, often including Jack while sharing an evening cup of coffee. But none of their insecurities ever left that tent. They would win this war; they had no doubt. They refused to consider any other possibility; that was the face they presented to their men at all times. They would finish this war triumphantly together ... then pursue a normal family life with their beloved little girl.

Chapter Thirty-Three

Destiny Beckons

By mid-February, Cornwallis had set up a base of operation across the Deep River on the road to Wilmington. Kathryn and Jason were well aware that he was leaving himself a path for retreat to the coast should it become necessary. After establishing his camp, his lordship pressed northeastward again, preparing his men for battle. Jason's dragoons followed, as always maintaining a reasonably high level of health and enthusiasm, due greatly to Kathryn's unflagging efforts.

By the end of the second week in March, Kathryn's spirits had begun to soar without concentrated effort on her part. Yes, it was still cold and raw, incessant drizzle dampening the best of moods occasionally, yet signs of spring abounded: a hint of fresh color returning to fields and trees alike. Also, on a more positive note, they were gaining ground on Nathanael Greene and his retreating army. She and Jason were sure he would turn and fight, soon—very soon. Guilford Courthouse seemed a likely spot.

Having ridden throughout that area on several occasions, Kathryn remembered it well. Her last visit, a couple of years ago, had been in early fall. She could still picture the huge cornfields stretching along both sides of the road as she approached the courthouse, bundles of drying cornstalks standing propped together on rich, red Carolina earth. The dense foliage of surrounding woods had seemed alive, sparkling with splendor as sunshine played on brilliantly colored leaves, those which had already drifted to the ground making a colorful path that crunched under Beauty's hooves, releasing rich earthy aromas.

However, it was the bubbling brook meandering through those woods, the crystal clarity of its rippling water that retained such a special place in her memories. Perhaps someday after this war was over, she and Jason might enjoy its cool comfort on a hot summer day. That thought brightened her face in a smile.

Just two nights ago, she and Jason had discussed the pros and cons of a pitched battle in that area, over their evening meal with Jack. Kathryn expressed concern, wishing it were a dryer time of year to afford better footing for the horses. The thick woods surrounding the courthouse presented other obvious problems; they would tackle that situation when the time came. They needed this victory desperately; they must succeed—they would succeed. She steadfastly refused to have her spirits dampened by unpleasant thoughts, savoring every waking moment of each and every day.

"She is unbelievable, Jack," Jason confided after supper one night. "Her spirits never waver and her courage …" he trailed off shaking his head in admiration.

"She draws strength and courage from you, Jason, as you do from her." Jack smiled.

They pressed ever northward, sporadically encountering a few rebel bands: quickly defeating or dispersing them. Jamie always stayed out of their immediate view, remaining forever elusive despite having been sighted more than once.

Jason's thigh had thoroughly healed: again strong and causing negligible discomfort. Kathryn supposed Cornwallis had been correct in having them stay on the sideline at Cowpens. However, they both regretted his decision, and the discouraging outcome of that battle.

***

"Finally, they are getting what they deserve," Jamie gloated. Hunkering beside the campfire and chewing a piece of roasted rabbit he eyed his son. "Morgan sure gave 'em 'what for' at Cowpens. He's a brilliant strategist, you know. Too bad his health is so poorly; I sure hate to see him retiring."

Pausing to wipe his mouth before continuing, he eyed his son with growing irritation.

"But Greene can finish what he and Morgan started together. Look how his forces continue to lure Cornwallis deeper into North Carolina, always staying just out of reach. And the English think they're the ones in control. Ha!"

Jamie was gleeful for the first time in many months.

"They seem to be faring not quite so well, now. Worn uniforms, food and other supplies running low; of course we can take a lot of credit for that."

He grinned at Gabriel. "You are awful damned quiet, son."

Gabriel eyed his father in silence, unable to share his elation, his concerns for Kathryn, all too real and painful. Without saying a word he abruptly turned on his heel and walked away, leaving Jamie shrugging.

***

Tonight it was warmer than it had been for the past few days. The dragoons threw together a makeshift campsite as rain continued to fall—as it had for the better part of the day—finally beginning to slacken as they finished their set up.

Kathryn stepped from their tent in her fresh, dry uniform, relieved to see the rain lessened to heavy drizzle. Jason was at her side, walking with no apparent limp despite the long day's ride in damp weather. She hugged him, smiling up into his sparkling eyes.

After a light meal with the dragoons and a few rounds of songs, they walked Gabrielle back to her tent where Anna waited. Anna was a solitary individual who rarely joined the group, preferring to savor her privacy.

Tonight she seemed unusually restless, puttering about in a distracted fashion as Jason read poetry to his little girl. Kathryn watched quietly, imprinting the loving picture of the two of them in her mind, realizing how much more her daughter mimicked her father's mannerisms with each passing month. Her coloring was all his, her expressive facial expressions—definitely his. Gabrielle could communicate so much with a profound arch of an eyebrow, just as he could. Although the planes of her daughter's face were slightly more angular, she was almost a mirror image of Kathryn; how she loved them both.

They stayed longer than usual this evening, playing with their daughter, delighting in her antics, attributing Anna's disquiet to their newly acquired information about the next day's pending battle.

Outriders had arrived earlier in the day with new orders from his lordship, just as they were setting up camp. Nathanael Greene had dug in with his troops, as they had suspected he would sooner or later, and was awaiting the arrival of Cornwallis's forces near Guilford Courthouse. *Tomorrow will be the day of reckoning.*

"What are you writing, my pet?" he asked, watching his wife toiling diligently at his desk.

He stood naked to the waist, wiping the glistening droplets of water from his face and chest, pausing with the towel held to his chin, his eyes exuding warmth.

She looked up, tapping the pen against her pursed lower lip.

"I am writing to Grandmother. It has been too long since last we wrote; I feel somewhat guilty."

Moving to stand behind her, he leaned over her shoulder, breathing softly against her ear.

"It will be a very short letter, my love, if you continue doing that." She planted a kiss on his cheek, grinning.

"Let us see what you have had to say." He perused the letter, his hand resting lightly on her shoulder as he read. "God, how I hope you are right, love. If only the battle goes well tomorrow." He paused then continued softly, "I do so want to be done with this infernal war, so I can take you and Gabrielle home to England."

She reached up to hold his hand while she finished her part of the letter, then handed him the pen, squeezing aside so he could sit down and add a personal note of his own.

Yes, they had often discussed England, and she looked forward to the journey eagerly. Perhaps in time, Jamie would forgive her and come to tolerate Jason. If not ... well she would not dwell on that thought. England would be an exciting adventure. It would not be a new land of total strangers as Jack would be there with his large family. Besides, she could adapt to anyplace as long as she and Jason could be together with their little girl. There might even be another child someday, a companion for Gabrielle—perhaps a little boy.

"You are somewhere far away, my pet," he murmured, tracing his fingers softly along her cheek.

"Yes," she breathed, "in England with you and Gabrielle."

She arose, turning into his waiting embrace.

"Tomorrow will be ours," she stated firmly. "Your leg is strong, and we have kept our health through the long, cold winter months. Spring is in the air—I feel it." Her eyes came alive with enthusiasm, a sparkling deep green in the lantern light.

His mouth closed over hers gently. How he loved this brave, confidant woman, such an integral part of his being he could barely remember life before her. He inhaled the marvelous familiar scent of her, as his lips followed the arch of her neck downwards, opening her shirt to suckle a taut nipple, welcoming her sharp intake of breath. Each time she entered his arms, it became a fresh, new encounter ... even after all these years.

They both savored the indestructible connection of intense intimacy existing between them, neither one able to sate their incredible need for the other. He still took her breath away each time his electric blue eyes met hers, or she experienced his exquisite touch. It was an evening of sheer delight, the magnitude of their passion leaving them drifting sleepily content within the circle of each other's arms.

But Jason could not give in to restful sleep just yet, as his final thoughts turned to tomorrow's battle. Jamie was nearby; they both knew that for a fact. Perhaps tomorrow would be a day of reckoning—the day they would finally meet on the battlefield. Maybe neither one would walk away.

But if I kill Jamie ... Oh my beloved Kathryn, will you still be able to look at me, with the same unqualified love that speaks so eloquently in your every glance?

Yet, somehow he knew she would cope. She always did, this woman he loved more than life itself. The feel of her long, lean body snugged against him breathing softly, calmed his thoughts as he joined her in peaceful sleep.

Just before dawn she awoke with a sob, startled from a dream, quickly quieted and reassured by her husband's gentle touch as he molded himself comfortingly against her back.

"I am here, my love, you are safe," he breathed softly against her neck.

"Jason," a broken sob escaped as she turned, reaching for him.

She tried to speak, but he silenced her with a kiss.

"It was only a dream, my love, only a dream."

But something in his tone struck an odd chord. He had already been awake, of that she was sure. Had he sensed the import of the dream … or had he shared it?

He cupped her face tenderly, capturing her gaze. Stroking back her tawny, wild curls, he whispered words of comfort as he kissed the tears from her cheeks. Hands that knew her better than she knew herself caressed slowly and thoroughly, as he continued to murmur gentling words against her throat. "All will be well, my dearest wife."

She touched his cheek, searching his face—the handsome, gentle face of this man she loved so deeply. In the early glow of dawn, she saw the passion, endless devotion and indestructible strength of his love for her, and was comforted … her answering look returning those emotions in full measure.

"I will never go without you, my Kathryn, never."

"Promise me … oh, promise me, my love."

"Always … always, we are as one." His eyes held hers. "Never fear."

His hands moved to gently caress her, loving her with such exquisite tenderness she was struck by the fathomless depth and intense fulfillment of their joining … this incredible man, her beloved husband … her heart and soul.

Suddenly it struck her. *He knows … he knows.* Of that, she was sure.

As they stepped towards the tent opening, prepared to face the day's battle, she paused, speaking his name in a voice that almost failed her. Turning, his arms opened as she flung herself against him. For long moments, they clung in silence drawing strength from each other to do what must be done. He broke the embrace first, afraid of his own emotions. If he held her any longer, he would be sorely tempted to call it off.

"We must go, my love, duty calls." He touched her cheek gently.

"Yes, love." She smiled bravely as he tenderly kissed her once more.

"If we tarry longer, Banastre will complain loudly of his injured hand and our lack of back-up." He forced a grin, attempting to make light of the situation.

She took her cue from him. If he could face destiny with such courage … she could also.

"It will go our way," she stated firmly. "The dragoons are strong, ready for battle, and your leg is good as new."

Her words rang hollow even to her own ears, but he loved her all the more for her brave attempt at optimism. Both realized the importance of winning this encounter today—and the extreme odds they faced.

Squaring their shoulders, they locked eyes, each taking a deep breath. Side by side, they stepped proudly from their tent to greet Lieutenant Jackson and the waiting dragoons, their smiles bright, both exuding an aura of utmost confidence.

Jack was waiting, as always, with their morning coffee. To the dragoons, who counted on their spirit and enthusiasm to set the tone of the day, all was as it should be. But knowing them as he did, Jack recognized the tension behind the smiles, and experienced a momentary prick of fear. But his apprehension quickly receded as her warm greeting and infectious grin caught him up in their forced exuberance.

At Anna's tent, Jason held his daughter close, nuzzling her neck for several minutes before handing her to her mother. Kathryn hugged her child, inhaling the sweet smell of her, tousling her curly hair.

"Come back soon," a happy, little voice chirped.

"Poppa and I will always be with you, little one. Never forget how very much we love you. Now, be good and do as Anna tells you."

With a long hug, she set Gabrielle down amidst her toys, eyeing the little wooden horse that had been Jason's, allowing her thoughts to drift momentarily before forcing herself back to the present.

Nodding towards Anna, she headed from the tent to follow Jason, but Anna called her back. The look on her face left no doubt in Kathryn's mind.

"You shared the dream too," Kathryn said with certainty.

Anna nodded, her dark eyes imploring she reconsider.

"You need not accept this destiny, Ugilohi ..."

Ugilohi, 'Longhair', her Indian name. Fleeting memories of the Bird Clan flickered then dimmed. There was no time for that now; Jason was waiting.

"We love our daughter, Anna, *I* love my daughter." Her voice caught. She paused fighting for control. She would not cry, would not frighten her little girl.

Moving to where Gabrielle sat playing with a cloth doll Anna had made for her, she crouched down. Quickly removing the treasured necklace that had belonged to Jason's mother, she placed it around her daughter's neck. Stroking back her raven curls she whispered, "Take care of this for momma."

The little girl clutched it, smiling happily as Kathryn kissed her one last time.

"It is his destiny." She stood slowly, speaking softly to Anna. "It is our destiny."

Anna watched her eyes, noting deep sadness but firm resolve; no argument could alter the decision already made.

She hugged Anna tightly. "I will not have him go alone. I cannot ..." her voice trailed into silence as her dear friend nodded, accepting.

"Help Jack, he will need your strength."

With a final hug she swiftly left the tent without a backwards glance.

Jason stood by the horses watching her stride towards them, donning her black leather gloves and adjusting her helmet. There was no time for further discussion, but it was not necessary. Understanding what had transpired between Anna and Kathryn, he forced himself to refocus on what lay ahead, blocking all disconcerting thoughts.

The dragoons sat astride restless horses, waiting expectantly. Jack's eyes followed her every move closely as their traditional 'pre-battle ritual', so familiar to all, began. Her slender fingers gently grazed Jason's chest then curled into a fist against her heart, her gaze never wavering from his. As she murmured *'your heart and mine shall beat as one'*, his lips caressed her forehead, his thumb gently tracing its familiar path along the bridge of her nose down to her chin, then tipping her mouth up to meet his in a lightly brushed kiss ... a kiss that lasted longer than usual.

"Always," he breathed touching her cheek gently, "... always."

She stepped back, smiling. But as he turned to step into his stirrup, she touched his sleeve. Halting, he turned back to her, somewhat surprised.

As the dragoons watched, thoroughly entranced, she dropped to one knee, lowering her head in deference to her husband: a gesture of honor and deep devotion. Lifting her face to search his, her emerald eyes connected with his piercing blue gaze in a look of such pure love, he thought he would falter.

"I am deeply honored, sir, to be your wife and to ride at your side." Her voice wavered ever so slightly, but carried loud enough for all to hear.

He was awestruck—such a tremendous honor displayed for all to see. Would she never cease to amaze him? Squeezing her hand gently, voice hoarse with emotion he stated, "It is I who am honored on both counts, Mrs. Tarrington."

Assisting her to rise, he smiled as she stepped into her stirrup and mounted Beauty with a dignity befitting the moment, then moved to take her position beside him.

Mounting Diablo, he looked back over his band of faithful dragoons. "Give them hell," he shouted, and with a curt gesture of his gloved hand, they rode out in formation.

Jack pulled near silently observing, unable to curb the gnawing unease in the pit of his stomach. But as she turned to wink at him, her face displayed nothing but calm ... an inner serenity, or perhaps acceptance. He was not sure which.

As they drew nearer to Guilford Courthouse, the discordant beat of drums, skirling bagpipes and the familiar sounds of a raging battle grew louder. Jason and Kathryn eyed each other. Their orders had been specific as to time and place. Had Cornwallis changed the hour of the planned attack, or had there been a surprise ambush?

Beauty and Diablo pranced willfully, excited by the familiar sounds. Both faithful horses were eager to get into the fray, their indefatigable spirits displayed with tireless energy, despite the miles of arduous trails they had traveled over the last few months.

Jason signaled the dragoons to pick up the pace. But as they neared the cornfields Kathryn had described, aware they were close to the courthouse, Jason brought them to a halt. Pausing to assess the situation before charging directly into the foray, he made quick decisions and issued curt orders.

"Try to stay close today." Jason leaned towards Kathryn and Jack. "And be cautious."

He eyed his wife pointedly on that statement, stifling a smile as she flashed a wide grin and retorted, "Of course, sir."

The battle was fully engaged in the clearing surrounding the courthouse and along the approaching roadside. Cornwallis's three big artillery pieces were easily visible, although they stood in silence—for the moment. Disorganization and confusion prevailed: the field a mass of fighting, seething bodies swarming like ants in all directions. Guns blazed and sabres flashed in the sunlight amidst the screams of dying men and animals—the number of bloodied dead and injured increasing rapidly. Greene's first and second American lines were attempting to advance, but at the moment, Cornwallis's army seemed in control. As was his fashion, Banastre—always bold and brash—was easily visible.

Perhaps it was a dream after all, Kathryn reasoned as she scanned the field. Noticing the ground had been recently plowed in readiness for a spring crop of corn, she indicated the soggy red earth to Jason and Jack, cautioning them to watch their footing.

"Charge!" Jason bellowed, and with a sweeping gesture of his arm, ordered his dragoons into battle; all extraneous thoughts forcefully set aside, replaced by intense concentration on the job at hand.

Kathryn rode fearlessly into the fray, her senses fully alert. Aware of rebels approaching from several directions, she moved decisively forward—never seeking individual faces—blocking her mind to everything but what she must accomplish.

The fighting intensified as they took the field, preventing them from maintaining their originally planned, tightly knit battle formation. The frenzied confusion of attacks from ever changing sides drew Kathryn, Jason, and Jackson out into the battling masses—away from one another.

"Stay close," Jason had admonished. But that was becoming impossible in this wild melee. Both sides surged back and forth across the battlefield with increasing disorder—the victorious outcome seesawing from one side, then to the other.

Sensing a presence to her left, Kathryn swung about to see Captain Hodges grinning widely and touching his helmet in salute, having successfully blocked a blow to her back. Taking the rebel down had brought him extreme pleasure, proud to have protected his 'Lady Kathryn', glad to repay her in some small way for the times she had saved him.

"Thanks." She flashed a grin, their eyes meeting fleetingly as they urged their horses into the fray.

The rebel onslaught ebbed and flowed, converging to attack in small powerful groups, before flowing back towards the protective cover of dense woods—like an oily slick on water: pooling and regrouping. There appeared to be a concentrated effort by these rebel bands to keep the three of them separated. Their reputation as an unbeatable team was well known, this determined strategy was meant to even the playing field—and it worked.

Kathryn flung her leg over Beauty's saddle and nimbly dropped to the ground, bringing down an approaching rebel in a manner more comfortable to her: a well-placed tomahawk. Hodges followed her lead, turning so his back would be against hers in a protective move, unwilling to leave her until the colonel or Lieutenant Jackson could work back through the melee to be at her side.

As he met another screaming rebel head on, he slashed viciously—certain from their method of advance—these rebels had targeted them with a well thought-out purpose in mind.

General Cornwallis sat astride his large, white stallion observing the bloody battle from a distance, his confidence slowly returning. Although it had begun badly, this engagement so far, had all the earmarks of a much-needed British victory.

Over the last few weeks, Greene and his American army had been doggedly relentless in their efforts to draw him ever northward. Much to his chagrin, he had allowed himself to be lulled into a false sense of security created by that devilish man. Greene's army had caught him unprepared in an unexpected ambush. But Colonel Tarrington and Kathryn were here now, taking the field forcefully in their own inimitable fashion with their well-trained dragoons. All would be well.

As the battle raged on, he lost track of them in the frenzied melee, as dominance seesawed back and forth between the two sides. Greene's first two lines of defense had been driven back, but his third line was now advancing, the fighting: bloody, brutal—incredibly savage.

"Look, milord, the American cavalry has arrived," Cornwallis's accompanying officer exclaimed, gesturing wildly towards the road.

A well-trained formation of armed military men rapidly approached Guilford Courthouse astride galloping horses, their vigorous attack renewing the flagging spirits of the Americans on the battlefield—inspiring them with new determination.

Turning in the direction indicated, Cornwallis was surprised and disheartened to see their energetic advance. He had not been expecting fresh American troops. This could be the determining factor in another British defeat—he could not afford that. With a grim look, the general shook his head, swearing under his breath.

"Fire our artillery into their midst: grapeshot," he muttered, hating the distasteful command.

At the stunned look of his officer he stated painfully, "It is a harsh but necessary measure if we mean to save the bulk of our army. Carry out my order, now."

It was unnecessary to provide explanation to a lower officer, of that he was well aware. But he needed to hear the words aloud, for himself; needed to detect the validity of the grim judgment he had passed.

Again, the rebel tide ebbed, leaving Kathryn and Hodges unchallenged for the moment. But the battle raged further out, nothing as yet resolved.

Seeing Jackson approaching rapidly on horseback, Hodges grinned. "See you around the campfire tonight, 'Lady Kathryn'." Touching a salute to his helmet, he strode towards his patiently waiting charger.

She returned the salute, matching his grin. *What a good man, 'polite almost to a fault'.* Sucking in a deep breath, she moved to Beauty's side. With a quick pat and words of praise, she flung herself onto her saddle and rode out to meet Jack.

Rushed unexpectedly from her left, she turned slashing sideways with her sabre; a well-built colonial sagged backwards clutching his chest, a shocked expression frozen on his features. She rode on. One more confrontation and she reined in at Jack's side, ready to ride into the heavy fighting around the courthouse. His eyes met hers with grim respect as they quickly surveyed the field.

Suddenly she caught sight of Diablo, rider-less and milling nervously with a marked limp. *Where is Jason?* Her breath caught at the back of her throat, her heart pounding a ragged beat … she knew a moment of true fear.

Jack followed her anguished gaze. At wood's edge, many yards away, Jason could be seen engaged in heavy hand-to-hand combat with a lone rebel. Kneeing their horses, they moved to his aid as rapidly as the soggy ground would permit.

Two rebels rode out to confront them and Jackson veered off to intercept.

"Help Jason, I have these two," he yelled back over his shoulder, waving her on.

Crouching low over Beauty's withers, Kathryn urged her faithful mare to greater speed, even as she begged her to tread carefully, praying her delicate grace would allow her to fare better than most horses on the soggy field.

Another rebel burst from cover at the edge of the woods coming straight for her. Slowing Beauty, she braced her pistol against her arm and fired, the lead ball finding its mark. Again, she urged her mare towards Jason, slowly closing the space between them, beginning to sort out details of the heated encounter in which he was embroiled.

Jason was the better swordsman, the rebel—bloody and faltering. She could not discern the rebel's features as his back faced her, yet his fighting style seemed—familiar. At that moment, several rebels emerged from the woods, threading their way towards Jason and approaching from her right, but she would be there in time to intercept them. This was going to be a fight on the ground, just where she liked it—where she would be at complete ease. Loosening her helmet she flung it aside, never truly comfortable within its confinement, she wanted no distracting encumbrances. As the helmet left her head, her long curls came free and caught the breeze in a tangled, golden-honey mass.

"It's her, it's her," someone shrieked.

Dimly aware of their cry, she kept full focus on Jason and his combatant as she closed the distance. Jack had circled wide and was heading in from her left. The three of them together again would be able to make short work of this encounter.

Reining Beauty to a halt, she leaped to the ground while the little mare was still in motion; near enough now, to catch bits and pieces of angry words spewing from the rebel attacker. He was weakening visibly under Jason's onslaught, and staggered backwards from a well-placed blow.

As she struggled through the soggy mire to get to Jason, his eyes caught hers for a flickering moment, connecting on a deep inner level before refocusing on his foe.

Without warning, their world suddenly erupted in a fiery, deafening explosion. With the thunderous boom, Kathryn saw Jason stagger—hit by grapeshot fired from their own artillery, she realized with horror.

Reeling from the impact, a guttural moan escaped as he struggled to remain upright. With strength flagging, his sabre angled downward digging into the soft earth, his rugged face contorting in agony as a circle of blood widened around the ragged hole in his jacket.

His rebel antagonist quickly dropped to one knee, head hanging as if severely wounded, his hand clutching at his leg. Badly injured, to be sure, and bleeding heavily, there was strength in him yet. Instantly she recognized his tactic, one in which a mortal wound is feigned as you drop to retrieve a hidden dirk.

"*Come up quickly. Strike with accuracy. Catch your enemy off-guard.*"

Terse instructions echoed eerily from her past. She knew the deadly game and remembered the teacher who had instructed her so thoroughly—her worst fears were finally realized.

A small dirk filled his hand, sliding easily from his boot top. Head snapping up, he lunged, beginning a sweeping arc to plunge his blade deeply into Jason's abdomen.

"No, Jamie, no!" she screamed, as she raced towards them, bringing instant recognition to her brother—and momentary distraction.

His deadly strike fell slightly off target, the dirk slicing upwards along Jason's ribcage opening a deep gash for several inches. Jason lurched backwards clutching his side, crumpling slowly to the ground as Jamie, his last vestige of strength gone, collapsed where he stood, too exhausted to strike again.

Her scream filled the air as she raced the last few yards, trying desperately to get to her husband. A second deafening blast erupted as grapeshot peppered the battlefield again, striking both sides indiscriminately.

Burning agony, the likes of which she had never experienced before, flared in her chest as the impact drove her to her knees. Gulping air, trying to focus around the incredible pain, she staggered doggedly to her feet. With sheer willpower, she forced herself to take those last halting steps to Jason, her frantic need to touch him driving her forward.

"Jason, Jason, my love," she gasped, weakly dropping down beside him, distraught—his deathly pallor, the gaping wounds and so much blood. "Jason, Jason," she murmured over and over stroking his ashen face, brushing back wily strands of hair. "Do not go, do not leave me."

Ignoring her excruciating pain she caressed his cheek tenderly, tears falling freely, completely unaware the sounds of battle had almost ceased, as combat-weary men retreated into the woods … and oblivious of the two men standing beside her, immersed in their own personal grief as they watched her suffering.

Moaning softly, Jason struggled to reclaim reality from the red haze that engulfed him. *Kathryn needs me.* He felt her distress. *I must get to her.* His eyes fluttered open searching for her, trying to focus, and came to rest on her tear-streaked face. Recognition registered, his eyes speaking of undying love as he weakly touched her wet cheek with a trembling hand, and then reached to trail his fingers in her riotous blonde curls.

"My beautiful wife, do not cry," he barely whispered. "Remember … *always.*"

His last bit of strength was fading; she was losing him. *She was losing him.* She clung to him frantically, ignoring her own pain.

"Do not go, Jason. You are my heart … my soul." Bending low, she kissed him passionately. For a brief moment, there was response … then he was gone.

Her grief was insufferable, her mind surrendering to that anguish, and ceasing to function. Throwing her head back, a keening wail erupted from the depth of her soul, an agonized cry of such enormous despair it seemed more the howl of a mortally wounded animal, than anything remotely human.

"You promised you would not go alone, Jason, you promised …" she trailed into coughing sobs, crumpling back into arms that were ready—waiting to hold and comfort her when the inevitable collapse came.

Jack stared in horror at the amount of blood on her chest, and ghostly pallor. Clutching her to him, he murmured gentle words softly into her hair as he frantically pressed a large handkerchief against the gaping wound.

"Kathryn, oh Kathryn," his voice broke as he rocked her gently.

She shuddered slightly then roused, her eyes fluttering open to search his face.

"Jack, always there … for us." She spoke haltingly, with mounting difficulty as the insidious pain engulfed her.

Another spoke her name grabbing her attention. She angled her head painfully to see Gabriel, comforted by his presence. Her eyes met his briefly with such love he found it difficult to swallow.

Slowly and painfully, she returned her attention to Lieutenant Jackson.

"Take … care of … our little girl," she gasped, as an agonizing spasm enveloped her.

"I will do all you asked, my Kathryn," Jack assured, as he held her gently, attempting to absorb her agony.

Gabriel knelt down, resting his hand gently on her shoulder, then up to touch her tear stained cheek as he murmured his assurance that he, too, would fulfill her wishes.

"Gabrielle will not come to harm, you have my sworn word, Aunt … *Kathryn.*"

He stroked a golden curl, wonderful memories flooding over him, wishing he could turn back the hands of time.

"Thank you for ..." she trailed off, her attention suddenly diverted, her green eyes drifting away from them, focusing on something or *someone* ... but not either of them.

Her features relaxed, the pain falling away. Slowly she extended her hand as if reaching to touch someone, and then lowered to rest over her heart, her fingers curling weakly into a fist. A slight smile graced her lips and held momentarily.

"Always ... my love," with only the barest whisper, she was gone.

"She is with him now; he came for her as promised." Jack began to sob uncontrollably, holding her to him, rocking gently.

Gabriel did not have to ask. He had observed their 'signature salute' once long ago, when Kathryn was a new bride and he, in anger and misunderstanding, had tried to slay her husband.

So long ago ... so much love and pain ... so much lost forever.

Too weak to move closer, Jamie hitched himself up on one elbow to better see his sister. He watched with growing anguish, fighting to release his last shreds of anger, wanting to touch her, comfort her—as she had done for him so many times long ago.

Warring emotions raged—cling to stubborn MacLean pride or relent and forgive her? He still cared, still loved her. *Yes, loved her, despite all that had gone wrong between them.*

His last shreds of anger fell away as her life slipped from her ... too late to make amends.

"Kathryn," his voice broke.

Falling back, a sob escaped as hot tears began to fall; she was gone. He knew that beyond doubt as he saw his son place a comforting hand on the shoulder of the distraught dragoon lieutenant.

Lieutenant Jackson wept unashamedly as Gabriel touched his shoulder in an attempt at comforting him. But in his heart, knew his gesture to be futile, the lieutenant's love for Kathryn, so very obvious. Perhaps, even time could not heal pain of such magnitude.

Jack's desolation showed plainly in his anguished eyes and slumped shoulders. He wept for himself, knowing with certainty that Kathryn and Jason were together ... at peace, and was glad for them. He wept for Gabrielle, who would never truly know her parents and their abiding love for their little girl. He wept for the loss of Jason, an excellent commanding officer—a good man and true friend. *But he felt as if his heart had been torn from his chest with the loss of his Kathryn.*

Gabriel looked down sadly at his aunt, beautiful even in death. Suddenly, memory after memory cascaded freely, his mind awash with visions of the exuberant girl with a passion for life, whose laughter could fill the house. Always pretty, even as a young girl, she had grown into a beautiful, young woman of many talents, a woman who was proud, independent, compassionate and fair in judgment, a woman who had helped shape his life and make him the man he was today.

The bitterness and conflict his father had clung to with such grim determination, trying to force him to also accept, was suddenly no longer important. He looked over at the colonel, his face also peaceful in death, recalling that he had been treated fairly by this man, a man his aunt had loved *beyond all reason* ... and knew what he must do.

Jamie had been removed from the field, barely conscious, his wounds severe but not life threatening. Gabriel indicated to his men with quiet gestures, that he would follow later. Hamish had been there to help carry Jamie to safety, but paused for a few moments of sad contemplation, remembering when Kathryn had spared his life, not once but twice, glad to have known her for the individual she truly was.

As Gabriel began to remove his coat, lengthening rays of the early setting, late winter sun gleamed from the exquisite pair of gold Celtic wedding bands resting on their fingers.

He knelt, and lifting Kathryn's hand gently, began rubbing his thumb across her beautiful wedding ring, a symbol of eternal love. How appropriate he thought, awed by Jason's incredible sensitivity in making such a choice.

"They wanted to be so sure that anyone who met them would know they belonged solely to each other."

The lieutenant's quiet words broke through Gabriel's grief startling him; he had not realized the officer had been observing him. Jack's countenance remained bleak, but he was forcefully making an effort to regain some control, he had a promise to fulfill.

"Lieutenant, you must get away, now." Gabriel eyed Jack gravely as he placed his rebel greatcoat over the lieutenant's bright red uniform. "There are too many rebels milling about for you to be safe in that outfit."

Jack still cradled Kathryn, unable to set her aside. But his tortured gaze now turned to rest on his fallen commander.

"You must save your grieving for later … as must I," Gabriel added softly. "There are too many factions who would gladly see their child used as a pawn … or worse. There is danger here that increases as we talk. You must go now," Gabriel insisted.

"I will tend to everything that needs to be done, and see they are laid to rest together. You know you can trust me."

Jack searched the handsome young man's face, his strength of conviction so very like Kathryn's, and knew he would be good to his word.

Slowly, with great tenderness, Jack eased Kathryn to the ground. He turned for a last look at his dear friend, reaching to touch his sleeve, before his gaze drifted back to Kathryn.

"Be at peace now, with him, my love," he whispered as he bent low and kissed her with such tenderness, that tears welling behind Gabriel's eyes threatened to break free.

"Hurry, take Beauty, she will be of comfort to both you and Gabrielle."

With a nod of 'thanks', Jack slipped into Gabriel's greatcoat. His heart clenched: so similar to Kathryn's.

With one final glance at the two people he had tended and loved for the last five years, he quickly moved to where Beauty stood nervously fidgeting. As he stepped up into the saddle and turned, inclining his head in 'thanks' and shared sorrow, Gabriel was relieved to see the lieutenant's eyes focused with purpose. He watched as Jack disappeared into the woods, confident he had gained enough control to do what must be done.

Gabriel was alone with Kathryn, at last. Now he could allow himself to grieve openly. He had done as she had asked of him so long ago. Tears streamed down his cheeks as he knelt to hold her one last time, gulping in air with great wracking sobs.

From a distance, Cornwallis searched the destruction of the battlefield through a looking glass as he readied himself to lead his army northward. Abruptly he stopped scanning, his face paling. His military aide reached to steady him as he swayed slightly—confused by Cornwallis's obvious anguish. Yes, they had lost many of their own men with the firing of the artillery, but it had been a wise decision on the general's part. The Americans were retreating rapidly, the battle decidedly in favor of the British.

"Today we have lost more ..." Cornwallis's throat convulsed—several moments passing before he could continue to speak.

"They are both gone ..." Eyes dark with pain, he turned and walked away, leaving the young aide shaking his head in wonder.

Jack flung himself from Beauty, dropping her reins outside Anna's tent. But before he could reach the tent flap, she appeared. Gabrielle was dressed warmly, clasped within her arms. From her expression, and the neatly tied saddlebags sitting at the edge of the tent opening, Anna had been expecting him.

"You knew?" he accused, gaping incredulously. "And you allowed her to go?" As his voice rose in exasperation, Gabrielle started to cry, confused by her uncle's anger.

"I was unable to dissuade her." A single tear escaped, tracking slowly down her dark angular cheek. "It was his destiny ... she would not have him go alone," she murmured in a voice so soft Jack was hard pressed to hear the words.

As full realization set in, blinding fury came over him.

"How could she leave ...?" He stopped mid-sentence, realizing what he had been about to say.

Anna smiled sadly, her eyes warm with understanding.

"Do not cloud her memory with bitterness, Lieutenant. Without him she was incomplete ... one half of a whole being. You cannot truly have loved her, and wish that for her."

Gabrielle was crying in earnest, realizing something was very wrong. Jack reached to touch the little girl he adored, wanting to comfort her, ashamed by his selfish reaction.

But Anna reached out and squeezed his arm, understanding. "They will both live eternally in our hearts, our memories. Keep her love alive always, Lieutenant."

Gently shifting Gabrielle into his arms, she hurriedly slung the saddlebags over Beauty's rump.

"Go quickly now, there is great danger. She is their immortality ... and they entrusted her to you."

"Come with us, Anna," he pleaded, grasping desperately for some sense of sanity in his collapsing world.

"I return to my people, Lieutenant. But I carry you both in my heart. Guard my little one well, my precious little bird."

Clasping the sobbing child against his chest, he whispered comforting words and mounted Beauty. But there were no words to ease to the aching emptiness in his heart. He had given them his promise, and would fulfill it. This beautiful little girl was all that remained of his beloved Kathryn, and Gabrielle was in grave danger.

He searched Anna's anguished face one last time, their eyes connecting in shared sorrow, then wheeled Kathryn's faithful, little mare and fled into the night.

Epilogue

As Gabriel eased his arms under Kathryn, lifting her gently, an almost inaudible sound escaped her slightly parted lips. He pressed his cheek to hers as the softest breath barely whispered across the tracks of his tears. Grasping her wrist, he probed gently, seeking any sign of life. Could it be? A light flutter: weak but definitely there. His tears began afresh.

"Kathryn, oh Kathryn, live … live," he choked.

Shifting slightly, he reached to touch the colonel's neck. Lingering warmth … unbelievably so, but was he still alive? He pressed trembling fingers firmly against his throat. Yes, there was a definite pulse, albeit thready; there was still life.

"Kathryn, Jason is alive, fight to live—fight," he whispered frantically against her ear.

Could they survive long enough for him to get help, to get them to safety? Who had the skills to tend them? Only Anna, her face flashed through his mind as if she had heard his desperate thoughts and somehow answered. He must remove them from the battlefield immediately, before it was discovered they were still alive: just barely, but alive. *I must find Anna, then perhaps, just perhaps …*

"Lay her down gently and back away," a rough, barely controlled voice, commanded.

Gabriel's head snapped up, his eyes coming to rest on a pistol aimed at his head. He recognized Captain Hodges, a man he remembered for his sensibilities and unusual devotion to both the colonel and Kathryn. The captain stepped closer, never lowering his pistol. He crouched down, leaning to touch the colonel's jacket before turning his concentration on Kathryn.

"They are both still alive, Captain," Gabriel stated with quiet assurance. The captain eyed him suspiciously. *Was this a ploy to catch him off-guard and escape?*

"Her heart still beats; see for yourself," Gabriel said calmly, indicating Kathryn's lolling wrist, encouraging him to touch her.

Never taking his eyes from Gabriel, he leaned forward and gently probed her wrist.

"My God," his words caught on a sob, "and the colonel?"

"Yes; impossibly so but yes."

Gabriel watched as the captain tore the jabot from around his neck and pressed it carefully under Kathryn's shirt to help staunch her bloody wound.

"We must get them away, Captain, there is no time to lose."

"And you would have me believe you are willing to risk your life to save them?" Captain Hodges appeared skeptical as he gingerly felt his colonel's wrist seeking life signs, a look of relief flooding his face within seconds.

"Yes," Gabriel avowed fiercely. "She is my aunt and I love her dearly." He stroked her hair with great tenderness. "And I have nothing but respect for the colonel. He is her heart, her soul."

He gazed down at her pale face with open love. "I only regret that we are on opposite sides of this infernal war."

Gabriel glanced back to the captain, beseeching that he believe him, his gaze so intensely riveting it startled Hodges.

"Trust me, Captain, but decide quickly. We have no time to waste," he said, his anxiety growing.

Captain Hodges searched Gabriel's face, noting the strong family resemblance, the same open-faced honesty that Kathryn had always displayed, remembering a time, not so long ago, when Gabriel had saved her life from his own rebel followers. Yes, he must trust him. There was no other choice if Kathryn and her colonel were to have a chance at life.

Decision made, Hodges holstered his pistol.

"All right, Lieutenant, I will trust your judgment." Hodges nodded with a grim smile.

"Do you have some men you can trust implicitly?" Gabriel asked anxiously.

The captain inclined his head towards the two men who had come up behind him.

Gabriel looked them over, somewhat taken aback. With complete attention focused on the desperate situation at hand, he had not heard their approach.

Taking a deep breath, Gabriel gathered Kathryn into his arms and stood slowly, cradling her gently as the dragoons lifted their colonel.

"Live, Kathryn, live for Jason … as I will beg him to live for you," Gabriel whispered fervently as he brushed a light kiss against her forehead, praying she would have the strength to recover.

"They are young and strong, with a passion for life … and for each other. But their injuries …" Gabriel trailed off, shaking his head sadly.

As he headed into the woods, he eyed Captain Hodges. "I do not know if we have a chance to save them, Captain …"

His young face was grim, but held that certain spark of determination and stubbornness which Hodges had so often seen twinkle in Kathryn's eye.

"But I have a plan."

The 'Beyond' Trilogy

Novels by **J. Winfield Currie**

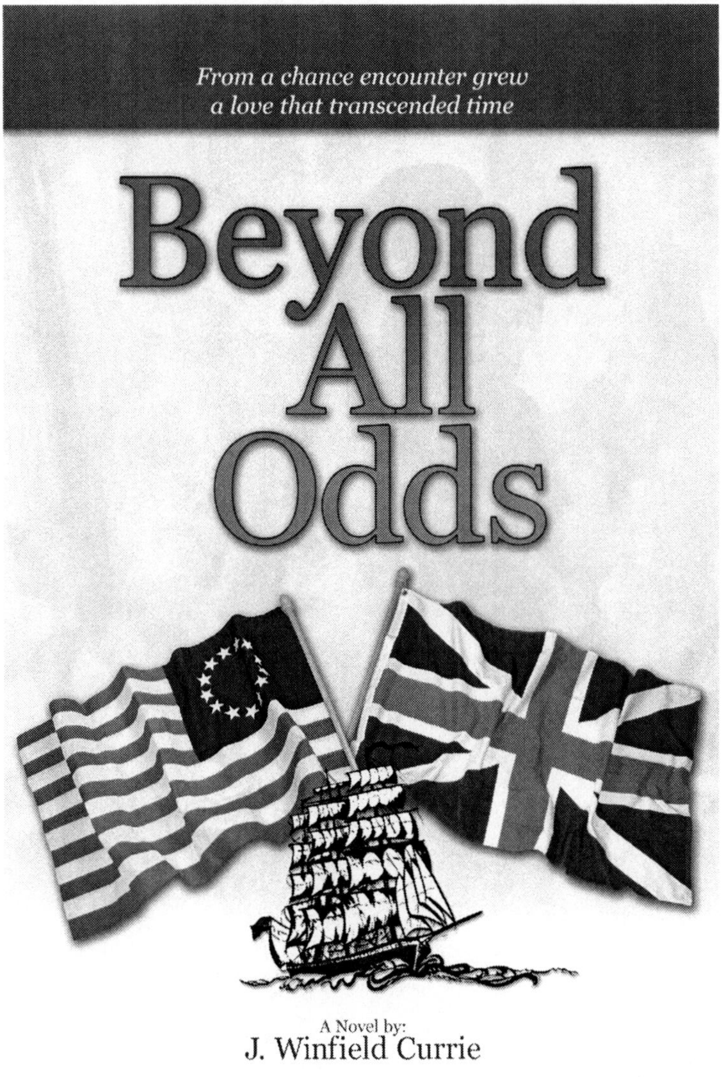
From a chance encounter grew
a love that transcended time
Beyond
All
Odds
A Novel by:
J. Winfield Currie

Beyond All Odds

Book II

Rebuilding Shattered Lives

Chapter One

Frantic Flight

With a final glance at the two people he had tended and loved for the last five years, Lieutenant Jackson moved to where Beauty stood nervously fidgeting. Stepping up into the saddle he turned, inclining his head in 'thanks' and shared sorrow to Gabriel—Kathryn's adored nephew, so like her in many ways. With a soft word to the little mare, he spun away and disappeared into the woods.

Clutching Gabriel's rebel greatcoat tightly about him to cover his telltale red jacket, he hunkered low over Beauty's withers. He must not be recognized, must not be taken by the rebels … must not be stopped … *must not* … or all would be lost. Gabrielle needed him; he was all she had now.

Gabrielle, oh Gabrielle, how will I ever explain? How could this have happened? We were all so sure. Your parents, Kathryn and Jason are … He could not bring himself to think the thought. *Where am I to go? What am I to do? You both depended on me and I always knew what needed to be done. But not now … not now.*

Diablo suddenly appeared out of nowhere—moving cautiously, limping slightly. Anxious and unsure, he approached with tentative, measured steps. Despite his skittish manner, he moved undauntedly towards his master's inert form, nickering softly. Craning his neck, the faithful steed gently nosed his master's legs as Captain Hodges settled the colonel against himself, readying to ease him onto his own charger. He paused for a long moment, eyeing the big stallion thoughtfully.

"What of Diablo, sir?" Sergeant Newcombe asked.

"Bring him with us," Hodges replied as he continued settling their unconscious colonel onto his horse with Simms's assistance. "Best to remove all traces of them from this place."

Reluctantly following instructions, the sergeant reached for Diablo's reins. As feared, the stallion immediately reared back, flashing sharp teeth.

"I will take him," Captain Hodges said calmly, and reached for the reins just as the sergeant quickly sidestepped, barely avoiding a well-aimed bite.

Diablo then immediately quieted and moved closer to his master.

"He will not let the colonel go either," he commented grimly, and nudged his mount to follow Gabriel.

Diablo fell in step, pacing Hodges's steed in a well-mannered gait, his uncomfortable limp all but forgotten.

Captain Hodges hugged his colonel close, repeating over and over: "Live, sir, live. Live for Kathryn … for all of us. Fight … all is not lost."

On and on he coaxed, pleaded, fervently presenting myriads of reasons to live, but mostly for his Kathryn … who needed him desperately.

Gabriel led the way with Kathryn cradled protectively in his arms—obviously well aware of the dragoon encampment, as Hodges suspected he would be. Thankfully it was not too far. Raindrops had begun to fall in fitful spatters, but ominous, black clouds building along the horizon, promised severe weather to come.

***

Anna wept, her shoulders shaking with racking sobs of all-consuming grief that threatened to overwhelm her. *'Anna'*: her name, so familiar and yet—not her own. A name lovingly awarded by her beloved Kathryn—so long ago that she could no longer recall why, or even the significance. But it had stuck.

Ugilohi—*'Long hair'*—Kathryn, her Cherokee name had fit perfectly. Her smiling image slipped easily into Anna's mind; her riotously tawny curls exploding around a flushed and grinning face as she crouched to pick up her adored little girl, Gabrielle. Lifting her high, she would kiss her soundly before turning, with love's fire burning in her eyes, to her husband ... her soul mate ... and invariably whisper, "Poppa and I have missed our little girl."

How eagerly he would then take the child, nuzzling her neck, breathing my poppet, as he hugged her close. They wore their love and pride like a badge for all to see; this tall, fierce dragoon colonel whose fervor in battle was exceeded only by his enduring passion for his wife.

So very right for my Kathryn.

They had been of one spirit, one mind—driven by a common goal and fierce, unquenchable passion for each other. It was difficult to determine where one existence left off and the other began. He had been a good man and he, too, had called her Anna.

Kuniakati, Anna's designated Cherokee title, the revered name of a healer and seer. But she had not been able to heal this ... unable to change their destiny despite her abilities. Anna flung her head back and moaned a sorrowful, guttural animal sound that built in crescendo to a howl of complete anguish.

The few dragoons, who had limped back into camp, were busily salvaging whatever supplies they could before moving on, but each paused as the mournful wail echoed eerily—individual grief written openly on their faces.

Their esteemed colonel and his incredible wife were gone. They had valued this woman as they had her husband, admiring her indomitable courage in the face of all odds, her unflagging spirit and unusual abilities. They stood in awe of the dynamic partnership she had forged with her husband: a colonel renowned for his violent, exacting battle abilities. Yet when off the battlefield, he had but to glance at her, eyeing his Kathryn with unashamed tenderness, abiding love and deepest respect, as her emerald eyes answered in kind.

Yes, they all wanted to throw their heads back and wail—howl their grief and anger like Anna—scream themselves into peaceful oblivion. But that would change nothing. Where were they to go from here? More than one of these hardened dragoons swiped an errant tear, fighting to maintain proper British dignity. But one or two, as Anna's anguished wailing continued echoing throughout the campsite, gave in to racking sobs; 'protocol be damned'!

Tears tracked the sharp planes of her dark, angular cheeks as she stuffed a few items into a blanket satchel. She must return to her Cherokee Bird Clan—to her former life.

Life? Can there ever be life without my Kathryn?

She felt as if she were suffocating. Nothing mattered ... nothing.

Pausing a moment in packing, she stared morosely off into space. Abruptly her head snapped up, the final piece of clothing clutched in her hand slipping to the floor unnoticed. Drawing herself up to her full height, she slowly turned, listening intently, angling her head in an attempt to discern tiny changes she unexpectedly perceived: a shifting breath of air, the minutest sound, a tentative new *feeling*.

Ugilohi—Kathryn's presence drifted across her thoughts bringing a confused furrowing of her brow. Anna sensed her ... barely tangible ... yet her spirit lingered. Tilting her head in the opposite direction, she strained to *sense* the spirit, struggling to comprehend. *Yes!* Her essence was stronger now, nearer, and yet another presence: seeking ... searching ... crying out for its other half, its other self. *Could it be? Was I mistaken?*

Suddenly Gabriel's agonizing need slammed through her with pain so intense she gasped, his desperation overwhelming.

Kathryn lives ... she lives, a choked sob escaped as tears began anew.

Tossing her satchel aside, swiping tears absentmindedly, Anna knew what she must do. Ducking through the tent opening, she headed for Cook's wagon. They were coming in, and she must be ready. Cook would help. They must prepare warmed stones, fir bark and willow bark tea? No, that would not be strong enough for their pain. Black cherry: yes, that would do. There was much to be done and little time to waste.

As more battle weary dragoons drifted back into camp, some with minor injuries, some unhurt, a few slung over their saddles beyond all earthly woes, Anna stopped her feverish preparations, and regarded them thoughtfully. She felt Gabriel's approach, understood his desperation—these last stragglers must be gone. Their numbers were less now, many lost or dead. These remaining few would defend their colonel and his wife at all cost, of that she had no doubt. But a carelessly spoken word, heard by the wrong ears, could be deadly.

They stood in a quiet group talking in hushed whispers—confused, unsure. Where was Colonel Tarrington? Where was Kathryn? Lieutenant Jackson? Captain Hodges? To whom should they turn?

Anna stepped forward. *What words? What words?* Catching sight of Sergeant Tibbs, she gestured him to her. She had cured his dysentery just three weeks earlier, capturing his abiding faith and devotion. He would heed her.

"Go to Tarleton." She eyed him authoritatively. "He will know what to do. Go as a group, his surgeons will heal your wounds. I am needed elsewhere. Go now, and tell Tarleton I have sent you."

Tibbs nodded, gesturing to the others to get mounted as he eyed Anna, openly curious. However, the look she flashed made it obvious—she would brook no questions.

"God go with you, Anna ... with all of us," he choked.

Anna mouthed a soft blessing in Cherokee, and stood back watching as the men remounted and headed out of camp into the dusk ... for the last time.

Spatters of rain touched her cheek, drawing her attention.

I must hurry. She sensed them more strongly. *They are near.*

With a last glance at the retreating dragoons, she pulled her cloak more tightly about her thin shoulders and headed towards Cook's wagon.

Chapter Two

Anna

"Live, Kathryn, live. I command it!" Gabriel had begged, coaxed, cajoled; now he commanded.

He hugged her close, relieved to feel the continued whisper of shallow breaths as he tugged his saddle blanket more securely around her.

She has not given up yet.

"You can do it, Kathryn. You may be Mrs. Tarrington now, but you will always be a MacLean. Never forget that; we are a stubborn, feisty lot. You said that yourself. Remember?" His voice faltered as the memories began to build.

"Your daughter needs you," he continued softly. "Your husband lives; *he* needs you. Even your brother, stubborn fool that he is, lives—and he, too, needs you. And Kathryn," his words caught on a barely controlled sob. "*I* need you."

Bending low, he kissed her forehead. "You have never been one to quit—not even when all the odds were stacked against you." He paused momentarily. "Do not begin now," he finished on an angry command.

Captain Hodges, although unable to detect his exact words, was well aware of all that transpired between Gabriel and his aunt's unconscious form. They very likely mimicked those he chanted incessantly to his colonel, and would continue to do so until they arrived at the dragoon encampment. Thank God, they were almost there. Darkness was closing in, and icy splats of rain were falling more steadily.

May Anna be ready for us … and have the incredible skills necessary.

Hodges mouthed a small prayer as he turned to speak quietly to Diablo. At his kind word, the big stallion moved closer and snuffled softly against his master's leg. Without being told, he then obediently moved back into his paced step.

Shaking his head, a grim smile crossed the captain's lips at the animal's incredible devotion.

"Just over the next rise," he raised his voice for Gabriel's hearing and was greeted with an answering nod.

Gabriel reined to a stop beside Anna's tent. Although situated far at the back of the dragoon encampment, the young lieutenant found it with ease, his familiarity with their camp, not surprising.

Captain Hodges admired the astute, young lieutenant in many ways, especially his handling of this dire situation. His unwavering composure, a quality rarely possessed by one so young, was admirable. But again, this fact came as no surprise; many of his abilities so very like … *Kathryn's.*

Hodges eyed him with interest, taking careful note of Gabriel's strength and agility as he stepped down from his horse, unassisted, while carefully cradling Kathryn's limp frame tenderly against his chest. As she was built long and lean, not a small woman, it was not an easy feat to accomplish, and he was impressed.

For a brief moment, he contemplated attempting the same with his commanding officer, a fleeting thought immediately dashed. Placing his colonel at risk of further injury merely to assuage his need for a show of bravado, would be an unconscionable act.

His moment of self-reproach was quickly relieved as Corporal Simms and Sergeant Newcombe dismounted and came to his side; the latter giving wide berth to Diablo. But other than flattening his ears and snorting, the black stallion made no threatening moves, allowing the dragoons to continue assisting his fallen master.

Without warning, Anna stepped from the tent, gesturing curtly for them to enter.

"Come in quickly," she said sharply. "Do not allow the warmth to escape. Place Kathryn there." She indicated a spot to Gabriel. "And you, Captain, place my colonel there." She pointed to an adjoining pile of blankets. "Where they may see each other if they awaken."

In the well-lighted interior of the tent, Gabriel noticed several buckets of hot steaming water, bunches of herbs, jars of pulpy, mashed fir bark and piles of cloth bandaging, all placed for easy accessibility. Anna had known—as he knew she would—and was ready.

As he gently lowered Kathryn, the rising heat of warmed stones reached out in welcoming comfort to her. A slight groan escaped as her body touched the warmth, her eyes flickering open momentarily, and then closing once more as her head lolled sideways.

Anna was immediately at her side, nudging Gabriel out of the way so as to examine Kathryn's injuries. Her barely concealed gasp left no doubt as to their severity. But he dared not phrase any questions, just looked on in worried silence.

Rising, Anna moved to the colonel's side. After a few moments of gentle probing, during which his eyes flickered open but immediately shut, she turned to Gabriel.

"You and Captain Hodges help the colonel. His wounds are severe, but I have taught you both well. I must help my Ugilohi, she is ..." her voice trailed into silence as she moved back to Kathryn's side.

As she began sponging the puddled blood from her chest, she spoke over her shoulder to Simms and Newcombe.

"Go to Cook's wagon. Tell him: bring all that is ready; make haste." She gestured curtly.

Within minutes, Cook entered quietly, his hands full of dripping poultices and strips of clean linen. But as his eyes fell upon the gaping wound in Kathryn's chest, a sob caught at the back of his throat and tears sprang forth.

"No time for tears or all will be lost," Anna growled, continuing angry words in Cherokee, returning to English at Cook's obvious confusion and hurt look. "Go now; bring the rest I requested." Her voice softened as she nodded encouragement to the grieving man.

Without further admonition, Cook set his supplies carefully beside Anna, gulped softly, turned and rushed from the tent.

Anna worked feverishly, alternately coaxing and commanding Kathryn to fight for her life: partially in English, a great deal in Cherokee. On and on, incessantly she alternated between crooning unintelligible words and garbled chanting.

Gabriel eyed Captain Hodges as the two worked together tending the colonel's many wounds. They had questions; both needing answers, but neither was fool enough to make a sound until Anna was ready. Only Anna could determine that moment, and it was a long time in coming.

"I have sent the dragoons to Tarleton." Anna finally started to speak.

Although addressing them, she did not turn, her eyes never leaving Kathryn's inert form.

"Too many eyes, too many wagging tongues." She paused, deep in thought, before continuing. "Cook is to be trusted. Besides, he refused to go."

As she turned to face them, a slight smile lifted the corners of her mouth at the remembrance of having strongly suggested he leave once the preparations had been made—and his stubborn retort that 'she would have to kill him first'.

"We need his help." She eyed Gabriel and then Hodges. "His size and strength alone will move them without further danger and—he knows his wagon team." Both men nodded agreement.

"What of Gabrielle and Lieutenant Jackson?" Gabriel asked sharply, concerned and unable to await Anna's slowly forthcoming explanations.

For a brief second, she eyed Gabriel confrontationally. But he met her glare with an equally icy one of his own, making her proud.

"They are gone—seeking safety. He is distraught, but in control, I believe," she added quickly, seeing the anxious expression on his face. "Gabrielle is confused, frightened. Beauty will help them both."

"Do you know where he will go?" Captain Hodges asked.

"Perhaps to Cornwallis, there is no time to think on that now," Anna stated with finality as she once again turned full attention to Kathryn.

She gently finished the final bandaging and covered her with warm blankets. Eyeing the roof of the tent with disgust, she moved to make final adjustments to the colonel's wounds, pleased to discover the two men's abilities had served him well.

"Rain, harrumph!" she grumbled. "We must move them quickly. I sense a heavy storm coming in."

At both men's questioning stare, she replied, "We must move them to Cherokee country. If they survive ..."

She quickly amended what she had been about to say.

"They *will* survive the journey and have a chance to mend their wounds. Soaring Eagle will work his magic with their mindset. And your beautiful Silver Fox," she regarded Gabriel warmly, "has the heart and hands of a true healer. Together we will mend their torn bodies and tormented souls."

When neither man spoke, she reiterated: "There is no safety here—you both know the danger. This is their only chance." She inhaled a deep breath and slowly released it. "And when they are well, they will find their daughter ... my precious little bird."

With an abrupt wave of her arm, she gestured them out of her tent.

"Now go! Do as I bid you. Tell Cook we are ready."

Gabriel sent Hodges a long, silent look before glancing back to Anna. With respectful nods, they pushed aside the tent flap and headed out into the rain to fulfill her orders.

Chapter Three

Lord Cornwallis

Rain pounded upon the flimsy material of the tent, rushing off the canvas roof in torrents—filling crudely dug trenches to overflowing—red mud seeping ceaselessly under sagging sides of the hurriedly erected shelter, as a steady drip plopped a slow, monotonous splat into a bucket in the center of the confined structure.

Lord Cornwallis sat with shoulders slumped, watching in morose concentration. His was one of the few tents left, after he had burned all excess supplies last week in an effort to travel light and fast. He had chased the elusive Nathanael Greene—or so he had thought at the time—in an attempt to corner his ragtag army and trounce them soundly. What with the disasters at Cowpens and King's Mountain, he had needed that decisive win. But Greene, that wily son-of-a-bitch, had set an exhausting pace, luring him ever onward into a cleverly sprung trap of his own.

Cornwallis sank more deeply into his misery, his mind reliving the debacle over and over. His well thought out plan had held all the earmarks of a much-needed success, or so it had seemed. But that was not to be. He had been forced to turn his own artillery and fire into the masses, spewing deadly grapeshot in a killing spree. Yes, he had been the victor at Guilford Courthouse—at least technically. But what a savage price to pay—for grapeshot had no conscience. It killed indiscriminately, taking down everything and everyone in its path.

He shivered with a deep, bone-rattling chill caused by far more than the raw weather that howled outside. Hunkering down on his cot, he pulled a damp blanket around his shoulders. But even exhaustion would not allow him to sink into the peaceful oblivion of sleep he so desperately sought. The incessant pounding of driving rain set up a cadence reminiscent of a funeral dirge, and he grimaced.

So many good men lost, both Colonel Tarrington and Kathryn. He swallowed convulsively, trying desperately to force the memory of their torn bodies to the back of his mind. He knew beyond doubt, the grapeshot had been their undoing ... and *he* had ordered it. He had killed them as surely as if he had lit the fuse himself. Jason and Kathryn: an incredible team with unbelievable passion for their cause—and each other.

He wrung his hands wishing he had a drink—but remembered somewhat ruefully, he had ordered all rum casks smashed on the trail, to hasten their forced march. Suddenly he recalled a flask he had secreted away in his saddlebags. Rising somewhat unsteadily, he searched frantically, finally locating his bag in the corner of the tent. Rummaging through the sodden, leather satchel, he found what he sought, unscrewed the cap, and without hesitation, gulped the fiery liquid. Its burning warmth sent an immediate flush to his face and heat to his belly. He took another deep swallow, more slowly this time, enjoying the immediate sense of calm and relaxation that it brought—albeit false. But he needed that right now.

What am I to do?

Tarleton had become less and less effective. Colonel Tarrington, on the other hand was, *had been* he corrected himself, a powerhouse. And Kathryn: what an incredible woman.

His hand shook as he brought the flask once again to his lips.

What of their child, Gabrielle?

He had promised that he would keep her safe. But, in all reality, could he?

Where is she? What must I do for final arrangements for Kathryn and Jason? Should they be laid to rest here ... together? Or should I try to send them back to England to the colonel's family?

As to his once magnificent army, only fourteen hundred men were left: tired, hungry, almost without ammunition. There was no answer but to turn towards Wilmington, where supplies would be waiting and he could regroup once again. But it was almost a three-week march from here.

His head began to pound. He took another swig from the flask.

What in hell will Nathanael Greene do next—that elusive bastard? Will he head south to attack Rawdon and try to reclaim Camden for the rebel colonials?

Camden was the last hold the British had in the South. All had begun so well. What had happened?

Cornwallis felt sick at heart. If he turned south and went to Rawdon's aid in his presently weakened state, all could be lost. The war would then be over, much to King George's distress.

No. Rawdon will have to handle the situation by himself.

If Rawdon was successful in taking Greene's army, then Cornwallis would not have been needed after all. And if Rawdon lost ... *ah well.*

Better that I be the one to put myself in a position to bring the South down hard.

And Cornwallis knew he could accomplish that feat if he continued northwards and attacked the supply depots in Virginia. If he destroyed their supply line, he could virtually bring the southern colonies to their knees; the rest would then follow in short order.

With another swig from his flask, he began to pace. He needed to be able to think clearly, to sort it all out. However, that, he would do on the morrow. Tonight he wanted only to be numb, senseless, to feel no pain. Draining the last of the flask, he lay down on his cot, and pulling a blanket snuggly around him, dropped into an agitated slumber.

***

Lieutenant Jackson clutched Gabrielle's small form closer. Feeling her shivering, he wrapped her more securely within his coat: a rebel greatcoat that would have to be abandoned in favor of his bright red dragoon jacket once he neared Lord Cornwallis's camp.

God, how I pray his lordship remained close at hand after the battle. He must still be there ... must be.

Greene's troops had retreated by now, of that he was sure. But he still needed to be extremely careful, and avoid meeting any of Jamie's straggling rebel militia. They would kill him without hesitation once they realized he was not one of them. The very British cut of his attire beneath Gabriel's greatcoat, and Beauty's harnessing were a dead give away. Perhaps Gabrielle would be spared, but only if Gabriel heard of their capture ... and could intervene on her behalf.

He must get to his lordship, must get papers granting both of them amnesty to board a ship and escape this repugnant land that had destroyed all he had ever truly loved ... all except Gabrielle. At least he still had this beautiful child and his memories.

Perhaps, the memories will eventually provide ease to my sorrow or I shall go mad. But there was no time to think of that now.

A violent shiver instantly drew his attention to Gabrielle, her raven curls now slicked and clinging from rain that fell ever more insistently. Gently stroking her hair, he murmured encouragement. As his eyes lifted to the roiling clouds gathering strength in the encroaching darkness, he realized it would not be long now, a Carolina deluge was building. He must find shelter immediately.

"Hush, my little princess. Hush, little one. You are safe. I will not allow anything to harm you," he whispered in a tone he hoped sounded confident.

Oh, how I wish ... If only ... I could do nothing to help your parents, but I will not fail you.

He brushed a kiss to the top of her head. Her uncontrollable sobs had reduced to a soft snuffling, her drooping shoulders evidence of her exhaustion.

What am I to do? Anna, Anna, how could you not have told me? Or at least warned me? Kathryn, my beloved Kathryn ... why? But he knew the answer. Kathryn and Jason: so passionate, so driven to succeed. All they had fought for ... died for. A sob caught at the back of his throat as tears began anew.

Suddenly images of the horrendous devastation ballooned in his mind. He relived the fearful roar of artillery as grapeshot pelted their midst.

Our own guns, for God's sake! What was Cornwallis thinking?

Kathryn and Jason, their battered forms lying close, peaceful in death, their beautiful Celtic wedding bands displayed so proudly in life ... now glinting on lifeless fingers in the dying light of a late spring afternoon.

With a ragged sob, he forced himself to focus on finding a solution for his immediate plight. Now was not the time to dwell on sorrow. There would be plenty of time for that later. Leaning protectively over Gabrielle, attempting to shelter her from the steadily pouring rain, he murmured a quiet promise.

"I will not fail you, little one," and small arms hugged him close in answer.

Rain began pummeling harder as he hunkered lower over Beauty's withers, urging her gently to make haste. Despite her confusion and sense of loss, Kathryn's beloved, little mare leaned into the storm, obeying Lieutenant Jackson's instructions without hesitation.

***

"General—General Cornwallis."

A loud, distressed voice pierced his troubled sleep.

Rolling over, ignoring the grating sound, he pulled his blanket tighter, chilled despite the quantity of alcohol he had consumed earlier.

"Your Lordship—General. I must talk to you." The tent flap raised as a rain soaked head thrust its way inside.

"For the love of God—quiet, man!" Cornwallis thundered, grimacing as throbbing pain pounded across his forehead.

"But your Lordship ..."

With grudging effort and a muffled curse, he rolled to face the intruder. Groaning, he swung his legs slowly over the edge of the cot. Forcing himself into an upright position, he raked a shaky hand back through his still damp hair.

"What in God's name could be so blasted important that you wake me from a sound sleep on such a godforsaken night?" he demanded.

"There is a man requesting—no, demanding to see you, your Lordship," the young corporal stammered.

Having stepped fully inside the tent, at risk of facing the formidable wrath of his commander he hesitated, suddenly bewildered, distinctly uncomfortable and eager to be gone.

Cornwallis pierced the young corporal with an icy glare.

"Tell whomever it is that I am occupied. I have no desire, *or need*, to speak with anyone on this dreary night. Send him away!"

"But, sir," he continued doggedly, "He has a young child with him, rather wet and cold, and bids me show you this."

He thrust a small wooden horse with the grimy remnants of a blue ribbon towards his lordship.

The general's eyes went wide, his face draining of all color. He would know that toy horse anywhere—had seen it so many times over the last few months clutched tightly in a pair of small hands.

"Bring them in quickly, Corporal. Not one word to anyone or you will draw your last breath tonight. Do I make myself absolutely clear?" Without waiting for an answer he added, "And bring whatever is available: hot broth, tea—anything providing warmth and sustenance. Be quick about it!"

With a clipped nod and pledge to silence, the corporal ducked under the tent flap and disappeared into the storm.

Within moments, puddles of water spilled inside as the flap lifted once again, and a tall man stepped into the dim light clutching a bedraggled child to his chest. Lieutenant Jackson, pale and drenched to the bone, faced Cornwallis eyeing him in silence. A tiny sob escaped as Gabrielle twisted in Jack's arms to face the general.

"Grampa," she hiccupped, reaching a small hand out to touch him.

Cornwallis stifled a gasp and lurched to his feet—stone cold sober.

"Gabrielle," he rasped, taking her into his arms and clutching her to him. Cupping her sodden curls, he hugged her with a light kiss, leaned back to look at her, and hugged her again.

He held her gently as she buried her face against his chest and cried, murmuring her parents' names broken-heartedly. And he could say nothing … nothing that could possibly begin to explain, or make things right.

"Your Lordship …" Cornwallis's young corporal poked his head cautiously into the tent, bravely interrupting once more.

"I will not be interrupted again, Corporal," Cornwallis growled at the thoroughly abashed young man as he quickly backed out into the pouring rain.

But before the tent flap could drop down into the oozing mud, a dripping hand flung it aside, and Banastre Tarleton stepped in, water puddling at his feet, rain beading the bright red wool of his jacket. His long hair, always dressed to perfection, clung in sodden plaits, and his habitually arrogant, smiling face had settled into grim lines of annoyance.

Swiping disgustedly at the heavy droplets that rolled reluctantly to the floor, he stood amidst a growing puddle of muddy water, his customarily immaculate uniform drenched and hanging slightly askew, his typical arrogance momentarily dashed as he digested the sorrowful scene before him.

Despite the dim light, Lord Cornwallis's pallor was obvious, emotional devastation overpowering his usually stoic features. He seemed a broken man as he sat holding a bedraggled little girl.

Gabrielle? Tarleton looked more closely at the disheveled child. Yes, Gabrielle. *My God, she is still alive.*

Banastre cleared his throat loudly, his eyes narrowing as he continued to take in the dismal scene. Gabrielle sat quietly on the general's lap, observing him in silence, her sad face conveying a look of hope as she gazed up at the dragoon colonel.

Lord Cornwallis rose slowly, cursing softly as he set the little girl on his cot and turned to face his officer.

"Whatever it is that brought you here tonight can wait, Tarleton." He gestured curtly towards the tent flap, ushering the irritating man out.

"I think not, your Lordship." Banastre stood his ground with cool confidence. The firm edge to his voice grabbed the earl's attention causing him to become silent, and raise a questioning eyebrow.

"I think perhaps *it* cannot wait. Time is valuable and of the essence."

Turning to face Lieutenant Jackson, he silently observed the man's fraught countenance for a long moment, before crouching down and extending a hand towards Gabrielle. Large eyes watched him—scrutinizing with a maturity far beyond her years—her recently shed tears still glistening on dark lashes as she stifled a sob.

Jack observed Tarleton warily, as Gabrielle, somewhat unsure of herself, hesitated before gathering her courage and going to him.

"So like your mother," he breathed, his hand extending to touch a damp curl.

Suddenly the glint from the gold necklace at her throat caught his eye, the beautiful pearl centered within a delicate golden heart that he recognized so well. Fingering it gently, he peered into crisp, blue eyes that held his gaze without faltering. Abruptly her small hand moved to protect it as she continued to eye him—judging him—so very like her mother. *So very like Kathryn.*

"Precious child," he murmured, hugging her to him, brushing a kiss to her forehead. A muscle twitched along the edge of his jaw, and Jack perceived the tiniest wince.

Allowing himself a moment of weakness, Banastre gently hugged Gabrielle to him, caressing her black, curly hair, savoring the smell and feel of her—surrendering to the memories of Kathryn. He felt no shame at this temporary departure from his normal icy control. Kathryn would have understood, and would never have ridiculed or betrayed him to fellow officers. She had protected him once before, not so long ago, when he had grieved uncontrollably over his friend Ferguson's death at King's Mountain.

Yes, Kathryn would understand.

Cornwallis watched in dumbstruck silence. This cruel man, branded 'butcher' for his callous violence, actually did have a very human side. But before he could think longer on that revelation, Banastre abruptly stood and turned to him.

"I believe, sir, I may be of some help." Not allowing his lordship to interrupt, he rushed on, once again in full control. "It is imperative we move quickly before the rebels, or God forbid even our very own, discover the colonel's daughter is alive and decide to make a coin or two on that discovery."

"Lieutenant," he stated curtly, abruptly turning to scrutinize the distressed man. "Do not eye me so balefully. It would seem you have no alternative *but* to trust me." Piercing him with an icy glare, he added, "As far as I can see, you have no one else to turn to. However," he softened his tone a bit, "if it makes you feel any better, and helps in your decision, I also respected Colonel Tarrington—and I owe Kathryn a favor."

Squaring his shoulders, Jackson advanced angrily towards Tarleton, incensed with his overly familiar use of her name.

"How dare you?" he spat.

"Because," Tarleton interrupted in his liquid honey voice, "contrary to popular belief, I do genuinely care … in this instance, at least."

Jack regarded Tarleton through tear-swollen eyes, struggling to decide, knowing he must trust someone. Time, so terribly important to Gabrielle's safety, was rapidly becoming their enemy.

Oh, Jason, Kathryn. Help me make the correct decision.

"Well, Lieutenant?" The sharp edge retuned to Tarleton's voice, betraying his own distress. "What will it be?"

He eyed Lieutenant Jackson, but reached to tousle Gabrielle's black curls, suddenly crouching down to her level.

"It will be all right, little one," he said quietly as he ran a single finger down the contour of her cheek. His comforting smile held compassion and—perhaps even trustworthiness.

"Can you find us a ship, Tarleton?" Jack asked, realizing this would be their only chance.

Aware that an escape route to the sea had been planned by Cornwallis during their recent march northwards, he assumed at least one ship should be ready and waiting on the coast. As his lordship had voiced no suggestions, or objections, he too must feel their wellbeing depended on this man's abilities. Perhaps, after all, Banastre's self-assured audacity was perfect for this situation. Jack remained deep in thought, the continued silence stretching out between them.

"Well?" Tarleton pushed—more gently this time.

"Do you know the status of our ships, Banastre?" Cornwallis interrupted, suddenly pulling himself up from his chair and moving closer. He was well aware of the man's questionable talents, Banastre usually having 'connections' where least expected—and when most needed.

"Commander Clinton and I have not spoken recently on the escape route," Cornwallis continued without waiting for his officer's answer. "However, all earlier conversations promised the presence of one or more vessels if needed. I shall draw up any letters of introduction necessary to carry them safely away from here. No eyebrows will be raised or questions asked."

He paused to take a deep breath, raising a hand to indicate he had not yet finished.

"I will then march the rest of my army to Yorktown and set up a center of action there. The fate of our cause now rests on my shoulders. You shall join our troops there when all is finished here."

He eyed Tarleton sternly and received a polite nod of agreement.

"All is not yet lost. If this damnable rain stops, we will be on the move early tomorrow. But Lieutenant Jackson and Gabrielle must be far from here at that time."

"They will be, sir. I have allies—friends."

"You must make arrangements for Beauty, too," Jack broke his silence.

"For Christ's sake, Lieutenant, she is merely a horse."

But those words rang hollow even to Tarleton. He knew how much Kathryn had loved the animal, knew of the mare's devotion to her. He remembered a rumor from long ago: when she had begged the colonel to take her life … but care well for her mare. He was unsure as to exactly how that interesting tidbit had ever surfaced, knowing the colonel would have protected her in a shroud of silence if at all possible.

He eyed the lieutenant's anxious face, hesitating another moment as he made his decision.

"It will take me a bit longer." He grimaced, shaking his head. "Be ready the moment I send for you—within the next hour."

Cornwallis noticed a distinct brittle edge to his voice. Was it to keep Jackson calm, or to keep himself from thinking too much and perhaps caring? Cornwallis was unsure, but he appraised the man more sharply, giving him the benefit of the doubt.

Banastre turned and headed for the tent flap. But a tug on his pant leg brought him to an abrupt stop. Looking down, his breath caught at the back of his throat. In the lamplight, Gabrielle's upturned face was illuminated: *Kathryn in miniature*. Her daughter, so very like her, yet carrying her father's raven hair and piercing blue eyes.

"Please, for momma." Frightened eyes pleaded.

Stooping quickly, he picked her up hugging her to him. With a last embrace, he set her down carefully and tousled her hair.

"For *you*, little one."

With a curt nod to Lieutenant Jackson, he spun on his heel and exited the tent. But not before Jack saw the unusual shimmer of his eyes and knew—the heartless bastard did actually have feelings. He would be good to his word, of that Jack was sure. He had loved Kathryn in his own way too.

"Where will you go, Lieutenant?" his lordship questioned softly.

Jack turned to face him. "To England, sir, my sister will welcome us with open arms."

"You must write. Keep me abreast of your plans. This war will not last forever. When I return home I shall wish to see how you both fare."

Jack nodded absently in answer, turning at a sudden sound. The corporal had stepped in quietly while they were talking. There was now a large bowl of steaming soup and hot tea on the general's small side table. With a nod from his lordship, Jack set to helping Gabrielle. There was little time now.

"Lieutenant," Cornwallis pulled him off to one side once Gabrielle was engaged in eating. "What of Kathryn and Jason?"

"Her nephew is caring for them. He is a good man and can be trusted. He will lay them to rest at her brother's farm."

"That is unacceptable. I will send a troop ..."

"No, your Lordship," Jack boldly interrupted. "Despite his rebel convictions, he was dedicated to Kathryn and respected the colonel. They are together, finally at peace. I beg of you, sir, let it be—for their child's sake, for my sake—for all of our sakes."

Cornwallis remained silent digesting this information.

"All right, Lieutenant." He nodded agreement. "Now, hasten quickly and take a bit of refreshment while I draft the necessary paperwork. It will be a long ride, and perhaps some time before you again taste warm food. Eat up; you must be ready to leave at a moment's notice. If I know Tarleton, *and I do*, he will return shortly. He will not want to be kept waiting as his patience is—somewhat lacking."

With that admonition, he nudged Jack towards the cot where Gabrielle sat dutifully sipping her hot broth. Moving to his side table, he opened a small drawer, and fishing out paper and pen, began to write in his bold, concise hand.

Gabrielle wriggled sideways allowing her 'Uncle Jack' enough space to sit down. With unusually steady hands, she offered him her still warm soup. The tiniest smile lifted the corner of her lips as she urged him to accept it.

If this little one has the courage to go on, then so must I.

Jack accepted the bowl she offered and returned her smile with a somewhat forced grin. He sipped the tasty broth, tentatively at first. But finding its warmth restorative, began eating in earnest.

Our fate now lies in Tarleton's hands—of all people. I wonder if Kathryn would be amused. No, more likely horrified. Ah well, the die is cast, little one.

At this point, Jack silenced all thoughts and proceeded to refill their bowls once again. They must not keep Tarleton waiting.

***

Lieutenant Jackson eyed the proud, little ship where it sat rocking in the dark, storm tossed water, tugging with angry vengeance at the taut rope lines securing it to the dock. To Jack, it seemed the sturdy vessel bumped the pier in a monotonous thumping, reminiscent of a demented soul pounding its ceaseless torment against an unmovable wall … and he could relate to that. But for his tremendous responsibility and lack of time, that could have been him.

Such a sleek, fast vessel, this must have required some strings being pulled. Tarleton, you never cease to amaze me. With a fair wind, we should be in England within three to four months time—maybe less.

Good to his word, Tarleton had returned within the hour. Issuing instructions at a staccato tempo, he paced impatiently, outlining his arrangements to Cornwallis.

Somehow they had survived the arduous journey. And here they stood, in the spitting rain, facing the beginnings of a new life with much trepidation. The trip had been strenuous, pushing onward at a relentless pace that left Jack and Tarleton short-tempered and snapping at each other, when not glowering in silence. There had been no time to think of anything, thank God, but survival.

Gabrielle's spirits actually lifted once they had gotten under way. It seemed a new kind of adventure to her, something she relished, so very like her mother. But here at dockside, after long days of endless riding, bone-chilling weather and a gnawing hunger in the pit of her belly, even her spirits were greatly diminished.

Beauty's exhaustion was also apparent. Jack's additional weight had provided an unaccustomed burden, and she was bone weary. Her usually spirited prancing had long since been reduced to resolute plodding, sheer will power pushing her doggedly onwards. Her head hung dejectedly, her once sparkling eyes now lackluster.

Jack leaned forward and patted Beauty's rain-slicked neck, murmuring a few words of encouragement and thanks, telling her their flight was now at an end. With a rattle of her harnessing, she bobbed her head, ears immediately pricking. This indomitable little creature would go further if urged. She would do whatever was requested of her.

Jackson dismounted somewhat unsteadily, the long hours in the saddle having left his legs cramped and a bit shaky. Turning, he extended his arms up to receive the exhausted, little girl as she slid limply down to him.

At Tarleton's curt instructions, he stepped tentatively onto the gangplank behind the man, glancing furtively to either side as he leaned into the steep assent. As Gabrielle uttered a muffled whimper, he clutched her tighter to his chest.

Do not betray us now, Tarleton, he prayed, suddenly unsure of why he had trusted this man in the first place. *Can a viper ever truly change?*

Whatever the answer, it was way too late to back out now. With a dubious shake of his head and a grim look of resolution, Jack lifted his eyes to the murky skies and forged purposefully up the gangplank.

Chapter Four

Creating Perfect Balance

Inadvertent jostling, as she was placed on a raised palette in Anna's lodging, sent shards of excruciating pain shattering throughout her chest, rousing her to semi-consciousness. She tried vaguely, to comprehend the devastating thoughts circling in her mind.

All is gone: Jason, my heart and soul; nothing is left ... nothing.

Her mewling whimper ceased as familiar sounds insinuated hazily upon her limited sensibilities. The comforting drone of chanting, familiar beat of leather-skinned drums and clattering hollow gourds relentlessly pulsing, building to a crescendo: *so familiar, welcoming, strangely comforting* ... calling her back home.

How odd. The chanting spoke of happiness and life ... *not of death.* Her mind swam.

But what of Jason? I saw him die ... and yet they sing of life.

Encouraging rhythmic sounds pounded over and over, urging her: *awake ... awake.* Incense wafting its heavy sweetness enveloped her, and though drifting in semi-awareness, she instinctively inhaled deeply.

"Focus, Kathryn, focus."

She heard the command and struggled to comply.

Reality ... or fleeting recollection of Jack's instructions as Gabrielle struggled to ...? Gabrielle? Jack? I must find you. Jason, my love, you promised me. Where are you?

A wave of unbearable pain sliced through her, dispersing all cohesive thoughts. Relinquishing her tentative grip on consciousness, she slipped back into shielding oblivion, blocking the dreadful reality surrounding her.

For days, Kathryn clung tenaciously to life as Anna worked tirelessly to heal her torn flesh. But of far greater concern ... a need to alleviate her emotional devastation. The trauma of believing her beloved husband dead, held greater threat than the insidious wound. Anna understood the necessity of bringing Kathryn's mind and body into perfect harmony to achieve full recovery: the ideal person to manage her spiritual healing—only Soaring Eagle.

While Anna tended her bodily injuries, Soaring Eagle labored long hours to mend Kathryn's distraught spirit. The deep resonance of his eloquent chanting drifted incessantly throughout the campsite conveying his message: *Live. Be at one with life.*

Over and over, virtually nonstop, he encouraged, cajoled, and at times loudly demanded, she not surrender to the peaceful void of death. That would be unacceptable, the way of a coward. Well aware of this brave woman's stubborn resilience, he was certain his taunting message would somehow penetrate her self-protective cocoon and spark renewed awareness.

Seemingly endless hours passed before Soaring Eagle paused in chanting to relieve his parched throat. As he sat sipping cool water, quietly watching her pale features for any sign of awakening, his thoughts drifted back to a day long ago when he and Kathryn had faced one another in a 'blood vengeance'.

He had purposefully hunted her down attempting to destroy her, and in so doing, honor his younger brother, slain in the prime of life by a British officer. He had loved Black Raven despite his hot-headed tantrums, and refused to acknowledge that in his drunkenness that day, he had brought premature death upon himself. At the time, Kathryn had been his wife. And although his physical abuses to her were common knowledge, he had looked the other way, a fact which now filled him with unremitting guilt.

Soaring Eagle vividly recalled biding his time—patiently planning, plotting obsessively. Eventually, he had lured her into a position whereby success—killing both her and her British husband—seemed assured, perhaps their child as well. For that was his familial obligation to his brother's memory.

But Kathryn had bravely met him face on, besting him before his warriors, who, as instructed—had looked on impassively. As was her right, she refused to take his life, demanding only that he end the 'blood vengeance'. Having injured him gravely, she allowed him time to mend, requesting only that he send Anna to her, when *his* physical danger had passed.

No, he had nothing but respect for this bold, out-spoken woman. He would do all within his power to heal her grief-stricken mind. He had much he wished to discuss once she was restored to full wellness. After all, she was the adored aunt of his son-in-law, Gabriel, husband of his first-born girl child, Silver Fox.

Kathryn is now family, a thought which pleased him.

Clearing his throat to resume chanting, he made a quick decision. When Kathryn's British husband recovered, he would befriend him. The colonel was a respected warrior chief of his people, renowned for his abilities in battle. Together, they had forged a formidable team, and he wished to understand the key to their success.

Perhaps, in time, he would comprehend the complex mind of the white man, for all was not as they would have him believe on the surface. Too many promises had already been broken, neither side speaking the complete truth. He was neither an ignorant man nor a simple fool; the future did not bode well for the Cherokee nation. With a young grandson to consider and another grandchild on the way, he wished to be prepared.

Anna leaned closer, cocking her head to catch the soft puffs of Kathryn's shallow breathing. She feared Kathryn's mental and physical agony to be almost more than humanly possible to bear. For hours she talked incessantly, occasionally slipping into her native Cherokee: beautiful words of encouragement, conveying her innermost thoughts, knowing if any could penetrate Kathryn's tortured mind … these would.

Anna worked resolutely for three days straight, refusing all food and rest, but finally, with Gabriel's persistent nagging, accepted a small amount of water. He remained nearby, occasionally napping fitfully, but ever ready to refresh supplies or tend wounds. His wife was large with their second child, concerning him sorely. But Silver Fox, imbued with the same dogged determination that sustained Anna, would not be denied her healing abilities—especially for Kathryn.

With Anna's continued prodding, and realizing the need to dispel any suspicions as to his whereabouts, Gabriel reluctantly left the Cherokee village, just long enough to check on his father's welfare. Although heartened to discover his injuries were slowly beginning to heal, his precarious mental state was of far greater concern. For with each brief visit in the days following the battle at Guilford Courthouse, he found Jamie grieving inconsolably for his lost '*baby*' sister: a grief that grew like a festering sore, increasing with each passing day.

Despite his concern, Gabriel experienced a modicum of relief. His father—so entangled in a self-pitying abyss of despair—barely noticed his son's comings and goings, and rarely questioned the length of time between visits.

There will be a day of reckoning when Kathryn is healed, he realized, blocking all other possibilities despite the gravity of her condition. And when that time arrived, he would have a difficult decision to make.

What will I tell my father? Can he be trusted not to betray them? Or will his mind lose its precarious grip on sanity before ...?

Shortly after their arrival, once Kathryn and Jason had been carefully settled on heated pallets within the safety of the Cherokee compound, Captain Hodges confronted Anna. Insisting loudly and vehemently, that he intended to remain in the Cherokee village with his colonel and 'Lady Kathryn', he faced her squarely with angry eyes and a stubborn, jutting chin; his typically quiet demeanor all but abandoned in his intense grief.

With a knowing look, Anna forgave his impertinence, but forbade him entrance. Out of respect for his sorrow, she allowed him a few moments of discussion. Then, with a promise of admission as soon as she deemed it safe, she turned abruptly and ducked inside, leaving him hovering nearby, quietly wringing his hands.

For two days he remained directly outside her lodge, barely eating—constantly pacing—while within, as she continued her feverish ministrations, Anna shook her head, grimacing. The constant plodding of his footsteps pacing back and forth—back and forth was ...

Mumbling strong epithets under her breath, she rose and stepped outside, quickly dropping the flap behind her to retain the warmth within.

"This accomplishes nothing," she spat. "I have done all within my earthly powers. Their destiny now lies in the hands of the Great Spirit ... and within their fierce, passionate hearts."

Her eyes locked on his, sending a wordless command: *time for you to leave.*

She was correct, as always, Hodges realized. He must locate Cornwallis's army, discover where Lieutenant Jackson had taken Gabrielle, and once assured of their safety, act as go-between both now, and in the future. There would be a future, for he refused to accept any alternative.

In truth, he wanted to be gone. He could no longer bear the few brief moments allowed him, watching Kathryn and Jason, once so vigorous and passionate, now lying pale and unresponsive side by side.

At Anna's quiet insistence, he conceded and packed his saddlebag.

"Go, now, Captain. Be eyes and ears, but no more," she warned. "You must be guardian of their secret. For they *will* live, of that I promise. Go, seek out Lieutenant Jackson. Find word of my precious little bird. Take your officers; swear them to silence."

She paused, narrowing her eyes in a warning look.

"If they are not to be trusted ..."

"They will say nothing. I give you that assurance, on my honor," he avowed. "If there is the slightest question, their lives will be forfeit; that I guarantee."

Following a few terse words with his junior officers, and a gentle pat to Diablo's long, sleek neck, Captain Hodges mounted his charger. With a quiet sigh and sorrowful glance backwards, he departed camp ... pledging himself to a silent promise.

In which direction would his lordship have headed? Hodges silently deliberated as he pressed ever northward alone. It had been several days since he bid farewell to Anna and two since parting with his men, cautioning them to hold fast to their oath of silence.

Cornwallis held the key to Lieutenant Jackson's passage to safety, of that he was sure. A dynamic man of power and influence who doted on Gabrielle ... *Yes, he would be the one Jackson had turned to—and he must be headed towards Yorktown.*

Control of the South, and a rapid end to the war, could be accomplished from that position if he moved with speed. And his lordship would never abandon such an ideal chance for recognition or glory.

Dusk fell as Hodges crossed the border into Virginia. His journey had been fast-paced and exhausting, but it was not much farther now. With an encouraging pat to his charger's sweat-slick neck, he leaned lower over its withers, and urged more speed from the huge beast.

***

"What of Kathryn and Colonel Tarrington?" Cornwallis asked curtly, breaking his stunned silence.

Hodges shook his head sadly, biting his lower lip.

"I do not know ..." he managed, momentarily choked-up. "They were alive when I left, your Lordship ... just barely. But to have survived the move from the battlefield is, in itself, beyond belief. Their stamina, sir, is incredible."

"What did I do to them?" Cornwallis's voice dropped to a barely audible whisper.

"It was a necessary action on your part, your Lordship. You need not ..."

"What did I do to them?" Cornwallis asked angrily, demanding truth—only truth.

"Their wounds were, are ..." Hodges faltered as the memories flooded back.

"Tell me, Captain, or you shall regret ..." Abruptly losing his composure, the general's face collapsed in grief.

"The colonel's wounds were taken mostly at the hands of the rebel militia leader: Kathryn's brother; extremely serious but not ..."

"What of Kathryn?" he interrupted impatiently.

"She took a severe wound to the chest, sir."

"Grapeshot?" he asked, but expected no answer—for he knew.

Tears leapt to his eyes as he faced the Loyalist captain apprehensively. But much to his relief, perceived only compassion, not accusation.

"Anna has created miracles before, sir, and she has assured me all will be well. She does have *the sight*," he added. "How else would she have known of our desperate need? She and Cook were ready when we arrived: blankets, medicine, bandaging, a small tent warmed with heated stones."

Cornwallis regarded him with sharp interest.

"And she made sure the campsite was deserted before we arrived: no prying eyes to jeopardize their ..."

"Ah, then it *was* Anna who sent the last stragglers to Tarleton," Cornwallis interrupted. "He claimed it so, but I often wonder at many of his statements."

He eyed the captain thoughtfully for a long moment.

"Then, at least there is hope. For that I am grateful, as it is far more than I have the right to ask. But you, Captain, are most likely tired and hungry. I suspect you have many questions, and perhaps I hold the answers you seek."

He placed his hand on Captain Hodges's shoulder and guided him to a small table.

"Come sit down, Captain. There are matters of great importance of which we must speak."

Chapter Five

Glimmer of Hope

Anna eyed the intricately woven Medicine Wheel hanging above Kathryn's inert form, taking careful note of Soaring Eagle's selection of feathers. *An excellent choice* she nodded, mouthing soft words of gratitude. The distinctive pattern of colors depicting the four segments of each day: the dark depths of night giving way to dawn, which then emerges into a new day, eventually yielding to twilight's cool indigo. *Cool.* She touched Kathryn's forehead, relieved to find her fever abating, and turned her gaze once again to the dangling talisman, a strong Medicine Wheel created with deep caring.

As the insidious fever finally lost its tenacious hold and began to recede, her coma slowly lifted, allowing fragments of reality to encroach upon the demons of her dementia. Flickering realities cascaded in her mind—slowly at first, then rapidly gaining momentum.

Kathryn floated in a hazy twilight of comprehension, often gripped by agonizing pain that threatened to crush her—yet at times eased—as she slipped in and out of fuzzy awareness. The black moments of terrifying horror occasionally receded, easing her torment but always returned.

Complete devastation: bloodshed, screaming horses wounded and dying, hundreds of soldiers—their torn bodies strewn carelessly, or staggering as grapeshot sprayed the battlefield indiscriminately. *My God, our own artillery!*

Jason … do not go … do not leave me! Her own tormented cries echoed in her ears.

Kathryn's eyes darted beneath her lids, a small cry escaping parched lips as the vicious kaleidoscope of images began to replay yet again: over and over.

Will it never end?

Another small cry, more piteous than the first, slipped into being.

Jason moved instantly to her side, reaching to grasp her hand where it lay limply on the blanket, his large hand cupping hers gently.

"For a moment I thought she would awaken. Something caught her attention."

Jason looked weakly towards Anna, hoping she would confirm his observations, or at least tell him he was slipping into fantasies and madness … finally succumbing to his own incredible grief.

How has my Kathryn survived this long? Can she find her way back?

For without her, he doubted he could go on.

Anna placed a gentle hand on his shoulder with an almost imperceptible nod.

"Soon Colonel, soon; she struggles to grasp reality, to chase the demons. Do not abandon her."

"Come to me, my Kathryn," he whispered, as he gently traced his fingers across the planes of her face.

He eyed the bright spots of color still lingering on her cheeks: telltale evidence of the fever which had gripped her mercilessly for days, but in the last few hours had lessened. She was cooler, he assured himself, and showed new awareness.

At Anna's nod, he edged aside allowing her to examine Kathryn more closely. His own strength still held precariously, threatening from moment to moment to abandon him. But he would do, or give, whatever his beloved wife needed. He would somehow find the strength.

Anna's knowledgeable hands skimmed over Kathryn's inert form, suddenly stopping and lingering. A smile lifted the corners of her mouth as she turned to Jason.

"Her slumber lightens; she will come back to us." Her hand paused over Kathryn's flat abdomen. "She carries new life, Colonel."

Jason's head snapped up. With a look of shocked horror, he stared at Anna, dumbfounded.

"No, she must not ..."

"Do not fear for her," she cut in. "It is a new life, barely begun, yet strong within her—so tiny it will take only what it requires to survive; not rob our Kathryn of the strength she will need to recover."

"But Kathryn never mentioned ..."

"She did not know. However, there *is* new life, of that I am sure," she said firmly. "She will struggle valiantly to live and return to you, Colonel ... but will fight like a lioness to protect your unborn child."

She pierced him with a commanding gaze.

"You must cast your sorrow aside and strive to regain your strength. Be strong for both of you, until she can reclaim her own vitality."

Placing her hand over his, she added, "She is frightened ... but does not yet realize."

Jason's brow wrinkled in confusion.

"When she awakens, her weakness will terrify her. However, I believe her greatest fear will be of losing you ..."

"Never," Jason cut her off, his voice stronger than it had been since that dreadful day at Guilford Courthouse.

Once again he turned full attention to his wife, coaxing and encouraging as he watched her chest slowly rise and fall, grateful for each and every shallow breath. But there was no further response.

"Kathryn ..." he rasped, his voice barely audible from continued exertion.

A hand came to rest lightly on his shoulder causing him to cast forlorn eyes upward.

Anna shook her head. "Enough for now, Colonel, you are weary and Ugilohi needs more time."

"But I thought ..." his pained expression bore witness to frustration and fatigue.

"Rest now."

Her stern look sent a silent command, daring him to refuse.

But his strength was done for the moment; no argument would be forthcoming. Grumbling under his breath, he moved to his cot, and within minutes dropped into an exhausted slumber.

Despair etched Jason's face as he slouched beside Kathryn, head hanging and arms dangling limply between his knees—scratching distractedly at a particularly bothersome spot on his leg.

He was barely beyond the merciless fever that had kept him muttering senselessly, half out of his mind for days, and despised the persistent weakness that dogged him. His wounds were finally beginning to heal, the itch of renewing flesh driving him to distraction and constant irritability.

And Kathryn ... how much more can she withstand? She is so near and yet, so distant. His own weakened state robbed him of all patience and understanding.

"When will she awaken?" he demanded of Anna as she moved to Kathryn's side and began dressing the deep, ugly wound in her chest.

"You are a healer, you must ..."

Low Cherokee epithets erupted as she speared him with an angry look, her tirade continuing for several lengthy sentences. Unwilling to dignify his cranky demands, she returned her attention to Kathryn, effectively dismissing him.

After eyeing her balefully for a long moment, he drew in a deep breath and began speaking with succinctly voiced irritation.

"Anna, I have often requested you speak in English when you curse me—in order that I may share your thoughts and better determine my response."

Anna concealed a grin, pleased at his mocking retort. *Yes, he will heal*, and with that surety she heaved a sigh of relief, for Kathryn would need his strength as well as her own.

"Well?" he grumbled, eyeing her confrontationally.

"I merely stated, Colonel, that you have the nasty temperament of a wild boar—and smell as badly."

With chin jutting, she shot him an undaunted look of defiance.

At his immediate affront she added, "It is time for you to take command. Kathryn needs that from you. You have indulged your grief long enough, making not even a feeble attempt to do otherwise. Bathe. Eat. Become strong."

Jason absorbed her angry tirade, taking heed of her sharp words. His pride was stung, but she spoke the truth. His hair *was* unkempt. He had not shaved for days, the grizzled result offensive even to himself. And yes, he had to admit, he did smell rather badly.

With a soft 'harrumph', he looked up, nodding in agreement.

"When you are done, bathe my Ugilohi. Your touch ... the intimacy will connect. She will respond in time. But *you* must have patience." She narrowed her eyes. "Talk to her. Convince her that you live, that you are not just a dream."

She held out a towel and strong soap, as well as colonial garments that she had obviously prepared for this moment. Her look dared him to argue, but he knew that to be useless; she would have the final word.

He rubbed his fingers over the rough muslin of the shirt; it would take some getting accustomed to. But perhaps not having to slick his hair with heavy pomade—well, that might be rather pleasant. Yes, he must learn to blend in for safety's sake.

With the briefest nod of compliance, allowing Anna to gloat with the knowledge she had won—he left to do her bidding.

Chapter Six

Awakening

"Kathryn is my life: my heart and soul. You know that, Anna."

"Then you must convince her of precisely that. She must hear your words over and over, stated without hesitation, in order to find the courage to return to this reality."

Jason winced as he hitched himself closer to rest heavily on the edge of her pallet. Brushing a tendril of hair behind her ear, he studied her face. Despite her pallor and dark circles etched beneath her eyes, she was beautiful.

Yes, he must reassure her. This feisty, bold wife of his harbored insecurities—as did he. He would never allow her cause to doubt. Brushing a kiss to her ear, he remained close, whispering fervent words that Anna could not discern, but easily sensed their significance.

Anna noted his steadfast resolve, and the toll it exacted. She had not misjudged in any way when she had chosen to join them many years ago; that knowledge pleased her.

As he sat up and turned to her, she filled the empty cup he held out with cool, fresh water. Slowly, he allowed a few drops to trickle over Kathryn's dry lips, watching as they followed the curve of her chin and then crept along the arch of her neck, noting her steady pulse—hoping for the tiniest reaction.

Unexpectedly, her lips moved, barely evident but they moved.

"Kathryn, my beloved," he crooned.

Her lips parted ever so slightly, the tip of her tongue catching a drop.

"Kathryn," he whispered, eagerly renewing his efforts to grab her attention. "I swore I would not leave you, I am here at your side ... my promise kept."

He trickled a few more drops of water, studying her slight, but distinct, response.

"My promise is kept," he repeated more forcefully. "Now *you* must keep your sworn vow to me. Live, Kathryn, live. I demand that of you as your commanding officer."

The firmness in his voice quickly softened into a frantic plea. "As your husband, I beg of you ... do not leave me, for I cannot bear it." He stifled a sob.

Should he risk mentioning the tiny, new life she carried: might the knowledge overwhelm her?

A low groan grabbed his attention.

"Talk to her, Colonel," Anna instructed. "Help her reach out to you, to break free of the terror that traps her.

Please, no more, her mind begged. But it had begun ... yet again. Pain—desperation—horror: a kaleidoscopic series of events clicking round and round, faster then slower, fragmenting momentarily before slipping into precise definition—its incessant hammering slowly eroding her will.

Stop; *no more*: a frantic entreaty as her face contorted with the agony welling in her chest. *This damnable pain ... I have known you before and beaten you! I will beat you now.* With mounting determination, she attempted to focus her sluggish mental powers.

"Anna, her pain …" Jason started to rise.

Quickly at her Ugilohi's side, she gently forced dark liquid drops between her lips—far less than usual.

"She is close to retaking her life, Colonel, and must bear her suffering to live—or remain in this state until …" she trailed off. "But she will not accept that."

With a light touch to Kathryn's cheek, she stood and slowly backed away.

"I believe she senses your earthly presence and dares to hope … but hesitates to embrace a reality so contrary to what she experienced."

"You must have patience, Colonel. Speak more to her; I recognize your exhaustion, but continue. Your strength will return with Kathryn's awakening."

Her reassurance renewed his flagging energy. Leaning in close, he gently grasped Kathryn's hand and began …

"As your commanding officer …"

She heard, and an inner spark caught, fanning into awareness.

"As your husband …"

Your husband: beautiful words echoing warmly, drawing her back.

Kathryn attempted to speak, but could manage no more than a garbled moan.

"You have the strength. Come to us Ugilohi," Anna encouraged.

For several moments, Jason eyed his wife thoughtfully, finally coming to a decision. *Patience,* Anna's use of that word stuck in his craw. *Patience? That is a virtue neither you nor I possess, my love. It is time to tell you of the new life you carry.*

Gently placing his hand on her taut belly he began, softly at first but building with intensity; speaking of the tiny new life, Gabrielle, Jack … and his undying love.

New life? Jason's words finally sank in creating absolute reality. Eagerly embracing that knowledge, she cast aside the last remnants of vagueness that had shrouded her for too long.

I am here, Jason, talk to me. I will follow your voice … my beloved.

With all the meager strength she could command, Kathryn forced her thoughts upward and outward, reaching for his presence, communicating in the unique fashion they shared. As the jumbled thoughts of the last few days clarified, her vitality began to build.

Jason is here, Jason is now, Jason is my heart and my soul.

Those words became her mantra to focus on living.

"Anna, I sense her thoughts, at long last she is with me," Jason exclaimed, his eyes shining with newfound hope.

"Kathryn." He turned back, bending low to brush a kiss against her lips, uttering terms of endearment and encouragement, stroking back tendrils of tawny hair, caressing her cheek: needing to touch her. Tears tracked the length of his gaunt face but he ignored them, unashamed even in front of Anna.

Kathryn's breathing deepened with purpose as she determinedly pulled air into lungs long deprived their full capacity of life's precious necessity. She reached out, her hand seeking blindly, relaxing its terrified search as Jason's warm fingers gently clasped hers and squeezed.

An audible sigh escaped as her eyes flickered open, closed, then flickered open again searching her surroundings, attempting to clear the blurry images.

"Kathryn, oh my Kathryn." He smothered her face in gentle kisses, interspersed with barely coherent words of love and reassurance.

Comforting sensations accosted her, reality slowly insinuating itself until abruptly—full comprehension dawned: *Jason, it really is you. You are alive!*

She labored to call his name with a parched throat that refused to make the smallest utterance, her cracked lips silently forming his name, all she could manage. Tears welled and overflowed as she tried to touch his face … needing to feel the reality of him.

Immediately understanding, Jason captured her hand, bringing it first to his lips and then to his cheek to linger there.

"I am here, my love. We are alive; it is no dream."

He appeared even more pale and thin than he had, after his severe leg wound at King's Mountain when their whole world had begun to collapse. But he was her adored husband … and he lived, their destiny not yet fully revealed.

She sobbed uncontrollably as the last vestiges of her murky world departed.

I am back. Here and now is reality. We will regain our strength: together. Then we will find our precious little girl and Jack.

A weary smile touched the corners of her mouth.

He returned the grin, knowing her every thought, nodding in agreement.

Suddenly her hand touched his chest and then curled against her own heart lightly.

"Your heart and mine shall always beat as one," she mouthed.

Kissing her forehead, he then traced his thumb down along the bridge of her nose to her chin, and tilting it upwards … gently kissed her.

"Always," they breathed in unison.

Their pledge of love, born on their wedding day, had sustained them through many difficult situations in their past, and it would now.

Their eyes met and held, exchanging wordless remembrances and promises, drawing strength from each other, as always.

Carefully he slid down beside her, cautious not to cause more pain. But she gave no indication of discomfort, her smile never fading as she watched him, smiling even as her eyes began to droop from exhaustion.

"Always, my love," he whispered softly as he placed his arm lightly across her waist.

"Always," she answered, placing her hand atop his as she slipped into healing sleep.

Chapter Seven

Gabrielle: Starting Over

Gabrielle grieved her sense of loss, devastating. No words of explanation, or years of maturity, were necessary for her to realize that all had gone terribly wrong. She missed her parents dreadfully, and ached for Anna's comforting touch.

She studied her Uncle Jack through sad, solemn eyes, watching as he tried to rise above his personal grief. But his attempted words of comfort fell short, and explanations were not forthcoming. He did his best, often gathering her in his arms and hugging her close, as he hummed one of her mother's favorite tunes.

Several days had passed since they had boarded the sleek, small vessel—days of merely existing—when suddenly Gabrielle rubbed her chest and winced, immediately drawing Jack from his quiet grief.

"Are you all right, little one?" he asked, concerned, as he lifted the edge of her blouse to check for bruises.

The sea had been rough, although she had not appeared upset. Sturdy on her feet, she actually enjoyed the tangy ocean spray and sharply angled pitch of the bow.

She nodded distractedly, remaining silent. Pulling her up beside him on to a stack of burlap-covered bales, he hugged her protectively. Unresisting, she leaned against him quietly content, remaining so for several minutes: her face serene, blue eyes focused afar.

Just as Jack became truly concerned, she abruptly slid to the deck, and bracing her small feet wide apart, stood swaying in rhythm with the rocking ship. With a loving smile, she reached to touch his cheek, and after a moment's scrutiny, followed with a kiss.

"All will be well, Uncle Jack," she whispered against his ear. "Of this I am sure."

Drawing herself up to her full height, she turned and proceeded to make her way to the railing of the rolling ship. Unnerved by her boldness, Jack quickly followed. But there was no need, Gabrielle was in complete control.

The little girl leaned against the railing, her small face pressed into the wind. With each sharp dip of the vessel, salt spray dashed her face and she laughed gleefully—excited, eager for adventure, so very like Kathryn.

Jack watched her, a sudden pang of grief overcoming him. He, too, embraced the salty spray, hoping any passerby would attribute the redness of his eyes to that.

Attempting to divert his attention away from sad memories, he searched the horizon, noting for the first time, threatening black clouds steadily rolling their way. The wind was picking up, and a few stinging rain spatters promised more to come.

Hoping he might lure Gabrielle back within the shelter of the ship without any argument, he moved to her side.

"With the ocean becoming so rough, perhaps Beauty will need reassurance, little one. And you know how she loves to see you."

As there was no immediate response, he reminded: "She will also expect you to comb her mane and rub her legs to keep them strong."

Gabrielle turned, angling her head to hold his gaze for a thoughtful moment, before taking his outstretched hand.

"She will want a lump of sugar too," she added, grinning widely, her look sending a succinct message; she understood him perfectly. And Jack smiled in spite of himself.

Having sensed their presence, well before they reached her tiny stall below deck, Beauty began nickering in welcome. Stomping her feet and tossing her head, she put on quite a display, eager to see them. Her existence was a far cry from her former life, and boredom weighed heavily.

Gabrielle threw her arms around her sleek neck, giggling at her huffing and snuffling as she sought the sugar lumps she so loved. But after a few minutes of welcomed patting, she settled into the roll of the ship and allowed Gabrielle and Jack to comb her mane, curry her shiny coat, and exercise her slender legs. They spent longer than usual with the little mare, but eventually headed for their small cabin, promising to return soon.

Jack groaned, rolling carefully to stay within the confines of his musty pallet, coming awake grudgingly, relieved the sea had finally ceased its furious rampage. It was the first time in three or four days—he had entirely lost track—that his stomach had not sat at the base of his throat threatening to spew unceremoniously into the slop pail wedged at the head of his pallet.

The pitch and roll of the little ship had lulled to a gentle rocking: manageable if he kept his mind focused on something, anything.

No, not that ... Do not think of that yet.

Dragging himself to an upright position on the edge of his rumpled pallet, he sat supporting his head between grimy palms.

At a soft sound his eyes drifted to the slight figure curled into herself on the opposite pallet. Dark lashes brushed cheeks lightly flushed from deep sleep. *So at ease, so like her mother and father.* He wished time would quickly elapse so that he might draw solace from watching their child, rather than living with this abysmal sense of loss.

Children recovered so quickly. Gabrielle had been almost inconsolable for days and then, he could not put his finger on it, everything changed. It seemed as if she sensed something, *but what?*

He had seen Kathryn: the vicious wound in her chest. And Jason, an ugly gash that traversed from hip to upper rib cage and the gaping hole in his shoulder. If only their child had the 'sight' like Anna and her mother. Perhaps then, he might grasp at a shred of hope. But he had seen them: observed their grief-stricken 'goodbye' on the battlefield.

Oh, God, I am driving myself crazy.

Forcefully, he turned his thoughts toward his sister, Eugenie, living in England. Although she had no inkling of their pending arrival, he had no doubt that she would welcome the two of them with open arms—or at least he hoped so.

He swiped at his cheeks absent mindedly, noting the moisture there.

Will this inner ache never cease?

Thankfully the seas were calmer this morning. It was a new day; time to begin planning what he would say to Eugenie.

After a light super, in consideration of his still rather queasy stomach, Jack took Gabrielle to their tiny room below deck. He sighed deeply as he brushed her long, black curls—glad for the small modicum of privacy provided through his lordship's connections and generosity. Unable to face prying eyes at this time, he needed that solitude. With a final brush stroke he patted her bottom, nudging her up onto her pallet and under the covers.

"There you go, my little princess, one quick story and then off to sleep."

He forced lightness into his voice that he did not truly feel, but strangely … tonight felt more at ease within Gabrielle's close proximity.

What does she know or sense? Her demeanor had changed.

Concerned for her warmth, he bent down and rummaged in the grubby knapsack shoved under his pallet, hoping that Anna had tucked away a small blanket, or perhaps, another warm shirt. Unexpectedly touching something firm amidst the clothes, he ceased his search, curious. Gabrielle watched with interest as Uncle Jack slowly wriggled the object free and held it up: a small, rectangular package, carefully wrapped in deer hide. Turning it to examine all sides, he raised an eyebrow and then with a smile, handed it to her to do the honors.

At her small gasp, Jack looked up, eyes brimming.

"Momma's," she murmured, running her small fingers over the well-worn books … turning them over and over, clasping them to her in a loving grip.

"Yes, little one, the poetry books your poppa brought from England."

"He read these to me too," she whispered happily.

Jack smiled, fighting for composure, warm memories flooding back. Along with Beattie's and MacPherson's books of poetry, Anna had included one or two well-worn parchments from her great grandmother. He knew these items well, especially the poetry books. When military demands had occasionally taken Jason from the encampment, he and Kathryn had spent many long hours amusing themselves, debating the validity of one poet or the other.

With Gabrielle's quiet insistence, he chose a short poem and read in his own distinct British accent. But at her eager request for another, he reminded her there would be many more days at sea, and to save some for another time. Her answering look displayed absolute understanding and compassion beyond her years.

She can read me just like her mother he realized, and felt oddly comforted.

However, Gabrielle, not ready for sleep just yet, remained wakeful, talkative. She spoke of Anna lovingly, and urged Uncle Jack to share all he could remember of her 'baby years'.

Placing a kiss on her forehead, it suddenly struck him how very mature she seemed tonight.

"Sleep now, little one, there will be plenty of time for that tomorrow."

Moving to his own pallet, he settled under the covers and slipped into an emotionally exhausted sleep.

Snug under her blanket, Gabrielle began to drift drowsily. Turning her thoughts upward and outward, as taught, her spirit floated into the ethers in search of Anna.

***

Suddenly Anna paused in dressing Kathryn's wound, and turned slowly—angling her head, scanning the empty space above her as if she had heard something.

"My little bird has the power," she mused, nodding approval. "Hmm, a power to rival mine: good … good."

With the slightest smile, she allowed herself a few moments of deep thought before turning attention back to Kathryn.

The die is cast … at last.

Anna mumbled a few words in Cherokee that Jason could not understand: yet, oddly enough, from which he derived a strong sense of comfort.

With renewed spirit, he bent low, and brushing a kiss to his wife's lips, encouraged her to live.

Chapter Eight

Recapturing Life

Jason sat beside Kathryn holding her hand as she slept, relieved to note returning strength in the steady, rhythmical breaths that raised and lowered her chest—somewhat less painfully today, he perceived.

Idly, he began rolling the wide, gold, Celtic wedding band adorning her slender finger—a perfectly matched, smaller version of his own. A smile lifted the corners of his mouth at the pleasant memories that began gently sifting back: welcome relief from all the previous horror.

He recalled having commissioned the matching pair from a Scottish craftsman who swore them to be unique: the only two of their kind. Kathryn's delightfully awed expression when he unveiled his gift still remained vividly etched in his mind, along with their impromptu wedding.

What a day that was!

A grin spread slowly across his face, easing the solemn features.

Sensing a quiet presence at his side, he looked up to see Anna, as always, silent in her approach, a fact that never ceased to amaze him. She paused briefly, her eyes bathing him with warmth. Then, with a reassuring touch to his shoulder, moved closer to Kathryn and crouched low. After a brief examination, she turned to Jason.

"Our Kathryn improves with every passing moment. Her life form flows in balanced harmony once again. The Medicine of the Four Directions, combined with Soaring Eagle's spiritual healing has worked its magic; the Earth Mother is pleased and graces her with bountiful blessings."

She scrutinized Jason silently, the long, quiet moments drawing out, causing him growing uneasiness.

What is she thinking?

"Passion, Colonel," she murmured thoughtfully, finally ending her silence, "is perhaps the final key and just possibly, most important."

Jason frowned, slightly confused.

"You and Kathryn share an incredible passion for life that equals or . . ." she hesitated, considering her next words, "may even supersede your incredible love for each other—a unique and rare blend, possibly the greatest healer of all."

At the clearing of a throat, both heads turned in unison. Gabriel, his face a mask of apprehension, stood holding the entry flap aside allowing his wife to enter.

"Is she . . ." his voice faltered.

"Kathryn is with us once more merely sleeping," Anna reassured.

Silver Fox stepped quickly into Anna's outstretched arms, hugging her joyously, the two women dropping easily into their native Cherokee to communicate details.

Gabriel's face flooded with relief as, without a split second of thought, he stooped down and hugged the colonel to him.

"Thank God," he murmured brokenly, "Thank God."

Both men quickly looked away as Gabriel stood, somewhat embarrassed—remaining so for only a moment, before slowly turning back to face each other, deciding tears of relief and a caring hug were not considered to be unmanly in common sharing.

"How fares your father?" Jason asked gruffly, clearing his throat in an attempt to regain composure.

"Although one day flows endlessly into the next, it would seem you have been gone for some time."

"The better part of two weeks," Gabriel agreed. "My father is not well, his mind more than body."

Jason nodded, well aware that Jamie had truly loved Kathryn and still did. There was no doubt of that. *But what to do?*

He eyed Gabriel, scrutinizing him sharply. Distress etched his youthful features, but something further troubled him. Catching him glancing furtively at his wife, he sensed she also played heavily in his concern.

"How fares Silver Fox?" he asked quietly.

Gabriel searched the face of this man his aunt loved dearly: a man he respected more with each passing day, a man he felt he could trust.

"Silver Fox is near to term. I fear complications, but she merely smiles sweetly and placates me with aimless prattle."

"Just as all women are wont to do, when they wish to distract us from worry," Jason declared, smiling slightly; thinking it one of Kathryn's more endearing, yet infuriating traits.

At that moment, Kathryn groaned and opened her eyes.

"We will talk later in private," Jason assured as he moved to his wife's side.

"I see we have company," Kathryn said softly. "And I—not dressed appropriately."

Her weary smile reached her eyes, and all present silently rejoiced. It would be only a matter of time before she was once again restored to full health.

Kathryn settled herself gingerly against the soft, folded deer hide that served as a pillow. Grimacing slightly, she inched herself into a more upright position. Pausing to regain her meager strength, she began idly stroking the sleek hair, suddenly remembering to give thanks to the animal's spirit for the food it had provided Anna's people, but more specifically, for the comfort it now afforded her.

She smiled at her instinctive reaction to the hide, realizing that Anna's teachings still remained such an integral part of her daily existence, that they often surfaced unbidden.

At the soft pad of moccasin-covered feet, she looked up to see Silver Fox entering the doorway with a wide grin.

"You grow stronger with each passing day, aunt. I fear that soon you will no longer need my services," she teased, her jet black eyes sparkling in merriment.

With a lopsided grin, working around her growing girth, she awkwardly lowered herself to set a bowl of medical necessities beside Kathryn.

"It soon will be my turn to help you," Kathryn said, touching the girl's arm. "You are very close to term," she added more seriously.

With those words, both statement and question, she hoped for a truthful answer.

"All will be well, I have both you and Anna," Silver Fox said, quickly averting her eyes and without further conversation, gently uncovered Kathryn's chest to began her work.

Chapter Nine

Healing Mind, Body and Soul

With her return to full awareness, Kathryn's incredible recuperative powers were quickly restored. Having healed rapidly in the past, she did so now. The arrival of spring had brought an abundance of fresh, healthful vegetables; that fact, combined with Anna's nagging, forced renewed interest into her lacking appetite.

However, it was to Jason's efforts that she attributed her regained strength. With his newly acquired hunting and fishing abilities, he quickly learned the preparation and cooking of wild game—often adding a creative, tantalizing twist to a meal, encouraging his wife to eat.

She worked the ill-used muscles of her torn shoulder determinedly, driving herself at a fever pitch that often earned a sharp reprimand from her husband. Even his gentle reminder of the new life she carried could not dissuade her.

"Our child will be strong—as will I," she ground out, after an exceptionally tiring workout.

Not wishing to share angry words, Jason walked away. He knew his Kathryn. She would drive herself—as would he. They understood each other; that was enough.

During her period of convalescence, Soaring Eagle often visited. Before he announced himself, he always lifted his face to the heavens, offering a chant for her continued healing: grateful for her progress and the part he had played.

In all their conversation, they had only touched once upon Black Raven and the 'blood vengeance'. They shared a newfound respect for each other: especially Soaring Eagle. He would never forget the day she had faced him down, grievously wounding him; yet laying aside her own needs, sent Anna to work her 'healing magic' on him.

"Look upon my wound," he said, drawing aside his chest adornments to bare a well-healed indentation; a lingering reminder of a well-placed bullet: *Kathryn's bullet.*

Kathryn moved closer, smiling.

"Anna worked her miracles with you, just as she has done with me. However …" she paused, merriment twinkling in her eyes, "I think we shall not compare scars today."

Soaring Eagle threw his head back and roared with laughter.

"Ah, Ugilohi, Ugilohi …" His eyes held hers. "My brother was such a fool. Would that he had come to know you, as I have."

He shook his head, momentary sadness seizing him, but quickly shifted the conversation lest the mood become solemn.

"My new grandchild thrives. You and the colonel—you and *Jason*," he corrected, "… must share our evening meal."

He moved towards the doorway and turned to face her, awaiting an answer.

"We are honored, my friend. When my husband returns from fishing, we will join you."

"Perhaps we will choose his Cherokee name tonight. His English surname so often eludes me." With that said, he turned and left.

Kathryn lay down on her soft pallet. She wanted to enjoy this evening's meal; a quick nap would do her good. Drifting sleepily, she thought of Jason fishing; something at which he had become quite adept, once he had moved past his initial argumentative denial.

This talented husband of mine ... she grinned and faded into sleep.

Spring's bounties provided a veritable feast at the dinner table that evening. Genuine warmth and camaraderie created a friendly combination of chatter and serious conversation, lightly sprinkled with occasional outbursts of sheer pleasure.

At Jason's request that his Cherokee name be easily understandable, they acknowledged him as 'Hunts with Spirit'. As the actual Cherokee terminology eluded him, he agreed to answer to 'Hunter'.

Gabriel and Silver Fox smiled happily, nodding agreement at Jason's new name. They sat a few feet away with their son, and the latest arrival: a little girl who had come into the world with some difficulty, but was now hale and hearty. The little boy sat proudly at their side prattling in a mixture of broken English and Cherokee.

Missing her own little girl, a momentary wave of sadness washed over Kathryn. Forcefully shutting her mind to all else, she forced a wide smile and shifted her focus to their son. It was the first time she had seen her nephew's little boy, a handsome child of about two years of age.

"Gabriel spoke of this young lad when I saw him last. What is his name?" she asked, reaching out as the toddler came to her without hesitation.

"Aunt Ug-hi-lo—Aunt Ka-ther-ryn ..." a long pause as he struggled around her name. "Auntie Kat," he dubbed her, beaming with pride. And so she was called from then on.

"And how shall I call you, little man?" she asked searching his chubby, smiling face.

"Raven," he answered proudly.

Kathryn's expression shifted slightly, unable to hide her surprise.

"My father loved his brother despite his faults," Silver Fox said softly. "Just as he loves and respects you, Kathryn."

Kathryn smiled affectionately, first at Silver Fox and then Soaring Eagle, hoping to ease any discomfort or lingering concern.

"I approve," she said firmly. "It is a good name, an appropriate name. Your son will make you proud someday."

She pulled the little boy onto her lap and hugged him.

"See my baby sister," Raven chortled, beginning to squirm and quickly sliding down off her lap, took rolling steps towards the sleeping baby.

"Have you decided her name?"

After a drawn out pause, as all waited expectantly, Gabriel spoke up. "We wish to name her after you, Kathryn, and Anna,"

But Kathryn immediately shook her head.

"Perhaps Anna, but also consider *your* mother's name, Gabriel. 'Mairi' was the love of your father's life, gone from us way too young. Jamie would be so proud."

"It should be so," Anna announced breaking her thoughtful silence. "So, little one, *Mairi*, you shall be."

As she picked up the tiny bundle and held her up for all to see, angry squalling erupted. With tiny flailing fists and a red, scrunched up face, *Mairi* proclaimed her indignation at being so rudely awakened.

Above the commotion, all agreed that the hour had grown late. With all proper pleasantries in place, the gathering was deemed successful and over.

Jason sat quietly watching Kathryn make preparations for bed. She hummed happily, lost somewhere in her own thoughts. Even with the party, her energy level had remained high and she seemed to be experiencing no discomfort. He mouthed a silent prayer of thankfulness. Her health continued to improve daily, and the recurring nightmares of their last battle were becoming less frequent.

Many nights he had cradled her against him crooning soft assurances, waiting for her racking sobs to cease, waiting for the fist of pain clenched in her chest to ease, allowing her to slip back into peaceful slumber. Of late, even those had faded into the past as she turned her thoughts towards the tiny new life she carried and finding their beloved Gabrielle.

At a loud clearing of her throat, Jason snapped out of his reverie and turned to her. She sat staring at him, a quizzical smile playing at the corners of her mouth.

"What are you looking at, my love?"

"You, my handsome husband." A twinkle sparkled in her eyes.

"Not so handsome now, I fear," he trailed off, indicating the area of wounds.

"I fear mine to be far more …" She stopped, abruptly turning away.

Instantly at her side, he turned her face up to meet his gaze.

"Wounds gained for a worthy cause are of no consequence, my love," he assured, pulling her into a warm embrace.

I wonder how fares our cause now? She forced the thought aside.

Jason's comforting touch—the nearness of him—too long apart. A slow burning spark kindled, quickly igniting into a hot, burning … Urgent need coiled in her belly as her eyes drifted to her husband's, eagerly met by his and filled with matching need.

"I am strong now," she reassured.

"Kathryn," he began, "you are barely …"

Her fingertips stopped his words mid-sentence.

"My body will not break, my love."

She nudged closer, the smell of her freshly washed curls instantly sending an intoxicating shiver across his abdomen.

"But my heart," her soft, warm exhalations brushed his cheek, "… is quite another matter."

The raw edge to her voice captured him; yet he hesitated, concerned.

"Jason …" she murmured more urgently.

As his finger gently traced the rough edges of her scar, his gaze drifted to her face. Wide, unblinking eyes searched his flashing desire, desperate need, and *fear*. Instantly, his finger ceased its aimless tracing, his hand moving to cup her cheek.

"Kathryn, my beautiful Kathryn," he whispered.

He brushed a gentle kiss to her lips before leaning back, his slight grin curving into a knowing smile. He understood her so very well, her fears were his also.

Fleetingly, he wondered if the day would ever come when she could finally cease to doubt. Probably not, nor could he. They shared the same insecurities, even after all their time together—and everything they had been through.

"Look at me, my Kathryn."

Raising himself up on one elbow he rolled slightly away, allowing the warm glow of the oil lamp to expose the ragged welt that traversed the full length of his chest in bold relief.

Looking down, he critically assessed the damage while tracing the wound's rough path with his finger.

A grin suddenly split her face as complete understanding dawned.

"My handsome husband—my love, my life."

No further words necessary, they fell to renewing their love and allaying any lingering fears or doubts.

Chapter Ten

What of Jamie?

Sitting across from each other the following morning, sharing a light breakfast, their eyes met … speaking volumes.

Smiling, they reached to touch lightly, and then hold hands.

"You have never been more beautiful, Kathryn."

"Nor you more handsome, my husband; you make me so very proud, as always."

Raising an eyebrow, he said lightly, "I am not sure I follow your train of thought, my love. But, that has never been an altogether uncommon occurrence in our lives."

At her pretty pout he added, "However, I am sure you will enlighten me."

She grinned, saying nothing until she could see his impatience growing.

"You have taken to a colonial lifestyle with apparent ease. You look the part quite convincingly in your new clothes. You hunt and trap almost as well as I." She winked.

He nodded, fully agreeing. "I do find the clothing a bit rough, but I never would have believed how much I appreciate the look and feel of my hair clubbed back loosely without pomade."

Hitching a bit closer, he draped an arm about her shoulder drawing her against him.

"It does seem strange not to be planning our next foray with our dragoons, not to be planning with Jack …"

"Not to be hugging our little girl," he finished.

She fought tears, eyes glistening.

"We must find them—somehow get word to his lordship, or Captain Hodges. Gabriel said he saved our lives, bringing us to safety while putting his own life at great risk.

They must know where Jack has gone. Someone must have seen him, or helped him."

She drew a deep breath and raced on. "Do you think they know we are alive? Do you think the war is more in England's favor by now? Do you …?"

"Hush, my love, too many questions all at once."

He placed his hand gently on her abdomen, hoping to feel the gentle 'kick of life' within.

"Gabriel's contacts have the ability to find answers for many of your questions, and he is ready to move ahead upon your instruction. After all, we *are* in his territory now."

"Would that I could be sure of Jamie, for he also has many influential contacts. But from what Gabriel has reported, I feel my brother needs me, or rather us, whether he realizes it or not."

"Your brother will not betray you *or me* at this point, of that I am sure. It is time for him to heal too. I bear him no grudge, my love. It was—or *is* war. But for us, my dearest Kathryn, it will remain over, for I will not risk losing you again. And in this matter *you will obey.* I remain your commanding officer, if you will recall."

Blowing a warm breath against her ear, he began placing nipping kisses.

"Do I have your complete understanding and compliance, my love?"

Eyeing him with annoyance, she muttered, "Yes, but …"

"Yes or no; what will it be?" His tongue played along the top of her ear.

"You cheat! You know I cannot resist …"

As his piercing blue eyes narrowed, she nodded like a chastised child.

"Yes."

"Yes what? I recall you have a habit of playing games with words and must be reminded to state precisely …"

"Yes, yes, yes! I will comply with your wishes."

She kissed his cheek and whispered, "I will not seek to get back into the fray, I need to hold our little girl, stay well for our new little one, find Jack and give him a big hug."

Suddenly her eyes went wide. "My God, he thinks us dead. He must be devastated. I had not really thought that through. As Anna senses that Gabrielle knows the truth, I …"

"Kathryn, you are just now well enough to start life again. One step at a time, and *slowly.* I will not have you becoming exhausted and losing hard-gained ground. Are we agreed?"

"You are right, my love; first things first. And I guess that would be handling Jamie."

"I agree, I will go talk to Gabriel, but I want you to rest." At the beginning of a protest, he added, "It seems to me that you had a rather, how shall I put it delicately, exciting evening last night. I would be pleased to find you …"

"Hmm, might I expect a promise for later, sir?" She grinned impishly.

"Always, my love." He returned her rakish grin.

"Then I shall nap. Do not be long."

Chuckling softly, he set out to find Gabriel.

"Ma hum a dig," Soaring Eagle rumbled his warm guttural welcome as Kathryn ducked to enter the low entrance of his lodge.

'Come, sit, and rest awhile'. Kathryn smiled at his greeting, her eyes sparkling.

He stood as she entered, but continued buffing an odd shaped piece of horn cupped in his hand.

Kathryn's curiosity was piqued, but she had come for a specific reason.

"You wish to speak with me, Ugilohi?"

Soaring Eagle's question squelched any further inquisitiveness.

"Yes, I have need of your advice."

He raised an eyebrow, pausing his buffing to give her a long look.

"Advice about Jamie."

"Ahh," he nodded slowly, pursing his lips thoughtfully. "My son-in-law's father, my friend and your—brother." He paused for several long moments, remaining silent.

As they had been on good terms for some time, and she wished to keep it so, she held her tongue. But he sorely tested her patience with his irritating way of constantly feeling the need to stretch out his conversations: never a simple *yes or no.*

Catching the brittle spark in her gaze, he abruptly sat back down.

"Such impatience," he grinned, enjoying her feisty nature. "Always eager, always hurried—passionate." He eyed her in solemn understanding.

"That is why you are still with the living. That is why …"

"No, that is more to do with you and Anna … and I shall always be grateful."

It more than likely bordered on bad manners to have interrupted, but patience had never been one of her virtues. She always wanted to 'just get on with it'. But the warmth in Soaring Eagle's eyes spoke of acceptance, not reproach.

"It is time for Jamie to know."

Kathryn snapped to alert, her eyes narrowing appreciatively at his perception. Would he never cease to surprise her?

"Yes," she answered, "whatever the consequences. His spirit is devastated and I fear for his mind, as well as the healing of his wounds."

"Yes, Gabriel has kept me aware of his condition, and it saddens me. He is lost in his grief … and guilt."

Turning, he gestured to a pile of animal skins draped over a small stool.

"Sit," he instructed, "I do not wish to tire you."

She shook her head, but gratefully accepted. Her strength returned more with each passing day, but she still had a way to go.

"Your heart has chosen wisely; what would you request of me?" he asked softly.

Kathryn hesitated, collecting her thoughts.

"He calls you dear friend, as do I." Their eyes met and held. "I would ask that you help him to understand *me*. For you possess great insight. Our souls have spoken and accepted each other through your healing of my spirit in my time of greatest of need."

She sat quietly, studying his angular face, his outward expression giving no indication as to what his mind was sorting out. After silently counting to twenty, *for the second time*, she felt her patience beginning to slip.

A knowing sparkle touched his eyes as he opened his mouth to speak.

"I know, I know," she murmured, shrugging at her inability to remain tolerant and quietly respectful.

Suddenly it came to her with a touch of regret—how deeply she must have offended Black Raven. He had never possessed the sensibilities of his older brother, had never understood her.

"We will heal him together. He loves you, Kathryn," Soaring Eagle said firmly, stressing her birth name.

"As I shall always love him," she whispered, as moisture sprang to her eyes.

Nodding, he stood and moved towards her. He had finally stopped polishing the item in his hand: a beautiful horn spoon, one of his more prized possessions.

"Go now, rest; all will be well, my Ugilohi."

As he assisted her to stand, he meaningfully pressed the spoon into her hand.

"I cannot accept this valued …" She shook her head, embarrassed by his selfless generosity.

Gently folding her fingers over the smooth roughness of its shape, he encased her hand within both of his.

"Jamie will understand when he sees this."

He squeezed her hand gently.

"But I …"

"No more," he said firmly, his eyes meeting hers. "Trust me." His voice softened as he added, "Rest, for *he* will need *your* strength as well as Hunter's, although he does not yet know that."

She moved towards the doorway, and with a final look of gratitude exited.

How strange, she thought as she wended her way back to the small shelter she and Jason shared. *Jason's Indian name flows as easily from Soaring Eagle's tongue as it does mine. He truly understands; he does.*

***

"Captain ...?" Lord Cornwallis looked up, eyeing the tall man standing patiently before him in his Yorktown headquarters, a curt reprimand for this annoying disturbance, on the tip of his tongue.

"At your request, sir," the captain answered smartly, forcing himself to stand taller in the general's presence.

Sudden recollection of a recent request, as well as vague recognition, stopped him. Looking over the nervous officer more carefully, he abruptly arose and leaned forward.

"Captain Hodges, is it not?"

"Yes your Lordship."

Hodges colored slightly, pleased that the general had remembered him from that awful night after Guilford Courthouse: a night no one should have to remember.

Cornwallis straightened, and then walked around his desk, coming to a stop before the uncomfortable captain. He recalled this particular man quite well: a Loyalist dedicated to the British cause, and devoted to ... He could not continue those thoughts, after all these weeks the memories still cut too deeply.

Forcing brightness to his tone he said, "Thank you for being so prompt, Captain. I trust Colonel Tarleton did not pressure your actions with too many questions."

"No, sir, I remained vague, as your orders stipulated. However, his curiosity is piqued—of that, I am sure."

"So be it, you will be gone before he has time to consider. I shall keep him busy across the bay, digging fortifications and making preparations for my next stage of action."

"Come, sit down, Captain Hodges."

Gesturing the captain to a seat near his desk, he again sat down. Eyeing the dragoon thoughtfully, he tented his fingers and leaned in close, the instructions he was about to impart, for the officer's ears only.

"Now, let me explain what I have in mind, Captain."

***

"Gabriel, thank heavens you have returned."

Kathryn quickly stood up, and moving to Jason's side, placed a hand on his shoulder. Quickly swallowing his mouthful of their evening meal and swiping his mouth, he also stood in greeting.

"I am sorry to interrupt, but I have urgent need to talk to you both."

"Your father ...?" Kathryn asked, afraid of the answer to her next question, but needing to know. "Is he worse? You have been gone so long this time that I feared ..."

"Yes," he said solemnly. "I fear he is slipping closer to the edge of ..." He hesitated and began again. "He is obsessed with your graves—pacing, fretting and talking to both of you, at times coherent but often no more than babbled gibberish."

"And what of his wounds?" Kathryn asked.

"His pain is constant, sometimes acute but more often a dull ache continually reminding him of that day. However, it is a festering sore on his leg which concerns me. I feel the heat of his forehead when I bend close."

He turned to Jason, shaking his head. "My father is a lost soul. Having been relieved of future militia duties, his men no longer need him. He has nothing pressing to draw him back to reality."

At that statement Jason arched a questioning brow.

"It would appear that Nathanael Greene has determined the local militia's reliability to be risky at best; informing them in no uncertain terms, they *are not* to rejoin him. All my father's former comrades have gone home to resume their previous lives."

"I expect Jamie feels his usefulness and purpose in life is over," Jason interjected.

Gabriel nodded. "It is the final blow; he has given up. Even my sisters cannot penetrate his depression, although to be honest, I think they tire of his illness. They are at an age when they wish to pursue their own lives, not be tied to a …"

"But they cannot be grown enough to live on their own. So I fail to …"

"Aunt Kathryn," Gabriel stopped her gently. "Time has moved on—no, rushed on. Remember how startled you were to find Ian full grown at the battle …"

Kathryn's eyes misted at the remembrance, instantly stopping Gabriel; he had no wish to hurt her further.

"Caitlin, my 'baby' sister, is now fifteen years and Annie—let me see—I would guess seventeen. She has several beaus and little desire to …"

Jason moved closer and gripped Gabriel's shoulder.

"It is time to tell your father."

Gabriel's eyes widened as he searched Jason's face.

"Are you sure?" he whispered hoarsely, afraid he had not heard correctly.

"Yes," Kathryn and Jason answered together, the firmness of their unified response leaving no question in his mind.

"Kathryn is strong enough now," Jason pointed out. "She has already spoken with Soaring Eagle."

"I have asked him to help Jamie … to understand *me*."

She reached down and picked up the horn spoon that had been hidden from Gabriel's view by the edge of the plate. "He gave me this as his answer."

Astonishment filled her nephew's eyes as he stared first at the treasured item—and then back to his aunt.

"Then all truly *will* be well."

In youthful exuberance and relief, he hugged Kathryn closely—carefully. Then quickly turning to Jason, he thrust out his hand.

"I must see Silver Fox and my wee ones first, for I have missed them sorely. But tomorrow I will return to my father's farm," he said excitedly.

"Bless you both, you, my dearest Aunt Kathryn, and you, Hunter—newfound friend."

With that, he spun on his heel and rushed from their lodge.

Jason murmured a satisfied sound as he pulled his wife gently against him, smiling.

"Now we may all heal, my love. Gabriel will know how to handle his father."

He bent to kiss her forehead, but her lips found his in a mutual quest. With his free hand, he damped the oil lamp, their dinner no longer of importance.

***

Gabriel called his father for breakfast—waited—and called again. No response.

Grabbing two mugs of steaming coffee, he kicked the porch screen door open, caught it with his elbow, sidled through without spilling a drop, and let the spring take it with a loud slam.

He paused, slowly scanning the fields, noting their neglect: almost June—and still no planting done. Voracious weeds had taken over where rows of corn had once stood. Somehow he must find time to help, or it would be a difficult winter for all of them.

Planting fields was hard work, a man's work—not an area he could justify pressing Annie and Caitlin for help. They had enough chores on their hands what with caring for the house and their father, a fact that they never allowed him to forget.

Enough, he muttered in angry undertones. *I am wasting time, hoping that somehow all will right itself: 'stalling'. Get it done; then it will be finished … one way or the other.*

Straightening his shoulders, he put aside frustration with his sisters and focused on his father. Jamie no longer cared about anything: his children, his farm, even his once tidy appearance that, at best, could only be described as disheveled. Life no longer held any joy.

What should I say? Gabriel fretted as he headed off across the backyard in search of his father. *Can I find the right words to pierce his depression; or is the risk of deepening his dementia too great?* Which words should he use: gentle, pleading or firmly demanding? *God, please help me choose wisely.*

He headed for the orchard, knowing exactly where his father would be: standing with his gnarled, wooden cane *talking to Kathryn.* Surprisingly, of late he had begun to mutter curt remarks in the direction of the colonel's resting place more often. He would stand for hours, staring fixedly at the slightly raised mounds, poking at the weeds insistently encroaching upon the fresh, new grass: the tip of his cane having become an instrument for venting hurt, anger and frustration.

After the battle of Guilford Courthouse, he had lain in a semi-conscious state, ranting and raving with a burning fever for three days: a result of numerous knife wounds. But Silver Fox, knowing Kathryn to be safe within Anna's healing care, had offered to help. It had been her ministrations that quickly defeated Jamie's fever, starting him on the path to recovery. She had healed most of his physical wounds, all but the one or two he refused her care, priding himself with medical capabilities of his own. But she could do nothing to heal his soul.

Silver Fox: his beautiful wife, his salvation. Gabriel prayed that his father, given time, would eventually come to love her, or at least accept her as part of their family. Perhaps her selfless caring, during his time of need, might be a beginning; for there would be no alternative.

From the moment Jamie had become fully cognizant, he had pleaded, "Tell me it is all a bad dream. Tell me, Kathryn …" But he knew, God help him, he knew.

For weeks he had wallowed in a mire of obsessive guilt, a state well deserved in Gabriel's opinion. But upon watching more closely, he noted a lessening of reality emerging in his father's logic: a fact that troubled him.

Jamie had adopted an air of self-righteous affront, cursing the undeserved position into which he had been thrust, demanding that no blame be laid at his feet. This tyrannical war that England had brought to their shore was at fault—*not him.* He stoutly denied any responsibility; none of it had been by his request. To have been designated as the determining factor in the execution of his … *Stop! I cannot bear it …* At that point he would collapse into fits of uncontrollable sobbing and take to his bed.

But as time passed, it became more obvious to Gabriel, that if he did not make his father aware of the actual facts soon, it would be too late to save his mind. The decision to tell him or not, had originally been placed on *his* shoulders. He had carried it as his personal torment for many weeks. But now, thanks to Kathryn and Hunter—he liked the sound of his friend's Indian name—he knew what he must do.

However, it would not necessarily be an easy task. Would his father allow them to continue to heal in safety, or would he betray them to the rebels? Had he lived with his guilt long enough to be trusted to protect them at all costs? Could he come to grips with his hatred for the colonel? Could he make a compromise, of sorts? Jason was part of the 'deal', *and that was non-negotiable.* If Jamie wanted Kathryn, he must accept the complete package.

His father was exactly where he expected him to be: at their gravesite. Gabriel paused before calling his name, quietly watching—deep sadness washing over him at the changes in this once robust man: stoop-shouldered and thin, his clothes disheveled, hair unkempt, and as he moved closer, definitely in need of a bath.

Jamie leaned forward to pick up a fallen branch leaning against the colonel's headstone, and tossed it aside. If he heard Gabriel's approach, he took no note; remaining where he was, muttering under his breath.

Leaning heavily on his cane, he inclined his head in a conversational manner and stated, "You were damned good, Colonel. You would ha' had me in another swipe of that sword of yours."

He paused, his mind reliving that moment in time, recalling something else.

"That crazy bastard, Cornwallis, turning his artillery on his own … Ah well, why tell you? You rode with him, you must've known first hand."

"I hate to admit it, Kathryn …" He turned towards his sister's grave. "The colonel, that son-of-a-bitch, almost had me. He should'na have died that way, and you …" He swallowed convulsively, overcome by paroxysms of grief.

Gabriel started forward to comfort his father, but stopped as Jamie abruptly regained control. Stepping to his sister's grave, he gently placed his palm on her stone marker.

"Kathryn, damn you, if ye were only here …" His words increased in intensity as he continued. "I would hug ye to me; protect ye for the rest o' yer life. Oh, hell …" He paused, testing his forthcoming words mentally.

"There were times when I was so proud of ye and yer abilities and yet, so damned embarrassed, outsmarted *by my own sister.*" He shook his head grimacing. "If I had got my hands on ye, I do not know for sure—even now—whether I would ha' hugged you, spanked you, or killed … Ahh, but I did just that, did I not? I killed …"

Gabriel moved forward and quickly set the coffee down.

"Father …" he said, touching his shoulder.

Jamie's head came up, startled, as he turned to his son, his face awash with tears. With a ragged sob, he fell into Gabriel's strong arms, accepting his comforting embrace as words tumbled out: broken, jumbled, almost incoherent. But Gabriel understood. He wept for his *own* unimaginable loss—angered by his stubborn idiocy. And he wept for Kathryn, acknowledging her inconsolable grief as she lay broken … suffering in agony on the muddy battlefield.

"When she needed me most … I, self-righteous bastard that I am, would not so much as move to her side to comfort her … beg her forgiveness."

He stopped as a sudden grudging revelation came to him: he also wept for the colonel. He could no longer deny that this man had brought his sister happiness, making her 'whole' for the first time in her life—and she had deserved that. He must not truly have been all bad, perhaps misguided, what with being on the wrong side of this damnable war, but not truly bad.

"Hush, father, look at me and listen very carefully," Gabriel demanded forcefully, immediately grabbing his father's full attention.

"They live," Gabriel said softly, and clutching him closer, repeated: "They live. Your sister loves you … and needs your help to heal. Will you help her?"

Jamie pushed back, standing somewhat shakily, his swollen eyes wide in disbelief. Searching Gabriel's face, seeking the truth of his statement, he mumbled startled words of doubt; question after question tumbling forth incoherently as he clutched Gabriel's arm.

"If this be false …"

"This *is* reality," Gabriel answered firmly. "I would never hurt you with falsehoods after what you have been through … after what *they* have endured. Now listen to me carefully. Can you do as I ask? No; … as I demand?"

He eyed his father solemnly.

"Kathryn has clung to life for weeks, suffering agonies most men could not withstand. If your intent is to harm her in anyway, either physically or by careless word …"

"No, never," Jamie interrupted, his arm sweeping in an abrupt gesture of denial. "Never," he whispered. "I could not lose her again."

"Her husband also lives; he, too, needs more time to heal. I want you …"

"They are as one," Jamie interrupted. "I had not wanted to think it, but I know the truth of it in my heart. They are just as my Mairi and I. We were as one, God rest her soul, and there is not a day goes by but …"

Gabriel listened patiently to his father's loving remembrances of his mother, then picking up the cups of coffee, nodded towards a small bench nearby.

"Come, sit with me, father. You and I have much to discuss over lukewarm coffee."

"But I wish to make myself presentable so that we may be on our way, so that I …"

"All in good time, but for once, my dearest father, you will listen to me—as I have been forced to listen to you in the past."

Jamie reluctantly sat down, and took the offered coffee.

"I have often wondered, father; which of you is the more stubborn: Kathryn or you? I think perhaps *you*."

He smiled, relieved by the outcome, and suddenly exhausted.

"We have numerous cautions to take in our preparations. And there is much I must tell you. You must understand what they have been through—more specifically what Kathryn has suffered. It is a miracle that she lived, but for God, Anna and—Soaring Eagle."

At the mention of his friend's name, Jamie's eyes narrowed, riveting on his son.

"Soaring Eagle has specifically requested your help in healing Kathryn, by *you* coming to understand her, or if necessary, finding forgiveness."

Gabriel scrutinized his father's face, pleased to see acceptance dawning in his rough features. *It will be all right.*

"Soaring Eagle? Of all people, I would not have thought …"

"Much has changed in the last few months. He now holds Kathryn in highest regard. By his own choice, he sat with her many long hours—begging, or more often demanding—that the Great Spirit allow her another chance at life; for he would consider it an honor to know her better and perhaps have the opportunity to request *her* forgiveness."

He allowed his father a few moments to digest all he had said before revealing the final bit of proof, conveying the truth of his words.

"Soaring Eagle has gifted her with his horn spoon as a token of his esteem."

"But that is his most prized possession," Jamie blurted, awestruck by the significance of that gift. "Well, then, I gather you and I have much to discuss, and plans to make, son."

Tossing his cane aside and squaring his shoulders, he took one tentative step, followed by another more firmly placed one; exuding newfound strength.

"Well, that is, after you take a nap. You look awful tired for someone so young. I guess, as always, it will be up to me to start setting this place in order so we can leave in a day or two."

With that statement and a devilish grin, he swallowed the last of his coffee, turned on his heel and headed towards the house, gesturing for his son to hurry up and follow.

Gabriel pushed himself up off the bench and stretched, smiling as he watched his father march towards the house. Barely limping, his stride strong and purposeful, he yelled back over his shoulder loudly, "Leave the cane there, son, I am done stomping out weeds."

Chapter Eleven

Captain Hodges Rides South

Captain Hodges reined his horse in with gentling words, and a pat to the noble charger's neck. They had ridden hard and fast, covering long miles at an exhausting pace. At first, he had pushed his faithful animal, eager to return to the area surrounding Guilford Courthouse in North Carolina; his orders, issued directly from Lord Cornwallis himself: discover, beyond all doubt, if they are still alive.

But now, merely a day or two away from his goal, he was beset by nagging dread. He almost wished Cornwallis had not sent for him. Did he have the courage to do this? His answer: a resounding *yes*. Had the general not sent for him, he probably would have gone on his own—at what consequence he could not guess—but definitely irrelevant. He was making this trip for himself—in a need to know. *And if my prayers have been answered …*

Nudging his horse to the edge of a small stream, he stepped down dropping the reins, allowing the animal to refresh itself. With a flick of his wrist, he snagged his canteen, drained it, refilled it with fresh stream water, and drained it again. Sagging down onto a large rock to rest a few minutes, his mind strayed back to Yorktown.

Unable to live with the situation any longer, and desperate to know the truth so as to alleviate his crippling guilt, or beg their forgiveness—*perhaps even attempt to forgive himself*—his lordship had sent for him: a curious, somewhat vague order, cloaked in secrecy.

One way or the other, the general needed to know. He was presently embroiled in an ongoing war that required his full concentration. However, for the past three months his focus had been somewhat lacking, a noxious situation he had never encountered before. This state of affairs *would not do*; he must address the problem immediately. That had been the impetus for calling in his Loyalist dragoon officer.

He had wondered, at the outset, if sending Captain Hodges was the best idea. Did he really want to know the truth? What if they were dead, or worse: what if they had lived and were horribly maimed? Could he forgive himself for having commanded the artillery to fire grapeshot into the masses, knowing full well he was responsible for the deaths of his own men—*and Kathryn?*

Cornwallis was not a coward, and could no longer live with not knowing the truth. Hodges had been successful at fading in and out of rebel territory undetected in the past; he could most assuredly do the same now. He was a Loyalist, born and bred in the Carolinas. No matter what his present status with family and friends might be, he could undoubtedly blend into the background far better than any of his other British officers. But more importantly, his undying devotion to Colonel Tarrington and Kathryn would not allow him to fail—regardless of reservations, doubts or fears he might harbor.

Guilford Courthouse: the closer Hodges neared his goal, the more his chest constricted. Yes, it *was* hot today: a far cry from that cold, raw, day this past March. But there was more to his malaise than that. Unwarranted visions accosted him, horrific scenes of total madness and …

"Enough," he yelled, shaking his fist skyward, startling his horse. "Enough," he pleaded. "Please …"

Emerging from the shadows of a woodsy path into bright sunlight, he halted. Row upon row of precisely laid out corn stretched as far as the eye could see. Suddenly a cheerful vision flared: Kathryn's beautiful smile. He could still hear her voice, as clearly as if she stood beside him, describing the rich, red soil, delicious sweetness of ripened corn, and the calming effect of swaying corn-silk tassels as you lay in their midst gazing up at the stars on a cool evening. The warm remembrance brought a smile to his lips.

"Come on old boy," he urged, gently kneeing his charger. "I know where our campsite was on that day; from there we will weave our way back into Cherokee land—and Anna's village."

An answering whicker caused him to smile. It was as if the animal understood, and perhaps he did—a rather comforting thought at that.

"But right now, my faithful friend," he murmured, "we are in the midst of rebel territory: time to disappear into the background and sort our directions out, later."

One minute he was quietly picking his way along a trail he vaguely remembered—the next, he was surrounded by a group of Indians astride agile ponies—their arrows nocked and aimed at him. Thankfully, their leader was easily recognizable.

"Soaring Eagle," he exclaimed, quickly raising his hands to show he held no threat.

However, as he gave no indication of recognition, remaining silent and stony-faced, Hodges attempted to explain. "I am Captain Hodges, come to seek Anna and …"

Soaring Eagle rode forward lowering his bow slightly, still more than ready to loose a killing shaft if necessary, while his companions held their positions, observing. Reining in close, he scrutinized Captain Hodges closely.

"Humph." Lowering his bow and nodding to the others to do likewise, he rumbled: "Follow me."

No further greeting. No explanations. No allowing him time to question. None was necessary Hodges surmised, as he obediently fell in behind Soaring Eagle—the other braves closing in tightly behind him.

They rode in silence for, what seemed to Hodges, an overly long time. He had thought himself to be closer, but had to admit his landmarks were somewhat hazy in recollection: perhaps due to having been under severe trauma at that time or—a thought popped into his head; mayhap Soaring Eagle had chosen a convoluted trail for the purpose of confusing him. He knew of Hodges's devotion to the colonel and Kathryn; he had proved that beyond doubt. But if they had not survived, was the big brave granting one last meeting with Anna, his secrecy thereby protecting their village after he was gone? His mind was awhirl with possibilities, none of which he wished to contemplate.

Wood smoke. He lifted his head inhaling deeply, picking up the scent of campfire smoke, its aroma rapidly growing in intensity as the forest abruptly thinned.

Just ahead lay a large opening dotted with a series of well-built structures: huts and canvas living quarters, laid out in an organized manner around a centrally located communal center of sorts; much as he remembered it. Several men and women moved about the campsite, busying themselves in daily tasks, while numerous children played happily off to one side. But no one took particular interest, almost as if he had been expected. Although a few glanced in his direction, they immediately returned their attention elsewhere. Dusk was now upon them.

Soaring Eagle raised his hand, quickly dismissing his companions. Beckoning Hodges forward, he gestured towards a small dwelling across the clearing, tucked well back into a low cluster of shrubbery. After eyeing the captain with a stony stare, so lacking in consideration that Hodges found him irritating, he finally spoke.

"Go," he stated gruffly. "Hunts with Spirit will talk to you."

"What of Anna?" Hodges asked.

He gave a non-committal shrug, reiterating with annoyance: "Hunts with Spirit has answers."

Hodges, knowing further questions to be futile, nodded a 'thank you' of sorts, and nudged his charger forward.

A sharp whinny bugled from beside the hut as Diablo suddenly moved into view. Throwing his head back, he emitted another high-pitched squeal of greeting which Hodges's charger immediately answered, snorting and prancing in recognition.

Hodges's stomach clenched, and for the briefest moment thought he might faint.

They must be gone. They must have ...

A tear spilled down his cheek, all hope abruptly dashed, as he realized that some unknown warrior now possessed Diablo. He held back, unsure whether he wanted to hear the details. But he could not leave without knowing the truth; without finding answers. Drawing a deep breath, he whispered a prayer for strength. At least he might finally find closure.

Swiping his cheek with a grubby sleeve, he nudged his charger forward, eager to be done with it. He would get his answers and start back tonight, despite the rapidly falling darkness. After taking his sad news back to Yorktown he would immerse himself in the war, throw himself back into his duties and hopefully ... peaceful forgetfulness.

"What has spooked Diablo, my love?" Kathryn asked as she sat brushing her hair.

"It sounds as if he is greeting an old friend, but I better check. Hopefully, not another one of his silly antics, which always annoys our neighbors."

With a teasing wink, he added, "I will also stoke the campfire—although *that* is not my duty." He then struck a beleaguered pose, his eyes sparkling with deviltry.

"I am well aware of *my* duties and of our 'deal', Hunter." Kathryn grinned, purposely stressing his appropriate new name.

"You catch it, I clean it and tonight, my love—since you are also starting the fire—I will cook your fresh game while you watch."

He raised a questioning brow, becoming serious.

"Do not fret over me so, my love, I feel strong tonight. But before we are asked to vacate our living arrangements, would you please go speak to your recalcitrant beast; convince him of the error of his ways?"

At Diablo's second more pronounced greeting, she frowned, deep in thought.

"Is it too soon for Gabriel to have returned? I am not sure what news he will bring or how to feel, what to expect, what to say or ... what if he will not come, what should I ..." Her troubled eyes sought his.

Jason silenced her with a kiss. "Do not worry yourself so. It will do harm to both you and our child." His hand slid protectively over her barely rounding belly.

"Anna has ridden out to meet them and …"

She grasped his arm tightly, eyeing him anxiously.

"All will be well," he said firmly. "She has assured me of that fact. A vision has …"

Stomping hooves, immediately outside their hut, indicated Diablo's rising agitation.

"I should have taken time to corral him after my hunt. I had best calm him before he creates havoc."

With a lightly placed kiss to Kathryn's forehead, he stepped quickly to the doorway.

Jason snagged Diablo's reins, yanking him in close with a firm command, and then turned to see the cause of his distraction. For a moment he was dumbstruck, questioning reality. *Could it possibly be?*

"Hodges? My God, it *is* you," he yelled, instantly recognizing the bold charger, but looking somewhat askance at the large, shabby form sitting astride.

Hodges sat momentarily paralyzed into silence, staring openly, awestruck. *Sweet Jesu …* He appeared pale and overly thin, his hair loosely clubbed rather than slicked back with pomade, and dressed in colonial apparel: not at all what he had expected. But there was no mistaking his colonel.

"Thank God, thank God," he murmured. Flinging himself to the ground, exhaustion immediately forgotten, he stepped rapidly towards his commanding officer.

Jason's hand shot out to clasp Hodges's, both men briefly speechless as they pulled each other into a firm back-slapping hug.

"Colonel," Hodges finally managed.

"No, Hodges. Here I am called Jason or Hunter: short for Hunts with Spirit."

"I thought you dead, sir."

At Jason's sharp look, Hodges corrected himself.

"Jason—Hunter, I thought you were gone when I saw Diablo standing there. Soaring Eagle gave no indication, one way or the other, merely told me to talk to Hunts with Spirit for answers. I assumed …"

"He has a rather unique personality, I must admit. But my Indian name is actually an accolade awarded to me by Soaring Eagle. He now holds me in highest regard, as he does Kathryn."

Tears welled and spilled freely as Hodges's eyes riveted on Jason.

"Come see her, my friend," he said softly, placing his arm on the captain's shoulder and guiding him towards the hut.

"Is she … well?" he asked, swallowing with difficulty, dreading the answer. He had seen her horrific wound, and found it nothing short of miraculous that she had survived.

"She is well, Captain, thanks to your incredible courage."

Kathryn appeared at the doorway smiling, her face awash with tears.

"My 'Lady Kathryn'," Hodges barely managed as he began to sob.

In three strides he reached her, and dropping to one knee took her hand and brought it to his lips. He searched her face, murmuring her name with trembling lips as tears spilled unashamedly. She, too, was thin and pale … but alive.

Kathryn moved close, touched his cheek and bent low to hug him. Quickly standing, and with nodded of approval from his former colonel—he must remember that term no longer existed—he enveloped her in a gentle bear hug.

"Thank you for my life, Captain. Without you …" For a moment she could not speak, powerful emotions overtaking her. But quickly recovering she asked, "What is your first name, Captain? We no longer stand on formalities in our new life." She stepped back eyeing him through her tears.

"Samuel, my lady."

"Samuel … such a pleasant name, yet after all our months together, I never knew it. May I call you so?"

He smiled widely, nodding vigorously, pleased by her request.

Jason moved to his wife's side, and sliding his arm around her waist, pulled her gently to him. "We owe you our lives, a debt we cannot begin to …"

Hodges shook his head. "I have forced myself to fulfill my duties, as if barely alive, for the last three months. You have given me back my life. There is no debt."

"I have forgotten my manners," Kathryn said lightly, needing to lighten the mood. "Come in, come in, you must be hungry. It is somewhat …" She stopped abruptly and peered closer, noticing his bruised face and a small gash over one eyebrow for the first time.

"What happened to you, Samuel? I was so shocked to see you that I failed to notice your injuries and your—how shall I put it—unusual attire?"

He shrugged sheepishly. "I am afraid I could not afford to be seen in my dragoon uniform, and found it necessary to *borrow* an outfit."

"But you are a large man, not easily …"

"Yes, my lady, and therein lies the problem. I eventually found a man large enough to fit my needs, unfortunately accompanied by three equally well-proportioned friends—all of whom objected, rather strongly, to my demands."

His eyes twinkled as he grinned first at one, and then the other. "However, after a bit of a 'discussion', we came to an agreement: although I am not so sure I received the better end of the bargain."

He wrinkled his nose at the unwashed body odor clinging to the outfit, and brushed a dirty spot off the lapel. "His cleanliness appears to have been somewhat lenient."

"Not to worry, Samuel, we shall change all that. Jason brought home a fine, fat rabbit which I was about to prepare when you arrived."

At Hodges's look of surprise, she added proudly, "He has become quite the huntsman, hence his new name. Now, you two go ready yourselves while I get to my 'woman's work'." She winked at her husband.

As Kathryn turned to enter their living quarters, a light touch on her shoulder caused her to pause.

"I am fine, my love," she whispered. "You and Samuel catch up with each other while I ready our meal. I will tend his cuts and bruises when you return."

With a light kiss to her cheek, he turned to his friend.

"I think we had best corral these two beasts, and perhaps a bath might be in order."

The two men returned, bathed and jovial, just as Kathryn put the finishing touches to their meal. Crouched by the campfire, she turned the spit holding the savory rabbit, judging the seasoning and browning with a critical eye, wanting it to be perfect.

"The aroma is incredible, my lady. It will be the best meal I have had in months." Hodges inhaled deeply, savoring the rich aroma.

"I do hope so; I want it to be special for you."

She poked in the embers, piercing several wrapped tubers, and finding them tender, smiled.

"I hope you have brought your appetite, for all is ready."

Jason helped her up, eyeing her carefully, but at her shushing wave, carried the food into their hut. This visit was the best medicine she had had in months; she would sleep well tonight.

They ate ravenously, even Kathryn—whose appetite was not always as good as it should be. No one spoke until they had polished off every last morsel. Setting down the last bone he had been gnawing, the captain searched for something to wipe his hands.

"Here, we lick our fingers. Try it," she coaxed, "I think you will find it quite a refreshing break from formality."

She also pushed a small bowl of clean water and a dry towel towards him before abruptly exiting the hut, returning shortly with willow bark tea.

"For your bruises, Samuel; I am sure you remember this favorite remedy of mine."

Grinning widely, he accepted the vividly painted bowl, sipping obediently while she tended his forehead.

"So, tell me, what brought you here? How is his lordship? What news do you have of Jack and Gabrielle?" Her voice faltered slightly with the mention of her daughter.

Before she could fire any more questions, he politely interrupted. "His lordship suffered greatly when he realized what had happened at Guilford Courthouse. At first, from what Tarleton indicated to me, his guilt almost incapacitated him. I think my returning to his campsite, after I left you both here, provided him solace … and hope."

"You have talked to Tarleton?" Kathryn asked.

"I am under his command at Gloucester Point, almost directly across the water from Cornwallis's headquarters in Yorktown. I am sure he has a good inkling of my whereabouts, although the general did all in his power to keep this trip secret."

Kathryn nodded, remembering the brash, insolent young man. They had shared many curt words when they all served together, but had developed a mutual respect after the death of his friend, Major Ferguson. Oh, that awful day, she could still see …

Samuel's next statement snapped her back to the present.

"His lordship sent me to find you, assuring me, that if you were both still clinging to life when I left, you would never give up the fight."

Reaching into his pocket, he pulled out a bar of English lavender soap and held it out.

"This is for you. He remembered how much you love it."

Kathryn smiled and inhaled deeply. "Hmmm, such a special treat. I *have* missed it sorely."

Putting the bar aside, she became serious. "What news of our daughter, Samuel?"

"Although Tarleton plays his hand very close to the chest, I know he is well aware of more than he admits. I believe he had much to do with their escape to safety."

Jason's eyes widened, amazed. "Tarleton actually helped?"

Hodges nodded. "I had picked up a few tidbits here and there, but his lordship finally confided, just before I left, that they took Beauty and sailed for England. I gather Jack felt it necessary to keep Gabrielle out of harm's way, by taking her to his family."

So far away and yet I sense her so often—as if she were almost here. Kathryn's mind formed the image of her bubbly, happy child.

"They must be almost there by now," she murmured.

"Samuel and I also discussed the war while tending the horses. It does not appear ..."

"I sensed problems almost from the minute you arrived, Samuel."

He nodded, wincing slightly. "Tarleton digs fortifications, as does his lordship. But at this point, all is lost in the South, what little remains will be gone shortly. Clinton still sends vague communiqués to his lordship and he replies in a like manner—neither willing to comply with the other's directives. There is no money forthcoming from England—no supplies, no reinforcements. And Nathanael Greene wreaks havoc at every turn."

"How serious ...? If Kathryn and I were to head for England, would there be safe passage at this point?"

"Yes, but you must go soon. Although Cornwallis believes the French will never consider bottling him in at Yorktown, thinking them too busy in the Indies to waste time on a young upstart country, I am not so sure. The French do not like us; that is an absolute fact. And this George Washington ..." He shook his head weighing the bits and pieces he had gleaned through careful observance and cautious eavesdropping. "The man definitely has a certain charisma."

He turned a grave eye to Jason. "It does not bode well. If the French blockade Chesapeake Bay, you must be long gone. Your reputations are well-known and I could not bear to lose you again." He hesitated, eyes misting briefly.

"Tomorrow I head north and return to Gloucester Point. I dare not be absent too long. Tarleton's curiosity will have driven him to investigate my whereabouts by now, and his lordship does not wish to pique his curiosity any more than necessary."

He glanced from Kathryn to the Jason.

"I shall inform Cornwallis that you will arrive by mid-August. That may be pressing our luck a bit with the French, but do not put your health at risk by pushing too hard. Your journey across the 'big pond' promises to be long and tedious; you will need your strength."

Catching Kathryn's uneasy expression, he reached out and took her hand.

"Do not fret, my lady. We found one ship, there will always be another, of that I am sure. I will get word to you if things become desperate."

"I do need Kathryn to be a little stronger," Jason said, turning to smile at her. "It seems my wife is going to make me a father once again, and I would have our family together and well for that event."

Hodges beamed as he gently hugged Kathryn, whispering his congratulations.

"Samuel. Kathryn and I would like you to be godfather to the newest Tarrington, when he or she arrives. Would you be willing to ...?"

"I am honored, sir ... Jason ... 'Lady Kathryn', I ..." he stuttered, a rush of pleasure washing vivid color to his cheeks.

"Maybe you men should check the horses while I clean up—talk over your 'manly affairs'." She winked, grinning at her husband. "I do regret, however, the lack of fine cigars and a good brandy to chat over."

A humorous glint touched Jason's eyes as he recalled the 'oh-so-proper' protocol his wife had been subjected to at one of their military dinners some time ago—when Archibald Campbell had come south in December of '78—and they had assisted him in the taking of Savannah.

"Perhaps tell Samuel where Gabriel and Anna have gone, and visit Soaring Eagle to assure him that all is well. And then, off to bed with you, Samuel. You have a long, hard ride ahead of you tomorrow."

"I feel new energy, and a sense of hope." Kathryn said, snuggling closer to her husband.

"And I would be delighted to show you just how much more energy I have, if it were not for our loudly snoring guest."

She kissed his chest, allowing a devilish flick of her tongue to graze a taut nipple.

"I will take you up on that offer tomorrow, Mrs. Tarrington," he sucked through clenched teeth. "Sleep well, my love, for you will need all your energy."

He smoothed her wildly curling hair, brushing kisses to her forehead, eyelids, cheeks and chin.

With a soft sigh of sheer pleasure, her hand curled against her heart, and their loving salute began.

"Always," they breathed, "Always."

Chapter Twelve

After Five Long Years: Healing

Kathryn sat by the glowing embers of their morning campfire sipping her second cup of coffee. It was not the same quality coffee they had shared daily with the dragoons: rather somewhat bitter chicory or perhaps another substitution of Anna's inclination, in an attempt to wean them from their old lifestyle.

"Whatever this concoction is brewed from, it renews and strengthens. I feel truly well for the first time in many weeks."

Jason smiled at his wife, noting her rosy coloring and sparkling eyes. Taking her hand, he gave a gentle squeeze.

"I think Hodges's visit answered some questions, and brought hope … at least for us; although not for the eventual outcome of the war," he said quietly.

"Ummm," she agreed. "I miss him already, and wish he could have stayed longer. There is so much I wanted to share with him. I do hope you told him of Gabriel and Anna and—Jamie."

"That I did, my love, when we had our 'man talk' last night." Winking, he leaned forward to steal a quick kiss.

"Men," she grumbled, returning his kiss, "so completely impossible and difficult to understand."

At his abruptly raised eyebrow, she chuckled. "For heaven's sake, look at Diablo, the way he carried on with Samuel's charger. I dread to imagine what his greeting to my Beauty might encompass."

"Yes, my pet. She is an enchanting, little tart, as are you: one of your more endearing characteristics, I might add."

Kathryn's smile abruptly faded.

"Beauty is with Gabrielle and Jack; she will be safe," Jason assured.

"Can she survive an ocean voyage in such cramped conditions? I have heard such awful things about …"

"Kathryn, you must have faith. Beauty is as resilient and stubborn as you, my love."

At that comment, she rolled her eyes. "You are right. I need to focus on becoming strong enough to make the trip to Yorktown, and then on to England."

"You and I both, and we shall do it together. Finish up here while I speak with Soaring Eagle. It seems he has chosen a rather pert pony for you. He feels you need a great deal of fresh air and exercise at this stage of your healing."

Talking around a last bit of biscuit she had just popped into her mouth, she began picking up the remains of their morning meal, ablaze with eager anticipation.

"Do not choke, my pet. I shall return shortly, and I really *do need* a riding partner."

It was a delightful ride, Soaring Eagle's choice of pony, commendable. She possessed an even temper, smooth gait and appeared tireless. Kathryn, feeling up to one or two jumps put the agreeable animal through her paces; keeping Jason's nerves on edge, lest harm come to his wife or their precious, new life within.

They walked back into their hut after toweling and feeding their horses. Kathryn, although a bit weary—in her own words—'felt marvelous'. Pouring a basin of water to freshen up before starting their evening meal, she commented: "How I miss Jack and his kind spoiling. There was always water waiting or a snack or ..." Her voice cracked. "Or he would have Gabrielle dandling on his knee and ..."

"Hush, my love. We now have people who will help us set our lives aright. We *will* all be together again. Let us share our evening meal quickly," he murmured suggestively, flashing a devilish look. "I believe you offered to demonstrate your newfound energy as soon as our guest left."

She leaned against the small table saying nothing, eyeing him seductively, purposely dragging out the moments. With a deep purr curling from the back of her throat, she abruptly pushed away from the table.

"Perhaps the evening meal should wait. I prefer your offer of ... *food for the soul*."

With that statement, she began working the laces of her shirt in earnest.

The next morning found them sharing a quickly thrown together repast as Kathryn was eager for her daily ride. She already sensed her stamina rebounding, the pain in her chest subsiding more each day, her appetite improving. She had peeked at her reflection in the washbasin this morning, happy to find her cheeks showing a bit of color from their previous day's ride.

As she picked up their plates, her head snapped up at a loudly yelled greeting.

"Halloo the camp." There was no mistaking Gabriel's booming voice.

Moving to the entrance of their hut together, Jason threw the cloth flap aside and stepped out.

Across the small clearing stood Jamie, flanked on either side by Gabriel and Anna—Soaring Eagle bringing up the rear.

Kathryn gasped, the breakfast plates clattering to the ground. Jason's arm immediately slid around her waist as she swayed slightly, her heart pounding. Drawing comforting circles in the small of her back, he whispered soft reassurance.

They were walking slowly towards her: Gabriel's smile confident, Anna's reserved but positive. Even Soaring Eagle's lips lifted slightly as his jet black eyes met hers.

And Jamie: flashing his customary devil-may-care grin she remembered so well.

But Kathryn detected a telltale quiver of lips belying his usually well-masked feelings—a roller coaster of emotions careening across his features—trepidation in his eyes. *Will she deny me? Has she changed her mind?*

Forcing himself not to think, urged with gentle nudges from both Anna and Gabriel, he put one foot in front of the other, moving doggedly forward.

"What shall I say? What shall I do?" Kathryn whispered frantically.

"Speak from your heart, my love. You will know the right words."

Jamie stopped directly in front of his sister, his eyes only for her. As the others stepped back, he searched her face, wringing his hands slightly, his features becoming suddenly still.

They stood facing each other, neither able to speak, silent communication flowing between them: old hurts, old promises, old expectations ... no longer of importance ... gone, put aside. New hope, new understanding, new acceptance of individuality and choices ... *can we do it?*

Suddenly Jamie's face crumpled. Dropping to one knee, he bowed his head for a long moment and then raised it, searching his sister's face, tears flowing down his cheeks.

"Forgive me, Kathryn … forgive me." His Scottish burr rolled unevenly in his distress. "Whatever ye ask of me … so be it. Whatever ye demand … so be it." He reached out to her. "I cannot …"

Instantly taking his hand, she crouched down, and cupping his cheeks, gently raised his face to meet her commanding gaze.

"Hush now, Jamie, it is over."

Her eyes caressed with sparkling warmth, a meaningful look of love and acceptance passing between them, sealing their new bargain. No further words were necessary: other than those he had needed to hear for so long, now given freely.

"I need you, my dearest brother," she whispered. "Never forget that, even for a moment. Aye?"

Rising slowly, he studied her, taking in every detail, his trembling fingers gently tracing the planes of her face. He had no words, awestruck by what she had accomplished in their time apart: the complete 'being' she had become, her strength, grace and self-confidence.

"I have missed ye so," he murmured, clutching her to him, but feeling her wince, quickly eased his grip.

"Pa would ha' been so proud—so verra proud."

She grinned. "However, not very ladylike, I fear."

Her remark brought a chuckle.

"Ma would ha' sent ye to yer room to rethink yer actions."

Her eyes twinkled with merriment as she moved to his side and turned to face her husband. Up until this point Jason had stood mute, absorbing the reunion of these two stubborn, proud individuals.

"Jamie, I would have you meet my *husband*," she stressed, gesturing Jason forward. "Forgive me, also, but understand me. Accept me as I am *now*—accept Jason, for he and I are as one. He is my life."

Jason stepped forward, hand extended in welcome, warmth flashing in his smile. "Brother-in-law," he said quietly, offering peace.

Jamie hesitated but a moment before grasping his hand.

"Aye, mon that ye are."

He searched Jason's face, sensing his strength of character; recalling his treatment of Gabriel long ago: knowing him to be honest and considerate in his dealings.

"We have much to talk over, you and I." He shrugged. "For we *must* be on the same side now. Greene has no further use for me—or my militia, so I am out of it. And you, Jason, surely cannot go back into the fray—cannot possibly take Kathryn …"

"Did you ever stop to think that perhaps *I* am the one who desires to return to the so-called 'fray', as you put it?"

With a disbelieving look, Jamie's mouth opened to comment, but Kathryn narrowed her eyes in silent warning. Knowing her brother only too well, she realized it would require time for him to understand, and accept, her husband. She and Jason would continue making their own decisions, just as they always had—*together*: period, end of discussion.

"We have something far more important to attend to at the moment," Kathryn said as she slid her arm easily around her husband's waist. "But first, you must all be in need of refreshment. Come inside everyone; we will eat and talk of the future. For much has happened since you left to bring Jamie here, and I doubt Soaring Eagle has had time to inform you."

For the better part of the afternoon they talked, rehashed and discussed, sometimes in animated fashion, occasionally emotional, and—as they began to tire—in a somewhat more heated manner, especially Jamie.

A sharp Cherokee epithet brought them up short, conversation ceasing abruptly as all attention riveted on Anna. With eyes narrowed, she planted herself directly in front of Jamie, fists balled at her sides.

"You *will* accept Hunter. I demand that from you, Jamie." She pierced him with a withering glare, daring him to defy her, knowing full well he would not.

"Complete respect will grow in time, as you come to know this man … as he will, *you*. For this is the way of all things. Hunter belongs with my Ugilohi. Theirs is a shared destiny, and you *will* understand that."

Jamie flinched, in the face of her wrath. He had not intended to lapse into a grudging attitude. A quick glance at Soaring Eagle and Gabriel brought further awareness: there would be no reinforcement coming from them.

Glancing at his sister, he suddenly caught sight of the sacred horn spoon cradled tightly in her cupped hand: awed by the enormous symbolism of the gift. *Enough*, his tired mind screamed. The ultimatum placed before him would be his only chance to share a life with his beloved sister. Understanding that, he finally conceded; his unanticipated reward: blessed relief and inner peace.

"Come with me, my friend." Soaring Eagle's deep, inviting tone interrupted Jamie's thoughts. Placing a hand on his shoulder he added, "We will visit your grandchildren and then find you a place to rest. It is time for healing on many levels, and I will help *you*, just as I have done for Ugilohi."

With a hug to Kathryn, and a firm handshake to Jason—*Hunter*—he must remember, Jamie followed the large warrior out the doorway.

Gabriel brushed a kiss to his aunt's cheek and clapped Jason on the back. "I think it went well, Kathryn, and will improve given time—as stubbornness gives way to growing familiarity. There will be rough edges to smooth over, but you have naught to fear from him. He will help *both* of you, of that I am confident."

With a kiss to Kathryn's cheek and handshake to Jason, Gabriel headed out the doorway.

So like his father—so like my beloved Kathryn. Jason breathed a sigh of relief.

Only Anna remained, her jet black eyes a-sparkle and a slight smile indicating her pleasure at the day's successful outcome.

Abruptly her expression changed. Lost in private thoughts, she stayed silent for several minutes, as Kathryn and Jason quietly watched … honoring her personal reverie.

"They have arrived." Anna released a long sigh.

"What is it, Anna?" Kathryn asked, moving to her friend's side.

"My little bird stands on solid ground," she said with solemn assurance.

"She is in England?" Jason asked anxiously, moving quickly to his wife's side.

Anna's eyes flicked to Jason and then back to Kathryn, as she nodded firmly.

"What of Jack? What of Beauty?" Kathryn's emotional words were barely audible.

"All stand on solid ground." Anna paused. "Lieutenant Jackson is finally home."

Chapter Thirteen

Brief Respite

"Home," Jack mouthed, as he watched the gangplank being lowered to the rustic pier. "Home," he murmured more forcefully in an attempt to find the old connection. *But so much had changed—so much.*

A sharp tug on his sleeve drew his attention to the little girl at his side: Gabrielle, looking hale and hearty. Much to his relief, she had weathered the sea voyage well in spite of heaving seas, heaving stomachs, weevils in their biscuits: *disgusting.* Towards the end of their journey, fresh water had been in such short supply that they had been forced to collect rainwater. He realized he should have been thankful for the four or five days of pelting rain, but its bleak gloominess quickly became unbearable … but not for Gabrielle.

A pleasant vision of the little girl came to mind, causing him to smile. With feet braced wide for balance, she stood amidst the pelting drops, swaying with the ocean's agitated swell. Steadying a small bucket against a large burlap-covered bale, she watched in fascination as it slowly filled for Beauty. Setting it down, she wrung out her sopping wet shift directly into her mouth. And as the trickling water diminished, sucked the shirttails dry, all the while thinking herself quite clever. Her spirit never seemed to falter, as if she somehow knew all would be well.

How does one so young have such unquestioning faith? But he knew the answer. *Because she is very much her mother's daughter*, he thought with a pang of grief. He had planned to arrive here when the war was over with … *Stop,* his mind, or what little was left of it, shrieked.

Abruptly he felt another tug on his sleeve, sharper than the first. Looking down, he was greeted by a beaming face and bouncy eagerness.

Forcing a half smile, he hugged her close. England had once been his home, but now? *Home* had been with … he quickly squelched that thought. This would be 'home', at least for now—or until he could sort things out.

A sudden thought created a moment's panic. There had been no way to make Eugenie aware of their pending arrival. She had always seemed loyal, but this was a lot to ask. He was no longer the soft-handed, foppish brother who had so boldly charged off to war seeking glory in the colonies: at present, not even remotely close to Eugenie's naïve image of a perfect 'gentleman' in society.

And how would she react to Gabrielle, this charming, bold child? Good Lord, her daily conversation is sprinkled with Cherokee; a language she often speaks fluently, as if it were her native tongue. She is vivacious, bold …

His drifting thoughts ceased abruptly as the gangplank dropped into place with a resounding 'thunk'. Grasping Gabrielle's hand firmly, and inclining his head to Smitty, he took a deep breath and stepped onto the gangplank.

As her foot touched the pier, Gabrielle turned and stood waiting expectantly, watching the opening at the top of the gangplank. At Jack's quizzical expression she smiled.

"We will wait for Beauty; she will be here soon."

"It is almost dark, little one. We stood offshore for so long, awaiting high tide to enter port that I am afraid others will be anxious to disembark. Beauty must wait her turn."

"Oh no, Uncle Jack, Smitty said he would bring her right along."

Jack actually smiled at that. Her mother had always had the ability to control almost any given situation. Thankfully, before unwanted images could rear their ugly heads, a soft whinny drew his attention back to the upper deck.

"See? I told you." Gabrielle hopped from one foot to the other, clapping her small hands with glee.

"You are amazing little one," he said softly, giving her a wink and returning his attention to the little mare. Watching Beauty dance lightly and surely down the gangplank with Smitty, he grinned in spite of himself.

"Step aside! Step aside! Valuable cargo coming through," Smitty growled as he elbowed his way, none too gently, through the few disembarking passengers.

Smitty: Jack shook his head in disbelief. How had he ever managed that?

From day one of their journey, he had been drawn to Gabrielle like a moth to flame, a fact which had made Jack uneasy at the outset. But constant watchfulness of the odd, little man reassured that he truly loved the little girl, and bore her no harm.

Perhaps he had lost a child to illness or, having had no children, wished for a little girl of his own flesh at some point in his life. But in all the weeks they had spent with him, he had divulged very little of his personal life: hiding behind tomfoolery and non-stop chatter.

And Gabrielle had been equally drawn to him, despite his somewhat intimidating appearance. Due to one slightly drooping eye, his grizzled features remained rather stern: a souvenir from '*an old battle with privateers*', he had once remarked offhandedly with pride radiating from every fiber of his body.

His rapidly balding head sported a very 'tired' old bandana, darkened from grease, sweat and just plain over use. In contrast, several well-polished, twinkling gold hoops of various sizes swung freely along the outer edges of both ears, fascinating Gabrielle. Although short in stature, he was built ruggedly—well muscled and 'beefy'—not one to be taken lightly; far better as a friend Jack decided early on.

As they watched Smitty make a cautious descent with his precious cargo, Jack noticed that several old tars immediately made themselves tight to the ropes allowing his passage.

"Move aside," Smitty yelled at a slower moving, much larger man blocking his progress.

Jack's eyes widened wondering if tempers would flare. But a grim scowl was the full extent of the big man's irritation.

Smitty flashed a generous grin baring a toothless expanse of pink gums, proudly acknowledging his command of the situation—as well as displaying his reward from a barroom brawl in his youth.

"You shoulda' seen the otha' guy when I waz finished," he guffawed.

Jack could still hear his accompanying peal of laughter, remembering it fondly; one of the few times the unique little man had shared a bit of himself with them.

"Here she is, sir, an' not likely a bit 'worse for wear' for all her weeks on board."

Smitty shoved the reins unceremoniously into his hands and turned immediately to Gabrielle. Sweeping her up into his strong arms, he hugged her close, brushing a kiss to her cheek.

"Ole Smitty's gotta go wet his whistle, my little princess."

Setting her astride the already saddled mare, he turned to Jack. "No goodbyes, sir. Yer last bag's tied to the saddle, but I'll be seein' you agin' someday."

He crushed Jack's hand in a mighty grip and then turned to Gabrielle, but not before Jack caught the brightness of his eyes.

"I love you, Smitty," she whispered, placing a kiss on his lips. "We *will* see you again." She hugged him close and said softly, "Please do not forget me."

"I will never forget *you*, little one," he said brokenly, and with a quick hug, ducked into the crowd and was gone.

Chapter Fourteen

Dubious Greeting

Well, here we are. Jack eyed the long, graceful driveway that wound its way to the portico of the elegant English Estate. Manicured gardens, privet hedges trimmed to perfection, shrubbery crafted into shapes of large animals—*what in the world do you call them ... topiary?*

He was now far removed, and happily so, from all this overwhelming, unnecessary excess. A sidewise glance at Gabrielle's awed expression and stunned silence indicated she viewed the estate in similar fashion.

Oh, what have I gotten us into? Jack groaned.

They had spent the previous night in a small untidy room at the back of a little pub, much to Jack's distress. He had fled the colonies with only a few coveted coins, which had quickly been spent during their long voyage, for one or two extras. He had no coin left, and the innkeeper—no compassion. Jack offered to sweep the floor, wash dishes, clean tables or whatever necessary to be allowed lodging for the night: a fair barter, apparently in his mind only. The fact that he was a British dragoon officer, returning home from fighting in the American colonies, gained nothing. Even pleading a heartfelt case—'for the little girl's sake'—through tightly gritted teeth, fell on deaf ears.

Throughout Jack's coaxing, the unpleasant man had eyed him sharply, looking him up and down repeatedly, until his gaze finally stopped on his red jacket. Wiping a grimy hand on his grease-spattered apron, he reached to finger several gold buttons before raising his glittering snake-like eyes.

"Those will do," he said matter-of-factly, ignoring Jack's shocked expression.

One musty pallet to share and two bowls of stew, the contents, of which, were questionable. Jack shook his head in disgust, well aware of who had gotten the better deal; but there had been no other choice.

Eugenie would have expected him to arrive in a carriage befitting his status as a 'gentleman' from a wealthy family. But astride Beauty would have to do, and lucky to have her at that or they would be walking.

Ah, Eugenie, my dear sister, I fear you are in for a rude awakening—as are we. May we all make this work—or at least survive until I can figure out what to do next.

With a slight nudge, Beauty began a slow prancing step, her delicate hooves picking their way nimbly along the cobble-stoned driveway. With head held high, silky mane swishing softly, she carried herself proudly. Her intelligence and understanding of any given situation never ceased to amaze him.

As they neared the front portico, he could see two or three of Eugenie's 'people', as she referred to them, pruning shrubs diligently off to one side of the manor. It was a lush, green maze, as he recalled: one with abrupt changes of direction, surprising dead ends, and a great deal of complexity. Memories of long hours spent in idle pleasure playing adult hide and seek came rushing back. Issuing a low sound of disgust, he shook his head. *How my life has changed.*

Gabrielle looked back over her shoulder, addressing him with sparkling blue eyes. "What are you thinking, Uncle Jack?"

"Nothing of importance, little one." But at her long, serious look added: "Actually, a few old memories are drifting back."

"Do we belong here?" she asked.

Struck by her astute awareness, he remained silent for a long moment, unsure of what to say. But he must be honest; she would expect that of him, as would her mother, he winced at that thought.

"Actually, I no longer know. But for the moment, it is all we have …"

"We have each other," she stated firmly, shifting in the saddle to hug him.

Jack inhaled a deep breath and released it slowly through pursed lips.

"Yes, princess, we do. And that will keep us strong."

Squaring his shoulders, he forced himself to sit straighter in the saddle as they reined Beauty to a stop under the portico. He had nothing for which to be ashamed, nor did Gabrielle. There was no reason to shrink before his sister's unwavering self-importance, and he would not. Perhaps she has changed; but that thought rang hollow in his ears.

By now their arrival had been noticed; a porter, having been summoned to their side, quickly appearing out of nowhere. Beauty flattened her ears, sidling away, but stopped her foolishness and stood quietly at Jack's command.

"Master … Jackson?" the liveried young man asked, staring at him with curiosity.

Jack nodded searching his memory, the name suddenly coming to him.

"Derek? You were but a boy when I left, and now grown to a fine young man."

A wide grin and bobbing head proved him right.

"Are you home from the war, sir? Is it over?"

"Yes and no. A rather long tale to be told at a later date," Jack answered as he dismounted and reached to lift Gabrielle down.

"I will stable your animal, sir." Derek said politely, but his attention remained riveted on Gabrielle.

"Thank you, but no. She will wait here until we can tend her. She is very particular in her ways."

Pulling Gabrielle forward, he introduced her. Although polite, she remained distant, observing the young man with a quiet thoughtfulness that made him uneasy.

"Please announce us, Derek. I trust Mrs. Beaumont is home."

The young man nodded and backed slowly away, obviously disappointed that no explanations were forthcoming, his curiosity left unanswered.

Mere moments passed before the front door opened and a tall, slender, austere woman stepped forward. Grasping Jack's shoulders, she gave him a polite hug.

"Dearest brother, it really *is* you. What an unexpected surprise." Somewhat hesitantly, she placed a kiss on each cheek, and then stood back eyeing him speculatively.

Momentarily nonplussed by his sister's understated greeting, Jack's mouth dropped open. But quickly gathering his senses, he pulled her into a rough hug. She barely returned his warmth before pushing away, reverting to her reserved fashion.

"Is that the best welcome you can offer after all these months, Eugenie? I had hoped you might have missed me."

His tone held a chastising edge that drew Gabrielle's attention to her Uncle Jack. Peering from her place of security a little behind him, she searched his face. Tightly hugging his pant leg, she watched with shy uncertainty.

She had occasionally seen her mother dressed lavishly in similar fashion: hair gathered to fall in long, curling ringlets, held in place with decorative pins and ribbons, and dangling earbobs swinging delicately—but *never* as daytime wear. It had not been her favorite attire: donned only when duty required and to please poppa. However, this woman appeared comfortable and in control.

How confusing, it is only mid-morning—way too early for a party. Does she always dress this way? Gabrielle clutched Jack's leg tighter in growing trepidation, listening as he explained their situation calmly and quietly. Throughout his tale, the woman stood stick-straight, her long, delicate hands folded in a precise pattern against the lace of her bodice, her face almost expressionless.

Why does she not hug him more, she wondered? *Why is she so—what did mama tell me to be, when I visited headquarters? Reserved? Yes—reserved.* The longer she watched Jack's sister, the greater her confusion. *How could she not miss her brother after all these months?* This woman caused her to feel unsure of herself and ill-at-ease. But she would do her best to fit in for her uncle's sake.

Suddenly Eugenie, that was the name he had called her, caught sight of the somewhat unkempt child clinging to her brother's leg and moved to get a better look, dousing Gabrielle's racing thoughts.

She sensed this woman found her appearance less than pleasing. Even with all Jack's effort to make them both presentable, their best outfits bore the trials and tribulations of long weeks at sea with only salt water for rare washings. However, their 'best' had never come close to this lady's elegant clothing. *Well, perhaps Uncle Jack's jacket did—before he sold the buttons to …*

"Well, now," Eugenie purred, bending to inspect Gabrielle. "And just what, or whom, do we have here? Such a charming little urchin."

Gabrielle's eyes went wide. She was not quite sure what that word meant, but it definitely did not sound complimentary.

"Eugenie, this is *their* child." Jack sounded tired.

Turning, he placed a comforting hand on Gabrielle's shoulder. Moving as unobtrusively as possible so as not to explicitly offend, he placed himself in a position to ward off his sister's grasping hand as she attempted to pull the little girl forward for a better look.

My God, how she has changed. He maintained a blank expression as he sought to find the correct words, but grimaced inwardly. There was no place for them to go; for the time being he had to make this work.

"I am Gabrielle Elizabeth Tarrington," announced a firm, proud voice, startling him slightly.

Moving into view, she took a deep breath and squared her small shoulders. Once again in control, she made full, unwavering eye contact with the severe woman. There was absolutely no reason to hide, or be ashamed. Her parents had taught her that, and she would never forget again—not even for a moment.

"Hmmph, a rather precocious chit, I might add."

"Eugenie, please." Jack bit his tongue, trying to remain civil to this woman he barely recognized. "I am sure you must recall my letters …"

"Oh, yes, I do recall you mentioning the colonel and his—*woman.*"

"His beloved *wife*, Eugenie," Jack corrected acidly, his patience with her cynicism rapidly waning. He needed an answer—now.

"Can you put us up for a while or not? We are exhausted and have been through …" His mouth snapped shut. He *would not* discuss details now, especially in front of the child.

"Of course we can always seek shelter at her grandmother's," he murmured, appearing to be deep in thought. Although *he* realized that situation to be impossible at the moment, Eugenie did not. "However, I thought you might prefer …"

"Yes, of course, dear brother," Eugenie interrupted, "you may both stay as long as you like," she trilled, gushing rather agreeably.

Her sudden change of demeanor came as no surprise, her shallowness so easily read. He suspected what she might be considering and wished they had gone elsewhere—*anywhere.*

Eugenie was momentarily struck silent. She now possessed a rather intriguing 'social plum'. Her brother obviously had first hand information on the war in the colonies, and this child … Her mind worked like a steel trap: oh, the endless possibilities for furthering her position in London's high society suddenly being handed to her on a platter. Such a brilliant stroke of luck, after all, one could never be too thin, too rich or too famous.

"Please do forgive me. I fear the shock of your arrival has caused me to forget my manners."

With a flourish of skirts and swish of numerous petticoats, she angled herself between Jack and Gabrielle, hugging each in turn and pressing a warm kiss.

"Do come in. You look as if a hot bath and clean clothes would be in order. By the time you have freshened up, the noon meal will be ready. I shall have another place setting arranged at the dining room table, and you, Miss Gabrielle," she pulled the little girl against her in a perfunctory squeeze, "may join Robert and Emiline at the children's table in the kitchen. And then …"

Afraid she would never stop, Jack interrupted. "First we must bed down Beauty. It will take no more than a few minutes," he assured. "Why not have our baths drawn, Eugenie—if it is not too much trouble? Then we will not keep anyone waiting at the table."

"Beauty?"

"My mama's horse," Gabrielle piped up. "She needs rest too."

A look of distaste shivered across Eugenie's features, and although quickly masked, Jack took note and understood. With a curt nod to both, she spun on her heel and disappeared into the house.

The mere thought of a *family* member, rather than servants, tending a horse was part of it, but the other fact had directly to do with Kathryn, of that he was sure. And he could not bear to go there at this point.

"Well, that certainly did not go as I had expected," he mumbled.

"She is not like you, Uncle Jack," Gabrielle said softly. Reaching to grasp his hand, she turned large, blue eyes to search his face. "Nor like me …" she added, concern flickering in their blue depth.

"We are safe, little one … and together. That will have to do for the moment, one day at a time, aye?"

Snatching Beauty's reins, he placed a hand on the little girl's shoulder and forced a reassuring smile.

"Come now, we must find a nice stall for Beauty, and we had best make haste."

"Aye, mate," she giggled. And mimicking one of Smitty's less than perfect salutes turned and headed for the outbuildings and paddock.

Gabrielle sat quietly eating her lunch—using the proper manners taught by her mother—and listening avidly to Robert share observations and comments in a lilting English accent tinged with humor.

Not wishing Robert to realize how closely she scrutinized him, she feigned concentration on her lunch, but silently observed him through lowered lashes. She could far more easily describe *him* in detail, if need be, than recite the numerous items served in their mid-day meal.

If this is called a 'light' meal, what ever will they serve at a full dinner? She wondered.

She recalled the stiff formality with which he had addressed his mother at their earlier introduction. Tall, slender and immaculately dressed, he had presented himself with hair brushed to perfection, and not so much as a single strand out of place.

How fascinating. At that time, he had also greeted her formally with a brief hug and light kiss to both cheeks in welcome. But now, sitting at the children's table in the kitchen with only his baby sister, Emiline, and the elderly cook rustling about in the background, she saw something quite different. Genuine warmth glowed in his rich, brown eyes as he smiled at her, but more—acceptance and perhaps—just a hint of deviltry. Time would tell, but she already liked him.

Thankfully, he seemed completely unlike his mother: totally lacking her rude, pretentious nature. She surmised he must be more like his father, although she had yet to meet him.

And Emiline, her thoughts drifted to Robert's three-year-old sister who sat to her left. With golden, corkscrew curls surrounding a cherubic face, she looked to be the absolute picture of innocence; and decidedly her mother's little 'pet'. However, when she thought she was unobserved, she narrowed her eyes and rudely darted her tongue, an absolute brat. Arrogant, even at this young age, she was definitely her mother's daughter.

Suddenly Robert looked over smiling, catching Gabrielle staring openly. As a flush of crimson raced across her cheeks, he reached and touched her hand.

"Enough about me." His grin widened; soft brown eyes encouraging. "I want to hear *everything, absolutely everything,* about *you*."

Emiline wrinkled her nose, interrupting with rude noises and a menacing scowl; the possibility that Gabrielle should be encouraged to speak, unacceptable.

"Emmie, you hush this minute. I will not allow you to be rude to our new friend," Robert hissed, lowering his face to within inches of hers. Turning back to Gabrielle, he nodded encouragement, anxious for her to begin.

Robert made her feel welcome and … *safe*, as if she had known him all her life. He could be trusted not to make fun of her, or belittle her feelings of self-worth, and to be there when she needed him, of that she had no doubt.

Taking a deep breath, she returned his smile and slowly began to talk.

With each passing day, Gabrielle found coping more difficult. So many new rules, a lifestyle very different from the one she had known. But she could see Uncle Jack's dreadful unhappiness, as he realized he no longer belonged here either. She would make a concerted effort to fit in; perhaps then, the ever-present tension between all of them might lessen.

To make things worse, Jack grieved continually for her parents. If only she could convince him that all truly *was* well. He wanted to believe, to grasp at any straw, but his sister's overbearing tutelage kept him much too rooted in everyday realities. Unfortunately, Gabrielle's fledgling abilities only allowed her to experience 'strong senses' of their well being but no specific details which might make her statements more believable. With each passing day she sensed their growing strength; knowing beyond doubt, that they would come to find her and Jack.

Robert's spoiled little sister, Emiline, was a fragile, pale child with blond hair that floated like fine-spun silken threads about her heart-shaped face. Those delicate looks concealed an angry, unpleasant, little girl consumed with jealousy; a tattletale, consummate liar and spiteful troublemaker: difficult to understand or like. In the beginning, Gabrielle had made an effort to find something likeable about her, but now merely stayed out of her way.

Mr. Beaumont seemed pleasant enough, the few times she saw him. He actually treated her in a friendly manner if his wife was not around. But when in the presence of her overpowering personality, he became stiff and somewhat severe.

Gabrielle pondered many grown-up thoughts as she drifted off to sleep at night, one of which concerned Mr. Beaumont. He seemed to be a fine, decent man, and had followed in his father-in-law's footsteps learning the banking business. Whether he enjoyed it or not, he had remained, always uncomplaining, and providing well for his family. Why, then, did he practically cower when in his wife's presence?

Enough about him, I will take mama aside and ask her to help when she gets here. Having solved that problem in her child's mind, her thoughts invariably drifted to Robert … *Robbie.* He was special. Although he played 'the role' in front of his mother, he was definitely 'his own man'.

Having completely convinced his mother that he was teaching Gabrielle about proper English etiquette, she allowed them to spend a great deal of time together. Gabrielle grinned at that, for more often than not they were actually just having fun: fishing in the pond, visiting the stables, even walking the grounds and talking. And most of the time, he handled Emmie's selfish tantrums, maintaining temporary peace.

But even with Robert's warmth and caring, she found her present existence too much—way too much. All she ever heard was: *Do not touch that. Be careful or you will break that.* And the nastiest of all: *Never forget, young lady—that is not yours.* Rules, rules, rules: her head ached with the noxious things.

It was the end of a very long day as she lay quietly listening to Jack talk of their life here. He never spoke of the past, although she wished he would. There was so much she wanted to ask him about that last battle and …

But tonight he was intent upon reliving this morning's latest infraction, one that she had already put behind her as trivial. It was the most recent of her on-going capers and obviously amused him. As so little pleased him, she grinned and gave him her full attention.

"I doubt Eugenie will ever recover, little one, and I shall see the look on her face forever." He actually laughed out loud, and at her quizzical expression continued. "When you tromped into her study with your dress hiked up and tied in a knot about your waist, your boots coated with mud, your silk hose baggy with water and filth … Well, I thought she would choke on her tea."

"Well, I did try to stay as clean as I could but …"

"You were priceless, my princess. Grinning from ear-to-ear and proud as a peacock, you stood there with a string of Eugenie's prized—and *renowned* I might add—Koi. Straight from her garden pool with one or two pond lilies still clinging …"

At her look of embarrassment he quickly hugged her.

"You have absolutely nothing of which to be ashamed. Nothing," he whispered. "I love you dearly, and admire your *joie de vivre*, so like …" He stopped short, recovered himself quickly, and added: "But the very best part of all, little one, was when you handed them to Eugenie and proudly announced: *Dinner!*"

With a shrug, Gabrielle started giggling into her hand and Jack, his shoulders shaking with mirth, struggled for silence so as not to be overheard in their shared glee.

Finally, with tears of laughter streaming down their cheeks, he tucked her into bed with another hug and a light kiss to her forehead.

"How long do you suppose we have been here, my little princess?" he asked quietly.

Without hesitation, she sat bolt upright, folded her arms across her chest and quipped, "Too long."

That feisty remark brought a chuckle and more smiles, the first true joy she had seen him express in weeks.

"You are so like your mother." He shook his head, amused, his statement finally seeming to bring inner pleasure. Brushing a stray lock behind her ear he added, "She would not have put up with this; it is about time I started to think about other options."

Tucking her back under the covers, he touched her cheek gently. "I will find something for us. *I will.*"

Twinkling blue eyes met his as a broad smile engulfed her face. "It *will be* all right, Uncle Jack. It *will be.*" With her dark lashes fluttering sleepily, she curled onto her side, and with a barely smothered yawn, drifted into sleep.

Chapter Fifteen

Time to be Away

Kathryn shaded her eyes against the late afternoon sun with a slender, tanned hand. Scanning the rapidly growing rows of healthy, young corn stalks, she smiled. Jason and Jamie conversed amiably as they strode across the field, each lifting a hand in greeting as they approached. Both men looked tanned and healthy, Jamie's limp no longer noticeable.

The reins of Old Joe, the family plow horse, draped casually over her brother's shoulder as the majestic beast plodded slowly at his side. With an occasional light slap of leather against his rump, he encouraged: "Make haste, old boy, y'er almost home. A warm stall and good meal await ye."

Turning to Jason, he eyed him with a devilish glint.

"And if we are in luck, and your Kathryn remembers her womanly duties, we will have a good meal waiting, or at least ready in short order." A broad grin spread across his face as he winked.

Jason flashed an answering grin, well aware that Kathryn, while refusing to subject herself to the edicts of so-called duty, never let them down: faithful to their needs through directives created out of *love;* self-devised rules which *she* chose to live by.

Kathryn smiled contentedly. *Time really does heal,* she thought. For when they had first left Anna's community and traveled north to stay at Jamie's farm, there had been obvious tension between the two proud men. But quickly realizing Kathryn's need to heal, they held their tempers in most incidents: self-restraint becoming easier with each passing day. In time, a distinct bond of trust and friendship had developed; they actually liked each other quite well—truly a blessing. Thanks to Jamie's coaching, Jason could quite convincingly be taken for a colonial. And that was important.

Soon, *very soon,* they must head towards Yorktown. Bits and pieces drifted back to them about ongoing fighting, news boding ill for the British: a fact continuing to eat at Kathryn.

This George Washington they were hearing so much about held a great deal of charisma with the French. If Hodges had been correct, they must be on their way to England soon, before it was too late. At this point they were ready: able to 'blend' into whichever side any given situation might demand, of that she was sure.

She continued watching as the two men stopped mid-way across the last field. Watching Jamie idly scratching Old Joe's ears as the two men talked, her mind began to wander.

Several weeks had passed since they left the Cherokee village. Anna's firm instructions still echoed clearly. "Heal and rebuild your strength and 'colonize' Hunter." Her important underlying meaning: "Prod Jamie into taking care of his farm and getting the crops into the ground." All this had been accomplished, *Anna would be proud.*

Getting to know her two young nieces, Annabelle and Caitlin, had been an eye-opener: they were no longer the cute little girls she remembered. The former detested her birth name, and flatly refused to answer to anything other than 'Annie'. They were masters of the typical MacLean trait: stubbornness. *Perhaps da would have been proud, but somehow …* Kathryn grimaced, rolling her eyes.

Having grown into unusually pretty young women, both realized their power to dazzle the young locals. And Annie, having several beaus, wasted no time in flaunting her conquests over her younger sister. Their day-to-day existence was not considered worthwhile unless lived as a competition—both vying to be victor. When not actually fulfilling their few daily obligations around the house, they made sure to be 'out and doing'.

Annie taught for a few hours a week at the small schoolhouse just outside town. In Kathryn's observation, she truly loved the children and appeared more than capable in her duties. Life came more easily to her. She made it so, by seizing what she wanted whenever possible—often giving little or no thought to consequences. In fairness to the girl, perhaps that was her way of coping with the aching losses of war. Kathryn hesitated to judge.

Caitlin, on the other hand, helped out in the general store, a job not particularly to her liking, but it provided pretty dresses and 'little extras'. She *wanted* material 'things', and constantly complained of having been cheated in life. She was a quiet girl with a tendency towards sullenness. In appearance she resembled Kathryn somewhat, but all other similarities stopped there.

Understanding her nieces, in general, came as a challenge, but one thing was clearly obvious: neither wanted to be involved in the maintenance of the farm or their father, unless he could take care of himself.

Startled by Old Joe's happy whinnying as he neared the barn, she quickly set aside her 'wool gathering'. Jason and Jamie had closed the distance between them, and hailed her loudly. Close enough now for her to distinguish warmth and devotion in her husband's gaze; close enough to rouse an immediate surge of pleasure … and an eagerness to touch him.

"Stay in the sun and continue your thoughts for a bit longer, my beautiful wife. Your brother and I still have the animals to bed down and feed." He winked knowingly, causing her to grin, her thoughts turning to the previous night.

They had dined together, Jamie having pulled out all the remaining pieces of china from a once bountiful set. Misuse, carelessness and a few roving militia requesting sustenance had taken its toll. However, the table looked elegant.

Gabriel and Silver Fox had been visiting for a week or perhaps more, with young Raven and his baby sister. It had been a wonderful time, long hours of catching up with one another, entertaining Gabriel's little ones and sharing an abundance of joyful laughter. In deference to both Jason and Jamie, talk of the war was kept to a minimum: the current status, how their colonial troops faired, even the possible outcome. For both men still harbored strong sensitivities.

Jason's were decidedly more obvious. But Jamie's, although seemingly subtle on the surface, caused him deep inner turmoil: the questioning of his personal abilities, insulting and undeserved. His pride still smarted from having been told, in no uncertain terms, that he and his rebel militia were no longer wanted or needed due to their lack of reliability. Nathanael Greene had not made even the slightest attempt at softening the blow when he had informed him, merely stating the fact bluntly and then heading off to regroup his troops and wade back into the southern fray.

At about that same time, Cornwallis had also regrouped his army and moved northwards leaving Jamie with no battles to fight or supply wagons to intercept forcing him to grudgingly pick up his life and remain on the sidelines. But he would adjust in time, of that she was sure. He became more at ease with his new life each passing day.

Kathryn smiled, remembering how embroiled their conversations had become during dinner on more than one occasion. Despite attempting to remain calm and neutral, heated discussions had arisen as all parties talked loudly over one another, fighting to present their individual sides. As this would be their last meal together before Gabriel and his family headed home, she had come prepared.

"Enough," Kathryn said loudly, rising from her chair and holding up a stick adorned with an upright feather. "I invoke the use of my Cherokee 'Talking Stick'." She speared each individual with a look that dared defiance. "And each one of you *will* comply so that we may all be heard."

Silver fox chortled gleefully as Kathryn folded the feather down and handed it to her. Then, raising the feather to indicate it was her turn to talk, she added her thoughts. And so it had gone throughout their after-dinner coffee: each individual taking an allotted turn with the 'Talking Stick'.

After all the dishes were washed and put away, Annie and Caitlin having actually helped without complaint, the women sat on the floor and played with Raven and his little sister. Kathryn held the tiny, delicate Mairi, realizing that she was actually beginning to feel some excitement over the tiny babe *she* carried.

Even with the obstacles of its conception and early weeks of clinging to life, the child's kicking was strong and becoming more frequent. But an even deeper sense of yearning for her daughter and Jack rapidly blossomed, likening itself to the all-pervasive growling of a hungry stomach.

She was once again strong, healthy and back to her original weight, time to feed the ache in her heart and perhaps a last bit of adventure. For even when Gabrielle and Jack returned to the colonies with them, Jason—in a heated argument—had forbidden her.

"You are *not* going to return to this war. On that subject there will be absolutely no discussion. If you will kindly recall, my love, I *am* your commanding officer. I care not whether it is the demands of your husband—or those of your colonel that you finally heed and accept, but you *will* do as you are told in this instance."

His terse words as they had readied for bed, still echoed from the previous night. She *had* pushed him to the limits of his patience, as she often did, merely testing—never giving in easily. However, with infinite tolerance, he had described convincing possibilities for an exciting future that they would build *together*, one requiring hard work and numerous challenges. That had caught her full attention, as he had known it would. He understood her as well as he did himself, their needs identical—settled farm life would never be a consideration.

Besides, who could tell what direction the war might take? Which side, under present circumstances, would they be drawn to support? Captain Hodges had hinted at changes looming on the horizon in his recent message, urging them to make haste in coming north. He would make preparations, and notify them of the time and meeting place shortly.

Tonight, with all the company gone and both girls attending a barn dance at the neighbors, they would make plans with Jamie for their departure. By weeks end they must be gone.

Abruptly yanked back to the present by Jamie's warning yell: '*Look out below,*' she grinned. Hurling a pitchfork-full of hay from the loft, he chortled devilishly as Jason quickly sidestepped to miss the sweet-smelling pile, allowing it to fall at his feet.

Within moments, Jamie joined him and stood watching as he tossed the last of the dried grass into the pigpen. Setting his pitchfork aside, Jason slapped dust from his trousers and grinned at his brother-in-law.

"Be wary of 'pay backs', my friend, for I now owe *you* one."

"Aye, that ye do, and I shall be prepared."

Laughing companionably, they stripped off their shirts beside the watering trough and proceeded to remove the top layer of dirt from their perspiring bodies. The sun striking Jason's tanned chest drew her attention to the long raised scar that traversed the full length of his abdomen and disappeared beneath his belt. It was less angry looking now, having paled and tightened with each passing week.

He had originally feared she would be repulsed by his hideous scars, just as she feared he would be unable to look upon her disfigurement: both needing reassurance, as always. But he had laid that worry to rest often and vehemently, just as she did for him.

A flush having nothing to do with the sunlight, or her tan, touched her cheeks as memories of last night flickered warmly. Jason's tongue trailing tenderly along the rippled edges of her wound before moving lower to flick deliciously at a taut nipple. Not stopping there, he proceeded to trace small circles on her rounding belly, momentary teasing before seductively heading lower. With a small, shuddering gasp, she forced all such thoughts aside. She wanted him desperately. But one could not tell Jamie that dinner would be held up … indefinitely.

With a small sigh, she headed for the house to start dinner, determinedly repeating each individual item she planned to prepare, over and over in an attempt to divert attention away from the aching need that had settled lower in her belly.

"Not bad, Sis." Jamie wiped his mouth, tossed the napkin on the table, tented his fingers and added, "I certainly taught you well." Leaning in close, he flashed a smug grin.

Jason could not hide his smile, thoroughly enjoying the playful banter between these two, often wondering how Kathryn had given this up for so long—*and just for him.*

Kathryn pursed her lips eyeing her brother speculatively. "Hmmph." Long pause. "Well …"

"Speechless, she is." Jamie turned to Jason. "Now, there's a triumph. Heed it well, my good man, Kathryn: actually speechless."

Laughter erupted from both men as Kathryn speared each with an evil eye and shook her head feigning disgust. Abruptly, without a hint of warning, Jamie's happy features collapsed, his smile and laughter vanishing. So like him Kathryn noted, always flitting from one mood to the next.

"It is so quiet tonight, what with everyone having gone back to their own lives," he said softly, reaching to take his sister's readily offered hand.

So in tune to each other Jason realized.

She nodded. "I miss them too." Squeezing his hand she added, "Would that all …" She stopped, leaving what she had been about to say unsaid. Words would accomplish nothing in changing bold facts. *Only time*, she acknowledged.

"Oh," Suddenly Jamie brightened again. "I almost forgot to tell you. A package arrived yesterday while you two were in the woods, doing whatever it is that ye are wont to do." He winked lasciviously at his brother-in-law, but at Kathryn's steely gaze continued. "It was rather oddly addressed, just to you, sis: *Kathryn Cameron McLean.*"

Jamie quickly stood and left the dining room, returning within moments with a compact, tightly wrapped package: its heavy brown paper secured with rough twine and bearing no notation as to origin or sender. He placed it between Kathryn and Jason, shrugging.

At Kathryn's hesitation, Jason moved aside dishes and nudged it in front of her. "It *is* addressed to you, my love."

Slowly, she began pushing the twine aside, carefully spreading the heavy, brown paper, pausing only long enough to cast a quizzical glance, first at Jason and then Jamie. Pushing the wrapping aside, she pulled forth one dark cloak and then another. A small parchment slipped from the folds and dropped to the table, the handwriting easily identifiable.

"From Captain Hodges?" Jason asked.

"Yes, our faithful Samuel," she breathed softly, running her fingers carefully over the thin paper, opening it to reveal his firm hand in a brief note. Passing it to Jason, she watched as he quickly scanned the two short paragraphs.

"He asks after our health and says we must come now. Situations grow more dangerous with each passing day. We must be away immediately, or it will be too late." He eyed his wife meaningfully, but at Jamie's loud throat clearing, turned to his brother-in-law.

"Hunter," Jamie said softly, "the man who delivered this is not known by me, and to my way of thinking asked far too many questions, showed way too much curiosity. I saved it until today, feeling it should not be shared even with the rest of the family; the fewer who know what's going on—the better."

He searched the face of his former foe with concern, before turning to his sister. "Ye must go. I hate to have it so, to lose you again so soon, but ye must."

"Aye," Kathryn said slowly. "These look to be capes fashioned in the Loyalist style to help us pass undetected."

"He gives us scant time and terse instructions, my pet." Jason touched his wife's cheek tenderly.

"Do what ye must and advise me of how to protect ye *both*," Jamie interrupted. Rising from his chair, he moved to Jason's side. "And lest ye worry, my friend, I *will* care well for that ill-tempered, four-legged black devil of yours until ye return."

Jason smiled, pulling Jamie into a bear hug.

"Find my niece," Jamie said huskily, as he quickly turned and began gathering dishes into a clattering pile. "Be gone by dawn. Go safe—and come back to me." With a swift hug and kiss to his sister, he turned quickly away and headed for the kitchen; unable to look back, not wishing them to see his face awash with tears.

An agonized cry brought Jamie out of a sound sleep. Flinging the bedclothes aside, he bolted upright, but stopped as his bare feet hit the cool pine boards of the bedroom floor bringing him fully awake.

"Ahh, lass," he sighed. "She relives it all yet again … and I am greatly to blame." He shook his head and mumbled, "I will ne'er hurt ye again! *Ye must* know by now, Kathryn. Ye must."

He ached to go to her, comfort her, as he should have on that awful day on the battlefield months ago. He paused listening intently, a smile of reassurance lifting the corners of his mouth.

Jason's rich, deep voice resonated softly in the adjoining room as he crooned comforting words to his wife, her muffled sobs lessening as the horrific scenes roiling in her head receded, and she knew beyond doubt, that it was but a bad dream. They were both here, alive and safe in each other's arms.

Such incredible devotion … and passion between them, their love just as Kathryn has explained over and over: exactly as it was between my Mairi and me. *Ah, my precious Mairi, I miss ye so.* Sighing deeply, he lay back against his pillow and pulled the covers up over him.

"I will protect ye both," he whispered into the darkness. "That I vow on my life."

And with that final thought, curled onto his side and dropped back into sleep.

"Sleep now, my love, I am here. Do not forget for a moment, I promised I would *never* leave you … and I *will not*." Jason crooned softly, rocking his wife tenderly as she slowly quieted and began drifting back to sleep.

"Heart of my heart …" His finger traced the bridge of her nose slowly down to her chin, raising it gently to meet the brush of his lips.

"Always …" she murmured, a smile curving her lips as she snuggled back into him, secure in his love.

Chapter Sixteen

Destination: Yorktown

"That smells delicious, my love." Jason moved to his wife's side and crouching down, dropped a kiss to her cheek.

Her smile was instantaneous, although her focus remained riveted on the spitted rabbit she slowly turned over the campfire. It was evenly roasted to a rich brown and, in Kathryn's expert opinion, would be done to perfection in a few more turns.

Jason watched in fascination, noting yams from Jamie's garden setting off to one side on heated rocks, their blackened crusts shielding the sweet orange pulp inside. Her ability to produce a delicious meal over a small wood fire never ceased to amaze him.

"This brings back old memories," she murmured. "On the trail once again, carrying your child and—as in the past—glad I am still able to crouch around my growing girth."

Jason brushed his fingers along her cheek; turning her to meet the warmth of his lips. Kissing him deeply, she relaxed but a moment before breaking the contact.

"Colonel, you would have me derelict in my duties?" She paused, turned the rabbit again and winked. "To put it more specifically, my *wifely* duties as it were?"

Chuckling softly, he stood up. Noticing dark massing clouds off his left he commented: "I had better tend the horses and see to the lean-to. It looks like rain coming in; perhaps heavy."

"You have about ten minutes and all will be ready."

With a nod, he disappeared into the dense brush surrounding them; a spot mutually chosen in order to remain inconspicuous.

Kathryn continued to turn the rabbit as her mind wandered. They had met no resistance up to this point, and were yet to encounter a single sole: stranger or otherwise. They had chosen to travel the back trails, which took somewhat longer, but afforded them safer progress.

The long riding skirt she had been forced to adopt, was bulky and much less comfortable than her former breeches: a necessary evil enabling her to blend into the background better. As both had been easily identifiable in their *former life*, they could not risk being discovered now—or all would be lost. Their luck had held this far; she prayed it would continue to do so. They were less than two day's ride from the assigned 'check- point'—and they were on time.

Drawing a deep breath, she gave the spit one last turn before twitching a crisp rabbit haunch to test it. Done to her liking, she reached for a tin plate, and with a practiced move of her hunting knife, deftly slid the meat neatly onto it.

The first tentative splats of rain began as she wiped the last piece of silverware: a completely unnecessary item when on the trail, but easier to have given in and taken them, than to argue further with her brother. She could still see his silly smirk, and hear the accompanying jest.

"I am afraid ye must act like a lady, my dear sister. After all, ye will be in the right proper company of a British general."

She had snatched the implements with a rough growl, and he winked.

"That was delicious, love." Jason hugged his wife, pausing in reciting one of her favorite Scottish poems from memory.

Tilting their heads, they listened to the heavy rhythm of falling rain on the thickly interwoven bows of their three-sided shelter, pleased to feel no errant drips invading their cozy abode.

"You are quiet tonight, my pet. What thoughts are running through that pretty head of yours?"

She made no answer; no eye contact.

"Kathryn, talk to me. We are close to our destination and, so far, all has been well. And it will continue to be; for we will travel cautiously, perhaps even at night from here on. But I …"

"What if no one is waiting at our appointed meeting place; not from lack of trying, but perhaps our plan discovered? What if there is no ship? What if no one has knowledge of our Gabrielle and Jack? What if his lordship is in trouble or …?"

"Hush, hush, my love, do not fret so, think of the babe."

Running his fingers through her thick curls, he drew her tightly against him, angling her face up gently, silently demanding that she make eye contact. In the flickering light of the dying campfire her eyes met his, searching for comfort she knew would be reflected there … and was not disappointed.

"Providence *did not* put us through sheer hell, and then save us, merely to end it all now. You have 'sensed' our little girl numerous times, have you not?"

She nodded dully.

"Then you must believe; for somehow, it *will* be."

He felt her nod in the ensuing darkness, the last embers finally sputtering out with the heaviest onslaught of rain. Thunder rumbled in the distance amidst flashes of lightening, quickly moving closer.

"I presume it is up to me to divert your concerns, my lady."

Nuzzling her ear, he slid his hand along the luscious curve of her calf … and higher, caressing her thigh with a soft chuckle.

"I do believe your riding skirt affords me far more devious pleasures than your breeches, my love. And I intend to take full advantage."

Pulling her against him, tightly aligning their bodies, he claimed her mouth insistently.

Without further hesitation, she sighed happily and met him with an aching need of her own.

***

"Lord Cornwallis?" Captain Hodges inclined his head politely. There had been no waiting, no questioning and no lack of recognition this time.

The general appeared tired but alert, his once robust arrogance no longer apparent as he sat behind his desk—rigid with tension—awaiting the Loyalist captain's news.

"What have you heard, Captain?" he snapped, aware he was being less than polite.

"I have heard naught, sir. However, that bodes well. If there had been trouble …" He paused, swallowing hard. "Bad news travels fast, as you well know, your Lordship, and I feel …"

"Is the appointed place ready to receive them? How soon? Does Colonel Tarleton know?"

"Yes, we are ready. They should arrive no later than tomorrow night. However, I expect it may be earlier in the day. And as to Colonel Tarleton …" He shrugged. "As you ordered, not even a casual word has slipped; and I have been careful in covering my tracks when meeting with you, sir. As he appears to be deeply engrossed in the barricades he is erecting at Gloucester Point, I doubt …"

"That is exactly what makes me nervous, Captain. He is *never* deeply immersed in anything, other than his dalliances. Do you think …?"

He stopped, not daring to voice his fears.

"I *will* bring good news shortly, your Lordship, but I must be gone. Prying eyes are ever present."

"Until tomorrow then." Cornwallis nodded, locking eyes with the captain as he politely backed away from his desk.

"Yes, milord, until then."

With a dignified salute, Captain Hodges drew a deep breath, spun on his heel and exited the general's headquarters.

***

Captain Hodges paced across the secluded meeting spot, then turned and paced in the opposite direction. He smiled to himself, remembering how it had been Kathryn's habit to do exactly that when waiting for her colonel to return from battle.

'Lady Kathryn' must be well now—and her babe growing strong and healthy. He would allow no other thought to enter his mind. As his colonel had been mending rapidly, well beyond the point of setbacks, he wasted no false worry on him.

Where are you his mind shrieked? *Where are you? You must be safe!*

A sharp twig snap, not of his making, brought him immediately alert: pistol drawn, free hand hovering over his sabre hilt in readiness. Turning slowly, circling in a half crouch, he scrutinized the low shrubbery, eyes searching for the slightest movement. Another snap of a branch: louder and closer this time. He tensed, waiting.

"Samuel." Kathryn's soft call drew him about. "Here," she called, peering out from under a low bush where she lay partially hidden. Grinning widely, she struggled to her feet, aided by the colonel who shook his head; first at his wife and then his former captain.

"She wanted to surprise you." He shrugged apologetically.

"Anna would chide me for the twig snapping, but I wished to give fair warning, Samuel." She smiled, hugging him tightly, then stepped back becoming serious. "No, actually I must admit the plush life I have lived at Jamie's has truly dulled my abilities. It is time for an adventure."

Snaking an arm around his wife's waist, Jason extended a hand in heartfelt greeting to his former captain.

"I *had* begun to worry, Colonel … Jason," he corrected. "I knew you would not be able to reply without risk of showing our hand. But problems are escalating in this damnable war, and as to his lordship's mood? An exceptionally low tolerance for lacking answers in any given situation—or being forced to wait."

He grinned and stood back, looking them both over with a keen eye.

"You certainly are a feast for sore eyes: restored to full health." His sparkling eyes met Kathryn's. "And how fares my godchild, milady?"

Kathryn swept the fronts of her cape aside and placed a hand against her rounding belly. "Growing by the minute—with a kick like a mule," she said, giggling as a flush of color dusted the captain's cheeks.

"Let us be on our way," Jason interjected, heartily slapping his friend's shoulder, "I imagine his lordship is pacing—as someone else is often wont to do." He winked at his wife.

"I see she has not changed one bit." Samuel chuckled, as he turned to fetch his horse.

"No, my friend, she has not. And for that I am thankful."

As the three rode quietly along a little-used cart path, they exchanged news of all that had occurred since they had last seen each other at Anna's campsite: Jamie's increasing good health, his farm, Banastre Tarleton's continued building of fortifications on Gloucester Point, and Lord Cornwallis's complete frustration in Yorktown. Hodges discussed the on-going lack of support and 'game-playing', suffered at the hands of their superior, General Sir Henry Clinton: accused by his lordship of sitting safely back in New York—so inept at his duties that he 'is unable to decide which coat to wear on any given day—although they are all alike'.

The sun was just setting as Hodges changed direction: leaving the cart path behind, and traveling a short distance through dense woods before entering a large field of waving grass and sweet-smelling wildflowers. Kathryn inhaled deeply, enjoying the rich aromas and dramatic colors of a brilliant sunset.

"Are we almost there, Samuel?" she asked, nudging her horse closer.

"We are near, but will stop for some refreshment, and await nightfall. Are *you* feeling well, Kathryn?"

"Yes, I could not be better." Weighing his words briefly, she nodded. "Arriving under cover of darkness makes sense. We have come this far—nothing will stop us now."

Dropping back beside Jason, she met his concerned look with a brilliant smile. "Soon," she whispered, and planted a kiss on his cheek.

Within minutes, as they crested a grassy knoll, a small cabin came into view, positioned protectively between two stands of tall trees. *Almost like guarding sentinels,* Kathryn perceived.

Lights glowed cheerily from two small windows on either side of the door. As they approached, the door opened, accompanied by protests of rusted hinges. A large, raw-boned woman emerged, and quickly wiping her hands on her apron, beckoned them in.

Dismounting quickly, both men moved to assist Kathryn. But with renewed strength, she gathered her voluminous riding skirt, swung her leg over the saddle, and slid into Jason's waiting arms, grinning from ear-to-ear.

"Show off," he whispered, brushing a kiss to her cheek as he propelled her towards the door.

"Margaret, these are my friends: Kathryn and Jason" He caught himself before *'Lady Kathryn'* slipped out. But this particular woman could be trusted.

As they shook hands and stepped into the cabin, Hodges added, "Margaret is a dear friend. We may talk freely, it will go no further."

Kathryn eyed him speculatively, her knowing look causing him to blush.

Margaret indicated basins of steaming water and towels off to one side, as she excused herself to help Samuel with the horses—affording them several minutes of privacy. An upstairs sleeping loft caught Kathryn's eye as she scanned the cabin's interior, impressed by the efficiency and comfort this woman's cozy home afforded.

Although small, her house was neat, tidy and hospitable. A leaping fire crackled in a large fieldstone fireplace, chasing the chilly evening air. Hanging from a large iron hook towards the back, a huge pot of bubbling stew caused Kathryn's stomach to rumble in anticipation. And the sight of two freshly baked loaves of bread, wrapped and peeking from a woven basket set on the small roughly hewn table started her salivating.

"This kind woman has gone to much trouble," Jason commented. "I am curious as to just how she fits into Samuel's life."

Kathryn nodded. She had taken careful note of Margaret: tall, buxom, but not overly heavy, seemingly independent and definitely self-assured—albeit somewhat quiet, perhaps even shy. Her tawny hair sat sensibly coiled in a large bun at the base of her neck. However, it was her soft brown, amber-flecked, eyes, following Samuel's every move that caught both Jason and Kathryn's attention.

Much to contemplate at a later time Kathryn decided, just as the door opened with a squeal of rusty protest.

"Remind me to fix that for you, Maggie." Samuel smiled, abruptly flushing as he realized his casual familiarity.

But Kathryn and Jason covered nicely for his perceived faux pas, commenting on her home and the marvelous aromas wafting throughout.

The meal was delightful—filling, refreshing and just what Kathryn had needed to restore her strength. Conversation with Margaret was genuine and caring—the fact that she already knew a great deal about them, apparent. But Kathryn perceived her to be no threat, rather quite the opposite. She felt somehow *protected* in this woman's presence; a meaningful look from Jason proving he agreed.

All too soon, Samuel excused himself and moved to the window. "The moon is high; we must go," he said, casting an apologetic glance at Margaret, before turning to face them, a gesture that did not escape Kathryn's notice.

Refusing help in tidying up, Margaret quickly ushered them towards the door. Standing on the small porch, she watched them mount their horses; smiling as Jason helped his wife with her cumbersome riding skirt.

"The time will come when I can wear my breeches again," she grumbled.

"That it will, my love." Jason patted her thigh and moved to his horse.

"Oh, wait one minute." Margaret rushed back into the cabin, promptly returning with a bulging bandana.

"Apples and fresh bread," she explained, handing the bundle up to Kathryn. "Do take care, milady, and come back as soon as you can. I would like to know both you and your good man, better. You are very special to Sam, and that means much to me."

As she stepped back, Samuel suddenly grasped her hand and leaning down, brushed a quick kiss to her forehead.

"Thank you, my Maggie," he whispered softly. "And I *will* fix your door."

In the light of the full moon, he turned to Kathryn and Jason and shrugged, a crooked grin creeping across his face, glad that they finally knew.

The moon had drifted lower in the sky as they waited in silence outside Cornwallis's headquarters, their horses sequestered nearby. The three of them had crept cautiously along a high stone wall, watching for any hint of detection, and now stood in a small courtyard adjoining the kitchen at the back of the manse: deserted and quiet at this hour.

"It is as promised, I see no guards," Samuel whispered tersely. "Wait here."

Standing in the shadows, they watched as he moved quietly to the door, and pausing, tapped a precise code on the heavy planking. Within moments it opened noiselessly; and after a hushed exchange of pre-arranged words, he was quickly pulled inside.

Kathryn nervously rocked from foot to foot, unable to stand still. Placing his hand against her lower back, Jason began tracing small circles, sending a silent message of support: *Courage, my love.*

Pausing, she leaned against him, finding solace within his embrace.

"Kathryn," he whispered against her forehead, "we are together, we …"

"Come quickly:" a sharply hissed command as the door opened again.

"Take my hand and watch your step. All is well, we are unobserved." Samuel led them inside, bolting the heavy door behind them before continuing in his hushed tone. "There are means of access allowing servants to pass undetected to different areas of the manor, even to their sleeping quarters in the loft. I will take you to his lordship via those passageways."

"How is his mind-set?" Kathryn asked as they stepped into a dimly lit corridor.

"He is beside himself with joy." Samuel shook his head, his upper lip twisting. "Although there are sides of this man that he never allows others to see, I truly believe he *does* have a heart."

With that comment, the three of them grasped hands and began wending their way through the dimly lit passage: down a long corridor, up a narrow flight of stairs, and Samuel stopped. Pressing his ear to a closed door, he rapped four staccato taps.

Immediately the small door, disguised as a decorative panel in the wainscoting, flew open and Lord Cornwallis, himself, stepped back searching the aperture apprehensively.

Barely wide enough to allow one person to enter at a time, Samuel slipped by his lordship with a polite nod; pulling Kathryn, followed by Jason, into the well-lit room. For a moment they stood blinking, their eyes adjusting to the bright lighting.

"Kathryn." Cornwallis's shoulders shook as he pulled her into his embrace, clutching her in a bear hug. "Kathryn," he choked. "I thought …"

"Hush, milord," she interrupted, freeing her hand to cup his cheek, her eyes warm and glistening.

"I hated what I had to do. I never dreamed …"

"It is over, done. We are both well." Kathryn stepped back pulling Jason forward.

"Colonel," Cornwallis's voice faltered, as he grasped both Jason's hands, trembling visibly.

"Believe me when I say how good it is to see you, milord." Jason's smile was genuine. "Allow me to quickly interject how grateful we are for any assistance you may be able to offer as we search for our daughter; and to also express our gratitude—for all you provided for her and Lieutenant Jackson, when we could not …"

Jason cleared his throat, glancing at his wife, before turning back to the general.

"I would also request, sir, if my charming wife, with her undying sense of duty, suggests ongoing responsibilities—please deny her."

Cornwallis turned to Kathryn, noting her frown and smiled. "Your work is done, Kathryn, and perhaps—mine also, in the near future."

As she opened her mouth to question, he added, "But none of that conversation now. It is late." Gesturing towards a table holding drinks and refreshments, he moved to pull a chair out for her to be seated.

"A light repast for all of you, and then sleep. There is much to be done tomorrow in readiness for your departure."

Kathryn and Jason watched the general's face intently, noting dark circles weighing heavily beneath his tired eyes and the gauntness of his usually robust features.

Hands clasped under the table, sipping their brandy, they listened politely to his idle prattle, which bordered on nonsensical at times. Occasionally they risked a surreptitious glance at Hodges, hoping to gather his perception of Cornwallis's somewhat odd behavior. But his features remained benignly blank.

So unlike the general, Kathryn worried. He had obviously suffered deeply from his perceived guilt. But she and Jason held no grudge. Hopefully their arrival and visibly good health would ease his stress—and it did. As they continued to talk, he became fully focused, returning to the man they had known before, and she felt heartened.

"You have news of Gabrielle and Lieutenant Jackson?" Jason asked.

"I am aware of their safe arrival in England." He hesitated, eyeing Kathryn. "And Beauty also," he added, grinning. "However, as I have not heard first hand, I can only surmise Lieutenant Jackson is at his sister's estate outside of London. That was what he indicated the night he left."

"Was he …" Kathryn started to question, but a gentle squeeze of Jason's hand stopped her.

It is unnecessary to worry about Jack's emotional status. He has Gabrielle and they are safe. That is enough to know for now. Receiving his silent message, she risked a slight smile, returning an answering squeeze.

As the hour grew late, the conversation became more informative: moving lightly from subject to subject in a rapid flow; no one wishing to retire. Some discussion allowed past regrets to heal, while other bits confronted the current disputes between Cornwallis and Clinton. Lighter moments touched upon past glories of specific battles, and then, in a more subdued tone: the concerns of the war and what lay ahead. Ferguson's untimely death at King's Mountain was also relived; his lordship clearly missing his former officer.

Cornwallis abruptly turned the conversation back to the most important aspect of their meeting: reuniting Kathryn and Jason with their daughter.

"Although it may surprise you both," Cornwallis paused shaking his head at the remembrance, "Colonel Tarleton actually played a strong role in getting them to safety and …"

"Not a strong role but the *complete* role!"

The wooden panel slammed back as Banastre Tarleton swept into the room.

"How in the blazes did you manage to …" Cornwallis spluttered, standing abruptly, red-faced and beyond furious, as all eyes riveted on the intruder.

With a curt bow and flourish of his cape, Tarleton faced the general grinning widely. "Your Lordship, I am sure you are well aware of my persuasive abilities, especially with the fairer sex." He winked quickly at Kathryn, and with a curt hand gesture, indicated for Jason and Hodges to relax.

Keep this light, Ban, or you may be pummeled to death as you pull her into your embrace, he reminded himself—so grateful to see her strong and restored to her former self, that he feared the urge to take her in his arms, to be almost overwhelming.

"How dare you enter unannounced, uninvited …"

"Because, General, once again you require my talents. And …" He held his hand up demanding silence. "Yet again, I have the answers … as I did before. Might I also mention, in addition to my *connections*, I possess the capability to 'make things happen': hence my knowledge of your arrival, and my ability to gain access to this room undeterred."

He flashed a warm smile at Kathryn, with a momentarily unguarded look, and then nodded to Jason.

Cornwallis opened his mouth to speak, but Tarleton continued on, undaunted. "You loathe my arrogance, but I *do* accomplish what I set my mind to—do I not?"

"How nice to see you again, Colonel," Kathryn said lightly, hoping to defuse the situation and halt the general's rising choler. "I understand that you were instrumental in helping our daughter and ..."

"What a dismal night that was. At least the weather is in our favor this time." Seeing Kathryn's inquisitive expression, he paused. "Ah, yes, as I recall you were in no condition to be aware of the pounding rain, the ... But I digress."

At Jason's icy glare, he quickly continued. "Actually, I *am* here for a reason." He turned full attention to his lordship, whose brilliant red countenance had faded to a mild blush of frustration, *and embarrassment,* Kathryn realized.

"The ship, on which you propose to send the colonel and his wife to England, although well armed, is a lumbering cow. She is top-heavy and unable to get out of her own way in a fight. That makes her an excellent target for the privateers presently plying these waters so successfully, as well as those surrounding England's ports."

Cocking his head with a boyish grin, he scanned all faces present, stopping at Captain Hodges. "Tisk, tisk, Captain: plotting behind my back." He wagged his finger, but said no more, continuing on in his usual rush of words. "I have even considered privateering myself: quite a lucrative career, you know. But I digress."

Leaning forward, he unhurriedly filled himself a brandy and stood sipping, focusing full attention on his drink.

"Not a bad year, your Lordship. I admire your exceptional taste." He continued to disregard them all for the moment, thoroughly enjoying Cornwallis's pique—satisfied in the knowledge that the man was powerless to curb him.

How he loves attention. He knows he is in full command—and is thrilled. Kathryn watched him closely, irritated by the fact that she must dance to his tune.

His next statement brought her abruptly back to the moment.

"Besides, if it would not be considered impertinence on my part, it would seem to me that Kathryn needs to arrive in England without any delaying confrontations." He smiled directly at her, before pointedly dropping his eyes to her rounding belly. "It appears you are again with child, my dear. Congratulations, Colonel."

With a sly grin, Tarleton turned full attention on Jason: sitting rigidly silent, his fists clenched, and barely able to control his fury; enraged even further by the fact that he *needed* this bastard's aide. And all it was to Tarleton: just another game.

"If it is a boy, would you do me the honor of naming him after me?"

Tarleton cocked his head waiting for an answer he knew would never come.

Jason forcefully shoved his chair back, almost knocking it over, breathing heavily from the effort of restraining himself.

Tarleton scanned the shocked, angry faces, tossed back his brandy, and setting his glass loudly on the table quickly stated: "Sorry; that last bit was definitely lacking sensitivity on my part."

He knew very well that he had almost pushed Jason to the edge of no return; and he had no desire to do that. He would not see Kathryn hurt again—*at least not by his hand.*

"All horseplay aside, privateering of English ships *is* extremely prevalent. It requires only a simple 'Letter of Marque', easily obtainable, and *voila* ... a new career awaits you. With that in mind," he paused for effect, "I have managed to find a sleek, fast, seaworthy beauty that will serve you far better."

"And just *how*, might I ask, did you manage this?" his lordship demanded.

"Do not ask, as it might indicate prior knowledge on your part. I purposely left you out of this, your Lordship."

At Cornwallis's somewhat surprised look, he added, "It would seem you have a great deal on your plate already. Therefore, I shall take full responsibility for my actions."

"Well, do go on, then, Colonel Tarleton." His voice had softened considerably. "You have our full attention."

Tarleton sat down, tenting his fingers as he explained tersely: "She is anchored off Gloucester Point—ready and waiting at this moment. It truly grieves me to cut your touching reunion short; but you must be ready to sail by dawn."

His statement was instantly greeted by startled looks and the beginnings of rebuttal. Throwing his hand up, dismissing all further discussion, he growled, "I realize this is short notice and the hour is late. Either you wish to depart in comparative safety—or you do not. Your choice, now what will it be?" He eyed first Kathryn and then Jason, in stony silence.

At their curt nods and mumbled assent, he added, "You may rest on board. But the tide will be right at that hour, and cover of darkness is essential, as you both well know."

Producing a folded parchment from an inner jacket pocket, he placed it on the table before the general.

"I have the details written out for you. Digest the information; then burn it. Further discussion is out of the question."

He speared each individual with a steely gaze. "Any questions ...? I thought not. Then read and memorize."

Opening the soiled paper, he spread it out before the general, as Jason and Hodges moved closer to study the instructions.

"Oh, in case I have neglected to mention it, there will be absolutely no transit of horses this time."

Kathryn chuckled as she slowly stood up. "May I speak with you a moment, Colonel Tarleton?"

At Jason's sharply raised eyebrow, she smiled, and with a knowing look he relaxed, turning his attention to absorbing the instructions spread out before him.

Tarleton followed Kathryn to the far corner of the room, where she turned, facing him with glowing warmth. For several long moments, his heart pounded so hard, he was relieved she asked no questions—for he doubted he could utter a word.

Kathryn, oh Kathryn, he stopped the onrushing thoughts, instantly blocking them.

"Ban," she said softly, knowing this to be the name he wished to be called by his friends. "You *are* a good man in spite of yourself, although you often choose to hide behind a façade of cruelty and callousness."

Arching her brow with a knowing smile, she captured his complete attention. "But I know there is much more to you than that."

Her emerald eyes sparkled in the lantern light captivating him. He could no more look away, despite his discomfort, than he could make either a weak denial—or agreement.

"However, that shall remain *our* secret." Reaching up, she brushed a kiss to his cheek. "I owe you perhaps more than I shall ever be able to repay."

"You owe me nothing, Kathryn," he managed softly. "Just consider for a moment. You may actually be the catalyst that puts me on a straighter, narrower path someday."

Smiling with a look bordering on a soft caress, he traced a finger lightly across her cheek.

"Although, do not hold your breath; for I do find that to be a rather repugnant thought."

Hugging her close, he inhaled her intoxicating aroma, embracing the complete essence of her—but quickly stepped back, needing to keep his wits about him.

"Contrary to the opinions of the 'powers that be', I have much to do, and barely enough time to accomplish it, for I *will not* fail you—or Jason for that matter."

To Kathryn's questioning look, he replied, "I see much from my vantage point at Gloucester Point, more than I wish to at times. I would have you gone from here immediately. I fear that …" He halted mid-sentence but quickly moved on with a businesslike terseness. "You and Jason must be ready at my signal. Answer to no others, I will come for you myself."

He was silent for several moments, deep in thought. Kathryn could almost see him visibly checking off the stages of their escape in his mind.

"Oh, do bid your farewells to Captain Hodges, he returns to camp with me tonight. Wagging tongues have begun to question his whereabouts."

Their eyes met, no words necessary, raw emotion saturating the surrounding air.

"Be ready."

Abruptly Tarleton turned away, only the glow of the oil lantern betraying a telltale brightness of his eyes.

"Thank you for Beauty," she added softly.

He stopped short, mid-stride, for no more than a heartbeat before continuing to the other side of the room to take his leave.

Watching him go, she grinned. From the shrug of his shoulders and curt shake of his head, she knew he was smiling, and it gave her pleasure.

After exchanging touching words with Samuel, conveying promises of coming together on their return, they watched him quietly leave through the same passageway by which they had arrived earlier.

It was not easy to bid goodnight to his lordship, as there was still much to be discussed: questions and answers they both wished to hear. But suddenly there was no more time. Perhaps that was for the best. Less than three hours before they would be on their way and Kathryn was tired.

Jason's arm draped lightly across his wife's waist as they lay fully dressed on the comfortable bed provided for them. Raising himself up on one elbow, he arched an inquisitive eyebrow, curious as to her conversation with Tarleton.

"There is not enough time to devote to a discussion of Banastre Tarleton in the brief moments left to us, my love. But it will provide great food for thought on our trip."

He kissed her tenderly, pulling her tightly against him. "I have something to show you."

Reaching behind him, he produced a little wooden horse on wheels, complete with a grimy blue ribbon to tug it with.

Kathryn gasped. "It is your …" Grasping it firmly, she turned it over several times, and then, end to end inspecting. "Where did you find it? Where did it come from? How did it get here?" Rapid-fire questions all directed at her husband.

"One question at a time, my love." He placed a shushing finger to her lips. "Lord Cornwallis gave it to me to return to Gabrielle. She was carrying it when she and Jack arrived seeking his help. Apparently Jack used it to gain audience, as his lordship had refused to see anyone after the battle. And that is another subject for a shipboard discussion.

"He forgot to give it to her when they left?"

"I gather it was an emotionally difficult meeting; one in which a small item could easily be forgotten."

Setting the toy horse aside, she cuddled back against her husband.

"Have I told you recently how very deeply I love you?" Jason murmured. "For if I have not I have been negligent."

"Always, my love, she whispered, her lips finding his.

"Tomorrow we embark on an adventure. We will bring our daughter home, and Jack, too, if he would like."

"Perhaps he is glad to be home sharing a life of ease with his family and will refuse," she said wistfully. "I recall him saying that he would return to England after the war."

"But that was in the beginning, before …"

"He will come with us too," they whispered, drifting hazily into much needed sleep.

Chapter Seventeen

Privateering: All for the Glory

John Paul Jones stepped slowly onto the ramp at Hackett's Boat Yard on the Piscataqua River and paused, momentarily spellbound. The cool, crisp spring day had nothing to do with goose bumps prickling the length of his spine: that tantalizing sensation, a result of a much deeper, more visceral pleasure … causing him to suck in a ragged breath.

She was beautiful—*absolutely beautiful*—all two hundred twenty feet of her. Although far from completion, her proud lines already boasted of grace and speed. He moved closer, taking care to memorize every detail: the exquisite choice of lumber, intricate craftsmanship and sleekness of her hull. Reaching up, he gently caressed her side, his fingers lingering in a lover's touch: for she was exactly that to him.

As he strolled slowly along the length of *his* ship, renewed pride swelled.

"Unqualified perfection," he whispered, eyeing her figurehead: 'Liberty'; a satisfied grin tugging his lips.

He paced the full length of *his* ship, casting a distracted glance briefly skyward at a screeching gull; but immediately returned to the beauty at hand. Rounding the stern he stopped short, awestruck by her exquisitely detailed carvings: Oppression and Tyranny chained under a Liberty Cap, and her name … *America.*

Oh, what I will do with this bold ship riding beneath me. I will terrorize British waters—bring back valuable prizes. The name of John Paul Jones will once again strike fear and respect.

As he rested his hand on the finely carved letters of her nameplate, a flicker of disquiet settled across his features, and he slipped back into his past. It had been a long, hard journey up to this point in his life. He was the son of a talented landscaper, recruited from Leith, Scotland to design and maintain all the gardens of William Craik's lush estate of Arbigland. But John Paul knew that was *not* to be his life. He wanted fame and glory: to be looked upon with admiration and praise.

He gazed at *America,* speaking in soft conversation, as if her lover.

"If only I had had *you* under me, rather than the old merchantman, *Bonhomme Richard.* The glory of capturing his Britannic Majesty's Ship, *Serapis,* would have been far greater. Oh, I will never forget that day."

His mind drifted back to that September day in 1779, reliving the battle as if it had occurred only yesterday. No other captain of an American navy ship had captured, or defeated, a British man-of-war before: *never.*

"But *I* did, despite all odds. Some called it blind luck, but *I* know the truth. My abilities are unparalleled, I am …"

With little effort, he brought the scene vividly to mind. Just off Flamborough Head on England's east coast, he and his squadron had encountered the dreaded *Serapis.* He immediately ran a blue flag up the foremast, followed by another blue up the main mast, and finally—a blue and yellow up the mizzen, ordering: "Form line of Battle".

Yet all three of his squadron had turned and fled leaving him to fend for his crew and his lumbering, aged ship. *Serapis* had been heavily laden with raw supplies from Scandinavia, slated for continued shipbuilding in England: a rich prize and *ours* for the taking.

Yet my squadron fled—in fear! Even Landais, that half-mad whoreson captaining the Alliance, sprayed my decks with grapeshot, meant for the Serapis, as he turned and deserted me. But I remained calm, undaunted. I, alone, captured the prize of the seas: justifiably according me renowned glory. Eventually, as luck would have it, the time did present itself to handle Landais.

Riding high on those laurels—as well as others accorded him between then and now—John Paul had hoped to be made admiral by the Continental Congress. However, it came as no surprise when they announced they did not care to create an outcry by favoring one captain over another, and therefore refused him.

"I did not gain flag rank but …" he paused, running a hand lovingly along *America's* side, "you, my beauty, are the consolation prize awarded instead."

His hand abruptly ceased motion, his smile fading, as he suddenly realized who was in charge of building this ship; and why it was so slow to reach completion.

John Langdon was *America's* builder, a man he neither liked nor respected. They had railed at each other—violent ongoing disagreements—over the *correct* rigging for the *Ranger* in fall of 1777.

"I may have been a bit forceful in my opinions at the time; after all, who should know better than *I* how the rigging of a ship should be constructed to work efficiently?" He cursed under his breath, regretting what that indiscretion had now cost him.

Right or wrong, while he impatiently waited for answers—unable to intercede in any way—the war had moved into the Southern colonies where at present, Lord Cornwallis was boldly striding through South Carolina. And here he stood, stuck in New Hampshire waiting for a ship which only the good Lord, and John Langdon, knew how long before it would actually sail.

All honor and acclaim are passing me by. I must rectify this sad state of affairs immediately.

Visibly fuming and muttering under his breath, he paced back along the length of *his* ship. Suddenly, it struck him. Not long ago, the *Alliance* had returned from L'Orient carrying very few of the supplies procured by Lafayette for the Continental Army, much to General Washington's disgust.

John Paul recalled that particular fiasco well. At that time, he had been enjoying acclaim in Paris, while successfully fielding urgent communiqués from Ben Franklin to sail for America. An even greater distraction, however, had been his constant effort to avoid Captain Landais: an excellent swordsman who had made it generally known he would not rest until he could end John Paul's life in an ignominious duel. He was, unfortunately, a far better swordsman, and despised John Paul for his scathing ridicule after the *Serapis* incident.

"I could have prevented Landais from taking …" he paused in confiding to *America*. "But truth be known, his decision to commandeer the *Alliance* served my purpose well; he was finally out of my life forever. With a bit of divine intervention, he arrived back in America—not only without cargo—but stark-raving mad. I, myself, could not have conceived a better ending for that vile man."

But what do I do now? I need to be out there. He gazed skyward, wracking his brain for answers.

Recently, he had brought the French frigate, *Ariel*, back to the colonies, filled to capacity with urgently needed gunpowder and arms. That patriotic act had salved his conscience somewhat, but severe ocean storms had almost sunk her on the way home: a frightening voyage he would not soon forget. Sadly, she now rested in dry-dock, probably damaged beyond repair.

He stood eyeing the figure of 'Liberty' on *America's* bow, deep in concentration. Suddenly his face lit up.

"*I* could make a quick run for more supplies—help thwart England's successful trouncing of the South. Word has it Cornwallis is in Yorktown preparing to blockade all trade and ring in the final 'deaths knell'." His eyes grew bright at the thought; renewed fame and glory were suddenly within his reach.

"What better place to stop Cornwallis? Washington will leap at my offer; the *Alliance* will be mine for the asking."

He straightened, throwing his shoulders back proudly, appearing noticeably taller.

"She is fast and sleek—however, not nearly as pretty as you, my lady, *America*."

He caressed her side again.

"I shall make a quick trip to L'Orient for supplies, waylaying any British ship that crosses my path on the way. And when I return to you, basking in the glory of yet another success, you will be ready."

Tipping his hat and whistling a bright tune, he spun on his heel and headed up the ramp. Time to round up his crew, and head the *Alliance* out to sea.

Chapter Eighteen

No Sanctuary This

Gabrielle stood at the paddock fence stroking Beauty's velveteen nose through the bars as she snuffled noisily into her palm: nipping softly, and looking for sugar. Like her mother, she never forgot the little mare: regularly filching a handful of sugar cubes as she passed the side-table on her way to the children's seating in the kitchen.

As she continued to scratch Beauty's neck, her thoughts drifted. She failed to understand why the children were rarely allowed to dine with the adults. But that was just one more item on a long list of topics never to be questioned.

Why must Robbie constantly pretend? This is such an unhappy place. She did not like it here—except for Robbie. She smiled at thoughts of him, but became serious as her attention turned to Jack. *He is so unhappy … and I cannot help. Momma, poppa, please get here … soon. I sense bad things about to happen.*

Emiline's high-pitched demand: "Pat the pony. Pat the pony. My turn, my turn, my turn," brought her back sharply.

Ignoring the spoiled little girl, she continued to stroke Beauty's nose, taking her time before acknowledging the 'fair-haired little gem'. If she thoroughly ignored Emmie, perhaps she would return to her dolls in the children's room. Then she and Robbie could enjoy each other's company without her interference.

Gabrielle hoped Robbie's daily lessons would be finished soon. As future owner of the Beaumont Estate, it was necessary that he learn every aspect of running the estate: its grounds, supervision and duties of servants, and more. Of equal or greater importance, he was expected to maintain high grades in his studies: a seat in Parliament being his mother's ultimate goal.

Today he was closeted with old Tobias learning about the stables. Who could guess what that entailed? She wanted him to be finished so that they might make a trip to the little brook that gently flowed along the perimeter of the Beaumont's property.

Gabrielle thought back to her arrival, wincing painfully. From the moment she arrived, the purposeful destruction of all she considered meaningful in her life … had been devastating. At that time, Robert's companionable presence had provided inner peace and courage. A spark of true friendship had ignited, increasing daily—steadfast and true.

He had taken her to the small brook teeming with freshly hatched tadpoles, to share one of his favorite adventures. It had been a late spring that year: the air and water still cool as gelatinous masses of frog's eggs clung to slender strands of grass waving gently in the slow current. She could vividly recall the frantic whipping tails of late hatchlings as she carefully prodded the gooey masses. Oh, how Robbie had laughed, thoroughly enjoying her delight—pleased to ease her pain.

"It is my turn to pat Beauty! My turn, my turn," Emmie whined loudly furious at being ignored by—*her.* Shoving rudely in front of Gabrielle, landing a sharp kick to her shin in passing, she began slapping at Beauty. The mare snorted, her ears flattening in irritation.

Attempting to make peace with the spoiled child, Gabrielle moved closer, crouching low so as not to 'talk down' to her.

"Emmie, when momma and poppa arrive, I am sure momma will be glad to show you dressage. That is the fancy name for the pretty steps that Beauty knows. My momma ..."

"They are dead!" Emmie spat. Angling her pert nose higher, she shoved Gabrielle, waited for a reaction and when none was forthcoming, shoved her again.

Gabrielle bit her tongue, stifling a sharp retort. Emmie's words hurt deeply, but they were, after all, only words as Uncle Jack had often reminded, begging her to hold her temper.

"Remember, she is much younger and smaller than you, my princess; and terribly spoiled. Please try to ignore her—for all our sake." At the time, he had hugged her tightly, pressing a kiss to her forehead. Sensing his unremitting feelings of hopelessness, she made continued efforts for his sake. But it was becoming more difficult with each passing day.

Saying nothing, she turned away, but a sharp yank on her hair brought her to an abrupt halt. Rubbing the back of her head, she spun to face her tormentor.

"They are dead," Emmie chanted. "Dead! Dead! Dead!" She sucked in a breath and scowled. "Your father was an English gentleman, but your mother and her unladylike ..."

Folding her arms across her chest with a smirk, she began a lilting, taunting chant.

"Your momma is dead, dead ... dead!"

Gabrielle turned aside, fighting back tears and the urge to strangle Emmie. Her eyes slid skyward as she mouthed a silent plea. "Please hurry, momma and poppa. Hurry, I have been brave so long, but ..."

"Dead, dead, dead! Your momma was no lady, no ..."

Having heard the commotion, Robbie suddenly emerged from the stable. Instantly dropping the saddle he held, he sprinted towards them.

"Emiline, you stop taunting Gabrielle!" he shouted. "Gabrielle, wait ..."

But it was too late. *Too late.* The dam had finally burst. With a war whoop, Gabrielle lowered her head and charged full force.

Emmie's eyes flew wide. Shocked, she stood rooted to the ground, unable to move. Gabrielle caught her mid-torso, flinging her backwards onto a freshly steaming pile of manure. Flailing and spluttering, she grabbed fistfuls of warm gobs and began flinging them in every direction, only making herself filthier.

As Emmie's fit of anger passed, Gabrielle moved closer. Standing over her with fists clenched, and rage darkened eyes, she lowered her face to within inches of the nasty child.

"Never say ill of my momma," she hissed. "Never again or I will ..." a devilish torment popped into her head. "... or else I will scalp you!"

As a look of pure dread suffused Emmie's face, she suffered a pang of guilt, which immediately gave way to utter joy at the success of her idle threat. With that, her fury fled. Standing back, arms folded, she began to laugh uproariously, tears of sheer joy streaming down her cheeks.

Robbie watched helplessly. There would be dire punishment for this, but he started to chuckle—then laughed out loud. What else could he do? No one had ever put Emiline in her place before; and in such an appropriate manner. He slid his arm around Gabrielle's shoulder giving her a squeeze of approval.

"We shall both pay for this one," he chortled. "But it will be more than worth it."

Their laughter was cut short as Emmie, with dawning awareness, noticed the smell and filth of her pretty pinafore. Filling her lungs, she let out a long, piercing wail, followed by a series of staccato shrieks, all sure to draw attention. And they did, very quickly.

In total disgust, Gabrielle wiped her hands briskly on her bodice, wishing the gesture would permanently rid her of the brat; then straightening, backed away. Casting a sad glance at Robert she whispered, "I guess there will be no trip to the brook today. But please make me feel good. Tell me it will be there … 'next time'."

"It will be, and *we will* be there." Compassion filled his brown eyes.

Tobias was rapidly approaching from the stables, and Eugenie had just flung the front door wide with an audible bang. Pausing just long enough to realize that once again, it was Gabrielle creating havoc, she strode angrily out to meet her.

Emmie, upon seeing an audience approaching, increased her frantic screeches: expressing herself with renewed vigor.

Sighing in resignation, Gabrielle strode quickly to where Beauty pressed anxiously at the fence: eager for her touch, uneasy in a situation she could not comprehend. After a calming hug, she turned and headed for the house.

Robert reached for her as she brushed past; but she did not stop.

"Do *not* strike that child one more time, Eugenie—or ever again for that matter. I forbid it," Jack warned icily.

Robert had run to find his uncle as his mother rushed by, shoving Gabrielle forcefully aside to get to her poor, little darling and comfort her. Her look of malevolence, unnerving in its intensity, was far more dangerous than any he had witnessed before. He found Jack in the farthest garden, reading from a worn poetry book, his constant companion. With urgency born of desperation, afraid for Gabrielle's safety, he had dragged Jack to her defense, explaining through gasped breaths as they went.

Eugenie's arm halted mid-strike, a stifled gasp the only betrayal of her shock. The deadly edge to her brother's demand was chilling, more threatening than an angry curse. This rash behavior was so unlike her usually quiet, gentle, easily led, brother.

Lowering her arm slowly, she raised narrowed, angry eyes. With stony silence, attempting to shatter his resolve, she searched his face for several long moments.

Jack's icy glare held hers, as he squared his shoulders defiantly, his irate warning neither subtle nor unwavering—in fact a very real threat.

Much to her annoyance, Eugenie faltered at his showing of newfound strength, astounded that he would dare 'command' her in any way. She would not tolerate this defiance in him, and would crush it immediately. Well aware of the cause, she knew exactly how to take care of it.

I fear that I have been too easy, but I will correct all that—soon, very soon.

Raising her face to meet her brother's steely gaze, her eyes flashed a haughty glint. Dropping the switch onto a nearby chair, she nudged Gabrielle to stand up and straighten her clothing.

Jack's gaze drifted to the two angry, red welts slashed across her small buttocks just as her petticoats dropped, preventing further scrutiny of her damaged flesh.

Turning quickly, he impaled Emmie with a withering glance that instantly wiped the smirk from her face, quelling her gloating delight.

He then turned to Gabrielle, taking note of her large, blue eyes—free of tears despite the pain she had bravely endured, and was proud. She had made no lame excuses or placed blame elsewhere. *Your mother would be so very proud, little one.*

"Go up to your room, Gabrielle, I will be up shortly."

Eugenie caught the loving caress in her brother's tone as he gently touched the child's shoulder, nodding with a reassuring smile.

Gabrielle curtsied dutifully to her aunt, but her beautiful eyes sought only her Uncle Jack's.

Robert stood quietly in the doorway, his eyes only for Gabrielle, sympathetic, caring.

"Emmie now sports a large, painful bruise on her arm that will not fade for days, and she dares not show it," he whispered as Gabrielle moved past him, slowing a bit so as to catch his words. The hint of a smile unexpectedly curved his lips as he grasped her hand and squeezed gently.

"Thanks, Robbie," she murmured, dipping her head in gratitude as she moved past him and headed for the stairs.

Jack watched her walking straight and proud, breaking his gaze only when she rounded the corner moving out of sight. Then, anger renewed itself and surged as he turned, skewering his sister with a look so intense, she realized she had gone too far.

"It *was* Emmie's fault, mother," Robert said loudly from the doorway.

Ignoring all propriety of his rearing, or possible consequences for his action, he interrupted his mother mid-sentence as she began more hateful retorts. In a quiet but forceful defense of Gabrielle's actions, he repeated his statement; wanting his uncle to understand that it was not her fault—no matter what his mother or Emmie said.

"You have lessons, do you not, young man?" she ground out in a low, even tone that promised future reprimand.

"It is the truth, mother." Robert stood his ground, facing his mother's wrath without faltering—fearless despite her angry glare.

Jack approved wholeheartedly. He loved his nephew, but harbored concerns for his future. The overly strict, structured existence his sister had created, demanding he adhere to was … He had no words.

"Robert …" With a low growl, his mother took a menacing step in his direction.

"I shall be finishing the weeding in the lower garden if you need me, mother," Robert interrupted politely.

Catching his uncle's nod of approval, he bowed slightly. Not waiting for his mother's dismissal, he spun on his heel, and grasping Emmie's hand in a vise-like grip, headed for the door tugging her forcefully with him—and she dared not make a 'peep'.

Eugenie turned on Jack sighing deeply, her haughty look returning.

"Do you see, my dear brother? This is exactly what I have tried to convey to you." As no answer seemed forthcoming, she continued. "My own son's manners are no longer pristine. You must take control of that child in your caring."

He said nothing, unsure of what he wanted or needed to say.

"What would you have me do, dearest brother of mine? Allow this bad mannered child to run rampant?"

"She grieves for her parents."

"I think not," Eugenie shot back. "She acts as if they are alive and well and will return any day."

"I can only pray she has the 'gift' … that perhaps she truly knows something."

"Balderdash, Beauregarde," she ridiculed. "Utterly absurd, you sound like a …"

"They will come back," a small voice interjected.

In their heated exchange, neither had seen Gabrielle quietly return.

"What are you down here for?" Eugenie snapped.

"I forgot to apologize. That is all."

Unmistakable sadness swam in her eyes, and it clutched at Jack's heart. Quickly moving to her side, he pulled her into a warm embrace, and stroking her silky, black curls murmured, "And we will be waiting for them." Turning her towards the stairs, he gave a gentle nudge. "I will be up, little one, very soon."

Eugenie noted the brightness of Jack's eyes.

"That incorrigible child, you will never put all that behind you and pick up your life as long as she is here—as long as she can conjure up old memories."

Seeing his defiance waning, she leaned in close and hissed: "Snap out of it, dear brother, for I find this whole arrangement becoming less tolerable with each passing day. This situation must—no, *will* be dealt with soon."

"Eugenie …"

"I shall begin looking into finishing schools and find a place that will handle her 'spirit' appropriately. If you ever intend to be rid of her, she must become a lady with qualities acceptable in proper society." She paused, taking a deep breath, gathering more possibilities. "Perhaps I might persuade Dame Agatha to …"

"Stop, Eugenie, I will hear no more. She is delightful and independent and …"

"Whose traits is she emulating anyway?" she rudely interrupted. "I cannot imagine her father's schooling and training having created this monster."

Shocked beyond belief, he took a menacing step toward her, balling his fists angrily.

"Oh, for heaven's sake, Beauregarde, why are you still moping about, constantly defending their honor? You act as if they were family. After all, he was only your commanding officer, and she—merely a camp follower—a commoner."

"Eugenie," Jack's tone turned deadly calm.

"If it makes you happier, *his wife,* if you must call her that, but certainly no lady."

Jack's mouth flew open then snapped shut. Once spoken, odious words could never be recalled, he hesitated.

Mistaking his silence for abject defeat, for one delightful moment Eugenie gloated triumphantly.

"Do not say one more word, Eugenie, or you will regret it for the rest of your life."

Murder shone dark in his eyes as his hand shot out, grasped her arm and squeezed painfully.

"Never go *there* again, Eugenie. Never," he snarled. "I have seen much—done much in the colonies—things that would appall you—unspeakable things …"

He left his statement opened ended, wanting her to feel threat and take it for exactly what it was—*very real threat.*

Shocked beyond belief, her eyes went wide; for once in her life she was speechless. Barely contained rage seethed menacingly beneath the surface of her once docile, easily duped brother: she experienced a moment's chilling fear.

"Gabrielle and I will take our dinner in my room tonight. That is, of course, if you choose to have it sent up. If not, it does not matter. However, we will *not* be joining you."

He released his iron grip but did not apologize.

"This is not necessary, dear," she said softly, rubbing her arm but unable to ease the ache; dumbfounded by his reaction.

"I believe we all need some space," he replied curtly, irritated by her condescending tone. "I need to make decisions."

"Beau," she pleaded, recognizing newly sprouting seeds of determination.

They stood eyeing each other in stony silence.

"Excuse me, if you will," Jack broke the tense truce, *of sorts*, as he brushed past her without further adieu and disappeared into the hallway.

Eugenie watched her brother go and sighed deeply. *I went way too far,* she realized. *But it is over five months, and yet he still grieves. We are British. It is well beyond the proper time for such display.*

He had become such an enigma—no longer the sweet, pliable brother who had sailed to the colonies so long ago. *I wonder just what atrocities he did encounter over there.* She rubbed her arm gingerly, knowing he had marked her. *No, perhaps better that I do not know. Ah, well, time to get on with life. I shall talk to Thomas tonight. Perhaps he can reason with him.* With a shake of her head, she squared her shoulders and marched out into the hallway almost colliding with the butler.

Snapping her fingers rudely, she shot him an icy look wondering exactly how much he had *'overheard'.*

"I shall take my tea in the Rose Room, Cornelius," she stated haughtily.

With a silent nod and prim smile, he turned towards the kitchen.

"Do be quick about it. Oh—and bring me one or two biscuits. I have much planning for Saturday's dinner party and may be late for the evening meal."

As he turned towards the kitchen, her final words interrupted yet again.

"Be sure I am not disturbed *until* the meal is fully served."

Jack entered Gabrielle's room quietly and paused, studying her delicate profile. She leaned, pressing her forehead to the windowpane, staring out into the garden where Robbie was weeding. Her elbows rested on the windowsill bearing much of her weight, pillows piled on the chair obviously not easing her pain as she winced and gingerly sought a more comfortable position.

His anger flared, renewing itself at her unnecessary discomfit.

"You did not defend yourself, Gabrielle, why?" he asked quietly.

She turned and shrugged, considering for a moment before answering softly, "I should have just walked away, Uncle Jack. I did try, I really did."

Her eyes held his, moist pools of brilliant blue exhibiting innate wisdom beyond her years.

"But when she started to say evil things about my momma ..." Her voice broke on a sob bringing Jack immediately to her side. Drawing her into his embrace, he held her gently as she cried.

"It is all right, little one, all right," he murmured, knowing all too well how one could be driven to rage by insult hurled at a loved one.

Oh, God, I must find the strength to make plans. Kathryn and Jason would expect it of me. This existence is not meant to be our life, but what? Where? Return to the colonies ... and perhaps risk Gabrielle's life?

He continued stroking her hair, as his mind drifted. *And how fares the war? I must ask my brother-in-law. With his political ties, he should have some inclination as to whether it has turned in our favor.*

And, what of Great-Grandmother? After all this time, he still had not found the courage to take Gabrielle to meet her, yet she lived less than a day's ride away.

Could I even consider leaving England without taking her great-grandchild to meet her? Yet, how could I ever explain her parents' deaths in any way that could possibly justify such an unspeakable loss?

Deeply engrossed in his private thoughts, he failed to notice that Gabrielle's tears had ceased, she was quietly observing him, deep concern etching her features.

"They are near, Uncle Jack."

"Gabrielle, my little love …" He shook his head sadly.

"I sense them here," she said fervently, placing a small hand against her heart.

Jack refused to refute her beliefs. There would be plenty of time for that later. For now, if it helped to overcome her dreadful loss and cope with this existence well, so be it. How he wished *he* could believe for just a few hours … or even a few minutes.

Sensing his reluctance to believe, she stretched up on tiptoe and touched his cheek, capturing his full attention.

"You *will* see. You *will* see," she assured, smiling up at him.

He kissed the top of her head, but did not answer immediately.

"Are you able to walk with me down to the kitchen?" he asked softly.

At her firm nod, he grinned. "Good, for I remember a remedy your mother showed me long ago, one that eases pain and bruising. We will get Cornelius to help us and in no time you will be comfortable."

Taking his hand, she smiled, her eyes sparkling. "Yes, my momma *is* a good healer."

"Ah, Mistress Gabrielle and Master Jack," Cornelius chirped brightly as they entered the kitchen, hand-in-hand. "I suspect I know right well why you have come to visit me. But first …"

He moved to the opposite side of the room, rummaged far back on the counter and then, concealing something behind his back, returned to her side with a secretive smile.

"A present has been left for you, young lady. My instructions, from a very concerned young gentleman, were to place it on your dinner tray. However, it may serve you better now."

At her curious expression he grinned, and producing a beautiful, yellow rose from behind his back, presented it with a flourish. It was unmistakably one of Eugenie's most prized and carefully guarded roses. All three noticed and began to chuckle in conspiratorial unison.

She reached cautiously for the beautiful rose.

"Not to worry, my lady, your young man removed all the thorns. He did not wish you to suffer further hurt today, or *any* other day for that matter. I gather he thinks you rather special." Giving her a quick hug, he held the rose out and added, "Most all of us here agree with the young master, and the others *do not* count."

Bringing the beautiful blossom to her nose, she inhaled deeply. Closing her eyes, she could see Robbie's encouraging, infectious grin, and suddenly all the day's upset seemed no longer of importance.

"Better now?" Cornelius asked softly.

"Yes," she whispered, inhaling deeply once again. "Oh, yes."

Cornelius caught Jack's eye over her head and winked, both men smiled.

The next few days passed quietly. Thankfully, there were no further encounters with Eugenie. Deeply immersed in finalizing all details for her forthcoming party, she rarely stepped outside her Rose Room.

As for nasty outbursts from Emmie; she seemed rather subdued. For one or two days she went about rubbing her arm, but when asked had nothing to say. Robbie had silenced her with fear of reprisal, and for the moment, at least, it worked.

Gabrielle kept to herself, remaining quietly aloof, but always watching for Robbie. Hopefully, he could find time to break free of lessons and chores—*for she missed him.*

Robert found, or made, time for a few stolen moments—a quick story, laughing words or a visit to Beauty. But this particular afternoon, he wanted to share a secret project with her. He found her wandering the garden maze and hurried her down to the brook: a place where they could talk, far away from prying eyes. His smiling exuberance made it obvious, whatever his project, it meant a great deal.

"I saw this done once, but I have had the devil of a time trying to figure it out."

She rolled her eyes, giggling into her hand at language his mother would frown upon.

"Ah, but my mother is not here now, is she?"

Without having to say a word, Robbie knew her thoughts, and what amused her. *As he always did,* she realized.

"As I said," he paused and winked, "I saw this done once, and I believe I have finally mastered the process. What do you think, Gabrielle?" In the flat of his hand he held an intricately carved wooden object. Anxious concern flashed in his eyes as he watched her, holding his breath awaiting approval.

She moved the connected pieces, one by one, completely fascinated as her fingers traced the smooth ovals of several wooden chain links.

"This is amazing, Robbie truly amazing. I have never seen anything like it." Her eyes met his, as she continued fingering the endless links. "It must all be made from one piece, for I cannot find any places that were cut and put together. How were you ever able to …?"

He released a long breath, as a bright smile lit his face, relieved that she was pleased.

"I have to admit, it has taken me some time to figure it out. Mostly, I guess, just lots of patience."

"Something which I usually lack," she giggled. "But will you teach me how someday?"

"To have patience, or how to make one of these?" He grinned affectionately. "You know I will, my little 'Gabbie'. But for now, I had best get back to my chores before I am missed."

"Gabbie?" she asked.

"Would you prefer 'Ellie'? I want a special name for you … that is just ours."

She thought for a moment, pursing her lips.

"Actually, now that I hear both roll off the tip of my tongue, I think I prefer 'Ellie', if that meets your approval. I *like* the sound: pretty, musical, happy—the way I see you."

"I like it very much, Robbie," she said softly, reluctantly placing the wooden 'chain' in the palm of his hand.

Curling his fingers around hers, he gave a light squeeze and darted off along the hedgerow, heading towards the back of the house. He looked back once grinning, then ducked out of sight.

Finally the weekend had arrived; all was in rehearsed readiness for Eugenie's lavish dinner party. The mansion gleamed in faultless perfection: both inside and out.

Elegant floral bouquets graced every available tabletop accompanied by bowls of fruit, appetizers and sweetmeats. Elegant crystal wine goblets were precisely placed on carved wooden racks, heavy tumblers and snifters flanking them in perfectly aligned rows: *the appropriate glass for the appropriate drink.*

Eugenie had spared no expense: imported Belgian table coverings, elegant china, silver servers and place settings, no corner of the house left untouched—*absolutely flawless.*

And the food: eight full courses of costly fare which caused Thomas to cringe at such outrageous expenditures. Fresh vegetables, potatoes, breads, venison, duck, pheasant, fresh salmon and numerous other delicacies, accompanied by extravagant after dinner sweets: pies, cakes, candies and so much more—a soiree to be remembered.

Her regular household servants, dressed immaculately, moved freely throughout the lower rooms, as did the few assigned to the second floor; each to be available upon a moment's notice to direct guests to the garderobe or attend any other need that arose. They had been strictly instructed: remain highly visible, smile readily and be overly gracious. *Proper decorum was to be maintained at all times.*

Several additional maids, possessing none but the best qualifications, had also been brought in for the evening, thereby assuring that even the idlest whim of any of her influential guests, would be accommodated without delay, their every need answered immediately.

Upon arrival early that morning, the temporary hires had been taken on a quick tour to familiarize themselves with the mansion and its grounds, followed by a thorough briefing with Cornelius. Eugenie had no doubt, that under his sharp-eyed scrutiny, and even sharper tongue, her soiree would be anything other than the ultimate success: the talk of London Society for some time to come.

All of Thomas's influential banking associates, members from her 'Lady's Society', several dignitaries from Parliament, two or three noted musicians, and anyone else perceived to be of Quality had been invited.

Having given a great deal of thought to specific subjects for conversation around the dinner table, she was well-prepared. One pertinent topic had the potential of raising her social status quite nicely. At the correct moment, she would bring up the war in the colonies. Having a family member with firsthand knowledge of the war would benefit her social standing immeasurably. With pointed questions, she would force Beauregarde into a position whereby he could not refuse to answer. Curiosity piqued, her guests would then drag him into—an *'oh, do tell all'*—situation.

She had no intention of allowing him to sit in silence, ignoring her guests and drawing questioning stares. She would pressure him to participate or purposefully cause her embarrassment. He would never dare humiliate her, despite his recent display of strength. *Oh, no, dear brother. Both you and that chit owe me a great deal. You will cooperate and be an object of great interest; I will make sure of that.*

Carriage after carriage arrived, guest after guest announced, drink after drink poured and served. During all this, the three children stood quietly well-behaved in the reception line beside Eugenie, Thomas and Uncle Jack: their manners remaining impeccable throughout the lengthy introductions, head patting and cheek pinching.

It was a lot to be subjected to, and Emiline was beginning to fidget, shifting from foot to foot. Gabrielle caught Robbie's attention just long enough for each to roll their eyes and grimace, but they remained perfect little angels.

At last, even the adult's hugging and cheek kissing came to an end with the arrival of the last guest. Every invited guest was in attendance, even those who had traveled from quite a distance. Eugenie was flattered and tremendously pleased—all signs bode well for this evening's success. Smiling graciously to her collective visitors, she raised her chin a notch higher.

She glanced at the children. Each one—even Beauregarde's brat—had behaved beautifully. And she freely admitted, *only* to herself, it had indeed been an exceptionally long greeting line, her own feet hurt. Glancing around the gracious splendor of her home, her mood lightened. Trepidation at having allowed the children to sit at the main table with her guests for the first course had all but disappeared. For there they sat, making her proud. Each wore a stylish new outfit, each sat with neatly folded hands, each displayed an almost beatific smile, and each spoke a few polite words, but only when spoken to first.

When she had originally decided to show them off to her peers, she questioned whether including Gabrielle would lead to trouble: a definite possibility, and one to consider seriously. She had repeatedly lectured all three about proper manners. But Gabrielle she had actually taken aside and threatened.

Well, it would appear my efforts worked. She is as well mannered as my own, thank the Lord. We only have to get through one more half hour before they retire.

With that thought, a soft organized clatter announced the first course as it emerged from the kitchen, allowing her to happily return focus to her guests. Delicious aromas wafted into the dining room upon exquisite serving trays, held high by an entourage of well-trained domestics moving about the table with swift, precise accuracy. Gracefully and efficiently they positioned plates, napkins and additional silverware as needed, removed empty glasses: whatever any guest deemed necessary.

Cornelius has everything under control; all is perfect. Eugenie breathed a relieved sigh, and flashing a beaming smile, relaxed enjoying her party.

The guests sat specifically placed around the huge rectangular table enjoying the first course, the idle talk bandied softly around the perimeter: politics and King George's latest fancy. The conversation had not begun to 'warm up' yet. But it *would* if his sister had any say. Jack prayed she would keep him out of it, but knew that to be a useless entreaty.

He glanced at the children, smiling at their excellent behavior; they hated this phoniness as much as he. The food *was* delicious, but finding it difficult to rise from his ongoing lethargy, he tasted nothing. Occasionally he succeeded, but for every step forward he allowed himself several steps backward. *Actually,* he admitted silently, *I have not made much of an effort. Only when Eugenie criticized Kathryn did I finally react as I should.* But now was not the time or place to revisit that event.

He sat idly pushing food around on his plate, making a half-hearted effort to enjoy his sister's banquet. As he continued poking at his plate, he scanned the length of the dinner table, a look of polite interest glued on his features. Out of the corner of his eye he noticed Gabrielle. Something in her expression gave him pause ... *something.* Abruptly, tales of her mother's good-natured deviltry as a child came to mind—ever present throughout young womanhood, *no, even until the day...* He forcefully stopped that thought.

Seeing her make a surreptitious motion, he hid his smirk behind a quickly grabbed napkin. Something was up, of that he was sure. But he had no intention of intervening *only thoroughly enjoying.*

"P-s-s-t," Gabrielle hissed, getting Robbie's immediate attention.

She had had enough; a sideways glance from him expressing identical feelings. With a look of conspiratorial mischief, she partially opened her hand under the edge of the fine linen tablecloth, extending it towards him. Robert sniggered in delight, but instantly covered his mouth so as not to alert the adults. Eyes bright with anticipation, he transferred the large frog from Gabrielle's hand to his, and quickly changing hands, leaned towards his baby sister seated just to his right.

"P-s-s-t! Emmie." He held his hand out, angling it low with palm down, concealing the slippery gift.

Emiline turned, eyeing her brother with open curiosity.

"A present for you," Robert urged in a low whisper, as he reached closer. Her small hand opened under his—and the deed was done.

As the cold lump of wetness plopped into her palm, an ear-splitting shriek erupted.

All heads turned in unison—as with a loud crash of shattering glass—a well laden tray hit Eugenie's exquisite Persian carpet.

Jack leaned back folding his arms lightly across his chest, observing the debacle, thoroughly amused.

The guest's expressions ranged from startled shock, to mild irritation, and outright annoyance as they skewered the children with icy glares. But it was Eugenie's dagger-like looks that amused him most. *Oh yes, my dear sister, you have finally grabbed the notice of high society. And a rather successful attempt it is, I might add. They will probably talk of nothing else for months.*

Gabrielle and Robert sat gazing towards the ceiling, a picture of quiet innocence, their hands folded neatly in their laps. But Emmie's shrieks had just begun; she was just warming up to enjoying her hysteria. Face a brilliant red, eyes screwed tightly shut, she hurled the hapless frog onto her mother's lavishly adorned table, where it landed with a loud splash—right in the center of the punch bowl.

Horrified guests glanced at one another before staring in open disbelief at their host and hostess—finally turning angry focus on the cause of the pandemonium: the children. Emmie suddenly realized she had an audience: the 'command performance' was on. Stomping her feet and pounding the table amidst staccato yelps was only the beginning.

Having seen this act before, Eugenie rushed from her end of the table, making embarrassed apologies along the way. Upon reaching her daughter, she scooped her up in one arm, and balancing her like a sack of potatoes on her hip, clamped a hand over her mouth finally silencing her. But her legs still flailed and continued to do so, even as her mother marched her from the room, spewing livid epithets under her breath, and refusing to make eye contact with anyone.

How appropriate, Jack thought, shaking his head in amusement, trying to control his facial expressions. But he was helpless. Grabbing his napkin, he pressed it to his mouth to stop from laughing out loud. As it was, his eyes watered with telltale glee, he had not felt this good in months.

Complete silence filled the dining room—no one made a move or dared make a sound. All but the hapless frog, Jack noticed. It bobbed quietly in the pink lemonade, blinking its large eyes—and as he watched—proceeded to paddle, unconcerned, in watery bliss.

Oh, there will be hell to pay for this night's work, Jack grinned. *But how perfect, how very perfect!*

Chapter Nineteen

Do I Know Ye, Lass?

Kathryn stood on the bottom rung of the ship's railing, head thrown back, hair whipping wildly, enjoying the delicious feel of sea spray spattering her tanned face. A brisk wind filled the sails causing a twang in the taut lines and a green curl to peel back along the prow. A sudden gust dashed spray higher, soaking the front of her light jacket, and she laughed. She leaned farther out, but at the touch of a restraining hand, a brilliant smile brightened her face.

"Do be cautious, my love. I have no wish to play hero by jumping in to save you."

Stepping down, she turned to her husband, arms open and welcoming. He pulled her to him, loving the feel of her rounded belly, and kissed her soundly before moving to stand beside her. Placing his hand atop hers on the railing, he gently traced her fingers with his thumb as they stood quietly, staring out into the distance.

"How I wish we would see a dark smudge on the horizon indicating land. I know it is still too soon but ..."

"I agree, my pet. I actually found three weevils in my biscuit this morning," Jason announced grimacing. "As they are quickly becoming frequent companions, perhaps we shall have to name them."

Kathryn laughed, her eyes crinkling in amusement. "I am impressed with your new-found sense of humor, my love—learned under Jamie's tutelage, I have no doubt."

"No, I take full credit. I am merely learning to find more humor in life, hopefully to make the days go faster. But if this trip becomes any less exciting, I may borrow a small knife and take up carving, like some of the crew."

He shook his head, biting his lower lip. "This boredom is deadly. *Deadly.*"

Kathryn nodded, turning back to watch the horizon. It had been six, more or less, seemingly endless weeks. She had lost exact count. With the winds constantly in their favor, the journey so far, had been fast and uneventful. They traveled light with no cargo to speak of; the two of them being the only passengers. It was a small ship and sleeping accommodations offered only a modicum of privacy.

With a sigh of longing, she leaned against her husband. "I miss you so, my love."

"Once again reading my mind," he chuckled, encircling her with a strong arm, his hand lightly touching her breast, pleased to feel her nipple instantly respond.

"I gather I have not completely lost my ability to gain your full attention," he whispered, brushing a kiss to her ear.

"Jason William Tarrington," she gasped, pulling away. "I will embarrass both of us, if you do not behave. You know I cannot resist ..."

"Thankfully so, nor can I. When we reach land ..." His eyes glistened with loving warmth as they held each other's gaze.

"I wonder how Tarleton managed this?" she said, trying desperately to move into another area of discussion that would not create further yearning. She ached—a visceral, physical ache that only he could heal.

"Banastre, somehow, demands favors: through blackmail, perhaps?"

"Do not ask, my pet. For some things are better left unanswered. But I *am* grateful. He is not the epitome of evil I had always thought him to be," Jason said dryly.

"No, though he certainly works hard at maintaining that image. Actually, I believe he truly cares for us, a fact he will never confess to, nor admit even to himself."

Both remained silent for a while, lost within their thoughts.

"This boredom," they stated together then laughed, their opinions so often voiced as one. Neither handled day-to-day idleness well.

"I do wish we had our poetry books." She slipped her arm around his waist. "But perhaps they are bringing Jack solace; and I imagine our little girl enjoys hearing him read." She gazed into his brilliant blue eyes. "Just as I always love to hear you read."

"You have not yet tired of my recitations? We have shared them so many times; I believe I recall every word by heart."

"*Never*, in answer to your question, and *perfectly*, in comment on your statement." She frowned, shaking her head. "Listen to us. In lieu of a specific focus or 'cause' our words have turned to no more than idle chatter, my love. Mere sounds in an attempt to fill the endless *quiet*."

"But that will change, Kathryn. We have serious decisions to make once we find our little girl and Jack. And do not forget—we have the baby to look forward to."

"Our son," she said firmly, placing his hand against her rounding belly.

"You seem very sure, my pet. I realize this child does not share similarities in size or kicking ability with our daughter, but ..."

"I just *know*. And though he is smaller, he is an active, healthy baby, actually more active than his sister was at the same stage."

"It would seem ..." He stopped abruptly, directing her attention to the horizon behind them.

They squinted, trying to discern the small dot that appeared to be coming closer; their eyes glued to the horizon as it slowly began to take shape.

"How fascinating," she murmured. "I believe it is a small ship: smaller but faster—and rapidly overtaking us." Suddenly, she turned and headed for the hatchway.

"And just where are *you* going, my love?"

"My dirk is in my boot as always, but my tomahawk ..." She ducked out of sight leaving him shaking his head, and within moments reappeared carrying her favored weapon and a pistol for him.

"Kathryn ..."

"How close are they?" she asked, hastily handing him the pistol, as she swept past to stand at the rail.

Snugging his pistol tight, he moved to her side.

"What do you see?" he asked, touching the small of her back—smiling at the familiar feel of her tomahawk. "This almost seems like old times."

"Although I have never seen one, Jason, I do believe *that* is a privateering ship flying American colors."

"*This* ought to be interesting," they mouthed simultaneously, both enjoying the rush of tingling excitement as they watched the sprightly vessel quickly close the distance.

Abruptly Kathryn turned, moving past her husband and over to a rope ladder hanging from the main mast.

"Kathryn, I forbid you to climb that ladder!" Jason glowered at her, truly angry.

"I wish to see better, and the seas are fairly calm."

But his stern look held.

With exaggerated slowness, she removed her foot from the bottom rung and turned to face him.

"You— *forbid me?*" Their eyes locked in a battle of wills, neither backing down.

How he loved this bold, brash, *stubborn* woman. But this was not the time to foolishly risk injury. Resolved to win the debate, he opened his mouth to reiterate more forcefully, just as the ship lurched, pitching her against him. Grabbing her and the ladder, he held on tightly.

With an easy grin, she leaned up and planted a firm kiss on his lips.

"You win, my love," she chortled, "… *this time.*"

The small privateer rapidly closed the gap between them. Their ship had no guns; there was but one choice. As they watched, tension escalating, their ship lowered its sails and prepared for boarding.

Jason moved behind his wife at the rail, and breathed softly into her ear, "I see quite clearly now, how our daughter comes by her boldness so naturally, my love."

Eyeing him over her shoulder she grinned, but quickly turned her attention to the pending interception.

"Be careful, Kathryn, we are *both* out of practice." He need say no more; she would understand his underlying concerns without their being voiced.

He was right, that she knew, but neither would she stand by allowing harm to come to him—or to herself, for that matter.

Their captain gestured them below deck; but they ignored him. Having too much to contend with at that moment, he refused to extend further worry, and headed at a run towards the bow.

Shouting crewmen raced along the deck as grappling hooks were flung over the rails, chunking into the wooden planking, skidding with abrasive complaint before digging in and holding. Cursing outbursts filled the air as flopping sails dropped, ropes were kicked out of the way, and both crews faced off at close range: one armed and in full command—the other, anxiously awaiting the outcome, and ultimately—their fate.

With a loud grunt, a grizzled character poked his head over the rail just a few feet to Kathryn's left. Scanning hastily to both sides, he heaved himself aboard. Moving with exceptional agility, despite his barrel belly, he focused on them: approaching warily and brandishing a small knife.

Without thought, reacting from sheer instinct, Kathryn dropped into a low crouch. Snatching the tomahawk from her belt, and bringing it to rest lightly in the palm of her hand, she balanced on the balls of her feet, riding the gentle ocean swell with ease.

Jason slid his pistol free, but would not interfere. Distraction at this point could be deadly; she needed to focus.

"Drop it, lassie," he growled, his snide grin displaying a toothless wasteland of gums. "I am verra gude at what I do."

"I am better," she snarled. "Try me, and I will see you over the rail: food for fish." They locked eyes, her icy stare causing him to hesitate.

"Put your knife away, Deacon. We are not here to do injury."

The man behind the authoritative voice was handsome almost to the point of prettiness. Dressed impeccably, slender of build and medium height, he had easily slipped on board unnoticed while her attention was focused on her attacker.

Although he was unarmed, Kathryn noted that his crew, standing astride the outer rail of his ship as it moved in unison with theirs, were all well prepared for—*anything.*

Deacon slipped his knife back into his belt and grudgingly stepped aside. "I only meant ta hav a bit o' fun, Capn'. No harm dun."

But Kathryn stood her ground, as did Jason, their shoulders touching.

"And you, milady ..." he began politely.

Fascinated by this rather imperious female, he found her unfaltering gaze impressive—for she stood watching *his* approach with unflinching resolve. Yielding without a fight would be absolutely out of the question where she was concerned—and as to her male companion? Certainly not to be taken lightly. *I wonder about this pair.* Something nagged at the back of his mind.

"It is far easier to talk without imminent threat of injury to myself or to you," he said quietly.

She relaxed her 'battle stance' lowering her tomahawk, but did not return it to its resting place at her back.

The jaunty captain seemed unflustered by her continued look of defiance as he strode slowly by her. Looking back over his shoulder, he stopped and turned. She had his complete attention as he scrutinized her thoughtfully—curiosity etching his tanned face.

Ahh, milady, what is it that nags at me so thoroughly as to just who might ye be? He took one tentative step and then another, returning to stand mere inches from her. Unable to take his eyes off her, he completely ignored Jason.

Jason tensed at the captain's close proximity, but with a light touch of Kathryn's hand, relaxed. Curiosity about this man's strange behavior delayed any immediate action, but he remained alert—scrutinizing intently. *Strangely,* he felt this impressive man offered them no particular threat.

The ornately dressed captain cast a quick glance at Jason, eyeing him in an almost friendly fashion before turning full focus back to Kathryn. She obviously puzzled him in some way. With head angled, one hand grasping his chin in consternation, he stood lost in thought. Suddenly a wide grin spread across his handsome face, displaying a brilliant flash of perfectly even teeth.

"I have it now. Ye seemed so familiar somehow."

As he released a satisfied sound, proud to have reached an answer, Kathryn and Jason tensed. *Does he know us?*

"Damned if ye do not have the look of a MacLean in a fit o' temper," he chuckled, stroking his chin. "Tell me ye are not a MacLean and I shall brand ye liar!"

Kathryn's eyes widened as she placed her tomahawk back into her belt thoroughly taken aback.

"What is your lineage, milady, if I might be so impertinent as to ask? Ye have the same look of someone I knew many years ago—when we were both but lads."

"My brother, Jamie, I imagine," she said lightly, chuckling.

He nodded vigorously. "Ye both have the look of yer grandma—here, about the eyes a bit." He pushed back wind-blown strands for a better look. "Yes, easily seen now; eyes like yer da's mother." His burr rolled easily as he continued to study her closely.

"I fear I have no remembrance of her." She smiled a bit wistfully. "I was born in the colonies and have never been to Scotland; but Jamie spoke of her often."

Abruptly he turned to Jason. "Do forgive my rudeness. It is rare, indeed, when I find someone who links me to my former life." With a flourish and dignified bow he added, "Allow me to introduce myself: Captain John Paul Jones, privateering for the American colonies under a Letter of Marque. Perhaps you have heard mention of my name?"

He is 'fishing' for flattery, Jason realized. He actually had heard of him at some point in time, excellent at what he did but in constant need of compliments.

"Yes, we have both heard of you and your abilities, Captain, but were not familiar with your face," Jason added quickly.

"Until now, that is." Kathryn jumped in. "Kathryn Cameron MacLean and ..." she proudly snaked her arm around Jason's waist pulling him close, "my husband, Jason."

She purposefully omitted her married name, although it pained her to do so. But Jason's hand, moving subtly to the small of her back, conveyed his message of complete understanding and agreement.

The captain would very likely have heard of them, and that would seal their doom. Although a privateer who usually confiscated cargo only, *and* an old friend of her brother, she knew he would never pass up the glory for their capture. She must move the conversation in another direction quickly.

But there was no need. John Paul had not achieved his status and position without guile and intelligence. With great sensitivity, he veered away from pursuing the possibility of *interesting information* immediately within his grasp. And his kind gesture did not go unnoticed.

"Will you be seeing Jamie again?" he asked. "For I have a message you may convey if you will. Unfortunately, my feet rarely see land long enough to visit old acquaintances."

"Yes, and I will gladly carry your message."

"Two things: ask if he remembers the time my da locked me in Mr. Craik's summerhouse at Arbigland and why? And does he still read James MacPherson's poetry? We used to argue about the validity of Ossian for hours." He smiled. "You MacLeans are a stubborn lot, I give you that."

Jason chuckled and gave his wife a wink.

She eyed him narrowly, and turned back to John Paul.

"You, read his poetry?" Her eyes were bright with surprise.

"One of my favorites," he assured. "Especially the quandary over Ossian."

"Jason and I find him fascinating ..."

Abruptly one of John Paul's crew approached, ending all further conversation.

Excusing himself politely, he stepped aside and conferred quietly with the man, words that try as she might, Kathryn could not hear anything worthwhile.

Momentarily, he returned and bowed slightly to both of them.

"I truly regret we must be on our way, for I would find it great conversation to talk poetry and *get to know you both better.* But I have duties to fulfill, promises to keep and obligations. Responsibilities, which I am sure you *both* understand well."

He knows us: realization struck both at the same time.

Taking Kathryn's hand he kissed it, smiling deeply, noting the incredible emerald green of her eyes.

"While you are in England, you might consider looking up the poetry of a dear friend of mine: Phillis Wheatley. She is a charming African-American poetess, highly touted by both Boston *and* London Society despite the fact she lives in the colonies."

He bowed to Jason. "Please forgive my intrusion on your journey, but truly, the pleasure has been all mine. I hope we may meet again someday; this war will not last forever." He gave Jason a knowing look.

"And Kathryn, may your child inherit all your incorrigible spirit—for that is the 'stuff' upon which new nations are born. It is exactly that type of brash, vitality that …" He stopped abruptly, emotion blurring his eyes, spun on his heel and moved to the railing to board his ship.

Loud yells accompanied a whirl of action and untamed energy, for what seemed to last mere moments. Grappling hooks splashed into the ocean as the two vessels drifted apart; there was no rush now. Sails were hoisted and unfurled, catching the stiff breeze with a resounding 'crack'.

John Paul stood proudly at the prow of his ship as it pulled away. He dipped his head ever so slightly in Kathryn and Jason's direction, and they returned the salute as his sleek ship picked up speed and rapidly disappeared into the horizon ahead of them: gone as fast as he had arrived—as if in a dream.

"That certainly broke the boredom," Kathryn said, kissing Jason's cheek.

"Guns and ammunition for the southern colonies, perhaps?" Jason arched his brow.

"I am afraid so, my love. It would seem that Samuel was correct; the war will be over by the time we return. A new nation will be born, as John Paul said. Yet I am not sure of my feelings: confusion, sorrow? I …"

"Do not worry, my love, for I have plans for you," he whispered softly. "Our life is just beginning. We have been given another chance."

"Yes, and I am eager to begin. No looking backward. No regrets."

He held her tight, cradling her against him. Dusk was falling and a distinct chill nipped the air. Jason guided his wife to the hatchway and stepping down, grasped her hand and winked.

"You and your brother certainly have ties to some very interesting people, my pet. I have heard a great deal about that man, and he is *not* one to be trifled with. He knows his business and does it efficiently."

"Yes," she said softly, stepping down into the lower sleeping area, fully aware of his meaning.

"He knows exactly who we are—yet I doubt he will ever say so."

"Another good man; I will not forget him. I will also remember to ask Jamie about Mr. Craik's summerhouse, for I cannot begin to figure out the answer."

"Something else he mentioned of interest: Phillis Wheatley. Perhaps she will be reciting poetry somewhere in the vicinity of Maidstone," Jason added. "I am sure Jack would also be interested.

"I find it truly unique, the number of incredible men in my life who love poetry."

"We are not insensitive boors *all* the time, my love—only upon occasion."

"I believe you told me something quite similar to that once very long ago; at about the same time I informed *you,* that we colonials were not just ignorant farmers carrying pitchforks," she chuckled.

"Umm, that seems so very long ago." With a quick tousle of her tawny hair, he took her hand. "I think the fresh air and excitement, have stirred my appetite. Perhaps we should see about some form of food, preferably *not* biscuits with weevils."

Chapter Twenty

Land at Last

"I see land, I see land!" Kathryn yelled, leaning as far over the railing as her well-rounded belly would allow. Day after day, she had stood grasping the railing, searching the horizon for the subtlest of changes. At long last, there it was.

"Look, Jason," she squeaked, pointing excitedly off to her left. "I see land."

Setting aside his whittling, he joined her, squinting in the direction she indicated.

"Although it seems we have not been at sea long enough to have arrived, I am more than ready to rest my feet on solid ground."

Shading her eyes, she continued pointing. Moving closer, he leaned down, sighting along her arm at the dot on the horizon.

"Right as always, my love," he chuckled, kissing her cheek. "You know, after we met John Paul, I actually gave some thought to a career in privateering. But ..."

They shook their heads together.

"If I see one more piece of salty, dried beef or peas as hard as pebbles ..." she said, wrinkling her nose.

"Or moldy biscuits alive with hidden surprises," he added.

"Washing my hair in salt water and toweling the rest of me with the same. It will be such luxury, Jason, to sink into a large tub of hot water with a bar of soap—and you." Her eyes flashed promise.

They stood arm-in-arm, swaying easily with the wake of the ship, watching the smudge on the horizon come into focus and begin to take a more distinct shape.

"Do you think we will be able to go ashore by tonight?" she asked, recalling how Tarleton had stressed the importance of the tide's height when they sailed out of Gloucester Point two months ago.

"I will ask the captain," he answered, heading off across the deck—gone for only a matter of minutes before reappearing.

"What did he say? When will we be ...?"

Placing a shushing finger against her lips, he smiled. "The captain said, my love, that if all goes well, we should be on the main pier at Dover just before tea time."

Kathryn became quiet, her mind busily working, but abruptly smiled. "Forgive me, my love. I have neglected to ask how your carving is coming. May I see the results before we get caught up in all the excitement once we land?" She put her hand out, quietly insistent.

Looking thoroughly pained, he shrugged and withdrew a roughly carved, primitive shape—of a *horse* she thought.

"I truly believe I am far better at carving up adversaries on the battlefield than this."

"I agree." Her eyes sparkled. "However, I suspect our daughter will be much happier if her parents stay off the battlefields from now on."

He grunted agreement, turning the object in his hand, eyeing it critically.

"I *do* detect a certain likeness to Diablo; Gabrielle will cherish it along with the little toy horse from your childhood. I imagine she has missed it sorely."

"I was deeply touched when my grandmother sent it to us in the colonies. After we find our little girl and Jack, she must be the first person we contact."

"I doubt Jack has been able to inform her of his sad news. We meant the world to him, as he does to us. I only hope …" Banishing that painful thought, she raised her eyes seaward.

Their small ship was rapidly approaching land. Spectacular, lofty cliffs were becoming more discernible. Although still too distant to distinguish much detail, great flocks of sea birds, shrieking and gliding through the crisp blue skies were highly visible. Soaring high, they missed one another by inches, before abruptly angling their wings and plunging into the dark, wind-tossed water—resurfacing within moments with silvery, wriggling fish clutched in needle-sharp beaks.

"What do they call this place?" she whispered, mesmerized.

"White Cliffs of Dover: a rather unique sight."

They sped closer, suddenly veering sharply to hug the coastline, the wind tugging even harder at their already full sails. Thankfully, Kathryn's sea legs helped keep her upright—along with her husband's firm grip around her waist. The vessel never slowed, seeming to barely kiss the ocean's surface as she raced on at breakneck speed.

Kathryn could now discern huge nests packed tightly into innumerable crevices, clinging tenaciously along the face of the cliffs. The inhabitants, perched along the craggy edges and soaring on high, eyed them through beady, black eyes, shrieking loudly—proclaiming their annoyance at the intrusion.

"Why does it suddenly occur to me, that our captain may have more talents than meet the eye?" Kathryn asked her knuckles white on the railing.

"I must admit, I felt more at ease in the midst of battle with the enemy approaching from all sides."

Jason agreed. "However, your question falls into one of those categories in which we had best not tread, nor ask specifics. Anyone who works, either with or for Colonel Tarleton, has—how shall I put it—many talents?"

Taking her hand, he headed towards the hatchway.

"Time for us to change our clothes and pack our few belongings, I do not wish to be seen in colonial garb as we approach the dock."

Jason preceded his wife up the steps to the deck, turning to offer his hand. Her new dress consisted of much more fabric than her riding skirt: he had no intention of having her trip. He eyed his wife appreciatively, one eyebrow arched in question. She stood on deck shaking out her petticoats, but stopped as she caught his look.

"What?" she said, trying to maintain stern decorum, but inwardly amused. "What?" She stifled a giggle as she caught his eyes drift to her hemline, and then back up—his smile widening. "Yes, I *have* my boots on, and my dirk."

"And I am glad, my pet, for it is a wise choice."

She stood, eyes sparkling devilishly, and suddenly burst into laughter.

"I recall Lord Cornwallis's party all too well, as if it were but yesterday—you and your boots," he chuckled, raising a hand to cup her cheek. Capturing her gaze, his voice softened. "But some things *have* changed, my Kathryn. You grow more beautiful with each passing day, and although I never believed it possible … I love you even more."

Kathryn's eyes misted. "You are my heart and soul, Jason."

"We are as one … always."

"Always," she murmured, gesturing that he turn, so she could study him from all sides. With an admiring sigh, she nodded complete approval at the handsome figure he presented. Every brass button had been polished to brilliance, his striking red jacket, immaculate. Her eyes followed its perfect lines down to his form-fitting black pants, continuing the length of his long, muscular legs to his highly polished black boots.

Reaching up, she cupped his face, her eyes flooding with warm tears.

"You take my breath away," she managed.

He eyed her with concern, knowing exactly where her thoughts had retreated to. With each familiar article he donned, his had done the same.

"You even pomaded your hair and braided your queue while I was fighting with my petticoats and skirts."

She ordered her mind to move forward, forcefully setting aside nagging memories.

"I fear I do not accomplish the task as precisely as you always did, my pet. But you were solving problems of your own at that moment. Therefore, I was duty-bound to rise to the occasion."

She grinned, brushing a kiss to his cheek; and stepping back, burst into cheerful laughter, all poignant reminiscences fleeing. This delightful facet of his wife never failed to awe him—her resilience and constant ability to meet all challenges head on.

"Now, let me look at you, my pet." He turned her gently. "Are you comfortable?"

"As comfortable as I will ever be in a dress. You always choose well; however, this particular gown would seem too dressy for daytime wear. Will I look out of place?"

"Kathryn, you know I would not put you in a position of embarrassment. This is England—not the colonies."

Her face fell slightly.

"How shall I act, Jason? I would not wish to embarrass you in any way."

"My beloved Kathryn," he murmured, drawing her head against his shoulder, wishing his statement had not been put quite so baldly for she suffered insecurities, as did he. "Be yourself, I ask no more or less from you."

"But …"

"No 'buts', my love, for …"

Flapping canvas, accompanied by the odd musicality of sliding metal rings, instantly drew his attention upwards.

"The sails are coming down, we must be almost there."

"Jason, look who is coming our way." She nudged him sharply.

Having left the duty of bringing his ship into port with his second in command, the captain advanced in their direction.

"Colonel and Mrs. Tarrington, I would gather?" He eyed them speculatively, awaiting an answer.

Jason gave the slightest nod: cautious.

"Captain Kirkland J. Farthingale, at your service." He swept a deep bow. "Parts of an interesting puzzle are beginning to fall into place," he said lightly, thoroughly pleased with himself.

"You do not seem surprised," Jason ventured.

He shook his head. "I have seen much and done much, Colonel. Very little surprises me any longer. It was said you had both died at Guilford Courthouse—a damned debacle that—but I had my doubts."

"We both had conversation with the angels more than once; thankfully, they seemed not ready for us just yet. But why did you doubt?" Jason asked.

"I had followed news of you both for many months, your numerous successes and incredible passion for the cause you both so strongly believed in."

His voice softened. "With your undying passion for each other, I was sure that ... *somehow* ... you would both survive."

He studied them both for a long moment, the silence drawing out between them. Then he spoke, his next statement stunning them.

"Moreover, I knew you must be of extreme importance, Colonel Tarleton demanded my absolute silence on pain of *something* more severe than death."

Jason's eyebrows rose, as Kathryn pierced him with a steady gaze.

"He threatened to *personally* neuter me and take great pleasure in doing so."

He quickly turned to Kathryn. "My apologies for speaking so crudely, milady."

"No offense taken. That *does* sound exactly like something Tarleton would threaten," she commented dryly.

Captain Farthingale took a long, searching look at her lovely face, impressed with her open honesty. *She is exactly as I was told,* he realized. *Even her guileless features do nothing to hide her true feelings.*

"Almost seven months ago, I was contacted by Colonel Tarleton." He spoke slowly, watching her face change, tension building as to his next words.

"I made a trip to this very same port, not because of easy access—for it is not—but because it was near my passenger's final destination. He was disheartened, perhaps desperate. I often thought he would have thrown himself into the ocean, on more than one occasion, if not for the beautiful little girl that he was protecting."

Kathryn's eyes opened wide upon a gasp.

"She was about five years old, milady: the spitting image of *you*, but with her father's coloring."

"And a spirited, little mare called Beauty?"

"Aye." He locked eyes with her, the last pieces of the puzzle coming together. "I believe I have had the pleasure of meeting your daughter and ..."

"Lieutenant Jackson and our child, Gabrielle," Jason filled in.

And with that last bit of information, the final piece slid into place.

Now all the pieces fit perfectly. He smiled, pleased with himself at having solved it.

Kathryn's mind was awhirl, her heart pounding, her breathing quick and shallow.

At the captain's concerned look, Jason said curtly, "This is somewhat of a shock to us both, Captain. All these weeks you have suspected, or known and yet have said nothing. Tell us more," he demanded, his cool façade beginning to crumble.

With a jolting thump the ship nosed against the pier.

"I am afraid our time for conversation has unfortunately come to an abrupt end. However, I will tell you, the lieutenant had a pretty rough time of it. But your daughter remained bubbly and happy despite the rougher weather we experienced, as if she refused to accept whatever had happened as fact."

Kathryn watched his eyes as Captain Farthingale thought back, recalling memories of them.

"And your mare: a feisty creature that one. That's most likely what brought her through it all. And now with your leave, it truly has been my pleasure."

As he started to turn away Jason thrust his arm out, stopping him. "Do you know where they went, Captain?"

He thought for a moment. "Not exactly; perhaps Maidstone. There is a character named Smitty, one of my crew who became close to your daughter, who may be of help if you can find him."

Kathryn and Jason both frowned.

"He did not sail back to the colonies with us last time. From what I gather, he got himself beaten up pretty badly in a bar brawl here in port. Nothing life threatening: a broken leg and a couple of snapped ribs."

"But, where …?"

He shrugged. "I will probably seek him out before I head back across the big pond. He is a good man when not brawling. But that will be several weeks from now as this young lady," he indicated his ship almost fondly, "is going in for refitting. It would seem Colonel Tarleton has other plans for us besides transporting mail."

Without further adieu, he spun on his heel and headed off to coordinate unloading and disembarking for dry-dock.

"As long as the price is right, I gather he asks no questions," Kathryn said, somewhat appalled. "Did I catch his last remark correctly?"

"That you did, my love. It would seem that we are being exposed to some rather interesting individuals."

At her silence he said firmly, "We *will* find them, my Kathryn, with or without this, 'Smitty'." Hugging her close, he guided her towards the gangplank. "I do recall that Jack's sister lives somewhere south of London. Maidstone sounds about right; we will start there."

"At least we know, first hand, that they arrived safely." She attempted a game smile, but it fell short of the mark. "I *am* worried about Jack."

She made her way slowly and carefully down the gangplank, held securely by her husband. As she placed her foot on the pier, the first solid footing in weeks, she moved aside so as not to hold up others. However, there was no need to rush; apparently they were the only two disembarking at this point.

A crewmember did come up rapidly behind them, handed Jason their large duffle bag, saluted and rushed back up on deck. Ropes were already being tossed back onto the pier releasing the vessel. Apparently, as the tide still remained in their favor for a bit longer, they were moving directly into dry-dock without further delay.

Kathryn inhaled deeply, wrinkling her nose. "The smell is no better on an English pier, than one in the colonies, how fascinating."

She grinned at Jason, picking up her step, eager to embark on their adventure—confidence restored. They were here at last.

Jason smiled, enjoying his wife's assessment of her new surroundings. The day was drawing to a close, the sun settling low in the sky. Many of the small shops lining the pier were already dropping their wooden shutters. Small vendors at the edge of the wharf were busily packing wares and loading them into their wooden carts, making ready to return home for the night.

Kathryn and Jason stood off to one side in silent fascination as a pair of dandies, unwilling to call it a day, continued strutting up and down the pier. Dressed foppishly in brilliant, ill-matched attire, they preened for their lady friends. Even the feathers in their over-sized hats appeared more outlandish than those of the women.

As they watched, the two began demanding immediate attention to the wants of themselves and their lady friends. They swore vehemently, hurling demeaning epithets at the vendors in nearest proximity, and pounding their canes on the wooden pier planking. Although they were ignored, they continued their outrageous act for several more minutes.

Kathryn shook her head. "Some things never change," she commented, angling her head towards the decadent couples. "I have often experienced this type of boorish behavior in the colonies. I gather arrogance knows no nationality—nor does fish smell any less in a grander setting."

Jason shook with unrepressed laughter, his eyes sparkling. Only his Kathryn could voice her opinions so succinctly. *Kathryn can only be herself at all times.* And for that he loved her dearly … grateful that she had chosen to 'belong' to him.

"I do wish the ground would stop swaying under my feet," she groused. "I feel as if I have partaken of one too many glasses of Lord Cornwallis's excellent brandy."

"That will stop soon, my pet, but for the moment, let us find a place to spend the night and enjoy a hearty meal."

"Biscuits without weevils, perchance?"

"Yes, hot baths, a comfortable bed and—some privacy." He winked suggestively.

"I think it would be best not to waste time hunting for this 'Smitty' character. I will arrange for an early carriage tomorrow. If Jack is staying within the area I suspect, and if the roads are good, we may find him by late afternoon; or at worst early the following morning."

"I wish we could …"

"Patience, my love, our wait is almost over. Besides, I have an idea that may help divert your attention; for I would not wish to allow you time to fret."

Desire shone in his eyes as he touched her cheek and kissed her, uncaring of anyone watching. They were safe. They might pique curiosity—a British Green Dragoon colonel and his 'lady'—but beyond that, nothing.

"Yes, I believe you just might have some *very* interesting ideas." She visibly relaxed. "Let us discuss them—at length." Taking his proffered elbow like a proper lady, they headed towards the main street of town.

The next morning found them at breakfast shortly after dawn. They had dressed quickly, Kathryn humming happily the whole time. Although neither had slept from excitement, *and other diversions*, both looked refreshed and none the worse for all the hardships of the last several weeks. With a delicious feast of bread, ham and eggs under their belts, they sat sipping hot tea, eagerly awaiting the arrival of a small carriage, arranged for them by their gracious innkeeper.

Jason's uniform had not gone unnoticed, but no one had spoken out of turn or bothered them. The innkeeper, proud they had chosen his inn for their stay, made sure every detail was handled personally by his wife or himself. Knowing he was desperate for a tidbit to share after they left, though too polite to ask, they gave him a few generalized statements: creating a reasonably believable tale of visiting a dying relative before returning to the war, supplying nothing which might divulge their identities.

Just as Kathryn was becoming anxious, their carriage arrived. With polite, but rushed 'goodbyes', their bag was put aboard, and they were handed up into their seats. The promise of a beautiful October day blossomed as the sun's glimmering rays kissed the treetops in welcome. Jason leaned over the side to confer with the driver as Kathryn watched, tapping her toe nervously.

"The roads are unusually clear for this time of year, Colonel. It has been exceptionally dry, no mud to speak of, and rather warm for my taste. I see no reason not to arrive there today," the young driver said lightly.

With a sideways glance at Kathryn he added thoughtfully: "Unless, of course, the missus tires—what with her condition and all. I mean ..." Unsure whether he had overstepped his position, he looked embarrassed, a bit ill-at-ease.

But Jason merely laughed. "My wife would push the carriage, herself, if she thought we might arrive sooner." Pressing a gold coin into the young man's hand, he smiled. "I trust your judgment completely, drive on."

Smiling a toothy grin, he hopped up onto his seat. Peeking at what had been pressed into his palm he whistled softly and quickly slid it into his vest pocket. Lacing the reins between his fingers, he settled himself comfortably for a long ride. A light snap of the whip, a few words of encouragement, and the carriage lurched forward.

The beautifully matched pair of grays shook their heads proudly, harness jingling, their creamy, silken manes floating airily, as they eagerly stepped off at a rapid pace.

Jason took his wife's hand gently in his. "Today," he whispered.

She smiled, settling back against his shoulder, humming a bright tune.

"You seem particularly happy this morning, Mrs. Tarrington. Might I inquire as to the reason?" He chucked her under the chin, enjoying her instant blush. "I do believe you just might begin to purr like a satisfied kitten at any moment."

"I just may, my handsome husband, I just may," she whispered.

Her emerald eyes sparkled passionately, capturing him completely—the eloquence she could convey with a mere look astounding him.

"Always," they breathed as one.

And the horses quickened their pace.

Chapter Twenty-One

Another Sad Anniversary

For several weeks after the 'horse manure' incident, followed rapidly by the 'frog affair', as Jack referred to them—to himself, only—an uneasy truce existed. At times the silence seemed almost deafening; meals being taken with little more than stilted civility. On occasion, Jack noticed that his nephew took his place at the kitchen table rather gingerly, his mother's tirades clearly more than verbal and on going. Jack assumed he was still trying to defend Gabrielle's character and her right to exist.

With your mother, you will never win, Robbie. It is up to me to find the strength to make the move ... and take her away from all this.

He recognized Eugenie's game, and the toll it had taken on all members of the family. His sister reveled in her power to control an individual, pretending deep concern while subtly shredding every feeling of self-worth, and newly emerging confidence. Even her poor husband had been all but neutered by her disdain.

What happened while I was away at war? Or did I actually grasp the reality of our shallow existence, and purposefully seek a new life with Jason and the dragoons? The past held no answers; only what he accomplished from here on would be of importance.

The deaths of Kathryn and Jason *had* crippled him emotionally, there was no denying that. But months had dragged on, as he stood by watching: doing nothing. However, on a slightly encouraging note, thoughts of correcting the situation had begun hammering incessantly, means of escape, his main focus. He could no longer disregard nor put aside the urgency. *I must be healing, but the healing is so incredibly painful.*

Two weeks had passed since the 'frog affair' and Jack still found humor. Replaying the fiasco in his mind, he often wondered if Eugenie's society friends had finally ceased making her the butt of their thoughtless jokes. But he would never ask. Lately her temper flared easily, often unprovoked, tension emanating from her like heat radiating off a sun-baked stone.

Perhaps his unanticipated mirth that day had created a crack in his protective shell. For a few minutes, he had been able to forget the self-deprecating misery in which he had been wallowing. It was only one small step, but it *was* a start. He began taking long, honest looks, assessing 'goings on' around him; and what he saw, made him sick at heart.

He watched Robert's eyes showering concern on Gabrielle whenever she was present. *He may be only eight years old, but he is harboring a much older feeling for that little girl.* He saw no solution for a future, and it saddened him.

Eugenie made continuous efforts to keep the two children apart; her inability to understand her son, or Gabrielle for that matter, making her totally inept. She would have been shocked to discover how often her son's clever resourcefulness allowed them stolen moments together.

Eugenie was consumed by jealousy, a fact of which Jack was well aware. She despised his devotion to Gabrielle—that *brat* was *Kathryn's* child, and Jack's *undying love for Kathryn* infuriated her. Although certain his sister would never dare inflict serious harm to the little girl, she would undoubtedly play the 'boarding school' card *soon.* They were here only by her good graces, and definitely on borrowed time. At the recollection of angry words the two of them had shared just two nights ago, he winced.

"That child *must* learn to accept her new life, brother. She is intelligent, surely she must be able to see the difference between *then*—and what is *now* expected of her." Eugenie stood regally aloof, arms folded across her chest, her foot tapping indignantly.

"Gabrielle loved her parents deeply, still loves *their* memory and *their* ways, as do I," he spat. "She embraces those customs, and their memories, as it gives her comfort."

"I am not attempting to cast aspersions on her parents nor their memory, Beauregarde." She smiled patronizingly.

Jack recognized where this conversation was going. Perhaps a softer version this time, in hopes he would see her side and comply; but again, the same old thing.

At times, I just want to ... Anger flared and he blocked the thought immediately, afraid that with the right provocation he might be powerless to stop. He had been in the war, had seen a great deal of man's inhumanity to man, had done what needed to be done without a shred of guilt—just as he had warned her.

"To be accepted by polite society and one day marry well, she must learn the genteel ways of a young lady. And *you* must return to our ways also."

Unbidden, the 'frog affair' flashed through his mind, causing him to stifle a chuckle. For that was a perfect example of 'polite society'. The corners of his mouth lifted.

Eugenie mistook his gentle smile for weakening, and stepped to his side. Resting a hand on his shoulder, she idly stroked an errant lock of thick, blonde hair back behind his ear, disgusted by its unruliness.

"This clubbing your hair back loosely, fashioned after the colonials, I gather, must really end, brother. Shall I speak to the wigmaker for you?" she prodded annoyingly. *You need* to take interest in your appearance again, Beauregarde. After all, *you* also reflect on our good family name."

At that remark, Jack stood abruptly, forcefully pushing her hand aside.

"No dear sister, when I am ready to resume the pompous airs of 'polite society', I will tend to the matter myself."

He turned and stalked from the room, ignoring her furious look as he strode past.

"I hardly know you any more, Beauregarde," she screeched, followed by several expletives and a sharp stamp of her heel.

"Well, that makes two of us, Eugenie," he muttered. "I hardly recognize myself any longer."

All he had once held dear was no longer valid—shallow at best. But Eugenie *had* taken them in, when they had no place else to go. He owed her gratitude for that bit of generosity. And now he was considered an embarrassment. He—more than likely true, but Gabrielle an embarrassment? Absolutely not, she is beautiful, vibrant, independent ... so like Kathryn. *She knows perfectly well what is expected of her in this life style.* He smiled. *She merely refuses to adopt their structured rules. And that is a MacLean trait through and through.*

They must leave, before he awakened one morning to find that Eugenie had spirited her away to boarding school in the middle of the night without allowing him to even say 'good bye'. She was more than capable of doing exactly that, and would do so with no regret, proud of her victory. *No more time for self pity, Jack.* He refused to let that happen. He had given Kathryn and Jason his word: it had been sacred before; it would remain so, now,

How strange; a specific event abruptly came to mind. *Three days ago, Gabrielle saved Emiline's life—yet she was shown no gratitude: not so much as a warm word.*

All three children had tromped into the house, soaking wet, with their shoes making muddy footprints across the kitchen floor. They had sneaked off to go fishing, including Emmie: an apology for the now infamous 'frog event'. That act of defiance sparked Eugenie's fury: they had dared to out and out disobey her.

On Robbie's forehead, a rapidly swelling lump slowly seeped blood, which he offhandedly swiped onto his once white shirt. Emmie, sporting a bruised cheek, stood with hands on hips, her lower lip thrust out in an irate pout.

"What have you done now, you vile child?" Eugenie screeched, grabbing Gabrielle's shoulder roughly.

"She saved Emmie's life mother!" Robert yelled, moving quickly to Gabrielle's side.

His words rushed out in a jumbled explanation: Emmie reaching too far for a pond lily, the boat rocking sharply—unbalanced—pitching all three into the pond, and Robbie, momentarily stunned as he struck his head, flailing to stay afloat. All of which, fell on deaf ears; Eugenie continued to clutch Gabrielle firmly, muttering furious words, pinching her arm painfully.

"But Emmie cannot swim, Mother." He yanked her skirt struggling to get her attention. "Gabrielle *saved her life*, and has promised to teach her to swim."

As Eugenie continued her tirade, ignoring Robert, he grabbed his sister, and with a rough shove, sent her stumbling against his mother. Taking a quick step backward, so as not to fall, she thrust Gabrielle aside.

"You tell Mother right now what happened," Robert ordered. But at her silence, he became furious. With a vicious shove, he sent her stumbling, causing Eugenie to grab for her, as well as the edge of the table to keep from falling.

"Emiline, you tell Mother the truth, you *spoiled brat.*" He flung the words, his underlying threat of retaliation, an absolute promise.

Emiline actually confessed, but it had done no good.

Ah, Gabrielle, if we could both walk on water, it would still fail to impress my sister.

Jack headed up to his room to think and make plans. Pulling out a piece of paper, a quill and ink from the desk, he began to jot down a few notes. His thoughts came sluggishly at first, but with perseverance began to flow. As he sat re-reading his last few lines, he paused. Some of his ideas actually had merit, even real possibilities. *We will both be all right,* he told himself firmly.

Eugenie would be taking all three children to tea at Dame Agatha's tomorrow, to spend several hours learning proper etiquette. He grimaced, thankful it was not *his* turn to learn how to 'crook' his little finger around a delicate teacup handle.

His thoughts began to wander, his outlook turning bleak as the next day's overwhelming heartbreak insinuated itself. *Seven months, to the day, that I lost them. Lord, please give me the strength to get through tomorrow, and I promise I will right all that is wrong in our lives.*

He sat at the desk, immersed in melancholy, his eyes lackluster. Pushing his notes aside, he reached idly for a bottle of brandy and poured himself a hefty glass. As the amber liquid warmed his insides, the past reared its ugly head. Once more, he unwittingly became its captive audience, reliving that horrific day … yet again.

Jack sat in the garden, its lush green of only a few weeks past now depleted, some of the trees already becoming skeletal with the chill of oncoming winter. However, today was unusually warm for this time of year, just like the previous day. He tried to take pleasure in the bright sun, warm earthy aromas and crisp blue sky.

Weather like this should be heralding good luck or happiness or ... almost anything but these memories, he murmured as he clutched a small, leather-bound book on his lap.

He had risen early, dressed presentably, and actually made the effort at breakfast to rise above it all. But the meal had been a solemn affair. Gabrielle remained quiet throughout, knowing what this day meant to him and respecting his grief. Or perhaps apprehension of a day spent under Dame Agatha's strict tutelage had something to do with it; for both Robbie and Emiline sat in silence too.

After they left, and the house was his to roam freely, he decided to read poetry for diversion. At least that might bring back some of the happy memories he treasured: days spent with Kathryn debating the validity of Ossian or ... Perhaps he might get through this anniversary without completely falling apart.

Upon entering Eugenie's Rose Room to borrow a volume of poetry from her library, he discovered her desk strewn with leaflets from several Boarding Schools. He made no attempt to look at them, forcing the unpleasant discovery aside. Only half-focused on why he had entered her office in the first place, he unenthusiastically searched the rows upon rows of books amassed on the shelves. Eventually, he located the works of Phillis Wheatley, an African-American poetess highly touted throughout London society, and surprisingly—Boston. He had not heard of her before but wondered: *Might her works have been something Kathryn and I could have enjoyed discussing?*

Momentarily lost in thought, he ran his fingers idly over the leather bound book on his lap and frowned. He had been sitting here in the garden for some time, in his usual spot, on his usual stone bench and with the book still lying closed—having suddenly lost all desire to read it. Any attempt at holding his emotions intact today had been dashed by the paperwork so deliberately displayed on Eugenie's desk.

With a groan, he hung his head, shaking it to dispel the miserable thoughts rapidly gathering there, but to no avail. Rules: so many unspoken rules and appearances to uphold. *Good Lord that was the reason I volunteered to fight in the colonies in the first place.*

"Oh, Kathryn," he murmured brokenly, "What shall I do? I always knew exactly how to handle any given situation when you were both here. I always felt in control, never doubting my abilities. But now ... now, I hardly feel competent to dress myself most mornings."

Dropping his face into his hands, he moaned. A tear formed, and he ignored its wet path tracking down his cheek. What did it matter if he cried? Would he be considered any less of a man than they already thought? *Who cares anyway?*

Seven months ago today, and he could still see their lifeless bodies as if it were only yesterday, the blood, raggedly torn flesh. Another tear slid assertively into the track of the previous one, and Jack knew more were coming.

They thought I was so strong, so capable of raising their child. He sighed sadly, lifting his head to stare out across the magnificently manicured lawns, gardens and pools of his sister's estate.

His mind drifted from one memory to another in a kaleidoscopic menu of subjects beyond his ability to control. He gazed at the lazily moving pond lilies, pushed gently by the breeze in one of her elegantly designed pools, and actually grinned. Pools once filled with prize Koi, now several less in number, thanks to Gabrielle. He could still see her proudly displaying her catch as Eugenie's face blanched—as white as her fine lace petticoats. And when she saw the child's filthy stockings and muddied shoes tracking clods of filth across one of her finest Persian rugs, he actually thought she might faint from apoplexy.

As quickly as the light moment blossomed, it withered and died, replaced by bleak visions of helplessness and unanswered questions. He had yet to find enough courage to seek out Gabrielle's great-grandmother. What could he tell her? *How* could he tell her?

And Jason, his true friend, a man's man who had always made him feel competent and accepted—a man of extraordinary understanding. Well aware of Jack's deep love for his wife, he had accepted it at face value, harboring no jealousy, feeling no threat—aware that an invisible line existed—one that would *never* be crossed.

And Gabrielle, another pleasant memory that occurred only a few weeks ago suddenly came to mind. During a rare day of peaceful interaction between them, Eugenie had asked the little girl to help weed her herb garden, the care of her precious herbs the *only* menial task she ever performed on the estate. Yanking the last cluster of weeds, Gabrielle had vigorously wiped her filthy hands on the front of her pinafore. Jack smiled wistfully remembering Kathryn—her child, exactly like her in so many ways.

At times, a simple gesture would shatter his heart. He could no longer look at Gabrielle without summoning memories of the past: at times wonderfully warm, but more often of late—heartbreaking. With each passing month, the roundness of her 'baby features' slowly changed into more slender lines. She had become an even closer mirror image of her mother, thankfully with her father's coloring. There never had been any great difficulty in figuring out her parentage, but now it was blatantly obvious.

When will this pain cease, allowing the memories to become a comfort? I look at this delightful, little girl and ... Another vision insinuated itself, pushing aside all other thoughts, a memory he relived over and over—still unable to stop. Completely at its mercy, lacking the strength to deny it, with a quiet sob, he buried his face in his hands.

His shoulders slumped, his face awash with tears as broken sobs racked his body. *Kathryn, oh Kathryn, I feel you in my arms, relaxing in death and going to him ... your beloved husband.* A loud groan erupted. *This must be my punishment for having loved you so dearly. Yet I would do it again, my Kathryn.*

For a few blessed moments no further thoughts roiled in his head ... he was calm. Inadvertently touching the forgotten poetry book at his side, he placed it in his lap. Swiping a sleeve across his face, he sniffed loudly and opened the book to a page—any page—it made no difference. With a soft sigh, he focused his tear-filled eyes and began to read. He would at least make an effort.

Chapter Twenty-Two

This is Home?

"I believe we are here, Colonel Tarrington," Theodore announced, slowing the carriage before turning into the driveway.

Large stone pillars flanked either side of a long crushed stone drive. Exquisite brass lanterns adorned the tops, and carefully chiseled into each post: the name BEAUMONT.

"Yes. Thomas Beaumont." Kathryn beamed, so excited she could hardly sit still. "That is Eugenie's husband."

It was mid-afternoon of the same day; they had made excellent time. Their driver, Theodore Artemis Oleander, had turned out to be a real character and extremely good at what he did. On one of their brief stops, he had informed them of his whole name, rolling his eyes as he pronounced it slowly and concisely.

"Call me Ted, that's what my friends catch me by."

He possessed an infectious grin and loved to tell tales about this area of England. As he managed his team, he tossed lengthy explanations back over his shoulder; his laughter floating easily back to them, as he related one story or another he thought to be rather humorous. With his jovial personality, there seemed very little that he viewed with other than infectious mirth.

They thoroughly enjoyed his light banter, and it had helped keep Kathryn's mind occupied. He knew the area like the back of his hand, often finding shortcuts. But he also knew his team. He spoke to them fondly in encouraging tones, and they responded, performing well for him. The two or three times they had stopped for Kathryn to refresh herself, under Ted's thoughtful pretense that he must rest his team, had been short.

"Thank heavens this little one of ours does not sit with his foot against my bladder," Kathryn had whispered to Jason. "That used to be one of Gabrielle's favorite resting spots."

He touched her face with concern. "Are you feeling ...?"

"Yes," she interrupted. "And I will continue to feel fine; do not worry so, my love, it will make your hair gray."

Settling himself comfortably beside her, he began rummaging through the large basket thoughtfully packed by the innkeeper. Producing a couple of apples, he handed one to Kathryn, who immediately began chomping delightedly, mentioning that the core would be for Beauty, along with a few sugar cubes.

Jason's eyebrow rose as he bit into his apple. With a giggle, she reached into her dress pocket and pulled out a handful of the goodies, filched from their breakfast.

"Our kind innkeeper packed a basket of bread, cheeses, wine and fruit—and you filched his sugar, Kathryn?"

Jason feigned horror, amused as the guilty look of a small child caught with its hand in the cookie jar, instantly flashed in her sparkling green eyes.

It had been a smooth trip, the hours speeding by rapidly. Ted had maintained a steady pace that failed to cause so much as a slick of sweat to break on the glossy necks of the matched grays. And now they were here. A ripple of excitement, bordering on apprehension, raced through Kathryn as she gripped her husband's hand tighter for courage.

"What if we find that …? What if they have …?"

"Hush, my love," Jason stopped her, squeezing her hand with reassurance.

"Are you ready, Missus?" Ted yelled back over his shoulder. But, sensing Kathryn's uneasiness, flicked his whip without waiting for an answer.

The carriage moved ahead at a slow leisurely pace, proper decorum obviously required in showing respect to the owner's of this wealthy estate, clearly people of Quality. Ted, well versed in the routine, accepted his lot in life without apparent grudge.

Kathryn and Jason were fascinated. Beautiful fields bordered both sides of the drive, still a lush green despite it being early Fall. An occasional cluster of rocks broke the softly waving grassy perfection, adding interest to the landscape; and miles of carefully built stonewalls boasted of clever craftsmen.

"And Jack left all this," Kathryn mused.

Up ahead, assorted outbuildings were beginning to emerge. Jason pointed sharply, and following the direction he indicated, she saw a sturdily built stable erected from fieldstones and wood. A large, fenced-in paddock was solidly attached at either end of the stable, and the heavy doors stood wide open.

As their carriage drew nearer, the pair of grays happily announced their arrival in high-pitched whinnies. Several well-groomed hunters nibbling grass close to the stable raised their heads, calling a welcoming answer before continuing their eating. They had seen comings and goings of the gentry many times, the carriage horses always being watered and fed before their return trip. There would be plenty of time to investigate the new visitors later.

Suddenly a small mare emerged from the open stable door, her ears pricked inquisitively, head held high and alert. Shaking her head, nostrils flared, tail switching side-to-side, she pranced nervously, her hooves dancing.

Kathryn gasped. *Beauty* Before she could put fingers to her lips to whistle, the mare let out a piercing whinny and bolted towards the drive.

"My God, can she make that height if she decides to jump?" Ted asked nervously.

"Oh, yes, just watch her." Pride rang in Kathryn's voice as she stood, holding onto the edge of the carriage.

Jason made no attempt to curb his wife, a useless waste of effort on his part, and merely steadied her.

"Beauty, oh my Beauty," she cried, tears starting down her cheeks.

"I think she knows you, missus. And I gather she's glad to see you," Ted tossed back over his shoulder, gripping his reins a bit tighter to command his team.

Beauty's hooves churned the dirt into puffs of dust as she raced the full length of the paddock, closing the distance within moments.

"Up and over she comes," Ted yelled appreciatively. "What a fine animal." He pulled his team to a halt having to fight them a bit in their excitement.

A picture of fluid motion, without a moment's hesitation she flung herself up and over the fence effortlessly, breaking to an abrupt halt at the side of the carriage. Pushing her soft nose into Kathryn's hand, she nibbled the waiting sugar cube, but quickly pushed forward into her embrace, nickering excitedly, snuffling soft moist breaths against her hair and cheek and neck.

Jason stood quietly, eyes misting at their reunion, awed by the adoration of this faithful mare despite all that had happened, and the substantial amount of time they had been apart.

Kathryn wept unashamedly, stroking her beautiful, little mare as jumbled words cascaded from her lips.

"Do you think she looks well, Jason?" she sniffled, wanting his opinion.

He nodded, eyes crinkling as his lips curved into a grin. "She has been well cared for."

"She is bloody beautiful," Ted exclaimed. "My grays are a pretty pair, but I have never seen the likes o' her!"

He tugged the reins to control his prancing pair. "Be still you blokes or you'll be making the long trip home *tonight!*" It was an idle threat, but they stood quiet at his order.

Beauty was beginning to calm her dancing hooves, enjoying the reunion but standing more quietly.

"Look." Jason gestured towards the paddock.

An older man barreled towards them with a rolling gait, progressing as rapidly as his marked limp allowed. Breathing heavily from the exertion, he coiled a rope awkwardly and cursed fluently as he advanced.

"That incorrigible piece of horseflesh," he growled, now only a few feet away.

Carefully watching her hindquarters, more than likely having been kicked before, if not by Beauty, probably one of the high-strung hunters, he edged cautiously closer readying a noose.

"My apologies, kind folks, this here piece of bad-humored horseflesh is the bane of my existence."

Guardedly approaching her side, he stepped back quickly as she flattened her ears and bared her teeth.

"Beauty," Kathryn spoke softly, "those are not the manners I have taught you."

Snorting her disgust, she pricked her ears and stood obediently.

"You certainly know how to handle that …"

Abruptly he stopped mouth agape. He had paid the visitors no heed up to this point, his focus having been on that *devilish beast.* But as his eyes met Kathryn's, all color drained from his face—as if seeing a ghost.

"We are Gabrielle's parents," Jason said quietly, wishing to calm the man.

"But it has been said that you both …"

Jason shook his head. "No, we are both hale and hearty, but tired after our long journey. So if you will be kind enough to take Beauty to the stable, we will proceed to the house."

He raised wide, skeptical eyes to the colonel, but at Kathryn's touch and soft words whispered against her mare's silky cheek, Beauty allowed herself to be led away.

"I will not leave without you, my Beauty," she promised loudly.

Beauty looked back more than once, her large, soft eyes following their progress as Ted's team moved ahead and rounded the huge circular entranceway to the manor.

Kathryn turned in her seat and waved across the yard as the wheels came to a stop. Beauty happily acknowledged the gesture, prancing with head held high as she disappeared into the stable.

Jason stepped quickly out of the carriage and around to Kathryn's side. Taking her hand, he assisted her to the ground, pulling her into an embrace and mopping her tear-streaked cheeks.

"Shall I announce you, Colonel?" Ted asked politely.

"Thank you, Ted, but no. As we were unable to give any advance warning, I think my wife might take great pleasure in watching their reactions."

"You told me they believed you both dead, sir. But as they have never met either of you, from what you said on the ride …" He paused, a frown settling across his brow. "Why would they think you ghosts?"

"Our daughter looks very much like me, but with her father's jet black hair and dazzling blue eyes, Ted." She eyed her husband with open devotion. "It is impossible not to know her parentage."

"Well then, I think I will just sit back and enjoy. And when you are ready for your luggage, give me a yell."

He liked these two. It made no difference that the gentleman was a colonel; he no more belonged in this society than did his delightful wife. They had told him so much of colonial lifestyles that he actually wondered if he might like to go abroad. His day-to-day existence here was, at best, a known quantity—most likely with little change for the rest of his life. But the colonies sounded like a true challenge, a place where a man would be limited only by his visions and the ambition to accomplish them. *I'll lay odds they go back at some point,* he thought, *and I would like to be the one to transport them to the pier, perhaps even … I will speak to the colonel about both possibilities.*

"Yes, and if I go I will take you, my beauties," he added lovingly to his grays.

The colonel, with arm tucked securely around his wife's waist, now stood on the doorstep rapping the elegant brass doorknocker loudly. Folding his arms across his chest, Ted settled back to watch.

It was only a minute or two before the heavy door swung open and a large, elegantly dressed man presented himself. His mouth opened on a greeting, but no words emerged. His eyes swept first over the colonel and then, in more lingering fashion over his wife.

Just as Jason started to make introductions, unsure as to whether the butler would restore himself to duty, he cleared his throat, gathered his wits and resumed his station.

"My sincere apologies, I fear you have startled me momentarily. You *must* be Colonel and Mrs. Tarrington."

At their surprised expressions, he said softly, "Gabrielle said you would come. But I would know you as her parents, anywhere."

"But Jack thought …" Kathryn hesitated, realizing the butler's befuddled expression indicated he was unsure of whom she was speaking. "Lieutenant Jackson, Mrs. Beaumont's brother." She looked directly at the butler, and as understanding lit his face she continued. "He thought us to be dead on the battlefield."

"How did Gabrielle know?" Jason turned to his wife.

"Anna was right. She *has* the sight, both a gift—and a curse at times," she said wryly. "At least she has had solace in the knowledge that we lived." Turning to the butler she asked, "But what of Jack? How has he fared?"

"Master Jackson needs you both. He has despaired all these long months. I need not color your perception. You will make your own judgment … about many things."

Kathryn shot him a look, but he would say no more. With a knowing smile and gracious bow, he ushered them into the main hallway.

"I fear I have been neglectful in welcoming you correctly. I am Cornelius, the Beaumont's butler. And if you would not consider it out of place, I must tell you what a delight your daughter is—such a breath of fresh air."

"Where is our little girl?" They asked. With pleasantries over, they were anxious.

"Mrs. Beaumont has taken the children: Robert, Emiline and Gabrielle, to Dame Agatha's for lessons in proper conduct at tea time."

Kathryn rolled her eyes and glanced at her husband, noting that he, too, was struggling to keep his face noncommittal. Not wishing to be offensive, she quickly asked, "And what time might they return?"

Cornelius, having caught their shared look, smiled to himself. This would be an extremely *interesting* visit. Too bad he was not a betting man, for he knew whose side he would champion. *Let the games begin.*

"I doubt they will be here until dinner time, milady. However, that will give you both some time to spend with Master Jackson, and rest after your journey. I will have a room readied, your bags brought in, and arrangements made for your carriage and driver." He winked, knowing they would not consider it an offense. "You see, I *can be* a very efficient butler when I put my mind to it."

He led them towards the back of the house where large French doors opened out onto an enclosed garden. It was easy to see that the flowers had been exquisite at the height of the growing season: many of the intricate plantings still retained much of that beauty, even now.

A beautifully sculpted knotwork garden was situated centrally, surrounded on one side by shrubs, and the other by a sparkling pool with splashing fountains that extended back into the far corner. Situated off to the far left sat a single stone bench, placed cozily under a tall tree. And there sat Jack, his back turned partially to them—shoulders slumped, head down, hands dangling limply between his knees.

At Kathryn's gasp Cornelius turned, concern etching his strong features. Jason pulled her closer, his warm strength lending courage. She searched the butler's face, but no coherent words would form. Jack's all consuming misery emanated in waves, patently obvious even from this distance.

"It is your seven month anniversary," he said softly, "and he grieves as though it all happened yesterday."

"Oh Jason," her voice caught. "I had lost track of time, but Jack has lived in hell all these long months." A tear slipped down her cheek, stopped by her husband's gentle touch.

"Go to him, Kathryn, I will be close behind."

Jack's hands hung loosely between his knees as he stared unseeing at the surrounding garden, his thoughts morose. *Seven months to the day, almost to the exact hour, when Jason and Kathryn ...* He forcefully stopped the thought as a tear spilled over his lower lashes. *Will this inner ache and devastating emptiness ever cease?*

In front of Gabrielle and his family he tried his best to appear to be regaining self-control, and making plans to get on with his life. He desperately needed to make a home for his precious godchild. She asked nothing of him, but deserved so much better than what he had provided up to this point.

And she believes they will come for her ... us. But Gabrielle, I saw your mother die. He wanted to scream, to strike out, smash things, to fade into a place of blissful, peaceful nothingness.

And your father: a man to be proud of, a man who made me what I ... was. What I should be even now, for I owe them better than ...

"Jack," Kathryn's voice caught on a sob as her hand touched her dear friend's shoulder.

"Back so soon, Eugenie?" He reached his hand to cover hers, realizing she was attempting as much warmth as she was capable of, as he mumbled distractedly, "I will take my tea later."

Not wanting her to see his red-rimmed eyes, he gently disengaged her hand from his shoulder, but did not turn. However, the hand returned, placed more firmly, and began slowly caressing. His face contorted in confusion. Eugenie had no such *loving* touch for him or anyone else for that matter—nor did she ever call him 'Jack'.

"Jack ... oh, Jack."

A beloved, familiar voice, ragged with emotion and barely able to utter his name, pierced his desolation.

God, what trick is my tortured mind playing now? It sounds so like her ... so like my Kathryn. He lifted his head, turning slowly, seeking the source of the words that sounded so like ... He stopped, mid-motion, his face draining of color.

Kathryn stood before him smiling, tears streaming down both cheeks, lips trembling in an attempt to stifle small sobs. And her hair—her glorious hair tumbled in riotous, tawny curls about her shoulders. And as he watched, this beautiful apparition reached to touch his face. *But the touch held warmth, tenderness ... and love.*

His trembling hand reached towards her, his mouth struggling to form her name, or any sound ... but nothing emerged.

She crouched down, cradling his face gently between her palms.

"It really *is* me, Jack," she choked, beginning to sob, nodding vigorously at his wide-eyed stare. "I am *alive* ... and here with you!" She leaned forward to kiss his forehead, then both cheeks in turn, and finally his lips.

"Kathryn," he barely managed, "oh, my beloved, Kathryn."

Standing slowly, he pulled her up into his arms, wrapping her in a fervent embrace. His eyes searched hers, seeking the bold sparkling love of life always present, wanting to believe. Perhaps if he touched her ... held her ... she would prove to be reality. Running his hands feverishly across her shoulders and down along her arms, he melted into the feel of her. Inhaling her familiar scent, he pressed his cheek to hers, their hot tears mingling as he fought to comprehend the reality of her presence. He dared not close his eyes for even the briefest second; frightened she would be gone ... no more than a ghost dredged up from his tormented soul.

As if sensing his thoughts, she pressed her lips to his ear. "Close your eyes, Jack, then open them. I will *still* be here, I promise." She paused, watching the fear of loss flicker in his eyes. "Do as I say," she insisted gently, and he complied. "Now, open your eyes and look at me." She touched his cheek.

Slowly he opened his eyes. "You *are* real. Oh thank God." His eyes swam with tears. "And Jason?" He was almost afraid to ask.

Kathryn stepped back, extending her arm to touch her husband's shoulder. He had been standing quietly, observing his wife in the arms of his best friend, participating vicariously in their joyous reunion. He *was* rather proud that he had experienced only the tiniest twitch of jealousy, a worthless emotion he easily pushed aside. But that had not always been the case.

"Be thankful I know you as well as I do, my friend. For I fear there would be hell to pay if it were anyone but you." Grinning widely, he moved quickly to Jack's side.

Both men crushed each other in a hearty embrace, tears falling unashamedly—Jack questioning brokenly, Jason answering with equal emotion.

Kathryn moved to the stone bench and sat down. Emotional exhaustion had finally caught up with her, and she needed to rest. She took note of her surroundings, pleased to see that dusk brought the same beautiful coloring experienced in the colonies, amused that she would even consider it might be different. Long shadows stretched closer as she listened to *her* men, questions and answers being asked and given from both sides.

Placing her hand on the bench, she felt a small book and picked it up, curious. In the dim light she could easily decipher its contents and author—the poetic works of Phillis Wheatley. A smile lit her face. "How fascinating," she mumbled.

"What is fascinating, my love?" Jason's hand touched her shoulder surprising her.

When she turned to look up, she realized both men were standing behind her. "I had not heard your approach, either of you. I am definitely losing my touch."

She stood slowly, each man taking an elbow, the book clutched in her hand. "Phillis Wheatley. Her poetry is one of John Paul Jones's favorites. I gather they are good friends."

At Jack's look of complete confusion, she giggled. "It is a long story, one of many. But I fear you and I will have more poetry to debate. And, as we will have a great deal of time on our hands, perhaps Jason will decide to join us."

"All well and good, my love, but right now I want you to take time for relaxation before our daughter returns."

She pouted prettily, noticing Jack's eyes glide to her rounding belly before returning to her face. "Do not fawn over me, either of you. I am fine, besides I have you, Jack, if I cannot bring this child into the world by myself."

"Eugenie will insist upon her doctor, and I doubt you will care for ..."

She shrugged, looking from one to the other, thoughtful as the sky began to color.

"What thoughts are rushing about in that pretty head of yours, my pet?"

Her eyes misted as she hugged them both.

"To see you two men together and have our precious daughter back, feels so right. Fear and sadness lie behind us, but opportunity lies ahead." She stepped back. "My brother, Jamie, actually calls Jason his *friend*. What more could one want?"

Taking their proffered elbows, they headed towards the manor to ready for dinner and Gabrielle's arrival.

Jack walked briskly at her side, feeling renewed, his confidence rebounding. The world would once again revolve as it always had—as it should. His mind raced ahead to dinner and he smiled. *Oh my dearest sister, you have no idea what awaits you. They are alive—and you will now have to contend with a fiercely proud, passionate woman, who could slash a man's throat without hesitation. Tread lightly, for she will protect her child at any cost.*

Darkness had completely fallen as Jack, Jason and Kathryn sat sipping brandy around a crackling fire in the den. A short nap, cool water splashed on her face, and she felt renewed.

Jack eyed her over his glass, ever amazed at her recuperative abilities. She was even more beautiful than he had remembered. Her eyes held new spiritual depth: as if she possessed an ethereal knowledge gained by having stared death in the face and shouted forcefully: *Not yet! I am not ready.*

And he studied the way she looked at Jason. *I thought they could never love more deeply … but I was wrong. One begins a thought … and the other completes it. They touch often, gently, unashamed of their devotion: two halves that make a whole.* And Jack was overjoyed, for they deserved all that and more.

"I hear a carriage," Kathryn exclaimed rising from her chair and going to the window.

Without waiting, she rushed from the room and headed towards the main entrance, completely missing Jack's ingrained statement: "Cornelius will bring them right in."

He shrugged at Jason as they both rose to follow. "I fear my sister, at long last, has someone who will undoubtedly question her strict protocol, someone who *will not* back down and submit to her whim of iron. Your stay should be somewhat *interesting.*"

They headed out of the den, Jason's mind momentarily distracted from the joy of reuniting with his child. *Something within this household is not right. I sense it in Jack's words, but feel it in every fiber of my body. Kathryn and I must talk of this later.*

Eugenie stepped down from the carriage, her hand delicately placed within Cornelius's supportive grip, ever aware of the 'graceful lady' image that must be portrayed at all times.

She turned back, watching the three children alight, a non-stop stream of commands erupting in bursts aimed at all of them. "Do not push! Do not shove one another! Go change immediately for dinner! We are late! Do not dawdle! Wash your hands and …"

With a gasp she was pushed aside as Gabrielle rushed past her.

"Gabrielle," she shrieked. "What have I told you about appropriate conduct, young lady? You may forget about having any dinner! I will see you …" Her mouth clamped shut. She stood aghast, her eyes narrowing.

Gabrielle was wrapped in the arms of a crouched woman, whose face she could not yet see, lost to view behind the child's unruly curls. Beauregarde stood in the doorway flanked by a dragoon colonel, obvious by his uniform, both observing the scene calmly, but with keen interest.

The colonel's eyes lifted to meet hers and held, flashing unmistakable warning. And Beauregarde's gleamed with an inner satisfaction she had never witnessed before. Eugenie struggled to retain her position of power, but a niggling fear crouched ready to pounce. *Who are these people?* But somehow, beyond all odds, she knew, and the knowledge was distressing.

"Momma, momma," Gabrielle wept, touching her mother's chest tenderly before sliding her small hand to cup her rounding belly. "I *knew* you would come for me; you and poppa and—my baby brother."

"Anna will be so proud of your abilities, little one." She gave her daughter a quick hug. "I would love to be selfish, for I have months of hugs to collect, but your poppa has missed you dearly."

As Gabrielle flung herself into her father's arms, Kathryn turned slowly to face Eugenie.

With an audible gasp, she swayed, her face going ashen. Cornelius, ever attentive, steadied her.

"Amazing likeness to her daughter, would you not agree?"

Eugenie said nothing, speechless: her normally controlled features, in the moment it took to regain composure, openly displaying nagging apprehension.

Jack grasped Kathryn's elbow, assisting her to stand, as she glared at Eugenie. She had heard her diatribe to the children, and did not like it in the least.

Jason pulled his poppet into a loving embrace, showering her in jumbled words of love while she babbled back at him in Cherokee, much to both parent's amusement. With unreserved adoration, he suddenly lifted her, swinging her in a wide circle. Shrieks of giddy glee bubbled from the child, as an accompanying rumble of delighted laughter erupted from her father.

Eugenie had recovered enough to find this open display of affection in extremely poor taste: surprising from of a man of his background. But she said nothing, biting her tongue, as Kathryn's steely gaze met her disapproving scowl.

Pulling the little carved horse from his pocket, Jason pressed it into her hand amidst squeals of joy. "For you, poppet, I have missed you dearly."

She held the wooden horse up, inspecting it carefully. "Diablo," she whispered nodding approval. Then, without uttering a word, she gently traced his scars along the outside of his jacket, knowing their exact placement although never having seen them. "You are healed, poppa."

"Yes," he whispered.

"Momma is healed too." Placing her small hand against her chest, she indicated the exact position of her mother's wound.

"Anna and Soaring Eagle," she stated solemnly, "healing the heart and soul—strong medicine."

He nodded, tousling her curly hair, awed by her revelations. He must talk to Kathryn. Their daughter had had no way of knowing. *Our poppet possesses extraordinary gifts.* And that thought gave him pleasure.

Robert and Emiline stood quietly, stunned by the spectacle before them. Her parents *were* alive, just as she had always said.

"This is my friend, Robbie and his sister, Emmie." Gabrielle turned in her father's arms acknowledging their presence; suddenly remembering that no one had introduced them yet.

Eugenie stood mute, slightly unsure of herself. But Robbie stepped forward and bowed politely, first to Kathryn and then the colonel.

"I am so pleased to meet both of you." He looked squarely at Kathryn and smiled. "Gabrielle has been waiting for so long." His eyes drifted to their daughter, conveying a depth of understanding and loyalty that startled Kathryn: *so young, yet such obvious devotion.*

"*Robert,*" Eugenie uttered succinctly, dashing any thoughts forming in Kathryn's mind, "is my eldest, and *Emiline* is the baby."

She nudged the little girl, who took one step forward and stopped, eyeing Kathryn with a scowl. *You are supposed to be dead* she thought, not at all happy with this turn of events.

"*Emmie,*" Kathryn said quietly, refusing to be intimidated by Eugenie. "You are a very pretty little girl, but if you continue to scowl, one day your face may suddenly freeze. How sad it would be for you to go through the rest of your life that way."

Indicating with her finger for Emmie to pirouette, she insisted: "Smile for me and turn, so that I may see your pretty pinafore."

And Emmie did so, rather pertly, with just the tiniest hint of a smile tugging at the corners of her mouth.

"Just as I thought," Kathryn chirped, "you are so pretty."

Jack caught her eye and winked; she always had a handle on any given situation, whether the involved parties were pleased or not.

Catching their exchange, Eugenie bristled. "Let us not stand out here in the dark any longer. I, for one, am hungry. Thomas shall arrive momentarily and expect his meal."

Jack hid a smile, well aware that his sister cared little if her husband's meal fit into his busy schedule or not. She spoke sharply, knowing she had met her match and did not like it. And she especially disliked her brother's newfound strength.

As Eugenie headed upstairs to freshen up, leaving Cornelius in charge of all else, she hustled the children ahead of her. But she cared not what they did at the moment: her mind was reeling. She would have to offer these people a place to stay as long as they liked, that thought unpleasant at best. She sensed trouble forthcoming with *that woman.*

However, the fact that Jason was a dragoon colonel held many possibilities. He had fought with Lord Cornwallis, a well liked general and friend of King George. Her Quality friends would be impressed, of that she was sure. *By now they have hopefully forgotten the last debacle, and there will never be another.* The children would be relegated to their rooms upstairs with the doors locked.

She smiled at her reflection in the mirror, pleased at the new possibilities which had just presented themselves. But as she curled a tress of hair to hang coyly along her cheek, she abruptly grimaced. A suddenly unattainable plan came to mind, and she was furious. She had so wanted to subject that brat to proper schooling.

"So much for educating *that* child," she sniped at her image as she pinched color back into her cheeks. "As she appears to be near to term, I imagine they will stay for some time. Why did she risk the voyage?" Shaking her head in disgust, she forced a smile and headed downstairs for dinner.

Eugenie arrived at the dinner table as a new person. She smiled a smile that failed to reach her eyes, and announced how delighted she would be to have them stay indefinitely. But Kathryn easily read deception in her gushing change of attitude, and made a mental note to be on her toes whenever in this shallow woman's presence.

The meal was a success, earlier tension having appeared to dissipate. Pleasant banalities were exchanged between the adults, all parties present quietly sizing each other up.

Jack caught both Kathryn and Jason in surreptitious glances. There were no questions to be answered as far as they were concerned. They had easily assessed the situation and were actively planning their next move, of that he was sure.

And the children, exhausted from their long day, had behaved perfectly, actually lacking effort to create deviltry. *No frogs.* Jack grinned to himself. He must remember to tell that story to Jason and Kathryn; they would appreciate the humor.

Eugenie's husband, Thomas, was an unpretentious, quiet man who rarely spoke up to his wife. Jack lived with them, and even he wondered if they ever actually conversed; suspecting that more than likely, Eugenie *informed.* He merely listened with unending patience, working long hours to support his family and keep his wife in the fineries she demanded.

Kathryn and Jason found Thomas to be a rather sad figure of a man. He was rarely home, by his own admittance, perhaps in an attempt to hide from his wife. He seemed well meant at heart, but lacked the backbone to thwart her strict demands.

Not a good father figure, Kathryn decided. *But I did not come all this way to cast judgment.* It had taken only these few hours of observation to know the answer. She and Jason and Jack had much to decide. But not *this* night; she was beginning to fade.

The adults adjourned from the dinner table and moved to sit beside the blazing fire in the den, enjoying a glass of brandy. All the children were tucked in bed, all but Gabrielle. Kathryn and Jason took longer in their 'good nights', eager to be with their child as she dropped into sleep cradling 'Diablo' to her chest.

Eugenie cast them an irritated look for their tardiness, but neither was fazed. There were far more important things than sitting down for a drink at a precise moment. *Tending to our child for one*, Kathryn thought, and returned her hostess's tart look. Perhaps more time given to *loving* Robbie and Emmie might be a consideration.

As Kathryn sat down, Eugenie decided to make mention of her condition.

"If you require anything for your comfort, do let us know, Kathryn."

Kathryn eyed her over the rim of her glass and smiled.

"I have found a marvelous doctor. He delivered Emiline, as a matter of fact, and he will gladly come at my request."

Will this woman never cease attempting to orchestrate our lives? Kathryn stiffened, irritated. But reading her well, Jason placed his hand in hand the small of her back, lending a calming effect.

Drawing a deep breath, she said politely, "Thank you, but I feel confident this will be an easy birth that I can handle myself."

Eugenie's horrified look was almost comical.

"My wife is a healer, all will go well," Jason said with a bit more forcefulness than he really felt; Gabrielle's birth had terrified him.

"But if there is a problem, your brother makes an excellent doctor. Gabrielle was a breech birth: a bit difficult, but we made it through quite well, did we not?" She turned a beaming face to Jack, amused as Eugenie's eyes widened even further.

"I understand you had a similar instance with Robbie's birth, and he helped you through that. I found that knowledge comforting when I had my difficulties. As a matter of fact …"

"You spoke of Robert's birth outside this house?" Eugenie rounded angrily on her brother, her eyes darkening with resentment.

Jack shrugged. "Not in detail of course, Eugenie." He smiled brightly adding, "Of course, if you wish me to, I will be more than happy to clarify the details."

Eugenie's cheeks flamed red, furious that he had shared such information. However, the fact that her spineless brother made no attempt at apology or explanation irked her even more. He was changing, becoming stronger right before her eyes, and she did not like the fact. Taking three deep breaths she calmed herself. She would thoroughly chastise her brother later. But at the moment, they were all sitting silently regarding her.

"Oh well, that is that," she quipped, attempting a smile. "Is anyone ready for a refill of their brandy?" She held the decanter out to her brother. "Beauregarde finds this his favorite part of the day."

Beauregarde? Caught off-guard, Kathryn inhaled a sip of brandy the wrong way: choking, laughing and trying to catch her breath. Jack and Jason were instantly at her side, deeply concerned as she gripped her chest. But as fast as she regained a modicum of control, she shook her head sending them back to their seats.

"It only hurts when I laugh." She grinned, spearing Jack with a probing look. "Beauregarde—*Beauregarde?*" she repeated, her eyes twinkling with glee.

"Thank you for noticing its uniqueness, Kathryn." He colored a bit, but his look held unmistakable mirth. "I *prefer*, Jack," he said firmly, turning a stern eye towards his sister. He had made his preference known months ago, but she had flatly refused, feeling it to be undignified.

"So do we," Jason and Kathryn said in unison.

Throwing her hands up in distinct aggravation, Eugenie made a low sound in her throat. But catching her husband's hapless glance, quickly attempted another insincere smile.

For the most part, the evening was over. Eugenie refused a second drink, professing it had been a long day. Agreement unanimous, they headed for their rooms.

At their bedroom door, Jack paused. "I cannot begin to tell you, for there are no words. You have saved me from …"

"Hush," Kathryn murmured, silencing him with a well-placed finger. "Words are such frail vehicles, but our hearts know and rejoice." Pulling him into a warm embrace, she held him for a long moment before breaking the contact.

Jason gripped Jack's shoulder firmly and grinned. "The feelings shall always remain the same, dear friend. However, in this particular household, perhaps we had best stop embracing, eyebrows may be raised."

They laughed uproariously. Their shattered world was beginning to come together at last—and it felt so right.

"Only our first night here, my love, and already our stay would seem too long."

Jason stretched out beside his wife, enjoying her nakedness pressed warmly against him. "Hmmm," he agreed. "When I wished Ted good night, he said we would not be here long."

"A rather discerning young man; I like him."

"Apparently he likes us." He eyed her steadily. "He wants to head to the colonies with us, when we return."

"Oh, does he now?" she chuckled.

"However, he has one stipulation: that he can bring his pair of grays."

He traced a finger along the ridge of her nipple, no longer noticing the puckered scar on her chest. Neither feared baring their wounds to the other, both blind to the disfigurements.

Kathryn sucked in her breath. "Jason, if you tease, you know I will demand payment—in full." Her emerald, green eyes flashed love … and need.

"I had hoped you would say that, my pet, for *I need you* desperately. I cannot even begin to think of staying here, for it depresses me. And we *must* talk of it but *not* tonight."

Her hands began to entice with knowing familiarity, causing a rippling thrill to tingle along his flesh.

"Tonight I must claim you as mine, and *mine alone*, for we are as one."

"Always," her fervent pledge, "as *you* are mine also."

"Always," his passionate answer.

He had thought all such feelings long since suppressed, but Jack's open devotion had caused a twinge of jealousy. However, Kathryn's wordless understanding never allowed him a moment's doubt. With gentle fingers she aroused, tempted and seduced, her eyes promising undying love.

He grasped her hands, capturing them firmly at either side of her head as his tongue flicked intimately along the rim of her ear. His tantalizing meanderings created molten trails of desire as he drifted lower. Heated breaths traced the arch of her neck, along her collarbone, but did not stop there. Hot wetness surrounded a taut nipple as his lips closed firmly, and she was his.

"Jason," she moaned."

He moved lower, his tongue so knowing of her every need. Breaking free of his grasp, she plunged her fingers into his long, black hair and rose to meet him. And with a throaty chuckle, he fell to loving her properly.

Chapter Twenty-Three

Much Ado About Everything

"Momma, poppa," a small voice chirped.

Kathryn cracked an eye and stretched, her movement causing Jason to roll over with a soft groan. Without opening his eyes, he tossed his arm over her shoulder and hugged her, placing a warm kiss against her neck.

"Momma, poppa," a slightly more insistent whisper from close proximity.

Both parents opened their eyes, yawning and smiling sleepily at their daughter.

"Good morning, poppet." Jason raised himself up on one elbow to see his daughter better. "And what brings you to visit so bright and early?"

"I must be prompt for children's breakfast, so that we may study our daily lessons while the adults eat."

Kathryn frowned. "You do not dine with the grown-ups?"

"No, the kitchen is where we usually sit."

Kathryn glanced over her shoulder, not surprised to see her husband frowning.

Gabrielle moved to the edge of the bed, but at her mother's open-armed invitation, hopped up and snuggled happily into the welcoming embrace. She had hugged herself on so many lonely nights, trying to imagine her mother's touch. But 'imagining' could not begin to compare to the reality … and tears sprang freely.

Jason gently caressed her small shoulder; becoming instantly alarmed by her shuddering sobs. *Who or what has hurt my child so?*

"What is it, little one?" Kathryn whispered, inching her fingers under her delicate chin and raising it: taken aback by the incredible sadness within her child's blue eyes.

"Tears? But we are all together now. Everything will finally be set right."

"Must we stay?" she asked mournfully.

"You have been unhappy here?" Jason asked.

Swinging his feet to the floor, he circled the bed and sat down, taking her small hand in his.

"I love Robbie and I shall miss him dearly," she whispered. "But I hate what they do to Uncle Jack."

"Hate is a very strong word, poppet." Jason tousled her unruly curls, so like her mother's.

"They say awful things to hurt his feelings. He is always in trouble because of me."

Tears welled anew as she glanced guiltily at her parents. "I am not like them, momma. I have tried—I truly have, but I am too different."

"Thank heavens," Kathryn whispered, pressing a kiss to the top of her head. "I am not surprised; it is those very qualities that make you so special. This is not meant to be your life."

"But poppa and Uncle Jack grew up here, and Great Grandmother is somewhere near too. You will want to stay, it is your home." She gazed up at her father with sad blue eyes.

Jason raised her chin to meet his vivid blue gaze. "*Home* is wherever you and momma are happy. And I *have* changed a great deal, poppet."

She blinked, sending a large tear rushing down her cheek, stopped gently by her father's thumb.

"I no longer belong here, nor does Uncle Jack," he said, giving her a comforting hug.

"How soon may we go?" she asked, relief flooding her face.

Kathryn chuckled. "After we bring your baby brother into this world, we will return to the colonies. Uncle Jamie, and cousins you have not yet met, eagerly await your return. And Anna sends her love, counting the number of sunsets until you reappear."

Jason nodded. "She and Soaring Eagle have awarded me an Indian name: 'Hunts with spirit'—Hunter, for short." He kissed her cheek. "We will go back, that I promise. But you must be patient for a while longer."

"Just as poppa and I must be," Kathryn interjected. "But we will make changes in this strict regime. And perhaps Great Grandmother would welcome a long visit, if it becomes too difficult here."

With a happy sigh, she leaned against her mother. "Show me, momma," she whispered, touching her mother's chest gently.

Kathryn's eyes widened as she searched her daughter's face.

"Show me, please. I need to see how they hurt you and poppa."

Wordlessly, Kathryn slid her chemise lower, baring the puckered scar: well healed but still bright against her creamy skin.

Gabrielle barely touched with her fingertips, running them lightly over the roughness. "I felt it, momma; here." She moved her hand to her own chest. "But I knew you still lived."

Turning to her father, she traced the long, uneven wound that ran the full length of his chest, and then pressed softly against the jagged healed tears in his shoulder, reminders of the grapeshot that had taken him down. Tears raced down her cheeks.

"Hush, little one, for *it is done*. Your father and I will not return to the war," Kathryn assured, gently mopping her daughter's face with the ample sleeve of her chemise.

"Promise me," she said firmly.

"Anything, my poppet."

"Never leave me behind again."

Jason's brow rose.

"I want to be with you—and momma—and Uncle Jack."

"I believe that to be a fair request. Done—done—and done."

Her blue eyes sparkled, a brilliant smile lighting her face. Reaching up, she lifted her hair. "Please undo my gold chain, poppa."

Pulling the golden necklace from beneath her nightgown, she handed it to her mother. At sight of the beautiful pearl set within a gold heart, a warm rush of memories flooded Kathryn.

Jason's eyes met hers, bright with emotion. It had belonged to his mother, and then passed down to him. He had placed it around Kathryn's neck, to wear in happiness, the delicate heart resting between her breasts until the day they rode out together, to face their final battle. That day, she had fastened it about her daughter's neck for 'safe keeping', bravely riding out with Jason to face their destiny at Guilford Courthouse. She had seen the dreadful outcome in a dream, but refused to have him go alone.

"You asked me to keep it safe, momma, and now it must rest where it truly belongs." She turned to her father with a wordless request.

Tears rolled down Kathryn's cheeks as Jason closed the clasp with a kiss.

"No tears, my love. Instead, consider its return a good omen for new beginnings."

Worrying at her quivering lip, unable to find adequate words, she hugged Gabrielle.

Needing to lighten the mood, Jason smiled at his daughter and rose from the bed.

"I have a thought, poppet. You have given momma a very special gift. And I have something that may bring you equal pleasure."

After rummaging in their large duffle bag for a moment, he pulled out her wooden pull toy. Instantly at his side, she crushed it to her chest, dancing in a circle.

"I thought it was lost forever. I forgot it, that night that Uncle Jack and I …"

"Grampa Cornwallis sends his love. He saved it for you."

Her eyes crinkled with joy. "It is a fair trade, poppa. Now momma and I both have our special gifts."

Suddenly the loud crowing of a barnyard rooster filled the air. Gabrielle froze for an instant then raced for the door. "I will be late," she flung back over her shoulder as she slammed the door, exiting before they could say a word.

Kathryn and Jason sat on the edge of the bed in silence. Jason ran his finger along the necklace chain and coming to the golden heart, toyed gently, smiling. Kathryn's hand closed over his, her lips parting to meet his kiss.

"This is unacceptable, Kathryn." He leaned back eyeing her thoughtfully. "Less than one day here and nothing seems right."

"I am afraid it is up to us to change it, at least where *our* daughter is concerned."

Swinging her legs over the edge of the bed, she gasped as a sharp pain caught her.

"Kathryn." Jason was immediately at her side.

She shook her head, waving him away with a sharp gesture. "Not today but soon: sooner than I had expected."

She rubbed her belly absentmindedly, her thoughts having turned to more pressing matters.

"Before we go down to breakfast, let us take a minute to discuss this, so that we may present a united front."

He nodded thoughtfully. "Yes, they offered us shelter for the duration of our stay, and whether graciously presented or not, we accepted—just by having spent one night."

"I am afraid our only other alternative would be an inn."

He shook his head, running different scenarios through his mind. "No, I fear that would leave Jack to take the brunt of Eugenie's constant temper." He eyed his wife. "Do you think that woman has ever truly lived a happy moment? One in which she has the courage to drop the ridiculous façade she hides behind?"

"I doubt that, but on another topic, did you see the way Robbie looked at our daughter? His young heart will be broken soon enough. I do not wish to separate them quite so soon, if at all possible."

"Have you thought of my grandmother? Jack admitted he had not found the courage to contact her as yet. I imagine she might be thrilled."

"Yes, and we *will* see her. But she is elderly now. Although she would be delighted to have you home, a crying infant and all that commotion …" She searched Jason's face.

"Besides, there is the problem of my miserable father to contend with and ..."

"And we *will* resolve that before we leave."

"Kathryn, I do not ..."

"*I will* resolve that situation before we sail. It is the last remaining ghost from your past—our past." She squeezed his hand soothingly.

"If I am reading you correctly, my pet, for all parties concerned, whether *they* realize it or not, it would be best if we stayed here?"

"Yes, my love, unfortunately, but I *have* given it a bit of consideration. Eugenie appears to be somewhat like Banastre. He and I have come to respect each other, although we seldom agree on most subjects."

"You are absolutely fearless, my beautiful wife."

Flashing a wide grin, she rose and began dressing. At Jason's concerned look, she rolled her eyes. "I am fine. The little one has decided: *not today.* So let us see if we must do battle this morning, or forestall until a later date. I believe that last night you mentioned a trip to town to purchase less dressy attire. Although my mind was not on anything but ..." Her hand slid seductively under his shirt, tantalizing playfully.

"Kathryn, if you do not wish me to demand immediate payment for teasing, I would advise ..."

Amidst lighthearted laughter, they readied themselves for a possible ensuing battle.

Surprisingly breakfast, although quiet, remained pleasant. Eugenie had apparently thought things through, deciding it would be better not to create an open rift—at least for the moment. But Kathryn read her all too well and was not fooled.

Speaking with her over a cup of tea in her Rose Room after breakfast, she explained that there would be no further need for Gabrielle to partake in such strictly structured daily lessons.

"However, if our daughter chooses to join your children in lessons while she is here, we will not stand in her way."

Eugenie's lips lifted, but the smile never reached her eyes.

"She *will* have adequate schooling back in the colonies. Jason and I both feel that learning is an important part of her upbringing."

Eugenie sniffed and turned aside; acting as if to add more honey to her tea, but Kathryn saw the sneer. She opened her mouth to defend her background, but stopped. *If I defend my schooling, she will tear me apart. No, Eugenie, silence is my power over you.* She smiled a secretive smile, causing Eugenie to stiffen; delighted to see confusion flickering in her eyes.

Kathryn stood and picked up her cup and saucer. "Thank you for the tea and conversation. Jason and I are going into town within the hour, and we *will* be taking Gabrielle."

Eugenie gave her a long look. "Enjoy your trip. Shall we expect you for dinner, then?"

"We look forward to it." Kathryn smiled.

"Do leave your cup and saucer, Cornelius or one of the maids will clear all this away."

"Oh, not to bother, I am heading in that direction anyway. In the colonies we were taught to pick up after ourselves."

Turning to leave, she caught Eugenie's fuming gaze. *My, my, I am afraid she and I really do not like each other very well.* Chuckling to herself, she headed for the kitchen and then out to greet Jack and Jason.

Their time spent together was a blessing, each needed healing. By sharing their grief, physical pain, and sorrow for all that had been lost, as well as that which had not—due to courage and blind luck—they would find consolation. Kathryn understood that men grieved differently than women, needing to share their sorrow with each other. Despite the incredible love she and Jason shared, he *needed* Jack, just as much as Jack needed him. Seeing them able to express their feelings freely, brought contentment: they would be fine.

They arrived back at the estate just in time for dinner. Jack had accompanied them to help choose the best shops for their needs. The hours they had shared had not caused complaint yet, but that would come. Kathryn and Jason had no intention of excluding Jack from anything they did. He had always been an integral part of their lives and would remain so—unless *he* saw fit to make a change.

As they sat down, Eugenie gasped. Although dressed more formally than colonial attire, their new garb fell far short of what Eugenie deemed appropriate at her dinner table. Besides the fact that Jack had also 'dressed down', what disgusted her further was the men's hair: both sporting a loosely clubbed style. She stared openly. Even Kathryn had failed to pull hers back into a fashionable bun, allowing her riotous, golden curls to cascade in billows about her shoulders.

The meal was tense, lacking in conversation and quickly over. The three conspirators winked at each other as they parted at their bedroom doors.

"Tomorrow will be another day, Jack," she giggled, as she and Jason said 'good night'.

The days passed quickly, some peaceful and entertaining, others bordering on open hostility between the warring parties. The children had been purposely kept out of the foray. They would learn this silly adult game-playing all by themselves—all in good time.

Many of the more pleasant days involved the children. Kathryn spent a great deal of time showing them Beauty's tricks, and helping to improve their riding abilities. However, Emmie was too little, too spoiled, and unfortunately not a 'natural' like her brother, to accomplish much.

Jason and Jack both enjoyed fishing, and could often be found with one or more children at the small brook. Of course chores and lessons had to be finished first, and then only after asking Eugenie's permission.

From the moment Robbie sat astride the mare, they were as one. He learned quickly and loved the beautiful animal as if she were his own. And he adored Kathryn.

Today he had asked to ride while the others, even Gabrielle, sat in the chilly air enjoying the brook. He wanted to speak with Kathryn, and Ellie had understood.

"I love Gabrielle," he admitted quietly, as the two of them worked together brushing Beauty's slick coat after putting her through her paces.

Kathryn eyed him silently, unsure of what to say.

"Do not think me too young. I may be only nine years old—well, I will be on my next birthday, but I have always been sure of what I wanted when it was presented."

"We must go home again, Robbie," she answered softly.

His words tugged at her heart, for she could see the truth of his statement revealed in his eyes. Gabrielle had expressed identical feelings to both parents some time ago.

Looking her straight in the eye, he added sadly: "My mother will never allow me to go. But *I will come* and find her. It is our destiny, Ellie and I."

Kathryn heard the devotion in her whispered nickname and pulled him to her, rocking him gently.

"Oh, Robbie, you two have chosen a difficult journey; for my daughter shares your feelings. But there is nothing that I can do."

"Yes, there is," he murmured. Giving her a quick hug, he stepped back. "Write to me. I will give you an address." His eyes searched hers. "And keep her safe, for *I will* come and find her. *I will.*"

He spun on his heel and left, but not before she saw the tears.

"Oh, Robbie," she whispered. "You are so young to be so old."

With a loving pat to her mare, she headed off to find Jason, an aching knot forming in her chest that had nothing to do with her wound.

Jason handed Kathryn carefully into the carriage and turned to assist his daughter. Seeing them smiling and settled, he stepped up to join Jack on the driver's seat.

"Eugenie's look was priceless," Jack chuckled as he slapped the reins and the carriage lurched ahead. "When Kathryn announced that I was going with you, she was a bit taken aback. But when you added that I was driving the carriage, rather than Tobias ..." He flashed a wide grin. "I doubt she will ever recover from the shame of it."

Jason eyed his friend. "Actually, Jack, it is truly sad. Having to constantly maintain such a flawless image must be a heavy burden to bear."

"That is why we are *all* going home," a small voice chirped from behind them.

Both men turned to smile at Gabrielle, nodding agreement. But Kathryn caught a look of sadness in Jack's eyes, and it troubled her. It quickly fled as he and Jason began happy, entertaining banter, but she would mention it to Jason later. She suspected the cause, but it would keep.

This was to be a day of pleasure, not marred by reality. Taking her daughter's hand, she settled back against the cushions to enjoy the sights and sounds and delightful fall aromas. It was a beautiful, sunny, crisp day and she felt marvelous.

Great Grandmother eagerly awaited their arrival. They had three or four hours to travel and would arrive by late morning, enjoy a light meal and then leave, allowing her to spend a quiet evening recuperating.

She lived a self-imposed life of contented solitude. As she had not seen Jason in many years, and never met his wife, child, or Jack, this visit would create a great deal of excitement. Jason insisted she came from sturdy stock, and had no intention of missing the occasion for any reason. Hopefully the shock would not be too great.

"You two handsome gentlemen are a delight," Kathryn yelled. "But I do miss Ted's ribald tales."

"You may get to hear more of those, my pet," Jason tossed back over his shoulder. "He sent news that he will be joining us, and has already contacted Captain Farthingale. Apparently, the refitting has taken a bit longer than originally planned. He expects to be in port for at least six more weeks."

"December," Kathryn murmured. "I wonder how the seas fare that time of year, for I doubt I can last until spring."

Gabrielle eyed her mother curiously.

"Just thinking out loud, little one, ignore me and enjoy the brisk fall air."

"Oh, by the way," Jason turned to give his wife a wink. "The captain sent his 'best' to the missus. I think he rather liked you, my pet."

"Only if he has a tendency towards pleasingly plump women," she retorted, causing them to laugh.

As if mention of her condition set things in motion, she suddenly experienced a gripping pain.

"Momma?" Gabrielle searched her mother's face.

"It is nothing, little one; we must not concern the men. The pain has passed."

"Great Grandmother will be thrilled." Her child's eyes reflected what she, herself, feared. "Tonight, momma, but it will be easy. My brother was tiny, but survived with your love. He understands, he lived through *your* pain and will make it easy."

Kathryn gathered her daughter into her arms, hugging her tight. "How I do love you little one," she whispered. "Your 'gift' is as powerful as Anna perceived."

"May I help?" she asked softly. "I am *not* too young."

Two of a kind they are—my daughter and her Robbie. "Yes, little one, if you will not be upset, I would like that very much."

"Will poppa mind?"

"I will speak to him. But I am afraid I shall have to stop referring to you as 'little one', for you and a certain young man both have maturity well beyond your years."

"I like 'little one'; you may always call me that."

She sparkled, her face absolutely aglow with happiness, and Kathryn took a long look at her daughter. No wonder people stared when they were seen together. Her plump, baby features had created a rounder similarity. But in the seven months they had been apart, the roundness had given way to a young girl's slightly more angular lines. *Even with her father's beautiful ebony hair and brilliant blue eyes, we look so alike.* She hoped her daughter would not consider that a curse someday.

"We have arrived," Jack yelled, as he pulled the team to a stop. Within moments, pandemonium broke out. Kathryn was catapulted into an emotional reunion, the likes of which only happened in storybooks: hugging, kissing, freely flowing tears and words tumbling erratically, trying to communicate the details of Jason's last five years.

It was exhausting, it was delightful. She laughed. She cried. She babbled incessantly trying to paint an accurate picture, searching for those elusive words which might begin to hint at all they had experienced, all they meant to each other, including Jack—for he *was* family.

Great Grandmother was a delightful lady, both she and Kathryn instantly bonding. When the elderly lady's arms wrapped around her, Kathryn felt blessed. It had been many years since experiencing the true meaning of a mother's love, and it filled an empty void. Just as Jason's mother, hers had also died when she was very young.

As Jack prepared to bring the carriage around, Kathryn experienced an agonizing spasm and sat quickly down, trying to conceal the fact. It would not be concealed for long as it escalated, coming faster and harder. Forcing a smile, she tried to focus. Jason and Jack stood talking by the door, unaware of her situation.

Perhaps we can find an inn before ...

"Great Grandmother, my momma is having her baby," Gabrielle whispered in the elderly lady's ear and received a delighted smile. "Right *now*," she added more forcefully.

"Really; right now?" She pushed herself up from her chair. "Then you and I have work to do—and quickly."

She moved to Kathryn's side with unusual agility. "Shall I have Jason help you into bed, my dear? Gabrielle and I have water to boil, and all that other necessary 'woman stuff'."

Kathryn eyed the delightful lady with a tight smile that rapidly turned into a grimace as another pain griped her unmercifully.

"I may need a little help," she ground out.

"Do you want a midwife, my dear?" But before she could gasp an answer, Great Grandmother, shook her head. "I think not, we can handle this, can't we now?"

She stood, announcing loudly: "Jason, you are about to become a father again. Come give your wife a hand to bed."

Jason's face drained of all color. "Jack, oh God, Jack ..."

"Do not even voice it, Jason. She will be all right, but not if we stand here."

"Kathryn." He knelt at her side as another spasm seized her, her breathing erupting in loud gasps.

"Perfect, Kathryn, I see you remember everything I taught you." Jack grinned. "Are you ready?" He stood up, poised to lift her. But Jason, abruptly gathering his wits, swept her into his arms and carried her into the guest bedroom.

"What can I do?" he asked, easing her clothing, attempting to make her comfortable.

With the next spasm, she grasped his hand in an iron grip, holding tightly until it eased. In the following moments of relief, she recognized the fear in his eyes.

"Please do something for me, my love," she said calmly.

"Anything, anything at all," he answered raggedly.

She gritted her teeth, panting, as he stared in guilty misery. "Have a drink with Jack and ..." she gasped, her contractions more rapid now. "Get ready for a sleepless night." She smiled weakly. "Now go. Gabrielle has asked to help." His eyes widened, startled. "Go, my love, Great Grandmother has everything under control. We will talk of this later."

"Go with it, Kathryn, I am here if you need me." With a gentle squeeze to her shoulder, Jack grasped Jason's arm and led him from the room.

The two men sat in the living room, each with a drink in hand. But Jason would only alight for a moment before he resumed pacing.

"You remind me of Kathryn," Jack chuckled.

"But Jack, what if ..."

"Stop looking so guilty, Jason. This is all part of loving each other. I recall she told me once, in the beginning, when you were at battle and she still relegated to remain in camp, that the passion you two share is, and always will be, a double-edged sword—incredible joy, acute heartache and worry."

Jason set his glass down hard on a table. "I feel so helpless and I ..."

Suddenly Gabrielle emerged from the bedroom and darted towards the kitchen, only to re-emerge with a small pan of hot water clutched between two carefully toweled hands. Swathed in a white apron, hitched up and tied snuggly so as not to trip her, she moved with authoritative purpose.

"Great Grandmother says not to worry," she informed him sternly, and without further adieu, disappeared back into the bedroom.

Jason rolled his eyes and sat down, clenching and unclenching his fists, trying to calm his inner fear. Within several minutes, seemingly an eternity, a loud, angry wail carried easily through the closed door.

Gabrielle came out grinning from ear to ear. "Do you hear my brother? He is little, but so strong." She pointed to her filthy apron proudly. "Momma let *me* cut his um-bil—his cord," she finished; annoyed that she could not pronounce the word correctly.

Jason stood dumbfounded, staring at his daughter.

"Congratulations, my princess, not every one could do what you have done," Jack applauded.

She beamed proudly, impatiently tugging his sleeve.

"Come see him. He has momma's light hair, but I am not really sure who he looks like."

"He looks like your poppa, little one."

Kathryn rested against pillows holding the wriggling infant, who continued his angry protest in spite of his mother's soothing tones. "He is hungry, but his poppa comes first." She smiled up at her husband, her eyes only for him.

Jason was instantly at her side, eyes misting, as he kissed her tenderly, murmuring jumbled words of love.

Jack looked on, pleased to see *this* birth had not robbed her of her strength—not like the last one, thank God, and smiled with adoration.

She beckoned him closer, including him, as she opened her son's blanket for his father's inspection. Great Grandmother and Gabrielle, hands folded neatly on their aprons, stood quietly observing, proud of their accomplishment.

Jason picked up his son, brought him to his face and kissed him. A small flailing fist grazed his cheek and stopped. Jason took the tiny hand, gently unfurling the perfectly shaped fingers as he proceeded to scan his small body, checking all the appropriate parts as he went.

"Look, Jack, he is so perfect." And for the second time in his life, was awestruck by their incredible creation.

"Gabrielle, my poppet," he said softly, handing his son to Jack and turning to his little girl, needing to assure her: his love for her would never be superseded by this newest addition to their family. "I am so proud of you, poppet. You and Great Grandmother helped make this easier for momma."

"I think we make an excellent team, Jason," Great Grandmother chimed in, wrapping her arm around her great grandchild.

"We did bring a bit more excitement than we planned, and I hope ..." Kathryn began.

"You have given me reason to live, my dear, and *you*, Jason, have healed my heart. If I were younger, I would beg to go with you to the colonies. But I will settle for long letters from you, and an occasional note from Jack. For he will always tell me the reality of a situation; not merely sell false comfort to an old lady." She gifted him with a warm smile.

Kathryn glowed, sitting comfortably propped against pillows and feeding the baby. Jack's eyes widened, fraught with pain at the sight of her angry wound—ugly memories stirring. She knew, and touched his hand squeezing gently, returning him to the present.

"That is all past," she whispered. "We must look ahead."

She was right—*perhaps. But what did his future hold?*

"And what name shall we give this wee bairn of ours?" Kathryn jumped in, scanning each person before focusing on her husband.

Jason rubbed his chin, deep in thought, as everyone waited for his decision. "Herkemeyer," he said firmly, a definite sparkle to his eyes.

"Poppa!" Gabrielle exclaimed, horrified.

But Jack and Great Grandmother merely grinned.

Jason frowned. "Perhaps not, my love, for I fear I cannot spell it."

In the silence following the outburst of laughter, Jason looked directly at his wife, eyes teeming with love, and stated quietly. "Then he shall be: James Beauregarde Tarrington, for your brother and our beloved Jack."

Jack swallowed convulsively, deeply honored.

But Kathryn, struck speechless, eyed her husband with tears welling. "For Jamie?"

"Yes, my Kathryn, for he loves you dearly, and is also my friend."

Four days passed, a happy, pleasurable coexistence as Kathryn regained her strength. The following morning, she urged the two men to take Gabrielle into London to see the city, commenting that, "Good or bad, there will be nothing like it in the colonies."

They had been gone no more than an hour, when a carriage pulled into the gravel drive. Kathryn sat holding her sleeping baby, but eyed the older woman curiously. Before she could walk to the window to see, the door was thrown open and a dark stranger entered, uninvited. Although disheveled, his face puffy from drink, she could detect a once strong, angular facial structure—so like that of her husband.

"And what is it this time, William? Short on rent again?" Great Grandmother spat.

"Oh, and a good day to you, my favorite mother-in-law," he sniped, swaying slightly, his rheumy eyes sending her a tart look.

"I have no money for you," she said crossly.

"You never have," he groused. "How about a hot meal and a bit of brandy?" he whined, wiping a dirty hand across his face.

"William, before you say anything more, and embarrass yourself further, I have company." She indicated Kathryn, rocking her baby and quietly studying him through narrowed eyes.

"Well, aren't you the pretty one," he snorted, moving closer for a better look, the reek of alcohol clinging to his clothing.

Perhaps his face had been handsome at one time, but that was long before overindulgence and an abusive nature had left their brand.

"Mind your manners or you shall leave this minute," Great Grandmother hissed. "This is Jason's wife and their new baby, and I will not have you insult her."

Kathryn smiled tightly, her eyes wary.

"Jason. Jason? And what is my useless son up to now?" He guffawed loudly.

Kathryn's eyes narrowed, spearing him with an icy glare. Rising slowly, she placed her son in Great Grandmother's waiting arms. "Would you please excuse us for a few minutes? Mr. Tarrington and I need to talk." And with that terse statement, she grabbed his arm, pulling him stumbling into the library.

The elderly lady held the infant gently, rocking and crooning softly, smiling with deep satisfaction. She had seen Kathryn's angry scar and understood her undying passion for her grandson. *William, you have finally met your match. My Kathryn will set you straight.* She moved a bit closer to where the door stood ajar.

Angry words erupted, Kathryn's diatribe not fully discernable, but her meaning, obvious. William's ugly retort, lilting with sarcasm, was instantly cut short by a violent slam of fists hitting the desk, accompanied by a coarse oath.

The baby whimpered, but light rocking and soft words calmed him. Sated and sleepy, as most wee babies, he easily became deaf to his surroundings.

Bits and pieces of Kathryn's angry tirade floated from the room, bringing a smile to Great Grandmother's face. "Oh, to have seen her in battle; you are truly blessed, Jason. This beautiful woman's undying love for you is a priceless gift," she murmured against the small blonde head cradled in her arms. Moving a little closer, staying just out of sight, the words became more recognizable.

"You forget yourself, sir. I *am nothing* like Jason's dear, departed mother! She was a gentle, timid soul, poor woman. But *I am not.* Do not think to threaten me, or treat me as you did her." Her fists slammed the desk, her tirade continuing.

William's sarcasm faded into occasional sulky bursts, but he did not cease his effrontery. Although Great Grandmother had not caught his last remark, she suspected it had involved added threat—for Kathryn erupted violently.

"Let this be fair warning," she ground out through gritted teeth. "Do *not* threaten me again. I have seen the atrocities of war and *participated* in them. I have slashed a man's throat clear to the bone without a moment's hesitation—*or regret.* Do not think to toy with me further."

Great Grandmother could see clearly, for she had inched even closer, fascinated by the scene unfolding before her. Liquor had made William fearless, or so he thought, and he dared counter with a series of semi-intelligible insulting remarks hurled at Jason's perceived failures, a serious mistake on his part.

Unleashing uncontrollable fury, she slammed both fists even more violently, following through with a vicious sweep of her arm, hurling books, candles, everything, onto the floor. Leaning in close, her face contorted with rage, she grabbed his lapels, yanking him upright, pulling him to within inches of her.

Great Grandmother cupped her mouth, silencing a gasp, as she watched, mesmerized. *She is like a lioness!* Jack had used those words in reference to her during one of their talks. At the time, she had not understood, but she did now.

Kathryn continued to rail, a growling tirade in English and a language she had never heard before. She shredded the man verbally, unmercifully, and was *not nearly* finished when his eyes suddenly cleared, her words striking a chord in his whiskey soaked brain.

He paled, a flicker of fear leaping to his eyes, for he had never seen another woman—or man for that matter—with such strength and untamed fury, and could not be sure what she might do.

Great Grandmother smiled a deep inner smile of satisfaction. *Oh, if only Jason's poor mother could have had but one half of Kathryn's spirit, you bastard. She would still be alive today.* She moved away from the door, crooning softly to Beau. A tear slid down her craggy cheek. *Justice has been served.* She turned back just in time to see Jason's father scrabbling to keep his chair upright—rocked backwards by an angry shove.

"Our discussion is over," Kathryn hissed fiercely.

She took a deep breath, centering herself, unsure how she had calmed her unmanageable fury without Jason, but thankful she had. *There are times when I wonder if I can …* she dropped the thought.

"Mark my words, Mr. Tarrington," she warned, her steely gaze skewering him unmercifully, "*Never* degrade Jason ever again, nor my children, nor Great Grandmother." She paused for effect. "Are we in complete understanding?"

Kathryn moved to the door and stood looking back over her shoulder at Jason's father. He sat slightly askew, his color slowly returning, a flickering look of disquiet remaining. His eyes were now clear, and he was sober.

"Do I have your complete understanding and agreement?" she repeated, slowly and precisely, her steely gaze unwavering.

"Yes," he answered softly. No more than that, but that was all she required.

"Then please make yourself presentable, Mr. Tarrington, for Jason should be returning shortly. He needs to lay old ghosts aside—as do you, I imagine. It would seem it is time for healing on all sides."

He nodded and rose from his chair, eyeing her with dawning respect. She smiled then, one of genuine warmth, and turning to leave added, "One thing you must know of me, William. I *never* hold a grudge once the situation is resolved."

As she stepped into the living room, Great Grandmother met her with a hug. "Oh, Kathryn …" But she had no words.

Kathryn lowered herself heavily into a chair. With the adrenaline rush over, she was tired. She reached for her sleeping son, peacefully oblivious and sucking his thumb.

"I do apologize for my rather unladylike display," she said softly, her eyes twinkling.

The elderly lady shook her head vigorously. "No, my dear Kathryn, you have corrected something that has needed correcting for a long time."

"Might I clean up a bit before my son arrives?" William asked quietly as he emerged from the library.

"Absolutely," Great Grandmother said lightly. "And I believe we will be having one more for dinner." With a wink to Kathryn, and a smile of genuine warmth for her son-in-law, she headed for the kitchen.

Kathryn settled back against a mound of pillows, enjoying the intimate connection as her son suckled contentedly, allowing her mind to drift. It was now three weeks since little *Beau's* birth, dubbed that nickname by his adoring big sister. There was never a moment when he was not fawned over, held, or loved by all the children. Even Emmie was pleased to be allowed to hold him—but only with Gabrielle's strictest instructions.

Jason and his father had buried old ghosts. The past could not be reclaimed, but they could save some of the future. They would never be close, but at least his father now held him in complete respect. Jason could not fully return those feelings, but he had gained insight into the demons which had controlled his father for so many years.

While in London, Jack and Jason had heard disheartening news. Captain Hodges's concern for their safe departure had been warranted. The French *had* sailed into Chesapeake Bay the first week in September, just shortly after their ship had sailed for England. As of mid-October, Lord

Cornwallis had surrendered in Yorktown, *the world turning upside down*, the war over. There were few details, but it seemed his lordship was unscathed and would return to England in late December or January.

Kathryn had said very little at that time, thoroughly shocked by the sad news. She had wished to see his lordship again, but that would be impossible. These last three weeks had dragged by, and not particularly pleasantly.

Three weeks ago, they had been informed that Captain Farthingale intended to sail in six weeks, only three weeks left to be ready. By then, it would be early December. Departing any later would be pressing their luck. They must be on board that ship, time to get word to the captain and reserve space for all of them—and Beauty.

She and Jason sat wrapped in each other's arms, resting against the plump pillows on their bed. Beau slept soundly in his crib, while Gabrielle slept soundly in her own room.

"I can hear your mind working, Kathryn."

"You always do, my love. I had hoped to see his lordship again," she said. "By estimated guess, he will not be in England before the end of December, possibly January. If we wait to greet him, we will not sail until spring. I cannot … We *must* sail now."

He gave her a long, thoughtful look. "But Beau is …"

"Beau will love the voyage, my love. He is both a MacLean and a Tarrington," she answered firmly, not allowing him to finish his thought.

"Such urgency; what has upset you, my pet?"

Her green eyes lacked their usual luster as she searched his face. "It is a brittle peace with Eugenie. I must be constantly on my guard, always waiting for the other shoe to drop—for it will."

He cradled her chin, studying her closely as she talked. "And …?" he prompted.

A tear started and he kissed it away, only to have it replaced by another.

"She is overcome with jealousy. I see the way she glowers at her children when they pay interest to Beau."

"I *have* noticed that myself."

"I see her physically cringe every time I call our son 'Beau', especially as it always brings happiness to Jack's face. And she despises me. I tread as lightly as I can but I think our daughter is a saint, for I cannot do it much longer."

"I must agree. I had hoped …" He shook his head. "I will send word to Captain Farthingale: one mare and four or hopefully five passengers. Will that set your mind at ease?"

A sparkle returned to her eyes as she kissed his cheek and then lips. "Yes, very much so, but there is one other favor you may grant me."

He arched an eyebrow, maintaining a blank stare for as long as he could. Finally he chuckled. "And just what might that favor be, my love?"

Sliding her hand down across his chest, she slipped it easily beneath his belt.

"Kathryn," he gasped, "It has been but three weeks since Beau's birth."

"Yes, and it *was* an easy birth at that."

The next morning he asked Jack to send a message to Captain Farthingale. "I *am* booking five passengers, Jack, and Beauty, of course."

"The war is over, Jason." He shrugged, not wanting to interfere with their lives.

Jason read him well. "Yes, but there is a bold, new world awaiting us, and it may require the two of us to keep that wife of mine from boredom. She finds all kinds of trouble when her hands are idle."

Jack laughed. "I fear I would be ..."

"I have booked your trip, Jack. Think about it, *we* want you to come."

Confirmation was received with a nice note of congratulations on their new son. Captain Farthingale gave them a date and time with specific instructions to travel lightly; he would be carrying more cargo.

That night Jason sat reading the captain's note to Kathryn in the privacy of their room. "He says, and I quote: 'A very persuasive young man pressed several gold coins into my palm, and two beautifully matched grays will be joining us for the voyage'. He also sends his best to you, my pet, and reminds us: 'Anything can be arranged if the price is right'."

She grinned. This would be a good trip; she felt it in her heart. "Jack *will* come, he must." Her face became serious.

Jason thought for a minute. "I believe so, but he has to sort it out for himself. And we should allow him to do that."

"Colonel, may I speak with you a moment—in here?" Eugenie beckoned him into her Rose Room.

He had been in the process of finishing his second cup of coffee when the children rushed in from the kitchen, impatient to see Beauty. Kathryn had kissed him and headed out to the stables, leaving him to finish in peace, and join them when ready. He had just dropped his napkin beside his plate and headed for the door when Eugenie caught him.

He followed her into the room and stood quietly, unwilling to open the conversation, waiting to see what she had in mind. She indicated a chair but he refused, politely, and remained standing.

"It would seem, Colonel ..." Eugenie's eyes met his, malice blazing. "My brother is overly fond of your wife." Her chin jutted at a self-satisfied angle as she smiled: a smile that quickly faded under the cautionary warning of his icy stare.

"Eugenie," he retorted, anger barely held at bay. "Jack loves my wife perhaps even more than I, a fact that has saved her life more than once, thankfully." His voice dripped pure venom, shocking her.

Realizing her error too late, she began spluttering shallow excuses, attempting to make light of the situation.

"You surprise me," Jason interrupted. "I would have thought that type of troublemaking beneath your dignity." Spinning on his heel, he headed for the door, but stopped and turned to face her. "My apologies for extending you the benefit of doubt, I *will not* allow that mistake to happen again."

He yanked the door shut with a loud slam. *Bitch! How has Jack stood her for this long?* He headed straight for the stable to find Kathryn and Gabrielle. They would be sailing within the week: Jack *must* be with them.

"Poppa!" Gabrielle thrust her currycomb towards her mother and rushed to greet her father.

Kathryn stood grinning, somewhat nonplussed, cradling Beau in one arm and the currycomb in her hand. Her heart filled with joy as she watched the two hugging, but today something was amiss.

"Poppet, let us saddle Beauty; you can show me what momma has taught you."

Within minutes, she was proudly cantering around the paddock as her parents stood by the fence watching.

"She is a natural, my love."

"Enough pleasantries; what has put that nettlesome frown on my handsome husband's brow?" She slid her arm around his waist, offering a comforting hug.

"Where are the children?" he asked, scanning the area to be sure they were not within earshot.

"As always, their lessons," she answered.

"Well, I *am* sorry that I cannot help them, they deserve better—especially young Robbie. But *we will be gone* shortly, and Jack *must* come."

Kathryn's eyes narrowed as she listened. "Bitch," she spat.

Jason actually laughed aloud. "We seem to use the same terminology in regards to her, my pet."

"Watch Gabrielle, love, so that she will not feel slighted." She shifted Beau into his arms and handed him a sugar teat. "In case he is hungry."

"I had not meant you to …" He looked startled.

"This is the last straw." She kissed him soundly. "I will be back shortly."

With long strides, she crossed the distance to the house and entered. Eugenie, looking quite out-of-sorts, was just coming from her Rose Room.

"Eugenie …" Kathryn grabbed her by the arm, stopping her. "Let us settle this situation between us and be done with it."

Eugenie pulled away, eyes glittering malice.

"*We* have been forced to accept your generosity due to obvious circumstances. And *you* …" she eyed her with equal dislike, "have been placed in the unfortunate position of having to put up with us, in order to save face within your social circles. Tisk, tisk; what deceptive webs one must weave to save appearances."

Eugenie made no effort to hide her hostility, annoyed by the fact that Kathryn was not the easily led country bumpkin she had presumed her to be.

"You and I do not like each other, Eugenie, nor do we have to. But your nasty attempt to create an irresolvable rift between Jason, Jack and me … *That is unacceptable!* And attempting to set your brother up for even greater hurt than he has already experienced these last months? You disgust me."

Glaring contemptuously, her face a mask of loathing, she growled: "Quite frankly, I would never have expected a woman of your so-called Quality to stoop so low, such a shabby, perverse trick, shame on you."

Eugenie maintained her haughty stance. "Well, I merely felt your husband should be aware …"

"You merely felt *nothing*, Eugenie. Do *not* do me further dishonor by considering me stupid. I know exactly what you planned," she snarled.

Eugenie stood speechless, knowing she had more than met her match.

"Never attempt to come between the three of us again. *Never!* For I have seen, and done, things that would horrify your oh-so-delicate nature, just to protect those *two* men I love."

Eugenie's eyes widened at her declaration.

"And I *will not* dishonor the unique relationship existing between the three of us, by discussing it with you. Be fair warned. Although I am grateful for your shelter, I will stop at *nothing* to protect *my* men."

Eugenie spluttered attempting to find words.

"Say nothing, for there is naught that I wish to hear from you. And let me leave you with some food for thought."

Eugenie stood dumbfounded, her eyes glittering angrily.

"*You* are a bully, tread *very* carefully. Anything you have heard rumored of me in battle is absolutely true. And *I do* mean this as a threat."

Eugenie's mind swam. Beauregarde had threatened her in the same way, but he was too gentle to possibly have meant it. But Kathryn ... She winced, wondering what they had seen and done, but not caring to know.

Kathryn held her ground in stony silence, her icy glare withering.

Eugenie faltered. With a swish of elegant petticoats, head held high, she sniffed loudly and marched upstairs.

"That went rather well." Jack applauded with a wide grin.

Kathryn whirled to face him with a gasp. "How much did you overhear?" she asked weakly.

"All of it, my Kathryn. And I am so very proud of you. I had no idea of what she was up to." He kissed her cheek. "I am so sorry. You have had way too much to cope with."

"Passage is booked for *all* of us, Jack. *All* of us."

He started to speak but she silenced him.

"Jason and I have not made plans beyond returning to the colonies, although we have discussed America's westward expansion, fur trading—even privateering. However, after meeting John Paul Jones and experiencing weeks at sea, we have definitely put that idea aside."

She rushed on before he could comment. "The war is over. We will all have to become, more or less, part of the scenery—invisible, so to speak. Jamie has vowed to help us, and he has many various *and unique* connections."

"I no longer belong here, and it would grieve me deeply to lose you again so quickly," he admitted hesitantly.

"Then it is settled. And we offer you nothing specific, other than it *will be* an adventure—that, I promise."

"There has *never* been a time, when life with the two of you *was not* an adventure," he chuckled, his eyes lighting with pleasure. "Let us go tell, Jason."

Arm in arm, they headed for the stables.

Chapter Twenty-Four

Homeward Bound

It was their last dinner together; they would be leaving at dawn the following morning, and sailing with the evening tide. Kathryn had one regret—*Robbie*. Her heart skipped a beat as his sad eyes met hers.

Eugenie had risen to the occasion, her Quality manners winning out. Deciding she could manage a few more hours pleasantly, she had allowed her children to be present. For once, the adults maintained a somewhat introspective silence, while the children bantered between themselves, unrestricted. Robbie and Gabrielle exchanged surreptitious glances throughout the meal, touching hands often.

"Excuse me for interrupting." Cornelius approached the table, holding out a silver salver to Kathryn. A battered parchment sat perfectly centered on the tray, its neatly tied bow arranged to face her.

Thanking him kindly, she picked up the letter, smiling, the bold, heavy strokes of her name, easily identifiable. "Jamie," she whispered.

"Excellent timing," Jack commented, and catching her flashing an amused grin at Jason, for once knew what she was thinking: British protocol its silver trays and perfectly placed letters, were definitely not requirements in her life—*or mine anymore*, he recognized.

"Are you going to read it now, momma?" Gabrielle asked.

"No, little one, that would be rude." Her eyes flicked to Eugenie. "Tomorrow night after we sail will be soon enough. The news will keep."

Perhaps it might provide diversion for her child. Thoughts of leaving Robbie pained *her*—she could barely imagine their heartbreak: *so young to have to face such an adult world*. Realizing her face more than likely reflected her solemn thoughts, she concentrated on finishing this last meal and being ready to travel the next morning.

"Our carriage is here," Jack announced.

Kathryn scanned the driveway for Beauty. Eugenie and the children not being present, was of no concern. But where was her mare?

A loud shout drew their attention to the barn. Trotting proudly, head held high, her mane swishing like freshly spun silk, Beauty emerged with Robbie sitting regally astride. He wore his Sunday best, and sat with the effortless grace Kathryn had encouraged. Emmie hugged her brother's waist, gripping Beauty's rump with short, stocky legs, a smile of accomplishment brightening her face. The mare's trappings sparkled against her shining, well-brushed coat as she performed her favorite gaits proudly.

Dipping into a graceful bow, she halted within six feet of Kathryn. Robbie remained stick straight, face beaming, as he elbowed Emmie to sit still, and then inclined his head in greeting.

"Bravo, Robbie," Kathryn said huskily. "You have honored me and my family."

Without further adieu, he inched his sister to the ground and quickly dismounted. Kathryn moved first, pulling the boy into a warm hug.

"Thank you, Robbie," she whispered, brushing a kiss to his cheek. "I will miss you." A tear welled in the corner of her eye. "Follow us someday, when the time is right. Gabrielle and I will write, as we spoke of. For you will remain in our hearts, and always be welcome."

He nodded biting his lower lip, but quickly turned aside, considering it unmanly to show emotion. But a sharp tug on his sleeve stopped him, as large blue eyes searched his.

"Gabrielle ... Ellie, I ... I ..." His voice broke. But as their eyes locked, he knew her heart as well as he knew his own and smiled. Reaching into his pocket, he brought out his prized wooden chain, now complete. "This is for you. It will be as if I were with you."

Tearfully Gabrielle handed him her lace handkerchief, a braided lock of her jet-black hair peeking from one end. "As I will be with you, Robbie," she whispered.

"Come, come, now. Time to be heading off or you will miss your ship." Eugenie's voice grated unpleasantly in the quiet early dawn, halting further emotional displays.

Thomas stood dutifully at her side, a non-committal, benign expression pasted on his face. Kathryn actually felt a moment's pity for the poor man.

"We have decided to accompany you," Eugenie stated primly. "The other carriage will be right out." She stood meticulously dressed with her customary formality.

Kathryn eyed Eugenie, curious as to her motivation for this decision. She and Gabrielle were dressed down to board the ship. Both Jason and Jack had discarded their brilliant jackets and all the accompanying trappings. There must be no trace of their former calling; although the war had been declared over, lingering memories of them could be dangerous.

Deciding not to waste effort figuring her out, Kathryn accepted pleasantly. "That is kind of you, Eugenie. Perhaps you might allow Robbie to ride Beauty. It would help keep her in line."

Eugenie was silent for a moment, studying her son. Seeing the bright excitement in his eyes, she softened. "I imagine I already know your answer, young man. But *do keep* your clothes clean."

It was late afternoon as they stood watching their ship rocking gently at the pier. She had new sails, a fresh coat of paint and semi-concealed cannon.

How interesting. Jason scrutinized every new detail, there would be much to discuss with the captain later. As if by cue, Captain Farthingale appeared at the rail, paused momentarily, and then proceeded nimbly down the gangplank.

He greeted them warmly, and after making a small 'to do' over Beau, turned full attention to Gabrielle, hugging her delightedly.

"You must like my sailing abilities, young lady. For I see you are back for a second trip. And, I found your friend, Smitty, rapscallion that he is. He is making your mare comfortable at the moment, but is eager to see you."

Gabrielle's eyes went wide, and clapping her hands with glee, she stretched up on tiptoe to plant a kiss on his cheek.

"And Jason," he adopted informality as it worked best on a long voyage. "Your young friend arrived with his grays. Thankfully, your mare is well behaved, for it is a bit of a tight fit."

With a curt bow to the women, he turned and marched up the gangplank.

"You have about twenty minutes before the tide turns. Say your goodbyes and get on board," he flung back over his shoulder.

Gabrielle headed slowly up the gangplank, bringing up the rear so she could watch Robbie. Suddenly turning, she ran back. Robbie broke from his parents and met her halfway, pulling her into a bear hug.

Eugenie started forward, aghast at his improper display, already regretting having come. The wharf area was full of noxious smells, and the people were so—*common.*

But Thomas abruptly grabbed her elbow, firmly pulling her back to his side. "Leave them be, Eugenie. They care deeply for each other."

"For heavens sake, Thomas, they are mere children and I find this ..."

"Hush, Eugenie, leave them be," he growled, gripping her elbow tighter.

Eugenie's mouth dropped open, horrified by his effrontery. As he continued to meet her indignant stare, unwilling to back down, her expression became one of confusion. Thomas had never once raised his voice, or dared command her, in all their time together. *Strangely,* considering the oddity, it almost felt good.

She turned just as Gabrielle placed a firm kiss on Robbie's forehead, and then began tracing an odd symbol with her thumb.

"You are part of me, Robbie," she murmured, tears she had tried to control, streaming down her cheeks.

"We are as one, my bold, little warrior, *my Ellie.*" He traced the identical pattern on her forehead. "I *will* find you," he whispered fervently. "Know that in your heart."

"What ever are they doing?" Eugenie turned to her husband. "They act so serious. But they are only children."

Thomas shook his head sadly. "Something *you* may never understand my dear, and regretfully—*your* loss."

With a toss of her head, she looked back just as Gabrielle stepped onto the deck, and moved to stand beside her mother.

They stood leaning against the rail, watching as the pier grew smaller. Waving to Jack's family, Kathryn felt her daughter's sharp loss. But for her—an exhilarating sense of freedom—as if a huge black cloud had lifted.

Jack and Eugenie had shared a few peaceful words at the dock, but no more than that, barely even a quick hug, a fact that further served to enforce the appropriateness of his decision to leave.

They were still standing on the pier, Eugenie's unrest easily read even from this distance. Thomas had apparently insisted they watch until the sails unfurled and caught the breeze. Robbie stood quietly beside his father, remaining stoic, but Emmie hopped from one foot to the other yelling, "Goodbye, Gabrielle."

"I believe you may have won her over, princess." Jack winked, squeezing her hand.

They continued to watch until the figures were no larger than ants before going below to inspect their accommodations. Someone's hand had definitely had a strong say. The cabin, although small, was clean and bright and appeared to have been recently added. Jack's accommodations were close by and just as pleasing.

"Great Grandmother or your father, do you think?" Kathryn asked.

"Perhaps my father's way of wishing to be remembered," Jason said thoughtfully.

"I am glad you both finally came to acceptance, if not complete forgiveness."

"You did the right thing, my love. From what my grandmother indicated, I must get you to give me all the details." He hugged her, talking softly against her ear. "And that subject is on the top of my list to cover over the next two months."

"You will find my unladylike behavior amusing and somewhat reminiscent of an afternoon spent with his lordship long ago." Baring her breast to suckle Beau as his whimpers elevated one notch higher, she smiled. "We *must* keep your grandmother involved in our lives, she is such a dear lady, and …"

With a slam, their cabin door flew open, startling them. But Beau, intent on one thing only, kept suckling. Kathryn eyed her daughter severely, before realizing that Jack stood braced in the doorway, shrugging helplessly and trying not to laugh.

"Momma. Poppa!" Even her parent's stern looks could not dampen her excitement.

"She is your daughter," Jason quipped, causing Kathryn to roll her eyes.

"I found him. He is here, just as the captain said, and all healed from his fight."

"Smitty?" Kathryn ventured.

"Yes. Yes. He gave apples to Beauty and both the pretty grays. And I met Ted, and he told me he would tell me lots of tales on our trip, and he will find you both later and …" She babbled excitedly.

"I imagine he will." Jason crouched down to her level. "But tell me about Smitty, poppet. Momma and I would like to meet him. It would seem that we owe him a bit of thanks."

"Well, he said he had chores, but maybe after supper." Kissing her father's cheek, she headed for the door, and squirreling around Jack's tall frame, disappeared.

As they sat enjoying the chill night air on deck, Smitty joined them, as promised. Noting his appearance, Kathryn's eyes flicked to Jason and then Jack.

"Just wait," Jack mouthed, and she relaxed.

Within moments, it became obvious why he meant so much to her daughter. He was delightful—his absolute devotion to their child, undeniable.

Smitty was immediately drawn to Kathryn, and turning to Gabrielle, said with a wink: "Ye have the look o' ye mum, little one. I guess ole Smitty will hafta watch out fer her too, aye?"

At Jason's sharp look, he flashed a gummy grin. "Well, of course by yer leave, sir. I means no offense."

Gabrielle began to giggle, trying to squelch it behind her hand, but to no avail. Jack merely grinned.

"I sees I am to be the butt o yer jokes, am I?" I don't hardly…"

"Not at all," Kathryn interrupted before misunderstandings arose. "Our daughter has exceptional judgment in knowing a *good man* when she meets him—of seeing a man's true value. She loves *you*, and that is all we need to know."

And he *was* delightful. When Ted peeked around Jack's shoulder and immediately joined in, Kathryn began to feel right at home. This would be a good trip, she sensed it.

The evening air was slowly becoming quite nippy and Beau had begun to complain.

"Time for me to say goodnight, it has been a very long day and I have a letter from my brother in the colonies which I have not yet read."

Without coaxing, Gabrielle waved goodnight to her friends and ducked into the hatchway, followed by Uncle Jack.

Kathryn and Jason lingered a moment longer.

"Cleverly done, my love," Jason chuckled, giving her a pat on the rump, as they headed towards the hatchway.

In the lantern light, Kathryn's face grew bright as she scanned the first few lines of Jamie's letter, returning to the top to read aloud.

Dearest Kathryn and Hunter,

The corn has grown well. Ye would be proud of me. I miss ye both, although I hate to admit it to that husband of yours. Tell him his black devil is alive and well, nasty beast that he is. I fear he is putting on weight. But I will not ride him, and he refuses to pull the harrow.

Knowing his contrary stallion, Jason grinned.

Annabelle wishes to marry the blacksmith, but he will never be able to afford to please her. Caitlin has been bitten by the green-eyed monster and wants a husband of her own—poor man.

I am hale and hearty, but find farm life … When ye come back, perhaps we will talk. Silver Fox is not as well as I would hope, with child again—too soon. Anna has had a disturbing vision of the future, something to do with tears and a long trail, and sends her blessings, eagerly awaiting your return.

Other than your note telling me of your safe arrival, I have no knowledge of your future plans. In the past I have tried to sway your decisions, but I will not now. Your life is yours, my dearest sister, to lead as you see fit. But I would have ye aware of certain situations. For ye will have to decide. Ye are a MacLean, need I say more?

"That is a very telling statement, my love," Jason teased. "I must concur."

"Hush now," she retorted, eyeing him over the top of the letter. Up to this point Jamie had said nothing of importance, meandering a bit as if girding himself to share … what? She tensed.

As to the war, the immediate fighting is over. I imagine you know of Cornwallis's surrender at Yorktown. However, sporadic fighting still continues in the Carolinas and I am glad ye are not here for that. There is more to discuss but the hour is late and there is another I wish to speak of.

A wide space followed, dotted with several dried splotches. "Tears," she whispered, her heart sinking. "Please …" she pushed the parchment into her husband's hand.

I have saved the worst for last. Gabriel has been captured by Rawdon, imprisoned on weakly fabricated charges.

Kathryn gasped, and Jack moved to her side. Jason placed a comforting hand on her shoulder and continued.

The bastard knows the war is done, but he also knows Gabriel is my son. As to Rawdon and I? There has never been any love lost between us. I fear …

Come home quickly. May God keep you safe until we meet again: you, Hunter and the children.

Your loving brother, Jamie

"Jamie's letter has taken so long to arrive, and we still have …" Kathryn choked, unable to continue as she raised a tear-streaked face to her husband.

Jason wrapped her in a warm embrace, eyeing Jack over the top of her head, as her broken sobs continued.

Jack grasped Gabrielle's hand and headed for the cabin door. But distressed by her mother's grief, she dug in her heels, refusing to leave. Bending down, he quietly explained, "Your momma needs your father right now. Come with me and I will give you all the details."

She stood firm, eyeing him suspiciously through narrowed eyes.

Easily reading her thoughts, he said softly, "No, my princess, I *will not* give you the children's version, for I fear you will be thrown into an adult world very soon. If you are old enough to bring a baby into this life, you are old enough to be told the truth."

With a comforting pat to her mother's arm, Gabrielle left the cabin with Jack.

The following morning broke clear and brisk. Full sails billowed and snapped on sharp gusts of salty air pushing the vessel forward, and forming frothy curls at the prow. A sudden gust dashed salty spray, misting Gabrielle's face and she chortled with glee.

Kathryn hugged Beau to her breast, but he seemed not to mind the chilly air, or the gentle pitch and roll of the ship. Jason stood at her side, his hand caressing the small of her back. She was calmer now. She must send positive thoughts out to the universe for her nephew's safety. She could not envision, even for a moment, the possibilities that awaited them.

Gabrielle and little Beau needed an attentive mother now—not later. Her pain would be hers, alone, to manage. She had endured that agonizing burden during many long years of war, keeping her heart protected deep within, and she would do so now.

"We have clear skies, a bracing breeze and constantly filled sails. If all holds well, my love, we will place our feet on land soon," Jason encouraged. Forcing a weak smile, she leaned closer, relishing his warmth.

"Yes, my love. Many challenges await us and *I am* ready."

Jason hugged her, loving her desperately, awed by her selfless determination to make it a pleasant voyage. He understood her fears, for he shared them equally.

Jack wrapped his arm around Gabrielle and hugged her. For the first time in months he felt whole, useful and loved.

Another brisk gust sent him leaning over the rail to welcome the bracing wetness, to embrace it. The stinging salt reddening his eyes, represented promise of a new life and 'freedom'—and felt good.

"Home, Uncle Jack," Gabrielle yelled into the wind, as she stepped up onto the rail, gripping him for security.

"Yes, my princess, finally we are headed for home."

Jack caught Jason's gaze, noting his barely concealed distress over Kathryn's sorrow.

They both knew Rawdon, better than either cared to. However, Jack held a possible trump card, information he had shared with Jason earlier. But it would be upwards of four months between the sending of Jamie's letter, and their arrival—a long time to be …

Jason hugged his wife as she stared at the horizon cradling little Beau against her breast. Catching Jack's look and knowing what was in his mind, he mouthed: *"Oh that we may still be in time."*

The 'Beyond' Trilogy

Novels by **J. Winfield Currie**

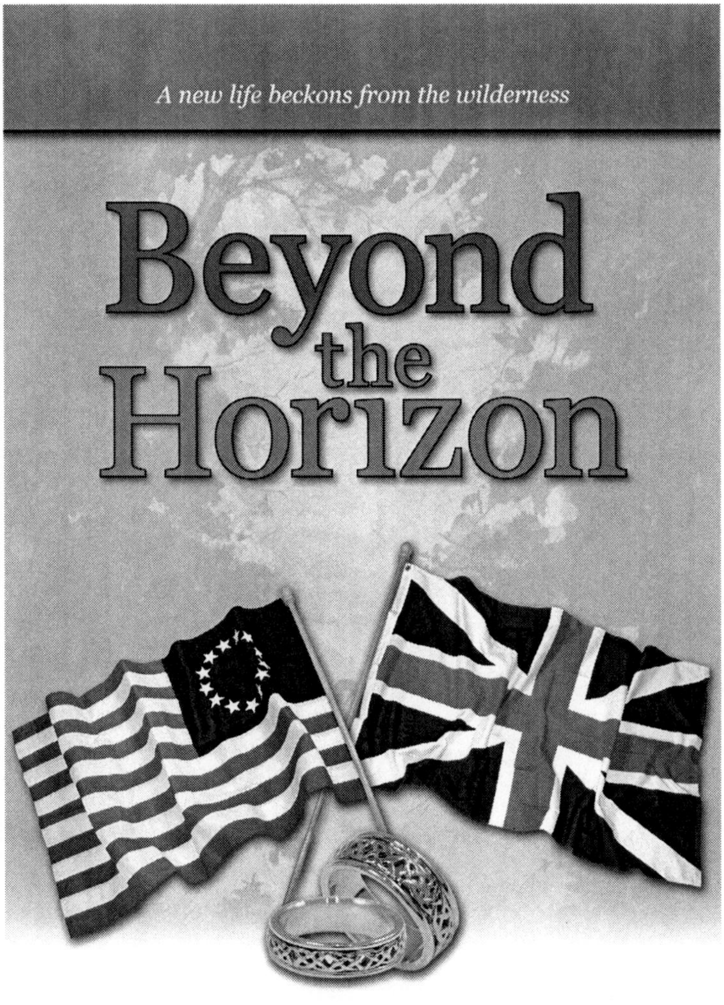

A new life beckons from the wilderness
Beyond the Horizon

A Novel by:
J. Winfield Currie

Beyond the Horizon

Book III

Life Comes Full Circle

Chapter One

Return to the Beginning

Anna stroked back wisps of jet black hair from the fitfully drowsing girl's forehead, continuing her chanting in low, measured tones: a mantra for complete healing, addressing both the physical and *spiritual* being. Her hand drifted gently over the girl's well-rounding abdomen sensing the life within. *She is cooler to the touch, the babe tenacious; but this child must be her last.*

"Would that it was another boy," Silver Fox said softly as her eyes flickered open. "But I believe it to be a little girl this time."

Anna's gaze shifted to the young woman's face, pleased to encounter alert black eyes. Making no response, she smiled enigmatically, well aware that she carried a lusty son.

"And 'she' *must be* your last," Anna said sharply, withholding the secret. "I have taught you ways to enjoy your pleasure without consequence; it is time you take heed."

The stinging edge of Anna's words caused Silver Fox to wince. A highly revered Cherokee healer, she spoke only truth. However, *truth* was not what she wished to hear at the moment. "Anna, I love Gabriel and …"

"And," she interrupted tartly, glaring icily. "He will want you alive. What good is a dead wife?" Her statement had been purposefully callous; she needed Silver Fox to use common sense—and had succeeded, acceptance flickered in the girl's eyes.

"But I so wanted to …" Silver Fox's lower lip quivered, her eyes brimming with tears.

"You have Raven, a fine lusty son, and Mairi, a delightful little girl—and now this precious child." She placed her hand once again on the girl's ever-rounding belly. "This little one is well, which is more than I can say for you at the moment."

Ignoring Anna's continued tartness, Silver Fox hitched herself up against a mound of animal skins and took the offered cup of water, gulping thirstily.

"I worry about my Gabriel," she said softly. "Would that we had not gone to town that day. The English officer's slur was not of importance, I have been called worse."

"Gabriel would not allow it, defending your honor in typical manly fashion. Now he is their prisoner, and *you* feel guilty." Anna candidly summed up the situation.

Silver Fox's eyes overflowed as she nodded hesitantly.

"He would do it again, what with his stubborn MacLean temperament. And he *does not* hold you to blame." Anna folded her arms across her chest in a striking pose of command. "Now it is time for you to be well and strong. Your birthing time draws near."

"But Gabriel has been in captivity for many long weeks and I fear …"

"Hush," Anna snapped, sounding and feeling more like her self. "I, too, have existed in a weakened state, ever since my devastating dreams foretelling the Cherokee's future. But it is yet many moons away. I am needed *today* in other ways, and must remain strong." She gave the younger woman a long look.

"Your husband *will* live—and he *will* be here for the birth of your last child."

Silver Fox eyed the venerable healer respectfully, wishing she could ask: '*are you certain*'? But Anna understood her questioning gaze and was not offended.

"Kathryn and Hunter *will* arrive in time, and they bring my precious little bird. I have seen it clearly—this *is* true," she said with a reassuring hug. Turning to leave, she issued one final instruction. "Rest today, tomorrow I shall expect your help in preparing venison. Your father brought in a large buck this morning, it will require several hours of your expertise, a perfect diversion for your worries, I believe."

Silver Fox nodded eagerly, feeling her energy beginning to rebound. "I will be ready."

Relaxing back onto her soft hides, she smiled contentedly, her thoughts drifting to Soaring Eagle with pride. *My father has helped two-fold: providing many meals for our people and helping me to concentrate on the 'now'.*

***

Jason emerged from the hatchway and stepped onto the gently rolling deck. Pausing, he blinked several times, adjusting his eyes to the brilliant, sunny day. Kathryn and Gabrielle stood side by side at the ship's railing, both wrapped in heavy woolen cloaks, their heads bare, allowing billowing curls to whip erratically in the cold December air.

His breath caught, and he found himself uttering words of gratitude to the 'powers that be'. Not a religious man by nature—nor was Kathryn for that matter—he studied his wife and the smaller version of her, his delightful little girl, feeling truly blessed.

As he approached, his son wriggled free of his blanket, gurgling happily. Kathryn tucked him more securely against her warm cloak and crooning softly, turned to flash a welcoming smile to her husband. She possessed a sixth sense—just as he did with her. During the war, their *gift* had saved them both on more than one occasion. Pulling her close, he kissed her soundly before turning to his daughter.

Picking Gabrielle up, he brushed a kiss to her forehead. "And how fares your baby brother?" he asked, knowing she would provide a full report as part of their daily ritual: his way of reminding her that she did not take second place, despite there being a male heir. He loved this child with a passion—second only to his wife—and always would.

"Now that you are here to keep my momma company, I will go help Jack and Ted with the horses. Beauty needs her legs rubbed and a piece of sugar."

"And remember …" Kathryn said, reaching into her pocket for several cubes of sugar. "I broke the pieces smaller so Beauty can share with Ted's grays."

"They have names you know," she said proudly. "Ted says his mares are the same color gray that appears just before dusk and dawn." She shrugged, grinning, waiting for their comment. "One is Dusk and one is Dawn, but I have a hard time telling which is which." With a giggle, she headed towards the hatchway.

Jason shook his head smiling and leaned against his wife. Fingering the blanket aside, he bid 'good morning' to his son. Blue-green eyes met his, observing him quietly. A brief smile curved his small mouth, followed by a huge belch.

"Well, such a way to greet your poppa, little man," Kathryn chuckled.

Pulling the blanket up around his face, Jason stroked the tawny head. But with a muffled complaint and flailing fists, he pushed it aside, watching his father intently.

"*He* is quietly assertive," Kathryn observed, "whereas our Gabrielle *is not*."

Jason laughed out loud. "I believe *her* more vocal 'self-expression' may have been inherited from the MacLean lineage—while his quiet, but just as adamant insistence, is more from my side." He shrugged. "Their personalities are quite different, and he is still but a wee babe. Things may change with one or the other and ..."

At Kathryn's amused look he stopped mid-sentence. He had been making idle talk, he knew it and so did she. Although she always smiled and her eyes sparkled, tiny lines crinkling the corners spoke of inner stress. He would not force her to talk, in that they were alike. She would speak of Gabriel when ready, and not before.

They stood in silence, enjoying each other's presence and the peacefulness of the gently rolling seas.

"Something has happened," she said softly.

He arched a dark brow but made no immediate comment.

"I have felt bereft, helpless, the tightness in my chest like a large fist crushing my heart." She searched his eyes, embracing the comforting compassion of his blue gaze. "But just now ... it has eased."

He stroked back wind-blown tawny tendrils, waiting for an explanation.

"Jamie and I ..." She became silent, considering her words. "You have long been aware that we 'read' each other upon occasion, when something of import has arisen. I have been in the clutches of my brother's distress, up until now. Something has happened to ease his anguish, but not death. I sense Gabriel's plight may have shifted for the better, not that he is necessarily free, but that his situation is no longer as dire."

Jason thought for a minute. "What might have changed? Yorktown has surrendered; the British are leaving but what of the Loyalists?" A thought struck simultaneously.

"Samuel—Captain Hodges," she breathed.

"Yes, my thoughts exactly. He would have left Gloucester Point by now and perhaps headed for home," he reasoned.

"I wish we had better knowledge of those remaining in that area. How did the surrender impact the English forces—and American Loyalists?"

"We will know soon enough, my love. But let us suppose, for sake of conversation, what if Samuel caught wind of Gabriel's capture?" He paused, running different thoughts through his mind, testing the plausibility of each. "Hodges has fought with Cornwallis. He would be readily accepted by any of our remaining forces. Even if he could not free your nephew, I believe he could intervene."

"And he would get word to Jamie," she reasoned.

"If only Hodges is able to stall for time. Jack knew Rawdon well at one point. He holds certain facts which could create serious problems for the man if brought into the open, and will divulge them without hesitation if necessary."

Sliding his arm about her waist, he drew her close. "Do not worry, my Kathryn. We *will* be there in time. *We will.*"

Chapter Two

Captain Hodges Steps In

"You requested to speak with me, sir?" Captain Hodges saluted smartly.

"I presume I must have—else you would not be here," Tarleton quipped. He sat on the corner of his desk swinging one leg idly.

Cocky bastard, Hodges thought, but maintained his noncommittal expression. Although curious as to why he had been sent for, there would be childish games to endure until Tarleton decided to get to the point: *his game—his rules.*

"What do you make of it, Captain?" Tarleton leaned forward resting an elbow on his knee and began nonchalantly slapping his gloves against his palm. "Well?" he growled.

"Make of what, sir?"

"Oh, for God's sake, stop being so obtuse, Captain. You have, upon occasion, proven your ability to handle complex thought processes—even an astute observation now and then." He paused, spearing the captain with a steely gaze. "I will ask you once again …"

"I assume you are referring to French ships recently arrived in Chesapeake Bay, sir."

Tarleton nodded. "Very good, Captain. Now what do you make of the situation?"

Captain Hodges, at that precise moment, wished he could knock the supercilious grin from his superior officer's face, preferably taking a few perfectly chiseled teeth along with it. However, that act would gain only a long stay in jail. Besides, despite his 'unique' personality quirks, Tarleton *had* stepped in not once, but twice, saving Lieutenant Jackson and Gabrielle several months ago, and more recently, her parents—despite risk to himself. *The man does have connections and uses them generously,* he had to admit.

Tarleton appeared to want honesty—*so be it.* "I fear it is all done, but for the shouting, sir. The unexpected arrival of French ships means we are effectively cut off from Commander Clinton and his reinforcements coming from Rhode Island. We are short-handed, low on supplies and our soldiers: suffering from assorted illness."

He eyed Tarleton awaiting any comment, as none was forthcoming he continued. "I believe Lord Cornwallis will be forced to surrender at Yorktown and …"

Grinning widely, Tarleton slapped his knee sharply with his gloves. "By God, Hodges," he interrupted chortling gleefully, "it *is* as I said! You *do* have the ability to make astute observations."

Hodges eyed him sharply, but remained silent. *None* of what he had said was news to this man. *Just what is his actual purpose?* He wondered.

"And I will guarantee you," Tarleton sneered, "his Lordship will be on a fast ship to England before the year is out. He will take his sad tale home to King George: Clinton's refusal to take his advice, failure to send supplies, infrequent communication and conflicting orders—all of which tied his poor, beleaguered hands, ultimately resulting in British defeat."

Tarleton's icy gaze returned. "He will go home and be vindicated, declared faultless, placing all the blame on Clinton. After all, it is a well-known fact that Cornwallis and the King are old friends. Mark my words, Captain, a new position of even greater appeal, *and reward,* will await his return."

Hodges nodded thoughtfully.

"Would you like to make a bet?"

"Thank you, but no, sir. It is impossible to bet when both parties are in accord."

"Well said, Captain." Tarleton tossed his gloves on the desk, a devilish grin spreading across his boyish face. "From the moment you walked through that door, you have been curious as to my true purpose in sending for you, have you not?"

"Yes sir," Hodges said with extreme patience.

"Well, you have allowed me to play my games, Captain. So I will reward you with ..." He paused, testing. Even junior officers eventually betrayed irritation by stance or expression—but *not* Captain Hodges. The man had definite merit.

"I have information which I believe will be of interest to you, a rather problematical situation as it were. *I* shall provide the means by which you may accomplish whatever *you* deem necessary to correct it."

Hodges arched an eyebrow, curious and interested.

"Allow me to put it to you plainly, for I actually *do* have other commitments that require my attention." He drew in a long breath. "Gabriel MacLean is imprisoned in Charleston."

Hodges's eyes went wide.

"Yes, Captain. Originally captured by Rawdon, but turned over to Stewart when he abruptly relinquished command and returned to England. Bad health? Bored? Disheartened? Who knows?" Tarleton shrugged, disinterested as to Rawdon's reason for departure.

Hodges's face became grim. "You mean Kathryn's nephew?"

"None other," he quipped.

"It is difficult *not* to love Kathryn," Hodges murmured thoughtfully.

Caught off-guard, twin patches of color blossomed on Tarleton's fair cheeks. "Her nephew means a great deal to her," he said brusquely, resuming his callous indifference.

Captain Hodges pretended not to have noticed, his respect increasing somewhat.

"I have in mind, killing two birds with one stone," Tarleton rushed on. "You were raised in South Carolina, were you not? A Loyalist, I gather."

Hodges nodded.

"Good. I intend to send you to Stewart under the auspices of providing forewarning, revealing unfortunate events here. He will consider himself honored that you endangered your person to alert him. Are you following me, Captain?"

Hodges nodded, his mind working rapidly.

"I will ask that—as a favor to me—you be assigned to his company." Eyes narrowing he added, "He owes me a favor or two, and will not deny you. *You* will be safely out of whatever happens here and in a position to help Gabriel. I will open the door, but the rest is up to you, Captain. I am assigned to defend Gloucester Point, and to absent myself now would be disastrous."

"I understand, sir, and I thank you."

Banastre Tarleton's smile was genuine, for once. "Be ready to leave tonight." He reached into his desk and pulled out a sheaf of folded papers.

"Your orders, Captain. Are there any questions?"

"No, sir, I have a long ride ahead—plenty of time to formulate a plan."

"I have faith in you, Captain. For you would never disappoint …"

"No, I *will not* fail Kathryn, sir. And she will wish to be remembered to you."

At his commanding officer's curt gesture of dismissal, Hodges started to turn away but paused, noting his faraway look, warm memories flickering openly. But with Tarleton's typical icy control, he abruptly returned to the moment and refocused, a slight smile lifting his lips as he added, "Please tell her when she returns …" He stopped, weighing his words before proceeding. "Rather, as one can rarely *tell* Kathryn, please *convey to her* …"

Hodges bristled, but a quick look confirmed that his words implied no criticism.

"Convey my deepest thanks."

At Hodges's questioning look, he added softly, "She will understand. Ask her to give Gabrielle a hug from me, such a bold, brave child …"

His final words, as he abruptly turned and stalked from the room were barely audible, but Captain Hodges caught them—and the sheen in Tarleton's eyes. "So very like her mother." With a curt nod and sucked in breath, Captain Hodges stepped into the empty hallway, pulling the door closed behind him.

***

"Captain Hodges, I believe you requested a meeting with me," Colonel Alexander Stewart mumbled somewhat distractedly. Sitting behind a large desk, he idly scratched notes on a grimy sheet of paper. Several long moments passed before he raised his head, awarding the ever-patient Hodges with polite eye contact. His immediate thoughts, upon first meeting the Loyalist Captain recently, could be summed up in three words: intelligent, dedicated and reliable. Nothing in his actions since then, had given cause to alter his initial impression.

"Yes, Colonel, so as not to waste your valuable time, I will come directly to the point."

Welcoming his directness, Stewart pushed the paperwork aside, folding his hands neatly. "I appreciate that, Captain. What seems to be of concern?" A glance at his knitted brow indicated he felt something to be amiss: if not in actuality, at least in *his* mind.

"Although the war is technically over, we still hold Charleston and Savannah and will continue to do so indefinitely."

Stewart gave a slight nod, his gaze remaining steady. *Where is this conversation going?* But he remained silent.

"We house six prisoners, sir, five resulting from ongoing hostilities after Eutaw Springs—the sixth due to physical battery charges resulting in an English officer's death."

"Yes," Stewart nudged. "Your problem—or shall I say *concern*—being?"

"Five captives have received no undue ill treatment, and may be released in the near future. The sixth, however, may not live, due to the severity of beatings inflicted, and lack of nourishment," Hodges answered conversationally, maintaining a non-judgmental tone of voice. He must not arouse suspicion if his plan was to succeed.

"He killed a British officer with his bare hands," Stewart retorted curtly.

"An act no different than those committed by the other five prisoners, sir," Hodges stated doggedly. "Why has *he* been singled out for a slow, painful death? Why not just shoot him and be done with it?"

Stewart studied Captain Hodges thoughtfully, scrutinizing his mood and intent. Having heard very little concerning him, neither good nor bad, he was curious: what is the importance of this particular prisoner to him? He stood slowly and moved around the desk to stand directly facing the captain, deciding honesty to be the best approach.

"I am sure you are aware, Captain, that I inherited these prisoners from Lord Rawdon when he stepped down from command. And you *are* correct. The man of whom you speak is Gabriel MacLean, I believe."

"Yes, sir." He started to say more but Stewart rushed on, allowing him no opening.

"His treatment was a result of a personal vendetta between Rawdon and the young man's father, the details of which are unknown to me. I fear that with all the turmoil of these last few weeks, I had given him no further thought."

"He is of no use to us dead, sir," Hodges stated succinctly.

Stewart's eyes snapped to the captain's face, scrutinizing for hidden purpose.

"And just why, might I inquire, is this young man's welfare of particular interest to you, Captain?" He kept his question even toned, precise. *Is his honesty merely a ruse? Will he admit the truth?*

Hodges hesitated but a moment, deciding truth was for the best. "I have never met Gabriel MacLean's father, nor seen him other than on the battlefield, the last time being at Guilford Courthouse, when he was carried off the field. We are both aware that he was the rebel militia leader at that time. We also know Nathanael Greene forced him to the sidelines in the aftermath."

"So far our sources agree, Captain." He smiled grimly. "However, you may not have heard, Greene has chosen to remain in the South until he sees proof of the Peace Treaty. This mess—*intermittent ongoing slaughter*—is far from over, but I digress, do go on."

"Then, possibilities of trading captives are definitely *not* over. Actually, MacLean's familial status may be of more importance than the side he fought for."

Stewart nodded, waiting for Hodges to lay all his cards on the table.

"*My* reasons are more of a personal nature, Colonel." Hodges drew in a deep breath. "Gabriel MacLean is Kathryn MacLean Tarrington's nephew. I speak for his welfare out of respect ..." his voice softened to a whisper, "for Kathryn and her colonel."

"Yes ... a tragic loss. Although I did not know them personally, their reputation is well known, larger than life and understated from all I hear."

Hodges eyes misted. "Gabriel once saved Kathryn from two of his own militia, placing himself at extreme risk. Perhaps for now, we should allow him life and sort it all out later."

"I agree, Captain, I appreciate your honesty. Henceforth, I will have ill treatment of MacLean forbidden. I put you in charge of his recovery. However, if I hear of him becoming fat and favored ..."

"I am a fair man," Hodges interrupted, "but I *do not* play favorites."

"I thought not, Captain. Thank you for bringing our options to light. It is a shame, in some ways, that the war will not continue on. A man of your stature and precise observations would be in line for a higher rank in short order."

"I am well satisfied with my place and rank, sir. As I have nothing further to discuss, please allow me to return to duty."

Colonel Stewart grasped Hodges's hand, shaking it firmly, surprising him. *This has gone better than expected,* he thought, but hid a smile.

"Good day to you, Captain. Keep me apprised of this situation, and any others that require my attention. Henceforth, you shall be my eyes and ears."

With a smart salute, Captain Hodges stepped out into the hallway, closing the door quietly behind him. "Do not be so sure, Stewart," he muttered under his breath. "I am not *your* man."

As he trod smartly back to the prisoner's holding area, his thoughts raced. His months spent under Tarleton's command had turned out to be a blessing in disguise; for he had watched and learned well from the man's devious abilities.

Jamie must be made aware of the situation immediately, or his tendency to be a hot-head could inadvertently create disaster. Hodges would assign him the task of contacting Kathryn and Jason. Hopefully, that important task would keep him focused and out of the way. Careful coordination would be required, but nothing insurmountable.

His first priority: heal Gabriel. At present, he lay in his own filth, barely aware of his surroundings, more than half-starved. Hodges doubted he had even recognized him the times he sat cradling his head, dripping water on his parched lips, urging him to drink.

At that time, he could not show preference without risk of being discovered. But as of this moment, things were different. Stewart had given his blessing for the healing of Lieutenant Gabriel MacLean, son of James Douglas MacLean, former Southern rebel militia leader. For that healing, would provide a valuable pawn—or so he thought.

However, Captain Hodges *did not* share Stewart's vision—his agenda quite different—and with a somewhat more radical outcome. And Stewart, with a firm handshake and freely given blessings, had just unwittingly handed him all the necessary tools required to accomplish *his* goals.

"I believe I owe you a bit of thanks, Tarleton, although it scares me to admit it. I now understand one of the 'keys' to your success," Hodges mouthed softly to himself. "To you, life is a game with only one acceptable outcome. Win by *any means* available: unmercifully bending the truth or out and out dishonesty."

Hodges paused, becoming thoughtful. "Of course, the other 'key' to success is a heavy purse, of which, unfortunately, I have not. Although I have been forced to take the more difficult route, I have succeeded—so far. I do believe you would be proud, Banastre."

No time for gloating, Samuel. There is much yet to be done. But the hardest part I have now accomplished. With the twitch of a smile, concealing his thoughts, he hummed a bright rebel tune softly—one of Kathryn's favorites, and picked up his pace.

Chapter Three

Solid Ground

Two days later, Kathryn sat happily ensconced amidst several well-secured boxes on deck, cradling her sleeping son. Pulling her cloak more tightly around them, she leaned back into the protective barrier of stacked crates. Although the wind remained fairly calm, its icy bite spiked goose bumps along her exposed lower arm.

"Missus, might I have a word with you?"

Kathryn turned, startled, but instantly smiled at Smitty's grin and sparkling eyes.

"It would seem Miss Gabrielle is a wee bit sad of late," he said, using his very best diction and manners.

"I fear she misses her young friend, Robbie," she said, sensing he wished to say something of a questionable nature. *Spit out whatever is on your mind.* She raised a curious brow.

"I thought I might take her up into the crow's-nest for a look-see." Flashing an innocent smile, he waited for her answer.

Kathryn's eyes drifted upwards. "All the way up there?" she asked, somewhat aghast.

"Yessum. No harm will come ta her, I promise. She'll be in a rope harness secured ta me. Ye've seen me up an' down the mast a dozen times or more. Ye know I would never risk her …" He sucked a quick breath, prepared to spew more convincing reasons.

Kathryn flipped her hand in a silencing gesture. "And what does her father say?"

As he gave no answer, appearing quite uncomfortable, she pressed more insistently.

"He says he sleeps in real close quarters wit' you, missus. So's I best git yer blessins lest his ballocks be forfeit." He grinned lopsidedly.

Kathryn eyed him sternly, but suddenly burst into laughter. "That *does* sound like something my dear husband would say."

"Yessum and Master Jack agreed and …" He clamped a hand over his mouth belatedly realizing that last bit of information should have remained unshared.

"Oh, did he now?" she said, skewering him with a long look, thoroughly enjoying his discomfiture. "Well, I gather I am to be out-voted."

Smitty rushed off leaving Kathryn mouthing a small prayer. After all the dangers she had shared with her father, how could she deny her child that thrill?

"Look, momma!" a delightful yell from above pierced her reverie.

Watching Smitty making his way quickly and surely up the ropes, despite his boxy stature, she had to admit it looked to be fun.

"Would you like to be next?" a soft voice whispered as caressing lips brushed her ear.

Kathryn turned, briefly eyeing her husband with feigned consternation, before turning an evil eye on Jack—his partner in crime—and then back to Jason.

"I understand you fear for your ballocks, my pet." She began to grin. "If I were you, I would, especially if you sneak up on me like that again." Turning quickly, she pointed an accusing finger towards his accomplice. "And as for you, Uncle Jack: *beware.*"

They laughed with genuine pleasure, happy to see Kathryn more at ease. When they looked skyward again, Smitty and Gabrielle were ensconced safely in the crow's-nest.

"She is like her parents, fearless," Jack commented.

"And her Uncle Jack," Kathryn reminded. "What you did for us after Guilford Courthouse …" For a moment she grew serious. "*Never* sell yourself short, Jack, *never.*"

He blushed at her words and glanced skyward, uncomfortable, yet deeply pleased.

"All's well below," Ted yelled as he walked briskly towards them. "The horses are doing well: fed, fresh bedding and water." Staring up towards the rigging, he began to chuckle. "It would seem all is well up here too."

A happy yell split the air as Gabrielle waved vigorously with both hands.

"No terror in that little one," Ted said appreciatively.

"She is just like her mother." Jason brushed a kiss to her cheek and winked.

Six weeks had passed since sailing from Dover, the seas remaining unusually calm for this time of year. Baby Beau thrived, a happy child who easily adapted to whatever Mother Nature sent their way. Gabrielle loved the ocean and was busily entertained by Smitty, Uncle Jack and her newfound friend, Ted; her few moments of sadness eased by reliving the precious times she and Robbie had shared. Exactly like her mother, if she could not change a situation, she treasured the best remnants and moved on.

Their days fell into a pattern, as did their evenings, when the adults gathered for a sip of coveted brandy and talked speculatively of what lay ahead—a good way to pass time, but open-ended and vague. As no amount of discussion, from where they sat rocking at sea, would change or solve the situation back home, they turned to future possibilities—where to go and what to do? Much of that also depended on existing circumstances upon arrival. They talked, shared poetry, relived some of the worst and best moments spent in England, and prayed for a speedy arrival.

Being on board ship was dissatisfying at best, unacceptable at worst, constantly at the mercy of Mother Nature, who proceeded on an undisclosed course charted by her alone, leaving all involved subject to her whim. Kathryn, Jason and Jack had always shared input, creating tactics that swayed the outcome of any given situation—their success depending on well thought out actions, over which they enacted a certain amount of *control.* None of that applied now, and they did not like this new set of rules.

"You two must bring me luck," Captain Farthingale yelled heartily as he approached at a rapid pace. "We should sight land by tomorrow. Even with all our cargo and cannon, we have made excellent time. I had expected at least one Nor'easter, common for December, you know. However, I do not bemoan that lacking in the least."

"Will we be docking at Gloucester Point?" Jason asked.

"No. As we have spoken of during the voyage, Banastre alerted me to the surrender. That was the reason for my ships new appearance and changed name—none of which had been originally planned. Consequently, I was held up longer."

"And that served our purpose well, but are you concerned that we may …"

"Absolutely not, Kathryn. I have taken precautions *not* to draw attention. We will be sailing into Charleston with bolts of brocades and linens for the fine southern ladies. I am a merchant trader who was merely prevailed upon to bring you to the colonies."

"There *is* truth to that statement," Jason added dryly as he turned to his wife. "And that is a better departure point for us, too. But tell me, Captain ..." his attention riveted on Farthingale as a thought crossed his mind. "Have you had word from Lord Cornwallis or Tarleton?"

"Well," he pursed his lips, "I imagine his Lordship passed us in the dark at some point, for he should arrive in England soon. As to Banastre? No word as yet. I sadly fear our lucrative business deals are all but over. Though I have *no doubt* that he will survive, he always does." With a wink, he added, "As will I."

Jason grasped the captain's hand, thanking him heartily for his goodwill.

"I detest strung out goodbyes, but I may say with utmost honesty, both encounters with your family have truly been *my pleasure.* And do not hesitate to call on me if I may be of service in the future. Although I will be easy to find, I shall make it *my* purpose to know of your well-being."

With a quickly placed kiss on Kathryn's cheek, he spun on his heel and disappeared.

Kathryn leaned against the ship's railing staring at the fuzzy line separating sea and sky.

"What are you thinking, my pet?" Jason kissed his wife and brushed a wisp of hair off his sleeping son's cheek. "You are unusually quiet today," he added softly.

She turned, her emerald eyes capturing his; alive with the sparkling intensity he knew and loved so well.

"*Beyond the horizon*, my love, awaits our new life, *our destiny,*" she answered, a slow smile nudging the corners of her mouth.

"I am as eager as you, my Kathryn. I have no idea what awaits, or what we have yet to accomplish in this life, but we have been given another chance." Drawing her into his embrace, he held her close, sharing the quiet pleasure of each other's company.

The next day dawned clear and bright as they sailed into port. Their few belongings were quickly unloaded and set in a small pile on the pier. Having gotten past her willful prancing, Beauty stood quietly, delighted to be on solid ground once again.

Kathryn grasped Gabrielle's hand and squeezed gently. Tears streamed down her daughter's cheeks as she stifled sobs, staring at Smitty unblinking. This was the second time she had had to leave him behind, and she thought her heart would break.

"Ole Smitty'll be in town for a few days, little one. Please don't cry. I'll not go wit'out givin' ye a hug."

The little man stood holding Beauty, readying to stable her for the night, tears welling. This unhappy scene would never end until someone made a move. Smitty broke first, nudging Beauty towards the barn at the far end of the pier.

It had been difficult to walk away from the little girl after the first voyage, when she and her 'Uncle Jack' had arrived in England and then disappeared from his life. He loved this child as if she were his own; she had helped ease the festering sore that had haunted him for years—one he had been unable to heal or put aside. And now this, he felt as if his heart would break. *What am I to do?* He had grown close to her parents, yet another factor. They felt like family, *his family.* But if he left the sea, could he survive? What talents did he have other than being pretty good in a brawl? They had not asked him to join them; did they think he loved the ocean? Countless unsettled thoughts chased in his mind, making him physically ill. Swallowing convulsively, he turned to Beauty, heartened as she gave his shoulder a nudge and began snuffling against his cheek.

"Ahh, lass, *you* understand Ole Smitty's grief, don'tcha?" He pulled a cube of sugar from his pocket and smiled as she gently mouthed it from his hand. "I'll miss *ye* too. Well, come along now, lassie. A good brushing, some oats and a clean stall for you—and jest mayhaps ye can help me think me way through this muddle."

Knowing the city well, Kathryn had chosen a small country inn on the outskirts that she and Jamie had occasionally visited. Although a bit of a walk, she felt the sights and people would give her daughter other things to think about. She ached for her little girl, but had no answers; their lives were about to change drastically. She, also, felt at a loss, an unaccustomed feeling she did not like. The knowing warmth of her husband's hand creating small circles in the small of her back conveyed his feelings to be identical.

They headed off in silence, each immersed in private thoughts. Ted led his matched grays proudly, enjoying their company as he worked his way towards a stable located farther down the main boulevard. Stanton's Livery had been highly recommended to him by a well-dressed gentleman on the dock who had stopped to admire his horses.

"With that gorgeous pair of animals, you will likely be hired on the spot, young man. As a matter of fact, I may be your first fare," he chortled, pressing a lavishly printed business card into Ted's hand—and then, with an elegant bow, went on his way.

As they walked, Ted quietly absorbed the wealth and lushness of Charleston, despite the war, knowing he could happily call this place home: no problem finding employment or living *very well*. Decision made, he broke the silence. "I really *do* prefer city life to that of the country and …" interrupting himself, he tipped his cap to a buxom young girl. "My grays are hale and hearty and ready to work and …"

Jason and Jack flashed knowing smiles; Kathryn rolled her eyes, shaking her head.

"What?" Ted demanded beginning to color.

"You like the pretty city girls," Gabrielle snorted, giggling into her hand.

"There is absolutely *nothing* wrong with that," Jack commented. "Sights for sore eyes, I might add."

Grinning sheepishly, Ted continued his previous train of thought. "I'm sure I can purchase or lease a carriage with no trouble. So, if you need me I won't be far. Besides, I can be your eyes and ears here in Charleston—an important factor what with the likes of these English blokes still here." He jerked his head towards a group of soldiers strolling along the sidewalk. "Uhh, no offense meant, Jason. I forgot for …"

"None taken, Ted." Jason retorted, offering his hand. "We are grateful for all you have done. Join us later at the inn; there is much we wish to discuss with you."

With a curt nod, he tousled Gabrielle's hair and headed in the opposite direction.

Gabrielle cast a wistful look after him as Jack grasped her hand. "Finally, I have you all to myself, young lady. It would seem I must vie for your attention on all sides."

Brilliant blue eyes sparkled up at him and she smiled coyly. "You will always be my favorite, Uncle Jack. We *are* family."

As they crossed the inns wide verandah, Kathryn turned to her men sighing happily. "My legs are still a bit shaky, but we are here, none the worse for wear after a delightful, trouble-free voyage. Our disembarkation was accomplished with ease, not one eyebrow raised. That bodes well for all of us."

"Charleston, or Charles Town, as the inhabitants call it, has always taken greater interest in the British side. If we can elude detection here ..." Jason paused, thinking.

"Then we should be 'home free'," Jack added as he held the door, ushering Kathryn into the rustic entrance hall.

As they approached the main desk, the innkeeper looked up flashing a well-practiced, mindless, welcoming smile. Before a word could be voiced, his bland look changed to one of open interest, his attention riveting on the newcomers—studying Kathryn openly.

"Excuse my impolite stares, milady, but I *do* believe I recognize you."

All three tensed. Jason and Jack concerned, their firearms were packed in their bags, and Kathryn—*how can I hand Beau to his father so I might reach the dirk in my boot?* It galled her to feel so utterly naked.

"Forgive me for staring, but are you perhaps Mr. and Mrs. Cameron?"

Kathryn touched Gabrielle's shoulder sending a subtle warning.

"Yes," Jason replied, his brow furrowing, tense. "My wife and children and a dear friend—just arrived from England."

"Then I have the right family." He smiled, relieved. "My wife was absolutely sure when she saw you coming across the boulevard."

They smiled but offered no further information. Kathryn noted proudly that Gabrielle stood silently, no longer the bubbly child who blurted whatever came to mind.

"A week or two past, a gentleman stopped in and gave me this." He rummaged under the counter, and finding a rather crumpled parchment, placed it in front of Jason.

Kathryn angled her head attempting to read the names. It was definitely Jamie's hand and clearly addressed to: *Mr. and Mrs. Jason Cameron.*

Jason tucked it into the inner pocket of his coat, and thanked the innkeeper kindly. The disappointed look washing across the man's face did not go unmissed. The letter would have provided him excellent gossip to share with his wife and others.

Realizing no further information would be forthcoming, the innkeeper added, "He never gave his name, but I see a strong family resemblance." He smiled pointedly at Kathryn.

"I have been told that before, sir, and I thank you," she answered, smiling prettily.

As even his last subtle tactic had fallen on apparently deaf ears, he snapped his fingers for the 'bell boy' and wished them a pleasant stay at his inn.

"Well, that caught me a bit off-guard," Jason said, closing the door to their room and handing his wife the letter. He and Jack stood flanking Kathryn in the center of the room, as Gabrielle cuddled her baby brother on the ample bed.

For a long moment Kathryn remained silent, making neither comment nor jest about the neatly tied ribbon that actually was a little askew, so typical of Jamie. "That *was* rather clever of my brother, the way in which he addressed the envelope to us." She eyed both men.

"He would do nothing to risk hurting us, my love. He is now *my* brother also."

"I look forward to meeting him," Jack said.

"Me too," Gabrielle chirped, bouncing her brother as he began a low, grumbling complaint—quickly ended by a sugar teat plopped into his pouting mouth.

"I am sure Jamie has been anxious for our arrival. He trusted us to come as soon as we could," Jason said, "and so we have." Realizing Kathryn's trepidation over the parchment's contents, he slipped the ribbon and broke the wax seal. "Why did he leave the note here? What would cause him to think we might choose this inn over another?"

"There certainly are much fancier spots, and closer to the pier," Jack chimed in.

"He *knows* my momma," Gabrielle said softly, a perceptive look shining in her eyes.

Kathryn eyed her daughter sharply and smiled. *How astute of you, little one. You have never met your uncle and yet you already understand him.*

"My brother knew I would choose to be here, as I prefer a simpler style devoid of fancy trappings." She grinned at both men. "I am sure, if you think about our past life, you will understand completely."

They nodded, grinning, no further comment necessary.

"What does Uncle Jamie have to say?" Gabrielle asked impatiently. Adults always took too long to get to the point. If they waited much longer, a sugar teat would not quiet Beau's ever-demanding appetite.

"He says," Jason eyed his daughter somewhat sternly. "He writes," he corrected.

Dearest Kathryn and Hunter,

If I have guessed correctly, this letter will find you happily arrived very soon. In order to help you become settled in your newly chosen life here in the colonies, I have discovered information of interest. I am staying with acquaintances and eagerly await your arrival. I have enclosed a map.

My regards to all.

Jamie

"How extremely well-written." Jack said appreciatively. "It says *everything* and yet *nothing.*"

"He wanted to give nothing away, if it was intercepted or read by the innkeeper," Jason said, eyeing Kathryn approvingly. "That is one reason the 'devil's spawn' was such a thorn in my side, and so successful. Besides his ability to push beyond the limits of endurance, he is intelligent, shrewd and possesses innate knowledge of human nature. Just like his sister, my incredible wife." He touched her cheek gently.

Kathryn's eyes shone with gratitude as her smile widened.

"Who is the 'devil's spawn'?" Gabrielle piped up, bouncing her baby brother more vigorously as he started a grating, meaningful complaint.

"That is a story for another time, little one," Jack explained, giving her a warm hug.

"Jamie's words, and the map, are sketchy for safeties sake. But I know where he is, a well-concealed spot in close proximity to our goal. Now that I know the news is not dire, I am eager to sink my teeth into some real food," Kathryn exclaimed.

"Jack and I will share a brandy in the great room while we await our two lovely ladies. However, do not be long as we are both ravenous, and that fact may outweigh good manners." With a wink and a light kiss, he headed for the door chuckling.

Sighing softly, she pulled her son into her arms, released her bodice and set him to suckling.

Chapter Four

Smitty Saves the Day

Beauty pranced willfully, tossing her head contemptuously. Having been penned up in a confined space on board ship, she had no intention of going willingly into another narrow stall. It was not so much the size of the stall, but her 'neighbors: ill-tempered beasts on either side, who flattened their ears, baring yellow teeth in greeting.

"Ahh, lass, it's been a long time for the likes o' you to curb yer energies. I understand yer grievance," Smitty cajoled. Pulling her head down gently, he whispered in her ear. "If I take ye for a nice walk down to the dock and back, would ye consider behaving yerself in front o' the otha' rude blokes? Yer manners are so much better. Show them up, eh?"

Eyeing him calmly through knowledgeable brown eyes, she accepted a sugar cube and started towards the barn door.

"Now there's a good lass. I knew ye would give in ta sound reasoning. Whistling a bright tune, he upped his pace to keep abreast of the mare as she strutted along the wharf, head held high and delicate hooves striking a staccato beat on the aged timbers. "A bit like yer mistress ye are, with a mind o' yer own. And no offense meant—I always liked my girls to be of a strong opinion. "Smitty grinned and trotted on at Beauty's side.

"Sweet Jesus, Gilson, look over there."

Belching loudly, Gilson swung about to stare in the direction O'Reilly was pointing. Narrowing his eyes, he swiped his mouth on the back of his sleeve and belched louder. There had been a time when he would never have made such a boorish gesture, but that was before Guilford Courthouse, before … He quickly stopped the painful thought.

"By God, that sure looks like …" he sucked in a ragged breath, wishing he had not downed that last drink.

They had barely been assigned to Rawdon's forces, when the duty was handed to Stewart. The duty was not distasteful, merely boring. They missed their former dragoon comrades, their colonel and his wife. They requested, and had been granted, a weekend leave. Immediately upon arrival, they had begun drinking at a small pub near the dock. Their entertainment of the moment, drinking and watching the docking of a ship or two, later they would search out female companionship and a warm bed. They had yet to put any solid food in their stomachs, and both were a bit giddy.

"Come on, Gilson, drunk or not, we both know Beauty when we see her." Standing abruptly, O'Reilly pushed his chair aside and flung a coin on the table. Hauling Gilson up, he shoved him towards the door and headed, a bit unsteadily, towards the wharf. "See, Gilson? I *was* right. It *is* Beauty!"

At their approach, Beauty slowed to a stop, eyeing them with interest. Smitty tensed, unsure of their purpose. They were British soldiers, a bit in their cups, but soldiers nevertheless. He did not wish a fight, but fight he would, if it became necessary.

O'Reilly nodded a quick greeting and reached a shaky hand to touch the mare. Beauty stood her ground nickering softly, obviously knowing both men.

A prick of concern tightened Smitty's gut. *No one must know they're here, absolutely no one.* "Back off, gents," he growled, moving confrontationally between the two inebriated dragoons and the mare.

Gilson, swaying slightly, reached for his sabre.

"Fer gawd's sake man," Smitty lightened his tone, shaking his head. "I'm as British as both of ye. And ye're both too drunk to risk my wrath." Patting Beauty's rump, he flashed a wide grin. "Nice piece o' horse flesh, wouldna' ye say?"

Smitty stalled for time, his mind working busily to craft a believable story. He knew enough of Gabrielle's family background to realize the danger in these men being aware of the truth, even if they wished to help. *No, way too dangerous for word to get out yet.*

"Where's the owner?" O'Reilly asked pointedly, interrupting Smitty's deliberation.

"Ye're lookin' at 'im. Me!" He thumped his chest proudly.

A befuddled look crossed the officers' faces, but quickly changed to angry accusation as they turned full attention to the pugnacious little man.

"Explain yourself!" Gilson demanded, having finally found his tongue.

"Won her fair and square I did, in a shipboard card game," he said smugly.

"When? Where? You are a …"

"Do *not* call me liar," Smitty interjected, jabbing his forefinger sharply against the belligerent officer's chest, "or you will be in a box headed for home on the next tide." If they had not been so drunk, he more than likely would be dead. But—*so far, so good.* He was on a 'roll' and thoroughly enjoying himself.

Smitty studied them silently, weighing his odds of success. Perhaps he better soften his tactics before he overplayed the game. With a noncommittal shrug, he said, "I can see ye gents want answers. Well, ye caught ole Smitty in a good frame o' mind, so I'll share me tale. Let me see, what month is it now?" As no immediate answer was forthcoming, he counted slowly on his fingers, as if lost in deep thought. "No matter anyhow. Guess it wuz about the end o' March last year that me ship took on cargo and guests, a couple of horses, a cow, some chickens. Not here though, further north."

"Yes, yes, yes. Get on with it," Gilson said testily.

Smitty cleared his throat and began again. "It's a long voyage, endless nights and no pretty temptresses to wile away the hours."

Their impatient stares urged Smitty to hurry it up. *No sense ruinin' whut I got goin',* he realized and picked up the pace. "So we gamble and play cards. One evening a tall man dressed in a jacket just like yours joined us."

A sudden spark of interest flickered in their bloodshot eyes.

"What did he look like?" O'Reilly asked, struggling to concentrate.

"Tall, blond, nice looking I guess, although not *my* type, if ye catch ma drift." At their scowls, he continued. "His luck wuz never particularly good."

"That sounds like Lieutenant Jackson." Gilson elbowed O'Reilly, recalling many evenings spent around the campfire playing cards. "Jack never did have much luck, but he never was ill-tempered over his losses. A good man," he added wistfully.

"He should have borrowed Kathryn's lucky rabbit's foot like she offered," O'Reilly said softly, enjoying the memory. "But what about the mare? What about Beauty?"

"Well, we wuz almost ta England, our last big card game before we landed. This Jack, as you calls 'im, lost badly and he waz outta funds. I told 'im he'd hafta go to sea to work the debt off. But he hated the ship, sick all the time, ya know."

"And ...?" Sergeant Gilson gestured curtly, his patience wearing thin. To hell with food, he wanted another drink—now!

"That's when he told me the mare waz his and now mine." He said, irritated by their impatience. It was a damn good story, and he was just beginning to really have fun.

Both men were silent for a long moment. Gilson finally stood, swaying slightly. "Did he have a little girl with him? Pretty little thing with jet black curls?"

"Dunno," Smitty shot back. "Didn't see 'im come on board. Didn't see 'im disembark. Spent my days up in the riggin' doin' me job, and me nights playin' cards."

"Were there any children on board?" Gilson pressed, sure that Gabrielle would have been noticed.

"Several," Smitty replied, "But from high in the riggin' they all look alike. And not too many kids seek me out afta' all—can't blame 'em, can yuh?" Indicating his motley appearance, he laughed raucously.

"Well, I agree with your assessment, buddy." O'Reilly slapped him on the back. The odd, little man had shared his story, providing considerable food for thought. He and Gilson could chew it all over, but not *this* weekend. They had a full agenda: *none* of it requiring *thinking*. "Well, Beauty, glad to see you hale and hearty."

They turned to leave, but Gilson stopped, eyeing Smitty. "Why did you bring Beauty back here?" he asked tartly. It was a strange tale, providing much to think about—later.

Smitty's mind raced. *Mustn't ruin it now, think fast, ole boy.* "Well, afta our rough trip to England, there wuz no way he wuz comin' back here. Especially if he had a kid wit' 'im, but that I don't know." He turned and patted Beauty affectionately. "But one thing I *do* know gents, I wasn't givin' 'im the chance ta win 'er back wit' a lucky hand."

"Don't blame you," the dragoons agreed and headed back to the pub.

Smitty watched them go, exhaling on a long sigh. "Well, ma pretty, little lady, I thinks I'd best get you outta sight and go warn yer people. Thankful I am that they went straight to the inn and didna' linger here."

Grasping Beauty's halter, he led her back towards the stable, explaining the whole situation as they walked. He would not rush. He must not draw undue attention. And he must be ready with more answers if the two dragoons returned. He doubted they would, at least not in the next couple of days: weekend leaves were few and far between. They had 'issues' of far greater importance on their docket. *They'll not draw a sober breath for the next two days. Sometime next week they'll remember—and maybe question.*

Beauty stepped into her stall, offering him no trouble.

"Ye are such a smart lass, ye know whut's goin' on I'm sure." With a light pat to her cheek and another lump of sugar, he headed towards the inn.

Smitty crossed the verandah of the fashionable inn, eyes darting furtively—relieved. No one had spared him a curious glance, so far. During the time taken to secure Beauty, he had considered many thoughts, finally making an important decision.

As he had never given thought to a wife and family—his looks, even before barroom brawling, not particularly notable—the sea had provided a good life. But Sadie had somehow found him, loved him, and born him a beautiful daughter. But his love had failed to protect them from the dreaded fever. Returning home after a long voyage, he was greeted with devastating loss and emptiness. Guilty remorse had driven him back to sea; he had lost his soul to this capricious mistress—until Gabrielle, who in her unwavering love had taught him to feel, to remember, rekindling his desire to live. He *would not* return to the sea, his life finally had purpose.

"You cannot come in here," the innkeeper stated flatly, confronting Smitty at the door. "Look at you. Be gone, you wharf rat."

"They *will* wish to speak with me." Smitty spoke distinctly, abandoning his customary lingo in an effort to convince the man and draw as little attention as possible. His mother had taught him excellent manners and proper speech at one point in his life; he merely chose not to waste his time in keeping up the practice.

In the great room, Jack sat facing the main entrance conversing quietly with Kathryn and Jason. At the disturbance, he glanced towards the inn door just as Gabrielle tugged his sleeve sharply. Jason and Kathryn turned, but Jack was out of his chair and heading towards the vestibule. "I shall handle this, Jason. You two stay put."

Kathryn picked at her food, frustrated that her back faced whatever was happening. It was Smitty, Gabrielle had indicated that much. *Why would he have come here unless there is trouble?*

"Kathryn," Jason said softly, taking her hand. "Jack will handle this. Trust him to …"

"I do, Jason, but …"

"You hate not knowing what is going on, momma."

"Out of the mouths of babes, my love, and well put at that." Jason grinned as she skewered them with a scowl.

"And just *when* did you become so discerning and grownup, young lady?"

Hunching her shoulders, she pointed to her sleeping baby brother and grinned.

Warmth filled Kathryn's eyes. "Yes, you and Great Grandmother helped so much."

"Jason, Kathryn, look who we have here." Jack stood with his arm draped about Smitty's shoulders, his features remaining bland, but his eyes bright and serious. "You need to hear what Smitty has to say."

Their table sat in the far corner of the great room, remote enough for private conversation. Jason pulled a chair and extra place setting over, gesturing Smitty to join them. Despite his misgivings, with Jason's firm insistence he sat down, his eyes widening at the delicious repast spread before him: at last, 'real' food after all the months at sea.

"Eat," Kathryn insisted, spooning stew into his bowl.

"I doubt it will make much difference if your news waits a little longer," Jason added, placing a basket of bread beside Smitty's bowl.

"There's more truth ta' that statement than ye know, Jason." He talked around mouthfuls. "The gents involved are either drunk or in bed wit' ..." He stopped mid-sentence looking embarrassed. "Excuse me; I forgot meself in front of the young'uns."

As Gabrielle burst into giggles he raised an eyebrow eyeing her briefly, and then continued his tale between bites.

"Well, it would seem we have *immediate* decisions to make." Kathryn leaned forward, smiling at each in turn. "Let us finish here and move the conversation upstairs. But first, I have a request of Smitty, for much depends on him." This request needed to come directly from her, she understood Smitty better than he did himself.

"Anything, missus. How may I help ye?"

"Must the sea be your home—or might you be lured ashore?"

"What are ye askin', missus? Speak clear for ole Smitty's heart is startin' to pound."

"Give up yer sea legs, me hearty," she said lightly, but her look conveyed volumes.

"We want you to watch our backs," Jason added.

"If you need more convincing, Smitty, let me offer you the pledge they gave me."

Kathryn and Jason grinned at Jack's inner wisdom.

"We have no idea what the future holds, but we promise it *will be* an adventure."

Gabrielle was up out of her chair, around the table and into his lap. "Say 'yes' please," she begged, planting a wet kiss on his cheek.

Smitty ceased his polite refusals. He had not dared to hope that they might ask him to join them. "Yes ... I ... Yes," he stammered.

"Good, now that we are all in agreement, we have much to discuss. Come to our room in about an hour," Jason advised.

Smitty set Gabrielle down and headed towards the door.

"And just where might you be going?" Jack asked.

"Headin' fer the ship to tell Farthingale he is finally rid o' me, and then to the stable to see Beauty. I'll visit her fer a bit and relax me tired old body—oh, and make arrangements for the night."

"You will find it difficult to watch our backs from there, my friend, you are rooming with me. Let me show you where you'll be resting 'yer tired old body' before you head off on errands." Jack stood and pushed his chair in. At Smitty's surprised look, he added, "I'll take no refusals; you are part of the team now." Clapping Smitty heartily on the back, he elbowed him towards the stairs. Winking over his shoulder at Kathryn and Jason, he leaned close and said lightly, "Cuddle if you must tonight, but be careful where you place your hands."

Smitty's head snapped up. Eyeing Jack with a mischievous grin, he chortled, "I might advise you to do the same, Jack, although I realize the temptation bein' thrown yer way to be almost overrpowerin."

The two men started up the stairs, their shoulders shaking in combined mirth.

"Now what do you suppose set them to laughing so?" Kathryn asked.

"Do not ask, my pet. Do not ask."

Chapter Five

Decisions

"What shall we do about Gilson and O'Reilly?" Kathryn asked.

Not risking being seen by his former comrades, Jack arrived at their room early. Drunk or sober, they would easily spot him; the sooner they left Charleston, the better.

"Well," he weighed his thoughts, "there are several ways of looking at this situation."

Kathryn and Jason held their opinions, wanting Jack's input first.

"Even blind drunk, they would recognize the three of us, alone or together. Would they be thrilled to find you both alive? Absolutely—however, if those two are this far south, and still in uniform as Smitty indicated, they have been reassigned here: probably to Rawdon. Obviously they know of Gabriel's incarceration. But would they help or hinder our plans? Would their commanding officer look the other way, allowing a prized prisoner to escape, even with the information I hold over him? If so, what might he expect in return; for us to rejoin and risk becoming dangerously visible?"

"And if we tell them nothing?" Jason asked.

"There is a strong possibility they may create trouble inadvertently, asking too many questions. Neither one is stupid. When they sober up, they will reconsider the unlikely tale told by Smitty, although I admit it took quick thinking on his part."

"He is a good man," Kathryn said thoughtfully. "He will be an asset in many ways."

"I like his sense of humor." Jack grinned, Jason merely rolled his eyes.

"So what is *your* answer, Jack?" Kathryn pushed.

"Unfortunately, this is a 'lose—lose' situation. Tell them or not, either way we lose. My gut feeling is to get out of town early tomorrow, find Jamie, and move on from there. Jamie's information will help determine our next step."

Kathryn nodded. "I agree; you have always had excellent analytical abilities."

"Thank you for coming with us, Jack, *we* need you," Jason added.

At his flush of color and pleased look, it suddenly struck Kathryn: *We must remind him often of his value to us and himself. He is as troubled by insecurities as Jason and I.*

A soft sound drew their attention to the far side of the room. Gabrielle stretched, yawning and smiling. In their serious conversation, her presence had been all but forgotten. *How much did she overhear?* Their daughter's next statement answered that.

"Gabriel knows you are coming for him. He is well enough to ride. He is in good hands," she said in choppy, firm sentences.

They eyed her with questioning stares, but she offered nothing further. With a knowing look, and secretive smile she added, "This is true; I just *know.*"

"Believe her," Jack sighed softly. "Some day ask me how I can be so sure."

With a sharp rap on the door, Smitty entered.

"Smitty," Gabrielle squeaked, jumping up from the chair and throwing her arms around him. "Let me look at you."

"Let us *all* take a look at you," Jason exclaimed.

Smitty bowed low and turned slowly for their approval. He had bathed, shaved his wiry whiskers, and replaced his filthy bandana with a nicely clubbed, colonial hairstyle. Dark breeches, tunic vest and shiny boots completed his new looks.

"Oh, Smitty …" was all Gabrielle could manage.

As the others remained speechless Smitty frowned, concerned. "Am I appropriately attired?" he asked formally. "I could not quite make meself give up me hoops just yet." He flicked the gold rings in his ears. "But I will if ye feels it to be necessary."

"What an incredible transformation," Jason said, finally finding his voice.

"And what do *you* think, missus? If I am to be part of the team, I hafta' look the part."

"I am overwhelmed, Smitty. You were never an embarrassment, there is no need …"

"Oh, but there is. Though I thank ye for yer kind words. I have had naught to care about fer years, but I do now." He knelt beside Gabrielle and gave her a long look. "Do you approve little one?" At her energetic nod, he asked, "Will ye help me in relearning the correct way o' speakin'? I knew it once, and can learn again."

"I will even teach you Cherokee; but you must promise *not* to give up your hoops."

Smitty smiled at each in turn. "I picked up a bit o' information which may be of interest. It seems that Nathanael Greene is here in Charleston. He has no intention of leavin' 'til he sees a peace treaty and holds it in his hand—not too trustin' if ye ask me."

He watched their faces become serious. "I was afraid o' that, so I made a decision," he said, stroking his chin, liking the smooth feel. "Where better to keep abreast of goings on than a blacksmith shop: rich or poor, yer horse regularly needs shoes or harnessing?"

Seeing nodded approval, he continued. "Ted's going to work with his horses, driving well-heeled customers about. He gathers one type of gossip, but I gathers another because of a different clientele."

"Excellent idea," Jason murmured.

"Good, because I've already been hired. I'm good at it too. Did it fer years to help out me mam. That's why they call me Smitty."

"What is your real name," Gabrielle asked.

"I was afraid ye would ask, but ye must never tell a soul beyond these doors." As she quickly crossed her heart in promise, he admitted shyly: "Chester Abernathy, and don't ask the middle name as I put it out of me mind years ago—hated it, I did."

"What is your plan?" Kathryn wanted him to dictate the rules.

Smitty noticed Gabrielle's stricken look and tousled her hair.

"I *will* be joining ye before ye know it. But I must help watch fer danger here. I can gather lots of information if you give me a few days—or longer if ye like."

"Good thinking, Smitty. You should join us as soon as our most pressing 'goal' is accomplished. There is no better man to have in a fight than you, so I am told."

Smitty puffed his chest out proudly, jerking a sharp nod of agreement.

"Ted can bring you to the appointed place in four or five days, unless you decide to stay with your *new trade*."

"City life is not to me liking, I can pick up any news of importance in that amount of time. Nathanael Greene piques my interest. I'd like to see if I kin get a feel for his game."

Jack speared him with a solemn look. "Do not risk life or limb doing anything foolish, Smitty. We have all grown accustomed to your company. Besides, carelessness on your part would break a certain young lady's heart."

"I'd not have made meself this handsome if I meant to be foolish. Me only true concern is learning to ride, I fear me arse—oops—me backside may blister." Becoming serious he added, "Go early while your '*friends*' have yet to find the time, or desire, to sort it all out. For they will," Smitty cautioned. "And there's another bit of information I picked up, mayhaps o' interest—Rawdon is gone, went home sick. Alexander Stewart is now in charge." He raised an inquisitive brow.

"Well, that definitely *is* interesting news. We must see how that fits into our thoughts, my Kathryn." With a kiss to her forehead and a hug to his daughter, Jason joined Jack and Smitty as they headed downstairs for brandy.

Amidst their light male banter, Jason's rich, resonant chuckle drifted back to her from the hallway, bringing a smile to her face. Their amiable camaraderie bonded them in a common cause.

We will need this mutual caring to succeed. For what lies ahead tomorrow is ... Kathryn forced the thought aside and turned to tend her son.

Chapter Six

Thwarted Attempt

"Kathryn," he murmured sternly, startling her.

Drawing a sharp breath, she wobbled slightly and jammed her foot down into her boot. Regaining her balance, she guiltily turned to face him.

Soft moonlight cascaded through their bedroom window playing across his angular features, highlighting the sparkle in his striking blue eyes—eyes conveying curiosity, irritation and hurt. *But this is not his problem* she reasoned.

"This *is not* your problem, my love," she said sheepishly, her statement sounding profoundly stupid even to her.

Tossing aside the covers, he swung his feet to the floor and stood. Soft blue iridescence caressed his muscular form and absolute maleness, creating the likeness of a superb marble statue. Kathryn gasped, unable to look away, deep longing claiming her.

"If Gabriel were *my* nephew, would you accept that advice from me?" he asked softly.

Her eyes met his guiltily.

"Would you?" he asked more firmly, quickly donning his pants. "No, you would not—nor will I." In three strides he was at her side, pulling her into his embrace. "We are in this together and *all* decisions will be made *together.* One person may not take the task secretly into *her* own hands. You need not explain, my love, I know you well."

"I …"

He silenced her with a lingering kiss and stepped back, meeting her gaze dead-on.

"As you may recall, after supper I disappeared with the men, to secure Beauty, view Ted's new carriage, and coordinate tomorrow's departure. We also drifted by a couple of pubs less apt to be frequented by Gilson and O'Reilly." He now had her full attention. "We mingled casually, asking a few discrete questions. I had expected this discussion would keep until dawn, but I see it can not. There are situations *you* need to be aware of."

He studied her changing expressions and alluring emerald eyes carefully. "You and I must make decisions. One of the fiercest battles, I gather the last, was fought at Eutaw Springs in South Carolina this past September."

"Yes, on the Santee River, shortly before his Lordship's surrender. By then both Jamie and Gabriel had been put aside by Nathanael Greene and were not involved in any way."

"Very true, but be that as it may, they are both equally well known and recognizable as you and I. Gabriel's capture occurred because he was in the wrong place at the wrong time, and recognized."

"I doubt his MacLean temper helped," she added.

Jason squeezed her hand lightly but made no comment. "We know that Rawdon is no longer in charge; he fell ill and stayed only long enough for Stewart to arrive before sailing for England."

"Is that better or worse for Gabriel?" she asked.

Jason remained thoughtful for a long moment. "Better, I believe. Jack told me Rawdon could be a surly bastard, tough and single-minded in pursuit of duty. However, Jack's information would have easily called his bluff."

"Does he know Stewart?" Kathryn asked, concerned by this turn of events.

"He does not, but *I* do. He is young, a bit more malleable perhaps. But as to exactly where he is holding Gabriel, I am not sure. To have asked such a pointed question could have attracted unwanted attention."

"I had it in mind to set out and see what I could find but ..."

"So I gather, my love. A bit of the proud, stubborn valor of a MacLean winning out over better judgment, I might add."

Kathryn murmured apologies and frowned, annoyed at herself. "You are right, my love, as always. We need to meet Jamie where indicated and see what news he has."

"Yes, from the sound of his letter it appears that he has done nothing rash up to this point. Thankfully, he did not muster some of his cronies and attempt a rescue. The British still hold Savannah and Charleston and are in no rush to leave. They would have run him to ground, burned the farm and taken the girls, searched out Silver Fox ..."

"No more, Jason, please. Those are my thoughts too."

"You and I can make suppositions all night, my pet; however our answers lie with Jamie. And they will have to wait until tomorrow."

"I wonder if Banastre ..."

"Kathryn," he said sharply. "I do hope Tarleton has had no hand in this. If he has helped us a third time, I fear he will demand heavy favors, if you catch my meaning."

Touching his cheek, she started to grin. "I gather *you* would feel it your husbandly duty to kill him where he stood for the mere suggestion."

"Absolutely," he chuckled. "Ahh, I knew ye to be a smart lass when I married ye."

Abruptly her thoughts turned to Jack. "Is Jack disappointed at this turn of events?"

Jason shrugged. "Jack wants to help in decision-making but lacks confidence."

"I agree, but what do we do?"

"Gently push him to take command, he has the ability—else you and I would have been in our graves long past. In answer to your question, yes, I believe he is disappointed. But he will have other opportunities. This war *is not* over Kathryn, despite the fact that his lordship surrendered at Yorktown. It will be another year, possibly more, before all the troops return to England." He shrugged, eyeing her sharply. Noting the spark of excitement flashing in her eyes, he sucked in a sharp breath; it was exactly as he had feared.

"And *which* side shall we support this time, my love?" His question caught her off guard.

She opened her mouth to comment, but closed it. Studying him through narrowed eyes, she remained silent, attempting to gauge his mood before formulating an answer.

"Which side, my love?" he pushed more insistently.

"Well, I felt we ..." she began, hedging slightly.

"And what of your brother and his loyalties?" he asked quietly, well aware of her dilemma.

Burying her face in her hands, she shook her head. "I do not know," she said mournfully.

Touching her cheek, he moved closer, crouching to capture her full attention.

"If, when we settle this situation with Gabriel ..." she began.

"Rescuing Gabriel is our first priority, and *will be* accomplished before any other decisions are made. But once he is safe," he said firmly, skewering her with a long look, "I ask you again—*which* side my love?"

"At that time, I guess our place must be on ..."

"The rebel's side," he answered.

She eyed him uneasily. "But how will you or I, or even Jack feel about that abrupt change? Some of our former allies may still be ..." Tears of confusion welled in her eyes, an errant drop escaping to drift the length of her cheek.

With a tender swipe of his thumb, he captured it.

"I intend to take it one step at a time, my Kathryn," he said softly. "I *will do* what I must do, to protect *you,* first and foremost, our children, and Jack. We have come *home* by choice and we *will* protect our new home if necessary."

He tilted her chin up, brushing her lips with a meaningful kiss.

"Is that an acceptable answer, my love? For it is the best I can give at the moment."

At her nod he smiled, his gaze showering her with warmth.

"You and I must adapt, step back from our former existence, and become an integral part of life in our new *home.* But do not fret, my Kathryn, our choices will include danger and adventure—as life always does. There will be skirmishes, perhaps a heated confrontation upon occasion. You *will* have a chance to become involved."

In the pale moonlight she glowed with contentment.

"I gather I need not ask again *which side*?"

"No, but it will seem odd if there is an occurrence when we must ...." She hesitated, struggling with her words. "I only hope we will not confront a former ..."

He silenced her with a shake of his head. "You think too much, my pet. We must take one step, one day at a time. Shall I repeat exactly where I stand?" he asked patiently.

With a firm shake of her head, her smile finally reached her sparkling, green eyes.

"Then we are as one in this?"

"Always," she murmured.

"Always," his familiar answer as he loosened his breeches, allowing them to drop.

She reached for him, just as he pulled her into a crushing embrace. Her breath came in short, measured bursts, his arousal, obvious and demanding.

"Yes, yes," she gasped.

In a well-practiced move, he pinned her beneath his muscular frame, her teasing fingers matching his. His tongue flicked tantalizingly along the edge of her ear, imprisoning the lobe within a soft bite, but abruptly released on a sharp intake of breath as her teeth found a sensitive spot and nipped.

"I see there is no further need for sleep," he choked. "Much like the old days ..." He could say no more. *She* wielded the power this night. "Kathryn, my God, Kathryn."

But she was relentless. *Her* demands would be met later, her needs satiated as only he could accomplish. But for the moment he was hers, and she glowed in that knowledge.

It would be a long, gratifying night of passionate 'give and take', their insatiable physical passion a form of rebirth and new beginnings every time they entered the circle of each other's arms.

Chapter Seven

In Search of Jamie

Mewling cries escalated as Kathryn lifted her son from his bed: a large bureau drawer padded with a pillow and blanket. She yawned loudly; dawn had yet to break.

"Hush, Beau, you will wake everyone; we will not be asked back."

Jason chuckled from where he lay, propped on one elbow, enjoying the interplay between his wife and child. Hitching himself up against the pillows, he beckoned her to join him while the baby nursed. She went eagerly, loving these precious minutes ensconced within his warm embrace as he nuzzled her ear, sharing his thoughts.

"Eutaw Springs is north of us," he said, thinking out loud.

She had not pressed him for further discussion after their rather spirited *talk* of the previous night. Quite frankly, after his exquisite love making, her dreamily euphoric state had left her struggling to focus, and in no mood for further words.

"Umm," she managed a nonsensical, agreeable sound.

He chuckled against her throat. "Might I expect you to purr at any moment, Mrs. Tarrington?"

"More than likely," she grumbled. "You are a demanding devil without conscience."

"Do you find that a problem, my love?"

"Absolutely not," she giggled, turning to kiss his cheek. "However, give me a moment to regain my focus." She paused, weighing her words before speaking. "Yes, Eutaw Springs *is* north of us. As Charleston is one of only two British strongholds left, I have a feeling Gabriel may be housed somewhere in between."

"You have no problem focusing, Kathryn. That was my exact thought. You seem familiar with Jamie's hideaway and …"

With a sharp rap, the door opened. "Good morning," Gabrielle greeted, as Jack stood braced in the doorway grinning.

Jason eyed his daughter, a slow smile spreading. "You certainly have grown up over the past months, poppet. I gather we can expect no more shrieked greetings and I shall miss them."

"Well, I can always change that, poppa." Her eyes twinkled devilishly. "But Uncle Jack and I thought Beau might be sleeping—or perhaps even you, after our long journey. May I?" She reached out and Kathryn placed Beau in her arms.

His belly full and barely awake, as Gabrielle pressed him to her shoulder patting his back, he belched loudly, eyes fluttering open but quickly closing as his thumb found his mouth. Burbling a soft contented sigh, he snuggled into his sister's shoulder.

"He is a little piglet just like I was, or still am now and then," she added, giggling.

"I see nothing wrong with thoroughly indulging oneself upon occasion," Jack chuckled. "Did you sleep well?" he asked, stepping into the room.

The spark of deviltry in their eyes was the answer he expected. Barely hiding a smirk, he cleared his throat. "And what is today's battle plan?"

"I think you and Jason should roust Ted out for breakfast. The later it gets the more people out and about. Gabrielle and I will meet you downstairs with Beau shortly."

"That means clean his bottom first." Gabrielle rolled her eyes, wrinkling her nose.

Jason tousled his daughter's raven curls. "One day you will have your own, poppet, and you will be well trained by then."

Breakfast was a light happy affair, albeit somewhat forced on Kathryn's part. As they were the only customers, they had no wish to pique the innkeeper's curiosity by sharing overly serious conversation. Ted and Smitty joined them shortly, Smitty needing to hug Gabrielle and assure her he would follow soon. *Perhaps more to assure meself, little one.* He wrapped her in another quick hug.

A pale winter sun had yet to lighten the sky as they parted, heading in different directions to make last minute preparations.

With a quick rap, the door opened and Jason peeked in. "Are you decent, my pet? The boys and I are back with the carriage and Beauty, and the innkeeper's wife is packing a lunch basket for us."

"You are amazing, my love. A quick dab of wax and we are done." Putting the final crease in Gabrielle's letter, she smiled at her daughter.

"I wrote it myself, poppa, with almost no help," she said proudly.

Stepping quickly into the room, he lifted her high, swinging her in an arc as she giggled happily. "And who will be the lucky recipient of your mail, poppet?" Setting her down, he crouched to communicate on her eye level.

"Robbie, if they will allow him to have it." Sadness misted her brilliant, blue eyes.

"Cornelius will see to it, my princess. Remember the secret rose?"

She nodded, *remembering*, and blew a kiss to her Uncle Jack as he stepped into the room, followed by Smitty and Ted.

"Will you make sure it gets on the right ship?" Her eyes drifted to Smitty.

"Of course I will. Anything for you, little one. That's whut pals are for."

She threw her arms around him, murmuring 'thanks', and orders to find her soon.

Kathryn tugged her cloak about her and turned to Ted. "I gather you had no trouble in finding employment."

"None, I merely pointed out that my team is mannerly and fully trained. Of course it didn't hurt to flash that gentleman's card, seems he's a regular customer. Besides, when I said I had my first client booked for today, how could he refuse? His wife even offered me an attic room in trade for doing small chores—a bit of good luck there I might add."

"And ..." Jack nudged.

Ted hesitated, blushing. "He also has two lovely young daughters." He glanced at Gabrielle and tousled her hair. "But you, my little pal, will always be my favorite girl."

"Well then, I would say we are ready to find Uncle Jamie. Our bags are packed, Beau is fed and dry-bottomed at least for the moment; shall we be off? Our new life is about to unfold and present itself."

With encouraging words, Ted urged his team to a brisk walk. The pale sun barely peeped over the lowest buildings and the streets were almost empty—their timing perfect.

"We'll let 'em work into the pace. They still have a bit of lingering sea legs and I ..."

"No need for explanations, Ted. Beauty will appreciate the pace too."

At mention of her name, Beauty nickered and drew closer.

Kathryn turned to Jason and Jack, sitting opposite. Foot warmers and lap robes had been supplied with their lunch basket; they rode in comfort. The wind held a wintry chill, and heavy clouds warned of pending changes. But the distance could be covered well before dark if they maintained a brisk pace.

"Does Ted know our destination?" she asked.

"I believe he has a vague idea, my love, but I am sure you have a precise one."

"That I do. I know exactly where Jamie is. It has been a long time, but I remember. It's an old cabin we used to stay in on our trips to Keowee: off the beaten path and well-hidden. With the way vegetation grows around here, I may actually have to search a bit."

"Abandoned?" Jack asked.

"As far as we could determine, but we made any small repairs our time would allow."

"Do you know what happened to the owner?"

"There was a rumor about a man who built it for his fiancée, expecting her to arrive from Kentucky to settle here, but she never made it. Perhaps she changed her mind, or died on the trail. Whatever the reason, he just walked away, never to return."

Gabrielle's eyes were bright with unshed tears. "I know how he felt," she mouthed.

Kathryn easily read the wordless comment in Jason's eyes. Their beloved little girl was growing up too fast, so many mature thoughts running through her head.

"Life presents itself without warning or even a 'by your leave'," she said softly, and both men nodded solemnly.

They stopped to rest the horses and enjoy the delicious basket of bread, cheese, dried meat, and a flask of rum: for warding off the cold. However, after sailing through wintry ocean weather which left hoarfrost clinging to the rigging, this seemed delightful.

"Do you think Uncle Jamie will like me?" Gabrielle abruptly asked, catching both parents off-guard.

"He will adore you, poppet. Why do you ask?"

She stared at her father for a long moment. "I remember some of what happened. But when I ask, you only fill in bits and pieces. I want to understand."

Kathryn looked perplexed. What did her child wish to know, and how to answer? As silence seemed to be all that was forthcoming from Jason and Jack, she forged ahead.

"I believe you *are* old enough now, but that subject requires a great deal of time to discuss, and we are almost there." Taking a deep breath, she gathered her thoughts. "War is an ugly business, little one. It tears apart friends and family and hurts those we love."

"And loving a person deeply, in and of itself, can divide families," Jack added softly.

"Yes," she sighed on a soft exhalation, "Robbie loves me, but his parents hate me."

"They do not hate you, Gabrielle," he declared firmly. "They do not understand you, your parents or *me*, for that matter. We are different, the 'rules' we live by are different. I believe that fact scares them." At her questioning look, he continued. "Think about it for a minute. If *our* lifestyle is the 'right' way, it questions the validity of *their* choices. As they feel their way to be correct, *we are the ones* in the wrong." He reached for her hand, hoping she could fully grasp his meaning.

Jason and Kathryn followed every word, fascinated by his astute logic.

"But Robbie understands," she said softly, searching their faces.

"He does not cast judgment, poppet, an unusual quality in such a young lad. I am confident he will grow to be a good man someday."

Cradling Beau as he sucked his fist noisily, Kathryn started to repack the lunch basket. "We have heard very few of your delightful tales this trip, Ted."

"I know when it is important to listen, missus. But never fear, I will tell a tale or two before we arrive," he said, helping her into the carriage.

Settling herself comfortably, she hugged her daughter and began feeding Beau. Sensing her little girl's disquiet, she smiled sympathetically. "Gabrielle, there will be plenty of time to sort out the last five years. Many new people will be coming into your life. Ask questions and you will receive honest answers. However, always remember: answers are given from each individual's *perception* of what happened." She paused, expecting questions. "Do you understand that word, little one?"

Gabrielle flashed a brilliant smile. "We each judge through our own eyes. Every person sees his own truth, and there will be *some* truth in what each person says."

Kathryn glanced at both men, speechless.

"Anna taught me that long ago. I *will* ask questions and sort out what *I* see as truth."

"And you can help your brother to understand as he gets older."

"Time for one o' my tales," Ted yelled back over his shoulder. "After that bit o' conversation, we need to share a smile or two."

Kathryn had thought to say more, but Ted was right. It was time to smile, a serious venture lay ahead. With that she relaxed, enjoying Ted's light repartee.

As the sun's rays grew longer, Kathryn's leaned forward, searching intently. She had been alert but extremely quiet for some time, a fact that had not gone unnoticed.

"Ted, do you see that dense grouping of shrubs off to your right?" She broke her silence, drawing Jason's immediate interest.

"That I do, missus."

"Watch for a very tight opening. It is denser than I remember, and will be barely wide enough to accommodate us, *but it will.* Pull your team in just off the roadway and stop."

Ted cast a curious glance and nodded. Slowing his team, he searched for an opening.

"I see it now," he said, gently urging his team forward and ducking to shield his face from low hanging branches. Within a few feet a roomy space opened, and he pulled his grays to a stop—close to the road yet well concealed from any passersby.

"Are we here?" He turned a quizzical eye on Kathryn.

"I believe we are." Jason stepped down, extending a hand to his wife.

Placing Beau in his sister's arms, she grabbed the small bag beside her feet and began unbuttoning her riding skirt. Her cape already lay in a crumpled heap on the seat.

Jack eyed Jason, and at his non-committal shrug, remained quiet, both observing.

Kathryn wriggled out of the long garment exposing familiar breeches beneath. Pushing the skirt and cape into her bag, she pulled out her tomahawk, tucked it into her belt and donned a heavy, hip-length vest.

"You look more like my momma, now," Gabrielle applauded excitedly.

Kathryn touched her cheek, and taking Jason's waiting hand, nimbly stepped down.

"I feel alive again," she whispered, kissing his cheek.

Before he could comment, she cupped her mouth, shrilling a unique warbling birdcall. Angling her head, she listened, and then repeated the call. All waited expectantly, eyeing one another. Just as she placed her hands to her mouth again, a similar call answered, paused and answered again.

"Wait here, everyone. I will take Beauty to save time."

Touching Jason's shoulder in a light caress, she released her mare's reins. He felt her tremble, noted the excitement blazing in her eyes, and placing his hand gently over hers stilled it for a moment.

"We *are* home, my Kathryn."

"That we are, my love." They *connected*, shared thoughts cascading in unison for a long moment before she stepped aside.

"Come, my Beauty." Crooning softly, she moved around her, running a knowing hand the length of each leg, checking for sensitivity. Beauty merely snuffled into her hair, nickering, as eager to go as she.

Jason stooped to offer her a leg up, but flashing her widest grin, she flung herself into the saddle in a graceful, fluid motion.

"My God, Kathryn," Jack whistled appreciatively.

"Still our Kathryn, you *have not* lost your edge, my love."

Gabrielle clapped vigorously, causing Beau to gurgle happily. Ted merely sat agape.

Beauty reared pawing the air, before settling into a sidling dance. Shaking her head, mane floating silkily on the light breeze, she set her harness to jingling. As two more birdcalls sounded, Kathryn placed a quieting hand on her withers. "Time for showing off is over, my Beauty." Snorting a final gust of pent up enthusiasm, she stood still.

After answering with two shrill calls, she kissed Jason. "Ten minutes, my love."

"I have *never* seen anything like that." Ted made no attempt to hide his admiration.

"Believe me, Ted. To put it in Smitty's vernacular, you ain't seen nuttin' yet." Jack's eyes shone with pride as he shook his head chuckling.

Kathryn slid to the ground as the cabin door was thrown wide. Even in twilight's dim lighting, and backlit by oil lamps from within, there was no mistaking her brother's robust health. Despite a distinct tightness about the eyes and dark smudges beneath, he appeared hale and hearty.

"Kathryn!" He reached her in three strides and pulled her into a crushing embrace.

"Oh, Jamie." She hugged him tight, kissing him soundly. "We are finally *home*."

"Such music to my ears, lass. I feared you might find polite society a strong pull to …"

"Are ye daft?" She stood back, hands on hips, eyeing him with a crooked grin.

His smile turned devilish as he lowered his face closer to hers. "But then I recalled it was me sweet, ladylike Kathryn, I was thinking of and …"

"I would box yer ears, dear brother, and take ye to task, but I have others waitin' yonder to see if we be welcomed or no."

Jamie's face grew serious, a tear sliding down his cheek, all playful chatter set aside.

"Welcomed? Oh God, Kathryn. Ye are such a sight for sore eyes," he said huskily, pulling her back into his embrace. "I have prayed so hard for your safe arrival, hoping my letters had found you and Hunter. Praying they would bring you directly *here* for I fear time is ..." he gulped. "Hunter, is he well? He *is* here with you."

Kathryn nodded, pleased he had asked for Jason. "We are *all* here: Jason, Gabrielle, Beau and Jack; Ted, a trusted accomplice, and Smitty, our ears in Charleston, who will join us shortly." At Jamie's confused look she added, "There was an *interesting occurrence* shortly after we landed. We will discuss all that and more, but first—I will return in moments." Before he could say another word, she strode to Beauty's side, swung up into the saddle and trotted into the darkening shadows of dense foliage.

"We are *home,* my brother." Jason pulled Jamie into a lion's embrace.

"My God, but ye are strong now, Hunter. Remind me not to anger you. I fear the outcome would be dire—for me," he chortled, turning at a sharp tug on his pant leg.

"I am Gabrielle, Uncle Jamie."

"Although our daughter is a bit shy, I am sure it will pass," Kathryn assured, winking.

Jamie crouched to see his niece better in the lamplight, releasing a startled gasp as he drew her to him, hugging her with a sound kiss.

"I look like my momma, but I have my poppa's black hair and blue eyes," she announced proudly.

"Oh, that is the very truth of it, little one. Ye are as pretty as your momma. I have watched ye for many years, never close enough to see ye well, yet I feel as if I know ye."

As she started to speak, Jamie placed a silencing finger against her lips. "You and I have much to talk of Gabrielle, and I *will* answer all ye ask. Thankfully, we will be seeing much of each other from now on. Aye?"

Her face lit up, eyes sparkling.

"Well, that is if *you* are agreeable to those terms."

"Yes," she answered firmly, head bobbing eagerly. "Oh ... and I have a new baby brother for you to meet." Reaching to take Beau from her mother, she gently placed him in Jamie's outstretched arms. "James Beauregarde Tarrington," she recited slowly and distinctly.

Jamie's eyes widened, searching his sister's smiling face.

"He is named for you and Uncle Jack," Gabrielle explained.

With that, Beau gurgled happily, clasping Jamie's extended finger and holding it.

Jamie grinned at his nephew. "Ye look like your da, but with my Kathryn's coloring. *I am proud* that ye are of my bloodline."

He turned. "Welcome to the family, Jack." Shifting around Beau's wriggling form, he extended his hand. "Sorry ye must be left until last. But I fear ye are neither a bouncing baby boy nor pretty, wee lass, and therefore relegated to the end of the line."

Jack shrugged. "Always a bridesmaid but—alas—never a bride." Catching Kathryn's eye, he winked at his jest, but understanding him all too well, she experienced a momentary pang of sadness.

"Be careful where you mention such as that, Jack," Jamie broke in playfully. "I have a young daughter who would run ye to ground like a hound-chased deer if you allow it."

Jack's color rose, but a brisk rap on the door saved him further embarrassment.

"Meet our friend and carriage driver: Theodore Artemis Oleander." Jason swept him into the room with an exaggerated flourish.

"Call me, Ted." He rolled his eyes. "A name like that means one of two things." He eyed his audience for effect. "Either your parents have grandiose plans for yer future—or they hate you." He gulped laughter, hesitating long enough to add, "I have yet to decide which it is in my case."

Easy laughter rolled around the room as Jason reached for Kathryn's hand and squeezed. "*It will all work out.*" His silent message brought an answering smile.

During the distraction of Ted's banter, Beau directed Jamie's finger into his mouth. He was now sucking insistently, as a look of discomfort spread across his uncle's face.

Kathryn disengaged Beau gently. "Alas, you cannot help, Jamie. That is my chore."

He grinned looking relieved. "Well, at least I can put together a meal for all of you. Of course, I might have need of your help, Gabrielle." Taking her eagerly offered hand, he grabbed an oil lamp and headed for the door. "I have fish in a weir at the edge of the brook, in safe keeping for your arrival. Tell me, young lady, can you catch fish?"

She started to giggle, eyeing Jack and then her father. Even her mother smirked from the far corner of the room where she nursed a ravenous child.

But Jack burst into unreserved laughter; the happiest Kathryn had seen him in a long time. "Tell Uncle Jamie the tale of Eugenie's prized Koi, he will love it."

As the laughter subsided and the door closed behind the two fishermen, Jack wiped tears of joy from his eyes. "Thank you for insisting I come along for the journey. There truly *is* life—after life."

"What do you know for fact?" Jason presented his brother-in-law with a direct question.

Dinner over, Gabrielle and Beau slept soundly in the loft while the adults sat around the table, each with a small cup of rum.

Jamie's eyes drifted to Ted. Kathryn opened her mouth to speak on his behalf, but he shook his head with an understanding smile. "I will check on the horses," he suggested, and tossing back the last of his rum, pushed away from the table.

Ted knew what they were up to, but would never betray them. During their weeks together, he had come to know them and care deeply. He would disavow anything other than a business relationship if ever questioned. He owed them that and more, although they firmly denied obligation on his part. They had made his new life possible; but of greater importance: he treasured their honest, heartfelt friendship, and deep caring.

He thought back, vividly recalling an incident on board ship. Upon introductions, while explaining that he was no more than a carriage hack, angry sparks had flashed in Kathryn's eyes. "*Never* apologize for who you are, Ted. And *never* listen to others who question *your* self-worth, for it is *they* who are lacking." Kathryn's outspoken vehemence had shocked him, but Jason pulled him quietly aside, and shared a painful incident from their past. "Heed my Kathryn," he had advised. "She cares about you and has no wish to see you hurt." *I can be trusted my dear friends. You are more than family to me.*

"Do stay, Ted, if you will," Jason said, interrupting his moments of reverie. Turning to Jamie he added firmly: "He is to be trusted. Perhaps with a basic knowledge of our plans, he can more easily fabricate a believable tale if caught off-guard."

"Yes, poor Smitty was approached by two of Jason's dragoons as he took Beauty to stable her after we landed yesterday morning. They recognized her of course. If not for his fast thinking …"

Jamie gave Ted a long, thoughtful look and refilled his glass. "All right, young man, we shall need a trusted friend to watch our backs. This war is declared over—but *it is not.* Not by a long shot." He tossed back his rum. "The British still hold Savannah and Charleston—as I am sure you have heard by now. Who knows for how long? And the bastard's have my son."

"Sorry, Hunter, I mean no offense to you or the others."

"None taken, Jamie. And we *will* rectify that situation shortly.

"Where is he being held? Have you seen him? Are there others, in the same cell, or adjoining? How many guards? How fares his health?" Kathryn paused for breath.

Jamie rolled his eyes. "One question at a time, Kathryn, have mercy." He turned to Jason. "I fear I have not given you enough credit, Hunter. Ye are a strong and patient man, and glad I am that she is *all yours.*"

Kathryn scowled, scanning the table for something to throw.

"Truce …" He quickly, raised his hands to ward off any flying objects. "In answer to your first question, it is an aged building north of the city on the old Peachtree Road."

"It is as we thought," Kathryn nodded.

"And no, I have not seen him since his capture. I believe there are five others, but not in the same cell, from what I am told."

Kathryn eyed her brother, not sure she liked other prisoners being present. Should they risk freeing them? She must talk to Jason at length, but in private.

"How have you come by this information, Jamie?" Jason asked.

He had been quietly observing, analyzing from a more objective point of view than his wife's. She was too close to the situation to be impartial, despite her incredible abilities. Gabriel had placed himself in danger, saving her life, during the height of war hostilities. Her emotions could easily override sensibility and caution—a risk he would not take. Without a moment's hesitation, she would gladly smash down doors and go in swinging: tomahawk, dirk, whatever it took to bring him home safely.

A daunting task lay before them. Was it possible to free Gabriel without divulging their identities? Ongoing conditions in the war's aftermath, made it imperative that they remain hidden—at least for now. Gazing at his wife's eager face, flushed with excitement, he realized a long night lay ahead. As much as he wanted her at his side on this mission, he must disappoint her, a fact she would not accept easily and requiring utmost diplomacy on his part. But that would come later, in the privacy of their room.

"How have you come by such precise information, Jamie?" he asked again.

Jamie turned a long, steady look towards his brother-in-law.

"Through a most interesting bit of luck—a unique individual to whom several of us owe an incredible debt *for different reasons.*"

All attention riveted on Jamie.

"Captain Samuel Hodges," he stated softly amidst a large room filled with uncommon silence.

Chapter Eight

Plans Set in Motion

"Pssst, Gabriel."

Silence.

"Gabriel," a more insistent whisper.

Shuffling steps approached the heavy, wooden-planked door and stopped. A dirty, blonde head leaned forward and pressed against the metal bars. Clutching the bars with both hands, he rolled his head to one side slowly, eyeing the tall guard.

"What good news?" he rasped. "Or just the usual?"

The low-lying moon, barely visible through the small window in the fieldstone wall, indicated that the hour was late, or extremely early—depending upon one's point of view.

"Well?" he snapped.

"They will arrive any day now," came the terse response, purposely stated softly so as not to awaken the other prisoners. "Your father left a note for them at the inn."

"And how can he be so sure they will sail into Charleston? Or go to that specific inn? Or even bother to return *here,* where discovery could mean their death? *Another* death," he added sarcastically. "They will have heard the news of the war in England by now, far safer to remain there than to risk coming back here. For Christ's sake, Cornwallis surrendered two months ago, and still we fight. Those poor bastards in the other cells were taken at Eutaw Springs well before that and yet they are still here, although the war is declared over. And I ..."

"Are you quite done?" The guard's patience finally gave out on an angry expletive. "You know as well as I, Savannah and Charleston still remain British strongholds, *here,* it will not be over soon."

Gabriel opened his mouth to grumble more but was harshly cut off.

"Listen to me and listen closely. I have not risked *my* neck to have you turn sullen, giving up so close to the end." He reached a large hand through the bars and squeezed a sagging shoulder. "You *know* they will come. But it is a very long journey, the time of year dictating the seas, and winter not always friendly. But quite honestly, Gabriel, do you truly think Kathryn could ever adopt or fit into English society?"

Gabriel actually managed a chuckle at that. "No, she will hate every moment."

"As will Jason. You saw him before he left and noticed the distinct changes."

"You are right, Samuel. But I have been here so long it seems a lifetime. My wife is unwell with this pregnancy and I worry. My father's hands are tied in attempting to free me; they would as gladly kill him for his former position in this war. He was responsible for numerous empty English saddles in many battles. By holding me, they had hoped to lure him in. But that has not happened, and I question my longevity at this point."

"Trust me, you have great value. I will explain it to you some other time."

"But what of my father? The stress he must endure, unable to lift a finger. He does not handle impotence well at all."

"But he *is* handling the situation well, Gabriel, as you must also."

Gabriel dropped his forehead to the cell bars with a soft groan.

"They *will* sail into Charleston, an English favoring harbor, on an *English* ship. They *will* go to that inn because its simplicity always appealed to Kathryn and her brother. The innkeeper *will* recognize her, for who but a blind man could fail to notice the incredible family resemblance?"

Gabriel raised sad eyes and nodded.

"Do not give up on me now when we are so near the end."

"At least I am finally healed, thanks to you. But there is much I wish to hear in an uninterrupted telling someday. Short, secretive bursts of information are difficult to piece together."

"You need know nothing more than: they *will* be here. You will be home before Silver Fox gives birth." He squeezed the young man's shoulder with assurance. "Besides, you will finally meet your cousin, Gabrielle, and her new little brother or sister." He hesitated for a moment smiling proudly. "And *I* will be a godfather."

He abruptly stepped away, leaving Gabriel shaking his head, amazed at how quietly such a big man could move. *Ahh, Hodges, I knew you were a good man the day you helped save their lives.*

It was extremely late as they readied for bed, Kathryn having wanted to set out for the rescue this very night. However, her brother's reasoning had been sound. Far better that Samuel be forewarned and ready for them. And Hamish: of all people to reappear in the guise of a regular messenger to Hodges. He had been but a young lad when he last crossed her path, and she was anxious to see him. Tomorrow night would be the night. She was excited, restless, and unable to think about sleeping.

Jason lay on the wide bed observing his wife, vividly aware of the energy emanating from her in waves, gearing himself for a long night of logical reasoning and ultimately—Kathryn's understanding and acceptance without rancor.

"Do you suppose Banastre put Samuel in a position to help Gabriel?" she asked.

"Of course, my love. He *is* a callous bastard, but he would not see you hurt if it fell within his power to prevent it. However," he winked seductively, "if he crosses our path in the future, he had best not mention how many favors *you* now owe him. For, I fear—grateful or not—I would kill him where he stood." His statement set her to giggling. Now was the time to broach the subject at hand. Patting the bed he urged her to join him.

"Kathryn, you and I must talk."

"I know," she mumbled softly. "You have allowed me to live my fantasy for long enough. You *will not* take me with you tomorrow and I understand, but my disappointment is a bitter pill to swallow. May we at least talk; help me drum the logic into my head?"

He was awestruck. When had she ever failed to realize the full import of any given situation, or fail to step back when absolutely necessary for a successful outcome? This incredibly intuitive woman was his wife. She belonged to him, as he belonged to her. Pulling her against him, he settled her into the warmth of his shoulder with a quick kiss.

"Have I told you recently, my beloved Kathryn, how very deeply I love you?"

"Yes," she whispered. "And I you … always."

Both remained silent for several contemplative moments. Understanding completely, Jason waited for her to voice her thoughts first. She processed decisions by *hearing* their strength or weakness spoken aloud, her final assessment a combination of intuition and the 'hearing' of it.

"You have no intention of confronting Stewart," she stated firmly, breaking her silence.

"No, my love."

"Success in our past was through our visibility."

"Yes."

"But now? Stewart *must not* realize we are alive. He would easily put the puzzle together, understanding Samuel's ulterior motives, especially with Gilson and O'Reilly's input." She grimaced. "Even Beauty must not play a part in the rescue. Although drunk when they saw her, neither is stupid or gullible. All would be lost before it is begun."

Jason nodded but made no comment.

"Stewart would make our presence well known, throwing us into the position of rejoining the British or being declared traitors. War or no war, we ultimately lose. Samuel would be hanged for his kindness to Gabriel, and I, most likely forced to watch my nephew's execution to prove my loyalty." She shook her head sadly. "Ahh, what an evil web has been spun."

"Yes, my pet, you are right on target; that is the crux of the matter."

She eyed him knowingly. "No, my love, this 'maneuver' must involve Jack."

He nodded, eyebrows rising. *When has she ever failed to grasp any situation?*

"Jack's only purpose during the war was to 'attend' without question: in the beginning to *your* needs—and later to *ours*. It is time for him to discover his true self."

Jason held her, hugging her close, listening as she sorted things out.

"We must continue pushing him to make decisions and participate. He is intelligent, loyal, exceptionally capable and a dear friend to us both. Eugenie hurt him deeply, trying her best to destroy his self-worth." She paused, deep in thought. "Perhaps that was for the best, he *survived*, growing and becoming stronger. That is what life is all about."

"Kathryn ..."

"No," she made a silencing gesture. "No need for further discussion, my love. Although the situation does not make me happy, I understand and agree. However, I shall more than likely pace until you and Jack and Gabriel return safely."

"I shall feel that a most important part of me is missing and ..." he began.

"Well then," she bent low to nip his ear and purred seductively, "you had best start soothing my *deeply hurt* feelings." Flashing a wide grin, she rolled astride his muscular form.

"I believe it is *I* who has the appropriate penance to justify your forgiveness, my love." In an abrupt practiced motion, he moved atop her taking control, and with a contented groan, ended any further discussion.

"Well, I see ye have finally deemed it time to join us," Jamie chuckled, eyeing them with a knowing look. "Gabrielle has such excellent command with the sugar teat; I doubt young Beau has even missed you."

They sat around the big table finishing their breakfast and smiling at the latecomers. Jamie quickly placed well-laden plates and steaming cups of coffee on the table, gesturing them to 'sit and enjoy'.

"Where is Ted?" Kathryn asked.

"He left before dawn," Jamie replied. "He felt it best to be far from here before daylight. The lad has a good head on his shoulders, if you ask me."

"He will bring Smitty back in a few days," Gabrielle chirped, clapping happily.

Catching Kathryn's quizzical look, Jack explained. "When we have Gabriel safely back here, it will be necessary to 'lay low' for a few days. In the aftermath, if Gilson and O'Reilly decide Smitty's story unlikely, and attempt to find and question ..."

"He must be long gone," Jason interjected. "Smitty is excellent in a fight; it would be best to have him right here with us."

"As Ted is virtually unknown, he will raise far less suspicion as our liaison. He also has the useful knack of appearing to pay little heed when, much to the contrary, he is highly alert," Kathryn murmured as she pulled Beau onto her lap.

Eyeing his sister's bare breast somewhat uneasily, Jamie announced tersely, "Hamish will arrive shortly."

"And he has never seen a bare breast before?" Kathryn gave her brother a long look.

"Not one near so nice, lass. Let us not send him home feeling bereft at his loss."

Hamish arrived within the hour, a strapping, well-built young man with no lingering traces of his former youthful awkwardness. Kathryn wrapped him in a welcoming embrace amidst garbled words of greeting cascading around them.

"I owe ye thanks for me life twice over," he said, eyeing her with heartfelt sincerity.

Kathryn smiled, recalling both instances as if they had occurred just recently.

"Are ye trying to rile me, ye feisty sprat?" Jamie demanded, feigning indignation, and causing Hamish to color for having brought up a sore spot.

"All is over and done," Jason interjected. "The past *is* the past. We are all on the same side now." Clapping the young man on the back, he pulled him into a bear hug.

Jack introduced himself next, greeting Hamish with a hearty welcome, followed by Gabrielle who took it upon herself to bring her brother into the conversation. Glancing around the room at her men-folk sharing camaraderie, reinforced the fact that they had truly *come home.* And Kathryn felt blessed.

Although Hamish did not stay long, as arrangements with Hodges needed to be finalized, he took time to provide a curious piece to the puzzle, explaining the ruse which had allowed him an occasional visit to Samuel to pass on important information.

"Maggie," he softly explained. "Maggie is the key."

At mention of her name, Kathryn's thoughts drifted back to Hodges's kindhearted lady friend who had welcomed them into her home for a brief respite many months ago.

"Is she here?" Jason asked.

"Nearby," he said. "Yet far enough away for safety. I am allowed to visit Samuel under the guise of bringing messages from my mother—to my *stepfather.*"

Kathryn's eyes widened. "How much truth is there in that statement?"

"There is *some* truth in any statement; but allow Hodges to tell you the details. I must be on my way. Tonight, when I return with word from Samuel, we will coordinate the final plans." With a curt nod, and wink to Gabrielle, he spun on his heel and left.

It would be a long day: none of them handled inertia well. Gabrielle entertained her baby brother while the adults talked and talked, most of their conversation of little interest as it revolved around their ocean voyage. Having experienced that first hand, she blocked the words; preferring to shower attention on Beau, playing clever games to amuse him.

Kathryn and Jason shared their unusual meeting with John Paul Jones, much to Jamie's delight. He easily recalled their youthful adventures and shared deviltry, experiencing a fleeting moment of nostalgia. "So long ago, sis, and yet I see it vividly."

"He knew who we were, Jamie; that was obvious. Yet he made not the slightest indication. I am still curious over that. He could have claimed our capture for personal glory but did not. However, he *did* request that when we saw you, we were to ask two very specific questions."

"And just what might those be, Hunter? For I have no answer, nor understand John Paul's reaction to you both, though he is known to harbor respect for courageous loyalty—no matter which side of a cause. He is a somewhat unique individual."

Jason smiled wryly. "He also asked if you remember what happened in Mr. Craik's summer house."

At that, Jamie burst out laughing. "How could I ever forget? John Paul's father was a noted landscaper, hired by Mr. Craik to beautify his estate. He was so obsessed with balance and uniformity, he near to drove us both crazy." He paused, remembering. "A common thief was once caught and held in one of the two small summer houses that sat on either side of the driveway. That left one empty; John Paul's da immediately imprisoned *him* in the other one, for the sake of 'balance'. And no amount of yelling on his part got him freed any sooner than the thief."

Catching that story, Gabrielle giggled. "You see, lass," Jamie said attempting to sound serious, "you knowing about that bit of foolishness makes your parents' punishments seem all the more proper."

He turned back to Jason. "The second question is?"

"Do you still read MacPherson?"

"But of course—as do all of you, I suspect." Winking at his sister, he reached to the top of the small bookshelf and handed her the well-worn little book of poetry. "I imagine John Paul also made mention of Phillis Wheatley."

At their looks of amazement, he smiled. "Well, that must be a topic for another time. Gabrielle and I have dinner to catch. You three amuse yourselves anyway you see fit. However, some of us around here have work to do." Taking her small hand, he grabbed two rods and an empty bucket and guided her out the back door.

With the long shadows of dusk, Hamish reappeared. Supper was quickly dispensed with: the moment had arrived. Gabrielle, aware that important details needed to be discussed, headed up stairs to the loft with Beau.

Jamie wiped his mouth and stood. Resting both hands on the back of his chair, he announced: "I have no wish to be a part of the planning. I fear I cannot be unbiased if there is need. *You* will have far better knowledge of how the English think and react, Hunter and …" he trailed into silence.

Kathryn stared at her brother, taken aback, but realized he was right, a brave admission on his part.

"How about a bedtime tale, Gabrielle?" Jamie sat down on the top step and placed his arm around her slender shoulders.

"Oh, yes." Her eyes lit up. "I wish I were older, Uncle Jamie. Then I could be of help."

"*You* are doing what must be done, little one. You know, sometimes the smallest jobs—the ones that seem not to matter—actually *are* the ones of greatest importance."

Kathryn pushed her chair back quietly and stood, unsure, well aware that she played no part in this.

"Kathryn, please stay." Jason held out his hand. "Your input is sorely needed. You have the innate ability to often see a clear solution amidst the *unobvious.*"

"You know this area like the back of your hand, Kathryn. You have said so in the past, and proven it many times over," Jack added firmly. "We need your input."

"But Hamish is going with you and ..." she trailed off, fighting to keep her disappointment from showing.

"No, my love, he only goes as far as the 'split' that leads south to Keowee. He will wait there for our return. When we have Gabriel safely in *our* hands, he will ride south and carry the good news to Silver Fox and Anna."

"*We* will then come directly here, and wait for any furor we stirred up to die down, before taking your nephew home," Jack said, signaling her to take a seat.

Noting strength and confidence in Jack's attitude, she sat down, grateful to be included, pleased that she and Jason had made the right decision.

Within a matter of minutes it became apparent from Hamish's details that all was in readiness on Samuel's end. Putting their heads together, they went over their plan in careful detail, agreeing on alternate possibilities if the need arose.

When all discussion came to a mutual halt, Jason stood slowly. Reaching for Kathryn's hand, he pulled her into his embrace, whispering words for her hearing only.

Jack's look showed obvious disappointment as she hugged him. It struck her suddenly: he and Jason were equally unhappy at having to leave her out of this 'battle'. With that realization she forced a stoic smile. "God go with both of you. Return to me safely with my nephew."

Jason stopped her, his eyes intense. "I shall not leave ..."

Tears glistening, sensing an urgent need, she placed her hand against her heart and began their *salute.*

"Always," he whispered.

"Always," she assured.

And with a final embrace, he was gone.

Kathryn paced as Jamie eyed her quizzically.

"How many pairs of boots have ye worn out in the last few years, lass?"

She spun on him scowling, but quickly repented. "Too many," she confessed. "Especially at the cost of good leather."

"Come, sit down," he said softly, holding out his hand.

"No matter what the outcome tonight, I am beholding to both Hunter and Jack, for the danger they have willingly shouldered to help my son. But especially to you, Kathryn, for *allowing*, despite the necessity that ye must sit on the sidelines and not take part."

Taking his hand, she rested her head on his shoulder. They sat amiably side by side on a small settee—very old and well worn, yet comfortable.

"I *do* understand, Kathryn, 'tis a feeling akin to abandonment, is it not?"

Her eyes met his, glistening with unshed tears.

"*I* am also a MacLean, if ye may recall. Need I go into a lengthy explanation?"

At that she could not conceal a grin. "Ahh, the burdens we share, my dear brother."

Abruptly, Jamie's features became serious and pained. "On more than one occasion I actually *did* approach Nathanael Greene to help me with Gabriel's release. After all, I fought side by side with him; I felt I had served him well and that he …"

Shaking his head, he stood up and walked to a cabinet. Filling two glasses with amber liquid, he returned and sat beside her.

"Here's to tonight's success." He took a long swallow and Kathryn matched him. "It matters not what I expected of *him*—he abides only by his own agenda. He's here in Charleston, stirring up a bit of trouble now and then, and intends to remain until the peace treaty is signed—and proven to *him* personally. Apparently rescuing Gabriel would risk raising his visibility and be inconvenient, it was not a covert enough plot."

"In a few hours it will all be over, Jamie. It *will* go well."

He pursed his lips, giving her a long look. "Aye, that it will. But Greene is a troubling sort. When we talked, he suddenly asked me if it were true—the rumors of your death, you know. And *glad* he was of your demise. When he realized the callousness of his statement, although I could see by his expression he had no real concern, he gave me a long look and said: 'Ahh, but she was a traitor, sister or no. You would have taken her down yourself if the opportunity had been present, aye?' "

Jamie slugged the last of his drink and wiped his mouth on his sleeve. "Do you have any idea, Kathryn, of how difficult it was *not* to scream the truth to that bastard, as I joyfully slit his throat?"

Shortly before dawn, Kathryn roused from a troubled sleep, an unaccustomed noise having startled her. Suddenly it came again: the snapping of a twig. With dirk in one hand and tomahawk in the other she edged towards the door, only to be met by Jamie.

"I have checked the back, sis. All is as it should be. They are coming to the front." He lifted the latch quietly.

Before she could form a retort, the door opened and Gabriel stepped into the room, terribly thin, apparent even in the light of a dying moon, but very much alive.

"Gabriel," she murmured with relief, as Jamie wrapped his son in an iron embrace, weeping unashamedly.

Where was Jason? Jack? She peered into the darkness, panic rising. Abruptly, strong arms pulled her into a bear hug, an insistent mouth capturing hers.

"Jason," she gasped, tears streaming, "Jason."

Leaning back, he pulled Jack into the cabin. "Jack was indispensable, actually saved Hodges's back."

"Jack, thank God, you must tell me everything." She hugged him close, instantly concerned by warm stickiness on his cheek.

"Merely a scratch," he laughed, taking her hand. "You may tend it later if you like, but there is someone who has worried about you for months."

With that introduction, Samuel Hodges stepped into the room, pulling the door closed behind him.

"My 'Lady Kathryn', you are a sight for sore eyes. If it would cause no offense, might I hug you?" He eyed the men and at their smiles, turned to Kathryn.

She welcomed him into her arms, murmuring, "We can never thank you enough. I …"

"The look on your face, milady, and theirs …" Bending down, he placed a kiss on her forehead, immediately followed by a flush of color as he stepped back, self conscious.

"It is my turn," Gabriel insisted, pulling her against him. "Oh, Kathryn ..."

They both dissolved into tears.

"Welcome home, Gabriel," a small voice piped up.

All heads turned. Gabrielle sat on the top step of the loft stairs, holding her baby brother. Mouthing prayers of thanks, she had quietly observed the homecoming with Beau, who happily entertained himself—sucking on his sister's thick braid.

Suddenly she stood up and blew kisses to everyone below. "You all look so tired," she said softly. "I will wait until later to hear the story."

"Out of the mouths of babes," Kathryn commented, scanning the men's exhausted faces. "Everyone get some sleep, there will be plenty of time to share details when you are rested. Depending on the amount of objection aroused by Gabriel's release, we may have several days to get to know one another better. And I, for one, want to hear it *all*."

Relaxation rested more easily on the shoulders of all concerned when they gathered for a late breakfast, early that afternoon. Their mission successfully accomplished nothing more could be done until the furor died, and there would be that. Stewart's indignation and embarrassment at being duped by Hodges—especially as he prided himself in being a good judge of character—would become widely known, producing deadly repercussions. In Jamie's hideaway, they were safe, at least for a few days.

Kathryn sat sponging Jack's forehead, plying him with her famous willow bark tea.

"It is nothing, Kathryn," he grumbled, but loved the attention.

Hodges held his godson, thrilled and proud at the honor. "He is *so perfect*, Kathryn. I imagine this is the way I will feel when I hold my own child."

"Well, gentlemen, I cannot wait any longer. What happened?" Kathryn asked.

Bit by bit, their story of the previous night unfolded.

"There are not many details, Kathryn," Hodges said. "Gabriel and I were ready, his cell unlocked and Gabriel armed with my extra pistol. I believe suspicion had begun to arise. However, we did not give Stewart time to think it through and post extra guards."

"Input from Gilson and O'Reilly?" Kathryn asked.

Hodges nodded. "There is no way of being sure, but having known them for years, I believe they would not have helped in Gabriel's escape, and will likely be horrified when they learn the truth—their British sense of duty overriding caring for both of you."

"By now, I expect they are back in Charleston looking for Smitty," Jack commented.

At Kathryn's concerned look, he shook his head. "Do not worry about Smitty. He knows how to handle himself. We talked at length and both agree: once Gilson and O'Reilly sober up, they will realize his story was bogus. I would *never* give up your beloved Beauty—especially not in a hand of cards."

"By now, Stewart has sent them to Charleston with orders to find Smitty and bring him in for questioning," Jason said, joining the conversation.

Jack took a swig of his drink. "Smitty is smart. He will lie low until he can leave without raising eyebrows. Ted is dropping him here shortly, but will immediately return to the city under cover of darkness. They are using a roundabout route, but should be here tonight."

Hodges picked up the story. "Jason and Jack came in so quietly they startled me. We rushed Gabriel out and got him onto my big charger. All was well until the prisoner in the next cell set up a commotion that brought guards on the run."

"Hell, that rebel bastard was supposedly on my side," Gabriel growled, breaking his silence. "He resented my being the only one freed and sought possible 'reward' for sounding an alarm."

"There is little more to tell." Hodges wrapped up the remaining details. "Jack took down the first guard to arrive on the scene, giving me time to get Gabriel away. He and Jason stalled, taking two more guards down, before meeting us at the 'split'."

"Thankfully timing was in our favor. Had we waited one more day, Gilson and O'Reilly would have presented a different picture to Stewart." Kathryn sighed, turning to her husband. "Although you and I were not seen together, it will only be a matter of time before niggling suspicion becomes reality, my love. It is good that we head to Keowee shortly. With distance and no further sightings, we should be able to buy time."

"Do not be concerned about Nathanael Greene setting his cap to be a hero. "By the time suspicions filter down to him, we will be long gone," Jamie assured.

"Samuel, how did you happen to be sent here from Gloucester Point?" Kathryn asked, voicing a nagging question.

His steady look and crooked grin was all she needed to know.

"Would you care for details, 'Lady Kathryn'?" He hesitated and at her low chuckle began. "Tarleton was truly concerned. He made arrangements to transfer me to Rawdon and ultimately Alexander Stewart. As a Loyalist, it made sense for me to head homeward and bypass the surrendering process. But he also placed me in a position to be of help to Gabriel, the means by which left up to me—and that, I did."

"Quite cleverly, I might add, but I would hie thee to the hills in haste, Hodges, if you ever see Stewart again," Gabriel said.

"Just as I had thought, my Kathryn; but hopefully Banastre has returned to England by now."

"That he has," Samuel said. "From what he indicated, he intends to write his memoirs. However, on a serious note, had he not intervened, Gabriel would not be with us today. Strangers who assist—not necessarily seeking reward—astound me. Occasionally, a given situation also dictates direction. I am a good example. As a Loyalist my lands have been seized; all that I once had—gone."

"And Maggie stepped in," Kathryn murmured, "carrying messages and playing mother to Hamish."

Samuel gave her a long look, nodding. "Yes, Maggie and I are married and expecting a baby any moment. She will be relieved to know I am safe."

"And Hamish will carry the news?"

"Yes, after he visits Silver Fox. Hopefully news of her husband's well-being will bring relief and improved health."

"We head there next and you are welcome to come, but …"

"Thank you, Kathryn, but I will go home to my Maggie. I miss her sorely and wish to be there for the new babe's arrival. We have a small place not far from Jamie's farm. We will see you both when you come north again. Maggie is eager to get to know you, and by then we will have the newest Hodges member to introduce."

"We look forward to that visit and many more, Samuel. A new life awaits us *all*."

"We shall go in different directions, in smaller numbers," Jamie spoke up. "Stewart may not let this drop. Being made to look foolish *will not* be taken lightly."

"How long dare we remain here? Are we safe?" Kathryn asked.

A slow grin crept across her brother's face. "Now that ye have *finally* chosen the correct side, ye will find many new friends appearing out of nowhere."

"Yes, is your answer, I gather," she growled.

"Aye, and *you*, James—such an uncomplaining and patient man while you waited for us to come to our senses." Jason laughed, his lilted Scottish burr causing Jamie to shake his head appreciatively.

With all the 'telling' done, they settled into light talk to while away the hours. Eventually light banter ceased, replaced by quiet anxiety as they awaited Smitty's arrival.

Jamie eyed the silent group, the tension so thick it could be cut with a knife. Taking Gabrielle's hand, he sat her down—not part of the group—yet well within their hearing.

"Mistress Gabrielle, you and I have done much talking while fishing, have we not?"

Gabrielle studied him with sparkling eyes. This uncle was filled with a bit of deviltry, different from Uncle Jack, yet she liked him, not a disappointment in any way. "Yes," she answered softly, wondering what mischief he was up to now.

"I have been a great help in your education, have I not? We talked of the highland darters that will hatch from wee, slimy things in the spring and …"

"Dragonflies." she nodded.

"At dusk, the sky becomes a certain color gray. Might ye know its proper name?"

She shook her head.

"Why, that be called 'groglin gray'," he answered smartly.

"Groglin gray?" she exclaimed, scrunching her nose, and eyeing him with disbelief.

Kathryn stiffened, knowing exactly what was coming next, yet unable to stop it.

"Why, little lass, yer education be lacking fer sure. Groglin gray is, of course …" he paused for emphasis, "the exact color of a she mouse's fart." Chortling gleefully, he watched proudly as his niece burst into uncontrolled fits of giggles.

Hearing the warning scrape of a chair, he turned to meet his sister's icy glare. "Have ye taught yer daughter nothing, dear sister?"

All heads turned as *both* Kathryn and Jamie burst into laughter.

"Now I suppose you will feel it necessary to teach her to …" She stopped abruptly, hoping she had not put the thought in his head. But the answering glint in his eyes announced it was too late.

Jamie extended his finger towards his niece.

"James Douglas MacLean, *do not* …" Kathryn warned.

"Pull my finger, lass." He ignored his sister. "T'is a bit o' magic."

Gabrielle, unsure of the outcome, but knowing it would be funny, gave a stout yank.

A resounding fart set her into fits of giggles, hiccupping hysterically into her cupped hand, tears rolling down both cheeks.

For a moment the adults struggled to maintain decorum, but quickly gave in to raucous laughter, enjoying themselves—any lingering shreds of tension finally gone.

"Well now," Kathryn said lightly, eyeing her brother sternly, "Although I *do* find male preoccupation with flatulence a somewhat amusing curiosity, I doubt that particular bit of education was included in Dame Agatha's schooling of our daughter in England."

Another round of laughter echoed in the cabin.

"I fear we had best head south soon, before my brother destroys all possibility of instilling delicate manners in our child." Tears of laughter rolled down Kathryn's cheeks, negating her prim declaration and setting everyone to laughing.

"You *must* show Smitty and Ted, Uncle Jamie. Promise me you will."

"Aye, lass, that I will," he chuckled, glancing at his sister, who merely rolled her eyes.

As Jamie placed a heaping plate of roasted rabbit on the table, a shrill whistle erupted once—and in a few seconds—sounded again.

"My God, Kathryn, did you teach them nothing?" They could be shot for mimicking the sound of the magical filli-loo bird."

"Jamie," she snapped, rising to go to the door, accompanied by Jason and Jack.

"What is a filli-loo bird?" Gabrielle arched a puzzled brow.

"Oh, very magical he is lass, and one of a kind. He sticks his head in the sand and whistles out his …"

"Jamie," Kathryn snarled. "Enough lessons for one day! Do you hear me?"

He smiled serenely, the picture of innocence, and nodded agreeably. "Further lessons will wait for another day." With that pledge, he winked at Gabrielle and opened the door.

Within seconds, soft curses erupted near at hand.

"Me arse is so sore, Ted. Was there truly a need to see so much of the countryside?" Smitty limped into view, leading his horse. "Agreeable beast, but a back, so bony …"

"Hush up, Smitty. I got you here, didn't I?"

"And just in time," Jason beckoned them in. "Dinner is on the table, and by now Gilson and O'Reilly are searching every nook and cranny for you."

"Smitty! Ted!" Having placed pillows on either side of her, she patted the bench indicating they both sit.

Dinner was delicious, restful, filled with chitchat and camaraderie, but over too soon. While Smitty's horse was brushed down and fed, Ted caught up on important news. Keowee was their next destination. He had no idea where that was, but could find it in a hurry if necessary.

He would be their eyes and ears in the city; no one could connect them *personally* in any way. Hiring his carriage to leave Charleston had been purely a business deal, and he never divulged details of former clients. Even Captain Farthingale would deny all knowledge of their identity, they were in safe hands.

With hugs all around, he mounted his horse. As he nudged the animal towards the hidden path, Gabrielle stepped to his side.

"Ted, will you …?"

"I *will* watch for letters from England and …" He leaned down to kiss the top of her head and tousle her riotous curls. "And I *will* watch for Robbie."

With a slap of reins, he clucked to his horse and disappeared into the darkness.

Chapter Nine

"Run Them to Ground!"

"Well?" Gilson demanded. "What did you find out?"

O'Reilly's chin jutted defiantly. "Do *not* use that tone of voice, Gilson—as if *I* was the one derelict in my duties. For God's sake, *neither* of us should be considered derelict. After all, we had a weekend pass, supposedly ours to do with as we pleased."

Sergeant Gilson gave him a long look, softening his tone. "If we had been less drunk, we might have questioned that little man further. We both know Lieutenant Jackson would *never* have given up Kathryn's mare under any circumstances. Besides, with his terrible luck, he would not have risked losing her in a card game."

O'Reilly nodded. "But where is the little bastard now? And where is Beauty? And why is it that nobody remembers either of them?"

"Even sober, I find too many possibilities to come up with easy answers. Is Jackson here? Does he have Gabrielle? Where did he disappear to? And if he has returned—why?"

"Damned if I know; but why would he deliberately stay out of sight? We hold both Charleston and Savannah; there would be no threat to him here."

"We could debate this all day long, O'Reilly. Jackson poses no threat either, unless he has in mind to rescue Kathryn's nephew. But why would he do that? To what purpose? Both she and the colonel are dead." He paused for a moment's reflection. "Let's report back to Stewart. Maybe he will have thoughts about the situation by now."

"I doubt that. Hodges seemed befuddled when I ran the scenario by him after we returned. He was closer to Jackson than you or I. If he is unaware, I fail to see why ..."

With a shrug, the two mounted their horses and headed back to camp.

"Goddamn it! What the hell happened here?" Alexander Stewart thundered his face suffusing deep beet red in frustrated rage.

Sergeants Gilson and O'Reilly stood at attention, painfully aware they were in serious trouble. Any accusations as far as they were concerned, were unjust and undeserved.

"Our most valuable prisoner: *gone*. Sergeant Hodges: *gone*. He was beside himself. "Why was MacLean released, but not the others? Are not all of them rebels?"

Both officers wished they could disappear into thin air. In Stewart's frame of mind he might shoot them where they stood, foregoing the time and length of rope for a hanging.

"I spoke with the prisoner in the next cell. Despite the dim light, he was able to give me a brief description of the two men," Gilson began.

"And?" Stewart prodded rudely.

"He was asleep, and if not a light sleeper by his own admission, might not have awakened. There was no apparent scuffle. Hodges appeared to be expecting them and *helped*, rather than trying to thwart the rescue."

"What did they look like? Was this Lieutenant Jackson one of them?"

"Both men were tall, dressed in colonial attire. One had loosely clubbed blonde hair, perhaps Jackson. It sounded a bit like him."

"And the other?"

Gilson cleared his throat, hedging, color rising to his cheeks.

Stewart stood abruptly, moved around his desk, stopping directly in front of him. Exactly Gilson's height but stockier, his anger radiated in virulent waves. Bringing his face to within inches of the nervous sergeant's, he demanded, "What of the other?"

"Therein lies a bit of confusion, sir," Gilson managed, swallowing convulsively.

Stewart skewered him with an acid glare.

"He was tall ..."

"You already stated that!"

"Dressed as a colonial and ..."

"Get to something I *do not* already know," he growled.

"The prisoner said that the few hushed words he spoke had a British accent."

Stewart backed off a step, deep in thought. "What did he say?"

"Apparently words of greeting to MacLean."

"Did anyone get a glimpse of his face?"

"Not clearly but ..." he hesitated, uneasy with what he had to relate. "He possessed angular good looks, a well-muscled frame and exacting control. The prisoner's description almost fits that of Colonel Tarrington," he finished, shifting uneasily.

Stewart's eyebrows shot upwards. "Are you suggesting perhaps a *ghost*?"

"I do not know *what* I am suggesting, sir." Gilson winced, uncomfortable and edgy.

"Might Colonel Tarrington have lived?" Stewart stroked his chin, deep in thought.

O'Reilly broke his silence. "If it was the colonel, why would he help MacLean escape? Unless Kathryn still lives and ..." Speechless at the thought, his heart skipped a beat.

"I *do not* believe in ghosts," Stewart stated firmly. "But I *do believe* in miraculous healing—even under appalling conditions—and allegedly trusted officers who protect by partial omission of the truth."

He scowled openly. "I felt Captain Hodges to be dedicated and loyal ..."

"Obviously not in this instance, sir," Gilson said. "I, too, believed in him completely."

"You are wrong, Sergeant Gilson. Captain Hodges is *exactly* the dedicated type I mentioned. But in this instance, not loyal to me *or* to *our* cause—but rather to that of another: perhaps Colonel Tarrington?"

Gilson and O'Reilly stared blankly.

Stewart strode back to his desk and sat down. Folding his hands, he pierced each officer with an unforgiving icy stare: first Gilson and then O'Reilly.

"Find him," he growled. "If it truly was Lieutenant Jackson and Colonel Tarrington, I will hang them as traitors despite their impeccable pasts. But *I will* know the truth of this incident. You two, now have a chance to redeem yourselves."

Gilson was affronted. *Redeem ourselves for doing what?* But he dared not voice that thought, or make eye contact with O'Reilly lest his features betray him.

"Get to the crux of this fiasco. Do *not* return without answers *and* the traitors, or you will live only long enough to regret it. Do I make myself absolutely clear?" he snarled.

With smart salutes, Gilson and O'Reilly backed from the room.

"Sweet Jesus," O'Reilly muttered as they headed for the stable. "If the colonel *is* alive and maybe Kathryn, what will …? I mean, how can we bring them back as traitors?"

"Get ready to ride, O'Reilly, and keep your thoughts to yourself," Gilson barked.

"But …"

"I am going say this *once only.* If it comes down to *them* or me—I *will* save myself. You may do as you see fit. But if I have to take you down too, *I will.*"

O'Reilly gulped, giving Gilson a long look.

"Nothing personal, O'Reilly, and no hard feelings. Do we have an understanding?" He turned a stony face on his former 'pal'.

Speechless, O'Reilly nodded dumbly. Numerous disconcerting thoughts swirled in his head. He wished he had never gone into Charleston that weekend, gotten drunk with Gilson, never seen that odd little man—and *never* seen Beauty.

O'Reilly sat astride his patient charger, watching Gilson make final adjustments to his cinch strap and re-check the saddle bags. They had packed enough provisions to last several days—weeks actually, if they were frugal and hunted along the way—well prepared to travel fast and far if need be. During the time taken to prepare—time in which he attempted to calm himself and reassess—he felt no better about Gilson's statements. *Gilson never used to think like this. For God sakes, Kathryn tended his wounds and cared for him after …*

"What are you thinking?" Gilson growled, swinging up into his saddle. Eyeing his partner caustically, he added, "Your mind is miles away and I *do not* care for the lack of conviction I see in your face."

"What if," he gulped, "by some miracle they lived? I never saw them up close, and I hear it was pretty gruesome. But what if …?"

"Make your point, O'Reilly, we are losing daylight."

Shrugging, he went silent. Discussion would not solve this; better to say nothing.

Gilson scowled, ignoring him, but suddenly skewered him with an icy look and terse question. "Where would *you* go to hide once you rescued your nephew?"

"Take him back to his wife; back to her people. Gabriel MacLean is married to a Cherokee girl; Soaring Eagle's daughter, Silver Fox, if memory serves me."

"Well now, I *am* impressed, O'Reilly. I never paid much attention to that part of Kathryn's life. They would most likely head for Keowee."

Kicking his horse sharply, he headed off at a canter. Gesturing sharply for O'Reilly to follow, he yelled: "Let's find Anna. She'll have answers."

"You dumb bastard, Gilson, I was just about to tell you—Anna will *never* give them up, nor will the Cherokees for that matter. We might as well shoot ourselves now and get it over," he muttered. Gilson had picked up speed, leaving him much farther behind.

O'Reilly urged his horse into a canter. Gilson's attitude distressed him. *He's out for blood. Why? I doubt Stewart would actually have us hanged. Is he embarrassed or covering feelings of guilt? What ever will I do if we find them alive?*

The war was over, but in truth—it *was not.* Perhaps he still owed allegiance to Alexander Stewart and the British cause until dismissed and sent home. But did he owe anything beyond that? His mind clicked repetitively: a kaleidoscope of debatable questions. Could he bring himself to take part in capturing Kathryn and the colonel and Jack, if they found them alive? *Gilson has named them traitors—but I cannot.*

Kneeing his horse sharply, he pulled abreast of Gilson, matching his horse's gait—maintaining complete silence. *I hope we do not find them or I will have to make a serious decision and I …*

He quickly dropped the thought, emptied his mind and focused on the narrow trail.

Chapter Ten

Time to be Away

Two days later, they packed their few belongings and tidied the cabin. Dusk had fallen, time to be away. They would ride under cover of darkness, until they put distance between them and Charleston. Jamie had disappeared for several hours earlier in the day, returning mid-afternoon with two horses, saying only: "I told ye I have friends."

As they mounted to leave, Jamie pulled abreast of Jason. "I wish I could have brought that black devil of yours for *his* sake, certainly not ours. When you return to the farm, I demand you ride him hard and restore some manners to the beast. He nipped me arse more than once, ungrateful bastard that he is."

"I will take that under advisement, brother." Jason gripped his brother-in-law's hand tightly, bidding him 'goodbye'. Jamie was heading to his farm in Georgetown. He had been away too long and duty called: a terse explanation to avoid thinking.

Hamish galloped in at the last minute to accompany Jamie, especially as Hodges would be traveling with them part way. It had been Jamie who had initially brought them together, part of his plan to heal and rescue Gabriel. Through long weeks, several risky visits and working together in absolute secrecy, he had come to like and respect Hodges. This would be a chance to get to know him better.

Hamish had kept his eyes and ears open as he headed north to the cabin. Stopping at a small pub the previous evening, he settled into a quiet corner with a pint of ale, and blending into the shadows, listened carefully to the excited buzz. "As we are about to go our separate ways, let me touch lightly upon what I heard." He glanced around making sure he had their attention.

"Alexander Stewart is on a tear. Being informed that both the 'odd, little man' and Beauty had disappeared without a trace, fanned the flames of his fury and raised more questions. Had they actually existed, other than in the besotted minds of his sergeants?"

"Gilson even approached the ship's captain about Beauty. However Farthingale, furious at being delayed as he prepared to set sail, was uncooperative. Apparently he claimed that *all* horses looked alike to him, and Gilson could either get off his ship or get ready to climb the rigging. I find that last bit highly amusing."

"To sum it up, Stewart blames this debacle on Gilson and O'Reilly's drunkenness. But conjuring up ghosts from their past is the least of it. If they actually saw what they claimed, and failed to follow through with immediate action … That offense has him ready to hang them both—and not surprisingly," he winked at Hodges. "Stewart is incensed by your betrayal, no matter what your reason, he wants you brought in."

"He believed me to be entirely loyal; and having come to know the man, he *will not* take this lightly." Hodges shrugged, unconcerned. "As I am headed north and will travel part of the way with you and Jamie, we can watch each other's back."

"Neither Gilson nor O'Reilly are stupid," Kathryn said hesitantly. "I worry …"

"They *will* eventually figure it out," Jason commented. "We shall move quickly and remain alert. With any luck, we will be far from here before any organized search is formed. Their confusion and ineptitude plays to our side."

Hamish turned to Gabriel and clasped his hand firmly. "Silver Fox sends her love. Both she and your two little ones are well, and eagerly await your arrival. Until we meet again, dear friend ..."

He then turned a wide grin on the captain. "And Samuel," your Maggie looks forward to your return. I am not sure why she misses your scruffy countenance but ..." He ducked as Hodges aimed a playful jab.

Hamish eyed each, smiling. "Unless I have forgotten anything, we had best be on our individual journeys. Until we meet again: ride safe and be well."

Kathryn watched with a touch of melancholy, as her brother prepared to ride away with Hamish, Captain Hodges and Smitty. At the last moment, Jamie had insisted that Smitty accompany him back to the farm. "Ye need to familiarize yourself with the ways of a landlubber, Smitty. Besides, it's a shorter distance to my farm than where they're heading, and a large bottle of liniment awaits ye," he cajoled.

More importantly, he doubted that Anna's people would be up to *experiencing* the little man's 'uniqueness' unannounced. *You certainly are one of a kind, Smitty. We share the same sense of humor; that fact gains you points. You are a welcome addition.*

Eyeing his horse, Smitty rubbed his backside and groaned.

"Stop yer complaining. He's a gentle, old, carriage horse and will give ye a smooth ride. Ye may have a few calluses on yer arse by the time we arrive, but I shall make a horseman out of you yet." Slapping his thigh, Jamie burst into loud guffaws.

Before Smitty could utter any protest, he was boosted into the saddle and left to sort out the reins and stirrups. Jamie moved to his own mount and flung himself into the saddle. "There is but one way to learn, my good man—just do it."

Smitty spewed a colorful stream of epithets aimed directly at Jamie's questionable 'parentage', as he struggled to wrap his short legs around the horse's broad back.

Jamie's grin broadened. "I fear me mother would take umbrage at that accusation." Without further adieu, he nudged his horse into a fast trot. Looking back, he was pleased to see Smitty rapidly closing the gap between them. Having given up trying to stretch his short legs to reach the stirrups, he grasped the saddle pommel for dear life. A wild-eyed grin accompanied his look of sheer determination—he refused to be beaten.

Ye are a good man, friend Smitty, ye have guts. Perhaps I'll not sic Diablo on ye after all. Kneeing his horse he quickened the pace, grinning.

With forced smiles, vigorous waves and words of coming together before spring, Jason and his family rode south with Jack and Gabriel.

Gabrielle insisted upon riding behind her father, holding him snuggly around the waist. "I shall not let you leave me behind again, poppa. I shall hold on tightly."

"Do not worry, poppet. I will also have you ride in front of me at times, so that *I* may have the pleasure of holding *you* tightly. I missed you dearly."

Kathryn observed their devotion with quiet pleasure. *To think I wasted a minute of concern over Jason's acceptance of this beautiful child. He has doted on her since the day she announced herself with a lusty pair of lungs.* She smiled contentedly, thankful for the numerous blessings in her life—despite the war—and hugged little Beau tighter.

For a time, each rode in silence, immersed in personal thoughts. The moon shone bright in a cloudless, brisk sky making the trail easier to follow.

Gabrielle rode with her head resting against the warmth of her father's broad back. She rolled her face skyward, mesmerized by its deep indigo tones and endless tiny bright specks. Many were familiar and comforting: the little dipper, the big dipper, the North Star—ever constant. Taking her time, enjoying this pleasant diversion, she identified the main constellations, murmuring each by name.

Staring at the horizon, she noted a much larger, luminous orb barely clearing the treetops—a planet for sure. She did not know its name, but momma would. Suddenly a brilliant trail flashed across the sky, disappearing as quickly as it had come. *A shooting star for love and luck,* she breathed, her small heart pounding. *It is a sure sign. My letter will reach Robbie. Captain Farthingale will not fail me.* "Come to me, my Robbie. I know not how, but please come," she whispered against the loving strength of her father's back as a tear slipped willfully onto her cheek.

With dawn breaking, they left the trail. Gabriel had chosen a spot where they would be undetected: a small cavern concealed by a thick tangle of vines and closely set trees. If they had planned to stay for any length of time, it would have been uncomfortable. But for their purpose—a quick meal and much needed sleep—the accommodations served well. Exhaustion quickly overtaking them, they drifted into deep slumber, leaning against one another for warmth under an old blanket.

They had met no one on the trail, but dared not light a fire. Keowee was situated one hundred miles from 'The 96', a former British post commanded by Jason's Loyalist friend, John Cruger. They had no direct news of the redoubt's present status, but could not risk being seen by hangers-on. Savannah represented absolute danger. They would skirt both areas and proceed with utmost caution.

"Knowledge of the enemy is power," Kathryn muttered, eyeing her husband. "We have *no* knowledge at the moment—a situation not to my liking."

"Nor mine, my pet. We shall remain vigilant and move quickly."

"How long shall we stay?" she asked, eyeing him speculatively, her question left unanswered as Jack and Gabriel returned from checking the horses.

"Gabriel and I have talked." Jack said directly to Jason, but glanced at Kathryn, including her in what he was about to say.

"As a group, we are too easily detected, even under cover of dark," Gabriel stated evenly. "The farther south we go, at least for a bit, the greater our danger of meeting British reconnaissance and I …"

"Very true," Kathryn laughed, "but there is more to it than that, my dearest nephew. You are a MacLean through and through, Gabriel. I read you easily."

Striking an innocent pose, he gave no immediate answer.

"You are healthy and eager to see Silver Fox, and can travel much faster alone."

"Not totally alone, Kathryn. I am riding with Gabriel," Jack said casually.

"We shall miss your company and make haste to join you," Jason approved heartily. "As a small family, we are also less likely to draw attention. Good thinking, men."

As dusk fell, Jack and Gabriel mounted their horses. Gabrielle's sad eyes tugged at Jack's heart. "Gabriel and I *will be* safe, my princess. Take care of momma and poppa and little Beau. It is a large responsibility, but you can do it. I will tell Anna you are on your way."

"Jack," Kathryn's soft voice caught his attention. "Do not be angry with Anna, for it is *I* who am to blame. I forbade her ..."

Jack smiled, love flashing openly in his eyes. "I will see all of you soon, ride safely."

Jason pulled his wife and daughter close, holding them quietly. He knew Kathryn's thoughts as if they were his own. Jack was adapting and growing. He would have a good life here, and they were glad. Within a few minutes, they urged their horses into a gentle trot, once again picking up the trail. The weather had remained in their favor for several days. If it continued—crisp, clear and dry—they would be no more than three days behind Jack and Gabriel. Smiling, Kathryn began humming an old English ditty, picked up around the campfire from what seemed a lifetime ago, and hunkered over Beauty's withers for a long night's ride.

Two days out from Keowee they set up camp for the day beside a small brook. It was one of Kathryn's favorite spots, a place she and Beauty had often visited in her frequent meandering travels in the past, *before there was Jason*. Happy memories flitted back as she nursed Beau. Contented with life, she savored the new challenges their future promised.

After a quickly swallowed meal of bread and cheese, they relaxed into much needed sleep, finally waking by late afternoon.

"Gabrielle and I are going upstream, my love."

Kathryn eyed Jason inquisitively as she finished changing Beau's linen.

"A small fire will not draw attention, and fresh fish is welcomed at this point."

"I remember the rules, sir," she quipped. "You catch it and I cook it. I shall have a fire ready when you both return."

Beaming happily, Gabrielle rushed to kiss her mother and then headed into the brush along the edge of the stream, calling back over her shoulder, "Come on, poppa. Let's see who catches the biggest fish."

Gabrielle walked at her father's side smiling proudly. In one hand she gripped her coiled fishing string with its sharp barb, in the other swung a string of four plump trout.

Suddenly her father's hand shot out, halting her. With curt gestures he instructed: be silent, crouch low, and move out of sight—then wait. As frightened eyes met his, he nodded reassuringly, but placed a silencing finger to his lips. Bending low, he disappeared into the brush.

As Jason crept nearer to their campsite, he could hear voices. He inched closer, needing to see his target better, so as not to risk Kathryn or Beau.

They stood facing each other—Kathryn and a tall man, his immediate identity hidden by a thick branch. Both had pistols drawn and firmly aimed—neither backing down. Jason's gaze swept the perimeter of the small clearing, assessing the danger, relieved to see Beau shaking a twig and kicking happily, off to one side.

He inched closer—there was no time for weighing additional possibilities. Finding a better angle was not an option with the dense shrubbery; proximity would have to suffice.

Kathryn was livid, obvious even from his limited point of view. *But who is the man facing her down?* He crept closer, and within three steps reached a position from where he could see clearly. Even from the back, he recognized Sergeant Gilson. That knowledge brought rage and a silent curse.

"Gilson, do *not* put me in a position which will be harmful only for *you*." Kathryn's voice lowered to a threatening purr.

Gilson's shock at discovering Kathryn alive had hindered his initial decisiveness, providing her time to set Beau aside and bring her pistol up—aimed directly at his chest.

Forcefully pushing aside lingering memories, he hardened his heart. *It's them or me.* His eyes turned cold, unfeeling—a look Kathryn had never seen in all their years of riding together—and it startled her. This was no joke, this was for real.

"Kathryn," he said softly, attempting to throw her off-guard by using guilt as a ploy. "After all we have been through, how can you …?"

"Do not play that card, Tobias. I do not wish to think any less of you, than I do."

Startled by her use of his birth name, and derisive words, he eyed her speculatively, weighing his odds carefully.

"Why are you putting yourself at risk of becoming a primary target for the masses, Kathryn? Bounty hunters will eagerly seek the prize of a lifetime when news gets out. Hell, they would take you down merely for the glory, and as to Gabriel's rescue? Don't fool yourself. The British *will not* look the other way out of consideration for past performance. The war, in theory, is over. But we *are still here* and will remain so."

He sucked in a long breath, checking his cocked pistol hammer, readjusting his aim for a shot between her eyes. "You are a bloody traitor. For God's sake, why? What would Colonel Tarrington say?"

"Colonel Tarrington would say: drop that gun, you son-of-a-bitch or I will see my wife through the hole in your skull as you drop." Jason stabbed his pistol painfully into the back of Gilson's head.

His former sergeant's face paled, his hand shaking slightly, but he remained silent, refusing to drop his gun—the final mistake of his life.

As Jason's pistol roared, Kathryn lurched sideways, rolling up onto her feet safely off to one side. Her eyes met her husband's in shared grief and mutual understanding. *One does what one must in life. Grieve momentarily—but abandon guilt and move on.*

Jason stooped, felt for a pulse on Gilson's throat and quickly moved to his wife's side. Pulling her into his embrace, he held her as she comforted their mewling son.

"Why?" she managed, as her face collapsed in sorrow.

"His heart *changed*."

Jason and Kathryn spun about, startled by the statement—and its source.

Gabrielle knelt at Gilson's side, her hand placed gently on his chest. Her solemn eyes met theirs displaying sadness and incredible maturity, shocking both parents.

"I told you to stay back," Jason barked, his misplaced anger forcing curtness he immediately regretted.

"I am no longer a baby with a nursemaid to protect me from life, poppa," she answered softly, reaching out to him for understanding.

Taking her hand, he pulled her into his arms as Kathryn placed a loving hand on her shoulder. Serene, blue eyes met her mother's concerned gaze, addressing her wordlessly.

"Life is not always pretty, poppa, but it is ours to accept—and deal with."

Jason gaped, speechless. Kathryn lifted brilliant, green eyes to his, smiling grimly. With a barely perceptible nod he sighed, finally comprehending what Kathryn had known, and tried to explain months ago while they were in England. This beautiful child was no longer his 'baby' ... and the loss grieved him.

"I *will always* be your baby, poppa."

His eyes riveted on her adoring, upturned face. She could read him just like her mother, a rather unsettling fact, yet somehow comforting.

"For that, I will always be grateful, poppet." He tousled her silky, black curls. "You help momma with Beau. I will handle this. We need to be gone as quickly as possible."

"Sergeant O'Reilly *is not* our enemy," Gabrielle mumbled, appearing distant—lost in thought. "He feels confused and sad. We will see him again."

Exchanging concerned glances, Kathryn and Jason stared openly at their daughter. Suddenly her faraway look receded, returning her to the present. "Sergeant Gilson did not fear Stewart's threats because he had assurance of several gold pieces with his success." Gabrielle shrugged. "His heart turned to ice."

"Anna spoke truth, Jason, our daughter *is* unique."

Mid-afternoon the following day, Sergeant O'Reilly stopped to water his horse in a small clearing beside a quiet brook. He and Gilson had split up to cover a wider search area two days ago, a fact which pleased him. He did not like what his former friend was becoming—*had* become, he corrected.

O'Reilly had made no effort in the search. Giving up quickly, he backtracked and followed Gilson's trail to discover what, if anything, he had learned. They were not far from Keowee, and he was nervous. When Anna had been part of their lives, they might have been welcome; without her—questionable. If Soaring Eagle was any example, they would be skewered with arrows and asked questions later.

He crouched beside his horse, splashing cold water on his face, attempting to renew his energy. He must present an image of having tried. For who knew what Stewart's mood might be when they returned empty handed? It was a 'lose—lose' situation no matter how he looked at it. Drying his face on his sleeve, he scanned the surroundings, suddenly noticing the ground immediately to his right. *Someone has been here recently,* he murmured. Signs of one or more people were evident. Leaving his horse to nibble the meager, grassy stubble, he searched the area carefully.

His eyes drifted to remnants of what appeared to be drying blood. Heart pounding, breathing raggedly, he hesitated—unsure whether he wanted to find the cause. Perhaps only an animal slain for a meal, but he doubted that. Hastily covered evidence of a heavy object being dragged off to one side was easy to follow.

Just beyond the shrubbery he discovered another clearing, and in the middle, a stone covered mound and small cross. Hanging from one arm was a heavy gold chain—a chain and medallion he knew well. Moving closer, he examined the burial site, its method of construction familiar. There was only one person who set stones at the head of a grave in such unique fashion—her personal way of honoring the dead.

"Kathryn," he murmured, as tears of relief cascaded down his cheeks.

"Gilson, you stupid …" He stopped the thought. If Kathryn could place stones 'honoring' *him* after what he had attempted … Taking the chain, he tucked it carefully into his pocket. Gilson had no family that he was aware of, but that made no difference; he wanted it. *I'll take this as a remembrance of better times, Gilson. And for once, you are in no shape to argue, ole buddy.*

Remounting his horse, he scanned the surrounding area. With a sigh, he urged his horse southwards. *I cannot return to Charleston, nor do I wish to see Savannah. Stewart will raise the alarm. What shall I do?* A deep frown settled across his brow.

Recalling Kathryn's love of nature and positive outlook, he glanced upwards at the rich, winter-blue sky, dotted with crisply defined white clouds, and smiled. *They are both alive, thank God.* They were likely in Keowee by now, but they would eventually leave. And when they did—he would be waiting.

"Come on, my faithful charger, time to find me some colonial attire and you, old boy—less fancy trappings." He was no longer scared. He had finally made a decision, right or wrong, it was made. *Whether they accept me or not, I embrace this opportunity for a new beginning. I know nothing of farming or hunting or … Who cares? I will learn.* Whistling a bright tune, one of Kathryn's favorites, he urged his charger into a canter.

Chapter Eleven

Keowee

Sitting amidst her 'family' Anna smiled contentedly, enjoying their playful banter. A full week had passed since Kathryn and Jason's welcome arrival. After their encounter with Sergeant Gilson they picked up their pace. If Gilson had found them, O'Reilly could do the same. They had pushed harder, traveling by night and staying well concealed during daylight hours, arriving only two days behind Gabriel and Jack.

What a delightful but exhausting week it had been: reacquainting themselves with old friends and greeting new ones. The Cherokees' unique style of living set an easier pace, and knowing they were safe was a blessing. Keowee provided a secure hideaway, a place to sort their lives out without pressure. Anna had her 'precious little bird' under her tutelage, and wished them to stay indefinitely. Kathryn and Jason shared concerns over Jack. Could he find contentment and adapt to a lifestyle so different? Perhaps the cheerless existence at his sister's estate had laid good groundwork for change; he seemed happy and had been well received.

Not surprisingly, Silver Fox's health improved immediately upon her husband's safe return. Gabriel, in a shared moment with Kathryn, expressed his gratitude for Jack's quiet words to his wife. "Our daughter's birth last year was ... difficult. But Jack's gentle reassurance and sharing details of Gabrielle's successful 'event' has greatly restored her confidence." He reached for his aunt's hand. "He *is a* good man, Kathryn, a man of tremendous courage," he said softly, holding her gaze, both in complete accord.

"Yes, he *is* an incredible man," she answered quietly.

Before Kathryn could broach the subject, he quickly said: "My Silver Fox is not yet as strong as she should be, and *I* am well aware it is too soon for another child."

Kathryn merely grinned. Enough said.

Two weeks later, much to her delight, Silver Fox gave birth to another healthy son, with only her husband in attendance. After the birth, she rebounded rapidly, her life settling happily back into place. They introduced their newest family member at a huge feast, honoring Jason by naming the lusty infant: Jason Eagle MacLean—Gabriel's way of giving thanks for his freedom. Kathryn saw the brightness of her husband's eyes, reading his thoughts, as he held the wriggling infant. Much had changed in the last two years.

As Anna's eyes came to rest on her in thoughtful observation, Kathryn smiled. They read each other well. *Patience, my Kathryn. Slow the pace; enjoy life's journey.* Anna's message, though easily understood, was not easy to live by. But she would try for a while.

"Tell a story, Auntie Kat. My turn to sit on your lap," Raven demanded, his pout smoothing into a wide smile as she reached for him. *Your baby gibberish has become quite understandable, little Raven.* Kathryn sighed. *Time stands still for no one—he is growing up as I watch.* A pair of shiny, black eyes skewered her, demanding she begin a tale of magic, mystery and daring-do. Scanning the area around her, she discovered a captivated group of small children hanging on every word, and smiled.

Jason stepped into their hut quietly, halting mid-step at the scene before him. Facing the back wall, Kathryn sat cross-legged on the floor, head down, shoulders slouched. Rocking slowly, she read one of James Beattie's poems aloud in ragged, hushed tones.

He stood staring in silent confusion. His wife always remained upbeat despite inner heartache. During the war she had coped with agonies most could not have withstood, holding personal sorrow within. He could count on one hand the few times he had seen her actually cry, but she was crying now. Her voice caught on a sob at a particularly loving phrase. "Oh, Jason," she murmured, "my love, my life."

"Kathryn." Placing his hands gently on her shoulders, he turned her to face him, pulling her up into his warm embrace. Stroking her unruly curls back, he searched her face, gently palming tears from her cheeks.

"I thought you had gone hunting with …" she began haltingly.

His lips closed over hers, his tongue seeking readily given access, his body pressed firmly against hers speaking openly of his need. With a groan, he stepped back. Cupping her cheeks, he said softly, "I begged off, I felt your need. At least I hoped it was *your need,* rather than my rutting male demands. I have missed …"

"My heart, my body, aches for you, Jason. We have *never* been so apart in all our years together."

"I can attest to that, my love, from personal experience." Eyeing her with a lopsided grin, he added: "Having *handled* the problem so often out of sheer necessity, I have come to fear it unnatural in its excess." He looked embarrassed at his confession.

Her lower lip quivered, a devilish giggle escaping in spite of her attempts to curb it.

"It *is not* a matter of humor, Kathryn," he stated curtly.

"Forgive me, my love, but thankfully *your* need has been as *mine.* I thought perhaps I suffered alone."

"Kathryn, you truly shock me. You know I …"

"We need to heal each other, Jason. And there are matters of which we must speak."

"Where are our children?"

"Gabrielle, as always, is with Anna. Silver Fox is caring for Beau. She felt my unhappiness and wished to help."

"Good, for *we* are going for a ride: *now.* I will be right back and you are to be *ready.*"

"Yes, sir." She snapped a quick salute, grasping his innuendo, a slow grin spreading as her pulse quickened.

Kathryn leaned back against a tree within the secluded copse, running her fingers through her hair, shaking it out to coil wildly on her shoulders. Opening her blouse, she watched her husband approach, his desire blatant.

"Make the time, Colonel," she purred her green eyes dark and smoldering.

"I am a busy man, madam," he growled. He had missed their role-playing, so much a part of their daily existence.

The tip of her tongue slid seductively across her upper lip, leaving glistening moisture. "Make the time, sir—I promise you will have no regrets."

"Sweet Jesus, Kathryn …" The throbbing ache in his groin threatened to drop him to his knees. In two steps he reached her. Breathing heavily, barely in control, he thrust her blouse off her shoulders. Caressing her breasts, he brought their lush fullness to his lips, suckling each in turn, relishing the milky drops.

Groaning, she struggled to loosen the stubborn rawhide laces of his shirt. Annoyed with their resistance, she moved lower, quickly releasing his breeches to hungrily grasp the heat of him, unable to continue role playing, her willpower abruptly collapsing.

"Rough," she gasped.

"Like the first time, madam?" he panted, able to 'play' their game, though just barely.

"Yes," she ground out. *Damn his iron control.*

Some time later, he rested above her, searching her face, concerned. In his incredible need, he had been rougher than intended.

"Have I hurt you, my Kathryn?" he asked softly.

"Never, my love." Her eyes met his—alive, sparkling, her desire obvious. "We have had so few stolen moments, I …"

"Good," he interrupted. "Now I shall love you properly, gently and completely until you beg for mercy: mercy that *shall not* be granted, until I have given you absolute pleasure. And *I* shall be the one to determine when that moment is fulfilled." His eyes shone dark, smoldering. The years *had not* diminished their mutual passion, merely heightened it.

"Jason, my love …" were her last intelligible words as he began a heated trail of nipping kisses the length of her taut body.

"It is near dusk despite spring's lengthening days," she commented as they cantered along the wooded path heading back to Keowee.

Seeing her glowing features Jason smiled, his face reflected the same inner peace. Neither had felt this 'complete' in months; they vowed to keep it so henceforth. Lying in each other's arms, basking in the afterglow, reality abruptly insinuated itself.

"We must move on," they said in unison, then burst into laughter.

"We still think as one, my Kathryn, a fact that will never change."

She made no immediate comment, somewhere lost in thought.

"Talk to me," he said, slowing his horse to hear her.

"I feel caged," she answered, hoping he would follow her line of thought; he nodded, reading her easily, pleasing her.

"We *are* caged, Kathryn, shut away from the outside world: no word from Ted, Jamie or Hodges—and what of Stewart? There are situations of which we should be aware."

"But there is one other person we must …"

"My poppet," he whispered, eyes softening at thoughts of his beloved little girl. "We have stayed longer than we planned, Kathryn. I have no wish to upset our child, but I doubt I have the strength to leave her behind."

"Good grief, the children. I hope they are not creating trouble …"

"Sorry, my pet, your lush body took precedence. Never worry, they are well attended." A wry grin and twinkling eyes provided the suspected answer.

"Poor Jack. Will the day ever arrive when he *is not* called upon to generate unlimited time for our pleasure?"

"Probably not, but I have never heard a complaint."

She chuckled shaking her head but suddenly tensed, reining Beauty to an abrupt halt. "I smell a campfire." Angling her head, she sniffed deeply. "Coming from that direction."

"Yes, but little smoke, maybe an attempt at not being detected?"

Sharing a look of understanding, they left the trail. Leaving the horses nearby, they crept through the brush, pistols drawn. As they drew close, the smell of roasting rabbit wafted enticingly. Whoever had taken time to catch and cook a rabbit was *not* apt to be seeking them specifically. But they kept pistols at the ready as they separated, approaching from opposite sides of the small campsite.

"Sit tight, stranger," Jason instructed as he stepped into the clearing.

Sitting on a rough log facing away from Jason, the man instantly stiffened a rabbit haunch halfway to his mouth. Immediately raising his hands, still clutching his dinner, he kept his eyes forward until told to do otherwise. Scanning the perimeter, Jason noted a small, sturdy lean-to: he had been camped here for several days.

Kathryn emerged from the opposite side of the clearing, pistol drawn, wary. Eyes narrowing, she searched the man's face in the gloom of approaching dusk. "O'Reilly?"

The rabbit haunch dropped to the ground, forgotten, as his hands began to shake uncontrollably.

"Kathryn?" he gasped. "Jason?" He spun about, heart pounding, and came face-to-face with his former colonel.

"I understand you are looking for us," Jason snarled, keeping his pistol at the ready.

"Yes—no, at least not the way you think, sir. Are you real—or ghosts?" he stammered, turning the sickly, grayish-white of old tallow.

"*Very real*," Kathryn added tartly, moving closer but keeping O'Reilly's chest in her sights. "Stand up," she ordered.

"Truth be known, milady, I am not sure I *can* stand, my knees are …."

"Allow me to assist you." Jason seized him roughly, hauling him to his feet.

Kathryn quickly patted him down, and removing his knife tucked it into her waistband, along with his pistol.

"Talk to us, O'Reilly, or I will be creating a burial cairn for you similar to Gilson's." Her singsong delivery implied danger … he froze.

"I saw Gilson's grave. He *changed*. I have my suspicions, though no explanation. But *I can* tell you about me," he rushed on, nervous: they might kill him too. "I have adopted colonial dress, just as you. I *am* a dead man if I return to Stewart empty-handed, but I would never harm either of you." His words tumbled out in repetitive, nonsensical babble, trying to convince them of his honesty.

He is an emotional mess, she realized. *No danger to us—rather more to himself perhaps*. Jason met her look, agreeing with her silent assessment.

Holstering their pistols, Kathryn moved forward and pulled O'Reilly into a warm embrace. "Let's talk," she murmured.

With that, he crumpled onto the log in a sobbing mass.

"I fear reality has been a bit of a shock to our former sergeant. Shall we give him a few moments to collect himself?" She raised a quizzical brow to her husband.

Leaning down, she eyed O'Reilly. "May I?" She indicated the perfectly cooked rabbit.

O'Reilly made an inarticulate sound, swiping at his cheeks.

"I will take that as a 'yes', O'Reilly." Smiling cordially, she broke two hunks of meat from the rabbit. Handing one to Jason, she sat down and began munching contentedly.

It was well after dark as they entered Keowee.

"You are late," Soaring Eagle grumbled, greeting them at the outskirts of the village. He would never admit to having begun to worry. "There *is* a limit to pleasure ..."

"There *is not*," Kathryn said firmly. "However, we found Sergeant O'Reilly."

Soaring Eagle's expression changed dramatically. "He *is* dead, I presume."

"No," Jason answered. "Kathryn and I are not quite sure what to do with him."

Cherokee expletives erupted intermixed with chastising words.

"He *is not* our enemy. We shall talk in council," Kathryn retorted crisply. Kneeing Beauty, she preceded Jason into the campsite, ending all further discussion.

Another two weeks passed uneventfully with no firm decisions made. Kathryn and Jason were in a quandary as to what to do with O'Reilly. He had insisted upon waiting until they left Keowee, and then intended to join them. No matter how long he had to wait, he would remain out of sight—ready to travel on a moments notice.

But Kathryn and Jason were not about to head into the wilderness with a 'follower'. Having promised Jamie they would help him plant his crops this spring, their first obligation was to him. Besides, Gabrielle and Beau had yet to meet their cousins.

"Whatever will we do with him?" Kathryn moaned.

Jason looked perplexed and shrugged. "He feels he owes us protection for Gilson's betrayal. He is just one more item on our list to deal with, sooner or later." His answer lent no comfort, adding to her frustration. With each passing day her dissatisfaction grew. Gabrielle spent almost no time with them, training long hours with Anna, returning to their hut well after dusk—to sleep. *She is a little girl. Must she learn everything before she is seven?* Kathryn was not sure what her daughter's 'required knowledge' entailed. Each time she inquired, Anna reproached her silently with penetrating looks. Gabrielle's sacred path was not to be questioned nor discussed. Kathryn loved and revered her mentor, but she had questions that ached to be answered.

The previous evening Gabrielle had said softly, "Anna and I are at an important stage of my learning, momma." With a quick kiss to both parents, she quietly left.

Too much, too much, Kathryn's mind screamed. Forcing a weak smile for her daughter's sake, she turned attention to her son as he suckled greedily. She dared not make eye contact with Jason, his rising resentment easily felt from across the room. His emotional turmoil shrouded her in a weighty cloak of doubtfulness. *He will demand answers.* Would *he* accept the response he regularly gave her: "I guess that is one more item on our list to deal with." She shook her head. *No, I think not.*

"Damn it," Kathryn swore vehemently, overcome by frustration. "Where did I put that rattle?" She continued shoving aside the clutter in their small hut, searching wildly. This small structure had been adequate for Jason and her—but two children in addition? No, even with the little amount of time Gabrielle spent there, it was overcrowded.

Beau continued to gripe, his intermittent squalls escalating. "I know you are cutting teeth, but that has never troubled you before. What is your complaint now?" she groused.

"He feels your tension, momma," came an astutely observant answer.

Kathryn spun about to find her daughter standing quietly near the door.

"I admit I am a bit …" she began, embarrassed by her display of bad temper.

Gabrielle smiled as she crossed the hut, pushed aside a pile of deerskins and pulled out a colorful gourd rattle: a present from Silver Fox. Shaking it rapidly, she dipped from side to side, crooning. As she zigzagged towards him his eyes followed her, his angry squalls ceasing, a wide grin spreading across his plump face.

"Ahh, a new tooth." She poked a finger into his mouth prodding the gums gently. "And more coming rapidly. Beau, no biting," she ordered, pulling her finger back quickly.

Turning, she found her mother smiling at last. Her parents worried her. Idleness had created tension between them for as long as she could remember. But, inactivity was not the problem today. *This is about me; we must talk now.* Kissing her brother's blonde head she instructed, "Hush, little man, entertain yourself; momma and I must talk."

Kathryn shot her daughter a piercing look, mystified by her demeanor.

"Come sit beside me, momma," she urged, moving to the bench covered with pelts.

Kathryn sat down, pulling her daughter close.

"Hold me tight please; I want to be your baby again for just a moment."

Kissing the top of her little girl's head, she rocked soothingly, willing her to feel the love. "I am sorry you saw me …"

"*I* am to blame momma—not you."

Kathryn was truly bewildered. "Gabrielle, you …"

"Please listen, momma. Let me tell you while I have the courage."

Mesmerized, she stared into her daughter's sparkling blue eyes, unable to look away, certain she would be sucked into their incredible depth at any moment—the same sensation she experienced when gazing at indigo heavens on a star-speckled evening. Her breath caught her chest constricting, unable to bear the words she expected to hear. *Jason, lend me your strength. God help me.*

"I am not going to say what you fear," she said softly, touching her mother's cheek with a gentle caress. "I must disappoint Anna, at least for now—perhaps forever."

Kathryn released her breath on a long sigh, as tears welled and overflowed. Wet channels raced along her cheeks as she began to sob.

Gabrielle mopped her mother's face with her sleeve, a concerned frown settling across her brow. "That *is not* what you wished to hear, momma?"

Kathryn struggled for control. Pulling her daughter against her, she tried to form sensible words. "After all these weeks of your endless studying under Anna's tutelage, I was certain—or *we* were poppa and I …" She stopped to collect her thoughts and began again. "When you touch my hand, or my shoulder, or hug me, I feel the energy pouring from you. You sense events before …"

"As do you, momma," she interrupted.

"But nothing comparable to your skills, little one."

"The choice is for each of us to decide; ability improves with practice."

"There are times I wonder if I really want to know."

"Me too, momma. I see too much sometimes," she said, surprising her mother.

"I know what Anna fears, for I have shared her vision: years from now—a 'trail of tears' for her people and too many deaths to count. By then, Anna will rest with the elders. At that time I will be older than you and poppa. Can you imagine it?" she giggled. "Perhaps too old to cause trouble, or be of much help." Deviltry sparkled in her eyes.

Kathryn burst into laughter. "Thank you for your delightful observation. However, I *do* feel we may have a few more good years left."

Gabrielle's grin faded. "I am still young—and yet *very old*, momma. For I *understand* Anna's words, her teachings. I am also a healer, channeling energies of the universe to help others. I have seen it for myself."

"Do you mean to give this up, at least for now?" Kathryn needed to know.

"I do not have to give it up, my gifts lie within me—mine to use as I see fit."

"I am confused, little one."

"I shall use my abilities so as not to appear ungrateful to the Great Spirit. But I am not ready to dedicate my life, to live as Anna does—at least not yet. There is much I want to learn *outside* the Cherokee family. Each time I return it will feel like coming home. But I have a great deal to see, feel and learn before I come home for good."

Kathryn searched her child's face, feeling as if she were conversing with a long lost friend, completely taken aback.

"I have silenced you," she giggled. "Poppa will wish me to teach him how it is done."

Hugging her mother, she said softly, "I want to love a man, to touch him, experience the incredible passion you and poppa share. When I can do that, perhaps I will be ready to consider Anna's passionate way of life: seer, psychic and healer—a large responsibility. I will need strength to stand tall, perhaps alone, and not be swallowed into nothingness."

"I do not know what to say, little one."

"Do I make sense, momma? For I have yet to tell Anna, and I dread the telling."

"You will find appropriate words; though I am sure she is aware and understands. This ordeal is part of your training: knowing when the timing is right or wrong. No matter what you choose, poppa and I will always love you and rejoice in your happiness."

"Would you have missed me, just a little, if I had chosen to stay?"

Kathryn winked. "Of course, who else has the ability to humor her brother when he is crotchety? Or her mother for that matter?"

They sat side by side in silence, watching Beau gurgle happily as he wriggled on his belly, pushing his rattle under the pelts—losing it and finding it—enjoying his game.

"I see how he lost his toy," Kathryn laughed, expecting a cute comment from her daughter, but instead received an unexpected statement on a totally different matter.

"It is time to head for Uncle Jamie's farm. I am not sure we will remain there very long, but long enough for Robbie to find me. He is on his way, momma."

"Well, now ..." Again she had no words. This would create an interesting situation: Robbie coming to the colonies. *How can he manage that,* she wondered? *He is so young.*

"He will stow away, or perhaps Captain Farthingale ... I have no clear vision yet."

"Gabrielle," Kathryn eyed her uncomfortably. "Would you please *not* practice your gift of reading my mind too often? Many thoughts may be inappropriate at your age."

Gabrielle merely grinned. "Your secrets are *always* safe with me, momma."

"Are you going to tell poppa?"

"Yes, right now. I want to see him smile. He has been so serious of late."

"And Uncle Jack?"

She hung her head, eyes downcast. "I told him earlier."

Kathryn giggled. "You love him dearly, I understand."

Gabrielle nodded. "If he were younger, Robbie would find it hard to catch my eye."

"Somehow I doubt that, little one. Go see poppa; he needs to hear your words."

With the burden of a difficult decision lifted from her slender shoulders, she beamed. Blowing a kiss to her baby brother, she headed out the door.

She had finally experienced her first important adult understanding in life. Although informing loved ones of complex personal choices is difficult, the initial *decision-making* challenges the very soul.

After spending time with her father and Anna, Gabrielle headed to their hut for the evening meal, Anna's words echoing in her mind.

"Your poppa loves another as deeply as his beloved Kathryn, although he thought that never to be possible—*you,* little Gabrielle. However, with incredible love comes a shared burden of pain: a double-edged sword. Your poppa needs you now, little bird. You will continue to grow and learn on your own, for I have sown the seeds of knowledge within you—a beginning and an understanding of basic rules. Only *you* will know when the time is right."

Gabrielle fingered the delicate medicine wheel hanging around her neck. Anna had placed it there as she whispered a Cherokee prayer in soft, lilting tones. Pressing a light kiss against her forehead, the venerable healer leaned back and smiled, nodding acceptance of her decision, and promise of her *everlasting love.*

I am blessed, Gabrielle announced quietly to the universe, pausing momentarily before entering the hut to break bread with her family.

Chapter Twelve

A Momentous Decision

With barely a 'swish' of warning, a switch snapped painfully across Robbie's hand.

"Master Beaumont!"

Robert turned to eye the headmaster, knowing full well that his total lack of emotion would only frustrate and anger him more. With a well-controlled, carefully guarded look, he relaxed back in his chair, observing him through cold eyes.

Nigel Wallingford stood eyeing Robert, annoyed that the boy did not so much as flinch, did not move to protect his hand, nor rub it to ease the ache, although a red welt had already begun to rise. "And just what are we day-dreaming of today, young man?"

No answer.

The switch struck again with greater force. Wallingford prided himself with choosing a freshly cut, green switch to dole out his daily punishments: far better 'snap'—inflicting greater pain than the wide, flat side of a wooden rule.

Robert eyed him silently—hatred glinting openly—yet did not grimace as a second angrier welt rose along the back of his hand.

"Do you have any idea which lesson I just taught?"

"No, sir," Robert answered tartly, staring unblinking at his professor '*emeritus*', as he was so often reminded.

Snickering erupted, rolling in waves about the room, but ceased immediately as Wallingford skewered each member of the class with a venomous look.

"Do you have last nights lesson prepared?" He sniffed haughtily, snapping the green reed against the palm of his hand.

"No sir." Leaning back casually in his chair, he flashed a disdainful look.

Wallingford took three deep calming breaths, and leaned close. At the stale offensive odor, Robert scowled, wrinkling his nose. The headmaster's face suffused a brilliant red, his barely controlled fury rippling just beneath the surface. The classroom went silent, each pupil holding his breath, fearful of the outcome for Robbie's insubordination.

Wallingford knew he could beat this boy senseless and suffer no guilt or caring. However, his mother traveled in prestigious circles. Although she had personally expressed her bewilderment and anger with Robert to him, she would never allow serious injury to come to her *precious,* only son.

"Master Beaumont," he ground out, willing himself to be calm. "You will remain after class and wash the slates, clean erasers, dust thoroughly, refill ink jars, cut new quills, and scrub the floor on your hands and knees."

Relief flooded the faces of his classmates for Robbie was well liked: quick to laugh, quick to share in each individual's joys or sorrows. Yet he was a constant target for the headmaster's ire, a curious situation that no one but Robbie understood.

"And when you are done, you shall go to your room. Tomorrow you shall come to class prepared with, not only your lessons from yesterday and today, but also a letter of sincere apology to me." He paused, breathing heavily directly into Robert's face. "Do *we* have an understanding, young man?"

"As you wish, sir."

The headmaster clapped his hands sharply. "Class dismissed." He watched until the room emptied before addressing his delinquent. "And you *will* have plenty of time for lessons and your letter, Master Beaumont, for you *may not* attend your evening meal nor will food be sent to your room. A growling stomach will serve as a good reminder of the error of your ways. Now, take your books to your room and return immediately. You have much to accomplish."

Giving Wallingford a long look, he stalked to the door leaving him fuming.

"By God that little bastard has no respect for me. I wish … If only I had met that ill-mannered chit from the colonies who had such a horrible influence over him; perhaps I could better judge how to break his stubborn independence without killing him."

Mrs. Beaumont had spoken with him, on more than one occasion, about that 'awful child' and her parents from the wilds of the southern colonies. He could still hear her whining reproach echoing in his mind. "My son was a polite, dutiful young man until that …" She spluttered, momentarily at a loss for words. "She is a rude, ill-mannered troublemaker just like her mother. Surprisingly, her father is an English gentleman, born and bred, but has unfortunately sunk to the same level as his wife. My God, they even ruined my poor, dear brother, Beauregarde, robbed him of his good upbringing. I am just thankful they are gone. But my son needs strong discipline and I entrust him to the capabilities of both *you* and this fine school."

Wallingford stood staring at the ceiling, deep in thought, as he awaited Robert's return. *I wonder if he is too young for a pressgang. He is large for his size and well muscled. Mayhap he should be sent to sea. I may just use that premise to instill the fear of God in the little prick.* Thinking that to be a rather brilliant idea he smiled, formulating threatening words to drive fear into the boy. He would have two or three hours alone with him: plenty of time. He actually experienced a rush of pleasure at the thought of frightening this over-privileged young man.

At that moment, the classroom door opened and Robert entered.

"Do come in, Master Beaumont. You have much to accomplish before you start your lessons. Let us hurry. I understand tonight's meal is especially good: meat pastries followed by clotted cream and gingerbread. I would certainly hate to be late."

Robert's gaze remained icy but he said nothing, merely rolled up his sleeves and headed towards the blackboard.

Robert sat on the edge of his bed, pressing a cold, wet cloth to the back of his wrist, hoping to ease the throbbing. Scanning his cubicle, he smiled. Two biscuits sat on the trunk at the end of his mattress. *Probably Timothy,* he decided, a stalwart pal. Quickly picking them up, he devoured one and tucked the other under his pillow, unwilling to have any of his school companions put at risk if Wallingford chose to check on him.

He massaged his hand noticing it felt better, more aggravation than actual pain. His mind shifted, recalling some of Wallingford's ranting discourse about the sea: alone, abandoned with no monies, no well-heeled family to come to his rescue. His last words still echoed clearly amusing him. "Rotten meat and weevils in your biscuits, so many you may decide to name them as pets."

Pausing in his tirade, Wallingford had grinned maliciously. Abruptly moving closer, he grabbed Robbie by the collar, yanking him to within inches of his face. "With a pretty face like yours, laddie, even with the scowl you will make a special pet for some filthy, rutting, old tar." He laughed nastily, shoving Robbie backwards against a desk.

But none of it had scared him, although he did not let Wallingford know, for that could be dangerous. As a matter of fact, he felt himself to be quite an accomplished actor—showing just enough fear to be convincing, yet not overplaying his part. On the contrary, he found his headmaster's fearful diatribe quite informative. He *had* been running that precise thought through his mind of late. It was always good to be aware of things that could very well happen and be prepared. Ellie had often reminded him that *knowledge of the enemy was power*: one of her parents' favorite sayings.

Moving to the door he listened carefully, and hearing nothing, moved back into the far corner. Digging inside his shirt, he withdrew a crumpled, soiled parchment. Holding it to his heart he closed his eyes, seeing *his* Ellie—vibrant and smiling back at him. He sensed her, felt her closeness. At this hour, she would be coming awake in the colonies: a special time of day for both, a pre-agreed time of sharing inner thoughts, moments when he felt sure he could reach out and almost 'touch' her. His fingers caressed her letter. As young as she was, she wrote small, neat letters forming words in a distinctive hand.

His mother's butler, Cornelius—his 'partner in crime'—had thoughtfully intercepted the letter and secreted it away, waiting until an appropriate moment when no prying eyes might question. Presenting the parchment with a wide grin, he told Rob that he had instructed the man delivering the letter: to never mention it under any circumstances. Robert smiled, remembering that day. Cornelius always watched out for him, going so far as to tell the post rider that any mail from the colonies must be placed directly into his hands and *no other.* "One of cook's apple pies sealed the deal, Master Robbie, our secret is safe." He laughed with a deep, throaty rumble.

Robbie's father had unknowingly burst in on them, discovering what they were up to one afternoon. But rather than give them away, he became a willing partner. *I will actually miss you father;* that fleeting thought saddened him.

Months had passed with not so much as one request for him to come home for a visit. He had received a quickly dashed note from his father with generous monies enclosed, but nothing further from family or … Ellie. *Ahh well, I must travel on good faith and what little I know for fact.* He began mentally ticking off what Ellie had said. They arrived in Charleston in January and found it held by the English, although the war was allegedly over. Sporadic fighting flared, but they were safely out of it. *Somehow I doubt that.* Ted had found employment amidst the hustle, bustle and *wealth* of the city. He would make Charleston his home: an excellent spot to blend in and *observe* the comings and goings of importance. *That is useful knowledge; he will know where they went.*

Robbie's mind raced. With his decision made, only timing was left to be decided. He had no intention of doing his lessons or writing a letter of apology to Wallingford. Reaching under his pillow, he withdrew the second biscuit and scoffed it down, munching and savoring the taste as he worked out a strategy. Getting to the port would not be too difficult. Wagons full of wares were constantly coming and going: easy to hide in, or if necessary, pay a half penny. He patted one of several well-hidden pouches, mouthing words of thanks to his father.

Which ship? Suddenly the thought struck: *I am large for my age; should I hire on or stowaway?* Scanning his clothing, he groaned. *Way too rich in appearance, making me a prime target for robbery. Put that on my list: 'borrow', or buy common apparel.*

He sat deep in thought, idly tapping his bottom lip. There was much to be addressed, but none of it overwhelming. *I can do this,* he realized and grinned. The night was slowly slipping away. Soon the clock tower bell would peal. Dawn was less than two hours away.

Suddenly Gabrielle's face blossomed into view, her vibrant, blue eyes gazing warmly into his. "Approaching each day with a sense of adventure is to be alive my Robbie, but to *accept* that adventure is to *truly live.*" Her sage advice whispered in his mind, accompanied by a light kiss to his cheek.

When? He tucked her letter safely inside his shirt. *Now,* thundered in his ears, and Ellie smiled. Without further hesitation he moved to the door, listened carefully and opened it. Empty corridors and silence met his cautious gaze. Without a backwards glance, and nothing but the clothes on his back, he pulled the door quietly shut and tip-toed down the hall.

***

"That damnable bitch!" Eugenie erupted, cold fury flashing in her eyes.

Thomas regarded her with feigned innocence, his face remaining bland, emotionless, although well aware of whom she meant.

"Who has offended you now, Eugenie?"

"Kathryn, of course," Eugenie spat, rolling her eyes at his stupidity.

He eyed his wife silently, puzzled, as Kathryn and her family had sailed months ago.

"Our son has run away from boarding school." Yanking an officious looking parchment from her desk, she waved it rudely in her husband's face.

That news, although not altogether unexpected, *did* come as a bit of a shock. "And just *how* would Kathryn play a part in his delinquency?" he asked quietly, not wishing to send Eugenie into one of her fits of shrieking diatribes.

"She obviously *lured* him away."

"And just how might she have managed that? Communication between England and the colonies does not occur weekly, or even monthly, to the best of my knowledge."

His impertinence infuriated her, setting venomous accusations into motion. However, he was not in the mood to listen. "Consider this, Eugenie," he interrupted, grasping her shoulder painfully. Her reaction was instantaneous: a closed fist came up without warning, but was quickly restrained in his vice-like grip. "If he *has* fled to the colonies, my dear wife, it is because he seeks, *and will find,* a haven of loving warmth: something sadly missing in this household," he snarled, and turning abruptly left.

Heated invective followed him down the long hallway, her final words: "I *will* contact that grandmother of hers and ..."

The last of it died as he closed the study door with a slam. *Is it any wonder that our daughter, Emiline, is such a selfish, arrogant, difficult child?* Thomas sat down at his desk and stared out at the knotwork gardens. Their precise symmetry fascinated him and eased his troubled mind.

It distressed him that Robert—*Robbie*—had fled, for he would worry. Although a large lad, looking older than his actual age, he was only eleven. During Robbie's first, and only, visit home from school he had entered the kitchen unannounced, discovering Cornelius in whispered conversation with his son. "Whatever this is about I am to be trusted," Thomas had assured. He knew the money he had secretly sent his son had allowed him to make his 'leap of faith' sooner than expected, yet he had no regrets.

Thomas sat staring at the garden, a deeper shade of green in the on-coming dusk, appalled at how quickly the hours had sped by as he sat deeply lost in thought. His eyes misted with a mixture of joy, sadness and relief. *He told me of his plans that day and without prearranged planning or cognizant thought, I sent him the funds to accomplish his wish.* "Be safe, my son, be happy, live your life as you see fit, I love you," he murmured to the quiet room. Pushing his chair back, he headed for the kitchen to confer with Cornelius.

***

Robbie lurched from side to side as the small oxen cart rumbled along the rutted path. As the left wheels suddenly struck a rut, he was pitched against a huge sow who wriggled her tail in rapid circles, grumbling her annoyance. *Funny, I thought a wriggling tail meant happiness.* Robbie smiled, thrilled to have a ride despite his unusual companions. *Mother would have a fit if she could see me. She could never hold her head up in polite society again.* He stifled a giggle.

The cart then lurched abruptly to the right. Unable to brace himself, Robbie was launched against a large ram. The ram, however, sent no mixed signals. Bleating angrily, he swiped his horned head in retaliation, catching Robbie a glancing blow on his shoulder. "Sorry, old man," he muttered.

Rubbing his shoulder gingerly, he began inching his way along the floorboards to the rear of the cart; where he squirreled himself between two wooden crates: one filled with cackling hens, the other geese. Easing his feet through the slat-work gate, he allowed them to dangle. "This *is* rather unique. Facing this way, I can enjoy where I have been. I must tell Gabrielle," he whispered to the geese.

Apparently unimpressed with his observation, with a loud *'splat'*, a wet, green glob struck his thigh. Wrinkling his nose, he grabbed a handful of straw and scrubbed his leg. "Thanks," he quipped, grinning. "Good luck intended, I presume." Absolutely *nothing* could dampen his spirits today, or any day, from here on for that matter.

By the time they reached the market area near the wharf, Robbie had two or three more 'gifts of abundance' from his noisy companions. As he hopped off the back of the cart, he eyed the hens more respectfully. They apparently lacked the desire, or perhaps ability, to shoot a wad of effluence with any efficiency. *Probably the latter* he figured, for they had pecked him viciously several times, obviously vexed by his uninvited proximity.

He rubbed his sore rump. Two days of that bumpy ride had made him appreciative of the riding horses available at the *Beaumont Estate.* He no longer thought of it 'home'. "However," he murmured softly as he waited for the Brewsters to lumber down from their higher perch on the wagon seat, "No horse of mother's came close to the quality of Beauty. I hope to ride her again someday."

It was late Friday afternoon, the Brewster's timing having been *perfect* in their estimation: early enough to pick a prominent spot to display their stock and grab a few hours of rest. Saturday would entice some eager customers, but Sunday should bring a constant bustle of interesting people from all walks of life. Most people of religious faith congregated at the large stone church just outside town every Sunday, eager to receive their weekly atonement. Once accomplished, they headed to town, or down onto the wharf to sample the wide variety of wares available at market.

Robbie smiled. His mother had always insisted on Sunday worship at their local parish for inappropriate reasons, her primary mission: flaunting her well-mannered, family in their Sunday finest for all her peers to appreciate and covet. *Religious concepts amaze me. Do whatever you choose all week, for you shall be forgiven every Sunday.* He had observed the same offenders arriving faithfully each week, over and over. At that thought he chuckled out loud.

"You seem in fine spirits, young man," Mrs. Brewster quipped as she unfastened the wood-slat gate at the back of the wagon.

"That I am, Mrs. Brewster, and grateful for the ride. Show me where to put those animals and I shall secure them for you."

With a gesture of her meaty arm, she marched towards the coveted spot her husband was guarding, dragging the protesting sow behind her. Robbie quickly snatched the crate of hens and followed. He would leave the geese until last; he needed to gear up courage for that. This was his only pair of pants, which at the moment needed cleaning.

The Brewsters were old hands at this; in short order all was precisely arranged, including the wagon being angled into position to act as living quarters. Robbie was impressed. *I know so little of how life is truly lived; but I shall correct all that.*

"We're headed for the pub for a pint and a bite," Mr. Brewster announced, clapping Robbie on the shoulder, pleased for the help. "Care to join us?"

"No thank you, sir. I shall remain here and watch your spot until you return."

Brewster's eyebrows rose somewhat skeptically.

"I *can* handle myself, sir," he said, fingering the hilt of a dirk tied under his tunic.

"I just bet you can, lad, you got spunk." Grasping his wife by the arm, he marched off.

Robbie leaned against the wheel of the cart, observing the vendors as they arrived and chose their spots, occasionally with a bit of coarse language and idle threats. Apparently many knew each other, the thread of camaraderie easily sensed in their ribald tales and light banter. Volunteering to stay with the cart had served two purposes: the obvious, which he had stated, and time to dig out a penny from one of his well-concealed pouches. Even after purchasing his present clothing, he had four pouches tied snuggly in different spots so as not to create an obvious bulge.

He intended to beg or barter for the most part, to save what coin he had to get started in the colonies. *Started? Doing what exactly?* He pursed his lips, eyes rolling skyward. *That, Robbie, shall be determined at the appropriate time, my good man.* He grinned, feeling giddily happy. *Perhaps the day will come when I awake some morning and wonder: what have I done?* He shook his head and whispered, "I doubt it."

When the Brewsters returned, Robbie headed to the tavern. Mrs. Brewster had kindly offered him a hen to trade for dinner, which he politely declined; explaining that he would be offering to work for meals and lodging from here on out. He was delighted to help them with their two-day market stay, after which he would bid 'goodbye'.

"You say you wish to go to sea, laddie?" Mrs. Brewster had cornered him in a quiet moment alone. "I'll ask ye no questions about yer business, nor offer any uncalled for advice. But I see true quality beneath those rough garments. Ye are a good lad, from good stock, with a long life ahead of you."

"Mrs. Brewster, you are dying to ask if my cause is worth the risk, and all I must forfeit." He grinned knowingly and she nodded, embarrassed. "Yes—absolutely."

"Well, I see determination and happiness written all over your face. I need no further details. May God be with you each and every day." Placing a wet kiss on his cheek, she turned to greet a prospective buyer who stood eyeing the recalcitrant ram.

Robbie wandered the length of the pier and back before turning to scan the horizon. Shading his eyes against the glare he searched for sails, or even a hazy bit of dark fuzz on the horizon that would indicate a ship arriving. But still nothing.

Captain Farnham? Farraday? What did Gabrielle tell me? He fumed, his face scrunching into an irritated frown. "I know," he said jubilantly, snapping his fingers. "Captain Farthingale, Captain Kirkland J. Farthingale, that's it. I must find him or at least hear of his whereabouts. He made sure the letter from Gabrielle reached me, actually paid a lad to bring it directly to the butler at the Beaumont Estate." Robbie looked about quickly, aware he was carrying on a conversation, *out loud,* with himself. Relieved to find he was not within hearing distance of the few people wandering the pier, he promised never to tease about his grandfather's similar idiosyncrasy again.

His original plan had been to stow away until well out to sea, before announcing his presence. He had no experience with ships, sailing, or anything else about that life. Better to find Captain Farthingale; he had been fond of Gabrielle and her parents. Perhaps in deference to her, he would make Robbie's 'training period' at least *gentler.*

Rob had remained close to the pier, working in the pub for two weeks now. The Brewsters would not be returning soon; they had sold all their stock, and at a good profit. For that, he was pleased. But he did wish a ship would dock soon. He had asked repeatedly after Captain Farthingale and his ship, but had received no specific answers. His continued questioning eventually won him a few vague ramblings and odd looks from some 'old salts', their lopsided grins and rolling eyes causing Rob to wonder what he was missing. Obviously they felt he was either too young for explanations or that it was none of his business. *Most likely both.*

Curiosity overcoming common sense, Robbie spent the day roaming the small back allies of the seedier end of town. Everyone he asked gave him the same reaction. *They all know something. Farthingale has been here recently or is still here—somewhere.* His feelings leaned towards the latter, although not through logical deduction.

Lost in thought, he failed to remain alert. "Get 'im!" all he heard as he was roughly grabbed from behind, arms pinned, and gut-punched. Air whooshing painfully from his lungs, he dropped to his knees gasping. A rank smelling sack was quickly yanked over his head and snugged around his neck. Thrown effortlessly over a beefy man's shoulder, he was carried into an alleyway. Yelling would be useless, the thick sack made simple breathing difficult—yelling would be impossible. His only recourse was to kick, and *kick* he did, thrashing arms and legs wildly.

Heaved to the ground amidst coarse epithets, he landed with a hard 'thump' on his back. Two pairs of rough hands quickly trussed him like a holiday turkey. With arms *and* legs imprisoned, further attempts at struggle were useless. He actually found the image of himself as a 'trussed turkey' quite amusing. He had no time to contemplate the idiocy of that vision, *or* his future, as he felt himself carried up a long set of stairs, a feat accomplished effortlessly without so much as heavy breathing. His captor was a huge man, able to have killed him easily and yet he had not. Neither one had removed his dirk, yet Robbie knew they were aware of it: as the smaller man had tied his arms he commented: "Nice little pig-sticker. Should we …?"

"Nah, he's well-trussed. The boss said to bring him *as is*—and *as is*—is what he is." He guffawed at his own humor.

They stopped at the top of the stairs, and apparently having reached their destination, rapped a staccato beat on the door. His captor waited and then repeated the same series of raps. A shifting slide bolt could be heard, accompanied by the rattle of a released chain guard. The door opened soundlessly on well-oiled hinges.

"Have you brought the package?" an authoritative voice asked.

"Yes, sir."

"Drop it there. Any weapons?"

"Yes, sir."

Robbie felt a finger jab his side indicating the dirk, yet he still did not remove it.

"Shall I stay, sir?"

"No. Time for *you* to begin sobering up the ranks."

Robbie heard the door open—then close, and the slap of receding footsteps fading and blending with the distant sounds of the alley. The bolt lock was slid into place as the chain guard rattled, *both* reset for security. He lay still, curious more than frightened. A hand slid up under his tunic, quickly relieving him of his dirk. Unsheathing it, his captor slit the rope around his ankles, paused, and when no struggle ensued, proceeded to free his arms and wrists. In a practiced move, the knife then slid quickly under the rope around his neck, its sharp point piercing the offensive sack and resting precariously against the vulnerable flesh under his jaw. Robbie held his breath remaining motionless.

"You've got brains, boy. You learn rapidly."

A large hand grasped the coarse sack and with a swift 'yank,' the hood peeled back. He drew in a deep breath, ridding his lungs of the filthy stench, but stayed motionless—waiting. The point of the dirk lingered at his throat—he was not about to do anything foolish. As his eyes accustomed themselves to the well-lit room, he found himself facing a large, well-dressed, authoritative man.

"Stop frightening the lad," purred a soft voice from somewhere behind him.

Startled, Robbie turned towards the source, stopping abruptly as the dirk broke his skin painfully. His captor stood, keeping the blade leveled at Robbie's chest as he flashed a chastising glance at whoever was in the far corner.

"You may stand up, boy. Slowly, no fast moves."

"Yes, sir," he said politely, as he slowly stood and stretched to his full height.

His captor moved about him unhurriedly, judging him through narrowed eyes, looking him up and down thoroughly. Robbie felt his teeth might be checked at any moment, perhaps worse—like Mrs. Brewster's ram: eyed, petted and fingered before sale.

"My, my, my …" an appreciative, seductive female purr issued.

Ignoring her, his captor moved to a large chair and sat down, casually dangling one leg over the arm, but the dirk stayed at the ready.

"Face me, boy."

Robbie turned to find himself also facing the source of the lilting, feminine voice. She was—no appropriate words came to mind. She lounged on the bed amidst satin sheets and mounds of frilly pillows, her red pouting lips forming an alluring smile. Sparkling, amber eyes impaled him seductively as she flounced golden, corkscrew curls. Swinging bare feet to the floor, she plumped her breasts and smoothed her lacy chemise, allowing her upper thigh to remain exposed.

Robbie feared his shocked innocence doubtless registered openly on his face and was embarrassed. Yes, he *was* young, but not totally unaware of the lures of women, especially *certain ones.* Older classmates had related ribald tales on a regular basis, bawdy stories he attributed to bragging. Perhaps he had judged too quickly.

A slow smile spread across the handsome face of his captor. "Sheathe your claws, my dear. He is but a boy. And I am *not* done with you just yet."

Although unsure as to exactly why, the man's last remark served to embarrass him even more. He often awoke to stiff discomfort *down there*—more and more often as a matter of fact and …

"I understand you have been looking for Captain Farthingale," the man stated firmly.

"Yes, sir." Robbie's mind leaped back to business, halting further *'thoughts'.*

"Why?" Icy, blue eyes bored through him.

"I *must* get to the colonies. I considered stowing away with the first ship going there, but I …"

"Perhaps, if my abilities to judge character have not been impaired by too much idle time and …" He shot a look at his companion and winked. "I gather you wish to work your way across the ocean, and become a man in the doing, eh boy?"

Robbie gaped, astounded that a stranger could understand him better than his parents. He nodded, but found no words.

"Why specifically, Farthingale?"

"I owe him for a kind favor, and would work hard in return."

"What favor might that be?" he asked, a frown creasing his forehead.

"He made sure I received a letter that came from the colonies. It was a special …"

"My God, you are Gabrielle's *Robbie.* Now what are the odds of that?"

"Yes, sir."

The woman on the bed took a sudden interest, standing up and adjusting her chemise more appropriately. But a stern look sat her back down.

He's the one with the talons, Robbie decided. *He merely sheathes them well.*

"Well then, young Robbie, I *am* Captain Farthingale, as I am sure you have guessed. My question to you is: *why?*"

"Why am I running away, to put it more bluntly?"

"Yes, you obviously come from wealth, fine schooling, probably a large estate. What more could you possibly desire?"

"A chance to live my life as *I* choose, one not chosen for me in order to fulfill my obligation for the act of having been born."

Farthingale threw back his head and laughed. "Exactly the same reasons I left home many years ago."

He stood, walked over to Robbie and handed him his knife.

"From my limited observation, you appear intelligent and brave; and more than likely, extremely determined and stubborn or you would not have gotten this far. So I will make no attempt to send you home, nor will I turn you over to the authorities." He looked Robbie in the eye, his gaze harsh. "However, I *will* warn you, the sea is a cruel mistress—crueler even than this one." He winked at his lady friend. "I *will* work you hard, but I will also be fair. Long hours, rough seas, rotten food, calloused hands and aching backs, and that is just the beginning. Have I dissuaded you yet?"

At Robbie's vigorous shake of his head, he laughed. "I thought not. Therefore, I will promise you one thing. By the time we hit port in Charleston, you *will* be a man. Now, what say you?"

"When do we sail, Captain?"

"In three days time, young man. My ship has been in dry-dock for minor repairs, but will be ready to leave on the full tide. Be on the dock at dawn, not a moment later. Keep your money tucked snuggly and watch yourself closely. You will have to prove yourself to the crew, earn their respect. They *are* a hard lot, but you have merit. There is one thing I absolutely forbid on my ship and will intervene on your behalf: no buggery of young lads—or the cows for that matter—if you get my meaning. What the older men do on their own time is not my concern. But you? You will be safe."

"For heaven's sake, why scare the lad?" she asked, her rich, sultry voice bringing Robbie to understand some of her appeal to the captain.

"I am not scared, miss," he said politely. "Merely warned. Gabrielle's mother told me that knowledge of the 'enemy' is a form of power." Turning back to the captain he added, "I thank you for this opportunity. I *will not* disappoint you or myself for that matter."

"You will do just fine, lad. Now, do you think you can get back to the other side of town unscathed?"

"Absolutely, sir. I shall not daydream this time. *That* is a job better assigned to the fairer sex." With a jaunty grin and quick wink, he took his leave amidst raucous laughter.

"In three days time I will be on my way, Ellie. Wish me the strength to make both you and myself proud," he murmured and hurried down the stairs. Focusing on what he was about this time, he moved deftly along the streets and alleys, steering clear of all dark corners. But try as he might, he could not stop humming a bright tune.

Chapter Thirteen

By Land or By Sea

"Jason, over here," Jack jerked his head towards the woods. "We need to talk."

Jason shot him a curious look, but followed him.

Stopping behind some low underbrush, Jack turned to face his friend. They were far enough from the village, out of view and beyond any possibility of being overheard. "I am not sure we can trust O'Reilly." Jack got directly to the point. "We will be leaving Keowee shortly, and O'Reilly, by his own words, will be watching for us."

"Unfortunately so." Jason frowned. "Kathryn and I have talked of this problem, but have yet to find a solution. We do not need 'hangers on'."

"From what you both said, he insists that he tag along to help ensure your safety."

"So he claimed, but we have reservations."

"And so you should. O'Reilly is not a bad man, but can be easily led, *that* could be dangerous. As a fellow officer, he and I interacted more closely. I have seen his determination falter under duress, a fact which worries me."

"Good point, Jack. Astute observation is one of your talents, but what specifically bothers you?"

"He *knew* Gilson had become a rabid dog, and yet joined him. In his defense, he was threatened by Stewart to produce you or face dire consequences. But look at him. He would be in no worse position had he shown some courage and taken Gilson down. Jack watched Jason absorb his words, his expression becoming stony, unreadable. "He could have spared you that dangerous altercation with Gilson. Thankfully, neither of you was injured, but if the timing had been off …" He shook his head.

Jason paused considering the possibilities. "You have no faith in his vow to us?"

"*He* believes what he promised, and made his vow in good faith. However, at the time he was in shock over Gilson's death." Jack eyed Jason for a moment before continuing." I am sure he feels the same now, but no one has challenged him as yet. It is one thing to make vows when there is no immediate threat—but quite another when imminent danger is present. Apparently Stewart has not sent soldiers to find out why the two of them disappeared, but he may. Somehow I doubt O'Reilly would maintain the courage of his convictions when faced with the possibility of his own death."

"Unfortunately your scenario rings of truth."

"As I said, he is not a *bad* man, Jason, merely a *weak* one."

"You have given this a great deal of thought, Jack. What are you proposing? I know you would not have spoken unless you were prepared to …"

"I am prepared to *handle* the situation," Jack interjected.

Jason smiled, pleased at Jack's self-confident, quietly assertive demeanor.

"May I ask what you plan?"

"I am riding to Charleston to see if Ted can bring his carriage to Jamie's hideaway. As we travel north, we are less apt to draw attention as a family traveling by carriage. Hopefully, he can get us closer to Georgetown before we relegate ourselves to horseback. I will also find out what he knows of remaining hostilities—and Stewart. Several months have passed; all could be changed by now."

"What about O'Reilly?"

"That part of the plan will evolve depending on my meeting with him and what I sense at the time. I could read him easily in the past. However, I promise you—he *will not* be traveling with us."

Jason arched a black brow, his eyes narrowing.

"You, Kathryn and the children shall meet me at Jamie's hideaway one week from tomorrow. I will have current information to help make decisions, even if I cannot get the carriage. Wait for me without fail. I *will* meet you there."

"And O'Reilly?" Jason pushed.

Jack's eyes darkened, his gaze turning stony.

"Don't give him a second thought. Enjoy your remaining time here and travel safely."

Both children were asleep. Kathryn turned to her husband, knowing he and Jack had met earlier." We will soon have to hold our private conversations, as well as other 'diversions', in the wee hours, what with Beau's growing demands and Gabrielle keeping later hours." She heaved a sigh, shaking her head disconsolately.

With a caress to her cheek, Jason smiled warmly. "From here on, my love, we *will have* more privacy. I shall see to it." Snaking an arm about her waist, he nudged her quietly out the door.

They stood in the warm darkness conversing in low voices. Kathryn listened intently, eyes widening as Jason related his conversation with Jack almost verbatim.

"Jack has become his own man, now that he has been given the chance," Kathryn commented. "His assessment of O'Reilly disturbs me a bit, but I did not know the man that well. He tended to be a loner and rather quiet," she mused, testing Jack's harsh judgment but unable to fault him.

"Nor I, my pet. However, I have always had absolute faith in Jack's decisions, trusting him implicitly, even in the beginning when I barely knew him."

She muttered a sound of agreement, remaining deep in thought for several long moments before raising her eyes. Even in the dim light of a partial moon, her expression was *unusual … unreadable* as she asked softly, "Does Jack plan to kill him?"

"I did not ask, Kathryn. Jack will do whatever he must. The decision lies in *his* hands. He came to me and …"

"And *we* have packing to accomplish and many 'goodbyes' if we are to meet him at the appointed time," she said firmly, forcing a thin smile.

Jason cupped her face, kissing her with deep feeling. "I love you."

"Always," she answered fervently. Arm-in-arm, they re-entered their hut.

"Jesus, he is in the exact place Kathryn and Jason left him weeks ago," Jack muttered, shaking his head. "He truly means to attach himself to us."

Jack studied O'Reilly from a secluded spot, watching as he prodded his campfire into activity, throwing pieces of wood into the burning embers. Adjusting a dented pan over the flames, he sat back on his haunches, sipping what appeared to be coffee.

No surprise, he never could make decisions without guidance. Jack frowned as it dawned on him: *much like my former self.* He thought back to Kathryn's quiet advice, given shortly after another of Eugenie's thoughtless, humiliating putdowns. "When you discover your true self, Jack, you will embrace the good and change what is not to your liking no matter the difficulty, or how long it takes." *I am finally doing that, my Kathryn.* He smiled at the memory. *To think that at one time, we actually considered you to be nothing more than an ignorant colonial. We were the ignorant ones, I fear.*

O'Reilly stretched and belched loudly, quickly refocusing Jack. "Well, O'Reilly, let's see exactly what you are up to," he mouthed and crept nearer.

"Greetings, O'Reilly," Jack said lightly, stepping from behind a tree, his pistol holstered but easily accessible.

O'Reilly's head spun towards the sound. Dropping his cup, he reached for his gun.

"Leave it holstered," Jack advised, as *his* pistol neatly cleared the holster and leveled on O'Reilly's chest.

"Jack? Jesus you took me by surprise. Damn you, you always did have that talent. You just took ten years off my life," he swore softly.

Perhaps more, Jack thought grimly as he smiled and moved into the small clearing. As O'Reilly displayed open hands, proving them empty, he re-holstered his gun.

"I hardly recognize you, Jack. Where in hell did you disappear to? What have you been doing? What are you …?"

"*That* is my question to *you*, O'Reilly."

"Well, Gilson and I," he began somewhat uncomfortably.

"I know all that and could care less," Jack interrupted tartly.

"Then you know I can't return to Charleston. So I decided my best chance is to go with the colonel." He shrugged his pleading expression pathetic. Jack did not 'buy it'.

"You have camped here for many weeks. Even after your meeting with Kathryn and Jason you stayed. Why? Did they give you any false hope or promises?"

"Well, no," he admitted.

"You should have moved on. By now you would have been headed for home or more likely, long since back in England."

"Nothing awaits me there either, Jackson."

"Has anyone ever been honest enough to tell you, that you are a parasite?"

O'Reilly scowled and stood. Clenching his fists he hissed, "Why do you insult me so? I will travel with them and I *will* protect them."

Jack eyed him intently. "When difficulties arise—what then?"

"I will, I will …"

"*Falter,* as you have done in the past, more than once," Jack snapped. "You thought your actions undetected, but I have seen Gilson cover for you so often it has permanently stuck in my craw. Perhaps that is why he turned on you."

"That is not fair," he whined.

"Save it, O'Reilly. You are to pack up and head in any direction you choose. Just *do not* be here, or anywhere close, by nightfall. Do we have complete understanding?"

"Yes, I guess. But not really." His mind spun, weighing his options. *I'll let him think I'm moving out and catch him off-guard. After this bullshit, I can take that son-of-a-bitch without guilt. I'll join the colonel; deny I saw Jack and act surprised if asked.*

"All right, all right. Don't look so impatient," O'Reilly said, kicking dirt onto the fire.

He made a series of ineffectual attempts at appearing to break camp, but Jack was not fooled. *You read like an open book, O'Reilly. Just force the issue.*

"Good luck, O'Reilly. I'll be on my way."

As Jack turned, he saw O'Reilly's hand edge towards his holster. *Go for it you weak bastard. Go for it.* Jack spun back as O'Reilly's thumb cocked the hammer. He never knew what hit him, a shocked expression transfixing his features as a blossom of brilliant red spread across his chest. He dropped like a stone, without as much as a twitch.

"Sorry, O'Reilly. You *never* were cut out for this lifestyle."

Holstering his pistol, he grasped O'Reilly by the ankles and dragged him into the thicket. He would make him a quick grave, he owed him that much.

For a moment he wished he had misjudged, but quickly put his guilt aside. "Let's make this quick, O'Reilly. I have a lot of ground to cover and little time to do it."

***

The first two weeks had been rougher than Robbie could possibly have imagined. He quickly discovered his worst fears were nothing compared to the reality he faced daily in his new life at sea with toughened old tars. Captain Farthingale, good to his word, did not intervene to halt the taunting or the physical abuse he dealt with—a rough shove or overly hardy slap on the back. In fairness to Farthingale, Robbie realized his life would be even worse if the crew viewed him as the captain's favorite. He made no complaints, ignoring those who ridiculed and called him a 'whiner', doing as told, without complaint.

Within his first two days on board, just as dusk fell, a grizzled tar had approached him. Leaning close he leered suggestively, relating lurid details of his proposed plan, disgusting and embarrassing him. Thinking quickly, Rob answered, "No thanks, friend. The captain keeps me way too busy to find time. But I appreciate your warm thoughts."

The man burst out laughing, slapping his thigh in wholehearted glee. "That's the best put-down I've ever received. Relax, laddie, I never takes anyone by force." He stood back, hands on hips, eyeing Robbie thoughtfully. "As a matter of fact, I like you. Call me Fish."

"I like you too, Fish. I'll be pleased to call you my first friend. Do you have a nickname for me to help me fit in better?" Robbie grinned.

Fish looked him over, scratching his whiskered chin vigorously, whether deep in thought or scratching a louse, Robbie was unsure. Finally a smile flashed across his face. "For the time bein', Brat will do."

"Brat, it is. I'll see you at chow."

With a mock salute, Fish swaggered off chortling to himself; Robbie breathed a sigh of relief. *That went better than first appearances promised. May all my 'encounters' go as smoothly, but he sincerely doubted it.*

That night Robbie secreted himself behind wooden crates on deck. Within a few minutes, his talented carving abilities provided him with a wooden shiv: small enough to easily conceal, yet strong enough to cause painful damage. He had no desire to pull his dirk on one of these hardened tars for fear it would be forcefully taken away or worse.

He chuckled to himself as he ran his fingers over the rounded top edge. He had given extra attention to the smoothing, making it easier to hold without risk of splinters, allowing a firmer thrust. *My God, I've begun to think like them already. And my precisely spoken English has gone to hell.*

Several days passed without major upset or further suggestive moves aimed in his direction. He did his work, asking questions if unsure rather than creating problems through ignorance. He was not a slacker, only ate his share of allotted meals, and had not gotten seasick—at least so far. When his palms bled from the rough manila rope, he accepted a fingers worth of lard that Fish filched from the galley, pleased to find him good to his word. After rubbing it into his abrasions, he wrapped his hands with muslin torn from his shirttails. *Asking for bandaging would be unacceptable.*

They watched him relentlessly seeking to discredit him, as they did with all new members—especially an untried 'Brat'. With any luck, a situation might eventually present itself; one in which he could earn their respect. With no unpleasant confrontations of late, he became lulled into a false sense of security.

Dusk seemed to be the 'magic hour': a time ripe for small crimes to be carried out with the least reprisal. Robbie stood at the rail near the prow, coiling the slack lines neatly, as instructed. Bending down, he grabbed the heavy manila hawser and straightened. Gazing out across the gently, rolling swells of the ocean, mesmerized by her beauty, he idly ran one hand down the rope and effortlessly snagged it into a neat coil.

Suddenly a pair of strong hands slammed down on the railing—one on either side of him—pinning him there. A large, unkempt body insinuated itself firmly against his back, noticeable desire pressing firmly into the cleft of Robbie's buttocks.

"Don't fuss, laddie, it'll go easier for you."

Robbie froze—his mind awhirl. Struggle? Scream? Attempt reasoning? *No, all bad ideas.* It was Black Dog, the sound of his voice and particularly offensive smell a dead giveaway. *Think quickly or it'll be too late.* "Black Dog, I'll not fight you. At least allow me to ease my breeches," Robbie said calmly, amazing himself.

"Now there's a good lad," he chortled. Although surprised, he agreeably moved back enough to accommodate the boy. *Delicious, sweet thing: a virgin to be sure.* His mind already lived the 'act', his breath coming in ever-quicker gasps.

Robbie's hand slid towards the front of his baggy breeches, fingers slipping quickly into his pocket; grasping the wooden shiv he spun, and in one fluid motion scribed an arcing slash along the side of the large man's neck, upwards across his cheek.

"You fucking, little bastard," he screamed, cupping his cheek, shocked as blood poured around his fingers. "You just barely missed me eye!"

"I *did not* miss, Black Dog," Robbie growled, fury fueling his determination. "I decided to be generous is all—at least *this one time.*"

"Wait until I tell …"

"You'll tell *no one,* you son-of-a-bitch."

"Who says?" Pulling a grimy rag from his pocket, he dabbed his neck gingerly.

"Your pals would *never* let you live it down, sneering at a raw youth besting you, and Captain Farthingale might just get wind of it." Robbie held his gaze fearlessly. "Both you and I know that buggery is the one bit of savagery he forbids on his ship."

Black Dog's snarling facade began to ease, his icy fury fading. Robbie detected a change of attitude towards him, as the big man stared fixedly. *Respect* and it shocked him. This man's reputation was notorious: a cruel, callous, bully who demanded and received as he saw fit—up until today. Robbie would pinch himself later to be sure it had actually happened. But right now he needed to say something.

"I wish to be just one more shipmate, working together as comrades. But I *shall have* personal boundaries—*never* to be crossed. Do we have an understanding, Black Dog?" Robbie boldly ran the shiv across the palm of his hand.

Black Dog eyed him briefly. "Agreed, lad. You got big balls for one so young."

Turning away, he froze in his tracks. Captain Farthingale was approaching at a fast clip. "Sweet, everlovin' Jesus," he muttered, turning to Robbie, who stood nonchalantly recoiling the rope.

Robbie glimpsed a flicker of fear. He could make or break this man here and now.

Black Dog whipped a quick salute to his captain, noticing that Robbie immediately dropped the rope and followed suit. *Plucky lad,* he applauded silently.

"Good evening, gentlemen. Neat coils, lad, you learn quickly."

He peered closer at the big sailor's face to see better in the dim light. "What happened to you, Black Dog? Catch yourself on a spike?"

He knows, Robbie realized, applauding his attentiveness.

"Carelessness, sir, and I'll not make the same mistake again."

Farthingale pursed his lips, casting a knowing eye at Black Dog. "I would wash that gash with sea water, along with the rest of you—then splash it with rum. Now, come along, let the lad finish his work so he can get a bite to eat. Cookie is almost ready to lay out ham and biscuits."

He stood back, gesturing Black Dog to precede him down the narrow walkway. With a quick wink to Robbie, he said: "Make haste, lad. We'll not hold your meal." And then more quietly added, "Well done."

***

Kathryn shifted uncomfortably in Beauty's saddle. Traveling with Beau was no longer the pleasure it had been when he was an infant. At almost seven months, he grew heavier daily, fidgeted endlessly and demanded constant attention in never-ending gibberish which, after all these hours in the saddle, bordered on unbearable.

Gabrielle smiled encouragingly at her mother from her perch astride her father's large gelding. "Was I like that too, momma?"

But Gabrielle already knew that answer. Beau's personality was very different from hers. If he had been first-born, she wondered if her mother could have played such a dynamic part in her father's former life. *Would she have been on the battlefield at Guilford Courthouse that day, following poppa's destiny, or safe back at the campsite trying to control Beau?* Gabrielle continued playing 'what if' to entertain herself. It was a long, boring ride with little conversation shared between them, partially due to the necessity of traveling undetected, but more so, life had become 'so daily', as her mother put it. *I wonder if Jack and I would have gone to England. Probably not, but then, I would never have met Robbie.* She veered from that discomforting thought, taking her game in another direction.

Kathryn's eyes drifted to her daughter, riding straight and proud in front of her father. Her child's thoughts were miles away, her eyes fixed, eyeing the full moon.

"Such a serious face, little one," she commented softly. "Heavy thoughts?" Nudging Beauty closer, she silenced her son sharply, wanting to hear Gabrielle's answer.

Gabrielle faced her mother, her blue eyes still distant. "Playing 'what if', momma."

Jason brushed a kiss to the top of her head and hugged her. "Does your game allow you happy endings, poppet?"

"Sometimes. But more often just a different set of problems to handle."

"Do you wish to discuss …?" Kathryn asked, concerned by her melancholy.

A sad smile fought its way to her child's lips. "Not tonight, momma, but maybe sometime." Their life had always consisted of changes, excitement, a congenial 'family' of dragoons and ever-lurking danger. Even now, riding at night to avoid being stopped and questioned seemed bland. She understood her parents' unrest all too well. Suddenly she looked up at her father. "What is to become of us?" she whispered.

Jason shot his wife a startled look, unsure how one tells their child that he has no answers for her or her mother. He likened himself to the captain of a ship tossed on a stormy sea without mast or sails. Drifting blindly, he prayed for dead calm to overcome the challenges that threatened to leave their lives becalmed.

Gabrielle turned in the saddle, eyeing her father, expecting him to say something—*anything*.

"With luck, your Uncle Jamie's farm will be a safe port in a storm, at least for awhile, poppet. Sometimes, when it seems impossible to know what to do or where to go, change your approach. Instead of choosing from the *positive* opportunities available, consider the *negatives*. Dismiss those you never want to do, or be." He cupped her cheek gently. "And pray that the remaining one or two opportunities, may hold possibilities."

Gabrielle rewarded him with a brilliant answering smile, and a quick glance at his wife reassured him. As always, Kathryn's eyes spoke of understanding and undying love.

Just as the glowing, orange rays of sunrise burst forth highlighting the treetops, Jason indicated a copse of dense, scrubby-growth. Kathryn forced a tired smile and nudged Beauty in that direction. Completely exhausted, she wanted nothing more than to curl into her woolen cape and sleep. Unfortunately, that would be a while in coming.

She blew an exasperated breath, watching in detached fashion, as it created wispy fog in the cool dawn air. They would all want a bite to eat. Beau had slept for the last three hours; he would demand entertainment after his feeding, and then loudly voice displeasure at having his bottom cleaned. He rather enjoyed sitting in unkempt clouts, kicking and flailing when his mother wrinkled her nose and completed the 'evil deed'.

"This particular whim of his had best be temporary, my love. Very shortly, he will find his bottom giving him difficulty in sitting," Jason grumbled.

"Aye," she muttered, as she met her husband's concerned gaze. "I never dreamed I would voice this sentiment, Jason, but in many ways Guilford Courthouse was easier than this."

For a brief moment, he thought she might burst into tears. With a light touch to her shoulder, he murmured sympathetically, "If you can manage our son, Gabrielle and I will put together a light repast and prepare the bedding."

Gabrielle threw her arms around her mother and hugged. Searching her tired face, she gently chided: "The only person who expects you to do everything is *you*, momma. Perhaps someday you will learn to accept help more *gracefully*." A beaming smile softened the rebuke and Kathryn smiled. Rolling her eyes at her husband, she asked, "Your family traits or mine?" A question which left him chuckling and shaking his head.

"Here at last," Kathryn announced, pushing the cabin door open.

"Phew!" She wrinkled her nose at the musty, dank aroma assailing her nostrils.

"Well, I gather that delightful odor indicates Jamie's hideaway has remained unused since we were here," Jason commented, bouncing his son in the crook of his arm.

"I can fix that smell quickly, momma. Anna shared some of her secrets." Gabrielle headed out into the sheltering overgrowth. "I will not go far and shall be right back," she added before they could caution her.

Jason chuckled. "She has our number, my pet."

"She is truly a delight and a godsend. At times I wonder how I could manage without her. Then I become concerned that I am pressuring her too much."

"Do not fret, my love. Our daughter does not allow herself to be pressured in any way. Hence she is with *us*, rather than back in Keowee."

Kathryn kissed his cheek whispering softly: "I love you so."

Chucking her son under the chin, she whispered the same to him but added, "even when you are difficult, little man."

After looking around the large main room, assuring there was nothing of danger to Beau, she placed him on the floor with his gourd rattle. "You entertain yourself while momma and poppa open windows and shake out bedding. A little fresh air will help until your sister returns with herbs and sweet grasses."

In order to make Jack's deadline they had traveled longer hours than usual the previous night, even well into dawn, daylight having just broken as they arrived.

Kathryn yawned loudly. "I certainly hope Jack has children of his own someday so he can better determine the length of traveling time necessary. I find myself actually glad he is not here yet, as I would love to get some sleep."

"Me too, we have pushed hard these last few days, my Kathryn. I hope he brings ..." Jason shrugged. "Whatever he brings, he brings."

Within an hour, the cabin had taken on a new look. Gabrielle's armloads of fresh reeds and sweet grasses adorned the floor, much to Beau's delight as he crawled, happily content, playing unattended and uncomplaining.

"We must remember this trick," Kathryn commented, finishing the last bite of her meal. "Also, Miss Gabrielle, your fish was much appreciated and delicious."

Gabrielle beamed as she scooped up all the tin plates and headed for the sideboard to clean them. "You and poppa get some sleep. I will care for Beau and wait for Uncle Jack."

As Kathryn opened her mouth to speak, Gabrielle shook her head. "I am not sleepy right now." She stared at her parents with a bit of awkwardness. "I am excited to hear what Jack knows, who he has seen, and if Ted could come with his team and—I am not sleepy." She shrugged.

Kathryn gave her a kiss and with a knowing look, headed towards the bedroom. Jason yanked the covers up over them, and had barely pulled her into his arms to nuzzle her neck when she felt his deep, even breathing. *Thank heavens he is as tired as I. I thought perhaps I was losing my touch.* She smiled, drifting easily into much needed sleep.

A familiar birdcall just at dusk heralded Jack's arrival. Gabrielle rushed from the campfire and flung herself into Jack's open arms as he stepped down from his saddle.

"Oh, that all the lassies should greet me as you do, my princess." At Gabrielle's feigned pout he quickly added, "However, none will ever capture my heart and replace you." He hugged her soundly.

She stepped back smiling, searching for Ted. A pretty piebald mare stood tethered to Jack's big gelding, eyeing the greeting with curiosity.

"Where is ...?" Gabrielle's question was silenced as the little pinto stepped forward and boldly pushed a velvety nose against her cheek, snuffling and blowing softly.

"Well, *hello* to you too," she giggled, scratching her ears and tugging her forelock gently. "And what is your name?"

"Whatever name you give her, Gabrielle. I can see she loves you already."

Gabrielle spun to face Jack. She had been forced to leave her pony behind when they fled to England. But this was a full-grown horse—pretty, delicate, well mannered, a little on the small side just like her mother's Beauty—but a real horse.

"For me?" she gasped.

Jack nodded his eyes bright at her delighted pleasure.

"But, why, what have I done to deserve ...?"

Jack pulled her into his arms and held her, smiling over her head at her parents surprised faces. He could make light chatter, thereby diminishing the importance of his gift, or say what was in his heart and bear the embarrassed flush that would brand his cheeks. *I need her to know how much I love her, how much she has always meant to me, and how she saved me in England.* He opted for the latter.

Jack crouched down, and taking her hand, cradled it in his. Stroking the hair back from her forehead, he studied her face as her sparkling, blue eyes riveted on him.

The little mare determinedly snuffled against her cheek again, interrupting. With a slight gesture of Gabrielle's hand, she ceased her snuffling and stepping back, stood quietly attentive, astounding everyone at the instant bond between the two.

"I love her, Uncle Jack, she is beautiful, but why?" Her eyes captured his, questioning.

"*You, and only you*, saved me on that damnable ship and kept me sane during our hellish stay in England. Words are inadequate, my princess, but I know you understand both *me* and my meaning completely."

Gabrielle nodded her gaze unblinking.

"And also because she will be a constant reminder that I shall always love you, and carry you in my heart, even when we must be apart."

At that point an unbidden tear trickled down her cheek, stopped by Jack's thumb. Throwing herself into his welcoming embrace she clung tightly, her shoulders shaking in silent sobs. She knew of no words to convey her feelings. This wonderful, incredible man, whom she loved dearly, had forced aside personal devastation, risking everything to save *her* life.

Jason's arm slid around his wife's waist, pulling her close. He swiped her tears with his sleeve, glad he did not have to say anything at the moment; he doubted he could. Even Beau behaved, seemingly mesmerized by the beautifully patterned horse.

"She is so sweet mannered and elegant, Uncle Jack," she hiccupped.

"Do you need time to think of a name?" he asked.

With a vigorous shake of her head, she clucked to the mare, patting her cheek as she moved in close. "I shall reward you in a moment," she paused, feeling in her pocket for an ever-present sugar cube. "But first I must name you." She gently moved the mare's forelock aside to reveal an odd-shaped white patch hidden there. "I think you shall be called North Star—ever constant." Scanning their faces, she was pleased to see smiling agreement. But she laughed out loud as the small mare shook her head enthusiastically, setting the delicate strands of her silken mane afloat. Two cubes of sugar later, Gabrielle headed for the shed to introduce her mare to the other horses, make room for her, and be sure all were watered and fed.

They sat around the table, well satisfied by the delicious meal Kathryn prepared: roasted rabbit, fish, crisp greens, bread and piping hot coffee. The table conversation now turned to a serious nature. Gabrielle was invited to join them for a while as much of what Jack had to relate would ultimately impact on her.

The subject of O'Reilly was tabled until later. In a private moment earlier, well away from small ears, Jack spoke briefly to Jason of O'Reilly. "He will *never* be a problem. I presented options, he made the fateful decision." Jack shrugged no guilt apparent. "We will speak of it later. I will discuss the details so you may judge the necessity of what I did. However, I leave the details shared with Kathryn up to you. It may be disturbing."

"You always know what must be done, Jack. Neither Kathryn nor I will ever question your judgment, but she will want to know the truth. We will talk *after* Gabrielle is asleep. There is much in life she does not need to share yet. Come, let's get something to eat."

Jason pushed his chair back from the table, cupping his coffee in both hands, inhaling its fresh aroma deeply.

"Why didn't Ted come with his carriage and team?" Gabrielle asked, eager for news, her disappointment showing.

"We talked the pros and cons, my princess. He wanted to come, but it was not a good idea. I will explain in a minute, but first, of far greater importance, he asked that I give you an extra hug and this." Pulling a wrapped package out of his vest, he placed it in her hands and hugged her. With a giggle, she tore the paper aside to reveal a delicate lace-trimmed handkerchief.

"Something for a proper, young lady," Kathryn smiled.

"It smells so good," she gushed, inhaling deeply and handing it to her parents.

"Lavender," Kathryn breathed appreciatively. "That is a very thoughtful gift."

As Gabrielle tucked it in her sleeve, Jack continued. "Ted is well. He has been an asset to his employer, pleasing him by broadening his regular client base. Although he is allowed leeway in customer choices, neither of us could come up with a believable reason for him to take a fare that required such a long absence. He felt he risked angering his regular customers, as well as his employer."

"He is in too valuable a position to risk losing it," Jason explained, eyeing his daughter sympathetically.

"I understand, poppa. He is our eyes and ears and must remain so. I had just wished … Well, I wanted to ask him to watch for Robbie," she said softly, casting her eyes downward, discomforted.

Jack's large hand slid over hers and squeezed gently. "He knows, my princess."

"Thank you, Uncle Jack." Standing up, she hugged him and turned to face her parents. "You have much to discuss, and I know you will share anything I need to know when the time is right. Besides, I have the information I wanted." Lifting her sleeping brother from her mother's arms, she whispered, "I shall take care of 'his lordship'. You and poppa enjoy your evening with Uncle Jack." She headed for the rear door, causing her mother to send her a questioning look. "I must say 'goodnight' to North Star and the others." Dipping her free hand into her pocket she withdrew several cubes of sugar and held them up.

Kathryn merely smiled and turned her attention back to the table conversation.

Jack's news held some interest. But the unexpected letter he brought took precedence: addressed to *Mr. and Mrs. Jason Cameron* and written with the easily recognizable flourishes of his lordship.

"How did you come by this, Jack?" she asked, astounded.

""I do not ask Ted the 'how or why', but am thankful for his watchfulness."

Kathryn nodded, concentrating as Jason started to read. *Dearest Kathryn and Jason,* it began in a relaxed and personal nature—mentioning his children, a visit with Great Grandmother, and congratulations on the birth of their son. His lordship then proceeded to points of interest and tidbits about Banastre's marriage to an actress and pending book: his memoirs, of all things. Finally he got to the crux of the matter: *King George is not displeased and will soon determine an appropriate placement for me—possibly an ambassadorship, but too soon to give specifics. He is extremely impressed with your abilities and spoke of future possibilities, of which I shall keep you apprised, and ...*

Kathryn had heard barely a word, her swirling memories dashed. She riveted her gaze on her husband. *Do I detect an odd tone in his voice? Would he consider? Oh dear God ...*

At his wife's stricken look, Jason said firmly: "No, my love; that *is not* our future. Though, I *do* propose we stay in contact for ongoing news of Great Grandmother, Banastre's forthcoming book, and the new political atmosphere Britain must adopt."

Kathryn's face eased as Jack spoke up. "Politics will have an ongoing impact on the colonies. From what news I picked up in Charleston, it seems Savannah is close to evacuation. English troops will depart sometime in July, about a month from now."

"And Charleston?" Kathryn asked.

"That remains uncertain, although word has it, not until the end of the year. Nathanael Greene skirts the area ready to pounce, refusing to leave until the Treaty of Paris is presented directly to him, preferably on a golden platter." Jack laughed, amused.

"What of Alexander Stewart?" Jason asked.

"He is furious at the disappearance of Gilson and O'Reilly—doubtful about their drunken tale—and cannot find any explanation for Captain Hodges's odd departure. As the British status remains unclear, he finds himself unable to pursue the whereabouts of his own officers. Nathanael Greene would be delighted to build accusations of malice on Stewart's part. True or false, he would not hesitate to take matters into his own hands."

"Just what is *our* status at this point?" Kathryn eyed Jack.

"Stewart's stand is obvious, but as to Greene, despite Jamie's aid to his militia, there is no love lost between them. Jamie's favorable words would fall on deaf ears. We need to move further out, at least for now, Kathryn. Ted is too valuable right where he is, to risk coming here. He knows where we will be." He paused, a smile brightening his face. "He will know how to direct Robbie."

"And what of that situation?" Jason asked. How would they possibly handle that too?

"Nothing more than what Gabrielle assures. But she *does* know things that you or I would not be aware of, until they happened. Had I believed her words long ago, I would not have …" He stopped, refusing to relive that sadness again. "Thankfully, she is her mother's daughter," he said softly. "I think we should all get some sleep, spend tomorrow relaxing and leave at dusk. One more night of traveling, should put us far enough from Charleston to risk riding during daylight hours from that point on. Do you both agree?"

***

Kathryn sat on Jamie's porch steps watching her son crawl in the dirt.

"Your poppa will roll his eyes and think me daft, Beau."

Beau looked up, gurgling unintelligible words, and plopping himself over onto his plump bottom, shoved a grimy hand into his mouth. Kathryn smiled. She would never understand this child, but she loved him dearly. His precious existence had given her the strength to reclaim life, when it had hung precariously in the balance; over a year ago now. *How fast time is moving on.* She was filled with contentment. This was where they should be, at least for now.

Sad thoughts of O'Reilly crossed her mind briefly. Jack had advised, "You do not need to hear the details." But she had insisted—his description appalling her. Jack's recent changes, the sudden hard edge … *May he never set aside warmth and caring; this wonderful man I love … second only to Jason.*

A loud hailing from the nearest field brought her up sharply. Gabrielle, her hair billowing in an unruly mass, crouched low over North Star's withers as the mare galloped towards her, mane and tail flying.

Kathryn held her breath; *the fence is too high, the small mare will not …*

In a single fluid motion of elegance, the mare's sleek muscles bunched and sprang, carrying them effortlessly over the rickety fence. *My God, she is so like me.*

Gabrielle reined to a stop. North Star pranced, snorting loudly—obvious pride shining in her intelligent eyes. "Almost as good as you and Beauty, momma," Gabrielle exclaimed, dismounting.

"No longer 'almost', little one; you are just as good, perhaps gaining on *better.*

Gabrielle laughed and picked up her baby brother. Kathryn grinned, but her insides clenched. *Oh mother, now I understand what you went through with me.*

The friendly teasing of multiple voices drew her attention back to the road, where Jack and Jason flanked Jamie, following Old Joe, while Smitty happily brought up the rear of the procession. Jamie yelled his usual threats to the faithful, old plow horse as he flicked the leather reins gently on his back. "Get on there now or there'll be no food left, ye ornery beast." The tireless energy in their quick gait indicated the planting of the last field was finished: a little later than usual, but well within the growing season.

Kathryn's eyes raked hungrily over her husband's muscular frame, as she waved excitedly. A customary burst of inner warmth brought instant pleasure. *Thankfully, we now have a room to ourselves.* Her mind moved quickly ahead to tonight.

Lifting Beau from her daughter's arms, she gave North Star several appreciative pats.

"She is such a patient animal. What a marvelous gift, little one."

"Uncle Jack …" Gabrielle whispered softly, her mind revisiting another place and time, ignoring her brother's escalating clamor. "I love him so, momma. He truly wanted to die after … But he pushed on, just for me."

Hushing Beau sharply, she managed a smile at her little girl. Memories of Jack's pain tugged at her heart, for she understood the cause of his devastation; each revisited memory bringing renewed guilt.

"Time to clean up the little piglet before poppa sees him." With that statement, the heavy mood broke as both giggled conspiratorially. Kathryn headed for the house to tidy her son and begin the evening meal, as Gabrielle marched North Star towards the stable, praising her softly as they went.

Yes, life for the time being is perfect ... almost.

Chapter Fourteen

'Land Ho'

Robbie relaxed into the safety restraints of the crow's-nest, completely at ease, no longer nervous about either the height or constant motion. His spirits were exceptionally high. The sky was a cloudless brilliant blue, strong winds filled taut sails, a continuous curl of froth peeled along the prow, and gulls soared effortlessly. *We are close;* he smiled, excitement building in his chest. *He* would be the one to have first sighting, the one to experience the privilege of shouting 'Land ho' and he was proud.

Shading his eyes against the sparkling glare dancing atop blue-green waves, he searched the horizon. "Nothing yet, but soon; the gulls are proof." A twinge of melancholy struck, surprising him. He would actually miss these men: cutthroats, braggarts, even swaggering liars, if it served their purpose. Yet, after all these often painful weeks spent in close quarters, most were his friends; at least none were outright enemies.

His mind drifted—a kaleidoscope of recent events—pausing longer on memorable moments and shifting over those of little import. Captain Farthingale remained an enigma. *He acts the dandy ashore, but there is more to him than that. He is strict, tough, yet is fair; principled after a fashion.* That thought made him grin. After taking another quick scan along the horizon, he allowed individual faces to float through his memory as he ticked off various events: some good, some painful.

Fish would hold a special place as his first *friend.* But, oddly, Black Dog would be the one he would truly miss. They had gotten off to a wretched start, but in time had become fast friends, mutual respect the key to their friendship. "He saved my life and my legs," Robbie explained to the swirling gulls, wanting to share his tale with *someone.*

After another careful search along the horizon he relaxed, recalling one particular incident. The day had dawned dark, ill-omened in his opinion, and gone rapidly downhill from there. By late morning there was no mistaking the huge, dark patch looming on the horizon—ominous danger directly in their path and bearing down rapidly. All they could do was pray and hold steady to their course—if possible. Ink-black clouds roiled, the sea answering in kind—rolling and bucking as if wind and sea challenged each other to a contest to ascertain which had superior strength.

Crew members scuttled up the ropes crablike, hanging on for dear life, fighting the fierce gales, attempting to secure the sails from ripping free. Robbie moved quickly to secure the wooden crates lashed on deck. Struggling to stay upright, he stumbled against a crate just as the lashings gave way. Thrown onto his back, the air knocked from his lungs, he was helpless to avoid the huge crate that toppled precariously—then landed painfully pinning his legs.

Gulping air, he fought to get free. Another crate teetered precariously; the second one would kill him for sure. He thrashed futilely, his eyes blinded by sleeting rain.

"Cease yer struggles, lad, else you'll bring 'em all down," a harsh voice growled, as a stilling hand clutched his shoulder.

Robbie fought the intense pain, attempting to stay still. *Black Dog?* His mind swam, consciousness flickering, yet aware of the large form that slowly inched itself between him and the teetering crate.

With grunts of effort, audible over the howling gale, he secured it. Bellowing a colorful curse, he then turned full attention on Robbie. Crouching at the boy's side, he pushed his sodden hair back and peered closely into his ashen face.

"Don't quit on me now, laddie. You gotta help with this, I cain't do it alone." He shook Robbie into awareness. "You *can* do this. When I lift the crate, you scuttle out."

Mired in a red haze of agony, Robbie stared blankly: completely unaware of the cold rain cascading across his face, and heedless of Black Dog's gruff voice.

"Goddamit, you little bastard, do as I say *now!* Else I may renegotiate our deal." He shook him harder, pleased to see his idle threat achieving what he had hoped.

Robbie's eyes cleared, awareness returning. "No way," he ground out. "I'm listening."

"Wait for my instructions." Despite Black Dog's massive strength, it took immense effort to lift the corner of the crate, but he refused to give up.

"Now," he grunted. "Roll free."

The pain had been excruciating. To this day he could not recall dragging his legs free just as the ship lurched, wrenching the crate from Black Dog's grip and sending it crashing to the deck mere inches from his feet. Robbie struggled to sit up, but a firm hand on his chest forced him flat.

"Stay put until I see the damage," Black Dog yelled over the wind and rain as he proceeded to gently prod and bend Robbie's legs. He worked systematically up and down each leg, refusing to be rushed. When sure of his findings, he leaned close and assured: "Your legs are whole, lad, but you'll hurt for a day or two."

Without warning, he lifted Robbie effortlessly. Ignoring the boy's sharp gasp of pain, he headed below deck, fighting to stay upright in the pitching, storm-tossed ship.

"Brave lad," he said softly, placing him carefully on his berth. Grabbing dry rags, he patted Robbie down. The stuffy warmth, ever present below deck, was welcoming; it would ward off a chill. "I seen lotsa men who screamed like a babe for far less, lad."

Robbie's attempted smile became a grimace.

Black Dog lit an oil lamp and snapped it snuggly closed as the ship continued its choppy pitch and roll. "Let's take a better look." He gently nudged the boy's soggy pant legs up above his knees. Robbie immediately tensed.

"Relax, Brat. It was necessary to git yer attention. I got over *that* particular urge long ago—no offense meant." He grinned and returned to his methodical gentle prodding. "Scrapes, bruising, a pretty good cut here."

Abruptly disappearing, he returned shortly with a dented flask. He gave no warning; just unscrewed the cap and poured amber liquid into the wound. Robbie's eyes flew open on a gasp as he fought for control. "Payback you son-of-a-bitch?" he ground out through gritted teeth. But his blossoming grin matched Black Dog's.

Black Dog chuckled as he tightened a clean rag around the wound. Sitting on the opposite berth, he threw his head back and swallowed deeply from the flask. Then, swiping his mouth with a grubby sleeve, offered it to Robbie. "Where's me manners, lad? Ye have greater need than I." He raised Robbie's head, gently forcing the flask against his lips as the boy muttered denial. "I said *drink*, lad, nothing more than that."

Burning warmth tore down his throat and into his gut bringing immediate warmth and relaxation. Two or three more swigs and his eyelids drooped heavily.

"Feels better, don't it? Now, do you think you can keep yerself in this berth without me lashing you in?"

Robbie made a soft guttural sound.

"I'll take that as *yes*. I'm goin' back up on deck to help, but I expect *you* to stay put. You got bone bruisin', but you're a tough one. You'll be fine."

He turned, stopping abruptly. Captain Farthingale stood motionless, observing him intently. Braced under the low entrance, he held the casement for balance. His eyes blazed and Black Dog knew exactly what was in his mind.

"And just *what* do we have here, Black Dog?" he growled tersely.

"One tough lad, sir, albeit a bit drunk at the moment," he quipped lightly.

Farthingale's eyebrows shot upwards and Black Dog sobered, eyeing his captain with guiltless honesty.

"Banged his legs up a bit, sir; but they're sound. By yer leave, sir, I'll go above and do me job." At the Captain's firm nod, Black Dog moved around him and headed up the narrow steps.

Farthingale moved to Robbie's side, studying his bare legs carefully. Scanning the boy's face, he smiled. With eyes closed and bright color in his cheeks, he snored softly, occasionally releasing bursts of boozy breath. "I promised you an education, lad. May you still feel it worth the pain, when we finally reach land." Turning away, he headed topside, amused. "There is far more *'man'* to Black Dog than I would have imagined," he muttered aloud. Glancing at Robbie's prone figure, he could have sworn the lad smiled.

"Look lively up there, Brat! Whadya see?"

Robbie snapped back to the present, and leaned over the edge to see who had yelled.

"What would you like me to see, Fish?" he asked innocently.

"Smart ass right to the end, eh boy?" Fish chortled. "Are we there yet? All me natural urges are screamin' fer release, even a few of the unnatural ones is yellin' too!"

Raucous guffaws erupted, ceasing abruptly at the grating sound of a throat being cleared. Fish spun about and tipped his cap to the captain apologetically. Farthingale shook his head in feigned annoyance, but in reality could care less. They were now only a few hours from Charleston: one more successful crossing. He had much to be thankful for, and often voiced his appreciation when within the privacy of his cabin. To date, he had never been dealt a disappointment that could not be easily swept aside.

He smiled a private, unreadable smile as he scanned the horizon. An extremely lucrative venture awaited his arrival, and he was ready. His crew worked well together, a vital part of any success. A luscious warm body, eagerly anticipating his arrival, lounged on a thick feather bed, piled with satin comforters and lace-covered pillows to ease his aching bones. His bedside table would sport a glass decanter filled with the best brandy money could buy, and a dish of his favorite sweetmeats. *Yes, life was good.*

"What do you see, lad?" he bellowed upwards, cupping his hands to carry the sound. "Do you know what to look for?"

Robbie nodded vigorously, holding a finger up for patience as he searched the horizon, scrutinizing to the left and then the right. He jerked his head back, the tiniest 'difference' having caught the edge of his eye. Leaning as far as his restraints allowed he stared, unblinking, off to his far left.

"Well?" Farthingale demanded.

"Smudge on the horizon, sir; growing larger as I watch."

Curious faces looked skyward, eyeing him eagerly, mumbling questions and encouragement. "Come on, young eyes, what's ahead?"

Robbie ignored everything but the fuzzy shape on the horizon, focusing intently. "Are you real or are you a wishful vision? Just what are you?" he muttered, annoyed by the shape's continued lack of definition. He leaned farther out, straining to see more clearly. "Yes!" he screamed standing and waving his cap. "Land ho, boys! Land ho!" Tossing his cap into the air, he watched as it drifted over the railing and onto a passing wave.

More bodies gathered on deck, shouting and cavorting, expressing their pleasure. Robbie inhaled deeply, smiling in satisfaction. Snapping a smart salute to his captain, he started down the ropes. Farthingale flashed him a satisfied grin as he headed back to the wheelhouse to check his charts, leaving Robbie to fend for himself as he joined the celebration. *By God, it's taken the whole voyage, but I am finally one of them.* Robbie congratulated himself, feeling *that* to be his greatest accomplishment.

Robbie gripped the railing, watching the pier grow larger, excitement thrumming in his veins. He had never felt such elation in his whole life. They had been forced to lay off shore for several hours until the tide turned in their favor. As excitement escalated amongst the crew, eager to go ashore after eight weeks at sea and frustrated with the additional wait, small spats arose. But that was over, the tide was in. As they pulled anchor and nosed slowly towards the huge wharf, Robbie was amazed at the bustling masses. *This is my new home,* he realized. Blood pounded in his ears, his heart hammered a ragged beat, and for a second he felt light-headed.

Charleston appeared to be a magnificent city, its wealth and grandeur more evident the closer they came. Fancy carriages sat parked in a neat line, the well-groomed teams patiently awaiting their next command. Elegantly dressed men and women strolled proudly, displaying their ostentatious finery. Robbie had seen a great deal of 'display' when Gabrielle had embarked for the colonies, but nothing to match this performance. Scanning his apparel, he drew a sharp breath and shrugged. 'Gutter rat' would be the only applicable term at the moment. But that would change shortly. He began making mental notes of his needs and their order of priority once his feet touched ground. His whole life lay ahead of him, and he was eager to begin.

Excited cheers erupted as their ship nudged the pier with a gentle bump; an excellent landing on Captain Farthingale's part. In a matter of moments, the ship's lines were secure and eager sailors rushed down the gangplank. With a salute to their captain and promises to return on time, they yelled hasty goodbyes to one another—and to Robbie, wishing him well. He waited until last to disembark, avoiding the crush and allowing himself to absorb the contagious excitement. *Everything was a new experience and he reveled in each moment.*

As the last of the crew rushed past, Robbie stepped onto the gangplank, but immediately stopped at Captain Farthingale's curt hailing.

"Wait up, Rob."

The captain approached at his usual snappy pace. Robbie stepped back eyeing him with open curiosity. They had said their 'goodbyes', what could this be about?

"Remember men, three days only. Drunk or sober be here!" he yelled after his crew. He issued no idle threats; they knew from experience what was expected of them. With Captain Farthingale there was no such thing as an *idle threat.* A ragged but respectful chorus of 'aye Captain' echoed back and he smiled.

Robbie and Captain Farthingale stood alone on deck. Farthingale indicated a spot farther back from curious eyes on the pier, gesturing Robbie to join him. Leaning against the main mast, he crossed his arms, a smile spreading across his handsome features.

"Have I kept my promise to you, Rob?"

"Aye, Captain. If not yet a full grown man, I am well on my way."

"You handle yourself better than many of my regular crew, son."

Robbie smiled, his tan cheeks coloring, embarrassed by such singular praise.

"Is *this* truly where you wish to be?" Farthingale swung his arm in a sweeping gesture encompassing the city of Charleston.

"Not exactly in the city, sir, I will stay only long enough to make inquiries and …"

"Gabrielle is yet a child, Rob," he interrupted. "Come to sea with me; allow her to grow up and be ready for you. Perhaps another year or two," he shrugged noncommittally.

Robbie was curious. He had his own plans but why not see what kept Farthingale on the move. Obviously he had found a lucrative means of support compensating for Tarleton's 'retirement'; their former enterprise had been the topic of many tales at sea. Farthingale's ship had been delayed in port while in England. Numerous bunks with evenly spaced chains and cuffs had been installed on the lowest level. Robbie had seen them for himself, and did not like the implications—especially when Black Dog had painted a graphic description of how the 'captives' were to be shipped.

"You are a bright lad, and curious."

Robbie's eyes met the captain's knowing gaze. *Does he ever miss anything*? He forced himself not to shrink from his steely gaze.

"Although I shall miss the intrigue of partnering with Tarleton, the monies of my present venture make it *very easy* to move on." He paused, eyeing Rob closely, noting a spark of interest perhaps—or merely curiosity? The lad was good at hiding his true feelings, a valuable trait in successful business deals.

"Triangle Trade, Rob. Ever hear mention of it?"

"Not enough to completely understand, sir."

"My actual destination is New England. I merely dropped anchor here to renew old friendships."

His explanation was too simplistic. There was more to it than that, but none of his business and remained quiet.

"I will fill my hold with grains, textiles and rum. Rhode Island or Boston will be my next stop, I await final instructions. From there to Africa to exchange my cargo for …"

"For slaves," Robbie supplied, fully understanding the changes below deck, horrified. It required all his willpower to keep his outward expression neutral, non-judgmental. Obviously this business meant nothing more to Farthingale than 'business as usual'. But Robbie could never compartmentalize his mind into making that career acceptable.

Farthingale's eyes narrowed as he searched the lad's face for telltale feelings, not surprised to find nothing revealed or accusing. "In the Caribbean I sell my 'cargo' to the sugar plantations for—what else? Sugar and molasses to be made into rum back in New England. And the cycle begins all over." He studied Robbie. "Do you follow me, lad?"

Robbie nodded, but said nothing, any comment he made would be totally offensive.

"Occasionally I return to England to deliver much sought after sugar, at an excellent price I might add. This last layover I needed more berths. That is why you and I were able to 'hook up'. Perhaps you should take that as a positive sign, an opportunity not to be quickly denied. Consider it, lad. Numerous possibilities are being laid at your feet."

"Thank you for your show of confidence, sir, but I ..."

"Rob, although the concept is disconcerting at first, you *will* become accustomed."

"I am privileged to have sailed under your command and honored by your request, sir. However, I have a knot in my belly which must be tended first."

Farthingale chuckled, clapping Robbie on the shoulder. "Well-spoken Rob, always the diplomat and ever honest—those traits will take you far." He headed towards the gangplank, indicating Robbie to follow. Stopping at the top step, he turned and winked. "I have a lady friend awaiting my arrival, eagerly I trust."

Robbie grinned, recalling their first meeting on the docks in England.

"When you find Miss Gabrielle and her family, and you *will*," he said softly, his face taking on a serious expression. "Give her a hug from me. Don't hurt her, lad. She deserves far better than what I provide to my ..." He stopped abruptly, realizing he had inadvertently exposed too much of himself to this *mere lad* and was shocked. He had never opened up with any other person, nor would he again. He felt *naked* in the youth's eyes. Rob was a unique, young man. He wished he might reconsider his offer but knew there would be no possibility, he was far too principled. However, he would follow the lad's chosen path in life, from afar by necessity.

"I will never hurt her, sir. I love her too much," he said, his voice trailing to a whisper. "I will also tell her *you* delivered me safely and made me a man, as promised."

"No, lad, I merely provided you the *means. You* accomplished the rest. Take pride in yourself; you have earned it," he said, a brilliant smile lighting his stern countenance.

Final words unnecessary, Farthingale stepped onto the gangplank, and moving with practiced agility, quickly made his way to the bottom and stepped onto the wharf. With a quick wave to Robbie, he yelled: "If ever things change, talk to Ted." Without waiting for an answer, he turned and disappeared into the milling crowd.

***

General Nathanael Greene, flanked by two aides, walked the Charleston wharf with a rapid, ground-eating stride. His troops were not within the city borders—as yet. They would be, however, as soon as the British departed. At that time, he would move his troops closer, remaining until the arrival of a valid Peace Treaty. Although not soon enough for his liking, all signs pointed to the English being gone by the end of the year.

He paid no attention to the occasional soldier pacing the main streets, maintaining a low profile and minding his own business. At this point, they would not create trouble, nor would he. He merely wanted to see the 'lay' of the land, absorb the city's general atmosphere, and observe day-to-day customs of the Charlestonians.

Born and raised in Rhode Island amidst hustle-bustle lives, guarded brevity and the standoffish nature of New Englanders, he had come to appreciate the slower paced, more genteel elegance of the South. He drank in the city's bustling hum, completely at ease. It would be a difficult transition, but he would make his home in Georgia once the Treaty was signed, sealed and delivered. He chatted casually with his aides, actually enjoying his first few hours of leisure in many months, a 'gift' he had granted himself, finally admitting he needed a few hours of freedom from interpreting ambiguous orders, settling petty squabbles and hearing valid complaints from his troops, the latter—not within his power to alleviate.

As he skirted a crouched figure bent over examining several canvas satchels, the man stood, recognizing him immediately.

"Good morning, General Greene, Postmaster Artemis Jenkins at your service and pleased to make your acquaintance. Your fame has preceded you."

Greene paused, returned a polite greeting and continued on.

"Sir, I have information that may be of interest," Jenkins called after him.

Greene turned and faced the man, his eyebrow arching.

"I handle all incoming and outgoing mail between here and the other colonies, as well as countries overseas—one of them, of course, being England."

To Greene, the man's obtuse presentation was obvious. Having cornered the American General's attention, he intended to string out their encounter as long as possible. Any other time, he would have flayed the man with an impatient tongue, but today he was relaxed—more or less. "And just what might that information be?" he asked a bit curtly, humoring him.

"Two or three weeks ago a letter arrived from somewhere north of Dover, England. Oddly enough, it was addressed to *Colonel and Mrs. Jason Tarrington.* I dare say, sir, most people here know of their fate at Guilford Courthouse. After all these months, news of their demise should have reached any relatives over seas, sir—if you catch my meaning. It just seems a bit *odd.*"

"Oh? Where is the letter, Mr. Jenkins?" Greene's interest was piqued.

He had been advised of Alexander Stewart's 'folly', as he liked to refer to it, and the still unsolved disappearance of his two sergeants. *Could it possibly be true? Might they have lived?* He was here to keep peace, not open a can of worms that could wreak considerable havoc. Breaking up small skirmishes or busting a few skulls was to be expected. But order an all out search for these two *villains*? And if he did find them alive, then what? This was Loyalist territory. He let thoughts of involvement drop.

"What of the letter?" he repeated, noting Jenkins had yet to answer.

"I, uh, gave it to the young man who drives a carriage for Stanton's Livery. Ted has become a friend of James MacLean. I gather he has hired their carriage once or twice."

Greene regarded Jenkins coolly, his scrutiny making him extremely uncomfortable.

"Well, Mrs. Tarrington *was* his sister, after all," he blurted. "I felt he should …" He stopped abruptly. "I am sure I could get the letter back, sir, if you would prefer to take it to him. I know you both fought together at one time."

"That will not be necessary. I have …"

"Oh, there's Ted now. Excuse me for interrupting, sir. But see that magnificent team of grays?" He pointed across the street. "That's Ted and his carriage."

"Thank you, Mr. Jenkins." Flanked by his aides, General Greene swept past the flustered postal clerk and hastened across the street, curiosity getting the better of him. "Hold up there, young man." Greene signaled Ted.

Gently pulling back his reins and speaking softly to his team, Ted brought them to a stop. Looking over his shoulder, he eyed the general with mild interest. *General Greene, I presume. I heard you were close by, but not actually here in the city.* "I have time for one short 'hire' if you like, sir," he said politely, flashing a winning smile, all business.

Greene ignored his comment and stated brusquely, "I understand you have a certain letter of interest in your possession."

"I have many letters of interest in my hand from time to time," Ted replied, stalling to see where this was going, but knew with certainty. *Damn Jenkins and his big mouth!*

"The particular letter in question was addressed to *Colonel and Mrs. Jason Tarrington*," he ground out, annoyed at the lad's impudence.

"Oh, *that* letter. I did have it, sir," Ted hedged. "But I sent it on to Mr. MacLean with one of his friends. I don't happen to recall his name at the moment." He was glad he had the gift of thinking fast on his feet. "He has many friends, sir, as he was the local rebel militia leader for a time. I am sure you know that," he added, wishing to tweak the general, well aware the relationship had been a sore spot, particularly for Jamie. Playing the innocent had worked for him in the past; it would now.

Greene scowled openly. "Your accent indicates you are from England."

"Yes, sir." Ted made a mental note to work on softening his accent to blend in better. "I heard tell of ample opportunities awaiting anyone with the courage to relocate to the colonies. With nothing to lose I came here, and glad I am that I did."

"You seem to be doing well for yourself, young man," Greene observed dryly.

"I have no complaints, sir, and I am no threat. I am pleased to be here in the American colonies, and able to call myself *friend* to the likes of Jamie MacLean," he added, hoping to quickly rid himself of the tiresome man. *Why is the matter of Jason and Kathryn of interest to him anyway? The damnable war is supposed to be over.*

"If ever I have need of a carriage, I will send word. Your team is magnificent," Greene commented tightly and started to move away.

Ted's barbs had struck true, but he was not done with him yet. He liked to live on the edge—push his luck on occasion. "Oh, by the way, sir, would you like me to save any future letters, so that you might have the opportunity of renewing your relationship?"

Greene turned, facing him with a steely gaze. "No, I will not be back for several weeks. Send them on if more arrive. However, I believe it to be a *dead* issue," he stated tightly, a sneer curling his lip. Piercing Ted with one last icy look, he spun on his heel and moved away at an exacting pace. "That little bastard knows something," he growled to his aides. "He is aware I am here to *keep* the peace, not create a greater rift. So he tweaks me, knowing I am in no position to do anything—a smart, aggravating, young bastard."

"Shall we arrange for …?"

"He's not worth our effort, Lieutenant. Let us enjoy the rest of our day and put this matter to rest." As he walked, he analyzed the last few minutes of confrontation. He would love to make it his personal vendetta to discover the truth of that pair. As a dynamic team, they had been vicious in battle, tearing into his troops unmercifully and wreaking devastating havoc. *I refuse to acknowledge their unbelievable passion to win—and unquestionable talent. They were just one more aggravation in a detestable war.* But that statement was as idiotic as it was untrue, giving him no satisfaction. "I wonder if we shall ever know for sure," he said softly. "In death they have become as formidable as they were in life."

Ted watched them disappear into the milling populace of the street. Smiling at his successful encounter, he touched his vest, feeling the soft crinkling of parchment in his inner pocket. *Our small victory today, Jamie: yours and mine.* Clucking to his team, he moved away to pick up his next appointment.

Ted sat on his bed, tapping the sealed parchment against the palm of his hand. The address, in and of itself, would raise questions to those seeking information. Jason had told him to watch specifically for mail addressed to *Mr. and Mrs. Jason Cameron*—Kathryn's mother's maiden name. *How strange. Who did they miss in the telling?*

If it had not been for Artemis Jenkins's open curiosity, he might have missed the letter all together. Depending on the contents, it could contain important information. He thought back to the previous week's ship arrival.

"I'll be damned," Jenkins had exclaimed, holding the parchment out to Ted as he sorted the mail. "Ain't they both supposed to be dead?"

"As far as I know," Ted responded casually. "But I'll see it gets to Jamie MacLean. She was his sister, after all." He had quickly tucked the letter into his vest and asked, "Anything for Cameron, today? No time to chat, I must be on my way to an early appointment." And that had provided enough diversion to end further conversation.

Now he sat, comfortably ensconced against his pillows, tapping the thing as if it might somehow willingly divulge its contents. "Well, should I open you?" he asked, debating the issue aloud. "This is definitely out of the ordinary. Might it carry information of Robbie? Jack mentioned he might be on his way. There's no return address for a hint. Open it or not?"

Pulling a coin from his pocket he flipped it high, catching it effortlessly. Opening his hand, he grinned. "Yup, open it. However, I would have opened it no matter what the toss," he admitted, chuckling. "I can always apologize later to Jason and Kathryn. After all, I lied—quite convincingly I might add—to a general today. What's a bit of 'invasion of privacy' added to my sins?"

Opening the letter with care, he scanned the page and whistled softly. Muttering a prayer of 'thanks' for good timing; he tucked it back into his inner vest pocket.

This is definitely not for general knowledge—especially not Greene. Who knows what his reaction might have been despite his avowal of peace. Besides, being forewarned, I will be ready for young, master Robbie's arrival.

With a loud yawn, Ted leaned back against his pillow and immediately fell into a sound sleep.

Chapter Fifteen

Robbie's Search Begins

Robbie stood for a long moment absorbing the sights and sounds of the bustling wharf. *Mother would have considered this so common, despite the rich fineries.* That honest appraisal forced him to consider his appearance; however, it had been a well-dressed gentleman's rude string of epithets, which had hammered the truth home.

"Well, I see that making me presentable has become my top priority," he muttered.

Instead of heading to the main boulevard, he skirted the masses, working his way towards a side alley stacked with crates of cargo—whether coming or going, he was unsure. Scanning the waiting carriages along the far side of the wharf, he hoped he might spot Ted. According to Ellie's letter, he had remained in Charleston, loving the lifestyle and lucky enough to have a good position at Stanton's Livery, if memory served him correctly. If he could not locate him on the pier, he would check the livery once he looked more respectable. He was here at last, and refused to be discouraged.

He eyed each rig carefully. If Ted had changed in appearance, his team would still be easily recognizable. Just then a handsome carriage with a pair of grays caught his eye. With some difficulty, he worked his way closer only to discover, that although pretty from afar, they were not the magnificent pair he had met in England. Not allowing that to dampen his spirits, he headed for the alley. Crowds had never been to his liking, anyway. Besides, unlike his experience in England where narrow alleys held constant threat—here, the cutthroats, pickpockets and common riff-raff were former crewmembers and friends. That brought a smile.

He could see a stable at the end of the alley, a good place to splash water on his face and slick back his unkempt hair. Hopefully, he would then be allowed into one of the smaller, less ostentatious inns to make a thorough job of it. Despite the hot August day, the idea of a warm tub of soapy water beckoned deliciously. It had been eight long weeks since his last bath—he wanted it badly. "Besides, I actually need to shave," he said proudly to the empty air as he rubbed his stubbled chin.

"I surely doubt that, lad." An amused chuckle accompanied the teasing statement.

Robbie spun about coming face-to-face with Ted, smirking and in high good humor.

"I thought you'd never get here, Robbie. Whatcha' been doing since you docked?"

Robbie grinned, taking the outstretched hand and shaking vigorously. "Discussing an *interesting* subject with the captain and fighting my way to carriages only to discover the team of grays was not nearly as magnificent as yours."

"When I heard the *Lucifer* was coming in, I took the day off to look for you."

"How did you ...?"

"Long story, lots to catch up on, but first," he wrinkled his nose, "we need to make you acceptable in polite surroundings."

"Is Gabrielle ...?" Robbie asked hesitantly, not sure he was up to hearing anything unsettling just yet.

"Jack said to tell you that she eagerly awaits your presence. I gather *you* will grasp her 'knowing' of your arrival." Robbie's face lit up, pure joy washing over his features.

"Once we clean you up, I want to hear everything about your voyage. It must have been some experience, Rob. You were only a boy when I last saw you, but that's no longer true." Draping his arm loosely over Robbie's shoulder, they headed towards the end of the alley. "By the way, my employer said you are welcome to stay with me, cousin." He winked. "I always wanted some relatives, and you'll do rather nicely."

Robbie chuckled. "By the sounds of your lifestyle, you have a great deal to share with me too."

"That I do, Rob. Lest you grow eager and press me as to *where, when and how*, let me say that all has been set in motion. But give me the pleasure of your company for a day or two so we might come to know each other better."

"Agreed, this *is* the beginning of the rest of my life. Let's get it off to a good start."

One or two days blossomed into a full week. Robbie regaled Ted with all the details of his 'coming of manhood', omitting nothing: relating his last day at Boarding School, unique meeting with the Captain Farthingale prior to sailing, and the incredible learning curve experienced while at the beck and call of cutthroats.

Ted introduced him to life in Charleston, taking him on one or two livery jobs. Robbie could appreciate the valuable service he provided Ellie's family by making the city his home. Much of Ted's information about Nathanael Greene, Alexander Stewart and the status of Colonel and Mrs. Jason Tarrington was startling. The war being technically declared over, yet in actuality was not, a fascinating and disconcerting fact. He had never realized what an insulated life he had lived in England.

"How long must they constantly look back over their shoulders?" he asked Ted while sharing ale in the local pub one evening.

Ted shook his head, shrugging, and Robbie detected a note of sadness as he quietly said, "Who knows? Maybe forever, their reputation is such that it will never die. And *it is* one to be proud of. Whichever side you backed, if you were honest, you could not help but admire their incredible abilities … and their *passion*."

Robbie sat astride his big, bay gelding at the crossroads just outside the city proper, and looked back for a long, thoughtful moment. He and Ted had become fast friends during their brief visit; he would miss him.

"All right, Sampson, show me the stuff you are made of. We have a long trip ahead," Robbie informed his edgy horse.

Ted had chosen the animal for his agreeable nature and eagerness to be 'going', and purchased him for Robbie: a fact resulting in a rather vehement discussion between the two. After a lengthy pushing and shoving of money between them, Ted stated firmly, and with obvious finality: "I do well here, Rob. I chose Sampson as a gift from me to you, and will consider it a personal insult if you fail to accept."

Robbie gave in gracefully, ending further discussion. He loved the large animal's pleasant, non-complaining personality, and looked forward to sharing this adventure and many more in years to come. Well-stocked canvas satchels hung on both sides of his saddle. A pistol was tucked into the top of his new breeches, his familiar dirk snugged into sturdy, new boots. His clothing would never draw undue attention while riding alone over long trails. He was clean and neat, and appeared to be a farm lad: exactly what he would claim if asked.

Stashed securely inside his vest pocket was a well-drawn map of the safest and easiest route to Georgetown, along with the letter from Great Grandmother to be read after he arrived at Jamie's farm. As his journey might take one or two weeks, he would have enjoyed Ted's company. But traveling alone did not make him ill-at-ease. Life with Captain Farthingale and his motley crew had prepared him well for this, and much more.

With a final look at the city of Charleston, he smiled—glad to have been there, but eager to be on his way. With words of encouragement, Sampson responded setting a leisurely pace of his own making, one that he sustained effortlessly as he devoured the miles at a steady, ground-eating pace.

Patting Sampson's shoulder, Robbie settled into his saddle, riding completely at ease, becoming an integral part of the animal, just as Kathryn had taught him. This would ease Sampson's burden over the long miles and build a permanent friendship between them by journeys end. Kathryn's instructions echoed in his memory. "In order to achieve a lasting partnership between 'man and beast', it is of utmost importance to be properly introduced from first encounter—easing the animal's burden, your main concern." Having often observed the incredible devotion shared between Kathryn and her beloved Beauty; her words rang true.

Throwing his arms wide, he threw his head back, embracing the sun's warmth, inhaling deeply of summer aromas. At one with the world and deeply satisfied with life, he eagerly welcomed his new beginning.

"I am on my way, my Ellie … to *you*," he whispered fervently.

Sensing his master's high spirits, Sampson shook his head setting his heavy mane to dancing, and picked up the pace.

Chapter Sixteen

A Deceitful Game

Enjoying the dimly lit solitude of Jamie's huge barn, Jack hummed a familiar tune as he flicked the pitchfork with practiced ease, spreading fresh hay in the last stall. He had insisted upon this specific chore, for it offered a peaceful haven in which to reflect amidst pleasant, welcoming aromas. He paused, glancing upwards as a barn swallow swished past heading for its nest in the eaves. A startled squeak informed him of his callously placed foot and Jack grinned—at peace with the world and himself, for the moment.

Beauty snuffled against his shoulder as he moved closer, impatient to join Diablo in the paddock. Once outside, she always joined the black charger in a side-by-side gallop around the fenced perimeter, both tossing silky manes, nipping playfully and whinnying loudly, their unique bond, a delight to watch.

Kathryn and Jason preferred to tend their horses, when children or other duties did not interrupt, relishing the peacefulness of the old barn, a place for private conversation, shared intimacy and quiet moments expressing love for their animals. Jack always coordinated *'appropriate timing'*—his duty-like attentiveness a carryover from prior years of serving the colonel and his wife. Although no longer required or expected, he derived great pleasure from his 'duties' and would continue them until informed otherwise.

"Let me get the others out, Beauty, and I will give you my full attention." Jack knuckled her nose, slipping her a cube of sugar.

Stepping over a steaming pile of manure, he made a circuitous route to her stall, stopping to fetch the wheelbarrow and move it closer. As he grabbed his pitchfork, a brilliant shaft of light pierced the dimly lit haven, shattering his reverie. Swinging towards the source of interruption, he noted an abundance of dust motes drifting on the draft of a slowly closing barn door. Despite temporary blindness from unaccustomed brilliance, he easily recognized the backlit silhouette of *Caitlin*.

Eyeing her sternly, he uttered a soft curse and set his pitchfork aside. What could she possibly want now? But he knew. This confrontation promised to be what Jamie surely had known, yet only hinted at when Jack first arrived. "Be prepared, Jack. That lass will run you to ground like a hound chased deer, if given the chance." He had laughed raucously, thinking himself clever. Unfortunately, Jack had paid no heed

He recalled setting eyes on the girl for the first time—startled speechless—her dramatic likeness to Kathryn unnerving. Slightly shorter, she was gifted with the same tawny curls, wide grin and radiant green eyes. *How could she be a problem?* Many a night he had lain awake, the intensity of his physical need forcing him to consider, *Could she ever be …?* But he knew the answer. *No, there would never be another Kathryn.* Thankfully, lingering considerations for Caitlin were soon dashed. Beyond sharing similarities in appearance, Kathryn and Caitlin had *nothing else* in common.

Jack watched her sultry approach, annoyed. Caitlin had desired him from the moment she set eyes on him, and had openly pursued. Apparently, she had chosen this moment to press the issue. Caitlin approached, delighting in his wary gaze and obvious discomfiture. Good looking, well built, polite and soft-spoken—Caitlin, could and *would,* bend him to her desires. Initial attempts of coy flirtation and simpering coquettishness had failed. Jack had remained uninterested, avoiding her at all times.

She moved slowly, building anticipation. *He is only a man after all* and she was well aware of a man's body, its needs and what to do. She had the reputation to prove it. She delighted in teasing a man and bringing him to the *edge*, only to dash his hopes with haughty denial—proud of the power her woman's body wielded, and never lacking for eager volunteers. After all, she had only to look in the mirror to see what they saw and gloat.

Recently 'awakened', Caitlin understood the commanding drive of physical need and its power to control. Regretfully, *she* had been the one forced to come to grips with 'need'. Her downfall, so to speak, had been at the hands of Buddy Bleaker, the local barfly. Half gone with liquor, furious as her teasing turned to arrogant denial, he 'took' her forcefully behind the pub, on display for any passersby to see. But her protests had quickly subsided into urgent sighs. Not only had she begged for *more*, she had sought him out on several occasions. Until then, she had prided herself with iron control—*her* lacking, still infuriating her. *For my indiscretion, I carry his bastard.*

She *wanted* Jack and would have him. Only two monthly courses had been missed. It would be easy to dupe sweet, naïve Jack into believing she bore *his* child, albeit somewhat prematurely. *Not uncommon for a first birth after all.* Even as her mind wandered, her focus never flickered as she continued her swaying approach, pleased to note Jack had begun to pale. When the act was done, she would sob uncontrollably at having been coerced by an older man. Playing the soiled, innocent victim would be delightful. The barn door was closed and bolted for privacy, no interruptions. *Dear, foolish, Jack. Today you will be mine.*

Jack watched her approach, sensing *danger*. Her hips swayed in a provocative rhythm, the hems of her petticoats swishing seductively in the freshly strewn hay. Her eyes captured his, holding his gaze as she stopped in front of him, so close her breasts touched his folded arms, her décolletage concealing nothing. Fearing she would accuse him of lewd touching, he stepped back.

"Jack," she purred, allowing her mint-sweetened breath to accost his senses. "I had hoped I might find you here." Her voice was light and tinkling, musical: sweetness and light—*forced* and *fake*. She nudged closer, and with a sudden move, pressed her firm lushness tightly against him.

"What do you want, Caitlin?" he ground out, annoyed by his inane question; they both knew *that* answer.

"Oh, Jack," her tone held pretended hurt as she pouted prettily. "You have been avoiding me, and it breaks my poor, little heart."

Turning aside, he reached for the pitchfork. "I have work, Caitlin. You *must* have chores ..."

"Jack," she interrupted, pressing closer, forcing him against the wall. Firmly grasping his buttock, she massaged its soft curve, squeezing seductively.

"Damn it, Caitlin." Jack plunged the pitchfork into a mound of hay and spun to face her—just as she had planned.

Her impertinent hand deftly moved to cup his crotch in a wrenching grip.

"Jesus," he hissed, stumbling backwards against the wall.

Having thrown him off-guard, she used his shocked disbelief to her advantage. Flinging her arms around his neck, she yanked his head forward, covering his mouth in a panting gasp. Abruptly drawing back, she eyed him savagely. "*I* am the one in control, Jack, do not fight me," she hissed, covering his mouth again, biting his lip painfully.

Dumbfounded, he was slow to react. He actually welcomed the stabbing pain in his testicles; saving him the embarrassment of uncontrollable male physiology. *That would be all she needed.* Wrenching sideways, he threw off her imprisoning arms.

"Stop this instant, Caitlin. You …" His sentence ended upon a choked gasp as she brought her knee up viciously, right on target. Spots of color exploded behind his eyes as he fought to stay upright.

"Jack, Jack, Jack," she purred. "Do not deny me, do not deny yourself."

He gaped: stunned. "Nothing of the sort," he managed.

Without warning, she slammed her weight against his chest, forcing the air from his lungs. He had yet to hurt a woman, but he would now, *Jamie be damned*. As she yanked him forward to meet her insistent mouth, he grabbed her wrists and squeezed, exerting unmerciful pressure. Tears of anguish welled in her eyes as he twisted downwards and back, inflicting severe pain as he forcibly thrust her away. "Never touch *any* part of my body again, Caitlin," he spat.

"You bastard, you hurt me. How dare you treat me so?"

At that statement, Jack burst out laughing, infuriating her further.

"You are no man," she sneered. "I felt not the slightest bit of interest. Is it perhaps sheep—or maybe little boys that entice you?"

Realizing her game, Jack bit his tongue. He had won; she would likely never forgive him—thank God. Slowly, on a deep breath, he inclined his head and smiled slightly. Picking up his pitchfork, he strode towards the last stall. Turning abruptly, he leveled a long look at her. "I trust a *lady* of your unique abilities is able to find her way out," he said caustically, adding insult to injury.

Muttering vulgar expletives and numerous threats, she marched to the barn door; after a brief battle with the stubborn slide bolt, she yanked it open and stormed out. A brilliant slice of sunlight turned the inner barn bright. Dust motes danced as if in celebration. Through the partially open door, Jack could see Caitlin marching across the yard, her haughty stride oozing raw fury.

But there was something else, other than his sore bollocks, which bothered him. *What brought on such a desperate attempt to capture me,* he wondered? He was no fool, she had tried to force him into a position in which he would have to comply. She would surely use this confrontation to create dissention between Jamie, his sister and brother-in-law. *I am truly sorry Kathryn. But what could I have done differently?*

Suddenly it struck him. She displayed glowing color, a slightly rounding belly and full breasts: like Kathryn, when she had carried Gabrielle. *Pregnant,* he realized. He thrust another pile of manure into the wheelbarrow. He needed to think. What would be Caitlin's reaction? *A woman scorned …* He groaned. Just last week, Jason had teased: "Be careful of that one, Jack. There's many a lusty, agreeable wench in town that has no desire to *own* your name. With Caitlin, the shroud of entrapment would weigh heavily on your shoulders—and I guarantee you would like it not." Jack could still hear their combined laughter. He smiled, but quickly sobered. *Who knows what she will claim to Jamie. I may have more than painful bollocks to worry about. Being Jamie, he may try removing them with a dull knife. Now there's a bit of grim humor*—but he did not smile.

A soft nickering drew his attention. "Ahh, Beauty, you have been so patient; sorting this out can wait." Stabbing the pitchfork into a pile of hay, he walked to her stall.

Kathryn sat on the bottom porch step, yet again. *If nothing changes, I may soon become permanently attached,* she fumed, frustration escalating as the picture of her life replayed over and over *and over.* At least she had varied it this time: she was barefoot. She wriggled her toes in the cool grass, the only thing *cool* on this steamy day.

Beau had grown into a sturdy child, crawling, standing, walking with almost no assistance and creating constant deviltry that frayed his mother's nerves. "I don't ever recall feeling the heat as much as I do this summer, Beau. Come here now—not in the mud." A fast moving thunderstorm the previous night had dumped heavy rains, creating mushy puddles, a tempting allure for a *willful* child.

"Beau," she growled, sifting his name through gritted teeth, hoping to sound threatening. She should have remembered: *this* child loved to do anything forbidden, constantly testing how far he could push her. She groaned as recognition dawned. *This is one of my traits. Your father will gleefully remind me that you come by that naturally.* Chortling happily, Beau teetered precariously on chubby legs and headed for the nearest quagmire.

"Damn it," she breathed, heaving herself up from the step and grabbing her son, just as he bent to play. But not quite fast enough as one small hand successfully reached the muddy goo—which he then joyfully applied to his mother's cheek, pleased to have won again.

"Beau," she snapped, grabbing his hand, anger flaring. She was instantly sorry for her sharp tone, but need not have been; he seemed unimpressed and definitely not upset.

Oh Smitty, I wish you spent more time here at Jamie's. You are so good with children. She knew he loved helping Annie and her husband on their small farm nearby as it made him feel useful. *Something we all need to feel,* she admitted, and Annie's personality had improved with his continual company. She sat down on the porch step, pulling Beau onto her lap. Uncurling his chubby fist, she pressed a kiss into his palm.

"Momma loves you, little man, but you do try her patience." Even at his young age, he had picked up on her unrest and emotional distance, 'tweaking' her to get attention, any acknowledgment, even angry, being better than nothing.

Completely in tune to her mother's distress, Gabrielle helped without complaint. It was not *her* place to be a nursemaid for her baby brother. She would have her own children to cope with someday. *Admittedly, she will handle motherhood better than I.*

"Here we are, Beau, sitting in the cool shade, gazing across the fields of this beautiful farm, far from pounding guns and skirling bagpipes; yet I miss all that: the excitement, the danger." Kathryn suddenly realized her son was sitting quietly, engrossed in listening to her talk, not understanding her grownup rambling but drawn to the sound of her voice—and the attention. She tousled his blonde head, noticing his baby curls were becoming more like his father's sleek, thick locks.

Kathryn talked on, reliving her former life with his beloved father, knowing Beau would not be distressed. *Jason … oh, how I need you.* She brought his image to mind and smiled. She wanted desperately to be in the fields, helping with planting and weeding—anything but cleaning the house, cooking and tending children. *Anything!* And try to find time to love her husband? They had their own room with a lock. But it required an appointment to be alone, what with all the constant comings and goings of family members and numerous curious neighbors, wishing to welcome her home and meet her once 'notorious' husband.

She envied Jason's ability to escape into 'man's work'. Yet even *he* showed tension, his irritability flaring, the outbursts coming more often. Although regretting his ill humor once it had passed, he was unable to curb on-going frustration.

She loved her brother. Having miraculously survived the devastating war years—torn apart emotionally and physically—it was delightful to share his home, enjoying the laughter and playful teasing flowing freely amongst them. Even Jack was considered to be family, *and who could not love him?*

But the key words of importance were: *Jamie's house—not ours. Not ours, we are only guests here.* That thought brought a smile. *What is that old saying about family, guests and fish? Something to do with the aroma after a few days stay, I believe.* She attempted pulling warm visions forth; thinking back to their day of arrival always brought pleasure. Beauty had trumpeted, announcing them as soon as her hooves touched the dirt drive. Within seconds a bellowing answer sounded. Diablo burst from cover and thundered towards them. Once sure Beauty was real, he turned to Jason, nuzzling his master, refusing to leave his side, openly annoyed when returned to the stable as the 'human beings' moved to the house, continuing their greetings.

Jason and Jack had immediately thrust themselves into farm life, testing whether this might answer the question: *What shall we do now that the war is over?* It had all seemed wonderful at first. But now? She no longer 'fit' this lifestyle, even though she had been raised here. Not wishing to offend or appear ungrateful, Jason and Jack carefully hid their feelings, but she read them easily. She paused in her meandering recollections to hug Beau—snuggled against her, perfectly content as he sucked his fist. His warm presence brought inner happiness, and she allowed her mind to continue drifting.

Jamie's two daughters came to the forefront, difficult to understand and leaving much to be desired. Annabelle had married the blacksmith, Thomas Kinkade, as Jamie had surmised. Kind, generous and completely besotted, he was blind to her contrary nature. *As long as he keeps his blinders on it will be a marriage made in heaven, poor man.* Kathryn liked him and enjoyed their weekly visits. Annabelle seemed to truly love him, albeit she had a strange way of showing it. Despite her faults, Annie—as she insisted on being called—could not begin to compare with her sister. Caitlin was obnoxious and possessed a deceitful, hateful streak—never doing anything without an ulterior motive: one that benefited herself first and foremost.

And Jamie, God love him, was either oblivious or unable to cope. *He would never have let me get away with that behavior.* But it was Caitlin's looking so much like her that bothered most. Abruptly a disquieting thought struck. *Please see her for what she truly is, Jack. I would not have you hurt, especially for the wrong reasons.*

Beau gurgled and chirped "Momma," startling her; she had all but forgotten he was there. "You are an angel today, Beau, and momma needed that." She kissed him soundly.

With the grating of rusty hinges, the screen door opened and Gabrielle emerged. Draped in a voluminous apron, she wiped her hands vigorously on the bib, and then swept damp hair back from her perspiring forehead. "I have baked bread for tonight's meal," she announced proudly.

"So I see, little one," Kathryn teased, gesturing to the white powder sprinkled liberally on her apron and smudges decorating both cheeks.

Swiping half-heartedly at her cheeks, Gabrielle scooped up her skirts and plopped down beside her mother. Beau immediately flung himself at her, clamoring to be held. "Missed me, did you?" She pulled him onto her lap, and after a quick search in her apron pocket, handed him his favorite rattle. "With this heat, I wish *we* could go bare-chested like the men."

Kathryn eyed her daughter. "At risk of shocking your poppa's delicate sensibilities, I would not make *that* particular suggestion in front of him, but I definitely agree."

She heard her mother's light words, but could not miss the telltale sadness in her eyes. "Blue day, momma?" she asked quietly, shaking the rattle to divert Beau. "Changes are coming, have patience."

The slam of the barn door abruptly drew their attention. Caitlin flounced out the door and stalked towards the back of the house. High color and muttered epithets spoke of uncontrolled fury. Kicking several stones in her path, and taking a thoughtless swipe at old Percy, the barn cat, reinforced the fact.

"Whatever is she up to now?" Gabrielle shook her head, disgusted. "Poor Percy; thankfully she missed, him or *I* would be dealing with her," she snarled.

"Will you watch Beau for a bit, little one? I hate to ask but I need to see …"

"We'll stay out of that witch's way, you find out what she tried to pull with Jack."

Kathryn forced a weak smile and set off for the barn. Everyone knew this was the hour of day he tended stalls and cleaned the horse's gear. Although Jamie teased him unmercifully that well-shined saddles were not a necessary part of farm life, Jack's years of ingrained military perfection found that unacceptable. Truth be known, he enjoyed the process. This duty was his alone, and expected, making him feel part of the family rather than an intruder or 'taker'.

"What in hell has Caitlin forced on Jack?" Kathryn mumbled angrily as she marched towards the barn. "She has played on his feelings for me with her looks, chasing him like a bitch in heat since he first arrived." Ceasing all thoughts, fearing the worst, she tugged the barn door fully open just in time to hear an angry oath, and a fist slamming the wall.

"Jack," she called softly, not immediately seeing him. She stood still, the door partially open, waiting for her eyes to adjust before pulling it closed. "Jack," she called again, attempting to sound calm, forcing down rising panic; still no response.

Just as she opened her mouth to speak louder, he answered. "Brushing Beauty; in the last stall." His voice held a raw edge.

Kathryn started forward, pleased that Beauty was acting as solace for him too, the peaceful 'scritch-scratch' of the currycomb carrying to her as she drew closer. At least he was not indisposed, that fact bringing immediate relief—for several reasons.

Beauty nickered providing an opening for a discussion, or a few words, or just *one* word—anything to break the unbearable tension hanging like a heavy cloud. But Jack remained silent.

"Beauty," Kathryn called softly as the mare turned, expecting a lump of sugar. She fished in her pocket, but for once came up empty.

Jack reached across Beauty's back, handing her a lump. "I never thought to see you, of all people, unprepared, Kathryn." He forced a grin, but anxiety radiated from his tall frame in waves, his beautiful amber eyes displaying confusion, pain and sadness.

Kathryn's eyes swam. *What shall I say?* Finally she managed: "Are *you* all right, Jack? I could care less about Caitlin, but I need to know you …"

"I was unprepared for Caitlin's—bluntness." He turned and began brushing Beauty, not wishing to face Kathryn, needing to quell his sudden rush of desire.

Thankfully, Caitlin's attempt at seduction had turned excruciatingly painful when it did. He had been on the verge of giving in for all the wrong reasons. It would have been so easy to pretend—just for the moment—though he knew better. He brushed and brushed until Beauty's mane was glorious, yet he continued. He brushed with a vigor that would normally have caused complaint, snorting and restless sidling. However, she remained quiet, standing patiently as if she understood, and perhaps she did. Jack had not expected Kathryn to enter the barn, and was not ready to look her in the eye—not until sure of being in control.

If ever there was a situation demanding humor to break the tension, this was it, Kathryn thought. But there was no humor in this. She understood all too well what had gone on, and the price Jack had paid.

She remained so quiet, that Jack began to wonder what thoughts must be racing through her mind. Eventually his 'brushing' slowed and he found the courage to hazard a look across Beauty's withers. As if sensing his gaze she looked up, her eyes meeting his. "Jack," his name caught on a sob as a tear slid down her cheek. "I am so sorry that …"

Dropping the brush, he moved quickly around Beauty, pulling her into a tender embrace he struggled to keep 'brotherly', as he thumbed her tear aside. It took but one look at her beautiful eyes to realize: *she knows and understands completely, as always. Has there ever been a time when she did not?* He accepted the fact that she was exactly where she should be, *must be*, in her life—Jason's soul mate. *If only it would not hurt quite so much upon occasion*, but he would never attempt to change it nor break the 'trust' shared by the three of them. For she loved him too, a fact of which Jason was well aware, and yet bore no grievance. *I can accept this; I will accept this.*

"Do you wish to talk about it with me? Or perhaps you and Jason would …" she began tentatively.

"Not the details, Kathryn," he chuckled, attempting to keep their conversation 'light'. "However, I *did not* touch her in any inappropriate way, no matter what she claims. Rest assured she *will* attempt to make trouble and claim that I—who knows how she will present her 'case' to Jamie? For she needs a husband very soon." He paused, eyeing Kathryn.

"She is pregnant," Kathryn stated solemnly. "I had wondered at her robust health of late. She reminds me of …"

"*You*, when you were first carrying Gabrielle," he filled in, nodding firmly.

Kathryn groaned. "I think I had best talk to her immediately, Jack. Caitlin will never walk away, nor take your refusal lightly. I fear that old adage *is* true." At his quizzical look she added, "The one about a 'woman scorned'."

It was now Jack's turn to groan. "I wish no trouble for you with your brother, Kathryn. But I have no idea what else I could have done under the circumstances. I have no wish to marry the girl, pregnant or not."

"Things are coming to a head on several levels, Jack, as I am sure you are aware, or at least sense. That is a conversation the three of us will have shortly. For now, please talk to Jason so he will not be blindsided if Jamie starts yelling before his brain engages."

Jack smiled warmly, deeply relieved.

"Beauty looks especially beautiful today, and I thank you." A spark of deviltry reached her eyes at this point. Winking, she spun on her heel and headed for the door. "I shall *handle* Miss Caitlin right now. See you at supper," she yelled cheerily over her shoulder as she closed the barn door behind her.

"Breeding are ye?" Kathryn's fury deepened her brogue as she grabbed Caitlin roughly by the arm, ignoring her stormy protest and haughty affront. "Breeding and placing blame on another? Ye nasty bitch!"

Amidst shock and attempted denial, Caitlin allowed herself to be forcefully propelled to the potting shed behind the house. With her aunt's strength there would be no use fighting. Her mind worked feverishly.

Shoving the shed door open with a loud slam, Kathryn pushed her niece inside, and spun her about to face her.

"What ever are you babbling about?" Caitlin spat, deciding on haughty innocence. Having nothing to lose at this point, she refused to admit her charade. "Are you referring to Jack's refusal to take responsibility for …?"

"Do *not* play the innocent with me," Kathryn growled.

Caitlin merely shrugged.

A vicious slap jerked her head sideways, introducing her to a 'take no nonsense' side of her aunt she had never experienced before. *You bitch!* Caitlin recoiled, heated color washing her face into mottled splotches as she stumbled backwards, tripped over a low stool and sprawled indelicately on the dirty floor. Gingerly fingering the angry red mark, she stubbornly elbowed her way upwards; only to be stopped by a booted foot, set none too gently on her abdomen, shoving her flat.

Kathryn leaned in close. "Lie there and make no move or I *will* knock ye down again—as many times as it takes."

"How dare you?" Caitlin spat, elbowing herself up again, but quickly dropping back, barely evading her aunt's furious lunge.

"Now, the fact that ye appear to be breeding *must* be dealt with. That condition, although careless on your part, may be forgiven. You have every right to pursue your own pleasure, but *not* at the expense of another."

Caitlin's eyes drifted towards the door, praying no one else would see or hear.

"Listen to me, Caitlin," she hissed. "Pay attention, for my patience is all but lacking at this point. Look me in the eye."

The deadly quiet of her aunt's tone held danger and Caitlin complied, knowing she had more than met her match. *My God she must have been formidable in battle.* Full comprehension stuck and she visibly shrank back.

"I fear ye had no mother to teach ye the ways of protecting yourself from pregnancy while answering *your* needs," she said firmly. However, had her mother lived, Kathryn knew she would never have taught her daughter. Despite being frail all her life, Mairi had tried to fulfill Jamie's wish for a house full of children, and died for her selfless effort.

Eyeing her niece, lying amidst tumbled flowerpots and loose soil, flushed with embarrassment, she felt growing sympathy. At the girl's obvious confusion, she allowed the briefest hint of a smile to slowly cross her lips. "Women, as well as men, have needs," she said matter-of-factly. "Although some would say us nay."

She now had Caitlin's full attention.

"Enduring physical passion is difficult to define, even by those who have experienced it, your father and mother—Jason and I, for example. There are also lesser levels of gratification shared between a man and woman: appropriate and fulfilling as long as respect is involved." She paused allowing time for the information to sink in. "Are you following what I am saying, Caitlin?"

Caitlin stared in fixed silence. No one had ever talked to her so openly. She was both aghast and pleased. Besides intense emotion, her aunt's eyes held compassion *for her*, confusing her more.

Kathryn read her well, sensing she had actually reached the girl on some level. Leaning down, she grasped her hand and pulled her to her feet. "When you try to force blame for *your* dilemma on an innocent man," she said slowly, allowing no chance for misunderstanding. "Then, and only then, are ye a slut. And I shall allow no kin of mine to be such."

"I … I," Caitlin stuttered, on the verge of tears, unsure of what she was expected to say or how to say it.

"It would seem you owe Jack an apology," Kathryn suggested.

"Why did he tell? How did he know anyway?" she retorted spitefully, an angry pout blooming on her lips.

"Would you like me to start this lesson from the beginning?" Kathryn growled beginning to doubt there was any hope for this nasty child. Leaning in close, she raised her hand threateningly.

Caitlin shrank back, shaking her head. She was beaten for the time being.

"Jack is an incredibly decent man." Kathryn's eyes narrowed to slits as she angled her head meaningfully. "You *will not* set your sights on him again, lest ye wish to deal with me, aye?"

Caitlin nodded, not wishing to affront her aunt further.

"You must understand, Caitlin, your inconsideration could create tremendous tension between *all* of us. Jack, Jason and I have protected each other throughout a hurtful war, suffering heartache well beyond your comprehension. We *will* protect each other now. I *will not* risk losing my brother again, over *this*. Do we have an understanding?" she finished softly.

Caitlin caught the shimmer in her eyes as she looked away. Suddenly it dawned on her; there was immense depth to this barely known aunt, obviously acquired through incredible pain, loss and *love*. Kathryn wore passion for her husband proudly, openly and unashamedly. Neither did she attempt to hide the devotion shared between Caitlin's father and herself. She was honest, passionate—and a very real threat when protecting her own. She also loved Jack. He must be considered dangerous territory and off-limits.

"I *will* apologize to Jack. He need not fear further advances from me. But please tell me how he knew."

At that, a wide grin split Kathryn's face. "You look the way I did when I was carrying Gabrielle. Although he feels sorry for your plight, he can not be the answer."

Tears filled the girl's eyes. "What shall I do, Aunt? The man who sired him is …"

Kathryn brushed the soil from the back of Caitlin's dress and pulled her into a warm embrace.

"As it is almost time to begin the evening meal, you and I have chores to do."

"But Aunt Kath …"

"Tomorrow, after you have had time to think more on the father of the innocent babe ye carry, and sort out any redeemable qualities he may possess, then you and I will talk."

Caitlin stretched up to place a kiss on Kathryn's cheek, surprising her.

"Jack will be coddling Old Joe right about now. I will go speak to him."

Kathryn shot her niece a stern look, her eyes narrowing in warning. "Make it quick."

She did not buy Caitlin's turn around by any stretch of the imagination. She was what she was: a headstrong, selfish brat who gained what she wanted through wheedling, or out and out deceit. At least she would no longer pursue Jack.

Kathryn quickly picked up the last of the toppled flowerpots, wanting to get to the porch. From there she would be able to keep an eye on the barn. She would not allow Caitlin more than a few minutes alone with Jack; it would take several days for residual tension to dissipate.

"And what of the babe?" she muttered, pulling the shed door closed. "I guess tomorrow will be soon enough to address *that* issue; tonight I have no answers." Her mind reeled. None of this bode well. Jamie's moods were questionable at best: irascible one minute, benevolent the next, changing daily … sometimes hourly. *Gabriel is the only one who knows best how to handle his father, but he is not here. Caitlin's problem will not be going away.* Kathryn forcefully stopped her thoughts. *For the moment, we will make it work until we see where our next step leads us.*

Heading for the house, she hummed a nameless tune, stopping as a thought abruptly struck. Her tune had the somber resonance of a *dirge*—and she grimaced.

The following day all seemed peaceful, at least on the surface. Obviously no one had made mention to Jamie as yet. Jack, always a complete gentleman, had not breathed a word of Caitlin's rude advances and gave no outward indication of lingering annoyance.

As Kathryn had hoped, Jack talked to Jason, of possible ramifications when Jamie either heard of it, or Caitlin's situation became obvious. For the time being, life at the farm would remain stable, a good thing as Gabrielle's excitement grew daily, sensing Robbie's forthcoming arrival.

At least Robbie's welcome presence and tales of his daring adventure, might buy them some time to calm Jamie once he realized, like it or not, he was about to become a grandfather.

Kathryn could already hear his furious ranting and raving heavily intermingled with curses. "A damned little bastard in me house? I'll nae ha' it."

Ahh, young Robbie, I fear this may be quite an education. Kathryn gave the situation a long thought. *Although maybe not—after two months at sea with …? No, perhaps this will not daunt you in the least. Stop worrying, Kathryn, and concentrate on today,* she chastised. *For we have yet to deal with Miss Caitlin.*

The next day Kathryn, as promised, made time to talk to Caitlin in private. She spoke at length of the pros and cons of her 'delicate' situation, placing no pressure nor making suggestions, the decision *hers* alone to make. Caitlin then piously informed her aunt that she refused to inform or marry the father, but had discovered a *sudden love* for this baby she carried, and rejected the idea of ridding herself of the burden. At least that came as a relief, Kathryn had feared the worst. She met Caitlin's claims of newfound responsibility with mixed emotion, she knew her niece. By the time Caitlin finally faced up to the mess she had created, it would be too late to alter her fate. Kathryn exhaled on a deep sigh, shaking her head. *I pray we will be long gone by then; this one is Jamie's problem. I have enough of my own.*

Knowing the men would love a glass of iced tea when they returned from the fields, she decided to brew a fresh pot. Lemon mint from the herb garden would add a nice touch; along with Gabrielle's plateful of freshly baked cookies.

Forcing a smile, she instructed herself to think positive thoughts and work diligently at finding some form of contentment while they remained on Jamie's farm. However, as she headed towards the back of the house to pick lemon mint, forcing a sense of 'joy' into her stride, the only tune that came to mind was a repetition of the previous day's *dirge.*

Chapter Seventeen

A Disconcerting Discovery

Two days later, everything still remained quiet. Daily life carried on as if nothing out of the ordinary had occurred, everyone going about their daily rituals as usual. Even shared meals were pleasant, astounding Kathryn. She had feared the worst, once they faced one another across a narrow table in a confined area. Although Caitlin seemed somewhat subdued, no one paid her particular attention. Never possessed of a 'chatty' nature, her conversations usually consisted of infractions or complaints she wished address. To Jason and Jack her silence *was* noticeable, but gratefully accepted.

Jamie seemed distracted, but with good reason. Earlier that day, the three men had ridden for miles, circling his huge corn and grain fields, assessing the quality and judging what could be expected at year's end. After a long day of careful observation, they unanimously agreed that all crops showed healthy, lush growth promising an excellent year-end bounty. Jamie would be able to repay the previous year's debts, incurred while he was laid up. That would give him peace of mind and security.

He talked excitedly about the prospects of adding two more fields devoted strictly to wheat, and described a new piece of machinery he wanted to purchase. Although secondhand, it was in good condition and would make life easier. He could hire fewer hands at harvest, saving considerable money and increasing the farm's profitability. Filled with exciting ideas, Jamie could care less about his daughter's silence.

Kathryn watched her brother's face, relieved to see him happy and planning new improvements for the following year. That bode well for her sanity. At one point, he had openly suggested leaving everything behind and tagging along with them; the thought still gave her recurring nightmares.

Glancing at Gabrielle, she caught her winking and rolling her eyes, reading her perfectly. The wordless understanding they shared was such a blessing. Kathryn had discussed Caitlin's folly with open honesty, well aware her child possessed perception far beyond her years. To tell her less than the truth would be an insult.

Glancing across the table, Kathryn watched Caitlin idly toying with her food, eating little. *I suspect she is having misgivings. You had best find ways to make your life easier, Jamie. You will be a very busy man in a few months.* The aftermath of their evening meal was just as pleasurable as the food, finishing with mugs of coffee, cookies warm from the oven and a few bright tunes on the tin whistle.

Meals shared over the next day or two miraculously held to the same pleasant ease. *But life is not always what it seems*, Kathryn realized, feeling uneasy, hating the nagging sense of pending doom— waiting for the other shoe to drop. And it *would* drop, she had no doubt.

Caitlin eventually found a quiet moment to talk with her alone, late one morning after the men headed for the fields. "What am I to do?" she asked pitifully. "Who will take care of me?"

Kathryn bit her tongue so as not to reply tartly. "Take it one day at a time, Caitlin. Things have a way of sorting themselves out."

"Is it too late to …?"

"Yes," Kathryn replied firmly. "Perhaps *now* is the time to tell your father and give him time to become *accustomed* to the idea." *For he will surely need it,* she added silently. Angling her head in pointed suggestion, she faced her niece's sullen glare unflinchingly.

Abruptly, with no word of thanks, Caitlin spun on her heel and departed.

"Well that certainly went rather well," Kathryn mouthed cynically. For a moment she stared after the girl in a detached fashion, then shrugged and headed towards the house. Caitlin was not now, nor would she ever be, *her* emotional burden to bear.

Caitlin steered clear of her aunt, remaining aloof and coolly polite when forced to be within close proximity. If she thought Kathryn considered this punishment, she was sorely mistaken. Kathryn breathed a sigh of relief, her *second* reprieve, and all within the same week. *Perhaps this is a good omen.* Their so-called 'new life' had failed to produce a perfect fit for any of them so far. *Are we trying too hard?* They were about to be pushed in a new direction, *perhaps this time …*

Jamie discovered the truth, late the following afternoon, quite by accident. While they sat on the porch enjoying a glass of tea and a bit of idle conversation, Jamie's gaze drifted out across the fields. Caitlin emerged from the paddock at just that moment, crossing his path of vision.

Abruptly, he sucked in a sharp breath, eyes narrowing as he leaned forward to scrutinize his daughter's overly rosy countenance. As the soft breeze pressed her cotton shift against her usually flat abdomen, there was no missing the soft rounding now present. Drawing in another sharp breath, he quickly stood and headed out to meet his daughter, without saying so much as one word to those left sitting, sipping their tea.

Kathryn rolled her eyes, glancing at Jason and then Jack. No one uttered a word, hoping to overhear the confrontation; there would be no difficulty in that, if Jamie reacted as expected.

Jamie stepped directly into Caitlin's path preventing her from sidestepping and moving past, forcing her to confront him, or risk his wrath. She smiled brightly, willing herself to remain calm, saying nothing until she could sense her father's mood and purpose. *It could be nothing or …* She chose not to speculate.

"Are ye breeding, Caitlin?" he asked, coming directly to the point.

Caitlin swallowed convulsively fighting down panic. Of all the trouble she regularly embroiled herself in this was by far the worst. If her father threw her out …

"What makes you ask that, poppa?" she asked with quiet innocence, stalling for time.

"Yer inner glow." He gestured towards her face. "Yer rounding belly." He gestured lower. "Do not insult my intelligence with yer false innocence, lass. I know ye too well."

"He knows," Kathryn groaned, having easily read her brother's gestures.

Jack and Jason continued to watch, curious as to what would follow. Kathryn took a long swallow of tea, settling deeper into her chair—observing.

"I, I …" Caitlin began uneasily.

"Do ye at least have *any* idea of who the father might be?" he asked sarcastically.

Caitlin cringed at her father's underlying inference, angry that he could believe the cheap talk of drunken sots. *How could he possibly think I slept with all of them?* Indignant, she replied haughtily, "Of course I know the father. What kind of …?"

"Don't ask," Jamie growled, interrupting her. "For I may just tell ye in words so clear ye'll not possibly misunderstand."

One look at his icy, forbidding countenance and she hung her head contritely.

"I gather *your knowing* the father is supposed to bring me relief and pleasure." He flashed a supercilious grin, wanting to throttle her where she stood. Rocking back on his heels, he took a deep breath and exhaled slowly. "However, at this moment, I feel neither relief nor pleasure—nor will I ever." He spun away and strode back towards the porch. Maintaining his forceful pace, he yelled back over his shoulder: "Go begin supper preparations, Caitlin. We will talk of this later."

Jamie plunked himself heavily into his chair, picked up his tea, and after a long swig, resumed the conversation exactly where he had left off, as if nothing out of the ordinary had occurred.

Each played their part admirably, showing no curiosity or understanding of what had just transpired. Jason and Jack breathed a sigh of relief, but Kathryn knew her brother all too well. Far better that he erupts violently today at the moment of discovery: better for him—better for them. He would seethe incessantly, building internal rage until he 'exploded', lashing out indiscriminately in all directions.

Which form might his fury take this time? Violent rage, sarcasm, on-going petty quarrels or perhaps hateful accusations—whatever form it took, and she had seen them all over the years, it would not be pleasant, and no one would survive unscathed.

Chapter Eighteen

A Memorable Arrival

"I love you, poppet, sleep well," Jason whispered, kissing his daughter's cheek.

As the door closed silently behind him, Gabrielle's hand slid under the edge of her pillow, her fingers moving in searching sweeps. At the familiar contact of smooth, wooden links she stopped, grasping tenderly, enjoying her immediate 'connection' to Robbie. He had pressed it into her hand when they parted, with the promise: "I *will* find you someday." It filled her with comfort, its precious 'connection' growing stronger with each passing day.

Rolling onto her back, she fingered the individual links, pressing them against her heart, whispering prayers and speaking Robbie's name repeatedly. Over the past two days, she had sensed his *presence,* certain he was near. She wished she could share this knowledge with her mother, but at the moment, she had more than enough to deal with. Gabrielle kept the knowledge to herself.

As she floated sleepily, her fingers caressed the smooth wooden links, appreciating the difficulty and loving patience required in its creation—four wooden links carved from one piece of birch, accomplished without cutting or gluing. This treasured gift symbolized the two of them, their unbroken 'connection' and the challenges that lay ahead. Recollections of her months spent in England suddenly blossomed. Reliving only delightful experiences, she forced all else aside. Whispering his name one last time, she drifted into sleep.

Kathryn sat on the edge of their bed brushing her hair with brisk strokes that caused it to fall in shiny coils about her face and shoulders, the way Jason loved to see it. She had already bid *her* goodnights to their children and eagerly awaited Jason's return from adding his blessings—moments of quietly shared love with their children that neither ever missed.

Tonight, perhaps tonight, she hummed a bright tune in anticipation, adjusting the collar of her unexciting chemise lower. *I need all the help I can muster with this old rag my only aid in seduction.* She frowned into the mirror. Although free from lace and ribbons as preferred, her chemise had held a bit more attraction when new and bright white. As she pulled the loose garment snug against her back to reveal her form, her spirits rebounded. She had never been prone to vanity, but when one shared as little private time with their husband as she did, she wanted to look her best. An honest appraisal of her reflection in the lantern light did not disappoint. After having borne two children, and adopting a far less active lifestyle, her stomach still remained pleasingly flat, her legs long and shapely, her breasts a bit fuller yet firm and …

The bedroom door opened quietly, Jason poking his head in and catching her mid-observation. "I see you are still awake, my pet." He entered, shut the door firmly behind him, and latched it securely. Turning to face her, he pretended not to have noticed her self-appraisal. "Are you aware that our daughter—*paces?*"

Kathryn quickly straightened her chemise and sat down on the edge of the bed eyeing him with obvious yearning, her breathing escalating. She shrugged, unsure of his exact question—more pressing thoughts filled her mind. *Please, my love, time is so precious. Ask me later…*

"I wonder where she comes by that habit," he pressed nonchalantly, seemingly unaware as he moved closer, unlacing his shirt slowly and deliberately, allowing anticipation to build, keeping her on edge, enjoying his charade.

Kathryn shrugged again, unsure if she could utter a complete sentence without gasping. Burning desire coiled low in her belly, sending tingling ripples cascading throughout every fiber of her body. It had been far too long. She had no idea what he wished to discuss, and could care less. Her eyes fastened hungrily on his lean, muscular form as he shrugged his shirt upwards over his head and flicked it carelessly on the chair.

He stood silently appraising her as he *ever so slowly* released the buttons of his breeches—first one, then another, then—"I fear I did not hear your answer, my love," his voice trailed into a seductive groan as he stretched languorously, thoroughly enjoying himself.

"Jason," a whispered plea. Her eyes devoured him, raking over his powerfully-built form as his breeches slid to the floor exposing his obvious need.

In one stride he reached her, pulled her forcefully into his arms, a rich throaty chuckle erupting. "Our daughter's pacing can wait," he managed.

With a violent yank, her chemise sheared down the front, his nimble fingers peeling it back off her shoulders to bare her luscious contours. "Kathryn," he murmured, his hand trembling as he touched lightly, here—there—frantic in his need to 'experience' her. "I have missed you so, *needed* you urgently." His mouth closed over hers in a demanding kiss. "I claim you as mine alone, *mine*. And fear I cannot be gentle; it has been too long."

Tears of joy threatened to spill as her mouth devoured his. She caressed his shoulders, chest, the taut flatness of his abdomen, her hands roving frantically in her need to reacquaint herself. Reaching lower, she found the delicious heat of him and grasped firmly, her nimble fingers stroking rhythmically, pleased at the resulting tremors. "Thankfully so," she replied amidst sporadic breaths, "For *nothing* shall be gentle in my reclaiming of you."

She had no idea of the hour when they awoke, replete and rejuvenated. For them, as always, their passionate *reclaiming* served as a soothing balm of re-connecting and re-energizing, as it had since the day they first met. As Kathryn reached to caress his cheek, he shifted, pinning her beneath him, sliding the length of her body. Grasping her hands by her sides, ignoring protests of wanting to *share* the experience, his tongue began a delicious investigation. *She was his—they both knew it.*

"For you, my love. I have neglected my husbandly duties too long, and it has truly been *my* loss."

No further words were necessary, nor could she convey any.

Gabrielle jerked awake, clutching Robbie's wooden chain against her heart. She listened intently for a repeat of whatever sound had roused her, but it did not repeat itself. A quick glance towards the window showed a gray sky, night receding and fading into dawn. Projecting her thoughts outward, she concentrated on Robbie, just as Anna had taught her.

"Robbie, not that road. Not that road!" she cried fearfully. She sat bolt upright seeing through *his* eyes. Having ridden all night and exhausted, he had misjudged—the path chosen taking him directly into notorious Braxton Woods. He was riding into danger.

Throwing the covers back, she tossed on a shirt, breeches and long vest. Stuffing the precious links into her pocket and sliding a small dirk into her boot, she took a quick detour to Beau's cradle. Assured he was sleeping soundly, she headed out the bedroom door, closing it softly behind her.

As she tiptoed past Uncle Jack's room, his door suddenly opened. He stood eyeing her with an odd look. He was fully dressed, his pistol belted firmly around his waist, a sheathed knife adorning either side. Gabrielle stopped and stared, stunned into silence.

"I am ready if you are, but we must tell your parents first," he said lightly.

Gabrielle grabbed his outstretched hand and hurried her shorter steps to match his.

"How did you know?" she whispered.

Glancing down, he grinned. "Purely gut intuition. He *is* my nephew after all."

A loud rap sounded on their door, then another somewhat more frantic. Kathryn groaned as Jason pulled his breeches on and headed to lift the latch. They had just fallen asleep, both still drifting in the satisfying aftermath of passion. *What in the world would be so important it could not wait?* Kathryn struggled to focus.

Jason stepped back as Gabrielle rushed in. Jack stood braced in the doorway, an appreciative smile spreading across his face as he drank in Kathryn's sleepy, tousled appearance in the soft glow of the bedside lamp.

A few rapid words of explanation, assurances of necessity, and Kathryn swung her feet to the floor—wrapped in the sheet but ready to join them.

"*I* am the one to go this time," Jack addressed Jason. "I am not her 'parent' and can more easily distance …" He allowed the rest of the explanation to drop, aware they followed his line of thought and agreed.

"Jack will protect me, momma. But we *must* go now. Robbie's in Braxton Woods."

Kathryn swallowed a gasp.

"Finish your 'goodbyes', princess, and meet me in the barn. I will begin saddling the horses, but you must help," Jack instructed as he headed towards the door, giving Jason a firm, reassuring nod in passing.

"Give me a kiss, poppet, and be off." He pulled her into his arms with a firm hug, quickly freeing her to rush into her mother's open arms.

"Be safe, both of you," was all she could manage as Gabrielle darted after Jack, calling soft assurances over her shoulder.

Jason shut the door quietly and moved towards the bed. "I do believe I like the new Jack. I have never seen him so …"

"In charge," Kathryn added, actually smiling.

Jason crawled in beside his wife, his hands beginning to rove relentlessly.

"Jason, I …" she hesitated.

"Gabrielle is in safe hands, my pet," he insisted, nuzzling her neck, his breathing taking on a staccato rhythm. "Jack will bring both children home safely."

"But how can I …?"

"You must trust me to divert your worries, my love." His fingers moved deftly, insistently. Fully understanding her needs, he took a forceful lead, allowing no further discussion. He needed her for selfish reasons—though he would not voice it. He could not—*would not*—allow himself to think of his beloved daughter risking such danger, or he would shatter. *I am her father; I could not allow … Jack knows best.* He fell to loving his wife in earnest before he would have to *think*—losing himself, burying himself, in the comforting sanctuary of his beloved Kathryn.

Gabrielle rushed into the barn. North Star's saddle had been placed on her back, waiting for her mistress to adjust the cinch. Jack smiled as he finished the final tightening to his own saddle.

Grabbing the bridle, Gabrielle fitted it over her mare's ears as the intelligent animal lowered her head to accommodate the little girl's height. She seemed to have caught the sense of urgency and pawed the straw, anxious to be on the way.

"Braxton Woods, Uncle Jack, he's heading into Braxton Woods," she reiterated, her voice tremulous, eyes wide with worry.

"We *will* be in time, princess," Jack assured, stepping to her side and basketing his hands to assist her.

Shaking her head, she said, "Watch me," and flung herself up onto the saddle. "Almost as good as momma." With a sassy wink, she kneed North Star into a trot.

Jack exhaled a long breath. *Just like her mother.* Quickly mounting, he nudged his horse sharply, catching up with her at the edge of the road. Pulling abreast, he gently touched her shoulder, narrowing his eyes meaningfully. "Do nothing rash, little one. That is *my* job."

She locked eyes, grinning. "Follow me, Uncle Jack; I know a shortcut to the clearing."

Having her in the lead made him nervous. Who knew what they might be riding into? Braxton Woods was noted for harboring cutthroats and thieves who preyed upon hapless victims by day, or more preferably, under the greater safety of darkness.

Immediately urging North Star into a gallop, Gabrielle cleverly escaped any chance of discussion. Kneed sharply, Jack's horse lunged ahead, quickly coming apace.

"Let's go," he yelled as the two of them thundered down the dirt road at a pounding pace, leaving nothing but flying grit and dust in their wake.

Robbie *sensed* danger long before he saw it. The back of his neck prickled, hair standing upright at the nape, sweat beading his forehead. *Intuition*, a sixth sense more finely honed after weeks at sea amidst less than scrupulous companions. Scanning the trail, he swore softly. In his exhaustion, with only the dim light of a crescent moon for guidance, he had taken the wrong trail. This one, which had appeared wide and fairly smooth at the beginning, had turned into a narrow cow path, fenced on both sides by dense shrubbery and thick forest—claustrophobic in its restriction.

Luckily, he had ridden this far without confrontation, but now his senses screamed: *danger.* He was being watched, of that he was sure. Sliding his hand surreptitiously into his pocket, he assured himself the wooden shiv was easily accessible, but did not check his concealed weapons or money pouches—proceeding on cautiously. Above the tops of dense trees, a pale gray announced dawn. *If the path stays tight, I may be all right,* he reasoned. *But if there is the smallest clearing ...* He clucked to Sampson to pick up the pace. Even *he* seemed alert and concerned, his ears pricking and scanning erratically to catch the slightest sound.

Suddenly the thick stands of shrubs fell away, a bright area opening into a moderate-sized clearing; perfect for an attack. They were upon him in an instant, two burly thugs reeking of stale sweat, filth and the previous night's rum.

Fighting down panic, Robbie pretended defeat—neither resisting nor protesting—as the larger of the two yanked him from Sampson's back. He hoped they would see him as nothing more than a non-threatening, over-sized child, and they did.

Shoved unceremoniously to the ground, Robbie lay with hands raised defensively, cowering in frightened innocence. The larger thug quickly straddled him, deciding to toy with his victim before taking whatever he had to offer.

"T'is but a gangling lad," the smaller commented. "Did ye run away from home, boy?"

Robbie nodded, gasping as if winded from his fall, his eyes wide, feigning fear.

"Catch yer breath, laddie, me and Butch, here, got questions ta ask."

Robbie elbowed his way up to a slouched position, rolling a bit to one side, concealing the shiv in his palm. "Yessir, I runned from me mam—stole pa's fav'rite horse. Hell to pay fer shur, iffen they catch me." Robbie spoke slowly, hiccupping air as if still needing more to recover.

The big one seemed unimpressed. "Whadya' got with you, boy?"

Robbie shrugged. "Jist pa's horse and a loaf of mam's fresh made bread. Thought I'd sell the horse soon as I hit town. Git me a small boat and head up river. Don't much care where—jist far frum here." *Rather convincing if I do say so,* Robbie thought, smiling with beguiling innocence, playing them for all he was worth.

Apparently the two men had nothing pressing and no particular place to go. While thoroughly enjoying taunting their innocent victim, they failed to notice orange fingers of sunlight inching forth. *Better for me. Relax fellows; this'll make it easier to take you unawares.*

"Voices ahead," Jack whispered, placing a warning hand on Gabrielle's shoulder.

She nodded, and crouching low began a crab-walk motion, inching closer to the sounds. She had, indeed, known a direct route to the clearing, shaving the better part of an hour off their time. Jack made mental note to find out *why* and *how* later.

As the underbrush was too thick for their horses to make quiet headway, they had been left some distance back. Both understood stealthy approach and both were good at it. Surprise was on their side. As they drew near enough to see the clearing, Jack touched Gabrielle's arm, signaling he would go first. She shook her head, stubbornly moving forward, stopped short by a restraining hold on her shoulder.

Gabrielle turned, glaring in shocked anger at her 'uncle'.

"You *will* mind me in this," he hissed, the stern set of his face brooking no argument.

With a slow, apologetic nod, she inched aside. This was a new side of Uncle Jack, one she had never witnessed and was fascinated.

"Enough," the big man growled, abruptly aware their game-playing had delayed them—the protection of darkness vanished.

Both knew this route to be occasionally patrolled during daylight hours. Overzealous vigilantes, commissioned by local citizens preferring to use this shortcut to town, delighted in breaking heads.

"I tire of the game, laddie." He swiped his dirty sleeve across his mouth. "Let's jist see what ye took when ye ran." His arm shot out, but Robbie was quicker, rolling aside eluding his grasp. With two angry steps and numerous curses, the big man closed in, grabbing his shoulder and sinking large fingers painfully into his flesh. Yanking his innocent victim backwards, he was unprepared as Robbie's arm swooped in a vicious arc, slashing a deep, gaping wound from cheek to jaw.

Shrieking in pain, he leaped back, swiping his cheek with the heel of his hand. Blood dripped heavily from his fingers as he screamed obscenities, staring first at his hand and then at Robbie, shocked by what faced him. This was no 'innocent' child menacing in a low crouch, brandishing a large knife as if it were an integral part of him. They had been duped by a mere boy.

"Don't jist stand there gawking, kill the little bastard. Kill him," he screeched at his dumbfounded partner.

"I wouldn't do that," Jack growled, stepping from cover, one pistol aimed on the smaller man's chest, the other tucked firmly in the back of his pants, readily accessible.

Paying no heed, the smaller ruffian's gun swung up—the hammer not fully cocked when Jack's pistol roared, dropping him in a heap.

"Now you," he snarled, turning towards the big brute, his hand resting on his second pistol.

With a wild yell, the big man lunged at Jack, hoping the lad had flashed his knife for show only. That was his final mistake. With a dull 'thunk' Robbie's knife buried itself to the hilt in his back. Screaming louder, he stumbled in a frantic circle, hands flailing futilely, attempting to grasp the handle and dislodge it.

Jack held his pistol at the ready as he and Robbie watched dispassionately: clumsy circling, slowing to staggering, choppy steps—and then a final collapse.

Robbie walked forward, rocked his knife free, stabbed it into the dirt several times to remove the gore, and re-sheathed it.

Silence prevailed as Jack watched his nephew's casual actions, surprised, impressed or horrified, he was not quite sure which.

Hazarding a glance at his uncle, seeing open shock at what his *innocent* nephew had done, Robbie chose humor.

"What kept you, Uncle Jack? I thought you would never get here."

Jack holstered one gun, tucked the other into his belt, and moved forward shaking his head, a wry grin playing at the corners of his mouth.

"I left you as an innocent lad, Robbie. You come to me now as a man. You do both of us proud." Pulling his nephew into a manly embrace, he added, "I will never embarrass you in front of others, nephew, but just this once I need to feel the reality of you to be sure you are not a dream."

Robbie wrapped his arms about his uncle, hugging him tight, unashamed that his tears wet Jack's shirt as he uttered brokenly: "There were times when I thought never to see you again, never to find my Ellie."

"I am here," a small voice announced.

Robbie spun, swiping wetness from his cheeks. "Ellie," he croaked hoarsely. "This should not be a scene for your eyes." Hugging her close as she sobbed, he attempted to regain composure. "You should not have come, little one," he murmured.

"It was Gabrielle who brought me, Robbie," Jack volunteered. "She knew you were in trouble, knew the shortcut that got us here in time." He tousled her curly, raven hair and winked. "And that, my princess, is a topic you and I will discuss later."

Jack's humor centered and calmed her. "I have seen pain and death before, Robbie, just not quite so close." Stepping back, she squared her small shoulders and stated curtly, "I am no longer a little girl, Robert Beaumont. Do not treat me as one."

Jack squelched a grin, delighted: *a handful, just as her mother must have been—and thankfully still is.*

Robbie's eyebrows shot upwards on a laugh of delight. Pulling her against him, he planted a kiss on her forehead, followed by tracing an intricate symbol with his thumb. "Still my bold, little warrior my Ellie."

Reaching up on tiptoe, she finished their ritual before hugging him again with a softly whispered question. "Are ye all right, my Robbie?"

Jack groaned softly, so like Jason and Kathryn—but way too young. Time and distance had not diminished their connection in any way. *Ahh, Robbie, I fear you have chosen a long, difficult road.*

"Shall we bury them, Uncle Jack?" Robbie broke into his thoughts.

Jack shook his head. "Not now, first we need to let others know you are safe. These two will keep until later."

Sampson had stood riveted to the same spot throughout the whole goings on. Robbie strode to his side, gave him a quick pat and picked up his dangling reins.

"Not a war horse, I gather." Gabrielle grinned as she fished in her pocket and pulled out a cube of sugar. "But he is gentle and handsome and I like him."

Robbie led Sampson, skittish and complaining, through the tangled underbrush to where the other two stood patiently waiting. They set a rapid pace that brought the three of them racing into Jamie's yard just as Jason and Kathryn, well-armed and ready for battle, emerged from the barn on horseback with Jamie right behind.

"Just as I warned," Jack yelled, causing ready smiles as they drew to a dusty halt, obviously unharmed.

"Thank God," Kathryn murmured, inordinate relief starting a tear which Jason leaned to kiss away.

"Look what I found yonder," Jack announced, using light words to cover his relief.

Kathryn's eyes met Jack's with gratitude and pride, which he gratefully acknowledged with a long, meaningful look.

Momentary silence prevailed as they dismounted, but quickly gave way to loud greetings. Sharing hugs, kisses, and murmured words of welcome, each worked at sorting out raw emotion.

At that instant, Beau interrupted with a demanding wail of complaint, annoyed at being trapped in a sling on his mother's back. Gabrielle burst out laughing, and quickly relieving her mother's burden, carried him chattering happily to meet Robbie.

Robbie moved into better view, cuddling Beau and talking nonsense to him. Kathryn's eyes widened, his once slender, boyish figure had been replaced with a muscular, tanned frame exuding maturity and confidence. Her breath caught raggedly, her eyes drifting towards her husband. Catching his serious expression she groaned, knowing they shared identical thoughts.

In short order, Robbie began to visibly fade, hollow smudges under his eyes attesting to his fatigue. Kathryn sent Gabrielle and Beau with him to the house, where a room was ready and waiting. There would be much to talk of when he was better rested at supper tonight.

She had missed the lad and was glad to have him as a member of their family. Robbie would provide a pleasurable addition, tales of his trials and tribulations acting as an excellent diversion while they set their final plans. Having something other than Caitlin to think about, Jamie might control his growing resentment until after they were gone, allowing them to depart unscathed—perhaps even friends.

As to Caitlin, she would most assuredly share words with her shortly. Rob—no longer Robbie unless he wished it—was very young. Although possessing the height, good looks and appearance of a man full-grown, he was not. *Rob will not be her next target; I will not have my daughter hurt.*

Kathryn had no intention of creating a problem where none existed *yet*. She would watch carefully for the slightest interest on her niece's part, and handle it. *She may grow accustomed to the potting shed floor before I'm done with her.*

Kathryn watched Jamie's large bay gelding trot out to the paddock, happily joining the others. During their unsaddling, the handling of the two bodies in Braxton Woods was discussed, a decision finally agreed upon after a few curt words with Jamie. Putting that behind her, Kathryn turned to Jack, listening intently as he described what had taken place. Jamie commented approvingly. "Such a plucky lad—bravo." But the other three exchanged meaningful glances. This was not the little boy they had left in England. What had he been subjected to onboard ship that had caused him to 'grow up' so rapidly?

Kathryn doubted she cared to know, especially after Jack mentioned softly, on their way to the house: "I am glad you were not there—either of you. It was somewhat of a rude awakening even to me."

Chapter Nineteen

An Innocent Game's Success

His welcome had been boisterous—overwhelming and emotionally exhausting—so unlike the strictly upheld composure of British greetings. Rob kept Gabrielle at his side, unwilling to claim the limelight by himself. Caitlin fawned over him asking numerous questions, cooing in delight or feigning shock, depending on his answer. Robbie begged off as quickly as good manners would allow, relieved to have Gabrielle lead him up stairs to the promised escape of his room.

"Sleep well, my Robbie," she whispered, stretching on tiptoe to kiss his cheek.

At his welcoming gesture, urging her to come in and talk, she shook her head.

"I have so much to share with *you*, my Ellie."

"And I, with you, but tonight I am sure Uncle Jamie will hold a welcoming party. You will need your strength."

From what he had already been subjected to, that seemed an understatement. His eyes locked on hers. "I have missed you so, and *will not* ever lose you again."

With eyes asparkle, she blew him a kiss, pulling the door shut behind her. As she reached the stairs, she spotted Caitlin lingering on the top step. Refusing to allow her to dampen the evening's celebration, she stepped around her and headed downstairs to help her mother with preparations.

Robbie slept deeply, dreamlessly, lost in exhaustion. Several hours later he came suddenly awake, startled by his strange surroundings. His eyes darted around the room taking it all in, his sluggish mind slow to respond—a sudden smile curving his lips as a wave of relief washed over him.

"I'm here," he whispered. "I *am* home." Swinging his feet to the floor, he stretched cat-like, yawning, and headed for the door, desperately wanting time with Gabrielle. He peeked out into the hallway, looking both ways. At the far end, Gabrielle sat curled in a large chair, reading. Her head snapped up, a wide grin spreading across her face, as he stepped out his doorway and came towards her. Tossing the book into the chair, she rushed to meet him.

"Are you more rested, Robbie?"

Nodding, he said apologetically, "I had not meant to ..."

"You *will* need your strength, Robbie. My uncle has done as I expected. He has taken the carriage and gone to pick up Cousin Annie, her husband, and my friend Smitty. He means this to be a fine party in your honor."

"I remember you telling me of Smitty. Since he and I have both sailed with Captain Farthingale, we'll have much to discuss; lots of 'notes' to compare." He paused, searching her face. "But first, I want to talk to *you*. There is so much I *need* to share, questions I *must* ask."

"Soon," she promised. Taking his hand, they headed downstairs and into a roomful of guests, all eager to meet him. *The celebration was on.* Jamie's party, so like him, was raucous: everyone talking at once, interrupting one another in an attempt to capture Robbie's attention. They sat in the living room, Gabrielle pressed against Robbie's side on the settee, forced into a narrow space by Caitlin's demanding presence on his far side.

Annie was bright and cheerful despite the unannounced evening out. The closer she neared her delivery date the more Thomas shielded her, keeping her home under his watchful eye. Smitty was her savior. His delightful outlook on the world, and his place in it, kept her sane. He made her laugh, and at this point in her pregnancy, that was a difficult accomplishment. Tonight Smitty was at his best, dancing a little jig, humming sea shanties and promising Robbie they would have lots to discuss.

As a lavish meal was set on the huge dining table, Jamie loudly instructed everyone to 'sit and enjoy', indicating for Robbie to take the seat immediately to his right. Robbie acknowledged him and moved to politely hold the adjoining chair for Gabrielle. Before she could sit, Caitlin cleverly squeezed in front of her, and flashing a brilliant smile, *she* slid into the chair. Gabrielle narrowed her eyes, but graciously moved aside, unwilling to spoil Robbie's party. But she need not have worried.

Robbie had dealt with all types in his travels, manipulative bullies his least favorite. Caitlin reminded him a bit of Captain Farthingale's mistress—shallow, a pretty bit of fluff using seduction to wheedle pleasures. He also recalled Farthingale's quiet reprimand. "Sheath your claws." And she had done so. Seemingly reserved and gentlemanly, the captain ruled with an iron fist, *softly* demanding obedience, *and got it.* Robbie could handle Caitlin without so much as raising his voice. Saying nothing, he pushed her chair in, waiting until she was comfortable.

"Miss Gabrielle, please allow me to treat you to my very best British manners while I can still recall them," he said in a lilting British tone.

He now had everyone's attention. Making an exaggerated display of pulling the next chair out, he elegantly gestured for her to be seated, his eyes capturing hers with unspoken deviltry. Caitlin's grin faded, irritated by the composure of this—*boy.*

Gabrielle immediately rose to the game afoot. "Why thank you, Mr. Beaumont." Her eyes sparkled as she primly sat down, allowing herself to be nudged into position.

Jack recognized the 'game' and winked at her parents.

"Are you ladies comfortable?" Robbie inquired in courtly fashion. He stood between their two chairs, appearing ready to edge his way back to his assigned seat.

Even Jamie narrowed his eyes suspiciously.

With their nodded approval, he announced, "I will now take my seat, so every one can begin this delicious meal." And he did so, moving to the chair *beyond* Gabrielle and plunking himself down, increasing his distance from Caitlin—infuriating her. Taking his napkin, he made a lavish display of elegantly shaking it open. Folding his hands politely, he looked up and down the length of the table, catching each individual's eye before innocently inquiring, "May I ask what is for dinner? It smells absolutely marvelous."

Gabrielle's heart thumped with pride and joy as Caitlin scowled.

"Bravo, Rob," Kathryn mouthed. "Well handled."

Jason and Jack, exchanging amused glances, began passing heaped plates of venison, fish, rabbit, vegetables, sweet yams, bread and more.

Breaking into conversation to cover the cool silence coming from Caitlin's end of the table, Robbie addressed Smitty, the two of them swapping tales and fascinating everyone. Smitty was impressed to hear that the notorious Black Dog had befriended him.

"Oh, there was a bit o' discussion between us as to the terms of the friendship," Robbie laughed. "*My* terms won." He paused briefly. "Actually, I am grateful to him for saving my life. But it was Fish who befriended me first, and gave me the nickname: Brat."

While others occasionally added their own bits of conversation, time and again the talk gravitated back to life aboard ship. "Farthingale's quite the captain, eh? Comes across as a sweet-talking dandy, but rules his ship with a fist of iron. I always thought the ship's name most appropriate: *Lucifer*." Smitty sniggered.

"Yup," Robbie retorted. "The only thing *not* allowed on Farthingale's ship was bug—" His mouth slammed shut. "Beg your pardon. I fear I have lived too long with crude men. This is not table talk for ladies." He went silent, concentrating on his dinner.

"I imagine you have many other tales," a small voice encouraged.

His eyes drifted to Gabrielle's, a smile lifting his lips. "Would you like to hear how Black Dog saved my life?"

Gabrielle's smile flattened into concern.

"I am *here*, Ellie, *safe and* sound, and it *is* a good tale."

The evening was a huge success, even Caitlin eventually participating. The hour was late as everyone headed upstairs to bed, Annie, Thomas and Smitty staying for the night. Breakfast promised to be another 'party' and Jamie was beside himself with pleasure.

At the top of the stairs, Jack gave his nephew a warm hug. "Nicely handled tonight," he said. "I see I no longer have to worry about you in *any* situation. I can't tell you how glad I am to have you here, Rob. However, I bet your family is frantic. Shall we write your mother tomorrow?"

"Aye, Uncle Jack. Frantic or relieved, I am not sure which. But I do owe them a letter. Although my mother's arm has a long reach, at this distance I believe I am safe." With a boyish grin, he winked and moved down the hall to his room.

Jason nuzzled his wife's ear. "What a day, my love. Jack was …"

"Yes," she murmured," He has truly come into his own, finally free from the confines of military rule: both real and perceived."

Jason nodded. "But there is another who bears watching."

"Spoken like the father of a beloved daughter," she teased, but heartily agreed.

"He is no longer a boy, Kathryn. I see his love for our daughter shining in his eyes."

"Our Gabrielle is young to love so deeply. Yet I will not make light of her feelings, nor suggest it is nothing more than puppy love. The looks she shares with him are exactly as I share with you, my beloved. It is as I feared in England. A long difficult road lies ahead of them, and us."

Jason sighed, drawing her close. "I was afraid you would say that, my love."

Chapter Twenty

Disastrous Accident

"Come now, Hodges," Hamish chided, holding up a string of fish. "I've been with you two days now, and I fear t'is a lacking in British talents—at least on your part."

He grinned as Hodges sheepishly held up two small fish, shaking his head in disgust. "I believe you are right, Hamish. It would be a skimpy meal if not for you."

Hamish laughed. "Perhaps if ye beg, I will stay a day or two longer and try to teach ye. That is, if the missus has no objections."

"Do stay; however I doubt my abilities will improve."

Hamish picked up his fishing gear and turned. "I doubt that ... What is that glow just over the trees, Sam?" He stopped mid-sentence, a prick of concern nagging.

"My God, that is no sunset. That is my house!" Hodges charged past Hamish, shoving him aside as he broke into a pounding run, dropping gear and fish in his fearful haste.

Hodges broke from the woods, gasping for breath, Hamish immediately behind him. They stopped, awestruck by the scene before them, dumfounded into silence.

"Maggie," Hodges's voice caught on a ragged sob as he broke into a run.

Roiling smoke blurred the sky as brilliant flames, well beyond control, leaped from windows and doors. Dancing along the roof peak at a spectacular rate, the flames took on a life of their own—insatiable living beings caring nothing for the sorrow and devastating disaster they wrought.

Against the flames brilliance, Maggie's heavily rounded form appeared in silhouette as she staggered a few steps, their son grasped tightly against her, hurrying to safety.

"Maggie, my Maggie," Hodges panted, rushing to her side, lifting her effortlessly as Hamish snatched young William and hurried him farther back from the blistering heat.

Maggie sobbed, struggling to form sensible words, garbled syllables of unintelligible gibberish all that resulted.

"Hush, my love, hush, you and our son are safe, that is all that matters." Hodges had never seen his staunch, reliable, Maggie incapacitated. Fear registered as he held her, realizing no amount of wishes or prayers could change anything.

Hodges eyed Hamish shaking his head. At this point, nothing could control the inferno—merely douse the ashes when all was done. *All we worked so hard to create for our new life, all ...* His thoughts abruptly ceased. Maggie's gasped sob was not distress, she was in agony. Settling her on a soft mound of grass, he began a closer examination.

"The babe?" he asked, caressing her cheek, hoping her labor had not begun.

"No," she managed.

Despite Hamish's attempts at calming him, Willie sobbed pitifully off to one side.

"Is he hurt?" Hodges asked, struggling to focus.

"Not physically that I can see, Sam."

"William, you must be silent while I tend your momma." He reached to touch his son's cheek before turning back to Maggie.

Suddenly he saw the cause of her pain, obvious even in the dim light of ensuing nightfall. "Maggie," he swallowed a gasp, he must remain calm for her.

Up until now, he had failed to notice her right arm, completely bare and ... In anguished terror, she had yanked her burning sleeve off, tearing the bodice in her desperation. The cloying odor of lamp oil told the tale. Angry blisters ran the length of her arm and down onto her hand. Sloughing flesh bore telltale witness to her frantic efforts in saving their son. Snatching Willie from the spreading, burning oil, she had snugged him tightly against her and carried him to safety, heedless of her intense pain.

Hodges's mind swam in fear and frustration, his precious Maggie was in agony and he could do nothing. *What did Kathryn give her colonel for his excruciating leg wound?* He wracked his memory. *Nothing*: His mind went blank. He had never learned as there had been no need. Kathryn or Anna had always been there.

Hamish inched closer to Maggie, holding the quietly sniffling lad. At the sight of her arm, his eyes went round, shocked. Sucking in a breath he suggested, "Cold water will help, Sam. T'is about all I know, but I'll fetch it."

Setting the boy down, he headed to the small barn for a bucket. The recently erected structure was all that remained standing, as the house settled slowly into burning rubble.

"It was my fault, poppa," a small voice hiccupped.

Hodges's attention snapped to his son.

"It was an accident," Maggie managed, drawing his attention back to her.

"You are both alive, Willie. We will build a bigger house, with room for your new baby brother or sister," Hodges said, trying to instill courage—especially in himself.

Hamish returned shortly and began slowly trickling water over Maggie's arm, as she buried her face against her husband's chest, fighting not to scream. "My shirt was clean this morning, Maggie," he stated, the absurdity of his words drawing an incredulous look. "Linen strips kept constantly wet, so's not to stick, will keep out the dirt, and makes your skin feel better," he explained, taking no offense at Hodges's questioning look.

Hamish quickly stripped off his shirt, begging Maggie's pardon as he did so—a request that actually brought a weak smile—and within moments had deftly wrapped her arm in wet strips. Standing, he reached a hand down to the boy. "Come, Willie; you and I are going to make your barn into a temporary home."

The boy's eyes brightened at the prospect of doing something helpful, his two year old mind easily diverted if kept busy. As they headed towards the barn, Hamish called back over his shoulder, "I will ride for Kathryn as soon as ye are settled," his firm tone leaving no opening for discussion. But Hodges had no argument left in him, only fright for his Maggie.

Within the hour, Hamish had retrieved the fish, created a small campfire and cooked them. Plenty of fresh water stood at the ready. Maggie had been made as comfortable as possible on a bed of fresh hay. The cow and her calf were safely corralled and would provide a source of milk for the lad, or all of them, if the fish ran out.

Hamish and Hodges stood gazing at the once cozy house, now reduced to one or two beams standing staunchly upright amidst the smoking ashes. With a brief handshake, Hamish heaved himself into his saddle.

"Thank you," Sam said softly.

"Keep courage," he answered. "And keep the bandaging freshened and wet." Fishing in his saddle pouch, he pulled out a small deerskin flask. "Willow bark tea," he explained. "Not real fresh, but perhaps it will help a little."

Hodges took the flask. "*Kathryn,*" they murmured in unison.

"I will push this faithful beast for all he's worth. It may take two days, but don't give up."

Hodges took a deep breath and nodded.

"Promise me, Sam. Swear on whatever ye hold dear."

"I promise," he said slowly, reaching to seal his pledge with a handshake. He knew what Hamish was thinking. But as long as his Maggie could go on, he would too.

With a curt nod, Hamish dug his heels sharply into his unsuspecting horse. Lunging forward, the surprised animal quickly disappeared into the growing darkness, leaving a spray of swirling dust in his wake.

A tear slid down Samuel's cheek as he bit his quivering lower lip. *It will be a very long two days.*

Chapter Twenty-One

Final Affront

With hands clasped behind his head, Jamie leaned back. Sighing contentedly, he scanned the faces around his dinner table, observing their lighthearted exchanges amidst mouthfuls of the delicious fare. His gaze came to rest on Robbie, leaning in close to Gabrielle, imparting something he wished to quietly share. Such a delightful lad—uncomplaining, polite, a hard worker—Jamie liked him.

His eyes drifted the length of the dinner table to where Annie sat smiling contentedly, thanks to Smitty. Her husband, a slave to his blacksmith shop, lacked time—or ability—to keep up with household repairs. She loved her husband but, raised as a spoiled child, was in constant need of entertaining; Smitty fit the bill on both counts.

Smitty, God love him, clever, outspoken, witty, and prone to tomfoolery. He understood Annie's moods, accepting her as she was. Although not sure why, Jamie sensed she helped ease some sadness from his past, but would never ask. *I wonder what he'll make light of tonight,* he mused, his gaze drifting to Caitlin. *Damn her.* He forced himself not to think.

Jason, Jack, and *Kathryn*, jealousy reared its ugly head and he forced it down. She represented *freedom*, the ability to come and go at will, something he had coveted—but was ever denied. It had been *his* lot in life to be the *dutiful* son, the *responsible* son, the one who did what was expected of him. Though much of his assumed duty was self-imposed, he seemed unaware of the fact. He studied his sister's animated conversation fixedly, fighting rising irritation. *How can I begrudge ye, Kathryn? Ye have suffered for yer choices just as I have.*

A grating complaint from Caitlin drew his attention, nothing of import, merely expressing her usual caustic observations. *And I allowed her to become what she is.* He cringed, angry at himself, angry at her, angry at Kathryn. *Damn you, Kathryn.* His annoyance was beginning to smolder dangerously. Again, he forcefully tamped it down.

Kathryn would be moving on soon, he sensed her urgency. Despite good intentions, his thoughts churned relentlessly: *And on that day she will face me and say: "It is time, Jamie." And with no more than a kiss and our customary parting salute, she will be gone, and I? Left to await an unwanted grandchild, obliged yet again, to wear the heavy cloak of responsibility.* Forcing a smile, he pushed his feelings aside and stood to address his guests. "T'is truly a delight to break bread with all of you." He took his time, making individual eye contact.

Smitty, as vocal as ever, was the first to speak up. "A toast to ye for the excellent fare, Jamie." He lifted his glass in salute, first to his host and then to Annabelle. "And to ye, Miss Annie, ye're lovely as ever with round belly and rosy cheeks."

Annie stiffened, her eyes darting to Caitlin's rounding form and back to Smitty, not daring to catch her father's eye. Drawing focus to a rounding belly was a touchy subject at this point. Smitty often trod on dangerous territory; not from spite, merely saying whatever came to mind. Her sister's pregnancy, and refusal to name or marry the father, had stuck in Jamie's craw. To date, no amount of threats had broken Caitlin's stubborn willfulness.

Smitty's eyes roved around the table as he tipped his glass to one and all before drinking deeply. His face glowed in happy innocence. Annie often wondered if this was an act; it made no difference. She had adored him from the moment they first met. He made her laugh, helping her to bridge occasional 'gaps' in her marriage. She adored her husband, but being complete opposites, they had their moments.

Her mind drifted to the day he had agreed to come live with them. Smitty had shaken her hand flamboyantly, sealing the bargain. She could still hear him chuckling as he said, "Promise me one thing, Miss Annie. Make it right with yer pa or he'll force me to ride that black devil of Jason's. It's that threat what's kept me in line so far."

Abruptly her mind whipped back to the present. The party's tone had changed during her *mental absence.* Her father's delightful mood had fled. Unsmiling, he toyed with his food, no longer hungry. Intentional, or not, Smitty's *innocent* comment had struck deep. Everyone present felt the sudden chill, each making exaggerated efforts to concentrate on eating or forcing light talk, hoping to defuse the rapidly building tension.

Jamie stewed, uncontrollable anger rising. *Damn Kathryn, she'll leave me to tend this alone.* As his attention fastened on Caitlin, she smiled demurely, as if without a care in the world, and something inside him exploded—his misplaced fury aimed at Kathryn.

"Ye are extremely quiet tonight, dearest sister," he spat.

Attention instantly riveted on Jamie, surprised and shocked by the hard edge to his tone. Kathryn turned a steely gaze to meet his, but remained silent.

"Is it the old wanderlust rearing its ugly head? Impatient are ye with the lack of *doing*? Miss the war, do ye?" he hissed.

Jason cleared his throat loudly and began to rise.

"This conversation is between me and my sister, Jason. She's been a thorn in me side that has festered for years."

At Kathryn's light touch, Jason settled back into his chair; his appetite gone.

"I asked ye a question, Kathryn, and I expect an answer. I had thought, obviously mistakenly, perhaps with age ye might soften yer hard edges. Be content to live like most wives and *mothers*—learn to stay put and rear yer children in an appropriate manner."

"You bastard," she mouthed clearly.

All guests focused on their meals in uncomfortable silence.

Furious beyond words, Kathryn bit her lower lip, fearful she might fling spiteful words that once said, especially in front of all these witnesses, unable to be recalled.

"Excuse me. I have need for some fresh air," she stated tartly, wiping her mouth and pushing back her chair.

"My momma *is* a lady, and a good mother," Gabrielle hurled defiantly into the hushed silence, drawing an icy stare from her uncle.

"I would chastise you for impertinence, Gabrielle. However, *that* should be a mother's duty." His attention again riveted on his sister.

Jason stood abruptly, tossing his napkin onto his plate. Jack followed suit.

"Enough, Jamie. Say what you wish and be done with it quickly. You have already spoiled dinner for all concerned." Kathryn's eyes narrowed in warning.

Jamie's mouth opened for rebuttal just as Kathryn's fists slammed against the table, clattering dishes, silverware and glasses, startling all but Jason, who grinned—recalling other occasions which had provoked the same well-deserved reaction, and was proud.

"I said that is enough, Jamie," she growled.

Jamie, looking slightly affronted, folded his arms across his chest. With chin jutting smugly he retorted, "I merely thought if ye have need of adventure—and as there seems no possibility of conjuring another war for your convenience—why not cleave to the latest cause? Help curb Indian atrocities."

A heavy frown settled across her brow, anger rekindling. She was well aware of events happening in the so-called aftermath of the war. *Indian atrocities be damned.* There were two sides to that story, neither of which would be discussed with one as narrow-minded as her brother, and definitely not at an allegedly pleasant dinner gathering.

"Jamie," she ground out threateningly.

"I hear the Shawnees and Delaware caught up with Crawford—roasted him over a nice, warm fire after gutting him like a pig. Seems he was *done to a turn* ye might say."

Hushed gasps erupted.

"Now *there's* a cause. Embrace that adventure, Kathryn. And if ye take the Indian's side, ye are a *damned Brit.* No, wait ..." With a disparaging curse, he swept his arm in Jason and Jack's direction. "They're the damned Brits. Ye're nothing more than a goddamned Loyalist. And I don't know which sticks in me craw worse!"

Audible gasps erupted, followed by shocked silence.

"Uncalled for, James, and in front of young ears." Jack's lip curled in disgust as he shoved his chair against the table.

Jason tensed, impaling his brother-in-law with a steely glare. Observing closely, he was aghast. *I do believe that son-of-a-bitch is slipping over the edge.*

"I think it is past time for *all* to say 'good night'," Kathryn said calmly, drawing herself up to her full height, forcing herself to maintain a level tone, and control her fury. If she weakened for an instant, she would kill him without hesitation, and regret it for the rest of her life.

Gabrielle shoved away from the table so abruptly, her chair crashed to the floor, ignored. Whisking her brother out of his basket, she and Robbie headed up the stairs without so much as a backwards glance, or polite 'by-your-leave'.

Kathryn turned away. Flanked by Jason and Jack, she headed for the stairs, leaving Thomas and Annie eyeing each other uncomfortably; and Caitlin gaping in horror at her father's unwarranted attack.

Jamie watched them go, nonplussed and unsure of his next words or actions.

Smitty merely mumbled under his breath, "Stubborn Scotsman. I had not yet finished me dinner." With a shake of his head, he picked up his fork and dove into his meal.

Jack paused at their bedroom door. "Unacceptable behavior," he said solemnly, shaking his head in disbelief.

"I thought you might see it that way." Kathryn forced a smile.

"Give us a few minutes to ease the children's worries and come to our room, Jack. Decisions will be made tonight. If my wife has the fortitude to withstand this type of treatment, I salute her. *I*, however, do not," Jason said tartly.

Arm in arm Kathryn and Jason headed down the hall to Gabrielle's open doorway, and rapping lightly entered. Robbie sat on the bed with his arms wrapped around his Ellie, caressing her hair, crooning softly as she wept against his chest. Looking up, he smiled and tousled her hair, getting her attention. Gabrielle swiped at her tears and rushed into her father's open arms.

"Why, poppa?" she asked, her voice breaking. "Why does Uncle Jamie wish to hurt momma? He almost lost her *forever.* Does he not understand how precious and short life can be?" She reached for her mother's hand and held tightly to both parents.

"I doubt I can explain my brother's actions, little one. At least not convincingly. He is unhappy at the tasks life has assigned him, and strikes out in anger and fear."

"Even grownups find themselves occasionally scared, poppet." Jason's hand caressed her cheek, catching a tear. "Unfortunately, there are no manuals to teach us how to cope with problems in life; it is done by trial and error."

"Tomorrow morning your uncle will act as if none of this happened."

"Until the next time, momma."

Out of the mouth of babes. Kathryn glanced at her husband.

"It *is* time to go," she said in a small voice before either parent could answer. "Robbie and I have discussed this and we are ready."

With quick hugs, her parents stood back. Kathryn quickly checked their son, tucking him in with a kiss as she smoothed his covers.

"Momma and I need to talk to Jack, poppet. Perhaps Rob will stay for awhile and tell you more tales of his voyage." Rob nodded enthusiastically as Gabrielle plunked herself down beside him, the beginnings of a smile just starting. "I won't keep her up late," he assured.

Rob was decidedly a *member* of the family, a family not so different from the one he had fled in England. "T'is a good lesson for young Rob," Kathryn said, hugging her husband, as they gave a sharp rap on Jack's door. "Most families are quite similar. Some merely hide it better." She stifled a giggle.

"And just what might you find amusing on *this* particular evening, Kathryn?" Jack stepped into the hallway, pulled his door closed, and joined them.

"Come share a coveted brandy, Lieutenant, and we shall talk. I believe it is time to rally the troops and make a foray into new territory," Jason stated firmly.

"Yes, sir, might I suggest a destination far from here?"

They sat sipping brandy, no one speaking for a long moment. Jack broke the silence first. "What happened down there?"

"I fear *that* display of idiocy is my brother, Jamie, when not at his best." She shrugged. "When overwhelmed, feeling guilty, or hurt, he strikes out. I just happened to be the one in his line of fire tonight, exactly where he likes me to be."

"Wasn't the war enough?" Jason's temper flared. "Is his memory so short that he has forgotten his inconsolable grief at your apparent death? As well as his promises to never hurt you again when he discovered you were still alive?"

"To Jamie, I represent all he ever wanted in life—*freedom*. He taught me well, self-sufficiency, independence and a deeply ingrained sense of wanderlust. I came and went as I pleased, free of the responsibilities placed on his shoulders, a fact which has irritated him for years. Running the farm after our da's death, and raising four small children after his wife died, has been difficult for a man such as Jamie."

"You credit your brother for so many of your abilities, Kathryn," Jack said softly.

"Absolutely, we were close at one time. He was my revered, older brother. What a pair we were, we drove our parent's daft with our escapades. Unfortunately, an over abundance of responsibility eventually put pressure on our relationship. We fought and made up so many times we created our own 'good bye' ritual to tide us over until *I* returned. Jamie was never able to curb the independent nature *he* had so proudly instilled in me."

"And thankfully so, it was one of your flights into adventure that brought you to me," Jason murmured. "And for that, I will always be grateful."

"Caitlin is the problem. Jamie denounces *you* for *his* guilty sense of failure with her," Jack said firmly.

Kathryn's eyes held sorrow. "The three of us could analyze Jamie and me all night, and still come to no resolution. His stubborn self-righteousness is part of our ancestry, passed down through the ages, a heritage we *both* share, I might add."

"Aye, lass," a well-learned burr rolled easily from Jason's tongue. "Ye are stubborn, independent, brave and honest. Ye are a MacLean, after all, and I thank the Heaven's for their precious gift, each and every day."

"Enough," she retorted, the telltale brightness of her eyes sending a wordless message. "I fear we become maudlin in drink, and we still have much to discuss."

"What's the hurry? Are you considering going down to say 'good night', my love?"

"Absolutely not," she shot back. "He can stew a bit. *Distance* is the only answer with my brother, and that is what we shall give him."

"*I* have some thoughts on this situation if you care for my in put," Jack interjected. "Fall is now upon us, and winter not far behind—influential elements I have taken into consideration."

Kathryn and Jason leaned forward, resting elbows on knees and nodded.

"Help us out here, Jack," Jason encouraged.

"Yes, please do," Kathryn added.

Jack took a swig of brandy, leaned closer, and began to lay out his plan.

Chapter Twenty-Two

Self-Revelation

Maggie swallowed the last of the willow bark tea, wishing there were more. It had helped get her through the long night, just barely—a night of agonizing pain more insidious than childbirth. At least in childbirth there were moments when cramps eased, temporarily releasing pain's steady grip, allowing one to prepare for the next onslaught. *My reward in giving birth was my handsome Willie—more than worth the discomfort. But this? Nothing but a reminder of more pain to come.*

Steeling herself with courage, she attempted brightness. "The sun is high on the barn wall, time for us to take a look *together.*"

Willie began to sniffle as he gazed at his mother with sad eyes. "Willie does not want …" he began in a small voice.

"Willie needs to rid himself of guilt for an *accident,*" she said softly, eyeing her husband, sending an important message he must heed.

"But momma, I tossed the ball."

"And momma was not quick enough. It was *I,* who knocked the lamp over in trying to catch it." That was perhaps slight exaggeration, but she refused to have her two year old bear this burden for the rest of his life.

Sam understood, proud of his Maggie, but not altogether in agreement. However, he would soften his lecture. "Willie, we have talked about appropriate play in the house."

"Your father was a boy once too," she interjected. "I am sure, if he tries, he can remember that far back." Her words were tart, but a wink softened Sam's scowling face. "You are like your father, Willie: healthy, happy and prone to a bit of deviltry upon occasion. And for that I am grateful. I would have you no other way." She tousled his hair lovingly. "Now before I lose my courage, let's see what we have left."

Samuel loved this feisty, strong woman. Even in pain, her concern turned to them first. Mouthing a quick prayer of thanks, he snaked his arm about her waist as they stepped out into the stark reality of daylight.

Even her worst imaginings had not prepared Maggie. Stifling a shocked gasp, she leaned into her husband's embrace—smoldering ashes, nothing more. Even the stalwart uprights had fallen victim to the power of gravity during the night. Tears streamed down her cheeks, beyond her ability to control.

"Oh, my Samuel, first your lovely farmhouse and fields were taken, forfeited for your Loyalist participation. Shunned by so-called, former friends, we came here and built the beginnings of a beautiful, new life, and now this." Her eyes searched his, grieving for him, at yet another devastating loss.

Samuel remained silent for so long she became worried. *Is this more than he can bear?* "Maggie," he began slowly, acceptance of the hand dealt adding strength and resignation to his voice. "I refused to be intimidated when I was stripped of my farm and shunned. I simply moved farther out and rebuilt another small farm. I should have taken heed with the first warning."

"Are you daft from distress, my husband? For you are making no sense to me."

"I am not meant to be a farmer, Maggie, t'is as simple as that. The first time, I ignored the unseen 'powers that be', the hint was somewhat more subtle, but this I understand perfectly. Farming is not meant to be our lot in life."

"Then what, pray tell, Sam?"

He shrugged. "At least I know what I *am not* supposed to do. We have but to determine our destiny *together.* That is the key—*together.*"

"I love you, my Sam," was all she could manage as tears sprang fresh. "My brave, brave, Sam."

"Momma, poppa," Willie yelled excitedly. Having stayed well back from the rubble, as sternly warned by his father, he had inched his way to a place where he could see along the side of what had been their house.

"What is it, Willie?" Sam asked.

"I see momma's flower box—not burned." His face happily animated with the discovery, he rushed towards his parents, launching himself into his father's outstretched arms.

"Ahh, Maggie, a good omen if there ever was one, your marigolds survived," he said lightly.

Maggie forced down several mouthfuls of rabbit, knowing she needed to keep her strength up to help fight infection; but the real reason was to please her husband. Samuel, after much reassurance earlier, had disappeared just long enough to kill a rabbit and dig sweet yams for the evening meal. Cooked to perfection, it was a meal she would normally have relished and eaten heartily. But the agony in her arm hammered nonstop. Even immersing the bandages in cool spring water gave little relief. She tried distraction, watching Willie attempt to milk their cow, Millie. More liquid sprayed him than landed in the bucket, a scene that any other time would have delighted her. *I must think beyond the pain, I must.* She fought down another bout of nausea. *I will not vomit and upset my men. I will not.*

Samuel's eyes caressed. He sat holding her hand gently, willing her courage, wishing he could absorb her pain. *If only I could find a willow tree, but I know not …*

"I will beg Kathryn to teach me about medicine." Maggie's statement startled him from his thoughts. "I should know how …" With a stifled gasp, her hand flew to her rounding belly.

"Not the baby," Sam's voice sounded strangled.

After a long moment of silence she smiled, relief flooding her pinched features. "No, not yet, merely a sturdy kick from this second son of yours." She managed a weak smile.

"T'is late, Maggie, let me get you settled. I thought of something that may help."

He stepped away, but returned quickly with Hamish's empty deerskin flask. Slicing lengthwise, he opened it, handing her half. At her questioning expression, he instructed: "Chew on the leather; suck it. There *must be* some residue of the willow concoction left. Perhaps enough to allow you brief respite and a bit of sleep."

"It *does* actually help," she whispered, pleased by his clever resourcefulness.

He caressed her back as she began to drift.

"Kathryn will be here tomorrow," he began in an encouraging tone.

"We have no idea where they are, Sam. I *will* heal in time."

"Kathryn *will be* here—late in the day, but she *will* come. Mark my words, Maggie, she has *never* let me down," he stated firmly, adding to himself, *except for the day I thought her gone from my life forever.*

As Maggie's eyes closed with pain-induced exhaustion, her mind drifted back to the only time she had met Kathryn and her husband, the memory brought a pleasant recollection and *hope.*

Yes, she will come if Hamish finds her, and if it is within her power.

"Lord, please give me strength."

"Amen, my love," Samuel answered, bending to kiss her, startling her. She had not realized she spoke her prayer out loud.

Chapter Twenty-Three

Hamish Arrives

Kathryn yawned and stretched, swinging her feet over the edge of the bed. It had been a lengthy night of talk with Jack: his ideas well thought out and similar to theirs. Kathryn would pack today; that would not take long. They had few belongings, traveling as if still with the dragoons and constantly on the move. Despite Jason's lofty upbringing in England, he preferred this lifestyle.

"It is early yet, my pet." Jason yawned loudly. "Might I entice you?"

She pouted, sighing. "I would prefer an hour or two spent in your arms, my love. However, I should test the waters downstairs. I would not have Gabrielle and Robbie step into another of Jamie's hissy-fits. Actually, I am more than likely protecting him."

Jason chuckled. "I agree. I fear those two would need no encouragement to impart their thoughts loudly, a fact which makes me rather proud."

Kathryn walked slowly down the stairs, pleased to have her senses accosted by the rich aroma of coffee, ham, eggs and grits. At the sound of footsteps, Jamie poked his head from the kitchen, his customary grin flashing—again restored to his humorous self. Although pleased, Kathryn knew this would not last, not with Caitlin's belly rounding more fully with each passing day. *Our plans will not change.*

Jason and Jack had informed her that out of gratitude for all Jamie had done, they would help him with the final loading of his corncribs for winter. That job would be accomplished today. Tomorrow they would head south. Hoping their last day could be spent without additional angry words, she took a deep breath and smiled.

Jamie poured a steaming mug of coffee and extended it in greeting. Accepting it with mouthed 'thanks', she sat down. Noting the quiet plea in his tired eyes she said gently, but firmly, "It *is* time, Jamie," a statement, not open for discussion.

His face fell, it was as he feared. He had *hoped* right up until this moment.

"May we discuss this?" He would try, though he knew his sister, once her mind was set.

She shook her head.

"I will apologize."

"That is not necessary, nor is it expected." She shook her head.

"But I can explain to them t'is merely family ado. It'll settle itself out soon."

Her look said it all, and his heart sank. *Will I ne'er stop bein' the fool?*

"You are goin'? Fer sure?" he managed. "Ye'll leave me to deal with *her* alone?" His face exhibited an odd mixture of trepidation, anger and endless sadness.

"T'is of yer own making, brother. Ye must deal with *your* problems, as *I* must with mine. We have o'er stayed our welcome, clinging to the fringes of *your* life." *Please do not plead to come with us, Jamie. I have no wish to hurt you, but the answer is—no.*

"But I am not sure I can deal ..." he began pathetically, hoping to touch her 'softer' side with guilt.

"Jamie," she growled. "Ye are as stubborn and strong as me—like two peas in a pod."

"But …"

"What does not kill you makes you tougher."

"Spoken as crisply as our da," he commented dryly. He had lost the battle this time, but all was not over and done. *You will be back, Kathryn, just as in the past.* "Where will ye go?"

"Today we will finish filling the corncrib. That is the least we can do."

Briefly he thought of pressing for more favors due. But that would only create more ugliness, and he did not want that. *I will miss ye, my little Kathryn,* but could not bring himself to say it aloud. "I thank ye for that. And then?"

"T'is fall now and we head south."

With no further comment, he headed back to the kitchen, pausing to whistle loudly up the stairs and yell: "Come and get it, or I'll throw it to the pigs."

It was late afternoon as Kathryn headed towards the barn to see how the men's task was proceeding. Earlier in the day, she had found them working quietly and efficiently without their usual chatter—the atmosphere stilted. By mid-day, tension had begun to ease. She was packed and ready; *nothing* would stop tomorrow's departure.

Beau sat straddled on her hip, chattering non-stop, as they headed up the long dirt drive towards the barn. Her thoughts drifted to Gabrielle and Rob. They had voluntarily taken on working with the men; both strong enough to actually be of help.

"This is assurance the job *will* be done today. Nothing can hold us here one day longer," Gabrielle had informed her mother as she and Rob headed across the yard that morning. Blessed with several of her parent's traits, she also wished to move on.

Kathryn's mind meandered pleasantly. Abruptly a loud yell drew her attention to the end of the road. A lone rider galloped wildly towards them—his arms flailing, and legs kicking savagely. Even from this distance, it was apparent the poor beast was giving his all, but near to collapsing from exhaustion. Foam slicked his neck in dark rivulets and froth drooled copiously from the corners of his bloody mouth, spattering his chest and legs. The rider was in no better shape.

"Hamish," she yelled, breaking into a run.

"Kathryn," he shouted. "Thank God." Sawing the reins wildly, he brought his sweat-slicked horse skidding to a trembling stop beside her, spewing dust and grit into the air. Kathryn swung aside protecting Beau, as she placed a gentling hand on the exhausted animal's nose, crooning soothing words.

"Poor beast," she murmured, delving into her pocket for sugar. Despite heaving sides, he nipped the cubes gently from her outstretched hand.

Hamish slouched, sucking in deep breaths. Black smudges dashed beneath his eyes spoke of extreme fatigue, he looked ready to collapse.

"Hossie, Hossie," Beau chirped, delighted at this new game.

Kathryn's eyes darted towards the barn pleased to see Jason and Jack running towards her. Rob and Gabrielle were in close pursuit. Somewhat spent from the day's labor, Jamie brought up the rear, taking his time.

Jason lurched to a stop beside Hamish. Quickly taking in the young man's exhaustion, he reached up instructing: "Leg over and slide down. Jack and I will support you until your legs steady a bit."

Rob reached for Beau, relieving Kathryn.

"Drink this, Hamish." Gabrielle held out a dipperful of cool, fresh water.

Mouthing 'thank you', he gulped eagerly, spilling some with shaking hands.

"I'll get more." With a ready smile, she sped off.

"What in hell brings you in such a rush, boy?" Jamie growled. "You've damn near broke your poor horse."

Kathryn deliberately ignored her brother, turning to address Jason and Jack instead. "Let's get him into the house so he can catch his breath. The news will keep for a few more minutes." She gave him a quick hug.

Gabrielle returned with water, splashing some into her hand and cupping it against his horse's lips before handing it to Hamish. Reaching for the reins she asked, "What is his name?"

"Champion," he managed between eager gulps.

"Well, he certainly is that. Robbie and I will care well for him, Hamish." Flanking the tired beast, Gabrielle and Rob encouraged the worn out animal to make it as far as the barn, then his duties were over. Beau sat astride Rob's shoulders, babbling gibberish and flailing his arms in glee.

Hamish flopped onto the settee, and raking shaky fingers back through his hair began his tale.

"How serious are Maggie's injuries?" Kathryn asked.

"You will know better than I. But to me, the worst I've seen—heavy blistering and sloughing skin where she held her squirming son, carrying him to safety." A grief-stricken expression crossed his face. "She was in terrible pain. All I had to offer was my pouch of willow bark tea—and none too fresh at that."

Kathryn's mind worked rapidly, ticking off a mental list of necessary herbs, while Gabrielle and Rob, having returned from the barn, stood nearby catching enough detail to understand—ready to make themselves of use.

Kathryn glanced at her daughter; aware she was making a mental inventory of their medicine kits and moved to her side.

"I have linen bandaging, feverwort," she eyed her mother guiltily, "and a fresh infusion of black cherry."

Kathryn's eyes narrowed, smiling approvingly. "A dangerous choice, but exactly what I will need."

"It is no more dangerous than putting a loaded gun into *competent* hands," Gabrielle said calmly, standing her ground.

Kathryn agreed. "You make me proud, Gabrielle. *You* are in charge of readying my medicine bag." Wishing to speak with Hamish before he fell asleep, she paused beside Rob, and tousling her son's hair, leaned close. "Thank you, Rob, I entrust *both* my children to your care." He understood completely and smiled.

"Exactly where is Samuel's place?"

"Let me rest for fifteen minutes and I'll …" Hamish began.

"Jason and I will travel faster without worrying over you. Now, where?"

He had barely begun his directions when she interrupted. "He must have built his house in the field near Cobbler's Brook, where all the big trout are. A large oak tree stands at the far corner of the field as you face the woods."

Hamish nodded vigorously.

"Good, I know exactly where they are."

In short order, Jason and Kathryn stood beside their horses, the additional weight of canvas travel bags doing nothing to deter their eagerness as they sidled and pranced.

"Jack ..."

"No words are necessary, Kathryn. We will meet you in two days time. Hamish has insisted on acting as guide. I will have *all* our belongings with us." His gaze sent a silent message. *We move on from Hodges's place when all is settled there.*

Kathryn hugged her daughter. "Maggie will need your healing energy, travel safe."

Dressed in her favorite style: men's breeches, linen shirt and long vest, Kathryn flung herself onto Beauty's back. Jason sat astride Diablo, grinning, his hand taut on the rein as the huge stallion pawed.

"I see some things never change, my pet, tomahawk resting in the small of your back, two loaded pistols tucked in your belt and ..."

"A dirk in her boot," Jack added.

Kathryn shrugged innocently. "One should always be prepared."

With a signal to their mounts, they galloped at a ground-eating pace down the road and into the woods. The sun's rays were just beginning to settle into low shimmering colors. Kathryn's eyes met Jason's in wordless understanding. They would arrive at Hodges's place within twenty-four hours, perhaps less. This magnificent pair of horses delighted in running, and possessed the stamina to hold a punishing pace indefinitely.

The following morning, Jamie stood quietly observing Kathryn's family as they sat patiently astride their horses, waiting for Jack to re-check all cinch straps and saddle pouches. He took his time, unwilling to be rushed. When pleased that all was secure, he stepped up into his saddle.

Gabrielle sat astride North Star with Beau cradled in a sling across her shoulders, smiling as he cooed and waved his arms happily. She and Robbie exchanged frequent glances, their eyes bright, eager to be on their way.

"Ye will come back this way before ye head south?" Jamie asked, but knew the answer.

Jack shook his head firmly, irritated at the stubborn Scot's refusal to accept 'no' for an answer.

"But ye are leaving so quickly, my Annie and yer good friend Smitty will not ..." Jamie gave it one more attempt.

"This *is* goodbye for now," Jack softened the blow. "We are truly thankful for your generosity." He reached down to shake Jamie's hand.

"But how will I hear of Maggie's health?"

"Jamie," Hamish interrupted, his patience fading rapidly. "We *must* be going."

Jamie shot him a steely gaze; but had no more to say.

Jack forced a patient smile. "Hamish will bring news, I assure you."

Caitlin had stood silently in the background, but now stepped forward. "Thank you, Jack." She did not reach to touch him, nor did he reach out to her.

Sensing her Uncle Jack's discomfort, Gabrielle took matters into her own hands. Nudging North Star forward, she leaned down to kiss Uncle Jamie 'good bye'. *Let's hurry this along, we are losing valuable daylight.* She met Caitlin's stare with a nod and polite smile, nothing more. *Momma will be proud of me.*

Kneeing her prancing piebald into a fast trot she headed off, yelling back over her shoulder, "We will write, Uncle Jamie."

Robbie gave a curt nod and brief smile. Prodding Sampson, he quickly brought him apace with North Star. Jack, with a soft sigh of relief, fell in pace behind them. No one looked back. They knew Jamie's stoic façade had crumbled by now, and sensed his sadness with a bit of regret. But for them? *Freedom.*

"The road is wide enough to accommodate all of us traveling abreast," Rob yelled back over his shoulder.

Hamish and Jack smiled and guided their horses up beside them. With no further adieu, they picked up the pace, hoping to put several miles under their belts before stopping for a break.

Once beyond the borders of Jamie's fields, Kathryn and Jason altered their horses' gait to the loping, ground-eating stride the two animals loved so well, a pace they could hold indefinitely, retaining plenty of energy if necessity required it of them.

It was well after dark when they made their first stop at a small brook. Neither horse was overheated or breathing hard.

"Shall we take time for a light repast of bread and cheese?" Jason asked, draping a strong arm around his wife's shoulder as she refilled her canteen.

She grinned up at him, with a devilish glint, highlighted by the light of a full harvest moon. "I can think of other diversions, my love. But I fear they must wait."

"You always were one to adhere strictly to duty when necessary, Kathryn." He shook his head and kissed her firmly. "I *will* make it up to you."

The repast was brief but refreshing for all involved. Kathryn had also brought plenty of grain. As they headed off, Kathryn slowed the pace. Jason eyed her curiously; the road appeared to be in good condition. "Why slow our pace, my love?"

"It's been a long while since I traveled this road. I do not wish to miss the turn off. It may be well-hidden after all these years, but if I can find it we will cut off many miles."

"Hamish never mentioned …"

"Hamish, poor lad, either has no knowledge of it, or was in such a dither it never came to mind. Jamie and I used to wander through here many years ago. I am positive the path is still here somewhere."

"I will follow your lead, my pet."

Kathryn searched a bit, pushing back overgrowth, encouraging Beauty to use her bulk to break through. On their third try, Beauty broke through dense overgrowth and disappeared out of sight.

"Persuade Diablo. It's a bit snug, but he can make it," Kathryn instructed softly.

With snapping twigs and a loud grunt, Diablo's head and broad chest broke through, allowing him to sidle to Beauty's side.

"The full moon plays to our advantage; the path is narrow but looks sound."

"It used to be rough in certain areas. But I knew them well, and have not forgotten. We should get to Maggie by late morning, early afternoon at the latest."

Dawn broke as they emerged from the forest. A huge meadow lay before them, beautiful amidst slowly rising strings of mist, and absolute silence. They paused taking it all in. Three deer stood on the far side in the long, golden grass, ears twitching, alert but not yet startled by their presence. Venison would be welcome, but the timing was bad. Suddenly the ruckus of crows announced their presence; the deer fled in graceful leaps and bounds.

In the light of a new day, Kathryn ran soft hands over Beauty, checking her legs and hooves individually. Jason followed suit despite Diablo's impatience. This battle-trained pair was just reaching their stride. A few cubes of sugar, some fresh grain and cold water, and they were on the move again.

Just shy of noon, Kathryn reined to a halt. Inhaling deeply, she swiveled her head slowly, wrinkling her nose at the acrid smell still lingering in the air.

"We are almost there. Shortly, we will come out into a large field beside the huge oak tree I spoke of." Growing apprehension added an edge to her tone.

Jason reached for her hand, grasping it firmly, ignoring her impatient attempt to pull free. Eventually she raised her eyes to meet his, knowing he had something he wished to say—aware her hand would not be released until he had done so.

"Kathryn, you *are not* God. Do you understand me, or shall I waste another few minutes of time lecturing?"

She bit her lower lip and nodded. "But may God give me the strength, and judgment, to heal her," she murmured.

With a warm kiss to lend courage, they rode into the field by the big oak.

"Sweet Jesus," Jason blurted as Kathryn stifled an audible gasp. "There is not one timber left."

Kathryn drew in a deep breath closing her eyes, collecting her thoughts and setting her expression.

"Ready?" Jason asked.

"As ready as I'll ever be," she replied and nudged Beauty towards the small barn.

"Maggie, Samuel," Jason shouted.

They quickly dismounted just as Hodges's huge frame appeared, filling the doorway. Tears of joy, worry, frustration and grief rushed down his face as Jason pulled him into a bear hug. "I did not know if ..." he began brokenly.

"*Nothing* would stop us, Samuel," Kathryn said firmly. She stood holding her medicine bag, eager to see Maggie.

Hodges pulled her into a bear hug, whispering words of greeting and gratitude.

"How bad, Sam?" Kathryn stood back, her eyes fixing on his.

"She is so brave, so very brave."

"How bad, Sam?" she repeated.

Calming himself, he tried to give the details as best he could.

"Where is your son?" she asked.

"With his mother. He feels such guilt."

"I will need time alone with Maggie. Jason and I have discussed what needs to be done, most of it man's work," she said lightly, "and will keep Willie distracted."

Willie peeked around the door with fear-filled eyes, but dutifully stepped forward at his father's insistence. *I will not fail them* she vowed as she hugged him. "I hurt my momma," he hiccupped, needing to confess.

Kathryn ruffled his hair. "Accidents are another way of learning, Willie. *Learn well* from a mistake and put it behind you." He looked disbelieving, but she nodded firmly. "I am going to go help your momma. Your poppa and Uncle Jason will explain while you *men* go fishing." With a quick hug, she steeled herself for the worst and entered the barn.

"Maggie," Kathryn called softly, hoping she might be sleeping; doubting that possibility after Samuel's input of the hideous injury.

"Kathryn," a soft, painful response sounding mildly surprised.

Kathryn swept to her side, and crouching down, set her bag close by. Lightly resting her palm against Maggie's forehead, she smiled confidently, but detected warmth building: fever setting in. Eyeing the moist linen wrapping on Maggie's arm, and noting discolored seepage, she steeled herself. Maggie's gaunt face spoke of her agony; little remained of the robust, raw-boned woman they had met several months back.

Chronic pain is more debilitating than the injury. She reached for her bag. *We will deal with that first.* Taking a small vial from her bag, she removed the stopper. As she pressed it to her lips, Maggie stopped her. "Tell me, Kathryn. *Truth only.*"

"Do you trust me, Maggie?"

Her distraught eyes leveled on Kathryn as she nodded slowly.

"Implicitly?"

Another slow nod.

"You need to be *unaware* during all that I must do."

"My babe?" Her hand drifted to her rounding belly.

"You *will* cradle your healthy child in your arms, Maggie," she assured, blocking all thoughts of doubt. Raising Maggie's head, she pressed the vial to her lips. "Just a few drops until I see how it affects you." Crooning words of assurance, she held Maggie's hand as she began to slowly fade. When sure she was beyond the clutching fingers of pain, Kathryn carefully peeled back the linen bandaging.

Brilliant sunlight streaming through the barn window hid nothing—charred, blistered skin and 'sheets' of flesh hanging loosely. *My God,* she muttered wishing Anna was there, relieved that she and Gabrielle had judged accurately and prepared well.

Kathryn had no idea how much time had passed as she sloshed her hands with whiskey and picked up after re-bandaging Maggie's arm. The sun's rays slanted at a much lower angle through the window, the 'tending' process having been long, slow and tedious. She was exhausted but content. Although Maggie would carry scars the rest of her life, she would have full use of that arm.

The infected areas were contained, all dead tissue removed, but it would be a painful battle for several more days. She would keep Maggie just on the edge of awareness for at least the next two days while she forced fluids and reapplied healing oils and antiseptics.

Suddenly she recalled having seen the fallen window-boxes of golden-orange marigolds all that remained amidst the blackened timbers. Knowing how well they worked with burns, she decided to ask Willie to pick what was left, involve him with the 'healing' of his mother. *That will help him more than any amount of talking.*

At her softly called name, she roused from her thoughts. "We are done for now, come in," Kathryn answered.

Jason stepped in first, Samuel holding back, fearful.

"We have fires built, fish and sweet yams cooking, water heating and freshwater stored for drinking. Did we forget anything, my pet?" Jason offered his hand and pulled his wife up into his warm embrace. She leaned against him, shaking her head with a whispered 'thanks', appearing exhausted but content.

"Willie," she called out, and his small, anxious face peeked around the door. "I want you to pick all the marigolds left in the flower-boxes. I need *you* to help me make medicine for your momma. Can you do that for me?"

With a vigorous, relieved jerk of his head, he spun about and raced off.

"Sam, please come in and bring water for Maggie."

He had the bucket and dipper in his hand as he stepped through the door. His eyes showed it all: fear of asking, fear of being told. Kathryn had never seen him so pale and exhausted. "She *will* mend and be well. While your son is busy, let me tell you what to expect."

Kathryn fought to stay awake but was rapidly losing the battle. Lack of sleep she could deal with, it was the emotional turmoil. She ate sparingly, asleep as soon as her head touched the blanket Samuel had laid out for her.

Maggie roused long enough to take some liquid, and Willie was encouraged to help. Being included in his mother's healing, he had come to grips with his guilt, working it out in his two year old mind, and moving on.

Jason and Sam eyed each other tiredly. Quickly banking the coals in their cooking fire, they fed the animals and brought them into the far side of the small barn. Pulling the door shut and bolting it firmly, Sam stumbled to his wife's side, touched her cheek gently and was immediately asleep.

The next two days passed quickly. By the end of the second day, Kathryn eased Maggie's dose of black cherry. Keeping her heavily sedated was just as debilitating as the intolerable pain. Willow bark tea would make the pain tolerable from now on. The infected areas were responding well, her fever almost gone. She was a strong-willed, robust individual who had duties to her husband and son. She vowed she *would be* well.

"Hellooo, the house," Jack yelled, reining to a stop just outside the barn door.

It was late afternoon and a well-banked fire smoked and crackled from dripping fat. The delightful aroma of a roasting haunch of venison filled the air.

"Hellooo," Hamish echoed loudly as he dismounted.

Gabrielle and Robbie chimed in as Beau chattered loudly, spewing unintelligible gibberish, none the worse for his long journey and sleeping in the open.

A loud hailing came from within, but it took a few more minutes before anyone appeared. Millie was in the middle of being milked, Kathryn was just finishing final administrations to Maggie's arm, and Jason was trying to make space in the cramped quarters for their visitors.

"This should be fun," Maggie grinned. "We may get to know one another *very* well."

It was a noisy, happy series of introductions and questions, similar to their arrival at Jamie's. Everyone flowed into distinctive areas needing attention, working as a team. Kathryn stood watching, leaning against her husband, at ease and content.

"Amazing, isn't it?" Jason whispered.

Kathryn smiled. "Happiness is where you create it despite the difficulties."

Jason nodded, blowing out a frosty breath. "We *must* press on soon. I would not be surprised to see frost on the fields within a week."

Kathryn made a low sound in her throat. "These quarters will be a challenge, but if we can give Maggie a few more days it would be better."

Jason's hand slid slowly down her back, his hand caressing her bottom, sending a private message. "I miss you too," she whispered. Pulling his head down she kissed him soundly, uncaring of anyone watching.

There was little elbow room, but no one complained, their personalities adapting effortlessly to the unusual situation thrust upon them. They stayed fairly warm in the tight little barn, the horses sharing their sleeping area and adding more heat. But the days were becoming cold.

Gabrielle approached her mother early the next morning. "Robbie and I will tend the little ones. You grownups need to talk." She flashed a look of ageless knowledge.

"I believe you are old enough to have a say, little one, both you and Robbie."

"I do have a suggestion, momma. Robbie and I have talked at length. For now, perhaps Uncle Jamie's cottage would make a good home for Sam and Maggie."

"And what else?" Kathryn nudged. "Say all that is on you mind and I will discuss it with your poppa."

"It would be good for us to be in Keowee to help Anna's people with winter preparations, and, I miss Gabriel and Anna—and my training. I would like Anna to also ..."

"Give her blessings for you and Rob," Kathryn finished, delighted by her daughter's shy sideways glance.

"We will talk later, little one." With a quick kiss, Kathryn headed off to gather the men. *Yes, the time has finally come to speak of future destinations before our family becomes any larger.* Kathryn hummed a bright tune and smiled.

Chapter Twenty-Four

Futures Set in Motion

"Winter is approaching. This small barn will never hold all of us until next spring, if we hope to remain on speaking terms." Kathryn grinned. "Samuel is talking with his wife and will join us shortly. But while we have a few moments of privacy …"

"It is time for you to decide, Jack," Jason broke in. "We have interfered in your life so many times, and your friendship is invaluable."

"The happiest time of my life, despite everything, has been the years spent with the two of you." Jack glanced from one to the other. "*I* do not wish to change that. A request for me to leave would have to come from you."

Kathryn's eyes sparkled as she glanced to her husband, relieved. They wanted and *needed* Jack, and had included him in their plans. "Briefly, we are thinking of building a general store or trading post. We have no idea where, as yet."

Jack stroked his chin thoughtfully. "Far enough out so as not to encroach upon Cherokee lands but within easy accessibility for trappers and the likes, I imagine.

Jason nodded. "We intend to buy or build, keeping expansion in mind, in order to accommodate customer needs, possibly a cooper, furniture maker, or harness-maker."

"You sound as if you're thinking of a spot near a good road or easily accessible river." Jack caught their enthusiasm, expanding upon it. "Perhaps we might consider shipping merchandise between here and the New England colonies."

"Exactly, Jack," Jason clapped his friend on the back. If we don't propose something to keep my delightful wife busy, she has threatened to consider rum-running."

Kathryn chuckled. "Do you wish to captain a ship, Jack?"

It was Jack's turn to laugh. "I must have covered my seasickness rather well. I spent more than enough time leaning over a bucket on *both trips*. Thank you, but I think not. Actually, I thought *you* were the one who loved the sea, Kathryn."

She shook her head. "After a few days of fresh air and salty sea spray, it grew old."

"Why not Captain Farthingale?" A satisfied smile crept across Jason's face. "He told us specifically to leave word in Charleston, if we had need of his services. Our possibilities of success would be endless with that man on our side."

"I gather we should risk stopping in Charleston." Kathryn eyed her husband.

"In less than two months, the British will have evacuated, leaving only General Greene to contend with …" Jack left his statement hanging. "Here comes Sam. Is he part of this?"

Jason shook his head. "Although he would make an excellent addition, it would perhaps be better to ask him next year when his life has settled somewhat."

Jack's eyebrows raised in question.

"We hope, for now, he will stay at Jamie's hideaway until we return next spring."

"For the birth of Caitlin's baby?"

"Always on the same page with us, Jack. We have much to plan, but finally with a sense of direction. Not a word to Sam. We will break it to him when the time is right," Jason said quietly, as he turned a smile of greeting on Hodges.

"May I help you, Maggie?" Gabrielle moved to her side, reaching to grab the opposite edge of the blanket she was shaking out.

Maggie refused to play the invalid, her pain was now tolerable. "I am almost done, little one, but stay and chat awhile if you have a mind to."

"I would like that very much, but first. May I help *you*?"

Maggie stared openly, her face twisting into a quizzical expression.

Ignoring her look, Gabrielle gently led her, unresisting out of curiosity, to a hay bale, and gestured for her to sit. She then knelt, and holding both hands barely touching the bandaging, began chanting a soft, wordless, series of relaxing tones.

Suddenly Maggie gasped.

"Have I hurt you in any way?" Gabrielle asked calmly.

"No, no," she murmured, looking amazed and a bit confused. "I feel warmth and healing energy." She stopped, her mouth closing abruptly.

Gabrielle merely smiled, closed her eyes and continued her soft, lilting tones.

"What are *your* plans, Sam?" Jason confronted his friend.

Sam shrugged uncomfortably. He no longer had any idea of what to attempt. "I have been so *lost*, Jason. Up until you arrived, I could barely focus on surviving one more day. Maggie and I invested everything in this." He grimaced, making a futile gesture in the direction of the charred remains. "There is not so much as a kettle or pan left, all melted in the heat—along with the few coins we had set aside."

At Kathryn's raised eyebrow, he grumbled, "Believe me; I have looked more than once. This is the second house I have lost."

She pursed her lips. "We have decided to winter in Keowee, but plan to return north in April, to help Caitlin with the birth of her baby."

At Hodges's sharp look, she shook her head. "That is a long tale for another time, Sam. We need to get you and Maggie and Willie to shelter before the baby comes."

"Where?"

"Jamie's hideaway near Charleston."

"But will he allow that?"

"It is Jamie's in name only, Sam," Kathryn said. "He discovered it, fixed it up a bit, and used it— squatter's rights, so to speak." She shrugged. "Better to have it put to good use than left empty. On his way home, Hamish will stop by the farm to inform Jamie of how pleased you are at his *incredible* generosity."

"Will it suffice at least for the winter?"

"Suffice? My God, Jason, I had expected to somehow manage, here in the barn until I could find work. That is an incredible gift."

"Not a complete gift, Sam. I recall the back steps need fixing and—I can provide a wee list." Kathryn burst into laughter. *Everything is coming together.*

"My Maggie is a brave woman, and would face whatever she had to for my sake. It will be a joy to tell her." His eyes were suddenly awash with shimmering brightness.

"Go tell your good wife," Jason urged. "We will join you shortly."

The following day, after bidding a tearful 'goodbye' to Hamish, they set off—an odd caravan of assorted components. Jason and Jack took the lead with Robbie and Gabrielle directly behind them. Kathryn rode in the small wagon with Maggie and the two little ones, in case needed. Millie and her calf, resentful at being tied to the tail-gate, plodded unenthusiastically. Understanding her mare's disquiet, Kathryn had released her to follow at will, and Samuel brought up the rear.

As they set off down the dirt road he forced himself not to look back. Maggie turned, blowing him a kiss. All would be well as long as they had each other and their children.

"Why are you gripping your stomach, Maggie?" Kathryn asked, concerned. She had no wish to deliver a baby in the middle of nowhere, and with the cows it would take almost two weeks to arrive. Kathryn groaned.

"Not yet, Kathryn; but possibly sooner than planned," she said apologetically.

Although somewhat stressful, it was an uneventful trip: cold nights, drizzling rain, soggy campfires requiring creative oaths to light, huddling under the wagon for communal warmth, and makeshift covers of boughs to shed the icy wetness.

On the positive side, Maggie's arm continued to mend rapidly, the scarred tissue smoothing and softening with Kathryn's herbal salves. Willie and Beau were on best behavior, enjoying each other's company. Millie complained loudly and often, but kept on plodding. The adults, quickly adapting to the ebb and flow of their journey, actually found much to enjoy in the adventure.

However, the greatest joy witnessed, was that shared between Gabrielle and Rob.

"Your nephew may have been raised to the finer life, Jack. But he certainly is at ease here," Kathryn commented softly.

"Aye, an adaptable young man he is at that. Takes after his uncle, I believe." Jack's face split in an ear-to-ear grin as he winked.

"I do believe there is a certain *incentive* that spurs him on," Jason said, leaning in so as not to be overheard.

"Aye, so it would seem. You and I will speak of it at a later time, Jason." Jack's expression turned thoughtful. Glancing at Kathryn, he could see the escalating 'caring' between the two young people, also caused her concern. *Yes, much lies ahead of us,* he thought. *But I am where I should be, and I am ready.*

He smiled to himself. One look at Jason and Kathryn gave him to realize they read him well, knew his thoughts and agreed.

Chapter Twenty-Five

Temporary Sanctuary

"We are finally here," Kathryn shouted gleefully, her words pushing out small, misty clouds on the chilly afternoon air.

It was mid-afternoon of the sixteenth day, the end of November—and it was cold. Gathering black clouds on the horizon promised precipitation: icy rain more than likely.

"It will be wonderful to be warm tonight." Maggie smiled.

After her bout with stomach cramps, she seemed fine, at least to all outward appearances. She may have fooled the men, but not Kathryn. *Give us two or three days to settle in,* she prayed. There was much to be done to make the cabin habitable. Like the well-rehearsed team they had become, everyone pitched in. Windows were thrown open, blankets shaken out, small critters shooed outside and encouraged to make their homes elsewhere, firewood gathered, the horses and two cows fed and safely sheltered.

Maggie pitched in with the rest, nicely holding her own until firmly informed she was to do no more—just 'sit and direct'. She appeared peaked, drawing Kathryn's concern. *It is not her arm that bothers.* She made a mental note of the remaining contents of her depleted medicine bag. *Gabrielle and I must replenish our supplies with whatever we can find this time of year.*

However, Maggie's discomfort seemed to abate for the moment. By the time they sat down for their evening meal, the house smelled of fresh pine, a cheery fire leaped in the fieldstone fireplace, and the smell of roasting rabbit had all their stomachs growling.

Samuel, never known to show any inclination towards religion, requested a moment's silence, speaking emotionally of good friends, his wife's healing and new hope. He added a meaningful prayer at the end, paying no heed to tears trickling down his cheeks, as he made eye contact with each individual, mouthing a soft '*thank you*'.

Kathryn glanced around the table adding her own silent prayers. *This will work.* For the first time in months, they were on an appropriate path. They would sleep well tonight, in comfort.

After their meal, they talked of the next day's foray into Charleston for supplies. Kathryn and Gabrielle wanted desperately to visit the city, but concerns for Maggie would keep them at the hideaway.

"Actually, poppet, the fewer that go, the less attention we draw. The British have not left yet." Jason attempted soothing his daughter's disappointment.

Forcing a smile, she settled herself beside Rob on the stairwell, watching him whittle. The fact that her father was right did not make the decision easier to accept.

"Samuel cannot risk being seen after his part in Gabriel's escape either," Kathryn added, pressing for further input.

"Jack, Rob, and I will go," Jason stated summarily.

Gabrielle turned to Rob and smiled, unwilling to dampen his spirits with her selfishness, but hoping that the next time they visited the city, she would be allowed to join them.

The next morning Kathryn stood at the wooden tub washing dishes, her thoughts drifting, wishing she could accompany Jason, Jack and …

"Why, Gabrielle?"

Rob's sharp question, and use of her daughter's full name, grabbed her attention. Although out of sight, he sounded to be just outside the back door.

"I would like very much to see Ted again," she answered softly.

"Why? Why is he so important?"

Kathryn knew she should step away; their conversation was private, but Rob's tone struck an old and deep chord within, and she remained riveted.

"He is a friend, Robbie, *nothing more,*" she said firmly, adding in tones so low Kathryn was hard-pressed to hear. "Jealousy *is not* to be part of who we are, or what we mean to each other."

"I am *not* jealous, Ellie, merely attempting to understand the connection between you two."

Kathryn detected a softening of tone as he tried to conceal strong feelings, and hide insecurities.

"*Friendship* only, my Robbie, no more than I would expect of you with Caitlin, or any other *woman* for that matter." Those words caught his full attention.

"My heart belongs to you alone, Ellie. You know that."

"I am but a child experiencing a child's 'puppy love'."

Kathryn almost choked: different circumstances perhaps, and different words, but identical inference. *My God, Jason and myself.* She shook her head, disconcerted.

"That is not true, Gabrielle. Do not toy with me."

Seeing hurt flickering in his eyes, she ceased 'the game'. "From the moment I set eyes on you, Robbie, I understood our destiny—not the how or why—only the undeniable truth. *You* are my 'connection', no other."

"As you are mine, Ellie, and no other."

"I will miss you; come back to me safely."

There was a long silence. Kathryn waited, refusing to let her mind run rampant.

"I *will* convey your greetings to Ted," he said softly.

Another lingering silence and Kathryn bit her lower lip. Age was nothing but a number as one grew older. Neither was it now; her daughter was *old* beyond her years.

"Bring poppa and Uncle Jack home safely too. I am more concerned that they may find old disagreements to settle."

Both laughed and a long silence followed. Kathryn hoped they had moved farther away from the house. She refused to consider other possibilities. *Oh, momma,* she sighed, missing *her* mother. *How I wish you were here to advise me.* With a shake of her head, she hung the towel up and headed outside to give her husband a farewell kiss.

***

"It would appear Nathanael Greene enjoys flaunting his presence," Jason observed dryly, shielding his eyes from the sun's glare for a better look. He gestured toward the pier where the well-dressed American General strolled slowly, accompanied by two aides and six officers. Head held high, he seemed at ease with his surroundings, and himself.

"I do recall Ted saying that the man has a particular affinity for the wharf. Perhaps the ships and their cargos or ..." Jack shrugged.

The three of them stopped and stood casually observing. Rob's eyes swept the area, disconcerted. Hair prickled on the back of his neck, something was amiss. A glint of sunlight flashed off metal, abruptly catching his attention.

"Holy shite!" Leaping off the boardwalk, he raced towards the far end of the pier.

Jason's eyes darted after Rob, then back to the general. "Sweet Jesus," he cursed, bolting towards Greene.

Reality came together in a flash. "Oh Christ, Rob," Jack muttered, sprinting after his nephew. Jason would be fine for a few minutes; best to help Rob.

Jason lunged, his shoulder slamming into Greene's side, throwing him to the ground as a loud report echoed across the waterfront.

It all happened so fast, no one had made any attempt to stop Jason's charge. But they did now. The public stood awestruck, mouths agape. But Greene's officers reacted instantly, pummeling Jason as he struggled to deflect their blows, regain his feet and explain. The rifle shot seemed of no importance, their efforts placed on subduing the perpetrator—although he had no rifle or visible weapons.

"You son-of-bitch, how dare you? We will hang your sorry arse ..." Angry epithets rang in Jason's ears as he allowed himself to go limp, appearing to surrender. By the time he was dragged to his feet, he was bloodied and cursing softly.

General Greene, assisted to his feet, swiped angrily at his uniform attempting to rid it of filth while his aides fluttered about ineffectually. With a rude swing of impatience, he pushed them aside and strode forward to meet his attacker. He stood glowering—his face suffused deep red, and outraged that *anyone* would have the balls to strike *him*—of all people. "Look at me, you son-of-a-bitch," he spat, grabbing Jason's hair and yanking his head up.

Meeting the general's gaze, Jason said nothing, but prayed for a bit of luck.

Rob sped along the side alley, cutting through in time to catch the sniper making final adjustments to his aim. Sure of his target, confident of being undetected, he took his time. Intensely focused, he never heard Rob's stealthy approach.

"Whoreson bastard," Rob snarled, slamming into the sniper, shoving the rifle aside to fire harmlessly into the air.

Surprise having given him the upper hand, he quickly overpowered the slimly built figure. "Damn it." Rob rubbed his aching knuckles, scanning the area for rope.

"Rob," Jack panted, reaching his nephew's side slightly out of breath. Quickly taking in the scene, he retraced his steps, returning shortly with two lengths of rope. "This will do." He handed a piece to Rob.

A quick flip had the groaning man on his stomach. As Jack trussed his hands behind his back he looked up; his *sweet, young nephew* was just fastening a slip noose around the hapless fellow's neck. Inhaling deeply, he gave Rob a long, intense look. *My God, do I know you, nephew?* He gathered he need not worry over the lad's abilities to look out for himself any longer. "How are your knuckles?" he asked, at a loss for words.

"They'll do, Uncle Jack." He grinned.

"Well then, we had best go bail Jason out of trouble."

Yanking the dazed sniper to his feet, they each grabbed a shoulder, supporting and shoving him towards the wharf. Rob snagged the rifle in passing, tucking it snuggly under his arm. Their prisoner, now fully aware and fearful, began cursing fluently. With a sharp yank, his ranting ceased. Choking, eyes watering, he began to falter, his face slowly suffusing purple.

Rob waited until he began to stagger before loosening the rope. With deep, wracking coughs, he sucked in air, his vivid color fading slowly back to sallow. "One more word and I shall forget how to loosen the rope. Do we have an understanding?"

The sniper nodded dumbly, muttering under his breath.

"What did you say?" Rob growled.

"I'll be hanged anyway," he murmured.

"Likely a firing squad, but even hanging is faster than this." Rob tugged the rope as reminder.

Jack eyed his nephew. "Someday you must tell me more about your life at sea, Rob."

Rob merely grinned.

General Greene stepped back, fury flashing in his eyes as he searched Jason's face. Despite his greatly changed appearance, recognition struck.

"Colonel Tarrington is it not?" he asked curtly, slightly shaken and unsure as to what had just taken place.

"No, sir," Jason retorted. He stood a bit shakily, wiping blood from his nose and mouth, fighting down anger. "I *am* Jason William Tarrington—husband and father— attempting to raise my family in our *freely adopted* country, in peace and *obscurity.* I have no wish for trouble, General."

Greene appraised him intently sensing no deceit, and detecting nothing of the former villainous colonel of repute. It suddenly dawned on him, this former archenemy had apparently saved his life, the utter irony of that causing him to smile, surprising Jason.

"It would appear that I *may* owe you a debt of thanks, as well as an apology for the rough handling my men dealt you. However, until the circumstances have been verified, would you mind?"

"My pistol and knife, General." Without hesitation, Jason slid his hand into his boot retrieving a knife, and then snagged his pistol from its resting place snug against the small of his back. Holding both out, he smiled, easily reading the general's body language. He had caused Greene a bit of embarrassment.

Jason decided that making mention of his officers' ineptitude, would be undiplomatic and likely to create more trouble, for the sake of 'tweaking'. Albeit his weapons were partially concealed, Greene had not missed them. If true to his reputation, there would be more than harsh words doled out later. *Kathryn will be fascinated.*

"You—interest me, sir." Greene took the weapons, eyeing him sharply, understanding why he had been such an astute enemy.

At that moment, Jack and Rob pushed through the gathered crowd, and with a hard shove, Rob sent the sniper stumbling to his knees at the general's feet.

"This is the culprit you seek, General Greene." Rob stepped forward proudly. He had prevented the attempted murder; it was his privilege to set things straight.

Jack caught Jason's eye and shrugged. *Rob was no longer a boy; he was a man.*

That evening, after having shared cordials and sweetmeats over lengthy conversation with General Greene, they sat together at a long table in the old inn. Although later than planned and off schedule, they agreed it would have been unwise to refuse. Greene and his army had no intention of leaving Charleston for many months—better to have him on their side, if possible, if future plans forced them to become more visible.

Having remembered them, the innkeeper greeted them warmly. "Master Ted has a couple of letters for you, sir," he informed as he set a huge crock of stew in front of them, delighted to see them dig in hungrily.

Jason was first to realize the innkeeper was still there, standing quietly off to one side. "Delicious," he managed around a mouthful, turning to address him. But he made no move, smiling benignly, too polite to make open inquiries, but itching for news.

"My wife and children are well and wish to be remembered. Our seafaring friend, Smitty, I am sure you recall him, has adapted well to dry land." That seemed to be all he required. Bowing from the shoulders, he said pleasantly, "I will inform Master Oleander that you are here, gentlemen. If I may be of service, please call on me."

Rob grinned as he dipped a wide slab of fresh bread, warm from the oven, into the rich stew and began chewing contentedly. Youthful exuberance over the day's success provided 'heady' self-confidence. Neither Jason nor Jack asked the status of his knuckles. No one 'hovered' over Jason's swollen face. Rob would not allow anyone to 'hover' over him.

"You certainly learned a great deal at sea, nephew," Jack commented edgily.

Rob stopped chewing and eyed his uncle. *He is making a pertinent comment, about what?* The language he used earlier had been a bit *colorful.* "Yes sir," he replied contritely. "I regret my use of coarse words. They came without thought in the heat of the moment, I fear."

Jason tried unsuccessfully to hide a grin behind his swollen lip, proud of the young man his daughter had chosen.

"I will not promise it will never happen again, but I will try to refrain in the presence of ladies."

"Please at least do that," Jack said, trying to keep his voice firm, but failing miserably.

Jason nodded agreeably, holding the boy's gaze. "This is not the time or place, but another situation concerns me. I will broach the subject, but we will speak of it later."

"Ellie," he answered softly. "You are the father of a beautiful daughter, sir. You owe me no apologies for concern over my motives, or my ability for restraint."

At his forthright statement, Jason sucked in a sharp breath and glanced at Jack, who sat there avoiding eye contact, maintaining a blank expression.

Rob frowned, choosing his words. "We may be young sir, but we know our hearts."

"You *may* call me Jason, Rob. I am not—*sir.*"

"When I speak to you of serious matters, I shall address you as *sir.* Unless of course, that is offensive to you."

Jason shook his head. "Please go on, Rob."

"We found each other very young. But however long it takes, the prize is more than worth the wait. Watching Ellie grow into womanhood is a precious treat in itself. How many men have experienced the gift of watching their beloved move through the stages of maturity? Isn't that a rare and precious gift?"

Jack and Jason both nodded, struck by the young man's maturity.

"I will *never* hurt Ellie, never. You have my sworn oath in front of a witness." His eyes drifted to his uncle and then back to Ellie's father. "I learned much on board ship, not from personal experience, though one or two tried, but from observing and listening." He looked Jason squarely in the eye. "*Yes*, to your unasked question. I *do* have adult urges. A man's body *reacts* without thought, perhaps our only true weakness." He chuckled, but quickly became serious. "My language is one thing, but *that* particular urge I can, and *will* control. I will never hurt your daughter, sir. I have too much respect for her—and her parents."

"Thank you, Rob," Jason managed, glancing away to gather his thoughts.

"You and I will talk later, nephew," Jack assured, leaning closer. "Not to worry Jason, I will teach him to cope with restraint and the myriad complexities of a celibate man's life." He grinned. "Celibate for the most part anyway."

After readying for the night, they sat on their beds discussing the next day's plans. Ted had sent word via his new partner that he looked forward to meeting them for breakfast. He had one 'hire' to fulfill late this evening, but would be at the inn early.

"It would seem that Ted chose wisely. He must be doing well to have found a partner so soon." Jason commented, pleased for the young man.

"After breakfast we will shop for our necessities. Unless anyone has other reasons to stay longer, we shall be on the road and arrive back at Jamie's by midnight."

"My thoughts too, Jack. Maggie worries me a bit. If Farthingale is not expected in port right away, Ted will get word to him the moment he lands. Besides, we have plenty of time and much to accomplish before then."

Rob eyed Jason with open curiosity.

"We have a proposition for your friend Captain Farthingale, Rob. You know him better than either of us. It is too long a topic to begin tonight; we'll discuss it on the way back to the hideaway. Your input will be helpful."

Jason turned to Jack. "I have written a detailed outline of our proposal."

"His fertile mind will fill in the blanks and probably expand upon them," Jack added with a smirk.

"Captain Farthingale never fails to miss an opportunity. Did I tell you the details of what he had in mind for me?" Both men shook their head. "This won't take long, and you may find it of interest." Rob began his tale.

"Farthingale is our man," Jason said as he pulled the blanket up around his shoulders, missing Kathryn's warmth. "Your comments support our earlier suspicions, Rob. He's a dedicated fanatic when pursuing money—an excellent trait for a business partner."

As Jason reached to douse the oil lamp a resounding fart broke the silence. Guffaws erupted from the innocent parties and Jack sent his nephew a long sideways glance.

"What?" Rob pretended affront. "I take it neither of you fart? I may be a proper born Englishman, but even well-raised, we boarding school lads have gas upon occasion. It was a rich beef stew with lots of onions and ..."

"My God, Rob, if only your mother could see you now and know what your father's hard-earned money paid for."

"Oh," Rob interrupted, his expression becoming serious. Tossing his blanket aside he moved to his saddlebag, rummaged for a moment and brought out a well-worn leather pouch. Handing it to his uncle, he explained. "My father sent this to me at school—atonement for my mother's bad behavior, perhaps. I was to use it for something that would make me happy. My original thoughts were to invest in a business. But I am young and healthy and can earn more."

"What do you wish to do with it, Rob?"

"I want you to help buy clothing, food, whatever a new baby needs. Maggie and Sam have been treated badly, first by his government and then fate."

At the beginning of protest, he raised a silencing hand. "I have set aside a little for clothes or anything I might need, so as not to have to ask. And I will always work hard for the gift of a roof over my head. But they *need* help."

"All right," Jack said, tucking the pouch under his pillow, "if you are sure."

"I *am* sure," he stated. "I would not be here, but for the kindness of others. It is my turn now." Rob crawled back into his bed and pulled up the blanket.

As Jason doused the lamp Rob added, "I would request this be *our* secret. I would never have Sam think he is beholding to a *boy,* nor feel shamed or inadequate in his family's eyes. He is a good man and, would take the gift the wrong way."

Jason drifted sleepily. *You have chosen well, poppet. Rob is a good man.*

Breakfast with Ted had been delightful and informative. Captain Farthingale was due in port within the month and Ted would be sure to give him their outline. Their ideas appeared solid, exciting, and only moderate 'risk' involved. It should definitely appeal to the captain.

"Kirkland *never* turns down a venture that lines his pockets. Scruples or danger are no problem either," Ted declared. "As you recall, he trained under Tarleton." With that remark, Ted suddenly handed Jason two rather soiled letters the captain had brought from England on his last voyage: parchments which Jason tucked into his pocket to share with Kathryn later. One bore the decorative script of Great Grandmother, the other the heavy, bold hand of Lord Cornwallis.

A tense moment occurred when Rob, as promised, conveyed greetings from Gabrielle. Ted made a smart remark about wishing she had eyes only for *him,* rather than Rob. Though he handled himself well, his irritation and forced restraint were obvious. Jason groaned. *Good luck with conquering 'jealousy', lad. Even after all these years there are moments when I ...*

Rob had started off with the men, accompanying them for awhile, but soon left on investigations of his own, returning in time to help carry the staples up to their room. Having downed their dinner quickly, they now sat pondering the bundles attempting to organize for the next morning's early departure. The hours had flown by, the choosing and purchasing of supplies taking longer than planned. They would be forced to spend one more night in Charleston.

Jack stopped contemplating long enough to send his nephew a curious look. "You have seen rural areas, and now one of the major cities in the colonies. What do you think? Is city life for you?"

"Not for me, Uncle. But there *is* good money to be made from the wealthy living here. Tonight we must pack, but I will share my ideas on the ride tomorrow. I am *fascinated* by this country, similar and yet so very different from England."

"Well, you will find Keowee unlike anything you have known, a true *experience*, Rob." Jason grinned at the young man's youthful élan.

"Anywhere that Ellie is happy is …" He quickly caught himself.

Jason smiled in complete understanding. "The women in our lives seem to keep us here, willingly and happily I might add."

Jack agreed, his thoughts meandering. Pulling himself back to the moment he asked, "Well, do we hire a wagon? It will slow us down and have to be returned, but I …"

"I have an old mule," Rob broke in.

Both men eyed him sharply.

"I won him fair and square in a game of dice. As the man was no challenge I felt badly. I stayed and cleaned his barn and stacked hay."

"How *old* is old?" Jason asked.

Rob shrugged. "He seems fit, merely stubborn. He was really scruffy, so I cleaned him up and brushed him. I am sure the man just wished to be rid of him, for no one can be that bad at dice. But he claimed he is still strong and steady once you get him going."

"You never cease to amaze me, Rob," Jack said proudly.

"Praise me when we see how he takes to his load tomorrow."

"Cornelius is a likeable enough creature," Jason admitted a few hours into their ride, lumps of sugar the only incentive the mule needed to cooperate fully. "How did he come by that name?"

"Well, I thought the women might be offended by the name he came with."

At their curious glances, he chuckled. "He answered, somewhat inappropriately, to Shitehead. His personality reminds me of my mother's butler: calm, co-operative and good humored. He was good to me and Gabrielle, and I miss him. This noble beast is named in his honor."

"You must write him of that," Jack said. "He would be thoroughly amused." Cornelius was a good man; he thought of him often. He had helped Jack hold on to his sanity during those awful months in England.

The conversation eventually turned to future plans, and they did not sugarcoat it for the lad: constant hard work, long days, no assurance of financial security, the ever present danger from irascible trappers, Indians and wild animals.

Rob's eagerness astonished them. "Carving is one of my strengths—wood or stone. Here in the colonies, it is not necessary to waste long years on apprenticeship and journeyman training to become a master in that trade. My ability will speak for itself. After seeing the wealth of Charleston, high-end furniture could be perfect. However, I *am* realistic enough to know that it will take time and perseverance to be 'discovered'. But I have plenty of that." After a moment of silence he announced: "A cooper will be my main trade for now. Everyone needs barrels, chests—and coffins."

Jack and Jason smiled, exchanging looks of approval at his sound thoughts and mature observations.

Cornelius's loud braying negated the need for announcement. The cabin door flew open. Rushing down the steps, Gabrielle yelled a loud greeting just as Rob swung down from Sampson. Pulling her into his arms, he hugged her tight and swung her in a circle, smiling as she giggled gleefully.

Kathryn emerged with Beau tucked under one arm. Her eyes caught Jason's steady gaze and held, relief flooding throughout her body. She quickly flashed a smile at Jack and returned her attention to her husband, noting the bruises and swollen lip.

"I see you have walked into a door, my love. I thought your companions might make you more careful of your person."

"T'is a long but interesting tale, my pet, and General Greene sends his regards."

"Where is the Hodges family?" Jack asked.

"We are here, hale and hearty," a loud voice rumbled from the front porch.

All attention turned towards the cabin. Samuel stood eyeing them happily with a small, blanketed bundle in the crook of one arm and the other around his wife. Maggie held Willie's hand as he grinned proudly from ear-to-ear.

"I have a new sister," he announced.

Questions, answers, congratulations, the retelling of events from the last few days, everyone talking at once alternating with stunned silence, a joyous reunion.

"Maggie went into labor shortly after you left—an easy birth, quickly over. Thankfully, the baby *is* beautiful; Maggie had worried. Felicity is a perfect name, meaning *happiness*."

"How are her burns?" Jason asked.

"The skin is tender but well-healed. I made her a soft cotton sleeve for protection, and Gabrielle mixed large amounts of salve and willow bark tea. The wound will be sensitive for a long time to come, but there is no risk of further infection."

Much later, ensconced in their bed, Kathryn reached to the side table, filled a cup with willow tea and handed it to her husband with a long sigh. "For *your* pain, my love."

He brushed it aside gently, but at her insistent look complied: always a futile gesture to refuse his wife. They had shared *everything* from the past three days over a brandy with Jack, and now relished the peacefulness of their room.

"I have letters, my love." He reached into his pocket and handed her the parchments.

Her eyes widened. "Great Grandmother and his lordship—which shall we read first?"

"I am curious as to what Cornwallis has to say. We can then linger over my grandmother's and savor it."

"It is a very generous offer he makes you, Jason," Kathryn said tentatively as she handed the letter back to him. "Joining him on a post in India would place you in good favor with King George and …"

"And I would detest it. There will be no further discussion of this matter. Agreed?"

She smiled with relief.

"Now let us enjoy my grandmother's letter. Scanning quickly over your shoulder, it appears to speak only of happiness other than the fact she misses us."

It *was* a delightful letter bearing good tidings. Jason's father, having conquered his drinking, had become a rather decent human being. Rob's father had recently surprised her, visiting without his wife's knowledge. He sent his love and asked to hear about Rob's new life through her, explaining that Cornelius was watched too closely to intercept any further letters without discovery. "It would seem Eugenie's anger is on-going. What a fool she is; life is too short for such nonsense." Jason's grandmother had written.

Turning to her husband, she proceeded to gently rub salve into his scrapes and bruises. Dipping her finger again, she traced a gentle trail down his bare chest.

"Kathryn," he sucked in a breath, "I was *not* touched there by the general's men."

"That is a good thing," she purred, sliding slippery fingers lower. "That is for me to do."

With a low growl he flipped her, pinning her firmly beneath him. "There is no time for games tonight, my love," he rasped. "My need is too great."

Filling one hand with the full lushness of her, he reached to douse the lamp.

One week later, they sat astride their horses bidding warm farewells to Sam and his family. The look on his face expressed all their feelings, sadness at the 'going', yet contentment for the gift of new beginnings.

Sam's protestations, that none of this was a gift and *would be repaid,* were ignored. Jason and Jack, good to their word, never divulged Rob's part in the gift.

"Cornelius is on 'loan' for now," Rob announced, reaching down to shake Sam's hand. "He can be stubborn and contrary, but give him a lump of sugar and he'll do your bidding without complaint."

Sam's eyes locked on Rob's. "I value your friendship, young Rob; stay well."

As they turned their horses and trotted down the dirt path, Jason twisted in his saddle and called back over his shoulder: "We will be back in March. Stay well, friends."

Jason shared Rob's enthusiastic plan for himself with Kathryn. She had been thrilled, even more so after seeing his gift for Felicity, an exquisitely carved rattle created from a single piece of poplar. The long elaborate handle was topped with an open egg-shape, and within its open slats rattled a smooth round ball. Rob loved the challenge of creating without assembly or glue to achieve an end product. *And he was good at it.*

"Two more hours," Kathryn announced.

"They know we are close," Jason added, pleasing his wife with how attuned he had become to the Cherokees.

"How would they know that?" Rob asked, taken aback.

Jack gestured toward the sky where several white puffs drifted. At his nephew's look of confusion he added, "Smoke—not clouds, lad."

They dismounted to refill canteens and refresh themselves. Kathryn took their last piece of bread and broke off pieces, handing one to each of them. "This will keep us going for a little bit. Enjoy."

Suddenly they were surrounded by warriors: unsmiling, tattooed faces, painted ponies, bows at the ready with arrows nocked—*fearsome.* This was the 'stuff' of lurid tales read back in England—tales of the wild colonies across the ocean that Rob had read, but never dreamed of experiencing. Rob's hand slid towards his knife.

"Wait," Jack hissed, stopping his nephew with a firm grip on his wrist.

"Ahh, t'is only Ugilohi," came a loud shout followed by laughter, as the braves resheathed their arrows.

It was but a game, as Kathryn well knew. She smiled as a well-muscled warrior tossed his leg over his pony's neck, dropped to the ground and quickly approached. Pulling her into a bear hug, he kissed her soundly.

Bursting into laughter, she kissed him back. "How you take my breath away, Gabriel," she teased.

Rob stood in shock, eyes wide, mouth agape.

"That's momma's nephew," Gabrielle whispered, snaking a comforting arm about Rob's waist.

"Her—nephew?" he asked, incredulous.

"That's Gabriel, Uncle Jamie's son. I am named after him. He is married to Silver Fox, the daughter of Soaring Eagle and ..."

"More slowly please, Ellie. This is very new to me as yet."

"As a matter of fact, *there* is Soaring Eagle, Gabriel's father-in-law." She pointed with pride at the magnificent warrior, watching in silence with the barest hint of a smile. Seeing confusion lingering in Rob's eyes, she hugged him. "I will teach you, Robbie."

Jason and Jack stood back enjoying Kathryn's warm greeting and Rob's awestruck reaction.

Kathryn reached up to touch her nephew's face, tracing the decorative tattoos, appreciating the beauty of his design. He now sported the Cherokee's distinctive hair style: pulled into a topknot and adorned with a single feather and small beads. His ears were pierced in several places and held small shells which tinkled softly against each other, adornment and musical sounds, favorites of the '*People*'. His flesh was dyed to a rich golden tone, his bare arms decorated with extensive, intricate tattooing. Despite the cold, much of his skin remained exposed. He looked well, happy, and complete. And he deserved no less.

"You are thinking of how to express your concerns without offending me, my dear aunt," Gabriel said curtly.

Jack shifted uneasily; Jason merely laughed.

"You are wrong, Gabriel. I approve wholeheartedly. I meant it when I said you truly take my breath away. I was merely acknowledging and absorbing the import of such action on your part."

"*This* is now *your* life." Jason moved closer nodding approval.

"Ahh, Hunter, you know me well."

"That is true, Gabriel. However, we had also noticed that you have not come to the farm in many months and now understand why. It was much easier to walk in both worlds when you still retained much of the white man's dress and habits, but now?"

"I have no desire to do so any longer," Gabriel stated resolutely. "My heart lies here with my wife and children. With atrocities being committed on both sides, I *will not* risk their well-being by dragging them back and forth between the two worlds. Although my father will not be happy, we *do* have a right to live our own lives—a lesson I learned from my aunt. But there will be plenty of time to talk of this later. A meal is being prepared in honor of your return. Let us not be late." He eyed them, flashing a wry grin.

"As I recall, if one was late for a special occasion, they were told to fight the dogs for scraps," Jack chuckled, extending his hand, and Gabriel grasped it in firm welcome.

Gabriel smiled at Beau's wide-eyed wonder, touched his cheek tenderly, and with a quick hug to Gabrielle, a hearty handshake to Rob, signaled the braves and flung himself onto his pony.

"You and I will talk later, lad, for I wish to know you better," he informed Rob as he spun away.

Gabrielle pulled abreast of Rob and squeezed his hand.

"He wants to meet *me*," he whispered, his eyes dancing with anticipation.

Searching his face, she was pleased to see his shock had been replaced by healthy, growing excitement.

You will be fine, my Robbie, she mouthed, and kneed North Star to pick up the pace.

Chapter Twenty-Six

Return to Keowee

Well before they arrived in camp, they could smell the welcoming aromas of wood smoke and wild game cooking. By the time they stepped down from their horses, their stomachs growled in anticipation.

Soaring Eagle stepped forward. Murmuring personal greetings, and promising time to talk later, he quickly took charge of caring for the horses and unloading their gear.

Gabriel strode forward and showed them to their housing. He had enlarged Kathryn's home, adding another room for more privacy. Jack's hut had always been more than adequate and would easily house Rob.

"Become familiar again. Prepare for the evening meal. The drums will call."

As he turned to leave, he stopped beside Rob. "Do I frighten you?"

"Not in the least," Rob answered.

"Good," Gabriel said and headed for his house.

"Did I pass my first test?" he asked.

Kathryn laughed. "Does anything frighten you, Rob?"

"Very little," he stated honestly and turned to follow Jack.

"What an incredible evening," Kathryn exclaimed.

Lying within her husband's arms in the privacy of their newly built addition, she felt truly happy. "Anna looks well and Silver Fox—every one, as a matter of fact. I had forgotten the peacefulness that exists here."

Jason nuzzled her neck. "Were you surprised by Gabriel?"

She thought for a minute before answering. "No, not really. I think my first thoughts were of happiness for him, but sorry for *our* loss."

"You had hoped he would come with us."

"You read me well, my love."

"As you do with me, and such a delight—fewer words and more time to ..."

She set that remark aside for a moment. "Gabriel knows this area like the back of his hand. Perhaps he will help us choose an appropriate place and advise us, so we may remain in good standing with the Cherokees and other 'Nations' as well. Possibly our trading post could sell the Bird Clan's goods if they were agreeable."

Jason's lips found the rim of her ear. "The pieces are slowly coming together, my love. This *is* what we are meant to do. However, as we cannot talk to Gabriel at this late hour, might I interest you in slightly more *carnal* entertainment?"

She rolled to place the full length of her naked body against him, brushing a kiss to his chest.

"How well do you read me now, sir?"

"Perfectly, milady." And he doused the lamp.

The days flowed easily, one into another, as their lives adjusted to the beautiful rhythm of Anna's Bird Clan. When Kathryn unpacked her few belongings, she stopped and smiled at the lace handkerchief tucked inside one of her shirts. Lavender fragrance still clung tenaciously and she inhaled deeply. Gabrielle, wise beyond her years, had passed Ted's gift on to her mother. *Relationships between the sexes are always unique and often puzzling.* She shook her head and tucked it deeper into her belongings.

"Why is it that fathers are so overly protective of daughters?" Kathryn asked one evening, recalling Jason's recent outburst over Rob's audacity of kissing their daughter, not only soundly, but within his sight.

Jason eyed her for a long moment before a smile crept across his handsome face. "Ahh, lass, t'is simple. Callous bastards that we are, we ..."

She burst out laughing, ending whatever further nonsense he had meant to impart with a deep kiss.

Rob had the greatest amount of adapting in Keowee, but seemed happy to work at it. One evening, he and Gabrielle arrived at the door of her parent's hut in high good humor. Kathryn wrinkled her nose, scrunching her face into a mask of disgust.

"What in the world have you two been doing?"

"Soaring Eagle is allowing us to tan the hide of the big buck he shot," Gabrielle explained.

"It truly is amazing, Auntie Kat." Rob adopted little Raven's assigned title for her.

Kathryn had no objection; she was *definitely not* ready to be called *mom.*

"As small as the animal's brain appears to be in relation to the size of the whole hide, there is always enough *stuff to* complete the job. But you really have to mash it into the skin; practically push it *through* to the other side of the hide to do a good job."

Kathryn smiled at Rob's enthusiasm. Nothing seemed to daunt the lad. She was familiar with tanning, had worked with hides herself, but it was not a job for everyone; especially if one was squeamish. Glancing at her daughter's beaming face, she was glad for her, glad for both of them.

"Tomorrow we will hang it to age over a smoky, oak wood fire to keep it soft. Soaring Eagle has promised to teach me the next stage," Rob stated proudly. He glanced at Gabrielle and then back to her mother. "I suspect Ellie already knows the system, but she remains silent, allowing me to learn." He shot her a sideways glance.

Somehow, despite the incredibly strict lifestyle in which he had been raised, Rob seemed open to everything and eager to learn.

As Gabrielle's body rounded into the soft fullness of oncoming maturity, her parents noticed that Rob forced himself not to stare, attacking whatever task was nearest as diversion. He purposely worked hard in an effort to burn off excess energy, hoping to dampen his desire. Thankfully, Gabrielle's intense training with Anna had begun almost immediately upon arrival. Although he missed her constant companionship, being apart made his life easier—or so he told himself repeatedly.

If no specific task was pressing, he created one—hunting, fishing, tending the animals, building or mending huts and whittling. Most of the children within the village were proud owners of one of his intricate, wooden rattles. With each request, he eagerly began another. It had been obvious from the beginning that he was well-liked, but the day Soaring Eagle invited him into the privacy of his quarters to sit and talk, Rob knew he had found unreserved 'welcome'.

Each morning he participated in the ritual of cleanliness so revered by the Cherokees. No matter how frigid the weather, their honor demanded they bathe in the river. This time of year, Rob found it took extreme courage to wade right in. Goosebumps spiked along his arms and across his chest, chills rippling his flesh. He vowed he *would* become accustomed no matter what it took. He despised the embarrassment he experienced in Gabriel's presence. If Gabriel and Hunter could wade right in, then he would too.

This particular morning was especially cold as the three of them waded into the water, splashing handfuls of icy wetness across their chests, arms and faces, as wisps of frosty air spiraled skyward with each spoken word.

Invited to accompany Soaring Eagle on a trek into the woods for deer, Jack had bathed much earlier. As the winter months had dragged on, food had become low. Jack, Soaring Eagle and three other braves would be gone for the better part of the day, maybe even the next. With the ongoing encroachment of white settlers, once abundant game had moved farther out, and they refused to return empty handed. Jack had informed Rob the previous evening, "If I must chill my bones well before dawn, so be it. I am flattered to have been asked."

"You claim to be a man, young Rob," Gabriel taunted. Standing knee-deep in icy water, he casually glanced up and down the lad's tall frame. "I gather you judge by *smaller* standards in England." His gaze then swept casually over Jason. "Ahh, Hunter, I see it is obviously an English standard."

As Gabriel's apparent disdain turned on Jason, Rob tensed. Clenching his fists, he made ready to go to his defense. But Jason abruptly reached out, placing a hand on his shoulder in a calming gesture. "Relax, son, I see you have never experienced the delight that men take in comparing their *attributes*."

"*Never*, in my household and *definitely not* on board the *Lucifer*. Rob forced a smile, but remained unsettled.

"Your tattoos are well-done, Rob," Jason commented, wishing to break the tension and relieve the lad's disquietude until he could get him aside and explain. There were times when Gabriel took far too much pleasure in another's embarrassment—somewhat like his father.

"Gabriel designed them," Rob gave credit freely.

"Cried like a baby while I worked on him," Gabriel chided.

"I did no such …" Rob began, his temper flaring. But catching Jason's meaningful look changed his response. "I fear I did, but will not again. I am learning to be a man." He played the game, but felt no joy.

As they parted, Gabriel grinned at Rob, eyes appraising, but made no comment. Rob waited until he was well out of earshot before he spoke.

"Hunter, may I speak plainly?"

"Of course, Rob." He felt the lad's distress, knowing what to expect.

"Why does Gabriel dislike me so? I have shown nothing but respect."

Jason snorted. "Rob, I shared many weeks within the narrow confines of *your* British upbringing, and a *lifetime* within my own. In the colonies, especially back in the woods, forget all former instructions on propriety and refinement and *always* keep an open mind. Cities like Charleston will be much closer to what you were raised with, but not out here—most especially *not* in Gabriel's home territory."

"But his words are derisive. He mocks me unmercifully. I have begun to question my ..."

Placing a comforting hand on his shoulder, Jason's expression changed, his amusement replaced by open honesty and deep caring. "Rob, you will *never* have reason to apologize for your manhood, on any level. You *are* a good man. I consider you *my son.*"

Rob blinked rapidly, fighting overwhelming emotion at Hunter's words.

"Then I fail to ..."

"I know Gabriel likes and respects you, it is merely his way, nothing more."

Abruptly Rob smiled, for as inane as the situation was, he understood. "However, I gather I must not return the *favor,* no matter what his words."

"I knew my daughter had chosen wisely." With a long look, which spoke more than words, he turned towards his hut.

"Good morning, my love." He kissed her soundly before picking Beau up and swinging him overhead.

A resounding belch, followed by fits of hysterical giggles, brought a ready smile. "I see our son has already eaten his breakfast. I am thankful not to be *wearing* it. Has the little pig left anything for his poppa?"

After Jason ate his fill, he and Kathryn lingered over coffee. In the far corner of the room Beau sat happily amusing himself with rattles, strings of beads and a cornhusk doll. Having thankfully passed his 'clinging' stage, he entertained himself contentedly, allowing his parents more appreciated time to themselves.

Jason took a long swallow of coffee and mentioned casually, "Rob has handsome new tattoos across his shoulders."

Kathryn stopped in the midst of taking a sip. "Does he wish to remain here, to follow in Gabriel's footsteps?"

Jason caught her panicked tone. "No, I think not. It appears to be more a test of his manhood meted out by Gabriel. He truly likes Rob and wishes him to stay—using reverse psychology on the lad, and I question it."

"I don't follow you, Jason."

"He mocks Rob unmercifully, hoping he will dig in his heels and remain here, in order to prove he *is not* what Gabriel claims."

"He is like his father in some ways, but to point that fact out would only make matters worse. I do hope Rob will not be hurt by his games."

Jason pressed a kiss to her forehead. "I have taken care of that, my pet. Rob is a very intelligent, young man."

Gabriel tired quickly of his game when it became apparent that Rob understood the rules. He had no wish to truly hurt the lad. If he chose to move on when the time came, so be it.

They spent long hours discussing the new trading post. Georgia was suggested for a possible site, the Savannah River providing an excellent means of moving product to the coast. But would Farthingale be willing to make an additional stop? Building immediately south of the former Loyalist fort, 'The 96', would put them nearer to the Edisto River and Charleston—convenient for the captain, but not for them—requiring a wagon to get to the river, then switching to flatboat, and returning to land to continue on to Charleston. Would this be worth the inconvenience and risk?

Gabriel listened to their suppositions, refraining from input. Lacking facts upon which to make a sound judgment was frustrating. *His* idea would take them in a different direction—solve lingering questions and put them as close to safety as possible. But first he must be sure of his information so as not to disappoint them again. Soaring Eagle would have the means of securing important answers; he would talk to him.

March arrived far too quickly. Like it or not, having promised Jamie they would return to help Caitlin, they must head north. Kathryn hoped her niece had decided to marry the father of her child. Jamie might despise the man, but would perceive their marriage better for maintaining *his* good standing in the community; eventually he might come to accept him.

Anxious over delaying the pursuit of their new life, Kathryn rued having made the offer; but a promise was a promise. They would ride straight through to Jamie's, remain only long enough to help Caitlin with the birth, and immediately turn southwards. Stopping first in Charleston to connect briefly with Ted, they would then head to the hideaway and lay out their plans with Samuel.

"Everything appears to be coming together smoothly, Jason, once this duty is done."

Jason agreed, but a nagging sense of *something*—he was unsure exactly what—troubled him. He had experienced this exact feeling the night before Guilford Courthouse, and was uneasy.

"Stop that," Kathryn said sharply. "I *feel* it too, but we must put it aside. I foresee no possibility of reneging on our promise."

Turning a solemn face to his wife, he forced a smile. But the disquieting feeling prevailed. "Who is coming to Jamie's with us?" he asked, attempting diversion.

"Jack is staying here to keep an eye on Rob and Gabrielle."

"I thought our daughter wished to stop in Charleston to see Ted."

"That appears to be no longer important." A knowing look passed between them. "Silver Fox *asked specifically* to care for Beau." Kathryn rolled her eyes and shrugged. "She is up for sainthood or has taken leave of her senses, I am not sure which. You and I shall have much time alone," she purred.

"I wish that were true, my love, but Gabriel will be riding with us. He just informed me this morning that he feels it is time to face his father."

"Does he intend to make his appearance any less *unusual*?"

"No, and I respect him for that. But it should be a *very interesting* visit. Perhaps *that* is what nags with such misgivings."

"I hope so, Jason." *But I doubt it*, she added to herself.

"That took far less time than expected," Kathryn commented as they trotted along the dirt road approaching Jamie's farm.

"When you do not travel with an entourage you move faster." Gabriel's tart response indicated growing foreboding.

Jason flashed her a meaningful look, conveying similar feelings: trepidation. Something *was not* right. The air hung heavy with tension, becoming more so with each step the horses took. "Thank heavens the children are not with us," Kathryn murmured and Jason nodded.

As they stepped down from their horses and looped the reins around the fence, the front door flew open, slamming back against the house.

Jamie stood there, his face suffused with bright color eyeing each of them balefully. Before anyone gathered their wits to comment, he attacked verbally—his son first.

"Christ Jesus, was it not enough that ye marry one of them? Now ye must become one of them?" he flung nastily.

Gabriel tensed, eyes narrowing, furious but refusing to fight with his father. *He is what he is,* and remained silent.

His silence infuriated Jamie more. With a muttered curse, he spun towards Kathryn. "And *you,* my dear sister, come to pay yer condolences have ye?" His eyes flashed hatred.

Kathryn jerked back as if struck a physical blow, color draining from her face—shocked, confused, cut deeply by her brother's vicious attack. *Of what is he speaking?* Her mind raced.

"Caitlin died in the birthing, Kathryn. Had *you* been here as ye should ha' been, rather than scratchin' yer itches elsewhere, she might still be here. Rather than me left alone with her bastard to rear." Lip curled derisively, he advanced threateningly—like a panther stalking prey.

With lightening speed, Jason lunged, his large fist smashing into Jamie's jaw. Down he went with a surprised grunt and fluent curses.

"You son-of-a-bitch," Jason spat. Yanking his pistol from the back of his pants, he thumbed the hammer back and thrust it against his brother-in-law's chest.

Attempting to curb his fury, Kathryn's hand slid to the small of his back sending a calming message: *They are only words, my love, only* words. Despite the gravity, his speed in protecting her provided a moment's pause: *just as in the old days.*

Jamie's face paled instantly at the raw fury exuding from Jason's body. A lethal message sparked in those icy, blue eyes, one that pierced him, held him captive. This 'black villain' was no longer his friend, Hunter. *This* was none other than his former enemy, the notorious Colonel Jason William Tarrington; he experienced an instant prick of fear.

As abruptly as the fury seized Jason, it dissipated with no more than a gentle touch from his wife. In that instant, Jamie saw what this man *had been* capable of—what he *remained* capable of—and for the first time since he had known them as a couple, truly understood their complexity and passion: a dynamic team which had defied all odds … and survived.

Jason's fury was contained, but by no means over. "If you *ever* speak to my wife again in such a manner, I *will* kill you James Douglas MacLean, and somehow manage to live with Kathryn's inconsolable grief." His voice shook slightly.

Jamie lay there—speechless.

"*Never* again," he reiterated icily. "Do I have your clear understanding, James?" His pistol nudged Jamie's chest.

Jamie turned a pleading eye to his son. "Have ye nothing to say at this affront to yer father, Gabriel?"

Gabriel gave his father a long, thoughtful look. "No, father, I do believe everything that needs to be said—has been."

Jason eased the hammer down, slid the pistol back into the belt of his pants and extended his hand to assist Jamie in rising. *This gesture I make for you only, my Kathryn.*

Jamie remained sprawled, stubbornly refusing with jutting chin and icy silence.

Jason shrugged and stepped aside. Turning to his wife, he asked softy, "Would you care to see your newest family addition before we leave?"

"No," she whispered. Tears filled her eyes and spilled over as she looked sorrowfully at her brother. "I am truly sorry for your loss, Jamie." Flicking Beauty's reins free, she slowly mounted and headed towards the road. Within a few yards, she halted Beauty and sat staring across the fields to the distant forest.

As Jason drew up beside her, her hand reached blindly and he grasped it, deeply relieved. He had feared she might …

Her eyes were dry when she turned to meet his compassionate gaze, but the depth of her sorrow dimmed their customary luster. "*Thank you, my love*," she whispered.

He cradled her cheek in the palm of his hand, searching her face. But there were no words to ease this agony.

"As long ago as Keowee, when Jamie first came to us," she began shakily, "I realized it was too good to last. I prayed I was wrong but …" she trailed into silence.

As they sat watching the forest holding hands, neither wishing to break the contact, Jamie's acid accusations echoed across the field.

"Are ye not goin' to stay and comfort me son? After all yer months hidin' what ye've become you *owe me better.* Ye need to take some responsibility in helping raise yer new cousin. How can I be expected to raise this—*bastard*?"

Gabriel shook his head firmly. "I see nothing to be gained from any amount of conversation between us, father. You fail to learn from your mistakes, always repeating the same." He shook his head unable to finish, tears glistening as he moved to his horse.

Kathryn and Jason heard Gabriel's sharp shout to his piebald, and waited for him to pull abreast. "All is truly lost, Jason. Jamie has forsaken his only son." Swiping an errant tear with her shirt sleeve, she turned to offer a comforting smile to her nephew.

Bits and pieces of his continued diatribe, damning them all to hell, fell away as the three of them kneed their horses into a flat out gallop to put distance between them and Jamie. *None of them looked back.*

Immersed in their own thoughts they rode in silence for long hours, not stopping to make camp until well after dark. Jamie's name never came up. They had come north to Georgetown to celebrate a birth, and had left mourning the death of not one, but *two* family members.

When they arrived in Charleston, Gabriel declined accompanying them into the city. Kathryn immediately rose to his defense.

"Not for the reasons you think, Aunt. The Brits supposedly left several weeks ago, but if anyone lingers, who might remember me from my months in prison—that would be taking an uncalled for risk. We have experienced enough upset for one trip, no need to press our luck, merely to make a point over my appearance."

Kathryn grinned. "You read me well, Gabriel. Where shall we find you?"

"Don't worry, *I* will find you."

After sharing warm greetings, Kathryn and Jason joined Ted for dinner, conversing leisurely over a light repast in the old inn.

"I have two letters for you, Jason." Ted pushed one towards him. "Read this one first, it's more apt to be to your liking," he said. Captain Farthingale had arrived in port recently, remaining long enough to study their intriguing proposal—amongst other *things* on his agenda. Ted grinned wickedly and winked before continuing.

"He's extremely interested, and has enclosed a list of items that would be of *value* and *interest* in both New England and England. He will not return to port any sooner than late fall, but plans to winter here in Charleston. He insists you all meet at that time to finalize the deal."

Jason held the letter out to share with Kathryn. After scanning the short message she smiled. It was friendly and informative and said in part: ... *Your venture has merit and piques my interest. I wish you the best. We will have much to discuss upon my return to port.*

> *I look forward to seeing all of you, and will send word upon my arrival. Please give my regards to young Rob and Ellie. Invite them to accompany you on your next visit and we shall make a party of it. By then Rob may have reconsidered my lucrative offer—or perhaps not. I believe he has a far greater interest than money.*
>
> *With Sincerest Regard,*
> *Captain Kirkland J. Farthingale*

After folding the parchment and tucking it into an inner pocket, Jason's gaze riveted on the second letter Ted pushed towards him. The address was inked in a bold, easily read flourish: *Colonel and Mrs. Jason William Tarrington.*

"Damn it," Kathryn and Jason swore in unison.

"Nathanael Greene: how in hell did he know we would come through here at this time?" Jason's eyebrows shot upwards.

Ted winced, visibly embarrassed. "The general put a great deal of pressure on me as to information about your whereabouts. That's the reason I like to know as little as possible at all times. However, he did seem sincere, raving about Jason having saved his life. It seems he wants to speak to *both* of you. Sounds a bit irregular to me, but who am I to know?"

"I imagine he alluded to your business success depending upon your delivery of this." Jason slapped the parchment against his palm.

Ted swallowed, looking visibly ill.

"Duplicitous bastard," Kathryn spat, "using Jason's name so openly, damn him. He obviously has no concern for *our* safety."

"He brought the letter directly to me, and I put it out of sight immediately. But where it has been, I cannot say." Ted shook his head, upset.

"Not to worry, Ted. Two can play at this game." Jason opened the parchment, read it and passed it to Kathryn, who in turn read it and pushed it towards Ted.

"He offers you a position and quarters for your family, for the duration of his stay." Ted was puzzled. "Why?"

Kathryn and Jason laughed, amused at the absurdity of the offer, easily seeing through the general's ruse. At Ted's obvious confusion, Jason explained. "Greene may have more than one thought in mind. If he can coax us into accepting his offer, we would be close at hand, easy to keep an eye on. Be assured, *that* information would 'leak out'. For our past misdeeds, perhaps unforgiving Charlestonians would take matters into their own hands. Or if all else failed; a regrettable accident just before he evacuates his troops."

Ted was shocked. "General's *do not* play so low, do they?"

Again, Jason and Kathryn burst into laughter, surprising him. He was horrified: they acted as if it were no more than a rude joke.

"Oh, the tales we could tell you if we had more time," Kathryn said, becoming serious at Ted's continued discomfort.

"Nothing will change as a result of Greene's charade, other than readjusting a few details which will be worked out before we meet with Farthingale this fall." Jason eyed Ted thoughtfully. "Rest easy, *we* will be the ones to contact you. However, you do know how to find us if there is a true emergency?"

"Absolutely. Be safe."

With quick handshakes and hugs they were gone, leaving Ted far wiser, and somewhat disillusioned.

The visit with Maggie and Samuel and their children lifted their spirits. Maggie's arm was strong and no longer giving her discomfort. The children were hale and hearty and fascinated by Gabriel's dramatic physical appearance.

Kathryn and Jason spoke at length of their plans for the future. However, Sam and Maggie were not ready to pick up and move on. The hideaway was a perfect size for them; they had planted two gardens: a large vegetable garden and a smaller one filled with flowers.

"Would it be possible to speak with Jamie?" Hodges began.

"I can promise nothing at this point" Kathryn said softly, then explained the sad situation briefly. "Stay as long as you like. If a problem arises, Gabriel will know how to find us."

"Our offer will always be open," Jason said firmly, shaking his former captain's hand.

Bidding them a fond farewell, they headed south to Keowee one last time.

Two weeks had passed since Kathryn and Jason's visit. Ted sat sipping coffee at the dining table in the old inn. He rubbed his full stomach delightedly; breakfast had been delicious. He had thirty minutes to linger over a second cup of coffee before picking up his first 'hire' of the day; he smiled contentedly.

Abruptly the morning 'buzz' silenced. Ted looked up to see the cause. General Greene, flanked by two officers, stood at the entrance of the dining area. He paused a moment, scanning the room rapidly; spotting Ted seated in the middle of the room, he strode deliberately towards his table.

Ted pushed his chair back to rise, but a curt gesture from Greene informed him to remain seated. Resting both hands firmly on the table, Nathanael Greene pierced him with a steely glare.

"Have they arrived yet?" he demanded.

"Yes, sir; come and gone."

Startled and angry at the bold response, the general clenched his fists and retorted, "You informed me they would be here."

"Yes, sir, apparently their plans changed unexpectedly." Ted shrugged apologetically.

"Did you give them my letter?" Greene's jaw clenched, irritation building. "Did they read it?"

"Yes, sir."

The dining room remained noticeably—and uncomfortably—silent.

"And *what* was their reaction?" He flushed noticeably, struggling to maintain civility.

Ted looked extremely uncomfortable.

"Oleander, I asked you a specific question."

"They laughed sir."

"Damn them!" A muscle twitched along his jaw.

"Might I relay a message if I see them again?" Ted asked with feigned innocence, thoroughly enjoying himself.

"Damn them and damn you, you smart-mouthed, little bastard," Greene exploded, drawing furtive glances. In a fit of uncontrolled anger, he slammed both fists on the table, causing Ted's cup to dance in its saucer. Pinning him with an icy glare, Greene cursed softly and spun on his heel. Brushing past his officers, he stalked towards the door in complete disgust.

Quickly regaining their composure, his officers hustled after him. Looking neither left nor right, heads held high, they marched out of the dining room.

"I take that as a firm 'no'." Ted brought his coffee cup to his lips and swallowed deeply, breathing a sigh of relief. *I must remember to tell Jason and Kathryn when they return this fall.*

Within minutes, the customary morning chatter resumed as if nothing out of the ordinary had taken place.

Chapter Twenty-Seven

Another New Beginning

As promised, Gabriel appeared out of nowhere just as Kathryn was becoming concerned. After relating the day's events in Charleston, the three of them rode south in companionable silence. There would be plenty of time to discuss long-reaching problems over the next several days. The pall of Jamie's debacle still hung heavily: silence the best means of healing for now. By the next day spirits had lifted, the weather—perfect. Light talk slowly gravitated towards the 'heart' of what needed to be discussed.

"We must reassess," Jason began. "What is our ultimate goal, Kathryn? Success? Absolutely. Achieve riches? Perhaps, but that may require adopting a lifestyle similar to that of city folk: dressing for polite society, attending the theater and numerous galas—perhaps drinking tea with a little finger crooked." He looked pointedly at his wife, suppressing the urge to laugh at her horrified expression.

"Such a ridiculous statement does not dignify an answer," she snorted. "However, our grandiose idea of a huge trading post may have to be sized down for affordability, at least in the beginning."

"Now that Greene has virtually announced to Charleston that you are both alive, it will be difficult for you to make regular trips to the wharf with goods," Gabriel mentioned casually. "Although not impossible by any means," he added.

"That may actually have been Greene's ultimate goal. He would feel justice had been served with our demise, but in failing to accomplish that, might settle for making things difficult for us to start over."

Jason gave his wife a long speculative look before glancing to Gabriel. Both nodded, grinning at Kathryn, impressed by her intuitiveness.

"She is right, Hunter. Charleston will neither forgive nor forget what you both did to them, nor Lord Cornwallis's huge celebration given at the expense of their pride." Gabriel's words were a statement of truth issued without rancor—and neither took offense.

"When we return to Keowee, we will go ahead as planned, perhaps on a smaller scale," Jason announced.

Kathryn smiled, excitement setting her thoughts racing. "For some reason, I feel everything will work out. But as I bring each of us to mind, knowing Charleston to be unsafe for anything other than an occasional appearance, I wonder who?"

"Young Rob," Gabriel offered. "He has the ability—honest, intelligent, a *man* despite his age." He glanced meaningfully at Jason, understood his *knowing* smile, and vowed to soften his approach. There was nothing unmanly about the lad; he would no longer taunt him. Rob would stay or go by his own choice, and had no need to prove himself to Gabriel or any other.

Kathryn pursed her lips, not particularly happy with that idea no matter what Rob's abilities. "That won't be necessary. I sense change is coming," she said, and left it at that.

As they rode in silence, Gabriel's thoughts turned to his conversation with Soaring Eagle the night before they headed north to his father's farm. For a man of composed, stern countenance, he had been receptive and excited, surprising Gabriel. If feasible, his proposed venture would be profitable for everyone involved, but most importantly—the Cherokees.

"We are ready?" Soaring Eagle eyed Jack sharply. Scrutinizing his full saddle packs and blanket roll, he nodded approvingly. He had liked this man from the beginning. He learned quickly, wasted no words beyond those necessary for a given situation, and displayed patience, something his revered Ugilohi had yet to learn.

Turning his attention to Rob, his lips curved in a tight smile. The young man sat astride his large mount, his demeanor serious and alert, maintaining proper decorum in the presence of this venerable warrior.

A rich chuckle rumbled up from the back of Soaring Eagle's throat. "Gabrielle, *little bird*, do tell your young man I rarely bite, and only when provoked." With that bit of parting *humor*, they headed off down the well-worn Charleston Path.

Soaring Eagle *was* excited, although that fact would never be determined by looking at him. From the moment Gabriel first confided his idea, Soaring Eagle had begun to make plans. Taking Jack into his confidence, he explained the previous success, and excellent chance of renewed potential, in a venture he planned to divulge. As Jack was well aware of Jason and Kathryn's interests, he could give 'yea or nae' before they revealed the surprise.

Kathryn, Jason and Gabriel had barely ridden out of sight when Soaring Eagle's little group headed for 'The 96'.

Smitty sat slouched on an overturned barrel. It was an absolutely beautiful day, but he felt no joy. Leaning back against the paddock fence, deep in thought, he felt velvet lips nibble gently against his ear, coarse chin hairs tickling.

"You're a good pal, Horse." Smitty scratched the stubbly chin, glad for the diversion.

Thomas had taken Annie, and their infant daughter to visit her father, in an attempt to pull him out of his black mood. Smitty finally felt confident about their marriage. Through compromise they had come to genuine caring, the baby being the catalyst for new beginnings. Mellowing Annie, and a few pointed talks with Thomas, had also helped. Annie adored Smitty, but had turned to her husband for companionship, as it should be, the rewards of their combined efforts: a doting husband and wife, young son, baby daughter and another on the way.

Smitty had accomplished all he could here—time to move on. Caitlin's death had been a sad waste of potential. Although a bitter, unhappy girl, she had deserved a better death than that. Jamie's anger was loud and on going; not so much at the injustice of her death, but the fact that *he* now had to raise the 'little bastard'.

The little boy was an *innocent*. Smitty took offense at Jamie's callousness, but was in no position to raise a child, and therefore had no say. *Perhaps Annie and Thomas might consider …* He dropped the thought. It was none of his business.

He had been exposed to a new, to him, and unpleasant side of Jamie's personality. His bitter story of Kathryn and Jason's hateful treatment of him did not ring true, nor did disinheriting his only son as a negligent ingrate, carry authenticity. Smitty attempted a bit of leeway in judging Jamie, but the crass epithets he had hurled at Gabriel, followed by vile ranting that his sister cared nothing about *his* personal pain, was unacceptable. After five minutes of angrily pacing and spewing non-stop invective in his self-righteous retelling, Jamie suddenly 'shut down'. Turtle-like, he withdrew into a self-made shell of denial, retreating from the outside world.

Hamish had been present at the time and advised him: "T'is exactly *this* type of pious nonsense, which has torn them apart all their lives, Smitty; you can do naught to help. Move on with *your* life. Jamie must sort this out for himself."

Hamish's words echoed as he stood scratching his horse's ears. He worried about Kathryn; she was honest to a fault, often to the point of self-deprecation. It had been a long trip from Keowee to Georgetown, and to have come all that way in hopes of helping, only to have been met by that? He would have fled Jamie's idiocy too. *Poor lass,* he mused. *She has never known how she would be received by her brother. He is as changeable as the wind and just as erratic.* Smitty understood the situation more clearly than he wished to, the knowledge failing to bring relief. "Ahh, James," he murmured, "Ye have been good to me and I like you, but ye *are* yer own worst enemy."

Reaching through the fence, he rubbed the angular cheek affectionately. Horse shook his head and snorted, turning large, thoughtful eyes on his master and pressing closer.

"Give me a few minutes, friend, I must leave a note of farewell. Anything less would be ill-mannered. As ye know, Ole Smitty may be a bit rough around the edges, but he's got manners." With that statement, he actually smiled. This felt 'right'. With a quick pat to Horse's cheek, he headed for the house. Horse whinnied and moved along the fence after him, but a curt wave stopped the big animal; he stood patiently waiting as ordered.

After gathering his few possessions, not enough to even fill a canvas sack full, he sat down at Annie's desk. *What words to convey all I feel? There are no words, but Annie will understand; she has grown into a compassionate woman right before my eyes.*

Within a few more minutes, Smitty and Horse plodded the dirt trail towards the woods. He had remembered to grab a few slices of bread and cheese to tide him over at least for the day. "I hope you recall the way, Horse. I'm a bit hazy on directions but I figure Keowee is our best bet."

Horse snorted in answer, and Smitty smiled.

"How good to be back," Kathryn hugged each member of her family in turn.

"You are home sooner than expected." Gabrielle eyed her mother, reading her sadness.

"Things we will speak of later, little one."

Gabrielle immediately understood and asked no further. "See how Beau has grown," she quickly changed the subject, stepping aside to reveal her little brother.

Up to this point, Beau had been clinging quietly to the back of his sister's long tunic but now, unable to conceal his glee longer, lurched forward. "Momma, Poppa," he chirped, his small arms pin-wheeling as he took several wobbly steps towards them.

"Look at our little man." Kathryn beamed as she crouched with outstretched arms, catching her son as he abruptly lost his balance and tottered sideways.

Jason tousled his son's tawny hair, and lifting him from his mother's arms swung him up and held him, giggling and squirming above his head.

"You are truly brave, my love," Kathryn chuckled. "I do hope he has not just eaten."

Gabriel stood quietly watching the reunion, somber faced; but with that statement, a smile crept across his face to actually reach his eyes. It was the first break in his quiet introspection in days, and Kathryn was relieved. Despite avowal to the contrary, his father's unwarranted tirade had cut deeply, and his sister's death: just one more needless tragedy.

Joyous chattering addressed him, and he spun about. His wife stood gently assessing, her eyes bright with love. As his children rushed forward, it was then that Gabriel's face lit up with unmistakable joy. Quickly moving to them, he embraced his family with outstretched arms.

This is where he belongs. You are such a fool, Jamie … yet again.

They sat in Anna's lodge enjoying a lengthy meal. Anna had put together a veritable feast, insisting they eat slowly and relish the flavor. She refused to be rushed, basking in the warmth and joy of being surrounded by those she cherished dearly.

Kathryn was impatient for the meal to be done. "Something is afoot," she hissed.

Jason shared her anxiety. A quick glance at the smiling faces surrounding them left no doubt; everyone, except them, was part of *something*—even Gabrielle and Rob. Soaring Eagle appeared to be the spokesperson; surreptitious glances being aimed towards him.

"Relax, my love, all in good time; Soaring Eagle will *not* be rushed. He enjoys watching you fidget far too well." With those whispered words, he placed a calming hand in the middle of her back, circling his fingers slowly.

Eventually, after the smallest children were put down for the evening, and Soaring Eagle deemed the time appropriate, he stood and addressed Anna in Cherokee.

"He thanks Anna and asks to share his meeting with her, or move to his hut if she wishes," Kathryn quietly interpreted for Jason. Though he knew many words, even some lengthy sentences, Soaring Eagle's rapid-fire delivery was difficult to decipher.

Anna moved to sit beside Soaring Eagle, and with a sharp nod the meeting began. His face was stern as he eyed each person present, but the twinkle in his piercing, black gaze made quite a different statement: he was deeply pleased.

Kathryn noticed that Gabriel made no attempt at hiding *his* excitement and was a bit irked. *What is this about? How long have you known? If we are involved, why have you not …?* Irritation flared.

"Patience my love, he will explain all in his own good time," Jason whispered.

Kathryn shot him a startled look. *He reads me so clearly.*

"What are you waiting for, Gabriel?" Soaring Eagle rumbled, a smile flickering briefly, thoroughly enjoying.

"While we were away," Gabriel indicated Kathryn and Jason with a broad sweep of his arm, "Soaring Eagle and Jack rode out to 'The 96' along with Gabrielle and Rob." He now had their avid attention; questions were formulating in Kathryn's mind. Quickly moving on, he gestured there would be no discussion until he was done.

"I have heard you comment, more than once, about the veritable highway the Cherokee Path has become, Aunt."

Kathryn nodded.

"There is a valid reason." He decided it unnecessary and bordering on bad manners, to mention that, at the time, they had been entrenched *on the wrong side* of a bloody war and therefore likely unfamiliar. "The town around 'The 96' consisted of about a dozen houses, a courthouse, a *Trading Post* and a small inn."

"We were never there long enough to …" Jason began.

"I doubt you are aware that Nathanael Greene burned most of the town when he gave up the siege on the fort, and headed for the coast in May of 1781."

Kathryn shrugged, shaking her head. "I fear we were not well enough to have cared one way or the other."

"It is of no matter, Aunt. John Cruger finished the job, burning anything still standing when he finally evacuated. Although, for reasons known only to him, he left 'The 96' unscathed. All is *not* lost. Gouedy's Trading Post is still there and remains empty. It needs work, but nothing insurmountable."

"What about Gouedy?" Jason asked. The trading post was perfectly positioned for high volume trade between the western settlements beyond the Saluda River, and Charleston. "Although lifestyle in the colonies is still somewhat new to me—and I have much to learn—this makes perfect sense." He turned to Kathryn, pleased to see complete concurrence. But of far greater importance: unmistakable enthusiasm sparkling in her eyes. A quick glance at Jack and the young people indicated they were excited and eager to commit to this new venture.

Soaring Eagle abruptly added, "Robert Gouedy was a friend to the Cherokee for many years. He took our deerskins and furs in trade for items we needed: ammunition, trinkets, tools, blankets, beads and much more. Unfortunately for us, Gouedy died six years past. Two others have tried and failed since: as much *our* loss as theirs. The last man met a rather *unfortunate* ending this past year."

Kathryn's eyebrows shot up.

Soaring Eagle shrugged, gracing her with a long, meaningful look. "Let us say, he had a problem with *honesty*."

At Soaring Eagle's nod, Jack pointed out: "There are no living relatives holding claim to the trading post, or the inn for that matter. Although rumor has it that Gouedy's son is still alive, he apparently has no personal interest. He sold it shortly after his father's death. 'The 96' remains abandoned, open to any who wish to use it, and houses an excellent water supply, within what was called Stockade Fort. A unique two-story brick jail stands in excellent condition amidst the ruins of the town—a good beginning."

"We could all be housed there while we build and repair," Rob added, wishing to offer his approval. "The inn needs almost no repairs and stands only a few yards from the trading post. It is smaller but better placed for convenience."

Gabrielle moved to her mother's side and hugged her. "We have been secretive because we did not want to dash your hopes again. It was Gabriel's idea." She glanced gratefully at her cousin. "But Soaring Eagle searched for the necessary answers, making it possible."

Kathryn remained silent for a long moment, allowing comprehension of the incredible *gift* to sink in. At long last, the potential to accomplish all they had planned and more lay within their grasp, she was awestruck.

"There is also an inn?" she asked.

"The Black Swan: small but always busy in the past," Jack answered.

With quiet confidence, Gabriel stepped forward to address the underlying importance of this venture. "Bringing Gouedy's old trading post back to life would be, first and foremost, a direct advantage for the Cherokees—specifically the Bird Clan. But the white settlements farther west will also welcome you with open arms. Think of all the time and effort you will save them."

"We have saved the best for last," Jack said. "There are four or five large Loyalist plantations within a day's ride of the trading post. It is not necessary to remember their names at the moment, but we will meet them and make our plans known shortly. We are the answer to their continued success. They raise grain, cattle, tobacco and more."

"A Loyalist area," Kathryn murmured.

"Yes, my Ugilohi, you and your family will do well here, *welcome and safe* on all sides." Soaring Eagle's eyes embraced Kathryn and Jason with open warmth. "Will you both ride with me? Allow me to show you?" He stood and slowly folded his arms across his chest.

"Yes," they replied eagerly.

Soaring Eagle grinned at Gabriel. "I do believe they like your idea." Then, in customary fashion, he abruptly signaled the meeting was over.

As they made ready to file from Anna's lodge, she spoke up for the first time. "We will help you repair or build as necessary, Ugilohi. Success for all of us will be the reward. And to have you and my little bird but two days ride, is a gift I had hardly dared ask for." Her eyes drifted speculatively to Kathryn's. "I see it clearly now. It was *Hunter's* destiny at Guilford Courthouse, not yours. Your willingness to *share* called him back to heal you. The Universe has a higher purpose for you both, here and now."

For once, Kathryn had no words, remaining quietly thoughtful, knowing she would have much to think on later.

As they moved past Soaring Eagle he stated firmly, "Tomorrow at dawn—be ready. *All* of you are to come for a united decision." He individually nodded at Gabrielle, Rob, Jack and—*most especially*—Gabriel.

Gabriel, his respected son-in-law, was of extreme importance for he walked in both worlds—the white man's and the Cherokee's. He understood the ways of their thinking on both sides, his input invaluable. Soaring Eagle fully understood that the success of this venture would have a direct effect on the Cherokee people as a whole. But of greater importance to him, his beloved daughter, Silver Fox, and his grandchildren. Therefore, Gabriel *must* embrace the plan, and be a working part of it. Signs for the future did not bode well. Incredible changes were in the works. The world as the Cherokee People had known it—in all its regal beauty—was starting to crumble, and this was only the beginning.

"Although 'The 96' looks the same, I never realized all this was here," Jason commented as he strode through the charred remains, noticing the overgrowth of tenacious weeds. "The courthouse looks to have been of substantial size," he added, glancing along the remaining foundation.

Kathryn shook her head. "Only a few months ago, this village must have been quite lovely." The sweep of her arm indicated woods, open fields and a few remaining timbers which stood stalwartly, as if to deny such a rude ending.

Beauty and Diablo paced themselves, following Soaring Eagle in well-mannered fashion as he led the tour. From time to time, Jack or one of the young people would point out something of interest. Although eager to see the trading post, Jason and Kathryn allowed the day to unfold as it would. Nothing came from attempting to *nudge* Soaring Eagle.

"Over there is the brick jail I told you about, none the worse for the fire," Rob pointed off to the right. "It's large enough to make a good shop downstairs, with family living quarters on the second floor."

Kathryn smiled, momentarily taken aback. It was what Rob *was not* saying, his underlying hint, that caught her attention. She and Jason *must* talk.

Eventually Soaring Eagle, having decided that Kathryn had shown patience, gestured sharply indicating they follow him as he entered a wide trail disappearing into the woods. It was a pretty road, flanked by an assortment of tall trees, oak and fir most prevalent, and obviously still well-traveled.

"This is Gouedy's Trail," Jack said. "I don't believe I mentioned that his son is Major James Gouedy. Did you ever meet him?"

"That name sounds familiar," Jason replied giving it thought. "I believe we did meet when I last visited John Cruger at 'The 96'. However, as I recall, it was nothing more than a brief greeting, we were both just 'passing through' at the time."

As they rounded a bend in the trail, the path opened into a large clearing. There it stood—the trading post and just beyond, The Black Swan. The trading post looked in need of a few repairs, mostly of a cosmetic nature. But other than a few over-grown weeds, The Black Swan was in excellent condition, small but elegant. A huge Dutch oven, set off to one side, immediately caught Kathryn's eye, it was perfect.

"Oh Jason," she whispered.

"I gather it is to your liking," Soaring Eagle chuckled, watching with satisfaction, as they dismounted to explore.

They spent the night quite comfortably within the solid walls of the inn, curling up in their saddle blankets after sharing a delicious brace of roasted rabbits.

With dawn's first light, Soaring Eagle stood over the children, hands on hips, chin jutting. "It is far past time to be up, and on Keowee path. We will eat on the trail."

Catching the warrior's eye, Jack announced: "I will accompany Soaring Eagle." Seeing no hint of disagreement he added, "We will assemble the necessities for building and return shortly."

"What of our helping with spring planting? We had planned to be there."

"Kathryn, you will serve the Bird Clan better by quickly having all in place here," Soaring Eagle rumbled.

"While we are gone, you two will be making the acquaintance of the four nearest plantation owners: Zacharias Gibbs, David George, John Mayfield and Stephen Mayfield—just as we discussed last night," Jack said, as he swung up onto his horse.

"Do you feel we will be able to fulfill our promises to them, Jack? To be ready to accept their grain, tobacco and cattle so soon will be—difficult."

"Kathryn," Jack chided gently, "Has there ever been anything that you and Jason did not accomplish, once you set your minds to it?" Jack turned to Jason. "Talk to her, nothing will stop us now. This is *our* destiny." Kneeing his horse into a trot, he closed the gap between himself and the others. Having grown tired of on-going discussion, they were now a fair distance ahead of him. With a wide wave, he yelled back over his shoulder, "Be ready to report your success. You have seven days before we return."

It was the end of the fifth day. Kathryn crouched beside the campfire turning a rabbit, checking every few minutes to see if it was done. She was tired and hungry, as was Jason, yet both were thoroughly elated. They had been astonished by their unanimous welcome. All four plantation owners, pleased to have them as new neighbors, eagerly embraced their business propositions, inviting them to join their social lives as well.

Kathryn and Jason explained this first visit to their prospective customers as one of introduction only. They would sit down and create letters of intent well before harvest, *after* they had accomplished the necessary repairs to the trading post. The fact that they intended to reopen The Black Swan had been received with equal interest. As many of their business and social contacts had enjoyed the warmth and camaraderie of the solid, little inn over the years, they would spread the word.

Jason's polite hedging as to their joining the 'back woods' social whirl had not been accepted, and Kathryn groaned. She had hoped all that supercilious rubbish would have been over with the war, apparently naiveté on her part. *I fear I will have to bring my one or two dressy gowns out of retirement.* She would do whatever it took to make their venture successful.

"We look forward to doing business, Jason." Zacharias Gibbs thumped him on the back chuckling. "It's got to be good for both of us, as you well know. But after meeting your delightful wife, I have no doubts."

They were received with almost identical words of greeting at each of the other plantations. "Does no one here have an individual thought, Jason?" Kathryn had asked, shaking her head, mildly amused.

"It is your luscious figure draped in a seductive riding habit that bedazzles them, my love. I fear I may have to fend off suitors."

They had successfully introduced themselves to all but Thomas Fletchall, a noted Tory leader situated up on Fairforest Creek. They planned to make his acquaintance the following day. It had been a complete success, accomplished within Jack's time frame; they would be ready and waiting when he returned.

As Kathryn bit into a haunch of rabbit she smiled at her husband. "Do you think they suspect who we are, my love?"

"Absolutely, my pet, they savor the notoriety of naming us as 'friends' and business associates.

"Who would ever have thought it?" she laughed.

Chapter Twenty-Eight

Laying Groundwork

"Smitty!" Ted managed around a mouthful of ham and grits, eagerly waving him to his table. Ever since Nathanael Greene had startled him during his meal several weeks ago, he had chosen to dine at the table in the back corner, facing outwards towards the doorway.

As Smitty sat down, Ted caught the innkeeper's attention. "Please make it the same for my friend, George."

Before Smitty could stop grinning, a heaping plate of vittles was set in front of him, along with a steaming mug of coffee.

"That ought to fill the empty hole hugging your backbone," Ted chuckled. "What in hell happened to you? My God, ye are but a mere wisp of yer old self."

"Me overly muscled and far thinner physique makes me look quite a bit taller, wouldn't you agree?" Smitty patted his flat stomach proudly.

"Taller? Perhaps a bit, but taller or not you will draw the attention of the delightful, young ladies of Charleston like a magnet. How long are you staying and where?"

Smitty's smile faded. "As glad as I am to see you, Ted, I hope you have news of Jason and Kathryn. City life is not for me, nor is the sea. I hope to find them."

"Do you have any details of what happened at Jamie's?" Ted interrupted. "Gabriel refused to come into Charleston. That seemed strange, but they gave no specific reason. Jason said quietly that Jamie's daughter, Caitlin, had died. But Kathryn was so *quiet*, so unlike her. I was a bit worried."

"I fear it was another 'blow' for our Kathryn. But if ye wish to hear the details, I have some."

They spent the morning walking the city streets and catching up.

"I have a surprise that may come in handy." Ted smiled as he led Smitty out in back of the stables. "What do you think?"

"It's not real pretty, but sure looks to be sound. How did you ever come by this?" Smitty scratched his chin, frowning slightly.

"Quite the wagon, don't you think? And it comes with a team."

Smitty cocked his head, astounded.

"A client left this with me to pay a long overdue debt. It seems his high-rolling mistress had expensive demands which left him short on my fees. I was sure Kathryn and Jason could use it, but had no way of getting it to them. So please do me the favor of taking it off my hands."

A smile spread across Smitty's face. "It *is* perfect, Ted, and I thank you."

"Your timing is *perfect,* Smitty. It is *I,* who thank you."

"Don't mention it, lad, just another of my *many* outstanding qualities." He winked, flashing an idiotic grin.

***

"Hellooo the house," Smitty yelled through cupped hands. He was impressed with all the work Hodges had accomplished on outside repairs to the hideaway, and the addition of gardens. "Hellooo the house," he yelled again.

Ted had provided Smitty with the information on Kathryn and Jason's current plans. He also mentioned that they intended to visit Maggie and Sam before returning to Keowee. Smitty vaguely recalled how to find the hideaway, and with Ted's help clarified hazy areas of his memory. However, finding Keowee would be somewhat more of a challenge. None of the Cherokees knew him, and if Kathryn or Jason were not present to vouch for him—well, he did not even want to think about that. Hopefully, the Cherokees would at least be reasonable and question first, before performing any over-zealous greeting.

Having yet to hear any haling from the house, Smitty stepped down from the wagon and wrapped the team's reins around the fence. With a quick pat to Horse, he headed around to the back.

"Christ, Smitty, you startled me," Hodges swore, almost dropping the large crate he was carrying, as he came around the corner of the house.

Smitty's eyebrows shot up apologetically as he offered to take the box.

"Sorry, Smitty. It *is* good to see you, but we're in a bit of a mess and my temper is ..." He sucked a sharp breath through his teeth.

At Smitty's curious look, he set the heavy crate down. "Jamie just left here. That son-of-a-bitch sure has a short memory for past favors. He came down on us in a fury, for no good reason that I can see. My poor Maggie's inside trying to console our son, but *she's* the one more in need of a good shoulder to cry on. She loves this place. I offered to buy it from Jamie on installments, but he would hear nothing of it."

"Where has he gone?" Smitty asked.

"Don't know and don't care. But we are to be out of here when he returns in three days. I have no idea how we will move all we have accumulated in the last few months."

Smitty stared at him open-mouthed. "I think Caitlin's *death* must have 'titched' his mind." He paused. "Well, I'm here to help, and as fate would have it, I have a team and an empty wagon."

"Really?" Hodges was stunned.

"Yup, I'm on my way to bring it to Jason and Kathryn. Having no future plans of me own, I hoped that whatever they are doing might just fit the bill—and maybe an answer for you too." Smitty broke into his wide grin. "Never a door closes but a new one opens. At least now I'll have company on the road. Besides, *you* know how to find Keowee. We'll get through this, Samuel, trust me. Now, let me go greet your good woman. Organize what needs to be done and I'll be back shortly."

***

As Kathryn leaned to pick up her mallet, a large hand came to rest seductively on her bottom.

"You do not so much as 'start', Mrs. Tarrington." The words were gently teasing.

"I will know and cherish *your* touch until the day I die, my love." Kathryn turned into his eager arms, kissing his smiling mouth passionately.

"Sweet Jesus, Kathryn," Jason broke the connection, stepping back. "It has been too long."

"So I see, my love." Her eyes raked down his muscular frame, lingering on the blatancy of his statement. An ache of purling need coiled in her lower belly, and she sighed. "If you touch me like that again, I shall not care who enters and sees."

"*That* is no threat, my Kathryn." His blue eyes threw out a challenge.

"Prove it," she whispered in a smoky, seductive purr as her hand slid the length of his taut abdomen.

"Oh God, Kathryn," he sucked through gritted teeth, his head rolling back on a low groan. With two strides, he grabbed the heavy wooden gate, slammed it forcefully, and turned on her.

"I will brook *no* denial on your part, madam."

"There will be *none*, my colonel, *none*." With that smoky statement, their long overdue *game* was on. *Yes, it had been way too long.*

"You brought Beau," Kathryn smiled weakly at her daughter; *so much to be accomplished and so little time to accomplish it in.*

"*I* had to learn, so must he," Gabrielle replied. "He must be able to entertain himself for whatever length of time is necessary. I will not allow him to get hurt, but I will no longer spend hours amusing him."

"Remember, I can help too," Rob added.

Kathryn took a deep breath and exhaled slowly at her child's firm declaration. "I guess there's no time like the present." She lifted her son into her arms and hugged him. "I *am* glad you are here, little man." Actually, having her children and Jack back home filled her with happiness. Although life seemed more complex when all were present, it was worth any minor inconvenience.

Jack moved to Kathryn's side and grinned. "Jason informed me that you two have become 'the toast of the backwoods' while I was gone. You have set the business wheels in motion quite successfully from what I understand." He looked pleased.

"We had no other choice. *You* left specific instructions, a veritable taskmaster."

He grimaced, grasping his chest. "Cut to the core with yer sharp tongue, milady. If you will kindly recall, *you* have repeatedly encouraged me to take part."

"Hush." Fighting an urge to laugh at his antics, she narrowed her eyes menacingly. "Men!" With a quick hug, she whispered, "You have been sorely missed."

Over the next several days, Jack accompanied them on successive trips to the neighboring plantations. They became especially friendly with Zacharias; he seemed to have influence with the other plantation owners. Although it galled her, Kathryn acted the role perfectly, using her best manners in playing the appropriately politic games of society. Zacharias loved to show off his possessions, especially for her: two prized stallions, six magnificent chestnut hunters and a massive black bull that held several prestigious blue-ribbons.

"Your Beauty and Diablo are such magnificent animals; I don't suppose you might consider breeding them." Jason and Kathryn dashed that idea with vehement head shakes. Zacharias merely shrugged and moved on to his next topic, very little seemed to fluster him.

They rode out through his fields of newly planted grain, corn and tobacco, before continuing across acres of grazing cattle, keeping Zacharias chatting idly so that Jack's keen eye could take careful note of detail. He needed to determine the size and number of wagons necessary to convey such large amounts of product into Charleston.

"This is almost frightening in its enormity," Kathryn frowned over dinner.

"Do you know how one devours a whole elephant?" Jack smiled at Kathryn's quizzical look, and Gabrielle giggled into her cupped hand. "One bite at a time, as we will do in learning this—one step, *or bite*, at a time."

They laughed uproariously, he was right. *When is Jack not right?* This fall they would make a test run with a small load, to work out possible difficulties. By next year the system would be operating smoothly and efficiently.

"There is one thing that all these plantations have in common, which seems to add to their success. They make use of black slaves. Although they appear to be well-treated, for the most part, I do not care for that." Jack shook his head.

Kathryn and Jason agreed. "Those people have feelings, as we do. They eat, sleep, and bleed as we do. They are as maligned and mistreated as the Cherokees," Jason said. "Any man, woman or child who works with us, does so of their own volition—*free men*."

Jason turned to Rob. "Rob, when Captain Farthingale takes Africans on board, does he keep the families together?"

"Farthingale is better than most from what I have been told. He *does* attempt to keep them together. But once left in the Caribbean, and sold to the sugar plantations it is beyond his control."

Kathryn frowned. "Perhaps we might prevail upon Kirkland to rescue two or three families. We'll explain what we seek; at least allow them some choice over their future."

"Once they arrive here, fresh off the *Lucifer*, there will be no record linking them to anyone in the colonies; there can be no insistence upon servitude," Jason reasoned.

Jack agreed. "That would work. However, as we become successful, people will begin rebuilding the original village over by 'The 96'. I give it four or five years and you will begin to see an influx. It may take a bit to lure robust souls to the area, but it *will* be rebuilt. After all, there is a sturdy jail, what more could they possibly need for a beginning?"

"As *we* are not *the norm*, so to speak," Kathryn said softly, mulling over thoughts that came to mind. "Let us consider keeping the village *always* separate from us."

"Are you suggesting we build a *compound* around the trading post, where *misfits* the likes of us will be allowed to live unprovoked?" Jason's eyes sparkled as he searched his wife's thoughtful face.

"Yes, that's exactly what I mean."

"Then I second it," Jack stated firmly.

"What shall we call our new trading post?" Rob asked.

"Tarrington's Trading Post," Jack said. "It is more than appropriate and well-deserved. Does anyone object?"

Cheers and clapping echoed in the inn. As the noise faded, a loud belch sounded. All eyes riveted on Beau. "Me too," he hiccupped in his baby voice.

"I gather the vote is unanimous," Jack summed up, and burst into laughter.

"What do you think, Ellie?" Rob stood holding her hand in the doorway of the empty brick building. "I thought, perhaps a store for my woodworking downstairs, and a home for us upstairs."

At her shrug his face fell. Quickly cupping his cheeks, she forced him to meet her sparkling, blue gaze. "When Gabriel arrives, he will bring his braves to help build. Would you be unhappy if we built *our* house nearer the Trading Post?"

"No, little one, whatever makes you happy."

"We *are not* like the other plantation owners, my Robbie. Like it or not, a town *will* be rebuilt here. *Our* village will be made up of Cherokees, or free black men, or men like *our* Smitty." She abruptly paused, deep in thought. Angling her head as if listening, she added, "Smitty is searching for us as we speak."

"Wonderful, I like him. And Ellie, please understand, I *am not* like my parents."

"You would not love me if you were," she whispered, kissing him shyly. Linking her arm in his she suggested, "Let's find the perfect spot for our house, and bring it up at tonight's meal."

Chapter Twenty-Nine

Swelling Ranks

Three more weeks had passed. All necessary groundwork had been set in place. Rob's elaborately carved sign adorned the front porch of the trading post proudly announcing it to be: Tarrington's Trading Post.

Now they could devote time to building homes before summer heat settled about them in stifling waves. By October they would be on their way to Charleston to meet with Captain Farthingale. They planned to surprise him with their first tentative load of deerskin, furs and tobacco: items that would keep well. One wagon, better yet several, was on their list, but *one bite at a time* as Jack often reminded.

It was late afternoon as a loudly whooped greeting announced Gabriel's arrival. They had been working together, laying out Rob's proposed home on the edge of the woods, and turned in unison to gape. It looked like a parade: warrior after warrior on horseback, travois after travois of precut lumber, numerous tools, and—just coming into view—two huge wagons heavily laden with supplies.

"Smitty!" Gabrielle yelled, taking off at a run and waving frantically.

Smitty was up and out of the wagon racing to greet her, hugging her, and swinging her in a circle. "Ahh, little lass, ye and yer parents have led me on a merry chase. Ye never even said goodbye." Tears streamed freely as he hugged her, kissing her tear-stained cheeks."

"We were never able to," she began chokingly.

"I understand the truth o' the situation now, my princess. But I'll not let ye leave me again. Ye had best explain that to yer man." He jerked his chin towards Rob, standing at her side.

"Do not over-step proper boundaries and we'll have no problem," Rob said firmly, bursting into laughter. Rushing forward he enfolded his buddy in a manly bear hug.

Kathryn, Jason and Jack all stood waiting to greet their friend, but he had more to say. "Look who I brought with me." He made a sweeping gesture with his arm. "Don't be shy now, Samuel. Ye're amongst the dearest of friends as ye well know."

With a snap of reins Hodges urged his team out of line and into view. Maggie sat proudly at his side, smiling bravely and cradling their little girl, Felicity. Willie stood behind his father holding the back of the wagon seat, waving and grinning from ear to ear.

"Our prayers are answered." Kathryn's eyes filled as her husband's arm snaked around her waist, pulling her to his side.

Jason understood her tears, wishing he could personally strangle her brother.

"With all these new recruits, we may just be able to devour *our elephant* in record time," Jack said, resting his arm casually on Jason's shoulder. "Let's speak to Gabriel. We had best get hunting. It looks like we suddenly have many mouths to feed. We'll finish the greetings later."

At that moment Gabriel rode forward and swung down from his horse. Silver Fox had accompanied him, and sat proudly astride her pony beside their son, Raven. Mairi was strapped to her back, and little Jason in her lap. She looked happier and healthier than she had in months, as did her husband. *They heal in the presence of each other as do Jason and I,* Kathryn noticed and was glad.

"Is there anyone left to guard the Bird Clan's village?" Jason hailed his friend.

"I was firmly instructed by Anna to build strong homes for you, and convey her love and esteem. *She* and Soaring Eagle will guard the village in our absence." They smiled and clasped hands.

"She is well?"

"Yes, your new venture has given her hope. In serving yourselves, you are serving our people. According to her, the wheel of life is properly at work."

"Come hunt with us, Gabriel, there are many mouths to feed."

"First allow me to speak to Kathryn and soothe her hurt. Once again it is *not* of her making, or ability to heal."

Gabriel swept Kathryn into his comforting arms. She had known the moment she saw the Hodges family. *Is there no end to Jamie's misdirected hatred and anger?*

With soft words, he comforted her, made her understand. "Set it aside and think no more on the subject. I love you, my Kathryn, and would not see you hurt further. Would you do me the honor of making my family comfortable while I hunt with the men?"

With a nod, she bit her lip to stop the trembling. "Now go, I will handle all the rest. May your aim be accurate, for we are very hungry." She forced a smile.

With the heel of his hand he swept her tears aside. "Smile," he whispered as he brushed a light kiss to her forehead. Spinning on his heel, he joined the men in three quick strides.

The next two months passed so quickly Kathryn was astounded. Ted's gift of a team and wagon had been a welcome surprise. They would be able to take blankets, baskets and deerskins with them when they went into Charleston to meet Farthingale.

Their compound was taking shape nicely at the hands of Gabriel's capable warriors—hard-working, precise in building abilities, and an eye for including beauty even in utilitarian structures.

"We should not be surprised," Jack commented. "We have lived in the Bird Clan's village. Such pride, dedication and willingness to help one another, we could all learn from them."

Moving into their new homes as fast as each was completed, they no longer used the inn for themselves. The Black Swan had actually welcomed several visitors, their numbers increasing weekly. As word continued to spread rapidly about the gracious, little resting spot, monies began to come in.

Maggie and Samuel chose to build just beyond the inn. It was a small plot by choice, but with enough room for Maggie's three gardens: herbs, vegetables and her well-loved flowers. The house was two stories, strongly built, and with room for a growing family.

"I carry Samuel's second son," she confided proudly to Kathryn one day while they chatted over coffee. "I insist it is a boy, although my Sam stubbornly wishes for another little girl. One thing we do agree upon is the name. This will be the first child born in our new village, and represents our new life. He shall be named Freedom Hodges."

Kathryn hugged her, thrilled. She and Samuel had coped with a great deal of sadness over the last two years and deserved happiness. As they continued to chat, Maggie asked to become hostess of The Black Swan. She was a strong woman, and at ease with all types of people. Gregarious by nature, she was gifted with the knack of balancing a small child on one hip, while changing linen and baking bread. Maggie never became flustered. The busier the circumstances, the more at ease she became. Kathryn admired her patience and unique abilities, but had no regrets at lacking such talents herself.

"I must admit, Kathryn, when we were first told we had to leave," she trailed into silence. "I thought my life was over. But Providence came to our rescue in a most unlikely form—Smitty. How I love that insistent little man. Thankfully, he refused to take 'no' for an answer. I could not be happier with our new friendships and new life—and we thank you."

"It is *we* who are grateful, Maggie. Hunting, fishing and skinning animals is far more to *my* liking, although I *do* attempt to be a lady upon occasion." Kathryn grinned. "And your help with Beau …"

"Enough," Maggie said softly. "The happiness we all share is beyond words. I had never thought to see a smile work its way up to my Sam's eyes again. Yet it is now a daily occurrence. By the way, has he mentioned he wishes to take the back of the big barn and set up a blacksmith shop? Do you think that would be a suitable addition?"

"Truly? How wonderful. Tell him to speak to Jason and Jack. They will be ecstatic. There is so much work to be done here, and we have just begun to *eat our elephant*."

At her confused look, Kathryn giggled. "Ask Jack, it was *he* who explained the concept to me."

Smitty was a delightful shock. His abilities with erecting new buildings and repairing old ones were surprising. The little man *was* more than bluster, and he had a heart as big as all outdoors.

"I miss Annie and Thomas and the children," he told Kathryn. "But they are happy with each other now, and have another child on the way. I accomplished all I had set my mind to. It was time to move on to a place where I'm needed, even if *ye're* not yet aware of that fact." He laughed uproariously, dunking his biscuit in his coffee. Munching contentedly around the soggy sweet, he outlined what he perceived to be his abilities.

"I thought not to like driving the team and wagon, but I do. Surprised myself, actually. Perhaps that might be my forte: driving the supplies to and from Charleston. Although I'll do whatever ye have need of being done here, missus."

Kathryn merely grinned. "Ye are a mind reader, Smitty, and such a joy."

As he wished to be home to help with the corn harvest, Gabriel returned to Keowee with his warriors and family in late August.

"You still have much to accomplish here, Hunter. *We* can handle the harvest; we have been doing so quite successfully for years, long before you came into our lives."

Jason smiled at the gentle ribbing. "Did you happen to consider that perhaps we shall miss you and your family?"

"Then plan a longer visit with us on your return from Charleston." He eyed his aunt, saw her face brighten and began to make plans for entertainment.

"Ahh, Jason," she sighed snuggling into the warmth of him, cherishing the scent of him as her heart slowed to a manageable pace. "Do you recall, many months ago, when you asked me which side we would fight for this time?"

He nodded. "A difficult question—a difficult answer."

"At that point in time, yes, but fate has blessed us once more."

He remained silent for a long moment, enjoying her warmth.

"Soaring Eagle and Gabriel are incredible friends. We are living in an area that is *safe.* The Treaty of Paris actually may be signed at long last, and Nathanael Greene gone to retirement. However, strong feelings will take some time to die. Patriots and Loyalists are both pig-headed. You have had more than enough dealings with *my* family to understand."

He chuckled. "We will do well with our Trading Post. Like it or not, the Patriot's have need of us too, and *will not* cut their noses off to spite their faces. And we will treat them fairly. Those who have heard of us must admit that we, too, have had our share of miseries in this war. You have but to look at my chest …" He stopped abruptly as she tensed.

"Kathryn, my Kathryn." He rolled her gently towards him to trace the sunken wound in her chest. "Have I *ever* caused you a moment's doubt?"

She shook her head, but he did not miss the shimmer in her eyes.

"Nor will I, *ever.* I no longer see it. Upon occasion, when I am in a contemplative mood, I *do* see, and realize the incredible odds you fought and triumphed over for me."

His mouth found hers gently at first, then more insistently.

"I thought you and Jack were going hunting early, my love," she finally managed.

"Have you *ever* known Jack to complain?"

His fingers slid up along her rib cage to caress a full breast.

She gasped, and with no further hesitation, reached for him.

Towards the end of September, Gabriel rode in unannounced, other than by his whooping cry of greeting, flanked by Soaring Eagle, four sturdy warriors and Anna.

"I wished to see for myself, Ugilohi. It *is* as Gabriel has said, more than adequate and quite lovely." She sat astride her pony, eyes sweeping the compound approvingly, noting that young Rob's house was yet to be finished. "Why is young Rob's …?" She purposely left the sentence unfinished, waiting for an explanation.

"He lives with me, Anna, awaiting bricks to finish the front," Jack explained.

"Bricks?" she gave Rob a long, searching look.

"It must be special for my Ellie."

"I approve; it *must be ready soon.*"

Kathryn gulped, but tried to hide it. Jason's hand crept to the small of her back and circled. If he, as her father, could approve of Rob *loving* his daughter, then Kathryn must also give her consent. Jason knew Rob's vow had been kept, so far, knew the difficulty with which the lad struggled to maintain it, but also saw the way his little girl watched him, yearning for his touch. *It is well beyond time for them to be married. Age is merely a number. Kathryn and I must talk and settle this immediately.*

Jason glanced at Anna, surprised to see she had been observing him carefully. Her eyes sent an unmistakable message as her lips lifted imperceptibly.

Kathryn's eyes met Anna's and then his, startled. *My God, is there anyone who cannot read my mind?*

When he looked back, Anna was smiling openly. Jason stepped forward offering his hand, an unnecessary gesture which pleased Anna. As she slid down from her pony into his arms, she mentioned his fringed deerskin shirt. "Silver Fox has a gift for working with needle and hide. Are you used to the feel of the animal's presence against your body?"

"Butter-soft and far more comfortable than my English shirts. I am spoiled for life."

"Ahh, Ugilohi," Anna murmured, pulling her into a warm hug. "You and I have much to discuss." She shot Jason a knowing look. "And I wish to rest."

That night, Gabriel and Soaring Eagle sat down with Jason and Jack while Anna closeted herself in another room with Kathryn. Jason maintained a blank mind, unsure if he wanted to know how their discussion was going.

"I have it on good word that Nathanael Greene and his troops left Charleston in August. The Treaty of Paris arrived, and he was more than eager to leave. He has gone into retirement at his mansion in Georgia and refuses to budge. I gather he prefers the genteel life of the South, and will not return to the 'chilly airs' of New England." Grinning at his cleverness he added, "Thankfully we have seen the last of him." Gabriel swallowed deeply of his rum. "I have left the *best* until last. Greene left without becoming aware of your new venture. Be cautious for awhile, but I would not stay out of the city."

Jack and Jason grinned. "It would seem the fates smile at long last."

"In more ways than you know, Hunter," Gabriel said. "Farthingale reached port two weeks ago, earlier than expected. He struck a coral reef, sustained minor damage to the hull, and decided to put into port in Charleston rather than risk a run to New England."

"The wagon has been filled with deerskins and ready to go for a week. Smitty saw to that," Jack replied.

"My advice is to send him and the wagon ahead tomorrow with Rob riding shotgun," Soaring Eagle interjected. "They will be safe; my people will be close, but out of sight. Farthingale will wait for you, I have been assured. Ted also has two more wagons and teams ready."

Jack's eyes went wide with surprise. "This is wonderful, but how can we keep Maggie and the children safe and …?"

"Everything is set, Jackson," Soaring Eagle rumbled. He loved calling Jack by his last name, and delighted in being in charge.

The following morning they turned east towards Charleston. Smitty had pulled out with his loaded wagon, accompanied by Gabrielle and Rob, well before dawn.

"Damn it, Jason, our daughter …"

"Hush, my Kathryn, it is time for you to think deeply, think beyond *your* needs. Stop being a *mother* holding your child protectively to your breast. She *is* an adult. Set her *free*, my love, age is of no consequence here. If I, as an overly protective father can *release* my child, trusting in her ability to sort out what is right in life—so can you." He would be stern if necessary, but did not wish angry words, not when all was coming together so well.

She did not care for his words, especially after Anna's lecture, a lecture she had chosen *not* to share with Jason. She read him well, aware of the reasoning he presented so adamantly. But she did not have to like it.

"Kathryn," he nudged.

"I still recall the night I donned the uniform of the Green Dragoons. Jack was so frightened for me, so unhappy. Yet in the end, he smiled. He said he could accept, but did not have to like the decision. Aye?" Her beautiful eyes answered wordlessly.

His lips found hers, claimed them without reservation, tasting the salt of her tears. When he leaned back, she smiled warmly, her eyes again bright and happy in the sunny, clear day. "You are correct, my love, as *always*."

His slow, easy smile was one of sheer pleasure. Quickly kneeling, he basketed his hands to assist her in mounting. "Please allow me, Mrs. Tarrington, just this once—in honor of our new beginning."

Struck by the enormity of his gesture, she felt the sting of hot tears begin. *Was there ever a time when I did not love this incredible man?*

He stepped up into his stirrup and settled himself astride. Kathryn nudged Beauty close, leaning to kiss him. With gentle words, they set off at a fast trot. The new adventure was afoot, no more time would be wasted on fear, or doubt, or regrets.

Chapter Thirty

Captain Farthingale at Your Service

They sat around a large, central table chatting amiably in the old inn: Ted, Smitty, Gabrielle, Rob, Jack, Jason, Kathryn and Captain Kirkland J. Farthingale. Trenchers laden with pheasant, venison and fresh trout sat amongst baskets of soft rolls, sweet yams, potatoes, greens, and of course: grits.

"To good friends and success," Farthingale announced, tossing his brandy down and quickly refilling his glass. "You all look well and happy, your new life obviously agrees with you."

Amidst tales of the sea and the captain's ribald adventures, they eventually worked into the true 'meat' of their meeting. Kathryn remained quietly attentive, listening to Jason and Jack put forth their concerns. Jason had urged her to participate, but she knew better. Although Farthingale never hid the fact that he respected her intelligence, he was a 'man's man' preferring to do business directly with the men.

She had been forced to learn a *woman's place* years ago, during officers' meetings, a few even held at 'The 96' in its heyday. Relegated to the 'ladies hour', talking of such innocuous subjects as baby's colic or which color favored their individuality, she had *itched* to join the men. But with light, nonsensical pleasantries to their women, they closeted themselves behind closed doors: smoking over-sized cigars and downing numerous brandies as they sorted out all the problems of the world.

"It would seem," she recalled having told Jason somewhat tartly after one overly long session, "If men would cease merely *talking* about the problems, and finally *do* something about them, we might *all* be better off." She accepted the situation for what it was, a battle she could never win, and gave in gracefully. To make her point, she occasionally allowed herself the liberty of a caustic remark, much to Jason's amusement.

"Hell, Jason—please excuse me, Kathryn." Farthingale's explosive laughter snapped her back to the present. "I have exactly what you're looking for."

Jason had just explained their need for volunteers to live as *free men*.

"I have a man and his wife that I brought here with me—haven't decided what to do with them yet. He's a big, strapping buck and she's round with child. He broke his leg in heavy seas while trying to help secure the on-deck cargo."

He paused to look directly at Rob. "I couldn't very well leave him on a sugarcane plantation in that condition, now could I? Well I could, of course, but would have a bit of a problem looking myself squarely in the eye. I am not *all* bad am I, Rob? Sure you haven't changed your mind about my offer?" He stopped at Gabrielle's stern look and wagging finger, a ready smile spreading across his handsome features. "I fear not, unfortunately—my loss." He winked. "Ahh, the things we men do for the strong women in our lives, and *actually* enjoy the doing."

He glanced at Jack, absorbing the obvious changes since they had last met. *He appears to be 'whole' in both body and mind,* and was glad. "Jack, while these good people finish their meal, come meet Jedediah and Sukie. If the three of you reach a common agreement, they will ride out with you when you leave. As Ted has two more teams and wagons waiting, you could use the help. I am truly impressed with all that you have accomplished in such short time. Jason has indicated that *you* will be my contact; therefore, it is your decision as to the Cousins."

"Cousins?" Jack frowned.

"He had a last name so damned difficult to pronounce, I dubbed him 'Cousins'. He seemed not to mind and it stuck."

"Is his leg healed?"

"Still a bit tender but seems strong again. Jedediah hates the ocean with a passion, but agreed to ship out with me in March. For some reason he feels he owes me a debt of gratitude, truly a fine man. But gratitude to me? Ask young Rob. If Jedediah's leg had been sound, he'd be chopping sugarcane on the islands as we speak."

Jack grinned. He understood why Captain Farthingale and Banastre Tarleton had gotten along so well—both full of bluff and bluster to mask true feelings, each having a soft spot they guarded well. *I like the man,* Jack admitted. *This will work.*

Three days later, they headed back along the Charleston Path. Smitty took the lead as wagon master, yelling instructions and grinning happily. He had been assigned an important and permanent job, his personal responsibility in the building of their new community.

Sukie and Jedediah Cousins followed closely in the second wagon. Jedediah spoke English quite fluently, and Sukie was rapidly learning. It was obvious she loved this big, jovial man, and they were happy to be *free.* Having a gentle hand the horses easily responded to, he handled the team competently after one practice session along the wharf. Rob and Gabrielle sat side by side in the third wagon sharing companionable silence, at peace with the day and each other, as Rob deftly handled his team.

Kathryn, Jason and Jack brought up the rear on horseback.

"Farthingale is in for the long haul, I gather," Jason commented, turning to Jack.

"Yes, he has requested I return by the end of October with three wagons well-filled. He advised I leave the packing to Smitty; he apparently knows how to fit ten pounds of shite in a five pound bag." He shook his head, grinning. "He had a specific terminology for that, though I can't quite bring it to mind at the moment … oh, wait!" He held up a finger. "Blivot! That's it."

"Goodness, Jack. I doubt I'll be able to sleep tonight for thinking about your rapidly expanding education," Kathryn giggled. "He is a true 'piece of work', but I like him."

"I gather he is not going to winter here as originally planned," Jason said. "I noticed he has already repaired the damage to his hull."

"His holds will be filled to bursting once we arrive with our three additional wagon loads. As he has final obligations to fulfill in New England, he will put into port there before heading for England. The impression he gives me, is that he'll sail as soon as we have loaded his ship. The waters off the rocky coast of New England are noted to be treacherous during winter months. In truth, I believe it is the lure of a full purse taking precedence. He told me not to expect him back until spring."

The three of them continued tossing several ideas back and forth entertaining different possibilities. "Something is cooking in the back of that creative mind of his. Perhaps he'll be ready to enlighten us in October." Jack took a long pull on his canteen. It was a delightful, warm September day and the initial 'dealings' had begun well.

Jack pulled the barn door open, almost colliding with Kathryn.

"I am daydreaming as usual, Jack," she said apologetically, moving aside so he could enter. "I thought you and Rob and Jason were busy discussing how many levels of bricks are necessary for his house."

"That we were, however the discussion was becoming heated. I decided it best for Rob to work it out with his future father-in-law."

"Aye," she muttered. "I fear that event will happen all too soon. For if they wait ..."

"Do you have reservations for their union?"

"None, Jack, but they are so young."

"Their age has nothing to do with it, Kathryn. Let us be honest with each other."

She flashed a wry grin. "Leave it to you to make me face reality." After a moment's hesitation, she tossed the question back to him. "What have you determined to be the cause then?" *Spit it out, Jack, I am not in the mood for games.* She felt a bit testy this morning, tired from the long trip to Charleston, and worried about Beauty.

He regarded her warmly. "You fear growing older." She sucked in a sharp breath as he continued. "You are the mother of a daughter on the verge of marriage, and a son who already demonstrates his independence."

"I *do not* fear death, Jack. I *have been there,* if you will recall," she declared tartly, as a tear began to track down her cheek.

Jack's thumb caught it gently. "Do you know how many times I have wanted to do that for you over the years?" he asked softly. He was not angry, he understood her better than she did herself. "I made no mention of *death,* my Kathryn. In death we *shall all be together,* eternally young."

"Old age," she murmured as another tear followed in the wet track of the first.

Again Jack caught it. "Old age happens one day at a time, easing us into it. You *will not* just wake up one day and be *old.* I promise you that."

"But if the day comes when ..."

"Do you truly believe Jason or I, for that matter, are that shallow? For if so, we had best all sit down and speak honestly with one another."

She saw *hurt* flicker and felt guilt. "I know you both, love you both, and never wish to become a disappointment."

"Kathryn!" Frustrated, he turned away, afraid he might give in to the urge to shake some *sense* into her. Bracing his hands against the wall he shook his head, sighing deeply. "Jason is right," he muttered.

"About what?" she asked softly.

"There are times," he turned slowly to face her, "when there are no appropriate words to ease the pain of the one closest to your heart."

"What did he advise as an alternative, Jack?"

He shrugged, giving her a quick hug. "Love them, simple as that; love them *desperately* until the moment passes."

"Thank you," she whispered, her lower lip quivering.

"Come take a look at Beauty." Needing to break the *mood*, Jack took her arm and guided her to the end stall.

"After all these years, she is pregnant," Kathryn said with mixed feelings of shock, joy, fear and disbelief.

"That she is, and quite far along. She has covered it well until just this week."

"I thought so a few weeks ago. Jason feels that without the rigors of war, Diablo merely allowed nature to take its course."

"So that's how it happens," he laughed, pleased to see her smile.

She slipped into the stall and ran her hands lightly over her mare's rounding belly. "Do you think she is too old?"

"I do not wish to hear that word uttered from your lips again, Mrs. Tarrington, else I must bring your husband in to discuss the problem, and take you to task—a fearsome threat I might add." He gave her a long, steady look. His words were teasing, but he meant it.

"Forget I asked," she giggled. "Just love me, the mood will pass."

His eyes expressed words he dared not utter and she smiled, loving him too.

"You have been seeing John Mayfield's daughter," she blurted, needing to change the subject. Maybe this time he had found someone to bring him comfort and solace in life. "Might there be ...?"

"Kathryn ..." He shook his head, frowning.

She wished she had not brought the subject up, his discomfort was obvious.

"I am content with my life," he began slowly, softly. "I accept it the way it is. Upon occasion, I slake my need with the young lady." He made a curt gesture, silencing her. "The answer to the question nagging in your mind, and which you are too polite to ask, is a resounding—*no.* She expects no more from me, than I do from her. We fulfill a need for each other, no more—no less than that. She, too, *accepts.*"

Kathryn nodded. *Yes, acceptance is what life is all about and Jack has mastered it better than most.*

She reached out, grasped his hand and squeezed. "Let's go see who is winning in the 'brick discussion'."

***

"I am truly impressed, Jack. I suspected this would be lucrative, but this is beyond my wildest estimation." Captain Farthingale refilled his brandy and topped off Jack's. They had left Smitty, Rob and Jedediah filling the holds on the *Lucifer.* It would be tricky, as there was still Caribbean sugar slated for New England, but Smitty had assured it would fit.

"There may not be much room in your cabin when I'm done, Captain" Smitty chortled. "But it *will all* be on board."

"How shall we handle this demand, Jack? I gather Kathryn and Jason have no wish to turn away customers anymore than I do." He pursed his lips, his mind working feverishly. "What kept them from coming?" he asked abruptly.

"Kathryn's mare is ready to foal. Looks to be twins and she is justifiably nervous. Jason stayed to give support."

"He is a good man, they are an unusual couple. And I *do* recall how dear that animal is to *all* of you." He grinned. "You know, Jack, money *does not* appear to rule them in any way. Perhaps therein, lies the answer to their personal success and happiness in life."

Jack said nothing, merely smiled.

"Ahh, well, filthy lucre has always been my mistress. She may occasionally provide a cold bed, but she *never* complains of my faults." He caught Jack's look. "But I digress. We have decisions to make. I did speak with Captain Jenkins of the *Hawk.* He seemed *mildly* interested. Mild interest *never* breeds success. *Desire* and *personal drive* are required—as well as a talent for occasionally bending the rules."

Jack nodded but withheld comment. He understood Farthingale's need to talk all options aloud, the hearing of them his means of choosing appropriately.

"Ahh, here you are, Rob." Farthingale looked up, greeting his former crew member. "I was beginning to wonder where you and the others had drifted off to. Your name was on the tip of my tongue. I see you've kept Jedediah on the straight and narrow too."

"Errands," was all Rob offered, but with a wide smile added, "Smitty will join us shortly. His 'errands' required time for *dessert*."

Farthingale guffawed loudly, tossing out a ribald comment, and then indicated the two chairs beside him. "Care for a brandy, son?"

Rob eyed his uncle, noted his non-judgmental look and nodded. Might as well see what it's all about he decided, but vowed to pace himself. He would never hurt Ellie by doing something foolish and having a callous word find its way back to her. However, there was no chance of that. It took but one sip, brandy was not to his liking.

Before talk could resume in earnest, Smitty entered and sat down with a self-satisfied grin spreading from ear-to-ear.

"Good God, man, you smell like a French whore house," Farthingale commented dryly. "Hopefully she has not gifted you with a dose of the pox."

Smitty shrugged. "What have I missed in me absence?" He wished to divert attention elsewhere.

Farthingale rocked back in his chair and tossed down his drink; refilling his glass from Rob's he began. "As I was telling Jack, Captain Jenkins seems to lack the drive I require from a fellow businessman. I am considering dropping 'The Trade'." He sat stroking his chin thoughtfully.

So that's the idea he was toying with when we last saw him, Jack smiled to himself, he had read him well.

"That would please you, young Rob, would it not?"

Rob smiled, casting him a quizzical glance. *What's up with him?*

"I actually *do* have some principles, contrary to popular belief. 'The Trade' has never been my first choice, but when my stint with Tarleton ended—well, that's another long story better left untold."

He abruptly speared Jack with an intense gaze. "How many wagon loads do you feel you can bring to the coast annually?"

"Whatever it takes to make *you* agree to be our staunch, reliable partner," Jack retorted. "I have a contract right here." He patted his vest.

Farthingale regarded him with newfound respect.

"A handshake will suffice?" he asked, as Jack pushed the heavy papers towards him.

"Only if you ride back to the compound and seal the deal with the Tarringtons in person." He smiled, but his look demanded compliance.

Yes, Farthingale liked the new Jack. "Christ *no*, Jack. Can you picture me on horseback, or in an old wagon—every evening crouched beside a campfire waiting for raw flesh to cook? Absolutely not! Let me sign that damned thing, and we'll drink to our new deal."

"What do you offer us in return for *our* hard work?" Jack asked quietly. It would all be spelled out to his liking and understanding, before any signatures were set to paper by either of them.

Farthingale was further impressed. "I propose to give up 'The Trade'. Henceforth, I will work solely with you. I will have to hustle to fulfill your needs, but they *will be* met, that I vow in front of witnesses." He scanned all present at the table. "I will plan to make three or more trips between New England and England each year, depending on the weather. However, the market which fills the coffers faithfully will be our priority. If New England fulfills that requirement, and I forego England, I will be able to make more trips. Do you follow my thoughts and agree?"

"Perfectly, and I agree."

"We shall work out storage and timing of shipments after our meal. I hate to rush, but I must leave port immediately. As heavily laden as my ship is, I do not wish to risk running aground on the shoals along the coast."

He took the two copies of the contract, scanned both, signed them, and handed them back to Jack. The contract was explicit: Jack clearly named part-owner in Tarrington's Trading Company.

"I regret I will no longer be able to find you more good men like Jedediah. But I will keep my eyes open around Boston. Occasionally a good man tires of beans and codfish."

He snapped his fingers for George, signaling him to bring their evening meal. "As a matter of fact, Jack, as an act of good faith on my part ..." He wrestled a leather pouch from his belt and dropped it with a dull 'thunk' in front of him.

Jack's eyebrows shot up.

"I recall, quite clearly, money shortage can be a vicious demon when beginning a venture. Just a small payment in advance. I will bring the items requested for the Bird Clan in spring, sooner if circumstances permit. Fair?" he asked.

"Fair," Jack concurred.

"Then let's enjoy our meal. High tide is at 8 AM, and I must be sailing with the tide."

Chapter Thirty-One

First Winter in Their New Home

"Beauty is restless," Kathryn commented, stroking her mare's silky forelock. She dug in her pocket for a cube of sugar. "I hope all is going well with Jack and the captain."

"He shall likely strike a better deal than we would have, my love." Jason stroked his hand gently along the underside of Beauty's distended belly.

Beauty nibbled at the proffered cube without interest, allowing it to drop in the fresh hay. Kathryn frowned, fear nagging, as she eyed her husband. "I do wish Jack had not had to go," she mumbled.

Jason handed his wife a fresh cup of coffee. "Relax, my pet, Beauty is strong and healthy. I fear more for my poor Diablo." He jerked his head toward the end stall where the big stallion paced non-stop, furtively 'grousing'. Jason's comment was perfect.

"What in the world is *he* agitated about? *His* job is done, Beauty's is just beginning."

"We men are such callous bastards," he whispered, nuzzling her ear seductively.

"That ye are. Thankfully, however, ye *do* have one or two redeeming qualities."

"How fares my Beauty?"

Jason and Kathryn both spun about, startled by the unexpected question. Anna stood in the doorway, black eyes sparkling. Without waiting for an answer she strode into the barn, eagerly greeted by Beauty's soft nicker of welcome.

With a perfunctory hug to Kathryn, and quick nod to Jason, she moved to Beauty's side. As she moved her hands lightly over the mare's huge belly, gently pressing and prodding, she asked, "Hot water? Clean linen? Fresh oats?"

"All is ready, Anna. How is my Beauty?"

"In better condition than *you* at the moment," she snapped. "You worry too much. Show confidence; instill that confidence in your mare. She senses your *mood*."

Kathryn flinched under the acid criticism. Jason observed silently, well aware one *never* confronted or questioned Anna. He had made that mistake only once, long ago, yet the memory still clung.

"Come," she beckoned sharply. "Let me show you." Slowly placing and moving Kathryn's hands, she patiently explained what she was feeling, what to expect; a sharp kick caused Beauty to suddenly groan and side-step.

"Soon," Anna murmured. "Bring the water and linens, Hunter."

As the words left her lips, Beauty abruptly dropped to her knees, rolling gracelessly onto her side, her breathing heavy and labored, but she did not thrash.

"She knows by instinct what to do." Kathryn stared in amazement.

Jason set the kettle and clean rags by Anna's side. "How may I be of help, Anna?"

"Stay out of the way and silence that rutting stallion of yours," she stated tartly; but her eyes held humor, and he grinned.

Beauty grunted loudly as a set of long legs and perfectly shaped head emerged and slid smoothly into the fresh hay. She started to rise to tend her foal, but quickly flopped back onto her side as heavy contractions began again.

"So soon, my girl? You are eager to be done with it." Anna stroked the mare's sweaty neck as she turned to Kathryn. "Quickly now, clean away the sac, help the little one breath. Beauty is busy."

Jason helped, toweling and buffing the sleek, dark form. The leggy, black colt would be a stallion in his father's image. But at the moment, he struggled to stand on splayed legs which wobbled precariously. Down he went in a tangled heap. Stubbornly righting himself, he stood complaining loudly, nudging his mother's belly, only to be shooed aside by Anna.

"A bit like his father, I fear."

Loud whinnies and stomping brought smiles, as Diablo kicked his stall impatiently. Beauty ignored his foolishness. Having been at his side for years, she was accustomed to his ill-tempered nature.

"This is as wondrous as my children's births," Jason managed, but catching Kathryn's sharp look, amended, "Almost, at least."

"I admit *I* am finding it far easier," she chuckled.

With another loud grunt a second foal, smaller and more delicate, slid free. Beauty then struggled to her feet and began her motherly duties, pausing once or twice, to answer Diablo's petulant calls.

The black colt broke free, shoved his way to her side and began head-butting her belly. A quick snap of her teeth sent him back to wait. Kathryn smiled. She had wasted time and energy for nothing. *Remember this* she chastised, and rocked back on her heels to watch the new babies feed.

Jack returned three weeks later with enough supplies to set all the shelves in the Trading Post. They would have plenty of stock to handle their needs until spring. She and Jason were surprised and pleased. Jack had left for Charleston with what limited amount of coin they had been able to scrape together. They had anticipated this to be a lean year out of necessity, but would have a few products to offer. By the time Farthingale returned in the spring, they hoped to have saved enough to stock all the shelves; he had assured Jack that their products were of excellent quality and in great demand.

"How in the world ...?" Kathryn began.

With that, Jack pulled out the leather pouch and emptied it onto the kitchen table.

"Good grief," she exclaimed, lightly fingering the gleaming pile spread out before her.

"In advance with promises of more to come—and these." He pushed the signed contracts towards Jason.

"Good work, Jack." Jason filled a brandy and slid it towards him.

"It seems that Smitty wishes the responsibility of wagon master; *that* does not displease me in any way. Jedediah did well: handled the team with caring, worked hard, did as told and proved reliable. He and Sukie are actually very happy here."

"Do you feel they can handle the spring load alone?"

"Not this time. I will drive the third wagon, but I intend to put full responsibility in Smitty's hands, and see how he manages. Every second or third trip, I will go along to sit down with Farthingale."

"To keep him on the straight and narrow?"

"Absolutely, Kathryn. He likes us a lot, but temptation can be a dangerous mistress."

Kathryn glanced at Jason, smiling. Jack had represented them well.

"Who do you propose to drive the third wagon if you remain here?"

"Let's worry about that at the time. We are still feeling our way, still in the developmental stages."

Jason gathered the coins and slid them back into the pouch, leaving five shimmering pieces on the table. Jack raised an eyebrow.

"One each for Rob, Smitty and Jedediah. Two for you."

"That is not …" he began.

"You have earned it. The rest will be used to build our coffers, help the Bird Clan or whatever is voted necessary by the three of us. Agreed?" Jason eyed his wife and then Jack, each nodding approval.

Jack headed for the door. "I'll help them unload the wagons."

"I'll join you and convey our 'thanks'," Jason added, and headed after him.

"Get the stock undercover for the night, and bring everyone back here for dinner. We have a haunch of venison from Jason's big buck. Oh, stop and compliment Beauty and Diablo on their new offspring. Beauty basks in the praise," she yelled after them as they strode towards the heavily laden wagons parked in front of the Trading Post.

Both men turned and grinned.

As she bent to stir the grits, she felt a cold draft caress the backs of her legs. Before she could turn and detect the source—splat! A crudely made snowball struck her squarely on the rump.

Kathryn spun to see her son, face scrunched with impish laughter, giggling into his mittened hands.

When did you grow so big without my notice? She feigned an irritated scowl, which only brought more laughter. Plunking her balled fists on her hips, she advanced towards him growling, "Your penance, for such an affront, shall be *six* perfectly formed snow angels, Master Tarrington."

He knew the game and shrieked with joy. Grabbing his mother's hand, he tugged her towards the open door. *I doubt he has ever closed a door in his life.* Beau was a free spirit, delightful but irresponsible.

He confounded and irritated his father regularly. "Damn it, Kathryn, he does what *he alone* pleases without regard for the rest of us. If it pleases *him* to please us, he does so. But *only if it pleases him personally.*"

She remembered reaching up to kiss him, her exact words being, "Have you noticed that *real* punishment does not get his attention, or break his spirit or nudge him towards consideration of others?"

He had shaken his head in disgust.

"Well, my love, until you can find a successful solution, and 'beating him bloody' is not an acceptable suggestion, I fear we are stuck with his *unique* behavior." Even now, she smiled at the remembrance. To date, no solution had been discovered.

She stood on their front porch surveying the dusting of new snow, delighting in the fluffy flakes still fluttering to the ground, and could not be angry. She laughed giddily, childlike, catching snowflakes on her tongue. Head thrown back, arms flung wide, she spun slowly, inhaling deeply of the clean, crisp, frosty smell. She would be sure to hang all the bedding out to air later.

Across the open common, Jack glanced up from his coffee and looked out through their kitchen window. He nudged Rob, who in turn nudged Gabrielle, and they all broke into smiles. Jack's gaze remained on the playful scene, unable to take his eyes off Kathryn. He watched, eyes misting, his thoughts far away.

"Who could *not* love her?" Rob whispered, snapping his uncle back to the moment, slightly embarrassed.

"No, no, Beau, that is unacceptable, it is messy. Remember how I taught you," she giggled, enjoying his answering frown.

Carefully he lowered himself onto a fresh patch of snow, lay back and slowly began swinging arms and legs in a wide pattern. When sure he had a perfect angel, he lay there deep in thought.

"May I help?" she offered.

"Nope, I can do it," he stated stubbornly.

With that he slowly sat up, determined his bearing, levered himself up to a standing position, and carefully leaped aside, leaving a perfectly formed angel. He stood regarding his mother with a smug grin, waiting for her response.

"Wonderful," she applauded, clapping her hands. "Now only five more."

Beau grinned. "I may do more than that, momma. Payment in advance for the next time." A devilish glint flashed in his eyes.

She shook her head and smiled. This son of hers was so different from his sister. Although he puzzled her on a regular basis, she loved him a bit more each day. Independent, feisty and headstrong, he would do things *his way*. Period, end of discussion.

"Yer grand da would have been proud, son. You have taken our natural family traits to new heights. Why even Uncle Jamie …" She stopped all thoughts forcefully.

Pulling her shawl tightly closed against the chill air, she slowly lowered herself onto the snow, lay back and began swinging arms and legs slowly. As she carefully inched herself up, working at preserving her angel, a large hand reached down.

"Might I assist you, my love?" Jason pulled her up into his embrace, nuzzling her hair, relishing the hint of clinging lavender.

Lord Cornwallis, remembering her delight, had recently sent another box of mixed 'goodies': soaps, fine linens and a delightful china tea set.

"Ahh, Kathryn, my desire for you, my *need* for you, never diminishes even after all these years. I think of you and …"

"Poppa," a sharp tug on his pant leg drew his attention to his son, breaking the mood.

"Later," he whispered.

"Later," she answered softly, her emerald eyes revealing matching desire and promise as he turned to his son.

"Six perfect angels, poppa. Not a bad penance for a well-aimed snowball." With a joyous laugh, he spun on his heel and raced towards Jack's house, probably looking for Rob to pester.

Rolling his eyes, Jason headed for the house. Perhaps he and Kathryn could find a few minutes alone before any further interruptions occurred—but he doubted it.

This year the snow had fallen more often than in previous winters, but followed by unusually warm spells, it quickly melted away. The Black Swan's reputation was growing rapidly. Maggie's excellent cooking and warm cordiality was single-handedly responsible for that success. Although Kathryn's praise brought a flush of self-consciousness to her cheeks, inwardly she was thrilled. Samuel looked on proudly. People constantly traveled the Charleston Path, no matter what the season, and the small inn stayed busy.

Maggie's condition was obvious, her quickly rounding belly a dead giveaway. But with each month she grew stronger, healthier. She doted on her husband, her children and her work. Being a good wife and mother was fulfilling on many levels, and Samuel never failed to lavish praise. But her position at The Black Swan reinforced well-deserved feelings of self-worth and competence—filling her with even greater inner joy.

Cheerful and even-tempered by nature, Maggie loved holidays, or any excuse to celebrate. She instructed Samuel to cut down two fir trees: one large tree for the inn and one slightly smaller for their home. The choosing and cutting became a family event. Clasping his son's hand, Samuel took the lead as they marched into the woods. Willie's specific assignment was to help choose the perfect trees, then standby and watch as he cut them down. Maggie's responsibility was to gather winter greens. As she cut, trimmed and bagged the tangy-smelling fir boughs, Felicity cooed contentedly from her sling, snuggly secured across her mother's back.

"Look, Sam, mistletoe," she exclaimed, pointing upwards to a large tree branch.

"I need no little plant to instruct me to kiss you, my Maggie." A throaty chuckle arose as he promptly demonstrated, kissing her soundly.

"Tisk tisk, in front of the boy," she scolded, but her eyes twinkled with merriment.

Samuel quickly snagged a large cluster and carefully placed it in his wife's hand.

"Even the berries are still intact," she whispered, admiring the perfection of the plant and kissing his cheek shyly.

"We have never had a holiday tree," Kathryn said, awestruck at the huge tree Jason and Jack had set up in their main room. There it stood: majestic, fresh smelling and almost reaching the ceiling.

Decorating was to be a joyous occasion. Everyone who wished to help was welcome: cookies, mulled cider, music and camaraderie their reward. The house was bustling with happy laughter as the tree came slowly to life: small clay ornaments, colorful beads, unusual trinkets, candle stubs and strings of popcorn.

Smitty sat watching Gabrielle and Kathryn trim the tree. He sipped mulled cider and munched popcorn kernels by the fistful.

"You are to thread them in a long string, *not* eat them," Gabrielle chastised, grinning.

"Ahh, little lass, look at me. I am but a mere shadow of the man I used to be when we first met. I'll fade into nothing."

"I fail to see that has made you less attractive to the females, Smitty," she shot back. "As a matter of fact, I hear ye have yer eye on Mr. Fletchall's oldest daughter, and *she*, completely mesmerized by yer silver tongue, has set her cap for *you*."

The room went silent, everyone listening for Smitty's retort. However, he went oddly quiet, his usual glibness failing, a sign of how important she actually was.

"T'is true," was his only answer as began threading popcorn onto the string. Smitty had been taken by the girl, from the moment he set eyes on her. She was buxom and somewhat plain, with a ready smile and tart tongue—as drawn to him as he was to her.

"She's not a young lass, Kathryn, but is still of childbearing years. She confided she wishes to bear my children—as many as I would like." He ducked his head in embarrassment before adding, "I truly love the lass. Her father is less than pleased with the match, though I fail to understand his reasoning. But she's feisty that one, told her father straight up, she *would* have me and no other, and set the date for the end of January. She'll not even wait for spring—says that at her age we must get to work on making wee babes verra soon." He lifted his shoulders in an amused shrug and grinned. "What man in his right mind could refuse such a fine offer, I ask ye now?" And the two of them collapsed into fits of giggling.

The tree decorating was a complete success. Along with singing, dancing and tasty holiday delights, small gifts were exchanged, making it a fun-filled afternoon. At Jason's request, Kathryn brought out her tin whistle, and loud yells erupted. With quiet but firm insistence from all present, she performed her entire repertoire of English and rebel tunes, the highlight of the evening.

Eventually, as the hour grew late, the guests returned to their individual homes leaving peaceful quietude in their wake. Kathryn began setting the kitchen to rights while Jack and Jason sat sipping brandy. Their conversation soon turned to the new twins.

"Satan is the spitting image of his sire, Jason, but will certainly surpass him in height and strength: a truly magnificent animal."

"Jezebel holds my heart," Jason answered. "She is so perfectly shaped, slender legs and fine, proud carriage. She's independent, but more than willing to please."

Jack nodded. "Have you noticed Diablo? He remains aloof when around his son, waiting until he thinks no one is watching before he takes interest, obviously feeling he's *above* the mundane chores of parenting."

"Beauty will teach him, mark my words." Kathryn joined them, sitting down and taking the brandy Jason offered. The expensive decanter had arrived in their last package from Lord Cornwallis, an excellent year and of fine sipping quality.

They sat for a few moments, sipping and talking lightly of business prospects for spring. At a slight nod from Jason, Kathryn slipped a small package from her pocket and handed it to Jack.

"I fear brown paper and simple twine is the best I could do, Jack."

Jack looked uncomfortable. "Kathryn, we all agreed not to exchange gifts."

"I found it in Charleston and could not resist, dear friend," Jason interrupted. "However, it is perhaps more a gift to the three of us."

Jack slowly untied the ribbon and peeled the paper back, revealing a small, leather-bound copy of the complete works of the African poetess, Phillis Wheatley. With a soft gasp, he clutched the book to his chest, touched by the gift's implications. Regaining composure, he stated hoarsely, "I shall treasure this *always*."

No further words were necessary.

"For you, my love, I have a small memento that may take us both back to our beginnings."

Kathryn eyed her husband curiously, ceasing her busy rummaging in the back of her bureau drawer.

Jason held a small package in his hand and beckoned her to him. Happily ensconcing herself on his lap, she opened the gift.

"Oh," she sighed, eyes misting. "James MacPherson's works bound beautifully in leather and gold trim. Will you read to me, my love?"

"Look underneath, Kathryn."

Wrapped in soft tissue, she could feel a small lump and opened it carefully, sensing it to be delicate. At her sharp intake of breath, Jason smiled. Tears coursed down her cheeks as she held the delicate necklace up with trembling hands. "*Our* exquisite Celtic wedding rings in miniature. Oh, Jason ..."

"Say no more, my love, I see you are pleased."

"But how? When?"

"Must I tell you all my secrets?" he chuckled.

"When you are this extravagant; *yes*."

His lips began to nip gently along the edge of her ear.

"Wait," she instructed, sliding nimbly from his lap. "I do have a gift for you, but not nearly so fine, I fear." Reaching into the far recesses of the bureau drawer, she pulled out the package she had been seeking, and placed it in his hands.

"Kathryn, how incredible," he said, holding the buckskin breeches up, turning them from front to back, examining the fine needlework and craftsmanship.

"When did you ever find time to tan and ..."

"Must I tell you all my secrets?"

He quickly stood and donned his new breeches.

"I do believe they hug you quite nicely, displaying you at your very best, my love." Her hand slid to caress the bold announcement of his intent.

"Never in my life have I experienced such delightful comfort—while enduring such painful need. I am speechless, but well able to demonstrate my utmost gratitude." With a low growl, he swept her into his arms, onto their bed and began the demonstration.

"Happy first winter," she whispered.

"Happy first winter," he answered, "the first of many."

Chapter Thirty-Two

Rites of Passage

As avowed, Miss Marlissa Fletchall became Mrs. Alasdair Abernathy at the end of January. As all brides, she was lovely, absolutely glowing; Smitty could not take his eyes from her. Kathryn had never seen him so content, and rejoiced. Having survived great losses in his life, he deserved this happiness. *None of us are unscathed,* she realized.

The girl's parents, eventually agreeing to the match, attended the festivities with notable reserve. Kathryn was gracious, but had no liking for either: her father hot-headed, her mother, superficial and shallow.

"Their acceptance of Smitty came about upon realizing the success of our business," she commented in an aside to Jack and Jason.

"They live so far out, it will be inconvenient to visit. I overheard Fletchall complaining of the distance and our 'vulgar' means." Deeply affronted, Kathryn's temper flared. With an amused grin, Jason calmed her surging indignation, reminding her, "Kathryn, be *thankful* for small blessings."

Smitty's house had been quickly finished in time for the nuptials, thanks to Maggie's abilities at management. Winter greens festooned every room filling the house with a pungent aroma, fresh linens adorned their bed, and a warm fire roared in cheery welcome. The look on his bride's face, as she gazed into her new husband's eyes said it all. They loved each other deeply. Smitty, a sturdy man despite his small stature, easily lifted his new bride amidst giggles, raucous laughter and loud cheering—and carried her over the threshold into their new home making it official. Little was seen of them for the next few days. Life in the compound commenced as usual.

Dawn arrived displaying the promise of a brilliant, cerulean blue sky. The welcome aroma of blooming flowers and rich, musky smell of freshly turned earth wafted through their open doorway; spring planting was well underway.

Kathryn and Jason, having finished breakfast, sat idly gazing across the compound enjoying their second cup of coffee. Suddenly Jason nudged his wife, directing her attention across the enclosure to Jack's house. Rob and Gabrielle had just closed the front door and were loping towards the woods. Each clutched a rifle in one hand and an empty haversack flung loosely over their shoulder.

"They certainly love to hunt," Kathryn commented lightly, but Jason detected tension in her tone. *Something about them seems different today.*

Jason read his wife well, knowing her thoughts. "She has grown into a beautiful young *woman* right before our eyes, like an exquisite butterfly emerging from its chrysalis—no longer the little girl we dandled on our knee singing nonsense songs to."

Kathryn turned a solemn gaze in his direction.

"Ahh, my beloved wife, I see I have surprised ye with my sensitivity. Apparently ye still think me to be the callous, ill-bred boor of my past. When we met, I admit I was that man. However, you have trained me well, broken me of my evil ways." He winked.

She burst out laughing, her temporary *mood* dissipating. He understood the complexity of her, and moving closer murmured softly, "She is almost as beautiful as her mother."

"Far *more* beautiful with the bloom of youth, my love," she answered simply.

"You are mistaken, Kathryn. I see you *today,* as you were when we first met, as you will *always* appear to me. Lord Cornwallis was correct when he talked of his beloved Jemima. As she was to him, *you* are to me, you *never* change. If possible, I love ye *more* with each passing day." With a lingering kiss, he encased her within his arms, separating only when Jack rapped on the open doorframe, clearing his throat loudly.

"I fear we have much to accomplish today. In three weeks time our wagons must be in Charleston, dropping off and picking up." Gesturing for them to cease their idle play and pay attention, he chuckled. "I am afraid all *that* must wait until later."

"Always the taskmaster," Kathryn grumbled playfully.

Pouring Jack a fresh cup of coffee, she sat down, and folding her hands in her lap, adopted a contrite expression. Concerns for Rob and Gabrielle were set aside, business needs taking precedence. Jason smiled, relieved.

Gabrielle and Rob edged their way quietly around the outer perimeter of a large field. Gabrielle's haversack was full: three rabbits, two squirrels, one grouse. Rob's was equally full, but a fat squirrel, high in an old oak tree, had just caught his eye. Drawing a careful bead, he squeezed the trigger slowly and smoothly. An almost deafening report, a puff of acrid smoke, and the squirrel toppled. Knowing Ellie would be fast on his heels Rob took off at a run, bounding across the field to retrieve his quarry. Picking the fat, well-fed squirrel up by a hind leg, he looked it over. His head shot had not damaged any edible meat. He was justifiably proud. It had been a long shot. As he turned to show Ellie, they almost collided, startling him at her sudden proximity.

"You come through the brush silent as a deer, Ellie." Pride showed openly as he held the squirrel out for her approval.

She gave it a cursory glance and looked up, capturing his gaze. A soft breeze pressed her light shirt against the pleasing shapeliness of her breasts.

Against his will his eyes lowered, flicked back to hers and lowered again, unable to resist. Full roundness, pert nipples, he sucked in a ragged breath. He had lived many difficult months maintaining restraint, forbidding himself to look, forcing lustful thoughts aside. Although easier in the beginning, the last year had been sheer torture and Jack's counsel no longer helped. *His* slender, leggy filly had grown into her body, filling out in all the appropriate places and almost as tall as he. He forced his eyes back to her face, embarrassed. But her expression, the look in her eyes, startled him.

"It is time, my Robbie," she said softly, but with definite firmness.

"Time?" he asked weakly.

"Teach me how to *love* you." Dropping her haversack, she set her rifle down in the soft moss beneath the spreading branches of the old oak.

"Gabrielle …" He resorted to her full name when upset or confused.

"Robert," she answered equally formal, her lips curving into a grin as she tentatively touched the pronounced fullness of his breeches.

"Ellie," he managed through gritted teeth, dropping the squirrel, haversack and rifle. Weak-kneed and unsure, he eyed her hesitantly.

Her touch inflamed him, brought aching desire threatening to bring him to his knees.

"Ellie, please don't, for I cannot …"

"Teach me," she caressed gently, meaningfully, no longer tentative.

Groaning deeply he stepped back; she moved forward, maintaining closeness, refusing to relinquish their *contact.*

"I barely know myself, Ellie. I have *never* …" he let the statement drop, embarrassed to admit he was a virgin himself.

Her eyes widened in surprise.

"When I told you that I had chosen *you* and no other, *I meant it.* They were not idle words," he said almost apologetically. "But I *will* wait until …"

Her face broke into a happy, relieved smile as she cupped his cheeks and kissed him deeply. He resisted but a moment, then pulled her to him, hunger building. Unable to control his need, he stumbled backwards with a moan of abject torment.

"Are ye sure, my Ellie, for I …"

"I have a woman's body with a woman's needs. I need *you* to make me *your woman.*"

"Ellie," he murmured huskily, "Ellie."

She grasped his hand, placing it firmly against her breast.

He trembled—just as he had dreamed, but so much more—he was lost. Engulfed by new emotions, over-powered with desire, he pulled her close inhaling the scent of her, reveling in the touch of her soft, pliant body. Months of desire had been sheer torture, at times almost beyond endurance. The sweet agony of her touch sent him spiraling out of control. Too late for pleasant denial, well beyond restraint, his control fled, replaced by all-consuming need which would surely kill him, if not answered—*now.* Pressing her back into the soft, thick moss his hand slid slowly into her breeches.

"Are you sure?" he gasped.

Smiling, she pulled his head down to meet the warm insistence of her mouth.

He *sensed her* need, *her* desire, and questioned no further. With a low moan, he clumsily opened the buttons of his breeches as she watched her blue eyes alive, sparkling with intensity and *filled with love.*

Plans for the Charleston trip organized, they stood leaning against the paddock fence watching the 'youngsters' play at irritating their mother. Well beyond time for nursing, the stubborn, black colt nagged his dam. Almost her size, and stubbornly determined, he maneuvered her into a corner and head-butted her empty dugs insistently. Sharp, nipping teeth sent him scampering the length of the paddock, to where his sire stood regarding him with mild interest.

"They are like over-grown children," Jack laughed. "Speaking of which," He gestured towards the woods where Gabrielle and Rob were just emerging.

All three adults watched as they approached, noting an imperceptible, yet distinct, change in the two.

"Is it always that obvious the *first time?*" Jason asked.

"Well," Jack said, removing his booted foot from the lower railing, "I believe my nephew may have a question to ask of you both. I'll go speak with Jedediah and Smitty and begin readying the wagons."

"You are leaving *us* to face them alone?" Kathryn's eyes narrowed, her brow wrinkling in irritation.

"Absolutely, milady," he quipped. "I have many responsibilities and little time before we leave." With a curt bow and quick aside to Jason, "Does that sound believable?" he strode across the common, briefly greeting the two young people in passing.

"Good hunting?" Jason asked.

Despite sparkling eyes, Rob looked distinctly uncomfortable, a fact both Kathryn and Jason found contrary to his nature and amusing. Nothing frightened this young man, *absolutely nothing*, except the question he obviously feared asking.

"Excellent, sir."

"Sir? This sounds serious."

Taking a deep breath, Rob stared at his feet. "It is—*sir*." Pausing, he gathered his courage before looking up at Jason, holding his gaze. Jason struggled to keep his features bland so as not to insult the young man.

"I ask your permission, your blessings …" He stopped. "I fear I am doing this badly."

Gabrielle elbowed his side, stifling a giggle.

"Just spit it out, son, I have fine brandy waiting in the house."

"I would humbly request the hand …"

"We wish to be married," Gabrielle blurted. "There, did I handle *that* well?" Her eyes sparkled with deviltry.

"It depends on their answer." Rob shot her a stern look.

Kathryn burst out laughing. "Don't keep young Rob hanging, Jason."

"Our daughter will have no other, nor will we. *Welcome* to the family *officially*." Jason clasped Rob's hand in a warm grip.

"We shall stop in Keowee on our return from Charleston and make the necessary invitations there." Kathryn began listing names of guests on her finger tips. "Maggie will make a beautiful cake or Scottish bannock if ye prefer, little one." Now that all was said and done, she was thrilled with the prospect.

"Samuel can build the bower and …" Jason smiled tenderly at his daughter. Abandoning the light *play* of planning, he reached for Kathryn's hand and pulling her to his side, addressed his future son-in-law. "Love each other passionately, with quiet desperation, Rob. When rough times cross your path, *and they will*, cling to each other. *Together* you can weather all storms, just as Kathryn and I have."

Three days later, amidst jingling harness and the sounds of creaking wheels from over-burdened wagons, the small entourage moved out, heading to the main pier in Charleston and Captain Farthingale's *Lucifer*.

Smitty blew a kiss and waved vigorously as his wagon creaked and groaned its way past their house. Marlissa stood at the doorway, a brave smile pasted on her face.

"T'is no more than morning sickness," she had assured him, raising her head from the bucket sitting before her. Her face was pale, her forehead beaded with perspiration.

"How can I leave ye?" His eyes misted with tears.

"Gabrielle has promised to stay with me, and hold my hand in your absence. Not as comforting as yours by far, but will do until you return. You have an important job, Mr. Abernathy. *Duty comes first*."

He had held her overly long in their 'goodbyes', feeling an immediate sense of loss, missing her tender companionship long before she disappeared beyond his sight a few minutes later. Her last words echoed in his mind. "When you return, my Smitty, this part will be over. I'll be glowing with health and a rounding belly. You will be able to feel your son's sturdy kicks for the first time." Smitty smiled to himself, slapped the reins sharply across his team's backs and began whistling an old sea shanty.

Jason and Kathryn flanked Jack's wagon on horseback, bringing up the rear. Beau sat stick-straight beside Jack, excited at being included and feeling quite grownup. He remained quiet, absorbing everything around him, surprising his parents at how well-mannered he could be when subjected to something *he* considered of interest.

Gabrielle and Rob waved vigorously, yelling loud 'goodbyes'. Kathryn waved and smiled until they disappeared around the first bend, then became quiet, introspective.

"Kathryn." Jason touched her sleeve, capturing her attention. He knew her *concerns.*

She turned solemn eyes on him.

"If Gabrielle is with child, before her marriage ..." Kathryn tensed, her expression changing sharply.

"*If she is,* she will be no further along than *you* were on *our* wedding day. As this is to be our last trip to Charleston for some time, *please* relax and enjoy it."

Jack gazed towards the woods, suddenly interested in a tall cluster of pines, attempting not to smile. The many changes in Jason over the years were remarkable. *You have become one hell of a man, my friend.* And he smiled.

A sudden burst of laughter grabbed his attention. Jason's crisp remark *had* stung, but Kathryn knew he was right. "If not Jack chastising, it is *you,* my love, keeping me focused, drawing me back from foolish worries. However, I feel she may be with child soon."

Both men eyed her curiously.

"T'is easy to read, they love each other deeply, she will refuse using 'protection'. We may have to come to grips with being grandparents all too soon."

Jason smiled benignly at her rapid change of mood, eyeing Jack as a pink blush crept up the back of his neck.

"There's Captain Farthingale's ship, Beau," Kathryn pointed out, as the wagons drew down into the unloading area.

Beau stood on the seat to see better as Jack steadied him. He had been well-behaved during the journey, even helpful and co-operative—gathering wood for the campfire without being asked, doing as told and remaining cheerful, even when clouds of mosquitoes were particularly noisome. Jason and Kathryn, pleasantly surprised, hoped this change would last, but were realistic. That would be unlikely.

Beau leaped down and headed at a fast clip towards the vessel, fearless and eagerly embracing the strange smells, sights and unusual people roaming about.

Jason leaped from his saddle and grabbed his son's shoulder, reprimanding him curtly and advising him of the dangers of the big city. But he could see his words were falling on deaf ears.

"Jason, Kathryn," Captain Farthingale shouted, advancing rapidly towards them, all smiles. With quick handshakes and words of greeting all around, he turned to Beau. "And just who do I have the pleasure of meeting?" He leaned down and shook the child's hand.

"James Beauregard Tarrington," he stated with pride. "But you may call me Beau."

"Beau, it is then," he answered, swinging the boy up onto his shoulder to provide him a better view. "This lad of yours is the perfect blend of you both: handsome and fearless." He liked their son and made no attempt to hide it. "Jack will manage the wagons. You two head for the inn and arrange for everyone's rooms—perhaps grab a little *down* time." His leering grin left nothing to the imagination. "Our business can wait until later. First *I* must introduce your son to the city and my ship." Without giving them time for comment, he turned and strode towards the *Lucifer.*

Jack shrugged. "It would appear that Beau has found a kindred spirit."

"I fear so. Inadvertently or not, I sense he will set Beau on a new path." Kathryn stared after them, frowning.

"Gabrielle had *direction* in her life, almost from the moment she could toddle across our campsite. Beau, on the other hand ..." Jason shook his head. "However, if our son can be shown a path that pleases him enough to make him pleasant and respectful when in our presence, then I will embrace it."

By late afternoon, Kathryn was becoming concerned. Everything necessary had been accomplished; they sat enjoying tea in the main dining room of the old inn. *Where is Farthingale with our son?* Their wagons had been unloaded and all stock carefully stowed on board the *Lucifer*. New supplies for the Trading Post were packed in heavily laden wagons secured under paid guard, and the teams bedded down for the night.

With a cheerful, overly loud greeting, Captain Farthingale entered the room with Beau ensconced on his shoulder. "Shall you tell everyone what we have been doing, or shall I?"

"I will tell," Beau announced and slid to the floor. "I want to be *here in the city*," he stated adamantly. "I love the harbor and the ship and the people and Ted's carriage and beautiful horses and fine clothes," he rattled off his list non-stop, took a deep breath and grinned at both parents.

"What impressed you most?" Farthingale nudged.

"The pub," he grinned.

Kathryn's eyes widened, but the worst was yet to come.

"Neither of *you* showed me how much fun it is to play dice, board games and cards," he accused, scowling at both parents.

"No, I guess we have been negligent in your lessons," Jason stated tersely.

"The boy's good, he plays with passion," Farthingale applauded.

"More likely *obsessively*," she muttered to her husband. They had both seen that side of their son at one time or another. "I pray the die *is not* yet cast," she added softly, but deep in her heart, knew the truth and groaned.

"How did you like Captain Farthingale's ship?" Jack asked, aware of his friend's feelings.

"Someday I shall travel over the land by water—by rivers," Beau said specifically, eyeing Jack. "When we get back to the compound, I wish to start practicing with rafts. Rob will make me one, or perhaps a canoe. I'll talk to Gabriel about that."

"Now there's a young man who knows his own mind," Farthingale chuckled. Sitting down, he quickly indicated a round of brandy for everyone present.

Now he does, thanks to you, Kirkland. Kathryn wished she could wring his neck.

Years later, Kathryn, Jason and Jack would think back on this day and curse. They would be sitting around Kathryn's kitchen table going over records. Beau was off somewhere yet again, and the question arose quite naturally—where and for how long would he be gone this time?

"Who knows?" Kathryn grumbled. "Thank you very much, Captain Farthingale. Do you think, if we had left Beau home on that fateful trip, things would be different?"

"Stop blaming yourselves," Jack said. "You both know the answer. Your son has always marched to the beat of a different drum, from the minute he stood on two solid legs. He has grown into a good man, and is excellent at what he does. Be glad for that."

Kathryn raised her eyebrows, eyeing him curiously.

"He never cheats at cards—he does not have to."

The following morning Captain Farthingale gave good accounts of all that had transpired, went over the product they had brought, and placed a heavy bag of coin in Jason's hand.

"Do not forget, Kirkland, you gave us a generous advance last time," Jason began.

"I have taken that into account, but thanks for the honesty. I knew we would make good partners. I am sure you are aware we have a very successful business going here, one that will continue to grow. I am headed to England on this trip, but will stop in Boston before returning to Charleston."

Jack leaned closer. "Did you find us a family or two?"

"Ask and ye shall receive. Of course, that is why I am stopping in Boston. I found two eager families, much like the Cousins. They needed time to settle affairs, but will be with me this fall. I'll send word."

Kathryn and Jason veered off the main path and headed for Keowee. Jack volunteered to continue on, taking the loaded wagons back to the Trading Post. They had already left Hodges too long, with too much to handle and little backup.

The area had turned busy with the influx of newcomers, some of questionable background, staking claims around the remains of the old town by 'The 96'. They drifted in and out of the Trading Post, bragging of their new municipality dedicated to higher education, and named after the famous college in England: *Cambridge*. In a recent fit of pique Kathryn had exclaimed, "There are already too many people elbow-to-elbow here. If they wished to mimic the mother country, why didn't they stay there?" Sadly, there was no stopping *progress*.

"This will be a quick visit to make wedding plans and no more, Jack. We will be one day behind you. Do not kill yourself trying to get everything settled." Jason admonished.

Jack's answer was a wide grin and quick salute, as he snapped the reins and the wagon headed out, slowly at first then rapidly picking up speed.

Kathryn and Jason arrived in Keowee later that night to loud greetings. The happy news they brought was met with wild whoops of good tidings. Beau remained quiet throughout the trip. When they had separated from their wagons, and he was swung up onto the saddle behind his father, he made no comment, seemingly deep in thought. Even in Keowee, as they shared the evening meal surrounded by good food and good company, he remained quiet, politely ignoring even Gabriel's children.

Anna scrutinized the boy, leaning to confer with Soaring Eagle for several minutes before righting herself and nodding solemnly.

"I doubt we will care to hear her comments," Jason whispered, and Kathryn silently agreed.

But Anna surprised them, speaking only of the forthcoming nuptials.

As they made ready to head for home, Anna hugged Kathryn, holding her overly long. "Ahh, Ugilohi, this child is *unique*."

A nice way of putting it, Kathryn thought, causing the older woman to grin. Anna *always* read her thoughts and worries, never missing anything.

"He will be what he will be. It is already determined. Nothing you or Hunter, say or do, will change this. Enjoy what he offers of himself *freely,* and ask no more, otherwise you will drive him away."

"I was afraid you would see that in him too." Kathryn kissed her cheek.

"Do not despair. There will be *excellent* shared moments ... but very few. *Love means acceptance,* my Kathryn, *not* control."

Kathryn mounted Beauty and started to turn, but Anna reached up and touched her sleeve, signaling her to lean down. "Gabrielle and Rob are your salvation—the bridge of understanding between you and your son. All will be well."

Although close on Jack's heels, he had already unloaded the wagons and almost filled the shelves in the Trading Post, by the time they arrived at the compound.

Without warning Beau slid to the ground causing Diablo to sidle sideways—and drawing muttered curses from his father. Jason chastised his son, but could see his words were perceived as nothing more than babbled nonsense. Beau remained silent, however, adhering to his parents' inane rules. Needing to talk to Rob about building his raft, he stood quietly respectful and was quickly released to pursue his own interests.

Smitty waved from his front porch where he sat beside his wife smiling contentedly, his hand resting on her belly. Even from across the compound, Kathryn could see Marlissa was glowing, her morning sickness now behind her.

Maggie actually waddled with her bulk. "My God, Kathryn, if I do not have this child soon, I fear I'll not be able to get through the inn door."

"Do either you or Samuel have twins in your family?" she asked.

Maggie's eyes went wide. "Do not be thinking *that thought,* Kathryn. We only have one name."

"You'll think of another one, Maggie." Kathryn gave her a hug and headed towards Rob's house.

Gabrielle emerged from the back of Rob's house, wiping her hands on her heavy apron. "Robbie's coming too, but Beau has him cornered, describing the raft he wants him to build. He has not stopped babbling about Charleston since he walked into our yard."

"Oh, there is much to discuss about your brother and Captain Farthingale, but glad tidings from Anna and the Bird Clan are of far more importance at the moment."

"Momma, do not waste your breath on regrets. Beau's destiny is set. Let him be whatever he seems to think he *needs* to be."

Will this delightful daughter never cease to amaze me?

Sliding her arm around her mother's waist, she guided her towards the back of the house. "Come see the project Rob and I are working on."

They met Rob as they reached the corner. Beau had yet to stop chattering.

"Beau," Gabrielle said firmly, "You may talk with Rob later. Momma and poppa have just arrived home—*you* must wait your turn."

He eyed her sharply, considering a tart retort, but thought better of it. He had never been able to control his sister; he had tried many times and failed miserably. "All right, Gabbie."

She spun on him. "And what have I said to you about that?" Anger flared, her fists balling at her sides.

He had pushed too hard and provoked her. "Sorry, Gabrielle," he retorted. He hung his head and made small circles with his boot toe in the dirt, acting dutifully contrite.

Jason, just joining them, had caught most of the exchange. "Anna is correct," was all Kathryn said as they headed around the back of the house.

"This is amazing, Rob." Jason stood looking at the fine stonework he had produced in the short time they had been in Charleston. "Tell me about it."

"It is to be a fish pond for my wife." He grinned at her. "We may not be able to stock it with prized Koi, but there will be pond lilies, frogs and toads amongst the damp rocks. Who knows where I'll stop."

Gabrielle giggled. "I doubt Rob will ever allow me to forget my embarrassment at catching his mother's prized fish for dinner. It most likely galls her to this day. But is this not beautiful? He is planning a carved stone bench so we may sit and read."

"My sister's English garden and its pool was the one place that brought me solace," Jack interjected, startling them; no one had heard his approach.

"Well, I have planned a special addition," Rob stated. "I wish to carve a beautiful standing stone for the center of the pond, richly embellished with Celtic knotwork representing *our* eternal love," he said almost shyly. "We will have but to gaze on it and ..." His eyes met Ellie's. She was all he wanted, all he needed in life. "It will be done in time for our wedding if I must work day and night to accomplish it." *There, I have finally been man enough to say it out loud.* He felt proud and suddenly at ease.

All misgivings suddenly fled. Kathryn slid her arms around Jack and Jason. "We are truly blessed with the gift of your nephew, Jack."

"Did I not tell ye both he is a good lad?"

Plans for the wedding progressed on schedule. The weather was delightful, the fish pond completed and the granite standing stone close to being finished. The Trading Post and The Black Swan were both bustling with business, and Kathryn found herself spending a great deal of time helping Maggie.

"Any cramping yet?" she asked hopefully.

"None," Maggie said, disgusted. "And by the way, there *are* twins in my Sam's family." She rolled her eyes. "Let's pray it *is* twins or else I fear it will be born full grown."

Kathryn was grinning when she heard a faint sound from outside.

"Did you hear that, Maggie?"

She shook her head, listening carefully.

"There it is again, a small cry perhaps?"

"Yes, let me get Sam."

"No time," Kathryn hissed, "Stay here!" She flew out the door, yanking her tomahawk from her belt as she ran, heading towards Sukie's house.

A lone horse stood patiently, with reins tied to a small tree at the side of the Cousins' house. *Too many new, scurrilous people coming and going, mixing with the good,* Kathryn cursed as she slowed. Listening to ascertain the situation inside, she quietly crept through the open doorway.

Sukie faced towards the door with fear in her eyes, forced back against the far wall by a large, burly man. Kathryn shook her head, indicating *silence.* Sukie made no outward indication of her presence.

The big man leaned forward across the dining room table, able to touch Sukie if he tried, but in no hurry to press her, enjoying the threat he presented, and his bullying power. Both hands were braced for balance as he alternately threatened and enticed her to partake. Engrossed in his game, he never heard Kathryn's approach.

Kathryn's tomahawk slammed into the table no more than an inch from his fingers.

"You bitch," he yelled, grabbing his hand away and spinning to confront her.

Kathryn rocked the weapon free, her angry narrowed eyes never leaving his. Tapping her tomahawk against the flat of her hand in a rhythmic motion of warning, she moved closer. "Unless ye wish to see how well I handle my tomahawk, ye had best get out of here. Do not attempt to draw a weapon, for I am even better with my knife."

"I recognize you," he said suddenly, beginning to look a bit uneasy. "I've heard tales of ye, ye nasty bitch—how ye love to cut throats."

"All true," she purred dangerously, "and each time was *sheer pleasure.*" Grabbing the front of his shirt, she yanked him forward, and following with a hard shove, sent him stumbling backwards. "If you *ever* give Sukie—or anyone else—cause for *concern*, I shall wear your finger bones on a rawhide strip about my neck. Do you understand me?"

"You crazy bitch," he spat. Surprised at her strength and obvious ability, he decided not to press his luck. Heading sullenly for the door, he continued his insulting diatribe.

At Sukie's fearful look, Kathryn smiled. "Jason is just outside," she whispered, heading for the door smiling.

Dodging through the doorway, spewing continuous invectives over his shoulder, he never saw the board Jason swung at his shins. Down he went, sprawled in the dirt, startled and frantically trying to sort out what had just occurred. Before he could collect his wits, he was grabbed by the shoulder and flung over onto his back.

The bully gasped, shocked by the impressive figure confronting him. Although older, he was in no way diminished in stature. Colonel Jason William Tarrington stood silently glaring at him with icy, blue eyes. *He will kill me without thought or regret* he realized and trembled, much to his embarrassment. He had been no more than a green lad at the battle for Charleston and, by nothing short of a miracle, had escaped with his life that day. He would *never* forget *this* man: the demon of his nightmares for many months after the battle—and still now, upon occasion.

Jason's eyes narrowed. "Would you care to apologize to my *wife* and our friend, Mrs. Cousins?"

As he did not reply quickly enough, a large, booted foot stomped down on his chest, exerting increasing pressure. Death stared him in the face—an apology required, if he wished to live. Although the colonel's request had been offered lightly, he knew otherwise.

Kathryn moved to her husband's side, and stood staring down at the man with a look akin to mild amusement, a fact making him even more nervous.

"I am sorry," he mumbled.

"Speak up, I cannot hear you," Jason said tersely.

"I apologize," he said loudly and distinctly.

Kathryn made a low sound in her throat and shrugged. "There are plenty of willing *ladies* in the new town. Seek what you need there; *never* bother us here again."

"Is there any part of what my wife has said that you do not understand?"

The man shook his head vigorously.

"Then go." Jason removed his foot and stepped aside.

With a sharp intake of breath, grateful to be intact, for the most part, despite aching shins, he struggled upwards and sidled towards his horse.

Sukie came out of the house at this point, fully recovered from her fright. "How did you know I had trouble?"

"Kathryn knew, I just picked up on her emotions," Jason said simply as they turned and headed back to Maggie's.

"You never cease to amaze me, my love." Jason stroked back damp curls, kissing her forehead as they lay in the comfortable afterglow. "I wish to hear no more complaints about losing your touch." He nuzzled her neck. "There are times, when I must admit, I actually miss the old ..."

"Kathryn, please come quickly." Samuel yelled at the top of his lungs as he approached their house at a run.

Kathryn swung her feet to the floor, grabbed her shirt and breeches and flung them on. "Timing *is* everything," she giggled, blowing a kiss to her husband. "I'm coming Samuel," she yelled and headed for the door.

"Would you ..." she turned to Jason.

"I'll bring Gabrielle and Jack, you go ahead."

He always knows what I need, she grinned, loving him deeply as she rushed to Sam's side. The poor man was ashen.

"Please hurry, Kathryn. I hate to be a bother, but ..."

"Sam," she grabbed his hand and started off at a fast trot. "Maggie has had two children before, she will be fine."

"This one does not seem to be coming as it should. She chastised me for waking you, but something is different."

"I was still awake, my friend." She squeezed his hand.

At that remark he attempted a weak smile, forcing down his panic.

"Is all in readiness?"

He nodded, stepping back, allowing her to enter first. Willie stood at his mother's side bathing her forehead, fear written openly on his young features. His father had sternly told him to remain in his room. But fearful for his mother, he had sneaked downstairs again. Willie needed to be with his mother, to help keep her safe—*somehow.*

Kathryn instantly understood the situation. As Sam opened his mouth to scold, she squeezed his arm, shooting him a stern look. "Willie, would you like to help?"

Samuel sucked in a sharp breath, but said nothing.

Gabrielle was just coming through the door with Jack and Rob behind her.

"I see we are having a party," Maggie groaned.

"A coming out party," Gabrielle quipped and waved 'hello'. She reached for Willie's hand, nodding to her mother, and led him out into the kitchen.

"Go outside, Sam, anywhere but here," Kathryn instructed. It was obvious he would be of no help. With a look of silent communication, from his wife, Jason took Rob and headed out the door to divert Sam's frantic worry.

"Do you need me?" Jack asked softly.

"Maybe," Kathryn pursed her lips thoughtfully. "Let me see how she's progressing." She moved to Maggie's side and took her hand. It felt clammy and she perspired heavily, holding her breath with each contraction.

"Maggie," she said softly: no response. "Maggie," she barked sharply. "Breathe as I have taught ye. Breathe. Do not hold your breath, it makes it worse."

Maggie gave a low sob.

"How long have ye been in labor?"

"I, I, for hours," she managed.

Kathryn did not chastise, merely looked up at Jack, frowning slightly. Signaling to him, she stood and walked to where they could talk without being overheard.

"The babe is turned a bit, but I believe I can manage. Maggie is so incredibly shy. But will you stay close?" With a nod he headed for the kitchen to help Gabrielle, if needed.

It was not an easy birth for the first child, thankfully a lusty boy who would recover quickly. But the second, a delicate little girl, came into the world rapidly and smoothly once her recalcitrant brother had made up his mind. When Maggie was settled, the babies cleaned and swaddled and cuddling at her breast, Samuel was allowed to enter.

"Two, my Maggie?"

She smiled wanly, nodding happily. "I think Freedom would be an appropriate name for your son, but …"

"A little girl too?" At her nod, he grinned from ear-to-ear, proud as could be.

Rob helped Gabrielle return the kitchen to normalcy, remaining so quiet she finally addressed him firmly. "You have seen the babes and thought them amazing."

He nodded, unable to meet her eyes.

"What troubles you, my Rob?" There was no need to ask, she knew. It was he who needed to state his fears, and put them aside.

"I fear … Will I cause you such pain?"

"T'is soon forgotten with the joyous gift of new life. Do not worry; I will bear your child gladly and easily."

"What are you saying, Ellie?" His eyes widened, shock, fear or excitement, she was not sure which—perhaps all three.

"Are you hinting at what I think you are?"

"No," she whispered. "Not yet, my Rob, but that time *will* come, when we are ready."

He looked instantly relieved and she smiled "Let's finish up here and get some sleep. We have a great deal to accomplish before everyone arrives in just one week."

"You have not changed your mind?"

"Never," she whispered. "With or without a ceremony, we belong to each other."

"I knew from the moment we met. Remember our first lunch in the kitchen, when you kept peeking from under your long lashes to look at me?"

"I never did," she giggled.

"You did, because you felt our *connection* at the same moment as I. I saw it in your eyes and rejoiced."

"I am sure you will tell that tale and many others to our children someday."

"Children?" he gulped.

"Twins, I believe."

Brushing a light kiss to his cheek, she scooped up the last of the soiled linen and headed for the door, leaving him staring after her, speechless.

Chapter Thirty-Three

The Future is Present

Rob and Gabrielle's wedding day dawned sunny and bright; the air filled with myriads of rich floral scents, summer was upon them. Kathryn was pleased the service had been planned for late afternoon; some of the day's heat should have subsided. Their reception would last well into the cool of evening. *Perfect,* as far as she was concerned.

The young people had written their own vows: beautiful words of heartfelt simplicity, creating a ceremony of profound meaning. Anna officiated, partnering with the town's recently arrived pastor.

Gabrielle wore a beautiful white deerskin dress made especially for the occasion by Anna. With long hours of loving dedication, she had fashioned delicate fringing and exquisite beadwork. The garment was truly beautiful. She had not neglected Rob. His shirt and leggings matched Gabrielle's in design and decoration, but of a darker shade. "More manly," she said as she proudly presented her gift.

Throughout the ceremony, Jason's arm remained around his wife's waist, more for *his* sake than hers. *My little girl, my little girl …* he could not finish the thought.

Jack stood on Kathryn's opposite side, and turned to smile at both, from time-to-time. At one point he leaned close making the soft comment, "It is good to see Silver Fox looking hale and hearty, glowing—perhaps with child." Kathryn nodded, holding up four fingers, ticking off names in her mind, wiggling the fourth for emphasis.

She turned to Jason and hugged him, sharing mixed emotions, allowing her thoughts to flow freely. *Standing before us is proof of each family's legacy being carried on—the blends of different cultures, languages, and skin tones of intermixed nationalities: English, Scot, Cherokee, American and who knows what else,* a fulfilling thought.

A delightful reception followed: trenchers of food, pitchers of ale, rum punch and entertainment. Hugging, kissing and well-wishing, followed by night-long singing and dancing, a celebration they would talk of for months to come. No one had been excluded, even the Loyalist plantation owners from north of the Saluda River were in attendance, invited to stay at The Black Swan as a gift from the bride and groom. Jack produced his wedding cake specialty, similar to the one he had created for Jason and Kathryn. The sentimentality of his gesture was not lost on Kathryn, who fought back tears.

As the evening grew late, the bride and groom headed for their new house amidst rounds of ribald teasing. Gabrielle seemed at ease but Rob, even in the soft glow of lamp light, displayed a distinct flush of color.

Eventually, the guests departed for their homes, the inn, or the campsite created on the common by Soaring Eagle. A few remained to talk and solve the problems of the world—Gabriel, Jason, Jack, Samuel, Kathryn, and even Smitty, who stayed for a spell but wishing to keep an eye on his wife, bid an early 'good night'.

Talk turned to the new town by 'The 96' trying to rise from the ashes of its predecessor. Some newcomers stayed for a short while and then moved on, only to be quickly replaced by others—a constant coming and going—not the basis for a strong foundation. Kathryn likened them to shooting stars, a momentary flash of brilliance quickly gone.

Tarrington's Trading Post, and its surrounding village, had been established on strong principles of acceptance and consideration for each individual's uniqueness They had planned carefully, putting down strong roots that would withstand any storm—somewhat like sturdy trees that bent with the gale, but again stood tall when the worst had passed.

Kathryn was lost in her own thoughts, capturing the essence of what was discussed, but feeling no need to participate.

"Look what you and Jason have created here." Jack's soft words startled her.

She searched his face, embarrassed, but he nodded sharply, making a firm, but silent, statement. After all this time, *he* read her as easily as her husband. "No, Jack, it took *all* of us to accomplish this. You must accept credit too."

"Unlike that new town, *our* community will remain long after they're gone. In a few more years, Cambridge should be complete. But I'll lay you odds that within fifteen years after completion, give or take a few, it will be no more." Jack commented, shrugging.

"Although you are beginning to embrace the interesting speech of our son," Jason said dryly, "I *do* agree. These newcomers lack the dedication of a unified cause, grasping what each personally needs with little or no consideration for others."

"By that time, I hope you realize the Cherokee people will have moved farther west." Gabriel, who up to this point had been listening but not participating, abruptly changed the topic, presenting another factor sure to create impact in the future.

At questioning stares, he added solemnly, "By the year 1800, not five years hence, we will begin relocating to New Echota, once again attempting to rebuild our lives. That move will be just the beginning of many changes. However, it is a topic for another time, one that I am sure Anna desires to participate in, sharing her insight for the future of the Bird Clan and all other Cherokees."

The talk lightened, returning to the ceremony and reception. Eventually Kathryn stood, stretching stiffened limbs and yawned. "It has been delightful, and we thank all of you. However, I for one, am exhausted."

With that statement everyone dispersed, heading for their individual beds.

"What an incredible day, my love," Kathryn sighed, yawning.

Jason's hands moved gently, caressing the length of her long, bare back as he kissed her deeply, his anticipation building. "I am sorry for your state of exhaustion, my pet, I had thought just perhaps . . ." *Those* were the last words he was able to speak until much later.

"Our son was well behaved today," she whispered, as they relaxed in the afterglow.

"Where was he most of the day?"

"I know he spent some time teaching Willie tricks with the dice. But it was Soaring Eagle who spent a great many hours with him. We spoke alone earlier. It seems he is impressed with our son's unique abilities. Beau challenged all 'comers' with no regard to size or age, and won, thoroughly annoying his elders. They had been sure they could teach him a thing or two. But none of their attempts fazed our child. He merely smiled."

"What have we created, Kathryn?"

"It makes no difference what we may think or wish, my love, he *is* becoming his own man. He appears to love us, and is honest to a fault. However, his life runs by *his* dictates and no other."

With a deep sigh he moved closer and within moments slept deeply.

"Good morning, Mrs. Beaumont," Rob greeted softly as he entered their kitchen.

Gabrielle had breakfast and coffee ready and waiting. "Mrs. *Robert* Beaumont has never felt happier or more complete in her life," she answered, setting his heaped plate of ham and grits in front of him. She served herself and then sat down beside him, pushing a large cup of coffee in his direction.

"I believe there is an opposite side of the table where you might sit and allow me to stare at my beautiful wife."

She recognized his game; she would play.

"As you wish." Abruptly she stood and grabbed her plate.

Rob grasped her wrist gently, frowning slightly. "It seems you are too willing to comply, my delightful wife."

"Just for today, I will attempt being a dutiful wife and do as *you* request. However, please do not get used to it."

He quickly stood, and taking her plate, set it on the table. Encircling her in his strong arms, he pulled her against his firm body. "Never move away from me, my Ellie, not even for a moment. I could not bear it."

"Nor could I," she murmured.

Breakfast could wait. They shared a far more pressing urge that would not be denied.

"You and I have a great deal to accomplish, Ellie."

They sat at the kitchen table eating their re-warmed breakfast with great relish.

"I want children, once I have *means*." At her sharp look, he added, "Means *beyond* the Trading Post."

Understanding blue eyes met his. "Woodworking or stonecutting: which is your greater love?"

After a long moment of deep thought he replied, "I enjoy making intricately carved boxes and chests, and even larger pieces of furniture." His arm swept in an arc encompassing the pieces he had created especially for his Ellie. "Children's toys are also enjoyable, but a cooper's trade? Barrels are a necessity, but not particularly to my liking, although Samuel loves making the retaining hoops in his blacksmith shop."

"You love stonecutting." It was not a question.

He nodded. "Carving a block of stone, coaxing the beauty from within the depth of each individual piece of granite with my own bare hands—*that* is what brings joy and a sense of accomplishment."

"I can be of help too," she reminded, "selling my dried medicinal herbs and oils, and helping Maggie at The Swan, even …"

"Giving me children, Ellie? With all that work and the care of little ones, will you have enough time for …?"

"For you, my Rob? You know the answer, but I will say it so you never forget. You will always be my life, my greatest joy. You always come first, there is no other way."

In early September, just before their wagons began the trek into Charleston to meet the eagerly awaiting Captain Farthingale, Jason and Jack reined to a stop at the Beaumont's front door. Rob and Gabrielle, having left their workbenches in the shed, were in the middle of sharing a light midday meal. After hugged greetings, two place settings were quickly added. Although they managed a few quick bites, it was obvious that both were excited about something. Within a few minutes, Gabrielle excused herself, allowing them to talk privately, but they insisted she stay.

"Jack has made the most interesting discovery," Jason announced, broaching the news, unable to wait until they finished their meal.

"We both did," Jack said firmly, sharing the honors.

Like two overgrown children they elbowed each other—each urging the other to tell.

"For heavens sake," Gabrielle teased, "Choose between yourselves and *tell* before Rob and I die of curiosity."

"We have just discovered a cave," Jack said excitedly.

"I don't know why we never found it sooner," Jason added.

"It is nearby, but quite well hidden by overgrowth. An odd glint of sunlight caused me to look more carefully and ..." Jack dropped a small, natural point quartz crystal into Gabrielle's hand.

"*That* is a healing crystal, Uncle Jack," she exclaimed. "You place the base against the body of your patient with the point facing outwards to draw the illness away."

"You are a healer, it is the perfect gift." He was pleased, a special gift for his godchild.

"There are artifacts, remnants of clay pots, arrowheads, semi-precious stones and so much more. But best of all, Rob, there are numerous boulders of all sizes, as well as smaller uniquely shaped stones which look perfect for carving," Jason added.

"It appears to extend far back into the side of the cliff. We have barely begun to see what treasures it holds. Knowing your love of working with stone, we wanted to share the discovery with both of you before we took lanterns and explored any further."

Rob was instantly on his feet, his face alive with excitement. "Will you come, Ellie?"

She began a soft protest, not wishing to interfere.

"I expect no silly 'woman's' games from you, Gabrielle. You want to come, excitement is clearly written on your face," Jack said lightly. "Besides, your father is heading off to tell your mother of our exciting find. Do you think she'll give it a moment's hesitation before saddling Beauty? You have just enough time to get lanterns and old breeches. Rob and I will get picks and chisels, and your father ..."

Jack turned to where Jason had been sitting, to find he had left. Looking out through the open door, he could be seen jogging across the compound, headed towards the Trading Post.

The old cave was all Jack and Jason had claimed it to be and more. The five of them made a solemn pact that day: keep the discovery quiet, share the knowledge with just a few close, chosen friends—but not immediately. For if word got out, it would all be over. They had seen first hand what happens when large numbers of people flock to a newly discovered spot. This cave would provide long hours of relaxing pleasure, interesting treasures and more unique chunks of stone than Rob could possibly handle in a lifetime. *It was their secret.*

Chapter Thirty-Four

Caitlin's Bastard

Beau sat at a small table in the far corner of the Trading Post, rolling the dice over and over until Kathryn thought she would scream. She stood behind the main counter in front of floor-to-ceiling shelves heavily laden with stock. It was the end of month tally, a noisome job, but had to be done. Bracing herself on her elbows, she chewed the end of the quill as she rechecked her figures for the third time. She would have liked to suggest, that it would be nice if he could find elsewhere to practice. But his silent presence *was* his form of companionship. He actually felt he was doing his mother a favor. She refused to nag or scold, for as soon as the weather broke, he would again be on his way.

Just the previous night his father had cornered him, a bit testily.

"Beau, we are all getting older. What if we need you? And what if some family member becomes ill?"

"I am *always* with you *in spirit,* father," he said, adopting a look of innocence as he left the room, leaving Jason fuming.

Unannounced as always, Beau had arrived two weeks ago just before the first substantial snowfall of the season, more than happy to enjoy his mother's good cooking and sleep in his own comfortable bed. It never ceased to amaze her how much he *delighted* in their compound, when inclement weather threatened, hampering his lifestyle. Just exactly *what* his lifestyle involved, she never knew. He was never forthcoming with detail, and went stubbornly silent when questioned.

Abruptly the door opened, sending a cold draft and snowflakes sweeping across the room. On the following gust, the door slammed back loudly against the wall. It had been snowing off and on at a fairly steady pace for several hours. This was her first and only *customer* of the day. A tall, slender, young man quickly grabbed the door and closed it firmly, mouthing sincere apologies. He was soaked to the bone and shivering. Several days growth of beard, such as it was at his young age, darkened his chin and upper lip, supporting several small icicles. A woolen hat, tugged down over his ears, was heavily caked with snow. After acknowledging Beau in the far corner, he approached her slowly, leaving a track of instantly melting snow in his wake.

Beau adopted a benign stare and sat back to observe. Something about this young man instantly appealed, he sensed him to be somewhat of a kindred spirit.

Kathryn watched him approach, vague familiarity nagging—looks, mannerisms, tone of voice. *What is it about him?*

"Are ye perhaps, Kathryn Cameron MacLean?" He struggled to keep his voice even around chattering teeth.

"Perhaps—and just who might *you* be?"

He shrugged. "*Caitlin's Bastard* is what my grand da calls me, but I *prefer* Josh or Joshua MacLean."

Kathryn's eyes widened in shock as she quickly came around the counter, took his arm, and led him to a bench near the huge fieldstone fireplace. She glanced up to ask Beau to help, but surprisingly, he was already on his feet.

"I'll bed your horse down, Josh, and inform my sister we have a guest for dinner. "By the way, I'm Beau, it appears we're cousins, I guess. I think you and I just may become fast friends." With an amiable backslap he slipped out the door.

Josh raised tired eyes to Kathryn, forcing a weak smile as she helped him out of his soaking coat and wrapped a thick blanket about his shoulders.

"Drink," she ordered, placing a mug of steaming cider in his hand.

He sipped, enjoying the warmth beginning to curl in his belly. She added a dollop of brandy. "For preventive medicinal purposes," she grinned.

"Ye have the look of yer brother, but far prettier." His eyes held warmth. "I had to see for myself if ye truly are the evil banshee he claims ye to be." He swallowed deeply. "No, ye are an angel, Aunt Kathryn, if I may call ye that. I had no control over my birth and ..."

"Ye are family, young Josh. Welcome."

The door opened again as Jason and Jack walked in.

"I understand we have a well-mannered, new family member to welcome," Jason stuck out his hand. "Did you give the lad enough brandy, my love? He appears half frozen to death."

"My nephew is about your size, Josh. Rob has dry clothes waiting, and I believe Gabrielle is warming them by the fire as we speak." Jack stuck his hand out.

Josh was overwhelmed at the welcome, speechless. Taking a deep breath, he eyed all of them. "Family or no, we *are* strangers. But ye have received me far better than the family that raised me. I came looking for you because," his voice faltered.

"Because ye had no where else to go, Jamie's treatment has been most likely callous and unacceptable, and Annie? I suspect she has several more children by now and wishes only those of her own birthing."

Josh eyed her in surprise. "How did you know?"

Kathryn shook her head. "Put it aside, Josh. You have a home for as long as you wish. Now, toss down that cider and go get some dry clothes."

"There is always work to be done here, lad, and we'll not have you sick abed *on our time.*" Jason's smile belied his teasing words and a wide grin spread across Josh's face. "Watch that he does not trip, I do believe he's a might tipsy," Jason commented as Jack grasped the swaying boy's arm to steady him.

Placing a firmly sensuous kiss on his wife's lips Jason asked, "Have I told you *today* how deeply I love you?"

And she smiled.

Over the next few weeks, Beau and Josh became fast friends. Beau seemed to commiserate with his cousin's less than ideal upbringing. He did not always appreciate his own, ever-constant parents and their often inane rules, but to have no one?

Josh was drawn to Beau's world of fancy clothes, easy living and lovely women; although he admitted he had yet to 'test the waters' in that particular area. Although his hands were usually clean, they bore numerous calluses from heavy farm labor—unlike Beau's smooth agile fingers.

Beau spent hours with Josh, sharing his obsession of one day traveling on the rivers in elegant boats, playing cards and ... quickly dropping the subject if either of his parents came within ear shot. Kathryn suspected that Beau's most convincing argument in persuading Josh to 'partner' with him was a promise to take him on trial runs with his raft and canoe as soon as the weather warmed up, so he could get a 'taste' for the idea.

In one of his more recent escapades the previous fall, Beau had discovered news of an inventor working on an innovative vessel powered by huge steam turbines. Fascinated by the possibilities he decided this would be his new life, no matter how long it took for the vessel to be built, or where her home port was based. Although the inventor's full name escaped him at the moment, he had prattled excitedly to his parents about a Mr. Something, Something Fulton. After staying three short days, Beau packed his saddle bags readying for another disappearance, no destination disclosed, nor the length of time he would be gone. Irritated beyond silence, Jason met his son head-on with a stern commentary on his callous, inconsiderate lifestyle, but to no avail.

Beau merely shrugged, flashing his boyish grin. "Bad news travels rapidly father. You *will* hear if I am in trouble. Otherwise, don't waste time fretting. I will drop by from time-to-time so you can both remember my inherited good looks."

Jason took a deep breath, fighting the urge to slap the smug grin from his son's face. Kathryn stood silently, her hand caressing the small of his back, refusing to take part in an argument they could not win.

With a light kiss to his mother's cheek, he flung himself into the saddle and kicked his horse into a loping canter.

"*That* reprimand went rather well, don't you think, my love?" She shook her head, a wry grin curving her lips. "He will bow to no code but his own, much like Jamie, unfortunately. At least with me, my love, you can sometimes attempt *reasoning*."

Her statement had drawn a slow smile, but he cursed under his breath and glowered at the rapidly disappearing backside of his son.

Now that the weather had turned much colder, he was back. Happily unconcerned and oblivious to all that went on around him until Josh arrived.

"I'll not run young Josh's life," Kathryn said firmly. "He is not my child, nor do I wish him to be. He is of an age to be on his own, if he so chooses, Jason."

Things remained surprisingly smooth throughout Beau's stay. Inclement weather kept both young men at the small corner table practicing dice for long hours every day. Josh, obviously having had manners beaten into him under Annie's demanding rules, did offer to help. Many times, he even nagged Beau into helping with the convincing promise, "I'll get back to the dice and cards much faster if you pitch in."

This particular afternoon, as Kathryn worked at straightening shelves, she listened to Beau carefully refresh Josh's memory, repeating his lessons for the third time. "Backgammon, although interesting, is not for me. Dominoes have long been popular in France and just now gaining popularity here, but again … And draughts, popular but not one of my favorites."

"One of your favorites is lanterloo, played with 3 or 5 cards, and counters you call *fish*. Your fish are made of ivory and are really quite nice," Josh said, proud to have retained what he had been taught.

"Don't get ahead of me," Beau said tartly, momentarily irritated. *He* was the teacher. "Yes, lanterloo *is* my favorite game. You either lose or win lots of gold, because the stakes double with each hand. Watch closely, I'll teach you how to *never* lose." Winking at the younger lad, he began shuffling the deck.

Kathryn paused to watch, the now familiar soft slap of the cards drawing her attention. She had to admit he was truly gifted. The cards cascaded with lightening speed in her son's confident hands, *effortless perfection.* He became an integral part of the deck, carrying on conversation and making eye contact elsewhere, all the while shuffling—never accidentally dropping, flipping, or missing a card.

"Many are wary of the game as the stakes are high, Josh. But lure them in with 'put'. Lose one or two hands to build their confidence before you *strike.* Especially if they're in their cups, it's like shooting fish in a barrel." Beau laughed.

I believe Banastre would have liked our son, she groaned.

The door suddenly opened and Jason walked in.

Beau looked up from dealing the cards. "Hey, mom," he quickly caught himself, his father's stern look stopping him short. His shoulder still ached from where his father had slammed him against the barn wall the previous day.

"Damn it Beau. You *will* show respect for *both* your parents. We have *never* asked more than that of you. You *will* at least allow us that. Your mother *is not* 'mom' and I *am not* ..."

"Yes, *father,* if it pleases you," he quickly replied. There was no sense in cutting ones nose off to spite his face. They never made unfair demands. He could give them that.

"Mother, father," Beau began again, and watched his father relax.

During an early January thaw, the boys left together. Josh would never be as adept at gambling as Beau. Although he did not have the same inherent talent, he *was* very good. Kathryn was sure he would be successful if he chose that particular lifestyle. But as a contingency plan, she offered him permanent work driving the wagons for them. Even though Captain Farthingale had brought new people from Boston as promised, there was always room for one more competent driver.

It had been a good visit, a peaceful truce existing between father and son for the duration. Kathryn breathed a sigh of relief, glad the young men had moved on. She no longer had to tread on eggshells, wondering when one would break. She loved to see her son arrive, but was equally glad to see him leave—preferably with he and his father still on speaking terms. And one less concern for Kathryn this winter? Gabrielle was not pregnant. *I will adore her children, but I am not ready to be a grandmother just yet,* she admitted only to herself with a touch of guilt.

The first week in March, Gabriel rode up to the front of the Trading Post, announcing himself with his customary whooping call. He sat astride his piebald pony, straight and tall. He sported new, intricate tattoos across his broad shoulders, upper arms, neck, forehead, cheeks—and Kathryn dared not think where else. She was amazed at how much exposed skin he showed despite the crispness of early spring air.

"Bear grease and slowly accustoming oneself, my dear aunt," he said, answering her question before she could ask. Kathryn's thoughts were so easily read, and he smiled.

"I have come to see how all of you fared over the winter, especially my namesake and the 'Brat'." He used Rob's shipboard nickname affectionately.

Any time Gabriel arrived, it was cause for a celebration. Everyone at the compound was invited to the huge community feast put on by the women. Smitty even managed to coax his rather shy wife to show off their baby daughter, as he proudly and playfully rubbed her gently rounding belly, openly announcing she was again with child. Slapping his hand away, she blushed but was obviously pleased.

Eventually, as the hour grew late and guests returned to their homes, a smaller more intimate group gathered at Kathryn and Jason's for brandy: Gabrielle, Rob, Jack and Gabriel.

"What news have you brought?" Jason asked. "As pleased as we are to see you, you always have a purpose."

"Ahh, Hunter, you have grown more like us with each passing year," Gabriel raised his glass in salute.

Pleasantries had been taken care of earlier, time to broach the purpose of his visit. He had already been away from his wife and family too long. This must be a short stay.

"I have met Joshua MacLean."

"Just like Soaring Eagle, you have become a master of few words. Tell us how and where, Gabriel," Kathryn ground out.

Jack leaned back, enjoying his brandy, watching Gabriel's facial expressions intently, hoping whatever he was about to divulge would not impact too heavily. With each passing year, new *'things'* were constantly being thrown at all of them, as if life was designed as an ongoing test, which only the stoutest of heart could endure.

"The two boys arrived in Keowee shortly after they left here. Beau has always enjoyed playing dice with Soaring Eagle and wanted Josh to have more learning," Gabriel began.

"Josh is a good lad," Rob added.

"Surprisingly so, learned under my sister's caustic tutelage, I imagine."

Kathryn hid a smirk, but agreed on that issue.

"What else did he have to say, Gabriel?" Gabrielle asked. "Josh spoke very little to us of your father and his *problems*. Being considerate by nature, I believe there is more that he *did not* share, out of respect for my mother."

Gabriel's thoughtful gaze met hers and held. "You are just as Anna portrays you, little one, extremely sensitive and *knowing*."

He turned to Kathryn. "Josh shared *things* that caused me concern for your safety."

With that statement, he had everyone's attention.

"Of lesser importance, Annie *did* grow tired of having the boy under foot. She has six children of her own to tend: one married and one engaged I believe." Gabriel shrugged, unsure and uncaring. "They are no longer family, neither is my father." His last words were soft and filled with sadness.

"What of my brother?" Kathryn asked, unsure she wished to know.

"My father greeted me with a rifle clenched in his fists and a pistol tucked in his belt. For a moment I wished I had not gone there to see for myself. I knew *I* would leave alive, but could I bear the guilt of slaying my own father? I gave him more than enough time to spew his vile words of what I have become, what you and Hunter are, even Jack is now included in his *blessings*." He smiled ruefully at Jack.

"Do not soften the truth to save my feelings, Gabriel, I *need* to know."

"I shall soften nothing, Kathryn. You must move on without guilt. His mind borders on dementia, and has perhaps taken that final plunge into depravity as we speak. He guards the hideaway as if the war were still raging on all sides, watching for British soldiers or Loyalists to cross his path. He cares little, one way or the other, which crosses his path first. He will kill either."

He glanced toward Gabrielle and noting her stricken look, turned to Rob. "Perhaps your wife need not hear all this."

"It hurts deeply, but I must know too," she replied as Rob's arm slid comfortingly around her waist.

"He mumbles incessantly, wishing that 'perhaps with luck, that prick of misery, Colonel Tarrington, will cross his sights so he can finally bring him down, along with that bitch he calls *wife*.' He is well beyond reasoning." Gabriel shook his head sadly.

Kathryn gasped as a tear spilled onto her cheek. She fought to stop the rest and succeeded, at least for the moment, as Jason's hand found hers and squeezed gently.

"Then he is truly *lost*?"

"Yes, Hamish brings food and supplies to him, God knows why."

"You are absolutely certain that he is no threat to my parents?" Gabrielle demanded, fisting her eyes to stop the inevitable.

"I stayed one night with him, listened patiently to his diatribe of caustic 'goodbyes' as I left, and then moved to a place where I could observe from afar for five more days. He *never* wanders more than 50 feet in any direction from the hideaway. Like a dog guarding a bone, he dares not get beyond quick striking distance. I am grieved for all our sakes, but most especially for Josh. Somehow, he has grown up well, despite all of it. But one can only take being called 'a little bastard who has destroyed my life' for just so many years."

"Would a visit help?" It was Jason who asked first.

Gabriel shook his head. "He is no danger to you and yours, but *it is* too late. There is *nothing* left to save."

Gabriel was fascinated by Rob's skill with stone, and praised him openly. By mutual decision, they shared their 'secret', taking him quietly to the cave. His face lit up in wonder, once again an innocent child removed from the rigors of life—at least while here sharing Mother Nature's secrets.

"Do you think your parents might enjoy my family and me on a somewhat more permanent basis?" Gabriel asked at dinner that evening.

"You would actually come live here?" Gabrielle clapped her hands gleefully.

"Sometime soon, by next spring, everything will begin to change rapidly. We reach 1800 at years end, and welcome in a *new* century with so many … Would you visit Anna?" He abruptly changed the subject.

Gabrielle nodded. "She will live to see *our* twins, but I fear not much beyond that. She has no wish to leave Keowee. Her life has been long and fulfilling, and she does not feel cheated in any way. We have talked at length."

"Ellie," Rob's eyes went wide, but he managed control until his wife finished speaking. "What are you saying?"

"I had meant to tell you tonight, my Rob, but the timing seemed appropriate for this moment."

"Gabriel, I am to be a father," Rob exclaimed his face wreathed in smiles. "Might I need another tattoo?"

"Only if I may create the design and place it on your body with my own hand, my Rob," Gabrielle warned, smiling devilishly.

The next morning Gabriel accompanied Gabrielle on a walk to the nearby brook. The sun was warm on her face, and she loved sharing her cousin's close companionship.

With obvious disappointment, Rob had begged off. He had two large orders of buckets and barrels that must be ready for delivery by weeks end. *There is no challenge to the work, but the money is good,* he kept reminding himself. *Twins*—he was still attempting to wrap reality around that exciting information and no longer begrudged the tiresome labor.

Gabrielle sat in the sunlight quietly observing Gabriel. Although he appeared a bit withdrawn he seemed content, or more likely *relieved,* she thought. He had dreaded the telling of his father's irrevocable decline and the fact that *nothing* could be done. But there was something else he was *digesting.*

"Your mother seems ..."

"Sad," she finished for him as they sat in a sunny spot beside the brook.

"Am *I* the cause," he asked.

Gabrielle shook her head. "It is her beloved Beauty that worries her, as well as Diablo. They are no longer young and their legs stiffen with the cold damp of winter."

"I have seen grey hair creeping farther up their muzzles with each visit," he admitted, "but have you tried wrapping her legs?"

"Yes, momma and I massage Beauty's legs with special ointments Anna suggested, and wrap them with warm compresses. I sometimes wonder if it truly helps, or she just likes the attention. Spring will tell."

"And Diablo?"

"He and I finally came to an understanding," she giggled. "One day, his flattened ears and snorted complaints truly irritated me. No amount of coaxing worked, nor did Beauty's well-mannered example. I merely placed my hands on either side of his face, looked him directly in those intelligent, black eyes and spoke firmly in Cherokee."

"And that was the last of his stubbornness?"

"Aye. I am truly surprised ye must ask, cousin, for t'is obvious. The blood of a stubborn MacLean running in my veins and speaking Cherokee—the poor animal was too confused to fight me longer."

They laughed together, enjoying the moment.

"Diablo and Beauty now share the huge stall in the middle of the barn. They spend long hours standing shoulder-to-shoulder in quiet companionship, seemingly unaware that time has become an enemy."

"That is an animal's gift that I wish we too, could share. They never project ahead, nor do they fear. But what of Satan?" he asked, wishing to keep their visit 'light'.

"Satan is as feisty, stubborn and recalcitrant as his sire and now resides in his former stall. Poppa recently made a deal with Zacharias Gibbs, stud for stud, as it were." She blushed at the bluntness of her statement, but Gabriel threw his arm around her hugging firmly.

"Will you blush further if you explain? You are even more beautiful when you blush." He brushed a kiss to her forehead. *Beau is unique and somewhat of a disappointment, but this child is such a blessing.*

"Probably—if you tease me like that." Her eyes twinkled as she smiled. "Jezebel will bear a foal in late spring, sired by Mr. Gibb's prize hunter. In return, one of his best brood mares now carries Satan's foal."

"That sounds like quite a bargain, and carries on both Beauty and Diablo's blood lines. Gibbs must be happy."

"Not completely, for many years he has wanted Diablo to sire a feisty colt for him, but poppa would have none of it. Satan is his second choice."

"I can assure you, he *will not* be disappointed. Rarely has there been born an offspring that so completely mimics its parent."

"Must you return to Keowee so soon?" she abruptly changed topics.

"I miss my own family, and need to keep an eye on Anna. She refuses to go to New Echota next year, and I worry."

"She will begin the journey, fretting and arguing, but will not finish."

Gabriel stood, offering a hand up. "*That* is next year. I cannot think on it now."

"Come join momma, poppa and Jack. They insist I must share you. Besides, I am preparing a special meal for you. I have also put aside pemmican, dried venison strips and biscuits for your trip home."

"If the blood lines were not so close, I do believe you would have made me the perfect wife." He tousled her black curls, and at that, she blushed in rosy brilliance.

As an encouraging after-thought he added, "Do not give up on Beauty just yet, she has such a bold heart. See how she reacts to the rejuvenating warmth of spring."

"What in the world has spooked Cornelius?" Kathryn threw the blanket aside and swung her feet to the cool floorboards of their bedroom.

Jason was up in a flash, tugging the ties on his breeches closed and slamming his feet into his boots. "Wait here," he cautioned, gesturing Kathryn curtly, but too late.

Grabbing his rifle, he strode out the door in Kathryn's wake, shaking his head in annoyance and pride. She was armed as if for war, right down to the tomahawk tucked into the back of her breeches. They had just barely dropped off to sleep after a long night of enjoying Gabriel's companionship and his shared thoughts for the future. And loving his wife properly? Well, admittedly, that had taken a bit more delightful time.

Catching her at the bottom of the stairs, he grabbed her sleeve, pulling her firmly to his side. "This will be done *jointly*. Do you understand?"

She had seen that look many times during the war and their life together. There was no mistaking his firm, "You *will do* as I say in this matter." With no time to waste, she nodded sharply, and they rushed towards the barn.

Loud, angry braying intermingled with frightened squeals echoed through the night. Rob's mule, in an end stall close to the door, had sounded the alarm. As Kathryn and Jason closed the gap, a chorused cadence of unrest was beginning amongst the horses. Jason approached, working his way at a low crouch along the far side of the barn, but suddenly halted. Kathryn followed, snugging herself against the outer wall just behind him, tomahawk grasped firmly at her side.

A huge black bear stood on hind legs, nose pressed to the barred window of Cornelius's stall. Her claws raked the bars repeatedly in a frantic attempt to reach this much-needed meal. The inner shutter stood open allowing fresh spring air to circulate, and although safe, the bear's growling and grasping claws had the poor mule cowering against the far wall, squealing in abject terror.

As Jason stepped into the open, the full moon shone on her once silky, black fur highlighting the gnarled, matted hunks and her gaunt frame. She swung towards him, wobbled almost losing balance, and dropped to all fours with a groan of pain. Rearing up unsteadily, claws slashing harmlessly, she issued staccato grunts and threats, trying to decide what to do.

"She is badly hurt," Kathryn whispered.

With a curt nod, Jason brought her down with one clean shot, no more than a soft, guttural sigh issuing as she settled in a lifeless heap.

By now they were surrounded by an apprehensive audience. *Whatever concerns one in our community, concerns all,* she acknowledged. Gabriel's wide grin flashed pride as he braced himself against the fence, making no move to interfere.

Upon closer inspection of the carcass, they discovered her foot had been badly mangled, making her hunting abilities practically futile.

"It looks to have been a steel trap," Jack commented, crouching low. "I hate those damn things."

"Poor girl, she has a cub," Kathryn murmured, eyeing the jutting nipples.

"Twins," Gabrielle piped up as she emerged from the bushes with Rob.

A loose rope around the neck of the first, kept him from racing to his mother. The second cub, more timid and terribly frightened, followed closely refusing to be separated from its sibling. From a cursory once-over, they seemed to be in good health. Their clean coats shone in the moonlight, proof that even as the mother's health failed, she had cared well for them. They mewled and grunted, crying softly—realizing something was very wrong but unable to comprehend.

"Head back home and get some rest. Jack and I will skin and gut her. It would be a shame to waste this good meat."

As Gabrielle passed her father with the cubs in tow, he added softly, "Leave the cubs, little one, I will take care of it."

Kathryn said nothing, waiting to see the outcome, knowing the difficulty and impracticality of raising small cubs, yet sure of what *she* would do.

Gabrielle touched her father's arm and gave him a long look. A slow smile spread across her beautiful features.

Almost as tall as her father and so very like him, Kathryn observed, awestruck at how fast the years were slipping away.

"Sally's kid died two days ago. She bleats from sadness and the discomfort of over abundant milk. Let us give them a chance at life."

Jason frowned and turned to Rob who merely shrugged, picked up the smaller cub, gentling her with soft words, and turned to follow his wife. *Twins*, he thought, *how appropriate.*

Kathryn nodded silent approval, noting the flush that crept across her husband's cheeks at his 'baby girl' speaking so plainly.

"Kathryn?" Jason turned to her, looking for support as none had been forthcoming from either Jack or Gabriel.

She grinned. He had not yet become accustomed to his daughter's new status. "I am afraid, my love, that *that* decision is between Gabrielle and *her husband.* And it appears he has no problem with her choice."

Jason frowned, muttering under his breath.

"Suitable words and well-said I imagine, though I missed some of it," she chuckled. "You now have the distinction of understanding my displeasure upon occasion." Her eyes sparkled as he moved to her side and pulled her against his bare chest.

"Be thankful, my love. Those wee cubs are a far better choice than her alternative."

"Oh?" Jason arched an eyebrow.

"She had been considering a panther cub."

Jason groaned. "At least their temperament is better."

"Strong women bring delight into a man's life," Jack grinned.

Having stayed just long enough to establish there was no lingering danger, all compound members drifted back to their individual homes. Gabriel walked to the fence, stepped up on the bottom rail and shouted: "Wise choice, cousin. Might you consider parting with one?"

As Gabrielle turned to wave, the larger cub, now held protectively in her arms, licked her cheek.

"I will take that as a '*no*'." He turned and smiled pointedly at Jason and Kathryn. "It *is* a very appropriate choice in this instance—*twins*."

Kathryn gaped. Jason and Jack seemed befuddled.

"You'll figure it out," Gabriel chuckled as he headed back to his bed. He had a long ride ahead of him and dawn was not far off.

Chapter Thirty-Five

Life's Many Facets

It was the first week in April. Finally, spring was here to stay. Delightful aromas of flowers and sweet green grass filled the air. Gabriel had been gone almost a month, and was sorely missed.

Beauty and Diablo pranced in their stall, impatient to be outdoors. Kathryn, Jason and Jack, each in turn, gently trailed knowledgeable fingers over each animal's legs, their undisputed agreement—no perceptible stiffness or lingering discomfort. Having spent a long winter in their stall, they pushed at the wide gate, eager to set their hooves in the soft dirt. Jason swung the gate wide with a friendly pat as each rushed out.

Gabrielle suddenly came to stand beside her mother at the fence. "I am almost late, but I needed to remove any traces of the cubs' scent on my skin before I joined you."

"Good thought. Perhaps in time they will all become accustomed to …"

Gabrielle's attention riveted on the paddock as her mother turned, suddenly uneasy.

Beauty and Diablo trotted the full length of the paddock, appearing almost *youthful.*

"Maybe," Kathryn sighed, "just maybe."

"Gabriel told me we must not give up on Beauty. She has a bold heart." As the words left her mouth Gabrielle gasped, grabbed by a prick of fear.

Her mother's ashen face said it all.

In a sudden burst of energy, feeling like her old self, Beauty raced the length of the paddock with Diablo close on her heels. She eyed the fence as she approached, her bold heart telling her *you can do it.* Without breaking her stride, she launched herself into the air.

"No, my Beauty," Kathryn shrieked as she broke into a run.

Beauty lay on her side, legs flailing helplessly, the delicate bones of her front legs shattered when she could not scale the top rail. Diablo nuzzled her neck, attempting to calm her, bleating his fear. Something was very wrong.

Kathryn reached her first, and bent to her with tears streaming.

Jason spoke softly to his frightened stallion, finally calming him enough for Jack to lead him back to his stall. Quickly moving to his wife's side, he placed a comforting hand on her back. As Kathryn caressed Beauty's chestnut cheek, speaking in the softly musical tones of Cherokee, she ceased her struggling. When she rested both hands lightly on her beautifully sculpted forehead, she lay still. Soft brown eyes focused on her beloved mistress, unwavering and fearless—comprehending and trusting Kathryn to do what must be done. Having survived all those years on the battlefield … *she knew.*

"How can one little mare say so much without speaking a word?" Kathryn searched the faces of her loved ones.

A tear splashed on Beauty's cheek and she nickered softly.

Jason's hand came to rest on her shoulder, as he pressed his pistol into her hand, knowing she would have it no other way.

They buried Beauty beneath a small cluster of slender oaks. Rob's granite headstone was exquisitely carved, a veritable monument to the faithful animal. They grieved profoundly. In time, the pleasure of seeing Jezebel and Satan cavort, so like their dam and sire, would help ease the constant ache, but not now. Kathryn watched Jezebel, praying the sturdy hunter's bloodlines would give the new foal's delicate legs … She could not complete the thought. The loss cut too deeply.

They grieved, but Diablo's life was over. The *light* went out of his eyes. He refused to eat, barely drank, and had to be physically dragged from the far end of the paddock into his stall every night.

"In all my life, I have never seen an animal mourn so deeply," Jason said sadly, as the three of them watched him standing at the end of the paddock, staring forlornly.

"*I* understand the depth of his grief," Jack said softly. He headed across the paddock to where the old stallion stood, knees shaking visibly. With drooping head he pressed his angular face through the fence, reaching towards Beauty's resting place. Suddenly he went down. He did not fight, merely gave up. Exhaling on a soft sigh, he was gone.

Kathryn and Jason broke into a run, reaching Jack as he crouched beside the once fierce stallion. He shook his head sadly. "He is gone, brought down by grief," he murmured as he lovingly stroked the jet black mane for the last time.

Diablo was laid to rest beside his beloved mare, his headstone equally intricate—equally majestic.

"At least, if time must move so rapidly, it eventually brings some solace," Kathryn commented softly. She sat on the front porch, sharing brandy with Jason and Jack. Another winter had come and gone, and they had yet to hear from Gabriel. *What about New Echota?*

"This is one of my favorite times of the day, sitting and sharing a brandy. It reminds me of the war, at least some of the more pleasant aspects," Jack said as he relaxed back in his chair, bracing his feet on the porch railing. "The Trading Post is a huge success and continues to grow." He winked at Kathryn. "You see, I told you 'one bite at a time'. Have I ever misled either of you?"

She shook her head, grinning, and gestured across the compound to where the full-grown cubs were just coming into sight. Samantha loped towards home, followed closely by her brother, Big Boy.

"By the amount of grass and twigs stuck to their feet, I fear they've hit Maggie's beehives again. She will have a fit."

"They really are fun to watch," Jason admitted. "They never tire of each other's company, and I am amazed at how gentle they are with Gabrielle's two little ones."

"Our special Christmas gift: little Thomas, named after Rob's father, and Catherine after me—although spelled properly, as my daughter so cutely pointed out." She turned to Jack. "Well, we've successfully welcomed in the new century. What have you got to say about that, Mr. Jackson?"

"I, for one am ecstatic. We have plenty of honest help to relieve me from driving those damn wagons to and from Charleston. I have bounced so much on that hard seat, I feared for my …" he stopped, eyeing Kathryn out of the corner of his eye. Her joyous laughter was wonderful to hear.

Kathryn had frightened Jason and him this past winter. Insisting on hunting during a snowstorm, she had caught a chill, which eventually settled into her lungs. A wracking cough and fever hung on for several weeks, despite all her medicinal abilities.

Gabrielle visited several times a day, dosing her mother with tinctures, placing warm compresses to her chest and demanding she inhale wisps of steam rising from a pan infused with healing herbs. Being Kathryn, she stubbornly refused until whatever odoriferous herbs had been added, were removed.

This was a new, unsettling concern. The horrendous wound she had taken at Guilford Courthouse almost twenty years ago was beginning to cause ongoing weakness in her chest. When alone, Jason and Jack often discussed the situation, hoping one or the other would disagree, but they both understood the cold truth of the matter.

"What else," Kathryn interrupted the silence brightly, sensing the men were lapsing into less than happy thoughts.

"We are surrounded by dear friends who keep adding to our numbers. There will never be a shortage of help."

"And …" she nudged.

"And Captain Farthingale's retirement did not leave us 'high and dry'. His replacement is an acquaintance of Smitty's, a former cabin boy from many years past, and now a grown man—with a *passion* for money. Smithfield is his name, and honest to a fault according to Smitty."

"Lady Luck must be gifting us with her presence," Jason chuckled.

"I never thought to hear those words issuing from your mouth, my love. Too bad Beau is not here to chide you."

Their light banter continued until Kathryn suddenly rose and sniffed the air. "I believe our beef stew is ready. I know Maggie left a basket of fresh rolls from her Dutch oven, along with a tub of churned butter."

"There *is* something else we all enjoy, which I'd like to mention before we dine: *the cave*, its abundant secrets and treasures—one of my deepest pleasures," Jack said.

As Jason and Jack rose to follow Kathryn, she turned eyeing Jack thoughtfully. "You mentioned *passion*, Jack. I have thought on that a great deal of late, while struggling to accept the inevitable."

"Oh? And what have you decided?"

She sighed, sliding an arm around each of them. "Passion *does not* diminish or die with the passing of years; it merely learns to pace itself out of necessity."

"Well said, Kathryn. We must remind ourselves often and fervently—perhaps adopt it as our mantra. We can't fight it, fighting merely saps our energy."

As they sat eating their meal, Kathryn laid her spoon down. "Tomorrow I have two things I would like to do; spend the day at the cave with both of you and in the evening, to justify having spent the day thoroughly enjoying myself in idle pleasure—perhaps discuss the problems I see looming with our newly, acclaimed neighbor, *Cambridge*."

Kathryn strode in from the paddock and grinned appreciatively. Jason and Jack were working companionably at the kitchen counter preparing the evening meal. Two rabbits, gutted and skinned, were just being spitted to hang over the fire, and a grouse was in the works. Freshly washed yams and greens indicated they had been digging in her garden.

Jason paused, leaning across the table to kiss her. "How is Jezebel's filly? Do you like the way her lines are developing?"

"Katrina has such a delightful personality, and thankfully is built from sturdier stock than my Beauty." She could finally speak her name without tears welling. "She's broad of chest with sturdy, well-muscled legs and thighs like her sire. She'll be a 'jumper' for sure. However, her placid nature is all Beauty's." Her eyes grew distant for the briefest moment, the little mare's beautiful image drifting in her thoughts.

"Pour the brandy, Kathryn," Jack said as he placed the rabbits over the fire and poked the yams into the ashes at the base. "I believe we're going to solve, or at least discuss, the problems of the world tonight."

After setting the spitted grouse towards the back of the fire, Jason moved to the table. Placing a box in the center, he smiled. "More treasures, our 'finds' from today's work in the cave."

Kathryn moved closer. She loved the beautiful stones, even in their raw form. "Oh, how exquisite," she breathed, fingering a round rough stone. "What do you imagine its inner secret will display?"

"It may be amethyst," Jack said, handing her a large mallet. "We saved it for you."

Kathryn knelt, placing her unique stone on the hearth. Closing her eyes, she whispered several sing-song words in Cherokee and slammed the hammer down. Inhaling on an awestruck gasp, she held the two halves up for their inspection.

"Two perfect halves of equal beauty. Amethyst, as we suspected." Jack pulled a small book from his pocket and quickly thumbing through it, stopped to share the information. "Geodes are fascinating, and no two are alike."

"I want to go with you on the next visit. Maybe I'll find a stone shining prettily even before I polish it."

"Jack and I are in the process of making a simple machine that will tumble the stones endlessly, polishing them into lustrous brilliance without your hard labor, my love.

"We had thought to surprise you, Kathryn, when it was done." Jack turned a chastising glance to Jason before bursting into laughter. "Neither of us keeps a secret well, I was about to tell you myself."

"Our numbers increase to keep pace with those of Cambridge," Kathryn stated. "We have cleared many acres to house our growing masses, planted new fields of corn and grain, built larger stables and paddocks." Acknowledging their success, born from the tiniest seed of an idea and flourishing with *their* efforts, she felt inner satisfaction.

"Cambridge is … I know not what," Jack mused as Jason refilled his brandy.

"Perhaps my words will sound self-righteous," Kathryn said softly, "but I feel our compound has been built on finer values."

Jack had made it his business to drift through the town on a regular basis, to stay familiar with the goings on there. Jason had once said, 'Knowledge of the *enemy* is power.' Cambridge was neither friend nor enemy, but bore watching.

"The last time I visited, they had just completed the new courthouse, a large church—I did not bother to ask the denomination—and added more space in the jailhouse. The atmosphere is one of arrogant snobbery, for what reason I can not imagine. Their numbers largely consist of 'nouveau riche' who deem themselves high-classed."

"Tell her about 'Les Jeune Filles de la Nuit', Jack."

Jack frowned at Jason's grinning face. He had not wished to mention that place, but Kathryn's piercing gaze demanded he explain; best to do so, and move on. "It is a high-classed whorehouse, to put it plainly."

"I gathered as much from the name, what else?"

"It is also a pub with nightly gambling, a favorite watering hole of your son."

Kathryn burst out laughing, not the reaction he had expected. "I imagine he is also a regular customer at that charming brick jailhouse."

"Yes, but not due to bad behavior or cheating. His constant winning draws false accusations from the less fortunate. Innocent or not, when you bloody another man's face and relieve him of a few teeth—even in self-defense—you rest your heels on a hard bunk for a night." Jack shrugged. "Beau could care less. He usually comes out of brawls almost unscathed. He possesses a unique combination of both your abilities: strongly built and well-muscled like you, Jason—lithe and quick on his feet like you, Kathryn."

"The whorehouse, is it at least … *clean*?" Kathryn cringed.

Jack gulped as Jason struggled to hide a delighted smirk. Taking a deep breath he answered, "To the best of my knowledge," and abruptly changed the subject.

***

"Anna, please try to understand," Gabriel's words fell on deaf ears. She refused to acknowledge or be swayed. Silver Fox had also pleaded and cajoled but to no avail.

"We *are Ani'-Yun' wiya*, 'the Principal People', come from the far lakes to the north many moons ago to settle *here. Here* is where I have lived. *Here* is where I shall rest in peace with the Great Spirit, *soon*." Her angular chin jutted in stubborn determination. "The Cherokee Nation is the largest of the Five Civilized Tribes. We are a beautiful people of proud Iroquoian lineage. We live in log homes, not teepees. We have our own government—far better than that of the greedy newcomers. Since we began assimilating White culture in 1800, we have adopted *their* form of government, *their* style of clothing, *their* style of farming, and *their* style of home-building. We lose more of that which is uniquely us, 'the Principal People', with each passing day." She swore vehemently, too tired to resist longer. "I will go if you insist." Her voice faltered as she turned away, hiding tears.

Despite advanced years, Anna was sharp of mind. Gabriel agreed; she *was* correct in her summation. Perhaps he should stall their move. Talk of New Echota, as yet, amounted to little more than proposals. However, he wanted to be included in structuring a new foundation for the Cherokee's future seat of government. His family's future was involved; he must do all in his power to make it safe for them, if that were possible. That night he discussed Anna's thoughts, as well as his own, with Silver Fox.

His wife's lip quivered as she quietly said, "That is Anna's way of acceptance. She knows it is the future—but not *her* future. We will go as planned, my husband."

The following week they left for New Echota. Anna remained quiet, introspective. They had traveled less than halfway and were stopped by a small brook to relax, eat berries and slake their thirst.

Anna smiled, murmuring loving words to each of them. Having said her 'goodbyes', she lay down on a soft, mossy patch, closed her eyes, and within a few hours was gone.

***

"It is an unexpected delight to see you and your family," Kathryn said, hugging her nephew and then his family, each in turn.

The children's sad faces and Silver Fox's hollow eyes warned of foreboding news. Suspecting the reason for this impromptu visit, Kathryn's family quietly gathered.

Gabriel, for once, was helpless. "I fear we come with sad news," he said solemnly, quickly telling of Anna. "My beautiful Silver Fox grieves so, she frightens me."

Before Gabriel could ask it of Kathryn, Jason spoke up. "You must join us, for as long as you like. We have many helping hands. Your house will be completed in no time, and you will stay with us until it is ready." He allowed Gabriel no leeway for debate.

"Allow Silver Fox to choose the site and create a design for your new home. It may help to divert her mind," Jack suggested.

Moved by Jack's compassion, Gabriel gave him a long look … *remembering.*

And so it was that Gabriel's immediate plans changed. He built his home in the compound with his wife's dedicated help, creating her gardens for food, herbs and flowers. In time, with sadness shared, the inner ache lessened. Speaking of the happy years, shared with the venerable healer and seer, came more easily. Despite forewarning of Anna's death, Gabrielle grieved fiercely, concerning her mother. She withdrew within herself, seeking seclusion. But much to her mother's relief rejoined daily routines within a day or two, apparently having come to grips with her sorrow. Her daughter displayed new inner strength, honoring all that had been *Anna* and her teachings. Quietly and unannounced, Gabrielle rededicated herself to Anna's training, making it *her* personal duty to pick up the flame of knowledge and carry it forth in Anna's memory. Decision made, she discovered the strength and ability to move on.

"This is where we placed her," Gabriel pointed to the small, temporary marker beside a babbling brook just outside Keowee. "It was one of her favorite spots to meditate."

With great care, Rob's magnificent headstone was nudged into position. In time it became an established shrine, welcoming travelers. Set beneath towering pine trees beside the crystal clear waters of a fast-running brook, tired travelers stopped to enjoy the shade and slake their thirst. They would pause for a few moments, absorbing the magnificence of the marker—reflecting. Anna, renowned seer and healer, had been respected both near and far, a fact which would have embarrassed the extremely *private* woman if she had known. To all her loving family it provided solace for their loss—*that,* she would have allowed and understood.

Silver Fox and Kathryn wordlessly shared their heartache. Anna had been a major part of both their lives. Comforting each other on many levels came naturally.

Gabriel, as perhaps all men do, experienced his sorrow quite differently. He honestly admitted that being near his beloved aunt and Hunter was something *he* desperately needed. They were all the family he had left.

Within no time, life settled into a regular pace. Gabriel and his family were a delightful addition, welcomed by all. With his somewhat *unusual* appearance, Gabriel had the good sense to rarely visit the elitist town of Cambridge. Upon occasion, however, a devilish gleam entered his eyes, and with an amused smirk he would disappear.

"We may have to visit Cambridge tomorrow," Kathryn announced during super. "Once again we, or more likely *I*, will have to remind the jailor that Gabriel truly is my nephew. They do not seem to appreciate his sense of humor."

"I wonder why," Jason chuckled.

"Who knows, my love, maybe we will find our son cooling his heels in the next cell. It is about time for another visit from him."

"What has placed such a disconcerting frown on your handsome brow, my husband?"

Kathryn looked up from her sewing, breaking the thread with her teeth and folding his shirt neatly on her lap. Her eyes sparkled with humor and warmth.

"Did I not purchase a pair of sharp, trimming scissors?" he quipped, eyeing her with amusement.

"Yes, and they are lovely," she said, leaning to close her mending basket.

"Then why, might I ask …?" He arched a regal brow, piercing her with a curious gaze.

Several tart responses came to mind, but she disregarded them. Something troubled him, something he was hesitant to speak of. She recognized his ploy. Holding to old habit, he played a game of diversion.

"Kathryn?" Impatience flared at her slow response.

My but you are in a nettlesome mood today. With a slow grin she stood and moved towards him. "Because, my love, to tend your shirt in *this* manner reminds me of years ago when …"

"When we first came to know each other, to love each other fiercely," he answered, pulling her into a crushing embrace and holding her, breathing softly into tawny curls, now sprinkled with streaks of gray. "Our lives were so different then."

"Yes," she mouthed against his chest, thrilling to his touch, the strength of him and delightful familiarity of his scent. "The color of my hair may be changing, but this—this *never* changes, *never* diminishes." She sighed happily, almost forgetting her purpose.

Abruptly she pushed away and raising her chin, eyed him speculatively. "You almost succeeded, my love." She pouted prettily. "What troubles you, Jason?" Her hand slid to his cheek and cupped in a loving caress.

Taking her hand, he turned away, not wishing to face her with what he had to say.

"Jason?" she urged quietly, insistently.

"I fear our son, or perhaps more correctly *my* son, has failed to inherit any of your remarkable qualities."

"What *are* you talking about?" She moved around him, forcing him to face her as she attempted to gauge the true meaning of his odd statement.

His eyes flicked evasively sideways, but quickly returned, meeting her curious gaze.

"What has *our* son done?" she asked, almost adding, '*this time*'.

"Not so much what he has done at the moment, rather his attitude. He is rude, arrogant and a rapscallion with no intent to earn an honest days wage. He has apparently found this Mr. Fulton and his wonderful steamboat. He plies the river, preying on the innocent, fleecing them of their monies. He dresses like the fops we saw in Dover, for God's sake. Do you remember them?"

"I do." She thought to remind him of her rude remark at the time, but decided better.

"He has mastered every gambling trick ever created, and proudly added a few devious ones of his own. He drinks overly much and treats women callously." He paused reading her thoughts. "Yes, he is just as *I* was once."

"But changed, my love, perhaps he will too—when the time is right. He is young yet."

"That is no excuse."

"No," she replied firmly. "We will council him, alone or together, as you see fit."

"I dread that he is a throwback to my father," he spat.

She had no reply, Jason was right. Their son had been a challenge from the beginning, and no amount of words naming Jason faultless could convince him otherwise. *Was it my incredible pain and horrific injuries that caused this?* That thought had crossed her mind often over the years. She had had no answer in the beginning, she had no answer now.

"He is *our* son, Jason. We have raised our children, hoping they would adhere to some of the principles we value. However, if they toss it all aside, *we* are not to blame. *They* are their own person. We have expressed our disfavor loudly and angrily over the years. But he is of age. He makes his own choices whether we agree or not, and may someday be forced to suffer the consequences of his decisions."

Jason watched her expressive face, recognizing she claimed equal blame, if there were fingers to be pointed accusingly.

"How do we manage *our* feelings, my Kathryn?" he asked softly. "I look at our Gabrielle and my heart swells with pride and joy. Yet, I regard our son and ..."

"Do not judge him, or hold him up to Gabrielle's principles with derision. It will only drive him farther from us, and place a huge wedge between those two."

"Then what, how?" Jason's eyes were troubled, confused.

"*We love him*. I know of no other way. Our door must always remain open to him. We need not accept or approve his actions, but as long as he is assured of welcome and our love, there is hope."

"You make it sound easy, my love." He touched her cheek.

Shaking her head, a tear spilled over, quickly stopped by his thumb. "It will be one of the more difficult jobs we have faced, but we will work on it together."

Sighing deeply, he pulled her to him.

"Where is our son at this moment?" she asked, surprising him.

Jason stepped back, eyeing his wife. "He is at the barn entertaining Jack with his stories. But I never said he was here, how did you know?"

"To have caused such anxiety, it was one of two things. Either a traveler had arrived with news of his escapades—and I have seen no unknown travelers today—or he was actually here charming his father with braggadocio."

"You never miss a thing, Kathryn."

"Come with me." She took his hand and, smoothing her apron, started for the door. "We can always hope that Jack will provide council that he might finally take to heart. There is always that possibility."

"Not bloody likely," he growled.

"How very British of you, my lord husband." Looping her arm around his waist, she matched his stride as they headed across the yard. "Let's see how long he intends to stay. Perhaps he will teach you a trick or two."

"*You* are the only one allowed to teach me a trick or two." He nipped the rim of her ear and chuckled. His mood had passed and she relaxed, holding high hopes for a peaceful visit.

"Who knows, Jason, it might be a good idea for you to learn a bit about cards. It would be a good way to *connect* with our son. Someday, before we get too long of tooth, our curiosity might get the better of us, and we could take a journey on one of those smoke-belching, pot-bellied vessels. It would be far better for us, if you were *not* an innocent traveler ripe for the pickings."

With a curt epithet, he pasted a smile on his face, and picked up the pace.

Kathryn sat in her comfortable, padded chair, a gift from Rob and Gabrielle the previous Christmas. The carvings were of intricate Celtic knotwork, matching their wedding rings, lovingly designed by her son-in-law. Gabrielle had added the soft, deerskin cushions, wishing her mother to be comfortable. It was Kathryn's pride and joy. No one, even Jason, sat on it unless first requesting permission.

It had been almost two years since Beau's last visit, and they had heard nothing from him. *He told us that no news is good news. I refuse to worry.* She sat idly fingering a small crystal Gabriel had dug from the cave, rereading one of Phillis Wheatley's poems. Although the crystal sparkled brilliantly when sunlight struck its inner depth, it had an odd lean and broken tip, she liked it. *I must ask Gabrielle to tell me about it. Anna would have enjoyed interpreting it too.* A brief pang of loss struck.

The front door suddenly slammed back against the wall as two boisterous children rushed through the opening. Kathryn looked up and smiled at her grandchildren. Willie also stood politely in the doorway, hands folded in front of him. He had informed her on many occasions, he now 'felt himself to be a man with proper manners', at least in front of adults. Felicity, always quiet, stood smiling shyly at his side. The rambunctious new twins were nowhere to be seen at the moment. As Willie did not volunteer their whereabouts, she thought it better not to ask. *Lack of knowledge can be a good thing sometimes.*

"Come in, come in." She gestured them into the room. "And what brings my favorite guests to visit?" she asked, closing her poetry book and smiling, well aware of the reason.

"We smelled the fresh cookies across the whole compound." Catherine spread her arms wide, illustrating her statement.

"No, we did not," her brother corrected.

"Yes, we did." She stamped her foot angrily.

"I hope you didn't bring Samantha and Big Boy," Kathryn warned.

"Nope, left them in the barn," Thomas said proudly, having remembered without being reminded.

"Then help yourselves." Kathryn chuckled and pointed towards the kitchen table where a plateful of warm cookies sat waiting.

Her grandchildren rushed to the table, immediately snatching two for each hand. Willie approached more slowly, dignified and proper, helping himself to one cookie. Felicity, observing closely, mimicked her brother.

"Willie, you fill your pockets. The twins will want cookies too. And don't forget your parents, I made plenty." She sat watching them as they munched, trying to talk around mouthfuls of cookie, thoroughly enjoying their company. She wished Jason and Jack could be here, but they were at the cave. She had been torn, wishing to be with them, but was still fighting a nagging cough. *Damn your artillery, Lord Cornwallis. Its memory lives on, in more ways than one.* She forced the remembrance aside.

"Catherine, how old are you and Thomas? You grow so fast, it's hard to keep up."

"Ten," she stated proudly, wriggling the fingers of both hands. "I'm older by three minutes, and that makes *me* smarter."

"Does not," Thomas countered defensively.

"Does too."

Kathryn burst into laughter. "Outside with your arguments, you are *both* smart—end of discussion." She gazed after the foursome as they bounded out of the house, slamming the door in their wake. "At least they remembered to close it," she sighed. *Shades of Jamie and me growing up,* she mused. *We never could agree on anything.* Warm memories flooded back, only to be replaced by nagging concern. *Take care of yourself Jamie; be well.* But that would not happen, prayers or no.

"Who is coming into the compound at this late hour," Kathryn asked.

Jason and Jack stopped sorting their new collection of stones from the cave, and turned to follow her gaze. Jason frowned. The last light of day silhouetted the rider, making it impossible to see his face clearly, and Jack's input—a non-committal shrug.

Whoever it was, swung down from his horse outside the Trading Post. Securing the reins, he turned scanning the compound, and whistling softly under his breath, smiled.

"Always the fool, Jamie, look what ye've missed," he muttered. "Hello, anybody here?" he yelled.

"Right behind you. Who's asking?" Jason shouted from their porch.

The tall figure spun about. "I'll be damned, Jason. Ye are as fit as ever."

"Hamish?" Kathryn joined them on the front porch.

"Aye," he shouted, moving quickly towards them. "Ye are a sight for sore eyes, lovely as ever, and if not for the missus back home I might be tempted." He scooped her into his embrace, kissing her soundly.

He then shook Jason's hand vigorously and turned to Jack. Clapping him on the back, he exclaimed: "My God, what is in the water ye all drink? Ye are unchanged too."

Kathryn saw through his robust, good humor. He carried bad news. The evening was young yet and she wished to enjoy his banter, hear of his family. Whatever sad news he brought could wait. She looked him over, smiling. "Ye have the same look as the lad ye once were, but you are now full grown. Ye ask about *our* drinking water, but look at you—a full head taller, broad of shoulder, and well-muscled."

"Kathryn, my pet, have ye tired of me so quickly?" Jason feigned deep hurt.

"Never, my love, only *you* could have put up with all my frailties this long." She thought for a long moment. "There is one other—but I fear he might find the reality a bit ..." She gave Jack a quick hug, and he smiled.

"Come in and sit down, you must be tired. There is plenty of time to talk of serious matters later. I sense it might be appropriate to ask Gabriel to join us."

"Aye," he answered softly.

Jason pulled a chair out and set a brandy in front of him. "Is that to your liking, Hamish? We do have whiskey, but usually save it for wounds."

An easy grin spread across Hamish's face. "Nectar of the Gods, this will do just fine."

"I'll bed your horse down," Jack said as he headed for the door.

"The hell you will," Jason laughed. "It is *your* turn to begin supper." Whistling a bright tune, he started out the door.

After tending Hamish's horse, Jason headed towards Gabriel's house, intercepting him midway. Before he could offer a greeting, Gabriel placed a hand on his shoulder quietly stating, "More trouble I gather, I saw Hamish ride in."

"I suspect so. Join us for a bite and enjoy the calm before the storm."

It was a delightful meal. They ate heartily, cleared the table, and Jason poured brandy all around—for fortification Kathryn suspected.

"Well, that's my life up until now." Hamish was almost at the end of his tale. "However, I have saved the best for last. I bought your old homestead from Annie, and have restored its weed-infested fields and broken-down fences. Over time, I have added milk cows, horses, pigs and chickens. We are, for the most part, self-sufficient." He eyed Gabriel hoping he would be pleased.

"Thank you for that, Hamish. It grieved me to see it going downhill, but I have no wish to be there, nor does Annie obviously."

Hamish breathed a sigh of relief. "Annie and her family love their small farm. She and Thomas have filled it to the point of overflowing with children. Her six are fully grown, and three are married. I believe there are also eight grandchildren."

"I am glad she is happy, but what about you, Hamish?" Kathryn asked.

"I hesitate to put it into words lest it sound corny, but I have never felt happier or more content in all my life. My wife is a treasure, always putting up with me. Mayhap ye know the lass, Sally McKenna. She's pretty and plump and has the most beautiful brown eyes—and I miss her sorely at the moment." He was working up to the purpose he had come for. "The only reason she's plump is because she allows me to keep her that way." He smiled shyly. "Eight children already and *she* asks for more."

Kathryn's anxiety was rising, a sword hung over her head waiting to drop. *I can no longer stand the suspense.* "I have only one request, Hamish," Kathryn said abruptly. "Before you tell us the reason for your visit, will you stay for awhile to soften the blow?"

"I will," he said solemnly. Light conversation ceased, his tone taking on a distinct edge of sadness. Pouring himself a drink, he began. "The hideaway is gone, completely destroyed by fire." He dared a quick look at Kathryn's ashen face and quickly moved on. "I could not allow ye to hear through gossip. Ye deserve better than that."

Jason's arm snaked about her waist in a comforting touch and Jack, edging closer, felt her hand slide into his as he reached for her.

"An accident?" Kathryn was having difficulty with the question she needed to ask.

"I have no answer, Kathryn, other than to say *everything* burned: house, shed, and barn, even his horse, *lost.*"

"Jamie *set* the fire?" Jack ventured.

"So it would seem, but will it hurt any more to allow him the benefit of doubt?" Hamish's handsome face looked pained.

"Did they find him?" Kathryn managed huskily, her eyes awash with tears.

Hamish inhaled a sharp breath. "It was an inferno, not so much as a small trinket left to remember him by. Nothing for me to bring ye." There was a long pause as he gathered himself to tell the last. "I took Jamie home as best I could, and buried him beneath the huge oak where he thought *you* had been laid to rest. I hope he has finally found the peace that always seemed to elude him in life." He met Kathryn's sad gaze. "He was a good man, Kathryn, never be ashamed. His illness was his destruction, *not you* or any other," he said firmly, his eyes reinforcing his firm message.

Kathryn nodded, biting her lower lip attempting not to cry. Jason's gentle hug gave her strength. Jack's soft pressure on her hand brought her peace.

"Have you met Josh MacLean yet?" Hamish felt the sting behind his eyelids, needing to move on. "I know he went in search of ye months ago."

"We did, and he is traveling with our son as we speak. They struck up quite a friendship," Jason said.

Kathryn finally found her voice. "He *is* a good lad. If only Jamie could have realized that fact, it might have saved him. Caitlin would have been proud of her son, and rightfully so. We may never know his father, at least not by the lad's looks. His strong facial characteristics firmly announce he is a MacLean. But the man that sired him must have had some good qualities to have produced such a fine, young lad."

As promised, Hamish stayed for two more days. Jamie was not discussed further. He dedicated his short visit to renewing old acquaintances, enjoying all the children, and walking the compound with Kathryn, Jason and Jack. He found the loving strength of their relationship, a bond of rare beauty and indefinable in its uniqueness.

The morning of the third day, Hamish said his 'goodbyes'. Setting his foot into his stirrup, he suddenly stopped. Turning to Kathryn, he wrapped her in a bear hug, whispering into the wild curls surrounding her ear. "Thank you Kathryn."

"For what?" she asked softly.

"For my life; two times over and at great risk to your person. I have never forgotten."

She began a denial.

"Hush, Kathryn. Accept my thanks, knowing that I care deeply and will do whatever I can to help all of you, if the need ever arises." He broke the contact, swung into his saddle and without looking back, galloped away. Unshed tears finally burst free. Sobbing uncontrollably, he urged his horse to a faster pace. He wanted—no *needed*—his wife's comforting arms wrapped about him tightly, and to be sitting with her sharing the pleasure of watching their children's babbling play.

Kathryn sucked in a sharp breath. "Oh Rob, Jamie would be so pleased if he could but see." She traced the letters of her brother's name engraved on the large granite marker resting in the back of the wagon. "I don't know what to say."

"Words are not necessary, mother." He kissed her cheek. "I would do anything in my power for you. You and Hunter have been my *true* parents for many years, as ye well know. But remember too, Jamie was good to me and treated me well. Hold to all the *good* memories." Rob turned to his father-in-law and Jack, pleased to see pride shining in their eyes. "Are we ready for our *adventure*?"

A loud cheer erupted from the twins, ensconced on either side of the large marker.

"At ten years old, the twins have rarely set foot outside the safety of our compound, momma. It is time they discover that a big world awaits them." Gabrielle smiled lovingly at her children as she grabbed Rob's hand, hoisting herself up onto the seat beside him.

'The Trio', as Gabrielle had dubbed them, sat astride their horses. Jason rode Satan, Kathryn on Jezebel and Jack, smiling happily, atop Katrina. He loved Jezebel's foal and rode her often. Recently he had taken to allowing her to *jump* with him on her back, something he had sworn he would never do. But it took no effort on his part. *She* chose the downed tree or fence of her choice and sailed cleanly over it. *Never say never,* he reminded himself often.

"This family journey is a celebration honoring life in its many facets," Kathryn raised her voice for all to hear. "Enjoy." Breaking out her tin whistle, she piped a bright tune as they headed north.

Chapter Thirty-Six

The Shimmering Crystal

With each passing year, the neighboring town of Cambridge drifted farther from the academic center of higher education originally proposed—becoming a ship without a rudder—as more divergent opinions forced the solidarity of the original plan to fail. That fact did not particularly upset Kathryn. Their Trading Post had been formed and supported by a sturdy base of business from elsewhere: the Loyalist plantations, Cherokees, frontiersmen and local hunters. Most of the townspeople made no attempt to hide their disdain. In their judgment, stacks of dried skins, raw pelts and gutted animals, hanging to age behind the Trading Post, created a disgusting way of life. Everyone residing at the compound seemed immune to their neighbor's criticism—everyone but Silver Fox. The tension and occasional verbal ugliness bothered her delicate nature, slowly taking its toll on her health.

"Ugilohi," Silver Fox called softly, "May I speak with you?"

The use of her Cherokee name brought a smile. "Of course, anytime. Is all well?"

"Yes—and no."

Kathryn shot her a confused look.

"My children wish to take active part in their heritage. They hear talk of Sequoyah and his development of a syllabary which will eventually increase literacy amongst the Cherokee. My Gabriel taught me learning and I, in turn, our children. But reading is not yet common with our people. Although Sequoyah's quest is still in its infancy, he has captured my children's interest."

Kathryn poured a cup of tea and placed cookies on the table, already feeling the loss their departure would create, but they must follow the dictates of their heart—as she had.

"Gabriel says they speak of a *newspaper.* Can you imagine it? My biggest 'child'—my adored husband—champs at the bit. He has no love for Cambridge or its inhabitants."

"Nor do I." Kathryn took Silver Fox's hand and held it. "I shall miss you, and give thanks for the years we *have* shared, truly a gift. But you must follow your husband and your children."

"We will visit often," Silver Fox said, trying to convince herself of the possibility.

"Of course we will, but in the interim my heart and thoughts will accompany you always."

"Thank you for bringing me to this beautiful place before I go," Gabriel's voice caught.

"It will be here when you return," Jack said, as he ducked inside the cave.

"I am torn with my decision, Hunter." Gabriel ducked to enter after Jack.

"You have chosen, Gabriel, and it *is* the best decision for your family and its future. It is a choice requiring more courage than I believe I would have. The world of the Cherokee is not an easy one. Their future will depend on such courage as yours."

Gabriel laughed. "I will not waste time arguing courage with either of you. I know the truth of *true courage*." He speared both men with a piercing look. "As do *both* of you."

"Will any of the trading change?" Jack broke the emotional tension.

"I see no reason that it should. Participating in the building of our town government at New Echota will provide me a place of prominence, or *control*—perhaps more politely stated—a position more apt to conveniently *sway* outcomes."

With that final statement, business was set aside. They scrabbled through the cave for several hours, enjoying the camaraderie and bidding a silent *farewell*.

Gabriel's last words to both men were of a cautionary note, startling them equally. "Take care of Kathryn. She is so impetuous, so delightfully full of passion for life, and led by a bold heart that fails to accept subtle changes. Please assure her often of how very much I love her."

Perhaps it had been partially premonition, but Gabriel's choice to leave the compound proved to be a wise one. By the following year, 1815, many more townspeople had drifted away, their numbers dwindling to the point that conversation over a pint of watered-down ale usually turned to the question—'should we stay or go?' As life would have it, *fate* stepped in to make their decision.

When the powerful epidemic struck, Jason feared he would have to forcibly restrain Kathryn in order to keep her from harms way. He refused to have her expose herself to the virulent illness laying waste to Cambridge. Knowing his Kathryn, she would likely offer her healing knowledge at great risk to her own well-being. However, when confronted by her husband, she shook her head sadly. "I have no intention of going there, Jason. Years ago I offered to help, but was turned away. Do you recall the fever which claimed several children several years ago?"

"I never knew you went there," he said, startled. "It was extremely unsafe, as I recall."

"I never mentioned my visit to Cambridge—too embarrassed to admit my folly."

As he listened, anger tightened his jaw.

"My offer was received with haughty refusals as to my abilities. Rude smirks were the final straw. The town's two *finest* doctors were powerless to curb the fever—forced to helplessly watch as it ran its course. Perhaps I could not have saved lives, but I have watched Anna use boiled cedar berries and herbal decoctions quite successfully in similar situations. I would have at least liked to try. What would it have hurt?"

"By God, if I had known," Jason thundered.

"*That* angry outburst is another reason I stayed silent. I feared what you might do. It is the *only* thing that I have ever withheld from you, my love. To this day, I feel my decision was for the best."

"Gabrielle never offered her services." Jack had been silent up to this point.

"I *did* tell my daughter of my insulting treatment. In retrospect, I did so for selfish reasons. I would not allow her to be demeaned, nor did I wish to put her health at risk." Kathryn's chin jutted in remembered anger.

In a few short weeks, Cambridge, the town that had risen phoenix-like from the ashes of the former village at 'The 96', slowly began settling into the nothingness from which it had originally sprung. The few tenacious survivors, after burying their dead, loaded their belongings into wagons and crept away into the wilderness.

Kathryn made only one comment, as she surveyed the eerie silence of the abandoned buildings.

"I fear our Beau may no longer pass through to visit, as often as he once did."

The cave became their fetish—their magnificent obsession. In all types of weather, they spent long pleasurable hours, reading poetry and reliving old tales of Banastre and Lord Cornwallis. Jack, ever aware of their needs, made sure they had plenty of opportunities to share time alone.

Kathryn giggled impishly. It was an early fall afternoon as she and Jason sat by the little brook. As she listened to her husband read Beattie's poems, enunciating in the crisp British lilt she loved so well, she splashed her feet playfully and watched the sunlight set rainbow colors shimmering in the crystal droplets.

"Tell me if you become chilled, my pet."

"Chilled, my love? You have not lost your ability to warm me to my utmost."

"Thank you for your assurances, my Kathryn. I *do* still have my moments—just somewhat fewer and farther in between."

"Does this happen to be one of those moments?" she whispered against his ear, flicking her tongue playfully.

"I do believe it just may be."

He closed the poetry book and tossing it aside, set to proving his statement.

On cold, damp days, Kathryn was firmly instructed to remain within the warmth of the house. Gabrielle often visited with the twins on those days. Now in their teens, they took great joy in relating their delightful tales of deviltry to 'Granny'. She did not particularly care for the title they had bestowed, but it was a new generation and she tried to adapt. Their visits helped to make the hours pass more quickly. She missed her two men when she could not join them.

Throughout the winter, she had had only one bout with her wracking coughs and fever, much to Jason and Jack's relief. It had been warmer than usual with far less snow—customarily delightful snowfalls having been replaced by days of cold, lashing rain. But the gloomy days had finally relented, giving way to spring in all its typical warmth and floral glory.

"The flowers are so abundant this year. Do you suppose it might be due to all the rainy winter weather we suffered through?" Kathryn asked, inhaling deeply of the fresh spring scents.

Jack shrugged, and bowing from the waist, extended his hand as a spark of deviltry twinkled in his eyes. In his long-lost, crisp British accent he asked formally, "Would you care to join us for a day at the cave, milady?"

"Thank heavens, I thought you'd never ask" She did not have to be asked twice.

Jack ducked his head, entering the cave slowly, inhaling the earthy aroma he so thoroughly enjoyed. An odd shimmer instantly caught his attention, shining from a place on the inner wall which had never sparkled before—not that he had noticed.

With a small knife, he carefully scraped around it, exposing more of its beauty, excitement building. "Strange," he mused. "How have we missed *this* treasure? Has something shifted or moved?" he asked under his breath. Looking down at the base of the wall, he frowned. A small pile of fresh rubble seemed odd, but the lure of the crystal reclaimed his attention, and he gave it no further thought. *I must have that crystal.*

Ever so carefully, he coaxed and nudged the surrounding stone aside, prying gently to free the multi-faceted crystal. With a soft 'plop', it suddenly dropped into the palm of his eagerly awaiting hand. "Absolutely beautiful," he murmured, as he held it up towards the bright light at the entrance, impressed by its increased sparkle. Brushing away any remaining dirt, he dropped it into his shirt pocket and smiled. *Kathryn will love this.* There was never a moment when she was not in his thoughts and prayers.

"You are late today, Jason, otherwise this might have been *your* gift. But I will not relinquish it. Finders, keepers, you know," he chuckled to himself. No doubt, they were still tarrying over a second cup of coffee. *He hates to be apart from her, as much as I.*

Abruptly, the ground shuddered; erratic tremors shook beneath his feet throwing him off balance, jolting him from his reverie. Loose pebbles, rocks and dirt fell all around him.

"Sweet Jesus," he gasped and lunged for the cave opening.

Jason sat holding his wife's hand, sipping the last of his second cup of coffee.

"Poor, Jack, has there ever been a time when you, or *we,* have not kept him waiting?"

"Occasionally," he answered, squeezing her hand and leaning to kiss her forehead.

"What is today's adventure? Fishing?"

"Not today, my pet. We are heading up to the cave. He is more than likely coaxing small treasures from the walls as we speak."

"I wish I had not promised the twins I would make them a batch of cookies. I do so love to roam through the cave with you and …"

With a growling rumble, the house shook violently—only for a moment—but her cup rattled in its saucer and outreaching rings rippled across the top of her coffee.

"Oh God, no." She pushed back forcefully, her chair flying backwards. "Not Jack, not our Jack."

Jason rushed for the door.

"I'll saddle Jezebel and …"

"No time, Kathryn. He lifted her onto the shying Satan, cursing the frightened steed to stand and behave. Flinging himself up behind her, he kneed sharply, sending the high-strung animal at a pounding pace towards the woods.

"Rob, come quickly," Gabrielle screamed as her parents raced by.

Rounding the house at a run, he yanked aside his heavy, leather apron and headed for the barn. The sharp tremor and horrified panic in his wife's voice filled him with dread. Rob leaped onto his horse as his wife reached his side.

"Stay here with the children my, Ellie. *Please.*"

Her lips met his firmly in a kiss for courage. Then sawing the reins, he forced his terrified horse sideways and galloped towards the woods.

Jack lay flat on his back, arms flung wide, his body covered in rubble from mid-chest down. He had cleared the entrance just barely, safety almost within his grasp, when the collapsing cave sent rock from its jagged face tumbling down upon him.

"Hold on, Jack, we'll get you out." Jason rushed to his side and began flinging rocks away in crazed fear. He worked feverishly, at a pace driven by desperation.

"Stop, Jason, come talk to me," Jack whispered weakly.

"When I have removed all this," he answered stubbornly, fearing that if he allowed Jack to say 'goodbye' it would truly be over.

Kathryn knelt at his side, tenderly stroking back his graying hair. Easing his hand free of the few remaining rocks, she brought it to her lips. "Anna taught me well, you will …"

"Kathryn, my beloved." His eyes sought hers. *So much I want to say … so little time.*

She cradled his head, gently wiping dirt from his face. Pressing Jason's canteen to his lips she talked softly, reassuringly as he slowly sipped.

Breathing heavily from his exertion, Jason heaved the last rock aside and knelt by his dear friend's side. "Jack, you will be fine. We will get you back to our …"

"No, there is no cure for this," he sad sadly.

"Are you in pain, Jack?" Jason lifted his hand, cradling it in both of his, upset at the lack of warmth.

"No, thankfully. My spine is … I have no feeling in my legs. But I can feel the loving warmth of both your hands, t'is what gives me courage. This is as it should be; I could not bear to watch either of you leave me a second time."

Kathryn turned away, lost in grief, lost to the words of the two men saying their 'goodbyes'. Her mind and body went numb. She felt close to suffocating, her heart pounding fiercely and chest constricting painfully. Her tears were barely held at bay, but she would not cry, *would not* until …

Jason's hand startled her as he placed it tenderly on her shoulder. "Say 'goodbye', my love, there is little time left." He leaned closer, urging in a soft whisper, "Tell him what he so desperately needs to hear. I will understand. He needs to say 'goodbye' to *you* … needs your love for courage. Do so with my blessings." With a squeeze to her hand, he stepped away. "I will always understand, my Kathryn."

Kathryn moved closer, her hip touching Jack's side. At her touch his beautiful, amber eyes opened, coming to rest on her.

"Do not cry, my Kathryn." He reached to cup her cheek; thankful his arms still worked—still had feeling. "Reach in my pocket … a gift for *you*."

Oh Jack," she gasped, clasping the beautiful crystal against her. "It is exquisite."

"It is for you, my beloved. I cannot remember a time when I have not loved you." His words were breathy, and perspiration beaded his brow.

"Nor I, you, Jack." She cradled his head gently on her lap embracing him, stroking his hair, caressing his cheeks, placing light kisses to his forehead and cheeks. "What will *I* do without you? Who will teach me to be sensible? You must not go."

"I will be at your side … always. I *will* be there … when it is your time, and Jason's." It took effort to talk now. His hand slid the length of her arm, caressing softly, moving upwards to rest weakly on her shoulder.

She leaned down, her lips finding his, kissing gently and then more firmly.

He returned her kiss … fully, deeply, cherishing each moment. He had not dared ask, but she had known, as she always did, and he loved her more *if that was possible*. Losing himself to the sublime tenderness of her kiss, he ignored the encroaching darkness.

"T'would be wurth dyin' jist ter feel her gentle touch." Lieutenant McCrae's dying words echoed softly from the past, startling Jack with the stark simplicity of their *truth*.

"I will love you throughout eternity, my beloved Kathryn," he whispered fervently against her lips, as his fingers slowly eased their light grip, sliding gradually to his side.

Kathryn's keening wail of anguish brought Jason instantly to her side. Pulling her up into his arms, he held her as they sobbed in combined grief. No words, no amount of time, could ease this pain. How had Jack managed to cope after their *death*? She raised her tear-streaked face to her husband's as he gently cupped her cheek, searching her eyes. Jason had given Jack the greatest gift imaginable through her, selflessly putting his own feelings aside. She must now reassure him.

"You are my complete life, my heart and soul, *always*, my beloved husband. We *have* each other and always will have," she sobbed.

"We have each other," he answered, "or I could not go on. I could not bear this agony alone." Jason held her tightly, afraid for her, afraid for himself. Emptiness engulfed him. Jack had been such an indispensable part of their lives—more than he had even realized. How could they manage ...?

Rob knelt at Jack's side, tears streaming. They had not heard him arrive, did not know how long he had been there, or how long they had wept in each other's arms.

Jason placed his hand on his son-in-law's shoulder. "Would you help me take him home, Rob? Not slung like a sack of grain ..." his voice broke. "I will carry him ... like the *man* he is."

They headed back to the compound with Jack cradled in Jason's arms. Kathryn sat astride Jack's Katrina flanking one side, and Rob on the other. As they approached the compound, Jason turned to Rob. He was in better control now, at least for the moment. "Your uncle will be buried here."

Rob nodded. "Yes, I know, he wanted to be sure I understood."

"I still recall the day he told me his final wishes, Rob. He laughed, demanding that I not waste a perfectly good keg of rum to ship him back to England. I hear his words so clearly." Jason almost smiled with the memory. "He told me he wished his final resting place to be here in his new home, surrounded by the people he loved dearly—and we shall do that for him."

"That sounds so like our Jack," Kathryn whispered as tears began afresh. She now understood how *he* had felt, and the realization did nothing to ease her pain.

Jack was buried in the compound's cemetery, beside a bench he often sat upon to read Phillis Wheatley's poetry.

"He will rest easy here," Rob assured. "His memorial stone will be ready by the time the family gathers for his 'celebration of life' ceremony."

Although there was little time, and Jason wondered if that would be possible, Rob was good to his word. He set all orders aside, working day and night with his wife at his side providing food and encouragement. His uncle would be honored appropriately, with a magnificent headstone which *would be* completed on time.

The whole compound attended, wishing to show respect for this wonderful man that so many had shared the last forty years of their life with. Jack was well-loved, his loss creating a huge void that could not be filled. He would not be forgotten, and remain *alive* within their hearts.

Gabriel and his family made the long journey. They would not forego Jack's 'celebration of life' for any reason. Although appearing stoic on the surface, Gabriel's heart was filled with anguish. Waiting until everyone had left, and they could be alone, he and Jason sat down and sobbed, sharing their sorrow.

Rob's magnificent headstone, created for his beloved Uncle Jack, was his finest piece of work to date—a design of magnitude and intricacy—crafted with a selfless act of love.

Gabrielle caught her mother in a quiet moment alone. She was concerned at her parents' intense grief, more especially her mother's. The weakness in her lungs worried her, it had seemed to worsen. She sat holding her hand, brushing back her tawny, gray-streaked curls.

"Momma, you know as well as I, that Jack *is not* gone. He is here with us now, waiting in the ethers—watching, caring, and loving you both. He *will be* here when it is your time. But not yet, your time is *not* yet. He survived—so can you."

It was an unexpected lecture from her daughter, catching her completely off-guard.

"I will try little one … for *you* I will try."

Chapter Thirty-Seven

Following his Heart

Kathryn and Jason succumbed to their inconsolable loss. Just as if a limb had been severed, nothing felt right and no amount of words brought comfort.

"How did Jack ever manage to survive when …?" She could not finish as tears sprang fresh.

"Duty, so aptly instilled in dragoons—and a promise to us," Jason said softly. "He had Gabrielle to protect. We have each other and our family."

"We were so dynamic, so successful in battle together, the infamous 'Trio' who instilled fear at the mention of their names." A crooked smile curved her lips. "Look at us now—or rather, look at *me*. Jack was right, my love. I *do fear* old age. Jack has beaten it, but you and I?"

"We will face it together, my Kathryn. I am sure there are humorous moments to aging. I recall when you were carrying Gabrielle. At first you fought the changes: less energy, growing girth, heightened emotions and, always one of your favorites, a constant need to relieve yourself behind the nearest bush."

That actually brought a giggle. "I survived because I knew many others had gone before me. If they could do it, so could I."

"I want you to hold that thought, my love, especially when you are feeling particularly blue." He cupped her cheeks, kissing her gently. "This," he whispered, "kissing you, touching you, making love to you—none of *this* fades nor ever grows old, nor will it."

"But Jack …" she kept returning to him, unable to exclude him from her thoughts.

"Kathryn," Jason skewered her with a pointed look, "do you feel *guilt?*"

"Of course not," her anger flared momentarily.

Jason knew, as always. Suddenly tears brimmed over, spilling willfully beyond her control. Pulling the beautiful crystal from her pocket—where she always carried it—she held it up to her husband.

"Jack died for …"

"Kathryn," he cut her off sharply. "*Your* gift was *our* blessing."

Confusion distorted her face.

"Had Jack not stopped to collect the gift for you, he would have gone to our regular digging spot—in the *very back* of the cave."

He held her until her sobs quieted—the horrific realization almost more than either could bear. He continued to hold her, quietly allowing her to sort things out. His statement *had* struck home.

"There is nothing to feel guilty about, my Kathryn. Towards the end, Jack and I spoke often *of everything.* By his own words, if he had been given a choice, he would have changed *nothing.*"

She drew in a ragged breath and raising her eyes, searched his face for the truth of his statement.

"I have *never* lied to you, Kathryn." His mouth found hers and lingered.

"I have *never* questioned your word, Jason, and I will not start now."

They never spoke of the crystal again, and life moved slowly forward.

Grief is a fickle jokester, lulling the mourner with bits of delightful memories to ease the inner ache, only to deliver a gut-punch of cruel reality, driving them to their knees when least expected.

The endless days plodded on.

One morning Kathryn looked across the breakfast table at her husband. Setting her coffee down so hard it sloshed into its saucer, she reached for his hand. "How does one recover from a broken heart?" she asked bitterly.

"The same way you eat an elephant, my love: one bite at a time."

That brought a smile. "Jack certainly had unique ways of supplying answers," she murmured.

"That he did, and was usually correct. Rob is much like him, in looks and temperament. We will never worry about our Gabrielle. Her marriage is as blessed as ours."

Edging his chair closer, Jason pulled her into his embrace. Quickly shoving the chair back, he eased her onto his lap, settling her against him as she became lost in thought. He worried about her more with each passing day. As fall approached, a dry cough began. At times he found her gasping from the strain. Gabrielle tended her mother, trying different combinations of healing herbs, but all seemed less and less effective.

Her health was failing; no amount of denial would change the facts. It was like watching a once brilliant flame slowly flicker and go out ... one day at a time.

Jason wept for her when alone, but encouraged and cajoled during their waking hours together. He rarely left her side for fear he would return to find all had been lost in his absence.

She had good days and bad as the winds of winter swept down upon the compound, but seemed to hold her own. She began to sing occasionally, to bake cookies for the twins, to force her mind outward from dwelling on inner sadness. She was still alive and things needed to be done.

As winter released its tenacious hold, the lengthening days had a restorative effect on Kathryn. There were a few lingering patches of snow, but perky snowbells—one of the first harbingers of spring—peeked stubbornly through, promising a fresh, new year.

This particular morning, she came from the kitchen and walked to where Jason sat by the fire sipping his coffee. Settling herself on the small stool beside him, she looked up and smiled. Her eyes sparkled, and a healthy touch of color brightened her face. "Why is it, Jason, that when we finally reach a point in life when the hours of leisure are *ours* to dictate for pleasure, the mind says '*yes*', but the body suggests emphatically—*later?*" She giggled. "We must ask Jack when next we see him."

For a second he eyed her sharply. *Her mind is clear. She is just saying ...* He refused to finish the thought. Giving her a hand-up he pulled her against him relishing her warmth, and brought his lips to the arch of her neck. She was just beginning an enticing caress, enjoying his eager response, when she caught motion through the window.

"I fear we are about to have company, my love. Please hold that thought, we *will* discuss it later."

With a hug and a *promise*, he went to the door to welcome Gabrielle and Rob.

"We have a surprise, momma." Gabrielle smiled, setting a pan of snow on the table.

"Thank you, I think—a rather unique gift it is."

"That is only part of the surprise, mother," Rob chuckled as he uncovered a steaming pan of liquid he had been carrying under a heavy towel.

"Whose turn, my Ellie?"

"Yours, and be quick before the snow melts. There is not much left."

Taking a spoon from his pocket, Rob dipped it into the gooey liquid. Licking a delicious drop from his wrist, he began dribbling the amber sweetness in intricate patterns across the snow-filled pan. "Celtic knotwork, stars and snowflakes," he said, concentrating on his designs.

"Maple syrup," Kathryn chirped, clapping her hands. "I had forgotten. Oh Jason, how absolutely delightful. Did you know?"

"No, they tell me little lest I give away the secret." Reaching into the pan, he chose a brittle piece of Celtic knotwork and held it out to Kathryn.

"Delicious," she mumbled around the last bit, licking the sticky sweetness from her fingers. "May I have more?"

"As much as you like, mother. If we need fresh snow, I'll find some." Rob was delighted to see her so happy. "Ellie, I don't think I heard you tell mother who cooked the maple syrup to such perfection."

"I failed to mention it, my Rob, hoping she would think it was *I* who was so talented."

They stayed the afternoon, and the rafters rang with laughter. Kathryn felt better than she had in months.

Kathryn chastised herself. There was so much to be thankful for and enjoy in life. Rob and Gabrielle had reinforced that fact with their delightful visit. She made a renewed effort to participate *joyfully* in daily routines. She took fresh delight in the children, interacted with the traders, helped Maggie at the Swan and spent much needed *happy* time with her husband.

Although more than a year had passed since Jack's death, she still found herself forming questions she wished to ask him on a regular basis. Quickly forcing the inner ache aside, she allowed warm memories to enter in its place. It truly *was* about surviving, one day at a time. In the beginning, it had been about surviving from minute to minute—yes, she was better.

Jason breathed a sigh of relief as life settled back into its former daily rhythm. When Kathryn insisted they ride to New Echota to visit Gabriel and Silver Fox, an inexplicable nagging fear settled around his heart. But she seemed strong, eager, much more like her self. Loving her so deeply, he would do whatever it took to make her happy.

Their journey to New Echota was taken at a leisurely pace. Feeling restored, Kathryn fished and hunted along the way. "I never realized how much I *truly* enjoy cooking over a campfire. Perhaps greater appreciation of the *moment*, no matter how simple or complex comes with age. I no longer feel the need to rush ahead, seeking the next thrill. What I have here and now, *shared with you*, is all I need, my love."

The early fall weather was invigorating. Crisp, fresh air, the changing colors of leaves, and brilliant fall sunsets were beyond description. It was a delightful time of year to travel—the swarming insects and unbearable humidity of summer long gone. They would be back, safely, at Tarrington's Trading Post long before wintry weather set in. With that knowledge, Jason relaxed somewhat, enjoying their journey thoroughly. Time alone with his Kathryn—without constant interruptions—was precious, and he savored it.

Kathryn and Jason stood eyeing Gabriel's new domain. New Echota was unique and beautiful, beyond all expectation. She and Jason must come back often, become an integral part of the—*future.*

"Will you join us, Ugilohi?" Gabriel asked, brushing a kiss to his aunt's cheek. Wishing to share ideas and seeking fresh input, he was taking Jason on a tour of their new town.

"I would love to, but Soaring Eagle has *requested* I visit him. It is a command performance as we all know." She laughed happily. "Perhaps you will include me tomorrow."

"I would like that," Gabriel answered softly. "But I am glad Soaring Eagle has asked to see you. He rarely leaves his home or visits. After all, he is a man of at least eighty years, although he admits to no more than that. Quite an accomplishment."

With a light kiss from both men, they went their separate ways.

Kathryn stood, waiting patiently outside Soaring Eagle's home. *Patience* now belonged to her, at least most of the time. It had come with age, *time* having solved that problem.

"Enter Ugilohi, and welcome." The deep resonance of his voice, although softer, held strength.

He sat facing her in a heavily built oak chair. Meaningful symbols had been carved in detail along the back, sides, arms and top edge, a gift created especially for him by Rob, and presented amidst much fanfare several years ago. On an earlier visit with his wife and children, Rob—always sharp of eye and soft of tongue—noticed that rheumatism was rapidly becoming a greater enemy to Soaring Eagle than the encroaching settlers. He was no longer able to stand unassisted for any length of time, and considered a bench below his dignity when counseling his people. Disdaining pitying attempts to help him rise or remain standing, he had withdrawn into a life of seclusion, rarely allowing visitors other than his children, and even *they*—only on specific occasions.

Soaring Eagle's daughter, Silver Fox, had been deeply saddened. His grandchildren changed daily. He was missing the joy of watching their personalities develop—each so different and delightful. Gabriel, as stubborn and vocal as his father-in-law, was the only one who visited on a regular basis—with or without invitation.

Rob's gift changed all that. He had constructed a regal throne, fit for a venerable warrior, finer than that of distant kings, he was sure. Soaring Eagle no longer needed assistance to rise, nor felt embarrassment, and with a glad heart reopened his life to one and all.

"Patience is finally yours, Ugilohi," he rumbled. "I thought never to see the day."

"Nor I," she answered, sharing his laughter.

His hair was brilliant white, dramatic in its stark contrast to his rich, burnished skin. His craggy face bore thick lines earned in a long life of hard work. To her, he seemed more handsome than he had in youth.

"Come close and sit by me," he said warmly, indicating a small bench.

She moved forward as asked, but as she began to sit, he stopped her.

"Ugilohi." His arms opened in welcome as he slowly arose.

Moving eagerly into his arms, she held him, inhaled the familiar scent of him, and in many ways felt she was *home*. He crushed her to him with strength belying the frail body existing beneath his long robe. They stood that way for many minutes, warm memories cascading freely. Intermingling tears streamed down their faces, neither wishing to break this precious moment, or contact. It would be for the last time … there was no need to rush.

Their talk touched upon their last forty years: moments of joy, nagging regrets, sadness, loss, their mutual success with the Trading Post. Lastly they turned to Anna.

"How proud she was of you." With a curt gesture he hushed her denial. "How proud *I am* of you."

She lowered her head, deeply embarrassed. Long fingers lifted her chin to face him. His eyes bored into her—through her—the depth of his emotion astounding.

"Be proud, my Ugilohi. *You* have followed your destiny."

This is goodbye, it suddenly struck, as deep inner calm settled into her heart. Rummaging in her pocket, she brought out an object and pressed it into his hand.

"For you," she whispered.

He gasped, unable to utter a single word. But no words were necessary. Closing his hand around his precious stag horn spoon, he clutched it to his heart.

"It will not be long," he murmured.

"No," she answered softly.

"Does eternity frighten you?"

"No."

They embraced one last time, sharing deep feelings of peace and understanding … and she thanked God she had come.

"How was your visit with Soaring Eagle?" Jason asked over their evening meal.

"Delightful," she responded, her face wreathed in smiles. "Now tell me all about your day with Gabriel, my love. I wish to hear of the *future*."

Their visit at New Echota had been wonderful. Kathryn felt brief sadness at Anna's lack of presence, but it quickly passed. "She would have liked it here, Silver Fox, of that I am sure. It *is* the future, and an exciting one at that," Kathryn assured.

"The progress you have made since we last saw each other is remarkable, Gabriel. Sometimes it takes a visitor to notice the changes. You are too close to the source, and *impatience* acts as your guide."

Gabriel smiled at Jason's words. "I do wish you could talk Kathryn into staying with us. The Cherokees will have many years of success and happiness before it all begins to change. The Trading Post and Inn all but run themselves. Smitty knows the ropes and …"

"As you follow your children, so do we. However, we have already begun plans to return and see your progress next spring."

They left on a high note, pleased with what they had seen, relaxed and content with each other and life.

On the second night, a sudden mountain storm struck, holding them in its icy grip for a full day before beginning to relent. It was too early for the icy rain which fell heavily, and Jason grimaced, wishing they had delayed their trip until spring. He constructed a warm, water-tight shelter, built a huge fire which he kept constantly burning—and watched Kathryn closely.

"Stay warm, my pet, you must not get chilled."

However, the afternoon of the second day, as he collected fire wood, Kathryn slipped quietly into the woods. She returned shortly carrying a brace of rabbits and grinning from ear-to-ear. Thinking herself quite clever, and delighted with her accomplishment, she failed to notice her husband's distress.

Jason had returned with an armload of firewood and finding her gone, was panic stricken. But one look at her glowing face as she handed him the rabbits, and he could not scold her. After helping her into dry clothes, he sat her close to the fire and chafed warmth into her delicate wrists. Grabbing his flask of brandy, he plied her with the warming liquid until she finally stopped shivering. But his fear escalated.

By the time they reached home, fever had set in, accompanied by a wracking cough. They were met at the door by a concerned and loving daughter and son-in-law. A trapper had come through the Trading Post the day before bringing disquieting news of the untimely storm.

Gabrielle settled her mother comfortably in her parents' big bed, making sure to first warm it with heated stones. After bringing tea and dosing her with a decoction of herbs, she tucked warm quilts snugly under her chin.

"Do not fuss so, little one. I have survived worse than this. Besides, it was worth it." She broke into a fit of harsh coughing. "Ask your poppa," she finally managed.

Gabrielle kissed her mother's forehead, and urging her to get some sleep, moved to the living room. Rob sat alongside her father on the big couch, attempting to console him. Hearing her footstep, he quickly slid over making room. Stifling a sob, her father looked up with fear filled eyes, and reached out to his daughter, needing to touch her.

"Poppa, it is *not* your fault," she said firmly as she sat down and pulled him, unresisting, into a loving hug. Momma *needed* to do what she did. Your unselfish caring allowed her that pleasure. I imagine it is the first time she has lost herself in complete enjoyment since …"

It took but one look at the depth of sorrow in his daughter's piercing, blue eyes to know the truth he feared. Tears fell unashamed as he sobbed within his *little girl's* arms, while Rob's firm, compassionate hand rested on his shoulder conveying *courage.*

He never left her side: feeding her, bathing her, urging her to eat, reading from her favorite poetry books—the same battered books that had accompanied them throughout the war. Phillis Wheatley's works had been added to their library long ago on John Paul Jones's suggestion. They had hoped to get to Boston someday and meet the talented woman—but the timing had never been quite right.

Maggie came by daily to sit and talk of everyday goings on, and preparations being started for winter. Samuel always accompanied her, and with a great amount of urging, would coax Jason to take a short walk or to hunt—anything to give him a temporary break. He never complained, but his gaunt face bore the stress of constant grief.

Gabrielle peeked in to say 'hi' several times each day, often with the twins or Rob, when he could leave his work. She always arrived with porridge or stew that she had prepared *way too much of,* making sure her father ate. She helped him in any way she could, often doing no more than sitting beside him with her arm draped lovingly over his shoulder. Words were unnecessary, her presence more than enough to keep him going.

"I fear your brother will arrive too …" he stopped as a tear slipped down his cheek.

Gabrielle sighed deeply. "Do *not* waste a moment fretting over him. T'is not worth the effort, for he is what he is." She knew of no words that would ease his pain. "Momma accepted long ago—she will not be distressed."

Rob closeted himself for long hours in his workshop. Jason never asked, but he knew the purpose of Rob's project, understood his feverish, driven pace to finish.

Days passed, perhaps weeks, time no longer mattered. Jason sat dozing, shoulders slumped, exhausted and desolate with the knowledge of what was to come.

Kathryn lay watching him, her eyes caressing his strong face, that magnificent, wonderful face she had cherished for so many years. Seeing sorrow etched so deeply, her heart ached, knowing she was the cause of his grief.

Jason sensed her watching and roused. His smile was tender as his eyes met hers, captured hers. *So frail now ... so very frail.*

"Make love to me, my beloved husband." Her voice was stronger, pleading. "I need you so." Within her pale, thin face, emerald eyes burned with the old passion.

"I am *yours* to command, my love," he whispered, brushing a kiss to her forehead. Quickly casting his clothing aside, he slid beneath the covers. As their flesh touched, he felt the heat of fever still gripping her relentlessly, and for a brief moment feared he could not. But his body would not deny her—or himself.

Resting in the aftermath, he gently kissed tears of joy from her face; sure he had never loved her more sweetly, more passionately or more thoroughly in all their years together. Tears spilled freely down his cheeks as she thumbed them away.

He held her close, willing strength and renewed health and ... *life.*

"You *will not* go alone, my beloved Kathryn," he mouthed against her forehead and felt her start—whether comprehending and accepting inevitability or readying an argument, he was unsure.

Weakly she placed her hand against his chest. "Your heart and mine beat as one," no more than a frail whisper. Her hand dropped, her fingers curling slowly against her heart. It took so much effort now. "You are my life, my heart, my soul."

Jason brushed a kiss to her forehead, and placing his thumb gently against her brow, began tracing it slowly along the bridge of her nose down to her chin. Tipping her face upwards, he kissed her with utmost tenderness in their final salute. "Always, my love ... always."

They both slept deeply. Just after dawn he jerked awake in panic, but quickly relaxed. Kathryn lay within his arms, breathing evenly, the fever broken at last. She yawned and stretched, coming awake slowly, an intimate smile curving her lips. "*That* was certainly a moment of incredible magnitude, my love. I feel restored."

She was particularly tired that evening. The long day filled with family visits had been wonderful but exhausting. She had no appetite, but was breathing without difficulty, and experiencing no apparent pain in her chest—at least nothing she would admit to.

Jason held her hand as he read MacPherson's works, her choice for the evening.

"Jack *is* here," she murmured, startling him mid-sentence.

"Where?" his voice faltered on a sob.

Her eyes drifted to the far corner of the room, and then slowly back to her beloved husband. "So young ... hale, and ... hearty ... reaching out in welcome." Struggling with the effort to form the words, she trailed into exhausted silence. "Damn this frail body," she cursed, a vivid spark of the old defiance he loved so dearly—but exhausting her further.

Tears welled, tracking down his angular cheeks. "Kathryn, my beloved Kathryn." There was no doubt in his mind as to the reality of her vision.

After a long pause to gather strength, she said again. "Jack *is* here ... smiling."

"Tell him to wait, my love. *We* will be with him shortly. You *shall not* go alone. I cannot bear it."

"Jason, my love ..." She coughed slightly.

She was fading before his eyes.

"Kathryn," he sobbed. Grasping her hand, he held tight as he bent to gently capture her mouth in a tender kiss.

"Always," she murmured.

"Always," he answered.

Her lips, suddenly alive in a moment of relived passion, slowly relaxed.

Miraculously there were no tears, only a kaleidoscopic display of beautiful memories clicking through his mind ... Kathryn, his incredible gift for over forty years.

Calmly he reached into the drawer of the bedside stand and withdrew his pistol. Fleeting recollections flickered as he held the familiar weapon—so much a part of his earlier life—of *their* earlier life together.

Grasping her hand, he eyed the wide, gold wedding band before glancing at his own—their rings a perfect match. Recalling her pleasure at his choice of intricate Celtic knotwork, commissioned especially for his Scottish lass so long ago, he smiled. Those rings, representing their eternal love, had *never* left their hands during all their rich, beautiful life together.

Enough, I cannot risk losing you now, my beloved.

"Wait for me, my love, I am right behind you."

Pulling the hammer back, he pressed the barrel firmly against his temple ... and squeezed the trigger.

Epilogue

Gabrielle stood in silence, staring down at the headstone with eyes that refused to focus. As the enormity of her devastating loss washed over her again and again, she swayed into the comforting strength of Rob's arms. She sighed softly, glancing up into warm eyes regarding her with deep concern. An errant tear escaped at last, cascading willfully the full length of her cheek, stopped by a large, gentle thumb brushed along her jaw.

Pulling her snuggly to him, he buried his chin amidst the raven curls rioting untamed about her face. *So like her mother,* he mused, hugging her closer.

Sighing softly again, she snaked her arm about his waist, returning his hug, glad for the quiet strength he provided. She breathed deeply struggling to refocus, her eyes drifting back to the huge, beautifully carved headstone bearing both their names, and their interwoven Celtic wedding rings.

She had felt like a fragile pane of glass on the verge of shattering into sparkling shards—and would have, if not for Rob. He was as precious to her, as her father had been to her mother. It was Rob's undying love for her parents, and his gifted hands that had wrought the intricately carved stone that marked their resting place. *He always understands,* she realized. "Eternal love," she breathed softly, her hand drifting to touch the two gold chains her mother had worn in life, now resting within the cleft of her breasts, warm and comforting against her heart. She felt her parents' presence, and drew strength from the knowledge that they were together … where they should be.

"He could not have survived without her," Rob whispered against her forehead, startling her, openly reading her thoughts. His uncanny ability no longer surprised her as it once had. He knew her far better than she knew herself.

"I know, my Rob," she answered turning into strong arms that instantly wrapped around her protectively. "It just seemed so sudden, so …" She could not finish as a wave of sadness washed over her anew.

Rob held her close, allowing the tears to soothe. "It has been a difficult few months what with Uncle Jack's death and now theirs—and Beau so far away.

Stifling a sob, she raised a tear-streaked face to her husband. "Beau does not even know, Rob, and may not for several weeks yet."

"He *will* know … he *does* know," Rob said softly.

Gabrielle eyed her husband sharply, confused by his words. "How?" she asked. "He never displayed signs of possessing momma's and my 'gift', nor did he show the least interest."

"Ahh, but he does, my Ellie, although in far more subtle ways. I doubt he's even aware of his 'gift'. Whereas you and mother 'envision' people and situations, he *sees* or *senses* his cards—always attributing success to *his* talent. Although I'm sure he would never admit it, it takes far more than luck or even *talent,* to be as consistently successful as he has been."

"But I fail to see how he will …"

"We have never been able to fathom your brother's actions," Rob interrupted. "But he loved them … in his own way. This loss will cut too deeply, he *will* know, and he will come home."

With a hiccupped exhalation, she pushed back swiping tears. Gently stilling her hands, he tipped her chin up to receive his lingering kiss. She swayed against him, eyes fluttering closed, relinquishing herself to the solace of his touch. *I am as blessed in my marriage as you were, momma. Rob is my heart and soul … my life.*

"You have had my heart from the first moment I set eyes on you, from the very first. We were both so young, but I knew, my Ellie."

She nodded slowly. "It seems as if it were just yesterday."

"*You*, my precious Ellie, are their immortality, their pride and joy. We still have much to accomplish in this life. But when our time is done here, they will be waiting with open arms. They *are* here with us now, as you well know."

"Remind me often, my Rob. In my *selfish wanting*, I tend to forget. I miss their earthly presence, but feel them lingering in the ethers, and it comforts me.

"Jack is with them," he said with soft assurance.

"Yes." She squeezed his hand.

"Are you all right, mother?" Hesitant clearing of throats and an anxious question interrupted her drifting thoughts. Catherine and Thomas stood regarding their parents with quiet concern.

Turning to her children, Gabrielle placed a loving hand on each child's cheek. "*Yes*, my precious children, *yes*."

Gabrielle gazed devotedly at her husband. "You are correct, my Rob. They are not gone, their immortality lives on in this delightful pair standing before our eyes."

***

The comforting thrum of engines and steady, gliding motion of the paddle-wheeler, usually so calming, did nothing to reduce Beau's increasing irritation.

"God damn it, Josh," he exploded angrily as his cousin fumbled the cards again. "Tonight's game is important. I'll not have you screw it up. For Christ's sake, my father plays better than that! Try that move again. You're sloppy, you need to …"

Without warning, his angry words ceased upon a strangled gasp. A stricken expression contorted his features, his normally robust coloring paling to a shade of old tallow. Shoving back from the table, he stumbled to the small bedside stand, opened the top drawer and pulled out a crumpled parchment. Dropping heavily onto his bed, he carefully unfolded it, and with shaking hands began reading for the—he had lost count of the number of times he had reread it.

> *My dearest son*, it began. *It has been over a year since Jack's accident … and I am finally able speak of him without breaking down.*

It was a long, loving letter conveying support for his chosen lifestyle—words expressing their pride and enduring love. However, it was the last lines that had moved him close to tears, added at the bottom in his father's distinctive script.

As we wish to appreciate your fascination for Mr. Fulton's steamship, your mother and I plan to visit you next spring. I have practiced the card moves you taught me so as not to embarrass you. But go easy on me, son. I do not begin to possess your talent.

Slowly he reread his father's words, words that amounted to a written declaration of love for *his* son, before carefully refolding the battered parchment and tucking it into his vest pocket.

"They're gone," he murmured brokenly. "They're both gone." Burying his face in his hands, he wept convulsively—guilt-ridden sobs of desolation and loss.

Watch for the Prequel "Before Jason"

A Novel by: J. Winfield Currie

In 'Beyond All Reason', you met Kathryn Cameron MacLean, a young woman in her early twenties. Independent, courageous, filled with good humor and indefatigable spirit, she wandered the back roads of the Carolinas, searching ... always searching.

What did she seek? The answer persistently eluded her, yet she was certain it lay just beyond the next hill. She had no idea what drove her, only a lingering sense of something missing in her life. She needed an answer or she could never rest easy.

Kathryn's father had survived the horrific Battle of Culloden in Scotland, only to find himself faced with the Highland Clearances. Like so many Scots, he fled his homeland, bringing his wife and young son to the southern colonies of America in the mid 1700s. However, the much promised 'land of milk and honey' presented its own set of challenges and rules: along with the threat of war with England looming on the horizon.

Ian Dougal MacLean was independent, hardworking, feisty, stubborn, and honest to a fault. Shortly after settling in North Carolina, his wife gifted him with a delightful baby daughter.

"Saints be praised," he whispered, awestruck. Staring into bold, unblinking, green eyes, he tousled her curling wisps of tawny hair. "She be the spittin' image o' meself, my Mairi, but with her great grandma's spunk and coloring. Now there's a formidable combination fer sich a wee lass."

Casting his gaze skyward, he raised his hand in salute. "Here's to ye, Great Grandma Kathryn, meet yer namesake. Mark me now, she'll do ye proud."

No truer or more prophetic words were ever spoken, for Kathryn was very much her father's daughter, with a wee splash of her great grandma's temperament thrown in for good measure.

Bitten by the wanderlust bug, teased and taunted by an older brother who wished she had been born a boy, she saw and lived more in her first few years of life, than most of us do in a lifetime.

The people, places and situations that formed her, all come to life in vivid detail. You will laugh, you will cry and you will come to love her ... just as Jason did.